I0763279

The Novels of Elizabeth Gaskell, Volume One

By

Elizabeth Cleghorn Gaskell

Cover Photograph: Patrick Metzdorf

ISBN: 978-1-78139-430-4

Contents

MARY BARTON:

CRANFORD

RUTH

NORTH AND SOUTH

MARY BARTON:

A TALE OF MANCHESTER LIFE.

"'How knowest thou,' may the distressed Novel-wright exclaim, 'that I, here where I sit, am the Foolishest of existing mortals; that this my Long-ear of a fictitious Biography shall not find one and the other, into whose still longer ears it may be the means, under Providence, of instilling somewhat?' We answer, 'None knows, none can certainly know: therefore, write on, worthy Brother, even as thou canst, even as it is given thee.'"

CARLYLE.

PREFACE.

Three years ago I became anxious (from circumstances that need not be more fully alluded to) to employ myself in writing a work of fiction. Living in Manchester, but with a deep relish and fond admiration for the country, my first thought was to find a frame-work for my story in some rural scene; and I had already made a little progress in a tale, the period of which was more than a century ago, and the place on the borders of Yorkshire, when I bethought me how deep might be the romance in the lives of some of those who elbowed me daily in the busy streets of the town in which I resided. I had always felt a deep sympathy with the care-worn men, who looked as if doomed to struggle through their lives in strange alternations between work and want; tossed to and fro by circumstances, apparently in even a greater degree than other men. A little manifestation of this sympathy, and a little attention to the expression of feelings on the part of some of the work-people with whom I was acquainted, had laid open to me the hearts of one or two of the more thoughtful among them; I saw that they were sore and irritable against the rich, the even tenor of whose seemingly happy lives appeared to increase the anguish caused by the lottery-like nature of their own. Whether the bitter complaints made by them, of the neglect which they experienced from the prosperous—especially from the masters whose fortunes they had helped to build up—were well-founded or no, it is not for me to judge. It is enough to say, that this belief of the injustice and unkindness which they endure from their fellow-creatures, taints what might be resignation to God's will, and turns it to revenge in too many of the poor uneducated factory-workers of Manchester.

The more I reflected on this unhappy state of things between those so bound to each other by common interests, as the employers and the employed must ever be, the more anxious I became to give some utterance to the agony which, from time to time, convulses this dumb people; the agony of suffering without the sympathy of the happy, or of erroneously believing that such is the case. If it be an error, that the woes, which come with ever-returning tide-like flood to overwhelm the workmen in our manufacturing towns, pass unregarded by all but the sufferers, it is at any rate an error so bitter in its consequences to all parties, that whatever public effort can do in the way of legislation, or private effort in the way of merciful deeds, or helpless love in the way of "widow's mites," should be done, and that speedily, to disabuse the work-people of so miserable a misapprehension. At present they seem to me to be left in a state, wherein lamentations and tears are thrown aside as useless, but in which the lips are compressed for curses, and the hands clenched and ready to smite.

I know nothing of Political Economy, or the theories of trade. I have tried to write truthfully; and if my accounts agree or clash with any system, the agreement or disagreement is unintentional.

To myself the idea which I have formed of the state of feeling among too many of the factory-people in Manchester, and which I endeavoured to represent in this tale (completed above a year ago), has received some confirmation from the events which have so recently occurred among a similar class on the Continent.

OCTOBER, 1848.

CHAPTER I - A MYSTERIOUS DISAPPEARANCE.

Oh! 'tis hard, 'tis hard to be working
  The whole of the live-long day,
When all the neighbours about one
  Are off to their jaunts and play.
There's Richard he carries his baby,
  And Mary takes little Jane,
And lovingly they'll be wandering
  Through field and briery lane.

MANCHESTER SONG.

There are some fields near Manchester, well known to the inhabitants as "Green Heys Fields," through which runs a public footpath to a little village about two miles distant. In spite of these fields being flat and low, nay, in spite of the want of wood (the great and usual recommendation of level tracts of land), there is a charm about them which strikes even the inhabitant of a mountainous district, who sees and feels the effect of contrast in these common-place but thoroughly rural fields, with the busy, bustling manufacturing town he left but half-an-hour ago. Here and there an old black and white farm-house, with its rambling out-buildings, speaks of other times and other occupations than those which now absorb the population of the neighbourhood. Here in their seasons may be seen the country business of hay-making, ploughing, &c., which are such pleasant mysteries for townspeople to watch; and here the artisan, deafened with noise of tongues and engines, may come to listen awhile to the delicious sounds of rural life: the lowing of cattle, the milk-maids' call, the clatter and cackle of poultry in the old farm-yards. You cannot wonder, then, that these fields are popular places of resort at every holiday time; and you would not wonder, if you could see, or I properly describe, the charm of one particular stile, that it should be, on such occasions, a crowded halting-place. Close by it is a deep, clear pond, reflecting in its dark green depths the shadowy trees that bend over it to exclude the sun. The only place where its banks are shelving is on the side next to a rambling farm-yard, belonging to one of those old-world, gabled, black and white houses I named above, overlooking the field through which the public footpath leads. The porch of this farm-house is covered by a rose-tree; and the little garden surrounding it is crowded with a medley of old-fashioned herbs and flowers, planted long ago, when the garden was the only druggist's shop within reach, and allowed to grow in scrambling and wild luxuriance—roses, lavender, sage, balm (for tea), rosemary, pinks and wallflowers, onions and jessamine, in most republican and indiscriminate order. This farm-house and garden are within a hundred yards of the stile of which I spoke, leading from the large pasture field into a smaller one, divided by a hedge of hawthorn and black-thorn; and near this stile, on the further side, there runs a tale that primroses may often be found, and occasionally the blue sweet violet on the grassy hedge bank.

I do not know whether it was on a holiday granted by the masters, or a holiday seized in right of Nature and her beautiful spring time by the workmen, but one afternoon (now ten or a dozen years ago) these fields were much thronged. It was an early May evening—the April of the poets; for heavy showers had fallen all the morning, and the round, soft, white clouds which were blown by a west wind over the dark blue sky, were sometimes varied by one blacker and more threatening. The softness of the day tempted forth the young green leaves, which almost visibly fluttered into life; and the willows, which that morning had had only a brown reflection in the water below, were now of that tender gray-green which blends so delicately with the spring harmony of colours.

Groups of merry and somewhat loud-talking girls, whose ages might range from twelve to twenty, came by with a buoyant step. They were most of them factory girls, and wore the usual out-of-doors dress of that particular class of maidens; namely, a shawl, which at mid-day or in fine weather was allowed to be merely a shawl, but towards evening, or if the day were chilly, became a sort of Spanish mantilla or Scotch plaid, and was brought over the head and hung loosely down, or was pinned under the chin in no unpicturesque fashion.

Their faces were not remarkable for beauty; indeed, they were below the average, with one or two exceptions; they had dark hair, neatly and classically arranged, dark eyes, but sallow complexions and irregular features. The only thing to strike a passer-by was an acuteness and intelligence of countenance, which has often been noticed in a manufacturing population.

There were also numbers of boys, or rather young men, rambling among these fields, ready to bandy jokes with any one, and particularly ready to enter into conversation with the girls, who, however, held themselves aloof, not in a shy, but rather in an independent way, assuming an indifferent manner to the noisy wit or obstreperous compliments of the lads. Here and there came a sober quiet couple, either whispering lovers, or husband and wife, as the case might be; and if the latter, they were seldom unencumbered by an infant, carried for the most part by the father, while occasionally even three or four little toddlers had been carried or dragged thus far, in order that the whole family might enjoy the delicious May afternoon together.

CHAPTER I - A MYSTERIOUS DISAPPEARANCE.

Sometime in the course of that afternoon, two working men met with friendly greeting at the stile so often named. One was a thorough specimen of a Manchester man; born of factory workers, and himself bred up in youth, and living in manhood, among the mills. He was below the middle size and slightly made; there was almost a stunted look about him; and his wan, colourless face gave you the idea, that in his childhood he had suffered from the scanty living consequent upon bad times and improvident habits. His features were strongly marked, though not irregular, and their expression was extreme earnestness; resolute either for good or evil; a sort of latent, stern enthusiasm. At the time of which I write, the good predominated over the bad in the countenance, and he was one from whom a stranger would have asked a favour with tolerable faith that it would be granted. He was accompanied by his wife, who might, without exaggeration, have been called a lovely woman, although now her face was swollen with crying, and often hidden behind her apron. She had the fresh beauty of the agricultural districts; and somewhat of the deficiency of sense in her countenance, which is likewise characteristic of the rural inhabitants in comparison with the natives of the manufacturing towns. She was far advanced in pregnancy, which perhaps occasioned the overpowering and hysterical nature of her grief. The friend whom they met was more handsome and less sensible-looking than the man I have just described; he seemed hearty and hopeful, and although his age was greater, yet there was far more of youth's buoyancy in his appearance. He was tenderly carrying a baby in arms, while his wife, a delicate, fragile-looking woman, limping in her gait, bore another of the same age; little, feeble twins, inheriting the frail appearance of their mother.

The last-mentioned man was the first to speak, while a sudden look of sympathy dimmed his gladsome face. "Well, John, how goes it with you?" and, in a lower voice, he added, "Any news of Esther, yet?" Meanwhile the wives greeted each other like old friends, the soft and plaintive voice of the mother of the twins seeming to call forth only fresh sobs from Mrs. Barton.

"Come, women," said John Barton, "you've both walked far enough. My Mary expects to have her bed in three weeks; and as for you, Mrs. Wilson, you know you're but a cranky sort of a body at the best of times." This was said so kindly, that no offence could be taken. "Sit you down here; the grass is well nigh dry by this time; and you're neither of you nesh[1] folk about taking cold. Stay," he added, with some tenderness, "here's my pocket-handkerchief to spread under you, to save the gowns women always think so much of; and now, Mrs. Wilson, give me the baby, I may as well carry him, while you talk and comfort my wife; poor thing, she takes on sadly about Esther."

These arrangements were soon completed: the two women sat down on the blue cotton handkerchiefs of their husbands, and the latter, each carrying a baby, set off for a further walk; but as soon as Barton had turned his back upon his wife, his countenance fell back into an expression of gloom.

---

[1] "Nesh;" Anglo-Saxon, nesc, tender.

"Then you've heard nothing of Esther, poor lass?" asked Wilson.

"No, nor shan't, as I take it. My mind is, she's gone off with somebody. My wife frets, and thinks she's drowned herself, but I tell her, folks don't care to put on their best clothes to drown themselves; and Mrs. Bradshaw (where she lodged, you know) says the last time she set eyes on her was last Tuesday, when she came down stairs, dressed in her Sunday gown, and with a new ribbon in her bonnet, and gloves on her hands, like the lady she was so fond of thinking herself."

"She was as pretty a creature as ever the sun shone on."

"Ay, she was a farrantly[1] lass; more's the pity now," added Barton, with a sigh. "You see them Buckinghamshire people as comes to work in Manchester, has quite a different look with them to us Manchester folk. You'll not see among the Manchester wenches such fresh rosy cheeks, or such black lashes to gray eyes (making them look like black), as my wife and Esther had. I never seed two such pretty women for sisters; never. Not but what beauty is a sad snare. Here was Esther so puffed up, that there was no holding her in. Her spirit was always up, if I spoke ever so little in the way of advice to her; my wife spoiled her, it is true, for you see she was so much older than Esther she was more like a mother to her, doing every thing for her."

"I wonder she ever left you," observed his friend.

"That's the worst of factory work, for girls. They can earn so much when work is plenty, that they can maintain themselves any how. My Mary shall never work in a factory, that I'm determined on. You see Esther spent her money in dress, thinking to set off her pretty face; and got to come home so late at night, that at last I told her my mind: my missis thinks I spoke crossly, but I meant right, for I loved Esther, if it was only for Mary's sake. Says I, 'Esther, I see what you'll end at with your artificials, and your fly-away veils, and stopping out when honest women are in their beds; you'll be a street-walker, Esther, and then, don't you go to think I'll have you darken my door, though my wife is your sister.' So says she, 'Don't trouble yourself, John. I'll pack up and be off now, for I'll never stay to hear myself called as you call me.' She flushed up like a turkey-cock, and I thought fire would come out of her eyes; but when she saw Mary cry (for Mary can't abide words in a house), she went and kissed her, and said she was not so bad as I thought her. So we talked more friendly, for, as I said, I liked the lass well enough, and her pretty looks, and her cheery ways. But she said (and at the time I thought there was sense in what she said) we should be much better friends if she went into lodgings, and only came to see us now and then."

"Then you still were friendly. Folks said you'd cast her off, and said you'd never speak to her again."

"Folks always make one a deal worse than one is," said John Barton, testily. "She came many a time to our house after she left off living with us. Last Sunday se'nnight—no! it was this very last Sunday, she came to drink a cup of tea with Mary; and that was the last time we set eyes on her."

---

[1] "Farrantly," comely, pleasant-looking.

"Was she any ways different in her manner?" asked Wilson.

"Well, I don't know. I have thought several times since, that she was a bit quieter, and more womanly-like; more gentle, and more blushing, and not so riotous and noisy. She comes in, toward four o'clock, when afternoon church was loosing, and she goes and hangs her bonnet up on the old nail we used to call hers, while she lived with us. I remember thinking what a pretty lass she was, as she sat on a low stool by Mary, who was rocking herself, and in rather a poor way. She laughed and cried by turns, but all so softly and gently, like a child, that I couldn't find in my heart to scold her, especially as Mary was fretting already. One thing I do remember I did say, and pretty sharply too. She took our little Mary by the waist, and—"

"Thou must leave off calling her 'little' Mary, she's growing up into as fine a lass as one can see on a summer's day; more of her mother's stock than thine," interrupted Wilson.

"Well, well, I call her 'little,' because her mother's name is Mary. But, as I was saying, she takes Mary in a coaxing sort of way, and, 'Mary,' says she, 'what should you think if I sent for you some day and made a lady of you?' So I could not stand such talk as that to my girl, and I said, 'Thou'd best not put that nonsense i' the girl's head I can tell thee; I'd rather see her earning her bread by the sweat of her brow, as the Bible tells her she should do, ay, though she never got butter to her bread, than be like a do-nothing lady, worrying shopmen all morning, and screeching at her pianny all afternoon, and going to bed without having done a good turn to any one of God's creatures but herself.'"

"Thou never could abide the gentlefolk," said Wilson, half amused at his friend's vehemence.

"And what good have they ever done me that I should like them?" asked Barton, the latent fire lighting up his eye: and bursting forth, he continued, "If I am sick, do they come and nurse me? If my child lies dying (as poor Tom lay, with his white wan lips quivering, for want of better food than I could give him), does the rich man bring the wine or broth that might save his life? If I am out of work for weeks in the bad times, and winter comes, with black frost, and keen east wind, and there is no coal for the grate, and no clothes for the bed, and the thin bones are seen through the ragged clothes, does the rich man share his plenty with me, as he ought to do, if his religion wasn't a humbug? When I lie on my deathbed, and Mary (bless her) stands fretting, as I know she will fret," and here his voice faltered a little, "will a rich lady come and take her to her own home if need be, till she can look round, and see what best to do? No, I tell you, it's the poor, and the poor only, as does such things for the poor. Don't think to come over me with th' old tale, that the rich know nothing of the trials of the poor. I say, if they don't know, they ought to know. We're their slaves as long as we can work; we pile up their fortunes with the sweat of our brows; and yet we are to live as separate as if we were in two worlds; ay, as separate as Dives and Lazarus, with a great gulf betwixt us: but I know who was best off then," and he wound up his speech with a low chuckle that had no mirth in it.

"Well, neighbour," said Wilson, "all that may be very true, but what I want to know now is about Esther—when did you last hear of her?"

"Why, she took leave of us that Sunday night in a very loving way, kissing both wife Mary, and daughter Mary (if I must not call her little), and shaking hands with me; but all in a cheerful sort of manner, so we thought nothing about her kisses and shakes. But on Wednesday night comes Mrs. Bradshaw's son with Esther's box, and presently Mrs. Bradshaw follows with the key; and when we began to talk, we found Esther told her she was coming back to live with us, and would pay her week's money for not giving notice; and on Tuesday night she carried off a little bundle (her best clothes were on her back, as I said before), and told Mrs. Bradshaw not to hurry herself about the big box, but bring it when she had time. So of course she thought she should find Esther with us; and when she told her story, my missis set up such a screech, and fell down in a dead swoon. Mary ran up with water for her mother, and I thought so much about my wife, I did not seem to care at all for Esther. But the next day I asked all the neighbours (both our own and Bradshaw's), and they'd none of 'em heard or seen nothing of her. I even went to a policeman, a good enough sort of man, but a fellow I'd never spoke to before because of his livery, and I asks him if his 'cuteness could find any thing out for us. So I believe he asks other policemen; and one on 'em had seen a wench, like our Esther, walking very quickly, with a bundle under her arm, on Tuesday night, toward eight o'clock, and get into a hackney coach, near Hulme Church, and we don't know th' number, and can't trace it no further. I'm sorry enough for the girl, for bad's come over her, one way or another, but I'm sorrier for my wife. She loved her next to me and Mary, and she's never been the same body since poor Tom's death. However, let's go back to them; your old woman may have done her good."

As they walked homewards with a brisker pace, Wilson expressed a wish that they still were the near neighbours they once had been.

"Still our Alice lives in the cellar under No. 14, in Barber Street, and if you'd only speak the word she'd be with you in five minutes, to keep your wife company when she's lonesome. Though I'm Alice's brother, and perhaps ought not to say it, I will say there's none more ready to help with heart or hand than she is. Though she may have done a hard day's wash, there's not a child ill within the street but Alice goes to offer to sit up, and does sit up too, though may be she's to be at her work by six next morning."

"She's a poor woman, and can feel for the poor, Wilson," was Barton's reply; and then he added, "Thank you kindly for your offer, and mayhap I may trouble her to be a bit with my wife, for while I'm at work, and Mary's at school, I know she frets above a bit. See, there's Mary!" and the father's eye brightened, as in the distance, among a group of girls, he spied his only daughter, a bonny lassie of thirteen or so, who came bounding along to meet and to greet her father, in a manner which showed that the stern-looking man had a tender nature within. The two men had crossed the last stile while Mary loitered behind to gather some buds of the coming hawthorn, when an over-grown lad came past her, and snatched a kiss, exclaiming, "For old acquaintance sake, Mary."

"Take that for old acquaintance sake, then," said the girl, blushing rosy red, more with anger than shame, as she slapped his face. The tones of her voice called back her father and his friend, and the aggressor proved to be the eldest son of the latter, the senior by eighteen years of his little brothers.

"Here, children, instead o' kissing and quarrelling, do ye each take a baby, for if Wilson's arms be like mine they are heartily tired."

Mary sprang forward to take her father's charge, with a girl's fondness for infants, and with some little foresight of the event soon to happen at home; while young Wilson seemed to lose his rough, cubbish nature as he crowed and cooed to his little brother.

"Twins is a great trial to a poor man, bless 'em," said the half-proud, half-weary father, as he bestowed a smacking kiss on the babe ere he parted with it.

CHAPTER II - A MANCHESTER TEA-PARTY.

Polly, put the kettle on,
  And let's have tea!
Polly, put the kettle on,
  And we'll all have tea.

"Here we are, wife; didst thou think thou'd lost us?" quoth hearty-voiced Wilson, as the two women rose and shook themselves in preparation for their homeward walk. Mrs. Barton was evidently soothed, if not cheered, by the unburdening of her fears and thoughts to her friend; and her approving look went far to second her husband's invitation that the whole party should adjourn from Green Heys Fields to tea, at the Bartons' house. The only faint opposition was raised by Mrs. Wilson, on account of the lateness of the hour at which they would probably return, which she feared on her babies' account.

"Now, hold your tongue, missis, will you," said her husband, good-temperedly. "Don't you know them brats never goes to sleep till long past ten? and haven't you a shawl, under which you can tuck one lad's head, as safe as a bird's under its wing? And as for t'other one, I'll put it in my pocket rather than not stay, now we are this far away from Ancoats."

"Or I can lend you another shawl," suggested Mrs. Barton.

"Ay, any thing rather than not stay."

The matter being decided, the party proceeded home, through many half-finished streets, all so like one another that you might have easily been bewildered and lost your way. Not a step, however, did our friends lose; down this entry, cutting off that corner, until they turned out of one of these innumerable streets into a little paved court, having the backs of houses at the end opposite to the opening, and a gutter running through the middle to carry off household slops, washing suds, &c. The women who lived in the court were busy taking in strings of caps, frocks, and various articles of linen, which hung from side to side, dangling so low, that if our friends had been a few minutes sooner, they would have had to stoop very much, or else the half-wet clothes would have flapped in their faces; but although the evening seemed yet early when they were in the open fields—among the pent-up houses, night, with its mists, and its darkness, had already begun to fall.

CHAPTER II - A MANCHESTER TEA-PARTY.

Many greetings were given and exchanged between the Wilsons and these women, for not long ago they had also dwelt in this court.

Two rude lads, standing at a disorderly looking house-door, exclaimed, as Mary Barton (the daughter) passed, "Eh, look! Polly Barton's gotten a sweet-heart."

Of course this referred to young Wilson, who stole a look to see how Mary took the idea. He saw her assume the air of a young fury, and to his next speech she answered not a word.

Mrs. Barton produced the key of the door from her pocket; and on entering the house-place it seemed as if they were in total darkness, except one bright spot, which might be a cat's eye, or might be, what it was, a red-hot fire, smouldering under a large piece of coal, which John Barton immediately applied himself to break up, and the effect instantly produced was warm and glowing light in every corner of the room. To add to this (although the coarse yellow glare seemed lost in the ruddy glow from the fire), Mrs. Barton lighted a dip by sticking it in the fire, and having placed it satisfactorily in a tin candlestick, began to look further about her, on hospitable thoughts intent. The room was tolerably large, and possessed many conveniences. On the right of the door, as you entered, was a longish window, with a broad ledge. On each side of this, hung blue-and-white check curtains, which were now drawn, to shut in the friends met to enjoy themselves. Two geraniums, unpruned and leafy, which stood on the sill, formed a further defence from out-door pryers. In the corner between the window and the fire-side was a cupboard, apparently full of plates and dishes, cups and saucers, and some more nondescript articles, for which one would have fancied their possessors could find no use—such as triangular pieces of glass to save carving knives and forks from dirtying table-cloths. However, it was evident Mrs. Barton was proud of her crockery and glass, for she left her cupboard door open, with a glance round of satisfaction and pleasure. On the opposite side to the door and window was the staircase, and two doors; one of which (the nearest to the fire) led into a sort of little back kitchen, where dirty work, such as washing up dishes, might be done, and whose shelves served as larder, and pantry, and storeroom, and all. The other door, which was considerably lower, opened into the coal-hole—the slanting closet under the stairs; from which, to the fire-place, there was a gay-coloured piece of oil-cloth laid. The place seemed almost crammed with furniture (sure sign of good times among the mills). Beneath the window was a dresser with three deep drawers. Opposite the fire-place was a table, which I should call a Pembroke, only that it was made of deal, and I cannot tell how far such a name may be applied to such humble material. On it, resting against the wall, was a bright green japanned tea-tray, having a couple of scarlet lovers embracing in the middle. The fire-light danced merrily on this, and really (setting all taste but that of a child's aside) it gave a richness of colouring to that side of the room. It was in some measure propped up by a crimson tea-caddy, also of japan ware. A round table on one branching leg really for use, stood in the corresponding corner to the cupboard; and, if you can picture all this with a washy, but clean stencilled pattern on the walls, you can form some idea of John Barton's home.

The tray was soon hoisted down, and before the merry chatter of cups and saucers began, the women disburdened themselves of their out-of-door things, and sent Mary up stairs with them. Then came a long whispering, and chinking of money, to which Mr. and Mrs. Wilson were too polite to attend; knowing, as they did full well, that it all related to the preparations for hospitality; hospitality that, in their turn, they should have such pleasure in offering. So they tried to be busily occupied with the children, and not to hear Mrs. Barton's directions to Mary.

"Run, Mary dear, just round the corner, and get some fresh eggs at Tipping's (you may get one a-piece, that will be five-pence), and see if he has any nice ham cut, that he would let us have a pound of."

"Say two pounds, missis, and don't be stingy," chimed in the husband.

"Well, a pound and a half, Mary. And get it Cumberland ham, for Wilson comes from there-away, and it will have a sort of relish of home with it he'll like,—and Mary" (seeing the lassie fain to be off), "you must get a pennyworth of milk and a loaf of bread—mind you get it fresh and new—and, and—that's all, Mary."

"No, it's not all," said her husband. "Thou must get sixpennyworth of rum, to warm the tea; thou'll get it at the 'Grapes.' And thou just go to Alice Wilson; he says she lives just right round the corner, under 14, Barber Street" (this was addressed to his wife), "and tell her to come and take her tea with us; she'll like to see her brother, I'll be bound, let alone Jane and the twins."

"If she comes she must bring a tea-cup and saucer, for we have but half-a-dozen, and here's six of us," said Mrs. Barton.

"Pooh! pooh! Jem and Mary can drink out of one, surely."

But Mary secretly determined to take care that Alice brought her tea-cup and saucer, if the alternative was to be her sharing any thing with Jem.

Alice Wilson had but just come in. She had been out all day in the fields, gathering wild herbs for drinks and medicine, for in addition to her invaluable qualities as a sick nurse and her worldly occupation as a washerwoman, she added a considerable knowledge of hedge and field simples; and on fine days, when no more profitable occupation offered itself, she used to ramble off into the lanes and meadows as far as her legs could carry her. This evening she had returned loaded with nettles, and her first object was to light a candle and see to hang them up in bunches in every available place in her cellar room. It was the perfection of cleanliness: in one corner stood the modest-looking bed, with a check curtain at the head, the whitewashed wall filling up the place where the corresponding one should have been. The floor was bricked, and scrupulously clean, although so damp that it seemed as if the last washing would never dry up. As the cellar window looked into an area in the street, down which boys might throw stones, it was protected by an outside shelter, and was oddly festooned with all manner of hedge-row, ditch, and field plants, which we are accustomed to call valueless, but which have a powerful effect either for good or for evil, and are consequently much used among the poor. The room was strewed, hung, and darkened with these bunches, which emitted no very fragrant odour in their process of drying. In one corner was a sort of broad hanging shelf, made of old planks, where some old hoards of Alice's were kept. Her little bit of crockery ware was ranged on the mantelpiece, where also stood her candlestick and box of matches. A small cupboard contained at the bottom coals, and at the top her bread and basin of oatmeal, her frying pan, tea-pot, and a small tin saucepan, which served as a kettle, as well as for cooking the delicate little messes of broth which Alice sometimes was able to manufacture for a sick neighbour.

After her walk she felt chilly and weary, and was busy trying to light her fire with the damp coals, and half green sticks, when Mary knocked.

"Come in," said Alice, remembering, however, that she had barred the door for the night, and hastening to make it possible for any one to come in.

"Is that you, Mary Barton?" exclaimed she, as the light from her candle streamed on the girl's face. "How you are grown since I used to see you at my brother's! Come in, lass, come in."

"Please," said Mary, almost breathless, "mother says you're to come to tea, and bring your cup and saucer, for George and Jane Wilson is with us, and the twins, and Jem. And you're to make haste, please."

"I'm sure it's very neighbourly and kind in your mother, and I'll come, with many thanks. Stay, Mary, has your mother got any nettles for spring drink? If she hasn't I'll take her some."

"No, I don't think she has."

Mary ran off like a hare to fulfil what, to a girl of thirteen, fond of power, was the more interesting part of her errand—the money-spending part. And well and ably did she perform her business, returning home with a little bottle of rum, and the eggs in one hand, while her other was filled with some excellent red-and-white smoke flavoured Cumberland ham, wrapped up in paper.

She was at home, and frying ham, before Alice had chosen her nettles, put out her candle, locked her door, and walked in a very foot-sore manner as far as John Barton's. What an aspect of comfort did his houseplace present, after her humble cellar. She did not think of comparing; but for all that she felt the delicious glow of the fire, the bright light that revelled in every corner of the room, the savoury smells, the comfortable sounds of a boiling kettle, and the hissing, frizzling ham. With a little old-fashioned curtsey she shut the door, and replied with a loving heart to the boisterous and surprised greeting of her brother.

And now all preparations being made, the party sat down; Mrs. Wilson in the post of honour, the rocking chair on the right hand side of the fire, nursing her baby, while its father, in an opposite arm-chair, tried vainly to quieten the other with bread soaked in milk.

Mrs. Barton knew manners too well to do any thing but sit at the tea-table and make tea, though in her heart she longed to be able to superintend the frying of the ham, and cast many an anxious look at Mary as she broke the eggs and turned the ham, with a very comfortable portion of confidence in her own culinary powers. Jem stood awkwardly leaning against the dresser, replying rather gruffly to his aunt's speeches, which gave him, he thought, the air of being a little boy; whereas he considered himself as a young man, and not so very young neither, as in two months he would be eighteen. Barton vibrated between the fire and the tea-table, his only drawback being a fancy that every now and then his wife's face flushed and contracted as if in pain.

At length the business actually began. Knives and forks, cups and saucers made a noise, but human voices were still, for human beings were hungry, and had no time to speak. Alice first broke silence; holding her tea-cup with the manner of one proposing a toast, she said, "Here's to absent friends. Friends may meet, but mountains never."

It was an unlucky toast or sentiment, as she instantly felt. Every one thought of Esther, the absent Esther; and Mrs. Barton put down her food, and could not hide the fast dropping tears. Alice could have bitten her tongue out.

It was a wet blanket to the evening; for though all had been said and suggested in the fields that could be said or suggested, every one had a wish to say something in the way of comfort to poor Mrs. Barton, and a dislike to talk about any thing else while her tears fell fast and scalding. So George Wilson, his wife and children, set off early home, not before (in spite of *mal-à-propos* speeches) they had expressed a wish that such meetings might often take place, and not before John Barton had given his hearty consent; and declared that as soon as ever his wife was well again they would have just such another evening.

"I will take care not to come and spoil it," thought poor Alice; and going up to Mrs. Barton she took her hand almost humbly, and said, "You don't know how sorry I am I said it."

To her surprise, a surprise that brought tears of joy into her eyes, Mary Barton put her arms round her neck, and kissed the self-reproaching Alice. "You didn't mean any harm, and it was me as was so foolish; only this work about Esther, and not knowing where she is, lies so heavy on my heart. Good night, and never think no more about it. God bless you, Alice."

Many and many a time, as Alice reviewed that evening in her after life, did she bless Mary Barton for these kind and thoughtful words. But just then all she could say was, "Good night, Mary, and may God bless *you*."

CHAPTER III - JOHN BARTON'S GREAT TROUBLE.

But when the morn came dim and sad,
   And chill with early showers,
Her quiet eyelids closed—she had
   Another morn than ours!

HOOD.

In the middle of that same night a neighbour of the Bartons was roused from her sound, well-earned sleep, by a knocking, which had at first made part of her dream; but starting up, as soon as she became convinced of its reality, she opened the window, and asked who was there?

"Me, John Barton," answered he, in a voice tremulous with agitation. "My missis is in labour, and, for the love of God, step in while I run for th' doctor, for she's fearful bad."

While the woman hastily dressed herself, leaving the window still open, she heard cries of agony, which resounded in the little court in the stillness of the night. In less than five minutes she was standing by Mrs. Barton's bed-side, relieving the terrified Mary, who went about, where she was told, like an automaton; her eyes tearless, her face calm, though deadly pale, and uttering no sound, except when her teeth chattered for very nervousness.

The cries grew worse.

The doctor was very long in hearing the repeated rings at his night-bell, and still longer in understanding who it was that made this sudden call upon his services; and then he begged Barton just to wait while he dressed himself, in order that no time might be lost in finding the court and house. Barton absolutely stamped with impatience, outside the doctor's door, before he came down; and walked so fast homewards, that the medical man several times asked him to go slower.

"Is she so very bad?" asked he.

"Worse, much worser than ever I saw her before," replied John.

No! she was not—she was at peace. The cries were still for ever. John had no time for listening. He opened the latched door, stayed not to light a candle for the mere ceremony of showing his companion up the stairs, so well known to himself; but, in two minutes was in the room, where lay the dead wife, whom he had loved with all the power of his strong heart. The doctor stumbled up stairs by the fire-light, and met the awe-struck look of the neighbour, which at once told him the state of things. The room was still, as he, with habitual tip-toe step, approached the poor frail body, whom nothing now could more disturb. Her daughter knelt by the bed-side, her face buried in the clothes, which were almost crammed into her mouth, to keep down the choking sobs. The husband stood like one stupified. The doctor questioned the neighbour in whispers, and then approaching Barton, said, "You must go down stairs. This is a great shock, but bear it like a man. Go down."

He went mechanically and sat down on the first chair. He had no hope. The look of death was too clear upon her face. Still, when he heard one or two unusual noises, the thought burst on him that it might only be a trance, a fit, a—he did not well know what,—but not death! Oh, not death! And he was starting up to go up stairs again, when the doctor's heavy cautious creaking footstep was heard on the stairs. Then he knew what it really was in the chamber above.

"Nothing could have saved her—there has been some shock to the system—" and so he went on; but, to unheeding ears, which yet retained his words to ponder on; words not for immediate use in conveying sense, but to be laid by, in the store-house of memory, for a more convenient season. The doctor seeing the state of the case, grieved for the man; and, very sleepy, thought it best to go, and accordingly wished him good-night—but there was no answer, so he let himself out; and Barton sat on, like a stock or a stone, so rigid, so still. He heard the sounds above too, and knew what they meant. He heard the stiff, unseasoned drawer, in which his wife kept her clothes, pulled open. He saw the neighbour come down, and blunder about in search of soap and water. He knew well what she wanted, and *why* she wanted them, but he did not speak, nor offer to help. At last she went, with some kindly-meant words (a text of comfort, which fell upon a deafened ear), and something about "Mary," but which Mary, in his bewildered state, he could not tell.

He tried to realise it, to think it possible. And then his mind wandered off to other days, to far different times. He thought of their courtship; of his first seeing her, an awkward, beautiful rustic, far too shiftless for the delicate factory work to which she was apprenticed; of his first gift to her, a bead necklace, which had long ago been put by, in one of the deep drawers of the dresser, to be kept for Mary. He wondered if it was there yet, and with a strange curiosity he got up to feel for it; for the fire by this time was well-nigh out, and candle he had none. His groping hand fell on the piled-up tea things, which at his desire she had left unwashed till morning—they were all so tired. He was reminded of one of the daily little actions, which acquire such power when they have been performed for the last time, by one we love. He began to think over his wife's daily round of duties; and something in the remembrance that these would never more be done by her, touched the source of tears, and he cried aloud. Poor Mary, meanwhile, had mechanically helped the neighbour in all the last attentions to the dead; and when she was kissed, and spoken to soothingly, tears stole quietly down her cheeks: but she reserved the luxury of a full burst of grief till she should be alone. She shut the chamber-door softly, after the neighbour had gone, and then shook the bed by which she knelt, with her agony of sorrow. She repeated, over and over again, the same words; the same vain, unanswered address to her who was no more. "Oh, mother! mother, are you really dead! Oh, mother, mother!"

At last she stopped, because it flashed across her mind that her violence of grief might disturb her father. All was still below. She looked on the face so changed, and yet so strangely like. She bent down to kiss it. The cold, unyielding flesh struck a shudder to her heart, and, hastily obeying her impulse, she grasped the candle, and opened the door. Then she heard the sobs of her father's grief; and quickly, quietly, stealing down the steps, she knelt by him, and kissed his hand. He took no notice at first, for his burst of grief would not be controlled. But when her shriller sobs, her terrified cries (which she could not repress), rose upon his ear, he checked himself.

"Child, we must be all to one another, now *she* is gone," whispered he.

"Oh, father, what can I do for you? Do tell me! I'll do any thing."

"I know thou wilt. Thou must not fret thyself ill, that's the first thing I ask. Thou must leave me, and go to bed now, like a good girl as thou art."

"Leave you, father! oh, don't say so."

"Ay, but thou must! thou must go to bed, and try and sleep; thou'lt have enough to do and to bear, poor wench, to-morrow."

Mary got up, kissed her father, and sadly went up stairs to the little closet, where she slept. She thought it was of no use undressing, for that she could never, never sleep, so threw herself on her bed in her clothes, and before ten minutes had passed away, the passionate grief of youth had subsided into sleep.

Barton had been roused by his daughter's entrance, both from his stupor and from his uncontrollable sorrow. He could think on what was to be done, could plan for the funeral, could calculate the necessity of soon returning to his work, as the extravagance of the past night would leave them short of money, if he long remained away from the mill. He was in a club, so that money was provided for the burial. These things settled in his own mind, he recalled the doctor's words, and bitterly thought of the shock his poor wife had so recently had, in the mysterious disappearance of her cherished sister. His feelings towards Esther almost amounted to curses. It was she who had brought on all this sorrow. Her giddiness, her lightness of conduct, had wrought this woe. His previous thoughts about her had been tinged with wonder and pity, but now he hardened his heart against her for ever.

One of the good influences over John Barton's life had departed that night. One of the ties which bound him down to the gentle humanities of earth was loosened, and henceforward the neighbours all remarked he was a changed man. His gloom and his sternness became habitual instead of occasional. He was more obstinate. But never to Mary. Between the father and the daughter there existed in full force that mysterious bond which unites those who have been loved by one who is now dead and gone. While he was harsh and silent to others, he humoured Mary with tender love; she had more of her own way than is common in any rank with girls of her age. Part of this was the necessity of the case; for, of course, all the money went through her hands, and the household arrangements were guided by her will and pleasure. But part was her father's indulgence, for he left her, with full trust in her unusual sense and spirit, to choose her own associates, and her own times for seeing them.

With all this, Mary had not her father's confidence in the matters which now began to occupy him, heart and soul; she was aware that he had joined clubs, and become an active member of a trades' union, but it was hardly likely that a girl of Mary's age (even when two or three years had elapsed since her mother's death) should care much for the differences between the employers and the employed,—an eternal subject for agitation in the manufacturing districts, which, however it may be lulled for a time, is sure to break forth again with fresh violence at any depression of trade, showing that in its apparent quiet, the ashes had still smouldered in the breasts of a few.

Among these few was John Barton. At all times it is a bewildering thing to the poor weaver to see his employer removing from house to house, each one grander than the last, till he ends in building one more magnificent than all, or withdraws his money from the concern, or sells his mill to buy an estate in the country, while all the time the weaver, who thinks he and his fellows are the real makers of this wealth, is struggling on for bread for their children, through the vicissitudes of lowered wages, short hours, fewer hands employed, &c. And when he knows trade is bad, and could understand (at least partially) that there are not buyers enough in the market to purchase the goods already made, and consequently that there is no demand for more; when he would bear and endure much without complaining, could he also see that his employers were bearing their share; he is, I say, bewildered and (to use his own word) "aggravated" to see that all goes on just as usual with the mill-owners. Large houses are still occupied, while spinners' and weavers' cottages stand empty, because the families that once occupied them are obliged to live in rooms or cellars. Carriages still roll along the streets, concerts are still crowded by subscribers, the shops for expensive luxuries still find daily customers, while the workman loiters away his unemployed time in watching these things, and thinking of the pale, uncomplaining wife at home, and the wailing children asking in vain for enough of food, of the sinking health, of the dying life of those near and dear to him. The contrast is too great. Why should he alone suffer from bad times?

I know that this is not really the case; and I know what is the truth in such matters: but what I wish to impress is what the workman feels and thinks. True, that with child-like improvidence, good times will often dissipate his grumbling, and make him forget all prudence and foresight.

CHAPTER III - JOHN BARTON'S GREAT TROUBLE.

But there are earnest men among these people, men who have endured wrongs without complaining, but without ever forgetting or forgiving those whom (they believe) have caused all this woe.

Among these was John Barton. His parents had suffered, his mother had died from absolute want of the necessaries of life. He himself was a good, steady workman, and, as such, pretty certain of steady employment. But he spent all he got with the confidence (you may also call it improvidence) of one who was willing, and believed himself able, to supply all his wants by his own exertions. And when his master suddenly failed, and all hands in that mill were turned back, one Tuesday morning, with the news that Mr. Hunter had stopped, Barton had only a few shillings to rely on; but he had good heart of being employed at some other mill, and accordingly, before returning home, he spent some hours in going from factory to factory, asking for work. But at every mill was some sign of depression of trade; some were working short hours, some were turning off hands, and for weeks Barton was out of work, living on credit. It was during this time his little son, the apple of his eye, the cynosure of all his strong power of love, fell ill of the scarlet fever. They dragged him through the crisis, but his life hung on a gossamer thread. Every thing, the doctor said, depended on good nourishment, on generous living, to keep up the little fellow's strength, in the prostration in which the fever had left him. Mocking words! when the commonest food in the house would not furnish one little meal. Barton tried credit; but it was worn out at the little provision shops, which were now suffering in their turn. He thought it would be no sin to steal, and would have stolen; but he could not get the opportunity in the few days the child lingered. Hungry himself, almost to an animal pitch of ravenousness, but with the bodily pain swallowed up in anxiety for his little sinking lad, he stood at one of the shop windows where all edible luxuries are displayed; haunches of venison, Stilton cheeses, moulds of jelly—all appetising sights to the common passer by. And out of this shop came Mrs. Hunter! She crossed to her carriage, followed by the shopman loaded with purchases for a party. The door was quickly slammed to, and she drove away; and Barton returned home with a bitter spirit of wrath in his heart, to see his only boy a corpse!

You can fancy, now, the hoards of vengeance in his heart against the employers. For there are never wanting those who, either in speech or in print, find it their interest to cherish such feelings in the working classes; who know how and when to rouse the dangerous power at their command; and who use their knowledge with unrelenting purpose to either party.

So while Mary took her own way, growing more spirited every day, and growing in her beauty too, her father was chairman at many a trades' union meeting; a friend of delegates, and ambitious of being a delegate himself; a Chartist, and ready to do any thing for his order.

But now times were good; and all these feelings were theoretical, not practical. His most practical thought was getting Mary apprenticed to a dressmaker; for he had never left off disliking a factory life for a girl, on more accounts than one.

Mary must do something. The factories being, as I said, out of the question, there were two things open—going out to service, and the dressmaking business; and against the first of these, Mary set herself with all the force of her strong will. What that will might have been able to achieve had her father been against her, I cannot tell; but he disliked the idea of parting with her, who was the light of his hearth, the voice of his otherwise silent home. Besides, with his ideas and feelings towards the higher classes, he considered domestic servitude as a species of slavery; a pampering of artificial wants on the one side, a giving-up of every right of leisure by day and quiet rest by night on the other. How far his strong exaggerated feelings had any foundation in truth, it is for you to judge. I am afraid that Mary's determination not to go to service arose from far less sensible thoughts on the subject than her father's. Three years of independence of action (since her mother's death such a time had now elapsed) had little inclined her to submit to rules as to hours and associates, to regulate her dress by a mistress's ideas of propriety, to lose the dear feminine privileges of gossiping with a merry neighbour, and working night and day to help one who was sorrowful. Besides all this, the sayings of her absent, her mysterious aunt, Esther, had an unacknowledged influence over Mary. She knew she was very pretty; the factory people as they poured from the mills, and in their freedom told the truth (whatever it might be) to every passer-by, had early let Mary into the secret of her beauty. If their remarks had fallen on an unheeding ear, there were always young men enough, in a different rank from her own, who were willing to compliment the pretty weaver's daughter as they met her in the streets. Besides, trust a girl of sixteen for knowing well if she is pretty; concerning her plainness she may be ignorant. So with this consciousness she had early determined that her beauty should make her a lady; the rank she coveted the more for her father's abuse; the rank to which she firmly believed her lost aunt Esther had arrived. Now, while a servant must often drudge and be dirty, must be known as a servant by all who visited at her master's house, a dressmaker's apprentice must (or so Mary thought) be always dressed with a certain regard to appearance; must never soil her hands, and need never redden or dirty her face with hard labour. Before my telling you so truly what folly Mary felt or thought, injures her without redemption in your opinion, think what are the silly fancies of sixteen years of age in every class, and under all circumstances. The end of all the thoughts of father and daughter was, as I said before, Mary was to be a dressmaker; and her ambition prompted her unwilling father to apply at all the first establishments, to know on what terms of painstaking and zeal his daughter might be admitted into ever so humble a workwoman's situation. But high premiums were asked at all; poor man! he might have known that without giving up a day's work to ascertain the fact. He would have been indignant, indeed, had he known that if Mary had accompanied him, the case might have been rather different, as her beauty would have made her desirable as a show-woman. Then he tried second-rate places; at all the payment of a sum of money was necessary, and money he had none. Disheartened and angry he went home at night, declaring it was time lost; that dressmaking was at all events a toilsome business, and not worth learning. Mary saw that the grapes were sour, and the next day set out herself, as her father could not afford to lose another day's work; and before night (as yesterday's experience had considerably lowered her ideas) she had engaged herself as apprentice (so called, though there were no deeds or indentures to the bond) to a certain Miss Simmonds, milliner and dressmaker, in a respectable little street leading off Ardwick Green, where her business was duly announced in gold letters on a black ground, enclosed in a bird's-eye maple frame, and stuck in the front parlour window; where the workwomen were called "her young ladies;" and where Mary was to work for two years without any remuneration, on consideration of being taught the business; and where afterwards she was to dine and have tea, with a small quarterly salary (paid quarterly, because so much more genteel than by the week), a *very* small one, divisible into a minute weekly pittance. In summer she was to be there by six, bringing her day's meals during the first two years; in winter she was not to come till after breakfast. Her time for returning home at night must always depend upon the quantity of work Miss Simmonds had to do.

And Mary was satisfied; and seeing this, her father was contented too, although his words were grumbling and morose; but Mary knew his ways, and coaxed and planned for the future so cheerily, that both went to bed with easy if not happy hearts.

CHAPTER IV - OLD ALICE'S HISTORY.

> To envy nought beneath the ample sky;
> To mourn no evil deed, no hour mis-spent;
> And, like a living violet, silently
> Return in sweets to Heaven what goodness lent,
> Then bend beneath the chastening shower content.
>
> ELLIOTT.

Another year passed on. The waves of time seemed long since to have swept away all trace of poor Mary Barton. But her husband still thought of her, although with a calm and quiet grief, in the silent watches of the night: and Mary would start from her hard-earned sleep, and think in her half-dreamy, half-awakened state, she saw her mother stand by her bed-side, as she used to do "in the days of long-ago;" with a shaded candle and an expression of ineffable tenderness, while she looked on her sleeping child. But Mary rubbed her eyes and sank back on her pillow, awake, and knowing it was a dream; and still, in all her troubles and perplexities, her heart called on her mother for aid, and she thought, "If mother had but lived, she would have helped me." Forgetting that the woman's sorrows are far more difficult to mitigate than a child's, even by the mighty power of a mother's love; and unconscious of the fact, that she was far superior in sense and spirit to the mother she mourned. Aunt Esther was still mysteriously absent, and people had grown weary of wondering and began to forget. Barton still attended his club, and was an active member of a trades' union; indeed, more frequently than ever, since the time of Mary's return in the evening was so uncertain; and, as she occasionally, in very busy times, remained all night. His chiefest friend was still George Wilson, although he had no great sympathy on the questions that agitated Barton's mind. Still their hearts were bound by old ties to one another, and the remembrance of former times gave an unspoken charm to their meetings. Our old friend, the cub-like lad, Jem Wilson, had shot up into the powerful, well-made young man, with a sensible face enough; nay, a face that might have been handsome, had it not been here and there marked by the small-pox. He worked with one of the great firms of engineers, who send from out their towns of workshops engines and machinery to the dominions of the Czar and the Sultan. His father and mother were never weary of praising Jem, at all which commendation pretty

Mary Barton would toss her head, seeing clearly enough that they wished her to understand what a good husband he would make, and to favour his love, about which he never dared to speak, whatever eyes and looks revealed.

One day, in the early winter time, when people were provided with warm substantial gowns, not likely soon to wear out, and when, accordingly, business was rather slack at Miss Simmonds', Mary met Alice Wilson, coming home from her half-day's work at some tradesman's house. Mary and Alice had always liked each other; indeed, Alice looked with particular interest on the motherless girl, the daughter of her whose forgiving kiss had so comforted her in many sleepless hours. So there was a warm greeting between the tidy old woman and the blooming young work-girl; and then Alice ventured to ask if she would come in and take her tea with her that very evening.

"You'll think it dull enough to come just to sit with an old woman like me, but there's a tidy young lass as lives in the floor above, who does plain work, and now and then a bit in your own line, Mary; she's grand-daughter to old Job Legh, a spinner, and a good girl she is. Do come, Mary! I've a terrible wish to make you known to each other. She's a genteel-looking lass, too."

At the beginning of this speech Mary had feared the intended visitor was to be no other than Alice's nephew; but Alice was too delicate-minded to plan a meeting, even for her dear Jem, when one would have been an unwilling party; and Mary, relieved from her apprehension by the conclusion, gladly agreed to come. How busy Alice felt! it was not often she had any one to tea; and now her sense of the duties of a hostess were almost too much for her. She made haste home, and lighted the unwilling fire, borrowing a pair of bellows to make it burn the faster. For herself she was always patient; she let the coals take their time. Then she put on her pattens, and went to fill her kettle at the pump in the next court, and on the way she borrowed a cup; of odd saucers she had plenty, serving as plates when occasion required. Half an ounce of tea and a quarter of a pound of butter went far to absorb her morning's wages; but this was an unusual occasion. In general, she used herb-tea for herself, when at home, unless some thoughtful mistress made her a present of tea-leaves from her more abundant household. The two chairs drawn out for visitors, and duly swept and dusted; an old board arranged with some skill upon two old candle-boxes set on end (rather ricketty to be sure, but she knew the seat of old, and when to sit lightly; indeed the whole affair was more for apparent dignity of position than for any real ease); a little, very little round table put just before the fire, which by this time was blazing merrily; her unlackered, ancient, third-hand tea-tray arranged with a black tea-pot, two cups with a red and white pattern, and one with the old friendly willow pattern, and saucers, not to match (on one of the extra supply, the lump of butter flourished away); all these preparations complete, Alice began to look about her with satisfaction, and a sort of wonder what more could be done to add to the comfort of the evening. She took one of the chairs away from its appropriate place by the table, and putting it close to the broad large hanging shelf I told you about when I first described her cellar-dwelling, and mounting on it, she pulled towards her an old deal box, and took thence a quantity of the oat bread of the north, the clap-bread of Cumberland and Westmoreland, and descending carefully with the thin cakes threatening to break to pieces in her hand, she placed them on the bare table, with the belief that her visitors would have an unusual treat in eating the bread of her childhood. She brought out a good piece of a four-pound loaf of common household bread as well, and then sat down to rest, really to rest, and not to pretend, on one of the rush-bottomed chairs. The candle was ready to be lighted, the kettle boiled, the tea was awaiting its doom in its paper parcel; all was ready.

A knock at the door! It was Margaret, the young workwoman who lived in the rooms above, who having heard the bustle, and the subsequent quiet, began to think it was time to pay her visit below. She was a sallow, unhealthy, sweet-looking young woman, with a careworn look; her dress was humble and very simple, consisting of some kind of dark stuff gown, her neck being covered by a drab shawl or large handkerchief, pinned down behind and at the sides in front. The old woman gave her a hearty greeting, and made her sit down on the chair she had just left, while she balanced herself on the board seat, in order that Margaret might think it was quite her free and independent choice to sit there.

"I cannot think what keeps Mary Barton. She's quite grand with her late hours," said Alice, as Mary still delayed.

The truth was, Mary was dressing herself; yes, to come to poor old Alice's—she thought it worth while to consider what gown she should put on. It was not for Alice, however, you may be pretty sure; no, they knew each other too well. But Mary liked making an impression, and in this it must be owned she was pretty often gratified—and there was this strange girl to consider just now. So she put on her pretty new blue merino, made tight to her throat, her little linen collar and linen cuffs, and sallied forth to impress poor gentle Margaret. She certainly succeeded. Alice, who never thought much about beauty, had never told Margaret how pretty Mary was; and, as she came in half-blushing at her own self-consciousness, Margaret could hardly take her eyes off her, and Mary put down her long black lashes with a sort of dislike of the very observation she had taken such pains to secure. Can you fancy the bustle of Alice to make the tea, to pour it out, and sweeten it to their liking, to help and help again to clap-bread and bread-and-butter? Can you fancy the delight with which she watched her piled-up clap-bread disappear before the hungry girls, and listened to the praises of her home-remembered dainty?

"My mother used to send me some clap-bread by any north-country person—bless her! She knew how good such things taste when far away from home. Not but what every one likes it. When I was in service my fellow-servants were always glad to share with me. Eh, it's a long time ago, yon."

"Do tell us about it, Alice," said Margaret.

"Why, lass, there's nothing to tell. There was more mouths at home than could be fed. Tom, that's Will's father (you don't know Will, but he's a sailor to foreign parts), had come to Manchester, and sent word what terrible lots of work was to be had, both for lads and lasses. So father sent George first (you know George, well enough, Mary), and then work was scarce out toward Burton, where we lived, and father said I maun try and get a place. And George wrote as how wages were far higher in Manchester than Milnthorpe or Lancaster; and, lasses, I was young and thoughtless, and thought it was a fine thing to go so far from home. So, one day, th' butcher he brings us a letter fra George, to say he'd heard on a place—and I was all agog to go, and father was pleased, like; but mother said little, and that little was very quiet. I've often thought she was a bit hurt to see me so ready to go—God forgive me! But she packed up my clothes, and some o' the better end of her own as would fit me, in yon little paper box up there—it's good for nought now, but I would liefer live without fire than break it up to be burnt; and yet it's going on for eighty years old, for she had it when she was a girl, and brought all her clothes in it to father's, when they were married. But, as I was saying, she did not cry, though the tears was often in her eyes; and I seen her looking after me down the lane as long as I were in sight, with her hand shading her eyes—and that were the last look I ever had on her."

Alice knew that before long she should go to that mother; and, besides, the griefs and bitter woes of youth have worn themselves out before we grow old; but she looked so sorrowful that the girls caught her sadness, and mourned for the poor woman who had been dead and gone so many years ago.

"Did you never see her again, Alice? Did you never go home while she was alive?" asked Mary.

"No, nor since. Many a time and oft have I planned to go. I plan it yet, and hope to go home again before it please God to take me. I used to try and save money enough to go for a week when I was in service; but first one thing came, and then another. First, missis's children fell ill of the measles, just when th' week I'd ask'd for came, and I couldn't leave them, for one and all cried for me to nurse them. Then missis herself fell sick, and I could go less than ever. For, you see, they kept a little shop, and he drank, and missis and me was all there was to mind children, and shop, and all, and cook and wash besides."

Mary was glad she had not gone into service, and said so.

"Eh, lass! thou little knows the pleasure o' helping others; I was as happy there as could be; almost as happy as I was at home. Well, but next year I thought I could go at a leisure time, and missis telled me I should have a fortnight then, and I used to sit up all that winter working hard at patchwork, to have a quilt of my own making to take to my mother. But master died, and missis went away fra Manchester, and I'd to look out for a place again."

"Well, but," interrupted Mary, "I should have thought that was the best time to go home."

"No, I thought not. You see it was a different thing going home for a week on a visit, may be with money in my pocket to give father a lift, to going home to be a burden to him. Besides, how could I hear o' a place there? Anyways I thought it best to stay, though perhaps it might have been better to ha' gone, for then I should ha' seen mother again;" and the poor old woman looked puzzled.

"I'm sure you did what you thought right," said Margaret, gently.

"Ay, lass, that's it," said Alice, raising her head and speaking more cheerfully. "That's the thing, and then let the Lord send what He sees fit; not but that I grieved sore, oh, sore and sad, when toward spring next year, when my quilt were all done to th' lining, George came in one evening to tell me mother was dead. I cried many a night at after;[1] I'd no time for crying by day, for that missis was terrible strict; she would not hearken to my going to th' funeral; and indeed I would have been too late, for George set off that very night by th' coach, and th' letter had been kept or summut (posts were not like th' posts now-a-days), and he found the burial all over, and father talking o' flitting; for he couldn't abide the cottage after mother was gone."

"Was it a pretty place?" asked Mary.

"Pretty, lass! I never seed such a bonny bit anywhere. You see there are hills there as seem to go up into th' skies, not near may be, but that makes them all the bonnier. I used to think they were the golden hills of heaven, about which my mother sang when I was a child,

'Yon are the golden hills o' heaven,
  Where ye sall never win.'

Something about a ship and a lover that should hae been na lover, the ballad was. Well, and near our cottage were rocks. Eh, lasses! ye don't know what rocks are in Manchester! Gray pieces o' stone as large as a house, all covered over wi' moss of different colours, some yellow, some brown; and the ground beneath them knee-deep in purple heather, smelling sae sweet and fragrant, and the low music of the humming-bee for ever sounding among it. Mother used to send Sally and me out to gather ling and heather for besoms, and it was such pleasant work! We used to come home of an evening loaded so as you could not see us, for all that it was so light to carry. And then mother would make us sit down under the old hawthorn tree (where we used to make our house among the great roots as stood above th' ground), to pick and tie up the heather. It seems all like yesterday, and yet it's a long long time agone. Poor sister Sally has been in her grave this forty year and more. But I often wonder if the hawthorn is standing yet, and if the lasses still go to gather heather, as we did many and many a year past and gone. I sicken at heart to see the old spot once again. May be next summer I may set off, if God spares me to see next summer."

"Why have you never been in all these many years?" asked Mary.

"Why, lass! first one wanted me and then another; and I couldn't go without money either, and I got very poor at times. Tom was a scapegrace, poor fellow, and always wanted help of one kind or another; and his wife (for I think scapegraces are always married long before steady folk) was but a helpless kind of body. She were always ailing, and he were always in trouble; so I had enough to do with my hands and my money too, for that matter. They died within twelve-

---

[1] A common Lancashire phrase. "Come to me, Tyrrel, soon, at after supper." SHAKSPEARE, Richard III.

month of each other, leaving one lad (they had had seven, but the Lord had taken six to Himself), Will, as I was telling you on; and I took him myself, and left service to make a bit on a home-place for him, and a fine lad he was, the very spit of his father as to looks, only steadier. For he was steady, although nought would serve him but going to sea. I tried all I could to set him again a sailor's life. Says I, 'Folks is as sick as dogs all the time they're at sea. Your own mother telled me (for she came from foreign parts, being a Manx woman) that she'd ha thanked any one for throwing her into the water.' Nay, I sent him a' the way to Runcorn by th' Duke's canal, that he might know what th' sea were; and I looked to see him come back as white as a sheet wi' vomiting. But the lad went on to Liverpool and saw real ships, and came back more set than ever on being a sailor, and he said as how he had never been sick at all, and thought he could stand the sea pretty well. So I telled him he mun do as he liked; and he thanked me and kissed me, for all I was very frabbit[1] with him; and now he's gone to South America, at t'other side of the sun, they tell me."

Mary stole a glance at Margaret to see what she thought of Alice's geography; but Margaret looked so quiet and demure, that Mary was in doubt if she were not really ignorant. Not that Mary's knowledge was very profound, but she had seen a terrestrial globe, and knew where to find France and the continents on a map.

After this long talking Alice seemed lost for a time in reverie; and the girls, respecting her thoughts, which they suspected had wandered to the home and scenes of her childhood, were silent. All at once she recalled her duties as hostess, and by an effort brought back her mind to the present time.

"Margaret, thou must let Mary hear thee sing. I don't know about fine music myself, but folks say Margaret is a rare singer, and I know she can make me cry at any time by singing 'Th' Owdham Weaver.' Do sing that, Margaret, there's a good lass."

With a faint smile, as if amused at Alice's choice of a song, Margaret began.

Do you know "The Oldham Weaver?" Not unless you are Lancashire born and bred, for it is a complete Lancashire ditty. I will copy it for you.

THE OLDHAM WEAVER.

I.

Oi'm a poor cotton-weyver, as mony a one knoowas,
Oi've nowt for t' yeat, an' oi've woorn eawt my clooas,
Yo'ad hardly gi' tuppence for aw as oi've on,
My clogs are boath brosten, an' stuckins oi've none,
    Yo'd think it wur hard,
    To be browt into th' warld,
To be—clemmed,[2] an' do th' best as yo con.

---

[1] "Frabbit," peevish.

[2] "Clem," to starve with hunger. "Hard is the choice, when the valiant must eat their arms or clem."—Ben Jonson.

II.

Owd Dicky o' Billy's kept telling me lung,
Wee s'd ha' better toimes if I'd but howd my tung,
Oi've howden my tung, till oi've near stopped my breath,
Oi think i' my heeart oi'se soon clem to deeath,
    Owd Dicky's weel crammed,
    He never wur clemmed,
An' he ne'er picked ower i' his loife.[1]

III.

We tow'rt on six week—thinking aitch day wur th' last,
We shifted, an' shifted, till neaw we're quoite fast;
We lived upo' nettles, whoile nettles wur good,
An' Waterloo porridge the best o' eawr food,
    Oi'm tellin' yo' true,
    Oi can find folk enow,
As wur livin' na better nor me.

IV.

Owd Billy o' Dans sent th' baileys one day,
Fur a shop deebt oi eawd him, as oi could na pay,
But he wur too lat, fur owd Billy o' th' Bent,
Had sowd th' tit an' cart, an' ta'en goods fur th' rent,
    We'd neawt left bo' th' owd stoo',
    That wur seeats fur two,
An' on it ceawred Marget an' me.

V.

Then t' baileys leuked reawnd as sloy as a meawse,
When they seed as aw t' goods were ta'en eawt o' t' heawse,
Says one chap to th' tother, "Aws gone, theaw may see;"
Says oi, "Ne'er freet, mon, yeaur welcome ta' me."
    They made no moor ado
    But whopped up th' eawd stoo',
An' we booath leet, whack—upo' t' flags!

VI.

Then oi said to eawr Marget, as we lay upo' t' floor,
"We's never be lower i' this warld, oi'm sure,

---

[1] To "pick ower," means to throw the shuttle in hand-loom weaving.

If ever things awtern, oi'm sure they mun mend,
For oi think i' my heart we're booath at t' far eend;
For meeat we ha' none;
Nor looms t' weyve on,—
Edad! they're as good lost as fund."

VII.

Eawr Marget declares had hoo cloo'as to put on,
Hoo'd goo up to Lunnon an' talk to th' greet mon;
An' if things were na awtered when there hoo had been,
Hoo's fully resolved t' sew up meawth an' eend;
Hoo's neawt to say again t' king,
But hoo loikes a fair thing,
An' hoo says hoo can tell when hoo's hurt.

The air to which this is sung is a kind of droning recitative, depending much on expression and feeling. To read it, it may, perhaps, seem humorous; but it is that humour which is near akin to pathos, and to those who have seen the distress it describes, it is a powerfully pathetic song. Margaret had both witnessed the destitution, and had the heart to feel it; and withal, her voice was of that rich and rare order, which does not require any great compass of notes to make itself appreciated. Alice had her quiet enjoyment of tears. But Margaret, with fixed eye, and earnest, dreamy look, seemed to become more and more absorbed in realising to herself the woe she had been describing, and which she felt might at that very moment be suffering and hopeless within a short distance of their comparative comfort.

Suddenly she burst forth with all the power of her magnificent voice, as if a prayer from her very heart for all who were in distress, in the grand supplication, "Lord, remember David." Mary held her breath, unwilling to lose a note, it was so clear, so perfect, so imploring. A far more correct musician than Mary might have paused with equal admiration of the really scientific knowledge, with which the poor depressed-looking young needle-woman used her superb and flexile voice. Deborah Travers herself (once an Oldham factory girl, and afterwards the darling of fashionable crowds as Mrs. Knyvett) might have owned a sister in her art.

She stopped; and with tears of holy sympathy in her eyes, Alice thanked the songstress, who resumed her calm, demure manner, much to Mary's wonder, for she looked at her unweariedly, as if surprised that the hidden power should not be perceived in the outward appearance.

When Alice's little speech of thanks was over, there was quiet enough to hear a fine, though rather quavering, male voice, going over again one or two strains of Margaret's song.

"That's grandfather!" exclaimed she. "I must be going, for he said he should not be at home till past nine."

"Well, I'll not say nay, for I've to be up by four for a very heavy wash at Mrs. Simpson's; but I shall be terrible glad to see you again at any time, lasses; and I hope you'll take to one another."

As the girls ran up the cellar steps together, Margaret said: "Just step in and see grandfather. I should like him to see you."

And Mary consented.

CHAPTER V - THE MILL ON FIRE—JEM WILSON TO THE RESCUE.

Learned he was; nor bird, nor insect flew,
But he its leafy home and history knew;
Nor wild-flower decked the rock, nor moss the well,
But he its name and qualities could tell.

ELLIOTT.

There is a class of men in Manchester, unknown even to many of the inhabitants, and whose existence will probably be doubted by many, who yet may claim kindred with all the noble names that science recognises. I said "in Manchester," but they are scattered all over the manufacturing districts of Lancashire. In the neighbourhood of Oldham there are weavers, common hand-loom weavers, who throw the shuttle with unceasing sound, though Newton's "Principia" lie open on the loom, to be snatched at in work hours, but revelled over in meal times, or at night. Mathematical problems are received with interest, and studied with absorbing attention by many a broad-spoken, common-looking, factory-hand. It is perhaps less astonishing that the more popularly interesting branches of natural history have their warm and devoted followers among this class. There are botanists among them, equally familiar with either the Linnæan or the Natural system, who know the name and habitat of every plant within a day's walk from their dwellings; who steal the holiday of a day or two when any particular plant should be in flower, and tying up their simple food in their pocket-handkerchiefs, set off with single purpose to fetch home the humble-looking weed. There are entomologists, who may be seen with a rude-looking net, ready to catch any winged insect, or a kind of dredge, with which they rake the green and slimy pools; practical, shrewd, hard-working men, who pore over every new specimen with real scientific delight. Nor is it the common and more obvious divisions of Entomology and Botany that alone attract these earnest seekers after knowledge. Perhaps it may be owing to the great annual town-holiday of Whitsun-week so often falling in May or June that the two great, beautiful families of Ephemeridæ and Phryganidæ have been so much and so closely studied by Manchester workmen, while they have in a great measure escaped general observation. If you will refer to the preface to Sir

J. E. Smith's Life (I have it not by me, or I would copy you the exact passage), you will find that he names a little circumstance corroborative of what I have said. Sir J. E. Smith, being on a visit to Roscoe, of Liverpool, made some inquiries from him as to the habitat of a very rare plant, said to be found in certain places in Lancashire. Mr. Roscoe knew nothing of the plant; but stated, that if any one could give him the desired information, it would be a hand-loom weaver in Manchester, whom he named. Sir J. E. Smith proceeded by coach to Manchester, and on arriving at that town, he inquired of the porter who was carrying his luggage if he could direct him to So and So.

"Oh, yes," replied the man. "He does a bit in my way;" and, on further investigation, it turned out, that both the porter, and his friend the weaver, were skilful botanists, and able to give Sir J. E. Smith the very information which he wanted.

Such are the tastes and pursuits of some of the thoughtful, little understood, working men of Manchester.

And Margaret's grandfather was one of these. He was a little wiry-looking old man, who moved with a jerking motion, as if his limbs were worked by a string like a child's toy, with dun coloured hair lying thin and soft at the back and sides of his head; his forehead was so large it seemed to overbalance the rest of his face, which had indeed lost its natural contour by the absence of all the teeth. The eyes absolutely gleamed with intelligence; so keen, so observant, you felt as if they were almost wizard-like. Indeed, the whole room looked not unlike a wizard's dwelling. Instead of pictures were hung rude wooden frames of impaled insects; the little table was covered with cabalistic books; and a case of mysterious instruments lay beside, one of which Job Legh was using when his granddaughter entered.

On her appearance he pushed his spectacles up so as to rest midway on his forehead, and gave Mary a short, kind welcome. But Margaret he caressed as a mother caresses her first-born; stroking her with tenderness, and almost altering his voice as he spoke to her.

Mary looked round on the odd, strange things she had never seen at home, and which seemed to her to have a very uncanny look.

"Is your grandfather a fortune-teller?" whispered she to her new friend.

"No," replied Margaret, in the same voice; "but you're not the first as has taken him for such. He is only fond of such things as most folks know nothing about."

"And do you know aught about them, too?"

"I know a bit about some of the things grandfather is fond on; just because he's fond on 'em I tried to learn about them."

"What things are these?" said Mary, struck with the weird looking creatures that sprawled around the room in their roughly-made glass cases.

But she was not prepared for the technical names which Job Legh pattered down on her ear, on which they fell like hail on a skylight; and the strange language only bewildered her more than ever. Margaret saw the state of the case, and came to the rescue.

CHAPTER V - THE MILL ON FIRE—JEM WILSON TO THE RESCUE.

"Look, Mary, at this horrid scorpion. He gave me such a fright: I'm all of a twitter yet when I think of it. Grandfather went to Liverpool one Whitsun-week to go strolling about the docks and pick up what he could from the sailors, who often bring some queer thing or another from the hot countries they go to; and so he sees a chap with a bottle in his hand, like a druggist's physic-bottle; and says grandfather, 'What have ye gotten there?' So the sailor holds it up, and grandfather knew it was a rare kind o' scorpion, not common even in the East Indies where the man came from; and says he, 'How did ye catch this fine fellow, for he wouldn't be taken for nothing I'm thinking?' And the man said as how when they were unloading the ship he'd found him lying behind a bag of rice, and he thought the cold had killed him, for he was not squashed nor injured a bit. He did not like to part with any of the spirit out of his grog to put the scorpion in, but slipped him into the bottle, knowing there were folks enow who would give him something for him. So grandfather gives him a shilling."

"Two shilling," interrupted Job Legh, "and a good bargain it was."

"Well! grandfather came home as proud as Punch, and pulled the bottle out of his pocket. But you see th' scorpion were doubled up, and grandfather thought I couldn't fairly see how big he was. So he shakes him out right before the fire; and a good warm one it was, for I was ironing, I remember. I left off ironing, and stooped down over him, to look at him better, and grandfather got a book, and began to read how this very kind were the most poisonous and vicious species, how their bite were often fatal, and then went on to read how people who were bitten got swelled, and screamed with pain. I was listening hard, but as it fell out, I never took my eyes off the creature, though I could not ha' told I was watching it. Suddenly it seemed to give a jerk, and before I could speak, it gave another, and in a minute it was as wild as could be, running at me just like a mad dog."

"What did you do?" asked Mary.

"Me! why, I jumped first on a chair, and then on all the things I'd been ironing on the dresser, and I screamed for grandfather to come up by me, but he did not hearken to me."

"Why, if I'd come up by thee, who'd ha' caught the creature, I should like to know?"

"Well, I begged grandfather to crush it, and I had the iron right over it once, ready to drop, but grandfather begged me not to hurt it in that way. So I couldn't think what he'd have, for he hopped round the room as if he were sore afraid, for all he begged me not to injure it. At last he goes to th' kettle, and lifts up the lid, and peeps in. What on earth is he doing that for, thinks I; he'll never drink his tea with a scorpion running free and easy about the room. Then he takes the tongs, and he settles his spectacles on his nose, and in a minute he had lifted the creature up by th' leg, and dropped him into the boiling water."

"And did that kill him?" said Mary.

"Ay, sure enough; he boiled for longer time than grandfather liked though. But I was so afeard of his coming round again. I ran to the public-house for some gin, and grandfather filled the bottle, and then we poured off the water, and picked him out of the kettle, and dropped him into the bottle, and he were there above a twelvemonth."

"What brought him to life at first?" asked Mary.

"Why, you see, he were never really dead, only torpid—that is, dead asleep with the cold, and our good fire brought him round."

"I'm glad father does not care for such things," said Mary.

"Are you! Well, I'm often downright glad grandfather is so fond of his books, and his creatures, and his plants. It does my heart good to see him so happy, sorting them all at home, and so ready to go in search of more, whenever he's a spare day. Look at him now! he's gone back to his books, and he'll be as happy as a king, working away till I make him go to bed. It keeps him silent, to be sure; but so long as I see him earnest, and pleased, and eager, what does that matter? Then, when he has his talking bouts, you can't think how much he has to say. Dear grandfather! you don't know how happy we are!"

Mary wondered if the dear grandfather heard all this, for Margaret did not speak in an under tone; but no! he was far too deep and eager in solving a problem. He did not even notice Mary's leave-taking, and she went home with the feeling that she had that night made the acquaintance of two of the strangest people she ever saw in her life. Margaret, so quiet, so common place, until her singing powers were called forth; so silent from home, so cheerful and agreeable at home; and her grandfather so very different to any one Mary had ever seen. Margaret had said he was not a fortune-teller, but she did not know whether to believe her.

To resolve her doubts, she told the history of the evening to her father, who was interested by her account, and curious to see and judge for himself. Opportunities are not often wanting where inclination goes before, and ere the end of that winter Mary looked upon Margaret almost as an old friend. The latter would bring her work when Mary was likely to be at home in the evenings and sit with her; and Job Legh would put a book and his pipe in his pocket and just step round the corner to fetch his grand-child, ready for a talk if he found Barton in; ready to pull out pipe and book if the girls wanted him to wait, and John was still at his club. In short, ready to do whatever would give pleasure to his darling Margaret.

I do not know what points of resemblance (or dissimilitude, for the one joins people as often as the other) attracted the two girls to each other. Margaret had the great charm of possessing good strong common sense, and do you not perceive how involuntarily this is valued? It is so pleasant to have a friend who possesses the power of setting a difficult question in a clear light; whose judgment can tell what is best to be done; and who is so convinced of what is "wisest, best," that in consideration of the end, all difficulties in the way diminish. People admire talent, and talk about their admiration. But they value common sense without talking about it, and often without knowing it.

So Mary and Margaret grew in love one toward the other; and Mary told many of her feelings in a way she had never done before to any one. Most of her foibles also were made known to Margaret, but not all. There was one cherished weakness still concealed from every one. It concerned a lover, not beloved, but favoured by fancy. A gallant, handsome young man; but—not beloved. Yet Mary hoped to meet him every day in her walks, blushed when she heard his name, and tried to think of him as her future husband, and above all, tried to think of herself as his future wife. Alas! poor Mary! Bitter woe did thy weakness work thee.

She had other lovers. One or two would gladly have kept her company, but she held herself too high, they said. Jem Wilson said nothing, but loved on and on, ever more fondly; he hoped against hope; he would not give up, for it seemed like giving up life to give up thought of Mary. He did not dare to look to any end of all this; the present, so that he saw her, touched the hem of her garment, was enough. Surely, in time, such deep love would beget love.

He would not relinquish hope, and yet her coldness of manner was enough to daunt any man; and it made Jem more despairing than he would acknowledge for a long time even to himself.

But one evening he came round by Barton's house, a willing messenger for his father, and opening the door saw Margaret sitting asleep before the fire. She had come in to speak to Mary; and worn out by a long working, watching night, she fell asleep in the genial warmth.

An old-fashioned saying about a pair of gloves came into Jem's mind, and stepping gently up he kissed Margaret with a friendly kiss.

She awoke, and perfectly understanding the thing, she said, "For shame of yourself, Jem! What would Mary say?"

Lightly said, lightly answered.

"She'd nobbut say, practice makes perfect." And they both laughed. But the words Margaret had said rankled in Jem's mind. Would Mary care? Would she care in the very least? They seemed to call for an answer by night, and by day; and Jem felt that his heart told him Mary was quite indifferent to any action of his. Still he loved on, and on, ever more fondly.

Mary's father was well aware of the nature of Jem Wilson's feelings for his daughter, but he took no notice of them to any one, thinking Mary full young yet for the cares of married life, and unwilling, too, to entertain the idea of parting with her at any time, however distant. But he welcomed Jem at his house, as he would have done his father's son, whatever were his motives for coming; and now and then admitted the thought, that Mary might do worse when her time came, than marry Jem Wilson, a steady workman at a good trade, a good son to his parents, and a fine manly spirited chap—at least when Mary was not by: for when she was present he watched her too closely, and too anxiously, to have much of what John Barton called "spunk" in him.

It was towards the end of February, in that year, and a bitter black frost had lasted for many weeks. The keen east wind had long since swept the streets clean, though on a gusty day the dust would rise like pounded ice, and make people's faces quite smart with the cold force with which it blew against them. Houses, sky, people, and every thing looked as if a gigantic brush had washed them all over with a dark shade of Indian ink. There was some reason for this grimy appearance on human beings, whatever there might be for the dun looks of the landscape; for soft water had become an article not even to be purchased; and the poor washerwomen might be seen vainly trying to procure a little by breaking the thick gray ice that coated the ditches and ponds in the neighbourhood. People prophesied a long continuance to this already lengthened frost; said the spring would be very late; no spring fashions required; no summer clothing purchased for a short uncertain summer. Indeed there was no end to the evil prophesied during the continuance of that bleak east wind.

Mary hurried home one evening, just as daylight was fading, from Miss Simmonds', with her shawl held up to her mouth, and her head bent as if in deprecation of the meeting wind. So she did not perceive Margaret till, she was close upon her at the very turning into the court.

"Bless me, Margaret! is that you? Where are you bound to?"

"To nowhere but your own house (that is, if you'll take me in). I've a job of work to finish to-night; mourning, as must be in time for the funeral to-morrow; and grandfather has been out moss-hunting, and will not be home till late."

"Oh, how charming it will be. I'll help you if you're backward. Have you much to do?"

"Yes, I only got the order yesterday at noon; and there's three girls beside the mother; and what with trying on and matching the stuff (for there was not enough in the piece they chose first), I'm above a bit behindhand. I've the skirts all to make. I kept that work till candlelight; and the sleeves, to say nothing of little bits to the bodies; for the missis is very particular, and I could scarce keep from smiling while they were crying so, really taking on sadly I'm sure, to hear first one and then t'other clear up to notice the sit of her gown. They weren't to be misfits I promise you, though they were in such trouble."

"Well, Margaret, you're right welcome as you know, and I'll sit down and help you with pleasure, though I was tired enough of sewing to-night at Miss Simmonds'."

By this time Mary had broken up the raking coal, and lighted her candle; and Margaret settled herself to her work on one side of the table, while her friend hurried over her tea at the other. The things were then lifted *en masse* to the dresser; and dusting her side of the table with the apron she always wore at home, Mary took up some breadths and began to run them together.

"Who's it all for, for if you told me I've forgotten?"

"Why for Mrs. Ogden as keeps the greengrocer's shop in Oxford Road. Her husband drank himself to death, and though she cried over him and his ways all the time he was alive, she's fretted sadly for him now he's dead."

"Has he left her much to go upon?" asked Mary, examining the texture of the dress. "This is beautifully fine soft bombazine."

"No, I'm much afeared there's but little, and there's several young children, besides the three Miss Ogdens."

"I should have thought girls like them would ha' made their own gowns," observed Mary.

"So I dare say they do, many a one, but now they seem all so busy getting ready for the funeral; for it's to be quite a grand affair, well-nigh twenty people to breakfast, as one of the little ones told me; the little thing seemed to like the fuss, and I do believe it comforted poor Mrs. Ogden to make all the piece o' work. Such a smell of ham boiling and fowls roasting while I waited in the kitchen; it seemed more like a wedding nor[1] a funeral. They said she'd spend a matter o' sixty pound on th' burial."

"I thought you said she was but badly off," said Mary.

"Ay, I know she's asked for credit at several places, saying her husband laid hands on every farthing he could get for drink. But th' undertakers urge her on you see, and tell her this thing's usual, and that thing's only a common mark of respect, and that every body has t'other thing, till the poor woman has no will o' her own. I dare say, too, her heart strikes her (it always does when a person's gone) for many a word and many a slighting deed to him, who's stiff and cold; and she thinks to make up matters, as it were, by a grand funeral, though she and all her children, too, may have to pinch many a year to pay the expenses, if ever they pay them at all."

"This mourning, too, will cost a pretty penny," said Mary. "I often wonder why folks wear mourning; it's not pretty or becoming; and it costs a deal of money just when people can spare it least; and if what the Bible tells us be true, we ought not to be sorry when a friend, who's been good, goes to his rest; and as for a bad man, one's glad enough to get shut[2] on him. I cannot see what good comes out o' wearing mourning."

"I'll tell you what I think th' fancy was sent for (Old Alice calls every thing 'sent for,' and I believe she's right). It does do good, though not as much as it costs, that I do believe, in setting people (as is cast down by sorrow and feels themselves unable to settle to any thing but crying) something to do. Why now I told you how they were grieving; for, perhaps, he was a kind husband and father, in his thoughtless way, when he wasn't in liquor. But they cheered up wonderful while I was there, and I asked 'em for more directions than usual, that they might have something to talk over and fix about; and I left 'em my fashion-book (though it were two months old) just a purpose."

"I don't think every one would grieve a that way. Old Alice wouldn't."

"Old Alice is one in a thousand. I doubt, too, if she would fret much, however sorry she might be. She would say it were sent, and fall to trying to find out what good it were to do. Every sorrow in her mind is sent for good. Did I ever tell you, Mary, what she said one day when she found me taking on about something?"

"No; do tell me. What were you fretting about, first place?"

"I can't tell you just now; perhaps I may sometime."

"When?"

---

[1] "Nor," generally used in Lancashire for "than." "They had lever sleep nor be in laundery."—Dunbar.

[2] "Shut," quit.

"Perhaps this very evening, if it rises in my heart; perhaps never. It's a fear that sometimes I can't abide to think about, and sometimes I don't like to think on any thing else. Well, I was fretting about this fear, and Alice comes in for something, and finds me crying. I would not tell her no more than I would you, Mary; so she says, 'Well, dear, you must mind this, when you're going to fret and be low about any thing, "An anxious mind is never a holy mind."' Oh, Mary, I have so often checked my grumbling sin'[1] she said that."

The weary sound of stitching was the only sound heard for a little while, till Mary inquired,

"Do you expect to get paid for this mourning?"

"Why I do not much think I shall. I've thought it over once or twice, and I mean to bring myself to think I shan't, and to like to do it as my bit towards comforting them. I don't think they can pay, and yet they're just the sort of folk to have their minds easier for wearing mourning. There's only one thing I dislike making black for, it does so hurt the eyes."

Margaret put down her work with a sigh, and shaded her eyes. Then she assumed a cheerful tone, and said,

"You'll not have to wait long, Mary, for my secret's on the tip of my tongue. Mary! do you know I sometimes think I'm growing a little blind, and then what would become of grandfather and me? Oh, God help me, Lord help me!"

She fell into an agony of tears, while Mary knelt by her, striving to soothe and to comfort her; but, like an inexperienced person, striving rather to deny the correctness of Margaret's fear, than helping her to meet and overcome the evil.

"No," said Margaret, quietly fixing her tearful eyes on Mary; "I know I'm not mistaken. I have felt one going some time, long before I ever thought what it would lead to; and last autumn I went to a doctor; and he did not mince the matter, but said unless I sat in a darkened room, with my hands before me, my sight would not last me many years longer. But how could I do that, Mary? For one thing, grandfather would have known there was somewhat the matter; and, oh! it will grieve him sore whenever he's told, so the later the better; and besides, Mary, we've sometimes little enough to go upon, and what I earn is a great help. For grandfather takes a day here, and a day there, for botanising or going after insects, and he'll think little enough of four or five shillings for a specimen; dear grandfather! and I'm so loath to think he should be stinted of what gives him such pleasure. So I went to another doctor to try and get him to say something different, and he said, 'Oh, it was only weakness,' and gived me a bottle of lotion; but I've used three bottles (and each of 'em cost two shillings), and my eye is so much worse, not hurting so much, but I can't see a bit with it. There now, Mary," continued she, shutting one eye, "now you only look like a great black shadow, with the edges dancing and sparkling."

"And can you see pretty well with th' other?"

---

[1] "Sin'," since. "Sin that his lord was twenty yere of age." Prologue to Canterbury Tales.

"Yes, pretty near as well as ever. Th' only difference is, that if I sew a long time together, a bright spot like th' sun comes right where I'm looking; all the rest is quite clear but just where I want to see. I've been to both doctors again, and now they're both o' the same story; and I suppose I'm going dark as fast as may be. Plain work pays so bad, and mourning has been so plentiful this winter, I were tempted to take in any black work I could; and now I'm suffering from it."

"And yet, Margaret, you're going on taking it in; that's what you'd call foolish in another."

"It is, Mary! and yet what can I do? Folk mun live; and I think I should go blind any way, and I darn't tell grandfather, else I would leave it off, but he will so fret."

Margaret rocked herself backward and forward to still her emotion.

"Oh Mary!" she said, "I try to get his face off by heart, and I stare at him so when he's not looking, and then shut my eyes to see if I can remember his dear face. There's one thing, Mary, that serves a bit to comfort me. You'll have heard of old Jacob Butterworth, the singing weaver? Well, I know'd him a bit, so I went to him, and said how I wished he'd teach me the right way o' singing; and he says I've a rare fine voice, and I go once a week, and take a lesson fra' him. He's been a grand singer in his day. He's led th' chorusses at the Festivals, and got thanked many a time by London folk; and one foreign singer, Madame Catalani, turned round and shook him by th' hand before the Oud Church[1] full o' people. He says I may gain ever so much money by singing; but I don't know. Any rate it's sad work, being blind."

She took up her sewing, saying her eyes were rested now, and for some time they sewed on in silence.

Suddenly there were steps heard in the little paved court; person after person ran past the curtained window.

"Something's up," said Mary. She went to the door and stopping the first person she saw, inquired the cause of the commotion.

"Eh, wench! donna ye see the fire-light? Carsons' mill is blazing away like fun;" and away her informant ran.

"Come, Margaret, on wi' your bonnet, and let's go to see Carsons' mill; it's afire, and they say a burning mill is such a grand sight. I never saw one."

"Well, I think it's a fearful sight. Besides I've all this work to do."

But Mary coaxed in her sweet manner, and with her gentle caresses, promising to help with the gowns all night long if necessary, nay, saying she should quite enjoy it.

The truth was, Margaret's secret weighed heavily and painfully on her mind, and she felt her inability to comfort; besides, she wanted to change the current of Margaret's thoughts; and in addition to these unselfish feelings, came the desire she had honestly expressed, of seeing a factory on fire.

---

[1] "Old Church;" now the Cathedral of Manchester.

So in two minutes they were ready. At the threshold of the house they met John Barton, to whom they told their errand.

"Carsons' mill! Ay, there is a mill on fire somewhere, sure enough, by the light, and it will be a rare blaze, for there's not a drop o' water to be got. And much Carsons will care, for they're well insured, and the machines are a' th' oud-fashioned kind. See if they don't think it a fine thing for themselves. They'll not thank them as tries to put it out."

He gave way for the impatient girls to pass. Guided by the ruddy light more than by any exact knowledge of the streets that led to the mill, they scampered along with bent heads, facing the terrible east wind as best they might.

Carsons' mill ran lengthways from east to west. Along it went one of the oldest thoroughfares in Manchester. Indeed all that part of the town was comparatively old; it was there that the first cotton mills were built, and the crowded alleys and back streets of the neighbourhood made a fire there particularly to be dreaded. The staircase of the mill ascended from the entrance at the western end, which faced into a wide dingy-looking street, consisting principally of public-houses, pawn-brokers' shops, rag and bone warehouses, and dirty provision shops. The other, the east end of the factory, fronted into a very narrow back street, not twenty feet wide, and miserably lighted and paved. Right against this end of the factory were the gable ends of the last house in the principal street—a house which from its size, its handsome stone facings, and the attempt at ornament in the front, had probably been once a gentleman's house; but now the light which streamed from its enlarged front windows made clear the interior of the splendidly fitted up room, with its painted walls, its pillared recesses, its gilded and gorgeous fittings up, its miserable, squalid inmates. It was a gin palace.

Mary almost wished herself away, so fearful (as Margaret had said) was the sight when they joined the crowd assembled to witness the fire. There was a murmur of many voices whenever the roaring of the flames ceased for an instant. It was easy to perceive the mass were deeply interested.

"What do they say?" asked Margaret, of a neighbour in the crowd, as she caught a few words, clear and distinct, from the general murmur.

"There never is anyone in the mill, surely!" exclaimed Mary, as the sea of upward-turned faces moved with one accord to the eastern end, looking into Dunham Street, the narrow back lane already mentioned.

The western end of the mill, whither the raging flames were driven by the wind, was crowned and turreted with triumphant fire. It sent forth its infernal tongues from every window hole, licking the black walls with amorous fierceness; it was swayed or fell before the mighty gale, only to rise higher and yet higher, to ravage and roar yet more wildly. This part of the roof fell in with an astounding crash, while the crowd struggled more and more to press into Dunham Street, for what were magnificent terrible flames, what were falling timbers or tottering walls, in comparison with human life?

There, where the devouring flames had been repelled by the yet more powerful wind, but where yet black smoke gushed out from every aperture, there, at one of the windows on the fourth story, or rather a doorway where a crane was fixed to hoist up goods, might occasionally be seen, when the thick gusts of smoke cleared partially away for an instant, the imploring figures of two men. They had remained after the rest of the workmen for some reason or other, and, owing to the wind having driven the fire in the opposite direction, had perceived no sight or sound of alarm, till long after (if any thing could be called long in that throng of terrors which passed by in less time than half an hour) the fire had consumed the old wooden staircase at the other end of the building. I am not sure whether it was not the first sound of the rushing crowd below that made them fully aware of their awful position.

"Where are the engines?" asked Margaret of her neighbour.

"They're coming, no doubt; but, bless you, I think it's bare ten minutes since we first found out th' fire; it rages so wi' this wind, and all so dry-like."

"Is no one gone for a ladder?" gasped Mary, as the men were perceptibly, though not audibly, praying the great multitude below for help.

"Ay, Wilson's son and another man were off like a shot, well nigh five minute agone. But th' masons, and slaters, and such like, have left their work, and locked up the yards."

Wilson! then, was that man whose figure loomed out against the ever increasing dull hot light behind, whenever the smoke was clear,—was that George Wilson? Mary sickened with terror. She knew he worked for Carsons; but at first she had had no idea any lives were in danger; and since she had become aware of this, the heated air, the roaring flames, the dizzy light, and the agitated and murmuring crowd, had bewildered her thoughts.

"Oh! let us go home, Margaret; I cannot stay."

"We cannot go! See how we are wedged in by folks. Poor Mary! ye won't hanker after a fire again. Hark! listen!"

For through the hushed crowd, pressing round the angle of the mill, and filling up Dunham Street, might be heard the rattle of the engine, the heavy, quick tread of loaded horses.

"Thank God!" said Margaret's neighbour, "the engine's come."

Another pause; the plugs were stiff, and water could not be got.

Then there was a pressure through the crowd, the front rows bearing back on those behind, till the girls were sick with the close ramming confinement. Then a relaxation, and a breathing freely once more.

"'Twas young Wilson and a fireman wi' a ladder," said Margaret's neighbour, a tall man who could overlook the crowd.

"Oh, tell us what you see?" begged Mary.

"They've gotten it fixed again the gin-shop wall. One o' the men i' th' factory has fell back; dazed wi' the smoke, I'll warrant. The floor's not given way there. God!" said he, bringing his eye lower down, "th' ladder's too short! It's a' over wi' them, poor chaps. Th' fire's coming slow and sure to that end, and afore they've either gotten water, or another ladder, they'll be dead out and out. Lord have mercy on them!"

A sob, as if of excited women, was heard in the hush of the crowd. Another pressure like the former! Mary clung to Margaret's arm with a pinching grasp, and longed to faint, and be insensible, to escape from the oppressing misery of her sensations. A minute or two.

"They've taken th' ladder into th' Temple of Apollor. Can't press back with it to the yard it came from."

A mighty shout arose; a sound to wake the dead. Up on high, quivering in the air, was seen the end of the ladder, protruding out of a garret window, in the gable end of the gin palace, nearly opposite to the doorway where the men had been seen. Those in the crowd nearest the factory, and consequently best able to see up to the garret window, said that several men were holding one end, and guiding by their weight its passage to the door-way. The garret window-frame had been taken out before the crowd below were aware of the attempt.

At length—for it seemed long, measured by beating hearts, though scarce two minutes had elapsed—the ladder was fixed, an aerial bridge at a dizzy height, across the narrow street.

Every eye was fixed in unwinking anxiety, and people's very breathing seemed stilled in suspense. The men were nowhere to be seen, but the wind appeared, for the moment, higher than ever, and drove back the invading flames to the other end.

Mary and Margaret could see now; right above them danced the ladder in the wind. The crowd pressed back from under; firemen's helmets appeared at the window, holding the ladder firm, when a man, with quick, steady tread, and unmoving head, passed from one side to the other. The multitude did not even whisper while he crossed the perilous bridge, which quivered under him; but when he was across, safe comparatively in the factory, a cheer arose for an instant, checked, however, almost immediately, by the uncertainty of the result, and the desire not in any way to shake the nerves of the brave fellow who had cast his life on such a die.

"There he is again!" sprung to the lips of many, as they saw him at the doorway, standing as if for an instant to breathe a mouthful of the fresher air, before he trusted himself to cross. On his shoulders he bore an insensible body.

"It's Jem Wilson and his father," whispered Margaret; but Mary knew it before.

The people were sick with anxious terror. He could no longer balance himself with his arms; every thing must depend on nerve and eye. They saw the latter was fixed, by the position of the head, which never wavered; the ladder shook under the double weight; but still he never moved his head—he dared not look below. It seemed an age before the crossing was accomplished. At last the window was gained; the bearer relieved from his burden; both had disappeared.

Then the multitude might shout; and above the roaring flames, louder than the blowing of the mighty wind, arose that tremendous burst of applause at the success of the daring enterprise. Then a shrill cry was heard, asking

"Is the oud man alive, and likely to do?"

CHAPTER V - THE MILL ON FIRE—JEM WILSON TO THE RESCUE.

"Ay," answered one of the firemen to the hushed crowd below. "He's coming round finely, now he's had a dash of cowd water."

He drew back his head; and the eager inquiries, the shouts, the sea-like murmurs of the moving rolling mass began again to be heard—but for an instant though. In far less time than even that in which I have endeavoured briefly to describe the pause of events, the same bold hero stepped again upon the ladder, with evident purpose to rescue the man yet remaining in the burning mill.

He went across in the same quick steady manner as before, and the people below, made less acutely anxious by his previous success, were talking to each other, shouting out intelligence of the progress of the fire at the other end of the factory, telling of the endeavours of the firemen at that part to obtain water, while the closely packed body of men heaved and rolled from side to side. It was different from the former silent breathless hush. I do not know if it were from this cause, or from the recollection of peril past, or that he looked below, in the breathing moment before returning with the remaining person (a slight little man) slung across his shoulders, but Jem Wilson's step was less steady, his tread more uncertain; he seemed to feel with his foot for the next round of the ladder, to waver, and finally to stop half-way. By this time the crowd was still enough; in the awful instant that intervened no one durst speak, even to encourage. Many turned sick with terror, and shut their eyes to avoid seeing the catastrophe they dreaded. It came. The brave man swayed from side to side, at first as slightly as if only balancing himself; but he was evidently losing nerve, and even sense: it was only wonderful how the animal instinct of self-preservation did not overcome every generous feeling, and impel him at once to drop the helpless, inanimate body he carried; perhaps the same instinct told him, that the sudden loss of so heavy a weight would of itself be a great and imminent danger.

"Help me! she's fainted," cried Margaret. But no one heeded. All eyes were directed upwards. At this point of time a rope, with a running noose, was dexterously thrown by one of the firemen, after the manner of a lasso, over the head and round the bodies of the two men. True, it was with rude and slight adjustment: but, slight as it was, it served as a steadying guide; it encouraged the sinking heart, the dizzy head. Once more Jem stepped onwards. He was not hurried by any jerk or pull. Slowly and gradually the rope was hauled in, slowly and gradually did he make the four or five paces between him and safety. The window was gained, and all were saved. The multitude in the street absolutely danced with triumph, and huzzaed and yelled till you would have fancied their very throats would crack; and then with all the fickleness of interest characteristic of a large body of people, pressed and stumbled, and cursed and swore in the hurry to get out of Dunham Street, and back to the immediate scene of the fire, the mighty diapason of whose roaring flames formed an awful accompaniment to the screams, and yells, and imprecations, of the struggling crowd.

As they pressed away, Margaret was left, pale and almost sinking under the weight of Mary's body, which she had preserved in an upright position by keeping her arms tight round Mary's waist, dreading, with reason, the trampling of unheeding feet.

Now, however, she gently let her down on the cold clean pavement; and the change of posture, and the difference in temperature, now that the people had withdrawn from their close neighbourhood, speedily restored her to consciousness.

Her first glance was bewildered and uncertain. She had forgotten where she was. Her cold, hard bed felt strange; the murky glare in the sky affrighted her. She shut her eyes to think, to recollect.

Her next look was upwards. The fearful bridge had been withdrawn; the window was unoccupied.

"They are safe," said Margaret.

"All? Are all safe, Margaret?" asked Mary.

"Ask yon fireman, and he'll tell you more about it than I can. But I know they're all safe."

The fireman hastily corroborated Margaret's words.

"Why did you let Jem Wilson go twice?" asked Margaret.

"Let!—why we could not hinder him. As soon as ever he'd heard his father speak (which he was na long a doing), Jem were off like a shot; only saying he knowed better nor us where to find t'other man. We'd all ha' gone, if he had na been in such a hurry, for no one can say as Manchester firemen is ever backward when there's danger."

So saying, he ran off; and the two girls, without remark or discussion, turned homewards. They were overtaken by the elder Wilson, pale, grimy, and blear-eyed, but apparently as strong and well as ever. He loitered a minute or two alongside of them, giving an account of his detention in the mill; he then hastily wished good-night, saying he must go home and tell his missis he was all safe and well: but after he had gone a few steps, he turned back, came on Mary's side of the pavement, and in an earnest whisper, which Margaret could not avoid hearing, he said,

"Mary, if my boy comes across you to-night, give him a kind word or two for my sake. Do! bless you, there's a good wench."

Mary hung her head and answered not a word, and in an instant he was gone.

When they arrived at home, they found John Barton smoking his pipe, unwilling to question, yet very willing to hear all the details they could give him. Margaret went over the whole story, and it was amusing to watch his gradually increasing interest and excitement. First, the regular puffing abated, then ceased. Then the pipe was fairly taken out of his mouth, and held suspended. Then he rose, and at every further point he came a step nearer to the narrator.

When it was ended, he swore (an unusual thing for him) that if Jem Wilson wanted Mary he should have her to-morrow, if he had not a penny to keep her.

Margaret laughed, but Mary, who was now recovered from her agitation, pouted, and looked angry.

CHAPTER V - THE MILL ON FIRE—JEM WILSON TO THE RESCUE.

The work which they had left was resumed: but with full hearts, fingers never go very quickly; and I am sorry to say, that owing to the fire, the two younger Miss Ogdens were in such grief for the loss of their excellent father, that they were unable to appear before the little circle of sympathising friends gathered together to comfort the widow, and see the funeral set off.

CHAPTER VI - POVERTY AND DEATH.

"How little can the rich man know
   Of what the poor man feels,
When Want, like some dark dæmon foe,
   Nearer and nearer steals!
He never tramp'd the weary round,
   A stroke of work to gain,
And sicken'd at the dreaded sound
   Telling him 'twas in vain.
Foot-sore, heart-sore, *he* never came
   Back through the winter's wind,
To a dark cellar, there no flame,
   No light, no food, to find.
He never saw his darlings lie
   Shivering, the flags their bed;
He never heard that maddening cry,
   'Daddy, a bit of bread!'"

MANCHESTER SONG.

John Barton was not far wrong in his idea that the Messrs. Carson would not be over much grieved for the consequences of the fire in their mill. They were well insured; the machinery lacked the improvements of late years, and worked but poorly in comparison with that which might now be procured. Above all, trade was very slack; cottons could find no market, and goods lay packed and piled in many a warehouse. The mills were merely worked to keep the machinery, human and metal, in some kind of order and readiness for better times. So this was an excellent opportunity, Messrs. Carson thought, for refitting their factory with first-rate improvements, for which the insurance money would amply pay. They were in no hurry about the business, however. The weekly drain of wages given for labour, useless in the present state of the market, was stopped. The partners had more leisure than they had known for years; and promised wives and daughters all manner of pleasant excursions, as soon as the weather should become more genial. It was a pleasant thing to be able to lounge over breakfast with a review or newspaper in hand; to have time for becoming acquainted with agreeable and accomplished daughters, on whose education no money had been spared, but whose fathers, shut up during a long day with calicoes and accounts, had so seldom had leisure to enjoy their daughters' talents. There were happy family evenings, now that the men of business had time for domestic enjoyments. There is another side to the picture. There were homes over which Carsons' fire threw a deep, terrible gloom; the homes of those who would fain work, and no man gave unto them—the homes of those to whom leisure was a curse. There, the family music was hungry wails, when week after week passed by, and there was no work to be had, and consequently no wages to pay for the bread the children cried aloud for in their young impatience of suffering. There was no breakfast to lounge over; their lounge was taken in bed, to try and keep warmth in them that bitter March weather, and, by being quiet, to deaden the gnawing wolf within. Many a penny that would have gone little way enough in oatmeal or potatoes, bought opium to still the hungry little ones, and make them forget their uneasiness in heavy troubled sleep. It was mother's mercy. The evil and the good of our nature came out strongly then. There were desperate fathers; there were bitter-tongued mothers (O God! what wonder!); there were reckless children; the very closest bonds of nature were snapt in that time of trial and distress. There was Faith such as the rich can never imagine on earth; there was "Love strong as death;" and self-denial, among rude, coarse men, akin to that of Sir Philip Sidney's most glorious deed. The vices of the poor sometimes astound us *here*; but when the secrets of all hearts shall be made known, their virtues will astound us in far greater degree. Of this I am certain.

As the cold bleak spring came on (spring, in name alone), and consequently as trade continued dead, other mills shortened hours, turned off hands, and finally stopped work altogether.

Barton worked short hours; Wilson, of course, being a hand in Carsons' factory, had no work at all. But his son, working at an engineer's, and a steady man, obtained wages enough to maintain all the family in a careful way. Still it preyed on Wilson's mind to be so long indebted to his son. He was out of spirits and depressed. Barton was morose, and soured towards mankind as a body, and the rich in particular. One evening, when the clear light at six o'clock contrasted strangely with the Christmas cold, and when the bitter wind piped down every entry, and through every cranny, Barton sat brooding over his stinted fire, and listening for Mary's step, in unacknowledged trust that her presence would cheer him. The door was opened, and Wilson came breathless in.

"You've not got a bit o' money by you, Barton?" asked he.

"Not I; who has now, I'd like to know. Whatten you want it for?"

"I donnot[1] want it for mysel, tho' we've none to spare. But don ye know Ben Davenport as worked at Carsons'? He's down wi' the fever, and ne'er a stick o' fire, nor a cowd[2] potato in the house."

"I han got no money, I tell ye," said Barton. Wilson looked disappointed. Barton tried not to be interested, but he could not help it in spite of his gruffness. He rose, and went to the cupboard (his wife's pride long ago). There lay the remains of his dinner, hastily put by ready for supper. Bread, and a slice of cold fat boiled bacon. He wrapped them in his handkerchief, put them in the crown of his hat, and said—"Come, let's be going."

"Going—art thou going to work this time o' day?"

"No, stupid, to be sure not. Going to see the fellow thou spoke on." So they put on their hats and set out. On the way Wilson said Davenport was a good fellow, though too much of the Methodee; that his children were too young to work, but not too young to be cold and hungry; that they had sunk lower and lower, and pawned thing after thing, and that now they lived in a cellar in Berry Street, off Store Street. Barton growled inarticulate words of no benevolent import to a large class of mankind, and so they went along till they arrived in Berry Street. It was unpaved; and down the middle a gutter forced its way, every now and then forming pools in the holes with which the street abounded. Never was the Old Edinburgh cry of "Gardez l'eau" more necessary than in this street. As they passed, women from their doors tossed household slops of *every* description into the gutter; they ran into the next pool, which overflowed and stagnated. Heaps of ashes were the stepping-stones, on which the passer-by, who cared in the least for cleanliness, took care not to put his foot. Our friends were not dainty, but even they picked their way till they got to some steps leading down into a small area, where a person standing would have his head about one foot below the level of the street, and might at the same time, without the least motion of his body, touch the window of the cellar and the damp muddy wall right opposite. You went down one step even from the foul area into the cellar in which a family of human beings lived. It was very dark inside. The window-panes were, many of them, broken and stuffed with rags, which was reason enough for the dusky light that pervaded the place even at mid-day. After the account I have given of the state of the street, no one can be surprised that on going into the cellar inhabited by Davenport, the smell was so fœtid as almost to knock the two men down. Quickly recovering themselves, as those inured to such things do, they began to penetrate the thick darkness of the place, and to see three or four little children rolling on the damp, nay wet, brick floor, through which the stagnant, filthy moisture of the street oozed up; the fire-place was empty and black; the wife sat on her husband's lair, and cried in the dank loneliness.

---

[1] "Don" is constantly used in Lancashire for "do;" as it was by our older writers. "And that may non Hors don."—Sir J. Mondeville. "But for th' entent to don this sinne."—Chaucer.

[2] "Cowd," cold. Teut., kaud. Dutch, koud.

"See, missis, I'm back again.—Hold your noise, children, and don't mither[1] your mammy for bread; here's a chap as has got some for you."

In that dim light, which was darkness to strangers, they clustered round Barton, and tore from him the food he had brought with him. It was a large hunch of bread, but it vanished in an instant.

"We mun do summut for 'em," said he to Wilson. "Yo stop here, and I'll be back in half-an-hour."

So he strode, and ran, and hurried home. He emptied into the ever-useful pocket-handkerchief the little meal remaining in the mug. Mary would have her tea at Miss Simmonds'; her food for the day was safe. Then he went up-stairs for his better coat, and his one, gay, red-and-yellow silk pocket-handkerchief—his jewels, his plate, his valuables, these were. He went to the pawn-shop; he pawned them for five shillings; he stopped not, nor stayed, till he was once more in London Road, within five minutes' walk of Berry Street—then he loitered in his gait, in order to discover the shops he wanted. He bought meat, and a loaf of bread, candles, chips, and from a little retail yard he purchased a couple of hundredweights of coals. Some money yet remained—all destined for them, but he did not yet know how best to spend it. Food, light, and warmth, he had instantly seen were necessary; for luxuries he would wait. Wilson's eyes filled with tears when he saw Barton enter with his purchases. He understood it all, and longed to be once more in work, that he might help in some of these material ways, without feeling that he was using his son's money. But though "silver and gold he had none," he gave heart-service and love works of far more value. Nor was John Barton behind in these. "The fever" was (as it usually is in Manchester) of a low, putrid, typhoid kind; brought on by miserable living, filthy neighbourhood, and great depression of mind and body. It is virulent, malignant, and highly infectious. But the poor are fatalists with regard to infection; and well for them it is so, for in their crowded dwellings no invalid can be isolated. Wilson asked Barton if he thought he should catch it, and was laughed at for his idea.

The two men, rough, tender nurses as they were, lighted the fire, which smoked and puffed into the room as if it did not know the way up the damp, unused chimney. The very smoke seemed purifying and healthy in the thick clammy air. The children clamoured again for bread; but this time Barton took a piece first to the poor, helpless, hopeless woman, who still sat by the side of her husband, listening to his anxious miserable mutterings. She took the bread, when it was put into her hand, and broke a bit, but could not eat. She was past hunger. She fell down on the floor with a heavy unresisting bang. The men looked puzzled. "She's well-nigh clemmed," said Barton. "Folk do say one mustn't give clemmed people much to eat; but, bless us, she'll eat nought."

"I'll tell yo what I'll do," said Wilson. "I'll take these two big lads, as does nought but fight, home to my missis's for to-night, and I'll get a jug o' tea. Them women always does best with tea and such-like slop."

---

[1] "Mither," to trouble and perplex. "I'm welly mithered"—I'm well nigh crazed.

So Barton was now left alone with a little child, crying (when it had done eating) for mammy; with a fainting, dead-like woman; and with the sick man, whose mutterings were rising up to screams and shrieks of agonised anxiety. He carried the woman to the fire, and chafed her hands. He looked around for something to raise her head. There was literally nothing but some loose bricks. However, those he got; and taking off his coat he covered them with it as well as he could. He pulled her feet to the fire, which now began to emit some faint heat. He looked round for water, but the poor woman had been too weak to drag herself out to the distant pump, and water there was none. He snatched the child, and ran up the area-steps to the room above, and borrowed their only saucepan with some water in it. Then he began, with the useful skill of a working-man, to make some gruel; and when it was hastily made he seized a battered iron table-spoon (kept when many other little things had been sold in a lot), in order to feed baby, and with it he forced one or two drops between her clenched teeth. The mouth opened mechanically to receive more, and gradually she revived. She sat up and looked round; and recollecting all, fell down again in weak and passive despair. Her little child crawled to her, and wiped with its fingers the thick-coming tears which she now had strength to weep. It was now high time to attend to the man. He lay on straw, so damp and mouldy no dog would have chosen it in preference to flags; over it was a piece of sacking, coming next to his worn skeleton of a body; above him was mustered every article of clothing that could be spared by mother or children this bitter weather; and in addition to his own, these might have given as much warmth as one blanket, could they have been kept on him; but as he restlessly tossed to and fro, they fell off and left him shivering in spite of the burning heat of his skin. Every now and then he started up in his naked madness, looking like the prophet of woe in the fearful plague-picture; but he soon fell again in exhaustion, and Barton found he must be closely watched, lest in these falls he should injure himself against the hard brick floor. He was thankful when Wilson re-appeared, carrying in both hands a jug of steaming tea, intended for the poor wife; but when the delirious husband saw drink, he snatched at it with animal instinct, with a selfishness he had never shown in health.

Then the two men consulted together. It seemed decided, without a word being spoken on the subject, that both should spend the night with the forlorn couple; that was settled. But could no doctor be had? In all probability, no; the next day an infirmary order might be begged, but meanwhile the only medical advice they could have must be from a druggist's. So Barton (being the moneyed man) set out to find a shop in London Road.

It is a pretty sight to walk through a street with lighted shops; the gas is so brilliant, the display of goods so much more vividly shown than by day, and of all shops a druggist's looks the most like the tales of our childhood, from Aladdin's garden of enchanted fruits to the charming Rosamond with her purple jar. No such associations had Barton; yet he felt the contrast between the well-filled, well-lighted shops and the dim gloomy cellar, and it made him moody that such contrasts should exist. They are the mysterious problem of life to more than him.

He wondered if any in all the hurrying crowd had come from such a house of mourning. He thought they all looked joyous, and he was angry with them. But he could not, you cannot, read the lot of those who daily pass you by in the street. How do you know the wild romances of their lives; the trials, the temptations they are even now enduring, resisting, sinking under? You may be elbowed one instant by the girl desperate in her abandonment, laughing in mad merriment with her outward gesture, while her soul is longing for the rest of the dead, and bringing itself to think of the cold-flowing river as the only mercy of God remaining to her here. You may pass the criminal, meditating crimes at which you will to-morrow shudder with horror as you read them. You may push against one, humble and unnoticed, the last upon earth, who in Heaven will for ever be in the immediate light of God's countenance. Errands of mercy—errands of sin—did you ever think where all the thousands of people you daily meet are bound? Barton's was an errand of mercy; but the thoughts of his heart were touched by sin, by bitter hatred of the happy, whom he, for the time, confounded with the selfish.

He reached a druggist's shop, and entered. The druggist (whose smooth manners seemed to have been salved over with his own spermaceti) listened attentively to Barton's description of Davenport's illness; concluded it was typhus fever, very prevalent in that neighbourhood; and proceeded to make up a bottle of medicine, sweet spirits of nitre, or some such innocent potion, very good for slight colds, but utterly powerless to stop, for an instant, the raging fever of the poor man it was intended to relieve. He recommended the same course they had previously determined to adopt, applying the next morning for an infirmary order; and Barton left the shop with comfortable faith in the physic given him; for men of his class, if they believe in physic at all, believe that every description is equally efficacious.

Meanwhile, Wilson had done what he could at Davenport's home. He had soothed, and covered the man many a time; he had fed and hushed the little child, and spoken tenderly to the woman, who lay still in her weakness and her weariness. He had opened a door, but only for an instant; it led into a back cellar, with a grating instead of a window, down which dropped the moisture from pigsties, and worse abominations. It was not paved; the floor was one mass of bad smelling mud. It had never been used, for there was not an article of furniture in it; nor could a human being, much less a pig, have lived there many days. Yet the "back apartment" made a difference in the rent. The Davenports paid threepence more for having two rooms. When he turned round again, he saw the woman suckling the child from her dry, withered breast.

"Surely the lad is weaned!" exclaimed he, in surprise. "Why, how old is he?"

"Going on two year," she faintly answered. "But, oh! it keeps him quiet when I've nought else to gi' him, and he'll get a bit of sleep lying there, if he's getten[1]

[1] "For he had geten him yet no benefice."—Prologue to Canterbury Tales.

nought beside. We han done our best to gi' the childer[1] food, howe'er we pinched ourselves."

"Han[2] ye had no money fra th' town?"

"No; my master is Buckinghamshire born; and he's feared the town would send him back to his parish, if he went to th' board; so we've just borne on in hope o' better times. But I think they'll never come in my day;" and the poor woman began her weak high-pitched cry again.

"Here, sup[3] this drop o' gruel, and then try and get a bit o' sleep. John and I'll watch by your master to-night."

"God's blessing be on you!"

She finished the gruel, and fell into a deep sleep. Wilson covered her with his coat as well as he could, and tried to move lightly for fear of disturbing her; but there need have been no such dread, for her sleep was profound and heavy with exhaustion. Once only she roused to pull the coat round her little child.

And now all Wilson's care, and Barton's to boot, was wanted to restrain the wild mad agony of the fevered man. He started up, he yelled, he seemed infuriated by overwhelming anxiety. He cursed and swore, which surprised Wilson, who knew his piety in health, and who did not know the unbridled tongue of delirium. At length he seemed exhausted, and fell asleep; and Barton and Wilson drew near the fire, and talked together in whispers. They sat on the floor, for chairs there were none; the sole table was an old tub turned upside-down. They put out the candle and conversed by the flickering fire-light.

"Han yo known this chap long?" asked Barton.

"Better nor three year. He's worked wi' Carsons that long, and were alway a steady, civil-spoken fellow, though, as I said afore, somewhat of a Methodee. I wish I'd gotten a letter he sent his missis, a week or two agone, when he were on tramp for work. It did my heart good to read it; for, yo see, I were a bit grumbling mysel; it seemed hard to be spunging on Jem, and taking a' his flesh-meat money to buy bread for me and them as I ought to be keeping. But, yo know, though I can earn nought, I mun eat summut. Well, as I telled ye, I were grumbling, when she (indicating the sleeping woman by a nod) brought me Ben's letter, for she could na read hersel. It were as good as Bible-words; ne'er a word o' repining; a' about God being our Father, and that we mun bear patiently whate'er He sends."

"Don ye think He's th' masters' Father, too? I'd be loath to have 'em for brothers."

"Eh, John! donna talk so; sure there's many and many a master as good or better nor us."

"If you think so, tell me this. How comes it they're rich, and we're poor? I'd like to know that. Han they done as they'd be done by for us?"

---

[1] Wicklife uses "childre" in his Apology, page 26.

[2] "What concord han light and dark."—Spenser.

[3] "And thay soupe the brothe thereof."—Sir J. Mandeville.

But Wilson was no arguer; no speechifier as he would have called it. So Barton, seeing he was likely to have it his own way, went on.

"You'll say (at least many a one does), they'n[1] getten capital an' we'n getten none. I say, our labour's our capital and we ought to draw interest on that. They get interest on their capital somehow a' this time, while ourn is lying idle, else how could they all live as they do? Besides, there's many on 'em as had nought to begin wi'; there's Carsons, and Duncombes, and Mengies, and many another, as comed into Manchester with clothes to their back, and that were all, and now they're worth their tens of thousands, a' getten out of our labour; why the very land as fetched but sixty pound twenty year agone is now worth six hundred, and that, too, is owing to our labour: but look at yo, and see me, and poor Davenport yonder; whatten better are we? They'n screwed us down to th' lowest peg, in order to make their great big fortunes, and build their great big houses, and we, why we're just clemming, many and many of us. Can you say there's nought wrong in this?"

"Well, Barton, I'll not gainsay ye. But Mr. Carson spoke to me after th' fire, and says he, 'I shall ha' to retrench, and be very careful in my expenditure during these bad times, I assure ye;' so yo see th' masters suffer too."

"Han they ever seen a child o' their'n die for want o' food?" asked Barton, in a low, deep voice.

"I donnot mean," continued he, "to say as I'm so badly off. I'd scorn to speak for mysel; but when I see such men as Davenport there dying away, for very clemming, I cannot stand it. I've but gotten Mary, and she keeps hersel pretty much. I think we'll ha' to give up house-keeping; but that I donnot mind."

And in this kind of talk the night, the long heavy night of watching, wore away. As far as they could judge, Davenport continued in the same state, although the symptoms varied occasionally. The wife slept on, only roused by a cry of her child now and then, which seemed to have power over her, when far louder noises failed to disturb her. The watchers agreed, that as soon as it was likely Mr. Carson would be up and visible, Wilson should go to his house, and beg for an Infirmary order. At length the gray dawn penetrated even into the dark cellar. Davenport slept, and Barton was to remain there until Wilson's return; so stepping out into the fresh air, brisk and reviving, even in that street of abominations, Wilson took his way to Mr. Carson's.

Wilson had about two miles to walk before he reached Mr. Carson's house, which was almost in the country. The streets were not yet bustling and busy. The shopmen were lazily taking down the shutters, although it was near eight o'clock; for the day was long enough for the purchases people made in that quarter of the town, while trade was so flat. One or two miserable-looking women were setting off on their day's begging expedition. But there were few people abroad. Mr. Carson's was a good house, and furnished with disregard to expense. But in addition to lavish expenditure, there was much taste shown, and many articles chosen for

[1] "They'n," contraction of "they han," they have.

their beauty and elegance adorned his rooms. As Wilson passed a window which a housemaid had thrown open, he saw pictures and gilding, at which he was tempted to stop and look; but then he thought it would not be respectful. So he hastened on to the kitchen door. The servants seemed very busy with preparations for breakfast; but good-naturedly, though hastily, told him to step in, and they could soon let Mr. Carson know he was there. So he was ushered into a kitchen hung round with glittering tins, where a roaring fire burnt merrily, and where numbers of utensils hung round, at whose nature and use Wilson amused himself by guessing. Meanwhile, the servants bustled to and fro; an out-door man-servant came in for orders, and sat down near Wilson; the cook broiled steaks, and the kitchen-maid toasted bread, and boiled eggs.

The coffee steamed upon the fire, and altogether the odours were so mixed and appetising, that Wilson began to yearn for food to break his fast, which had lasted since dinner the day before. If the servants had known this, they would have willingly given him meat and bread in abundance; but they were like the rest of us, and not feeling hunger themselves, forgot it was possible another might. So Wilson's craving turned to sickness, while they chattered on, making the kitchen's free and keen remarks upon the parlour.

"How late you were last night, Thomas!"

"Yes, I was right weary of waiting; they told me to be at the rooms by twelve; and there I was. But it was two o'clock before they called me."

"And did you wait all that time in the street?" asked the housemaid, who had done her work for the present, and come into the kitchen for a bit of gossip.

"My eye as like! you don't think I'm such a fool as to catch my death of cold, and let the horses catch their death too, as we should ha' done if we'd stopped there. No! I put th' horses up in th' stables at th' Spread Eagle, and went mysel, and got a glass or two by th' fire. They're driving a good custom, them, wi' coachmen. There were five on us, and we'd many a quart o' ale, and gin wi' it, to keep out cold."

"Mercy on us, Thomas; you'll get a drunkard at last!"

"If I do, I know whose blame it will be. It will be missis's, and not mine. Flesh and blood can't sit to be starved to death on a coach-box, waiting for folks as don't know their own mind."

A servant, semi-upper-housemaid, semi-lady's-maid, now came down with orders from her mistress.

"Thomas, you must ride to the fishmonger's, and say missis can't give above half-a-crown a pound for salmon for Tuesday; she's grumbling because trade's so bad. And she'll want the carriage at three to go to the lecture, Thomas; at the Royal Execution, you know."

"Ay, ay, I know."

"And you'd better all of you mind your P's and Q's, for she's very black this morning. She's got a bad headache."

"It's a pity Miss Jenkins is not here to match her. Lord! how she and missis did quarrel which had got the worst headaches; it was that Miss Jenkins left for; she would not give up having bad headaches, and missis could not abide any one to have 'em but herself."

"Missis will have her breakfast up-stairs, cook, and the cold partridge as was left yesterday, and put plenty of cream in her coffee, and she thinks there's a roll left, and she would like it well buttered."

So saying, the maid left the kitchen to be ready to attend to the young ladies' bell when they chose to ring, after their late assembly the night before.

In the luxurious library, at the well-spread breakfast-table, sat the two Mr. Carsons, father and son. Both were reading; the father a newspaper, the son a review, while they lazily enjoyed their nicely prepared food. The father was a prepossessing-looking old man; perhaps self-indulgent you might guess. The son was strikingly handsome, and knew it. His dress was neat and well appointed, and his manners far more gentlemanly than his father's. He was the only son, and his sisters were proud of him; his father and mother were proud of him: he could not set up his judgment against theirs; he was proud of himself.

The door opened and in bounded Amy, the sweet youngest daughter of the house, a lovely girl of sixteen, fresh and glowing, and bright as a rosebud. She was too young to go to assemblies, at which her father rejoiced, for he had little Amy with her pretty jokes, and her bird-like songs, and her playful caresses all the evening to amuse him in his loneliness; and she was not too much tired, like Sophy and Helen, to give him her sweet company at breakfast the next morning.

He submitted willingly while she blinded him with her hands, and kissed his rough red face all over. She took his newspaper away after a little pretended resistance, and would not allow her brother Harry to go on with his review.

"I'm the only lady this morning, papa, so you know you must make a great deal of me."

"My darling, I think you have your own way always, whether you're the only lady or not."

"Yes, papa, you're pretty good and obedient, I must say that; but I'm sorry to say Harry is very naughty, and does not do what I tell him; do you, Harry?"

"I'm sure I don't know what you mean to accuse me of, Amy; I expected praise and not blame; for did not I get you that eau de Portugal from town, that you could not meet with at Hughes', you little ungrateful puss?"

"Did you! Oh, sweet Harry; you're as sweet as eau de Portugal yourself; you're almost as good as papa; but still you know you did go and forget to ask Bigland for that rose, that new rose they say he has got."

"No, Amy, I did not forget. I asked him, and he has got the Rose, *sans reproche*; but do you know, little Miss Extravagance, a very small one is half-a-guinea?"

"Oh, I don't mind. Papa will give it me, won't you, dear father? He knows his little daughter can't live without flowers and scents."

Mr. Carson tried to refuse his darling, but she coaxed him into acquiescence, saying she must have it, it was one of her necessaries. Life was not worth having without flowers.

"Then, Amy," said her brother, "try and be content with peonies and dandelions."

"Oh, you wretch! I don't call them flowers. Besides, you're every bit as extravagant. Who gave half-a-crown for a bunch of lilies of the valley at Yates', a month ago, and then would not let his poor little sister have them, though she went on her knees to beg them? Answer me that, Master Hal."

"Not on compulsion," replied her brother, smiling with his mouth, while his eyes had an irritated expression, and he went first red, then pale, with vexed embarrassment.

"If you please, sir," said a servant, entering the room, "here's one of the mill people wanting to see you; his name is Wilson, he says."

"I'll come to him directly; stay, tell him to come in here."

Amy danced off into the conservatory which opened out of the room, before the gaunt, pale, unwashed, unshaven weaver was ushered in. There he stood at the door, sleeking his hair with old country habit, and every now and then stealing a glance round at the splendour of the apartment.

"Well, Wilson, and what do you want to-day, man?"

"Please, sir, Davenport's ill of the fever, and I'm come to know if you've got an Infirmary order for him?"

"Davenport—Davenport; who is the fellow? I don't know the name."

"He's worked in your factory better nor three year, sir."

"Very likely; I don't pretend to know the names of the men I employ; that I leave to the overlooker. So he's ill, eh?"

"Ay, sir, he's very bad; we want to get him in at the fever wards.

"I doubt if I have an in-patient's order to spare; they're always wanted for accidents, you know. But I'll give you an out-patient's, and welcome."

So saying, he rose up, unlocked a drawer, pondered a minute, and then gave Wilson an out-patient's order to be presented the following Monday. Monday! How many days there were before Monday!

Meanwhile, the younger Mr. Carson had ended his review, and began to listen to what was going on. He finished his breakfast, got up, and pulled five shillings out of his pocket, which he gave to Wilson as he passed him, for the "poor fellow." He went past quickly, and calling for his horse, mounted gaily, and rode away. He was anxious to be in time to have a look and a smile from lovely Mary Barton, as she went to Miss Simmonds'. But to-day he was to be disappointed. Wilson left the house, not knowing whether to be pleased or grieved. It was long to Monday, but they had all spoken kindly to him, and who could tell if they might not remember this, and do something before Monday. Besides, the cook, who, when she had had time to think, after breakfast was sent in, had noticed his paleness, had had meat and bread ready to put in his hand when he came out of the parlour; and a full stomach makes every one of us more hopeful.

When he reached Berry Street, he had persuaded himself he bore good news, and felt almost elated in his heart. But it fell when he opened the cellar-door, and saw Barton and the wife both bending over the sick man's couch with awe-struck, saddened look.

"Come here," said Barton. "There's a change comed over him sin' yo left, is there not?"

Wilson looked. The flesh was sunk, the features prominent, bony, and rigid. The fearful clay-colour of death was over all. But the eyes were open and sensible, though the films of the grave were settling upon them.

"He wakened fra his sleep, as yo left him in, and began to mutter and moan; but he soon went off again, and we never knew he were awake till he called his wife, but now she's here he's gotten nought to say to her."

Most probably, as they all felt, he could not speak, for his strength was fast ebbing. They stood round him still and silent; even the wife checked her sobs, though her heart was like to break. She held her child to her breast, to try and keep him quiet. Their eyes were all fixed on the yet living one, whose moments of life were passing so rapidly away. At length he brought (with jerking, convulsive effort) his two hands into the attitude of prayer. They saw his lips move, and bent to catch the words, which came in gasps, and not in tones.

"Oh Lord God! I thank thee, that the hard struggle of living is over."

"Oh, Ben! Ben!" wailed forth his wife, "have you no thought for me? Oh, Ben! Ben! do say one word to help me through life."

He could not speak again. The trump of the archangel would set his tongue free; but not a word more would it utter till then. Yet he heard, he understood, and though sight failed, he moved his hand gropingly over the covering. They knew what he meant, and guided it to her head, bowed and hidden in her hands, when she had sunk in her woe. It rested there, with a feeble pressure of endearment. The face grew beautiful, as the soul neared God. A peace beyond understanding came over it. The hand was a heavy, stiff weight on the wife's head. No more grief or sorrow for him. They reverently laid out the corpse—Wilson fetching his only spare shirt to array it in. The wife still lay hidden in the clothes, in a stupor of agony.

There was a knock at the door, and Barton went to open it. It was Mary, who had received a message from her father, through a neighbour, telling her where he was; and she had set out early to come and have a word with him before her day's work; but some errands she had to do for Miss Simmonds had detained her until now.

"Come in, wench!" said her father. "Try if thou canst comfort yon poor, poor woman, kneeling down there. God help her." Mary did not know what to say, or how to comfort; but she knelt down by her, and put her arm round her neck, and in a little while fell to crying herself so bitterly, that the source of tears was opened by sympathy in the widow, and her full heart was, for a time, relieved.

And Mary forgot all purposed meeting with her gay lover, Harry Carson; forgot Miss Simmonds' errands, and her anger, in the anxious desire to comfort the poor lone woman. Never had her sweet face looked more angelic, never had her gentle voice seemed so musical as when she murmured her broken sentences of comfort.

"Oh, don't cry so, dear Mrs. Davenport, pray don't take on so. Sure he's gone where he'll never know care again. Yes, I know how lonesome you must feel; but think of your children. Oh! we'll all help to earn food for 'em. Think how sorry *he'd* be, if he sees you fretting so. Don't cry so, please don't."

And she ended by crying herself, as passionately as the poor widow.

It was agreed that the town must bury him; he had paid to a burial club as long as he could; but by a few weeks' omission, he had forfeited his claim to a sum of money now. Would Mrs. Davenport and the little child go home with Mary? The latter brightened up as she urged this plan; but no! where the poor, fondly loved remains were, there would the mourner be; and all that they could do was to make her as comfortable as their funds would allow, and to beg a neighbour to look in and say a word at times. So she was left alone with her dead, and they went to work that had work, and he who had none, took upon him the arrangements for the funeral.

Mary had many a scolding from Miss Simmonds that day for her absence of mind. To be sure Miss Simmonds was much put out by Mary's non-appearance in the morning with certain bits of muslin, and shades of silk which were wanted to complete a dress to be worn that night; but it was true enough that Mary did not mind what she was about; she was too busy planning how her old black gown (her best when her mother died) might be spunged, and turned, and lengthened into something like decent mourning for the widow. And when she went home at night (though it was very late, as a sort of retribution for her morning's negligence), she set to work at once, and was so busy, and so glad over her task, that she had, every now and then, to check herself in singing merry ditties, that she felt little accorded with the sewing on which she was engaged.

So when the funeral day came, Mrs. Davenport was neatly arrayed in black, a satisfaction to her poor heart in the midst of her sorrow. Barton and Wilson both accompanied her, as she led her two elder boys, and followed the coffin. It was a simple walking funeral, with nothing to grate on the feelings of any; far more in accordance with its purpose, to my mind, than the gorgeous hearses, and nodding plumes, which form the grotesque funeral pomp of respectable people. There was no "rattling the bones over the stones," of the pauper's funeral. Decently and quietly was he followed to the grave by one determined to endure her woe meekly for his sake. The only mark of pauperism attendant on the burial concerned the living and joyous, far more than the dead, or the sorrowful. When they arrived in the churchyard, they halted before a raised and handsome tombstone; in reality a wooden mockery of stone respectabilities which adorned the burial-ground. It was easily raised in a very few minutes, and below was the grave in which pauper bodies were piled until within a foot or two of the surface; when the soil was shovelled over, and stamped down, and the wooden cover went to do temporary duty over another hole.[1] But little they recked of this who now gave up their dead.

---

[1] The case, to my certain knowledge, in one churchyard in Manchester. There may be more.

CHAPTER VII - JEM WILSON'S REPULSE.

"How infinite the wealth of love and hope
Garnered in these same tiny treasure-houses!
And oh! what bankrupts in the world we feel,
When Death, like some remorseless creditor,
Seizes on all we fondly thought our own!"

"THE TWINS."

The ghoul-like fever was not to be braved with impunity, and baulked of its prey. The widow had reclaimed her children; her neighbours, in the good Samaritan sense of the word, had paid her little arrears of rent, and made her a few shillings beforehand with the world. She determined to flit from that cellar to another less full of painful associations, less haunted by mournful memories. The board, not so formidable as she had imagined, had inquired into her case; and, instead of sending her to Stoke Claypole, her husband's Buckinghamshire parish, as she had dreaded, had agreed to pay her rent. So food for four mouths was all she was now required to find; only for three she would have said; for herself and the unweaned child were but reckoned as one in her calculation.

She had a strong heart, now her bodily strength had been recruited by a week or two of food, and she would not despair. So she took in some little children to nurse, who brought their daily food with them, which she cooked for them, without wronging their helplessness of a crumb; and when she had restored them to their mothers at night, she set to work at plain sewing, "seam, and gusset, and band," and sat thinking how she might best cheat the factory inspector, and persuade him that her strong, big, hungry Ben was above thirteen. Her plan of living was so far arranged, when she heard, with keen sorrow, that Wilson's twin lads were ill of the fever.

They had never been strong. They were like many a pair of twins, and seemed to have but one life divided between them. One life, one strength, and in this instance, I might almost say, one brain; for they were helpless, gentle, silly children, but not the less dear to their parents and to their strong, active, manly, elder brother. They were late on their feet, late in talking, late every way; had to be nursed and cared for when other lads of their age were tumbling about in the street, and losing themselves, and being taken to the police-office miles away from home.

Still want had never yet come in at the door to make love for these innocents fly out at the window. Nor was this the case even now, when Jem Wilson's earnings, and his mother's occasional charrings were barely sufficient to give all the family their fill of food.

But when the twins, after ailing many days, and caring little for their meat, fell sick on the same afternoon, with the same heavy stupor of suffering, the three hearts that loved them so, each felt, though none acknowledged to the other, that they had little chance for life. It was nearly a week before the tale of their illness spread as far as the court where the Wilsons had once dwelt, and the Bartons yet lived.

Alice had heard of the illness of her little nephews several days before, and had locked her cellar door, and gone off straight to her brother's house, in Ancoats; but she was often absent for days, sent for, as her neighbours knew, to help in some sudden emergency of illness or distress, so that occasioned no surprise.

Margaret met Jem Wilson several days after his brothers were seriously ill, and heard from him the state of things at his home. She told Mary of it as she entered the court late that evening; and Mary listened with saddened heart to the strange contrast which such woeful tidings presented to the gay and loving words she had been hearing on her walk home. She blamed herself for being so much taken up with visions of the golden future, that she had lately gone but seldom on Sunday afternoons, or other leisure time, to see Mrs. Wilson, her mother's friend; and with hasty purpose of amendment she only stayed to leave a message for her father with the next-door neighbour, and then went off at a brisk pace on her way to the house of mourning.

She stopped with her hand on the latch of the Wilsons' door, to still her beating heart, and listened to the hushed quiet within. She opened the door softly: there sat Mrs. Wilson in the old rocking-chair, with one sick, death-like boy lying on her knee, crying without let or pause, but softly, gently, as fearing to disturb the troubled, gasping child; while behind her, old Alice let her fast-dropping tears fall down on the dead body of the other twin, which she was laying out on a board, placed on a sort of sofa-settee in a corner of the room. Over the child, which yet breathed, the father bent, watching anxiously for some ground of hope, where hope there was none. Mary stepped slowly and lightly across to Alice.

"Ay, poor lad! God has taken him early, Mary."

Mary could not speak; she did not know what to say; it was so much worse than she expected. At last she ventured to whisper,

"Is there any chance for the other one, think you?"

Alice shook her head, and told with a look that she believed there was none. She next endeavoured to lift the little body, and carry it to its old accustomed bed in its parents' room. But earnest as the father was in watching the yet-living, he had eyes and ears for all that concerned the dead, and sprang gently up, and took his dead son on his hard couch in his arms with tender strength, and carried him upstairs as if afraid of wakening him.

The other child gasped longer, louder, with more of effort.

"We mun get him away from his mother. He cannot die while she's wishing him."

"Wishing him?" said Mary, in a tone of inquiry.

"Ay; donno ye know what wishing means? There's none can die in the arms of those who are wishing them sore to stay on earth. The soul o' them as holds them won't let the dying soul go free; so it has a hard struggle for the quiet of death. We mun get him away fra' his mother, or he'll have a hard death, poor lile[1] fellow."

So without circumlocution she went and offered to take the sinking child. But the mother would not let him go, and looking in Alice's face with brimming and imploring eyes, declared in earnest whispers, that she was not wishing him, that she would fain have him released from his suffering. Alice and Mary stood by with eyes fixed on the poor child, whose struggles seemed to increase, till at last his mother said with a choking voice,

"May happen[2] yo'd better take him, Alice; I believe my heart's wishing him a' this while, for I cannot, no, I cannot bring mysel to let my two childer go in one day; I cannot help longing to keep him, and yet he sha'not suffer longer for me."

She bent down, and fondly, oh! with what passionate fondness, kissed her child, and then gave him up to Alice, who took him with tender care. Nature's struggles were soon exhausted, and he breathed his little life away in peace.

Then the mother lifted up her voice and wept. Her cries brought her husband down to try with his aching heart to comfort hers. Again Alice laid out the dead, Mary helping with reverent fear. The father and mother carried him up-stairs to the bed, where his little brother lay in calm repose.

Mary and Alice drew near the fire, and stood in quiet sorrow for some time. Then Alice broke the silence by saying,

"It will be bad news for Jem, poor fellow, when he comes home."

"Where is he?" asked Mary.

"Working over-hours at th' shop. They'n getten a large order fra' forrin parts; and yo' know, Jem mun work, though his heart's well-nigh breaking for these poor laddies."

Again they were silent in thought, and again Alice spoke first.

"I sometimes think the Lord is against planning. Whene'er I plan over-much, He is sure to send and mar all my plans, as if He would ha' me put the future into His hands. Afore Christmas-time I was as full as full could be, of going home for good and all; yo' han heard how I've wished it this terrible long time. And a young lass from behind Burton came into place in Manchester last Martinmas; so after awhile, she had a Sunday out, and she comes to me, and tells me some cousins o' mine bid her find me out, and say how glad they should be to ha' me to bide wi'

---

[1] "Lile," a north-country word for "little." "Wit leil labour to live."—Piers Ploughman.

[2] "May happen," perhaps.

'em, and look after th' childer, for they'n getten a big farm, and she's a deal to do among th' cows. So many a winter's night did I lie awake and think, that please God, come summer, I'd bid George and his wife good bye, and go home at last. Little did I think how God Almighty would baulk me, for not leaving my days in His hands, who had led me through the wilderness hitherto. Here's George out o' work, and more cast down than ever I seed him; wanting every chip o' comfort he can get, e'en afore this last heavy stroke; and now I'm thinking the Lord's finger points very clear to my fit abiding place; and I'm sure if George and Jane can say 'His will be done,' it's no more than what I'm beholden to do."

So saying, she fell to tidying the room, removing as much as she could every vestige of sickness; making up the fire, and setting on the kettle for a cup of tea for her sister-in-law, whose low moans and sobs were occasionally heard in the room below.

Mary helped her in all these little offices. They were busy in this way when the door was softly opened, and Jem came in, all grimed and dirty from his night-work, his soiled apron wrapped round his middle, in guise and apparel in which he would have been sorry at another time to have been seen by Mary. But just now he hardly saw her; he went straight up to Alice, and asked how the little chaps were. They had been a shade better at dinner-time, and he had been working away through the long afternoon, and far into the night, in the belief that they had taken the turn. He had stolen out during the half-hour allowed at the works for tea, to buy them an orange or two, which now puffed out his jacket-pocket.

He would make his aunt speak; he would not understand her shakes of the head and fast coursing tears.

"They're both gone," said she.

"Dead!"

"Ay! poor fellows. They took worse about two o'clock. Joe went first, as easy as a lamb, and Will died harder like."

"Both!"

"Ay, lad! both. The Lord has ta'en them from some evil to come, or He would na ha' made choice o' them. Ye may rest sure o' that."

Jem went to the cupboard, and quietly extricated from his pocket the oranges he had bought. But he stayed long there, and at last his sturdy frame shook with his strong agony. The two women were frightened, as women always are, on witnessing a man's overpowering grief. They cried afresh in company. Mary's heart melted within her as she witnessed Jem's sorrow, and she stepped gently up to the corner where he stood, with his back turned to them, and putting her hand softly on his arm, said,

"Oh, Jem, don't give way so; I cannot bear to see you."

Jem felt a strange leap of joy in his heart, and knew the power she had of comforting him. He did not speak, as though fearing to destroy by sound or motion the happiness of that moment, when her soft hand's touch thrilled through his frame, and her silvery voice was whispering tenderness in his ear. Yes! it might be very wrong; he could almost hate himself for it; with death and woe so surrounding him, it yet was happiness, was bliss, to be so spoken to by Mary.

"Don't, Jem, please don't," whispered she again, believing that his silence was only another form of grief.

He could not contain himself. He took her hand in his firm yet trembling grasp, and said, in tones that instantly produced a revulsion in her mood,

"Mary, I almost loathe myself when I feel I would not give up this minute, when my brothers lie dead, and father and mother are in such trouble, for all my life that's past and gone. And, Mary (as she tried to release her hand), you know what makes me feel so blessed."

She did know—he was right there. But as he turned to catch a look at her sweet face, he saw that it expressed unfeigned distress, almost amounting to vexation; a dread of him, that he thought was almost repugnance.

He let her hand go, and she quickly went away to Alice's side.

"Fool that I was—nay, wretch that I was—to let myself take this time of trouble to tell her how I loved her; no wonder that she turns away from such a selfish beast."

Partly to relieve her from his presence, and partly from natural desire, and partly, perhaps, from a penitent wish to share to the utmost his parents' sorrow, he soon went up-stairs to the chamber of death.

Mary mechanically helped Alice in all the duties she performed through the remainder of that long night, but she did not see Jem again. He remained up-stairs until after the early dawn showed Mary that she need have no fear of going home through the deserted and quiet streets, to try and get a little sleep before work hour. So leaving kind messages to George and Jane Wilson, and hesitating whether she might dare to send a few kind words to Jem, and deciding that she had better not, she stepped out into the bright morning light, so fresh a contrast to the darkened room where death had been.

"They had
Another morn than ours."

Mary lay down on her bed in her clothes; and whether it was this, or the broad daylight that poured in through the sky-window, or whether it was over-excitement, it was long before she could catch a wink of sleep. Her thoughts ran on Jem's manner and words; not but what she had known the tale they told for many a day; but still she wished he had not put it so plainly.

"Oh dear," said she to herself, "I wish he would not mistake me so; I never dare to speak a common word o' kindness, but his eye brightens and his cheek flushes. It's very hard on me; for father and George Wilson are old friends; and Jem and I ha' known each other since we were quite children. I cannot think what possesses me, that I must always be wanting to comfort him when he's downcast, and that I must go meddling wi' him to-night, when sure enough it was his aunt's place to speak to him. I don't care for him, and yet, unless I'm always watching myself, I'm speaking to him in a loving voice. I think I cannot go right, for I either check myself till I'm downright cross to him, or else I speak just natural, and that's too kind and tender by half. And I'm as good as engaged to be married to another; and another far handsomer than Jem; only I think I like Jem's face best for all that; liking's liking, and there's no help for it. Well, when I'm Mrs. Harry Carson, may happen I can put some good fortune in Jem's way. But will he thank me for it? He's rather savage at times, that I can see, and perhaps kindness from me, when I'm another's, will only go against the grain. I'll not plague myself wi' thinking any more about him, that I won't."

So she turned on her pillow, and fell asleep, and dreamt of what was often in her waking thoughts; of the day when she should ride from church in her carriage, with wedding-bells ringing, and take up her astonished father, and drive away from the old dim work-a-day court for ever, to live in a grand house, where her father should have newspapers, and pamphlets, and pipes, and meat dinners every day,—and all day long if he liked.

Such thoughts mingled in her predilection for the handsome young Mr. Carson, who, unfettered by work-hours, let scarcely a day pass without contriving a meeting with the beautiful little milliner he had first seen while lounging in a shop where his sisters were making some purchases, and afterwards never rested till he had freely, though respectfully, made her acquaintance in her daily walks. He was, to use his own expression to himself, quite infatuated by her, and was restless each day till the time came when he had a chance, and, of late, more than a chance of meeting her. There was something of keen practical shrewdness about her, which contrasted very bewitchingly with the simple, foolish, unworldly ideas she had picked up from the romances which Miss Simmonds' young ladies were in the habit of recommending to each other.

Yes! Mary was ambitious, and did not favour Mr. Carson the less because he was rich and a gentleman. The old leaven, infused years ago by her aunt Esther, fermented in her little bosom, and perhaps all the more, for her father's aversion to the rich and the gentle. Such is the contrariness of the human heart, from Eve downwards, that we all, in our old-Adam state, fancy things forbidden sweetest. So Mary dwelt upon and enjoyed the idea of some day becoming a lady, and doing all the elegant nothings appertaining to ladyhood. It was a comfort to her, when scolded by Miss Simmonds, to think of the day when she would drive up to the door in her own carriage, to order her gowns from the hasty tempered yet kind dressmaker. It was a pleasure to her to hear the general admiration of the two elder Miss Carsons, acknowledged beauties in ball-room and street, on horseback and on foot, and to think of the time when she should ride and walk with them in loving sisterhood. But the best of her plans, the holiest, that which in some measure redeemed the vanity of the rest, were those relating to her father; her dear father, now oppressed with care, and always a disheartened, gloomy person. How she would surround him with every comfort she could devise (of course, he was to live with them), till he should acknowledge riches to be very pleasant things, and bless his lady-daughter! Every one who had shown her kindness in her low estate should then be repaid a hundred-fold.

Such were the castles in air, the Alnaschar-visions in which Mary indulged, and which she was doomed in after days to expiate with many tears.

Meanwhile, her words—or, even more, her tones—would maintain their hold on Jem Wilson's memory. A thrill would yet come over him when he remembered how her hand had rested on his arm. The thought of her mingled with all his grief, and it was profound, for the loss of his brothers.

CHAPTER VIII - MARGARET'S DEBUT AS A PUBLIC SINGER.

"Deal gently with them, they have much endured.
Scoff not at their fond hopes and earnest plans,
Though they may seem to thee wild dreams and fancies.
Perchance, in the rough school of stern experience,
They've something learned which Theory does not teach;
Or if they greatly err, deal gently still,
And let their error but the stronger plead
'Give us the light and guidance that we need!'"

LOVE THOUGHTS.

One Sunday afternoon, about three weeks after that mournful night, Jem Wilson set out with the ostensible purpose of calling on John Barton. He was dressed in his best, his Sunday suit of course; while his face glittered with the scrubbing he had bestowed on it. His dark black hair had been arranged and re-arranged before the household looking-glass, and in his button-hole he stuck a narcissus (a sweet Nancy is its pretty Lancashire name), hoping it would attract Mary's notice, so that he might have the delight of giving it her.

It was a bad beginning of his visit of happiness that Mary saw him some minutes before he came into her father's house. She was sitting at the end of the dresser, with the little window-blind drawn on one side, in order that she might see the passers-by, in the intervals of reading her Bible, which lay open before her. So she watched all the greeting a friend gave Jem; she saw the face of condolence, the sympathetic shake of the hand, and had time to arrange her own face and manner before Jem came in, which he did, as if he had eyes for no one but her father, who sat smoking his pipe by the fire, while he read an old "Northern Star," borrowed from a neighbouring public-house.

Then he turned to Mary, who, he felt by the sure instinct of love, by which almost his body thought, was present. Her hands were busy adjusting her dress; a forced and unnecessary movement Jem could not help thinking. Her accost was quiet and friendly, if grave; she felt that she reddened like a rose, and wished she could prevent it, while Jem wondered if her blushes arose from fear, or anger, or love.

She was very cunning, I am afraid. She pretended to read diligently, and not to listen to a word that was said, while, in fact, she heard all sounds, even to Jem's long, deep sighs, which wrung her heart. At last she took up her Bible, and as if their conversation disturbed her, went up-stairs to her little room. And she had scarcely spoken a word to Jem; scarcely looked at him; never noticed his beautiful sweet Nancy, which only awaited her least word of praise to be hers! He did not know—that pang was spared—that in her little dingy bed-room, stood a white jug, filled with a luxuriant bunch of early spring roses, making the whole room fragrant and bright. They were the gift of her richer lover. So Jem had to go on sitting with John Barton, fairly caught in his own trap, and had to listen to his talk, and answer him as best he might.

"There's the right stuff in this here 'Star,' and no mistake. Such a right-down piece for short hours."

"At the same rate of wages as now?" asked Jem.

"Ay, ay! else where's the use? It's only taking out o' the masters' pocket what they can well afford. Did I ever tell yo what th' Infirmary chap let me into, many a year agone?"

"No," said Jem, listlessly.

"Well! yo must know I were in th' Infirmary for a fever, and times were rare and bad; and there be good chaps there to a man, while he's wick,[1] whate'er they may be about cutting him up at after.[2] So when I were better o' th' fever, but weak as water, they says to me, says they, 'If yo can write, yo may stay in a week longer, and help our surgeon wi' sorting his papers; and we'll take care yo've your belly full o' meat and drink. Yo'll be twice as strong in a week.' So there wanted but one word to that bargain. So I were set to writing and copying; th' writing I could do well enough, but they'd such queer ways o' spelling that I'd ne'er been used to, that I'd to look first at th' copy and then at my letters, for all the world like a cock picking up grains o' corn. But one thing startled me e'en then, and I thought I'd make bold to ask the surgeon the meaning o't. I've gotten no head for numbers, but this I know, that by *far th' greater part o' th' accidents as comed in, happened in th' last two hours o' work*, when folk getten tired and careless. Th' surgeon said it were all true, and that he were going to bring that fact to light."

Jem was pondering Mary's conduct; but the pause made him aware he ought to utter some civil listening noise; so he said

"Very true."

"Ay, it's true enough, my lad, that we're sadly over-borne, and worse will come of it afore long. Block-printers is going to strike; they'n getten a bang-up union, as

---

[1] "Wick," alive. Anglo-Saxon, cwic. "The quick and the dead."—Book of Common Prayer.

[2] "At after." "At after souper goth this noble king." Chaucer; The Squire's Tale.

won't let 'em be put upon. But there's many a thing will happen afore long, as folk don't expect. Yo may take my word for that, Jem."

Jem was very willing to take it, but did not express the curiosity he should have done. So John Barton thought he'd try another hint or two.

"Working folk won't be ground to the dust much longer. We'n a' had as much to bear as human nature can bear. So, if th' masters can't do us no good, and they say they can't, we mun try higher folk."

Still Jem was not curious. He gave up hope of seeing Mary again by her own good free will; and the next best thing would be, to be alone to think of her. So, muttering something which he meant to serve as an excuse for his sudden departure, he hastily wished John good afternoon, and left him to resume his pipe and his politics.

For three years past, trade had been getting worse and worse, and the price of provisions higher and higher. This disparity between the amount of the earnings of the working classes and the price of their food, occasioned, in more cases than could well be imagined, disease and death. Whole families went through a gradual starvation. They only wanted a Dante to record their sufferings. And yet even his words would fall short of the awful truth; they could only present an outline of the tremendous facts of the destitution that surrounded thousands upon thousands in the terrible years 1839, 1840, and 1841. Even philanthropists who had studied the subject, were forced to own themselves perplexed in their endeavour to ascertain the real causes of the misery; the whole matter was of so complicated a nature, that it became next to impossible to understand it thoroughly. It need excite no surprise then to learn that a bad feeling between working-men and the upper classes became very strong in this season of privation. The indigence and sufferings of the operatives induced a suspicion in the minds of many of them, that their legislators, their magistrates, their employers, and even the ministers of religion, were, in general, their oppressors and enemies; and were in league for their prostration and enthralment. The most deplorable and enduring evil that arose out of the period of commercial depression to which I refer, was this feeling of alienation between the different classes of society. It is so impossible to describe, or even faintly to picture, the state of distress which prevailed in the town at that time, that I will not attempt it; and yet I think again that surely, in a Christian land, it was not known even so feebly as words could tell it, or the more happy and fortunate would have thronged with their sympathy and their aid. In many instances the sufferers wept first, and then they cursed. Their vindictive feelings exhibited themselves in rabid politics. And when I hear, as I have heard, of the sufferings and privations of the poor, of provision shops where ha'porths of tea, sugar, butter, and even flour, were sold to accommodate the indigent,—of parents sitting in their clothes by the fire-side during the whole night for seven weeks together, in order that their only bed and bedding might be reserved for the use of their large family,—of others sleeping upon the cold hearth-stone for weeks in succession, without adequate means of providing themselves with food or fuel (and this in the depth of winter),—of others being compelled to fast for days together, uncheered by any hope of better fortune, living, moreover, or rather starving, in a crowded garret, or damp cellar, and gradually sinking under the pressure of want and despair into a premature grave; and when this has been confirmed by the evidence of their care-worn looks, their excited feelings, and their desolate homes,—can I wonder that many of them, in such times of misery and destitution, spoke and acted with ferocious precipitation?

An idea was now springing up among the operatives, that originated with the Chartists, but which came at last to be cherished as a darling child by many and many a one. They could not believe that government knew of their misery; they rather chose to think it possible that men could voluntarily assume the office of legislators for a nation, ignorant of its real state; as who should make domestic rules for the pretty behaviour of children, without caring to know that those children had been kept for days without food. Besides, the starving multitudes had heard, that the very existence of their distress had been denied in Parliament; and though they felt this strange and inexplicable, yet the idea that their misery had still to be revealed in all its depths, and that then some remedy would be found, soothed their aching hearts, and kept down their rising fury.

So a petition was framed, and signed by thousands in the bright spring days of 1839, imploring Parliament to hear witnesses who could testify to the unparalleled destitution of the manufacturing districts. Nottingham, Sheffield, Glasgow, Manchester, and many other towns, were busy appointing delegates to convey this petition, who might speak, not merely of what they had seen, and had heard, but from what they had borne and suffered. Life-worn, gaunt, anxious, hunger-stamped men, were those delegates.

One of them was John Barton. He would have been ashamed to own the flutter of spirits his appointment gave him. There was the childish delight of seeing London—that went a little way, and but a little way. There was the vain idea of speaking out his notions before so many grand folk—that went a little further; and last, there was the really pure gladness of heart, arising from the idea that he was one of those chosen to be instruments in making known the distresses of the people, and consequently in procuring them some grand relief, by means of which they should never suffer want or care any more. He hoped largely, but vaguely, of the results of his expedition. An argosy of the precious hopes of many otherwise despairing creatures, was that petition to be heard concerning their sufferings.

The night before the morning on which the Manchester delegates were to leave for London, Barton might be said to hold a levée, so many neighbours came dropping in. Job Legh had early established himself and his pipe by John Barton's fire, not saying much, but puffing away, and imagining himself of use in adjusting the smoothing-irons that hung before the fire, ready for Mary when she should want them. As for Mary, her employment was the same as that of Beau Tibbs' wife, "just washing her father's two shirts," in the pantry back-kitchen; for she was anxious about his appearance in London. (The coat had been redeemed, though the silk handkerchief was forfeited.) The door stood open, as usual, between the houseplace and back-kitchen, so she gave her greeting to their friends as they entered.

"So, John, yo're bound for London, are yo?" said one.

"Ay, I suppose I mun go," answered John, yielding to necessity as it were.

"Well, there's many a thing I'd like yo to speak on to the Parliament people. Thou'lt not spare 'em, John, I hope. Tell 'em our minds; how we're thinking we've been clemmed long enough, and we donnot see whatten good they'n been doing, if they can't give us what we're all crying for sin' the day we were born."

"Ay, ay! I'll tell 'em that, and much more to it, when it gets to my turn; but thou knows there's many will have their word afore me."

"Well, thou'lt speak at last. Bless thee, lad, do ask 'em to make th' masters break th' machines. There's never been good times sin' spinning-jennies came up."

"Machines is th' ruin of poor folk," chimed in several voices.

"For my part," said a shivering, half-clad man, who crept near the fire, as if ague-stricken, "I would like thee to tell 'em to pass th' Short-hours Bill. Flesh and blood gets wearied wi' so much work; why should factory hands work so much longer nor other trades? Just ask 'em that, Barton, will ye?"

Barton was saved the necessity of answering, by the entrance of Mrs. Davenport, the poor widow he had been so kind to; she looked half-fed, and eager, but was decently clad. In her hand she brought a little newspaper parcel, which she took to Mary, who opened it, and then called out, dangling a shirt collar from her soapy fingers:

"See, father, what a dandy you'll be in London! Mrs. Davenport has brought you this; made new cut, all after the fashion.—Thank you for thinking on him."

"Eh, Mary!" said Mrs. Davenport, in a low voice. "Whatten's all I can do, to what he's done for me and mine? But, Mary, sure I can help ye, for you'll be busy wi' this journey."

"Just help me wring these out, and then I'll take 'em to th' mangle."

So Mrs. Davenport became a listener to the conversation; and after a while joined in.

"I'm sure, John Barton, if yo are taking messages to the Parliament folk, yo'll not object to telling 'em what a sore trial it is, this law o' theirs, keeping childer fra' factory work, whether they be weakly or strong. There's our Ben; why, porridge seems to go no way wi' him, he eats so much; and I han gotten no money to send him t' school, as I would like; and there he is, rampaging about th' streets a' day, getting hungrier and hungrier, and picking up a' manner o' bad ways; and th' inspector won't let him in to work in th' factory, because he's not right age; though he's twice as strong as Sankey's little ritling[1] of a lad, as works till he cries for his legs aching so, though he is right age, and better."

"I've one plan I wish to tell John Barton," said a pompous, careful-speaking man, "and I should like him for to lay it afore the Honourable House. My mother

---

[1] "Ritling," probably a corruption of "ricketling," a child that suffers from the rickets—a weakling.

comed out o' Oxfordshire, and were under-laundry-maid in Sir Francis Dashwood's family; and when we were little ones, she'd tell us stories of their gran-grandeur; and one thing she named were, that Sir Francis wore two shirts a day. Now he were all as one as a Parliament man; and many on 'em, I han no doubt, are like extravagant. Just tell 'em, John, do, that they'd be doing th' Lancashire weavers a great kindness, if they'd ha' their shirts a' made o' calico; 'twould make trade brisk, that would, wi' the power o' shirts they wear."

Job Legh now put in his word. Taking the pipe out of his mouth, and addressing the last speaker, he said:

"I'll tell ye what, Bill, and no offence, mind ye; there's but hundreds of them Parliament folk as wear so many shirts to their back; but there's thousands and thousands o' poor weavers as han only gotten one shirt i' th' world; ay, and don't know where t' get another when that rag's done, though they're turning out miles o' calico every day; and many a mile o't is lying in warehouses, stopping up trade for want o' purchasers. Yo take my advice, John Barton, and ask Parliament to set trade free, so as workmen can earn a decent wage, and buy their two, ay and three, shirts a-year; that would make weaving brisk."

He put his pipe in his mouth again, and redoubled his puffing to make up for lost time.

"I'm afeard, neighbours," said John Barton, "I've not much chance o' telling 'em all yo say; what I think on, is just speaking out about the distress that they say is nought. When they hear o' children born on wet flags, without a rag t' cover 'em, or a bit o' food for th' mother; when they hear of folk lying down to die i' th' streets, or hiding their want i' some hole o' a cellar till death come to set 'em free; and when they hear o' all this plague, pestilence, and famine, they'll surely do somewhat wiser for us than we can guess at now. Howe'er, I han no objection, if so be there's an opening, to speak up for what yo say; anyhow, I'll do my best, and yo see now, if better times don't come after Parliament knows all."

Some shook their heads, but more looked cheery; and then one by one dropped off, leaving John and his daughter alone.

"Didst thou mark how poorly Jane Wilson looked?" asked he, as they wound up their hard day's work by a supper eaten over the fire, which glowed and glimmered through the room, and formed their only light.

"No, I can't say as I did. But she's never rightly held up her head since the twins died; and all along she has never been a strong woman."

"Never sin' her accident. Afore that I mind her looking as fresh and likely a girl as e'er a one in Manchester."

"What accident, father?"

"She cotched[1] her side again a wheel. It were afore wheels were boxed up. It were just when she were to have been married, and many a one thought George would ha' been off his bargain; but I knew he wern't the chap for that trick. Pretty near the first place she went to when she were able to go about again, was th' Oud

[1] "Cotched," caught.

Church; poor wench, all pale and limping she went up the aisle, George holding her up as tender as a mother, and walking as slow as e'er he could, not to hurry her, though there were plenty enow of rude lads to cast their jests at him and her. Her face were white like a sheet when she came in church, but afore she got to th' altar she were all one flush. But for a' that it's been a happy marriage, and George has stuck by me through life like a brother. He'll never hold up his head again if he loses Jane. I didn't like her looks to-night."

And so he went to bed, the fear of forthcoming sorrow to his friend mingling with his thoughts of to-morrow, and his hopes for the future. Mary watched him set off, with her hands over her eyes to shade them from the bright slanting rays of the morning sun, and then she turned into the house to arrange its disorder before going to her work. She wondered if she should like or dislike the evening and morning solitude; for several hours when the clock struck she thought of her father, and wondered where he was; she made good resolutions according to her lights; and by-and-bye came the distractions and events of the broad full day to occupy her with the present, and to deaden the memory of the absent.

One of Mary's resolutions was, that she would not be persuaded or induced to see Mr. Harry Carson during her father's absence. There was something crooked in her conscience after all; for this very resolution seemed an acknowledgment that it was wrong to meet him at any time; and yet she had brought herself to think her conduct quite innocent and proper, for although unknown to her father, and certain, even did he know it, to fail of obtaining his sanction, she esteemed her love-meetings with Mr. Carson as sure to end in her father's good and happiness. But now that he was away, she would do nothing that he would disapprove of; no, not even though it was for his own good in the end.

Now, amongst Miss Simmonds' young ladies was one who had been from the beginning a confidant in Mary's love affair, made so by Mr. Carson himself. He had felt the necessity of some third person to carry letters and messages, and to plead his cause when he was absent. In a girl named Sally Leadbitter he had found a willing advocate. She would have been willing to have embarked in a love-affair herself (especially a clandestine one), for the mere excitement of the thing; but her willingness was strengthened by sundry half-sovereigns, which from time to time Mr. Carson bestowed upon her.

Sally Leadbitter was vulgar-minded to the last degree; never easy unless her talk was of love and lovers; in her eyes it was an honour to have had a long list of wooers. So constituted, it was a pity that Sally herself was but a plain, red-haired, freckled girl; never likely, one would have thought, to become a heroine on her own account. But what she lacked in beauty she tried to make up for by a kind of witty boldness, which gave her what her betters would have called piquancy. Considerations of modesty or propriety never checked her utterance of a good thing. She had just talent enough to corrupt others. Her very good-nature was an evil influence. They could not hate one who was so kind; they could not avoid one who was so willing to shield them from scrapes by any exertion of her own; whose ready fingers would at any time make up for their deficiencies, and whose still more convenient tongue would at any time invent for them. The Jews, or Mohammedans (I forget which), believe that there is one little bone of our body, one of the vertebræ, if I remember rightly, which will never decay and turn to dust, but will lie incorrupt and indestructible in the ground until the Last Day: this is the Seed of the Soul. The most depraved have also their Seed of the Holiness that shall one day overcome their evil, their one good quality, lurking hidden, but safe, among all the corrupt and bad.

Sally's seed of the future soul was her love for her mother, an aged bedridden woman. For her she had self-denial; for her, her good-nature rose into tenderness; to cheer her lonely bed, her spirits, in the evenings when her body was often woefully tired, never flagged, but were ready to recount the events of the day, to turn them into ridicule, and to mimic, with admirable fidelity, any person gifted with an absurdity who had fallen under her keen eye. But the mother was lightly principled like Sally herself; nor was there need to conceal from her the reason why Mr. Carson gave her so much money. She chuckled with pleasure, and only hoped that the wooing would be long a-doing.

Still neither she, nor her daughter, nor Harry Carson liked this resolution of Mary, not to see him during her father's absence.

One evening (and the early summer evenings were long and bright now), Sally met Mr. Carson by appointment, to be charged with a letter for Mary, imploring her to see him, which Sally was to back with all her powers of persuasion. After parting from him she determined, as it was not so very late, to go at once to Mary's, and deliver the message and letter.

She found Mary in great sorrow. She had just heard of George Wilson's sudden death: her old friend, her father's friend, Jem's father—all his claims came rushing upon her. Though not guarded from unnecessary sight or sound of death, as the children of the rich are, yet it had so often been brought home to her this last three or four months. It was so terrible thus to see friend after friend depart. Her father, too, who had dreaded Jane Wilson's death the evening before he set off. And she, the weakly, was left behind while the strong man was taken. At any rate the sorrow her father had so feared for him was spared. Such were the thoughts which came over her.

She could not go to comfort the bereaved, even if comfort were in her power to give; for she had resolved to avoid Jem; and she felt that this of all others was not the occasion on which she could keep up a studiously cold manner.

And in this shock of grief, Sally Leadbitter was the last person she wished to see. However, she rose to welcome her, betraying her tear-swollen face.

"Well, I shall tell Mr. Carson to-morrow how you're fretting for him; it's no more nor he's doing for you, I can tell you."

"For him, indeed!" said Mary, with a toss of her pretty head.

"Ay, miss, for him! You've been sighing as if your heart would break now for several days, over your work; now arn't you a little goose not to go and see one who I am sure loves you as his life, and whom you love; 'How much, Mary?' 'This much,' as the children say" (opening her arms very wide).

"Nonsense," said Mary, pouting; "I often think I don't love him at all."

"And I'm to tell him that, am I, next time I see him?" asked Sally.

"If you like," replied Mary. "I'm sure I don't care for that or any thing else now;" weeping afresh.

But Sally did not like to be the bearer of any such news. She saw she had gone on the wrong tack, and that Mary's heart was too full to value either message or letter as she ought. So she wisely paused in their delivery, and said in a more sympathetic tone than she had heretofore used,

"Do tell me, Mary, what's fretting you so? You know I never could abide to see you cry."

"George Wilson's dropped down dead this afternoon," said Mary, fixing her eyes for one minute on Sally, and the next hiding her face in her apron as she sobbed anew.

"Dear, dear! All flesh is grass; here to-day and gone to-morrow, as the Bible says. Still he was an old man, and not good for much; there's better folk than him left behind. Is th' canting old maid as was his sister alive yet?"

"I don't know who you mean," said Mary, sharply; for she did know, and did not like to have her dear, simple Alice so spoken of.

"Come, Mary, don't be so innocent. Is Miss Alice Wilson alive, then; will that please you? I haven't seen her hereabouts lately."

"No, she's left living here. When the twins died she thought she could, may be, be of use to her sister, who was sadly cast down, and Alice thought she could cheer her up; at any rate she could listen to her when her heart grew overburdened; so she gave up her cellar and went to live with them."

"Well, good go with her. I'd no fancy for her, and I'd no fancy for her making my pretty Mary into a Methodee."

"She wasn't a Methodee, she was Church o' England."

"Well, well, Mary, you're very particular. You know what I meant. Look, who is this letter from?" holding up Henry Carson's letter.

"I don't know, and don't care," said Mary, turning very red.

"My eye! as if I didn't know you did know and did care."

"Well, give it me," said Mary, impatiently, and anxious in her present mood for her visitor's departure.

Sally relinquished it unwillingly. She had, however, the pleasure of seeing Mary dimple and blush as she read the letter, which seemed to say the writer was not indifferent to her.

"You must tell him I can't come," said Mary, raising her eyes at last. "I have said I won't meet him while father is away, and I won't."

"But, Mary, he does so look for you. You'd be quite sorry for him, he's so put out about not seeing you. Besides you go when your father's at home, without letting on[1] to him, and what harm would there be in going now?"

---

[1] "Letting on," informing. In Anglo-Saxon, one meaning of "lætan" was "to admit;" and we say, to let out a secret.

"Well, Sally! you know my answer, I won't; and I won't."

"I'll tell him to come and see you himself some evening, instead o' sending me; he'd may be find you not so hard to deal with."

Mary flashed up.

"If he dares to come here while father's away, I'll call the neighbours in to turn him out, so don't be putting him up to that."

"Mercy on us! one would think you were the first girl that ever had a lover; have you never heard what other girls do and think no shame of?"

"Hush, Sally! that's Margaret Jennings at the door."

And in an instant Margaret was in the room. Mary had begged Job Legh to let her come and sleep with her. In the uncertain fire-light you could not help noticing that she had the groping walk of a blind person.

"Well, I must go, Mary," said Sally. "And that's your last word?"

"Yes, yes; good-night." She shut the door gladly on her unwelcome visitor—unwelcome at that time at least.

"Oh Margaret, have ye heard this sad news about George Wilson?"

"Yes, that I have. Poor creatures, they've been sore tried lately. Not that I think sudden death so bad a thing; it's easy, and there's no terrors for him as dies. For them as survives it's very hard. Poor George! he were such a hearty looking man."

"Margaret," said Mary, who had been closely observing her friend, "thou'rt very blind to-night, arn't thou? Is it wi' crying? Your eyes are so swollen and red."

"Yes, dear! but not crying for sorrow. Han ye heard where I was last night?"

"No; where?"

"Look here." She held up a bright golden sovereign. Mary opened her large gray eyes with astonishment.

"I'll tell you all how and about it. You see there's a gentleman lecturing on music at th' Mechanics', and he wants folk to sing his songs. Well, last night th' counter got a sore throat and couldn't make a note. So they sent for me. Jacob Butterworth had said a good word for me, and they asked me would I sing? You may think I was frightened, but I thought now or never, and said I'd do my best. So I tried o'er the songs wi' th' lecturer, and then th' managers told me I were to make myself decent and be there by seven."

"And what did you put on?" asked Mary. "Oh, why didn't you come in for my pretty pink gingham?"

"I did think on't; but you had na come home then. No! I put on my merino, as was turned last winter, and my white shawl, and did my hair pretty tidy; it did well enough. Well, but as I was saying, I went at seven. I couldn't see to read my music, but I took th' paper in wi' me, to ha' somewhat to do wi' my fingers. Th' folks' heads danced, as I stood as right afore 'em all as if I'd been going to play at ball wi' 'em. You may guess I felt squeamish, but mine weren't the first song, and th' music sounded like a friend's voice, telling me to take courage. So to make a long story short, when it were all o'er th' lecturer thanked me, and th' managers said as how there never was a new singer so applauded (for they'd clapped and stamped after I'd done, till I began to wonder how many pair o' shoes they'd get through a week at that rate, let alone their hands). So I'm to sing again o' Thursday; and I got a sovereign last night, and am to have half-a-sovereign every night th' lecturer is at th' Mechanics'."

"Well, Margaret, I'm right glad to hear it."

"And I don't think you've heard the best bit yet. Now that a way seemed opened to me, of not being a burden to any one, though it did please God to make me blind, I thought I'd tell grandfather. I only telled him about the singing and the sovereign last night, for I thought I'd not send him to bed wi' a heavy heart; but this morning I telled him all."

"And how did he take it?"

"He's not a man of many words; and it took him by surprise like."

"I wonder at that; I've noticed it in your ways ever since you telled me."

"Ay, that's it! If I'd not telled you, and you'd seen me every day, you'd not ha' noticed the little mite o' difference fra' day to day."

"Well, but what did your grandfather say?"

"Why, Mary," said Margaret, half smiling, "I'm a bit loath to tell yo, for unless yo knew grandfather's ways like me, yo'd think it strange. He were taken by surprise, and he said: 'Damn yo!' Then he began looking at his book as it were, and were very quiet, while I telled him all about it; how I'd feared, and how downcast I'd been; and how I were now reconciled to it, if it were th' Lord's will; and how I hoped to earn money by singing; and while I were talking, I saw great big tears come dropping on th' book; but in course I never let on that I saw 'em. Dear grandfather! and all day long he's been quietly moving things out o' my way, as he thought might trip me up, and putting things in my way, as he thought I might want; never knowing I saw and felt what he were doing; for, yo see, he thinks I'm out and out blind, I guess—as I shall be soon."

Margaret sighed, in spite of her cheerful and relieved tone.

Though Mary caught the sigh, she felt it was better to let it pass without notice, and began, with the tact which true sympathy rarely fails to supply, to ask a variety of questions respecting her friend's musical debut, which tended to bring out more distinctly how successful it had been.

"Why, Margaret," at length she exclaimed, "thou'lt become as famous, may be, as that grand lady fra' London, as we seed one night driving up to th' concert room door in her carriage."

"It looks very like it," said Margaret, with a smile. "And be sure, Mary, I'll not forget to give thee a lift now an' then when that comes about. Nay, who knows, if thou'rt a good girl, but mayhappen I may make thee my lady's maid! Wouldn't that be nice? So I'll e'en sing to mysel' th' beginning o' one o' my songs,

> 'An' ye shall walk in silk attire,
> An' siller hae to spare.'"

"Nay, don't stop; or else give me something a bit more new, for somehow I never quite liked that part about thinking o' Donald mair."

"Well, though I'm a bit tir'd, I don't care if I do. Before I come, I were practising well nigh upon two hours this one which I'm to sing o' Thursday. Th' lecturer said he were sure it would just suit me, and I should do justice to it; and I should be right sorry to disappoint him, he were so nice and encouraging like to me. Eh! Mary, what a pity there isn't more o' that way, and less scolding and rating i' th' world! It would go a vast deal further. Beside, some o' th' singers said they were a'most certain it were a song o' his own, because he were so fidgetty and particular about it, and so anxious I should give it th' proper expression. And that makes me care still more. Th' first verse, he said, were to be sung 'tenderly, but joyously!' I'm afraid I don't quite hit that, but I'll try.

'What a single word can do!
Thrilling all the heart-strings through,
Calling forth fond memories,
Raining round hope's melodies,
Steeping all in one bright hue—
What a single word can do!'

Now it falls into th' minor key, and must be very sad like. I feel as if I could do that better than t'other.

'What a single word can do!
Making life seem all untrue,
Driving joy and hope away,
Leaving not one cheering ray
Blighting every flower that grew—
What a single word can do!'"

Margaret certainly made the most of this little song. As a factory worker, listening outside, observed, "She spun it reet[1] fine!" And if she only sang it at the Mechanics' with half the feeling she put into it that night, the lecturer must have been hard to please, if he did not admit that his expectations were more than fulfilled.

When it was ended, Mary's looks told more than words could have done what she thought of it; and partly to keep in a tear which would fain have rolled out, she brightened into a laugh, and said, "For certain, th' carriage is coming. So let us go and dream on it."

CHAPTER IX - BARTON'S LONDON EXPERIENCES.

"A life of self-indulgence is for us,
  A life of self-denial is for them;
For us the streets, broad-built and populous,
  For them unhealthy corners, garrets dim,
  And cellars where the water-rat may swim!
For us green paths refreshed by frequent rain,
  For them dark alleys where the dust lies grim!

---

[1] "Reet," right; often used for "very."

CHAPTER VIII - MARGARET'S DEBUT AS A PUBLIC SINGER.

Not doomed by us to this appointed pain—
God made us rich and poor—of what do these complain?"

MRS. NORTON'S "CHILD OF THE ISLANDS."

The next evening it was a warm, pattering, incessant rain, just the rain to waken up the flowers. But in Manchester, where, alas! there are no flowers, the rain had only a disheartening and gloomy effect; the streets were wet and dirty, the drippings from the houses were wet and dirty, and the people were wet and dirty. Indeed, most kept within-doors; and there was an unusual silence of footsteps in the little paved courts.

Mary had to change her clothes after her walk home; and had hardly settled herself before she heard some one fumbling at the door. The noise continued long enough to allow her to get up, and go and open it. There stood—could it be? yes it was, her father!

Drenched and way-worn, there he stood! He came in with no word to Mary in return for her cheery and astonished greeting. He sat down by the fire in his wet things, unheeding. But Mary would not let him so rest. She ran up and brought down his working-day clothes, and went into the pantry to rummage up their little bit of provision while he changed by the fire, talking all the while as gaily as she could, though her father's depression hung like lead on her heart.

For Mary, in her seclusion at Miss Simmonds',—where the chief talk was of fashions, and dress, and parties to be given, for which such and such gowns would be wanted, varied with a slight whispered interlude occasionally about love and lovers,—had not heard the political news of the day: that Parliament had refused to listen to the working-men, when they petitioned with all the force of their rough, untutored words to be heard concerning the distress which was riding, like the Conqueror on his Pale Horse, among the people; which was crushing their lives out of them, and stamping woe-marks over the land.

When he had eaten and was refreshed, they sat in silence for some time; for Mary wished him to tell her what oppressed him so, yet durst not ask. In this she was wise; for when we are heavy laden in our hearts, it falls in better with our humour to reveal our case in our own way, and our own time.

Mary sat on a stool at her father's feet in old childish guise, and stole her hand into his, while his sadness infected her, and she "caught the trick of grief, and sighed," she knew not why.

"Mary, we mun speak to our God to hear us, for man will not hearken; no, not now, when we weep tears o' blood."

In an instant Mary understood the fact, if not the details, that so weighed down her father's heart. She pressed his hand with silent sympathy. She did not know what to say, and was so afraid of speaking wrongly, that she was silent. But when his attitude had remained unchanged for more than half-an-hour, his eyes gazing vacantly and fixedly at the fire, no sound but now and then a deep drawn sigh to break the weary ticking of the clock, and the drip-drop from the roof without, Mary could bear it no longer. Any thing to rouse her father. Even bad news.

"Father, do you know George Wilson's dead?" (Her hand was suddenly and almost violently compressed.) "He dropped down dead in Oxford Road yester morning. It's very sad, isn't it, father?"

Her tears were ready to flow as she looked up in her father's face for sympathy. Still the same fixed look of despair, not varied by grief for the dead.

"Best for him to die," he said, in a low voice.

This was unbearable. Mary got up under pretence of going to tell Margaret that she need not come to sleep with her to-night, but really to ask Job Legh to come and cheer her father.

She stopped outside their door. Margaret was practising her singing, and through the still night air her voice rang out like that of an angel.

"Comfort ye, comfort ye, my people, saith your God."

The old Hebrew prophetic words fell like dew on Mary's heart. She could not interrupt. She stood listening and "comforted," till the little buzz of conversation again began, and then entered and told her errand.

Both grandfather and grand-daughter rose instantly to fulfil her request.

"He's just tired out, Mary," said old Job. "He'll be a different man to-morrow."

There is no describing the looks and tones that have power over an aching, heavy laden heart; but in an hour or so John Barton was talking away as freely as ever, though all his talk ran, as was natural, on the disappointment of his fond hope, of the forlorn hope of many.

"Ay, London's a fine place," said he, "and finer folk live in it than I ever thought on, or ever heerd tell on except in th' story-books. They are having their good things now, that afterwards they may be tormented."

Still at the old parable of Dives and Lazarus! Does it haunt the minds of the rich as it does those of the poor?

"Do tell us all about London, dear father," asked Mary, who was sitting at her old post by her father's knee.

"How can I tell yo a' about it, when I never seed one-tenth of it. It's as big as six Manchesters, they telled me. One-sixth may be made up o' grand palaces, and three-sixths o' middling kind, and th' rest o' holes o' iniquity and filth, such as Manchester knows nought on, I'm glad to say."

"Well, father, but did you see th' Queen?"

"I believe I didn't, though one day I thought I'd seen her many a time. You see," said he, turning to Job Legh, "there were a day appointed for us to go to Parliament House. We were most on us biding at a public-house in Holborn, where they did very well for us. Th' morning of taking our petition we'd such a spread for breakfast as th' Queen hersel might ha' sitten down to. I suppose they thought we wanted putting in heart. There were mutton kidneys, and sausages, and broiled ham, and fried beef and onions; more like a dinner nor a breakfast. Many on our chaps though, I could see, could eat but little. Th' food stuck in their throats when they thought o' them at home, wives and little ones, as had, may be at that very time, nought to eat. Well, after breakfast, we were all set to walk in procession, and a time it took to put us in order, two and two, and the petition as was yards long, carried by th' foremost pairs. The men looked grave enough, yo may be sure; and such a set of thin, wan, wretched-looking chaps as they were!"

"Yourself is none to boast on."

"Ay, but I were fat and rosy to many a one. Well, we walked on and on through many a street, much the same as Deansgate. We had to walk slowly, slowly, for th' carriages an' cabs as thronged th' streets. I thought by-and-bye we should may be get clear on 'em, but as th' streets grew wider they grew worse, and at last we were fairly blocked up at Oxford Street. We getten across at last though, and my eyes! the grand streets we were in then! They're sadly puzzled how to build houses though in London; there'd be an opening for a good steady master-builder there, as know'd his business. For yo see the houses are many on 'em built without any proper shape for a body to live in; some on 'em they've after thought would fall down, so they've stuck great ugly pillars out before 'em. And some on 'em (we thought they must be th' tailor's sign) had getten stone men and women as wanted clothes stuck on 'em. I were like a child, I forgot a' my errand in looking about me. By this it were dinner-time, or better, as we could tell by th' sun, right above our heads, and we were dusty and tired, going a step now and a step then. Well, at last we getten into a street grander nor all, leading to th' Queen's palace, and there it were I thought I saw th' Queen. Yo've seen th' hearses wi' white plumes, Job?"

Job assented.

"Well, them undertaker folk are driving a pretty trade in London. Wellnigh every lady we saw in a carriage had hired one o' them plumes for the day, and had it niddle noddling on her head. It were th' Queen's Drawing-room, they said, and th' carriages went bowling along toward her house, some wi' dressed up gentlemen like circus folk in 'em, and rucks[1] o' ladies in others. Carriages themselves were great shakes too. Some o' th' gentlemen as couldn't get inside hung on behind, wi' nosegays to smell at, and sticks to keep off folk as might splash their silk stockings. I wondered why they didn't hire a cab rather than hang on like a whip-behind boy; but I suppose they wished to keep wi' their wives, Darby and Joan like. Coachmen were little squat men, wi' wigs like th' oud fashioned parsons. Well, we could na get on for these carriages, though we waited and waited. Th' horses were too fat to move quick; they'n never known want o' food, one might tell by their sleek coats; and police pushed us back when we tried to cross. One or two on 'em struck wi' their sticks, and coachmen laughed, and some officers as stood nigh put their spy-glasses in their eye, and left 'em sticking there like mountebanks. One o' th' police struck me. 'Whatten business have yo to do that?' said I.

"'You're frightening them horses,' says he, in his mincing way (for Londoners are mostly all tongue-tied, and can't say their a's and i's properly), 'and it's our business to keep you from molesting the ladies and gentlemen going to her Majesty's Drawing-room.'

---

[1] "Rucks," a great quantity.

"'And why are we to be molested?' asked I, 'going decently about our business, which is life and death to us, and many a little one clemming at home in Lancashire? Which business is of most consequence i' the sight o' God, think yo, our'n or them gran ladies and gentlemen as yo think so much on?'

"But I might as well ha' held my peace, for he only laughed."

John ceased. After waiting a little to see if he would go on of himself, Job said,

"Well, but that's not a' your story, man. Tell us what happened when yo got to th' Parliament House."

After a little pause John answered,

"If yo please, neighbour, I'd rather say nought about that. It's not to be forgotten or forgiven either by me or many another; but I canna tell of our down-casting just as a piece of London news. As long as I live, our rejection that day will bide in my heart; and as long as I live I shall curse them as so cruelly refused to hear us; but I'll not speak of it no[1] more."

> "That of no wife toke he non offering
> For curtesie, he sayd, he n'old non."

So, daunted in their inquiries, they sat silent for a few minutes.

Old Job, however, felt that some one must speak, else all the good they had done in dispelling John Barton's gloom was lost. So after awhile he thought of a subject, neither sufficiently dissonant from the last to jar on the full heart, nor too much the same to cherish the continuance of the gloomy train of thought.

"Did you ever hear tell," said he to Mary, "that I were in London once?"

"No!" said she, with surprise, and looking at Job with increased respect.

"Ay, but I were though, and Peg there too, though she minds nought about it, poor wench! You must know I had but one child, and she were Margaret's mother. I loved her above a bit, and one day when she came (standing behind me for that I should not see her blushes, and stroking my cheeks in her own coaxing way), and told me she and Frank Jennings (as was a joiner lodging near us) should be so happy if they were married, I could not find in my heart t' say her nay, though I went sick at the thought of losing her away from my home. Howe'er, she were my only child, and I never said nought of what I felt, for fear o' grieving her young heart. But I tried to think o' the time when I'd been young mysel, and had loved her blessed mother, and how we'd left father and mother and gone out into th' world together, and I'm now right thankful I held my peace, and didna fret her wi' telling her how sore I was at parting wi' her that were the light o' my eyes."

"But," said Mary, "you said the young man were a neighbour."

"Ay, so he were; and his father afore him. But work were rather slack in Manchester, and Frank's uncle sent him word o' London work and London wages, so he were to go there; and it were there Margaret was to follow him. Well, my heart aches yet at thought of those days. She so happy, and he so happy; only the poor

---

[1] A similar use of a double negative is not unfrequent in Chaucer; as in the "Miller's Tale":

father as fretted sadly behind their backs. They were married, and stayed some days wi' me afore setting off; and I've often thought sin' Margaret's heart failed her many a time those few days, and she would fain ha' spoken; but I knew fra' mysel it were better to keep it pent up, and I never let on what I were feeling. I knew what she meant when she came kissing, and holding my hand, and all her old childish ways o' loving me. Well, they went at last. You know them two letters, Margaret?"

"Yes, sure," replied his grand-daughter.

"Well, them two were the only letters I ever had fra' her, poor lass. She said in them she were very happy, and I believe she were. And Frank's family heard he were in good work. In one o' her letters, poor thing, she ends wi' saying, 'Farewell, Grandad!' wi' a line drawn under grandad, and fra' that an' other hints I knew she were in th' family way; and I said nought, but I screwed up a little money, thinking come Whitsuntide I'd take a holiday and go and see her an' th' little one. But one day towards Whitsuntide comed Jennings wi' a grave face, and says he, 'I hear our Frank and your Margaret's both getten the fever.' You might ha' knocked me down wi' a straw, for it seemed as if God told me what th' upshot would be. Old Jennings had gotten a letter, yo see, fra' the landlady they lodged wi'; a well-penned letter, asking if they'd no friends to come and nurse them. She'd caught it first, and Frank, who was as tender o' her as her own mother could ha' been, had nursed her till he'd caught it himsel; and she expecting her down-lying[1] every day. Well, t' make a long story short, Old Jennings and I went up by that night's coach. So you see, Mary, that was the way I got to London."

"But how was your daughter when you got there?" asked Mary, anxiously.

"She were at rest, poor wench, and so were Frank. I guessed as much when I see'd th' landlady's face, all swelled wi' crying, when she opened th' door to us. We said, 'Where are they?' and I knew they were dead, fra' her look; but Jennings didn't, as I take it; for when she showed us into a room wi' a white sheet on th' bed, and underneath it, plain to be seen, two still figures, he screeched out as if he'd been a woman.

"Yet he'd other childer and I'd none. There lay my darling, my only one. She were dead, and there were no one to love me, no, not one. I disremember[2] rightly what I did; but I know I were very quiet, while my heart were crushed within me.

"Jennings could na' stand being in th' room at all, so th' landlady took him down, and I were glad to be alone. It grew dark while I sat there; and at last th' landlady come up again, and said, 'Come here.' So I got up and walked into th' light, but I had to hold by th' stair-rails, I were so weak and dizzy. She led me into a room, where Jennings lay on a sofa fast asleep, wi' his pocket handkercher over his head for a night-cap. She said he'd cried himself fairly off to sleep. There were tea on th' table all ready; for she were a kind-hearted body. But she still said, 'Come here,' and took hold o' my arm. So I went round the table, and there were a

[1] "Down-lying," lying-in.

[2] "Disremember," forget.

clothes-basket by th' fire, wi' a shawl put o'er it. 'Lift that up,' says she, and I did; and there lay a little wee babby fast asleep. My heart gave a leap, and th' tears comed rushing into my eyes first time that day. 'Is it hers?' said I, though I knew it were. 'Yes,' said she. 'She were getting a bit better o' the fever, and th' babby were born; and then the poor young man took worse and died, and she were not many hours behind.'

"Little mite of a thing! and yet it seemed her angel come back to comfort me. I were quite jealous o' Jennings whenever he went near the babby. I thought it were more my flesh and blood than his'n, and yet I were afeared he would claim it. However, that were far enough fra' his thoughts; he'd plenty other childer, and as I found out at after he'd all along been wishing me to take it. Well, we buried Margaret and her husband in a big, crowded, lonely churchyard in London. I were loath to leave them there, as I thought, when they rose again, they'd feel so strange at first away fra Manchester, and all old friends; but it couldna be helped. Well, God watches o'er their grave there as well as here. That funeral cost a mint o' money, but Jennings and I wished to do th' thing decent. Then we'd the stout little babby to bring home. We'd not overmuch money left; but it were fine weather, and we thought we'd take th' coach to Brummagem, and walk on. It were a bright May morning when last I saw London town, looking back from a big hill a mile or two off. And in that big mass o' a place I were leaving my blessed child asleep—in her last sleep. Well, God's will be done! She's gotten to heaven afore me; but I shall get there at last, please God, though it's a long while first.

"The babby had been fed afore we set out, and th' coach moving kept it asleep, bless its little heart. But when th' coach stopped for dinner it were awake, and crying for its pobbies.[1] So we asked for some bread and milk, and Jennings took it first for to feed it; but it made its mouth like a square, and let it run out at each o' th' four corners. 'Shake it, Jennings,' says I; 'that's the way they make water run through a funnel, when it's o'er full; and a child's mouth is broad end o' th' funnel, and th' gullet the narrow one.' So he shook it, but it only cried th' more. 'Let me have it,' says I, thinking he were an awkward oud chap. But it were just as bad wi' me. By shaking th' babby we got better nor a gill into its mouth, but more nor that came up again, wetting a' th' nice dry clothes landlady had put on. Well, just as we'd gotten to th' dinner-table, and helped oursels, and eaten two mouthful, came in th' guard, and a fine chap wi' a sample o' calico flourishing in his hand. 'Coach is ready!' says one; 'Half-a-crown your dinner!' says th' other. Well, we thought it a deal for both our dinners, when we'd hardly tasted 'em; but, bless your life, it were half-a-crown apiece, and a shilling for th' bread and milk as were possetted all over babby's clothes. We spoke up again[2] it; but every body said it were the rule, so what could two poor oud chaps like us do again it? Well, poor babby cried without stopping to take breath, fra' that time till we got to Brummagem for the night. My heart ached for th' little thing. It caught wi' its wee mouth at our

---

[1] "Pobbies," or "pobs," child's porridge.

[2] "Again," for against. "He that is not with me, he is ageyn me."—Wickliffe's Version.

coat sleeves and at our mouths, when we tried t' comfort it by talking to it. Poor little wench! It wanted its mammy, as were lying cold in th' grave. 'Well,' says I, 'it'll be clemmed to death, if it lets out its supper as it did its dinner. Let's get some woman to feed it; it comes natural to women to do for babbies.' So we asked th' chamber-maid at the inn, and she took quite kindly to it; and we got a good supper, and grew rare and sleepy, what wi' th' warmth, and wi' our long ride i' th' open air. Th' chamber-maid said she would like t' have it t' sleep wi' her, only missis would scold so; but it looked so quiet and smiling like, as it lay in her arms, that we thought 'twould be no trouble to have it wi' us. I says: 'See, Jennings, how women-folk do quieten babbies; it's just as I said.' He looked grave; he were always thoughtful-looking, though I never heard him say any thing very deep. At last says he—

"'Young woman! have you gotten a spare night-cap?'

"'Missis always keeps night-caps for gentlemen as does not like to unpack,' says she, rather quick.

"'Ay, but young woman, it's one of your night-caps I want. Th' babby seems to have taken a mind to yo; and may be in th' dark it might take me for yo if I'd getten your night-cap on.'

"The chambermaid smirked and went for a cap, but I laughed outright at th' oud bearded chap thinking he'd make hissel like a woman just by putting on a woman's cap. Howe'er he'd not be laughed out on't, so I held th' babby till he were in bed. Such a night as we had on it! Babby began to scream o' th' oud fashion, and we took it turn and turn about to sit up and rock it. My heart were very sore for th' little one, as it groped about wi' its mouth; but for a' that I could scarce keep fra' smiling at th' thought o' us two oud chaps, th' one wi' a woman's night-cap on, sitting on our hinder ends for half th' night, hushabying a babby as wouldn't be hushabied. Toward morning, poor little wench! it fell asleep, fairly tired out wi' crying, but even in its sleep it gave such pitiful sobs, quivering up fra' the very bottom of its little heart, that once or twice I almost wished it lay on its mother's breast, at peace for ever. Jennings fell asleep too; but I began for to reckon up our money. It were little enough we had left, our dinner the day afore had ta'en so much. I didn't know what our reckoning would be for that night lodging, and supper, and breakfast. Doing a sum alway sent me asleep ever sin' I were a lad; so I fell sound in a short time, and were only wakened by chambermaid tapping at th' door, to say she'd dress the babby afore her missis were up if we liked. But bless yo', we'd never thought o' undressing it th' night afore, and now it were sleeping so sound, and we were so glad o' the peace and quietness, that we thought it were no good to waken it up to screech again.

"Well! (there's Mary asleep for a good listener!) I suppose you're getting weary of my tale, so I'll not be long over ending it. Th' reckoning left us very bare, and we thought we'd best walk home, for it were only sixty mile, they telled us, and not stop again for nought, save victuals. So we left Brummagem, (which is as black a place as Manchester, without looking so like home), and walked a' that day, carrying babby turn and turn about. It were well fed by chambermaid afore we left, and th' day were fine, and folk began to have some knowledge o' th' proper way o' speaking, and we were more cheery at thoughts o' home (though mine, God knows, were lonesome enough). We stopped none for dinner, but at baggin-time[1] we getten a good meal at a public-house, an' fed th' babby as well as we could, but that were but poorly. We got a crust too, for it to suck—chambermaid put us up to that. That night, whether we were tired or whatten, I don't know, but it were dree[2] work, and poor wench had slept out her sleep, and began th' cry as wore my heart out again. Says Jennings, says he,

"'We should na ha' set out so like gentlefolk a top o' the coach yesterday.'

"'Nay, lad! We should ha' had more to walk, if we had na ridden, and I'm sure both you and I'se[3] weary o' tramping.'

"So he were quiet a bit. But he were one o' them as were sure to find out somewhat had been done amiss, when there were no going back to undo it. So presently he coughs, as if he were going to speak, and I says to mysel, 'At it again, my lad.' Says he,

"'I ax pardon, neighbour, but it strikes me it would ha' been better for my son if he had never begun to keep company wi' your daughter.'

"Well! that put me up, and my heart got very full, and but that I were carrying *her* babby, I think I should ha' struck him. At last I could hold in no longer, and says I,

"'Better say at once it would ha' been better for God never to ha' made th' world, for then we'd never ha' been in it, to have had th' heavy hearts we have now.'

"Well! he said that were rank blasphemy; but I thought his way of casting up again th' events God had pleased to send, were worse blasphemy. Howe'er, I said nought more angry, for th' little babby's sake, as were th' child o' his dead son, as well as o' my dead daughter.

"Th' longest lane will have a turning, and that night came to an end at last; and we were foot-sore and tired enough, and to my mind th' babby were getting weaker and weaker, and it wrung my heart to hear its little wail; I'd ha' given my right hand for one of yesterday's hearty cries. We were wanting our breakfasts, and so were it too, motherless babby! We could see no public-house, so about six o'clock (only we thought it were later) we stopped at a cottage where a woman were moving about near th' open door. Says I, 'Good woman, may we rest us a bit?' 'Come in,' says she, wiping a chair, as looked bright enough afore, wi' her apron. It were a cheery, clean room; and we were glad to sit down again, though I thought my legs would never bend at th' knees. In a minute she fell a noticing th' babby, and took it in her arms, and kissed it again and again. 'Missis,' says I, 'we're not without money, and if yo'd give us somewhat for breakfast, we'd pay yo honest, and if yo would wash and dress that poor babby, and get some pobbies down its throat,

---

[1] "Baggin-time," time of the evening meal.

[2] "Dree," long and tedious. Anglo-Saxon, "dreogan," to suffer, to endure.

[3] "I have not been, nor is, nor never schal."—Wickliffe's "Apology," p. 1.

for it's well-nigh clemmed, I'd pray for yo' till my dying day.' So she said nought, but gived me th' babby back, and afore yo' could say Jack Robinson, she'd a pan on th' fire, and bread and cheese on th' table. When she turned round, her face looked red, and her lips were tight pressed together. Well! we were right down glad on our breakfast, and God bless and reward that woman for her kindness that day; she fed th' poor babby as gently and softly, and spoke to it as tenderly as its own poor mother could ha' done. It seemed as if that stranger and it had known each other afore, maybe in Heaven, where folk's spirits come from they say; th' babby looked up so lovingly in her eyes, and made little noises more like a dove than aught else. Then she undressed it (poor darling! it were time), touching it so softly; and washed it from head to foot, and as many on its things were dirty; and what bits o' things its mother had gotten ready for it had been sent by th' carrier fra London, she put 'em aside; and wrapping little naked babby in her apron, she pulled out a key, as were fastened to a black ribbon, and hung down her breast, and unlocked a drawer in th' dresser. I were sorry to be prying, but I could na' help seeing in that drawer some little child's clothes, all strewed wi' lavendar, and lying by 'em a little whip an' a broken rattle. I began to have an insight into that woman's heart then. She took out a thing or two; and locked the drawer, and went on dressing babby. Just about then come her husband down, a great big fellow as didn't look half awake, though it were getting late; but he'd heard all as had been said down-stairs, as were plain to be seen; but he were a gruff chap. We'd finished our breakfast, and Jennings were looking hard at th' woman as she were getting the babby to sleep wi' a sort of rocking way. At length says he, 'I ha learnt th' way now; it's two jiggits and a shake, two jiggits and a shake. I can get that babby asleep now mysel.'

"The man had nodded cross enough to us, and had gone to th' door, and stood there whistling wi' his hands in his breeches-pockets, looking abroad. But at last he turns and says, quite sharp,

"'I say, missis, I'm to have no breakfast to-day, I s'pose.'

"So wi' that she kissed th' child, a long, soft kiss; and looking in my face to see if I could take her meaning, gave me th' babby without a word. I were loath to stir, but I saw it were better to go. So giving Jennings a sharp nudge (for he'd fallen asleep), I says, 'Missis, what's to pay?' pulling out my money wi' a jingle that she might na guess we were at all bare o' cash. So she looks at her husband, who said ne'er a word, but were listening wi' all his ears nevertheless; and when she saw he would na say, she said, hesitating, as if pulled two ways, by her fear o' him, 'Should you think sixpence over much?' It were so different to public-house reckoning, for we'd eaten a main deal afore the chap came down. So says I, 'And, missis, what should we gie you for the babby's bread and milk?' (I had it once in my mind to say 'and for a' your trouble with it,' but my heart would na let me say it, for I could read in her ways how it had been a work o' love.) So says she, quite quick, and stealing a look at her husband's back, as looked all ear, if ever a back did, 'Oh, we could take nought for the little babby's food, if it had eaten twice as much, bless it.' Wi' that he looked at her; such a scowling look! She knew what he meant, and stepped softly across the floor to him, and put her hand on his arm. He seem'd as though he'd shake it off by a jerk on his elbow, but she said quite low, 'For poor little Johnnie's sake, Richard.' He did not move or speak again, and after looking in his face for a minute, she turned away, swallowing deep in her throat. She kissed th' sleeping babby as she passed, when I paid her. To quieten th' gruff husband, and stop him if he rated her, I could na help slipping another sixpence under th' loaf, and then we set off again. Last look I had o' that woman she were quietly wiping her eyes wi' the corner of her apron, as she went about her husband's breakfast. But I shall know her in heaven."

He stopped to think of that long-ago May morning, when he had carried his grand-daughter under the distant hedge-rows and beneath the flowering sycamores.

"There's nought more to say, wench," said he to Margaret, as she begged him to go on. "That night we reached Manchester, and I'd found out that Jennings would be glad enough to give up babby to me, so I took her home at once, and a blessing she's been to me."

They were all silent for a few minutes; each following out the current of their thoughts. Then, almost simultaneously, their attention fell upon Mary. Sitting on her little stool, her head resting on her father's knee, and sleeping as soundly as any infant, her breath (still like an infant's) came and went as softly as a bird steals to her leafy nest. Her half-open mouth was as scarlet as the winter-berries, and contrasted finely with the clear paleness of her complexion, where the eloquent blood flushed carnation at each motion. Her black eye-lashes lay on the delicate cheek, which was still more shaded by the masses of her golden hair, that seemed to form a nest-like pillow for her as she lay. Her father in fond pride straightened one glossy curl, for an instant, as if to display its length and silkiness. The little action awoke her, and, like nine out of ten people in similar circumstances, she exclaimed, opening her eyes to their fullest extent,

"I'm not asleep. I've been awake all the time."

Even her father could not keep from smiling, and Job Legh and Margaret laughed outright.

"Come, wench," said Job, "don't look so gloppened[1] because thou'st fallen asleep while an oud chap like me was talking on oud times. It were like enough to send thee to sleep. Try if thou canst keep thine eyes open while I read thy father a bit on a poem as is written by a weaver like oursel. A rare chap I'll be bound is he who could weave verse like this."

So adjusting his spectacles on nose, cocking his chin, crossing his legs, and coughing to clear his voice, he read aloud a little poem of Samuel Bamford's[2] he had picked up somewhere.

---

[1] "Gloppened," amazed, frightened.

[2] The fine-spirited author of "Passages in the Life of a Radical"—a man who illustrates his order, and shows what nobility may be in a cottage.

God help the poor, who, on this wintry morn,
  Come forth from alleys dim and courts obscure.
God help yon poor pale girl, who droops forlorn,
  And meekly her affliction doth endure;
God help her, outcast lamb; she trembling stands,
All wan her lips, and frozen red her hands;
Her sunken eyes are modestly down-cast,
Her night-black hair streams on the fitful blast;
Her bosom, passing fair, is half revealed,
And oh! so cold, the snow lies there congealed;
Her feet benumbed, her shoes all rent and worn,
God help thee, outcast lamb, who standst forlorn!
          God help the poor!
God help the poor! An infant's feeble wail
  Comes from yon narrow gateway, and behold!
A female crouching there, so deathly pale,
  Huddling her child, to screen it from the cold;
Her vesture scant, her bonnet crushed and torn;
  A thin shawl doth her baby dear enfold:
And so she 'bides the ruthless gale of morn,
  Which almost to her heart hath sent its cold.
And now she, sudden, darts a ravening look,
As one, with new hot bread, goes past the nook;
And, as the tempting load is onward borne,
She weeps. God help thee, helpless one, forlorn!
          God help the poor!
God help the poor! Behold yon famished lad,
  No shoes, nor hose, his wounded feet protect;
With limping gait, and looks so dreamy sad,
  He wanders onward, stopping to inspect
Each window, stored with articles of food.
  He yearns but to enjoy one cheering meal;
Oh! to the hungry palate, viands rude,
  Would yield a zest the famished only feel!
He now devours a crust of mouldy bread;
  With teeth and hands the precious boon is torn;
Unmindful of the storm that round his head
  Impetuous sweeps. God help thee, child forlorn!
          God help the poor!
God help the poor! Another have I found—
  A bowed and venerable man is he;
His slouched hat with faded crape is bound;
  His coat is gray, and threadbare too, I see.
"The rude winds" seem "to mock his hoary hair;"

His shirtless bosom to the blast is bare.
Anon he turns and casts a wistful eye,
  And with scant napkin wipes the blinding spray;
And looks around, as if he fain would spy
  Friends he had feasted in his better day:
Ah! some are dead; and some have long forborne
To know the poor; and he is left forlorn!
        God help the poor!
God help the poor, who in lone valleys dwell,
  Or by far hills, where whin and heather grow;
Theirs is a story sad indeed to tell,
  Yet little cares the world, and less 't would know
  About the toil and want men undergo.
The wearying loom doth call them up at morn,
  They work till worn-out nature sinks to sleep,
  They taste, but are not fed. The snow drifts deep
  Around the fireless cot, and blocks the door;
  The night-storm howls a dirge across the moor;
And shall they perish thus—oppressed and lorn?
Shall toil and famine, hopeless, still be borne?
  No! God will yet arise, and help the poor.

"Amen!" said Barton, solemnly, and sorrowfully. "Mary! wench, couldst thou copy me them lines, dost think?—that's to say, if Job there has no objection."

"Not I. More they're heard and read and the better, say I."

So Mary took the paper. And the next day, on the blank half sheet of a valentine, all bordered with hearts and darts—a valentine she had once suspected to come from Jem Wilson—she copied Bamford's beautiful little poem.

CHAPTER X - RETURN OF THE PRODIGAL

"My heart, once soft as woman's tear, is gnarled
With gloating on the ills I cannot cure."

ELLIOTT.

"Then guard and shield her innocence,
Let her not fall like me;
'Twere better, Oh! a thousand times,
She in her grave should be."

"THE OUTCAST."

Despair settled down like a heavy cloud; and now and then, through the dead calm of sufferings, came pipings of stormy winds, foretelling the end of these dark prognostics. In times of sorrowful or fierce endurance, we are often soothed by the mere repetition of old proverbs which tell the experience of our forefathers; but now, "it's a long lane that has no turning," "the weariest day draws to an end," &c., seemed false and vain sayings, so long and so weary was the pressure of the terrible times. Deeper and deeper still sank the poor; it showed how much lingering suffering it takes to kill men, that so few (in comparison) died during those times. But remember! we only miss those who do men's work in their humble sphere; the aged, the feeble, the children, when they die, are hardly noted by the world; and yet to many hearts, their deaths make a blank which long years will never fill up. Remember, too, that though it may take much suffering to kill the able-bodied and effective members of society, it does *not* take much to reduce them to worn, listless, diseased creatures, who thenceforward crawl through life with moody hearts and pain-stricken bodies.

The people had thought the poverty of the preceding years hard to bear, and had found its yoke heavy; but this year added sorely to its weight. Former times had chastised them with whips, but this chastised them with scorpions.

Of course, Barton had his share of mere bodily sufferings. Before he had gone up to London on his vain errand, he had been working short time. But in the hopes of speedy redress by means of the interference of Parliament, he had thrown up his place; and now, when he asked leave to resume work, he was told they were diminishing their number of hands every week, and he was made aware by the remarks of fellow workmen, that a Chartist delegate, and a leading member of a Trades' Union, was not likely to be favoured in his search after employment. Still he tried to keep up a brave heart concerning himself. He knew he could bear hunger; for that power of endurance had been called forth when he was a little child, and had seen his mother hide her daily morsel to share it among her children, and when he, being the eldest, had told the noble lie, that "he was not hungry, could not eat a bit more," in order to imitate his mother's bravery, and still the sharp wail of the younger infants. Mary, too, was secure of two meals a day at Miss Simmonds'; though, by the way, the dress-maker, too, feeling the effect of bad times, had left off giving tea to her apprentices, setting them the example of long abstinence by putting off her own meal until work was done for the night, however late that might be.

But the rent! It was half-a-crown a week—nearly all Mary's earnings—and much less room might do for them, only two.—(Now came the time to be thankful that the early dead were saved from the evil to come.)—The agricultural labourer generally has strong local attachments; but they are far less common, almost obliterated, among the inhabitants of a town. Still there are exceptions, and Barton formed one. He had removed to his present house just after the last bad times, when little Tom had sickened and died. He had then thought the bustle of a removal would give his poor stunned wife something to do, and he had taken more interest in the details of the proceeding than he otherwise would have done, in the hope of calling her forth to action again. So he seemed to know every brass-headed nail driven up for her convenience. One only had been displaced. It was Esther's bonnet nail, which, in his deep revengeful anger against her, after his wife's death, he had torn out of the wall, and cast into the street. It would be hard work to leave that house, which yet seemed hallowed by his wife's presence in the happy days of old. But he was a law unto himself, though sometimes a bad, fierce law; and he resolved to give the rent-collector notice, and look out for a cheaper abode, and tell Mary they must flit. Poor Mary! she loved the house, too. It was wrenching up her natural feelings of home, for it would be long before the fibres of her heart would gather themselves about another place.

This trial was spared. The collector (of himself), on the very Monday when Barton planned to give him notice of his intention to leave, lowered the rent threepence a week, just enough to make Barton compromise and agree to stay on a little longer.

But by degrees the house was stripped of its little ornaments. Some were broken; and the odd twopences and threepences wanted to pay for their repairs, were required for the far sterner necessity of food. And by-and-bye Mary began to part with other superfluities at the pawn-shop. The smart tea-tray and tea-caddy, long and carefully kept, went for bread for her father. He did not ask for it, or complain, but she saw hunger in his shrunk, fierce, animal look. Then the blankets went, for it was summer time, and they could spare them; and their sale made a fund, which Mary fancied would last till better times came. But it was soon all gone; and then she looked around the room to crib it of its few remaining ornaments. To all these proceedings her father said never a word. If he fasted, or feasted (after the sale of some article), on an unusual meal of bread and cheese, he took all with a sullen indifference, which depressed Mary's heart. She often wished he would apply for relief from the Guardian's relieving office; often wondered the Trades' Union did nothing for him. Once when she asked him as he sat, grimed, unshaven, and gaunt, after a day's fasting over the fire, why he did not get relief from the town, he turned round, with grim wrath, and said, "I don't want money, child! D——n their charity and their money! I want work, and it is my right. I want work."

He would bear it all, he said to himself. And he did bear it, but not meekly; that was too much to expect. Real meekness of character is called out by experience of kindness. And few had been kind to him. Yet through it all, with stern determination he refused the assistance his Trades' Union would have given him. It had not much to give, but with worldly wisdom, thought it better to propitiate an active, useful member, than to help those who were unenergetic, though they had large families to provide for. Not so thought John Barton. With him need was right.

"Give it to Tom Darbyshire," he said. "He's more claim on it than me, for he's more need of it, with his seven children."

Now Tom Darbyshire was, in his listless, grumbling way, a backbiting enemy of John Barton's. And he knew it; but he was not to be influenced by that in a matter like this.

Mary went early to her work; but her cheery laugh over it was now missed by the other girls. Her mind wandered over the present distress, and then settled, as she stitched, on the visions of the future, where yet her thoughts dwelt more on the circumstances of ease, and the pomps and vanities awaiting her, than on the lover with whom she was to share them. Still she was not insensible to the pride of having attracted one so far above herself in station; not insensible to the secret pleasure of knowing that he, whom so many admired, had often said he would give any thing for one of her sweet smiles. Her love for him was a bubble, blown out of vanity; but it looked very real and very bright. Sally Leadbitter, meanwhile, keenly observed the signs of the times; she found out that Mary had begun to affix a stern value to money as the "Purchaser of Life," and many girls had been dazzled and lured by gold, even without the betraying love which she believed to exist in Mary's heart. So she urged young Mr. Carson, by representations of the want she was sure surrounded Mary, to bring matters more to a point. But he had a kind of instinctive dread of hurting Mary's pride of spirit, and durst not hint his knowledge in any way of the distress that many must be enduring. He felt that for the present he must still be content with stolen meetings and summer evening strolls, and the delight of pouring sweet honeyed words into her ear, while she listened with a blush and a smile that made her look radiant with beauty. No, he would be cautious in order to be certain; for Mary, one way or another, he must make his. He had no doubt of the effect of his own personal charms in the long run; for he knew he was handsome, and believed himself fascinating.

If he had known what Mary's home was, he would not have been so much convinced of his increasing influence over her, by her being more and more ready to linger with him in the sweet summer air. For when she returned for the night her father was often out, and the house wanted the cheerful look it had had in the days when money was never wanted to purchase soap and brushes, black-lead and pipe-clay. It was dingy and comfortless; for, of course, there was not even the dumb familiar home-friend, a fire. And Margaret, too, was now so often from home, singing at some of those grand places. And Alice; oh, Mary wished she had never left her cellar to go and live at Ancoats with her sister-in-law. For in that matter Mary felt very guilty; she had put off and put off going to see the widow after George Wilson's death from dread of meeting Jem, or giving him reason to think she wished to be as intimate with him as formerly; and now she was so much ashamed of her delay that she was likely never to go at all.

If her father was at home it was no better; indeed it was worse. He seldom spoke, less than ever; and often when he did speak they were sharp angry words, such as he had never given her formerly. Her temper was high, too, and her answers not over-mild; and once in his passion he had even beaten her. If Sally Leadbitter or Mr. Carson had been at hand at that moment, Mary would have been ready to leave home for ever. She sat alone, after her father had flung out of the house, bitterly thinking on the days that were gone; angry with her own hastiness, and believing that her father did not love her; striving to heap up one painful thought on another. Who cared for her? Mr. Carson might, but in this grief that seemed no comfort. Mother dead! Father so often angry, so lately cruel (for it was a hard blow, and blistered and reddened Mary's soft white skin with pain): and then her heart turned round, and she remembered with self-reproach how provokingly she had looked and spoken, and how much her father had to bear; and oh, what a kind and loving parent he had been, till these days of trial. The remembrance of one little instance of his fatherly love thronged after another into her mind, and she began to wonder how she could have behaved to him as she had done.

Then he came home; and but for very shame she would have confessed her penitence in words. But she looked sullen, from her effort to keep down emotion; and for some time her father did not know how to begin to speak. At length he gulped down pride, and said:

"Mary, I'm not above saying I'm very sorry I beat thee. Thou wert a bit aggravating, and I'm not the man I was. But it were wrong, and I'll try never to lay hands on thee again."

So he held out his arms, and in many tears she told him her repentance for her fault. He never struck her again.

Still, he often was angry. But that was almost better than being silent. Then he sat near the fire-place (from habit), smoking, or chewing opium. Oh, how Mary loathed that smell! And in the dusk, just before it merged into the short summer night, she had learned to look with dread towards the window, which now her father would have kept uncurtained; for there were not seldom seen sights which haunted her in her dreams. Strange faces of pale men, with dark glaring eyes, peered into the inner darkness, and seemed desirous to ascertain if her father were at home. Or a hand and arm (the body hidden) was put within the door, and beckoned him away. He always went. And once or twice, when Mary was in bed, she heard men's voices below, in earnest, whispered talk.

They were all desperate members of Trades' Unions, ready for any thing; made ready by want.

While all this change for gloom yet struck fresh and heavy on Mary's heart, her father startled her out of a reverie one evening, by asking her when she had been to see Jane Wilson. From his manner of speaking, she was made aware that he had been; but at the time of his visit he had never mentioned any thing about it. Now, however, he gruffly told her to go next day without fail, and added some abuse of her for not having been before. The little outward impulse of her father's speech gave Mary the push which she, in this instance, required; and, accordingly, timing her visit so as to avoid Jem's hours at home, she went the following afternoon to Ancoats.

The outside of the well-known house struck her as different; for the door was closed, instead of open, as it once had always stood. The window-plants, George Wilson's pride and especial care, looked withering and drooping. They had been without water for a long time, and now, when the widow had reproached herself severely for neglect, in her ignorant anxiety, she gave them too much. On opening the door, Alice was seen, not stirring about in her habitual way, but knitting by the fire-side. The room felt hot, although the fire burnt gray and dim, under the bright rays of the afternoon sun. Mrs. Wilson was "siding"[1] the dinner things, and talking all the time, in a kind of whining, shouting voice, which Mary did not at first understand. She understood at once, however, that her absence had been noted, and talked over; she saw a constrained look on Mrs. Wilson's sorrow-stricken face, which told her a scolding was to come.

"Dear Mary, is that you?" she began. "Why, who would ha' dreamt of seeing you! We thought you'd clean forgotten us; and Jem has often wondered if he should know you, if he met you in the street."

Now, poor Jane Wilson had been sorely tried; and at present her trials had had no outward effect, but that of increased acerbity of temper. She wished to show Mary how much she was offended, and meant to strengthen her cause, by putting some of her own sharp speeches into Jem's mouth.

Mary felt guilty, and had no good reason to give as an apology; so for a minute she stood silent, looking very much ashamed, and then turned to speak to aunt Alice, who, in her surprised, hearty greeting to Mary, had dropped her ball of worsted, and was busy trying to set the thread to rights, before the kitten had entangled it past redemption, once round every chair, and twice round the table.

---

[1] To "side," to put aside, or in order.

"You mun speak louder than that, if you mean her to hear; she become as deaf as a post this last few weeks. I'd ha' told you, if I'd remembered how long it were sin' you'd seen her."

"Yes, my dear, I'm getting very hard o' hearing of late," said Alice, catching the state of the case, with her quick-glancing eyes. "I suppose it's the beginning of th' end."

"Don't talk o' that way," screamed her sister-in-law. "We've had enow of ends and deaths without forecasting more." She covered her face with her apron, and sat down to cry.

"He was such a good husband," said she, in a less excited tone, to Mary, as she looked up with tear-streaming eyes from behind her apron. "No one can tell what I've lost in him, for no one knew his worth like me."

Mary's listening sympathy softened her, and she went on to unburden her heavy laden heart.

"Eh, dear, dear! No one knows what I've lost. When my poor boys went, I thought th' Almighty had crushed me to th' ground, but I never thought o' losing George; I did na think I could ha' borne to ha' lived without him. And yet I'm here, and he's—" A fresh burst of crying interrupted her speech.

"Mary,"—beginning to speak again,—"did you ever hear what a poor creature I were when he married me? And he such a handsome fellow! Jem's nothing to what his father were at his age."

Yes! Mary had heard, and so she said. But the poor woman's thoughts had gone back to those days, and her little recollections came out, with many interruptions of sighs, and tears, and shakes of the head.

"There were nought about me for him to choose me. I were just well enough afore that accident, but at after I were downright plain. And there was Bessy Witter as would ha' given her eyes for him; she as is Mrs. Carson now, for she were a handsome lass, although I never could see her beauty then; and Carson warn't so much above her, as they're both above us all now."

Mary went very red, and wished she could help doing so, and wished also that Mrs. Wilson would tell her more about the father and mother of her lover; but she durst not ask, and Mrs. Wilson's thoughts soon returned to her husband, and their early married days.

"If you'll believe me, Mary, there never was such a born goose at housekeeping as I were; and yet he married me! I had been in a factory sin' five years old a'most, and I knew nought about cleaning, or cooking, let alone washing and such-like work. The day after we were married he goes to his work at after breakfast, and says he, 'Jenny, we'll ha' th' cold beef, and potatoes, and that's a dinner fit for a prince.' I were anxious to make him comfortable, God knows how anxious. And yet I'd no notion how to cook a potato. I know'd they were boiled, and I know'd their skins were taken off, and that were all. So I tidyed my house in a rough kind o' way, and then I looked at that very clock up yonder," pointing at one that hung against the wall, "and I seed it were nine o'clock, so, thinks I, th' potatoes shall be well boiled at any rate, and I gets 'em on th' fire in a jiffy (that's to say, as soon as I could peel 'em, which were a tough job at first), and then I fell to unpacking my boxes! and at twenty minutes past twelve he comes home, and I had th' beef ready on th' table, and I went to take the potatoes out o' th' pot; but oh! Mary, th' water had boiled away, and they were all a nasty brown mass, as smelt through all the house. He said nought, and were very gentle; but, oh, Mary, I cried so that afternoon. I shall ne'er forget it; no, never. I made many a blunder at after, but none that fretted me like that."

"Father does not like girls to work in factories," said Mary.

"No, I know he doesn't; and reason good. They oughtn't to go at after they're married, that I'm very clear about. I could reckon up" (counting with her fingers) "ay, nine men I know, as has been driven to th' public-house by having wives as worked in factories; good folk, too, as thought there was no harm in putting their little ones out at nurse, and letting their house go all dirty, and their fires all out; and that was a place as was tempting for a husband to stay in, was it? He soon finds out gin-shops, where all is clean and bright, and where th' fire blazes cheerily, and gives a man a welcome as it were."

Alice, who was standing near for the convenience of hearing, had caught much of this speech, and it was evident the subject had previously been discussed by the women, for she chimed in.

"I wish our Jem could speak a word to th' Queen about factory work for married women. Eh! but he comes it strong, when once yo get him to speak about it. Wife o' his'n will never work away fra' home."

"I say it's Prince Albert as ought to be asked how he'd like his missis to be from home when he comes in, tired and worn, and wanting some one to cheer him; and may be, her to come in by-and-bye, just as tired and down in th' mouth; and how he'd like for her never to be at home to see to th' cleaning of his house, or to keep a bright fire in his grate. Let alone his meals being all hugger-mugger and comfortless. I'd be bound, prince as he is, if his missis served him so, he'd be off to a gin-palace, or summut o' that kind. So why can't he make a law again poor folks' wives working in factories?"

Mary ventured to say that she thought the Queen and Prince Albert could not make laws, but the answer was,

"Pooh! don't tell me it's not the Queen as makes laws; and isn't she bound to obey Prince Albert? And if he said they mustn't, why she'd say they mustn't, and then all folk would say, oh no, we never shall do any such thing no more."

"Jem's getten on rarely," said Alice, who had not heard her sister's last burst of eloquence, and whose thoughts were still running on her nephew, and his various talents. "He's found out summut about a crank or a tank, I forget rightly which it is, but th' master's made him foreman, and he all the while turning off hands; but he said he could na part wi' Jem, nohow. He's good wage now: I tell him he'll be thinking of marrying soon, and he deserves a right down good wife, that he does."

Mary went very red, and looked annoyed, although there was a secret spring of joy deep down in her heart, at hearing Jem so spoken of. But his mother only saw the annoyed look, and was piqued accordingly. She was not over and above desirous that her son should marry. His presence in the house seemed a relic of happier times, and she had some little jealousy of his future wife, whoever she might be. Still she could not bear any one not to feel gratified and flattered by Jem's preference, and full well she knew how above all others he preferred Mary. Now she had never thought Mary good enough for Jem, and her late neglect in coming to see her still rankled a little in her breast. So she determined to invent a little, in order to do away with any idea Mary might have that Jem would choose her for "his right down good wife," as aunt Alice called it.

"Ay, he'll be for taking a wife soon," and then, in a lower voice, as if confidentially, but really to prevent any contradiction or explanation from her simple sister-in-law, she added,

"It'll not be long afore Molly Gibson (that's her at th' provision-shop round the corner) will hear a secret as will not displease her, I'm thinking. She's been casting sheep's eyes at our Jem this many a day, but he thought her father would not give her to a common working man; but now he's as good as her, every bit. I thought once he'd a fancy for thee, Mary, but I donnot think yo'd ever ha' suited, so it's best as it is."

By an effort Mary managed to keep down her vexation, and to say, "She hoped he'd be happy with Molly Gibson. She was very handsome, for certain."

"Ay, and a notable body, too. I'll just step up stairs and show you the patchwork quilt she gave me but last Saturday."

Mary was glad she was going out of the room. Her words irritated her; perhaps not the less because she did not fully believe them. Besides she wanted to speak to Alice, and Mrs. Wilson seemed to think that she, as the widow, ought to absorb all the attention.

"Dear Alice," began Mary, "I'm so grieved to find you so deaf; it must have come on very rapid."

"Yes, dear, it's a trial; I'll not deny it. Pray God give me strength to find out its teaching. I felt it sore one fine day when I thought I'd go gather some meadowsweet to make tea for Jane's cough; and the fields seemed so dree and still, and at first I could na make out what was wanting; and then it struck me it were th' song o' the birds, and that I never should hear their sweet music no more, and I could na help crying a bit. But I've much to be thankful for. I think I'm a comfort to Jane, if I'm only some one to scold now and then; poor body! It takes off her thoughts from her sore losses when she can scold a bit. If my eyes are left I can do well enough; I can guess at what folk are saying."

The splendid red and yellow patch quilt now made its appearance, and Jane Wilson would not be satisfied unless Mary praised it all over, border, centre, and ground-work, right side and wrong; and Mary did her duty, saying all the more, because she could not work herself up to any very hearty admiration of her rival's present. She made haste, however, with her commendations, in order to avoid encountering Jem. As soon as she was fairly away from the house and street, she slackened her pace, and began to think. Did Jem really care for Molly Gibson? Well, if he did, let him. People seemed all to think he was much too good for her

(Mary's own self). Perhaps some one else, far more handsome, and far more grand, would show him one day that she was good enough to be Mrs. Henry Carson. So temper, or what Mary called "spirit," led her to encourage Mr. Carson more than ever she had done before.

Some weeks after this, there was a meeting of the Trades' Union to which John Barton belonged. The morning of the day on which it was to take place he had lain late in bed, for what was the use of getting up? He had hesitated between the purchase of meal or opium, and had chosen the latter, for its use had become a necessity with him. He wanted it to relieve him from the terrible depression its absence occasioned. A large lump seemed only to bring him into a natural state, or what had been his natural state formerly. Eight o'clock was the hour fixed for the meeting; and at it were read letters, filled with details of woe, from all parts of the country. Fierce, heavy gloom brooded over the assembly; and fiercely and heavily did the men separate, towards eleven o'clock, some irritated by the opposition of others to their desperate plans.

It was not a night to cheer them, as they quitted the glare of the gas-lighted room, and came out into the street. Unceasing, soaking rain was falling; the very lamps seemed obscured by the damp upon the glass, and their light reached but to a little distance from the posts. The streets were cleared of passers-by; not a creature seemed stirring, except here and there a drenched policeman in his oil-skin cape. Barton wished the others good night, and set off home. He had gone through a street or two, when he heard a step behind him; but he did not care to look and see who it was. A little further, and the person quickened step, and touched his arm very lightly. He turned, and saw, even by the darkness visible of that badly-lighted street, that the woman who stood by him was of no doubtful profession. It was told by her faded finery, all unfit to meet the pelting of that pitiless storm; the gauze bonnet, once pink, now dirty white; the muslin gown, all draggled, and soaking wet up to the very knees; the gay-coloured barège shawl, closely wrapped round the form, which yet shivered and shook, as the woman whispered: "I want to speak to you."

He swore an oath, and bade her begone.

"I really do. Don't send me away. I'm so out of breath, I cannot say what I would all at once." She put her hand to her side, and caught her breath with evident pain.

"I tell thee I'm not the man for thee," adding an opprobrious name. "Stay," said he, as a thought suggested by her voice flashed across him. He gripped her arm—the arm he had just before shaken off, and dragged her, faintly resisting, to the nearest lamp-post. He pushed her bonnet back, and roughly held the face she would fain have averted, to the light, and in her large, unnaturally bright gray eyes, her lovely mouth, half open, as if imploring the forbearance she could not ask for in words, he saw at once the long-lost Esther; she who had caused his wife's death. Much was like the gay creature of former years; but the glaring paint, the sharp features, the changed expression of the whole! But most of all, he loathed the dress; and yet the poor thing, out of her little choice of attire, had put on the plainest she had, to come on that night's errand.

"So it's thee, is it! It's thee!" exclaimed John, as he ground his teeth, and shook her with passion. "I've looked for thee long at corners o' streets, and such like places. I knew I should find thee at last. Thee'll may be bethink thee o' some words I spoke, which put thee up at th' time; summut about street-walkers; but oh no! thou art none o' them naughts; no one thinks thou art, who sees thy fine draggle-tailed dress, and thy pretty pink cheeks!" stopping for very want of breath.

"Oh, mercy! John, mercy! listen to me for Mary's sake!"

She meant his daughter, but the name only fell on his ear as belonging to his wife; and it was adding fuel to the fire. In vain did her face grow deadly pale round the vivid circle of paint, in vain did she gasp for mercy,—he burst forth again.

"And thou names that name to me! and thou thinks the thought of her will bring thee mercy! Dost thou know it was thee who killed her, as sure as ever Cain killed Abel. She'd loved thee as her own, and she trusted thee as her own, and when thou wert gone she never held up head again, but died in less than a three week; and at the judgment day she'll rise, and point to thee as her murderer; or if she don't, I will."

He flung her, trembling, sickening, fainting, from him, and strode away. She fell with a feeble scream against the lamp-post, and lay there in her weakness, unable to rise. A policeman came up in time to see the close of these occurrences, and concluding from Esther's unsteady, reeling fall, that she was tipsy, he took her in her half-unconscious state to the lock-ups for the night. The superintendent of that abode of vice and misery was roused from his dozing watch through the dark hours, by half-delirious wails and moanings, which he reported as arising from intoxication. If he had listened, he would have heard these words, repeated in various forms, but always in the same anxious, muttering way.

"He would not listen to me; what can I do? He would not listen to me, and I wanted to warn him! Oh, what shall I do to save Mary's child? What shall I do? How can I keep her from being such a one as I am; such a wretched, loathsome creature! She was listening just as I listened, and loving just as I loved, and the end will be just like my end. How shall I save her? She won't hearken to warning, or heed it more than I did; and who loves her well enough to watch over her as she should be watched? God keep her from harm! And yet I won't pray for her; sinner that I am! Can my prayers be heard? No! they'll only do harm. How shall I save her? He would not listen to me."

So the night wore away. The next morning she was taken up to the New Bailey. It was a clear case of disorderly vagrancy, and she was committed to prison for a month. How much might happen in that time!

CHAPTER XI - MR. CARSON'S INTENTIONS REVEALED.

"O Mary, canst thou wreck his peace,
  Wha for thy sake wad gladly die?
Or canst thou break that heart of his,
  Whase only faut is loving thee?"

BURNS.

"I can like of the wealth, I must confess,
Yet more I prize the man, though moneyless;
I am not of their humour yet that can
For title or estate affect a man;
Or of myself one body deign to make
With him I loathe, for his possessions' sake."

WITHER'S "FIDELIA."

Barton returned home after his encounter with Esther, uneasy and dissatisfied. He had said no more than he had been planning to say for years, in case she was ever thrown in his way, in the character in which he felt certain he should meet her. He believed she deserved it all, and yet he now wished he had not said it. Her look, as she asked for mercy, haunted him through his broken and disordered sleep; her form, as he last saw her, lying prostrate in helplessness, would not be banished from his dreams. He sat up in bed to try and dispel the vision. Now, too late, his conscience smote him for his harshness. It would have been all very well, he thought, to have said what he did, if he had added some kind words, at last. He wondered if his dead wife was conscious of that night's occurrence; and he hoped not, for with her love for Esther he believed it would embitter Heaven to have seen her so degraded and repulsed. For he now recalled her humility, her tacit acknowledgment of her lost character; and he began to marvel if there was power in the religion he had often heard of, to turn her from her ways. He felt that no earthly power that he knew of could do it, but there glimmered on his darkness the idea that religion might save her. Still, where to find her again? In the wilderness of a large town, where to meet with an individual of so little value or note to any?

And evening after evening he paced those streets in which he had heard her footsteps following him, peering under every fantastic, discreditable bonnet, in the hopes of once more meeting Esther, and addressing her in a far different manner from what he had done before. But he returned, night after night, disappointed in his search, and at last gave it up in despair, and tried to recall his angry feelings towards her, in order to find relief from his present self-reproach.

He often looked at Mary, and wished she were not so like her aunt, for the very bodily likeness seemed to suggest the possibility of a similar likeness in their fate; and then this idea enraged his irritable mind, and he became suspicious and anxious about Mary's conduct. Now hitherto she had been so remarkably free from all control, and almost from all inquiry concerning her actions, that she did not brook this change in her father's behaviour very well. Just when she was yielding more than ever to Mr. Carson's desire of frequent meetings, it was hard to be so questioned concerning her hours of leaving off work, whether she had come straight home, &c. She could not tell lies; though she could conceal much if she were not questioned. So she took refuge in obstinate silence, alleging as a reason for it her indignation at being so cross-examined. This did not add to the good feeling between father and daughter, and yet they dearly loved each other; and in the minds of each, one principal reason for maintaining such behaviour as displeased the other, was the believing that this conduct would insure that person's happiness.

Her father now began to wish Mary were married. Then this terrible superstitious fear suggested by her likeness to Esther would be done away with. He felt that he could not resume the reins he had once slackened. But with a husband it would be different. If Jem Wilson would but marry her! With his character for steadiness and talent! But he was afraid Mary had slighted him, he came so seldom now to the house. He would ask her.

"Mary, what's come o'er thee and Jem Wilson? Yo were great friends at one time."

"Oh, folk say he's going to be married to Molly Gibson, and of course courting takes up a deal o' time," answered Mary, as indifferently as she could.

"Thou'st played thy cards badly, then," replied her father, in a surly tone. "At one time he were desperate fond o' thee, or I'm much mistaken. Much fonder of thee than thou deservedst."

"That's as people think," said Mary, pertly, for she remembered that the very morning before she had met Mr. Carson, who had sighed, and swore, and protested all manner of tender vows that she was the loveliest, sweetest, best, &c. And when she had seen him afterwards riding with one of his beautiful sisters, had he not evidently pointed her out as in some way or other an object worthy of attention and interest, and then lingered behind his sister's horse for a moment to kiss his hand repeatedly. So, as for Jem Wilson, she could whistle him down the wind.

But her father was not in the mood to put up with pertness, and he upbraided her with the loss of Jem Wilson till she had to bite her lips till the blood came, in order to keep down the angry words that would rise in her heart. At last her father left the house, and then she might give way to her passionate tears.

It so happened that Jem, after much anxious thought, had determined that day to "put his fate to the touch, to win or lose it all." He was in a condition to maintain a wife in comfort. It was true his mother and aunt must form part of the household; but such is not an uncommon case among the poor, and if there were the advantage of previous friendship between the parties, it was not, he thought, an obstacle to matrimony. Both mother and aunt he believed would welcome Mary. And oh! what a certainty of happiness the idea of that welcome implied.

He had been absent and abstracted all day long with the thought of the coming event of the evening. He almost smiled at himself for his care in washing and dressing in preparation for his visit to Mary. As if one waistcoat or another could decide his fate in so passionately momentous a thing. He believed he only delayed before his little looking-glass for cowardice, for absolute fear of a girl. He would try not to think so much about the affair, and he thought the more.

Poor Jem! it is not an auspicious moment for thee!

"Come in," said Mary, as some one knocked at the door, while she sat sadly at her sewing, trying to earn a few pence by working over hours at some mourning.

Jem entered, looking more awkward and abashed than he had ever done before. Yet here was Mary all alone, just as he had hoped to find her. She did not ask him to take a chair, but after standing a minute or two he sat down near her.

"Is your father at home, Mary?" said he, by way of making an opening, for she seemed determined to keep silence, and went on stitching away.

"No, he's gone to his Union, I suppose." Another silence. It was no use waiting, thought Jem. The subject would never be led to by any talk he could think of in his anxious fluttered state. He had better begin at once.

"Mary!" said he, and the unusual tone of his voice made her look up for an instant, but in that time she understood from his countenance what was coming, and her heart beat so suddenly and violently she could hardly sit still. Yet one thing she was sure of; nothing he could say should make her have him. She would show them all *who* would be glad to have her. She was not yet calm after her father's irritating speeches. Yet her eyes fell veiled before that passionate look fixed upon her.

"Dear Mary! (for how dear you are, I cannot rightly tell you in words). It's no new story I'm going to speak about. You must ha' seen and known it long; for since we were boy and girl, I ha' loved you above father and mother and all; and all I've thought on by day and dreamt on by night, has been something in which you've had a share. I'd no way of keeping you for long, and I scorned to try and tie you down; and I lived in terror lest some one else should take you to himself. But now, Mary, I'm foreman in th' works, and, dear Mary! listen," as she, in her unbearable agitation, stood up and turned away from him. He rose, too, and came nearer, trying to take hold of her hand; but this she would not allow. She was bracing herself up to refuse him, for once and for all.

"And now, Mary, I've a home to offer you, and a heart as true as ever man had to love you and cherish you; we shall never be rich folk, I dare say; but if a loving heart and a strong right arm can shield you from sorrow, or from want, mine shall do it. I cannot speak as I would like; my love won't let itself be put in words. But oh! darling, say you believe me, and that you'll be mine."

She could not speak at once; her words would not come.

"Mary, they say silence gives consent; is it so?" he whispered.

Now or never the effort must be made.

"No! it does not with me." Her voice was calm, although she trembled from head to foot. "I will always be your friend, Jem, but I can never be your wife."

"Not my wife!" said he, mournfully. "Oh Mary, think awhile! you cannot be my friend if you will not be my wife. At least I can never be content to be only your friend. Do think awhile! If you say No you will make me hopeless, desperate. It's no love of yesterday. It has made the very groundwork of all that people call good in me. I don't know what I shall be if you won't have me. And, Mary! think how glad your father would be! it may sound vain, but he's told me more than once how much he should like to see us two married!"

Jem intended this for a powerful argument, but in Mary's present mood it told against him more than any thing; for it suggested the false and foolish idea, that her father, in his evident anxiety to promote her marriage with Jem, had been speaking to him on the subject with some degree of solicitation.

"I tell you, Jem, it cannot be. Once for all, I will never marry you."

"And is this the end of all my hopes and fears? the end of my life, I may say, for it is the end of all worth living for!" His agitation rose and carried him into passion. "Mary! you'll hear, may be, of me as a drunkard, and may be as a thief, and may be as a murderer. Remember! when all are speaking ill of me, you will have no right to blame me, for it's your cruelty that will have made me what I feel I shall become. You won't even say you'll try and like me; will you, Mary?" said he, suddenly changing his tone from threatening despair to fond passionate entreaty, as he took her hand and held it forcibly between both of his, while he tried to catch a glimpse of her averted face. She was silent, but it was from deep and violent emotion. He could not bear to wait; he would not hope, to be dashed away again; he rather in his bitterness of heart chose the certainty of despair, and before she could resolve what to answer, he flung away her hand and rushed out of the house.

"Jem! Jem!" cried she, with faint and choking voice. It was too late; he left street after street behind him with his almost winged speed, as he sought the fields, where he might give way unobserved to all the deep despair he felt.

It was scarcely ten minutes since he had entered the house, and found Mary at comparative peace, and now she lay half across the dresser, her head hidden in her hands, and every part of her body shaking with the violence of her sobs. She could not have told at first (if you had asked her, and she could have commanded voice enough to answer) why she was in such agonised grief. It was too sudden for her to analyse, or think upon it. She only felt that by her own doing her life would be hereafter dreary and blank. By-and-bye her sorrow exhausted her body by its power, and she seemed to have no strength left for crying. She sat down; and now thoughts crowded on her mind. One little hour ago, and all was still unsaid, and she had her fate in her own power. And yet, how long ago had she determined to say pretty much what she did, if the occasion ever offered.

It was as if two people were arguing the matter; that mournful, desponding communion between her former self and her present self. Herself, a day, an hour ago; and herself now. For we have every one of us felt how a very few minutes of the months and years called life, will sometimes suffice to place all time past and future in an entirely new light; will make us see the vanity or the criminality of the bye-gone, and so change the aspect of the coming time, that we look with loathing on the very thing we have most desired. A few moments may change our character for life, by giving a totally different direction to our aims and energies.

To return to Mary. Her plan had been, as we well know, to marry Mr. Carson, and the occurrence an hour ago was only a preliminary step. True; but it had unveiled her heart to her; it had convinced her she loved Jem above all persons or things. But Jem was a poor mechanic, with a mother and aunt to keep; a mother, too, who had shown her pretty clearly she did not desire her for a daughter-in-law: while Mr. Carson was rich, and prosperous, and gay, and (she believed) would place her in all circumstances of ease and luxury, where want could never come. What were these hollow vanities to her, now she had discovered the passionate secret of her soul? She felt as if she almost hated Mr. Carson, who had decoyed her with his baubles. She now saw how vain, how nothing to her, would be all gaieties and pomps, all joys and pleasures, unless she might share them with Jem; yes, with him she harshly rejected so short a time ago. If he were poor, she loved him all the better. If his mother did think her unworthy of him, what was it but the truth, as she now owned with bitter penitence. She had hitherto been walking in grope-light towards a precipice; but in the clear revelation of that past hour, she saw her danger, and turned away resolutely and for ever.

That was some comfort: I mean her clear perception of what she ought not to do; of what no luring temptation should ever again induce her to hearken to. How she could best undo the wrong she had done to Jem and herself by refusing his love, was another anxious question. She wearied herself with proposing plans, and rejecting them.

She was roused to a consciousness of time by hearing the neighbouring church clock strike twelve. Her father she knew might be expected home any minute, and she was in no mood for a meeting with him. So she hastily gathered up her work, and went to her own little bed-room, leaving him to let himself in.

She put out her candle, that her father might not see its light under the door; and sat down on her bed to think. But after turning things over in her mind again and again, she could only determine at once to put an end to all further communication with Mr. Carson, in the most decided way she could. Maidenly modesty (and true love is ever modest) seemed to oppose every plan she could think of, for showing Jem how much she repented her decision against him, and how dearly she had now discovered that she loved him. She came to the unusual wisdom of resolving to do nothing, but try and be patient, and improve circumstances as they might turn up. Surely, if Jem knew of her remaining unmarried, he would try his fortune again. He would never be content with one rejection; she believed she could not in his place. She had been very wrong, but now she would try and do right, and have womanly patience, until he saw her changed and repentant mind in her natural actions. Even if she had to wait for years, it was no more than now it was easy to look forward to, as a penance for her giddy flirting on the one hand, and her cruel mistake concerning her feelings on the other. So anticipating a happy ending to the course of her love, however distant it might be, she fell asleep just as the earliest factory bells were ringing. She had sunk down in her clothes, and her sleep was unrefreshing. She wakened up shivery and chill in body, and sorrow-stricken in mind, though she could not at first rightly tell the cause of her depression.

She recalled the events of the night before, and still resolved to adhere to those determinations she had then formed. But patience seemed a far more difficult virtue this morning.

She hastened down-stairs, and in her earnest sad desire to do right, now took much pains to secure a comfortable though scanty breakfast for her father; and when he dawdled into the room, in an evidently irritable temper, she bore all with the gentleness of penitence, till at last her mild answers turned away wrath.

She loathed the idea of meeting Sally Leadbitter at her daily work; yet it must be done, and she tried to nerve herself for the encounter, and to make it at once understood, that having determined to give up having any thing further to do with Mr. Carson, she considered the bond of intimacy broken between them.

But Sally was not the person to let these resolutions be carried into effect too easily. She soon became aware of the present state of Mary's feelings, but she thought they merely arose from the changeableness of girlhood, and that the time would come when Mary would thank her for almost forcing her to keep up her meetings and communications with her rich lover.

So, when two days had passed over in rather too marked avoidance of Sally on Mary's part, and when the former was made aware by Mr. Carson's complaints that Mary was not keeping her appointments with him, and that unless he detained her by force, he had no chance of obtaining a word as she passed him in the street on her rapid walk home, she resolved to compel Mary to what she called her own good.

She took no notice during the third day of Mary's avoidance as they sat at work; she rather seemed to acquiesce in the coolness of their intercourse. She put away her sewing early, and went home to her mother, who, she said, was more ailing than usual. The other girls soon followed her example, and Mary, casting a rapid glance up and down the street, as she stood last on Miss Simmonds' door-step, darted homewards, in hopes of avoiding the person whom she was fast learning to dread. That night she was safe from any encounter on her road, and she arrived at home, which she found as she expected, empty; for she knew it was a club night, which her father would not miss. She sat down to recover breath, and to still her heart, which panted more from nervousness than from over-exertion, although she had walked so quickly. Then she rose, and taking off her bonnet, her eye caught the form of Sally Leadbitter passing the window with a lingering step, and looking into the darkness with all her might, as if to ascertain if Mary were returned. In an instant she re-passed and knocked at the house-door, but without awaiting an answer, she entered.

"Well, Mary, dear" (knowing well how little "dear" Mary considered her just then); "i's so difficult to get any comfortable talk at Miss Simmonds', I thought I'd just step up and see you at home."

"I understood from what you said your mother was ailing, and that you wanted to be with her," replied Mary, in no welcoming tone.

"Ay, but mother's better now," said the unabashed Sally. "Your father's out I suppose?" looking round as well as she could; for Mary made no haste to perform the hospitable offices of striking a match, and lighting a candle.

"Yes, he's out," said Mary, shortly, and busying herself at last about the candle, without ever asking her visitor to sit down.

"So much the better," answered Sally, "for to tell you the truth, Mary, I've a friend at th' end of the street, as is anxious to come and see you at home, since you're grown so particular as not to like to speak to him in the street. He'll be here directly."

"Oh, Sally, don't let him," said Mary, speaking at last heartily; and running to the door she would have fastened it, but Sally held her hands, laughing meanwhile at her distress.

"Oh, please, Sally," struggling, "dear Sally! don't let him come here, the neighbours will so talk, and father'll go mad if he hears; he'll kill me, Sally, he will. Besides, I don't love him—I never did. Oh, let me go," as footsteps approached, and then, as they passed the house, and seemed to give her a respite, she continued, "Do, Sally, dear Sally, go and tell him I don't love him, and that I don't want to have any thing more to do with him. It was very wrong, I dare say, keeping company with him at all, but I'm very sorry, if I've led him to think too much of me; and I don't want him to think any more. Will you tell him this, Sally? and I'll do any thing for you if you will."

"I'll tell you what I'll do," said Sally, in a more relenting mood, "I'll go back with you to where he's waiting for us; or rather, I should say, where I told him to wait for a quarter of an hour, till I seed if your father was at home; and if I didn't come back in that time, he said he'd come here, and break the door open but he'd see you."

"Oh, let us go, let us go," said Mary, feeling that the interview must be, and had better be anywhere than at home, where her father might return at any minute. She snatched up her bonnet, and was at the end of the court in an instant; but then, not knowing whether to turn to the right or to the left, she was obliged to wait for Sally, who came leisurely up, and put her arm through Mary's, with a kind of decided hold, intended to prevent the possibility of her changing her mind, and turning back. But this, under the circumstances, was quite different to Mary's plan. She had wondered more than once if she must not have another interview with Mr. Carson; and had then determined, while she expressed her resolution that it should be the final one, to tell him how sorry she was if she had thoughtlessly given him false hopes. For be it remembered, she had the innocence, or the ignorance, to believe his intentions honourable; and he, feeling that at any price he must have her, only that he would obtain her as cheaply as he could, had never undeceived her; while Sally Leadbitter laughed in her sleeve at them both, and wondered how it would all end,—whether Mary would gain her point of marriage, with her sly affectation of believing such to be Mr. Carson's intention in courting her.

Not very far from the end of the street, into which the court where Mary lived opened, they met Mr. Carson, his hat a good deal slouched over his face as if afraid of being recognised. He turned when he saw them coming, and led the way without uttering a word (although they were close behind) to a street of half-finished houses.

The length of the walk gave Mary time to recoil from the interview which was to follow; but even if her own resolve to go through with it had failed, there was the steady grasp of Sally Leadbitter, which she could not evade without an absolute struggle.

At last he stopped in the shelter and concealment of a wooden fence, put up to keep the building rubbish from intruding on the foot-pavement. Inside this fence, a minute afterwards, the girls were standing by him; Mary now returning Sally's detaining grasp with interest, for she had determined on the way to make her a witness, willing or unwilling, to the ensuing conversation. But Sally's curiosity led her to be a very passive prisoner in Mary's hold.

With more freedom than he had ever used before, Mr. Carson put his arm firmly round Mary's waist, in spite of her indignant resistance.

"Nay, nay! you little witch! Now I have caught you, I shall keep you prisoner. Tell me now what has made you run away from me so fast these few days—tell me, you sweet little coquette!"

Mary ceased struggling, but turned so as to be almost opposite to him, while she spoke out calmly and boldly,

"Mr. Carson! I want to speak to you for once and for all. Since I met you last Monday evening, I have made up my mind to have nothing more to do with you. I know I've been wrong in leading you to think I liked you; but I believe I didn't rightly know my own mind; and I humbly beg your pardon, sir, if I've led you to think too much of me."

For an instant he was surprised; the next, vanity came to his aid, and convinced him that she could only be joking. He, young, agreeable, rich, handsome! No! she was only showing a little womanly fondness for coquetting.

"You're a darling little rascal to go on in this way! 'Humbly begging my pardon if you've made me think too much of you.' As if you didn't know I think of you from morning to night. But you want to be told it again and again, do you?"

"No, indeed, sir, I don't. I would far liefer[1] that you should say you will never think of me again, than that you should speak of me in this way. For indeed, sir, I never was more in earnest than I am, when I say to-night is the last night I will ever speak to you."

"Yet had I *levre* unwist for sorrow die." *Chaucer; "Troilus and Creseide."*

"Last night, you sweet little equivocator, but not last day. Ha, Mary! I've caught you, have I?" as she, puzzled by his perseverance in thinking her joking, hesitated in what form she could now put her meaning.

"I mean, sir," she said, sharply, "that I will never speak to you again at any time, after to-night."

"And what's made this change, Mary?" said he, seriously enough now. "Have I done any thing to offend you?" added he, earnestly.

"No, sir," she answered gently, but yet firmly. "I cannot tell you exactly why I've changed my mind; but I shall not alter it again; and as I said before, I beg your pardon if I've done wrong by you. And now, sir, if you please, good night."

"But I do not please. You shall not go. What have I done, Mary? Tell me. You must not go without telling me how I have vexed you. What would you have me do?"

"Nothing, sir! but (in an agitated tone) oh! let me go! You cannot change my mind; it's quite made up. Oh, sir! why do you hold me so tight? If you *will* know why I won't have any thing more to do with you, it is that I cannot love you. I have tried, and I really cannot."

This naive and candid avowal served her but little. He could not understand how it could be true. Some reason lurked behind. He was passionately in love. What should he do to tempt her? A thought struck him.

"Listen! Mary. Nay, I cannot let you go till you have heard me. I do love you dearly; and I won't believe but what you love me a very little, just a very little. Well, if you don't like to own it, never mind! I only want now to tell you how much I love you, by what I am ready to give up for you. You know (or perhaps you are not fully aware) how little my father and mother would like me to marry you. So angry would they be, and so much ridicule should I have to brave, that of course I have never thought of it till now. I thought we could be happy enough without marriage." (Deep sank those words into Mary's heart.) "But now, if you like, I'll get a licence to-morrow morning—nay, to-night, and I'll marry you in defiance of all the world, rather than give you up. In a year or two my father will forgive me, and meanwhile you shall have every luxury money can purchase, and every charm that love can devise to make your life happy. After all, my mother was but a factory girl." (This was said half to himself, as if to reconcile himself to this bold step.) "Now, Mary, you see how willing I am to—to sacrifice a good deal for you; I even offer you marriage, to satisfy your little ambitious heart; so, now, won't you say you can love me a little, little bit?"

---

[1] "Liefer," rather.

He pulled her towards him. To his surprise, she still resisted. Yes! though all she had pictured to herself for so many months in being the wife of Mr. Carson was now within her grasp, she resisted. His speech had given her but one feeling, that of exceeding great relief. For she had dreaded, now she knew what true love was, to think of the attachment she might have created; the deep feeling her flirting conduct might have called out. She had loaded herself with reproaches for the misery she might have caused. It was a relief to gather that the attachment was of that low, despicable kind, which can plan to seduce the object of its affection; that the feeling she had caused was shallow enough, for it only pretended to embrace self, at the expense of the misery, the ruin, of one falsely termed beloved. She need not be penitent to such a plotter! That was the relief.

"I am obliged to you, sir, for telling me what you have. You may think I am a fool; but I did think you meant to marry me all along; and yet, thinking so, I felt I could not love you. Still I felt sorry I had gone so far in keeping company with you. Now, sir, I tell you, if I had loved you before, I don't think I should have loved you now you have told me you meant to ruin me; for that's the plain English of not meaning to marry me till just this minute. I said I was sorry, and humbly begged your pardon; that was before I knew what you were. Now I scorn you, sir, for plotting to ruin a poor girl. Good night."

And with a wrench, for which she had reserved all her strength, she was off like a bolt. They heard her flying footsteps echo down the quiet street. The next sound was Sally's laugh, which grated on Mr. Carson's ears, and keenly irritated him.

"And what do you find so amusing, Sally?" asked he.

"Oh, sir, I beg your pardon. I humbly beg your pardon, as Mary says, but I can't help laughing, to think how she's outwitted us." (She was going to have said, "outwitted you," but changed the pronoun.)

"Why, Sally, had you any idea she was going to fly out in this style?"

"No, I hadn't, to be sure. But if you did think of marrying her, why (if I may be so bold as to ask) did you go and tell her you had no thought of doing otherwise by her? That was what put her up at last!"

"Why I had repeatedly before led her to infer that marriage was not my object. I never dreamed she could have been so foolish as to have mistaken me, little provoking romancer though she be! So I naturally wished her to know what a sacrifice of prejudice, of—of myself, in short, I was willing to make for her sake; yet I don't think she was aware of it after all. I believe I might have any lady in Manchester if I liked, and yet I was willing and ready to marry a poor dress-maker. Don't you understand me now? and don't you see what a sacrifice I was making to humour her? and all to no avail."

Sally was silent, so he went on:

"My father would have forgiven any temporary connexion, far sooner than my marrying one so far beneath me in rank."

"I thought you said, sir, your mother was a factory girl," reminded Sally, rather maliciously.

"Yes, yes!—but then my father was in much such a station; at any rate, there was not the disparity there is between Mary and me."

Another pause.

"Then you mean to give her up, sir? She made no bones of saying she gave you up."

"No, I do not mean to give her up, whatever you and she may please to think. I am more in love with her than ever; even for this charming capricious ebullition of hers. She'll come round, you may depend upon it. Women always do. They always have second thoughts, and find out that they are best in casting off a lover. Mind! I don't say I shall offer her the same terms again."

With a few more words of no importance, the allies parted.

CHAPTER XII - OLD ALICE'S BAIRN.

"I lov'd him not; and yet, now he is gone,
    I feel I am alone.
I check'd him while he spoke; yet, could he speak,
    Alas! I would not check.
For reasons not to love him once I sought,
    And wearied all my thought."

W. S. LANDOR.

And now Mary had, as she thought, dismissed both her lovers. But they looked on their dismissals with very different eyes. He who loved her with all his heart and with all his soul, considered his rejection final. He did not comfort himself with the idea, which would have proved so well founded in his case, that women have second thoughts about casting off their lovers. He had too much respect for his own heartiness of love to believe himself unworthy of Mary; that mock humble conceit did not enter his head. He thought he did not "hit Mary's fancy;" and though that may sound a trivial every-day expression, yet the reality of it cut him to the heart. Wild visions of enlistment, of drinking himself into forgetfulness, of becoming desperate in some way or another, entered his mind; but then the thought of his mother stood like an angel with a drawn sword in the way to sin. For, you know, "he was the only son of his mother, and she was a widow;" dependent on him for daily bread. So he could not squander away health and time, which were to him money wherewith to support her failing years. He went to his work, accordingly, to all outward semblance just as usual; but with a heavy, heavy heart within.

Mr. Carson, as we have seen, persevered in considering Mary's rejection of him as merely a "charming caprice." If she were at work, Sally Leadbitter was sure to slip a passionately loving note into her hand, and then so skilfully move away from her side, that Mary could not all at once return it, without making some sensation among the work-women. She was even forced to take several home with her. But after reading one, she determined on her plan. She made no great resistance to receiving them from Sally, but kept them unopened, and occasionally returned them in a blank half-sheet of paper. But far worse than this, was the being so constantly waylaid as she went home by her persevering lover; who had been so long acquainted with all her habits, that she found it difficult to evade him. Late or early, she was never certain of being free from him. Go this way or that, he might come up some cross street when she had just congratulated herself on evading him for that day. He could not have taken a surer mode of making himself odious to her.

And all this time Jem Wilson never came! Not to see her—that she did not expect—but to see her father; to—she did not know what, but she had hoped he would have come on some excuse, just to see if she hadn't changed her mind. He never came. Then she grew weary and impatient, and her spirits sank. The persecution of the one lover, and the neglect of the other, oppressed her sorely. She could not now sit quietly through the evening at her work; or, if she kept, by a strong effort, from pacing up and down the room, she felt as if she must sing to keep off thought while she sewed. And her songs were the maddest, merriest, she could think of. "Barbara Allen," and such sorrowful ditties, did well enough for happy times; but now she required all the aid that could be derived from external excitement to keep down the impulse of grief.

And her father, too—he was a great anxiety to her, he looked so changed and so ill. Yet he would not acknowledge to any ailment. She knew, that be it as late as it would, she never left off work until (if the poor servants paid her pretty regularly for the odd jobs of mending she did for them) she had earned a few pence, enough for one good meal for her father on the next day. But very frequently all she could do in the morning, after her late sitting up at night, was to run with the work home, and receive the money from the person for whom it was done. She could not stay often to make purchases of food, but gave up the money at once to her father's eager clutch; sometimes prompted by savage hunger it is true, but more frequently by a craving for opium.

On the whole he was not so hungry as his daughter. For it was a long fast from the one o'clock dinner-hour at Miss Simmonds' to the close of Mary's vigil, which was often extended to midnight. She was young, and had not yet learned to bear "clemming."

One evening, as she sang a merry song over her work, stopping occasionally to sigh, the blind Margaret came groping in. It had been one of Mary's additional sorrows that her friend had been absent from home, accompanying the lecturer on music in his round among the manufacturing towns of Yorkshire and Lancashire. Her grandfather, too, had seen this a good time for going his expeditions in search of specimens; so that the house had been shut up for several weeks.

"Oh! Margaret, Margaret! how glad I am to see you. Take care. There, now, you're all right, that's father's chair. Sit down."—She kissed her over and over again.

"It seems like the beginning o' brighter times, to see you again, Margaret. Bless you! And how well you look!"

"Doctors always send ailing folk for change of air! and you know I've had plenty o' that same lately."

"You've been quite a traveller for sure! Tell us all about it, do, Margaret. Where have you been to, first place?"

"Eh, lass, that would take a long time to tell. Half o'er the world I sometimes think. Bolton, and Bury, and Owdham, and Halifax, and—but Mary, guess who I saw there! May be you know though, so it's not fair guessing."

"No, I donnot. Tell me, Margaret, for I cannot abide waiting and guessing."

"Well, one night as I were going fra' my lodgings wi' the help on a lad as belonged to th' landlady, to find the room where I were to sing, I heard a cough before me, walking along. Thinks I, that's Jem Wilson's cough, or I'm much mistaken. Next time came a sneeze and a cough, and then I were certain. First I hesitated whether I should speak, thinking if it were a stranger he'd may be think me forrard.[1] But I knew blind folks must not be nesh about using their tongues, so says I, 'Jem Wilson, is that you?' And sure enough it was, and nobody else. Did you know he were in Halifax, Mary?"

"No;" she answered, faintly and sadly; for Halifax was all the same to her heart as the Antipodes; equally inaccessible by humble penitent looks and maidenly tokens of love.

"Well, he's there, however; he's putting up an engine for some folks there, for his master. He's doing well, for he's getten four or five men under him; we'd two or three meetings, and he telled me all about his invention for doing away wi' the crank, or somewhat. His master's bought it from him, and ta'en out a patent, and Jem's a gentleman for life wi' the money his master gied him. But you'll ha' heard all this, Mary?"

No! she had not.

"Well, I thought it all happened afore he left Manchester, and then in course you'd ha' known. But may be it were all settled after he got to Halifax; however, he's gotten two or three hunder pounds for his invention. But what's up with you, Mary? you're sadly out o' sorts. You've never been quarrelling wi' Jem, surely?"

Now Mary cried outright; she was weak in body, and unhappy in mind, and the time was come when she might have the relief of telling her grief. She could not bring herself to confess how much of her sorrow was caused by her having been vain and foolish; she hoped that need never be known, and she could not bear to think of it.

"Oh, Margaret; do you know Jem came here one night when I were put out, and cross. Oh, dear! dear! I could bite my tongue out when I think on it. And he told me how he loved me, and I thought I did not love him, and I told him I didn't; and, Margaret,—he believed me, and went away so sad, and so angry; and now I'd do any thing,—I would, indeed," her sobs choked the end of her sentence. Margaret looked at her with sorrow, but with hope; for she had no doubt in her own mind, that it was only a temporary estrangement.

---

[1] "Forrard," forward.

"Tell me, Margaret," said Mary, taking her apron down from her eyes, and looking at Margaret with eager anxiety, "what can I do to bring him back to me? Should I write to him?"

"No," replied her friend, "that would not do. Men are so queer, they like to have a' the courting to themselves."

"But I did not mean to write him a courting letter," said Mary, somewhat indignantly.

"If you wrote at all, it would be to give him a hint you'd taken the rue, and would be very glad to have him now. I believe now he'd rather find that out himself."

"But he won't try," said Mary, sighing. "How can he find it out when he's at Halifax?"

"If he's a will he's a way, depend upon it. And you would not have him if he's not a will to you, Mary! No, dear!" changing her tone from the somewhat hard way in which sensible people too often speak, to the soft accents of tenderness which come with such peculiar grace from them; "you must just wait and be patient. You may depend upon it, all will end well, and better than if you meddled in it now."

"But it's so hard to be patient," pleaded Mary.

"Ay, dear; being patient is the hardest work we, any on us, have to do through life, I take it. Waiting is far more difficult than doing. I've known that about my sight, and many a one has known it in watching the sick; but it's one of God's lessons we all must learn, one way or another." After a pause. "Have ye been to see his mother of late?"

"No; not for some weeks. When last I went she was so frabbit[1] with me, that I really thought she wished I'd keep away."

"Well! if I were you I'd go. Jem will hear on't, and it will do you far more good in his mind than writing a letter, which, after all, you would find a tough piece of work when you came to settle to it. 'Twould be hard to say neither too much nor too little. But I must be going, grandfather is at home, and it's our first night together, and he must not be sitting wanting me any longer."

She rose up from her seat, but still delayed going.

"Mary! I've somewhat else I want to say to you, and I don't rightly know how to begin. You see, grandfather and I know what bad times is, and we know your father is out o' work, and I'm getting more money than I can well manage; and, dear, would you just take this bit o' gold, and pay me back in good times?" The tears stood in Margaret's eyes as she spoke.

"Dear Margaret, we're not so bad pressed as that." (The thought of her father, and his ill looks, and his one meal a day, rushed upon Mary.) "And yet, dear, if it would not put you out o' your way,—I would work hard to make it up to you;—but would not your grandfather be vexed?"

---

[1] "Frabbit," ill-tempered.

"Not he, wench! It were more his thought than mine, and we have gotten ever so many more at home, so don't hurry yoursel about paying. It's hard to be blind, to be sure, else money comes in so easily now to what it used to do; and it's downright pleasure to earn it, for I do so like singing."

"I wish I could sing," said Mary, looking at the sovereign.

"Some has one kind o' gifts, and some another. Many's the time when I could see, that I longed for your beauty, Mary! We're like childer, ever wanting what we han not got. But now I must say just one more word. Remember, if you're sore pressed for money, we shall take it very unkind if you donnot let us know. Good bye to ye."

In spite of her blindness she hurried away, anxious to rejoin her grandfather, and desirous also to escape from Mary's expressions of gratitude.

Her visit had done Mary good in many ways. It had strengthened her patience and her hope. It had given her confidence in Margaret's sympathy; and last, and really least in comforting power (of so little value are silver and gold in comparison to love, that gift in every one's power to bestow), came the consciousness of the money-value of the sovereign she held in her hand. The many things it might purchase! First of all came the thought of a comfortable supper for her father that very night; and acting instantly upon the idea, she set off in hopes that all the provision-shops might not yet be closed, although it was so late.

That night the cottage shone with unusual light, and fire-gleam; and the father and daughter sat down to a meal they thought almost extravagant. It was so long since they had had enough to eat.

"Food gives heart," say the Lancashire people; and the next day Mary made time to go and call on Mrs. Wilson, according to Margaret's advice. She found her quite alone, and more gracious than she had been the last time Mary had visited her. Alice was gone out, she said.

"She would just step to the post-office, all for no earthly use. For it were to ask if they hadn't a letter lying there for her from her foster-son Will Wilson, the sailor-lad."

"What made her think there were a letter?" asked Mary.

"Why, yo see, a neighbour as has been in Liverpool, telled us Will's ship were come in. Now he said last time he were in Liverpool he'd ha' come to ha' seen Alice, but his ship had but a week holiday, and hard work for the men in that time too. So Alice makes sure he'll come this, and has had her hand behind her ear at every noise in th' street, thinking it were him. And to-day she were neither to have nor to hold, but off she would go to th' post, and see if he had na sent her a line to th' old house near yo. I tried to get her to give up going, for let alone her deafness she's getten so dark, she cannot see five yards afore her; but no, she would go, poor old body."

"I did not know her sight had failed her; she used to have good eyes enough when she lived near us."

"Ay, but it's gone lately a good deal. But you never ask after Jem—" anxious to get in a word on the subject nearest her heart.

"No," replied Mary, blushing scarlet. "How is he?"

"I cannot justly say how he is, seeing he's at Halifax; but he were very well when he wrote last Tuesday. Han ye heard o' his good luck?"

Rather to her disappointment, Mary owned she had heard of the sum his master had paid him for his invention.

"Well! and did not Margaret tell yo what he'd done wi' it? It's just like him though, ne'er to say a word about it. Why, when it were paid what does he do, but get his master to help him to buy an income for me and Alice. He had her name put down for her life; but, poor thing, she'll not be long to the fore, I'm thinking. She's sadly failed of late. And so, Mary, yo see, we're two ladies o' property. It's a matter o' twenty pound a year they tell me. I wish the twins had lived, bless 'em," said she, dropping a few tears. "They should ha' had the best o' schooling, and their belly-fulls o' food. I suppose they're better off in heaven, only I should so like to see 'em."

Mary's heart filled with love at this new proof of Jem's goodness; but she could not talk about it. She took Jane Wilson's hand, and pressed it with affection; and then turned the subject to Will, her sailor nephew. Jane was a little bit sorry, but her prosperity had made her gentler, and she did not resent what she felt as Mary's indifference to Jem and his merits.

"He's been in Africa and that neighbourhood, I believe. He's a fine chap, but he's not gotten Jem's hair. His has too much o' the red in it. He sent Alice (but, maybe, she telled you) a matter o' five pound when he were over before; but that were nought to an income, yo know."

"It's not every one that can get a hundred or two at a time," said Mary.

"No! no! that's true enough. There's not many a one like Jem. That's Alice's step," said she, hastening to open the door to her sister-in-law. Alice looked weary, and sad, and dusty. The weariness and the dust would not have been noticed either by her, or the others, if it had not been for the sadness.

"No letters!" said Mrs. Wilson.

"No, none! I must just wait another day to hear fra my lad. It's very dree work, waiting!" said Alice.

Margaret's words came into Mary's mind. Every one has their time and kind of waiting.

"If I but knew he were safe, and not drowned!" spoke Alice. "If I but knew he *were* drowned, I would ask grace to say, Thy will be done. It's the waiting."

"It's hard work to be patient to all of us," said Mary; "I know I find it so, but I did not know one so good as you did, Alice; I shall not think so badly of myself for being a bit impatient, now I've heard you say you find it difficult."

The idea of reproach to Alice was the last in Mary's mind; and Alice knew it was. Nevertheless, she said,

"Then, my dear, I ask your pardon, and God's pardon, too, if I've weakened your faith, by showing you how feeble mine was. Half our life's spent in waiting, and it ill becomes one like me, wi' so many mercies, to grumble. I'll try and put a bridle o'er my tongue, and my thoughts too." She spoke in a humble and gentle voice, like one asking forgiveness.

"Come, Alice," interposed Mrs. Wilson, "don't fret yoursel for e'er a trifle wrong said here or there. See! I've put th' kettle on, and you and Mary shall ha' a dish o' tea in no time."

So she bustled about, and brought out a comfortable-looking substantial loaf, and set Mary to cut bread and butter, while she rattled out the tea-cups—always a cheerful sound.

Just as they were sitting down, there was a knock heard at the door, and without waiting for it to be opened from the inside, some one lifted the latch, and in a man's voice asked, if one George Wilson lived there?

Mrs. Wilson was entering on a long and sorrowful explanation of his having once lived there, but of his having dropped down dead; when Alice, with the instinct of love (for in all usual and common instances, sight and hearing failed to convey impressions to her until long after other people had received them), arose, and tottered to the door.

"My bairn!—my own dear bairn!" she exclaimed, falling on Will Wilson's neck.

You may fancy the hospitable and welcoming commotion that ensued; how Mrs. Wilson laughed, and talked, and cried, altogether, if such a thing can be done; and how Mary gazed with wondering pleasure at her old playmate; now a dashing, bronzed-looking, ringletted sailor, frank, and hearty, and affectionate.

But it was something different from common to see Alice's joy at once more having her foster-child with her. She did not speak, for she really could not; but the tears came coursing down her old withered cheeks, and dimmed the horn spectacles she had put on, in order to pry lovingly into his face. So what with her failing sight, and her tear-blinded eyes, she gave up the attempt of learning his face by heart through the medium of that sense, and tried another. She passed her sodden, shrivelled hands, all trembling with eagerness, over his manly face, bent meekly down in order that she might more easily make her strange inspection. At last, her soul was satisfied.

After tea, Mary, feeling sure there was much to be said on both sides, at which it would be better no one should be present, not even an intimate friend like herself, got up to go away. This seemed to arouse Alice from her dreamy consciousness of exceeding happiness, and she hastily followed Mary to the door. There, standing outside, with the latch in her hand, she took hold of Mary's arm, and spoke nearly the first words she had uttered since her nephew's return.

"My dear! I shall never forgive mysel, if my wicked words to-night are any stumbling-block in your path. See how the Lord has put coals of fire on my head! Oh! Mary, don't let my being an unbelieving Thomas weaken your faith. Wait patiently on the Lord, whatever your trouble may be."

CHAPTER XIII - A TRAVELLER'S TALES.

"The mermaid sat upon the rocks
All day long,
Admiring her beauty and combing her locks,
And singing a mermaid song.
"And hear the mermaid's song you may,
As sure as sure can be,
If you will but follow the sun all day,
And souse with him into the sea."

W. S. LANDOR.

It was perhaps four or five days after the events mentioned in the last chapter, that one evening, as Mary stood lost in reverie at the window, she saw Will Wilson enter the court, and come quickly up to her door. She was glad to see him, for he had always been a friend of hers, perhaps too much like her in character ever to become any thing nearer or dearer. She opened the door in readiness to receive his frank greeting, which she as frankly returned.

"Come, Mary! on with bonnet and shawl, or whatever rigging you women require before leaving the house. I'm sent to fetch you, and I can't lose time when I'm under orders."

"Where am I to go to?" asked Mary, as her heart leaped up at the thought of who might be waiting for her.

"Not very far," replied he. "Only to old Job Legh's round the corner here. Aunt would have me come and see these new friends of hers, and then we meant to ha' come on here to see you and your father, but the old gentleman seems inclined to make a night of it, and have you all there. Where's your father? I want to see him. He must come too."

"He's out, but I'll leave word next door for him to follow me; that's to say, if he comes home afore long." She added, hesitatingly, "Is any one else at Job's?"

"No! My aunt Jane would not come for some maggot or other; and as for Jem! I don't know what you've all been doing to him, but he's as down-hearted a chap as I'd wish to see. He's had his sorrows sure enough, poor lad! But it's time for him to be shaking off his dull looks, and not go moping like a girl."

"Then he's come fra Halifax, is he?" asked Mary.

"Yes! his body's come, but I think he's left his heart behind him. His tongue I'm sure he has, as we used to say to childer, when they would not speak. I try to rouse him up a bit, and I think he likes having me with him, but still he's as gloomy and as dull as can be. 'Twas only yesterday he took me to the works, and you'd ha' thought us two Quakers as the spirit hadn't moved, all the way down we were so mum. It's a place to craze a man, certainly; such a noisy black hole! There were one or two things worth looking at, the bellows for instance, or the gale they called a bellows. I could ha' stood near it a whole day; and if I'd a berth in that place, I should like to be bellows-man, if there is such a one. But Jem weren't diverted even with that; he stood as grave as a judge while it blew my hat out o' my hand. He's lost all relish for his food, too, which frets my aunt sadly. Come! Mary, ar'n't you ready?"

She had not been able to gather if she were to see Jem at Job Legh's; but when the door was opened, she at once saw and felt he was not there. The evening then would be a blank; at least so she thought for the first five minutes; but she soon forgot her disappointment in the cheerful meeting of old friends, all, except herself, with some cause for rejoicing at that very time. Margaret, who could not be idle, was knitting away, with her face looking full into the room, away from her work. Alice sat meek and patient with her dimmed eyes and gentle look, trying to see and to hear, but never complaining; indeed, in her inner self she was blessing God for her happiness; for the joy of having her nephew, her child, near her, was far more present to her mind, than her deprivations of sight and hearing.

Job was in the full glory of host and hostess too, for by a tacit agreement he had roused himself from his habitual abstraction, and had assumed many of Margaret's little household duties. While he moved about he was deep in conversation with the young sailor, trying to extract from him any circumstances connected with the natural history of the different countries he had visited.

"Oh! if you are fond of grubs, and flies, and beetles, there's no place for 'em like Sierra Leone. I wish you'd had some of ours; we had rather too much of a good thing; we drank them with our drink, and could scarcely keep from eating them with our food. I never thought any folk could care for such fat green beasts as those, or I would ha' brought you them by the thousand. A plate full o' peas-soup would ha' been full enough for you, I dare say; it were often too full for us."

"I would ha' given a good deal for some on 'em," said Job.

"Well, I knew folk at home liked some o' the queer things one meets with abroad; but I never thought they'd care for them nasty slimy things. I were always on the look-out for a mermaid, for that I knew were a curiosity."

"You might ha' looked long enough," said Job, in an under-tone of contempt, which, however, the quick ears of the sailor caught.

"Not so long, master, in some latitudes, as you think. It stands to reason th' sea hereabouts is too cold for mermaids; for women here don't go half-naked on account o' climate. But I've been in lands where muslin were too hot to wear on land, and where the sea were more than milk-warm; and though I'd never the good luck to see a mermaid in that latitude, I know them that has."

"Do tell us about it," cried Mary.

"Pooh, pooh!" said Job the naturalist.

Both speeches determined Will to go on with his story. What could a fellow who had never been many miles from home know about the wonders of the deep, that he should put him down in that way?

"Well, it were Jack Harris, our third mate last voyage, as many and many a time telled us all about it. You see he were becalmed off Chatham Island (that's in the Great Pacific, and a warm enough latitude for mermaids, and sharks, and such like perils). So some of the men took the long boat, and pulled for the island to see what it were like; and when they got near, they heard a puffing, like a creature come up to take breath; you've never heard a diver? No! Well! you've heard folks in th' asthma, and it were for all the world like that. So they looked around, and what should they see but a mermaid, sitting on a rock, and sunning herself. The water is always warmer when it's rough, you know, so I suppose in the calm she felt it rather chilly, and had come up to warm herself."

"What was she like?" asked Mary, breathlessly.

Job took his pipe off the chimney-piece and began to smoke with very audible puffs, as if the story were not worth listening to.

"Oh! Jack used to say she was for all the world as beautiful as any of the wax ladies in the barbers' shops; only, Mary, there were one little difference: her hair was bright grass green."

"I should not think that was pretty," said Mary, hesitatingly; as if not liking to doubt the perfection of any thing belonging to such an acknowledged beauty.

"Oh! but it is when you're used to it. I always think when first we get sight of land, there's no colour so lovely as grass green. However, she had green hair sure enough; and were proud enough of it, too; for she were combing it out full-length when first they saw her. They all thought she were a fair prize, and may be as good as a whale in ready money (they were whale-fishers you know). For some folk think a deal of mermaids, whatever other folk do." This was a hit at Job, who retaliated in a series of sonorous spittings and puffs.

"So, as I were saying, they pulled towards her, thinking to catch her. She were all the while combing her beautiful hair, and beckoning to them, while with the other hand she held a looking-glass."

"How many hands had she?" asked Job.

"Two, to be sure, just like any other woman," answered Will, indignantly.

"Oh! I thought you said she beckoned with one hand, and combed her hair with another, and held a looking-glass with a third," said Job, with provoking quietness.

"No! I didn't! at least if I did, I meant she did one thing after another, as any one but" (here he mumbled a word or two) "could understand. Well, Mary," turning very decidedly towards her, "when she saw them coming near, whether it were she grew frightened at their fowling-pieces, as they had on board, for a bit o' shooting on the island, or whether it were she were just a fickle jade as did not rightly know her own mind (which, seeing one half of her was woman, I think myself was most probable), but when they were only about two oars' length from the rock where she sat, down she plopped into the water, leaving nothing but her hinder end of a fish tail sticking up for a minute, and then that disappeared too."

"And did they never see her again?" asked Mary.

"Never so plain; the man who had the second watch one night declared he saw her swimming round the ship, and holding up her glass for him to look in; and then he saw the little cottage near Aber in Wales (where his wife lived) as plain as ever he saw it in life, and his wife standing outside, shading her eyes as if she were looking for him. But Jack Harris gave him no credit, for he said he were always a bit of a romancer, and beside that, were a home-sick, down-hearted chap."

"I wish they had caught her," said Mary, musing.

"They got one thing as belonged to her," replied Will, "and that I've often seen with my own eyes, and I reckon it's a sure proof of the truth of their story; for them that wants proof."

"What was it?" asked Margaret, almost anxious her grandfather should be convinced.

"Why, in her hurry she left her comb on the rock, and one o' the men spied it; so they thought that were better than nothing, and they rowed there and took it, and Jack Harris had it on board the *John Cropper*, and I saw him comb his hair with it every Sunday morning."

"What was it like?" asked Mary, eagerly; her imagination running on coral combs, studded with pearls.

"Why, if it had not had such a strange yarn belonging to it, you'd never ha' noticed it from any other small-tooth comb."

"I should rather think not," sneered Job Legh.

The sailor bit his lips to keep down his anger against an old man. Margaret felt very uneasy, knowing her grandfather so well, and not daring to guess what caustic remark might come next to irritate the young sailor guest.

Mary, however, was too much interested by the wonders of the deep to perceive the incredulity with which Job Legh received Wilson's account of the mermaid; and when he left off, half offended, and very much inclined not to open his lips again through the evening, she eagerly said,

"Oh do tell us something more of what you hear and see on board ship. Do, Will!"

"What's the use, Mary, if folk won't believe one. There are things I saw with my own eyes, that some people would pish and pshaw at, as if I were a baby to be put down by cross noises. But I'll tell you, Mary," with an emphasis on *you*, "some more of the wonders of the sea, sin' you're not too wise to believe me. I have seen a fish fly."

This did stagger Mary. She had heard of mermaids as signs of inns, and as sea-wonders, but never of flying fish. Not so Job. He put down his pipe, and nodding his head as a token of approbation, he said

"Ay, ay! young man. Now you're speaking truth."

"Well now! you'll swallow that, old gentleman. You'll credit me when I say I've seen a crittur half fish, half bird, and you won't credit me when I say there be such beasts as mermaids, half fish, half woman. To me, one's just as strange as t'other."

"You never saw the mermaid yoursel," interposed Margaret, gently. But "love me, love my dog," was Will Wilson's motto, only his version was "believe me, believe Jack Harris;" and the remark was not so soothing to him as it was intended to have been.

"It's the Exocetus; one of the Malacopterygii Abdominales," said Job, much interested.

"Ay, there you go! You're one o' them folks as never knows beasts unless they're called out o' their names. Put 'em in Sunday clothes and you know 'em, but in their work-a-day English you never know nought about 'em. I've met wi' many o' your kidney; and if I'd ha' known it, I'd ha' christened poor Jack's mermaid wi' some grand gibberish of a name. Mermaidicus Jack Harrisensis; that's just like their new-fangled words. D'ye believe there's such a thing as the Mermaidicus, master?" asked Will, enjoying his own joke uncommonly, as most people do.

"Not I! Tell me about the—"

"Well!" said Will, pleased at having excited the old gentleman's faith and credit at last. "It were on this last voyage, about a day's sail from Madeira, that one of our men—"

"Not Jack Harris, I hope," murmured Job.

"Called me," continued Will, not noticing the interruption, "to see the what d'ye call it—flying fish I say it is. It were twenty feet out o' water, and it flew near on to a hundred yards. But I say, old gentleman, I ha' gotten one dried, and if you'll take it, why, I'll give it you; only," he added, in a lower tone, "I wish you'd just gie me credit for the Mermaidicus."

I really believe if the assuming faith in the story of the mermaid had been made the condition of receiving the flying fish, Job Legh, sincere man as he was, would have pretended belief; he was so much delighted at the idea of possessing this specimen. He won the sailor's heart by getting up to shake both his hands in his vehement gratitude, puzzling poor old Alice, who yet smiled through her wonder; for she understood the action to indicate some kindly feeling towards her nephew.

Job wanted to prove his gratitude, and was puzzled how to do it. He feared the young man would not appreciate any of his duplicate Araneides; not even the great American Mygale, one of his most precious treasures; or else he would gladly have bestowed any duplicate on the donor of a real dried Exocetus. What could he do for him? He could ask Margaret to sing. Other folks beside her old doating grandfather thought a deal of her songs. So Margaret began some of her noble old-fashioned songs. She knew no modern music (for which her auditors might have been thankful), but she poured her rich voice out in some of the old canzonets she had lately learnt while accompanying the musical lecturer on his tour.

Mary was amused to see how the young sailor sat entranced; mouth, eyes, all open, in order to catch every breath of sound. His very lids refused to wink, as if afraid in that brief proverbial interval to lose a particle of the rich music that floated through the room. For the first time the idea crossed Mary's mind that it was possible the plain little sensible Margaret, so prim and demure, might have power over the heart of the handsome, dashing, spirited Will Wilson.

Job, too, was rapidly changing his opinion of his new guest. The flying fish went a great way, and his undisguised admiration for Margaret's singing carried him still further.

It was amusing enough to see these two, within the hour so barely civil to each other, endeavouring now to be ultra-agreeable. Will, as soon as he had taken breath (a long, deep gasp of admiration) after Margaret's song, sidled up to Job, and asked him in a sort of doubting tone,

"You wouldn't like a live Manx cat, would ye, master?"

"A what?" exclaimed Job.

"I don't know its best name," said Will, humbly. "But we call 'em just Manx cats. They're cats without tails."

Now Job, in all his natural history, had never heard of such animals; so Will continued,

"Because I'm going, afore joining my ship, to see mother's friends in the island, and would gladly bring you one, if so be you'd like to have it. They look as queer and out o' nature as flying fish, or"—he gulped the words down that should have followed. "Especially when you see 'em walking a roof-top, right again the sky, when a cat, as is a proper cat, is sure to stick her tail stiff out behind, like a slack-rope dancer a-balancing; but these cats having no tail, cannot stick it out, which captivates some people uncommonly. If yo'll allow me, I'll bring one for Miss there," jerking his head at Margaret. Job assented with grateful curiosity, wishing much to see the tail-less phenomenon.

"When are you going to sail?" asked Mary.

"I cannot justly say; our ship's bound for America next voyage, they tell me. A mess-mate will let me know when her sailing-day is fixed; but I've got to go to th' Isle o' Man first. I promised uncle last time I were in England to go this next time. I may have to hoist the blue Peter any day; so, make much of me while you have me, Mary."

Job asked him if he had ever been in America.

"Haven't I? North and South both! This time we're bound to North. Yankee-Land, as we call it, where Uncle Sam lives."

"Uncle who?" said Mary.

"Oh, it's a way sailors have of speaking. I only mean I'm going to Boston, U. S., that's Uncle Sam."

Mary did not understand, so she left him and went to sit by Alice, who could not hear conversation unless expressly addressed to her. She had sat patiently silent the greater part of the night, and now greeted Mary with a quiet smile.

"Where's yo'r father?" asked she.

"I guess he's at his Union; he's there most evenings."

Alice shook her head; but whether it were that she did not hear, or that she did not quite approve of what she heard, Mary could not make out. She sat silently watching Alice, and regretting over her dimmed and veiled eyes, formerly so bright and speaking; as if Alice understood by some other sense what was passing in Mary's mind, she turned suddenly round, and answered Mary's thought.

"Yo're mourning for me, my dear; and there's no need, Mary. I'm as happy as a child. I sometimes think I am a child, whom the Lord is hushabying to my long sleep. For when I were a nurse-girl, my missis alway telled me to speak very soft and low, and to darken the room that her little one might go to sleep; and now all noises are hushed and still to me, and the bonny earth seems dim and dark, and I know it's my Father lulling me away to my long sleep. I'm very well content, and yo mustn't fret for me. I've had well nigh every blessing in life I could desire."

Mary thought of Alice's long-cherished, fond wish to revisit the home of her childhood, so often and often deferred, and now probably never to take place. Or if it did, how changed from the fond anticipation of what it was to have been! It would be a mockery to the blind and deaf Alice.

The evening came quickly to an end. There was the humble cheerful meal, and then the bustling merry farewell, and Mary was once more in the quietness and solitude of her own dingy, dreary-looking home; her father still out, the fire extinguished, and her evening's task of work lying all undone upon the dresser. But it had been a pleasant little interlude to think upon. It had distracted her attention for a few hours from the pressure of many uneasy thoughts, of the dark, heavy, oppressive times, when sorrow and want seemed to surround her on every side; of her father, his changed and altered looks, telling so plainly of broken health, and an embittered heart; of the morrow, and the morrow beyond that, to be spent in that close monotonous work-room, with Sally Leadbitter's odious whispers hissing in her ear; and of the hunted look, so full of dread, from Miss Simmonds' door-step up and down the street, lest her persecuting lover should be near: for he lay in wait for her with wonderful perseverance, and of late had made himself almost hateful, by the unmanly force which he had used to detain her to listen to him, and the indifference with which he exposed her to the remarks of the passers-by, any one of whom might circulate reports which it would be terrible for her father to hear—and worse than death should they reach Jem Wilson. And all this she had drawn upon herself by her giddy flirting. Oh! how she loathed the recollection of the hot summer evening, when, worn out by stitching and sewing, she had loitered homewards with weary languor, and first listened to the voice of the tempter.

And Jem Wilson! Oh, Jem, Jem, why did you not come to receive some of the modest looks and words of love which Mary longed to give you, to try and make up for the hasty rejection which you as hastily took to be final, though both mourned over it with many tears. But day after day passed away, and patience seemed of no avail; and Mary's cry was ever the old moan of the Moated Grange,

"Why comes he not," she said,
"I am aweary, aweary,
I would that I were dead."

CHAPTER XIV - JEM'S INTERVIEW WITH POOR ESTHER.

"Know the temptation ere you judge the crime!
Look on this tree—'twas green, and fair, and graceful;
Yet now, save these few shoots, how dry and rotten!
Thou canst not tell the cause. Not long ago,
A neighbour oak, with which its roots were twined,
In falling wrenched them with such cruel force,
That though we covered them again with care,
Its beauty withered, and it pined away.
So, could we look into the human breast,
How oft the fatal blight that meets our view,
Should we trace down to the torn, bleeding fibres
Of a too trusting heart—where it were shame,
For pitying tears, to give contempt or blame."

"STREET WALKS."

The month was over;—the honeymoon to the newly-married; the exquisite convalescence to the "living mother of a living child;" the "first dark days of nothingness" to the widow and the child bereaved; the term of penance, of hard labour, and solitary confinement, to the shrinking, shivering, hopeless prisoner.

"Sick, and in prison, and ye visited me." Shall you, or I, receive such blessing? I know one who will. An overseer of a foundry, an aged man, with hoary hair, has spent his Sabbaths, for many years, in visiting the prisoners and the afflicted in Manchester New Bailey; not merely advising and comforting, but putting means into their power of regaining the virtue and the peace they had lost; becoming himself their guarantee in obtaining employment, and never deserting those who have once asked help from him.[1]

---

[1] Vide Manchester Guardian, of Wednesday, March 18, 1846; and also the Reports of Captain Williams, prison inspector.

Esther's term of imprisonment was ended. She received a good character in the governor's books; she had picked her daily quantity of oakum, had never deserved the extra punishment of the tread-mill, and had been civil and decorous in her language. And once more she was out of prison. The door closed behind her with a ponderous clang, and in her desolation she felt as if shut out of home—from the only shelter she could meet with, houseless and pennyless as she was, on that dreary day.

But it was but for an instant that she stood there doubting. One thought had haunted her both by night and by day, with monomaniacal incessancy; and that thought was how to save Mary (her dead sister's only child, her own little pet in the days of her innocence) from following in the same downward path to vice. To whom could she speak and ask for aid? She shrank from the idea of addressing John Barton again; her heart sank within her, at the remembrance of his fierce repulsing action, and far fiercer words. It seemed worse than death to reveal her condition to Mary, else she sometimes thought that this course would be the most terrible, the most efficient warning. She must speak; to that she was soul-compelled; but to whom? She dreaded addressing any of her former female acquaintance, even supposing they had sense, or spirit, or interest enough to undertake her mission.

To whom shall the outcast prostitute tell her tale? Who will give her help in her day of need? Hers is the leper-sin, and all stand aloof dreading to be counted unclean.

In her wild night wanderings, she had noted the haunts and habits of many a one who little thought of a watcher in the poor forsaken woman. You may easily imagine that a double interest was attached by her to the ways and companionships of those with whom she had been acquainted in the days which, when present, she had considered hardly-worked and monotonous, but which now in retrospection seemed so happy and unclouded. Accordingly, she had, as we have seen, known where to meet with John Barton on that unfortunate night, which had only produced irritation in him, and a month's imprisonment to her. She had also observed that he was still intimate with the Wilsons. She had seen him walking and talking with both father and son; her old friends too; and she had shed unregarded, unvalued tears, when some one had casually told her of George Wilson's sudden death. It now flashed across her mind, that to the son, to Mary's playfellow, her elder brother in the days of childhood, her tale might be told, and listened to with interest, and some mode of action suggested by him by which Mary might be guarded and saved.

All these thoughts had passed through her mind while yet she was in prison; so when she was turned out, her purpose was clear, and she did not feel her desolation of freedom as she would otherwise have done.

That night she stationed herself early near the foundry where she knew Jem worked; he stayed later than usual, being detained by some arrangements for the morrow. She grew tired and impatient; many workmen had come out of the door in the long, dead, brick wall, and eagerly had she peered into their faces, deaf to all insult or curse. He must have gone home early; one more turn in the street, and she would go.

During that turn he came out, and in the quiet of that street of workshops and warehouses, she directly heard his steps. Now her heart failed her for an instant; but still she was not daunted from her purpose, painful as its fulfilment was sure to be. She laid her hand on his arm. As she expected, after a momentary glance at the person who thus endeavoured to detain him, he made an effort to shake it off, and pass on. But trembling as she was, she had provided against this by a firm and unusual grasp.

"You must listen to me, Jem Wilson," she said, with almost an accent of command.

"Go away, missis; I've nought to do with you, either in hearkening, or talking."

He made another struggle.

"You must listen," she said again, authoritatively, "for Mary Barton's sake."

The spell of her name was as potent as that of the mariner's glittering eye. "He listened like a three-year child."

"I know you care enough for her to wish to save her from harm."

He interrupted his earnest gaze into her face, with the exclamation—

"And who can yo be to know Mary Barton, or to know that she's ought to me?"

There was a little strife in Esther's mind for an instant, between the shame of acknowledging herself, and the additional weight to her revelation which such acknowledgment would give. Then she spoke.

"Do you remember Esther, the sister of John Barton's wife? the aunt to Mary? And the Valentine I sent you last February ten years?"

"Yes, I mind her well! But yo are not Esther, are you?" He looked again into her face, and seeing that indeed it was his boyhood's friend, he took her hand, and shook it with a cordiality that forgot the present in the past.

"Why, Esther! Where han ye been this many a year? Where han ye been wandering that we none of us could find you out?"

The question was asked thoughtlessly, but answered with fierce earnestness.

"Where have I been? What have I been doing? Why do you torment me with questions like these? Can you not guess? But the story of my life is wanted to give force to my speech, afterwards I will tell it you. Nay! don't change your fickle mind now, and say you don't want to hear it. You must hear it, and I must tell it; and then see after Mary, and take care she does not become like me. As she is loving now, so did I love once; one above me far." She remarked not, in her own absorption, the change in Jem's breathing, the sudden clutch at the wall which told the fearfully vivid interest he took in what she said. "He was so handsome, so kind! Well, the regiment was ordered to Chester (did I tell you he was an officer?), and he could not bear to part from me, nor I from him, so he took me with him. I never thought poor Mary would have taken it so to heart! I always meant to send for her to pay me a visit when I was married; for, mark you! he promised me marriage. They all do. Then came three years of happiness. I suppose I ought not to have been happy, but I was. I had a little girl, too. Oh! the sweetest darling that ever was seen! But I must not think of her," putting her hand wildly up to her forehead, "or I shall go mad; I shall."

"Don't tell me any more about yoursel," said Jem, soothingly.

"What! you're tired already, are you? but I'll tell you; as you've asked for it, you shall hear it. I won't recall the agony of the past for nothing. I will have the relief of telling it. Oh, how happy I was!"—sinking her voice into a plaintive child-like manner. "It came like a shot on me when one day he came to me and told me he was ordered to Ireland, and must leave me behind; at Bristol we then were."

Jem muttered some words; she caught their meaning, and in a pleading voice continued,

"Oh, don't abuse him; don't speak a word against him! You don't know how I love him yet; yet, when I am sunk so low. You don't guess how kind he was. He gave me fifty pound before we parted, and I knew he could ill spare it. Don't, Jem, please," as his muttered indignation rose again. For her sake he ceased. "I might have done better with the money; I see now. But I did not know the value of money. Formerly I had earned it easily enough at the factory, and as I had no more sensible wants, I spent it on dress and on eating. While I lived with him, I had it for asking; and fifty pounds would, I thought, go a long way. So I went back to Chester, where I'd been so happy, and set up a small-ware shop, and hired a room near. We should have done well, but alas! alas! my little girl fell ill, and I could not mind my shop and her too; and things grew worse and worse. I sold my goods any how to get money to buy her food and medicine; I wrote over and over again to her father for help, but he must have changed his quarters, for I never got an answer. The landlord seized the few bobbins and tapes I had left, for shop-rent; and the person to whom the mean little room, to which we had been forced to remove, belonged, threatened to turn us out unless his rent was paid; it had run on many weeks, and it was winter, cold bleak winter; and my child was so ill, so ill, and I was starving. And I could not bear to see her suffer, and forgot how much better it would be for us to die together;—oh her moans, her moans, which money would give me the means of relieving! So I went out into the street, one January night—Do you think God will punish me for that?" she asked with wild vehemence, almost amounting to insanity, and shaking Jem's arm in order to force an answer from him.

But before he could shape his heart's sympathy into words, her voice had lost its wildness, and she spoke with the quiet of despair.

"But it's no matter! I've done that since, which separates us as far asunder as heaven and hell can be." Her voice rose again to the sharp pitch of agony. "My darling! my darling! even after death I may not see thee, my own sweet one! She was so good—like a little angel. What is that text, I don't remember,—that text mother used to teach me when I sat on her knee long ago; it begins, 'Blessed are the pure'"—

"Blessed are the pure in heart, for they shall see God."

"Ay, that's it! It would break mother's heart if she knew what I am now—it did break Mary's heart, you see. And now I recollect it was about her child I wanted so to see you, Jem. You know Mary Barton, don't you?" said she, trying to collect her thoughts.

Yes, Jem knew her. How well, his beating heart could testify!

"Well, there's something to do for her; I forget what; wait a minute! She is so like my little girl;" said she, raising her eyes, glistening with unshed tears, in search of the sympathy of Jem's countenance.

He deeply pitied her; but oh! how he longed to recall her mind to the subject of Mary, and the lover above her in rank, and the service to be done for her sake. But he controlled himself to silence. After awhile, she spoke again, and in a calmer voice.

"When I came to Manchester (for I could not stay in Chester after her death), I found you all out very soon. And yet I never thought my poor sister was dead. I suppose I would not think so. I used to watch about the court where John lived, for many and many a night, and gather all I could about them from the neighbours' talk; for I never asked a question. I put this and that together, and followed one, and listened to the other; many's the time I've watched the policeman off his beat, and peeped through the chink of the window-shutter to see the old room, and sometimes Mary or her father sitting up late for some reason or another. I found out Mary went to learn dress-making, and I began to be frightened for her; for it's a bad life for a girl to be out late at night in the streets, and after many an hour of weary work, they're ready to follow after any novelty that makes a little change. But I made up my mind, that bad as I was, I could watch over Mary and perhaps keep her from harm. So I used to wait for her at nights, and follow her home, often when she little knew any one was near her. There was one of her companions I never could abide, and I'm sure that girl is at the bottom of some mischief. By-and-bye, Mary's walks homewards were not alone. She was joined soon after she came out, by a man; a gentleman. I began to fear for her, for I saw she was light-hearted, and pleased with his attentions; and I thought worse of him for having such long talks with that bold girl I told you of. But I was laid up for a long time with spitting of blood; and could do nothing. I'm sure it made me worse, thinking about what might be happening to Mary. And when I came out, all was going on as before, only she seemed fonder of him than ever; and oh Jem! her father won't listen to me, and it's you must save Mary! You're like a brother to her, and maybe could give her advice and watch over her, and at any rate John will hearken to you; only he's so stern and so cruel." She began to cry a little at the remembrance of his harsh words; but Jem cut her short by his hoarse, stern inquiry,

"Who is this spark that Mary loves? Tell me his name!"

"It's young Carson, old Carson's son, that your father worked for."

There was a pause. She broke the silence.

"Oh! Jem, I charge you with the care of her! I suppose it would be murder to kill her, but it would be better for her to die than to live to lead such a life as I do. Do you hear me, Jem?"

"Yes! I hear you. It would be better. Better we were all dead." This was said as if thinking aloud; but he immediately changed his tone, and continued,

"Esther, you may trust to my doing all I can for Mary. That I have determined on. And now listen to me! you loathe the life you lead, else you would not speak of it as you do. Come home with me. Come to my mother. She and my aunt Alice live together. I will see that they give you a welcome. And to-morrow I will see if some honest way of living cannot be found for you. Come home with me."

She was silent for a minute, and he hoped he had gained his point. Then she said,

"God bless you, Jem, for the words you have just spoken. Some years ago you might have saved me, as I hope and trust you will yet save Mary. But it is too late now;—too late," she added, with accents of deep despair.

Still he did not relax his hold. "Come home," he said.

"I tell you, I cannot. I could not lead a virtuous life if I would. I should only disgrace you. If you will know all," said she, as he still seemed inclined to urge her, "I must have drink. Such as live like me could not bear life if they did not drink. It's the only thing to keep us from suicide. If we did not drink, we could not stand the memory of what we have been, and the thought of what we are, for a day. If I go without food, and without shelter, I must have my dram. Oh! you don't know the awful nights I have had in prison for want of it!" said she, shuddering, and glaring round with terrified eyes, as if dreading to see some spiritual creature, with dim form, near her.

"It is so frightful to see them," whispering in tones of wildness, although so low spoken. "There they go round and round my bed the whole night through. My mother, carrying little Annie (I wonder how they got together) and Mary—and all looking at me with their sad, stony eyes; oh Jem! it is so terrible! They don't turn back either, but pass behind the head of the bed, and I feel their eyes on me everywhere. If I creep under the clothes I still see them; and what is worse," hissing out her words with fright, "they see me. Don't speak to me of leading a better life—I must have drink. I cannot pass to-night without a dram; I dare not."

Jem was silent from deep sympathy. Oh! could he, then, do nothing for her! She spoke again, but in a less excited tone, although it was thrillingly earnest.

"You are grieved for me! I know it better than if you told me in words. But you can do nothing for me. I am past hope. You can yet save Mary. You must. She is innocent, except for the great error of loving one above her in station. Jem! you *will* save her?"

With heart and soul, though in few words, Jem promised that if aught earthly could keep her from falling, he would do it. Then she blessed him, and bade him good-night.

"Stay a minute," said he, as she was on the point of departure. "I may want to speak to you again. I mun know where to find you—where do you live?"

She laughed strangely. "And do you think one sunk so low as I am has a home? Decent, good people have homes. We have none. No, if you want me, come at night, and look at the corners of the streets about here. The colder, the bleaker, the more stormy the night, the more certain you will be to find me. For then," she added, with a plaintive fall in her voice, "it is so cold sleeping in entries, and on door-steps, and I want a dram more than ever."

Again she rapidly turned off, and Jem also went on his way. But before he reached the end of the street, even in the midst of the jealous anguish that filled his heart, his conscience smote him. He had not done enough to save her. One more effort, and she might have come. Nay, twenty efforts would have been well rewarded by her yielding. He turned back, but she was gone. In the tumult of his other feelings, his self-reproach was deadened for the time. But many and many a day afterwards he bitterly regretted his omission of duty; his weariness of well-doing.

Now, the great thing was to reach home, and solitude. Mary loved another! Oh! how should he bear it? He had thought her rejection of him a hard trial, but that was nothing now. He only remembered it, to be thankful he had not yielded to the temptation of trying his fate again, not in actual words, but in a meeting, where her manner should tell far more than words, that her sweeter smiles, her dainty movements, her pretty household ways, were all to be reserved to gladden another's eyes and heart. And he must live on; that seemed the strangest. That a long life (and he knew men did live long, even with deep, biting sorrow corroding at their hearts) must be spent without Mary; nay, with the consciousness she was another's! That hell of thought he would reserve for the quiet of his own room, the dead stillness of night. He was on the threshold of home now.

He entered. There were the usual faces, the usual sights. He loathed them, and then he cursed himself because he loathed them. His mother's love had taken a cross turn, because he had kept the tempting supper she had prepared for him waiting until it was nearly spoilt. Alice, her dulled senses deadening day by day, sat mutely near the fire; her happiness, bounded by the circle of the consciousness of the presence of her foster child, knowing that his voice repeated what was passing to her deafened ear, that his arm removed each little obstacle to her tottering steps. And Will, out of the very kindness of his heart, talked more and more merrily than ever. He saw Jem was downcast, and fancied his rattling might cheer him; at any rate, it drowned his aunt's muttered grumblings, and in some measure concealed the blank of the evening. At last, bed-time came; and Will withdrew to his neighbouring lodging; and Jane and Alice Wilson had raked the fire, and fastened doors and shutters, and pattered up stairs, with their tottering foot-steps, and shrill voices. Jem, too, went to the closet termed his bed-room. There was no bolt to the door; but by one strong effort of his right arm, a heavy chest was moved against it, and he could sit down on the side of his bed, and think.

Mary loved another! That idea would rise uppermost in his mind, and had to be combated in all its forms of pain. It was, perhaps, no great wonder that she should prefer one so much above Jem in the external things of life. But the gentleman; why did he, with his range of choice among the ladies of the land, why did he stoop down to carry off the poor man's darling? With all the glories of the garden at his hand, why did he prefer to cull the wild-rose,—Jem's own fragrant wild-rose?

His *own!* Oh! never now his own!—Gone for evermore!

Then uprose the guilty longing for blood!—The frenzy of jealousy!—Some one should die. He would rather Mary were dead, cold in her grave, than that she were another's. A vision of her pale, sweet face, with her bright hair all bedabbled with gore, seemed to float constantly before his aching eyes. But hers were ever open, and contained, in their soft, deathly look, such mute reproach! What had she done to deserve such cruel treatment from him? She had been wooed by one whom Jem knew to be handsome, gay, and bright, and she had given him her love. That was all! It was the wooer who should die. Yes, die, knowing the cause of his death. Jem pictured him (and gloated on the picture), lying smitten, yet conscious; and listening to the upbraiding accusation of his murderer. How he had left his own rank, and dared to love a maiden of low degree; and—oh! stinging agony of all—how she, in return, had loved him! Then the other nature spoke up, and bade him remember the anguish he should so prepare for Mary! At first he refused to listen to that better voice; or listened only to pervert. He would glory in her wailing grief! he would take pleasure in her desolation of heart!

No! he could not, said the still small voice. It would be worse, far worse, to have caused such woe, than it was now to bear his present heavy burden.

But it was too heavy, too grievous to be borne, and live. He would slay himself, and the lovers should love on, and the sun shine bright, and he with his burning, woeful heart would be at rest. "Rest that is reserved for the people of God."

Had he not promised with such earnest purpose of soul, as makes words more solemn than oaths, to save Mary from becoming such as Esther? Should he shrink from the duties of life, into the cowardliness of death? Who would then guard Mary, with her love and her innocence? Would it not be a goodly thing to serve her, although she loved him not; to be her preserving angel, through the perils of life; and she, unconscious all the while?

He braced up his soul, and said to himself, that with God's help he would be that earthly keeper.

And now the mists and the storms seemed clearing away from his path, though it still was full of stinging thorns. Having done the duty nearest to him (of reducing the tumult of his own heart to something like order), the second became more plain before him.

Poor Esther's experience had led her, perhaps, too hastily to the conclusion, that Mr. Carson's intentions were evil towards Mary; at least she had given no just ground for the fears she entertained that such was the case. It was possible, nay, to Jem's heart, very probable, that he might only be too happy to marry her. She was a lady by right of nature, Jem thought; in movement, grace, and spirit. what was birth to a Manchester manufacturer, many of whom glory, and justly too, in being the architects of their own fortunes? And, as far as wealth was concerned, judging another by himself, Jem could only imagine it a great privilege to lay it at the feet of the loved one. Harry Carson's mother had been a factory girl; so, after all, what was the great reason for doubting his intentions towards Mary?

There might probably be some little awkwardness about the affair at first: Mary's father having such strong prejudices on the one hand; and something of the same kind being likely to exist on the part of Mr. Carson's family. But Jem knew he had power over John Barton's mind; and it would be something to exert that power in promoting Mary's happiness, and to relinquish all thought of self in so doing.

Oh! why had Esther chosen him for this office? It was beyond his strength to act rightly! Why had she singled him out?

The answer came when he was calm enough to listen for it. Because Mary had no other friend capable of the duty required of him; the duty of a brother, as Esther imagined him to be in feeling, from his long friendship. He would be unto her as a brother.

As such, he ought to ascertain Harry Carson's intentions towards her in winning her affections. He would ask him, straightforwardly, as became man speaking to man, not concealing, if need were, the interest he felt in Mary.

Then, with the resolve to do his duty to the best of his power, peace came into his soul; he had left the windy storm and tempest behind.

Two hours before day-dawn he fell asleep.

CHAPTER XV - A VIOLENT MEETING BETWEEN THE RIVALS.

"What thoughtful heart can look into this gulf
That darkly yawns 'twixt rich and poor,
And not find food for saddest meditation!
Can see, without a pang of keenest grief,
Them fiercely battling (like some natural foes)
Whom God had made, with help and sympathy,
To stand as brothers, side by side, united!
Where is the wisdom that shall bridge this gulf,
And bind them once again in trust and love?"

"LOVE-TRUTHS."

We must return to John Barton. Poor John! He never got over his disappointing journey to London. The deep mortification he then experienced (with, perhaps, as little selfishness for its cause as mortification ever had) was of no temporary nature; indeed, few of his feelings were.

Then came a long period of bodily privation; of daily hunger after food; and though he tried to persuade himself he could bear want himself with stoical indifference, and did care about it as little as most men, yet the body took its revenge for its uneasy feelings. The mind became soured and morose, and lost much of its equipoise. It was no longer elastic, as in the days of youth, or in times of comparative happiness; it ceased to hope. And it is hard to live on when one can no longer hope.

The same state of feeling which John Barton entertained, if belonging to one who had had leisure to think of such things, and physicians to give names to them, would have been called monomania; so haunting, so incessant, were the thoughts that pressed upon him. I have somewhere read a forcibly described punishment among the Italians, worthy of a Borgia. The supposed or real criminal was shut up in a room, supplied with every convenience and luxury; and at first mourned little over his imprisonment. But day by day he became aware that the space between the walls of his apartment was narrowing, and then he understood the end. Those painted walls would come into hideous nearness, and at last crush the life out of him.

And so day by day, nearer and nearer, came the diseased thoughts of John Barton. They excluded the light of heaven, the cheering sounds of earth. They were preparing his death.

It is true, much of their morbid power might be ascribed to the use of opium. But before you blame too harshly this use, or rather abuse, try a hopeless life, with daily cravings of the body for food. Try, not alone being without hope yourself, but seeing all around you reduced to the same despair, arising from the same circumstances; all around you telling (though they use no words or language), by their looks and feeble actions, that they are suffering and sinking under the pressure of want. Would you not be glad to forget life, and its burdens? And opium gives forgetfulness for a time.

It is true they who thus purchase it pay dearly for their oblivion; but can you expect the uneducated to count the cost of their whistle? Poor wretches! They pay a heavy price. Days of oppressive weariness and languor, whose realities have the feeble sickliness of dreams; nights, whose dreams are fierce realities of agony; sinking health, tottering frames, incipient madness, and worse, the *consciousness* of incipient madness; this is the price of their whistle. But have you taught them the science of consequences?

John Barton's overpowering thought, which was to work out his fate on earth, was rich and poor; why are they so separate, so distinct, when God has made them all? It is not His will, that their interests are so far apart. Whose doing is it?

And so on into the problems and mysteries of life, until, bewildered and lost, unhappy and suffering, the only feeling that remained clear and undisturbed in the tumult of his heart, was hatred to the one class and keen sympathy with the other.

But what availed his sympathy? No education had given him wisdom; and without wisdom, even love, with all its effects, too often works but harm. He acted to the best of his judgment, but it was a widely-erring judgment.

The actions of the uneducated seem to me typified in those of Frankenstein, that monster of many human qualities, ungifted with a soul, a knowledge of the difference between good and evil.

The people rise up to life; they irritate us, they terrify us, and we become their enemies. Then, in the sorrowful moment of our triumphant power, their eyes gaze on us with a mute reproach. Why have we made them what they are; a powerful monster, yet without the inner means for peace and happiness?

John Barton became a Chartist, a Communist, all that is commonly called wild and visionary. Ay! but being visionary is something. It shows a soul, a being not altogether sensual; a creature who looks forward for others, if not for himself.

And with all his weakness he had a sort of practical power, which made him useful to the bodies of men to whom he belonged. He had a ready kind of rough Lancashire eloquence, arising out of the fulness of his heart, which was very stirring to men similarly circumstanced, who liked to hear their feelings put into words. He had a pretty clear head at times, for method and arrangement; a necessary talent to large combinations of men. And what perhaps more than all made him relied upon and valued, was the consciousness which every one who came in contact with him felt, that he was actuated by no selfish motives; that his class, his order, was what he stood by, not the rights of his own paltry self. For even in great and noble men, as soon as self comes into prominent existence, it becomes a mean and paltry thing.

A little time before this, there had come one of those occasions for deliberation among the employed, which deeply interested John Barton; and the discussions concerning which had caused his frequent absence from home of late.

I am not sure if I can express myself in the technical terms of either masters or workmen, but I will try simply to state the case on which the latter deliberated.

An order for coarse goods came in from a new foreign market. It was a large order, giving employment to all the mills engaged in that species of manufacture: but it was necessary to execute it speedily, and at as low prices as possible, as the masters had reason to believe a duplicate order had been sent to one of the continental manufacturing towns, where there were no restrictions on food, no taxes on building or machinery, and where consequently they dreaded that the goods could be made at a much lower price than they could afford them for; and that, by so acting and charging, the rival manufacturers would obtain undivided possession of the market. It was clearly their interest to buy cotton as cheaply, and to beat down wages as low as possible. And in the long run the interests of the workmen would have been thereby benefited. Distrust each other as they may, the employers and the employed must rise or fall together. There may be some difference as to chronology, none as to fact.

But the masters did not choose to make all these facts known. They stood upon being the masters, and that they had a right to order work at their own prices, and they believed that in the present depression of trade, and unemployment of hands, there would be no great difficulty in getting it done.

Now let us turn to the workmen's view of the question. The masters (of the tottering foundation of whose prosperity they were ignorant) seemed doing well, and like gentlemen, "lived at home in ease," while they were starving, gasping on from day to day; and there was a foreign order to be executed, the extent of which, large as it was, was greatly exaggerated; and it was to be done speedily. Why were the masters offering such low wages under these circumstances? Shame upon them! It was taking advantage of their work-people being almost starved; but they would starve entirely rather than come into such terms. It was bad enough to be poor, while by the labour of their thin hands, the sweat of their brows, the masters were made rich; but they would not be utterly ground down to dust. No! they would fold their hands, and sit idle, and smile at the masters, whom even in death they could baffle. With Spartan endurance they determined to let the employers know their power, by refusing to work.

So class distrusted class, and their want of mutual confidence wrought sorrow to both. The masters would not be bullied, and compelled to reveal why they felt it wisest and best to offer only such low wages; they would not be made to tell that they were even sacrificing capital to obtain a decisive victory over the continental manufacturers. And the workmen sat silent and stern with folded hands, refusing to work for such pay. There was a strike in Manchester.

Of course it was succeeded by the usual consequences. Many other Trades' Unions, connected with different branches of business, supported with money, countenance, and encouragement of every kind, the stand which the Manchester power-loom weavers were making against their masters. Delegates from Glasgow, from Nottingham, and other towns, were sent to Manchester, to keep up the spirit of resistance; a committee was formed, and all the requisite officers elected; chairman, treasurer, honorary secretary:—among them was John Barton.

The masters, meanwhile, took their measures. They placarded the walls with advertisements for power-loom weavers. The workmen replied by a placard in still larger letters, stating their grievances. The masters met daily in town, to mourn over the time (so fast slipping away) for the fulfilment of the foreign orders; and to strengthen each other in their resolution not to yield. If they gave up now, they might give up always. It would never do. And amongst the most energetic of the masters, the Carsons, father and son, took their places. It is well known, that there is no religionist so zealous as a convert; no masters so stern, and regardless of the interests of their work-people, as those who have risen from such a station themselves. This would account for the elder Mr. Carson's determination not to be bullied into yielding; not even to be bullied into giving reasons for acting as the masters did. It was the employer's will, and that should be enough for the employed. Harry Carson did not trouble himself much about the grounds for his conduct. He liked the excitement of the affair. He liked the attitude of resistance. He was brave, and he liked the idea of personal danger, with which some of the more cautious tried to intimidate the violent among the masters.

Meanwhile, the power-loom weavers living in the more remote parts of Lancashire, and the neighbouring counties, heard of the masters' advertisements for workmen; and in their solitary dwellings grew weary of starvation, and resolved to come to Manchester. Foot-sore, way-worn, half-starved looking men they were, as they tried to steal into town in the early dawn, before people were astir, or late in the dusk of evening. And now began the real wrong-doing of the Trades' Unions. As to their decision to work, or not, at such a particular rate of wages, that was either wise or unwise; all error of judgment at the worst. But they had no right to tyrannise over others, and tie them down to their own procrustean bed. Abhorring what they considered oppression in the masters, why did they oppress others? Because, when men get excited, they know not what they do. Judge, then, with something of the mercy of the Holy One, whom we all love.

In spite of policemen set to watch over the safety of the poor country weavers,—in spite of magistrates, and prisons, and severe punishments,—the poor depressed men tramping in from Burnley, Padiham, and other places, to work at the condemned "Starvation Prices," were waylaid, and beaten, and left almost for dead by the road-side. The police broke up every lounging knot of men:—they separated quietly, to reunite half-a-mile further out of town.

Of course the feeling between the masters and workmen did not improve under these circumstances.

Combination is an awful power. It is like the equally mighty agency of steam; capable of almost unlimited good or evil. But to obtain a blessing on its labours, it must work under the direction of a high and intelligent will; incapable of being misled by passion, or excitement. The will of the operatives had not been guided to the calmness of wisdom.

So much for generalities. Let us now return to individuals.

A note, respectfully worded, although its tone of determination was strong, had been sent from the power-loom weavers, requesting that a "deputation" of them might have a meeting with the masters, to state the conditions they must have fulfilled before they would end the turn-out. They thought they had attained a sufficiently commanding position to dictate. John Barton was appointed one of the deputation.

The masters agreed to this meeting, being anxious to end the strife, although undetermined among themselves how far they should yield, or whether they should yield at all. Some of the old, whose experience had taught them sympathy, were for concession. Others, white-headed men too, had only learnt hardness and obstinacy from the days of the years of their lives, and sneered at the more gentle and yielding. The younger men were one and all for an unflinching resistance to claims urged with so much violence. Of this party Harry Carson was the leader.

But like all energetic people, the more he had to do the more time he seemed to find. With all his letter-writing, his calling, his being present at the New Bailey, when investigations of any case of violence against knob-sticks[1] were going on, he beset Mary more than ever. She was weary of her life for him. From blandishments he had even gone to threats—threats that whether she would or not she should be his; he showed an indifference that was almost insulting to every thing that might attract attention and injure her character.

And still she never saw Jem. She knew he had returned home. She heard of him occasionally through his cousin, who roved gaily from house to house, finding and making friends everywhere. But she never saw him. What was she to think? Had he given her up? Were a few hasty words, spoken in a moment of irritation, to stamp her lot through life? At times she thought that she could bear this meekly, happy in her own constant power of loving. For of change or of forgetfulness she did not dream. Then at other times her state of impatience was such, that it required all her self-restraint to prevent her from going and seeking him out, and (as man would do to man, or woman to woman) begging him to forgive her hasty words, and allow her to retract them, and bidding him accept of the love that was filling her whole heart. She wished Margaret had not advised her against such a manner of proceeding; she believed it was her friend's words that seemed to make such a simple action impossible, in spite of all the internal urgings. But a friend's advice is only thus powerful, when it puts into language the secret oracle

[1] "Knob-sticks," those who consent to work at lower wages.

of our souls. It was the whisperings of her womanly nature that caused her to shrink from any unmaidenly action, not Margaret's counsel.

All this time, this ten days or so, of Will's visit to Manchester, there was something going on which interested Mary even now, and which, in former times, would have exceedingly amused and excited her. She saw as clearly as if told in words, that the merry, random, boisterous sailor had fallen deeply in love with the quiet, prim, somewhat plain Margaret: she doubted if Margaret was aware of it, and yet, as she watched more closely, she began to think some instinct made the blind girl feel whose eyes were so often fixed upon her pale face; that some inner feeling made the delicate and becoming rose-flush steal over her countenance. She did not speak so decidedly as before; there was a hesitation in her manner, that seemed to make her very attractive; as if something softer, more loveable than excellent sense, were coming in as a motive for speech; her eyes had always been soft, and were in no ways disfigured by her blindness, and now seemed to have a new charm, as they quivered under their white down-cast lids. She must be conscious, thought Mary,—heart answering heart.

Will's love had no blushings, no downcast eyes, no weighing of words; it was as open and undisguised as his nature; yet he seemed afraid of the answer its acknowledgment might meet with. It was Margaret's angelic voice that had entranced him, and which made him think of her as a being of some other sphere, that he feared to woo. So he tried to propitiate Job in all manner of ways. He went over to Liverpool to rummage in his great sea-chest for the flying-fish (no very odorous present by the way). He hesitated over a child's caul for some time, which was, in his eyes, a far greater treasure than any Exocetus. What use could it be of to a landsman? Then Margaret's voice rang in his ears; and he determined to sacrifice it, his most precious possession, to one whom she loved, as she did her grandfather.

It was rather a relief to him, when, having put it and the flying-fish together in a brown paper parcel, and sat upon them for security all the way in the railroad, he found that Job was so indifferent to the precious caul, that he might easily claim it again. He hung about Margaret, till he had received many warnings and reproaches from his conscience in behalf of his dear aunt Alice's claims upon his time. He went away, and then he bethought him of some other little word with Job. And he turned back, and stood talking once more in Margaret's presence, door in hand, only waiting for some little speech of encouragement to come in and sit down again. But as the invitation was not given, he was forced to leave at last, and go and do his duty.

Four days had Jem Wilson watched for Mr. Harry Carson without success; his hours of going and returning to his home were so irregular, owing to the meetings and consultations among the masters, which were rendered necessary by the turn-out. On the fifth, without any purpose on Jem's part, they met.

It was the workmen's dinner-hour, the interval between twelve and one; when the streets of Manchester are comparatively quiet, for a few shopping ladies and lounging gentlemen count for nothing in that busy, bustling, living place. Jem had been on an errand for his master, instead of returning to his dinner; and in passing along a lane, a road (called, in compliment to the intentions of some future builder, a street), he encountered Harry Carson, the only person, as far as he saw beside himself, treading the unfrequented path. Along one side ran a high broad fence, blackened over by coal-tar, and spiked and stuck with pointed nails at the top, to prevent any one from climbing over into the garden beyond. By this fence was the foot-path. The carriage road was such as no carriage, no, not even a cart, could possibly have passed along, without Hercules to assist in lifting it out of the deep clay ruts. On the other side of the way was a dead brick wall; and a field after that, where there was a sawpit, and joiner's shed.

Jem's heart beat violently when he saw the gay, handsome young man approaching, with a light, buoyant step. This, then, was he whom Mary loved. It was, perhaps, no wonder; for he seemed to the poor smith so elegant, so well-appointed, that he felt his superiority in externals, strangely and painfully, for an instant. Then something uprose within him, and told him, that "a man's a man for a' that, for a' that, and twice as much as a' that." And he no longer felt troubled by the outward appearance of his rival.

Harry Carson came on, lightly bounding over the dirty places with almost a lad's buoyancy. To his surprise the dark, sturdy-looking artisan stopped him by saying respectfully,

"May I speak a word wi' you, sir?"

"Certainly, my good man," looking his astonishment; then finding that the promised speech did not come very quickly, he added, "But make haste, for I'm in a hurry."

Jem had cast about for some less abrupt way of broaching the subject uppermost in his mind than he now found himself obliged to use. With a husky voice that trembled as he spoke, he said,

"I think, sir, yo're keeping company wi' a young woman called Mary Barton?"

A light broke in upon Harry Carson's mind, and he paused before he gave the answer for which the other waited.

Could this man be a lover of Mary's? And (strange, stinging thought) could he be beloved by her, and so have caused her obstinate rejection of himself? He looked at Jem from head to foot, a black, grimy mechanic, in dirty fustian clothes, strongly built, and awkward (according to the dancing-master); then he glanced at himself, and recalled the reflection he had so lately quitted in his bed-room. It was impossible. No woman with eyes could choose the one when the other wooed. It was Hyperion to a Satyr. That quotation came aptly; he forgot "That a man's a man for a' that." And yet here was a clue, which he had often wanted, to her changed conduct towards him. If she loved this man. If— he hated the fellow, and longed to strike him. He would know all.

"Mary Barton! let me see. Ay, that is the name of the girl. An arrant flirt, the little hussy is; but very pretty. Ay, Mary Barton is her name."

Jem bit his lips. Was it then so; that Mary was a flirt, the giddy creature of whom he spoke? He would not believe it, and yet how he wished the suggestive words unspoken. That thought must keep now, though. Even if she were, the more reason for there being some one to protect her; poor, faulty darling.

"She's a good girl, sir, though may be a bit set up with her beauty; but she's her father's only child, sir, and—" he stopped; he did not like to express suspicion, and yet he was determined he would be certain there was ground for none. What should he say?

"Well, my fine fellow, and what have I to do with that? It's but loss of my time, and yours, too, if you've only stopped me to tell me Mary Barton is very pretty; I know that well enough."

He seemed as though he would have gone on, but Jem put his black, working, right hand upon his arm to detain him. The haughty young man shook it off, and with his glove pretended to brush away the sooty contamination that might be left upon his light great-coat sleeve. The little action aroused Jem.

"I will tell you in plain words what I have got to say to you, young man. It's been telled me by one as knows, and has seen, that you walk with this same Mary Barton, and are known to be courting her; and her as spoke to me about it, thinks as how Mary loves you. That may be, or may not. But I'm an old friend of hers, and her father's; and I just wished to know if you mean to marry the girl. Spite of what you said of her lightness, I ha' known her long enough to be sure she'll make a noble wife for any one, let him be what he may; and I mean to stand by her like a brother; and if you mean rightly, you'll not think the worse on me for what I've now said; and if—but no, I'll not say what I'll do to the man who wrongs a hair of her head. He shall rue it the longest day he lives, that's all. Now, sir, what I ask of you is this. If you mean fair and honourable by her, well and good; but if not, for your own sake as well as hers, leave her alone, and never speak to her more." Jem's voice quivered with the earnestness with which he spoke, and he eagerly waited for some answer.

Harry Carson, meanwhile, instead of attending very particularly to the purpose the man had in addressing him, was trying to gather from his speech what was the real state of the case. He succeeded so far as to comprehend that Jem inclined to believe that Mary loved his rival; and consequently, that if the speaker were attached to her himself, he was not a favoured admirer. The idea came into Mr. Carson's mind, that perhaps, after all, Mary loved him in spite of her frequent and obstinate rejections; and that she had employed this person (whoever he was) to bully him into marrying her. He resolved to try and ascertain more correctly the man's relation to her. Either he was a lover, and if so, not a favoured one (in which case Mr. Carson could not at all understand the man's motives for interesting himself in securing her marriage); or he was a friend, an accomplice, whom she had employed to bully him. So little faith in goodness have the mean and selfish!

"Before I make you into my confidant, my good man," said Mr. Carson, in a contemptuous tone, "I think it might be as well to inquire your right to meddle with our affairs. Neither Mary nor I, as I conceive, called you in as a mediator." He paused; he wanted a distinct answer to this last supposition. None came; so he began to imagine he was to be threatened into some engagement, and his angry spirit rose.

"And so, my fine fellow, you will have the kindness to leave us to ourselves, and not meddle with what does not concern you. If you were a brother, or father of hers, the case might have been different. As it is, I can only consider you an impertinent meddler."

Again he would have passed on, but Jem stood in a determined way before him, saying,

"You say if I had been her brother, or her father, you'd have answered me what I ask. Now, neither father nor brother could love her as I have loved her, ay, and as I love her still; if love gives a right to satisfaction, it's next to impossible any one breathing can come up to my right. Now, sir, tell me! do you mean fair by Mary or not? I've proved my claim to know, and, by G——, I will know."

"Come, come, no impudence," replied Mr. Carson, who, having discovered what he wanted to know (namely, that Jem was a lover of Mary's, and that she was not encouraging his suit), wished to pass on.

"Father, brother, or rejected lover" (with an emphasis on the word rejected), "no one has a right to interfere between my little girl and me. No one shall. Confound you, man! get out of my way, or I'll make you," as Jem still obstructed his path with dogged determination.

"I won't, then, till you've given me your word about Mary," replied the mechanic, grinding his words out between his teeth, and the livid paleness of the anger he could no longer keep down covering his face till he looked ghastly.

"Won't you?" (with a taunting laugh), "then I'll make you." The young man raised his slight cane, and smote the artisan across the face with a stinging stroke. An instant afterwards he lay stretched in the muddy road, Jem standing over him, panting with rage. What he would have done next in his moment of ungovernable passion, no one knows; but a policeman from the main street, into which this road led, had been sauntering about for some time, unobserved by either of the parties, and expecting some kind of conclusion like the present to the violent discussion going on between the two young men. In a minute he had pinioned Jem, who sullenly yielded to the surprise.

Mr. Carson was on his feet directly, his face glowing with rage or shame.

"Shall I take him to the lock-ups for assault, sir?" said the policeman.

"No, no," exclaimed Mr. Carson; "I struck him first. It was no assault on his side; though," he continued, hissing out his words to Jem, who even hated freedom procured for him, however justly, at the intervention of his rival, "I will never forgive or forget your insult. Trust me," he gasped the words in excess of passion, "Mary shall fare no better for your insolent interference." He laughed, as if with the consciousness of power.

Jem replied with equal excitement—"And if you dare to injure her in the least, I will await you where no policeman can step in between. And God shall judge between us two."

CHAPTER XV - A VIOLENT MEETING BETWEEN THE RIVALS.

The policeman now interfered with persuasions and warnings. He locked his arm in Jem's to lead him away in an opposite direction to that in which he saw Mr. Carson was going. Jem submitted gloomily, for a few steps, then wrenched himself free. The policeman shouted after him,

"Take care, my man! there's no girl on earth worth what you'll be bringing on yourself if you don't mind."

But Jem was out of hearing.

CHAPTER XVI - MEETING BETWEEN MASTERS AND WORKMEN.

"Not for a moment take the scorner's chair;
While seated there, thou know'st not how a word,
A tone, a look, may gall thy brother's heart,
And make him turn in bitterness against thee."

"LOVE-TRUTHS."

The day arrived on which the masters were to have an interview with a deputation of the work-people. The meeting was to take place in a public room, at an hotel; and there, about eleven o'clock, the mill-owners, who had received the foreign orders, began to collect.

Of course, the first subject, however full their minds might be of another, was the weather. Having done their duty by all the showers and sunshine which had occurred during the past week, they fell to talking about the business which brought them together. There might be about twenty gentlemen in the room, including some by courtesy, who were not immediately concerned in the settlement of the present question; but who, nevertheless, were sufficiently interested to attend. These were divided into little groups, who did not seem unanimous by any means. Some were for a slight concession, just a sugar-plum to quieten the naughty child, a sacrifice to peace and quietness. Some were steadily and vehemently opposed to the dangerous precedent of yielding one jot or one tittle to the outward force of a turn-out. It was teaching the work-people how to become masters, said they. Did they want the wildest thing heareafter, they would know that the way to obtain their wishes would be to strike work. Besides, one or two of those present had only just returned from the New Bailey, where one of the turn-outs had been tried for a cruel assault on a poor north-country weaver, who had attempted to work at the low price. They were indignant, and justly so, at the merciless manner in which the poor fellow had been treated; and their indignation at wrong, took (as it so often does) the extreme form of revenge. They felt as if, rather than yield to the body of men who were resorting to such cruel measures towards their fellow-workmen, they, the masters, would sooner relinquish all the benefits to be derived from the fulfilment of the commission, in order that the workmen might suffer keenly. They forgot that the strike was in this instance the consequence of want and need, suffered unjustly, as the endurers believed; for, however insane, and without ground of reason, such was their belief, and such was the cause of their violence. It is a great truth, that you cannot extinguish violence by violence. You may put it down for a time; but while you are crowing over your imaginary success, see if it does not return with seven devils worse than its former self!

No one thought of treating the workmen as brethren and friends, and openly, clearly, as appealing to reasonable men, stating the exact and full circumstances which led the masters to think it was the wise policy of the time to make sacrifices themselves, and to hope for them from the operatives.

In going from group to group in the room, you caught such a medley of sentences as the following:

"Poor devils! they're near enough to starving, I'm afraid. Mrs. Aldred makes two cows' heads into soup every week, and people come several miles to fetch it; and if these times last we must try and do more. But we must not be bullied into any thing!"

"A rise of a shilling or so won't make much difference, and they will go away thinking they've gained their point."

"That's the very thing I object to. They'll think so, and whenever they've a point to gain, no matter how unreasonable, they'll strike work."

"It really injures them more than us."

"I don't see how our interests can be separated."

"The d——d brute had thrown vitriol on the poor fellow's ankles, and you know what a bad part that is to heal. He had to stand still with the pain, and that left him at the mercy of the cruel wretch, who beat him about the head till you'd hardly have known he was a man. They doubt if he'll live."

"If it were only for that, I'll stand out against them, even if it were the cause of my ruin."

"Ay, I for one won't yield one farthing to the cruel brutes; they're more like wild beasts than human beings."

(Well! who might have made them different?)

"I say, Carson, just go and tell Duncombe of this fresh instance of their abominable conduct. He's wavering, but I think this will decide him."

The door was now opened, and a waiter announced that the men were below, and asked if it were the pleasure of the gentlemen that they should be shown up.

They assented, and rapidly took their places round the official table; looking, as like as they could, to the Roman senators who awaited the irruption of Brennus and his Gauls.

Tramp, tramp, came the heavy clogged feet up the stairs; and in a minute five wild, earnest-looking men stood in the room. John Barton, from some mistake as to time, was not among them. Had they been larger boned men, you would have called them gaunt; as it was, they were little of stature, and their fustian clothes hung loosely upon their shrunk limbs. In choosing their delegates, too, the operatives had had more regard to their brains, and power of speech, than to their wardrobes; they might have read the opinions of that worthy Professor Teufelsdruch, in Sartor Resartus, to judge from the dilapidated coats and trousers, which yet clothed men of parts and of power. It was long since many of them had known the luxury of a new article of dress; and air-gaps were to be seen in their garments. Some of the masters were rather affronted at such a ragged detachment coming between the wind and their nobility; but what cared they?

At the request of a gentleman hastily chosen to officiate as chairman, the leader of the delegates read, in a high-pitched, psalm-singing voice, a paper, containing the operatives' statement of the case at issue, their complaints, and their demands, which last were not remarkable for moderation.

He was then desired to withdraw for a few minutes, with his fellow delegates, to another room, while the masters considered what should be their definitive answer.

When the men had left the room, a whispered earnest consultation took place, every one re-urging his former arguments. The conceders carried the day, but only by a majority of one. The minority haughtily and audibly expressed their dissent from the measures to be adopted, even after the delegates re-entered the room; their words and looks did not pass unheeded by the quick-eyed operatives; their names were registered in bitter hearts.

The masters could not consent to the advance demanded by the workmen. They would agree to give one shilling per week more than they had previously offered. Were the delegates empowered to accept such offer?

They were empowered to accept or decline any offer made that day by the masters.

Then it might be as well for them to consult among themselves as to what should be their decision. They again withdrew.

It was not for long. They came back, and positively declined any compromise of their demands.

Then up sprang Mr. Henry Carson, the head and voice of the violent party among the masters, and addressing the chairman, even before the scowling operatives, he proposed some resolutions, which he, and those who agreed with him, had been concocting during this last absence of the deputation.

They were, firstly, withdrawing the proposal just made, and declaring all communication between the masters and that particular Trades' Union at an end; secondly, declaring that no master would employ any workman in future, unless he signed a declaration that he did not belong to any Trades' Union, and pledged himself not to assist or subscribe to any society, having for its object interference with the masters' powers; and, thirdly, that the masters should pledge themselves to protect and encourage all workmen willing to accept employment on those conditions, and at the rate of wages first offered. Considering that the men who now stood listening with lowering brows of defiance were all of them leading members of the Union, such resolutions were in themselves sufficiently provocative of animosity: but not content with simply stating them, Harry Carson went on to characterise the conduct of the workmen in no measured terms; every word he spoke rendering their looks more livid, their glaring eyes more fierce. One among them would have spoken, but checked himself in obedience to the stern glance and pressure on his arm, received from the leader. Mr. Carson sat down, and a friend instantly got up to second the motion. It was carried, but far from unanimously. The chairman announced it to the delegates (who had been once more turned out of the room for a division). They received it with deep brooding silence, but spake never a word, and left the room without even a bow.

Now there had been some by-play at this meeting, not recorded in the Manchester newspapers, which gave an account of the more regular part of the transaction.

While the men had stood grouped near the door, on their first entrance, Mr. Harry Carson had taken out his silver pencil, and had drawn an admirable caricature of them—lank, ragged, dispirited, and famine-stricken. Underneath he wrote a hasty quotation from the fat knight's well-known speech in Henry IV. He passed it to one of his neighbours, who acknowledged the likeness instantly, and by him it was sent round to others, who all smiled and nodded their heads. When it came back to its owner he tore the back of the letter on which it was drawn, in two; twisted them up, and flung them into the fire-place; but, careless whether they reached their aim or not, he did not look to see that they fell just short of any consuming cinders.

This proceeding was closely observed by one of the men.

He watched the masters as they left the hotel (laughing, some of them were, at passing jokes), and when all had gone, he re-entered. He went to the waiter, who recognised him.

"There's a bit on a picture up yonder, as one o' the gentlemen threw away; I've a little lad at home as dearly loves a picture; by your leave I'll go up for it."

The waiter, good-natured and sympathetic, accompanied him up-stairs; saw the paper picked up and untwisted, and then being convinced, by a hasty glance at its contents, that it was only what the man had called it, "a bit of a picture," he allowed him to bear away his prize.

Towards seven o'clock that evening many operatives began to assemble in a room in the Weavers' Arms public-house, a room appropriated for "festive occasions," as the landlord, in his circular, on opening the premises, had described it. But, alas! it was on no festive occasion that they met there on this night. Starved, irritated, despairing men, they were assembling to hear the answer that morning given by the masters to their delegates; after which, as was stated in the notice, a gentleman from London would have the honour of addressing the meeting on the present state of affairs between the employers and the employed, or (as he chose to term them) the idle and the industrious classes. The room was not large, but its bareness of furniture made it appear so. Unshaded gas flared down upon the lean and unwashed artisans as they entered, their eyes blinking at the excess of light.

They took their seats on benches, and awaited the deputation. The latter, gloomily and ferociously, delivered the masters' ultimatum, adding thereunto not one word of their own; and it sank all the deeper into the sore hearts of the listeners for their forbearance.

Then the "gentleman from London" (who had been previously informed of the masters' decision) entered. You would have been puzzled to define his exact position, or what was the state of his mind as regarded education. He looked so self-conscious, so far from earnest, among the group of eager, fierce, absorbed men, among whom he now stood. He might have been a disgraced medical student of the Bob Sawyer class, or an unsuccessful actor, or a flashy shopman. The impression he would have given you would have been unfavourable, and yet there was much about him that could only be characterised as doubtful.

He smirked in acknowledgment of their uncouth greetings, and sat down; then glancing round, he inquired whether it would not be agreeable to the gentlemen present to have pipes and liquor handed round; adding, that he would stand treat.

As the man who has had his taste educated to love reading, falls devouringly upon books after a long abstinence, so these poor fellows, whose tastes had been left to educate themselves into a liking for tobacco, beer, and similar gratifications, gleamed up at the proposal of the London delegate. Tobacco and drink deaden the pangs of hunger, and make one forget the miserable home, the desolate future.

They were now ready to listen to him with approbation. He felt it; and rising like a great orator, with his right arm outstretched, his left in the breast of his waistcoat, he began to declaim, with a forced theatrical voice.

After a burst of eloquence, in which he blended the deeds of the elder and the younger Brutus, and magnified the resistless might of the "millions of Manchester," the Londoner descended to matter-of-fact business, and in his capacity this way he did not belie the good judgment of those who had sent him as delegate. Masses of people, when left to their own free choice, seem to have discretion in distinguishing men of natural talent; it is a pity they so little regard temper and principles. He rapidly dictated resolutions, and suggested measures. He wrote out a stirring placard for the walls. He proposed sending delegates to entreat the assistance of other Trades' Unions in other towns. He headed the list of subscribing Unions, by a liberal donation from that with which he was especially connected in London; and what was more, and more uncommon, he paid down the money in real, clinking, blinking, golden sovereigns! The money, alas, was cravingly required; but before alleviating any private necessities on the morrow, small sums were handed to each of the delegates, who were in a day or two to set out on their expeditions to Glasgow, Newcastle, Nottingham, &c. These men were most of them members of the deputation who had that morning waited upon the masters. After he had drawn up some letters, and spoken a few more stirring words, the gentleman from London withdrew, previously shaking hands all round; and many speedily followed him out of the room, and out of the house.

The newly-appointed delegates, and one or two others, remained behind to talk over their respective missions, and to give and exchange opinions in more homely and natural language than they dared to use before the London orator.

"He's a rare chap, yon," began one, indicating the departed delegate by a jerk of his thumb towards the door. "He's gotten the gift of the gab, anyhow!"

"Ay! ay! he knows what he's about. See how he poured it into us about that there Brutus. He were pretty hard, too, to kill his own son!"

"I could kill mine if he took part wi' the masters; to be sure, he's but a step-son, but that makes no odds," said another.

But now tongues were hushed, and all eyes were directed towards the member of the deputation who had that morning returned to the hotel to obtain possession of Harry Carson's clever caricature of the operatives.

The heads clustered together, to gaze at and detect the likenesses.

"That's John Slater! I'd ha' known him anywhere, by his big nose. Lord! how like; that's me, by G——, it's the very way I'm obligated to pin my waistcoat up, to hide that I've gotten no shirt. That *is* a shame, and I'll not stand it."

"Well!" said John Slater, after having acknowledged his nose and his likeness; "I could laugh at a jest as well as e'er the best on 'em, though it did tell again mysel, if I were not clemming" (his eyes filled with tears; he was a poor, pinched, sharp-featured man, with a gentle and melancholy expression of countenance), "and if I could keep from thinking of them at home, as is clemming; but with their cries for food ringing in my ears, and making me afeard of going home, and wonder if I should hear 'em wailing out, if I lay cold and drowned at th' bottom o' th' canal, there,—why, man, I cannot laugh at ought. It seems to make me sad that there is any as can make game on what they've never knowed; as can make such laughable pictures on men, whose very hearts within 'em are so raw and sore as ours were and are, God help us."

John Barton began to speak; they turned to him with great attention. "It makes me more than sad, it makes my heart burn within me, to see that folk can make a jest of earnest men; of chaps who comed to ask for a bit o' fire for th' old granny, as shivers in th' cold; for a bit o' bedding, and some warm clothing to the poor wife as lies in labour on th' damp flags; and for victuals for the childer, whose little voices are getting too faint and weak to cry aloud wi' hunger. For, brothers, is not them the things we ask for when we ask for more wage? We donnot want dainties, we want bellyfuls; we donnot want gimcrack coats and waistcoats, we want warm clothes, and so that we get 'em we'd not quarrel wi' what they're made on. We donnot want their grand houses, we want a roof to cover us from the rain, and the snow, and the storm; ay, and not alone to cover us, but the helpless ones that cling to us in the keen wind, and ask us with their eyes why we brought 'em into th' world to suffer?" He lowered his deep voice almost to a whisper.

"I've seen a father who had killed his child rather than let it clem before his eyes; and he were a tender-hearted man."

He began again in his usual tone. "We come to th' masters wi' full hearts, to ask for them things I named afore. We know that they've gotten money, as we've earned for 'em; we know trade is mending, and that they've large orders, for which they'll be well paid; we ask for our share o' th' payment; for, say we, if th' masters get our share of payment it will only go to keep servants and horses, to more dress and pomp. Well and good, if yo choose to be fools we'll not hinder you, so long as you're just; but our share we must and will have; we'll not be cheated. *We* want it for daily bread, for life itself; and not for our own lives neither (for there's many a one here, I know by mysel, as would be glad and thankful to lie down and die out o' this weary world), but for the lives of them little ones, who don't yet know what life is, and are afeard of death. Well, we come before th' masters to state what we want, and what we must have, afore we'll set shoulder to their work; and they say, 'No.' One would think that would be enough of hard-heartedness, but it isn't. They go and make jesting pictures of us! I could laugh at mysel, as well as poor John Slater there; but then I must be easy in my mind to laugh. Now I only know that I would give the last drop o' my blood to avenge us on yon chap, who had so little feeling in him as to make game on earnest, suffering men!"

A low angry murmur was heard among the men, but it did not yet take form or words. John continued—

"You'll wonder, chaps, how I came to miss the time this morning; I'll just tell you what I was a-doing. Th' chaplain at the New Bailey sent and gived me an order to see Jonas Higginbotham; him as was taken up last week for throwing vitriol in a knob-stick's face. Well, I couldn't help but go; and I didn't reckon it would ha' kept me so late. Jonas were like one crazy when I got to him; he said he could na get rest night or day for th' face of the poor fellow he had damaged; then he thought on his weak, clemmed look, as he tramped, foot-sore, into town; and Jonas thought, may be, he had left them at home as would look for news, and hope and get none, but, haply, tidings of his death. Well, Jonas had thought on these things till he could not rest, but walked up and down continually like a wild beast in his cage. At last he bethought him on a way to help a bit, and he got th' chaplain to send for me; and he telled me this; and that th' man were lying in th' Infirmary, and he bade me go (to-day's the day as folk may be admitted into th' Infirmary) and get his silver watch, as was his mother's, and sell it as well as I could, and take the money, and bid the poor knob-stick send it to his friends beyond Burnley; and I were to take him Jonas's kind regards, and he humbly axed him to forgive him. So I did what Jonas wished. But bless your life, none on us would ever throw vitriol again (at least at a knob-stick) if they could see the sight I saw to-day. The man lay, his face all wrapped in cloths, so I didn't see *that*; but not a limb, nor a bit of a limb, could keep from quivering with pain. He would ha' bitten his hand to keep down his moans, but couldn't, his face hurt him so if he moved it e'er so little. He could scarce mind me when I telled him about Jonas; he did squeeze my hand when I jingled the money, but when I axed his wife's name he shrieked out, 'Mary, Mary, shall I never see you again? Mary, my darling, they've made me blind because I wanted to work for you and our own baby; oh, Mary, Mary!' Then the nurse came, and said he were raving, and that I had made him worse. And I'm afeard it was true; yet I were loth to go without knowing where to send the money. ... So that kept me beyond my time, chaps."

"Did yo hear where the wife lived at last?" asked many anxious voices.

"No! he went on talking to her, till his words cut my heart like a knife. I axed th' nurse to find out who she was, and where she lived. But what I'm more especial naming it now for is this,—for one thing I wanted yo all to know why I weren't at my post this morning; for another, I wish to say, that I, for one, ha' seen enough of what comes of attacking knob-sticks, and I'll ha nought to do with it no more."

There were some expressions of disapprobation, but John did not mind them.

"Nay! I'm no coward," he replied, "and I'm true to th' backbone. What I would like, and what I would do, would be to fight the masters. There's one among yo called me a coward. Well! every man has a right to his opinion; but since I've thought on th' matter to-day, I've thought we han all on us been more like cowards in attacking the poor like ourselves; them as has none to help, but mun choose between vitriol and starvation. I say we're more cowardly in doing that than in leaving them alone. No! what I would do is this. Have at the masters!" Again he shouted, "Have at the masters!" He spoke lower; all listened with hushed breath.

"It's the masters as has wrought this woe; it's the masters as should pay for it. Him as called me coward just now, may try if I am one or not. Set me to serve out the masters, and see if there's ought I'll stick at."

"It would give th' masters a bit on a fright if one on them were beaten within an inch of his life," said one.

"Ay! or beaten till no life were left in him," growled another.

And so with words, or looks that told more than words, they built up a deadly plan. Deeper and darker grew the import of their speeches, as they stood hoarsely muttering their meaning out, and glaring, with eyes that told the terror their own thoughts were to them, upon their neighbours. Their clenched fists, their set teeth, their livid looks, all told the suffering their minds were voluntarily undergoing in the contemplation of crime, and in familiarising themselves with its details.

Then came one of those fierce terrible oaths which bind members of Trades' Unions to any given purpose. Then, under the flaring gaslight, they met together to consult further. With the distrust of guilt, each was suspicious of his neighbour; each dreaded the treachery of another. A number of pieces of paper (the identical letter on which the caricature had been drawn that very morning) were torn up, and *one was marked*. Then all were folded up again, looking exactly alike. They were shuffled together in a hat. The gas was extinguished; each drew out a paper. The gas was re-lighted. Then each went as far as he could from his fellows, and examined the paper he had drawn without saying a word, and with a countenance as stony and immovable as he could make it.

Then, still rigidly silent, they each took up their hats and went every one his own way.

He who had drawn the marked paper had drawn the lot of the assassin! and he had sworn to act according to his drawing! But no one save God and his own conscience knew who was the appointed murderer!

CHAPTER XVII - BARTON'S NIGHT-ERRAND.

"Mournful is't to say Farewell,
  Though for few brief hours we part;
In that absence, who can tell
  What may come to wring the heart!"

ANONYMOUS.

The events recorded in the last chapter took place on a Tuesday. On Thursday afternoon Mary was surprised, in the midst of some little bustle in which she was engaged, by the entrance of Will Wilson. He looked strange, at least it was strange to see any different expression on his face to his usual joyous beaming appearance. He had a paper parcel in his hand. He came in, and sat down, more quietly than usual.

"Why, Will! what's the matter with you? You seem quite cut up about something!"

"And I am, Mary! I'm come to say good-bye; and few folk like to say good-bye to them they love."

"Good-bye! Bless me, Will, that's sudden, isn't it?"

Mary left off ironing, and came and stood near the fire-place. She had always liked Will; but now it seemed as if a sudden spring of sisterly love had gushed up in her heart, so sorry did she feel to hear of his approaching departure.

"It's very sudden, isn't it?" said she, repeating her question.

"Yes! it's very sudden," said he, dreamily. "No, it isn't;" rousing himself, to think of what he was saying. "The captain told me in a fortnight he would be ready to sail again; but it comes very sudden on me, I had got so fond of you all."

Mary understood the particular fondness that was thus generalised. She spoke again.

"But it's not a fortnight since you came. Not a fortnight since you knocked at Jane Wilson's door, and I was there, you remember. Nothing like a fortnight!"

"No; I know it's not. But, you see, I got a letter this afternoon from Jack Harris, to tell me our ship sails on Tuesday next; and it's long since I promised my uncle (my mother's brother, him that lives at Kirk-Christ, beyond Ramsay, in the Isle of Man) that I'd go and see him and his, this time of coming ashore. I must go. I'm sorry enough; but I mustn't slight poor mother's friends. I must go. Don't try to keep me," said he, evidently fearing the strength of his own resolution, if hard pressed by entreaty.

"I'm not a-going, Will. I dare say you're right; only I can't help feeling sorry you're going away. It seems so flat to be left behind. When do you go?"

"To-night. I shan't see you again."

"To-night! and you go to Liverpool! May be you and father will go together. He's going to Glasgow, by way of Liverpool."

"No! I'm walking; and I don't think your father will be up to walking."

"Well! and why on earth are you walking? You can get by railway for three-and-sixpence."

"Ay, but Mary! (thou mustn't let out what I'm going to tell thee) I haven't got three shillings, no, nor even a sixpence left, at least not here; before I came here I gave my landlady enough to carry me to the island and back, and may be a trifle for presents, and I brought all the rest here; and it's all gone but this," jingling a few coppers in his hand.

"Nay, never fret over my walking a matter of thirty mile," added he, as he saw she looked grave and sorry. "It's a fine clear night, and I shall set off betimes, and get in afore the Manx packet sails. Where's your father going? To Glasgow, did you say? Perhaps he and I may have a bit of a trip together then, for, if the Manx boat has sailed when I get into Liverpool, I shall go by a Scotch packet. What's he going to do in Glasgow?—Seek for work? Trade is as bad there as here, folk say."

"No; he knows that," answered Mary, sadly. "I sometimes think he'll never get work again, and that trade will never mend. It's very hard to keep up one's heart. I wish I were a boy, I'd go to sea with you. It would be getting away from bad news at any rate; and now, there's hardly a creature that crosses the door-step, but has something sad and unhappy to tell one. Father is going as a delegate from his Union, to ask help from the Glasgow folk. He's starting this evening."

Mary sighed, for the feeling again came over her that it was very flat to be left alone.

"You say no one crosses the threshold but has something sad to say; you don't mean that Margaret Jennings has any trouble?" asked the young sailor, anxiously.

"No!" replied Mary, smiling a little, "she's the only one I know, I believe, who seems free from care. Her blindness almost appears a blessing sometimes; she was so downhearted when she dreaded it, and now she seems so calm and happy when it's downright come. No! Margaret's happy, I do think."

"I could almost wish it had been otherwise," said Will, thoughtfully. "I could have been so glad to comfort her, and cherish her, if she had been in trouble."

"And why can't you cherish her, even though she is happy?" asked Mary.

"Oh! I don't know. She seems so much better than I am! And her voice! When I hear it, and think of the wishes that are in my heart, it seems as much out of place to ask her to be my wife, as it would be to ask an angel from heaven."

Mary could not help laughing outright, in spite of her depression, at the idea of Margaret as an angel; it was so difficult (even to her dress-making imagination) to fancy where, and how, the wings would be fastened to the brown stuff gown, or the blue and yellow print.

Will laughed, too, a little, out of sympathy with Mary's pretty merry laugh. Then he said—

"Ay, you may laugh, Mary; it only shows you've never been in love."

In an instant Mary was carnation colour, and the tears sprang to her soft gray eyes; she was suffering so much from the doubts arising from love! It was unkind of him. He did not notice her change of look and of complexion. He only noticed that she was silent, so he continued:

"I thought—I think, that when I come back from this voyage, I will speak. It's my fourth voyage in the same ship, and with the same captain, and he's promised he'll make me second mate after this trip; then I shall have something to offer Margaret; and her grandfather, and aunt Alice, shall live with her, to keep her from being lonesome while I'm at sea. I'm speaking as if she cared for me, and would marry me; d'ye think she does care at all for me, Mary?" asked he, anxiously.

Mary had a very decided opinion of her own on the subject, but she did not feel as if she had any right to give it. So she said—

"You must ask Margaret, not me, Will; she's never named your name to me." His countenance fell. "But I should say that was a good sign from a girl like her. I've no right to say what I think; but, if I was you, I would not leave her now without speaking."

"No! I cannot speak! I have tried. I've been in to wish them good-bye, and my voice stuck in my throat. I could say nought of what I'd planned to say; and I never thought of being so bold as to offer her marriage till I'd been my next trip, and been made mate. I could not even offer her this box," said he, undoing his paper parcel and displaying a gaudily ornamented accordion; "I longed to buy her something, and I thought, if it were something in the music line, she would may-be fancy it more. So, will you give it to her, Mary, when I'm gone? and, if you can slip in something tender,—something, you know, of what I feel,—may-be she would listen to you, Mary."

Mary promised that she would do all that he asked.

"I shall be thinking on her many and many a night, when I'm keeping my watch in mid-sea; I wonder if she will ever think on me when the wind is whistling, and the gale rising. You'll often speak of me to her, Mary? And if I should meet with any mischance, tell her how dear, how very dear, she was to me, and bid her, for the sake of one who loved her well, try and comfort my poor aunt Alice. Dear old aunt! you and Margaret will often go and see her, won't you? She's sadly failed since I was last ashore. And so good as she has been! When I lived with her, a little wee chap, I used to be wakened by the neighbours knocking her up; this one was ill, or that body's child was restless; and, for as tired as ever she might be, she would be up and dressed in a twinkling, never thinking of the hard day's wash afore her next morning. Them were happy times! How pleased I used to be when she would take me into the fields with her to gather herbs! I've tasted tea in China since then, but it wasn't half so good as the herb tea she used to make for me o' Sunday nights. And she knew such a deal about plants and birds, and their ways! She used to tell me long stories about her childhood, and we used to plan how we would go sometime, please God (that was always her word), and live near her old home beyond Lancaster; in the very cottage where she was born if we could get it. Dear! and how different it is! Here is she still in a back street o' Manchester, never likely to see her own home again; and I, a sailor, off for America next week. I wish she had been able to go to Burton once afore she died."

"She would may be have found all sadly changed," said Mary, though her heart echoed Will's feeling.

"Ay! ay! I dare say it's best. One thing I do wish though, and I have often wished it when out alone on the deep sea, when even the most thoughtless can't choose but think on th' past and th' future; and that is, that I'd never grieved her. Oh Mary! many a hasty word comes sorely back on the heart, when one thinks one shall never see the person whom one has grieved again!"

They both stood thinking. Suddenly Mary started.

"That's father's step. And his shirt's not ready!"

She hurried to her irons, and tried to make up for lost time.

John Barton came in. Such a haggard and wildly anxious looking man, Will thought he had never seen. He looked at Will, but spoke no word of greeting or welcome.

"I'm come to bid you good bye," said the sailor, and would in his sociable friendly humour have gone on speaking. But John answered abruptly,

"Good bye to ye, then."

There was that in his manner which left no doubt of his desire to get rid of the visitor, and Will accordingly shook hands with Mary, and looked at John, as if doubting how far to offer to shake hands with him. But he met with no answering glance or gesture, so he went his way, stopping for an instant at the door to say,

"You'll think on me on Tuesday, Mary. That's the day we shall hoist our blue Peter, Jack Harris says."

Mary was heartily sorry when the door closed; it seemed like shutting out a friendly sunbeam. And her father! what could be the matter with him? He was so restless; not speaking (she wished he would), but starting up and then sitting down, and meddling with her irons; he seemed so fierce, too, to judge from his face. She wondered if he disliked Will being there; or if he were vexed to find that she had not got further on with her work. At last she could bear his nervous way no longer, it made her equally nervous and fidgetty. She would speak.

"When are you going, father? I don't know the time o' the trains."

"And why shouldst thou know?" replied he, gruffly. "Meddle with thy ironing, but donnot be asking questions about what doesn't concern thee."

"I wanted to get you something to eat first," answered she, gently.

"Thou dost not know that I'm larning to do without food," said he.

Mary looked at him to see if he spoke jestingly. No! he looked savagely grave.

She finished her bit of ironing, and began preparing the food she was sure her father needed; for by this time her experience in the degrees of hunger had taught her that his present irritability was increased, if not caused, by want of food.

He had had a sovereign given him to pay his expenses as delegate to Glasgow, and out of this he had given Mary a few shillings in the morning; so she had been able to buy a sufficient meal, and now her care was to cook it so as most to tempt him.

"If thou'rt doing that for me, Mary, thou may'st spare thy labour. I telled thee I were not for eating."

"Just a little bit, father, before starting," coaxed Mary, perseveringly.

At that instant, who should come in but Job Legh. It was not often he came, but when he did pay visits, Mary knew from past experience they were any thing but short. Her father's countenance fell back into the deep gloom from which it was but just emerging at the sound of Mary's sweet voice, and pretty pleading. He became again restless and fidgetty, scarcely giving Job Legh the greeting necessary for a host in his own house. Job, however, did not stand upon ceremony. He had come to pay a visit, and was not to be daunted from his purpose. He was interested in John Barton's mission to Glasgow, and wanted to hear all about it; so he sat down, and made himself comfortable, in a manner that Mary saw was meant to be stationary.

"So thou'rt off to Glasgow, art thou?" he began his catechism.

"Ay."

"When art starting?"

"To-night."

"That I knowed. But by what train?"

That was just what Mary wanted to know; but what apparently her father was in no mood to tell. He got up without speaking, and went up-stairs. Mary knew from his step, and his way, how much he was put out, and feared Job would see it, too. But no! Job seemed imperturbable. So much the better, and perhaps she could cover her father's rudeness by her own civility to so kind a friend.

So half listening to her father's movements up-stairs, (passionate, violent, restless motions they were) and half attending to Job Legh, she tried to pay him all due regard.

"When does thy father start, Mary?"

That plaguing question again.

"Oh! very soon. I'm just getting him a bit of supper. Is Margaret very well?"

"Yes, she's well enough. She's meaning to go and keep Alice Wilson company for an hour or so this evening; as soon as she thinks her nephew will have started for Liverpool; for she fancies the old woman will feel a bit lonesome. Th' Union is paying for your father, I suppose?"

"Yes, they've given him a sovereign. You're one of th' Union, Job?"

"Ay! I'm one, sure enough; but I'm but a sleeping partner in the concern. I were obliged to become a member for peace, else I don't go along with 'em. Yo see they think themselves wise, and me silly, for differing with them; well! there's no harm in that. But then they won't let me be silly in peace and quietness, but will force me to be as wise as they are; now that's not British liberty, I say. I'm forced to be wise according to their notions, else they parsecute me, and sarve me out."

What could her father be doing up-stairs? Tramping and banging about. Why did he not come down? Or why did not Job go? The supper would be spoilt.

But Job had no notion of going.

"You see my folly is this, Mary. I would take what I could get; I think half a loaf is better than no bread. I would work for low wages rather than sit idle and starve. But, comes the Trades' Union, and says, 'Well, if you take the half-loaf, we'll worry you out of your life. Will you be clemmed, or will you be worried?' Now clemming is a quiet death, and worrying isn't, so I choose clemming, and come into th' Union. But I wish they'd leave me free, if I am a fool."

Creak, creak, went the stairs. Her father was coming down at last.

Yes, he came down, but more doggedly fierce than before, and made up for his journey, too; with his little bundle on his arm. He went up to Job, and, more civilly than Mary expected, wished him good-bye. He then turned to her, and in a short cold manner, bade her farewell.

"Oh! father, don't go yet. Your supper is all ready. Stay one moment!"

But he pushed her away, and was gone. She followed him to the door, her eyes blinded by sudden tears; she stood there looking after him. He was so strange, so cold, so hard. Suddenly, at the end of the court, he turned, and saw her standing there; he came back quickly, and took her in his arms.

"God bless thee, Mary!—God in heaven bless thee, poor child!" She threw her arms round his neck.

"Don't go yet, father; I can't bear you to go yet. Come in, and eat some supper; you look so ghastly; dear father, do!"

"No," he said, faintly and mournfully. "It's best as it is. I couldn't eat, and it's best to be off. I cannot be still at home. I must be moving."

So saying, he unlaced her soft twining arms, and kissing her once more, set off on his fierce errand.

And he was out of sight! She did not know why, but she had never before felt so depressed, so desolate. She turned in to Job, who sat there still. Her father, as soon as he was out of sight, slackened his pace, and fell into that heavy listless step, which told as well as words could do, of hopelessness and weakness. It was getting dark, but he loitered on, returning no greeting to any one.

A child's cry caught his ear. His thoughts were running on little Tom; on the dead and buried child of happier years. He followed the sound of the wail, that might have been *his*, and found a poor little mortal, who had lost his way, and whose grief had choked up his thoughts to the single want, "Mammy, mammy." With tender address, John Barton soothed the little laddie, and with beautiful patience he gathered fragments of meaning from the half spoken words which came mingled with sobs from the terrified little heart. So, aided by inquiries here and there from a passer-by, he led and carried the little fellow home, where his mother had been too busy to miss him, but now received him with thankfulness, and with an eloquent Irish blessing. When John heard the words of blessing, he shook his head mournfully, and turned away to retrace his steps.

Let us leave him.

Mary took her sewing after he had gone, and sat on, and sat on, trying to listen to Job, who was more inclined to talk than usual. She had conquered her feeling of impatience towards him so far as to be able to offer him her father's rejected supper; and she even tried to eat herself. But her heart failed her. A leaden weight seemed to hang over her; a sort of presentiment of evil, or perhaps only an excess of low-spirited feeling in consequence of the two departures which had taken place that afternoon.

She wondered how long Job Legh would sit. She did not like putting down her work, and crying before him, and yet she had never in her life longed so much to be alone in order to indulge in a good hearty burst of tears.

"Well, Mary," she suddenly caught him saying, "I thought you'd be a bit lonely to-night; and as Margaret were going to cheer th' old woman, I said I'd go and keep th' young un company; and a very pleasant, chatty evening we've had; very. Only I wonder as Margaret is not come back."

"But perhaps she is," suggested Mary.

"No, no, I took care o' that. Look ye here!" and he pulled out the great house-key. "She'll have to stand waiting i' th' street, and that I'm sure she wouldn't do, when she knew where to find me."

"Will she come back by hersel?" asked Mary.

"Ay. At first I were afraid o' trusting her, and I used to follow her a bit behind; never letting on, of course. But, bless you! she goes along as steadily as can be; rather slow, to be sure, and her head a bit on one side as if she were listening. And it's real beautiful to see her cross the road. She'll wait above a bit to hear that all is still; not that she's so dark as not to see a coach or a cart like a big black thing, but she can't rightly judge how far off it is by sight, so she listens. Hark! that's her!"

Yes; in she came with her usually calm face all tear-stained and sorrow-marked.

"What's the matter, my wench?" said Job, hastily.

"Oh! grandfather! Alice Wilson's so bad!" She could say no more, for her breathless agitation. The afternoon, and the parting with Will, had weakened her nerves for any after-shock.

"What is it? Do tell us, Margaret!" said Mary, placing her in a chair, and loosening her bonnet-strings.

"I think it's a stroke o' the palsy. Any rate she has lost the use of one side."

"Was it afore Will had set off?" asked Mary.

"No; he were gone before I got there," said Margaret; "and she were much about as well as she has been this many a day. She spoke a bit, but not much; but that were only natural, for Mrs. Wilson likes to have the talk to hersel, you know. She got up to go across the room, and then I heard a drag wi' her leg, and presently a fall, and Mrs. Wilson came running, and set up such a cry! I stopped wi'

Alice, while she fetched a doctor; but she could not speak, to answer me, though she tried, I think."

"Where was Jem? Why didn't he go for the doctor?"

"He were out when I got there, and he never came home while I stopped."

"Thou'st never left Mrs. Wilson alone wi' poor Alice?" asked Job, hastily.

"No, no," said Margaret. "But, oh! grandfather; it's now I feel how hard it is to have lost my sight. I should have so loved to nurse her; and I did try, until I found I did more harm than good. Oh! grandfather; if I could but see!"

She sobbed a little; and they let her give that ease to her heart. Then she went on—

"No! I went round by Mrs. Davenport's, and she were hard at work; but, the minute I told my errand, she were ready and willing to go to Jane Wilson, and stop up all night with Alice."

"And what does the doctor say?" asked Mary.

"Oh! much what all doctors say: he puts a fence on this side, and a fence on that, for fear he should be caught tripping in his judgment. One moment he does not think there's much hope—but while there is life there is hope; th' next he says he should think she might recover partial, but her age is again her. He's ordered her leeches to her head."

Margaret, having told her tale, leant back with weariness, both of body and mind. Mary hastened to make her a cup of tea; while Job, lately so talkative, sat quiet and mournfully silent.

"I'll go first thing to-morrow morning, and learn how she is; and I'll bring word back before I go to work," said Mary.

"It's a bad job Will's gone," said Job.

"Jane does not think she knows any one," replied Margaret. "It's perhaps as well he shouldn't see her now, for they say her face is sadly drawn. He'll remember her with her own face better, if he does not see her again."

With a few more sorrowful remarks they separated for the night, and Mary was left alone in her house, to meditate on the heavy day that had passed over her head. Everything seemed going wrong. Will gone; her father gone—and so strangely too! And to a place so mysteriously distant as Glasgow seemed to be to her! She had felt his presence as a protection against Harry Carson and his threats; and now she dreaded lest he should learn she was alone. Her heart began to despair, too, about Jem. She feared he had ceased to love her; and she—she only loved him more and more for his seeming neglect. And, as if all this aggregate of sorrowful thoughts was not enough, here was this new woe, of poor Alice's paralytic stroke.

CHAPTER XVIII - MURDER.

"But in his pulse there was no throb,
Nor on his lips one dying sob;
Sigh, nor word, nor struggling breath
Heralded his way to death."

SIEGE OF CORINTH.

"My brain runs this way and that way; 'twill not fix
On aught but vengeance."

DUKE OF GUISE.

I must now go back to an hour or two before Mary and her friends parted for the night. It might be about eight o'clock that evening, and the three Miss Carsons were sitting in their father's drawing-room. He was asleep in the dining-room, in his own comfortable chair. Mrs. Carson was (as was usual with her, when no particular excitement was going on) very poorly, and sitting up-stairs in her dressing-room, indulging in the luxury of a head-ache. She was not well, certainly. "Wind in the head," the servants called it. But it was but the natural consequence of the state of mental and bodily idleness in which she was placed. Without education enough to value the resources of wealth and leisure, she was so circumstanced as to command both. It would have done her more good than all the æther and sal-volatile she was daily in the habit of swallowing, if she might have taken the work of one of her own housemaids for a week; made beds, rubbed tables, shaken carpets, and gone out into the fresh morning air, without all the paraphernalia of shawl, cloak, boa, fur boots, bonnet, and veil, in which she was equipped before setting out for an "airing," in the closely shut-up carriage.

So the three girls were by themselves in the comfortable, elegant, well-lighted drawing-room; and, like many similarly-situated young ladies, they did not exactly know what to do to while away the time until the tea-hour. The elder two had been at a dancing-party the night before, and were listless and sleepy in consequence. One tried to read "Emerson's Essays," and fell asleep in the attempt; the other was turning over a parcel of new music, in order to select what she liked. Amy, the youngest, was copying some manuscript music. The air was heavy with the fragrance of strongly-scented flowers, which sent out their night odours from an adjoining conservatory.

The clock on the chimney-piece chimed eight. Sophy (the sleeping sister) started up at the sound.

"What o'clock is that?" she asked.

"Eight," said Amy.

"Oh dear! how tired I am! Is Harry come in? Tea would rouse one up a little. Are not you worn out, Helen?"

"Yes; I am tired enough. One is good for nothing the day after a dance. Yet I don't feel weary at the time; I suppose it is the lateness of the hours."

"And yet, how could it be managed otherwise? So many don't dine till five or six, that one cannot begin before eight or nine; and then it takes a long time to get into the spirit of the evening. It is always more pleasant after supper than before."

"Well, I'm too tired to-night to reform the world in the matter of dances or balls. What are you copying, Amy?"

"Only that little Spanish air you sing—'Quien quiera.'"

"What are you copying it for?" asked Helen.

"Harry asked me to do it for him this morning at breakfast-time,—for Miss Richardson, he said."

"For Jane Richardson!" said Sophy, as if a new idea were receiving strength in her mind.

"Do you think Harry means any thing by his attention to her?" asked Helen.

"Nay, I do not know any thing more than you do; I can only observe and conjecture. What do you think, Helen?"

"Harry always likes to be of consequence to the belle of the room. If one girl is more admired than another, he likes to flutter about her, and seem to be on intimate terms with her. That is his way, and I have not noticed any thing beyond that in his manner to Jane Richardson."

"But I don't think she knows it's only his way. Just watch her the next time we meet her when Harry is there, and see how she crimsons, and looks another way when she feels he is coming up to her. I think he sees it, too, and I think he is pleased with it."

"I dare say Harry would like well enough to turn the head of such a lovely girl as Jane Richardson. But I'm not convinced that he is in love, whatever she may be."

"Well, then!" said Sophy, indignantly, "though it is our own brother, I do think he is behaving very wrongly. The more I think of it the more sure I am that she thinks he means something, and that he intends her to think so. And then, when he leaves off paying her attention—"

"Which will be as soon as a prettier girl makes her appearance," interrupted Helen.

"As soon as he leaves off paying her attention," resumed Sophy, "she will have many and many a heart-ache, and then she will harden herself into being a flirt, a feminine flirt, as he is a masculine flirt. Poor girl!"

"I don't like to hear you speak so of Harry," said Amy, looking up at Sophy.

"And I don't like to have to speak so, Amy, for I love him dearly. He is a good, kind brother, but I do think him vain, and I think he hardly knows the misery, the crimes, to which indulged vanity may lead him."

Helen yawned.

"Oh! do you think we may ring for tea? Sleeping after dinner always makes me so feverish."

"Yes, surely. Why should not we?" said the more energetic Sophy, pulling the bell with some determination.

"Tea directly, Parker," said she, authoritatively, as the man entered the room.

She was too little in the habit of reading expressions on the faces of others to notice Parker's countenance.

Yet it was striking. It was blanched to a dead whiteness; the lips compressed as if to keep within some tale of horror; the eyes distended and unnatural. It was a terror-stricken face.

The girls began to put away their music and books, in preparation for tea. The door slowly opened again, and this time it was the nurse who entered. I call her nurse, for such had been her office in by-gone days, though now she held rather an anomalous situation in the family. Seamstress, attendant on the young ladies, keeper of the stores; only "Nurse" was still her name. She had lived longer with them than any other servant, and to her their manner was far less haughty than to the other domestics. She occasionally came into the drawing-room to look for things belonging to their father or mother, so it did not excite any surprise when she advanced into the room. They went on arranging their various articles of employment.

She wanted them to look up. She wanted them to read something in her face—her face so full of woe, of horror. But they went on without taking any notice. She coughed; not a natural cough; but one of those coughs which ask so plainly for remark.

"Dear nurse, what is the matter?" asked Amy. "Are not you well?"

"Is mamma ill?" asked Sophy, quickly.

"Speak, speak, nurse!" said they all, as they saw her efforts to articulate, choked by the convulsive rising in her throat. They clustered round her with eager faces, catching a glimpse of some terrible truth to be revealed.

"My dear young ladies! my dear girls," she gasped out at length, and then she burst into tears.

"Oh! do tell us what it is, nurse," said one. "Any thing is better than this. Speak!"

"My children! I don't know how to break it to you. My dears, poor Mr. Harry is brought home—"

"Brought home—*brought* home—how?" Instinctively they sank their voices to a whisper; but a fearful whisper it was. In the same low tone, as if afraid lest the walls, the furniture, the inanimate things which told of preparation for life and comfort, should hear, she answered,

"Dead!"

Amy clutched her nurse's arm, and fixed her eyes on her as if to know if such a tale could be true; and when she read its confirmation in those sad, mournful, unflinching eyes, she sank, without word or sound, down in a faint upon the floor. One sister sat down on an ottoman, and covered her face, to try and realise it. That was Sophy. Helen threw herself on the sofa, and burying her head in the pillows, tried to stifle the screams and moans which shook her frame.

The nurse stood silent. She had not told *all.*

"Tell me," said Sophy, looking up, and speaking in a hoarse voice, which told of the inward pain, "tell me, nurse! Is he *dead*, did you say? Have you sent for a doctor? Oh! send for one, send for one," continued she, her voice rising to shrillness, and starting to her feet. Helen lifted herself up, and looked, with breathless waiting, towards nurse.

"My dears, he is dead! But I have sent for a doctor. I have done all I could."

"When did he—when did they bring him home?" asked Sophy.

"Perhaps ten minutes ago. Before you rang for Parker."

"How did he die? Where did they find him? He looked so well. He always seemed so strong. Oh! are you sure he is dead?"

She went towards the door. Nurse laid her hand on her arm.

"Miss Sophy, I have not told you all. Can you bear to hear it? Remember, master is in the next room, and he knows nothing yet. Come, you must help me to tell him. Now be quiet, dear! It was no common death he died!" She looked in her face as if trying to convey her meaning by her eyes.

Sophy's lips moved, but nurse could hear no sound.

"He has been shot as he was coming home along Turner Street, to-night."

Sophy went on with the motion of her lips, twitching them almost convulsively.

"My dear, you must rouse yourself, and remember your father and mother have yet to be told. Speak! Miss Sophy!"

But she could not; her whole face worked involuntarily. The nurse left the room, and almost immediately brought back some sal-volatile and water. Sophy drank it eagerly, and gave one or two deep gasps. Then she spoke in a calm unnatural voice.

"What do you want me to do, nurse? Go to Helen and poor Amy. See, they want help."

"Poor creatures! we must let them alone for a bit. You must go to master; that's what I want you to do, Miss Sophy. You must break it to him, poor old gentleman. Come, he's asleep in the dining-room, and the men are waiting to speak to him."

Sophy went mechanically to the dining-room door.

"Oh! I cannot go in. I cannot tell him. What must I say?"

"I'll come with you, Miss Sophy. Break it to him by degrees."

"I can't, nurse. My head throbs so, I shall be sure to say the wrong thing."

However, she opened the door. There sat her father, the shaded light of the candle-lamp falling upon, and softening his marked features, while his snowy hair contrasted well with the deep crimson morocco of the chair. The newspaper he had been reading had dropped on the carpet by his side. He breathed regularly and deeply.

At that instant the words of Mrs. Hemans's song came full into Sophy's mind.

"Ye know not what ye do,
  That call the slumberer back
From the realms unseen by you,
  To life's dim, weary track."

But this life's track would be to the bereaved father something more than dim and weary, hereafter.

"Papa," said she, softly. He did not stir.

"Papa!" she exclaimed, somewhat louder.

He started up, half awake.

"Tea is ready, is it?" and he yawned.

"No! papa, but something very dreadful—very sad, has happened!"

He was gaping so loud that he did not catch the words she uttered, and did not see the expression of her face.

"Master Henry is not come back," said nurse. Her voice, heard in unusual speech to him, arrested his attention, and rubbing his eyes, he looked at the servant.

"Harry! oh no! he had to attend a meeting of the masters about these cursed turn-outs. I don't expect him yet. What are you looking at me so strangely for, Sophy?"

"Oh, papa, Harry is come back," said she, bursting into tears.

"What do you mean?" said he, startled into an impatient consciousness that something was wrong. "One of you says he is not come home, and the other says he is. Now that's nonsense! Tell me at once what's the matter. Did he go on horse-back to town? Is he thrown? Speak, child, can't you?"

"No! he's not been thrown, papa," said Sophy, sadly.

"But he's badly hurt," put in the nurse, desirous to be drawing his anxiety to a point.

"Hurt? Where? How? Have you sent for a doctor?" said he, hastily rising, as if to leave the room.

"Yes, papa, we've sent for a doctor—but I'm afraid—I believe it's of no use."

He looked at her for a moment, and in her face he read the truth. His son, his only son, was dead.

He sank back in his chair, and hid his face in his hands, and bowed his head upon the table. The strong mahogany dining-table shook and rattled under his agony.

Sophy went and put her arms round his bowed neck.

"Go! you are not Harry," said he; but the action roused him.

"Where is he? where is the—" said he, with his strong face set into the lines of anguish, by two minutes of such intense woe.

"In the servants' hall," said nurse. "Two policemen and another man brought him home. They would be glad to speak to you when you are able, sir."

"I am able now," replied he. At first when he stood up, he tottered. But steadying himself, he walked, as firmly as a soldier on drill, to the door. Then he turned back and poured out a glass of wine from the decanter which yet remained on the table. His eye caught the wine-glass which Harry had used but two or three hours before. He sighed a long quivering sigh. And then mastering himself again, he left the room.

"You had better go back to your sisters, Miss Sophy," said nurse.

Miss Carson went. She could not face death yet.

The nurse followed Mr. Carson to the servants' hall. There, on their dinner-table, lay the poor dead body. The men who had brought it were sitting near the fire, while several of the servants stood round the table, gazing at the remains.

The remains!

One or two were crying; one or two were whispering; awed into a strange stillness of voice and action by the presence of the dead. When Mr. Carson came in they all drew back and looked at him with the reverence due to sorrow.

He went forward and gazed long and fondly on the calm, dead face; then he bent down and kissed the lips yet crimson with life. The policemen had advanced and stood ready to be questioned. But at first the old man's mind could only take in the idea of death; slowly, slowly came the conception of violence, of murder. "How did he die?" he groaned forth.

The policemen looked at each other. Then one began, and stated that having heard the report of a gun in Turner Street, he had turned down that way (a lonely, unfrequented way Mr. Carson knew, but a short cut to his garden-door, of which Harry had a key); that as he (the policeman) came nearer, he had heard footsteps as of a man running away; but the evening was so dark (the moon not having yet risen) that he could see no one twenty yards off. That he had even been startled when close to the body by seeing it lying across the path at his feet. That he had sprung his rattle; and when another policeman came up, by the light of the lantern they had discovered who it was that had been killed. That they believed him to be dead when they first took him up, as he had never moved, spoken, or breathed. That intelligence of the murder had been sent to the superintendent, who would probably soon be here. That two or three policemen were still about the place where the murder was committed, seeking out for some trace of the murderer. Having said this, they stopped speaking.

Mr. Carson had listened attentively, never taking his eyes off the dead body. When they had ended, he said,

"Where was he shot?"

They lifted up some of the thick chestnut curls, and showed a blue spot (you could hardly call it a hole, the flesh had closed so much over it) in the left temple. A deadly aim! And yet it was so dark a night!

"He must have been close upon him," said one policeman.

"And have had him between him and the sky," added the other.

There was a little commotion at the door of the room, and there stood poor Mrs. Carson, the mother.

She had heard unusual noises in the house, and had sent down her maid (much more a companion to her than her highly-educated daughters) to discover what was going on. But the maid either forgot, or dreaded, to return; and with nervous impatience Mrs. Carson came down herself, and had traced the hum and buzz of voices to the servants' hall.

Mr. Carson turned round. But he could not leave the dead for any one living.

"Take her away, nurse. It is no sight for her. Tell Miss Sophy to go to her mother." His eyes were again fixed on the dead face of his son.

Presently Mrs. Carson's hysterical cries were heard all over the house. Her husband shuddered at the outward expression of the agony which was rending his heart.

Then the police superintendent came, and after him the doctor. The latter went through all the forms of ascertaining death, without uttering a word, and when at the conclusion of the operation of opening a vein, from which no blood flowed, he shook his head, all present understood the confirmation of their previous belief. The superintendent asked to speak to Mr. Carson in private.

"It was just what I was going to request of you," answered he; so he led the way into the dining-room, with the wine-glass still on the table.

The door was carefully shut, and both sat down, each apparently waiting for the other to begin.

At last Mr. Carson spoke.

"You probably have heard that I am a rich man."

The superintendent bowed in assent.

"Well, sir, half—nay, if necessary, the whole of my fortune I will give to have the murderer brought to the gallows."

"Every exertion, you may be sure, sir, shall be used on our part; but probably offering a handsome reward might accelerate the discovery of the murderer. But what I wanted particularly to tell you, sir, is that one of my men has already got some clue, and that another (who accompanied me here) has within this quarter of an hour found a gun in the field which the murderer crossed, and which he probably threw away when pursued, as encumbering his flight. I have not the smallest doubt of discovering the murderer."

"What do you call a handsome reward?" said Mr. Carson.

"Well, sir, three, or five hundred pounds is a munificent reward: more than will probably be required as a temptation to any accomplice."

"Make it a thousand," said Mr. Carson, decisively. "It's the doing of those damned turn-outs."

"I imagine not," said the superintendent. "Some days ago the man I was naming to you before, reported to the inspector when he came on his beat, that he had had to separate your son from a young man, who by his dress he believed to be employed in a foundry; that the man had thrown Mr. Carson down, and seemed inclined to proceed to more violence, when the policeman came up and interfered. Indeed, my man wished to give him in charge for an assault, but Mr. Carson would not allow that to be done."

"Just like him!—noble fellow!" murmured the father.

"But after your son had left, the man made use of some pretty strong threats. And it's rather a curious coincidence that this scuffle took place in the very same spot where the murder was committed; in Turner Street."

There was some one knocking at the door of the room. It was Sophy, who beckoned her father out, and then asked him, in an awe-struck whisper, to come up-stairs and speak to her mother.

"She will not leave Harry, and talks so strangely. Indeed—indeed—papa, I think she has lost her senses."

And the poor girl sobbed bitterly.

"Where is she?" asked Mr. Carson.

"In his room."

They went up stairs rapidly and silently. It was a large, comfortable bedroom; too large to be well lighted by the flaring, flickering kitchen-candle which had been hastily snatched up, and now stood on the dressing-table.

On the bed, surrounded by its heavy, pall-like green curtains, lay the dead son. They had carried him up, and laid him down, as tenderly as though they feared to waken him; and, indeed, it looked more like sleep than death, so very calm and full of repose was the face. You saw, too, the chiselled beauty of the features much more perfectly than when the brilliant colouring of life had distracted your attention. There was a peace about him which told that death had come too instantaneously to give any previous pain.

In a chair, at the head of the bed, sat the mother,—smiling. She held one of the hands (rapidly stiffening, even in her warm grasp), and gently stroked the back of it, with the endearing caress she had used to all her children when young.

"I am glad you are come," said she, looking up at her husband, and still smiling. "Harry is so full of fun, he always has something new to amuse us with; and now he pretends he is asleep, and that we can't waken him. Look! he is smiling now; he hears I have found him out. Look!"

And, in truth, the lips, in the rest of death, did look as though they wore a smile, and the waving light of the unsnuffed candle almost made them seem to move.

"Look, Amy," said she to her youngest child, who knelt at her feet, trying to soothe her, by kissing her garments.

"Oh, he was always a rogue! You remember, don't you, love? how full of play he was as a baby; hiding his face under my arm, when you wanted to play with him. Always a rogue, Harry!"

"We must get her away, sir," said nurse; "you know there is much to be done before—"

"I understand, nurse," said the father, hastily interrupting her in dread of the distinct words which would tell of the changes of mortality.

"Come, love," said he to his wife. "I want you to come with me. I want to speak to you down-stairs."

"I'm coming," said she, rising; "perhaps, after all, nurse, he's really tired, and would be glad to sleep. Don't let him get cold, though,—he feels rather chilly," continued she, after she had bent down, and kissed the pale lips.

Her husband put his arm round her waist, and they left the room. Then the three sisters burst into unrestrained wailings. They were startled into the reality of life and death. And yet, in the midst of shrieks and moans, of shivering, and chattering of teeth, Sophy's eye caught the calm beauty of the dead; so calm amidst such violence, and she hushed her emotion.

"Come," said she to her sisters, "nurse wants us to go; and besides, we ought to be with mamma. Papa told the man he was talking to, when I went for him, to wait, and she must not be left."

Meanwhile, the superintendent had taken a candle, and was examining the engravings that hung round the dining-room. It was so common to him to be acquainted with crime, that he was far from feeling all his interest absorbed in the present case of violence, although he could not help having much anxiety to detect the murderer. He was busy looking at the only oil-painting in the room (a youth of eighteen or so, in a fancy dress), and conjecturing its identity with the young man so mysteriously dead, when the door opened, and Mr. Carson returned. Stern as he had looked before leaving the room, he looked far sterner now. His face was hardened into deep-purposed wrath.

"I beg your pardon, sir, for leaving you." The superintendent bowed. They sat down, and spoke long together. One by one the policemen were called in, and questioned.

All through the night there was bustle and commotion in the house. Nobody thought of going to bed. It seemed strange to Sophy to hear nurse summoned from her mother's side to supper, in the middle of the night, and still stranger that she could go. The necessity of eating and drinking seemed out of place in the house of death.

When night was passing into morning, the dining-room door opened, and two persons' steps were heard along the hall. The superintendent was leaving at last. Mr. Carson stood on the front door-step, feeling the refreshment of the cooler morning air, and seeing the starlight fade away into dawn.

"You will not forget," said he. "I trust to you."

The policeman bowed.

"Spare no money. The only purpose for which I now value wealth is to have the murderer arrested, and brought to justice. My hope in life now is to see him sentenced to death. Offer any rewards. Name a thousand pounds in the placards. Come to me at any hour, night or day, if that be required. All I ask of you is, to get the murderer hanged. Next week, if possible—to-day is Friday. Surely, with the clues you already possess, you can muster up evidence sufficient to have him tried next week."

"He may easily request an adjournment of his trial, on the ground of the shortness of the notice," said the superintendent.

"Oppose it, if possible. I will see that the first lawyers are employed. I shall know no rest while he lives."

"Every thing shall be done, sir."

"You will arrange with the coroner. Ten o'clock, if convenient."

The superintendent took leave.

Mr. Carson stood on the step, dreading to shut out the light and air, and return into the haunted, gloomy house.

"My son! my son!" he said, at last. "But you shall be avenged, my poor murdered boy."

Ay! to avenge his wrongs the murderer had singled out his victim, and with one fell action had taken away the life that God had given. To avenge his child's death, the old man lived on; with the single purpose in his heart of vengeance on the murderer. True, his vengeance was sanctioned by law, but was it the less revenge?

Are we worshippers of Christ? or of Alecto?

Oh! Orestes! you would have made a very tolerable Christian of the nineteenth century!

CHAPTER XIX - JEM WILSON ARRESTED ON SUSPICION.

"Deeds to be hid which were not hid,
Which, all confused, I could not know,
Whether I suffered or I did,
For all seemed guilt, remorse, or woe."

COLERIDGE.

I left Mary, on that same Thursday night which left its burden of woe at Mr. Carson's threshold, haunted with depressing thoughts. All through the night she tossed restlessly about, trying to get quit of the ideas that harassed her, and longing for the light when she could rise, and find some employment. But just as dawn began to appear, she became more quiet, and fell into a sound heavy sleep, which lasted till she was sure it was late in the morning by the full light that shone in.

She dressed hastily, and heard the neighbouring church-clock strike eight. It was far too late to do as she had planned (after inquiring how Alice was, to return and tell Margaret), and she accordingly went in to inform the latter of her change of purpose, and the cause of it; but on entering the house she found Job sitting alone, looking sad enough. She told him what she came for.

"Margaret, wench! why she's been gone to Wilson's these two hours. Ay! sure, you did say last night you would go; but she could na rest in her bed, so was off betimes this morning."

Mary could do nothing but feel guilty of her long morning nap, and hasten to follow Margaret's steps; for late as it was, she felt she could not settle well to her work, unless she learnt how kind good Alice Wilson was going on.

So, eating her crust-of-bread breakfast, she passed rapidly along the streets. She remembered afterwards the little groups of people she had seen, eagerly hearing, and imparting news; but at the time her only care was to hasten on her way, in dread of a reprimand from Miss Simmonds.

She went into the house at Jane Wilson's, her heart at the instant giving a strange knock, and sending the rosy flush into her face, at the thought that Jem might possibly be inside the door. But I do assure you, she had not thought of it before. Impatient and loving as she was, her solicitude about Alice on that hurried morning had not been mingled with any thought of him.

Her heart need not have leaped, her colour need not have rushed so painfully to her cheeks, for he was not there. There was the round table, with a cup and saucer, which had evidently been used, and there was Jane Wilson sitting on the other side, crying quietly, while she ate her breakfast with a sort of unconscious appetite. And there was Mrs. Davenport washing away at a night-cap or so, which, by their simple, old-world make, Mary knew at a glance were Alice's. But nothing—no one else.

Alice was much the same, or rather better of the two, they told her; at any rate she could speak, though it was sad rambling talk. Would Mary like to see her?

Of course she would. Many are interested by seeing their friends under the new aspect of illness; and among the poor there is no wholesome fear of injury or excitement to restrain this wish.

So Mary went up-stairs, accompanied by Mrs. Davenport, wringing the suds off her hands, and speaking in a loud whisper far more audible than her usual voice.

"I mun be hastening home, but I'll come again to-night, time enough to iron her cap; 'twould be a sin and a shame if we let her go dirty now she's ill, when she's been so rare and clean all her life-long. But she's sadly forsaken, poor thing! She'll not know you, Mary; she knows none on us."

The room up-stairs held two beds, one superior in the grandeur of four posts and checked curtains to the other, which had been occupied by the twins in their brief life-time. The smaller had been Alice's bed since she had lived there; but with the natural reverence to one "stricken of God and afflicted," she had been installed since her paralytic stroke the evening before in the larger and grander bed, while Jane Wilson had taken her short broken rest on the little pallet.

Margaret came forwards to meet her friend, whom she half expected, and whose step she knew. Mrs. Davenport returned to her washing.

The two girls did not speak; the presence of Alice awed them into silence. There she lay with the rosy colour, absent from her face since the days of childhood, flushed once more into it by her sickness nigh unto death. She lay on the affected side, and with her other arm she was constantly sawing the air, not exactly in a restless manner, but in a monotonous, incessant way, very trying to a watcher. She was talking away, too, almost as constantly, in a low, indistinct tone. But her face, her profiled countenance, looked calm and smiling, even interested by the ideas that were passing through her clouded mind.

"Listen!" said Margaret, as she stooped her head down to catch the muttered words more distinctly.

"What will mother say? The bees are turning homeward for th' last time, and we've a terrible long bit to go yet. See! here's a linnet's nest in this gorse-bush. Th' hen-bird is on it. Look at her bright eyes, she won't stir! Ay! we mun hurry home. Won't mother be pleased with the bonny lot of heather we've got! Make haste,

Sally, may be we shall have cockles for supper. I saw th' cockle-man's donkey turn up our way fra' Arnside."

Margaret touched Mary's hand, and the pressure in return told her that they understood each other; that they knew how in this illness to the old, world-weary woman, God had sent her a veiled blessing: she was once more in the scenes of her childhood, unchanged and bright as in those long departed days; once more with the sister of her youth, the playmate of fifty years ago, who had for nearly as many years slept in a grassy grave in the little church-yard beyond Burton.

Alice's face changed; she looked sorrowful, almost penitent.

"Oh, Sally! I wish we'd told her. She thinks we were in church all morning, and we've gone on deceiving her. If we'd told her at first how it was—how sweet th' hawthorn smelt through the open church-door, and how we were on th' last bench in the aisle, and how it were the first butterfly we'd seen this spring, and how it flew into th' very church itself; oh! mother is so gentle, I wish we'd told her. I'll go to her next time she comes in sight, and say, 'Mother, we were naughty last Sabbath.'"

She stopped, and a few tears came stealing down the old withered cheek, at the thought of the temptation and deceit of her childhood. Surely, many sins could not have darkened that innocent child-like spirit since. Mary found a red-spotted pocket-handkerchief, and put it into the hand which sought about for something to wipe away the trickling tears. She took it with a gentle murmur.

"Thank you, mother."

Mary pulled Margaret away from the bed.

"Don't you think she's happy, Margaret?"

"Ay! that I do, bless her. She feels no pain, and knows nought of her present state. Oh! that I could see, Mary! I try and be patient with her afore me, but I'd give aught I have to see her, and see what she wants. I am so useless! I mean to stay here as long as Jane Wilson is alone; and I would fain be here all to-night, but—"

"I'll come," said Mary, decidedly.

"Mrs. Davenport said she'd come again, but she's hard-worked all day—"

"I'll come," repeated Mary.

"Do!" said Margaret, "and I'll be here till you come. May be, Jem and you could take th' night between you, and Jane Wilson might get a bit of sound sleep in his bed; for she were up and down the better part of last night, and just when she were in a sound sleep this morning, between two and three, Jem came home, and th' sound o' his voice roused her in a minute."

"Where had he been till that time o' night?" asked Mary.

"Nay! it were none of my business; and, indeed, I never saw him till he came in here to see Alice. He were in again this morning, and seemed sadly downcast. But you'll, may be, manage to comfort him to-night, Mary," said Margaret, smiling, while a ray of hope glimmered in Mary's heart, and she almost felt glad, for an instant, of the occasion which would at last bring them together. Oh! happy night! when would it come? Many hours had yet to pass.

Then she saw Alice, and repented, with a bitter self-reproach. But she could not help having gladness in the depths of her heart, blame herself as she would. So she tried not to think, as she hurried along to Miss Simmonds', with a dancing step of lightness.

She was late—that she knew she should be. Miss Simmonds was vexed and cross. That also she had anticipated, but she had intended to smooth her raven down by extraordinary diligence and attention. But there was something about the girls she did not understand—had not anticipated. They stopped talking when she came in; or rather, I should say, stopped listening, for Sally Leadbitter was the talker to whom they were hearkening with intense attention. At first they eyed Mary, as if she had acquired some new interest to them, since the day before. Then they began to whisper; and, absorbed as Mary had been in her own thoughts, she could not help becoming aware that it was of her they spoke.

At last Sally Leadbitter asked Mary if she had heard the news?

"No! What news?" answered she.

The girls looked at each other with gloomy mystery. Sally went on.

"Have you not heard that young Mr. Carson was murdered last night?"

Mary's lips could not utter a negative, but no one who looked at her pale and terror-stricken face could have doubted that she had not heard before of the fearful occurrence.

Oh, it is terrible, that sudden information, that one you have known has met with a bloody death! You seem to shrink from the world where such deeds can be committed, and to grow sick with the idea of the violent and wicked men of earth. Much as Mary had learned to dread him lately, now he was dead (and dead in such a manner) her feeling was that of oppressive sorrow for him.

The room went round and round, and she felt as though she should faint; but Miss Simmonds came in, bringing a waft of fresher air as she opened the door, to refresh the body, and the certainty of a scolding for inattention to brace the sinking mind. She, too, was full of the morning's news.

"Have you heard any more of this horrid affair, Miss Barton?" asked she, as she settled to her work.

Mary tried to speak; at first she could not, and when she succeeded in uttering a sentence, it seemed as though it were not her own voice that spoke.

"No, ma'am, I never heard of it till this minute."

"Dear! that's strange, for every one is up about it. I hope the murderer will be found out, that I do. Such a handsome young man to be killed as he was. I hope the wretch that did it may be hanged as high as Haman."

One of the girls reminded them that the assizes came on next week.

"Ay," replied Miss Simmonds, "and the milk-man told me they will catch the wretch, and have him tried and hung in less than a week. Serve him right, whoever he is. Such a handsome young man as he was."

Then each began to communicate to Miss Simmonds the various reports they had heard.

Suddenly she burst out—

"Miss Barton! as I live, dropping tears on that new silk gown of Mrs. Hawkes'! Don't you know they will stain, and make it shabby for ever? Crying like a baby, because a handsome young man meets with an untimely end. For shame of yourself, miss. Mind your character and your work if you please. Or, if you must cry" (seeing her scolding rather increased the flow of Mary's tears, than otherwise), "take this print to cry over. That won't be marked like this beautiful silk," rubbing it, as if she loved it, with a clean pocket-handkerchief, in order to soften the edges of the hard round drops.

Mary took the print, and naturally enough, having had leave given her to cry over it, rather checked the inclination to weep.

Every body was full of the one subject. The girl sent out to match silk, came back with the account gathered at the shop, of the coroner's inquest then sitting; the ladies who called to speak about gowns first began about the murder, and mingled details of that, with directions for their dresses. Mary felt as though the haunting horror were a nightmare, a fearful dream, from which awakening would relieve her. The picture of the murdered body, far more ghastly than the reality, seemed to swim in the air before her eyes. Sally Leadbitter looked and spoke of her, almost accusingly, and made no secret now of Mary's conduct, more blameable to her fellow-workwomen for its latter changeableness, than for its former giddy flirting.

"Poor young gentleman," said one, as Sally recounted Mary's last interview with Mr. Carson.

"What a shame!" exclaimed another, looking indignantly at Mary.

"That's what I call regular jilting," said a third. "And he lying cold and bloody in his coffin now!"

Mary was more thankful than she could express, when Miss Simmonds returned, to put a stop to Sally's communications, and to check the remarks of the girls.

She longed for the peace of Alice's sick room. No more thinking with infinite delight of her anticipated meeting with Jem, she felt too much shocked for that now; but longing for peace and kindness, for the images of rest and beauty, and sinless times long ago, which the poor old woman's rambling presented, she wished to be as near death as Alice; and to have struggled through this world, whose sufferings she had early learnt, and whose crimes now seemed pressing close upon her. Old texts from the Bible that her mother used to read (or rather spell out) aloud, in the days of childhood, came up to her memory. "Where the wicked cease from troubling, and the weary are at rest." "The tears shall be wiped away from all eyes," &c. And it was to that world Alice was hastening! Oh! that she were Alice!

I must return to the Wilsons' house, which was far from being the abode of peace that Mary was picturing it to herself. You remember the reward Mr. Carson offered for the apprehension of the murderer of his son? It was in itself a temptation, and to aid its efficacy came the natural sympathy for the aged parents mourning for their child, for the young man cut off in the flower of his days; and besides this, there is always a pleasure in unravelling a mystery, in catching at the gossamer clue which will guide to certainty. This feeling, I am sure, gives much impetus to the police. Their senses are ever and always on the qui-vive, and they enjoy the collecting and collating evidence, and the life of adventure they experience: a continual unwinding of Jack Sheppard romances, always interesting to the vulgar and uneducated mind, to which the outward signs and tokens of crime are ever exciting.

There was no lack of clue or evidence at the coroner's inquest that morning. The shot, the finding of the body, the subsequent discovery of the gun, were rapidly deposed to; and then the policeman who had interrupted the quarrel between Jem Wilson and the murdered young man was brought forward, and gave his evidence, clear, simple, and straightforward. The coroner had no hesitation, the jury had none, but the verdict was cautiously worded. "Wilful murder against some person unknown."

This very cautiousness, when he deemed the thing so sure as to require no caution, irritated Mr. Carson. It did not soothe him that the superintendent called the verdict a mere form,—exhibited a warrant empowering him to seize the body of Jem Wilson, committed on suspicion,—declared his intention of employing a well-known officer in the Detective Service to ascertain the ownership of the gun, and to collect other evidence, especially as regarded the young woman, about whom the policeman deposed that the quarrel had taken place: Mr. Carson was still excited and irritable; restless in body and mind. He made every preparation for the accusation of Jem the following morning before the magistrates: he engaged attorneys skilled in criminal practice to watch the case and prepare briefs; he wrote to celebrated barristers coming the Northern Circuit, to bespeak their services. A speedy conviction, a speedy execution, seemed to be the only things that would satisfy his craving thirst for blood. He would have fain been policeman, magistrate, accusing speaker, all; but most of all, the judge, rising with full sentence of death on his lips.

That afternoon, as Jane Wilson had begun to feel the effect of a night's disturbed rest, evinced in frequent droppings off to sleep while she sat by her sister-in-law's bed-side, lulled by the incessant crooning of the invalid's feeble voice, she was startled by a man speaking in the house-place below, who, wearied of knocking at the door, without obtaining any answer, had entered and was calling lustily for

"Missis! missis!"

When Mrs. Wilson caught a glimpse of the intruder through the stair-rails, she at once saw he was a stranger, a working-man, it might be a fellow-labourer with her son, for his dress was grimy enough for the supposition. He held a gun in his hand.

"May I make bold to ask if this gun belongs to your son?"

She first looked at the man, and then, weary and half asleep, not seeing any reason for refusing to answer the inquiry, she moved forward to examine it, talking while she looked for certain old-fashioned ornaments on the stock. "It looks like his; ay, it's his, sure enough. I could speak to it anywhere by these marks. You see it were his grandfather's, as were gamekeeper to some one up in th' north; and they don't make guns so smart now-a-days. But, how comed you by it? He sets great store on it. Is he bound for th' shooting gallery? He is not, for sure, now his aunt is so ill, and me left all alone;" and the immediate cause for her anxiety being thus recalled to her mind, she entered on a long story of Alice's illness, interspersed with recollections of her husband's and her children's deaths.

The disguised policeman listened for a minute or two, to glean any further information he could; and then, saying he was in a hurry, he turned to go away. She followed him to the door, still telling him her troubles, and was never struck, until it was too late to ask the reason, with the unaccountableness of his conduct, in carrying the gun away with him. Then, as she heavily climbed the stairs, she put away the wonder and the thought about his conduct, by determining to believe he was some workman with whom her son had made some arrangement about shooting at the gallery; or mending the old weapon; or something or other. She had enough to fret her, without moidering herself about old guns. Jem had given it him to bring to her; so it was safe enough; or, if it was not, why she should be glad never to set eyes on it again, for she could not abide fire-arms, they were so apt to shoot people.

So, comforting herself for her want of thought in not making further inquiry, she fell off into another doze, feverish, dream-haunted, and unrefreshing.

Meanwhile, the policeman walked off with his prize, with an odd mixture of feelings; a little contempt, a little disappointment, and a good deal of pity. The contempt and the disappointment were caused by the widow's easy admission of the gun being her son's property, and her manner of identifying it by the ornaments. He liked an attempt to baffle him; he was accustomed to it; it gave some exercise to his wits and his shrewdness. There would be no fun in fox-hunting, if Reynard yielded himself up without any effort to escape. Then, again, his mother's milk was yet in him, policeman, officer of the Detective Service though he was; and he felt sorry for the old woman, whose "softness" had given such material assistance in identifying her son as the murderer. However, he conveyed the gun, and the intelligence he had gained, to the superintendent; and the result was, that, in a short time afterwards, three policemen went to the works at which Jem was foreman, and announced their errand to the astonished overseer, who directed them to the part of the foundry where Jem was then superintending a casting.

Dark, black were the walls, the ground, the faces around them, as they crossed the yard. But, in the furnace-house a deep and lurid red glared over all; the furnace roared with mighty flame. The men, like demons, in their fire-and-soot colouring, stood swart around, awaiting the moment when the tons of solid iron should have melted down into fiery liquid, fit to be poured, with still, heavy sound, into the delicate moulding of fine black sand, prepared to receive it. The heat was intense, and the red glare grew every instant more fierce; the policemen stood awed with the novel sight. Then, black figures, holding strange-shaped bucket shovels, came athwart the deep-red furnace light, and clear and brilliant flowed forth the iron into the appropriate mould. The buzz of voices rose again; there was time to speak, and gasp, and wipe the brows; and then, one by one, the men dispersed to some other branch of their employment.

No. B. 72 pointed out Jem as the man he had seen engaged in a scuffle with Mr. Carson, and then the other two stepped forward and arrested him, stating of what he was accused, and the grounds of the accusation. He offered no resistance, though he seemed surprised; but calling a fellow-workman to him, he briefly requested him to tell his mother he had got into trouble, and could not return home at present. He did not wish her to hear more at first.

So Mrs. Wilson's sleep was next interrupted in almost an exactly similar way to the last, like a recurring nightmare.

"Missis! missis!" some one called out from below.

Again it was a workman, but this time a blacker-looking one than before.

"What don ye want?" said she, peevishly.

"Only nothing but—" stammered the man, a kind-hearted matter-of-fact person, with no invention, but a great deal of sympathy.

"Well! speak out, can't ye, and ha' done with it?"

"Jem's in trouble," said he, repeating Jem's very words, as he could think of no others.

"Trouble!" said the mother, in a high-pitched voice of distress. "Trouble! God help me, trouble will never end, I think. What d'ye mean by trouble? Speak out, man, can't ye? Is he ill? My boy! tell me, is he ill?" in a hurried voice of terror.

"Na, na, that's not it. He's well enough. All he bade me say was, 'Tell mother I'm in trouble, and can't come home to-night.'"

"Not come home to-night! And what am I to do with Alice? I can't go on, wearing my life out wi' watching. He might come and help me."

"I tell you he can't," said the man.

"Can't; and he is well, you say? Stuff! It's just that he's getten like other young men, and wants to go a-larking. But I'll give it him when he comes back."

The man turned to go; he durst not trust himself to speak in Jem's justification. But she would not let him off.

She stood between him and the door, as she said, "Yo shall not go, till yo've told me what he's after. I can see plain enough you know, and I'll know too, before I've done."

"You'll know soon enough, missis!"

"I'll know now, I tell ye. What's up that he can't come home and help me nurse? Me, as never got a wink o' sleep last night wi' watching."

"Well, if you will have it out," said the poor badgered man, "the police have got hold on him."

"On my Jem!" said the enraged mother. "You're a downright liar, and that's what you are. My Jem, as never did harm to any one in his life. You're a liar, that's what you are."

"He's done harm enough now," said the man, angry in his turn, "for there's good evidence he murdered young Carson, as was shot last night."

She staggered forward to strike the man for telling the terrible truth; but the weakness of old age, of motherly agony, overcame her, and she sank down on a chair, and covered her face. He could not leave her.

When next she spoke, it was in an imploring, feeble, child-like voice.

"Oh, master, say you're only joking. I ax your pardon if I have vexed ye, but please say you're only joking. You don't know what Jem is to me."

She looked humbly, anxiously up at him.

"I wish I were only joking, missis; but it's true as I say. They've taken him up on charge o' murder. It were his gun as were found near th' place; and one o' the police heard him quarrelling with Mr. Carson a few days back, about a girl."

"About a girl!" broke in the mother, once more indignant, though too feeble to show it as before. "My Jem was as steady as—" she hesitated for a comparison wherewith to finish, and then repeated, "as steady as Lucifer, and he were an angel, you know. My Jem was not one to quarrel about a girl."

"Ay, but it was that, though. They'd got her name quite pat. The man had heard all they said. Mary Barton was her name, whoever she may be."

"Mary Barton! the dirty hussey! to bring my Jem into trouble of this kind. I'll give it her well when I see her: that I will. Oh! my poor Jem!" rocking herself to and fro. "And what about the gun? What did ye say about that?"

"His gun were found on th' spot where the murder were done."

"That's a lie for one, then. A man has got the gun now, safe and sound; I saw it not an hour ago."

The man shook his head.

"Yes, he has indeed. A friend o' Jem's, as he'd lent it to."

"Did you know the chap?" asked the man, who was really anxious for Jem's exculpation, and caught a gleam of hope from her last speech.

"No! I can't say as I did. But he were put on as a workman."

"It's may be only one of them policemen, disguised."

"Nay; they'd never go for to do that, and trick me into telling on my own son. It would be like seething a kid in its mother's milk; and that th' Bible forbids."

"I don't know," replied the man.

Soon afterwards he went away, feeling unable to comfort, yet distressed at the sight of sorrow; she would fain have detained him, but go he would. And she was alone.

She never for an instant believed Jem guilty; she would have doubted if the sun were fire, first: but sorrow, desolation, and, at times, anger took possession of her mind. She told the unconscious Alice, hoping to rouse her to sympathy; and then was disappointed, because, still smiling and calm, she murmured of her mother, and the happy days of infancy.

CHAPTER XX - MARY'S DREAM—AND THE AWAKENING.

"I saw where stark and cold he lay,
  Beneath the gallows-tree,
And every one did point and say,
  "Twas there he died for thee!'
    *   *   *   *
"Oh! weeping heart! Oh, bleeding heart!
  What boots thy pity now?
Bid from his eyes that shade depart,
  That death-damp from his brow!"

"THE BIRTLE TRAGEDY."

So there was no more peace in the house of sickness, except to Alice, the dying Alice.

But Mary knew nothing of the afternoon's occurrences; and gladly did she breathe in the fresh air, as she left Miss Simmonds' house, to hasten to the Wilsons'. The very change, from the in-door to the out-door atmosphere, seemed to alter the current of her thoughts. She thought less of the dreadful subject which had so haunted her all day; she cared less for the upbraiding speeches of her fellow work-women; the old association of comfort and sympathy received from Alice gave her the idea that, even now, her bodily presence would soothe and compose those who were in trouble, changed, unconscious, and absent though her spirit might be.

Then, again, she reproached herself a little for the feeling of pleasure she experienced, in thinking that he whom she dreaded could never more beset her path; in the security with which she could pass each street corner—each shop, where he used to lie in ambush. Oh! beating heart! was there no other little thought of joy lurking within, to gladden the very air without? Was she not going to meet, to see, to hear Jem; and could they fail at last to understand each other's loving hearts!

She softly lifted the latch, with the privilege of friendship. *He* was not there, but his mother was standing by the fire, stirring some little mess or other. Never mind! he would come soon: and with an unmixed desire to do her grateful duty to all belonging to him, she stepped lightly forwards, unheard by the old lady, who was partly occupied by the simmering, bubbling sound of her bit of cookery; but more with her own sad thoughts, and wailing, half-uttered murmurings.

Mary took off bonnet and shawl with speed, and advancing, made Mrs. Wilson conscious of her presence, by saying,

"Let me do that for you. I'm sure you mun be tired."

Mrs. Wilson slowly turned round, and her eyes gleamed like those of a pent-up wild beast, as she recognised her visitor.

"And is it thee that dares set foot in this house, after what has come to pass? Is it not enough to have robbed me of my boy with thy arts and thy profligacy, but thou must come here to crow over me—me—his mother? Dost thou know where he is, thou bad hussy, with thy great blue eyes and yellow hair, to lead men on to ruin? Out upon thee, with thy angel's face, thou whited sepulchre! Dost thou know where Jem is, all through thee?"

"No!" quivered out poor Mary, scarcely conscious that she spoke, so daunted, so terrified was she by the indignant mother's greeting.

"He's lying in th' New Bailey," slowly and distinctly spoke the mother, watching the effect of her words, as if believing in their infinite power to pain. "There he lies, waiting to take his trial for murdering young Mr. Carson."

There was no answer; but such a blanched face, such wild, distended eyes, such trembling limbs, instinctively seeking support!

"Did you know Mr. Carson as now lies dead?" continued the merciless woman. "Folk say you did, and knew him but too well. And that for the sake of such as you, my precious child shot yon chap. But he did not. I know he did not. They may hang him, but his mother will speak to his innocence with her last dying breath."

She stopped more from exhaustion than want of words. Mary spoke, but in so changed and choked a voice that the old woman almost started. It seemed as if some third person must be in the room, the voice was so hoarse and strange.

"Please, say it again. I don't quite understand you. What has Jem done? Please to tell me."

"I never said he had done it. I said, and I'll swear that he never did do it. I don't care who heard 'em quarrel, or if it is his gun as were found near the body. It's not my own Jem as would go for to kill any man, choose how a girl had jilted him. My own good Jem, as was a blessing sent upon the house where he was born." Tears came into the mother's burning eyes as her heart recurred to the days when she had rocked the cradle of her "first-born;" and then, rapidly passing over events, till the full consciousness of his present situation came upon her, and perhaps annoyed at having shown any softness of character in the presence of the Dalilah who had lured him to his danger, she spoke again, and in a sharper tone.

"I told him, and told him to leave off thinking on thee; but he wouldn't be led by me. Thee! wench! thou were not good enough to wipe the dust off his feet. A vile, flirting quean as thou art. It's well thy mother does not know (poor body) what a good-for-nothing thou art."

"Mother! oh mother!" said Mary, as if appealing to the merciful dead. "But I was not good enough for him! I know I was not," added she, in a voice of touching humility.

For through her heart went tolling the ominous, prophetic words he had used when he had last spoken to her—

"Mary! you'll may be hear of me as a drunkard, and may be as a thief, and may be as a murderer. Remember! when all are speaking ill of me, yo will have no right to blame me, for it's your cruelty that will have made me what I feel I shall become."

And she did not blame him, though she doubted not his guilt; she felt how madly she might act if once jealous of him, and how much cause had she not given him for jealousy, miserable guilty wretch that she was! Speak on, desolate mother! Abuse her as you will. Her broken spirit feels to have merited all.

But her last humble, self-abased words had touched Mrs. Wilson's heart, sore as it was; and she looked at the snow-pale girl with those piteous eyes, so hopeless of comfort, and she relented in spite of herself.

"Thou seest what comes of light conduct, Mary! It's thy doing that suspicion has lighted on him, who is as innocent as the babe unborn. Thou'lt have much to answer for if he's hung. Thou'lt have my death too at thy door!"

Harsh as these words seem, she spoke them in a milder tone of voice than she had yet used. But the idea of Jem on the gallows, Jem dead, took possession of Mary, and she covered her eyes with her wan hands, as if indeed to shut out the fearful sight.

She murmured some words, which, though spoken low, as if choked up from the depths of agony, Jane Wilson caught. "My heart is breaking," said she, feebly. "My heart is breaking."

"Nonsense!" said Mrs. Wilson. "Don't talk in that silly way. My heart has a better right to break than yours, and yet I hold up, you see. But, oh dear! oh dear!" with a sudden revulsion of feeling, as the reality of the danger in which her son was placed pressed upon her. "What am I saying? How could I hold up if thou wert gone, Jem? Though I'm as sure as I stand here of thy innocence, if they hang thee, my lad, I will lie down and die!"

She sobbed aloud with bitter consciousness of the fearful chance awaiting her child. She cried more passionately still.

Mary roused herself up.

"Oh, let me stay with you, at any rate, till we know the end. Dearest Mrs. Wilson, mayn't I stay?"

The more obstinately and upbraidingly Mrs. Wilson refused, the more Mary pleaded, with ever the same soft, entreating cry, "Let me stay with you." Her stunned soul seemed to bound its wishes, for the hour at least, to remaining with one who loved and sorrowed for the same human being that she did.

But no. Mrs. Wilson was inflexible.

"I've may be been a bit hard on you, Mary, I'll own that. But I cannot abide you yet with me. I cannot but remember it's your giddiness as has wrought this woe. I'll stay wi' Alice, and perhaps Mrs. Davenport may come help a bit. I cannot put up with you about me. Good-night. To-morrow I may look on you different, may be. Good-night."

And Mary turned out of the house, which had been *his* home, where *he* was loved, and mourned for, into the busy, desolate, crowded street, where they were crying halfpenny broadsides, giving an account of the bloody murder, the coroner's inquest, and a raw-head-and-bloody-bones picture of the suspected murderer, James Wilson.

But Mary heard not, she heeded not. She staggered on like one in a dream. With hung head and tottering steps, she instinctively chose the shortest cut to that home, which was to her, in her present state of mind, only the hiding place of four walls, where she might vent her agony, unseen and unnoticed by the keen, unkind world without, but where no welcome, no love, no sympathising tears awaited her.

As she neared that home, within two minutes' walk of it, her impetuous course was arrested by a light touch on her arm, and turning hastily, she saw a little Italian boy with his humble show-box,—a white mouse, or some such thing. The setting sun cast its red glow on his face, otherwise the olive complexion would have been very pale; and the glittering tear-drops hung on the long curled eyelashes. With his soft voice and pleading looks, he uttered, in his pretty broken English, the words

"Hungry! so hungry."

And, as if to aid by gesture the effect of the solitary word, he pointed to his mouth, with its white quivering lips.

Mary answered him impatiently,

"Oh, lad, hunger is nothing—nothing!"

And she rapidly passed on. But her heart upbraided her the next minute with her unrelenting speech, and she hastily entered her door and seized the scanty remnant of food which the cupboard contained, and retraced her steps to the place where the little hopeless stranger had sunk down by his mute companion in loneliness and starvation, and was raining down tears as he spoke in some foreign tongue, with low cries for the far distant "Mamma mia!"

With the elasticity of heart belonging to childhood he sprang up as he saw the food the girl brought; she whose face, lovely in its woe, had tempted him first to address her; and, with the graceful courtesy of his country, he looked up and smiled while he kissed her hand, and then poured forth his thanks, and shared her bounty with his little pet companion. She stood an instant, diverted from the thought of her own grief by the sight of his infantine gladness; and then bending down and kissing his smooth forehead, she left him, and sought to be alone with her agony once more.

She re-entered the house, locked the door, and tore off her bonnet, as if greedy of every moment which took her from the full indulgence of painful, despairing thought.

Then she threw herself on the ground, yes, on the hard flags she threw her soft limbs down; and the comb fell out of her hair, and those bright tresses swept the dusty floor, while she pillowed and hid her face on her arms, and burst forth into hard, suffocating sobs.

Oh, earth! thou didst seem but a dreary dwelling-place for thy poor child that night. None to comfort, none to pity! And self-reproach gnawing at her heart.

Oh, why did she ever listen to the tempter? Why did she ever give ear to her own suggestions, and cravings after wealth and grandeur? Why had she thought it a fine thing to have a rich lover?

She—she had deserved it all; but he was the victim,—he, the beloved. She could not conjecture, she could not even pause to think who had revealed, or how he had discovered her acquaintance with Harry Carson. It was but too clear, some way or another, he had learnt all; and what would he think of her? No hope of his love,—oh, that she would give up, and be content; it was his life, his precious life, that was threatened. Then she tried to recall the particulars, which, when Mrs. Wilson had given them, had fallen but upon a deafened ear,—something about a gun, a quarrel, which she could not remember clearly. Oh, how terrible to think of his crime, his blood-guiltiness; he who had hitherto been so good, so noble, and now an assassin! And then she shrank from him in thought; and then, with bitter remorse, clung more closely to his image with passionate self-upbraiding. Was it not she who had led him to the pit into which he had fallen? Was she to blame him? She to judge him? Who could tell how maddened he might have been by jealousy; how one moment's uncontrollable passion might have led him to become a murderer? And she had blamed him in her heart after his last deprecating, imploring, prophetic speech!

Then she burst out crying afresh; and when weary of crying, fell to thinking again. The gallows! The gallows! Black it stood against the burning light which dazzled her shut eyes, press on them as she would. Oh! she was going mad; and for awhile she lay outwardly still, but with the pulses careering through her head with wild vehemence.

And then came a strange forgetfulness of the present, in thought of the long-past times;—of those days when she hid her face on her mother's pitying, loving bosom, and heard tender words of comfort, be her grief or her error what it might;—of those days when she had felt as if her mother's love was too mighty not to last for ever;—of those days when hunger had been to her (as to the little stranger she had that evening relieved) something to be thought about, and mourned over;—when Jem and she had played together; he, with the condescension of an older child, and she, with unconscious earnestness, believing that he was as much gratified with important trifles as she was;—when her father was a cheery-hearted man, rich in the love of his wife, and the companionship of his friend;—when (for it still worked round to that), when mother was alive, and *he* was not a murderer.

And then Heaven blessed her unaware, and she sank from remembering, to wandering, unconnected thought, and thence to sleep. Yes! it was sleep, though in that strange posture, on that hard cold bed; and she dreamt of the happy times of long ago, and her mother came to her, and kissed her as she lay, and once more the dead were alive again in that happy world of dreams. All was restored to the gladness of childhood, even to the little kitten which had been her playmate and bosom friend then, and which had been long forgotten in her waking hours. All the loved ones were there!

She suddenly wakened! Clear and wide awake! Some noise had startled her from sleep. She sat up, and put her hair (still wet with tears) back from her flushed cheeks, and listened. At first she could only hear her beating heart. All was still without, for it was after midnight, such hours of agony had passed away; but the moon shone clearly in at the unshuttered window, making the room almost as light as day, in its cold ghastly radiance. There was a low knock at the door! A strange feeling crept over Mary's heart, as if something spiritual were near; as if the dead, so lately present in her dreams, were yet gliding and hovering round her, with their dim, dread forms. And yet, why dread? Had they not loved her?—and who loved her now? Was she not lonely enough to welcome the spirits of the dead, who had loved her while here? If her mother had conscious being, her love for her child endured. So she quieted her fears, and listened—listened still.

"Mary! Mary! open the door!" as a little movement on her part seemed to tell the being outside of her wakeful, watchful state. They were the accents of her mother's voice; the very south-country pronunciation, that Mary so well remembered; and which she had sometimes tried to imitate when alone, with the fond mimicry of affection.

So, without fear, without hesitation, she rose and unbarred the door. There, against the moonlight, stood a form, so closely resembling her dead mother, that Mary never doubted the identity, but exclaiming (as if she were a terrified child, secure of safety when near the protecting care of its parent)—

"Oh! mother! mother! You are come at last!"

She threw herself, or rather fell, into the trembling arms of her long-lost, unrecognised aunt Esther.

CHAPTER XXI - ESTHER'S MOTIVE IN SEEKING MARY.

"My rest is gone,
   My heart is sore,
Peace find I never,
   And never more."

MARGARET'S SONG IN "FAUST."

I must go back a little to explain the motives which caused Esther to seek an interview with her niece.

The murder had been committed early on Thursday night, and between then and the dawn of the following day there was ample time for the news to spread far and wide among all those whose duty, or whose want, or whose errors, caused them to be abroad in the streets of Manchester.

Among those who listened to the tale of violence was Esther.

A craving desire to know more took possession of her mind. Far away as she was from Turner Street, she immediately set off to the scene of the murder, which was faintly lighted by the gray dawn as she reached the spot. It was so quiet and still that she could hardly believe it to be the place. The only vestige of any scuffle or violence was a trail on the dust, as if somebody had been lying there, and then been raised by extraneous force. The little birds were beginning to hop and twitter in the leafless hedge, making the only sound that was near and distinct. She crossed into the field where she guessed the murderer to have stood; it was easy of access, for the worn, stunted hawthorn-hedge had many gaps in it. The night-smell of bruised grass came up from under her feet, as she went towards the saw-pit and carpenter's shed, which, as I have said before, were in a corner of the field near the road, and where one of her informants had told her it was supposed by the police that the murderer had lurked while waiting for his victim. There was no sign, however, that any one had been about the place. If the grass had been bruised or bent where he had trod, it had had enough of the elasticity of life to raise itself under the dewy influences of night. She hushed her breath with involuntary awe, but nothing else told of the violent deed by which a fellow-creature had passed away. She stood still for a minute, imagining to herself the position of the parties, guided by the only circumstance which afforded any evidence, the trailing mark on the dust in the road.

Suddenly (it was before the sun had risen above the horizon) she became aware of something white in the hedge. All other colours wore the same murky hue, though the forms of objects were perfectly distinct. What was it? It could not be a flower;—that, the time of year made clear. A frozen lump of snow, lingering late in one of the gnarled tufts of the hedge? She stepped forward to examine. It proved to be a little piece of stiff writing-paper compressed into a round shape. She understood it instantly; it was the paper that had served as wadding for the murderer's gun. Then she had been standing just where the murderer must have been but a few hours before; probably (as the rumour had spread through the town, reaching her ears) one of the poor maddened turn-outs, who hung about everywhere, with black, fierce looks, as if contemplating some deed of violence. Her sympathy was all with them, for she had known what they suffered; and besides this there was her own individual dislike of Mr. Carson, and dread of him for Mary's sake. Yet, poor Mary! Death was a terrible, though sure, remedy for the evil Esther had dreaded for her; and how would she stand the shock, loving as her aunt believed her to do? Poor Mary! who would comfort her? Esther's thoughts began to picture her sorrow, her despair, when the news of her lover's death should reach her; and she longed to tell her there might have been a keener grief yet had he lived.

Bright, beautiful came the slanting rays of the morning sun. It was time for such as she to hide themselves, with the other obscene things of night, from the glorious light of day, which was only for the happy. So she turned her steps towards town, still holding the paper. But in getting over the hedge it encumbered her to hold it in her clasped hand, and she threw it down. She passed on a few steps, her thoughts still of Mary, till the idea crossed her mind, could it (blank as it appeared to be) give any clue to the murderer? As I said before, her sympathies were all on that side, so she turned back and picked it up; and then feeling as if in some measure an accessory, she hid it unexamined in her hand, and hastily passed out of the street at the opposite end to that by which she had entered it.

And what do you think she felt, when, having walked some distance from the spot, she dared to open the crushed paper, and saw written on it Mary Barton's name, and not only that, but the street in which she lived! True, a letter or two was torn off, but, nevertheless, there was the name clear to be recognised. And oh! what terrible thought flashed into her mind; or was it only fancy? But it looked very like the writing which she had once known well—the writing of Jem Wilson, who, when she lived at her brother-in-law's, and he was a near neighbour, had often been employed by her to write her letters to people, to whom she was ashamed of sending her own misspelt scrawl. She remembered the wonderful flourishes she had so much admired in those days, while she sat by dictating, and Jem, in all the pride of newly-acquired penmanship, used to dazzle her eyes by extraordinary graces and twirls.

If it were his!

Oh! perhaps it was merely that her head was running so on Mary, that she was associating every trifle with her. As if only one person wrote in that flourishing, meandering style!

It was enough to fill her mind to think from what she might have saved Mary by securing the paper. She would look at it just once more, and see if some very dense and stupid policeman could have mistaken the name, or if Mary would certainly have been dragged into notice in the affair.

No! no one could have mistaken the "ry Barton," and it *was* Jem's handwriting!

Oh! if it was so, she understood it all, and she had been the cause! With her violent and unregulated nature, rendered morbid by the course of life she led, and her consciousness of her degradation, she cursed herself for the interference which she believed had led to this; for the information and the warning she had given to Jem, which had roused him to this murderous action. How could she, the abandoned and polluted outcast, ever have dared to hope for a blessing, even on her efforts to do good? The black curse of Heaven rested on all her doings, were they for good or for evil.

Poor, diseased mind! and there were none to minister to thee!

So she wandered about, too restless to take her usual heavy morning's sleep, up and down the streets, greedily listening to every word of the passers by, and loitering near each group of talkers, anxious to scrape together every morsel of information, or conjecture, or suspicion, though without possessing any definite purpose in all this. And ever and always she clenched the scrap of paper which might betray so much, until her nails had deeply indented the palm of her hand; so fearful was she in her nervous dread, lest unawares she should let it drop.

Towards the middle of the day she could no longer evade the body's craving want of rest and refreshment; but the rest was taken in a spirit vault, and the refreshment was a glass of gin.

Then she started up from the stupor she had taken for repose; and suddenly driven before the gusty impulses of her mind, she pushed her way to the place where at that very time the police were bringing the information they had gathered with regard to the all-engrossing murder. She listened with painful acuteness of comprehension to dropped words and unconnected sentences, the meaning of which became clearer, and yet more clear to her. Jem was suspected. Jem was ascertained to be the murderer.

She saw him (although he, absorbed in deep sad thought, saw her not), she saw him brought hand-cuffed and guarded out of the coach. She saw him enter the station,—she gasped for breath till he came out, still hand-cuffed, and still guarded, to be conveyed to the New Bailey.

He was the only one who had spoken to her with hope, that she might yet win her way back to virtue. His words had lingered in her heart with a sort of call to Heaven, like distant Sabbath bells, although in her despair she had turned away from his voice. He was the only one who had spoken to her kindly. The murder, shocking though it was, was an absent, abstract thing, on which her thoughts could not, and would not dwell; all that was present in her mind was Jem's danger, and his kindness.

Then Mary came to remembrance. Esther wondered till she was sick of wondering, in what way she was taking the affair. In some manner it would be a terrible blow for the poor, motherless girl; with her dreadful father, too, who was to Esther a sort of accusing angel.

She set off towards the court where Mary lived, to pick up what she could there of information. But she was ashamed to enter in where once she had been innocent, and hung about the neighbouring streets, not daring to question, so she learnt but little; nothing in fact but the knowledge of John Barton's absence from home.

She went up a dark entry to rest her weary limbs on a door-step and think. Her elbows on her knees, her face hidden in her hands, she tried to gather together and arrange her thoughts. But still every now and then she opened her hand to see if the paper were yet there.

She got up at last. She had formed a plan, and had a course of action to look forward to that would satisfy one craving desire at least. The time was long gone by when there was much wisdom or consistency in her projects.

It was getting late, and that was so much the better. She went to a pawn-shop, and took off her finery in a back room. She was known by the people, and had a character for honesty, so she had no very great difficulty in inducing them to let her have a suit of outer clothes, befitting the wife of a working-man, a black silk bonnet, a printed gown, a plaid shawl, dirty and rather worn to be sure, but which had a sort of sanctity to the eyes of the street-walker as being the appropriate garb of that happy class to which she could never, never more belong.

She looked at herself in the little glass which hung against the wall, and sadly shaking her head, thought how easy were the duties of that Eden of innocence from which she was shut out; how she would work, and toil, and starve, and die, if necessary, for a husband, a home,—for children,—but that thought she could not bear; a little form rose up, stern in its innocence, from the witches' cauldron of her imagination, and she rushed into action again.

You know now how she came to stand by the threshold of Mary's door, waiting, trembling, until the latch was lifted, and her niece, with words that spoke of such desolation among the living, fell into her arms.

She had felt as if some holy spell would prevent her (even as the unholy Lady Geraldine was prevented, in the abode of Christabel) from crossing the threshold of that home of her early innocence; and she had meant to wait for an invitation. But Mary's helpless action did away with all reluctant feeling, and she bore or dragged her to a seat, and looked on her bewildered eyes, as, puzzled with the likeness, which was not identity, she gazed on her aunt's features.

In pursuance of her plan, Esther meant to assume the manners and character, as she had done the dress, of a mechanic's wife; but then, to account for her long absence, and her long silence towards all that ought to have been dear to her, it was necessary that she should put on an indifference far distant from her heart, which was loving and yearning, in spite of all its faults. And, perhaps, she over-acted her part, for certainly Mary felt a kind of repugnance to the changed and altered aunt, who so suddenly re-appeared on the scene; and it would have cut Esther to the very core, could she have known how her little darling of former days was feeling towards her.

"You don't remember me I see, Mary!" she began. "It's a long while since I left you all, to be sure; and I, many a time, thought of coming to see you, and—and your father. But I live so far off, and am always so busy, I cannot do just what I wish. You recollect aunt Esther, don't you, Mary?"

"Are you aunt Hetty?" asked Mary, faintly, still looking at the face which was so different from the old recollections of her aunt's fresh dazzling beauty.

"Yes! I am aunt Hetty. Oh! it's so long since I heard that name," sighing forth the thoughts it suggested; then recovering herself, and striving after the hard character she wished to assume, she continued: "And to-day I heard a friend of yours, and of mine too, long ago, was in trouble, and I guessed you would be in sorrow, so I thought I would just step this far and see you."

Mary's tears flowed afresh, but she had no desire to open her heart to her strangely-found aunt, who had, by her own confession, kept aloof from and neglected them for so many years. Yet she tried to feel grateful for kindness (however late) from any one, and wished to be civil. Moreover, she had a strong disinclination to speak on the terrible subject uppermost in her mind. So, after a pause she said,

"Thank you. I dare say you mean very kind. Have you had a long walk? I'm so sorry," said she, rising, with a sudden thought, which was as suddenly checked by recollection, "but I've nothing to eat in the house, and I'm sure you must be hungry, after your walk."

For Mary concluded that certainly her aunt's residence must be far away on the other side of the town, out of sight or hearing. But, after all, she did not think much about her; her heart was so aching-full of other things, that all besides seemed like a dream. She received feelings and impressions from her conversation with her aunt, but did not, could not, put them together, or think or argue about them.

And Esther! How scanty had been her food for days and weeks, her thinly-covered bones and pale lips might tell, but her words should never reveal! So, with a little unreal laugh, she replied,

"Oh! Mary, my dear! don't talk about eating. We've the best of every thing, and plenty of it, for my husband is in good work. I'd such a supper before I came out. I couldn't touch a morsel if you had it."

Her words shot a strange pang through Mary's heart. She had always remembered her aunt's loving and unselfish disposition; how was it changed, if, living in plenty, she had never thought it worth while to ask after her relations, who were all but starving! She shut up her heart instinctively against her aunt.

And all the time poor Esther was swallowing her sobs, and over-acting her part, and controlling herself more than she had done for many a long day, in order that her niece might not be shocked and revolted, by the knowledge of what her aunt had become:—a prostitute; an outcast.

For she longed to open her wretched, wretched heart, so hopeless, so abandoned by all living things, to one who had loved her once; and yet she refrained, from dread of the averted eye, the altered voice, the internal loathing, which she feared such disclosure might create. She would go straight to the subject of the day. She could not tarry long, for she felt unable to support the character she had assumed for any length of time.

They sat by the little round table, facing each other. The candle was placed right between them, and Esther moved it in order to have a clearer view of Mary's face, so that she might read her emotions, and ascertain her interests. Then she began:

"It's a bad business, I'm afraid, this of Mr. Carson's murder."

Mary winced a little.

"I hear Jem Wilson is taken up for it."

Mary covered her eyes with her hands, as if to shade them from the light, and Esther herself, less accustomed to self-command, was getting too much agitated for calm observation of another.

"I was taking a walk near Turner Street, and I went to see the spot," continued Esther, "and, as luck would have it, I spied this bit of paper in the hedge," producing the precious piece still folded in her hand. "It has been used as wadding for the gun, I reckon; indeed, that's clear enough, from the shape it's crammed into. I was sorry for the murderer, whoever he might be (I didn't then know of Jem's being suspected), and I thought I would never leave a thing about as might help, if ever so little, to convict him; the police are so 'cute about straws. So I carried it a little way, and then I opened it and saw your name, Mary."

Mary took her hands away from her eyes, and looked with surprise at her aunt's face, as she uttered these words. She *was* kind after all, for was she not saving her from being summoned, and from being questioned and examined; a thing to be dreaded above all others: as she felt sure that her unwilling answers, frame them how she might, would add to the suspicions against Jem; her aunt was indeed kind, to think of what would spare her this.

Esther went on, without noticing Mary's look. The very action of speaking was so painful to her, and so much interrupted by the hard, raking little cough, which had been her constant annoyance for months, that she was too much engrossed by the physical difficulty of utterance, to be a very close observer.

"There could be no mistake if they had found it. Look at your name, together with the very name of this court! And in Jem's hand-writing too, or I'm much mistaken. Look, Mary!"

And now she did watch her.

Mary took the paper and flattened it; then suddenly stood stiff up, with irrepressible movement, as if petrified by some horror abruptly disclosed; her face, strung and rigid; her lips compressed tight, to keep down some rising exclamation. She dropped on her seat, as suddenly as if the braced muscles had in an instant given way. But she spoke no word.

"It is his hand-writing—isn't it?" asked Esther, though Mary's manner was almost confirmation enough.

"You will not tell. You never will tell," demanded Mary, in a tone so sternly earnest, as almost to be threatening.

"Nay, Mary," said Esther, rather reproachfully, "I am not so bad as that. Oh! Mary, you cannot think I would do that, whatever I may be."

The tears sprang to her eyes at the idea that she was suspected of being one who would help to inform against an old friend.

Mary caught her sad and upbraiding look.

"No! I know you would not tell, aunt. I don't know what I say, I am so shocked. But say you will not tell. Do."

"No, indeed I will not tell, come what may."

Mary sat still, looking at the writing, and turning the paper round with careful examination, trying to hope, but her very fears belying her hopes.

"I thought you cared for the young man that's murdered," observed Esther, half aloud; but feeling that she could not mistake this strange interest in the suspected murderer, implied by Mary's eagerness to screen him from any thing which might strengthen suspicion against him. She had come, desirous to know the extent of Mary's grief for Mr. Carson, and glad of the excuse afforded her by the important scrap of paper. Her remark about its being Jem's hand-writing, she had, with this view of ascertaining Mary's state of feeling, felt to be most imprudent the instant after she uttered it; but Mary's anxiety that she should not tell was too great, and too decided, to leave a doubt as to her interest for Jem. She grew more and more bewildered, and her dizzy head refused to reason. Mary never spoke. She held the bit of paper firmly, determined to retain possession of it, come what might; and anxious, and impatient, for her aunt to go. As she sat, her face bore a likeness to Esther's dead child.

"You are so like my little girl, Mary!" said Esther, weary of the one subject on which she could get no satisfaction, and recurring, with full heart, to the thought of the dead.

Mary looked up. Her aunt had children, then. That was all the idea she received. No faint imagination of the love and the woe of that poor creature crossed her mind, or she would have taken her, all guilty and erring, to her bosom, and tried to bind up the broken heart. No! it was not to be. Her aunt had children, then; and she was on the point of putting some question about them, but before it could be spoken another thought turned it aside, and she went back to her task of unravelling the mystery of the paper, and the hand-writing. Oh! how she wished her aunt would go.

As if, according to the believers in mesmerism, the intenseness of her wish gave her power over another, although the wish was unexpressed, Esther felt herself unwelcome, and that her absence was desired.

She felt this some time before she could summon up resolution to go. She was so much disappointed in this longed-for, dreaded interview with Mary; she had wished to impose upon her with her tale of married respectability, and yet she had yearned and craved for sympathy in her real lot. And she had imposed upon her well. She should perhaps be glad of it afterwards; but her desolation of hope seemed for the time redoubled. And she must leave the old dwelling-place, whose very walls, and flags, dingy and sordid as they were, had a charm for her. Must leave the abode of poverty, for the more terrible abodes of vice. She must—she would go.

"Well, good-night, Mary. That bit of paper is safe enough with you, I see. But you made me promise I would not tell about it, and you must promise me to destroy it before you sleep."

"I promise," said Mary, hoarsely, but firmly. "Then you are going?"

"Yes. Not if you wish me to stay. Not if I could be of any comfort to you, Mary;" catching at some glimmering hope.

"Oh, no," said Mary, anxious to be alone. "Your husband will be wondering where you are. Some day you must tell me all about yourself. I forget what your name is?"

"Fergusson," said Esther, sadly.

"Mrs. Fergusson," repeated Mary, half unconsciously. "And where did you say you lived?"

"I never did say," muttered Esther; then aloud, "In Angel's Meadow, 145, Nicholas Street."

"145, Nicholas Street, Angel Meadow. I shall remember."

As Esther drew her shawl around her, and prepared to depart, a thought crossed Mary's mind that she had been cold and hard in her manner towards one, who had certainly meant to act kindly in bringing her the paper (that dread, terrible piece of paper) and thus saving her from—she could not rightly think how much, or how little she was spared. So, desirous of making up for her previous indifferent manner, she advanced to kiss her aunt before her departure.

But, to her surprise, her aunt pushed her off with a frantic kind of gesture, and saying the words,

"Not me. You must never kiss me. You!"

She rushed into the outer darkness of the street, and there wept long and bitterly.

CHAPTER XXII - MARY'S EFFORTS TO PROVE AN ALIBI

"There was a listening fear in her regard,
As if calamity had but begun;
As if the vanward clouds of evil days
Had spent their malice, and the sullen rear
Was, with its stored thunder, labouring up."

KEATS' "HYPERION."

No sooner was Mary alone than she fastened the door, and put the shutters up against the window, which had all this time remained shaded only by the curtains hastily drawn together on Esther's entrance, and the lighting of the candle.

She did all this with the same compressed lips, and the same stony look that her face had assumed on the first examination of the paper. Then she sat down for an instant to think; and rising directly, went, with a step rendered firm by inward resolution of purpose, up the stairs;—passed her own door, two steps, into her father's room. What did she want there?

I must tell you; I must put into words the dreadful secret which she believed that bit of paper had revealed to her.

Her father was the murderer!

That corner of stiff, shining, thick writing-paper, she recognised as part of the sheet on which she had copied Samuel Bamford's beautiful lines so many months ago—copied (as you perhaps remember) on the blank part of a valentine sent to her by Jem Wilson, in those days when she did not treasure and hoard up every thing he had touched, as she would do now.

That copy had been given to her father, for whom it was made, and she had occasionally seen him reading it over, not a fortnight ago she was sure. But she resolved to ascertain if the other part still remained in his possession. He might, it was just possible he *might*, have given it away to some friend; and if so, that person was the guilty one, for she could swear to the paper anywhere.

First of all she pulled out every article from the little old chest of drawers. Amongst them were some things which had belonged to her mother, but she had no time now to examine and try and remember them. All the reverence she could pay them was to carry them and lay them on the bed carefully, while the other things were tossed impatiently out upon the floor.

The copy of Bamford's lines was not there. Oh! perhaps he might have given it away; but then must it not have been to Jem? It was his gun.

And she set to with redoubled vigour to examine the deal-box which served as chair, and which had once contained her father's Sunday clothes, in the days when he could afford to have Sunday clothes.

He had redeemed his better coat from the pawn-shop before he left, that she had noticed. Here was his old one. What rustled under her hand in the pocket?

The paper! "Oh! Father!"

Yes, it fitted; jagged end to jagged end, letter to letter; and even the part which Esther had considered blank had its tallying mark with the larger piece, its tails of *y*s and *g*s. And then, as if that were not damning evidence enough, she felt again, and found some bullets or shot (I don't know which you would call them) in that same pocket, along with a small paper parcel of gunpowder. As she was going to replace the jacket, having abstracted the paper, and bullets, &c., she saw a woollen gun-case made of that sort of striped horse-cloth you must have seen a thousand times appropriated to such a purpose. The sight of it made her examine still further, but there was nothing else that could afford any evidence, so she locked the box, and sat down on the floor to contemplate the articles; now with a sickening despair, now with a kind of wondering curiosity, how her father had managed to evade observation. After all it was easy enough. He had evidently got possession of some gun (was it really Jem's; was he an accomplice? No! she did not believe it; he never, never would deliberately plan a murder with another, however he might be wrought up to it by passionate feeling at the time. Least of all would he accuse her to her father, without previously warning her; it was out of his nature).

Then having obtained possession of the gun, her father had loaded it at home, and might have carried it away with him some time when the neighbours were not noticing, and she was out, or asleep; and then he might have hidden it somewhere to be in readiness when he should want it. She was sure he had no such thing with him when he went away the last time.

She felt it was of no use to conjecture his motives. His actions had become so wild and irregular of late, that she could not reason upon them. Besides, was it not enough to know that he was guilty of this terrible offence? Her love for her father seemed to return with painful force, mixed up as it was with horror at his crime. That dear father, who was once so kind, so warm-hearted, so ready to help either man or beast in distress, to murder! But, in the desert of misery with which these thoughts surrounded her, the arid depths of whose gloom she dared not venture to contemplate, a little spring of comfort was gushing up at her feet, unnoticed at first, but soon to give her strength and hope.

And *that* was the necessity for exertion on her part which this discovery enforced.

Oh! I do think that the necessity for exertion, for some kind of action (bodily or mental) in time of distress, is a most infinite blessing, although the first efforts at such seasons are painful. Something to be done implies that there is yet hope of some good thing to be accomplished, or some additional evil that may be avoided; and by degrees the hope absorbs much of the sorrow.

It is the woes that cannot in any earthly way be escaped that admit least earthly comforting. Of all trite, worn-out, hollow mockeries of comfort that were ever uttered by people who will not take the trouble of sympathising with others, the one I dislike the most is the exhortation not to grieve over an event, "for it cannot be helped." Do you think if I could help it, I would sit still with folded hands, content to mourn? Do you not believe that as long as hope remained I would be up and doing? I mourn because what has occurred cannot be helped. The reason you give me for not grieving, is the very and sole reason of my grief. Give me nobler and higher reasons for enduring meekly what my Father sees fit to send, and I will try earnestly and faithfully to be patient; but mock me not, or any other mourner, with the speech, "Do not grieve, for it cannot be helped. It is past remedy."

But some remedy to Mary's sorrow came with thinking. If her father was guilty, Jem was innocent. If innocent, there was a possibility of saving him. He must be saved. And she must do it; for was not she the sole depository of the terrible secret? Her father was not suspected; and never should be, if by any foresight or any exertions of her own she could prevent it.

She did not yet know how Jem was to be saved, while her father was also to be considered innocent. It would require much thought and much prudence. But with the call upon her exertions, and her various qualities of judgment and discretion, came the answering consciousness of innate power to meet the emergency. Every step now, nay, the employment of every minute, was of consequence; for you must remember she had learnt at Miss Simmonds' the probability that the murderer would be brought to trial the next week. And you must remember, too, that never was so young a girl so friendless, or so penniless, as Mary was at this time. But the lion accompanied Una through the wilderness and the danger; and so will a high, resolved purpose of right-doing ever guard and accompany the helpless.

It struck two; deep, mirk, night.

It was of no use bewildering herself with plans this weary, endless night. Nothing could be done before morning: and, at first in her impatience, she began to long for day; but then she felt in how unfit a state her body was for any plan of exertion, and she resolutely made up her mind to husband her physical strength.

First of all she must burn the tell-tale paper. The powder, bullets, and guncase, she tied into a bundle, and hid in the sacking of the bed for the present, although there was no likelihood of their affording evidence against any one. Then she carried the paper down stairs, and burnt it on the hearth, powdering the very ashes with her fingers, and dispersing the fragments of fluttering black films among the cinders of the grate. Then she breathed again.

Her head ached with dizzying violence; she must get quit of the pain or it would incapacitate her for thinking and planning. She looked for food, but there was nothing but a little raw oatmeal in the house: still, although it almost choked her, she ate some of this, knowing from experience, how often headaches were caused by long fasting. Then she sought for some water to bathe her throbbing temples, and quench her feverish thirst. There was none in the house, so she took the jug and went out to the pump at the other end of the court, whose echoes re-sounded her light footsteps in the quiet stillness of the night. The hard, square outlines of the houses cut sharply against the cold bright sky, from which myriads of stars were shining down in eternal repose. There was little sympathy in the outward scene, with the internal trouble. All was so still, so motionless, so hard! Very different to this lovely night in the country in which I am now writing, where the distant horizon is soft and undulating in the moonlight, and the nearer trees sway gently to and fro in the night-wind with something of almost human motion; and the rustling air makes music among their branches, as if speaking soothingly to the weary ones who lie awake in heaviness of heart. The sights and sounds of such a night lull pain and grief to rest.

But Mary re-entered her home after she had filled her pitcher, with a still stronger sense of anxiety, and a still clearer conviction of how much rested upon her unassisted and friendless self, alone with her terrible knowledge, in the hard, cold, populous world.

She bathed her forehead, and quenched her thirst, and then, with wise delibera-tion of purpose, went upstairs, and undressed herself, as if for a long night's slumber, although so few hours intervened before day-dawn. She believed she never could sleep, but she lay down, and shut her eyes; and before many minutes she was in as deep and sound a slumber as if there was no sin nor sorrow in the world.

She awakened, as it was natural, much refreshed in body; but with a con-sciousness of some great impending calamity. She sat up in bed to recollect, and when she did remember, she sank down again with all the helplessness of despair. But it was only the weakness of an instant; for were not the very minutes pre-cious, for deliberation if not for action?

Before she had finished the necessary morning business of dressing, and set-ting her house in some kind of order, she had disentangled her ravelled ideas, and arranged some kind of a plan for action. If Jem was innocent (and now, of his guilt, even his slightest participation in, or knowledge of, the murder, she acquit-ted him with all her heart and soul), he must have been somewhere else when the crime was committed; probably with some others, who might bear witness to the fact, if she only knew where to find them. Every thing rested on her. She had heard of an alibi, and believed it might mean the deliverance she wished to ac-complish; but she was not quite sure, and determined to apply to Job, as one of the few among her acquaintance gifted with the knowledge of hard words, for to her, all terms of law, or natural history, were alike many-syllabled mysteries.

No time was to be lost. She went straight to Job Legh's house, and found the old man and his grand-daughter sitting at breakfast; as she opened the door she heard their voices speaking in a grave, hushed, subdued tone, as if something grieved their hearts. They stopped talking on her entrance, and then she knew they had been conversing about the murder; about Jem's probable guilt; and (it flashed upon her for the first time) on the new light they would have obtained regarding herself: for until now they had never heard of her giddy flirting with Mr. Carson; not in all her confidential talk with Margaret had she ever spoken of him. And now Margaret would hear her conduct talked of by all, as that of a bold, bad girl; and even if she did not believe every thing that was said, she could hardly help feeling wounded, and disappointed in Mary.

So it was in a timid voice that Mary wished her usual good-morrow, and her heart sank within her a little, when Job, with a form of civility, bade her welcome in that dwelling, where, until now, she had been too well assured to require to be asked to sit down.

She took a chair. Margaret continued silent.

"I'm come to speak to you about this—about Jem Wilson."

"It's a bad business, I'm afeared," replied Job, sadly.

"Ay, it's bad enough anyhow. But Jem's innocent. Indeed he is; I'm as sure as sure can be."

"How can you know, wench? Facts bear strong again him, poor fellow, though he'd a deal to put him up, and aggravate him, they say. Ay, poor lad, he's done for himself, I'm afeared."

"Job!" said Mary, rising from her chair in her eagerness, "you must not say he did it. He didn't; I'm sure and certain he didn't. Oh! why do you shake your head? Who is to believe me,—who is to think him innocent, if you, who know'd him so well, stick to it he's guilty?"

"I'm loth enough to do it, lass," replied Job; "but I think he's been ill used, and—jilted (that's plain truth, Mary, hard as it may seem), and his blood has been up—many a man has done the like afore, from like causes."

"Oh, God! Then you won't help me, Job, to prove him innocent? Oh! Job, Job; believe me, Jem never did harm to no one."

"Not afore;—and mind, wench! I don't over-blame him for this." Job relapsed into silence.

Mary thought a moment.

"Well, Job, you'll not refuse me this, I know. I won't mind what you think, if you'll help me as if he was innocent. Now suppose I know—I knew he was innocent,—it's only supposing, Job,—what must I do to prove it? Tell me, Job! Isn't it called an *alibi*, the getting folk to swear to where he really was at the time?"

"Best way, if you know'd him innocent, would be to find out the real murderer. Some one did it, that's clear enough. If it wasn't Jem, who was it?"

"How can I tell?" answered Mary, in an agony of terror, lest Job's question was prompted by any suspicion of the truth.

But he was far enough from any such thought. Indeed, he had no doubt in his own mind that Jem had, in some passionate moment, urged on by slighted love and jealousy, been the murderer. And he was strongly inclined to believe, that Mary was aware of this, only that, too late repentant of her light conduct which had led to such fatal consequences, she was now most anxious to save her old play-fellow, her early friend, from the doom awaiting the shedder of blood.

"If Jem's not done it, I don't see as any on us can tell who did. We might find out something if we'd time; but they say he's to be tried on Tuesday. It's no use hiding it, Mary; things looks strong against him."

"I know they do! I know they do! But, oh! Job! isn't an *alibi* a proving where he really was at th' time of the murder; and how must I set about an *alibi*?"

"An *alibi* is that, sure enough." He thought a little. "You mun ask his mother his doings, and his whereabouts that night; the knowledge of that will guide you a bit."

For he was anxious that on another should fall the task of enlightening Mary on the hopelessness of the case, and he felt that her own sense would be more convinced by inquiry and examination than any mere assertion of his.

Margaret had sat silent and grave all this time. To tell the truth, she was surprised and disappointed by the disclosure of Mary's conduct, with regard to Mr. Henry Carson. Gentle, reserved, and prudent herself, never exposed to the trial of being admired for her personal appearance, and unsusceptible enough to be in doubt even yet, whether the fluttering, tender, infinitely-joyous feeling she was for the first time experiencing, at sight, or sound, or thought of Will Wilson, was love or not,—Margaret had no sympathy with the temptations to which loveliness, vanity, ambition, or the desire of being admired, exposes so many; no sympathy with flirting girls, in short. Then, she had no idea of the strength of the conflict between will and principle in some who were differently constituted from herself. With her, to be convinced that an action was wrong, was tantamount to a determination not to do so again; and she had little or no difficulty in carrying out her determination. So she could not understand how it was that Mary had acted wrongly, and had felt too much ashamed, in spite of all internal sophistry, to speak of her actions. Margaret considered herself deceived; felt aggrieved; and, at the time of which I am now telling you, was strongly inclined to give Mary up altogether, as a girl devoid of the modest proprieties of her sex, and capable of gross duplicity, in speaking of one lover as she had done of Jem, while she was encouraging another in attentions, at best of a very doubtful character.

But now Margaret was drawn into the conversation. Suddenly it flashed across Mary's mind, that the night of the murder was the very night, or rather the same early morning, that Margaret had been with Alice. She turned sharp round, with—

"Oh! Margaret, you can tell me; you were there when he came back that night; were you not? No! you were not; but you were there not many hours after. Did not you hear where he'd been? He was away the night before, too, when Alice was first taken; when you were there for your tea. Oh! where was he, Margaret?"

"I don't know," she answered. "Stay! I do remember something about his keeping Will company, in his walk to Liverpool. I can't justly say what it was, so much happened that night."

"I'll go to his mother's," said Mary, resolutely.

They neither of them spoke, either to advise or dissuade. Mary felt she had no sympathy from them, and braced up her soul to act without such loving aid of friendship. She knew that their advice would be willingly given at her demand, and that was all she really required for Jem's sake. Still her courage failed a little as she walked to Jane Wilson's, alone in the world with her secret.

Jane Wilson's eyes were swelled with crying; and it was sad to see the ravages which intense anxiety and sorrow had made on her appearance in four-and-twenty hours. All night long she and Mrs. Davenport had crooned over their sorrows, always recurring, like the burden of an old song, to the dreadest sorrow of all, which was now impending over Mrs. Wilson. She had grown—I hardly know what word to use—but, something like proud of her martyrdom; she had grown to hug her grief; to feel an excitement in her agony of anxiety about her boy.

"So, Mary, you're here! Oh! Mary, lass! He's to be tried on Tuesday."

She fell to sobbing, in the convulsive breath-catching manner which tells so of much previous weeping.

"Oh! Mrs. Wilson, don't take on so! We'll get him off, you'll see. Don't fret; they can't prove him guilty!"

"But I tell thee they will," interrupted Mrs. Wilson, half-irritated at the light way, as she considered it, in which Mary spoke; and a little displeased that another could hope when she had almost brought herself to find pleasure in despair.

"It may suit thee well," continued she, "to make light o' the misery thou hast caused; but I shall lay his death at thy door, as long as I live, and die I know he will; and all for what he never did—no, he never did; my own blessed boy!"

She was too weak to be angry long; her wrath sank away to feeble sobbing and worn-out moans.

Mary was most anxious to soothe her from any violence of either grief or anger; she did so want her to be clear in her recollection; and, besides, her tenderness was great towards Jem's mother. So she spoke in a low gentle tone the loving sentences, which sound so broken and powerless in repetition, and which yet have so much power when accompanied with caressing looks and actions, fresh from the heart; and the old woman insensibly gave herself up to the influence of those sweet, loving blue eyes, those tears of sympathy, those words of love and hope, and was lulled into a less morbid state of mind.

"And now, dear Mrs. Wilson, can you remember where he said he was going on Thursday night? He was out when Alice was taken ill; and he did not come home till early in the morning, or, to speak true, in the night: did he?"

"Ay! he went out near upon five; he went out with Will; he said he were going to set[1] him a part of the way, for Will were hot upon walking to Liverpool, and wouldn't hearken to Jem's offer of lending him five shilling for his fare. So the two lads set off together. I mind it all now; but, thou seest, Alice's illness, and this business of poor Jem's, drove it out of my head; they went off together, to walk to Liverpool; that's to say, Jem were to go a part o' th' way. But, who knows" (falling

[1] "To set," to accompany.

back into the old desponding tone) "if he really went? He might be led off on the road. Oh! Mary, wench! they'll hang him for what he's never done."

"No, they won't—they shan't! I see my way a bit now. We mun get Will to help; there'll be time. He can swear that Jem were with him. Where is Jem?"

"Folk said he were taken to Kirkdale, i' th' prison-van, this morning; without my seeing him, poor chap! Oh! wench! but they've hurried on the business at a cruel rate."

"Ay! they've not let grass grow under their feet, in hunting out the man that did it," said Mary, sorrowfully and bitterly. "But keep up your heart. They got on the wrong scent when they took to suspecting Jem. Don't be afeard. You'll see it will end right for Jem."

"I should mind it less if I could do aught," said Jane Wilson; "but I'm such a poor weak old body, and my head's so gone, and I'm so dazed-like, what with Alice and all, that I think and think, and can do nought to help my child. I might ha' gone and seen him last night, they tell me now, and then I missed it. Oh! Mary, I missed it; and I may never see the lad again."

She looked so piteously in Mary's face with her miserable eyes, that Mary felt her heart giving way, and, dreading the weakening of her powers, which the burst of crying she longed for would occasion, hastily changed the subject to Alice; and Jane, in her heart, feeling that there was no sorrow like a mother's sorrow, replied,

"She keeps on much the same, thank you. She's happy, for she knows nought of what's going on; but th' doctor says she grows weaker and weaker. Thou'lt may be like to see her?"

Mary went up-stairs: partly because it is the etiquette in humble life to offer to friends a last opportunity of seeing the dying or the dead, while the same etiquette forbids a refusal of the invitation; and partly because she longed to breathe, for an instant, the atmosphere of holy calm, which seemed ever to surround the pious good old woman. Alice lay, as before, without pain, or at least any outward expression of it; but totally unconscious of all present circumstances, and absorbed in recollections of the days of her girlhood, which were vivid enough to take the place of realities to her. Still she talked of green fields, and still she spoke to the long-dead mother and sister, low-lying in their graves this many a year, as if they were with her and about her, in the pleasant places where her youth had passed.

But the voice was fainter, the motions were more languid; she was evidently passing away; but *how* happily!

Mary stood for a time in silence, watching and listening. Then she bent down and reverently kissed Alice's cheek; and drawing Jane Wilson away from the bed, as if the spirit of her who lay there were yet cognisant of present realities, she whispered a few words of hope to the poor mother, and kissing her over and over again in a warm, loving manner, she bade her good-bye, went a few steps, and then once more came back to bid her keep up her heart.

And when she had fairly left the house, Jane Wilson felt as if a sun-beam had ceased shining into the room.

Yet oh! how sorely Mary's heart ached; for more and more the fell certainty came on her that her father was the murderer! She struggled hard not to dwell on this conviction; to think alone on the means of proving Jem's innocence; that was her first duty, and that should be done.

CHAPTER XXIII - THE SUB-PŒNA.

"And must it then depend on this poor eye
And this unsteady hand, whether the bark,
That bears my all of treasured hope and love,
Shall find a passage through these frowning rocks
To some fair port where peace and safety smile,—
Or whether it shall blindly dash against them,
And miserably sink? Heaven be my help;
And clear my eye, and nerve my trembling hand!"

"THE CONSTANT WOMAN."

Her heart beating, her head full of ideas, which required time and solitude to be reduced into order, Mary hurried home. She was like one who finds a jewel of which he cannot all at once ascertain the value, but who hides his treasure until some quiet hour when he may ponder over the capabilities its possession unfolds. She was like one who discovers the silken clue which guides to some bower of bliss, and secure of the power within his grasp, has to wait for a time before he may tread the labyrinth.

But no jewel, no bower of bliss was ever so precious to miser or lover as was the belief which now pervaded Mary's mind, that Jem's innocence might be proved, without involving any suspicion of that other—that dear one, so dear, although so criminal—on whose part in this cruel business she dared not dwell even in thought. For if she did, there arose the awful question,—if all went against Jem the innocent, if judge and jury gave the verdict forth which had the looming gallows in the rear, what ought she to do, possessed of her terrible knowledge? Surely not to inculpate her father—and yet—and yet—she almost prayed for the blessed unconsciousness of death or madness, rather than that awful question should have to be answered by her.

But now a way seemed opening, opening yet more clear. She was thankful she had thought of the *alibi*, and yet more thankful to have so easily obtained the clue to Jem's whereabouts that miserable night. The bright light that her new hope threw over all seemed also to make her thankful for the early time appointed for the trial. It would be easy to catch Will Wilson on his return from the Isle of Man, which he had planned should be on the Monday; and on the Tuesday all would be made clear—all that she dared to wish to be made clear.

She had still to collect her thoughts and freshen her memory enough to arrange how to meet with Will—for to the chances of a letter she would not trust; to find out his lodgings when in Liverpool; to try and remember the name of the ship in which he was to sail: and the more she considered these points the more difficulty she found there would be in ascertaining these minor but important facts. For you are aware that Alice, whose memory was clear and strong on all points in which her heart was interested, was lying in a manner senseless: that Jane Wilson was (to use her own word, so expressive to a Lancashire ear) "dazed," that is to say, bewildered, lost in the confusion of terrifying and distressing thoughts; incapable of concentrating her mind; and at the best of times Will's proceedings were a matter of little importance to her (or so she pretended), she was so jealous of aught which distracted attention from her pearl of price, her only son Jem. So Mary felt hopeless of obtaining any intelligence of the sailor's arrangements from her.

Then, should she apply to Jem himself? No! she knew him too well. She felt how thoroughly he must ere now have had it in his power to exculpate himself at another's expense. And his tacit refusal so to do had assured her of what she had never doubted, that the murderer was safe from any impeachment of his. But then neither would he consent, she feared, to any steps which might tend to prove himself innocent. At any rate, she could not consult him. He was removed to Kirkdale, and time pressed. Already it was Saturday at noon. And even if she could have gone to him, I believe she would not. She longed to do all herself; to be his liberator, his deliverer; to win him life, though she might never regain his lost love, by her own exertions. And oh! how could she see him to discuss a subject in which both knew who was the blood-stained man; and yet whose name might not be breathed by either, so dearly with all his faults, his sins, was he loved by both.

All at once, when she had ceased to try and remember, the name of Will's ship flashed across her mind.

The *John Cropper*.

He had named it, she had been sure, all along. He had named it in his conversation with her that last, that fatal Thursday evening. She repeated it over and over again, through a nervous dread of again forgetting it. The *John Cropper*.

And then, as if she were rousing herself out of some strange stupor, she bethought her of Margaret. Who so likely as Margaret to treasure every little particular respecting Will, now Alice was dead to all the stirring purposes of life?

She had gone thus far in her process of thought, when a neighbour stepped in; she with whom they had usually deposited the house-key, when both Mary and her father were absent from home, and who consequently took upon herself to answer all inquiries, and receive all messages which any friends might make, or leave, on finding the house shut up.

"Here's somewhat for you, Mary! A policeman left it."

A bit of parchment.

Many people have a dread of those mysterious pieces of parchment. I am one. Mary was another. Her heart misgave her as she took it, and looked at the unusual appearance of the writing, which, though legible enough, conveyed no idea to her, or rather her mind shut itself up against receiving any idea, which after all was rather a proof she had some suspicion of the meaning that awaited her.

"What is it?" asked she, in a voice from which all the pith and marrow of strength seemed extracted.

"Nay! how should I know? Policeman said he'd call again towards evening, and see if you'd getten it. He were loth to leave it, though I telled him who I was, and all about my keeping th' key, and taking messages."

"What is it about?" asked Mary again, in the same hoarse, feeble voice, and turning it over in her fingers, as if she dreaded to inform herself of its meaning.

"Well! yo can read word of writing and I cannot, so it's queer I should have to tell you. But my master says it's a summons for yo to bear witness again Jem Wilson, at th' trial at Liverpool Assize."

"God pity me!" said Mary, faintly, as white as a sheet.

"Nay, wench, never take on so. What yo can say will go little way either to help or to hinder, for folk say he's certain to be hung; and sure enough it was t'other one as was your sweetheart."

But Mary was beyond any pang this speech would have given at another time. Her thoughts were all busy picturing to herself the terrible occasion of their next meeting—not as lovers meet should they meet!

"Well!" said the neighbour, seeing no use in remaining with one who noticed her words or her presence so little; "thou'lt tell policeman thou'st getten his precious bit of paper. He seemed to think I should be keeping it for mysel; he's th' first as has ever misdoubted me about giving messages, or notes. Good day."

She left the house, but Mary did not know it. She sat still with the parchment in her hand.

All at once she started up. She would take it to Job Legh and ask him to tell her the true meaning, for it could not be *that*.

So she went, and choked out her words of inquiry.

"It's a sub-pœna," he replied, turning the parchment over with the air of a connoisseur; for Job loved hard words, and lawyer-like forms, and even esteemed himself slightly qualified for a lawyer, from the smattering of knowledge he had picked up from an odd volume of Blackstone that he had once purchased at a book-stall.

"A sub-pœna—what is that?" gasped Mary, still in suspense.

Job was struck with her voice, her changed, miserable voice, and peered at her countenance from over his spectacles.

"A sub-pœna is neither more nor less than this, my dear. It's a summonsing you to attend, and answer such questions as may be asked of you regarding the trial of James Wilson, for the murder of Henry Carson; that's the long and short of it, only more elegantly put, for the benefit of them who knows how to value the gift of language. I've been a witness before-time myself; there's nothing much to be afeared on; if they are impudent, why, just you be impudent, and give 'em tit for tat."

"Nothing much to be afeared on!" echoed Mary, but in such a different tone.

"Ay, poor wench, I see how it is. It'll go hard with thee a bit, I dare say; but keep up thy heart. Yo cannot have much to tell 'em, that can go either one way or th' other. Nay! may be thou may do him a bit o' good, for when they set eyes on thee, they'll see fast enough how he came to be so led away by jealousy; for thou'rt a pretty creature, Mary, and one look at thy face will let 'em into th' secret of a young man's madness, and make 'em more ready to pass it over."

"Oh! Job, and won't you ever believe me when I tell you he's innocent? Indeed, and indeed I can prove it; he was with Will all that night; he was, indeed, Job!"

"My wench! whose word hast thou for that?" said Job, pityingly.

"Why! his mother told me, and I'll get Will to bear witness to it. But, oh! Job" (bursting into tears), "it is hard if you won't believe me. How shall I clear him to strangers, when those who know him, and ought to love him, are so set against his being innocent?"

"God knows, I'm not against his being innocent," said Job, solemnly. "I'd give half my remaining days on earth,—I'd give them all, Mary (and but for the love I bear to my poor blind girl, they'd be no great gift), if I could save him. You've thought me hard, Mary, but I'm not hard at bottom, and I'll help you if I can; that I will, right or wrong," he added; but in a low voice, and coughed the uncertain words away the moment afterwards.

"Oh, Job! if you will help me," exclaimed Mary, brightening up (though it was but a wintry gleam after all), "tell me what to say, when they question me; I shall be so gloppened,[1] I shan't know what to answer."

"Thou canst do nought better than tell the truth. Truth's best at all times, they say; and for sure it is when folk have to do with lawyers; for they're 'cute and cunning enough to get it out sooner or later, and it makes folk look like Tom Noddies, when truth follows falsehood, against their will."

"But I don't know the truth; I mean—I can't say rightly what I mean; but I'm sure, if I were pent up, and stared at by hundreds of folk, and asked ever so simple a question, I should be for answering it wrong; if they asked me if I had seen you on a Saturday, or a Tuesday, or any day, I should have clean forgotten all about it, and say the very thing I should not."

"Well, well, don't go for to get such notions into your head; they're what they call 'narvous,' and talking on 'em does no good. Here's Margaret! bless the wench! Look, Mary, how well she guides hersel."

Job fell to watching his grand-daughter, as with balancing, measured steps, timed almost as if to music, she made her way across the street.

Mary shrank as if from a cold blast—shrank from Margaret! The blind girl, with her reserve, her silence, seemed to be a severe judge; she, listening, would be

---

[1] "Gloppened," terrified.

such a check to the trusting earnestness of confidence, which was beginning to unlock the sympathy of Job. Mary knew herself to blame; felt her errors in every fibre of her heart; but yet she would rather have had them spoken about, even in terms of severest censure, than have been treated in the icy manner in which Margaret had received her that morning.

"Here's Mary," said Job, almost as if he wished to propitiate his granddaughter, "come to take a bit of dinner with us, for I'll warrant she's never thought of cooking any for herself to-day; and she looks as wan and pale as a ghost."

It was calling out the feeling of hospitality, so strong and warm in most of those who have little to offer, but whose heart goes eagerly and kindly with that little. Margaret came towards Mary with a welcoming gesture, and a kinder manner by far than she had used in the morning.

"Nay, Mary, thou know'st thou'st getten nought at home," urged Job.

And Mary, faint and weary, and with a heart too aching-full of other matters to be pertinacious in this, withdrew her refusal.

They ate their dinner quietly; for to all it was an effort to speak, and after one or two attempts they had subsided into silence.

When the meal was ended Job began again on the subject they all had at heart.

"Yon poor lad at Kirkdale will want a lawyer to see they don't put on him, but do him justice. Hast thought of that?"

Mary had not, and felt sure his mother had not.

Margaret confirmed this last supposition.

"I've but just been there, and poor Jane is like one dateless; so many griefs come on her at once. One time she seems to make sure he'll be hung; and if I took her in that way, she flew out (poor body!) and said, that in spite of what folk said, there were them as could, and would prove him guiltless. So I never knew where to have her. The only thing she was constant in, was declaring him innocent."

"Mother-like!" said Job.

"She meant Will, when she spoke of them that could prove him innocent. He was with Will on Thursday night, walking a part of the way with him to Liverpool; now the thing is to lay hold on Will and get him to prove this." So spoke Mary, calm, from the earnestness of her purpose.

"Don't build too much on it, my dear," said Job.

"I do build on it," replied Mary, "because I know it's the truth, and I mean to try and prove it, come what may. Nothing you can say will daunt me, Job, so don't you go and try. You may help, but you cannot hinder me doing what I'm resolved on."

They respected her firmness of determination, and Job almost gave in to her belief, when he saw how steadfastly she was acting upon it. Oh! surest way of conversion to our faith, whatever it may be,—regarding either small things, or great,—when it is beheld as the actuating principle, from which we never swerve! When it is seen that, instead of over-much profession, it is worked into the life, and moves every action!

Mary gained courage as she instinctively felt she had made way with one at least of her companions.

"Now I'm clear about this much," she continued, "he was with Will when the—shot was fired (she could not bring herself to say, when the murder was committed, when she remembered *who* it was that, she had every reason to believe, was the taker-away of life). Will can prove this. I must find Will. He wasn't to sail till Tuesday. There's time enough. He was to come back from his uncle's, in the Isle of Man, on Monday. I must meet him in Liverpool, on that day, and tell him what has happened, and how poor Jem is in trouble, and that he must prove an *alibi*, come Tuesday. All this I can and will do, though perhaps I don't clearly know how, just at present. But surely God will help me. When I know I'm doing right, I will have no fear, but put my trust in Him; for I'm acting for the innocent and good, and not for my own self, who have done so wrong. I have no fear when I think of Jem, who is so good."

She stopped, oppressed with the fulness of her heart. Margaret began to love her again; to see in her the same sweet, faulty, impulsive, lovable creature she had known in the former Mary Barton, but with more of dignity, self-reliance, and purpose.

Mary spoke again.

"Now I know the name of Will's vessel—the *John Cropper*; and I know that she is bound to America. That is something to know. But I forget, if I ever heard, where he lodges in Liverpool. He spoke of his landlady, as a good, trustworthy woman; but if he named her name, it has slipped my memory. Can you help me, Margaret?"

She appealed to her friend calmly and openly, as if perfectly aware of, and recognising the unspoken tie which bound her and Will together; she asked her in the same manner in which she would have asked a wife where her husband dwelt. And Margaret replied in the like calm tone, two spots of crimson on her cheeks alone bearing witness to any internal agitation.

"He lodges at a Mrs. Jones's, Milk-House Yard, out of Nicholas Street. He has lodged there ever since he began to go to sea; she is a very decent kind of woman, I believe."

"Well, Mary! I'll give you my prayers," said Job. "It's not often I pray regular, though I often speak a word to God, when I'm either very happy or very sorry; I've catched myself thanking Him at odd hours when I've found a rare insect, or had a fine day for an out; but I cannot help it, no more than I can talking to a friend. But this time I'll pray regular for Jem, and for you. And so will Margaret, I'll be bound. Still, wench! what think yo of a lawyer? I know one, Mr. Cheshire, who's rather given to th' insect line—and a good kind o' chap. He and I have swopped specimens many's the time, when either of us had a duplicate. He'll do me a kind turn, I'm sure. I'll just take my hat, and pay him a visit."

No sooner said, than done.

Margaret and Mary were left alone. And this seemed to bring back the feeling of awkwardness, not to say estrangement.

But Mary, excited to an unusual pitch of courage, was the first to break silence.

"Oh, Margaret!" said she, "I see—I feel how wrong you think I have acted; you cannot think me worse than I think myself, now my eyes are opened." Here her sobs came choking up her voice.

"Nay," Margaret began, "I have no right to—"

"Yes, Margaret, you have a right to judge; you cannot help it; only in your judgment remember mercy, as the Bible says. You, who have been always good, cannot tell how easy it is at first to go a little wrong, and then how hard it is to go back. Oh! I little thought when I was first pleased with Mr. Carson's speeches, how it would all end; perhaps in the death of him I love better than life."

She burst into a passion of tears. The feelings pent up through the day would have vent. But checking herself with a strong effort, and looking up at Margaret as piteously as if those calm, stony eyes could see her imploring face, she added,

"I must not cry; I must not give way; there will be time enough for that hereafter, if—I only wanted you to speak kindly to me, Margaret, for I am very, very wretched; more wretched than any one can ever know; more wretched, I sometimes fancy, than I have deserved,—but that's wrong, isn't it, Margaret? Oh! I have done wrong, and I am punished; you cannot tell how much."

Who could resist her voice, her tones of misery, of humility? Who would refuse the kindness for which she begged so penitently? Not Margaret. The old friendly manner came back. With it, may be, more of tenderness.

"Oh! Margaret, do you think he can be saved; do you think they can find him guilty if Will comes forward as a witness? Won't that be a good *alibi*?"

Margaret did not answer for a moment.

"Oh, speak! Margaret," said Mary, with anxious impatience.

"I know nought about law, or *alibis*," replied Margaret, meekly; "but, Mary, as grandfather says, aren't you building too much on what Jane Wilson has told you about his going with Will? Poor soul, she's gone dateless, I think, with care, and watching, and over-much trouble; and who can wonder? Or Jem may have told her he was going, by way of a blind."

"You don't know Jem," said Mary, starting from her seat in a hurried manner, "or you would not say so."

"I hope I may be wrong; but think, Mary, how much there is against him. The shot was fired with his gun; he it was as threatened Mr. Carson not many days before; he was absent from home at that very time, as we know, and, as I'm much afeared, some one will be called on to prove; and there's no one else to share suspicion with him."

Mary heaved a deep sigh.

"But, Margaret, he did not do it," Mary again asserted.

Margaret looked unconvinced.

"I can do no good, I see, by saying so, for none on you believe me, and I won't say so again till I can prove it. Monday morning I'll go to Liverpool. I shall be at hand for the trial. Oh dear! dear! And I will find Will; and then, Margaret, I think you'll be sorry for being so stubborn about Jem."

"Don't fly off, dear Mary; I'd give a deal to be wrong. And now I'm going to be plain spoken. You'll want money. Them lawyers is no better than a spunge for sucking up money; let alone your hunting out Will, and your keep in Liverpool, and what not. You must take some of the mint I've got laid by in the old tea-pot. You have no right to refuse, for I offer it to Jem, not to you; it's for his purposes you're to use it."

"I know—I see. Thank you, Margaret; you're a kind one, at any rate. I take it for Jem; and I'll do my very best with it for him. Not all, though; don't think I'll take all. They'll pay me for my keep. I'll take this," accepting a sovereign from the hoard which Margaret produced out of its accustomed place in the cupboard. "Your grandfather will pay the lawyer. I'll have nought to do with him," shuddering as she remembered Job's words, about lawyers' skill in always discovering the truth, sooner or later; and knowing what was the secret she had to hide.

"Bless you! don't make such ado about it," said Margaret, cutting short Mary's thanks. "I sometimes think there's two sides to the commandment; and that we may say, 'Let others do unto you, as you would do unto them,' for pride often prevents our giving others a great deal of pleasure, in not letting them be kind, when their hearts are longing to help; and when we ourselves should wish to do just the same, if we were in their place. Oh! how often I've been hurt, by being coldly told by persons not to trouble myself about their care, or sorrow, when I saw them in great grief, and wanted to be of comfort. Our Lord Jesus was not above letting folk minister to Him, for He knew how happy it makes one to do aught for another. It's the happiest work on earth."

Mary had been too much engrossed by watching what was passing in the street to attend very closely to that which Margaret was saying. From her seat she could see out of the window pretty plainly, and she caught sight of a gentleman walking alongside of Job, evidently in earnest conversation with him, and looking keen and penetrating enough to be a lawyer. Job was laying down something to be attended to she could see, by his up-lifted fore-finger, and his whole gesture; then he pointed and nodded across the street to his own house, as if inducing his companion to come in. Mary dreaded lest he should, and she be subjected to a closer cross-examination than she had hitherto undergone, as to why she was so certain that Jem was innocent. She feared he was coming; he stepped a little towards the spot. No! it was only to make way for a child, tottering along, whom Mary had overlooked. Now Job took him by the button, so earnestly familiar had he grown. The gentleman looked "fidging fain" to be gone, but submitted in a manner that made Mary like him in spite of his profession. Then came a volley of last words, answered by briefest nods, and monosyllables; and then the stranger went off with redoubled quickness of pace, and Job crossed the street with a little satisfied air of importance on his kindly face.

"Well! Mary," said he on entering, "I've seen the lawyer, not Mr. Cheshire though; trials for murder, it seems, are not his line o' business. But he gived me a note to another 'torney; a fine fellow enough, only too much of a talker; I could hardly get a word in, he cut me so short. However, I've just been going over the principal points again to him; may be you saw us? I wanted him just to come over and speak to you himsel, Mary, but he was pressed for time; and he said your evidence would not be much either here or there. He's going to the 'sizes first train on Monday morning, and will see Jem, and hear the ins and outs from him, and he's gived me his address, Mary, and you and Will are to call on him (Will 'special) on Monday at two o'clock. Thou'rt taking it in, Mary; thou'rt to call on him in Liverpool at two, Monday afternoon?"

Job had reason to doubt if she fully understood him; for all this minuteness of detail, these satisfactory arrangements, as he considered them, only seemed to bring the circumstances in which she was placed more vividly home to Mary. They convinced her that it was real, and not all a dream, as she had sunk into fancying it for a few minutes, while sitting in the old accustomed place, her body enjoying the rest, and her frame sustained by food, and listening to Margaret's calm voice. The gentleman she had just beheld would see and question Jem in a few hours, and what would be the result?

Monday: that was the day after to-morrow, and on Tuesday, life and death would be tremendous realities to her lover; or else death would be an awful certainty to her father.

No wonder Job went over his main points again:—

"Monday; at two o'clock, mind; and here's his card. 'Mr. Bridgenorth, 41, Renshaw Street, Liverpool.' He'll be lodging there."

Job ceased talking, and the silence roused Mary up to thank him.

"You're very kind, Job; very. You and Margaret won't desert me, come what will."

"Pooh! pooh! wench; don't lose heart, just as I'm beginning to get it. He seems to think a deal on Will's evidence. You're sure, girls, you're under no mistake about Will?"

"I'm sure," said Mary, "he went straight from here, purposing to go see his uncle at the Isle of Man, and be back Sunday night, ready for the ship sailing on Tuesday."

"So am I," said Margaret. "And the ship's name was the *John Cropper*, and he lodged where I told Mary before. Have you got it down, Mary?" Mary wrote it on the back of Mr. Bridgenorth's card.

"He was not over-willing to go," said she, as she wrote, "for he knew little about his uncle, and said he didn't care if he never knowed more. But he said kinsfolk was kinsfolk, and promises was promises, so he'd go for a day or so, and then it would be over."

Margaret had to go and practise some singing in town; so, though loth to depart and be alone, Mary bade her friends good-bye.

CHAPTER XXIV - WITH THE DYING.

"O sad and solemn is the trembling watch
Of those who sit and count the heavy hours,
Beside the fevered sleep of one they love!
O awful is it in the hushed mid night,
While gazing on the pallid, moveless form,
To start and ask, 'Is it now sleep—or death?'"

ANONYMOUS.

Mary could not be patient in her loneliness; so much painful thought weighed on her mind; the very house was haunted with memories and foreshadowings.

Having performed all duties to Jem, as far as her weak powers, yet loving heart could act; and a black veil being drawn over her father's past, present, and future life, beyond which she could not penetrate to judge of any filial service she ought to render; her mind unconsciously sought after some course of action in which she might engage. Any thing, any thing, rather than leisure for reflection.

And then came up the old feeling which first bound Ruth to Naomi; the love they both held towards one object; and Mary felt that her cares would be most lightened by being of use, or of comfort to his mother. So she once more locked up the house, and set off towards Ancoats; rushing along with down-cast head, for fear lest any one should recognise her and arrest her progress.

Jane Wilson sat quietly in her chair as Mary entered; so quietly, as to strike one by the contrast it presented to her usual bustling and nervous manner.

She looked very pale and wan; but the quietness was the thing that struck Mary most. She did not rise as Mary came in, but sat still and said something in so gentle, so feeble a voice, that Mary did not catch it.

Mrs. Davenport, who was there, plucked Mary by the gown, and whispered,

"Never heed her; she's worn out, and best let alone. I'll tell you all about it, up-stairs."

But Mary, touched by the anxious look with which Mrs. Wilson gazed at her, as if awaiting the answer to some question, went forward to listen to the speech she was again repeating.

"What is this? will you tell me?"

Then Mary looked and saw another ominous slip of parchment in the mother's hand, which she was rolling up and down in a tremulous manner between her fingers.

Mary's heart sickened within her, and she could not speak.

"What is it?" she repeated. "Will you tell me?" She still looked at Mary, with the same child-like gaze of wonder and patient entreaty.

What could she answer?

"I telled ye not to heed her," said Mrs. Davenport, a little angrily. "She knows well enough what it is,—too well, belike. I was not in when they sarved it; but Mrs. Heming (her as lives next door) was, and she spelled out the meaning, and made it all clear to Mrs. Wilson. It's a summons to be a witness on Jem's trial—Mrs. Heming thinks, to swear to the gun; for, yo see, there's nobbut[1] her as can testify to its being his, and she let on so easily to the policeman that it was his, that there's no getting off her word now. Poor body; she takes it very hard, I dare say!"

Mrs. Wilson had waited patiently while this whispered speech was being uttered, imagining, perhaps, that it would end in some explanation addressed to her. But when both were silent, though their eyes, without speech or language, told their hearts' pity, she spoke again in the same unaltered gentle voice (so different from the irritable impatience she had been ever apt to show to every one except her husband,—he who had wedded her, broken-down and injured)—in a voice so different, I say, from the old, hasty manner, she spoke now the same anxious words,

"What is this? Will you tell me?"

"Yo'd better give it me at once, Mrs. Wilson, and let me put it out of your sight.—Speak to her, Mary, wench, and ask for a sight on it; I've tried, and better-tried to get it from her, and she takes no heed of words, and I'm loth to pull it by force out of her hands."

Mary drew the little "cricket"[2] out from under the dresser, and sat down at Mrs. Wilson's knee, and, coaxing one of her tremulous, ever-moving hands into hers, began to rub it soothingly; there was a little resistance—a very little, but that was all; and presently, in the nervous movement of the imprisoned hand, the parchment fell to the ground.

Mary calmly and openly picked it up without any attempt at concealment, and quietly placing it in sight of the anxious eyes that followed it with a kind of spell-bound dread, went on with her soothing caresses.

"She has had no sleep for many nights," said the girl to Mrs. Davenport, "and all this woe and sorrow,—it's no wonder."

"No, indeed!" Mrs. Davenport answered.

---

[1] "Nobbut," none-but. "No man sigh evere God no but the oon bigetun sone."—Wiclif's Version.

[2] "Cricket," a stool.

"We must get her fairly to bed; we must get her undressed, and all; and trust to God, in His mercy, to send her to sleep, or else,—"

For, you see, they spoke before her as if she were not there; her heart was so far away.

Accordingly they almost lifted her from the chair in which she sat motionless, and taking her up as gently as a mother carries her sleeping baby, they undressed her poor, worn form, and laid her in the little bed up-stairs. They had once thought of placing her in Jem's bed, to be out of sight or sound of any disturbance of Alice's, but then again they remembered the shock she might receive in awakening in so unusual a place, and also that Mary, who intended to keep vigil that night in the house of mourning, would find it difficult to divide her attention in the possible cases that might ensue.

So they laid her, as I said before, on that little pallet-bed; and, as they were slowly withdrawing from the bed-side, hoping and praying that she might sleep, and forget for a time her heavy burden, she looked wistfully after Mary, and whispered,

"You haven't told me what it is. What is it?"

And gazing in her face for the expected answer, her eye-lids slowly closed, and she fell into a deep, heavy sleep, almost as profound a rest as death.

Mrs. Davenport went her way, and Mary was alone,—for I cannot call those who sleep allies against the agony of thought which solitude sometimes brings up.

She dreaded the night before her. Alice might die; the doctor had that day declared her case hopeless, and not far from death; and at times the terror, so natural to the young, not of death, but of the remains of the dead, came over Mary; and she bent and listened anxiously for the long-drawn, pausing breath of the sleeping Alice.

Or Mrs. Wilson might awake in a state which Mary dreaded to anticipate, and anticipated while she dreaded;—in a state of complete delirium. Already her senses had been severely stunned by the full explanation of what was required of her,—of what she had to prove against her son, her Jem, her only child,—which Mary could not doubt the officious Mrs. Heming had given; and what if in dreams (that land into which no sympathy or love can penetrate with another, either to share its bliss or its agony,—that land whose scenes are unspeakable terrors, are hidden mysteries, are priceless treasures to one alone,—that land where alone I may see, while yet I tarry here, the sweet looks of my dead child),—what if, in the horrors of her dreams, her brain should go still more astray, and she should waken crazy with her visions, and the terrible reality that begot them?

How much worse is anticipation sometimes than reality! How Mary dreaded that night, and how calmly it passed by! Even more so than if Mary had not had such claims upon her care!

Anxiety about them deadened her own peculiar anxieties. She thought of the sleepers whom she was watching, till overpowered herself by the want of rest, she fell off into short slumbers in which the night wore imperceptibly away. To be sure Alice spoke, and sang, during her waking moments, like the child she deemed herself; but so happily with the dearly-loved ones around her, with the scent of the heather, and the song of the wild bird hovering about her in imagination—with old scraps of ballads, or old snatches of primitive versions of the Psalms (such as are sung in country churches half draperied over with ivy, and where the running brook, or the murmuring wind among the trees makes fit accompaniment to the chorus of human voices uttering praise and thanksgiving to their God)—that the speech and the song gave comfort and good cheer to the listener's heart, and the gray dawn began to dim the light of the rush-candle, before Mary thought it possible that day was already trembling on the horizon.

Then she got up from the chair where she had been dozing, and went, half-asleep, to the window to assure herself that morning was at hand. The streets were unusually quiet with a Sabbath stillness. No factory bells that morning; no early workmen going to their labours; no slip-shod girls cleaning the windows of the little shops which broke the monotony of the street; instead, you might see here and there some operative sallying forth for a breath of country air, or some father leading out his wee toddling bairns for the unwonted pleasure of a walk with "Daddy," in the clear frosty morning. Men with more leisure on week-days would perhaps have walked quicker than they did through the fresh sharp air of this Sunday morning; but to them there was a pleasure, an absolute refreshment in the dawdling gait they, one and all of them, had.

To be sure, there were one or two passengers on that morning whose objects were less innocent and less praiseworthy than those of the people I have already mentioned, and whose animal state of mind and body clashed jarringly on the peacefulness of the day; but upon them I will not dwell: as you and I, and almost every one, I think, may send up our individual cry of self-reproach that we have not done all that we could for the stray and wandering ones of our brethren.

When Mary turned from the window, she went to the bed of each sleeper, to look and listen. Alice looked perfectly quiet and happy in her slumber, and her face seemed to have become much more youthful during her painless approach to death.

Mrs. Wilson's countenance was stamped with the anxiety of the last few days, although she, too, appeared sleeping soundly; but as Mary gazed on her, trying to trace a likeness to her son in her face, she awoke and looked up into Mary's eyes, while the expression of consciousness came back into her own.

Both were silent for a minute or two. Mary's eyes had fallen beneath that penetrating gaze, in which the agony of memory seemed every moment to find fuller vent.

"Is it a dream?" the mother asked at last in a low voice.

"No!" replied Mary, in the same tone.

Mrs. Wilson hid her face in the pillow.

She was fully conscious of every thing this morning; it was evident that the stunning effect of the subpœna, which had affected her so much last night in her weak, worn-out state, had passed away. Mary offered no opposition when she indicated by languid gesture and action that she wished to rise. A sleepless bed is a haunted place.

When she was dressed with Mary's help, she stood by Alice for a minute or two, looking at the slumberer.

"How happy she is!" said she, quietly and sadly.

All the time that Mary was getting breakfast ready, and performing every other little domestic office she could think of, to add to the comfort of Jem's mother, Mrs. Wilson sat still in the arm-chair, watching her silently. Her old irritation of temper and manner seemed to have suddenly disappeared, or perhaps she was too depressed in body and mind to show it.

Mary told her all that had been done with regard to Mr. Bridgenorth; all her own plans for seeking out Will; all her hopes; and concealed as well as she could all the doubts and fears that would arise unbidden. To this Mrs. Wilson listened without much remark, but with deep interest and perfect comprehension. When Mary ceased she sighed and said, "Oh wench! I am his mother, and yet I do so little, I can do so little! That's what frets me! I seem like a child as sees its mammy ill, and moans and cries its little heart out, yet does nought to help. I think my sense has left me all at once, and I can't even find strength to cry like the little child."

Hereupon she broke into a feeble wail of self-reproach, that her outward show of misery was not greater; as if any cries, or tears, or loud-spoken words could have told of such pangs at the heart as that look, and that thin, piping, altered voice!

But think of Mary and what she was enduring! Picture to yourself (for I cannot tell you) the armies of thoughts that met and clashed in her brain; and then imagine the effort it cost her to be calm, and quiet, and even, in a faint way, cheerful and smiling at times.

After a while she began to stir about in her own mind for some means of sparing the poor mother the trial of appearing as a witness in the matter of the gun. She had made no allusion to her summons this morning, and Mary almost thought she must have forgotten it; and surely some means might be found to prevent that additional sorrow. She must see Job about it; nay, if necessary, she must see Mr. Bridgenorth, with all his truth-compelling powers; for, indeed, she had so struggled and triumphed (though a sadly-bleeding victor at heart) over herself these two last days, had so concealed agony, and hidden her inward woe and bewilderment, that she began to take confidence, and to have faith in her own powers of meeting any one with a passably fair show, whatever might be rending her life beneath the cloak of her deception.

Accordingly, as soon as Mrs. Davenport came in after morning church, to ask after the two lone women, and she had heard the report Mary had to give (so much better as regarded Mrs. Wilson than what they had feared the night before it would have been)—as soon as this kind-hearted, grateful woman came in, Mary, telling her her purpose, went off to fetch the doctor who attended Alice.

He was shaking himself after his morning's round, and happy in the anticipation of his Sunday's dinner; but he was a good-tempered man, who found it difficult to keep down his jovial easiness even by the bed of sickness or death. He had mischosen his profession; for it was his delight to see every one around him in full enjoyment of life.

However, he subdued his face to the proper expression of sympathy, befitting a doctor listening to a patient, or a patient's friend (and Mary's sad, pale, anxious face might be taken for either the one or the other).

"Well, my girl! and what brings you here?" said he, as he entered his surgery. "Not on your own account, I hope."

"I wanted you to come and see Alice Wilson,—and then I thought you would may be take a look at Mrs. Wilson."

He bustled on his hat and coat, and followed Mary instantly.

After shaking his head over Alice (as if it was a mournful thing for one so pure and good, so true, although so humble a Christian, to be nearing her desired haven), and muttering the accustomed words intended to destroy hope, and prepare anticipation, he went in compliance with Mary's look to ask the usual questions of Mrs. Wilson, who sat passively in her arm-chair.

She answered his questions, and submitted to his examination.

"How do you think her?" asked Mary, eagerly.

"Why—a," began he, perceiving that he was desired to take one side in his answer, and unable to find out whether his listener was anxious for a favourable verdict or otherwise; but thinking it most probable that she would desire the former, he continued,

"She is weak, certainly; the natural result of such a shock as the arrest of her son would be,—for I understand this James Wilson, who murdered Mr. Carson, was her son. Sad thing to have such a reprobate in the family."

"You say '*who murdered*,' sir!" said Mary, indignantly. "He is only taken up on suspicion, and many have no doubt of his innocence—those who know him, sir."

"Ah, well, well! doctors have seldom time to read newspapers, and I dare say I'm not very correct in my story. I dare say he's innocent; I'm sure I had no right to say otherwise,—only words slip out.—No! indeed, young woman, I see no cause for apprehension about this poor creature in the next room;—weak—certainly; but a day or two's good nursing will set her up, and I'm sure you're a good nurse, my dear, from your pretty, kind-hearted face,—I'll send a couple of pills and a draught, but don't alarm yourself,—there's no occasion, I assure you."

"But you don't think her fit to go to Liverpool?" asked Mary, still in the anxious tone of one who wishes earnestly for some particular decision.

"To Liverpool—yes," replied he. "A short journey like that could not fatigue, and might distract her thoughts. Let her go by all means,—it would be the very thing for her."

"Oh, sir!" burst out Mary, almost sobbing; "I did so hope you would say she was too ill to go."

"Whew—" said he, with a prolonged whistle, trying to understand the case, but being, as he said, no reader of newspapers, utterly unaware of the peculiar reasons there might be for so apparently unfeeling a wish,—"Why did you not tell me so sooner? It might certainly do her harm in her weak state; there is always some risk attending journeys—draughts, and what not. To her, they might prove very injurious,—very. I disapprove of journeys, or excitement, in all cases where the patient is in the low, fluttered state in which Mrs. Wilson is. If you take *my* advice, you will certainly put a stop to all thoughts of going to Liverpool." He really had completely changed his opinion, though quite unconsciously; so desirous was he to comply with the wishes of others.

"Oh, sir, thank you! And will you give me a certificate of her being unable to go, if the lawyer says we must have one? The lawyer, you know," continued she, seeing him look puzzled, "who is to defend Jem,—it was as a witness against him—"

"My dear girl!" said he, almost angrily, "why did you not state the case fully at first? one minute would have done it,—and my dinner waiting all this time. To be sure she can't go,—it would be madness to think of it; if her evidence could have done good, it would have been a different thing. Come to me for the certificate any time; that is to say, if the lawyer advises you. I second the lawyer; take counsel with both the learned professions—ha, ha, ha,—"

And laughing at his own joke, he departed, leaving Mary accusing herself of stupidity in having imagined that every one was as well acquainted with the facts concerning the trial as she was herself; for indeed she had never doubted that the doctor would have been aware of the purpose of poor Mrs. Wilson's journey to Liverpool.

Presently she went to Job (the ever-ready Mrs. Davenport keeping watch over the two old women), and told him her fears, her plans, and her proceedings.

To her surprise he shook his head doubtfully.

"It may have an awkward look, if we keep her back. Lawyers is up to tricks."

"But it's no trick," said Mary. "She is so poorly, she was last night, at least; and to-day she's so faded and weak."

"Poor soul! I dare say. I only mean for Jem's sake; as so much is known, it won't do now to hang back. But I'll ask Mr. Bridgenorth. I'll e'en take your doctor's advice. Yo tarry at home, and I'll come to yo in an hour's time. Go thy ways, wench."

CHAPTER XXV - MRS. WILSON'S DETERMINATION.

"Something there was, what, none presumed to say,
Clouds lightly passing on a smiling day,—
Whispers and hints which went from ear to ear,
And mixed reports no judge on earth could clear."

CRABBE.

"Curious conjectures he may always make,
And either side of dubious questions take."

IB.

Mary went home. Oh! how her head did ache, and how dizzy her brain was growing! But there would be time enough she felt for giving way, hereafter.

So she sat quiet and still by an effort; sitting near the window, and looking out of it, but seeing nothing, when all at once she caught sight of something which roused her up, and made her draw back.

But it was too late. She had been seen.

Sally Leadbitter flaunted into the little dingy room, making it gaudy with the Sunday excess of colouring in her dress.

She was really curious to see Mary; her connexion with a murderer seemed to have made her into a sort of *lusus naturæ*, and was almost, by some, expected to have made a change in her personal appearance, so earnestly did they stare at her. But Mary had been too much absorbed this last day or two to notice this.

Now Sally had a grand view, and looked her over and over (a very different thing from looking her through and through), and almost learnt her off by heart;—"her every-day gown (Hoyle's print you know, that lilac thing with the high body) she was so fond of; a little black silk handkerchief just knotted round her neck, like a boy; her hair all taken back from her face, as if she wanted to keep her head cool—she would always keep that hair of hers so long; and her hands twitching continually about."

Such particulars would make Sally into a Gazette Extraordinary the next morning at the work-room, and were worth coming for, even if little else could be extracted from Mary.

"Why, Mary!" she began. "Where have you hidden yourself? You never showed your face all yesterday at Miss Simmonds'. You don't fancy we think any the worse of you for what's come and gone. Some on us, indeed, were a bit sorry for the poor young man, as lies stiff and cold for your sake, Mary; but we shall ne'er cast it up against you. Miss Simmonds, too, will be mighty put out if you don't come, for there's a deal of mourning, agait."

"I can't," Mary said, in a low voice. "I don't mean ever to come again."

"Why, Mary!" said Sally, in unfeigned surprise. "To be sure you'll have to be in Liverpool, Tuesday, and may be Wednesday; but after that you'll surely come, and tell us all about it. Miss Simmonds knows you'll have to be off those two days. But between you and me, she's a bit of a gossip, and will like hearing all how and about the trial, well enough to let you off very easy for your being absent a day or two. Besides, Betsy Morgan was saying yesterday, she shouldn't wonder but you'd prove quite an attraction to customers. Many a one would come and have their gowns made by Miss Simmonds just to catch a glimpse at you, at after the trial's over. Really, Mary, you'll turn out quite a heroine."

The little fingers twitched worse than ever; the large soft eyes looked up pleadingly into Sally's face; but she went on in the same strain, not from any unkind or cruel feeling towards Mary, but solely because she was incapable of comprehending her suffering.

She had been shocked, of course, at Mr. Carson's death, though at the same time the excitement was rather pleasant than otherwise; and dearly now would she have enjoyed the conspicuous notice which Mary was sure to receive.

"How shall you like being cross-examined, Mary?"

"Not at all," answered Mary, when she found she must answer.

"La! what impudent fellows those lawyers are! And their clerks, too, not a bit better. I shouldn't wonder" (in a comforting tone, and really believing she was giving comfort) "if you picked up a new sweetheart in Liverpool. What gown are you going in, Mary?"

"Oh, I don't know and don't care," exclaimed Mary, sick and weary of her visitor.

"Well, then! take my advice, and go in that blue merino. It's old to be sure, and a bit worn at elbows, but folk won't notice that, and th' colour suits you. Now mind, Mary. And I'll lend you my black watered scarf," added she, really good-naturedly, according to her sense of things, and withal, a little bit pleased at the idea of her pet article of dress figuring away on the person of a witness at a trial for murder.

"I'll bring it to-morrow before you start."

"No, don't!" said Mary; "thank you, but I don't want it."

"Why, what can you wear? I know all your clothes as well as I do my own, and what is there you can wear? Not your old plaid shawl, I do hope? You would not fancy this I have on, more nor the scarf, would you?" said she, brightening up at the thought, and willing to lend it, or any thing else.

"Oh Sally! don't go on talking a-that-ns; how can I think on dress at such a time? When it's a matter of life and death to Jem?"

"Bless the girl! It's Jem, is it? Well now, I thought there was some sweetheart in the back-ground, when you flew off so with Mr. Carson. Then what in the name of goodness made him shoot Mr. Harry? After you had given up going with him, I mean? Was he afraid you'd be on again?"

"How dare you say he shot Mr. Harry?" asked Mary, firing up from the state of languid indifference into which she had sunk while Sally had been settling about her dress. "But it's no matter what you think as did not know him. What grieves me is, that people should go on thinking him guilty as did know him," she said, sinking back into her former depressed tone and manner.

"And don't you think he did it?" asked Sally.

Mary paused; she was going on too fast with one so curious and so unscrupulous. Besides she remembered how even she herself had, at first, believed him guilty; and she felt it was not for her to cast stones at those who, on similar evidence, inclined to the same belief. None had given him much benefit of a doubt. None had faith in his innocence. None but his mother; and there the heart loved more than the head reasoned, and her yearning affection had never for an instant entertained the idea that her Jem was a murderer. But Mary disliked the whole conversation; the subject, the manner in which it was treated, were all painful, and she had a repugnance to the person with whom she spoke.

She was thankful, therefore, when Job Legh's voice was heard at the door, as he stood with the latch in his hand, talking to a neighbour, and when Sally jumped up in vexation and said, "There's that old fogey coming in here, as I'm alive! Did your father set him to look after you while he was away? or what brings the old chap here? However, I'm off; I never could abide either him or his prim granddaughter. Goodbye, Mary."

So far in a whisper, then louder,

"If you think better of my offer about the scarf, Mary, just step in to-morrow before nine, and you're quite welcome to it."

She and Job passed each other at the door, with mutual looks of dislike, which neither took any pains to conceal.

"Yon's a bold, bad girl," said Job to Mary.

"She's very good-natured," replied Mary, too honourable to abuse a visitor who had only that instant crossed her threshold, and gladly dwelling on the good quality most apparent in Sally's character.

"Ay, ay! good-natured, generous, jolly, full of fun; there are a number of other names for the good qualities the devil leaves his childer, as baits to catch gudgeons with. D'ye think folk could be led astray by one who was every way bad? Howe'er, that's not what I came to talk about. I've seen Mr. Bridgenorth, and he is in a manner of the same mind as me; he thinks it would have an awkward look, and might tell against the poor lad on his trial; still if she's ill she's ill, and it can't be helped."

"I don't know if she's so bad as all that," said Mary, who began to dread her part in doing any thing which might tell against her poor lover.

"Will you come and see her, Job? The doctor seemed to say as I liked, not as he thought."

"That's because he had no great thought on the subject, either one way or t'other," replied Job, whose contempt for medical men pretty nearly equalled his respect for lawyers. "But I'll go and welcome. I han not seen th' oud ladies since their sorrows, and it's but manners to go and ax after them. Come along."

The room at Mrs. Wilson's had that still, changeless look you must have often observed in the house of sickness or mourning. No particular employment going on; people watching and waiting rather than acting, unless in the more sudden and violent attacks; what little movement is going on, so noiseless and hushed; the furniture all arranged and stationary, with a view to the comfort of the afflicted; the window-blinds drawn down to keep out the disturbing variety of a sun-beam; the same saddened, serious look on the faces of the in-dwellers; you fall back into the same train of thought with all these associations, and forget the street, the outer world, in the contemplation of the one stationary, absorbing interest within.

Mrs. Wilson sat quietly in her chair, with just the same look Mary had left on her face; Mrs. Davenport went about with creaking shoes, which made all the more noise from her careful and lengthened tread, annoying the ears of those who were well, in this instance, far more than the dulled senses of the sick and the sorrowful. Alice's voice still was going on cheerfully in the upper room with incessant talking and little laughs to herself, or perhaps in sympathy with her unseen companions; "unseen," I say, in preference to "fancied," for who knows whether God does not permit the forms of those who were dearest when living, to hover round the bed of the dying?

Job spoke, and Mrs. Wilson answered.

So quietly, that it was unnatural under the circumstances. It made a deeper impression on the old man than any token of mere bodily illness could have done. If she had raved in delirium, or moaned in fever, he could have spoken after his wont, and given his opinion, his advice, and his consolation; now he was awed into silence.

At length he pulled Mary aside into a corner of the house-place where Mrs. Wilson was sitting, and began to talk to her.

"Yo're right, Mary! She's no ways fit to go to Liverpool, poor soul. Now I've seen her, I only wonder the doctor could ha' been unsettled in his mind at th' first. Choose how it goes wi' poor Jem, she cannot go. One way or another it will soon be over, and best to leave her in the state she is till then."

"I was sure you would think so," said Mary.

But they were reckoning without their host. They esteemed her senses gone, while, in fact, they were only inert, and could not convey impressions rapidly to the over-burdened, troubled brain. They had not noticed that her eyes had followed them (mechanically it seemed at first) as they had moved away to the corner of the room; that her face, hitherto so changeless, had begun to work with one or two of the old symptoms of impatience.

But when they were silent she stood up, and startled them almost as if a dead person had spoken, by saying clearly and decidedly—"I go to Liverpool. I hear you and your plans; and I tell you I shall go to Liverpool. If my words are to kill my son, they have already gone forth out of my mouth, and nought can bring them back. But I will have faith. Alice (up above) has often telled me I wanted faith, and now I will have it. They cannot—they will not kill my child, my only child. I will not be afeared. Yet, oh! I am so sick with terror. But if he is to die, think ye not that I will see him again; ay! see him at his trial? When all are hating him, he shall have his poor mother near him, to give him all the comfort, eyes, and looks, and tears, and a heart that is dead to all but him, can give; his poor old mother, who knows how free he is from sin—in the sight of man at least. They'll let me go to him, maybe, the very minute it's over; and I know many Scripture texts (though you would not think it), that may keep up his heart. I missed seeing him ere he went to yon prison, but nought shall keep me away again one minute when I can see his face; for maybe the minutes are numbered, and the count but small. I know I can be a comfort to him, poor lad. You would not think it, now, but he'd alway speak as kind and soft to me as if he were courting me, like. He loved me above a bit; and am I to leave him now to dree all the cruel slander they'll put upon him? I can pray for him at each hard word they say against him, if I can do nought else; and he'll know what his mother is doing for him, poor lad, by the look on my face."

Still they made some look, or gesture of opposition to her wishes. She turned sharp round on Mary, the old object of her pettish attacks, and said,

"Now, wench! once for all! I tell yo this. *He* could never guide me; and he'd sense enough not to try. What he could na do, don't you try. I shall go to Liverpool to-morrow, and find my lad, and stay with him through thick and thin; and if he dies, why, perhaps, God of His mercy will take me too. The grave is a sure cure for an aching heart."

She sank back in her chair, quite exhausted by the sudden effort she had made; but if they even offered to speak, she cut them short (whatever the subject might be), with the repetition of the same words, "I shall go to Liverpool."

No more could be said, the doctor's opinion had been so undecided; Mr. Bridgenorth had given his legal voice in favour of her going, and Mary was obliged to relinquish the idea of persuading her to remain at home, if indeed under all the circumstances it could be thought desirable.

"Best way will be," said Job, "for me to hunt out Will, early to-morrow morning, and yo, Mary, come at after with Jane Wilson. I know a decent woman where yo two can have a bed, and where we may meet together when I've found Will, afore going to Mr. Bridgenorth's at two o'clock; for, I can tell him, I'll not trust none of his clerks for hunting up Will, if Jem's life is to depend on it."

Now Mary disliked this plan inexpressibly; her dislike was partly grounded on reason, and partly on feeling. She could not bear the idea of deputing to any one the active measures necessary to be taken in order to save Jem. She felt as if they were her duty, her right. She durst not trust to any one the completion of her plan; they might not have energy, or perseverance, or desperation enough to follow out the slightest chance; and her love would endow her with all these qualities, independently of the terrible alternative which awaited her in case all failed and Jem was condemned. No one could have her motives; and consequently no one could have her sharpened brain, her despairing determination. Besides (only that was purely selfish), she could not endure the suspense of remaining quiet, and only knowing the result when all was accomplished.

So with vehemence and impatience she rebutted every reason Job adduced for his plan; and of course, thus opposed, by what appeared to him wilfulness, he became more resolute, and angry words were exchanged, and a feeling of estrangement rose up between them, for a time, as they walked homewards.

But then came in Margaret with her gentleness, like an angel of peace, so calm and reasonable, that both felt ashamed of their irritation, and tacitly left the decision to her (only, by the way, I think Mary could never have submitted if it had gone against her, penitent and tearful as was her manner now to Job, the good old man who was helping her to work for Jem, although they differed as to the manner).

"Mary had better go," said Margaret to her grandfather, in a low tone, "I know what she's feeling, and it will be a comfort to her soon, may be, to think she did all she could herself. She would perhaps fancy it might have been different; do, grandfather, let her."

Margaret had still, you see, little or no belief in Jem's innocence; and besides, she thought if Mary saw Will, and heard herself from him that Jem had not been with him that Thursday night, it would in a measure break the force of the blow which was impending.

"Let me lock up house, grandfather, for a couple of days, and go and stay with Alice. It's but little one like me can do, I know" (she added softly); "but, by the blessing o' God, I'll do it and welcome; and here comes one kindly use o' money, I can hire them as will do for her what I cannot. Mrs. Davenport is a willing body, and one who knows sorrow and sickness, and I can pay her for her time, and keep her there pretty near altogether. So let that be settled. And you take Mrs. Wilson, dear grandad, and let Mary go find Will, and you can all meet together at after, and I'm sure I wish you luck."

Job consented with only a few dissenting grunts; but on the whole, with a very good grace for an old man who had been so positive only a few minutes before.

Mary was thankful for Margaret's interference. She did not speak, but threw her arms round Margaret's neck, and put up her rosy-red mouth to be kissed; and even Job was attracted by the pretty, child-like gesture; and when she drew near him, afterwards, like a little creature sidling up to some person whom it feels to have offended, he bent down and blessed her, as if she had been a child of his own.

To Mary the old man's blessing came like words of power.

CHAPTER XXVI - THE JOURNEY TO LIVERPOOL

"Like a bark upon the sea,
   Life is floating over death;
Above, below, encircling thee,
   Danger lurks in every breath.
Parted art thou from the grave
   Only by a plank most frail;
Tossed upon the restless wave,
   Sport of every fickle gale.
Let the skies be e'er so clear,
   And so calm and still the sea,
Shipwreck yet has he to fear,
   Who life's voyager will be."

RÜCKERT.

The early trains for Liverpool, on Monday morning, were crowded by attorneys, attorneys' clerks, plaintiffs, defendants, and witnesses, all going to the Assizes. They were a motley assembly, each with some cause for anxiety stirring at his heart; though, after all, that is saying little or nothing, for we are all of us in the same predicament through life; each with a fear and a hope from childhood to death. Among the passengers there was Mary Barton, dressed in the blue gown and obnoxious plaid shawl.

Common as railroads are now in all places as a means of transit, and especially in Manchester, Mary had never been on one before; and she felt bewildered by the hurry, the noise of people, and bells, and horns; the whiz and the scream of the arriving trains.

The very journey itself seemed to her a matter of wonder. She had a back seat, and looked towards the factory-chimneys, and the cloud of smoke which hovers over Manchester, with a feeling akin to the "Heimweh." She was losing sight of the familiar objects of her childhood for the first time; and unpleasant as those objects are to most, she yearned after them with some of the same sentiment which gives pathos to the thoughts of the emigrant.

The cloud-shadows which give beauty to Chat-Moss, the picturesque old houses of Newton, what were they to Mary, whose heart was full of many things? Yet she seemed to look at them earnestly as they glided past; but she neither saw nor heard.

She neither saw nor heard till some well-known names fell upon her ear.

Two lawyers' clerks were discussing the cases to come on that Assizes; of course, "the murder-case," as it had come to be termed, held a conspicuous place in their conversation.

They had no doubt of the result.

"Juries are always very unwilling to convict on circumstantial evidence, it is true," said one, "but here there can hardly be any doubt."

"If it had not been so clear a case," replied the other, "I should have said they were injudicious in hurrying on the trial so much. Still, more evidence might have been collected."

"They tell me," said the first speaker,—"the people in Gardener's office I mean,—that it was really feared the old gentleman would have gone out of his mind, if the trial had been delayed. He was with Mr. Gardener as many as seven times on Saturday, and called him up at night to suggest that some letter should be written, or something done to secure the verdict."

"Poor old man," answered his companion, "who can wonder?—an only son,—such a death,—the disagreeable circumstances attending it; I had not time to read the *Guardian* on Saturday, but I understand it was some dispute about a factory girl."

"Yes, some such person. Of course she'll be examined, and Williams will do it in style. I shall slip out from our court to hear him if I can hit the nick of time."

"And if you can get a place, you mean, for depend upon it the court will be crowded."

"Ay, ay, the ladies (sweet souls) will come in shoals to hear a trial for murder, and see the murderer, and watch the judge put on his black cap."

"And then go home and groan over the Spanish ladies who take delight in bull-fights—'such unfeminine creatures!'"

Then they went on to other subjects.

It was but another drop to Mary's cup; but she was nearly in that state which Crabbe describes,

"For when so full the cup of sorrows flows
Add but a drop, it instantly o'erflows."

And now they were in the tunnel!—and now they were in Liverpool; and she must rouse herself from the torpor of mind and body which was creeping over her; the result of much anxiety and fatigue, and several sleepless nights.

She asked a policeman the way to Milk House Yard, and following his directions with the *savoir faire* of a town-bred girl, she reached a little court leading out of a busy, thronged street, not far from the Docks.

When she entered the quiet little yard she stopped to regain her breath, and to gather strength, for her limbs trembled, and her heart beat violently.

All the unfavourable contingencies she had, until now, forbidden herself to dwell upon, came forward to her mind. The possibility, the bare possibility, of Jem being an accomplice in the murder; the still greater possibility that he had not fulfilled his intention of going part of the way with Will, but had been led off by some little accidental occurrence from his original intention; and that he had spent the evening with those, whom it was now too late to bring forward as witnesses.

But sooner or later she must know the truth; so taking courage she knocked at the door of a house.

"Is this Mrs. Jones's?" she inquired.

"Next door but one," was the curt answer.

And even this extra minute was a reprieve.

Mrs. Jones was busy washing, and would have spoken angrily to the person who knocked so gently at the door, if anger had been in her nature; but she was a soft, helpless kind of woman, and only sighed over the many interruptions she had had to her business that unlucky Monday morning.

But the feeling which would have been anger in a more impatient temper, took the form of prejudice against the disturber, whoever he or she might be.

Mary's fluttered and excited appearance strengthened this prejudice in Mrs. Jones's mind, as she stood, stripping the soap-suds off her arms, while she eyed her visitor, and waited to be told what her business was.

But no words would come. Mary's voice seemed choked up in her throat.

"Pray what do you want, young woman?" coldly asked Mrs. Jones at last.

"I want—Oh! is Will Wilson here?"

"No, he is not," replied Mrs. Jones, inclining to shut the door in her face.

"Is he not come back from the Isle of Man?" asked Mary, sickening.

"He never went; he stayed in Manchester too long; as perhaps you know, already."

And again the door seemed closing.

But Mary bent forwards with suppliant action (as some young tree bends, when blown by the rough, autumnal wind), and gasped out,

"Tell me—tell me—where is he?"

Mrs. Jones suspected some love affair, and, perhaps, one of not the most creditable kind; but the distress of the pale young creature before her was so obvious and so pitiable, that were she ever so sinful, Mrs. Jones could no longer uphold her short, reserved manner.

"He's gone this very morning, my poor girl. Step in, and I'll tell you about it."

"Gone!" cried Mary. "How gone? I must see him,—it's a matter of life and death: he can save the innocent from being hanged,—he cannot be gone,—how gone?"

"Sailed, my dear! sailed in the *John Cropper* this very blessed morning."

"Sailed!"

CHAPTER XXVII - IN THE LIVERPOOL DOCKS.

"Yon is our quay!
Hark to the clamour in that miry road,
Bounded and narrowed by yon vessel's load;
The lumbering wealth she empties round the place,
Package and parcel, hogshead, chest and case:
While the loud seaman and the angry hind,
Mingling in business, bellow to the wind."

CRABBE.

Mary staggered into the house. Mrs. Jones placed her tenderly in a chair, and there stood bewildered by her side.

"Oh, father! father!" muttered she, "what have you done?—What must I do? must the innocent die?—or he—whom I fear—I fear—oh! what am I saying?" said she, looking round affrighted, and seemingly reassured by Mrs. Jones's countenance, "I am so helpless, so weak,—but a poor girl after all. How can I tell what is right? Father! you have always been so kind to me,—and you to be—never mind—never mind, all will come right in the grave."

"Save us, and bless us!" exclaimed Mrs. Jones, "if I don't think she's gone out of her wits!"

"No, I'm not!" said Mary, catching at the words, and with a strong effort controlling the mind she felt to be wandering, while the red blood flushed to scarlet the heretofore white cheek, "I'm not out of my senses; there is so much to be done—so much—and no one but me to do it, you know,—though I can't rightly tell what it is," looking up with bewilderment into Mrs. Jones's face. "I must not go mad whatever comes—at least not yet. No!" (bracing herself up) "something may yet be done, and I must do it. Sailed! did you say? The *John Cropper*? Sailed?"

"Ay! she went out of dock last night, to be ready for the morning's tide."

"I thought she was not to sail till to-morrow," murmured Mary.

"So did Will (he's lodged here long, so we all call him 'Will')," replied Mrs. Jones. "The mate had told him so, I believe, and he never knew different till he got to Liverpool on Friday morning; but as soon as he heard, he gave up going to the Isle o' Man, and just ran over to Rhyl with the mate, one John Harris, as has friends a bit beyond Abergele; you may have heard him speak on him, for they are great chums, though I've my own opinion of Harris."

"And he's sailed?" repeated Mary, trying by repetition to realise the fact to herself.

"Ay, he went on board last night to be ready for the morning's tide, as I said afore, and my boy went to see the ship go down the river, and came back all agog with the sight. Here, Charley, Charley!" She called out loudly for her son: but Charley was one of those boys who are never "far to seek," as the Lancashire people say, when any thing is going on; a mysterious conversation, an unusual event, a fire, or a riot, any thing, in short; such boys are the little omnipresent people of this world.

Charley had, in fact, been spectator and auditor all this time; though for a little while he had been engaged in "dollying" and a few other mischievous feats in the washing line, which had prevented his attention from being fully given to his mother's conversation with the strange girl who had entered.

"Oh, Charley! there you are! Did you not see the *John Cropper* sail down the river this morning? Tell the young woman about it, for I think she hardly credits me."

"I saw her tugged down the river by a steam-boat, which comes to same thing," replied he.

"Oh! if I had but come last night!" moaned Mary. "But I never thought of it. I never thought but what he knew right when he said he would be back from the Isle of Man on Monday morning, and not afore—and now some one must die for my negligence!"

"Die!" exclaimed the lad. "How?"

"Oh! Will would have proved an *alibi*,—but he's gone, and what am I to do?"

"Don't give it up yet," cried the energetic boy, interested at once in the case; "let's have a try for him. We are but where we were if we fail."

Mary roused herself. The sympathetic "we" gave her heart and hope. "But what can be done? You say he's sailed; what can be done?" But she spoke louder, and in a more life-like tone.

"No! I did not say he'd sailed; mother said that, and women know nought about such matters. You see" (proud of his office of instructor, and insensibly influenced, as all about her were, by Mary's sweet, earnest, lovely countenance) "there's sand-banks at the mouth of the river, and ships can't get over them but at high-water; especially ships of heavy burden, like the *John Cropper*. Now, she was tugged down the river at low water, or pretty near, and will have to lie some time before the water will be high enough to float her over the banks. So hold up your head,—you've a chance yet, though may be but a poor one."

"But what must I do?" asked Mary, to whom all this explanation had been a vague mystery.

"Do!" said the boy, impatiently, "why, have not I told you? Only women (begging your pardon) are so stupid at understanding about any thing belonging to the sea;—you must get a boat, and make all haste, and sail after him,—after the *John Cropper*. You may overtake her, or you may not. It's just a chance; but she's heavy laden, and that's in your favour. She'll draw many feet of water."

Mary had humbly and eagerly (oh, how eagerly!) listened to this young Sir Oracle's speech; but try as she would, she could only understand that she must make haste, and sail—somewhere—

"I beg your pardon," (and her little acknowledgment of inferiority in this speech pleased the lad, and made him her still more zealous friend). "I beg your pardon," said she, "but I don't know where to get a boat. Are there boat-stands?"

The lad laughed outright.

"You're not long in Liverpool, I guess. Boat-stands! No; go down to the pier,—any pier will do, and hire a boat,—you'll be at no loss when once you are there. Only make haste."

"Oh, you need not tell me that, if I but knew how," said Mary, trembling with eagerness. "But you say right,—I never was here before, and I don't know my way to the place you speak on; only tell me, and I'll not lose a minute."

"Mother!" said the wilful lad, "I'm going to show her the way to the pier; I'll be back in an hour,—or so,—" he added in a lower tone.

And before the gentle Mrs. Jones could collect her scattered wits sufficiently to understand half of the hastily formed plan, her son was scudding down the street, closely followed by Mary's half-running steps.

Presently he slackened his pace sufficiently to enable him to enter into conversation with Mary, for once escaped from the reach of his mother's recalling voice, he thought he might venture to indulge his curiosity.

"Ahem!—What's your name? It's so awkward to be calling you young woman."

"My name is Mary,—Mary Barton," answered she, anxious to propitiate one who seemed so willing to exert himself in her behalf, or else she grudged every word which caused the slightest relaxation in her speed, although her chest seemed tightened, and her head throbbing, from the rate at which they were walking.

"And you want Will Wilson to prove an *alibi*—is that it?"

"Yes—oh, yes—can we not cross now?"

"No, wait a minute; it's the teagle hoisting above your head I'm afraid of;—and who is it that's to be tried?"

"Jem; oh, lad! can't we get past?"

They rushed under the great bales quivering in the air above their heads and pressed onwards for a few minutes, till Master Charley again saw fit to walk a little slower, and ask a few more questions.

"Mary, is Jem your brother, or your sweetheart, that you're so set upon saving him?"

"No—no," replied she, but with something of hesitation, that made the shrewd boy yet more anxious to clear up the mystery.

"Perhaps he's your cousin, then? Many a girl has a cousin who has not a sweetheart."

"No, he's neither kith nor kin to me. What's the matter? What are you stopping for?" said she, with nervous terror, as Charley turned back a few steps, and peered up a side street.

"Oh, nothing to flurry you so, Mary. I heard you say to mother you had never been in Liverpool before, and if you'll only look up this street you may see the back windows of our Exchange. Such a building as yon is! with 'natomy hiding under a blanket, and Lord Admiral Nelson, and a few more people in the middle of the court! No! come here," as Mary, in her eagerness, was looking at any window that caught her eye first, to satisfy the boy. "Here, then, now you can see it. You can say, now, you've seen Liverpool Exchange."

"Yes, to be sure—it's a beautiful window, I'm sure. But are we near the boats? I'll stop as I come back, you know; only I think we'd better get on now."

"Oh! if the wind's in your favour, you'll be down the river in no time, and catch Will, I'll be bound; and if it's not, why, you know, the minute it took you to look at the Exchange will be neither here nor there."

Another rush onwards, till one of the long crossings near the docks caused a stoppage, and gave Mary time for breathing, and Charley leisure to ask another question.

"You've never said where you come from?"

"Manchester," replied she.

"Eh, then! you've a power of things to see. Liverpool beats Manchester hollow, they say. A nasty, smoky hole, bean't it? Are you bound to live there?"

"Oh, yes! it's my home."

"Well, I don't think I could abide a home in the middle of smoke. Look there! now you see the river! That's something now you'd give a deal for in Manchester. Look!"

And Mary did look, and saw down an opening made in the forest of masts belonging to the vessels in dock, the glorious river, along which white-sailed ships were gliding with the ensigns of all nations, not "braving the battle," but telling of the distant lands, spicy or frozen, that sent to that mighty mart for their comforts or their luxuries; she saw small boats passing to and fro on that glittering highway, but she also saw such puffs and clouds of smoke from the countless steamers, that she wondered at Charley's intolerance of the smoke of Manchester. Across the swing-bridge, along the pier,—and they stood breathless by a magnificent dock, where hundreds of ships lay motionless during the process of loading and unloading. The cries of the sailors, the variety of languages used by the passers-by, and the entire novelty of the sight compared with any thing which Mary had ever seen, made her feel most helpless and forlorn; and she clung to her young guide as to one who alone by his superior knowledge could interpret between her and the new race of men by whom she was surrounded,—for a new race sailors might reasonably be considered, to a girl who had hitherto seen none but inland dwellers, and those for the greater part factory people.

In that new world of sight and sound, she still bore one prevailing thought, and though her eye glanced over the ships and the wide-spreading river, her mind was full of the thought of reaching Will.

"Why are we here?" asked she of Charley. "There are no little boats about, and I thought I was to go in a little boat; those ships are never meant for short distances, are they?"

"To be sure not," replied he, rather contemptuously. "But the *John Cropper* lay in this dock, and I know many of the sailors; and if I could see one I knew, I'd ask him to run up the mast, and see if he could catch a sight of her in the offing. If she's weighed her anchor no use for your going, you know."

Mary assented quietly to this speech, as if she were as careless as Charley seemed now to be about her overtaking Will; but in truth her heart was sinking within her, and she no longer felt the energy which had hitherto upheld her. Her bodily strength was giving way, and she stood cold and shivering, although the noon-day sun beat down with considerable power on the shadeless spot where she was standing.

"Here's Tom Bourne!" said Charley; and altering his manner from the patronising key in which he had spoken to Mary, he addressed a weather-beaten old sailor who came rolling along the pathway where they stood, his hands in his pockets, and his quid in his mouth, with very much the air of one who had nothing to do but look about him, and spit right and left; addressing this old tar, Charley made known to him his wish in slang, which to Mary was almost inaudible, and quite unintelligible, and which I am too much of a land-lubber to repeat correctly.

Mary watched looks and actions with a renovated keenness of perception.

She saw the old man listen attentively to Charley; she saw him eye her over from head to foot, and wind up his inspection with a little nod of approbation (for her very shabbiness and poverty of dress were creditable signs to the experienced old sailor); and then she watched him leisurely swing himself on to a ship in the basin, and, borrowing a glass, run up the mast with the speed of a monkey.

"He'll fall!" said she, in affright, clutching at Charley's arm, and judging the sailor, from his storm-marked face and unsteady walk on land, to be much older than he really was.

"Not he!" said Charley. "He's at the mast-head now. See! he's looking through his glass, and using his arms as steady as if he were on dry land. Why, I've been up the mast, many and many a time; only don't tell mother. She thinks I'm to be a shoemaker, but I've made up my mind to be a sailor; only there's no good arguing with a woman. You'll not tell her, Mary?"

"Oh, see!" exclaimed she (his secret was very safe with her, for, in fact, she had not heard it). "See! he's coming down; he's down. Speak to him, Charley."

But unable to wait another instant she called out herself,

"Can you see the *John Cropper*? Is she there yet?"

"Ay, ay," he answered, and coming quickly up to them, he hurried them away to seek for a boat, saying the bar was already covered, and in an hour the ship would hoist her sails and be off. "You've the wind right against you, and must use oars. No time to lose."

They ran to some steps leading down to the water. They beckoned to some watermen, who, suspecting the real state of the case, appeared in no hurry for a fare, but leisurely brought their boat alongside the stairs, as if it were a matter of indifference to them whether they were engaged or not, while they conversed together in few words, and in an under-tone, respecting the charge they should make.

"Oh, pray make haste," called Mary. "I want you to take me to the *John Cropper*. Where is she, Charley? Tell them—I don't rightly know the words,—only make haste!"

"In the offing she is, sure enough, miss," answered one of the men, shoving Charley on one side, regarding him as too young to be a principal in the bargain.

"I don't think we can go, Dick," said he, with a wink to his companion; "there's the gentleman over at New Brighton as wants us."

"But, mayhap, the young woman will pay us handsome for giving her a last look at her sweetheart," interposed the other.

"Oh, how much do you want? Only make haste—I've enough to pay you, but every moment is precious," said Mary.

"Ay, that it is. Less than an hour won't take us to the mouth of the river, and she'll be off by two o'clock!"

Poor Mary's ideas of "plenty of money," however, were different to those entertained by the boatmen. Only fourteen or fifteen shillings remained out of the sovereign Margaret had lent her, and the boatmen, imagining "plenty" to mean no less than several pounds, insisted upon receiving a sovereign (an exorbitant fare, by the bye, although reduced from their first demand of thirty shillings).

While Charley, with a boy's impatience of delay, and disregard of money, kept urging,

"Give it 'em, Mary; they'll none of them take you for less. It's your only chance. There's St. Nicholas ringing one!"

"I've only got fourteen and ninepence," cried she, in despair, after counting over her money; "but I'll give you my shawl, and you can sell it for four or five shillings,—oh! won't that much do?" asked she, in such a tone of voice, that they must indeed have had hard hearts who could refuse such agonised entreaty.

They took her on board.

And in less than five minutes she was rocking and tossing in a boat for the first time in her life, alone with two rough, hard-looking men.

CHAPTER XXVIII - "JOHN CROPPER, AHOY!"

"A wet sheet and a flowing sea,
  A wind that follows fast
And fills the white and rustling sail,
  And bends the gallant mast!
And bends the gallant mast, my boys,
  While, like the eagle free,
Away the good ship flies, and leaves
  Old England on the lee."

ALLAN CUNNINGHAM.

Mary had not understood that Charley was not coming with her. In fact, she had not thought about it, till she perceived his absence, as they pushed off from the landing-place, and remembered that she had never thanked him for all his kind interest in her behalf; and now his absence made her feel most lonely—even his, the little mushroom friend of an hour's growth.

The boat threaded her way through the maze of larger vessels which surrounded the shore, bumping against one, kept off by the oars from going right against another, overshadowed by a third, until at length they were fairly out on the broad river, away from either shore; the sights and sounds of land being lost in the distance.

And then came a sort of pause.

Both wind and tide were against the two men, and labour as they would they made but little way. Once Mary in her impatience had risen up to obtain a better view of the progress they had made, but the men had roughly told her to sit down immediately, and she had dropped on her seat like a chidden child, although the impatience was still at her heart.

But now she grew sure they were turning off from the straight course which they had hitherto kept on the Cheshire side of the river, whither they had gone to avoid the force of the current, and after a short time she could not help naming her conviction, as a kind of nightmare dread and belief came over her, that every thing animate and inanimate was in league against her one sole aim and object of overtaking Will.

They answered gruffly. They saw a boatman whom they knew, and were desirous of obtaining his services as steersman, so that both might row with greater effect. They knew what they were about. So she sat silent with clenched hands while the parley went on, the explanation was given, the favour asked and granted. But she was sickening all the time with nervous fear.

They had been rowing a long, long time—half a day it seemed, at least—yet Liverpool appeared still close at hand, and Mary began almost to wonder that the men were not as much disheartened as she was, when the wind, which had been hitherto against them, dropped, and thin clouds began to gather over the sky, shutting out the sun, and casting a chilly gloom over every thing.

There was not a breath of air, and yet it was colder than when the soft violence of the westerly wind had been felt.

The men renewed their efforts. The boat gave a bound forwards at every pull of the oars. The water was glassy and motionless, reflecting tint by tint of the Indian-ink sky above. Mary shivered, and her heart sank within her. Still now they evidently were making progress. Then the steersman pointed to a rippling line in the river only a little way off, and the men disturbed Mary, who was watching the ships that lay in what appeared to her the open sea, to get at their sails.

She gave a little start, and rose. Her patience, her grief, and perhaps her silence, had begun to win upon the men.

"Yon second to the norrard is the *John Cropper*. Wind's right now, and sails will soon carry us alongside of her."

He had forgotten (or perhaps he did not like to remind Mary) that the same wind which now bore their little craft along with easy, rapid motion, would also be favourable to the *John Cropper*.

But as they looked with straining eyes, as if to measure the decreasing distance that separated them from her, they saw her sails unfurled and flap in the breeze, till, catching the right point, they bellied forth into white roundness, and the ship began to plunge and heave, as if she were a living creature, impatient to be off.

"They're heaving anchor!" said one of the boatmen to the others, as the faint musical cry of the sailors came floating over the waters that still separated them.

Full of the spirit of the chase, though as yet ignorant of Mary's motives, the men sprang to hoist another sail. It was fully as much as the boat could bear, in the keen, gusty east wind which was now blowing, and she bent, and laboured, and ploughed, and creaked upbraidingly as if tasked beyond her strength; but she sped along with a gallant swiftness.

They drew nearer, and they heard the distant "ahoy" more clearly. It ceased. The anchor was up, and the ship was away.

Mary stood up, steadying herself by the mast, and stretched out her arms, imploring the flying vessel to stay its course by that mute action, while the tears streamed down her cheeks. The men caught up their oars and hoisted them in the air, and shouted to arrest attention.

They were seen by the men aboard the larger craft; but they were too busy with all the confusion prevalent in an outward-bound vessel to pay much attention. There were coils of ropes and seamen's chests to be stumbled over at every turn; there were animals, not properly secured, roaming bewildered about the deck, adding their pitiful lowings and bleatings to the aggregate of noises. There were carcases not cut up, looking like corpses of sheep and pigs rather than like mutton and pork; there were sailors running here and there and everywhere, having had no time to fall into method, and with their minds divided between thoughts of the land and the people they had left, and the present duties on board ship; while the captain strove hard to procure some kind of order by hasty commands given in a loud, impatient voice, to right and left, starboard and larboard, cabin and steerage.

As he paced the deck with a chafed step, vexed at one or two little mistakes on the part of the mate, and suffering himself from the pain of separation from wife and children, but showing his suffering only by his outward irritation, he heard a hail from the shabby little river-boat that was striving to overtake his winged ship. For the men fearing that, as the ship was now fairly over the bar, they should only increase the distance between them, and being now within shouting range, had asked of Mary her more particular desire.

Her throat was dry; all musical sound had gone out of her voice; but in a loud harsh whisper she told the men her errand of life and death, and they hailed the ship.

"We're come for one William Wilson, who is wanted to prove an *alibi* in Liverpool Assize Courts to-morrow. James Wilson is to be tried for a murder, done on Thursday night, when he was with William Wilson. Any thing more, missis?" asked the boat-man of Mary, in a lower voice, and taking his hands down from his mouth.

"Say I'm Mary Barton. Oh, the ship is going on! Oh, for the love of Heaven, ask them to stop."

The boatman was angry at the little regard paid to his summons, and called out again; repeating the message with the name of the young woman who sent it, and interlarding it with sailors' oaths.

The ship flew along—away,—the boat struggled after.

They could see the captain take his speaking-trumpet. And oh! and alas! they heard his words.

He swore a dreadful oath; he called Mary a disgraceful name; and he said he would not stop his ship for any one, nor could he part with a single hand, whoever swung for it.

The words came in unpitying clearness with their trumpet-sound. Mary sat down, looking like one who prays in the death-agony. For her eyes were turned up to that Heaven, where mercy dwelleth, while her blue lips quivered, though no sound came. Then she bowed her head and hid it in her hands.

"Hark! yon sailor hails us."

She looked up. And her heart stopped its beating to listen.

William Wilson stood as near the stern of the vessel as he could get; and unable to obtain the trumpet from the angry captain, made a tube of his own hands.

"So help me God, Mary Barton, I'll come back in the pilot-boat, time enough to save the life of the innocent."

"What does he say?" asked Mary wildly, as the voice died away in the increasing distance, while the boatmen cheered, in their kindled sympathy with their passenger.

"What does he say?" repeated she. "Tell me. I could not hear."

She had heard with her ears, but her brain refused to recognise the sense.

They repeated his speech, all three speaking at once, with many comments; while Mary looked at them and then at the vessel now far away.

"I don't rightly know about it," said she, sorrowfully. "What is the pilot-boat?"

They told her, and she gathered the meaning out of the sailors' slang which enveloped it. There was a hope still, although so slight and faint.

"How far does the pilot go with the ship?"

To different distances they said. Some pilots would go as far as Holyhead for the chance of the homeward-bound vessels; others only took the ships over the Banks. Some captains were more cautious than others, and the pilots had different ways. The wind was against the homeward bound vessels, so perhaps the pilot aboard the *John Cropper* would not care to go far out.

"How soon would he come back?"

There were three boatmen, and three opinions, varying from twelve hours to two days. Nay, the man who gave his vote for the longest time, on having his judgment disputed, grew stubborn, and doubled the time, and thought it might be the end of the week before the pilot-boat came home.

They began disputing, and urging reasons; and Mary tried to understand them; but independently of their nautical language, a veil seemed drawn over her mind, and she had no clear perception of any thing that passed. Her very words seemed not her own, and beyond her power of control, for she found herself speaking quite differently to what she meant.

One by one her hopes had fallen away, and left her desolate; and though a chance yet remained, she could no longer hope. She felt certain it, too, would fade and vanish. She sank into a kind of stupor. All outward objects harmonised with her despair.

The gloomy leaden sky,—the deep, dark waters below, of a still heavier shade of colour,—the cold, flat yellow shore in the distance, which no ray lightened up,—the nipping, cutting wind.

She shivered with her depression of mind and body.

The sails were taken down, of course, on the return to Liverpool, and the progress they made, rowing and tacking, was very slow. The men talked together, disputing about the pilots at first, and then about matters of local importance, in which Mary would have taken no interest at any time, and she gradually became drowsy; irrepressibly so, indeed, for in spite of her jerking efforts to keep awake she sank away to the bottom of the boat, and there lay couched on a rough heap of sails, rope, and tackle of various kinds.

The measured beat of the waters against the sides of the boat, and the musical boom of the more distant waves, were more lulling than silence, and she slept sound.

Once she opened her eyes heavily, and dimly saw the old gray, rough boatman (who had stood out the most obstinately for the full fare) covering her with his thick pea-jacket. He had taken it off on purpose, and was doing it tenderly in his way, but before she could rouse herself up to thank him she had dropped off to sleep again.

At last, in the dusk of evening, they arrived at the landing-place from which they had started some hours before. The men spoke to Mary, but though she mechanically replied, she did not stir; so, at length, they were obliged to shake her. She stood up, shivering and puzzled as to her whereabouts.

"Now tell me where you are bound to, missis," said the gray old man, "and maybe I can put you in the way."

She slowly comprehended what he said, and went through the process of recollection; but very dimly, and with much labour. She put her hand into her pocket and pulled out her purse, and shook its contents into the man's hand; and then began meekly to unpin her shawl, although they had turned away without asking for it.

"No, no!" said the older man, who lingered on the step before springing into the boat, and to whom she mutely offered the shawl.

"Keep it! we donnot want it. It were only for to try you,—some folks say they've no more blunt, when all the while they've getten a mint."

"Thank you," said she, in a dull, low tone.

"Where are you bound to? I axed that question afore," said the gruff old fellow.

"I don't know. I'm a stranger," replied she, quietly, with a strange absence of anxiety under the circumstances.

"But you mun find out then," said he, sharply, "pier-head's no place for a young woman to be standing on, gape-saying."

"I've a card somewhere as will tell me," she answered, and the man, partly relieved, jumped into the boat, which was now pushing off to make way for the arrivals from some steamer.

Mary felt in her pocket for the card, on which was written the name of the street where she was to have met Mr. Bridgenorth at two o'clock; where Job and Mrs. Wilson were to have been, and where she was to have learnt from the former the particulars of some respectable lodging. It was not to be found.

She tried to brighten her perceptions, and felt again, and took out the little articles her pocket contained, her empty purse, her pocket-handkerchief, and such little things, but it was not there.

In fact she had dropped it when, so eager to embark, she had pulled out her purse to reckon up her money.

She did not know this, of course. She only knew it was gone.

It added but little to the despair that was creeping over her. But she tried a little more to help herself, though every minute her mind became more cloudy. She strove to remember where Will had lodged, but she could not; name, street, every thing had passed away, and it did not signify; better she were lost than found.

She sat down quietly on the top step of the landing, and gazed down into the dark, dank water below. Once or twice a spectral thought loomed among the shadows of her brain; a wonder whether beneath that cold dismal surface there would not be rest from the troubles of earth. But she could not hold an idea before her for two consecutive moments; and she forgot what she thought about before she could act upon it.

So she continued sitting motionless, without looking up, or regarding in any way the insults to which she was subjected.

Through the darkening light the old boatman had watched her: interested in her in spite of himself, and his scoldings of himself.

When the landing-place was once more comparatively clear, he made his way towards it, across boats, and along planks, swearing at himself while he did so, for an old fool.

He shook Mary's shoulder violently.

"D—— you, I ask you again where you're bound to? Don't sit there, stupid. Where are you going to?"

"I don't know," sighed Mary.

"Come, come; avast with that story. You said a bit ago you'd a card, which was to tell you where to go."

"I had, but I've lost it. Never mind."

She looked again down upon the black mirror below.

He stood by her, striving to put down his better self; but he could not. He shook her again. She looked up, as if she had forgotten him.

"What do you want?" asked she, wearily.

"Come with me, and be d——d to you!" replied he, clutching her arm to pull her up.

She arose and followed him, with the unquestioning docility of a little child.

CHAPTER XXIX - A TRUE BILL AGAINST JEM.

"There are who, living by the legal pen,
Are held in honour—honourable men."

CRABBE.

At five minutes before two, Job Legh stood upon the door-step of the house where Mr. Bridgenorth lodged at Assize time. He had left Mrs. Wilson at the dwelling of a friend of his, who had offered him a room for the old woman and Mary: a room which had frequently been his, on his occasional visits to Liverpool, but which he was thankful now to have obtained for them, as his own sleeping-place was a matter of indifference to him, and the town appeared crowded and disorderly on the eve of the Assizes.

He was shown in to Mr. Bridgenorth, who was writing. Mary and Will Wilson had not yet arrived, being, as you know, far away on the broad sea; but of this Job of course knew nothing, and he did not as yet feel much anxiety about their non-appearance; he was more curious to know the result of Mr. Bridgenorth's interview that morning with Jem.

"Why, yes," said Mr. Bridgenorth, putting down his pen, "I have seen him, but to little purpose, I'm afraid. He's very impracticable—very. I told him, of course, that he must be perfectly open with me, or else I could not be prepared for the weak points. I named your name with the view of unlocking his confidence, but—"

"What did he say?" asked Job, breathlessly.

"Why, very little. He barely answered me. Indeed, he refused to answer some questions—positively refused. I don't know what I can do for him."

"Then you think him guilty, sir?" said Job, despondingly.

"No, I don't," replied Mr. Bridgenorth, quickly and decisively. "Much less than I did before I saw him. The impression (mind, 'tis only impression; I rely upon your caution, not to take it for fact)—the impression," with an emphasis on the word, "he gave me is, that he knows something about the affair, but what, he will not say; and so the chances are, if he persists in his obstinacy, he'll be hung. That's all."

He began to write again, for he had no time to lose.

"But he must not be hung," said Job, with vehemence.

Mr. Bridgenorth looked up, smiled a little, but shook his head.

"What did he say, sir, if I may be so bold as to ask?" continued Job.

"His words were few enough, and he was so reserved and short, that as I said before, I can only give you the impression they conveyed to me. I told him of course who I was, and for what I was sent. He looked pleased, I thought,—at least his face (sad enough when I went in, I assure ye) brightened a little; but he said he had nothing to say, no defence to make. I asked him if he was guilty, then; and by way of opening his heart I said I understood he had had provocation enough, inasmuch as I heard that the girl was very lovely, and had jilted him to fall desper-desperately in love with that handsome young Carson (poor fellow!). But James Wilson did not speak one way or another. I then went to particulars. I asked him if the gun was his, as his mother had declared. He had not heard of her admission it was evident, from his quick way of looking up, and the glance of his eye; but when he saw I was observing him, he hung down his head again, and merely said she was right; it was his gun."

"Well!" said Job, impatiently, as Mr. Bridgenorth paused.

"Nay! I have little more to tell you," continued that gentleman. "I asked him to inform me in all confidence, how it came to be found there. He was silent for a time, and then refused. Not only refused to answer that question, but candidly told me he would not say another word on the subject, and, thanking me for my trouble and interest in his behalf, he all but dismissed me. Ungracious enough on the whole, was it not, Mr. Legh? And yet, I assure ye, I am twenty times more inclined to think him innocent than before I had the interview."

"I wish Mary Barton would come," said Job, anxiously. "She and Will are a long time about it."

"Ay, that's our only chance, I believe," answered Mr. Bridgenorth, who was writing again. "I sent Johnson off before twelve to serve him with his sub-pœna, and to say I wanted to speak with him; he'll be here soon, I've no doubt."

There was a pause. Mr. Bridgenorth looked up again, and spoke.

"Mr. Duncombe promised to be here to speak to his character. I sent him a subpœna on Saturday night. Though after all, juries go very little by such general and vague testimony as that to character. It is very right that they should not often; but in this instance unfortunate for us, as we must rest our case on the *alibi*."

The pen went again, scratch, scratch over the paper.

Job grew very fidgetty. He sat on the edge of his chair, the more readily to start up when Will and Mary should appear. He listened intently to every noise and every step on the stair.

Once he heard a man's footstep, and his old heart gave a leap of delight. But it was only Mr. Bridgenorth's clerk, bringing him a list of those cases in which the grand jury had found true bills. He glanced it over and pushed it to Job, merely saying,

"Of course we expected this," and went on with his writing.

There was a true bill against James Wilson. Of course. And yet Job felt now doubly anxious and sad. It seemed the beginning of the end. He had got, by imperceptible degrees, to think Jem innocent. Little by little this persuasion had come upon him.

Mary (tossing about in the little boat on the broad river) did not come, nor did Will.

Job grew very restless. He longed to go and watch for them out of the window, but feared to interrupt Mr. Bridgenorth. At length his desire to look out was irresistible, and he got up and walked carefully and gently across the room, his boots creaking at every cautious step. The gloom which had overspread the sky, and the influence of which had been felt by Mary on the open water, was yet more perceptible in the dark, dull street. Job grew more and more fidgetty. He was obliged to walk about the room, for he could not keep still; and he did so, regardless of Mr. Bridgenorth's impatient little motions and noises, as the slow, stealthy, creaking movements were heard, backwards and forwards, behind his chair.

He really liked Job, and was interested for Jem, else his nervousness would have overcome his sympathy long before it did. But he could hold out no longer against the monotonous, grating sound; so at last he threw down his pen, locked his portfolio, and taking up his hat and gloves, he told Job he must go to the courts.

"But Will Wilson is not come," said Job, in dismay. "Just wait while I run to his lodgings. I would have done it before, but I thought they'd be here every minute, and I were afraid of missing them. I'll be back in no time."

"No, my good fellow, I really must go. Besides, I begin to think Johnson must have made a mistake, and have fixed with this William Wilson to meet me at the courts. If you like to wait for him here, pray make use of my room; but I've a notion I shall find him there: in which case, I'll send him to your lodgings; shall I? You know where to find me. I shall be here again by eight o'clock, and with the evidence of this witness that's to prove the *alibi*, I'll have the brief drawn out, and in the hands of counsel to-night."

So saying he shook hands with Job, and went his way. The old man considered for a minute as he lingered at the door, and then bent his steps towards Mrs. Jones's, where he knew (from reference to queer, odd, heterogeneous memoranda, in an ancient black-leather pocket-book) that Will lodged, and where he doubted not he should hear both of him and of Mary.

He went there, and gathered what intelligence he could out of Mrs. Jones's slow replies.

He asked if a young woman had been there that morning, and if she had seen Will Wilson. "No!"

"Why not?"

"Why, bless you, 'cause he had sailed some hours before she came asking for him."

There was a dead silence, broken only by the even, heavy sound of Mrs. Jones's ironing.

"Where is the young woman now?" asked Job.

"Somewhere down at the docks," she thought. "Charley would know, if he was in, but he wasn't. He was in mischief, somewhere or other, she had no doubt. Boys always were. He would break his neck some day, she knew;" so saying, she quietly spat upon her fresh iron, to test its heat, and then went on with her business.

Job could have boxed her, he was in such a state of irritation. But he did not, and he had his reward. Charley came in, whistling with an air of indifference, assumed to carry off his knowledge of the lateness of the hour to which he had lingered about the docks.

"Here's an old man come to know where the young woman is who went out with thee this morning," said his mother, after she had bestowed on him a little motherly scolding.

"Where she is now, I don't know. I saw her last sailing down the river after the *John Cropper*. I'm afeared she won't reach her; wind changed and she would be under weigh, and over the bar in no time. She should have been back by now."

It took Job some little time to understand this, from the confused use of the feminine pronoun. Then he inquired how he could best find Mary.

"I'll run down again to the pier," said the boy; "I'll warrant I'll find her."

"Thou shalt do no such a thing," said his mother, setting her back against the door. The lad made a comical face at Job, which met with no responsive look from the old man, whose sympathies were naturally in favour of the parent; although he would thankfully have availed himself of Charley's offer, for he was weary, and anxious to return to poor Mrs. Wilson, who would be wondering what had become of him.

"How can I best find her? Who did she go with, lad?"

But Charley was sullen at his mother's exercise of authority before a stranger, and at that stranger's grave looks when he meant to have made him laugh.

"They were river boatmen;—that's all I know," said he.

"But what was the name of their boat?" persevered Job.

"I never took no notice;—the Anne, or William,—or some of them common names, I'll be bound."

"What pier did she start from?" asked Job, despairingly.

"Oh, as for that matter, it were the stairs on the Prince's Pier she started from; but she'll not come back to the same, for the American steamer came up with the tide, and anchored close to it, blocking up the way for all the smaller craft. It's a rough evening too, to be out on," he maliciously added.

"Well, God's will be done! I did hope we could have saved the lad," said Job, sorrowfully; "but I'm getten very doubtful again. I'm uneasy about Mary, too,—very. She's a stranger in Liverpool."

"So she told me," said Charley. "There's traps about for young women at every corner. It's a pity she's no one to meet her when she lands."

"As for that," replied Job, "I don't see how any one could meet her when we can't tell where she would come to. I must trust to her coming right. She's getten spirit and sense. She'll most likely be for coming here again. Indeed, I don't know what else she can do, for she knows no other place in Liverpool. Missus, if she comes, will you give your son leave to bring her to No. 8, Back Garden Court, where there's friends waiting for her? I'll give him sixpence for his trouble."

Mrs. Jones, pleased with the reference to her, gladly promised. And even Charley, indignant as he was at first at the idea of his motions being under the control of his mother, was mollified at the prospect of the sixpence, and at the probability of getting nearer to the heart of the mystery.

But Mary never came.

CHAPTER XXX - JOB LEGH'S DECEPTION.

"Poor Susan moans, poor Susan groans;
   The clock gives warning for eleven;
'Tis on the stroke—'He must be near,'
Quoth Betty, 'and will soon be here,
   As sure as there's a moon in heaven.'
The clock is on the stroke of twelve,
   And Johnny is not yet in sight,
—The moon's in heaven, as Betty sees,
But Betty is not quite at ease;
   And Susan has a dreadful night."

WORDSWORTH.

Job found Mrs. Wilson pacing about in a restless way; not speaking to the woman at whose house she was staying, but occasionally heaving such deep oppressive sighs as quite startled those around her.

"Well!" said she, turning sharp round in her tottering walk up and down, as Job came in.

"Well, speak!" repeated she, before he could make up his mind what to say; for, to tell the truth, he was studying for some kind-hearted lie which might soothe her for a time. But now the real state of the case came blurting forth in answer to her impatient questioning.

"Will's not to the fore. But he'll may be turn up yet, time enough."

She looked at him steadily for a minute, as if almost doubting if such despair could be in store for her as his words seemed to imply. Then she slowly shook her head, and said, more quietly than might have been expected from her previous excited manner,

"Don't go for to say that! Thou dost not think it. Thou'rt well-nigh hopeless, like me. I seed all along my lad would be hung for what he never did. And better he were, and were shut[1] of this weary world, where there's neither justice nor mercy left."

---

[1] "Shut," quit.

She looked up with tranced eyes as if praying to that throne where mercy ever abideth, and then sat down.

"Nay, now thou'rt off at a gallop," said Job. "Will has sailed this morning for sure, but that brave wench, Mary Barton, is after him, and will bring him back, I'll be bound, if she can but get speech on him. She's not back yet. Come, come, hold up thy head. It will all end right."

"It will all end right," echoed she; "but not as thou tak'st it. Jem will be hung, and will go to his father and the little lads, where the Lord God wipes away all tears, and where the Lord Jesus speaks kindly to the little ones, who look about for the mothers they left upon earth. Eh, Job, yon's a blessed land, and I long to go to it, and yet I fret because Jem is hastening there. I would not fret if he and I could lie down to-night to sleep our last sleep; not a bit would I fret if folk would but know him to be innocent—as I do."

"They'll know it sooner or later, and repent sore if they've hanged him for what he never did," replied Job.

"Ay, that they will. Poor souls! May God have mercy on them when they find out their mistake."

Presently Job grew tired of sitting waiting, and got up, and hung about the door and window, like some animal wanting to go out. It was pitch dark, for the moon had not yet risen.

"You just go to bed," said he to the widow. "You'll want your strength for to-morrow. Jem will be sadly off, if he sees you so cut up as you look to-night. I'll step down again and find Mary. She'll be back by this time. I'll come and tell you every thing, never fear. But, now, you go to bed."

"Thou'rt a kind friend, Job Legh, and I'll go, as thou wishest me. But, oh! mind thou com'st straight off to me, and bring Mary as soon as thou'st lit on her." She spoke low, but very calmly.

"Ay, ay!" replied Job, slipping out of the house.

He went first to Mr. Bridgenorth's, where it had struck him that Will and Mary might be all this time waiting for him.

They were not there, however. Mr. Bridgenorth had just come in, and Job went breathlessly up-stairs to consult with him as to the state of the case.

"It's a bad job," said the lawyer, looking very grave, while he arranged his papers. "Johnson told me how it was; the woman that Wilson lodged with told him. I doubt it's but a wild-goose chase of the girl Barton. Our case must rest on the uncertainty of circumstantial evidence, and the goodness of the prisoner's previous character. A very vague and weak defence. However, I've engaged Mr. Clinton as counsel, and he'll make the best of it. And now, my good fellow, I must wish you good-night, and turn you out of doors. As it is, I shall have to sit up into the small hours. Did you see my clerk as you came up-stairs? You did! Then may I trouble you to ask him to step up immediately?"

After this Job could not stay, and, making his humble bow, he left the room.

Then he went to Mrs. Jones's. She was in, but Charley had slipped off again. There was no holding that boy. Nothing kept him but lock and key, and they did not always; for once she had him locked up in the garret, and he had got off through the skylight. Perhaps now he was gone to see after the young woman down at the docks. He never wanted an excuse to be there.

Unasked, Job took a chair, resolved to await Charley's re-appearance.

Mrs. Jones ironed and folded her clothes, talking all the time of Charley and her husband, who was a sailor in some ship bound for India, and who, in leaving her their boy, had evidently left her rather more than she could manage. She moaned and croaked over sailors, and sea-port towns, and stormy weather, and sleepless nights, and trousers all over tar and pitch, long after Job had left off attending to her, and was only trying to hearken to every step and every voice in the street.

At last Charley came in, but he came alone.

"Yon Mary Barton has getten into some scrape or another," said he, addressing himself to Job. "She's not to be heard of at any of the piers; and Bourne says it were a boat from the Cheshire side as she went aboard of. So there's no hearing of her till to-morrow morning."

"To-morrow morning she'll have to be in court at nine o'clock, to bear witness on a trial," said Job, sorrowfully.

"So she said; at least somewhat of the kind," said Charley, looking desirous to hear more. But Job was silent.

He could not think of any thing further that could be done; so he rose up, and, thanking Mrs. Jones for the shelter she had given him, he went out into the street; and there he stood still, to ponder over probabilities and chances.

After some little time he slowly turned towards the lodging where he had left Mrs. Wilson. There was nothing else to be done; but he loitered on the way, fervently hoping that her weariness and her woes might have sent her to sleep before his return, that he might be spared her questionings.

He went very gently into thc house-place where the sleepy landlady awaited his coming and his bringing the girl, who, she had been told, was to share the old woman's bed.

But in her sleepy blindness she knocked things so about in lighting the candle (she could see to have a nap by fire-light, she said), that the voice of Mrs. Wilson was heard from the little back-room, where she was to pass the night.

"Who's there?"

Job gave no answer, and kept down his breath, that she might think herself mistaken. The landlady, having no such care, dropped the snuffers with a sharp metallic sound, and then, by her endless apologies, convinced the listening woman that Job had returned.

"Job! Job Legh!" she cried out, nervously.

"Eh, dear!" said Job to himself, going reluctantly to her bed-room door. "I wonder if one little lie would be a sin as things stand? It would happen give her sleep, and she won't have sleep for many and many a night (not to call sleep), if things goes wrong to-morrow. I'll chance it, any way."

"Job! art thou there?" asked she again with a trembling impatience that told in every tone of her voice.

"Ay! sure! I thought thou'd ha' been asleep by this time."

"Asleep! How could I sleep till I knowed if Will were found?"

"Now for it," muttered Job to himself. Then in a louder voice, "Never fear! he's found, and safe, ready for to-morrow."

"And he'll prove that thing for my poor lad, will he? He'll bear witness that Jem were with him? Oh, Job, speak! tell me all!"

"In for a penny, in for a pound," thought Job. "Happen one prayer will do for the sum total. Any rate, I must go on now.—Ay, ay," shouted he, through the door. "He can prove all; and Jem will come off as clear as a new-born babe."

He could hear Mrs. Wilson's rustling movements, and in an instant guessed she was on her knees, for he heard her trembling voice uplifted in thanksgiving and praise to God, stopped at times by sobs of gladness and relief.

And when he heard this, his heart misgave him; for he thought of the awful enlightening, the terrible revulsion of feeling that awaited her in the morning. He saw the short-sightedness of falsehood; but what could he do now?

While he listened, she ended her grateful prayers.

"And Mary? Thou'st found her at Mrs. Jones's, Job?" said she, continuing her inquiries.

He gave a great sigh.

"Yes, she was there, safe enough, second time of going.—God forgive me!" muttered he, "who'd ha' thought of my turning out such an arrant liar in my old days?"

"Bless the wench! Is she here? Why does she not come to bed? I'm sure she's need."

Job coughed away his remains of conscience, and made answer,

"She was a bit weary, and o'er done with her sail; and Mrs. Jones axed her to stay there all night. It was nigh at hand to the courts, where she will have to be in the morning."

"It comes easy enough after a while," groaned out Job. "The father of lies helps one, I suppose, for now my speech comes as natural as truth. She's done questioning now, that's one good thing. I'll be off before Satan and she are at me again."

He went to the house-place, where the landlady stood wearily waiting. Her husband was in bed, and asleep long ago.

But Job had not yet made up his mind what to do. He could not go to sleep, with all his anxieties, if he were put into the best bed in Liverpool.

"Thou'lt let me sit up in this arm-chair," said he at length to the woman, who stood, expecting his departure.

He was an old friend, so she let him do as he wished. But, indeed, she was too sleepy to have opposed him. She was too glad to be released and go to bed.

CHAPTER XXXI - HOW MARY PASSED THE NIGHT.

"To think
That all this long interminable night,
Which I have passed in thinking on two words—
'Guilty'—'Not Guilty!'—like one happy moment
O'er many a head hath flown unheeded by;
O'er happy sleepers dreaming in their bliss
Of bright to-morrows—or far happier still,
With deep breath buried in forgetfulness.
O all the dismallest images of death
Did swim before my eyes!"

WILSON.

And now, where was Mary?

How Job's heart would have been relieved of one of its cares if he could have seen her: for he was in a miserable state of anxiety about her; and many and many a time through that long night he scolded her and himself; her for her obstinacy, and himself for his weakness in yielding to her obstinacy, when she insisted on being the one to follow and find out Will.

She did not pass that night in bed any more than Job; but she was under a respectable roof, and among kind, though rough people.

She had offered no resistance to the old boatman, when he had clutched her arm, in order to insure her following him, as he threaded the crowded dock-ways, and dived up strange bye-streets. She came on meekly after him, scarcely thinking in her stupor where she was going, and glad (in a dead, heavy way) that some one was deciding things for her.

He led her to an old-fashioned house, almost as small as house could be, which had been built long ago, before all the other part of the street, and had a country-town look about it in the middle of that bustling back street. He pulled her into the house-place; and relieved to a certain degree of his fear of losing her on the way, he exclaimed,

"There!" giving a great slap of one hand on her back.

The room was light and bright, and roused Mary (perhaps the slap on her back might help a little, too), and she felt the awkwardness of accounting for her presence to a little bustling old woman who had been moving about the fire-place on her entrance. The boatman took it very quietly, never deigning to give any explanation, but sitting down in his own particular chair, and chewing tobacco, while he looked at Mary with the most satisfied air imaginable, half triumphantly, as if she were the captive of his bow and spear, and half defyingly, as if daring her to escape.

The old woman, his wife, stood still, poker in hand, waiting to be told who it was that her husband had brought home so unceremoniously; but, as she looked in amazement the girl's cheek flushed, and then blanched to a dead whiteness; a film came over her eyes, and catching at the dresser for support in that hot whirling room, she fell in a heap on the floor.

Both man and wife came quickly to her assistance. They raised her up, still insensible, and he supported her on one knee, while his wife pattered away for some cold fresh water. She threw it straight over Mary; but though it caused a great sob, the eyes still remained closed, and the face as pale as ashes.

"Who is she, Ben?" asked the woman, as she rubbed her unresisting, powerless hands.

"How should I know?" answered her husband gruffly.

"Well-a-well!" (in a soothing tone, such as you use to irritated children), and as if half to herself, "I only thought you might, you know, as you brought her home. Poor thing! we must not ask aught about her, but that she needs help. I wish I'd my salts at home, but I lent 'em to Mrs. Burton, last Sunday in church, for she could not keep awake through the sermon. Dear-a-me, how white she is!"

"Here! you hold her up a bit," said her husband.

She did as he desired, still crooning to herself, not caring for his short, sharp interruptions as she went on; and, indeed, to her old, loving heart, his crossest words fell like pearls and diamonds, for he had been the husband of her youth; and even he, rough and crabbed as he was, was secretly soothed by the sound of her voice, although not for worlds, if he could have helped it, would he have shown any of the love that was hidden beneath his rough outside.

"What's the old fellow after?" said she, bending over Mary, so as to accommodate the drooping head. "Taking my pen, as I've had better nor five year. Bless us, and save us! he's burning it! Ay, I see now, he's his wits about him; burnt feathers is always good for a faint. But they don't bring her round, poor wench! Now what's he after next? Well! he is a bright one, my old man! That I never thought of that, to be sure!" exclaimed she, as he produced a square bottle of smuggled spirits, labelled "Golden Wasser," from a corner cupboard in their little room.

"That'll do!" said she, as the dose he poured into Mary's open mouth made her start and cough. "Bless the man! It's just like him to be so tender and thoughtful!"

"Not a bit!" snarled he, as he was relieved by Mary's returning colour, and opened eyes, and wondering, sensible gaze; "not a bit! I never was such a fool afore."

His wife helped Mary to rise, and placed her in a chair.

"All's right now, young woman?" asked the boatman, anxiously.

"Yes, sir, and thank you. I'm sure, sir, I don't know rightly how to thank you," faltered Mary, softly forth.

"Be hanged to you and your thanks." And he shook himself, took his pipe, and went out without deigning another word; leaving his wife sorely puzzled as to the character and history of the stranger within her doors.

Mary watched the boatman leave the house, and then, turning her sorrowful eyes to the face of her hostess, she attempted feebly to rise, with the intention of going away,—where she knew not.

"Nay! nay! who e'er thou be'st, thou'rt not fit to go out into the street. Perhaps" (sinking her voice a little) "thou'rt a bad one; I almost misdoubt thee, thou'rt so pretty. Well-a-well! it's the bad ones as have the broken hearts, sure enough; good folk never get utterly cast down, they've always getten hope in the Lord: it's the sinful as bear the bitter, bitter grief in their crushed hearts, poor souls; it's them we ought, most of all, to pity and to help. She shanna leave the house to-night, choose who she is,—worst woman in Liverpool, she shanna. I wished I knew where th' old man picked her up, that I do."

Mary had listened feebly to this soliloquy, and now tried to satisfy her hostess in weak, broken sentences.

"I'm not a bad one, missis, indeed. Your master took me out to sea after a ship as had sailed. There was a man in it as might save a life at the trial to-morrow. The captain would not let him come, but he says he'll come back in the pilot-boat." She fell to sobbing at the thought of her waning hopes, and the old woman tried to comfort her, beginning with her accustomed,

"Well-a-well! and he'll come back, I'm sure. I know he will; so keep up your heart. Don't fret about it. He's sure to be back."

"Oh! I'm afraid! I'm sore afraid he won't," cried Mary, consoled, nevertheless, by the woman's assertions, all groundless as she knew them to be.

Still talking half to herself and half to Mary, the old woman prepared tea, and urged her visitor to eat and refresh herself. But Mary shook her head at the proffered food, and only drank a cup of tea with thirsty eagerness. For the spirits had thrown her into a burning heat, and rendered each impression received through her senses of the most painful distinctness and intensity, while her head ached in a terrible manner.

She disliked speaking, her power over her words seemed so utterly gone. She used quite different expressions to those she intended. So she kept silent, while Mrs. Sturgis (for that was the name of her hostess) talked away, and put her tea-things by, and moved about incessantly, in a manner that increased the dizziness in Mary's head. She felt as if she ought to take leave for the night and go. But where?

Presently the old man came back, crosser and gruffer than when he went away. He kicked aside the dry shoes his wife had prepared for him, and snarled at all she said. Mary attributed this to his finding her still there, and gathered up her strength for an effort to leave the house. But she was mistaken. By-and-bye, he said (looking right into the fire, as if addressing it), "Wind's right against them!"

"Ay, ay, and is it so?" said his wife, who, knowing him well, knew that his surliness proceeded from some repressed sympathy. "Well-a-well, wind changes often at night. Time enough before morning. I'd bet a penny it has changed sin' thou looked."

She looked out of their little window at a weather-cock, near, glittering in the moonlight; and as she was a sailor's wife, she instantly recognised the unfavourable point at which the indicator seemed stationary, and giving a heavy sigh, turned into the room, and began to beat about in her own mind for some other mode of comfort.

"There's no one else who can prove what you want at the trial to-morrow, is there?" asked she.

"No one!" answered Mary.

"And you've no clue to the one as is really guilty, if t'other is not?"

Mary did not answer, but trembled all over.

Sturgis saw it.

"Don't bother her with thy questions," said he to his wife. "She mun go to bed, for she's all in a shiver with the sea air. I'll see after the wind, hang it, and the weather-cock, too. Tide will help 'em when it turns."

Mary went up-stairs murmuring thanks and blessings on those who took the stranger in. Mrs. Sturgis led her into a little room redolent of the sea and foreign lands. There was a small bed for one son, bound for China; and a hammock slung above for another, who was now tossing in the Baltic. The sheets looked made out of sail-cloth, but were fresh and clean in spite of their brownness.

Against the wall were wafered two rough drawings of vessels with their names written underneath, on which the mother's eyes caught, and gazed until they filled with tears. But she brushed the drops away with the back of her hand, and in a cheerful tone went on to assure Mary the bed was well aired.

"I cannot sleep, thank you. I will sit here, if you please," said Mary, sinking down on the window-seat.

"Come, now," said Mrs. Sturgis, "my master told me to see you to bed, and I mun. What's the use of watching? A watched pot never boils, and I see you are after watching that weather-cock. Why now, I try never to look at it, else I could do nought else. My heart many a time goes sick when the wind rises, but I turn away and work away, and try never to think on the wind, but on what I ha' getten to do."

"Let me stay up a little," pleaded Mary, as her hostess seemed so resolute about seeing her to bed. Her looks won her suit.

"Well, I suppose I mun. I shall catch it down stairs, I know. He'll be in a fidget till you're getten to bed, I know; so you mun be quiet if you are so bent upon staying up."

And quietly, noiselessly, Mary watched the unchanging weather-cock through the night. She sat on the little window-seat, her hand holding back the curtain which shaded the room from the bright moonlight without; her head resting its weariness against the corner of the window-frame; her eyes burning and stiff with the intensity of her gaze.

The ruddy morning stole up the horizon, casting a crimson glow into the watcher's room.

It was the morning of the day of trial!

CHAPTER XXXII - THE TRIAL AND VERDICT—"NOT GUILTY."

"Thou stand'st here arraign'd,
That, with presumption impious and accursed,
Thou hast usurp'd God's high prerogative,
Making thy fellow mortal's life and death
Wait on thy moody and diseased passions;
That with a violent and untimely steel
Hast set abroach the blood that should have ebbed
In calm and natural current: to sum all
In one wild name—a name the pale air freezes at,
And every cheek of man sinks in with horror—
Thou art a cold and midnight murderer."

MILMAN'S "FAZIO."

Of all the restless people who found that night's hours agonising from excess of anxiety, the poor father of the murdered man was perhaps the most restless. He had slept but little since the blow had fallen; his waking hours had been too full of agitated thought, which seemed to haunt and pursue him through his unquiet slumbers.

And this night of all others was the most sleepless. He turned over and over again in his mind the wonder if every thing had been done that could be done, to insure the conviction of Jem Wilson. He almost regretted the haste with which he had urged forward the proceedings, and yet until he had obtained vengeance, he felt as if there was no peace on earth for him (I don't know that he exactly used the term vengeance in his thoughts; he spoke of justice, and probably thought of his desired end as such); no peace either bodily or mental, for he moved up and down his bedroom with the restless incessant tramp of a wild beast in a cage, and if he compelled his aching limbs to cease for an instant, the twitchings which ensued almost amounted to convulsions, and he re-commenced his walk as the lesser evil, and the more bearable fatigue.

With daylight increased power of action came; and he drove off to arouse his attorney, and worry him with further directions and inquiries; and when that was ended, he sat, watch in hand, until the courts should be opened, and the trial begin.

What were all the living,—wife or daughters,—what were they in comparison with the dead,—the murdered son who lay unburied still, in compliance with his father's earnest wish, and almost vowed purpose of having the slayer of his child sentenced to death, before he committed the body to the rest of the grave?

At nine o'clock they all met at their awful place of *rendezvous.*

The judge, the jury, the avenger of blood, the prisoner, the witnesses—all were gathered together within one building. And besides these were many others, personally interested in some part of the proceedings, in which, however, they took no part; Job Legh, Ben Sturgis, and several others were there, amongst whom was Charley Jones.

Job Legh had carefully avoided any questioning from Mrs. Wilson that morning. Indeed he had not been much in her company, for he had risen up early to go out once more to make inquiry for Mary; and when he could hear nothing of her, he had desperately resolved not to undeceive Mrs. Wilson, as sorrow never came too late; and if the blow were inevitable, it would be better to leave her in ignorance of the impending evil as long as possible. She took her place in the witness-room, worn and dispirited, but not anxious.

As Job struggled through the crowd into the body of the court, Mr. Bridgenorth's clerk beckoned to him.

"Here's a letter for you from our client!"

Job sickened as he took it. He did not know why, but he dreaded a confession of guilt, which would be an overthrow of all hope.

The letter ran as follows.

DEAR FRIEND,—I thank you heartily for your goodness in finding me a lawyer, but lawyers can do no good to me, whatever they may do to other people. But I am not the less obliged to you, dear friend. I foresee things will go against me—and no wonder. If I was a jury-man, I should say the man was guilty as had as much evidence brought against him as may be brought against me to-morrow. So it's no blame to them if they do. But, Job Legh, I think I need not tell you I am as guiltless in this matter as the babe unborn, although it is not in my power to prove it. If I did not believe that you thought me innocent, I could not write as I do now to tell you my wishes. You'll not forget they are the wishes of a man shortly to die. Dear friend, you must take care of my mother. Not in the money way, for she will have enough for her and Aunt Alice; but you must let her talk to you of me; and show her that (whatever others may do) you think I died innocent. I don't reckon she will stay long behind when we are all gone. Be tender with her, Job, for my sake; and if she is a bit fractious at times, remember what she has gone through. I know mother will never doubt me, God bless her.

There is one other whom I fear I have loved too dearly; and yet, the loving her has made the happiness of my life. She will think I have murdered her lover; she will think I have caused the grief she must be feeling. And she must go on thinking so. It is hard upon me

> to say this; but she *must*. It will be best for her, and that's all I ought to think on. But, dear Job, you are a hearty fellow for your time of life, and may live a many years to come; and perhaps you could tell her, when you felt sure you were drawing near your end, that I solemnly told you (as I do now) that I was innocent of this thing. You must not tell her for many years to come; but I cannot well bear to think on her living through a long life, and hating the thought of me as the murderer of him she loved, and dying with that hatred to me in her heart. It would hurt me sore in the other world to see the look of it in her face, as it would be, till she was told. I must not let myself think on how she must be viewing me now. So God bless you, Job Legh; and no more from
>
> Yours to command,
>
> JAMES WILSON.

Job turned the letter over and over when he had read it; sighed deeply; and then wrapping it carefully up in a bit of newspaper he had about him, he put it in his waistcoat pocket, and went off to the door of the witness-room to ask if Mary Barton were there.

As the door opened he saw her sitting within, against a table on which her folded arms were resting, and her head was hidden within them. It was an attitude of hopelessness, and would have served to strike Job dumb in sickness of heart, even without the sound of Mrs. Wilson's voice in passionate sobbing, and sore lamentations, which told him as well as words could do (for she was not within view of the door, and he did not care to go in), that she was at any rate partially undeceived as to the hopes he had given her last night.

Sorrowfully did Job return into the body of the court; neither Mrs. Wilson nor Mary having seen him as he had stood at the witness-room door.

As soon as he could bring his distracted thoughts to bear upon the present scene, he perceived that the trial of James Wilson for the murder of Henry Carson was just commencing. The clerk was gabbling over the indictment, and in a minute or two there was the accustomed question, "How say you, Guilty, or Not Guilty?"

Although but one answer was expected,—was customary in all cases,—there was a pause of dead silence, an interval of solemnity even in this hackneyed part of the proceeding; while the prisoner at the bar stood with compressed lips, looking at the judge with his outward eyes, but with far other and different scenes presented to his mental vision;—a sort of rapid recapitulation of his life,—remembrances of his childhood,—his father (so proud of him, his first-born child),—his sweet little playfellow, Mary,—his hopes, his love,—his despair, yet still, yet ever and ever, his love,—the blank, wide world it had been without her love,—his mother,—his childless mother,—but not long to be so,—not long to be away from all she loved,—nor during that time to be oppressed with doubt as to his innocence, sure and secure of her darling's heart;—he started from his instant's pause, and said in a low firm voice,

"Not guilty, my lord."

The circumstances of the murder, the discovery of the body, the causes of suspicion against Jem, were as well known to most of the audience as they are to you, so there was some little buzz of conversation going on among the people while the leading counsel for the prosecution made his very effective speech.

"That's Mr. Carson, the father, sitting behind Serjeant Wilkinson!"

"What a noble-looking old man he is! so stern and inflexible, with such classical features! Does he not remind you of some of the busts of Jupiter?"

"I am more interested by watching the prisoner. Criminals always interest me. I try to trace in the features common to humanity some expression of the crimes by which they have distinguished themselves from their kind. I have seen a good number of murderers in my day, but I have seldom seen one with such marks of Cain on his countenance as the man at the bar."

"Well, I am no physiognomist, but I don't think his face strikes me as bad. It certainly is gloomy and depressed, and not unnaturally so, considering his situation."

"Only look at his low, resolute brow, his downcast eye, his white compressed lips. He never looks up,—just watch him."

"His forehead is not so low if he had that mass of black hair removed, and is very square, which some people say is a good sign. If others are to be influenced by such trifles as you are, it would have been much better if the prison barber had cut his hair a little previous to the trial; and as for down-cast eye, and compressed lip, it is all part and parcel of his inward agitation just now; nothing to do with character, my good fellow."

Poor Jem! His raven hair (his mother's pride, and so often fondly caressed by her fingers), was that too to have its influence against him?

The witnesses were called. At first they consisted principally of policemen; who, being much accustomed to giving evidence, knew what were the material points they were called on to prove, and did not lose the time of the court in listening to any thing unnecessary.

"Clear as day against the prisoner," whispered one attorney's clerk to another.

"Black as night, you mean," replied his friend; and they both smiled.

"Jane Wilson! who's she? some relation, I suppose, from the name."

"The mother,—she that is to prove the gun part of the case."

"Oh, ay—I remember! Rather hard on her, too, I think."

Then both were silent, as one of the officers of the court ushered Mrs. Wilson into the witness-box. I have often called her "the old woman," and "an old woman," because, in truth, her appearance was so much beyond her years, which might not be many above fifty. But partly owing to her accident in early life, which left a stamp of pain upon her face, partly owing to her anxious temper, partly to her sorrows, and partly to her limping gait, she always gave me the idea of age. But now she might have seemed more than seventy; her lines were so set and deep, her features so sharpened, and her walk so feeble. She was trying to check her sobs into composure, and (unconsciously) was striving to behave as she thought would best please her poor boy, whom she knew she had often grieved by her uncontrolled impatience. He had buried his face in his arms, which rested on the front of the dock (an attitude he retained during the greater part of his trial, and which prejudiced many against him).

The counsel began the examination.

"Your name is Jane Wilson, I believe."

"Yes, sir."

"The mother of the prisoner at the bar?"

"Yes, sir;" with quivering voice, ready to break out into weeping, but earning respect by the strong effort at self-control, prompted, as I have said before, by her earnest wish to please her son by her behaviour.

The barrister now proceeded to the important part of the examination, tending to prove that the gun found on the scene of the murder was the prisoner's. She had committed herself so fully to the policeman, that she could not well retract; so without much delay in bringing the question round to the desired point, the gun was produced in court, and the inquiry made—

"That gun belongs to your son, does it not?"

She clenched the sides of the witness-box in her efforts to make her parched tongue utter words. At last she moaned forth,

"Oh! Jem, Jem! what mun I say?"

Every one bent forward to hear the prisoner's answer; although, in fact, it was of little importance to the issue of the trial. He lifted up his head; and with a face brimming full of pity for his mother, yet resolved into endurance, said,

"Tell the truth, mother!"

And so she did, with the fidelity of a little child. Every one felt that she did; and the little colloquy between mother and son did them some slight service in the opinion of the audience. But the awful judge sat unmoved; and the jurymen changed not a muscle of their countenances; while the counsel for the prosecution went triumphantly through this part of the case, including the fact of Jem's absence from home on the night of the murder, and bringing every admission to bear right against the prisoner.

It was over. She was told to go down. But she could no longer compel her mother's heart to keep silence, and suddenly turning towards the judge (with whom she imagined the verdict to rest), she thus addressed him with her choking voice.

"And now, sir, I've telled you the truth, and the whole truth, as *he* bid me; but don't ye let what I have said go for to hang him; oh, my lord judge, take my word for it, he's as innocent as the child as has yet to be born. For sure, I, who am his mother, and have nursed him on my knee, and been gladdened by the sight of him every day since, ought to know him better than yon pack of fellows" (indicating the jury, while she strove against her heart to render her words distinct and clear for her dear son's sake) "who, I'll go bail, never saw him before this morning in all their born days. My lord judge, he's so good I often wondered what harm there was in him; many is the time when I've been fretted (for I'm frabbit enough at times), when I've scold't myself, and said, 'You ungrateful thing, the Lord God has given you Jem, and isn't that blessing enough for you?' But He has seen fit to punish me. If Jem is—if Jem is—taken from me, I shall be a childless woman; and very poor, having nought left to love on earth, and I cannot say 'His will be done.' I cannot, my lord judge, oh, I cannot."

While sobbing out these words she was led away by the officers of the court, but tenderly, and reverently, with the respect which great sorrow commands.

The stream of evidence went on and on, gathering fresh force from every witness who was examined, and threatening to overwhelm poor Jem. Already they had proved that the gun was his, that he had been heard not many days before the commission of the deed to threaten the deceased; indeed, that the police had, at that time, been obliged to interfere to prevent some probable act of violence. It only remained to bring forward a sufficient motive for the threat and the murder. The clue to this had been furnished by the policeman, who had overheard Jem's angry language to Mr. Carson; and his report in the first instance had occasioned the subpœna to Mary.

And now she was to be called on to bear witness. The court was by this time almost as full as it could hold; but fresh attempts were being made to squeeze in at all the entrances, for many were anxious to see and hear this part of the trial.

Old Mr. Carson felt an additional beat at his heart at the thought of seeing the fatal Helen, the cause of all—a kind of interest and yet repugnance, for was not she beloved by the dead; nay, perhaps in her way, loving and mourning for the same being that he himself was so bitterly grieving over? And yet he felt as if he abhorred her and her rumoured loveliness, as if she were the curse against him; and he grew jealous of the love with which she had inspired his son, and would fain have deprived her of even her natural right of sorrowing over her lover's untimely end: for you see it was a fixed idea in the minds of all, that the handsome, bright, gay, rich young gentleman must have been beloved in preference to the serious, almost stern-looking smith, who had to toil for his daily bread.

Hitherto the effect of the trial had equalled Mr. Carson's most sanguine hopes, and a severe look of satisfaction came over the face of the avenger,—over that countenance whence the smile had departed, never more to return.

All eyes were directed to the door through which the witnesses entered. Even Jem looked up to catch one glimpse before he hid his face from her look of aversion. The officer had gone to fetch her.

She was in exactly the same attitude as when Job Legh had seen her two hours before through the half-open door. Not a finger had moved. The officer summoned her, but she did not stir. She was so still he thought she had fallen asleep, and he stepped forward and touched her. She started up in an instant, and followed him with a kind of rushing rapid motion into the court, into the witness-box.

And amid all that sea of faces, misty and swimming before her eyes, she saw but two clear bright spots, distinct and fixed: the judge, who might have to condemn; and the prisoner, who might have to die.

The mellow sunlight streamed down that high window on her head, and fell on the rich treasure of her golden hair, stuffed away in masses under her little bonnet-cap; and in those warm beams the motes kept dancing up and down. The wind had changed—had changed almost as soon as she had given up her watching; the wind had changed, and she heeded it not.

Many who were looking for mere flesh and blood beauty, mere colouring, were disappointed; for her face was deadly white, and almost set in its expression, while a mournful bewildered soul looked out of the depths of those soft, deep, gray eyes. But others recognised a higher and stranger kind of beauty; one that would keep its hold on the memory for many after years.

I was not there myself; but one who was, told me that her look, and indeed her whole face, was more like the well-known engraving from Guido's picture of "Beatrice Cenci" than any thing else he could give me an idea of. He added, that her countenance haunted him, like the remembrance of some wild sad melody, heard in childhood; that it would perpetually recur with its mute imploring agony.

With all the court reeling before her (always save and except those awful two), she heard a voice speak, and answered the simple inquiry (something about her name) mechanically, as if in a dream. So she went on for two or three more questions, with a strange wonder in her brain, as to the reality of the terrible circumstances in which she was placed.

Suddenly she was roused, she knew not how or by what. She was conscious that all was real, that hundreds were looking at her, that true-sounding words were being extracted from her; that that figure, so bowed down, with the face concealed by both hands, was really Jem. Her face flushed scarlet, and then paler than before. But in her dread of herself, with the tremendous secret imprisoned within her, she exerted every power she had to keep in the full understanding of what was going on, of what she was asked, and of what she answered. With all her faculties preternaturally alive and sensitive, she heard the next question from the pert young barrister, who was delighted to have the examination of this witness.

"And pray, may I ask, which was the favoured lover? You say you knew both these young men. Which was the favoured lover? Which did you prefer?"

And who was he, the questioner, that he should dare so lightly to ask of her heart's secrets? That he should dare to ask her to tell, before that multitude assembled there, what woman usually whispers with blushes and tears, and many hesitations, to one ear alone?

So, for an instant, a look of indignation contracted Mary's brow, as she steadily met the eyes of the impertinent counsellor. But, in that instant, she saw the hands removed from a face beyond, behind; and a countenance revealed of such intense love and woe,—such a deprecating dread of her answer; and suddenly her resolution was taken. The present was everything; the future, that vast shroud, it was maddening to think upon; but *now* she might own her fault, but *now* she might even own her love. Now, when the beloved stood thus, abhorred of men, there would be no feminine shame to stand between her and her avowal. So she also turned towards the judge, partly to mark that her answer was not given to the monkeyfied man who questioned her, and likewise that her face might be averted from, and her eyes not gaze upon, the form that contracted with the dread of the words he anticipated.

"He asks me which of them two I liked the best. Perhaps I liked Mr. Harry Carson once—I don't know—I've forgotten; but I loved James Wilson, that's now on trial, above what tongue can tell—above all else on earth put together; and I love him now better than ever, though he has never known a word of it till this minute. For you see, sir, mother died before I was thirteen, before I could know right from wrong about some things; and I was giddy and vain, and ready to listen to any praise of my good looks; and this poor young Mr. Carson fell in with me, and told me he loved me; and I was foolish enough to think he meant me marriage: a mother is a pitiful loss to a girl, sir; and so I used to fancy I could like to be a lady, and rich, and never know want any more. I never found out how dearly I loved another till one day, when James Wilson asked me to marry him, and I was very hard and sharp in my answer (for indeed, sir, I'd a deal to bear just then), and he took me at my word and left me; and from that day to this I've never spoken a word to him, or set eyes on him; though I'd fain have done so, to try and show him we had both been too hasty; for he'd not been gone out of my sight above a minute before I knew I loved—far above my life," said she, dropping her voice as she came to this second confession of the strength of her attachment. "But, if the gentleman asks me which I loved the best, I make answer, I was flattered by Mr. Carson, and pleased with his flattery; but James Wilson I—"

She covered her face with her hands, to hide the burning scarlet blushes, which even dyed her fingers.

There was a little pause; still, though her speech might inspire pity for the prisoner, it only strengthened the supposition of his guilt. Presently the counsellor went on with his examination.

"But you have seen young Mr. Carson since your rejection of the prisoner?"

"Yes, often."

"You have spoken to him, I conclude, at these times."

"Only once to call speaking."

"And what was the substance of your conversation? Did you tell him you found you preferred his rival?"

"No, sir. I don't think as I've done wrong in saying, now as things stand, what my feelings are; but I never would be so bold as to tell one young man I cared for another. I never named Jem's name to Mr. Carson. Never."

"Then what did you say when you had this final conversation with Mr. Carson? You can give me the substance of it, if you don't remember the words."

"I'll try, sir; but I'm not very clear. I told him I could not love him, and wished to have nothing more to do with him. He did his best to over-persuade me, but I kept steady, and at last I ran off."

"And you never spoke to him again?"

"Never!"

"Now, young woman, remember you are upon your oath. Did you ever tell the prisoner at the bar of Mr. Henry Carson's attentions to you? of your acquaintance, in short? Did you ever try to excite his jealousy by boasting of a lover so far above you in station?"

"Never. I never did," said she, in so firm and distinct a manner as to leave no doubt.

"Were you aware that he knew of Mr. Henry Carson's regard for you? Remember you are on your oath!"

"Never, sir. I was not aware until I heard of the quarrel between them, and what Jem had said to the policeman, and that was after the murder. To this day I can't make out who told Jem. Oh, sir, may not I go down?"

For she felt the sense, the composure, the very bodily strength which she had compelled to her aid for a time, suddenly giving way, and was conscious that she was losing all command over herself. There was no occasion to detain her longer; she had done her part. She might go down. The evidence was still stronger against the prisoner; but now he stood erect and firm, with self-respect in his attitude, and a look of determination on his face, which almost made it appear noble. Yet he seemed lost in thought.

Job Legh had all this time been trying to soothe and comfort Mrs. Wilson, who would first be in the court, in order to see her darling, and then, when her sobs became irrepressible, had to be led out into the open air, and sat there weeping, on the steps of the court-house. Who would have taken charge of Mary on her release from the witness-box I do not know, if Mrs. Sturgis, the boatman's wife, had not been there, brought by her interest in Mary, towards whom she now pressed, in order to urge her to leave the scene of the trial.

"No! no!" said Mary, to this proposition. "I must be here, I must watch that they don't hang him, you know I must."

"Oh! they'll not hang him! never fear! Besides the wind has changed, and that's in his favour. Come away. You're so hot, and first white and then red; I'm sure you're ill. Just come away."

"Oh! I don't know about any thing but that I must stay," replied Mary, in a strange hurried manner, catching hold of some rails as if she feared some bodily force would be employed to remove her. So Mrs. Sturgis just waited patiently by her, every now and then peeping among the congregation of heads in the body of the court, to see if her husband were still there. And there he always was to be seen, looking and listening with all his might. His wife felt easy that he would not be wanting her at home until the trial was ended.

Mary never let go her clutched hold on the rails. She wanted them to steady her, in that heaving, whirling court. She thought the feeling of something hard compressed within her hand would help her to listen, for it was such pain, such weary pain in her head, to strive to attend to what was being said. They were all at sea, sailing away on billowy waves, and every one speaking at once, and no one heeding her father, who was calling on them to be silent, and listen to him. Then again, for a brief second, the court stood still, and she could see the judge, sitting up there like an idol, with his trappings, so rigid and stiff; and Jem, opposite, looking at her, as if to say, Am I to die for what you know your ——. Then she checked herself, and by a great struggle brought herself round to an instant's sanity. But the round of thought never stood still; and off she went again; and every time her power of struggling against the growing delirium grew fainter and fainter. She muttered low to herself, but no one heard her except her neighbour, Mrs. Sturgis; all were too closely attending to the case for the prosecution, which was now being wound up.

The counsel for the prisoner had avoided much cross-examination, reserving to himself the right of calling the witnesses forward again; for he had received so little, and such vague instructions, and understood that so much depended on the evidence of one who was not forthcoming, that in fact he had little hope of establishing any thing like a show of a defence, and contented himself with watching the case, and lying in wait for any legal objections that might offer themselves. He lay back on the seat, occasionally taking a pinch of snuff in a manner intended to be contemptuous; now and then elevating his eyebrows, and sometimes exchanging a little note with Mr. Bridgenorth behind him. The attorney had far more interest in the case than the barrister, to which he was perhaps excited by his poor old friend Job Legh; who had edged and wedged himself through the crowd close to Mr. Bridgenorth's elbow, sent thither by Ben Sturgis, to whom he had been "introduced" by Charley Jones, and who had accounted for Mary's disappearance on the preceding day, and spoken of their chase, their fears, their hopes.

All this was told in a few words to Mr. Bridgenorth—so few, that they gave him but a confused idea, that time was of value; and this he named to his counsel, who now rose to speak for the defence.

Job Legh looked about for Mary, now he had gained, and given, some idea of the position of things. At last he saw her, standing by a decent-looking woman, looking flushed and anxious, and moving her lips incessantly, as if eagerly talking; her eyes never resting on any object, but wandering about as if in search of something. Job thought it was for him she was seeking, and he struggled to get round to her. When he had succeeded, she took no notice of him, although he spoke to her, but still kept looking round and round in the same wild, restless manner. He tried to hear the low quick mutterings of her voice, as he caught the repetition of the same words over and over again.

"I must not go mad. I must not, indeed. They say people tell the truth when they're mad; but I don't. I was always a liar. I was, indeed; but I'm not mad. I must not go mad. I must not, indeed."

Suddenly she seemed to become aware how earnestly Job was listening (with mournful attention) to her words, and turning sharp round upon him, with upbraiding for his eaves-dropping on her lips, she caught sight of something,—or some one,—who, even in that state, had power to arrest her attention, and throwing up her arms with wild energy, she shrieked aloud,

"Oh, Jem! Jem! you're saved; and I *am* mad—" and was instantly seized with convulsions. With much commiseration she was taken out of court, while the attention of many was diverted from her, by the fierce energy with which a sailor forced his way over rails and seats, against turnkeys and policemen. The officers of the court opposed this forcible manner of entrance, but they could hardly induce the offender to adopt any quieter way of attaining his object, and telling his tale in the witness-box, the legitimate place. For Will had dwelt so impatiently on the danger in which his absence would place his cousin, that even yet he seemed to fear that he might see the prisoner carried off, and hung, before he could pour out the narrative which would exculpate him. As for Job Legh, his feelings were all but uncontrollable; as you may judge by the indifference with which he saw Mary borne, stiff and convulsed, out of the court, in the charge of the kind Mrs. Sturgis, who, you will remember, was an utter stranger to him.

"She'll keep! I'll not trouble myself about her," said he to himself, as he wrote with trembling hands a little note of information to Mr. Bridgenorth, who had conjectured, when Will had first disturbed the awful tranquillity of the life-and-death court, that the witness had arrived (better late than never) on whose evidence rested all the slight chance yet remaining to Jem Wilson of escaping death. During the commotion in the court, among all the cries and commands, the dismay and the directions, consequent upon Will's entrance, and poor Mary's fearful attack of illness, Mr. Bridgenorth had kept his lawyer-like presence of mind; and long before Job Legh's almost illegible note was poked at him, he had recapitulated the facts on which Will had to give evidence, and the manner in which he had been pursued, after his ship had taken her leave of the land.

The barrister who defended Jem took new heart when he was put in possession of these striking points to be adduced, not so much out of earnestness to save the prisoner, of whose innocence he was still doubtful, as because he saw the opportunities for the display of forensic eloquence which were presented by the facts; "a gallant tar brought back from the pathless ocean by a girl's noble daring," "the dangers of too hastily judging from circumstantial evidence," &c., &c.; while the counsellor for the prosecution prepared himself by folding his arms, elevating his eyebrows, and putting his lips in the form in which they might best whistle down the wind such evidence as might be produced by a suborned witness, who dared to perjure himself. For, of course, it is etiquette to suppose that such evidence as may be given against the opinion which lawyers are paid to uphold, is any thing but based on truth; and "perjury," "conspiracy," and "peril of your immortal soul," are light expressions to throw at the heads of those who may prove (not the speaker, there would then be some excuse for the hasty words of personal anger, but) the hirer of the speaker to be wrong, or mistaken.

But when once Will had attained his end, and felt that his tale, or part of a tale, would be heard by judge and jury; when once he saw Jem standing safe and well before him (even though he saw him pale and care-worn at the felon's bar); his courage took the shape of presence of mind, and he awaited the examination with a calm, unflinching intelligence, which dictated the clearest and most pertinent answers. He told the story you know so well: how his leave of absence being nearly expired, he had resolved to fulfil his promise, and go to see an uncle residing in the Isle of Man; how his money (sailor-like) was all expended in Manchester, and how, consequently, it had been necessary for him to walk to Liverpool, which he had accordingly done on the very night of the murder, accompanied as far as Hollins Greeb by his friend and cousin, the prisoner at the bar. He was clear and distinct in every corroborative circumstance, and gave a short account of the singular way in which he had been recalled from his outward-bound voyage, and the terrible anxiety he had felt, as the pilot-boat had struggled home against the wind. The jury felt that their opinion (so nearly decided half an hour ago) was shaken and disturbed in a very uncomfortable and perplexing way, and were almost grateful to the counsel for the prosecution, when he got up, with a brow of thunder, to demolish the evidence, which was so bewildering when taken in connexion with every thing previously adduced. But if such, without looking to the consequences, was the first impulsive feeling of some among the jury, how shall I describe the vehemence of passion which possessed the mind of poor Mr. Carson, as he saw the effect of the young sailor's statement? It never shook his belief in Jem's guilt in the least, that attempt at an alibi; his hatred, his longing for vengeance, having once defined an object to itself, could no more bear to be frustrated and disappointed than the beast of prey can submit to have his victim taken from his hungry jaws. No more likeness to the calm stern power of Jupiter was there in that white eager face, almost distorted by its fell anxiety of expression.

The counsel to whom etiquette assigned the cross-examination of Will, caught the look on Mr. Carson's face, and in his desire to further the intense wish there manifested, he over-shot his mark even in his first insulting question:

"And now, my man, you've told the court a very good and very convincing story; no reasonable man ought to doubt the unstained innocence of your relation at the bar. Still there is one circumstance you have forgotten to name; and I feel that without it your evidence is rather incomplete. Will you have the kindness to inform the gentlemen of the jury what has been your charge for repeating this very plausible story? How much good coin of Her Majesty's realm have you received, or are you to receive, for walking up from the docks, or some less creditable place, and uttering the tale you have just now repeated,—very much to the credit of your instructor, I must say? Remember, sir, you are upon oath."

It took Will a minute to extract the meaning from the garb of unaccustomed words in which it was invested, and during this time he looked a little confused. But the instant the truth flashed upon him, he fixed his bright clear eyes, flaming with indignation, upon the counsellor, whose look fell at last before that stern unflinching gaze. Then, and not till then, Will made answer.

"Will you tell the judge and jury how much money you've been paid for your impudence towards one who has told God's blessed truth, and who would scorn to tell a lie, or blackguard any one, for the biggest fee as ever lawyer got for doing dirty work? Will you tell, sir?— But I'm ready, my lord judge, to take my oath as many times as your lordship or the jury would like, to testify to things having happened just as I said. There's O'Brien, the pilot, in court now. Would somebody with a wig on please to ask him how much he can say for me?"

It was a good idea, and caught at by the counsel for the defence. O'Brien gave just such testimony as was required to clear Will from all suspicion. He had witnessed the pursuit, he had heard the conversation which took place between the boat and the ship; he had given Will a homeward passage in his boat. And the character of an accredited pilot, appointed by Trinity House, was known to be above suspicion.

Mr. Carson sank back on his seat in sickening despair. He knew enough of courts to be aware of the extreme unwillingness of juries to convict, even where the evidence is most clear, when the penalty of such conviction is death. At the period of the trial most condemnatory to the prisoner, he had repeated this fact to himself in order to damp his too certain expectation of a conviction. Now it needed not repetition, for it forced itself upon his consciousness, and he seemed to *know*, even before the jury retired to consult, that by some trick, some negligence, some miserable hocus-pocus, the murderer of his child, his darling, his Absalom, who had never rebelled,—the slayer of his unburied boy would slip through the fangs of justice, and walk free and unscathed over that earth where his son would never more be seen.

It was even so. The prisoner hid his face once more to shield the expression of an emotion he could not control, from the notice of the over-curious; Job Legh ceased his eager talking to Mr. Bridgenorth; Charley looked grave and earnest; for the jury filed one by one back into their box, and the question was asked to which such an awful answer might be given.

The verdict they had come to was unsatisfactory to themselves at last; neither being convinced of his innocence, nor yet quite willing to believe him guilty in the teeth of the alibi. But the punishment that awaited him, if guilty, was so terrible, and so unnatural a sentence for man to pronounce on man, that the knowledge of it had weighed down the scale on the side of innocence, and "Not Guilty" was the verdict that thrilled through the breathless court.

One moment of silence, and then the murmurs rose, as the verdict was discussed by all with lowered voice. Jem stood motionless, his head bowed; poor fellow, he was stunned with the rapid career of events during the last few hours.

He had assumed his place at the bar with little or no expectation of an acquittal; and with scarcely any desire for life, in the complication of occurrences tending to strengthen the idea of Mary's more than indifference to him; she had loved another, and in her mind Jem believed that he himself must be regarded as the murderer of him she loved. And suddenly, athwart this gloom which made life seem such a blank expanse of desolation, there flashed the exquisite delight of hearing Mary's avowal of love, making the future all glorious, if a future in this world he might hope to have. He could not dwell on any thing but her words, telling of her passionate love; all else was indistinct, nor could he strive to make it otherwise. She loved him.

And Life, now full of tender images, suddenly bright with all exquisite promises, hung on a breath, the slenderest gossamer chance. He tried to think that the knowledge of her love would soothe him even in his dying hours; but the phantoms of what life with her might be, would obtrude, and made him almost gasp and reel under the uncertainty he was enduring. Will's appearance had only added to the intensity of this suspense.

The full meaning of the verdict could not at once penetrate his brain. He stood dizzy and motionless. Some one pulled his coat. He turned, and saw Job Legh, the tears stealing down his brown furrowed cheeks, while he tried in vain to command voice enough to speak. He kept shaking Jem by the hand as the best and necessary expression of his feeling.

"Here! make yourself scarce! I should think you'd be glad to get out of that!" exclaimed the gaoler, as he brought up another livid prisoner, from out whose eyes came the anxiety which he would not allow any other feature to display.

Job Legh pressed out of court, and Jem followed unreasoningly.

The crowd made way, and kept their garments tight about them, as Jem passed, for about him there still hung the taint of the murderer.

He was in the open air, and free once more! Although many looked on him with suspicion, faithful friends closed round him; his arm was unresistingly pumped up and down by his cousin and Job; when one was tired, the other took up the wholesome exercise, while Ben Sturgis was working off his interest in the scene by scolding Charley for walking on his head round and round Mary's sweetheart, for a sweetheart he was now satisfactorily ascertained to be, in spite of her assertion to the contrary. And all this time Jem himself felt bewildered and dazzled; he would have given any thing for an hour's uninterrupted thought on the occurrences of the past week, and the new visions raised up during the morning; aye, even though that tranquil hour were to be passed in the hermitage of his quiet prison cell. The first question sobbed out by his choking voice, oppressed with emotion, was,

"Where is she?"

They led him to the room where his mother sat. They had told her of her son's acquittal, and now she was laughing, and crying, and talking, and giving way to all those feelings which she had restrained with such effort during the last few days. They brought her son to her, and she threw herself upon his neck, weeping there. He returned her embrace, but looked around, beyond. Excepting his mother there was no one in the room but the friends who had entered with him.

"Eh, lad!" said she, when she found voice to speak. "See what it is to have behaved thysel! I could put in a good word for thee, and the jury could na go and hang thee in the face of th' character I gave thee. Was na it a good thing they did na keep me from Liverpool? But I would come; I knew I could do thee good, bless thee, my lad. But thou'rt very white, and all of a tremble."

He kissed her again and again, but looking round as if searching for some one he could not find, the first words he uttered were still,

"Where is she?"

CHAPTER XXXIII - REQUIESCAT IN PACE.

"Fear no more the heat o' th' sun,
  Nor the furious winter's rages;
Thou thy worldly task hast done,
  Home art gone and ta'en thy wages."

CYMBELINE.

"While day and night can bring delight,
  Or nature aught of pleasure give;
While joys above my mind can move
  For thee, and thee alone I live:
"When that grim foe of joy below
  Comes in between to make us part,
The iron hand that breaks our band,
  It breaks my bliss—it breaks my heart."

BURNS.

She was where no words of peace, no soothing hopeful tidings could reach her; in the ghastly spectral world of delirium. Hour after hour, day after day, she started up with passionate cries on her father to save Jem; or rose wildly, imploring the winds and waves, the pitiless winds and waves, to have mercy; and over and over again she exhausted her feverish fitful strength in these agonised entreaties, and fell back powerless, uttering only the wailing moans of despair. They told her Jem was safe, they brought him before her eyes; but sight and hearing were no longer channels of information to that poor distracted brain, nor could human voice penetrate to her understanding.

Jem alone gathered the full meaning of some of her strange sentences, and perceived that by some means or other she, like himself, had divined the truth of her father being the murderer.

Long ago (reckoning time by events and thoughts, and not by clock or dial-plate), Jem had felt certain that Mary's father was Harry Carson's murderer; and although the motive was in some measure a mystery, yet a whole train of circumstances (the principal of which was that John Barton had borrowed the fatal gun only two days before) had left no doubt in Jem's mind. Sometimes he thought that

John had discovered, and thus bloodily resented, the attentions which Mr. Carson had paid to his daughter; at others, he believed the motive to exist in the bitter feuds between the masters and their work-people, in which Barton was known to take so keen an interest. But if he had felt himself pledged to preserve this secret, even when his own life was the probable penalty, and he believed he should fall, execrated by Mary as the guilty destroyer of her lover, how much more was he bound now to labour to prevent any word of hers from inculpating her father, now that she was his own; now that she had braved so much to rescue him; and now that her poor brain had lost all guiding and controlling power over her words.

All that night long Jem wandered up and down the narrow precincts of Ben Sturgis's house. In the little bed-room where Mrs. Sturgis alternately tended Mary, and wept over the violence of her illness, he listened to her ravings; each sentence of which had its own peculiar meaning and reference, intelligible to his mind, till her words rose to the wild pitch of agony, that no one could alleviate, and he could bear it no longer, and stole, sick and miserable down stairs, where Ben Sturgis thought it his duty to snore away in an arm-chair instead of his bed, under the idea that he should thus be more ready for active service, such as fetching the doctor to revisit his patient.

Before it was fairly light, Jem (wide-awake, and listening with an earnest attention he could not deaden, however painful its results proved) heard a gentle subdued knock at the house door; it was no business of his, to be sure, to open it, but as Ben slept on, he thought he would see who the early visitor might be, and ascertain if there was any occasion for disturbing either host or hostess. It was Job Legh who stood there, distinct against the outer light of the street.

"How is she? Eh! poor soul! is that her! no need to ask! How strange her voice sounds! Screech! screech! and she so low, sweet-spoken, when she's well! Thou must keep up heart, old boy, and not look so dismal, thysel."

"I can't help it, Job; it's past a man's bearing to hear such a one as she is, going on as she is doing; even if I did not care for her, it would cut me sore to see one so young, and—I can't speak of it, Job, as a man should do," said Jem, his sobs choking him.

"Let me in, will you?" said Job, pushing past him, for all this time Jem had stood holding the door, unwilling to admit Job where he might hear so much that would be suggestive to one acquainted with the parties that Mary named.

"I'd more than one reason for coming betimes. I wanted to hear how yon poor wench was;—that stood first. Late last night I got a letter from Margaret, very anxious-like. The doctor says the old lady yonder can't last many days longer, and it seems so lonesome for her to die with no one but Margaret and Mrs. Davenport about her. So I thought I'd just come and stay with Mary Barton, and see as she's well done to, and you and your mother and Will go and take leave of old Alice."

Jem's countenance, sad at best just now, fell lower and lower. But Job went on with his speech.

"She still wanders, Margaret says, and thinks she's with her mother at home; but for all that, she should have some kith and kin near her to close her eyes, to my thinking."

"Could not you and Will take mother home? I'd follow when—" Jem faltered out thus far, when Job interrupted,

"Lad! if thou knew what thy mother has suffered for thee, thou'd not speak of leaving her just when she's got thee from the grave as it were. Why, this very night she roused me up, and 'Job,' says she, 'I ask your pardon for wakening you, but tell me, am I awake or dreaming? Is Jem proved innocent? Oh, Job Legh! God send I've not been only dreaming it!' For thou see'st she can't rightly understand why thou'rt with Mary, and not with her. Ay, ay! I know why; but a mother only gives up her son's heart inch by inch to his wife, and then she gives it up with a grudge. No, Jem! thou must go with thy mother just now, if ever thou hopest for God's blessing. She's a widow, and has none but thee. Never fear for Mary! She's young and will struggle through. They are decent people, these folk she is with, and I'll watch o'er her as though she was my own poor girl, that lies cold enough in London-town. I grant ye, it's hard enough for her to be left among strangers. To my mind John Barton would be more in the way of his duty, looking after his daughter, than delegating it up and down the country, looking after every one's business but his own."

A new idea and a new fear came into Jem's mind. What if Mary should implicate her father?

"She raves terribly," said he. "All night long she's been speaking of her father, and mixing up thoughts of him with the trial she saw yesterday. I should not wonder if she'll speak of him as being in court next thing."

"I should na wonder, either," answered Job. "Folk in her way say many and many a strange thing; and th' best way is never to mind them. Now you take your mother home, Jem, and stay by her till old Alice is gone, and trust me for seeing after Mary."

Jem felt how right Job was, and could not resist what he knew to be his duty, but I cannot tell you how heavy and sick at heart he was as he stood at the door to take a last fond, lingering look at Mary. He saw her sitting up in bed, her golden hair, dimmed with her one day's illness, floating behind her, her head bound round with wetted cloths, her features all agitated, even to distortion, with the pangs of her anxiety.

Her lover's eyes filled with tears. He could not hope. The elasticity of his heart had been crushed out of him by early sorrows; and now, especially, the dark side of every thing seemed to be presented to him. What if she died, just when he knew the treasure, the untold treasure he possessed in her love! What if (worse than death) she remained a poor gibbering maniac all her life long (and mad people do live to be old sometimes, even under all the pressure of their burden), terror-distracted as she was now, and no one able to comfort her!

"Jem!" said Job, partly guessing the other's feelings by his own. "Jem!" repeated he, arresting his attention before he spoke. Jem turned round, the little motion causing the tears to overflow and trickle down his cheeks. "Thou must trust in God, and leave her in His hands." He spoke hushed, and low; but the words sank all the more into Jem's heart, and gave him strength to tear himself away.

He found his mother (notwithstanding that she had but just regained her child through Mary's instrumentality) half inclined to resent his having passed the night in anxious devotion to the poor invalid. She dwelt on the duties of children to their parents (above all others), till Jem could hardly believe the relative positions they had held only yesterday, when she was struggling with and controlling every instinct of her nature, only because *he* wished it. However, the recollection of that yesterday, with its hair's breadth between him and a felon's death, and the love that had lightened the dark shadow, made him bear with the meekness and patience of a true-hearted man all the worrying little acerbities of to-day; and he had no small merit in so doing; for in him, as in his mother, the re-action after intense excitement had produced its usual effect in increased irritability of the nervous system.

They found Alice alive, and without pain. And that was all. A child of a few weeks old would have had more bodily strength; a child of a very few months old, more consciousness of what was passing before her. But even in this state she diffused an atmosphere of peace around her. True, Will, at first, wept passionate tears at the sight of her, who had been as a mother to him, so standing on the confines of life. But even now, as always, loud passionate feeling could not long endure in the calm of her presence. The firm faith which her mind had no longer power to grasp, had left its trail of glory; for by no other word can I call the bright happy look which illumined the old earth-worn face. Her talk, it is true, bore no more that constant earnest reference to God and His holy Word which it had done in health, and there were no death-bed words of exhortation from the lips of one so habitually pious. For still she imagined herself once again in the happy, happy realms of childhood; and again dwelling in the lovely northern haunts where she had so often longed to be. Though earthly sight was gone away, she beheld again the scenes she had loved from long years ago! she saw them without a change to dim the old radiant hues. The long dead were with her, fresh and blooming as in those bygone days. And death came to her as a welcome blessing, like as evening comes to the weary child. Her work here was finished, and faithfully done.

What better sentence can an emperor wish to have said over his bier? In second childhood (that blessing clouded by a name), she said her "Nunc Dimittis,"—the sweetest canticle to the holy.

"Mother, good night! Dear mother! bless me once more! I'm very tired, and would fain go to sleep." She never spoke again on this side Heaven.

She died the day after their return from Liverpool. From that time, Jem became aware that his mother was jealously watching for some word or sign which should betoken his wish to return to Mary. And yet go to Liverpool he must and would, as soon as the funeral was over, if but for a single glimpse of his darling. For Job had never written; indeed, any necessity for his so doing had never entered his head. If Mary died, he would announce it personally; if she recovered, he meant to bring her home with him. Writing was to him little more than an auxiliary to natural history; a way of ticketing specimens, not of expressing thoughts.

The consequence of this want of intelligence as to Mary's state was, that Jem was constantly anticipating that every person and every scrap of paper was to convey to him the news of her death. He could not endure this state long; but he resolved not to disturb the house by announcing to his mother his purposed intention of returning to Liverpool, until the dead had been carried forth.

On Sunday afternoon they laid her low with many tears. Will wept as one who would not be comforted.

The old childish feeling came over him, the feeling of loneliness at being left among strangers.

By and bye, Margaret timidly stole near him, as if waiting to console; and soon his passion sank down to grief, and grief gave way to melancholy, and though he felt as if he never could be joyful again, he was all the while unconsciously approaching nearer to the full happiness of calling Margaret his own, and a golden thread was interwoven even now with the darkness of his sorrow. Yet it was on his arm that Jane Wilson leant on her return homewards. Jem took charge of Margaret.

"Margaret, I'm bound for Liverpool by the first train to-morrow; I must set your grandfather at liberty."

"I'm sure he likes nothing better than watching over poor Mary; he loves her nearly as well as me. But let me go! I have been so full of poor Alice, I've never thought of it before; I can't do so much as many a one, but Mary will like to have a woman about her that she knows. I'm sorry I waited to be reminded, Jem." replied Margaret, with some little self-reproach.

But Margaret's proposition did not at all agree with her companion's wishes. He found he had better speak out, and put his intention at once to the right motive; the subterfuge about setting Job Legh at liberty had done him harm instead of good.

"To tell truth, Margaret, it's I that must go, and that for my own sake, not your grandfather's. I can rest neither by night nor day for thinking on Mary. Whether she lives or dies I look on her as my wife before God, as surely and solemnly as if we were married. So being, I have the greatest right to look after her, and I cannot yield it even to—"

"Her father," said Margaret, finishing his interrupted sentence. "It seems strange that a girl like her should be thrown on the bare world to struggle through so bad an illness. No one seems to know where John Barton is, else I thought of getting Morris to write him a letter telling him about Mary. I wish he was home, that I do!"

Jem could not echo this wish.

"Mary's not bad off for friends where she is," said he. "I call them friends, though a week ago we none of us knew there were such folks in the world. But being anxious and sorrowful about the same thing makes people friends quicker than any thing, I think. She's like a mother to Mary in her ways; and he bears a good character, as far as I could learn just in that hurry. We're drawing near home, and I've not said my say, Margaret. I want you to look after mother a bit. She'll not like my going, and I've got to break it to her yet. If she takes it very badly, I'll come back to-morrow night; but if she's not against it very much, I mean to stay till it's settled about Mary, one way or the other. Will, you know, will be there, Margaret, to help a bit in doing for mother."

Will's being there made the only objection Margaret saw to this plan. She disliked the idea of seeming to throw herself in his way; and yet she did not like to say any thing of this feeling to Jem, who had all along seemed perfectly unconscious of any love-affair, besides his own, in progress.

So Margaret gave a reluctant consent.

"If you can just step up to our house to-night, Jem, I'll put up a few things as may be useful to Mary, and then you can say when you'll likely be back. If you come home to-morrow night, and Will's there, perhaps I need not step up?"

"Yes, Margaret, do! I shan't leave easy unless you go some time in the day to see mother. I'll come to-night, though; and now good-bye. Stay! do you think you could just coax poor Will to walk a bit home with you, that I might speak to mother by myself?"

No! that Margaret could not do. That was expecting too great a sacrifice of bashful feeling.

But the object was accomplished by Will's going up-stairs immediately on their return to the house, to indulge his mournful thoughts alone. As soon as Jem and his mother were left by themselves, he began on the subject uppermost in his mind.

"Mother!"

She put her handkerchief from her eyes, and turned quickly round so as to face him where he stood, thinking what best to say. The little action annoyed him, and he rushed at once into the subject.

"Mother! I am going back to Liverpool to-morrow morning to see how Mary Barton is."

"And what's Mary Barton to thee, that thou shouldst be running after her in that-a-way?"

"If she lives, she shall be my wedded wife. If she dies—mother, I can't speak of what I shall feel if she dies." His voice was choked in his throat.

For an instant his mother was interested by his words; and then came back the old jealousy of being supplanted in the affections of that son, who had been, as it were, newly born to her, by the escape he had so lately experienced from danger. So she hardened her heart against entertaining any feeling of sympathy; and turned away from the face, which recalled the earnest look of his childhood, when he had come to her in some trouble, sure of help and comfort.

And coldly she spoke, in those tones which Jem knew and dreaded, even before the meaning they expressed was fully shaped. "Thou'rt old enough to please thysel. Old mothers are cast aside, and what they've borne forgotten, as soon as a pretty face comes across. I might have thought of that last Tuesday, when I felt as if thou wert all my own, and the judge were some wild animal trying to rend thee from me. I spoke up for thee then; but it's all forgotten now, I suppose."

"Mother! you know all this while, *you know* I can never forget any kindness you've ever done for me; and they've been many. Why should you think I've only room for one love in my heart? I can love you as dearly as ever, and Mary too, as much as man ever loved woman."

He awaited a reply. None was vouchsafed.

"Mother, answer me!" said he, at last.

"What mun I answer? You asked me no question."

"Well! I ask you this now. To-morrow morning I go to Liverpool to see her, who is as my wife. Dear mother! will you bless me on my errand? If it please God she recovers, will you take her to you as you would a daughter?"

She could neither refuse nor assent.

"Why need you go?" said she querulously, at length. "You'll be getting in some mischief or another again. Can't you stop at home quiet with me?"

Jem got up, and walked about the room in despairing impatience. She would not understand his feelings. At last he stopped right before the place where she was sitting, with an air of injured meekness on her face.

"Mother! I often think what a good man father was! I've often heard you tell of your courting days; and of the accident that befell you, and how ill you were. How long is it ago?"

"Near upon five-and-twenty years," said she, with a sigh.

"You little thought when you were so ill you should live to have such a fine strapping son as I am, did you now?"

She smiled a little, and looked up at him, which was just what he wanted.

"Thou'rt not so fine a man as thy father was, by a deal!" said she, looking at him with much fondness, notwithstanding her depreciatory words.

He took another turn or two up and down the room. He wanted to bend the subject round to his own case.

"Those were happy days when father was alive!"

"You may say so, lad! Such days as will never come again to me, at any rate." She sighed sorrowfully.

"Mother!" said he at last, stopping short, and taking her hand in his with tender affection, "you'd like me to be as happy a man as my father was before me, would not you? You'd like me to have some one to make me as happy as you made father? Now, would you not, dear mother?"

"I did not make him as happy as I might ha' done," murmured she, in a low, sad voice of self-reproach. "Th' accident gave a jar to my temper it's never got the better of; and now he's gone where he can never know how I grieve for having frabbed him as I did."

"Nay, mother, we don't know that!" said Jem, with gentle soothing. "Any how, you and father got along with as few rubs as most people. But for *his* sake, dear mother, don't say me nay, now that I come to you to ask your blessing before setting out to see her, who is to be my wife, if ever woman is; for *his* sake, if not for mine, love her who I shall bring home to be to me all you were to him: and mother! I do not ask for a truer or a tenderer heart than yours is, in the long run."

The hard look left her face; though her eyes were still averted from Jem's gaze, it was more because they were brimming over with tears, called forth by his words, than because any angry feeling yet remained. And when his manly voice died away in low pleadings, she lifted up her hands, and bent down her son's head below the level of her own; and then she solemnly uttered a blessing.

"God bless thee, Jem, my own dear lad. And may He bless Mary Barton for thy sake."

Jem's heart leaped up, and from this time hope took the place of fear in his anticipations with regard to Mary.

"Mother! you show your own true self to Mary, and she'll love you as dearly as I do."

So with some few smiles, and some few tears, and much earnest talking, the evening wore away.

"I must be off to see Margaret. Why, it's near ten o'clock! Could you have thought it? Now don't you stop up for me, mother. You and Will go to bed, for you've both need of it. I shall be home in an hour."

Margaret had felt the evening long and lonely; and was all but giving up the thoughts of Jem's coming that night, when she heard his step at the door.

He told her of his progress with his mother; he told her his hopes, and was silent on the subject of his fears.

"To think how sorrow and joy are mixed up together. You'll date your start in life as Mary's acknowledged lover from poor Alice Wilson's burial day. Well! the dead are soon forgotten!"

"Dear Margaret!—But you're worn out with your long evening waiting for me. I don't wonder. But never you, nor any one else, think because God sees fit to call up new interests, perhaps right out of the grave, that therefore the dead are forgotten. Margaret, you yourself can remember our looks, and fancy what we're like."

"Yes! but what has that to do with remembering Alice?"

"Why, just this. You're not always trying to think on our faces, and making a labour of remembering; but often, I'll be bound, when you're sinking off to sleep, or when you're very quiet and still, the faces you knew so well when you could see, come smiling before you with loving looks. Or you remember them, without striving after it, and without thinking it's your duty to keep recalling them. And so it is with them that are hidden from our sight. If they've been worthy to be heartily loved while alive, they'll not be forgotten when dead; it's against nature. And we need no more be upbraiding ourselves for letting in God's rays of light upon our sorrow, and no more be fearful of forgetting them, because their memory is not always haunting and taking up our minds, than you need to trouble yourself about remembering your grandfather's face, or what the stars were like,—you can't forget if you would, what it's such a pleasure to think about. Don't fear my forgetting Aunt Alice."

"I'm not, Jem; not now, at least; only you seemed so full about Mary."

"I've kept it down so long, remember. How glad Aunt Alice would have been to know that I might hope to have her for my wife! that's to say, if God spares her!"

"She would not have known it, even if you could have told her this last fortnight,—ever since you went away she's been thinking always that she was a little child at her mother's apron-string. She must have been a happy little thing; it was such a pleasure to her to think about those early days, when she lay old and gray on her death-bed."

"I never knew any one seem more happy all her life long."

"Ay! and how gentle and easy her death was! She thought her mother was near her."

They fell into calm thought about those last peaceful happy hours.

It struck eleven. Jem started up.

"I should have been gone long ago. Give me the bundle. You'll not forget my mother. Good night, Margaret."

She let him out and bolted the door behind him. He stood on the steps to adjust some fastening about the bundle. The court, the street, was deeply still. Long ago had all retired to rest on that quiet Sabbath evening. The stars shone down on the silent deserted streets, and the soft clear moonlight fell in bright masses, leaving the steps on which Jem stood in shadow.

A foot-fall was heard along the pavement; slow and heavy was the sound. Before Jem had ended his little piece of business, a form had glided into sight; a wan, feeble figure, bearing, with evident and painful labour, a jug of water from the neighbouring pump. It went before Jem, turned up the court at the corner of which he was standing, passed into the broad, calm light; and there, with bowed head, sinking and shrunk body, Jem recognised John Barton.

No haunting ghost could have had less of the energy of life in its involuntary motions than he, who, nevertheless, went on with the same measured clock-work tread until the door of his own house was reached. And then he disappeared, and the latch fell feebly to, and made a faint and wavering sound, breaking the solemn silence of the night. Then all again was still.

For a minute or two Jem stood motionless, stunned by the thoughts which the sight of Mary's father had called up.

Margaret did not know he was at home: had he stolen like a thief by dead of night into his own dwelling? Depressed as Jem had often and long seen him, this night there was something different about him still; beaten down by some inward storm, he seemed to grovel along, all self-respect lost and gone.

Must he be told of Mary's state? Jem felt he must not; and this for many reasons. He could not be informed of her illness without many other particulars being communicated at the same time, of which it were better he should be kept in ignorance; indeed, of which Mary herself could alone give the full explanation. No suspicion that he was the criminal seemed hitherto to have been excited in the mind of any one. Added to these reasons was Jem's extreme unwillingness to face him, with the belief in his breast that he, and none other, had done the fearful deed.

It was true that he was Mary's father, and as such had every right to be told of all concerning her; but supposing he were, and that he followed the impulse so natural to a father, and wished to go to her, what might be the consequences? Among the mingled feelings she had revealed in her delirium, ay, mingled even with the most tender expressions of love for her father, was a sort of horror of him; a dread of him as a blood-shedder, which seemed to separate him into two persons,—one, the father who had dandled her on his knee, and loved her all her life long; the other, the assassin, the cause of all her trouble and woe.

If he presented himself before her while this idea of his character was uppermost, who might tell the consequence?

Jem could not, and would not, expose her to any such fearful chance: and to tell the truth, I believe he looked upon her as more his own, to guard from all shadow of injury with most loving care, than as belonging to any one else in this world, though girt with the reverend name of Father, and guiltless of aught that might have lessened such reverence.

If you think this account of mine confused, of the half-feelings, half-reasons, which passed through Jem's mind, as he stood gazing at the empty space, where that crushed form had so lately been seen,—if you are perplexed to disentangle the real motives, I do assure you it was from just such an involved set of thoughts that Jem drew the resolution to act as if he had not seen that phantom likeness of John Barton; himself, yet not himself.

CHAPTER XXXIV - THE RETURN HOME.

"*Dixwell.* Forgiveness! Oh, forgiveness, and a grave!
Mary. God knows thy heart, my father! and I shudder
To think what thou perchance hast acted.
Dixwell. Oh!
Mary. No common load of woe is thine, my father."

ELLIOTT'S "KERHONAH."

Mary still hovered between life and death when Jem arrived at the house where she lay; and the doctors were as yet unwilling to compromise their wisdom by allowing too much hope to be entertained. But the state of things, if not less anxious, was less distressing than when Jem had quitted her. She lay now in a stupor, which was partly disease, and partly exhaustion after the previous excitement.

And now Jem found the difficulty which every one who has watched by a sick bed knows full well; and which is perhaps more insurmountable to men than it is to women,—the difficulty of being patient, and trying not to expect any visible change for long, long hours of sad monotony.

But after awhile the reward came. The laboured breathing became lower and softer, the heavy look of oppressive pain melted away from the face, and a languor that was almost peace took the place of suffering. She slept a natural sleep; and they stole about on tip-toe, and spoke low, and softly, and hardly dared to breathe, however much they longed to sigh out their thankful relief.

She opened her eyes. Her mind was in the tender state of a lately-born infant's. She was pleased with the gay but not dazzling colours of the paper; soothed by the subdued light; and quite sufficiently amused by looking at all the objects in the room,—the drawing of the ships, the festoons of the curtain, the bright flowers on the painted backs of the chairs,—to care for any stronger excitement. She wondered at the ball of glass, containing various coloured sands from the Isle of Wight, or some such place, which hung suspended from the middle of the little valance over the window. But she did not care to exert herself to ask any questions, although she saw Mrs. Sturgis standing at the bed-side with some tea, ready to drop it into her mouth by spoonfuls.

She did not see the face of honest joy, of earnest thankfulness,—the clasped hands,—the beaming eyes,—the trembling eagerness of gesture, of one who had long awaited her awakening, and who now stood behind the curtains watching through some little chink her every faint motion; or if she had caught a glimpse of that loving, peeping face, she was in too exhausted a state to have taken much notice, or have long retained the impression that he she loved so well was hanging about her, and blessing God for every conscious look which stole over her countenance.

She fell softly into slumber, without a word having been spoken by any one during that half hour of inexpressible joy. And again the stillness was enforced by sign and whispered word, but with eyes that beamed out their bright thoughts of hope. Jem sat by the side of the bed, holding back the little curtain, and gazing as if he could never gaze his fill at the pale, wasted face, so marbled and so chiselled in its wan outline.

She wakened once more; her soft eyes opened, and met his over-bending look. She smiled gently, as a baby does when it sees its mother tending its little cot; and continued her innocent, infantine gaze into his face, as if the sight gave her much unconscious pleasure. But by-and-by a different expression came into her sweet eyes; a look of memory and intelligence; her white face flushed the brightest rosy red, and with feeble motion she tried to hide her head in the pillow.

It required all Jem's self-control to do what he knew and felt to be necessary, to call Mrs. Sturgis, who was quietly dozing by the fireside; and that done, he felt almost obliged to leave the room to keep down the happy agitation which would gush out in every feature, every gesture, and every tone.

From that time forward Mary's progress towards health was rapid.

There was every reason, but one, in favour of her speedy removal home. All Jem's duties lay in Manchester. It was his mother's dwelling-place, and there his plans for life had been to be worked out; plans, which the suspicion and imprisonment he had fallen into, had thrown for a time into a chaos, which his presence was required to arrange into form. For he might find, in spite of a jury's verdict, that too strong a taint was on his character for him ever to labour in Manchester again. He remembered the manner in which some one suspected of having been a convict was shunned by masters and men, when he had accidentally met with work in their foundry; the recollection smote him now, how he himself had thought that it did not become an honest upright man to associate with one who had been a prisoner. He could not choose but think on that poor humble being, with his downcast conscious look; hunted out of the work-shop, where he had sought to earn an honest livelihood, by the looks, and half-spoken words, and the black silence of repugnance (worse than words to bear), that met him on all sides.

Jem felt that his own character had been attainted; and that to many it might still appear suspicious. He knew that he could convince the world, by a future as blameless as his past had been, that he was innocent. But at the same time he saw that he must have patience, and nerve himself for some trials; and the sooner these were undergone, the sooner he was aware of the place he held in men's estimation, the better. He longed to have presented himself once more at the foundry; and then the reality would drive away the pictures that would (unbidden) come of a shunned man, eyed askance by all, and driven forth to shape out some new career.

I said every reason "but one" inclined Jem to hasten Mary's return as soon as she was sufficiently convalescent. That one was the meeting which awaited her at home.

Turn it over as Jem would, he could not decide what was the best course to pursue. He could compel himself to any line of conduct that his reason and his sense of right told him to be desirable; but they did not tell him it was desirable to speak to Mary, in her tender state of mind and body, of her father. How much would be implied by the mere mention of his name! Speak it as calmly, and as indifferently as he might, he could not avoid expressing some consciousness of the terrible knowledge she possessed.

She, for her part, was softer and gentler than she had ever been in her gentlest mood; since her illness, her motions, her glances, her voice were all tender in their languor. It seemed almost a trouble to her to break the silence with the low sounds of her own sweet voice, and her words fell sparingly on Jem's greedy, listening ear.

Her face was, however, so full of love and confidence, that Jem felt no uneasiness at the state of silent abstraction into which she often fell. If she did but love him, all would yet go right; and it was better not to press for confidence on that one subject which must be painful to both.

There came a fine, bright, balmy day. And Mary tottered once more out into the open air, leaning on Jem's arm, and close to his beating heart. And Mrs. Sturgis watched them from her door, with a blessing on her lips, as they went slowly up the street.

They came in sight of the river. Mary shuddered.

"Oh, Jem! take me home. Yon river seems all made of glittering, heaving, dazzling metal, just as it did when I began to be ill."

Jem led her homewards. She dropped her head as searching for something on the ground.

"Jem!" He was all attention. She paused for an instant. "When may I go home? To Manchester, I mean. I am so weary of this place; and I would fain be at home."

She spoke in a feeble voice; not at all impatiently, as the words themselves would seem to intimate, but in a mournful way, as if anticipating sorrow even in the very fulfilment of her wishes.

"Darling! we will go whenever you wish; whenever you feel strong enough. I asked Job to tell Margaret to get all in readiness for you to go there at first. She'll tend you and nurse you. You must not go home. Job proffered for you to go there."

"Ah! but I must go home, Jem. I'll try and not fail now in what's right. There are things we must not speak on" (lowering her voice), "but you'll be really kind if you'll not speak against my going home. Let us say no more about it, dear Jem. I must go home, and I must go alone."

"Not alone, Mary!"

"Yes, alone! I cannot tell you why I ask it. And if you guess, I know you well enough to be sure you'll understand why I ask you never to speak on that again to me, till I begin. Promise, dear Jem, promise!"

He promised; to gratify that beseeching face he promised. And then he repented, and felt as if he had done ill. Then again he felt as if she were the best judge, and knowing all (perhaps more than even he did) might be forming plans which his interference would mar.

One thing was certain! it was a miserable thing to have this awful forbidden ground of discourse; to guess at each other's thoughts, when eyes were averted, and cheeks blanched, and words stood still, arrested in their flow by some casual allusion.

At last a day, fine enough for Mary to travel on, arrived. She had wished to go, but now her courage failed her. How could she have said she was weary of that quiet house, where even Ben Sturgis' grumblings only made a kind of harmonious bass in the concord between him and his wife, so thoroughly did they know each other with the knowledge of many years! How could she have longed to quit that little peaceful room where she had experienced such loving tendence! Even the very check bed-curtains became dear to her under the idea of seeing them no more. If it was so with inanimate objects, if they had such power of exciting regret, what were her feelings with regard to the kind old couple, who had taken the stranger in, and cared for her, and nursed her, as though she had been a daughter? Each wilful sentence spoken in the half unconscious irritation of feebleness came now with avenging self-reproach to her memory, as she hung about Mrs. Sturgis, with many tears, which served instead of words to express her gratitude and love.

Ben bustled about with the square bottle of Goldenwasser in one of his hands, and a small tumbler in the other; he went to Mary, Jem, and his wife in succession, pouring out a glass for each and bidding them drink it to keep their spirits up: but as each severally refused, he drank it himself; and passed on to offer the same hospitality to another with the like refusal, and the like result.

When he had swallowed the last of the three draughts, he condescended to give his reasons for having done so.

"I cannot abide waste. What's poured out mun be drunk. That's my maxim." So saying, he replaced the bottle in the cupboard.

It was he who in a firm commanding voice at last told Jem and Mary to be off, or they would be too late. Mrs. Sturgis had kept up till then; but as they left her house, she could no longer restrain her tears, and cried aloud in spite of her husband's upbraiding.

"Perhaps they'll be too late for th' train!" exclaimed she, with a degree of hope, as the clock struck two.

"What! and come back again! No! no! that would never do. We've done our part, and cried our cry; it's no use going o'er the same ground again. I should ha' to give 'em more out of yon bottle when next parting time came, and them three glasses they had made a hole in the stuff, I can tell you. Time Jack was back from Hamburg with some more."

When they reached Manchester, Mary looked very white, and the expression on her face was almost stern. She was in fact summoning up her resolution to meet her father if he were at home. Jem had never named his midnight glimpse of John Barton to human being; but Mary had a sort of presentiment that wander where he would, he would seek his home at last. But in what mood she dreaded to think. For the knowledge of her father's capability of guilt seemed to have opened a dark gulf in his character, into the depths of which she trembled to look. At one moment she would fain have claimed protection against the life she must lead, for some time at least, alone with a murderer! She thought of his gloom, before his mind was haunted by the memory of so terrible a crime; his moody, irritable ways. She imagined the evenings as of old: she, toiling at some work, long after houses were shut, and folks abed; he, more savage than he had ever been before with the inward gnawing of his remorse. At such times she could have cried aloud with terror, at the scenes her fancy conjured up.

But her filial duty, nay, her love and gratitude for many deeds of kindness done to her as a little child, conquered all fear. She would endure all imaginable terrors, although of daily occurrence. And she would patiently bear all wayward violence of temper; more than patiently would she bear it—pitifully, as one who knew of some awful curse awaiting the blood-shedder. She would watch over him tenderly, as the Innocent should watch over the Guilty; awaiting the gracious seasons, wherein to pour oil and balm into the bitter wounds.

With the untroubled peace which the resolve to endure to the end gives, she approached the house that from habit she still called home, but which possessed the holiness of home no longer.

"Jem!" said she, as they stood at the entrance to the court, close by Job Legh's door, "you must go in there and wait half-an-hour. Not less. If in that time I don't come back, you go your ways to your mother. Give her my dear love. I will send by Margaret when I want to see you." She sighed heavily.

"Mary! Mary! I cannot leave you. You speak as coldly as if we were to be nought to each other. And my heart's bound up in you. I know why you bid me keep away, but—"

She put her hand on his arm, as he spoke in a loud agitated tone; she looked into his face with upbraiding love in her eyes, and then she said, while her lips quivered, and he felt her whole frame trembling:

"Dear Jem! I often could have told you more of love, if I had not once spoken out so free. Remember that time, Jem, if ever you think me cold. Then, the love that's in my heart would out in words; but now, though I'm silent on the pain I'm feeling in quitting you, the love is in my heart all the same. But this is not the time to speak on such things. If I do not do what I feel to be right now, I may blame myself all my life long! Jem, you promised—"

And so saying she left him. She went quicker than she would otherwise have passed over those few yards of ground, for fear he should still try to accompany her. Her hand was on the latch, and in a breath the door was opened.

There sat her father, still and motionless—not even turning his head to see who had entered; but perhaps he recognised the foot-step,—the trick of action.

He sat by the fire; the grate I should say, for fire there was none. Some dull, gray ashes, negligently left, long days ago, coldly choked up the bars. He had taken the accustomed seat from mere force of habit, which ruled his automaton-body. For all energy, both physical and mental, seemed to have retreated inwards to some of the great citadels of life, there to do battle against the Destroyer, Conscience.

His hands were crossed, his fingers interlaced; usually a position implying some degree of resolution, or strength; but in him it was so faintly maintained, that it appeared more the result of chance; an attitude requiring some application of outward force to alter,—and a blow with a straw seemed as though it would be sufficient.

And as for his face, it was sunk and worn,—like a skull, with yet a suffering expression that skulls have not! Your heart would have ached to have seen the man, however hardly you might have judged his crime.

But crime and all was forgotten by his daughter, as she saw his abashed look, his smitten helplessness. All along she had felt it difficult (as I may have said before) to reconcile the two ideas, of her father and a blood-shedder. But now it was impossible. He was her father! her own dear father! and in his sufferings, whatever their cause, more dearly loved than ever before. His crime was a thing apart, never more to be considered by her.

And tenderly did she treat him, and fondly did she serve him in every way that heart could devise, or hand execute.

She had some money about her, the price of her strange services as a witness; and when the lingering dusk drew on, she stole out to effect some purchases necessary for her father's comfort.

For how body and soul had been kept together, even as much as they were, during the days he had dwelt alone, no one can say. The house was bare as when Mary had left it, of coal, or of candle, of food, or of blessing in any shape.

She came quickly home; but as she passed Job Legh's door, she stopped. Doubtless Jem had long since gone; and doubtless, too, he had given Margaret some good reason for not intruding upon her friend for this night at least, otherwise Mary would have seen her before now.

But to-morrow,—would she not come in to-morrow? And who so quick as blind Margaret in noticing tones, and sighs, and even silence?

She did not give herself time for further thought, her desire to be once more with her father was too pressing; but she opened the door, before she well knew what to say.

"It's Mary Barton! I know her by her breathing! Grandfather, it's Mary Barton!"

Margaret's joy at meeting her, the open demonstration of her love, affected Mary much; she could not keep from crying, and sat down weak and agitated on the first chair she could find.

"Ay, ay, Mary! thou'rt looking a bit different to when I saw thee last. Thou'lt give Jem and me good characters for sick nurses, I trust. If all trades fail, I'll turn to that. Jem's place is for life, I reckon. Nay, never redden so, lass. You and he know each other's minds by this time!"

Margaret held her hand, and gently smiled into her face.

Job Legh took the candle up, and began a leisurely inspection.

"Thou hast getten a bit of pink in thy cheeks,—not much; but when last I saw thee, thy lips were as white as a sheet. Thy nose is sharpish at th' end; thou'rt more like thy father than ever thou wert before. Lord! child, what's the matter? Art thou going to faint?"

For Mary had sickened at the mention of that name; yet she felt that now or never was the time to speak.

"Father's come home!" she said, "but he's very poorly; I never saw him as he is now, before. I asked Jem not to come near him for fear it might fidget him."

She spoke hastily, and (to her own idea) in an unnatural manner. But they did not seem to notice it, nor to take the hint she had thrown out of company being unacceptable; for Job Legh directly put down some insect, which he was impaling on a corking-pin, and exclaimed,

"Thy father come home! Why, Jem never said a word of it! And ailing too! I'll go in, and cheer him with a bit of talk. I ne'er knew any good come of delegating it."

"Oh, Job! father cannot stand—father is too ill. Don't come; not but that you're very kind and good; but to-night—indeed," said she at last, in despair, seeing Job still persevere in putting away his things; "you must not come till I send or come for you. Father's in that strange way, I can't answer for it if he sees strangers. Please don't come. I'll come and tell you every day how he goes on. I must be off now to see after him. Dear Job! kind Job! don't be angry with me. If you knew all you'd pity me."

For Job was muttering away in high dudgeon, and even Margaret's tone was altered as she wished Mary good night. Just then she could ill brook coldness from any one, and least of all bear the idea of being considered ungrateful by so kind and zealous a friend as Job had been; so she turned round suddenly, even when her hand was on the latch of the door, and ran back, and threw her arms about his neck, and kissed him first, and then Margaret. And then, the tears fast-falling down her cheeks, but no word spoken, she hastily left the house, and went back to her home.

There was no change in her father's position, or in his spectral look. He had answered her questions (but few in number, for so many subjects were unapproachable) by monosyllables, and in a weak, high, childish voice; but he had not lifted his eyes; he could not meet his daughter's look. And she, when she spoke, or as she moved about, avoided letting her eyes rest upon him. She wished to be her usual self; but while every thing was done with a consciousness of purpose, she felt it was impossible.

In this manner things went on for some days. At night he feebly clambered up stairs to bed; and during those long dark hours Mary heard those groans of agony which never escaped his lips by day, when they were compressed in silence over his inward woe.

Many a time she sat up listening, and wondering if it would ease his miserable heart if she went to him, and told him she knew all, and loved and pitied him more than words could tell.

By day the monotonous hours wore on in the same heavy, hushed manner as on that first dreary afternoon. He ate,—but without relish; and food seemed no longer to nourish him, for each morning his face had caught more of the ghastly fore-shadowing of Death.

The neighbours kept strangely aloof. Of late years John Barton had had a repellent power about him, felt by all, except to the few who had either known him in his better and happier days, or those to whom he had given his sympathy and his confidence. People did not care to enter the doors of one whose very depth of thoughtfulness rendered him moody and stern. And now they contented themselves with a kind inquiry when they saw Mary in her goings-out or in her comings-in. With her oppressing knowledge, she imagined their reserved conduct stranger than it was in reality. She missed Job and Margaret too; who, in all former times of sorrow or anxiety since their acquaintance first began, had been ready with their sympathy.

But most of all she missed the delicious luxury she had lately enjoyed in having Jem's tender love at hand every hour of the day, to ward off every wind of heaven, and every disturbing thought.

She knew he was often hovering about the house; though the knowledge seemed to come more by intuition, than by any positive sight or sound for the first day or two. On the third day she met him at Job Legh's.

They received her with every effort of cordiality; but still there was a cobweb-veil of separation between them, to which Mary was morbidly acute; while in Jem's voice, and eyes, and manner, there was every evidence of most passionate, most admiring, and most trusting love. The trust was shown by his respectful silence on that one point of reserve on which she had interdicted conversation.

He left Job Legh's house when she did. They lingered on the step, he holding her hand between both of his, as loth to let her go; he questioned her as to when he should see her again.

"Mother does so want to see you," whispered he. "Can you come to see her to-morrow? or when?"

"I cannot tell," replied she, softly. "Not yet. Wait awhile; perhaps only a little while. Dear Jem, I must go to him,—dearest Jem."

The next day, the fourth from Mary's return home, as she was sitting near the window, sadly dreaming over some work, she caught a glimpse of the last person she wished to see—of Sally Leadbitter!

She was evidently coming to their house; another moment, and she tapped at the door. John Barton gave an anxious, uneasy side-glance. Mary knew that if she delayed answering the knock, Sally would not scruple to enter; so as hastily as if the visit had been desired, she opened the door, and stood there with the latch in her hand, barring up all entrance, and as much as possible obstructing all curious glances into the interior.

"Well, Mary Barton! You're home at last! I heard you'd getten home; so I thought I'd just step over and hear the news."

She was bent on coming in, and saw Mary's preventive design. So she stood on tip-toe, looking over Mary's shoulders into the room where she suspected a lover to be lurking; but instead, she saw only the figure of the stern, gloomy father she had always been in the habit of avoiding; and she dropped down again, content to carry on the conversation where Mary chose, and as Mary chose, in whispers.

"So the old governor is back again, eh? And what does he say to all your fine doings at Liverpool, and before?—you and I know where. You can't hide it now, Mary, for it's all in print."

Mary gave a low moan,—and then implored Sally to change the subject; for unpleasant as it always was, it was doubly unpleasant in the manner in which she was treating it. If they had been alone, Mary would have borne it patiently,—or so she thought,—but now she felt almost certain her father was listening; there was a subdued breathing, a slight bracing-up of the listless attitude. But there was no arresting Sally's curiosity to hear all she could respecting the adventures Mary had experienced. She, in common with the rest of Miss Simmonds' young ladies, was almost jealous of the fame that Mary had obtained; to herself, such miserable notoriety.

"Nay! there's no use shunning talking it over. Why! it was in the *Guardian*,—and the *Courier*,—and some one told Jane Hodson it was even copied into a London paper. You've set up heroine on your own account, Mary Barton. How did you like standing witness? Ar'n't them lawyers impudent things? staring at one so. I'll be bound you wished you'd taken my offer, and borrowed my black watered scarf! Now didn't you, Mary? Speak truth!"

"To tell truth, I never thought about it then, Sally. How could I?" asked she, reproachfully.

"Oh—I forgot. You were all for that stupid James Wilson. Well! if I've ever the luck to go witness on a trial, see if I don't pick up a better beau than the prisoner. I'll aim at a lawyer's clerk, but I'll not take less than a turnkey."

Cast down as Mary was, she could hardly keep from smiling at the idea, so wildly incongruous with the scene she had really undergone, of looking out for admirers during a trial for murder.

"I'd no thought to be looking out for beaux, I can assure you, Sally.—But don't let us talk any more about it; I can't bear to think on it. How is Miss Simmonds? and everybody?"

"Oh, very well; and by the way she gave me a bit of a message for you. You may come back to work if you'll behave yourself, she says. I told you she'd be glad to have you back, after all this piece of business, by way of tempting people to come to her shop. They'd come from Salford to have a peep at you, for six months at least."

"Don't talk so; I cannot come, I can never face Miss Simmonds again. And even if I could—" she stopped, and blushed.

"Ay! I know what you're thinking on. But that will not be this some time, as he's turned off from the foundry,—you'd better think twice afore refusing Miss Simmonds' offer."

"Turned off from the foundry! Jem?" cried Mary.

"To be sure! didn't you know it? Decent men were not going to work with a—no! I suppose I mustn't say it, seeing you went to such trouble to get up an *alibi*; not that I should think much the worse of a spirited young fellow for falling foul of a rival,—they always do at the theatre."

But Mary's thoughts were with Jem. How good he had been never to name his dismissal to her. How much he had had to endure for her sake!

"Tell me all about it," she gasped out.

"Why, you see, they've always swords quite handy at them plays," began Sally; but Mary, with an impatient shake of her head, interrupted,

"About Jem,—about Jem, I want to know."

"Oh! I don't pretend to know more than is in every one's mouth: he's turned away from the foundry, because folks don't think you've cleared him outright of the murder; though perhaps the jury were loth to hang him. Old Mr. Carson is savage against judge and jury, and lawyers and all, as I heard."

"I must go to him, I must go to him," repeated Mary, in a hurried manner.

"He'll tell you all I've said is true, and not a word of lie," replied Sally. "So I'll not give your answer to Miss Simmonds, but leave you to think twice about it. Good afternoon!"

Mary shut the door, and turned into the house.

Her father sat in the same attitude; the old unchanging attitude. Only his head was more bowed towards the ground.

She put on her bonnet to go to Ancoats; for see, and question, and comfort, and worship Jem, she must.

As she hung about her father for an instant before leaving him, he spoke—voluntarily spoke for the first time since her return; but his head was drooping so low she could not hear what he said, so she stooped down; and after a moment's pause, he repeated the words,

"Tell Jem Wilson to come here at eight o'clock to-night."

Could he have overheard her conversation with Sally Leadbitter? They had whispered low, she thought. Pondering on this, and many other things, she reached Ancoats.

CHAPTER XXXV - "FORGIVE US OUR TRESPASSES."

"Oh, had he lived,
Replied Rusilla, never penitence
Had equalled his! full well I know his heart,
Vehement in all things. He would on himself
Have wreaked such penance as had reached the height
Of fleshly suffering,—yea, which being told,
With its portentous rigour should have made
The memory of his fault, o'erpowered and lost
In shuddering pity and astonishment,
Fade like a feeble horror."

SOUTHEY'S "RODERICK."

As Mary was turning into the street where the Wilsons lived, Jem overtook her. He came upon her suddenly, and she started.

"You're going to see mother?" he asked tenderly, placing her arm within his, and slackening his pace.

"Yes, and you too. Oh, Jem, is it true? tell me."

She felt rightly that he would guess the meaning of her only half expressed inquiry. He hesitated a moment before he answered her.

"Darling, it is; it's no use hiding it—if you mean that I'm no longer to work at Duncombe's foundry. It's no time (to my mind) to have secrets from each other, though I did not name it yesterday, thinking you might fret. I shall soon get work again, never fear."

"But why did they turn you off, when the jury had said you were innocent?"

"It was not just to say turned off, though I don't think I could have well stayed on. A good number of the men managed to let out they should not like to work under me again; there were some few who knew me well enough to feel I could not have done it, but more were doubtful; and one spoke to young Mr. Duncombe, hinting at what they thought."

"Oh Jem! what a shame!" said Mary, with mournful indignation.

"Nay, darling! I'm not for blaming them. Poor fellows like them have nought to stand upon and be proud of but their character, and it's fitting they should take care of that, and keep that free from soil and taint."

"But you,—what could they get but good from you? They might have known you by this time."

"So some do; the overlooker, I'm sure, would know I'm innocent. Indeed, he said as much to-day; and he said he had had some talk with old Mr. Duncombe, and they thought it might be better if I left Manchester for a bit; they'd recommend me to some other place."

But Mary could only shake her head in a mournful way, and repeat her words,

"They might have known thee better, Jem."

Jem pressed the little hand he held between his own work-hardened ones. After a minute or two, he asked,

"Mary, art thou much bound to Manchester? Would it grieve thee sore to quit the old smoke-jack?"

"With thee?" she asked, in a quiet, glancing way.

"Ay, lass! Trust me, I'll ne'er ask thee to leave Manchester while I'm in it. Because I've heard fine things of Canada; and our overlooker has a cousin in the foundry line there.—Thou knowest where Canada is, Mary?"

"Not rightly—not now, at any rate;—but with thee, Jem," her voice sunk to a soft, low whisper, "anywhere—"

What was the use of a geographical description?

"But father!" said Mary, suddenly breaking that delicious silence with the one sharp discord in her present life.

She looked up at her lover's grave face; and then the message her father had sent flashed across her memory.

"Oh, Jem, did I tell you?—Father sent word he wished to speak with you. I was to bid you come to him at eight to-night. What can he want, Jem?"

"I cannot tell," replied he. "At any rate I'll go. It's no use troubling ourselves to guess," he continued, after a pause of a few minutes, during which they slowly and silently paced up and down the by-street, into which he had led her when their conversation began. "Come and see mother, and then I'll take thee home, Mary. Thou wert all in a tremble when first I came up with thee; thou'rt not fit to be trusted home by thyself," said he, with fond exaggeration of her helplessness.

Yet a little more lovers' loitering; a few more words, in themselves nothing—to you nothing, but to those two what tender passionate language can I use to express the feelings which thrilled through that young man and maiden, as they listened to the syllables made dear and lovely through life by that hour's low-whispered talk.

It struck the half hour past seven.

"Come and speak to mother; she knows you're to be her daughter, Mary, darling."

So they went in. Jane Wilson was rather chafed at her son's delay in returning home, for as yet he had managed to keep her in ignorance of his dismissal from the foundry; and it was her way to prepare some little pleasure, some little comfort for those she loved; and if they, unwittingly, did not appear at the proper time to enjoy her preparation, she worked herself up into a state of fretfulness which found vent in upbraidings as soon as ever the objects of her care appeared, thereby marring the peace which should ever be the atmosphere of a home, however humble; and causing a feeling almost amounting to loathing to arise at the sight of the "stalled ox," which, though an effect and proof of careful love, has been the cause of so much disturbance.

Mrs. Wilson had first sighed, and then grumbled to herself, over the increasing toughness of the potato-cakes she had made for her son's tea.

The door opened, and he came in; his face brightening into proud smiles, Mary Barton hanging on his arm, blushing and dimpling, with eye-lids veiling the happy light of her eyes,—there was around the young couple a radiant atmosphere—a glory of happiness.

Could his mother mar it? Could she break into it with her Martha-like cares? Only for one moment did she remember her sense of injury,—her wasted trouble,—and then, her whole woman's heart heaving with motherly love and sympathy, she opened her arms, and received Mary into them, as, shedding tears of agitated joy, she murmured in her ear,

"Bless thee, Mary, bless thee! Only make him happy, and God bless thee for ever!"

It took some of Jem's self-command to separate those whom he so much loved, and who were beginning, for his sake, to love one another so dearly. But the time for his meeting John Barton drew on: and it was a long way to his house.

As they walked briskly thither they hardly spoke; though many thoughts were in their minds.

The sun had not long set, but the first faint shade of twilight was over all; and when they opened the door, Jem could hardly perceive the objects within by the waning light of day, and the flickering fire-blaze.

But Mary saw all at a glance!

Her eye, accustomed to what was usual in the aspect of the room, saw instantly what was unusual,—saw, and understood it all.

Her father was standing behind his habitual chair, holding by the back of it as if for support. And opposite to him there stood Mr. Carson; the dark out-line of his stern figure looming large against the light of the fire in that little room.

Behind her father sat Job Legh, his head in his hands, and resting his elbows on the little family table,—listening evidently; but as evidently deeply affected by what he heard.

There seemed to be some pause in the conversation. Mary and Jem stood at the half-open door, not daring to stir; hardly to breathe.

"And have I heard you aright?" began Mr. Carson, with his deep quivering voice. "Man! have I heard you aright? Was it you, then, that killed my boy? my only son?"—(he said these last few words almost as if appealing for pity, and then he changed his tone to one more vehement and fierce). "Don't dare to think that I shall be merciful, and spare you, because you have come forward to accuse yourself. I tell you I will not spare you the least pang the law can inflict,—you, who did not show pity on my boy, shall have none from me."

"I did not ask for any," said John Barton, in a low voice.

"Ask, or not ask, what care I? You shall be hanged—hanged—man!" said he, advancing his face, and repeating the word with slow, grinding emphasis, as if to infuse some of the bitterness of his soul into it.

John Barton gasped, but not with fear. It was only that he felt it terrible to have inspired such hatred, as was concentrated into every word, every gesture of Mr. Carson's.

"As for being hanged, sir, I know it's all right and proper. I dare say it's bad enough; but I tell you what, sir," speaking with an out-burst, "if you'd hanged me the day after I'd done the deed, I would have gone down on my knees and blessed you. Death! Lord, what is it to Life? To such a life as I've been leading this fortnight past. Life at best is no great thing; but such a life as I have dragged through since that night," he shuddered at the thought. "Why, sir, I've been on the point of killing myself this many a time to get away from my own thoughts. I didn't! and I'll tell you why. I didn't know but that I should be more haunted than ever with the recollection of my sin. Oh! God above only can tell the agony with which I've repented me of it, and part perhaps because I feared He would think I were impatient of the misery He sent as punishment—far, far worse misery than any hanging, sir." He ceased from excess of emotion.

Then he began again.

"Sin' that day (it may be very wicked, sir, but it's the truth) I've kept thinking and thinking if I were but in that world where they say God is, He would, may be, teach me right from wrong, even if it were with many stripes. I've been sore puzzled here. I would go through Hell-fire if I could but get free from sin at last, it's such an awful thing. As for hanging, that's just nought at all."

His exhaustion compelled him to sit down. Mary rushed to him. It seemed as if till then he had been unaware of her presence.

"Ay, ay, wench!" said he feebly, "is it thee? Where's Jem Wilson?"

Jem came forward. John Barton spoke again, with many a break and gasping pause,

"Lad! thou hast borne a deal for me. It's the meanest thing I ever did to leave thee to bear the brunt. Thou, who wert as innocent of any knowledge of it as the babe unborn. I'll not bless thee for it. Blessing from such as me would not bring thee any good. Thou'lt love Mary, though she is my child."

He ceased, and there was a pause of a few seconds.

Then Mr. Carson turned to go. When his hand was on the latch of the door, he hesitated for an instant.

"You can have no doubt for what purpose I go. Straight to the police-office, to send men to take care of you, wretched man, and your accomplice. To-morrow morning your tale shall be repeated to those who can commit you to gaol, and before long you shall have the opportunity of trying how desirable hanging is."

"Oh, sir!" said Mary, springing forward, and catching hold of Mr. Carson's arm, "my father is dying. Look at him, sir. If you want Death for Death, you have it. Don't take him away from me these last hours. He must go alone through Death, but let me be with him as long as I can. Oh, sir! if you have any mercy in you, leave him here to die."

John himself stood up, stiff and rigid, and replied,

"Mary, wench! I owe him summut. I will go die, where, and as he wishes me. Thou hast said true, I am standing side by side with Death; and it matters little where I spend the bit of time left of Life. That time I must pass in wrestling with my soul for a character to take into the other world. I'll go where you see fit, sir. He's innocent," faintly indicating Jem, as he fell back in his chair.

"Never fear! They cannot touch him," said Job Legh, in a low voice.

But as Mr. Carson was on the point of leaving the house with no sign of relenting about him, he was again stopped by John Barton, who had risen once more from his chair, and stood supporting himself on Jem, while he spoke.

"Sir, one word! My hairs are gray with suffering, and yours with years—"

"And have I had no suffering?" asked Mr. Carson, as if appealing for sympathy, even to the murderer of his child.

And the murderer of his child answered to the appeal, and groaned in spirit over the anguish he had caused.

"Have I had no inward suffering to blanch these hairs? Have not I toiled and struggled even to these years with hopes in my heart that all centered in my boy? I did not speak of them, but were they not there? I seemed hard and cold; and so I might be to others, but not to him!—who shall ever imagine the love I bore to him? Even he never dreamed how my heart leapt up at the sound of his footstep, and how precious he was to his poor old father.—And he is gone—killed—out of the hearing of all loving words—out of my sight for ever. He was my sunshine, and now it is night! Oh, my God! comfort me, comfort me!" cried the old man aloud.

The eyes of John Barton grew dim with tears. Rich and poor, masters and men, were then brothers in the deep suffering of the heart; for was not this the very anguish he had felt for little Tom, in years so long gone by that they seemed like another life!

The mourner before him was no longer the employer; a being of another race, eternally placed in antagonistic attitude; going through the world glittering like gold, with a stony heart within, which knew no sorrow but through the accidents of Trade; no longer the enemy, the oppressor, but a very poor and desolate old man.

The sympathy for suffering, formerly so prevalent a feeling with him, again filled John Barton's heart, and almost impelled him to speak (as best he could) some earnest, tender words to the stern man, shaking in his agony.

But who was he, that he should utter sympathy or consolation? The cause of all this woe.

Oh blasting thought! Oh miserable remembrance! He had forfeited all right to bind up his brother's wounds.

Stunned by the thought, he sank upon the seat, almost crushed with the knowledge of the consequences of his own action; for he had no more imagined to himself the blighted home, and the miserable parents, than does the soldier, who discharges his musket, picture to himself the desolation of the wife, and the pitiful cries of the helpless little ones, who are in an instant to be made widowed and fatherless.

To intimidate a class of men, known only to those below them as desirous to obtain the greatest quantity of work for the lowest wages,—at most to remove an overbearing partner from an obnoxious firm, who stood in the way of those who struggled as well as they were able to obtain their rights,—this was the light in which John Barton had viewed his deed; and even so viewing it, after the excitement had passed away, the Avenger, the sure Avenger, had found him out.

But now he knew that he had killed a man, and a brother,—now he knew that no good thing could come out of this evil, even to the sufferers whose cause he had so blindly espoused.

He lay across the table, broken-hearted. Every fresh quivering sob of Mr. Carson's stabbed him to his soul.

He felt execrated by all; and as if he could never lay bare the perverted reasonings which had made the performance of undoubted sin appear a duty. The longing to plead some faint excuse grew stronger and stronger. He feebly raised his head, and looking at Job Legh, he whispered out,

"I did not know what I was doing, Job Legh; God knows I didn't! Oh, sir!" said he wildly, almost throwing himself at Mr. Carson's feet, "say you forgive me the anguish I now see I have caused you. I care not for pain, or death, you know I don't; but oh, man! forgive me the trespass I have done!"

"Forgive us our trespasses as we forgive them that trespass against us," said Job, solemnly and low, as if in prayer; as if the words were suggested by those John Barton had used.

Mr. Carson took his hands away from his face. I would rather see death than the ghastly gloom which darkened that countenance.

"Let my trespasses be unforgiven, so that I may have vengeance for my son's murder."

There are blasphemous actions as well as blasphemous words: all unloving, cruel deeds are acted blasphemy.

Mr. Carson left the house. And John Barton lay on the ground as one dead.

They lifted him up, and almost hoping that that deep trance might be to him the end of all earthly things, they bore him to his bed.

For a time they listened with divided attention to his faint breathings; for in each hasty hurried step that echoed in the street outside, they thought they heard the approach of the officers of justice.

When Mr. Carson left the house he was dizzy with agitation; the hot blood went careering through his frame. He could not see the deep blue of the night-heavens for the fierce pulses which throbbed in his head. And partly to steady and calm himself, he leaned against a railing, and looked up into those calm majestic depths with all their thousand stars.

And by-and-by his own voice returned upon him, as if the last words he had spoken were being uttered through all that infinite space; but in their echoes there was a tone of unutterable sorrow.

"Let my trespasses be unforgiven, so that I may have vengeance for my son's murder."

He tried to shake off the spiritual impression made by this imagination. He was feverish and ill,—and no wonder.

So he turned to go homewards; not, as he had threatened, to the police-office. After all (he told himself), that would do in the morning. No fear of the man's escaping, unless he escaped to the grave.

So he tried to banish the phantom voices and shapes which came unbidden to his brain, and to recall his balance of mind by walking calmly and slowly, and noticing every thing which struck his senses.

It was a warm soft evening in spring, and there were many persons in the streets. Among others, a nurse with a little girl in her charge, conveying her home from some children's gaiety; a dance most likely, for the lovely little creature was daintily decked out in soft, snowy muslin; and her fairy feet tripped along by her nurse's side as if to the measure of some tune she had lately kept time to.

Suddenly up behind her there came a rough, rude errand-boy, nine or ten years of age; a giant he looked by the fairy-child, as she fluttered along. I don't know how it was, but in some awkward way he knocked the poor little girl down upon the hard pavement as he brushed rudely past, not much caring whom he hurt, so that he got along.

The child arose sobbing with pain; and not without cause, for blood was dropping down from the face, but a minute before so fair and bright—dropping down on the pretty frock, making those scarlet marks so terrible to little children.

The nurse, a powerful woman, had seized the boy, just as Mr. Carson (who had seen the whole transaction) came up.

"You naughty little rascal! I'll give you to a policeman, that I will! Do you see how you've hurt the little girl? Do you?" accompanying every sentence with a violent jerk of passionate anger.

The lad looked hard and defying; but withal terrified at the threat of the policeman, those ogres of our streets to all unlucky urchins. The nurse saw it, and began to drag him along, with a view of making what she called "a wholesome impression."

His terror increased, and with it his irritation; when the little sweet face, choking away its sobs, pulled down nurse's head and said,

"Please, dear nurse, I'm not much hurt; it was very silly to cry, you know. He did not mean to do it. *He did not know what he was doing*, did you, little boy? Nurse won't call a policeman, so don't be frightened." And she put up her little mouth to be kissed by her injurer, just as she had been taught to do at home to "make peace."

"That lad will mind, and be more gentle for the time to come, I'll be bound, thanks to that little lady," said a passer-by, half to himself, and half to Mr. Carson, whom he had observed to notice the scene.

The latter took no apparent heed of the remark, but passed on. But the child's pleading reminded him of the low, broken voice he had so lately heard, penitently and humbly urging the same extenuation of his great guilt.

"I did not know what I was doing."

He had some association with those words; he had heard, or read of that plea somewhere before. Where was it?

Could it be—?

He would look when he got home. So when he entered his house he went straight and silently up-stairs to his library, and took down the great large handsome Bible, all grand and golden, with its leaves adhering together from the bookbinder's press, so little had it been used.

On the first page (which fell open to Mr. Carson's view) were written the names of his children, and his own.

"Henry John, son of the above John and Elizabeth Carson.
Born, Sept. 29th, 1815."

To make the entry complete, his death should now be added. But the page became hidden by the gathering mist of tears.

Thought upon thought, and recollection upon recollection came crowding in, from the remembrance of the proud day when he had purchased the costly book, in order to write down the birth of the little babe of a day old.

He laid his head down on the open page, and let the tears fall slowly on the spotless leaves.

His son's murderer was discovered; had confessed his guilt; and yet (strange to say) he could not hate him with the vehemence of hatred he had felt, when he had imagined him a young man, full of lusty life, defying all laws, human and divine. In spite of his desire to retain the revengeful feeling he considered as a duty to his dead son, something of pity would steal in for the poor, wasted skeleton of a man, the smitten creature, who had told him of his sin, and implored his pardon that night.

In the days of his childhood and youth, Mr. Carson had been accustomed to poverty; but it was honest, decent poverty; not the grinding squalid misery he had remarked in every part of John Barton's house, and which contrasted strangely with the pompous sumptuousness of the room in which he now sat. Unaccustomed wonder filled his mind at the reflection of the different lots of the brethren of mankind.

Then he roused himself from his reverie, and turned to the object of his search—the Gospel, where he half expected to find the tender pleading: "They know not what they do."

It was murk midnight by this time, and the house was still and quiet. There was nothing to interrupt the old man in his unwonted study.

Years ago, the Gospel had been his task-book in learning to read. So many years ago, that he had become familiar with the events before he could comprehend the Spirit that made the Life.

He fell to the narrative now afresh, with all the interest of a little child. He began at the beginning, and read on almost greedily, understanding for the first time the full meaning of the story. He came to the end; the awful End. And there were the haunting words of pleading.

He shut the book, and thought deeply.

All night long, the Archangel combated with the Demon.

All night long, others watched by the bed of Death. John Barton had revived to fitful intelligence. He spoke at times with even something of his former energy; and in the racy Lancashire dialect he had always used when speaking freely.

"You see I've so often been hankering after the right way; and it's a hard one for a poor man to find. At least it's been so to me. No one learned me, and no one telled me. When I was a little chap they taught me to read, and then they ne'er gave me no books; only I heard say the Bible was a good book. So when I grew thoughtful, and puzzled, I took to it. But you'd never believe black was black, or night was night, when you saw all about you acting as if black was white, and night was day. It's not much I can say for myself in t'other world, God forgive me; but I can say this, I would fain have gone after the Bible rules if I'd seen folk credit it; they all spoke up for it, and went and did clean contrary. In those days I would ha' gone about wi' my Bible, like a little child, my finger in th' place, and asking the meaning of this or that text, and no one told me. Then I took out two or three texts as clear as glass, and I tried to do what they bid me do. But I don't know how it was; masters and men, all alike cared no more for minding those texts, than I did for th' Lord Mayor of London; so I grew to think it must be a sham put upon poor ignorant folk, women, and such-like.

"It was not long I tried to live Gospel-wise, but it was liker heaven than any other bit of earth has been. I'd old Alice to strengthen me; but every one else said, 'Stand up for thy rights, or thou'lt never get 'em;' and wife and children never spoke, but their helplessness cried aloud, and I was driven to do as others did,—and then Tom died. You know all about that—I'm getting scant o' breath, and blind-like."

Then again he spoke, after some minutes of hushed silence.

"All along it came natural to love folk, though now I am what I am. I think one time I could e'en have loved the masters if they'd ha' letten me; that was in my Gospel-days, afore my child died o' hunger. I was tore in two often-times, between my sorrow for poor suffering folk, and my trying to love them as caused their sufferings (to my mind).

"At last I gave it up in despair, trying to make folks' actions square wi' th' Bible; and I thought I'd no longer labour at following th' Bible mysel. I've said all this afore, may be. But from that time I've dropped down, down,—down."

After that he only spoke in broken sentences.

"I did not think he'd been such an old man,—Oh! that he had but forgiven me,"—and then came earnest, passionate, broken words of prayer.

Job Legh had gone home like one struck down with the unexpected shock. Mary and Jem together waited the approach of death; but as the final struggle drew on, and morning dawned, Jem suggested some alleviation to the gasping breath, to purchase which he left the house in search of a druggist's shop, which should be open at that early hour.

During his absence, Barton grew worse; he had fallen across the bed, and his breathing seemed almost stopped; in vain did Mary strive to raise him, her sorrow and exhaustion had rendered her too weak.

So, on hearing some one enter the house-place below, she cried out for Jem to come to her assistance.

A step, which was not Jem's, came up the stairs.

Mr. Carson stood in the door-way. In one instant he comprehended the case.

He raised up the powerless frame; and the departing soul looked out of the eyes with gratitude. He held the dying man propped in his arms. John Barton folded his hands as if in prayer.

"Pray for us," said Mary, sinking on her knees, and forgetting in that solemn hour all that had divided her father and Mr. Carson.

No other words could suggest themselves than some of those he had read only a few hours before.

"God be merciful to us sinners.—Forgive us our trespasses as we forgive them that trespass against us."

And when the words were said, John Barton lay a corpse in Mr. Carson's arms.

So ended the tragedy of a poor man's life.

Mary knew nothing more for many minutes. When she recovered consciousness, she found herself supported by Jem on the "settle" in the house-place. Job and Mr. Carson were there, talking together lowly and solemnly. Then Mr. Carson bade farewell and left the house; and Job said aloud, but as if speaking to himself,

"God has heard that man's prayer. He has comforted him."

CHAPTER XXXVI - JEM'S INTERVIEW WITH MR. DUNCOMBE.

"The first dark day of nothingness,
The last of danger and distress."

BYRON.

Although Mary had hardly been conscious of her thoughts, and it had been more like a secret instinct informing her soul, than the result of any process of reasoning, she had felt for some time (ever since her return from Liverpool, in fact), that for her father there was but one thing to be desired and anticipated, and that was death!

She had seen that Conscience had given the mortal wound to his earthly frame; she did not dare to question of the infinite mercy of God, what the Future Life would be to him.

Though at first desolate and stunned by the blow which had fallen on herself, she was resigned and submissive as soon as she recovered strength enough to ponder and consider a little; and you may be sure that no tenderness or love was wanting on Jem's part, and no consideration and sympathy on that of Job and Margaret, to soothe and comfort the girl who now stood alone in the world as far as blood-relations were concerned.

She did not ask or care to know what arrangements they were making in whispered tones with regard to the funeral. She put herself into their hands with the trust of a little child; glad to be undisturbed in the reveries and remembrances which filled her eyes with tears, and caused them to fall quietly down her pale cheeks.

It was the longest day she had ever known in her life; every charge and every occupation was taken away from her: but perhaps the length of quiet time thus afforded was really good, although its duration weighed upon her; for by this means she contemplated her situation in every light, and fully understood that the morning's event had left her an orphan; and thus she was spared the pangs caused to us by the occurrence of death in the evening, just before we should naturally, in the usual course of events, lie down to slumber. For in such case, worn out by anxiety, and it may be by much watching, our very excess of grief rocks itself to sleep, before we have had time to realise its cause; and we waken, with a start of agony like a fresh stab, to the consciousness of the one awful vacancy, which shall never, while the world endures, be filled again.

The day brought its burden of duty to Mrs. Wilson. She felt bound by regard, as well as by etiquette, to go and see her future daughter-in-law. And by an old association of ideas (perhaps of death with church-yards, and churches with Sunday) she thought it necessary to put on her best, and latterly unused clothes, the airing of which on a little clothes-horse before the fire seemed to give her a not unpleasing occupation.

When Jem returned home late in the evening succeeding John Barton's death, weary and oppressed with the occurrences and excitements of the day, he found his mother busy about her mourning, and much inclined to talk. Although he longed for quiet, he could not avoid sitting down and answering her questions.

"Well, Jem, he's gone at last, is he?"

"Yes. How did you hear, mother?"

"Oh, Job came over here and telled me, on his way to the undertaker's. Did he make a fine end?"

It struck Jem that she had not heard of the confession which had been made by John Barton on his death-bed; he remembered Job Legh's discretion, and he determined that if it could be avoided his mother should never hear of it. Many of the difficulties to be anticipated in preserving the secret would be obviated, if he could induce his mother to fall into the plan he had named to Mary of emigrating to Canada. The reasons which rendered this secrecy desirable related to the domestic happiness he hoped for. With his mother's irritable temper he could hardly expect that all allusion to the crime of John Barton would be for ever restrained from passing her lips, and he knew the deep trial such references would be to Mary. Accordingly he resolved as soon as possible in the morning to go to Job and beseech his silence; he trusted that secrecy in that quarter, even if the knowledge had been extended to Margaret, might be easily secured.

But what would be Mr. Carson's course? Were there any means by which he might be persuaded to spare John Barton's memory?

He was roused up from this train of thought by his mother's more irritated tone of voice.

"Jem!" she was saying, "thou might'st just as well never be at a death-bed again, if thou cannot bring off more news about it; here have I been by mysel all day (except when oud Job came in), but thinks I, when Jem comes he'll be sure to be good company, seeing he was in the house at the very time of the death; and here thou art, without a word to throw at a dog, much less thy mother: it's no use thy going to a death-bed if thou cannot carry away any of the sayings!"

"He did not make any, mother," replied Jem.

"Well, to be sure! So fond as he used to be of holding forth, to miss such a fine opportunity that will never come again! Did he die easy?"

"He was very restless all night long," said Jem, reluctantly returning to the thoughts of that time.

"And in course thou plucked the pillow away? Thou didst not! Well! with thy bringing up, and thy learning, thou might'st have known that were the only help in such a case. There were pigeons' feathers in the pillow, depend on't. To think of two grown-up folk like you and Mary, not knowing death could never come easy to a person lying on a pillow with pigeons' feathers in!"

Jem was glad to escape from all this talking to the solitude and quiet of his own room, where he could lie and think uninterruptedly of what had happened and remained to be done.

The first thing was to seek an interview with Mr. Duncombe, his former master. Accordingly, early the next morning Jem set off on his walk to the works, where for so many years his days had been spent; where for so long a time his thoughts had been thought, his hopes and fears experienced. It was not a cheering feeling to remember that henceforward he was to be severed from all these familiar places; nor were his spirits enlivened by the evident feelings of the majority of those who had been his fellow-workmen. As he stood in the entrance to the foundry, awaiting Mr. Duncombe's leisure, many of those employed in the works passed him on their return from breakfast; and with one or two exceptions, without any acknowledgment of former acquaintance beyond a distant nod at the utmost.

"It is hard," said Jem to himself, with a bitter and indignant feeling rising in his throat, "that let a man's life be what it may, folk are so ready to credit the first word against him. I could live it down if I stayed in England; but then what would not Mary have to bear? Sooner or later the truth would out; and then she would be a show to folk for many a day as John Barton's daughter. Well! God does not judge as hardly as man, that's one comfort for all of us!"

Mr. Duncombe did not believe in Jem's guilt, in spite of the silence in which he again this day heard the imputation of it; but he agreed that under the circumstances it was better he should leave the country.

"We have been written to by government, as I think I told you before, to recommend an intelligent man, well acquainted with mechanics, as instrument-maker to the Agricultural College they are establishing at Toronto, in Canada. It is a comfortable appointment,—house,—land,—and a good per-centage on the instruments made. I will show you the particulars if I can lay my hand on the letter, which I believe I must have left at home."

"Thank you, sir. No need for seeing the letter to say I'll accept it. I must leave Manchester; and I'd as lief quit England at once when I'm about it."

"Of course government will give you your passage; indeed, I believe an allowance would be made for a family if you had one; but you are not a married man, I believe?"

"No, sir, but—" Jem hung back from a confession with the awkwardness of a girl.

"But—" said Mr. Duncombe, smiling, "you would like to be a married man before you go, I suppose; eh, Wilson?"

"If you please, sir. And there's my mother, too. I hope she'll go with us. But I can pay her passage; no need to trouble government."

"Nay, nay! I'll write to-day and recommend you; and say that you have a family of two. They'll never ask if the family goes upwards or downwards. I shall see you again before you sail, I hope, Wilson; though I believe they'll not allow you long to wait. Come to my house next time; you'll find it pleasanter, I daresay. These men are so wrong-headed. Keep up your heart!"

Jem felt that it was a relief to have this point settled; and that he need no longer weigh reasons for and against his emigration.

And with his path growing clearer and clearer before him the longer he contemplated it, he went to see Mary, and if he judged it fit, to tell her what he had decided upon. Margaret was sitting with her.

"Grandfather wants to see you!" said she to Jem on his entrance.

"And I want to see him," replied Jem, suddenly remembering his last night's determination to enjoin secrecy on Job Legh.

So he hardly stayed to kiss poor Mary's sweet woe-begone face, but tore himself away from his darling to go to the old man, who awaited him impatiently.

"I've getten a note from Mr. Carson," exclaimed Job the moment he saw Jem; "and man-alive, he wants to see thee and me! For sure, there's no more mischief up, is there?" said he, looking at Jem with an expression of wonder. But if any suspicion mingled for an instant with the thoughts that crossed Job's mind, it was immediately dispelled by Jem's honest, fearless, open countenance.

"I can't guess what he's wanting, poor old chap," answered he. "May be there's some point he's not yet satisfied on; may be—but it's no use guessing; let's be off."

"It wouldn't be better for thee to be scarce a bit, would it, and leave me to go and find out what's up? He has, perhaps, getten some crotchet into his head thou'rt an accomplice, and is laying a trap for thee."

"I'm not afeared!" said Jem; "I've done nought wrong, and know nought wrong, about yon poor dead lad; though I'll own I had evil thoughts once on a time. Folk can't mistake long if once they'll search into the truth. I'll go and give the old gentleman all the satisfaction in my power, now it can injure no one. I'd my own reasons for wanting to see him besides, and it all falls in right enough for me."

Job was a little reassured by Jem's boldness; but still, if the truth must be told, he wished the young man would follow his advice, and leave him to sound Mr. Carson's intentions.

Meanwhile Jane Wilson had donned her Sunday suit of black, and set off on her errand of condolence. She felt nervous and uneasy at the idea of the moral sayings and texts which she fancied were expected from visitors on occasions like the present; and prepared many a good set speech as she walked towards the house of mourning.

As she gently opened the door, Mary, sitting idly by the fire, caught a glimpse of her,—of Jem's mother,—of the early friend of her dead parents,—of the kind minister to many a little want in days of childhood,—and rose and came and fell about her neck, with many a sob and moan, saying,

"Oh, he's gone—he's dead—all gone—all dead, and I am left alone!"

"Poor wench! poor, poor wench!" said Jane Wilson, tenderly kissing her. "Thou'rt not alone, so donnot take on so. I'll say nought of Him who's above, for thou know'st He is ever the orphan's friend; but think on Jem! nay, Mary, dear, think on me! I'm but a frabbit woman at times, but I've a heart within me through all my temper, and thou shalt be as a daughter henceforward,—as mine own ewe-lamb. Jem shall not love thee better in his way, than I will in mine; and thou'lt bear with my turns, Mary, knowing that in my soul God sees the love that shall ever be thine, if thou'lt take me for thy mother, and speak no more of being alone."

Mrs. Wilson was weeping herself long before she had ended this speech, which was so different to all she had planned to say, and from all the formal piety she had laid in store for the visit; for this was heart's piety, and needed no garnish of texts to make it true religion, pure and undefiled.

They sat together on the same chair, their arms encircling each other; they wept for the same dead; they had the same hope, and trust, and overflowing love in the living.

From that time forward, hardly a passing cloud dimmed the happy confidence of their intercourse; even by Jem would his mother's temper sooner be irritated than by Mary; before the latter she repressed her occasional nervous ill-humour till the habit of indulging it was perceptibly decreased.

Years afterwards in conversation with Jem, he was startled by a chance expression which dropped from his mother's lips; it implied a knowledge of John Barton's crime. It was many a long day since they had seen any Manchester people who could have revealed the secret (if indeed it was known in Manchester, against which Jem had guarded in every possible way). And he was led to inquire first as to the extent, and then as to the source of her knowledge. It was Mary herself who had told all.

For on the morning to which this chapter principally relates, as Mary sat weeping, and as Mrs. Wilson comforted her by every tenderest word and caress, she revealed to the dismayed and astonished Jane, the sting of her deep sorrow; the crime which stained her dead father's memory.

She was quite unconscious that Jem had kept it secret from his mother; she had imagined it bruited abroad as the suspicion against her lover had been; so word after word (dropped from her lips in the supposition that Mrs. Wilson knew all) had told the tale and revealed the cause of her deep anguish; deeper than is ever caused by Death alone.

On large occasions like the present, Mrs. Wilson's innate generosity came out. Her weak and ailing frame imparted its irritation to her conduct in small things, and daily trifles; but she had deep and noble sympathy with great sorrows, and even at the time that Mary spoke she allowed no expression of surprise or horror to escape her lips. She gave way to no curiosity as to the untold details; she was as secret and trustworthy as her son himself; and if in years to come her anger was occasionally excited against Mary, and she, on rare occasions, yielded to ill-temper against her daughter-in-law, she would upbraid her for extravagance, or stinginess, or over-dressing, or under-dressing, or too much mirth or too much gloom, but never, never in her most uncontrolled moments did she allude to any one of the circumstances relating to Mary's flirtation with Harry Carson, or his murderer; and always when she spoke of John Barton, named him with the respect due to his conduct before the last, miserable, guilty month of his life.

Therefore it came like a blow to Jem when, after years had passed away, he gathered his mother's knowledge of the whole affair. From the day when he learnt (not without remorse) what hidden depths of self-restraint she had in her soul, his manner to her, always tender and respectful, became reverential; and it was more than ever a loving strife between him and Mary which should most contribute towards the happiness of the declining years of their mother.

But I am speaking of the events which have occurred only lately, while I have yet many things to tell you that happened six or seven years ago.

CHAPTER XXXVII - DETAILS CONNECTED WITH THE MURDER.

"The rich man dines, while the poor man pines,
   And eats his heart away;
'They teach us lies,' he sternly cries,
   'Would *brothers* do as they?'"

"THE DREAM."

Mr. Carson stood at one of the breathing-moments of life. The object of the toils, the fears, and the wishes of his past years, was suddenly hidden from his sight,—vanished into the deep mystery which circumscribes existence. Nay, even the vengeance which he had proposed to himself as an aim for exertion, had been taken away from before his eyes, as by the hand of God.

Events like these would have startled the most thoughtless into reflection, much more such a man as Mr. Carson, whose mind, if not enlarged, was energetic; indeed, whose very energy, having been hitherto the cause of the employment of his powers in only one direction, had prevented him from becoming largely and philosophically comprehensive in his views.

But now the foundations of his past life were razed to the ground, and the place they had once occupied was sown with salt, to be for ever rebuilt no more. It was like the change from this Life to that other hidden one, when so many of the motives which have actuated all our earthly existence, will have become more fleeting than the shadows of a dream. With a wrench of his soul from the past, so much of which was as nothing, and worse than nothing to him now, Mr. Carson took some hours, after he had witnessed the death of his son's murderer, to consider his situation.

But suddenly, while he was deliberating, and searching for motives which should be effective to compel him to exertion and action once more; while he contemplated the desire after riches, social distinction, a name among the merchant-princes amidst whom he moved, and saw these false substances fade away into the shadows they truly are, and one by one disappear into the grave of his son,—suddenly, I say, the thought arose within him that more yet remained to be learned about the circumstances and feelings which had prompted John Barton's crime; and when once this mournful curiosity was excited, it seemed to gather strength in every moment that its gratification was delayed. Accordingly he sent a message to summon Job Legh and Jem Wilson, from whom he promised himself some elucidation of what was as yet unexplained; while he himself set forth to call on Mr. Bridgenorth, whom he knew to have been Jem's attorney, with a glimmering suspicion intruding on his mind, which he strove to repel, that Jem might have had some share in his son's death.

He had returned before his summoned visitors arrived; and had time enough to recur to the evening on which John Barton had made his confession. He remembered with mortification how he had forgotten his proud reserve, and his habitual concealment of his feelings, and had laid bare his agony of grief in the presence of these two men who were coming to see him by his desire; and he entrenched himself behind stiff barriers of self-control, through which he hoped no appearance of emotion would force its way in the conversation he anticipated.

Nevertheless, when the servant announced that two men were there by appointment to speak to him, and he had desired that they might be shown into the library where he sat, any watcher might have perceived by the trembling hands, and shaking head, not only how much he was aged by the occurrences of the last few weeks, but also how much he was agitated at the thought of the impending interview.

But he so far succeeded in commanding himself at first, as to appear to Jem Wilson and Job Legh one of the hardest and most haughty men they had ever spoken to, and to forfeit all the interest which he had previously excited in their minds by his unreserved display of deep and genuine feeling.

When he had desired them to be seated, he shaded his face with his hand for an instant before speaking.

"I have been calling on Mr. Bridgenorth this morning," said he, at last; "as I expected, he can give me but little satisfaction on some points respecting the occurrence on the 18th of last month which I desire to have cleared up. Perhaps you two can tell me what I want to know. As intimate friends of Barton's you probably know, or can conjecture a good deal. Have no scruple as to speaking the truth. What you say in this room shall never be named again by me. Besides, you are aware that the law allows no one to be tried twice for the same offence."

He stopped for a minute, for the mere act of speaking was fatiguing to him after the excitement of the last few weeks.

Job Legh took the opportunity of speaking.

"I'm not going to be affronted either for myself or Jem at what you've just now been saying about the truth. You don't know us, and there's an end on't; only it's as well for folk to think others good and true until they're proved contrary. Ask what you like, sir, I'll answer for it we'll either tell truth or hold our tongues."

"I beg your pardon," said Mr. Carson, slightly bowing his head. "What I wished to know was," referring to a slip of paper he held in his hand, and shaking so much he could hardly adjust his glasses to his eyes, "whether you, Wilson, can explain how Barton came possessed of your gun. I believe you refused this explanation to Mr. Bridgenorth."

"I did, sir! If I had said what I knew then, I saw it would criminate Barton, and so I refused telling aught. To you, sir, now I will tell every thing and any thing; only it is but little. The gun was my father's before it was mine, and long ago he and John Barton had a fancy for shooting at the gallery; and they used always to take this gun, and brag that though it was old-fashioned it was sure."

Jem saw with self-upbraiding pain how Mr. Carson winced at these last words, but at each irrepressible and involuntary evidence of feeling, the hearts of the two men warmed towards him. Jem went on speaking.

"One day in the week—I think it was on the Wednesday,—yes, it was,—it was on St. Patrick's day, I met John just coming out of our house, as I were going to my dinner. Mother was out, and he'd found no one in. He said he'd come to borrow the old gun, and that he'd have made bold, and taken it, but it was not to be seen. Mother was afraid of it, so after father's death (for while he were alive, she seemed to think he could manage it) I had carried it to my own room. I went up and fetched it for John, who stood outside the door all the time."

"What did he say he wanted it for?" asked Mr. Carson, hastily.

"I don't think he spoke when I gave it him. At first he muttered something about the shooting-gallery, and I never doubted but that it were for practice there, as I knew he had done years before."

Mr. Carson had strung up his frame to an attitude of upright attention while Jem was speaking; now the tension relaxed, and he sank back in his chair, weak and powerless.

He rose up again, however, as Jem went on, anxious to give every particular which could satisfy the bereaved father.

"I never knew for what he wanted the gun till I was taken up,—I do not know yet why he wanted it. No one would have had me get out of the scrape by implicating an old friend,—my father's old friend, and the father of the girl I loved. So I refused to tell Mr. Bridgenorth aught about it, and would not have named it now to any one but you."

Jem's face became very red at the allusion he made to Mary, but his honest, fearless eyes had met Mr. Carson's penetrating gaze unflinchingly, and had carried conviction of his innocence and truthfulness. Mr. Carson felt certain that he had heard all that Jem could tell. Accordingly he turned to Job Legh.

"You were in the room the whole time while Barton was speaking to me, I think?"

"Yes, sir," answered Job.

"You'll excuse my asking plain and direct questions; the information I am gaining is really a relief to my mind, I don't know how, but it is,—will you tell me if you had any idea of Barton's guilt in this matter before?"

"None whatever, so help me God!" said Job, solemnly. "To tell truth (and axing your forgiveness, Jem), I had never got quite shut of the notion that Jem here had done it. At times I was as clear of his innocence as I was of my own; and whenever I took to reasoning about it, I saw he could not have been the man that did it. Still I never thought of Barton."

"And yet by his confession he must have been absent at the time," said Mr. Carson, referring to his slip of paper.

"Ay, and for many a day after,—I can't rightly say how long. But still, you see, one's often blind to many a thing that lies right under one's nose, till it's pointed out. And till I heard what John Barton had to say yon night, I could not have seen what reason he had for doing it; while in the case of Jem, any one who looked at Mary Barton might have seen a cause for jealousy, clear enough."

"Then you believe that Barton had no knowledge of my son's unfortunate,—" he looked at Jem, "of his attentions to Mary Barton. This young man, Wilson, had heard of them, you see."

"The person who told me said clearly she neither had, nor would tell Mary's father," interposed Jem. "I don't believe he'd ever heard of it; he weren't a man to keep still in such a matter, if he had."

"Besides," said Job, "the reason he gave on his death-bed, so to speak, was enough; 'specially to those who knew him."

"You mean his feelings regarding the treatment of the workmen by the masters; you think he acted from motives of revenge, in consequence of the part my son had taken in putting down the strike?"

"Well, sir," replied Job, "it's hard to say: John Barton was not a man to take counsel with people; nor did he make many words about his doings. So I can only judge from his way of thinking and talking in general, never having heard him breathe a syllable concerning this matter in particular. You see he were sadly put about to make great riches and great poverty square with Christ's Gospel"—Job paused, in order to try and express what was clear enough in his own mind, as to the effect produced on John Barton by the great and mocking contrasts presented by the varieties of human condition. Before he could find suitable words to ex plain his meaning, Mr. Carson spoke.

"You mean he was an Owenite; all for equality and community of goods, and that kind of absurdity."

"No, no! John Barton was no fool. No need to tell him that were all men equal to-night, some would get the start by rising an hour earlier to-morrow. Nor yet did he care for goods, nor wealth—no man less, so that he could get daily bread for him and his; but what hurt him sore, and rankled in him as long as I knew him (and, sir, it rankles in many a poor man's heart far more than the want of any creature-comforts, and puts a sting into starvation itself), was that those who wore finer clothes, and eat better food, and had more money in their pockets, kept him at arm's length, and cared not whether his heart was sorry or glad; whether he lived or died,—whether he was bound for heaven or hell. It seemed hard to him that a heap of gold should part him and his brother so far asunder. For he was a loving man before he grew mad with seeing such as he was slighted, as if Christ Himself had not been poor. At one time, I've heard him say, he felt kindly towards every man, rich or poor, because he thought they were all men alike. But latterly he grew aggravated with the sorrows and suffering that he saw, and which he thought the masters might help if they would."

"That's the notion you've all of you got," said Mr. Carson. "Now, how in the world can we help it? We cannot regulate the demand for labour. No man or set of men can do it. It depends on events which God alone can control. When there is no market for our goods, we suffer just as much as you can do."

"Not as much, I'm sure, sir; though I'm not given to Political Economy, I know that much. I'm wanting in learning, I'm aware; but I can use my eyes. I never see the masters getting thin and haggard for want of food; I hardly ever see them making much change in their way of living, though I don't doubt they've got to do it in bad times. But it's in things for show they cut short; while for such as me, it's in things for life we've to stint. For sure, sir, you'll own it's come to a hard pass when a man would give aught in the world for work to keep his children from starving, and can't get a bit, if he's ever so willing to labour. I'm not up to talking as John Barton would have done, but that's clear to me at any rate."

"My good man, just listen to me. Two men live in solitude; one produces loaves of bread, the other coats,—or what you will. Now, would it not be hard if the bread-producer were forced to give bread for the coats, whether he wanted them or not, in order to furnish employment to the other? That is the simple form of the case; you've only to multiply the numbers. There will come times of great changes in the occupation of thousands, when improvements in manufactures and machinery are made.—It's all nonsense talking,—it must be so!"

Job Legh pondered a few moments.

"It's true it was a sore time for the hand-loom weavers when power-looms came in: them new-fangled things make a man's life like a lottery; and yet I'll never misdoubt that power-looms, and railways, and all such-like inventions, are the gifts of God. I have lived long enough, too, to see that it is part of His plan to send suffering to bring out a higher good; but surely it's also part of His plan that as much of the burden of the suffering as can be, should be lightened by those whom it is His pleasure to make happy, and content in their own circumstances. Of course it would take a deal more thought and wisdom than me, or any other man has, to settle out of hand how this should be done. But I'm clear about this, when God gives a blessing to be enjoyed, He gives it with a duty to be done; and the duty of the happy is to help the suffering to bear their woe."

"Still, facts have proved and are daily proving how much better it is for every man to be independent of help, and self-reliant," said Mr. Carson, thoughtfully.

"You can never work facts as you would fixed quantities, and say, given two facts, and the product is so and so. God has given men feelings and passions which cannot be worked into the problem, because they are for ever changing and uncertain. God has also made some weak; not in any one way, but in all. One is weak in body, another in mind, another in steadiness of purpose, a fourth can't tell right from wrong, and so on; or if he can tell the right, he wants strength to hold by it. Now to my thinking, them that is strong in any of God's gifts is meant to help the weak,—be hanged to the facts! I ask your pardon, sir; I can't rightly explain the meaning that is in me. I'm like a tap as won't run, but keeps letting it out drop by drop, so that you've no notion of the force of what's within."

Job looked and felt very sorrowful at the want of power in his words, while the feeling within him was so strong and clear.

"What you say is very true, no doubt," replied Mr. Carson; "but how would you bring it to bear upon the masters' conduct,—on my particular case?" added he, gravely.

"I'm not learned enough to argue. Thoughts come into my head that I'm sure are as true as Gospel, though may be they don't follow each other like the Q. E. D. of a Proposition. The masters has it on their own conscience,—you have it on yours, sir, to answer for to God whether you've done, and are doing all in your power to lighten the evils that seem always to hang on the trades by which you make your fortunes. It's no business of mine, thank God. John Barton took the question in hand, and his answer to it was NO! Then he grew bitter, and angry, and mad; and in his madness he did a great sin, and wrought a great woe; and repented him with tears as of blood; and will go through his penance humbly and meekly in t'other place, I'll be bound. I never seed such bitter repentance as his that last night."

There was a silence of many minutes. Mr. Carson had covered his face, and seemed utterly forgetful of their presence; and yet they did not like to disturb him by rising to leave the room.

At last he said, without meeting their sympathetic eyes,

"Thank you both for coming,—and for speaking candidly to me. I fear, Legh, neither you nor I have convinced each other, as to the power, or want of power, in the masters to remedy the evils the men complain of."

"I'm loth to vex you, sir, just now; but it was not the want of power I was talking on; what we all feel sharpest is the want of inclination to try and help the evils which come like blights at times over the manufacturing places, while we see the masters can stop work and not suffer. If we saw the masters try for our sakes to find a remedy,—even if they were long about it,—even if they could find no help, and at the end of all could only say, 'Poor fellows, our hearts are sore for ye; we've done all we could, and can't find a cure,'—we'd bear up like men through bad times. No one knows till they've tried, what power of bearing lies in them, if once they believe that men are caring for their sorrows and will help if they can. If fellow-creatures can give nought but tears and brave words, we take our trials straight from God, and we know enough of His love to put ourselves blind into His hands. You say our talk has done no good. I say it has. I see the view you take of things from the place where you stand. I can remember that, when the time comes for judging you; I sha'n't think any longer, does he act right on my views of a thing, but does he act right on his own. It has done me good in that way. I'm an old man, and may never see you again; but I'll pray for you, and think on you and your trials, both of your great wealth, and of your son's cruel death, many and many a day to come; and I'll ask God to bless both to you now and for evermore. Amen. Farewell!"

Jem had maintained a manly and dignified reserve ever since he had made his open statement of all he knew. Now both the men rose and bowed low, looking at Mr. Carson with the deep human interest they could not fail to take in one who had endured and forgiven a deep injury; and who struggled hard, as it was evident he did, to bear up like a man under his affliction.

He bowed low in return to them. Then he suddenly came forward and shook them by the hand; and thus, without a word more, they parted.

There are stages in the contemplation and endurance of great sorrow, which endow men with the same earnestness and clearness of thought that in some of old took the form of Prophecy. To those who have large capability of loving and suffering, united with great power of firm endurance, there comes a time in their woe, when they are lifted out of the contemplation of their individual case into a searching inquiry into the nature of their calamity, and the remedy (if remedy there be) which may prevent its recurrence to others as well as to themselves.

Hence the beautiful, noble efforts which are from time to time brought to light, as being continuously made by those who have once hung on the cross of agony, in order that others may not suffer as they have done; one of the grandest ends which sorrow can accomplish; the sufferer wrestling with God's messenger until a blessing is left behind, not for one alone but for generations.

It took time before the stern nature of Mr. Carson was compelled to the recognition of this secret of comfort, and that same sternness prevented his reaping any benefit in public estimation from the actions he performed; for the character is more easily changed than the habits and manners originally formed by that character, and to his dying day Mr. Carson was considered hard and cold by those who only casually saw him, or superficially knew him. But those who were admitted into his confidence were aware, that the wish which lay nearest to his heart was that none might suffer from the cause from which he had suffered; that a perfect understanding, and complete confidence and love, might exist between masters and men; that the truth might be recognised that the interests of one were the interests of all, and as such, required the consideration and deliberation of all; that hence it was most desirable to have educated workers, capable of judging, not mere machines of ignorant men; and to have them bound to their employers by the ties of respect and affection, not by mere money bargains alone; in short, to acknowledge the Spirit of Christ as the regulating law between both parties.

Many of the improvements now in practice in the system of employment in Manchester, owe their origin to short, earnest sentences spoken by Mr. Carson. Many and many yet to be carried into execution, take their birth from that stern, thoughtful mind, which submitted to be taught by suffering.

CHAPTER XXXVIII - CONCLUSION.

"Touch us gently, gentle Time!
  We've not proud nor soaring wings,
Our ambition, our content,
  Lies in simple things;
Humble voyagers are we
O'er life's dim unsounded sea;
  Touch us gently, gentle Time!"

BARRY CORNWALL.

Not many days after John Barton's funeral was over, all was arranged respecting Jem's appointment at Toronto; and the time was fixed for his sailing. It was to take place almost immediately: yet much remained to be done; many domestic preparations were to be made; and one great obstacle, anticipated by both Jem and Mary, to be removed. This was the opposition they expected from Mrs. Wilson, to whom the plan had never yet been named.

They were most anxious that their home should continue ever to be hers, yet they feared that her dislike to a new country might be an insuperable objection to this. At last Jem took advantage of an evening of unusual placidity, as he sat alone with his mother just before going to bed, to broach the subject; and to his surprise she acceded willingly to his proposition of her accompanying himself and his wife.

"To be sure 'Merica is a long way to flit to; beyond London a good bit I reckon; and quite in foreign parts; but I've never had no opinion of England, ever since they could be such fools as take up a quiet chap like thee, and clap thee in prison. Where you go, I'll go. Perhaps in them Indian countries they'll know a well-behaved lad when they see him; ne'er speak a word more, lad, I'll go."

Their path became daily more smooth and easy; the present was clear and practicable, the future was hopeful; they had leisure of mind enough to turn to the past.

"Jem!" said Mary to him, one evening as they sat in the twilight, talking together in low happy voices till Margaret should come to keep Mary company through the night, "Jem! you've never yet told me how you came to know about my naughty ways with poor young Mr. Carson." She blushed for shame at the remembrance of her folly, and hid her head on his shoulder while he made answer.

"Darling, I'm almost loth to tell you; your aunt Esther told me."

"Ah, I remember! but how did she know? I was so put about that night I did not think of asking her. Where did you see her? I've forgotten where she lives."

Mary said all this in so open and innocent a manner, that Jem felt sure she knew not the truth respecting Esther, and he half hesitated to tell her. At length he replied,

"Where did you see Esther lately? When? Tell me, love, for you've never named it before, and I can't make it out."

"Oh! it was that horrible night which is like a dream." And she told him of Esther's midnight visit, concluding with, "We must go and see her before we leave, though I don't rightly know where to find her."

"Dearest Mary,—"

"What, Jem?" exclaimed she, alarmed by his hesitation.

"Your poor aunt Esther has no home:—she's one of them miserable creatures that walk the streets." And he in his turn told of his encounter with Esther, with so many details that Mary was forced to be convinced, although her heart rebelled against the belief.

"Jem, lad!" said she, vehemently, "we must find her out,—we must hunt her up!" She rose as if she was going on the search there and then.

"What could we do, darling?" asked he, fondly restraining her.

"Do! Why! what could we *not* do, if we could but find her? She's none so happy in her ways, think ye, but what she'd turn from them, if any one would lend her a helping hand. Don't hold me, Jem; this is just the time for such as her to be out, and who knows but what I might find her close at hand."

"Stay, Mary, for a minute; I'll go out now and search for her if you wish, though it's but a wild chase. You must not go. It would be better to ask the police to-morrow. But if I should find her, how can I make her come with me? Once before she refused, and said she could not break off her drinking ways, come what might?"

"You never will persuade her if you fear and doubt," said Mary, in tears. "Hope yourself, and trust to the good that must be in her. Speak to that,—she has it in her yet,—oh, bring her home, and we will love her so, we'll make her good."

"Yes!" said Jem, catching Mary's sanguine spirit; "she shall go to America with us; and we'll help her to get rid of her sins. I'll go now, my precious darling, and if I can't find her, it's but trying the police to-morrow. Take care of your own sweet self, Mary," said he, fondly kissing her before he went out.

It was not to be. Jem wandered far and wide that night, but never met Esther. The next day he applied to the police; and at last they recognised under his description of her, a woman known to them under the name of the "Butterfly," from the gaiety of her dress a year or two ago. By their help he traced out one of her haunts, a low lodging-house behind Peter Street. He and his companion, a kind-hearted policeman, were admitted, suspiciously enough, by the landlady, who ushered them into a large garret where twenty or thirty people of all ages and both sexes lay and dozed away the day, choosing the evening and night for their trades of beggary, thieving, or prostitution.

"I know the Butterfly was here," said she, looking round. "She came in, the night before last, and said she had not a penny to get a place for shelter; and that if she was far away in the country she could steal aside and die in a copse, or a clough, like the wild animals; but here the police would let no one alone in the streets, and she wanted a spot to die in, in peace. It's a queer sort of peace we have here, but that night the room was uncommon empty, and I'm not a hard-hearted woman (I wish I were, I could ha' made a good thing out of it afore this if I were harder), so I sent her up,—but she's not here now, I think."

"Was she very bad?" asked Jem.

"Ay! nought but skin and bone, with a cough to tear her in two."

They made some inquiries, and found that in the restlessness of approaching death, she had longed to be once more in the open air, and had gone forth,—where, no one seemed to be able to tell.

Leaving many messages for her, and directions that he was to be sent for if either the policeman or the landlady obtained any clue to her where-abouts, Jem bent his steps towards Mary's house; for he had not seen her all that long day of search. He told her of his proceedings and want of success; and both were saddened at the recital, and sat silent for some time.

After a while they began talking over their plans. In a day or two, Mary was to give up house, and go and live for a week or so with Job Legh, until the time of her marriage, which would take place immediately before sailing; they talked themselves back into silence and delicious reverie. Mary sat by Jem, his arm round her waist, her head on his shoulder; and thought over the scenes which had passed in that home she was so soon to leave for ever.

Suddenly she felt Jem start, and started too without knowing why; she tried to see his countenance, but the shades of evening had deepened so much she could read no expression there. It was turned to the window; she looked and saw a white face pressed against the panes on the outside, gazing intently into the dusky chamber.

While they watched, as if fascinated by the appearance, and unable to think or stir, a film came over the bright, feverish, glittering eyes outside, and the form sank down to the ground without a struggle of instinctive resistance.

"It is Esther!" exclaimed they, both at once. They rushed outside; and, fallen into what appeared simply a heap of white or light-coloured clothes, fainting or dead, lay the poor crushed Butterfly—the once innocent Esther.

She had come (as a wounded deer drags its heavy limbs once more to the green coolness of the lair in which it was born, there to die) to see the place familiar to her innocence, yet once again before her death. Whether she was indeed alive or dead, they knew not now.

Job came in with Margaret, for it was bed-time. He said Esther's pulse beat a little yet. They carried her upstairs and laid her on Mary's bed, not daring to undress her, lest any motion should frighten the trembling life away; but it was all in vain.

Towards midnight, she opened wide her eyes and looked around on the once familiar room; Job Legh knelt by the bed praying aloud and fervently for her, but he stopped as he saw her roused look. She sat up in bed with a sudden convulsive motion.

"Has it been a dream then?" asked she wildly. Then with a habit, which came like instinct even in that awful dying hour, her hand sought for a locket which hung concealed in her bosom, and, finding that, she knew all was true which had befallen her since last she lay an innocent girl on that bed.

She fell back, and spoke word never more. She held the locket containing her child's hair still in her hand, and once or twice she kissed it with a long soft kiss. She cried feebly and sadly as long as she had any strength to cry, and then she died.

They laid her in one grave with John Barton. And there they lie without name, or initial, or date. Only this verse is inscribed upon the stone which covers the remains of these two wanderers.

Psalm ciii. v. 9.—"For He will not always chide, neither will He keep His anger for ever."

I see a long, low, wooden house, with room enough and to spare. The old primeval trees are felled and gone for many a mile around; one alone remains to overshadow the gable-end of the cottage. There is a garden around the dwelling, and far beyond that stretches an orchard. The glory of an Indian summer is over all, making the heart leap at the sight of its gorgeous beauty.

At the door of the house, looking towards the town, stands Mary, watching for the return of her husband from his daily work; and while she watches, she listens, smiling;

"Clap hands, daddy comes,
With his pocket full of plums,
And a cake for Johnnie."

Then comes a crow of delight from Johnnie. Then his grandmother carries him to the door, and glories in seeing him resist his mother's blandishments to cling to her.

"English letters! 'Twas that made me so late!"

"Oh, Jem, Jem! don't hold them so tight! What do they say?"

"Why, some good news. Come, give a guess what it is."

"Oh, tell me! I cannot guess," said Mary.

"Then you give it up, do you? What do you say, mother?"

Jane Wilson thought a moment.

"Will and Margaret are married?" asked she.

"Not exactly,—but very near. The old woman has twice the spirit of the young one. Come, Mary, give a guess!"

He covered his little boy's eyes with his hands for an instant, significantly, till the baby pushed them down, saying in his imperfect way,

"Tan't see."

"There now! Johnnie can see. Do you guess, Mary?"

"They've done something to Margaret to give her back her sight!" exclaimed she.

"They have. She has been couched, and can see as well as ever. She and Will are to be married on the twenty-fifth of this month, and he's bringing her out here next voyage; and Job Legh talks of coming too,—not to see you, Mary,—nor you, mother,—nor you, my little hero" (kissing him), "but to try and pick up a few specimens of Canadian insects, Will says. All the compliment is to the earwigs, you see, mother!"

"Dear Job Legh!" said Mary, softly and seriously.

CRANFORD

CHAPTER I - OUR SOCIETY

In the first place, Cranford is in possession of the Amazons; all the holders of houses above a certain rent are women. If a married couple come to settle in the town, somehow the gentleman disappears; he is either fairly frightened to death by being the only man in the Cranford evening parties, or he is accounted for by being with his regiment, his ship, or closely engaged in business all the week in the great neighbouring commercial town of Drumble, distant only twenty miles on a railroad. In short, whatever does become of the gentlemen, they are not at Cranford. What could they do if they were there? The surgeon has his round of thirty miles, and sleeps at Cranford; but every man cannot be a surgeon. For keeping the trim gardens full of choice flowers without a weed to speck them; for frightening away little boys who look wistfully at the said flowers through the railings; for rushing out at the geese that occasionally venture in to the gardens if the gates are left open; for deciding all questions of literature and politics without troubling themselves with unnecessary reasons or arguments; for obtaining clear and correct knowledge of everybody's affairs in the parish; for keeping their neat maid-servants in admirable order; for kindness (somewhat dictatorial) to the poor, and real tender good offices to each other whenever they are in distress, the ladies of Cranford are quite sufficient. "A man," as one of them observed to me once, "is *so* in the way in the house!" Although the ladies of Cranford know all each other's proceedings, they are exceedingly indifferent to each other's opinions. Indeed, as each has her own individuality, not to say eccentricity, pretty strongly developed, nothing is so easy as verbal retaliation; but, somehow, good-will reigns among them to a considerable degree.

The Cranford ladies have only an occasional little quarrel, spirited out in a few peppery words and angry jerks of the head; just enough to prevent the even tenor of their lives from becoming too flat. Their dress is very independent of fashion; as they observe, "What does it signify how we dress here at Cranford, where everybody knows us?" And if they go from home, their reason is equally cogent, "What does it signify how we dress here, where nobody knows us?" The materials of their clothes are, in general, good and plain, and most of them are nearly as scrupulous as Miss Tyler, of cleanly memory; but I will answer for it, the last gigot, the last tight and scanty petticoat in wear in England, was seen in Cranford—and seen without a smile.

I can testify to a magnificent family red silk umbrella, under which a gentle little spinster, left alone of many brothers and sisters, used to patter to church on rainy days. Have you any red silk umbrellas in London? We had a tradition of the first that had ever been seen in Cranford; and the little boys mobbed it, and called it "a stick in petticoats." It might have been the very red silk one I have described, held by a strong father over a troop of little ones; the poor little lady—the survivor of all—could scarcely carry it.

Then there were rules and regulations for visiting and calls; and they were announced to any young people who might be staying in the town, with all the solemnity with which the old Manx laws were read once a year on the Tinwald Mount.

"Our friends have sent to inquire how you are after your journey to-night, my dear" (fifteen miles in a gentleman's carriage); "they will give you some rest to-morrow, but the next day, I have no doubt, they will call; so be at liberty after twelve—from twelve to three are our calling hours."

Then, after they had called—

"It is the third day; I dare say your mamma has told you, my dear, never to let more than three days elapse between receiving a call and returning it; and also, that you are never to stay longer than a quarter of an hour."

"But am I to look at my watch? How am I to find out when a quarter of an hour has passed?"

"You must keep thinking about the time, my dear, and not allow yourself to forget it in conversation."

As everybody had this rule in their minds, whether they received or paid a call, of course no absorbing subject was ever spoken about. We kept ourselves to short sentences of small talk, and were punctual to our time.

I imagine that a few of the gentlefolks of Cranford were poor, and had some difficulty in making both ends meet; but they were like the Spartans, and concealed their smart under a smiling face. We none of us spoke of money, because that subject savoured of commerce and trade, and though some might be poor, we were all aristocratic. The Cranfordians had that kindly *esprit de corps* which made them overlook all deficiencies in success when some among them tried to conceal their poverty. When Mrs Forrester, for instance, gave a party in her baby-house of a dwelling, and the little maiden disturbed the ladies on the sofa by a request that she might get the tea-tray out from underneath, everyone took this novel proceeding as the most natural thing in the world, and talked on about household forms and ceremonies as if we all believed that our hostess had a regular servants' hall, second table, with housekeeper and steward, instead of the one little charity-school maiden, whose short ruddy arms could never have been strong enough to carry the tray upstairs, if she had not been assisted in private by her mistress, who now sat in state, pretending not to know what cakes were sent up, though she knew, and we knew, and she knew that we knew, and we knew that she knew that we knew, she had been busy all the morning making tea-bread and sponge-cakes.

There were one or two consequences arising from this general but unacknowledged poverty, and this very much acknowledged gentility, which were not amiss, and which might be introduced into many circles of society to their great improvement. For instance, the inhabitants of Cranford kept early hours, and clattered home in their pattens, under the guidance of a lantern-bearer, about nine o'clock at night; and the whole town was abed and asleep by half-past ten. Moreover, it was considered "vulgar" (a tremendous word in Cranford) to give anything expensive, in the way of eatable or drinkable, at the evening entertainments. Wafer bread-and-butter and sponge-biscuits were all that the Honourable Mrs Jamieson gave; and she was sister-in-law to the late Earl of Glenmire, although she did practise such "elegant economy."

"Elegant economy!" How naturally one falls back into the phraseology of Cranford! There, economy was always "elegant," and money-spending always "vulgar and ostentatious"; a sort of sour-grapeism which made us very peaceful and satisfied. I never shall forget the dismay felt when a certain Captain Brown came to live at Cranford, and openly spoke about his being poor—not in a whisper to an intimate friend, the doors and windows being previously closed, but in the public street! in a loud military voice! alleging his poverty as a reason for not taking a particular house. The ladies of Cranford were already rather moaning over the invasion of their territories by a man and a gentleman. He was a half-pay captain, and had obtained some situation on a neighbouring railroad, which had been vehemently petitioned against by the little town; and if, in addition to his masculine gender, and his connection with the obnoxious railroad, he was so brazen as to talk of being poor—why, then, indeed, he must be sent to Coventry. Death was as true and as common as poverty; yet people never spoke about that, loud out in the streets. It was a word not to be mentioned to ears polite. We had tacitly agreed to ignore that any with whom we associated on terms of visiting equality could ever be prevented by poverty from doing anything that they wished. If we walked to or from a party, it was because the night was *so* fine, or the air *so* refreshing, not because sedan-chairs were expensive. If we wore prints, instead of summer silks, it was because we preferred a washing material; and so on, till we blinded ourselves to the vulgar fact that we were, all of us, people of very moderate means. Of course, then, we did not know what to make of a man who could speak of poverty as if it was not a disgrace. Yet, somehow, Captain Brown made himself respected in Cranford, and was called upon, in spite of all resolutions to the contrary. I was surprised to hear his opinions quoted as authority at a visit which I paid to Cranford about a year after he had settled in the town. My own friends had been among the bitterest opponents of any proposal to visit the Captain and his daughters, only twelve months before; and now he was even admitted in the tabooed hours before twelve. True, it was to discover the cause of a smoking chimney, before the fire was lighted; but still Captain Brown walked upstairs, nothing daunted, spoke in a voice too large for the room, and joked quite in the way of a tame man about the house. He had been blind to all the small slights, and omissions of trivial ceremonies, with which he had been received. He had been friendly, though the Cranford ladies had been cool; he had answered small sarcastic compliments in good faith; and with his manly frankness had overpowered all the shrinking which met him as a man who was not ashamed to be poor. And, at last, his excellent masculine common sense, and his facility in devising expedients to overcome domestic dilemmas, had gained him an extraordinary place as authority among the Cranford ladies. He himself went on in his course, as unaware of his popularity as he had been of the reverse; and I am sure he was startled one day when he found his advice so highly esteemed as to make some counsel which he had given in jest to be taken in sober, serious earnest.

It was on this subject: An old lady had an Alderney cow, which she looked upon as a daughter. You could not pay the short quarter of an hour call without being told of the wonderful milk or wonderful intelligence of this animal. The whole town knew and kindly regarded Miss Betsy Barker's Alderney; therefore great was the sympathy and regret when, in an unguarded moment, the poor cow tumbled into a lime-pit. She moaned so loudly that she was soon heard and rescued; but meanwhile the poor beast had lost most of her hair, and came out looking naked, cold, and miserable, in a bare skin. Everybody pitied the animal, though a few could not restrain their smiles at her droll appearance. Miss Betsy Barker absolutely cried with sorrow and dismay; and it was said she thought of trying a bath of oil. This remedy, perhaps, was recommended by some one of the number whose advice she asked; but the proposal, if ever it was made, was knocked on the head by Captain Brown's decided "Get her a flannel waistcoat and flannel drawers, ma'am, if you wish to keep her alive. But my advice is, kill the poor creature at once."

Miss Betsy Barker dried her eyes, and thanked the Captain heartily; she set to work, and by-and-by all the town turned out to see the Alderney meekly going to her pasture, clad in dark grey flannel. I have watched her myself many a time. Do you ever see cows dressed in grey flannel in London?

Captain Brown had taken a small house on the outskirts of the town, where he lived with his two daughters. He must have been upwards of sixty at the time of the first visit I paid to Cranford after I had left it as a residence. But he had a wiry, well-trained, elastic figure, a stiff military throw-back of his head, and a springing step, which made him appear much younger than he was. His eldest daughter looked almost as old as himself, and betrayed the fact that his real was more than his apparent age. Miss Brown must have been forty; she had a sickly, pained, careworn expression on her face, and looked as if the gaiety of youth had long faded out of sight. Even when young she must have been plain and hard-featured. Miss Jessie Brown was ten years younger than her sister, and twenty shades prettier. Her face was round and dimpled. Miss Jenkyns once said, in a passion against Captain Brown (the cause of which I will tell you presently), "that she thought it was time for Miss Jessie to leave off her dimples, and not always to be trying to look like a child." It was true there was something childlike in her face; and there will be, I think, till she dies, though she should live to a hundred. Her eyes were large blue wondering eyes, looking straight at you; her nose was unformed and snub, and her lips were red and dewy; she wore her hair, too, in little rows of curls, which heightened this appearance. I do not know whether she was pretty or not; but I liked her face, and so did everybody, and I do not think she could help her dimples. She had something of her father's jauntiness of gait and manner; and any female observer might detect a slight difference in the attire of the two sisters—that of Miss Jessie being about two pounds per annum more expensive than Miss Brown's. Two pounds was a large sum in Captain Brown's annual disbursements.

Such was the impression made upon me by the Brown family when I first saw them all together in Cranford Church. The Captain I had met before—on the occasion of the smoky chimney, which he had cured by some simple alteration in the flue. In church, he held his double eye-glass to his eyes during the Morning Hymn, and then lifted up his head erect and sang out loud and joyfully. He made the responses louder than the clerk—an old man with a piping feeble voice, who, I think, felt aggrieved at the Captain's sonorous bass, and quivered higher and higher in consequence.

On coming out of church, the brisk Captain paid the most gallant attention to his two daughters. He nodded and smiled to his acquaintances; but he shook hands with none until he had helped Miss Brown to unfurl her umbrella, had relieved her of her prayer-book, and had waited patiently till she, with trembling nervous hands, had taken up her gown to walk through the wet roads.

I wonder what the Cranford ladies did with Captain Brown at their parties. We had often rejoiced, in former days, that there was no gentleman to be attended to, and to find conversation for, at the card-parties. We had congratulated ourselves upon the snugness of the evenings; and, in our love for gentility, and distaste of mankind, we had almost persuaded ourselves that to be a man was to be "vulgar"; so that when I found my friend and hostess, Miss Jenkyns, was going to have a party in my honour, and that Captain and the Miss Browns were invited, I wondered much what would be the course of the evening. Card-tables, with green baize tops, were set out by daylight, just as usual; it was the third week in November, so the evenings closed in about four. Candles, and clean packs of cards, were arranged on each table. The fire was made up; the neat maid-servant had received her last directions, and there we stood, dressed in our best, each with a candle-lighter in our hands, ready to dart at the candles as soon as the first knock came. Parties in Cranford were solemn festivities, making the ladies feel gravely elated as they sat together in their best dresses. As soon as three had arrived, we sat down to "Preference," I being the unlucky fourth. The next four comers were put down immediately to another table; and presently the tea-trays, which I had seen set out in the store-room as I passed in the morning, were placed each on the middle of a card-table. The china was delicate egg-shell; the old-fashioned silver glittered with polishing; but the eatables were of the slightest description. While the trays were yet on the tables, Captain and the Miss Browns came in; and I could see that, somehow or other, the Captain was a favourite with all the ladies present. Ruffled brows were smoothed, sharp voices lowered at his approach.

Miss Brown looked ill, and depressed almost to gloom. Miss Jessie smiled as usual, and seemed nearly as popular as her father. He immediately and quietly assumed the man's place in the room; attended to every one's wants, lessened the pretty maid-servant's labour by waiting on empty cups and bread-and-butterless ladies; and yet did it all in so easy and dignified a manner, and so much as if it were a matter of course for the strong to attend to the weak, that he was a true man throughout. He played for threepenny points with as grave an interest as if they had been pounds; and yet, in all his attention to strangers, he had an eye on his suffering daughter—for suffering I was sure she was, though to many eyes she might only appear to be irritable. Miss Jessie could not play cards: but she talked to the sitters-out, who, before her coming, had been rather inclined to be cross. She sang, too, to an old cracked piano, which I think had been a spinet in its youth. Miss Jessie sang, "Jock of Hazeldean" a little out of tune; but we were none of us musical, though Miss Jenkyns beat time, out of time, by way of appearing to be so.

It was very good of Miss Jenkyns to do this; for I had seen that, a little before, she had been a good deal annoyed by Miss Jessie Brown's unguarded admission (*à propos* of Shetland wool) that she had an uncle, her mother's brother, who was a shop-keeper in Edinburgh. Miss Jenkyns tried to drown this confession by a terrible cough—for the Honourable Mrs Jamieson was sitting at a card-table nearest Miss Jessie, and what would she say or think if she found out she was in the same room with a shop-keeper's niece! But Miss Jessie Brown (who had no tact, as we all agreed the next morning) *would* repeat the information, and assure Miss Pole she could easily get her the identical Shetland wool required, "through my uncle, who has the best assortment of Shetland goods of any one in Edinbro'." It was to take the taste of this out of our mouths, and the sound of this out of our ears, that Miss Jenkyns proposed music; so I say again, it was very good of her to beat time to the song.

When the trays re-appeared with biscuits and wine, punctually at a quarter to nine, there was conversation, comparing of cards, and talking over tricks; but by-and-by Captain Brown sported a bit of literature.

"Have you seen any numbers of 'The Pickwick Papers'?" said he. (They were then publishing in parts.) "Capital thing!"

Now Miss Jenkyns was daughter of a deceased rector of Cranford; and, on the strength of a number of manuscript sermons, and a pretty good library of divinity, considered herself literary, and looked upon any conversation about books as a challenge to her. So she answered and said, "Yes, she had seen them; indeed, she might say she had read them."

"And what do you think of them?" exclaimed Captain Brown. "Aren't they famously good?"

So urged Miss Jenkyns could not but speak.

"I must say, I don't think they are by any means equal to Dr Johnson. Still, perhaps, the author is young. Let him persevere, and who knows what he may become if he will take the great Doctor for his model?" This was evidently too much for Captain Brown to take placidly; and I saw the words on the tip of his tongue before Miss Jenkyns had finished her sentence.

"It is quite a different sort of thing, my dear madam," he began.

"I am quite aware of that," returned she. "And I make allowances, Captain Brown."

"Just allow me to read you a scene out of this month's number," pleaded he. "I had it only this morning, and I don't think the company can have read it yet."

"As you please," said she, settling herself with an air of resignation. He read the account of the "swarry" which Sam Weller gave at Bath. Some of us laughed heartily. *I* did not dare, because I was staying in the house. Miss Jenkyns sat in patient gravity. When it was ended, she turned to me, and said with mild dignity—

"Fetch me 'Rasselas,' my dear, out of the book-room."

When I had brought it to her, she turned to Captain Brown—

"Now allow *me* to read you a scene, and then the present company can judge between your favourite, Mr Boz, and Dr Johnson."

She read one of the conversations between Rasselas and Imlac, in a high-pitched, majestic voice: and when she had ended, she said, "I imagine I am now justified in my preference of Dr Johnson as a writer of fiction." The Captain screwed his lips up, and drummed on the table, but he did not speak. She thought she would give him a finishing blow or two.

"I consider it vulgar, and below the dignity of literature, to publish in numbers."

"How was the *Rambler* published, ma'am?" asked Captain Brown in a low voice, which I think Miss Jenkyns could not have heard.

"Dr Johnson's style is a model for young beginners. My father recommended it to me when I began to write letters—I have formed my own style upon it; I recommended it to your favourite."

"I should be very sorry for him to exchange his style for any such pompous writing," said Captain Brown.

Miss Jenkyns felt this as a personal affront, in a way of which the Captain had not dreamed. Epistolary writing she and her friends considered as her *forte*. Many a copy of many a letter have I seen written and corrected on the slate, before she "seized the half-hour just previous to post-time to assure" her friends of this or of that; and Dr Johnson was, as she said, her model in these compositions. She drew herself up with dignity, and only replied to Captain Brown's last remark by saying, with marked emphasis on every syllable, "I prefer Dr Johnson to Mr Boz."

It is said—I won't vouch for the fact—that Captain Brown was heard to say, *sotto voce*, "D-n Dr Johnson!" If he did, he was penitent afterwards, as he showed by going to stand near Miss Jenkyns' arm-chair, and endeavouring to beguile her into conversation on some more pleasing subject. But she was inexorable. The next day she made the remark I have mentioned about Miss Jessie's dimples.

CHAPTER II - THE CAPTAIN

IT was impossible to live a month at Cranford and not know the daily habits of each resident; and long before my visit was ended I knew much concerning the whole Brown trio. There was nothing new to be discovered respecting their poverty; for they had spoken simply and openly about that from the very first. They made no mystery of the necessity for their being economical. All that remained to be discovered was the Captain's infinite kindness of heart, and the various modes in which, unconsciously to himself, he manifested it. Some little anecdotes were talked about for some time after they occurred. As we did not read much, and as all the ladies were pretty well suited with servants, there was a dearth of subjects for conversation. We therefore discussed the circumstance of the Captain taking a poor old woman's dinner out of her hands one very slippery Sunday. He had met her returning from the bakehouse as he came from church, and noticed her precarious footing; and, with the grave dignity with which he did everything, he relieved her of her burden, and steered along the street by her side, carrying her baked mutton and potatoes safely home. This was thought very eccentric; and it was rather expected that he would pay a round of calls, on the Monday morning, to explain and apologise to the Cranford sense of propriety: but he did no such thing: and then it was decided that he was ashamed, and was keeping out of sight. In a kindly pity for him, we began to say, "After all, the Sunday morning's occurrence showed great goodness of heart," and it was resolved that he should be comforted on his next appearance amongst us; but, lo! he came down upon us, untouched by any sense of shame, speaking loud and bass as ever, his head thrown back, his wig as jaunty and well-curled as usual, and we were obliged to conclude he had forgotten all about Sunday.

Miss Pole and Miss Jessie Brown had set up a kind of intimacy on the strength of the Shetland wool and the new knitting stitches; so it happened that when I went to visit Miss Pole I saw more of the Browns than I had done while staying with Miss Jenkyns, who had never got over what she called Captain Brown's disparaging remarks upon Dr Johnson as a writer of light and agreeable fiction. I found that Miss Brown was seriously ill of some lingering, incurable complaint, the pain occasioned by which gave the uneasy expression to her face that I had taken for unmitigated crossness. Cross, too, she was at times, when the nervous irritability occasioned by her disease became past endurance. Miss Jessie bore with her at these times, even more patiently than she did with the bitter self-upbraidings by which they were invariably succeeded. Miss Brown used to accuse herself, not merely of hasty and irritable temper, but also of being the cause why her father and sister were obliged to pinch, in order to allow her the small luxuries which were necessaries in her condition. She would so fain have made sacrifices for them, and have lightened their cares, that the original generosity of her disposition added acerbity to her temper. All this was borne by Miss Jessie and her father with more than placidity—with absolute tenderness. I forgave Miss Jessie her singing out of tune, and her juvenility of dress, when I saw her at home. I came to perceive that Captain Brown's dark Brutus wig and padded coat (alas! too often threadbare) were remnants of the military smartness of his youth, which he now wore unconsciously. He was a man of infinite resources, gained in his barrack experience. As he confessed, no one could black his boots to please him except himself; but, indeed, he was not above saving the little maid-servant's labours in every way—knowing, most likely, that his daughter's illness made the place a hard one.

He endeavoured to make peace with Miss Jenkyns soon after the memorable dispute I have named, by a present of a wooden fire-shovel (his own making), having heard her say how much the grating of an iron one annoyed her. She received the present with cool gratitude, and thanked him formally. When he was gone, she bade me put it away in the lumber-room; feeling, probably, that no present from a man who preferred Mr Boz to Dr Johnson could be less jarring than an iron fire-shovel.

Such was the state of things when I left Cranford and went to Drumble. I had, however, several correspondents, who kept me *au fait* as to the proceedings of the dear little town. There was Miss Pole, who was becoming as much absorbed in crochet as she had been once in knitting, and the burden of whose letter was something like, "But don't you forget the white worsted at Flint's" of the old song; for at the end of every sentence of news came a fresh direction as to some crochet commission which I was to execute for her. Miss Matilda Jenkyns (who did not mind being called Miss Matty, when Miss Jenkyns was not by) wrote nice, kind, rambling letters, now and then venturing into an opinion of her own; but suddenly pulling herself up, and either begging me not to name what she had said, as Deborah thought differently, and *she* knew, or else putting in a postscript to the effect that, since writing the above, she had been talking over the subject with Deborah, and was quite convinced that, etc.—(here probably followed a recantation of every opinion she had given in the letter). Then came Miss Jenkyns—Deborah, as she liked Miss Matty to call her, her father having once said that the Hebrew name ought to be so pronounced. I secretly think she took the Hebrew prophetess for a model in character; and, indeed, she was not unlike the stern prophetess in some ways, making allowance, of course, for modern customs and difference in dress. Miss Jenkyns wore a cravat, and a little bonnet like a jockey-cap, and altogether had the appearance of a strong-minded woman; although she would have despised the modern idea of women being equal to men.

Equal, indeed! she knew they were superior. But to return to her letters. Everything in them was stately and grand like herself. I have been looking them over (dear Miss Jenkyns, how I honoured her!) and I will give an extract, more especially because it relates to our friend Captain Brown:—

"The Honourable Mrs Jamieson has only just quitted me; and, in the course of conversation, she communicated to me the intelligence that she had yesterday received a call from her revered husband's quondam friend, Lord Mauleverer. You will not easily conjecture what brought his lordship within the precincts of our little town. It was to see Captain Brown, with whom, it appears, his lordship was acquainted in the 'plumed wars,' and who had the privilege of averting destruction from his lordship's head when some great peril was impending over it, off the misnomered Cape of Good Hope. You know our friend the Honourable Mrs Jamieson's deficiency in the spirit of innocent curiosity, and you will therefore not be so much surprised when I tell you she was quite unable to disclose to me the exact nature of the peril in question. I was anxious, I confess, to ascertain in what manner Captain Brown, with his limited establishment, could receive so distinguished a guest; and I discovered that his lordship retired to rest, and, let us hope, to refreshing slumbers, at the Angel Hotel; but shared the Brunonian meals during the two days that he honoured Cranford with his august presence. Mrs Johnson, our civil butcher's wife, informs me that Miss Jessie purchased a leg of lamb; but, besides this, I can hear of no preparation whatever to give a suitable reception to so distinguished a visitor. Perhaps they entertained him with 'the feast of reason and the flow of soul'; and to us, who are acquainted with Captain Brown's sad want of relish for 'the pure wells of English undefiled,' it may be matter for congratulation that he has had the opportunity of improving his taste by holding converse with an elegant and refined member of the British aristocracy. But from some mundane failings who is altogether free?"

Miss Pole and Miss Matty wrote to me by the same post. Such a piece of news as Lord Mauleverer's visit was not to be lost on the Cranford letter-writers: they made the most of it. Miss Matty humbly apologised for writing at the same time as her sister, who was so much more capable than she to describe the honour done to Cranford; but in spite of a little bad spelling, Miss Matty's account gave me the best idea of the commotion occasioned by his lordship's visit, after it had occurred; for, except the people at the Angel, the Browns, Mrs Jamieson, and a little lad his lordship had sworn at for driving a dirty hoop against the aristocratic legs, I could not hear of any one with whom his lordship had held conversation.

My next visit to Cranford was in the summer. There had been neither births, deaths, nor marriages since I was there last. Everybody lived in the same house, and wore pretty nearly the same well-preserved, old-fashioned clothes. The greatest event was, that Miss Jenkyns had purchased a new carpet for the drawing-room. Oh, the busy work Miss Matty and I had in chasing the sunbeams, as they fell in an afternoon right down on this carpet through the blindless window! We spread newspapers over the places and sat down to our book or our work; and, lo! in a quarter of an hour the sun had moved, and was blazing away on a fresh spot; and down again we went on our knees to alter the position of the newspapers. We were very busy, too, one whole morning, before Miss Jenkyns gave her party, in following her directions, and in cutting out and stitching together pieces of newspaper so as to form little paths to every chair set for the expected visitors, lest their shoes might dirty or defile the purity of the carpet. Do you make paper paths for every guest to walk upon in London?

Captain Brown and Miss Jenkyns were not very cordial to each other. The literary dispute, of which I had seen the beginning, was a "raw," the slightest touch on which made them wince. It was the only difference of opinion they had ever had; but that difference was enough. Miss Jenkyns could not refrain from talking at Captain Brown; and, though he did not reply, he drummed with his fingers, which action she felt and resented as very disparaging to Dr Johnson. He was rather ostentatious in his preference of the writings of Mr Boz; would walk through the streets so absorbed in them that he all but ran against Miss Jenkyns; and though his apologies were earnest and sincere, and though he did not, in fact, do more than startle her and himself, she owned to me she had rather he had knocked her down, if he had only been reading a higher style of literature. The poor, brave Captain! he looked older, and more worn, and his clothes were very threadbare. But he seemed as bright and cheerful as ever, unless he was asked about his daughter's health.

"She suffers a great deal, and she must suffer more: we do what we can to alleviate her pain;—God's will be done!" He took off his hat at these last words. I found, from Miss Matty, that everything had been done, in fact. A medical man, of high repute in that country neighbourhood, had been sent for, and every injunction he had given was attended to, regardless of expense. Miss Matty was sure they denied themselves many things in order to make the invalid comfortable; but they never spoke about it; and as for Miss Jessie!—"I really think she's an angel," said poor Miss Matty, quite overcome. "To see her way of bearing with Miss Brown's crossness, and the bright face she puts on after she's been sitting up a whole night and scolded above half of it, is quite beautiful. Yet she looks as neat and as ready to welcome the Captain at breakfast-time as if she had been asleep in the Queen's bed all night. My dear! you could never laugh at her prim little curls or her pink bows again if you saw her as I have done." I could only feel very penitent, and greet Miss Jessie with double respect when I met her next. She looked faded and pinched; and her lips began to quiver, as if she was very weak, when she spoke of her sister. But she brightened, and sent back the tears that were glittering in her pretty eyes, as she said—

"But, to be sure, what a town Cranford is for kindness! I don't suppose any one has a better dinner than usual cooked but the best part of all comes in a little covered basin for my sister. The poor people will leave their earliest vegetables at our door for her. They speak short and gruff, as if they were ashamed of it: but I am sure it often goes to my heart to see their thoughtfulness." The tears now came back and overflowed; but after a minute or two she began to scold herself, and ended by going away the same cheerful Miss Jessie as ever.

"But why does not this Lord Mauleverer do something for the man who saved his life?" said I.

"Why, you see, unless Captain Brown has some reason for it, he never speaks about being poor; and he walked along by his lordship looking as happy and cheerful as a prince; and as they never called attention to their dinner by apologies, and as Miss Brown was better that day, and all seemed bright, I daresay his lordship never knew how much care there was in the background. He did send game in the winter pretty often, but now he is gone abroad."

I had often occasion to notice the use that was made of fragments and small opportunities in Cranford; the rose-leaves that were gathered ere they fell to make into a potpourri for someone who had no garden; the little bundles of lavender flowers sent to strew the drawers of some town-dweller, or to burn in the chamber of some invalid. Things that many would despise, and actions which it seemed scarcely worth while to perform, were all attended to in Cranford. Miss Jenkyns stuck an apple full of cloves, to be heated and smell pleasantly in Miss Brown's room; and as she put in each clove she uttered a Johnsonian sentence. Indeed, she never could think of the Browns without talking Johnson; and, as they were seldom absent from her thoughts just then, I heard many a rolling, three-piled sentence.

Captain Brown called one day to thank Miss Jenkyns for many little kindnesses, which I did not know until then that she had rendered. He had suddenly become like an old man; his deep bass voice had a quavering in it, his eyes looked dim, and the lines on his face were deep. He did not—could not—speak cheerfully of his daughter's state, but he talked with manly, pious resignation, and not much. Twice over he said, "What Jessie has been to us, God only knows!" and after the second time, he got up hastily, shook hands all round without speaking, and left the room.

That afternoon we perceived little groups in the street, all listening with faces aghast to some tale or other. Miss Jenkyns wondered what could be the matter for some time before she took the undignified step of sending Jenny out to inquire.

Jenny came back with a white face of terror. "Oh, ma'am! Oh, Miss Jenkyns, ma'am! Captain Brown is killed by them nasty cruel railroads!" and she burst into tears. She, along with many others, had experienced the poor Captain's kindness.

"How?—where—where? Good God! Jenny, don't waste time in crying, but tell us something." Miss Matty rushed out into the street at once, and collared the man who was telling the tale.

"Come in—come to my sister at once, Miss Jenkyns, the rector's daughter. Oh, man, man! say it is not true," she cried, as she brought the affrighted carter, sleeking down his hair, into the drawing-room, where he stood with his wet boots on the new carpet, and no one regarded it.

"Please, mum, it is true. I seed it myself," and he shuddered at the recollection. "The Captain was a-reading some new book as he was deep in, a-waiting for the down train; and there was a little lass as wanted to come to its mammy, and gave its sister the slip, and came toddling across the line. And he looked up sudden, at the sound of the train coming, and seed the child, and he darted on the line and cotched it up, and his foot slipped, and the train came over him in no time. O Lord, Lord! Mum, it's quite true, and they've come over to tell his daughters. The child's safe, though, with only a bang on its shoulder as he threw it to its mammy. Poor Captain would be glad of that, mum, wouldn't he? God bless him!" The great rough carter puckered up his manly face, and turned away to hide his tears. I turned to Miss Jenkyns. She looked very ill, as if she were going to faint, and signed to me to open the window.

"Matilda, bring me my bonnet. I must go to those girls. God pardon me, if ever I have spoken contemptuously to the Captain!"

Miss Jenkyns arrayed herself to go out, telling Miss Matilda to give the man a glass of wine. While she was away, Miss Matty and I huddled over the fire, talking in a low and awe-struck voice. I know we cried quietly all the time.

Miss Jenkyns came home in a silent mood, and we durst not ask her many questions. She told us that Miss Jessie had fainted, and that she and Miss Pole had had some difficulty in bringing her round; but that, as soon as she recovered, she begged one of them to go and sit with her sister.

"Mr Hoggins says she cannot live many days, and she shall be spared this shock," said Miss Jessie, shivering with feelings to which she dared not give way.

"But how can you manage, my dear?" asked Miss Jenkyns; "you cannot bear up, she must see your tears."

"God will help me—I will not give way—she was asleep when the news came; she may be asleep yet. She would be so utterly miserable, not merely at my father's death, but to think of what would become of me; she is so good to me." She looked up earnestly in their faces with her soft true eyes, and Miss Pole told Miss Jenkyns afterwards she could hardly bear it, knowing, as she did, how Miss Brown treated her sister.

However, it was settled according to Miss Jessie's wish. Miss Brown was to be told her father had been summoned to take a short journey on railway business. They had managed it in some way—Miss Jenkyns could not exactly say how. Miss Pole was to stop with Miss Jessie. Mrs Jamieson had sent to inquire. And this was all we heard that night; and a sorrowful night it was. The next day a full account of the fatal accident was in the county paper which Miss Jenkyns took in. Her eyes were very weak, she said, and she asked me to read it. When I came to the "gallant gentleman was deeply engaged in the perusal of a number of 'Pickwick,' which he had just received," Miss Jenkyns shook her head long and solemnly, and then sighed out, "Poor, dear, infatuated man!"

The corpse was to be taken from the station to the parish church, there to be interred. Miss Jessie had set her heart on following it to the grave; and no dissuasives could alter her resolve. Her restraint upon herself made her almost obstinate; she resisted all Miss Pole's entreaties and Miss Jenkyns' advice. At last Miss Jenkyns gave up the point; and after a silence, which I feared portended some deep displeasure against Miss Jessie, Miss Jenkyns said she should accompany the latter to the funeral.

"It is not fit for you to go alone. It would be against both propriety and humanity were I to allow it."

Miss Jessie seemed as if she did not half like this arrangement; but her obstinacy, if she had any, had been exhausted in her determination to go to the interment. She longed, poor thing, I have no doubt, to cry alone over the grave of the dear father to whom she had been all in all, and to give way, for one little half-hour, uninterrupted by sympathy and unobserved by friendship. But it was not to be. That afternoon Miss Jenkyns sent out for a yard of black crape, and employed herself busily in trimming the little black silk bonnet I have spoken about. When it was finished she put it on, and looked at us for approbation—admiration she despised. I was full of sorrow, but, by one of those whimsical thoughts which come unbidden into our heads, in times of deepest grief, I no sooner saw the bonnet than I was reminded of a helmet; and in that hybrid bonnet, half helmet, half jockey-cap, did Miss Jenkyns attend Captain Brown's funeral, and, I believe, supported Miss Jessie with a tender, indulgent firmness which was invaluable, allowing her to weep her passionate fill before they left.

Miss Pole, Miss Matty, and I, meanwhile attended to Miss Brown: and hard work we found it to relieve her querulous and never-ending complaints. But if we were so weary and dispirited, what must Miss Jessie have been! Yet she came back almost calm as if she had gained a new strength. She put off her mourning dress, and came in, looking pale and gentle, thanking us each with a soft long pressure of the hand. She could even smile—a faint, sweet, wintry smile—as if to reassure us of her power to endure; but her look made our eyes fill suddenly with tears, more than if she had cried outright.

It was settled that Miss Pole was to remain with her all the watching livelong night; and that Miss Matty and I were to return in the morning to relieve them, and give Miss Jessie the opportunity for a few hours of sleep. But when the morning came, Miss Jenkyns appeared at the breakfast-table, equipped in her helmet-bonnet, and ordered Miss Matty to stay at home, as she meant to go and help to nurse. She was evidently in a state of great friendly excitement, which she showed by eating her breakfast standing, and scolding the household all round.

No nursing—no energetic strong-minded woman could help Miss Brown now. There was that in the room as we entered which was stronger than us all, and made us shrink into solemn awestruck helplessness. Miss Brown was dying. We hardly knew her voice, it was so devoid of the complaining tone we had always associated with it. Miss Jessie told me afterwards that it, and her face too, were just what they had been formerly, when her mother's death left her the young anxious head of the family, of whom only Miss Jessie survived.

She was conscious of her sister's presence, though not, I think, of ours. We stood a little behind the curtain: Miss Jessie knelt with her face near her sister's, in order to catch the last soft awful whispers.

"Oh, Jessie! Jessie! How selfish I have been! God forgive me for letting you sacrifice yourself for me as you did! I have so loved you—and yet I have thought only of myself. God forgive me!"

"Hush, love! hush!" said Miss Jessie, sobbing.

"And my father, my dear, dear father! I will not complain now, if God will give me strength to be patient. But, oh, Jessie! tell my father how I longed and yearned to see him at last, and to ask his forgiveness. He can never know now how I loved him—oh! if I might but tell him, before I die! What a life of sorrow his has been, and I have done so little to cheer him!"

A light came into Miss Jessie's face. "Would it comfort you, dearest, to think that he does know?—would it comfort you, love, to know that his cares, his sorrows"—Her voice quivered, but she steadied it into calmness—"Mary! he has gone before you to the place where the weary are at rest. He knows now how you loved him."

A strange look, which was not distress, came over Miss Brown's face. She did not speak for come time, but then we saw her lips form the words, rather than heard the sound—"Father, mother, Harry, Archy;"—then, as if it were a new idea throwing a filmy shadow over her darkened mind—"But you will be alone, Jessie!"

Miss Jessie had been feeling this all during the silence, I think; for the tears rolled down her cheeks like rain, at these words, and she could not answer at first. Then she put her hands together tight, and lifted them up, and said—but not to us—"Though He slay me, yet will I trust in Him."

In a few moments more Miss Brown lay calm and still—never to sorrow or murmur more.

After this second funeral, Miss Jenkyns insisted that Miss Jessie should come to stay with her rather than go back to the desolate house, which, in fact, we learned from Miss Jessie, must now be given up, as she had not wherewithal to maintain it. She had something above twenty pounds a year, besides the interest of the money for which the furniture would sell; but she could not live upon that: and so we talked over her qualifications for earning money.

"I can sew neatly," said she, "and I like nursing. I think, too, I could manage a house, if any one would try me as housekeeper; or I would go into a shop as saleswoman, if they would have patience with me at first."

Miss Jenkyns declared, in an angry voice, that she should do no such thing; and talked to herself about "some people having no idea of their rank as a captain's daughter," nearly an hour afterwards, when she brought Miss Jessie up a basin of delicately-made arrowroot, and stood over her like a dragoon until the last spoonful was finished: then she disappeared. Miss Jessie began to tell me some more of the plans which had suggested themselves to her, and insensibly fell into talking of the days that were past and gone, and interested me so much I neither knew nor heeded how time passed. We were both startled when Miss Jenkyns reappeared, and caught us crying. I was afraid lest she would be displeased, as she often said that crying hindered digestion, and I knew she wanted

Miss Jessie to get strong; but, instead, she looked queer and excited, and fidgeted round us without saying anything. At last she spoke.

"I have been so much startled—no, I've not been at all startled—don't mind me, my dear Miss Jessie—I've been very much surprised—in fact, I've had a caller, whom you knew once, my dear Miss Jessie"—

Miss Jessie went very white, then flushed scarlet, and looked eagerly at Miss Jenkyns.

"A gentleman, my dear, who wants to know if you would see him."

"Is it?—it is not"—stammered out Miss Jessie—and got no farther.

"This is his card," said Miss Jenkyns, giving it to Miss Jessie; and while her head was bent over it, Miss Jenkyns went through a series of winks and odd faces to me, and formed her lips into a long sentence, of which, of course, I could not understand a word.

"May he come up?" asked Miss Jenkyns at last.

"Oh, yes! certainly!" said Miss Jessie, as much as to say, this is your house, you may show any visitor where you like. She took up some knitting of Miss Matty's and began to be very busy, though I could see how she trembled all over.

Miss Jenkyns rang the bell, and told the servant who answered it to show Major Gordon upstairs; and, presently, in walked a tall, fine, frank-looking man of forty or upwards. He shook hands with Miss Jessie; but he could not see her eyes, she kept them so fixed on the ground. Miss Jenkyns asked me if I would come and help her to tie up the preserves in the store-room; and though Miss Jessie plucked at my gown, and even looked up at me with begging eye, I durst not refuse to go where Miss Jenkyns asked. Instead of tying up preserves in the store-room, however, we went to talk in the dining-room; and there Miss Jenkyns told me what Major Gordon had told her; how he had served in the same regiment with Captain Brown, and had become acquainted with Miss Jessie, then a sweet-looking, blooming girl of eighteen; how the acquaintance had grown into love on his part, though it had been some years before he had spoken; how, on becoming possessed, through the will of an uncle, of a good estate in Scotland, he had offered and been refused, though with so much agitation and evident distress that he was sure she was not indifferent to him; and how he had discovered that the obstacle was the fell disease which was, even then, too surely threatening her sister. She had mentioned that the surgeons foretold intense suffering; and there was no one but herself to nurse her poor Mary, or cheer and comfort her father during the time of illness. They had had long discussions; and on her refusal to pledge herself to him as his wife when all should be over, he had grown angry, and broken off entirely, and gone abroad, believing that she was a cold-hearted person whom he would do well to forget. He had been travelling in the East, and was on his return home when, at Rome, he saw the account of Captain Brown's death in *Galignani*.

Just then Miss Matty, who had been out all the morning, and had only lately returned to the house, burst in with a face of dismay and outraged propriety.

"Oh, goodness me!" she said. "Deborah, there's a gentleman sitting in the drawing-room with his arm round Miss Jessie's waist!" Miss Matty's eyes looked large with terror.

Miss Jenkyns snubbed her down in an instant.

"The most proper place in the world for his arm to be in. Go away, Matilda, and mind your own business." This from her sister, who had hitherto been a model of feminine decorum, was a blow for poor Miss Matty, and with a double shock she left the room.

The last time I ever saw poor Miss Jenkyns was many years after this. Mrs Gordon had kept up a warm and affectionate intercourse with all at Cranford. Miss Jenkyns, Miss Matty, and Miss Pole had all been to visit her, and returned with wonderful accounts of her house, her husband, her dress, and her looks. For, with happiness, something of her early bloom returned; she had been a year or two younger than we had taken her for. Her eyes were always lovely, and, as Mrs Gordon, her dimples were not out of place. At the time to which I have referred, when I last saw Miss Jenkyns, that lady was old and feeble, and had lost something of her strong mind. Little Flora Gordon was staying with the Misses Jenkyns, and when I came in she was reading aloud to Miss Jenkyns, who lay feeble and changed on the sofa. Flora put down the *Rambler* when I came in.

"Ah!" said Miss Jenkyns, "you find me changed, my dear. I can't see as I used to do. If Flora were not here to read to me, I hardly know how I should get through the day. Did you ever read the *Rambler*? It's a wonderful book—wonderful! and the most improving reading for Flora" (which I daresay it would have been, if she could have read half the words without spelling, and could have understood the meaning of a third), "better than that strange old book, with the queer name, poor Captain Brown was killed for reading—that book by Mr Boz, you know—'Old Poz'; when I was a girl—but that's a long time ago—I acted Lucy in 'Old Poz.'" She babbled on long enough for Flora to get a good long spell at the "Christmas Carol," which Miss Matty had left on the table.

CHAPTER III - A LOVE AFFAIR OF LONG AGO

I THOUGHT that probably my connection with Cranford would cease after Miss Jenkyns's death; at least, that it would have to be kept up by correspondence, which bears much the same relation to personal intercourse that the books of dried plants I sometimes see ("Hortus Siccus," I think they call the thing) do to the living and fresh flowers in the lines and meadows. I was pleasantly surprised, therefore, by receiving a letter from Miss Pole (who had always come in for a supplementary week after my annual visit to Miss Jenkyns) proposing that I should go and stay with her; and then, in a couple of days after my acceptance, came a note from Miss Matty, in which, in a rather circuitous and very humble manner, she told me how much pleasure I should confer if I could spend a week or two with her, either before or after I had been at Miss Pole's; "for," she said, "since my dear sister's death I am well aware I have no attractions to offer; it is only to the kindness of my friends that I can owe their company."

Of course I promised to come to dear Miss Matty as soon as I had ended my visit to Miss Pole; and the day after my arrival at Cranford I went to see her, much wondering what the house would be like without Miss Jenkyns, and rather dreading the changed aspect of things. Miss Matty began to cry as soon as she saw me. She was evidently nervous from having anticipated my call. I comforted her as well as I could; and I found the best consolation I could give was the honest praise that came from my heart as I spoke of the deceased. Miss Matty slowly shook her head over each virtue as it was named and attributed to her sister; and at last she could not restrain the tears which had long been silently flowing, but hid her face behind her handkerchief and sobbed aloud.

"Dear Miss Matty," said I, taking her hand—for indeed I did not know in what way to tell her how sorry I was for her, left deserted in the world. She put down her handkerchief and said—

"My dear, I'd rather you did not call me Matty. She did not like it; but I did many a thing she did not like, I'm afraid—and now she's gone! If you please, my love, will you call me Matilda?"

I promised faithfully, and began to practise the new name with Miss Pole that very day; and, by degrees, Miss Matilda's feeling on the subject was known through Cranford, and we all tried to drop the more familiar name, but with so little success that by-and-by we gave up the attempt.

CHAPTER III - A LOVE AFFAIR OF LONG AGO

My visit to Miss Pole was very quiet. Miss Jenkyns had so long taken the lead in Cranford that now she was gone, they hardly knew how to give a party. The Honourable Mrs Jamieson, to whom Miss Jenkyns herself had always yielded the post of honour, was fat and inert, and very much at the mercy of her old servants. If they chose that she should give a party, they reminded her of the necessity for so doing: if not, she let it alone. There was all the more time for me to hear old-world stories from Miss Pole, while she sat knitting, and I making my father's shirts. I always took a quantity of plain sewing to Cranford; for, as we did not read much, or walk much, I found it a capital time to get through my work. One of Miss Pole's stories related to a shadow of a love affair that was dimly perceived or suspected long years before.

Presently, the time arrived when I was to remove to Miss Matilda's house. I found her timid and anxious about the arrangements for my comfort. Many a time, while I was unpacking, did she come backwards and forwards to stir the fire which burned all the worse for being so frequently poked.

"Have you drawers enough, dear?" asked she. "I don't know exactly how my sister used to arrange them. She had capital methods. I am sure she would have trained a servant in a week to make a better fire than this, and Fanny has been with me four months."

This subject of servants was a standing grievance, and I could not wonder much at it; for if gentlemen were scarce, and almost unheard of in the "genteel society" of Cranford, they or their counterparts—handsome young men—abounded in the lower classes. The pretty neat servant-maids had their choice of desirable "followers"; and their mistresses, without having the sort of mysterious dread of men and matrimony that Miss Matilda had, might well feel a little anxious lest the heads of their comely maids should be turned by the joiner, or the butcher, or the gardener, who were obliged, by their callings, to come to the house, and who, as ill-luck would have it, were generally handsome and unmarried. Fanny's lovers, if she had any—and Miss Matilda suspected her of so many flirtations that, if she had not been very pretty, I should have doubted her having one—were a constant anxiety to her mistress. She was forbidden, by the articles of her engagement, to have "followers"; and though she had answered, innocently enough, doubling up the hem of her apron as she spoke, "Please, ma'am, I never had more than one at a time," Miss Matty prohibited that one. But a vision of a man seemed to haunt the kitchen. Fanny assured me that it was all fancy, or else I should have said myself that I had seen a man's coat-tails whisk into the scullery once, when I went on an errand into the store-room at night; and another evening, when, our watches having stopped, I went to look at the clock, there was a very odd appearance, singularly like a young man squeezed up between the clock and the back of the open kitchen-door: and I thought Fanny snatched up the candle very hastily, so as to throw the shadow on the clock face, while she very positively told me the time half-an-hour too early, as we found out afterwards by the church clock. But I did not add to Miss Matty's anxieties by naming my suspicions, especially as Fanny said to me, the next day, that it was such a queer kitchen for having odd shadows about it, she really was almost afraid to stay; "for you know, miss," she added, "I don't see a creature from six o'clock tea, till Missus rings the bell for prayers at ten."

However, it so fell out that Fanny had to leave and Miss Matilda begged me to stay and "settle her" with the new maid; to which I consented, after I had heard from my father that he did not want me at home. The new servant was a rough, honest-looking, country girl, who had only lived in a farm place before; but I liked her looks when she came to be hired; and I promised Miss Matilda to put her in the ways of the house. The said ways were religiously such as Miss Matilda thought her sister would approve. Many a domestic rule and regulation had been a subject of plaintive whispered murmur to me during Miss Jenkyns's life; but now that she was gone, I do not think that even I, who was a favourite, durst have suggested an alteration. To give an instance: we constantly adhered to the forms which were observed, at meal-times, in "my father, the rector's house." Accordingly, we had always wine and dessert; but the decanters were only filled when there was a party, and what remained was seldom touched, though we had two wine-glasses apiece every day after dinner, until the next festive occasion arrived, when the state of the remainder wine was examined into in a family council. The dregs were often given to the poor: but occasionally, when a good deal had been left at the last party (five months ago, it might be), it was added to some of a fresh bottle, brought up from the cellar. I fancy poor Captain Brown did not much like wine, for I noticed he never finished his first glass, and most military men take several. Then, as to our dessert, Miss Jenkyns used to gather currants and gooseberries for it herself, which I sometimes thought would have tasted better fresh from the trees; but then, as Miss Jenkyns observed, there would have been nothing for dessert in summer-time. As it was, we felt very genteel with our two glasses apiece, and a dish of gooseberries at the top, of currants and biscuits at the sides, and two decanters at the bottom. When oranges came in, a curious proceeding was gone through. Miss Jenkyns did not like to cut the fruit; for, as she observed, the juice all ran out nobody knew where; sucking (only I think she used some more recondite word) was in fact the only way of enjoying oranges; but then there was the unpleasant association with a ceremony frequently gone through by little babies; and so, after dessert, in orange season, Miss Jenkyns and Miss Matty used to rise up, possess themselves each of an orange in silence, and withdraw to the privacy of their own rooms to indulge in sucking oranges.

I had once or twice tried, on such occasions, to prevail on Miss Matty to stay, and had succeeded in her sister's lifetime. I held up a screen, and did not look, and, as she said, she tried not to make the noise very offensive; but now that she was left alone, she seemed quite horrified when I begged her to remain with me in the warm dining-parlour, and enjoy her orange as she liked best. And so it was in everything. Miss Jenkyns's rules were made more stringent than ever, because the framer of them was gone where there could be no appeal. In all things else Miss Matilda was meek and undecided to a fault. I have heard Fanny turn her round twenty times in a morning about dinner, just as the little hussy chose; and I sometimes fancied she worked on Miss Matilda's weakness in order to bewilder her, and to make her feel more in the power of her clever servant. I determined that I would not leave her till I had seen what sort of a person Martha was; and, if I found her trustworthy, I would tell her not to trouble her mistress with every little decision.

Martha was blunt and plain-spoken to a fault; otherwise she was a brisk, well-meaning, but very ignorant girl. She had not been with us a week before Miss Matilda and I were astounded one morning by the receipt of a letter from a cousin of hers, who had been twenty or thirty years in India, and who had lately, as we had seen by the "Army List," returned to England, bringing with him an invalid wife who had never been introduced to her English relations. Major Jenkyns wrote to propose that he and his wife should spend a night at Cranford, on his way to Scotland—at the inn, if it did not suit Miss Matilda to receive them into her house; in which case they should hope to be with her as much as possible during the day. Of course it *must* suit her, as she said; for all Cranford knew that she had her sister's bedroom at liberty; but I am sure she wished the Major had stopped in India and forgotten his cousins out and out.

"Oh! how must I manage?" asked she helplessly. "If Deborah had been alive she would have known what to do with a gentleman-visitor. Must I put razors in his dressing-room? Dear! dear! and I've got none. Deborah would have had them. And slippers, and coat-brushes?" I suggested that probably he would bring all these things with him. "And after dinner, how am I to know when to get up and leave him to his wine? Deborah would have done it so well; she would have been quite in her element. Will he want coffee, do you think?" I undertook the management of the coffee, and told her I would instruct Martha in the art of waiting—in which it must be owned she was terribly deficient—and that I had no doubt Major and Mrs Jenkyns would understand the quiet mode in which a lady lived by herself in a country town. But she was sadly fluttered. I made her empty her decanters and bring up two fresh bottles of wine. I wished I could have prevented her from being present at my instructions to Martha, for she frequently cut in with some fresh direction, muddling the poor girl's mind as she stood open-mouthed, listening to us both.

"Hand the vegetables round," said I (foolishly, I see now—for it was aiming at more than we could accomplish with quietness and simplicity); and then, seeing her look bewildered, I added, "take the vegetables round to people, and let them help themselves."

"And mind you go first to the ladies," put in Miss Matilda. "Always go to the ladies before gentlemen when you are waiting."

"I'll do it as you tell me, ma'am," said Martha; "but I like lads best."

We felt very uncomfortable and shocked at this speech of Martha's, yet I don't think she meant any harm; and, on the whole, she attended very well to our directions, except that she "nudged" the Major when he did not help himself as soon as she expected to the potatoes, while she was handing them round.

The major and his wife were quiet unpretending people enough when they did come; languid, as all East Indians are, I suppose. We were rather dismayed at their bringing two servants with them, a Hindoo body-servant for the Major, and a steady elderly maid for his wife; but they slept at the inn, and took off a good deal of the responsibility by attending carefully to their master's and mistress's comfort. Martha, to be sure, had never ended her staring at the East Indian's white turban and brown complexion, and I saw that Miss Matilda shrunk away from him a little as he waited at dinner. Indeed, she asked me, when they were gone, if he did not remind me of Blue Beard? On the whole, the visit was most satisfactory, and is a subject of conversation even now with Miss Matilda; at the time it greatly excited Cranford, and even stirred up the apathetic and Honourable Mrs Jamieson to some expression of interest, when I went to call and thank her for the kind answers she had vouchsafed to Miss Matilda's inquiries as to the arrangement of a gentleman's dressing-room—answers which I must confess she had given in the wearied manner of the Scandinavian prophetess—

"Leave me, leave me to repose."

And *now* I come to the love affair.

It seems that Miss Pole had a cousin, once or twice removed, who had offered to Miss Matty long ago. Now this cousin lived four or five miles from Cranford on his own estate; but his property was not large enough to entitle him to rank higher than a yeoman; or rather, with something of the "pride which apes humility," he had refused to push himself on, as so many of his class had done, into the ranks of the squires. He would not allow himself to be called Thomas Holbrook, *Esq.*; he even sent back letters with this address, telling the post-mistress at Cranford that his name was *Mr* Thomas Holbrook, yeoman. He rejected all domestic innovations; he would have the house door stand open in summer and shut in winter, without knocker or bell to summon a servant. The closed fist or the knob of a stick did this office for him if he found the door locked. He despised every refinement which had not its root deep down in humanity. If people were not ill, he saw no necessity for moderating his voice. He spoke the dialect of the country in perfection, and constantly used it in conversation; although Miss Pole (who gave me these particulars) added, that he read aloud more beautifully and with more feeling than any one she had ever heard, except the late rector.

"And how came Miss Matilda not to marry him?" asked I.

"Oh, I don't know. She was willing enough, I think; but you know Cousin Thomas would not have been enough of a gentleman for the rector and Miss Jenkyns."

"Well! but they were not to marry him," said I, impatiently.

"No; but they did not like Miss Matty to marry below her rank. You know she was the rector's daughter, and somehow they are related to Sir Peter Arley: Miss Jenkyns thought a deal of that."

"Poor Miss Matty!" said I.

"Nay, now, I don't know anything more than that he offered and was refused. Miss Matty might not like him—and Miss Jenkyns might never have said a word—it is only a guess of mine."

"Has she never seen him since?" I inquired.

"No, I think not. You see Woodley, Cousin Thomas's house, lies half-way between Cranford and Misselton; and I know he made Misselton his market-town very soon after he had offered to Miss Matty; and I don't think he has been into Cranford above once or twice since—once, when I was walking with Miss Matty, in High Street, and suddenly she darted from me, and went up Shire Lane. A few minutes after I was startled by meeting Cousin Thomas."

"How old is he?" I asked, after a pause of castle-building.

"He must be about seventy, I think, my dear," said Miss Pole, blowing up my castle, as if by gun-powder, into small fragments.

Very soon after—at least during my long visit to Miss Matilda—I had the opportunity of seeing Mr Holbrook; seeing, too, his first encounter with his former love, after thirty or forty years' separation. I was helping to decide whether any of the new assortment of coloured silks which they had just received at the shop would do to match a grey and black mousseline-delaine that wanted a new breadth, when a tall, thin, Don Quixote-looking old man came into the shop for some woollen gloves. I had never seen the person (who was rather striking) before, and I watched him rather attentively while Miss Matty listened to the shopman. The stranger wore a blue coat with brass buttons, drab breeches, and gaiters, and drummed with his fingers on the counter until he was attended to. When he answered the shop-boy's question, "What can I have the pleasure of showing you to-day, sir?" I saw Miss Matilda start, and then suddenly sit down; and instantly I guessed who it was. She had made some inquiry which had to be carried round to the other shopman.

"Miss Jenkyns wants the black sarsenet two-and-twopence the yard"; and Mr Holbrook had caught the name, and was across the shop in two strides.

"Matty—Miss Matilda—Miss Jenkyns! God bless my soul! I should not have known you. How are you? how are you?" He kept shaking her hand in a way which proved the warmth of his friendship; but he repeated so often, as if to himself, "I should not have known you!" that any sentimental romance which I might be inclined to build was quite done away with by his manner.

However, he kept talking to us all the time we were in the shop; and then waving the shopman with the unpurchased gloves on one side, with "Another time, sir! another time!" he walked home with us. I am happy to say my client, Miss Matilda, also left the shop in an equally bewildered state, not having purchased either green or red silk. Mr Holbrook was evidently full with honest loud-spoken joy at meeting his old love again; he touched on the changes that had taken place; he even spoke of Miss Jenkyns as "Your poor sister! Well, well! we have all our faults"; and bade us good-bye with many a hope that he should soon see Miss Matty again. She went straight to her room, and never came back till our early tea-time, when I thought she looked as if she had been crying.

CHAPTER IV - A VISIT TO AN OLD BACHELOR

A FEW days after, a note came from Mr Holbrook, asking us—impartially asking both of us—in a formal, old-fashioned style, to spend a day at his house—a long June day—for it was June now. He named that he had also invited his cousin, Miss Pole; so that we might join in a fly, which could be put up at his house.

I expected Miss Matty to jump at this invitation; but, no! Miss Pole and I had the greatest difficulty in persuading her to go. She thought it was improper; and was even half annoyed when we utterly ignored the idea of any impropriety in her going with two other ladies to see her old lover. Then came a more serious difficulty. She did not think Deborah would have liked her to go. This took us half a day's good hard talking to get over; but, at the first sentence of relenting, I seized the opportunity, and wrote and despatched an acceptance in her name—fixing day and hour, that all might be decided and done with.

The next morning she asked me if I would go down to the shop with her; and there, after much hesitation, we chose out three caps to be sent home and tried on, that the most becoming might be selected to take with us on Thursday.

She was in a state of silent agitation all the way to Woodley. She had evidently never been there before; and, although she little dreamt I knew anything of her early story, I could perceive she was in a tremor at the thought of seeing the place which might have been her home, and round which it is probable that many of her innocent girlish imaginations had clustered. It was a long drive there, through paved jolting lanes. Miss Matilda sat bolt upright, and looked wistfully out of the windows as we drew near the end of our journey. The aspect of the country was quiet and pastoral. Woodley stood among fields; and there was an old-fashioned garden where roses and currant-bushes touched each other, and where the feathery asparagus formed a pretty background to the pinks and gilly-flowers; there was no drive up to the door. We got out at a little gate, and walked up a straight box-edged path.

"My cousin might make a drive, I think," said Miss Pole, who was afraid of ear-ache, and had only her cap on.

"I think it is very pretty," said Miss Matty, with a soft plaintiveness in her voice, and almost in a whisper, for just then Mr Holbrook appeared at the door, rubbing his hands in very effervescence of hospitality. He looked more like my idea of Don Quixote than ever, and yet the likeness was only external. His respectable housekeeper stood modestly at the door to bid us welcome; and, while she led the elder ladies upstairs to a bedroom, I begged to look about the garden. My request evidently pleased the old gentleman, who took me all round the place and showed me his six-and-twenty cows, named after the different letters of the alphabet. As we went along, he surprised me occasionally by repeating apt and beautiful quotations from the poets, ranging easily from Shakespeare and George Herbert to those of our own day. He did this as naturally as if he were thinking aloud, and their true and beautiful words were the best expression he could find for what he was thinking or feeling. To be sure he called Byron "my Lord Byrron," and pronounced the name of Goethe strictly in accordance with the English sound of the letters—"As Goethe says, 'Ye ever-verdant palaces,'" &c. Altogether, I never met with a man, before or since, who had spent so long a life in a secluded and not impressive country, with ever-increasing delight in the daily and yearly change of season and beauty.

When he and I went in, we found that dinner was nearly ready in the kitchen—for so I suppose the room ought to be called, as there were oak dressers and cupboards all round, all over by the side of the fireplace, and only a small Turkey carpet in the middle of the flag-floor. The room might have been easily made into a handsome dark oak dining-parlour by removing the oven and a few other appurtenances of a kitchen, which were evidently never used, the real cooking-place being at some distance. The room in which we were expected to sit was a stiffly-furnished, ugly apartment; but that in which we did sit was what Mr Holbrook called the counting-house, where he paid his labourers their weekly wages at a great desk near the door. The rest of the pretty sitting-room—looking into the orchard, and all covered over with dancing tree-shadows—was filled with books. They lay on the ground, they covered the walls, they strewed the table. He was evidently half ashamed and half proud of his extravagance in this respect. They were of all kinds—poetry and wild weird tales prevailing. He evidently chose his books in accordance with his own tastes, not because such and such were classical or established favourites.

"Ah!" he said, "we farmers ought not to have much time for reading; yet somehow one can't help it."

"What a pretty room!" said Miss Matty, *sotto voce*.

"What a pleasant place!" said I, aloud, almost simultaneously.

"Nay! if you like it," replied he; "but can you sit on these great, black leather, three-cornered chairs? I like it better than the best parlour; but I thought ladies would take that for the smarter place."

It was the smarter place, but, like most smart things, not at all pretty, or pleasant, or home-like; so, while we were at dinner, the servant-girl dusted and scrubbed the counting-house chairs, and we sat there all the rest of the day.

We had pudding before meat; and I thought Mr Holbrook was going to make some apology for his old-fashioned ways, for he began—

"I don't know whether you like newfangled ways."

"Oh, not at all!" said Miss Matty.

"No more do I," said he. "My house-keeper *will* have these in her new fashion; or else I tell her that, when I was a young man, we used to keep strictly to my father's rule, 'No broth, no ball; no ball, no beef'; and always began dinner with broth. Then we had suet puddings, boiled in the broth with the beef: and then the meat itself. If we did not sup our broth, we had no ball, which we liked a deal better; and the beef came last of all, and only those had it who had done justice to the broth and the ball. Now folks begin with sweet things, and turn their dinners topsy-turvy."

When the ducks and green peas came, we looked at each other in dismay; we had only two-pronged, black-handled forks. It is true the steel was as bright as silver; but what were we to do? Miss Matty picked up her peas, one by one, on the point of the prongs, much as Aminé ate her grains of rice after her previous feast with the Ghoul. Miss Pole sighed over her delicate young peas as she left them on one side of her plate untasted, for they *would* drop between the prongs. I looked at my host: the peas were going wholesale into his capacious mouth, shovelled up by his large round-ended knife. I saw, I imitated, I survived! My friends, in spite of my precedent, could not muster up courage enough to do an ungenteel thing; and, if Mr Holbrook had not been so heartily hungry, he would probably have seen that the good peas went away almost untouched.

After dinner, a clay pipe was brought in, and a spittoon; and, asking us to retire to another room, where he would soon join us, if we disliked tobacco-smoke, he presented his pipe to Miss Matty, and requested her to fill the bowl. This was a compliment to a lady in his youth; but it was rather inappropriate to propose it as an honour to Miss Matty, who had been trained by her sister to hold smoking of every kind in utter abhorrence. But if it was a shock to her refinement, it was also a gratification to her feelings to be thus selected; so she daintily stuffed the strong tobacco into the pipe, and then we withdrew.

"It is very pleasant dining with a bachelor," said Miss Matty softly, as we settled ourselves in the counting-house. "I only hope it is not improper; so many pleasant things are!"

"What a number of books he has!" said Miss Pole, looking round the room. "And how dusty they are!"

"I think it must be like one of the great Dr Johnson's rooms," said Miss Matty. "What a superior man your cousin must be!"

"Yes!" said Miss Pole, "he's a great reader; but I am afraid he has got into very uncouth habits with living alone."

"Oh! uncouth is too hard a word. I should call him eccentric; very clever people always are!" replied Miss Matty.

When Mr Holbrook returned, he proposed a walk in the fields; but the two elder ladies were afraid of damp, and dirt, and had only very unbecoming calashes to put on over their caps; so they declined, and I was again his companion in a turn which he said he was obliged to take to see after his men. He strode along, either wholly forgetting my existence, or soothed into silence by his pipe—and yet it was not silence exactly. He walked before me with a stooping gait, his hands clasped behind him; and, as some tree or cloud, or glimpse of distant upland pastures, struck him, he quoted poetry to himself, saying it out loud in a grand sonorous voice, with just the emphasis that true feeling and appreciation give. We came upon an old cedar tree, which stood at one end of the house—

> "The cedar spreads his dark-green layers of shade."

"Capital term—'layers!' Wonderful man!" I did not know whether he was speaking to me or not; but I put in an assenting "wonderful," although I knew nothing about it, just because I was tired of being forgotten, and of being consequently silent.

He turned sharp round. "Ay! you may say 'wonderful.' Why, when I saw the review of his poems in *Blackwood*, I set off within an hour, and walked seven miles to Misselton (for the horses were not in the way) and ordered them. Now, what colour are ash-buds in March?"

Is the man going mad? thought I. He is very like Don Quixote.

"What colour are they, I say?" repeated he vehemently.

"I am sure I don't know, sir," said I, with the meekness of ignorance.

"I knew you didn't. No more did I—an old fool that I am!—till this young man comes and tells me. Black as ash-buds in March. And I've lived all my life in the country; more shame for me not to know. Black: they are jet-black, madam." And he went off again, swinging along to the music of some rhyme he had got hold of.

When we came back, nothing would serve him but he must read us the poems he had been speaking of; and Miss Pole encouraged him in his proposal, I thought, because she wished me to hear his beautiful reading, of which she had boasted; but she afterwards said it was because she had got to a difficult part of her crochet, and wanted to count her stitches without having to talk. Whatever he had proposed would have been right to Miss Matty; although she did fall sound asleep within five minutes after he had begun a long poem, called "Locksley Hall," and had a comfortable nap, unobserved, till he ended; when the cessation of his voice wakened her up, and she said, feeling that something was expected, and that Miss Pole was counting—

"What a pretty book!"

"Pretty, madam! it's beautiful! Pretty, indeed!"

"Oh yes! I meant beautiful!" said she, fluttered at his disapproval of her word. "It is so like that beautiful poem of Dr Johnson's my sister used to read—I forget the name of it; what was it, my dear?" turning to me.

"Which do you mean, ma'am? What was it about?"

"I don't remember what it was about, and I've quite forgotten what the name of it was; but it was written by Dr Johnson, and was very beautiful, and very like what Mr Holbrook has just been reading."

"I don't remember it," said he reflectively. "But I don't know Dr Johnson's poems well. I must read them."

As we were getting into the fly to return, I heard Mr Holbrook say he should call on the ladies soon, and inquire how they got home; and this evidently pleased and fluttered Miss Matty at the time he said it; but after we had lost sight of the old house among the trees her sentiments towards the master of it were gradually absorbed into a distressing wonder as to whether Martha had broken her word, and seized on the opportunity of her mistress's absence to have a "follower." Martha looked good, and steady, and composed enough, as she came to help us out; she was always careful of Miss Matty, and to-night she made use of this unlucky speech—

"Eh! dear ma'am, to think of your going out in an evening in such a thin shawl! It's no better than muslin. At your age, ma'am, you should be careful."

"My age!" said Miss Matty, almost speaking crossly, for her, for she was usually gentle—"My age! Why, how old do you think I am, that you talk about my age?"

"Well, ma'am, I should say you were not far short of sixty: but folks' looks is often against them—and I'm sure I meant no harm."

"Martha, I'm not yet fifty-two!" said Miss Matty, with grave emphasis; for probably the remembrance of her youth had come very vividly before her this day, and she was annoyed at finding that golden time so far away in the past.

But she never spoke of any former and more intimate acquaintance with Mr Holbrook. She had probably met with so little sympathy in her early love, that she had shut it up close in her heart; and it was only by a sort of watching, which I could hardly avoid since Miss Pole's confidence, that I saw how faithful her poor heart had been in its sorrow and its silence.

She gave me some good reason for wearing her best cap every day, and sat near the window, in spite of her rheumatism, in order to see, without being seen, down into the street.

He came. He put his open palms upon his knees, which were far apart, as he sat with his head bent down, whistling, after we had replied to his inquiries about our safe return. Suddenly he jumped up—

"Well, madam! have you any commands for Paris? I am going there in a week or two."

"To Paris!" we both exclaimed.

"Yes, madam! I've never been there, and always had a wish to go; and I think if I don't go soon, I mayn't go at all; so as soon as the hay is got in I shall go, before harvest time."

We were so much astonished that we had no commissions.

Just as he was going out of the room, he turned back, with his favourite exclamation—

"God bless my soul, madam! but I nearly forgot half my errand. Here are the poems for you you admired so much the other evening at my house." He tugged away at a parcel in his coat-pocket. "Good-bye, miss," said he; "good-bye, Matty! take care of yourself." And he was gone. But he had given her a book, and he had called her Matty, just as he used to do thirty years to.

"I wish he would not go to Paris," said Miss Matilda anxiously. "I don't believe frogs will agree with him; he used to have to be very careful what he ate, which was curious in so strong-looking a young man."

Soon after this I took my leave, giving many an injunction to Martha to look after her mistress, and to let me know if she thought that Miss Matilda was not so well; in which case I would volunteer a visit to my old friend, without noticing Martha's intelligence to her.

Accordingly I received a line or two from Martha every now and then; and, about November I had a note to say her mistress was "very low and sadly off her food"; and the account made me so uneasy that, although Martha did not decidedly summon me, I packed up my things and went.

I received a warm welcome, in spite of the little flurry produced by my impromptu visit, for I had only been able to give a day's notice. Miss Matilda looked miserably ill; and I prepared to comfort and cosset her.

I went down to have a private talk with Martha.

"How long has your mistress been so poorly?" I asked, as I stood by the kitchen fire.

"Well! I think it's better than a fortnight; it is, I know; it was one Tuesday, after Miss Pole had been, that she went into this moping way. I thought she was tired, and it would go off with a night's rest; but no! she has gone on and on ever since, till I thought it my duty to write to you, ma'am."

"You did quite right, Martha. It is a comfort to think she has so faithful a servant about her. And I hope you find your place comfortable?"

"Well, ma'am, missus is very kind, and there's plenty to eat and drink, and no more work but what I can do easily—but—" Martha hesitated.

"But what, Martha?"

"Why, it seems so hard of missus not to let me have any followers; there's such lots of young fellows in the town; and many a one has as much as offered to keep company with me; and I may never be in such a likely place again, and it's like wasting an opportunity. Many a girl as I know would have 'em unbeknownst to missus; but I've given my word, and I'll stick to it; or else this is just the house for missus never to be the wiser if they did come: and it's such a capable kitchen—there's such dark corners in it—I'd be bound to hide any one. I counted up last Sunday night—for I'll not deny I was crying because I had to shut the door in Jem Hearn's face, and he's a steady young man, fit for any girl; only I had given missus my word." Martha was all but crying again; and I had little comfort to give her, for I knew, from old experience, of the horror with which both the Miss Jenkynses looked upon "followers"; and in Miss Matty's present nervous state this dread was not likely to be lessened.

I went to see Miss Pole the next day, and took her completely by surprise, for she had not been to see Miss Matilda for two days.

"And now I must go back with you, my dear, for I promised to let her know how Thomas Holbrook went on; and, I'm sorry to say, his housekeeper has sent me word to-day that he hasn't long to live. Poor Thomas! that journey to Paris was quite too much for him. His housekeeper says he has hardly ever been round his fields since, but just sits with his hands on his knees in the counting-house, not reading or anything, but only saying what a wonderful city Paris was! Paris has much to answer for if it's killed my cousin Thomas, for a better man never lived."

"Does Miss Matilda know of his illness?" asked I—a new light as to the cause of her indisposition dawning upon me.

"Dear! to be sure, yes! Has not she told you? I let her know a fortnight ago, or more, when first I heard of it. How odd she shouldn't have told you!"

Not at all, I thought; but I did not say anything. I felt almost guilty of having spied too curiously into that tender heart, and I was not going to speak of its secrets—hidden, Miss Matty believed, from all the world. I ushered Miss Pole into Miss Matilda's little drawing-room, and then left them alone. But I was not surprised when Martha came to my bedroom door, to ask me to go down to dinner alone, for that missus had one of her bad headaches. She came into the drawing-room at tea-time, but it was evidently an effort to her; and, as if to make up for some reproachful feeling against her late sister, Miss Jenkyns, which had been troubling her all the afternoon, and for which she now felt penitent, she kept telling me how good and how clever Deborah was in her youth; how she used to settle what gowns they were to wear at all the parties (faint, ghostly ideas of grim parties, far away in the distance, when Miss Matty and Miss Pole were young!); and how Deborah and her mother had started the benefit society for the poor, and taught girls cooking and plain sewing; and how Deborah had once danced with a lord; and how she used to visit at Sir Peter Arley's, and tried to remodel the quiet rectory establishment on the plans of Arley Hall, where they kept thirty servants; and how she had nursed Miss Matty through a long, long illness, of which I had never heard before, but which I now dated in my own mind as following the dismissal of the suit of Mr Holbrook. So we talked softly and quietly of old times through the long November evening.

The next day Miss Pole brought us word that Mr Holbrook was dead. Miss Matty heard the news in silence; in fact, from the account of the previous day, it was only what we had to expect. Miss Pole kept calling upon us for some expression of regret, by asking if it was not sad that he was gone, and saying—

"To think of that pleasant day last June, when he seemed so well! And he might have lived this dozen years if he had not gone to that wicked Paris, where they are always having revolutions."

She paused for some demonstration on our part. I saw Miss Matty could not speak, she was trembling so nervously; so I said what I really felt; and after a call of some duration—all the time of which I have no doubt Miss Pole thought Miss Matty received the news very calmly—our visitor took her leave.

Miss Matty made a strong effort to conceal her feelings—a concealment she practised even with me, for she has never alluded to Mr Holbrook again, although the book he gave her lies with her Bible on the little table by her bedside. She did not think I heard her when she asked the little milliner of Cranford to make her caps something like the Honourable Mrs Jamieson's, or that I noticed the reply—

"But she wears widows' caps, ma'am?"

"Oh! I only meant something in that style; not widows', of course, but rather like Mrs Jamieson's."

This effort at concealment was the beginning of the tremulous motion of head and hands which I have seen ever since in Miss Matty.

The evening of the day on which we heard of Mr Holbrook's death, Miss Matilda was very silent and thoughtful; after prayers she called Martha back and then she stood uncertain what to say.

"Martha!" she said, at last, "you are young"—and then she made so long a pause that Martha, to remind her of her half-finished sentence, dropped a curtsey, and said—

"Yes, please, ma'am; two-and-twenty last third of October, please, ma'am."

"And, perhaps, Martha, you may some time meet with a young man you like, and who likes you. I did say you were not to have followers; but if you meet with such a young man, and tell me, and I find he is respectable, I have no objection to his coming to see you once a week. God forbid!" said she in a low voice, "that I should grieve any young hearts." She spoke as if she were providing for some distant contingency, and was rather startled when Martha made her ready eager answer—

"Please, ma'am, there's Jem Hearn, and he's a joiner making three-and-sixpence a-day, and six foot one in his stocking-feet, please, ma'am; and if you'll ask about him to-morrow morning, every one will give him a character for steadiness; and he'll be glad enough to come to-morrow night, I'll be bound."

Though Miss Matty was startled, she submitted to Fate and Love.

CHAPTER V - OLD LETTERS

I HAVE often noticed that almost every one has his own individual small economies—careful habits of saving fractions of pennies in some one peculiar direction—any disturbance of which annoys him more than spending shillings or pounds on some real extravagance. An old gentleman of my acquaintance, who took the intelligence of the failure of a Joint-Stock Bank, in which some of his money was invested, with stoical mildness, worried his family all through a long summer's day because one of them had torn (instead of cutting) out the written leaves of his now useless bank-book; of course, the corresponding pages at the other end came out as well, and this little unnecessary waste of paper (his private economy) chafed him more than all the loss of his money. Envelopes fretted his soul terribly when they first came in; the only way in which he could reconcile himself to such waste of his cherished article was by patiently turning inside out all that were sent to him, and so making them serve again. Even now, though tamed by age, I see him casting wistful glances at his daughters when they send a whole inside of a half-sheet of note paper, with the three lines of acceptance to an invitation, written on only one of the sides. I am not above owning that I have this human weakness myself. String is my foible. My pockets get full of little hanks of it, picked up and twisted together, ready for uses that never come. I am seriously annoyed if any one cuts the string of a parcel instead of patiently and faithfully undoing it fold by fold. How people can bring themselves to use india-rubber rings, which are a sort of deification of string, as lightly as they do, I cannot imagine. To me an india-rubber ring is a precious treasure. I have one which is not new—one that I picked up off the floor nearly six years ago. I have really tried to use it, but my heart failed me, and I could not commit the extravagance.

Small pieces of butter grieve others. They cannot attend to conversation because of the annoyance occasioned by the habit which some people have of invariably taking more butter than they want. Have you not seen the anxious look (almost mesmeric) which such persons fix on the article? They would feel it a relief if they might bury it out of their sight by popping it into their own mouths and swallowing it down; and they are really made happy if the person on whose plate it lies unused suddenly breaks off a piece of toast (which he does not want at all) and eats up his butter. They think that this is not waste.

Now Miss Matty Jenkyns was chary of candles. We had many devices to use as few as possible. In the winter afternoons she would sit knitting for two or three hours—she could do this in the dark, or by firelight—and when I asked if I might not ring for candles to finish stitching my wristbands, she told me to "keep blind man's holiday." They were usually brought in with tea; but we only burnt one at a time. As we lived in constant preparation for a friend who might come in any evening (but who never did), it required some contrivance to keep our two candles of the same length, ready to be lighted, and to look as if we burnt two always. The candles took it in turns; and, whatever we might be talking about or doing, Miss Matty's eyes were habitually fixed upon the candle, ready to jump up and extinguish it and to light the other before they had become too uneven in length to be restored to equality in the course of the evening.

One night, I remember this candle economy particularly annoyed me. I had been very much tired of my compulsory "blind man's holiday," especially as Miss Matty had fallen asleep, and I did not like to stir the fire and run the risk of awakening her; so I could not even sit on the rug, and scorch myself with sewing by firelight, according to my usual custom. I fancied Miss Matty must be dreaming of her early life; for she spoke one or two words in her uneasy sleep bearing reference to persons who were dead long before. When Martha brought in the lighted candle and tea, Miss Matty started into wakefulness, with a strange, bewildered look around, as if we were not the people she expected to see about her. There was a little sad expression that shadowed her face as she recognised me; but immediately afterwards she tried to give me her usual smile. All through teatime her talk ran upon the days of her childhood and youth. Perhaps this reminded her of the desirableness of looking over all the old family letters, and destroying such as ought not to be allowed to fall into the hands of strangers; for she had often spoken of the necessity of this task, but had always shrunk from it, with a timid dread of something painful. To night, however, she rose up after tea and went for them—in the dark; for she piqued herself on the precise neatness of all her chamber arrangements, and used to look uneasily at me when I lighted a bed-candle to go to another room for anything. When she returned there was a faint, pleasant smell of Tonquin beans in the room. I had always noticed this scent about any of the things which had belonged to her mother; and many of the letters were addressed to her—yellow bundles of love-letters, sixty or seventy years old.

Miss Matty undid the packet with a sigh; but she stifled it directly, as if it were hardly right to regret the flight of time, or of life either. We agreed to look them over separately, each taking a different letter out of the same bundle and describing its contents to the other before destroying it. I never knew what sad work the reading of old-letters was before that evening, though I could hardly tell why. The letters were as happy as letters could be—at least those early letters were. There was in them a vivid and intense sense of the present time, which seemed so strong and full, as if it could never pass away, and as if the warm, living hearts that so expressed themselves could never die, and be as nothing to the sunny earth. I should have felt less melancholy, I believe, if the letters had been more so. I saw the tears stealing down the well-worn furrows of Miss Matty's cheeks, and her spectacles often wanted wiping. I trusted at last that she would light the other candle, for my own eyes were rather dim, and I wanted more light to see the pale, faded ink; but no, even through her tears, she saw and remembered her little economical ways.

The earliest set of letters were two bundles tied together, and ticketed (in Miss Jenkyns's handwriting) "Letters interchanged between my ever-honoured father and my dearly-beloved mother, prior to their marriage, in July 1774." I should guess that the rector of Cranford was about twenty-seven years of age when he wrote those letters; and Miss Matty told me that her mother was just eighteen at the time of her wedding. With my idea of the rector derived from a picture in the dining-parlour, stiff and stately, in a huge full-bottomed wig, with gown, cassock, and bands, and his hand upon a copy of the only sermon he ever published—it was strange to read these letters. They were full of eager, passionate ardour; short homely sentences, right fresh from the heart (very different from the grand Latinised, Johnsonian style of the printed sermon preached before some judge at assize time). His letters were a curious contrast to those of his girl-bride. She was evidently rather annoyed at his demands upon her for expressions of love, and could not quite understand what he meant by repeating the same thing over in so many different ways; but what she was quite clear about was a longing for a white "Paduasoy"—whatever that might be; and six or seven letters were principally occupied in asking her lover to use his influence with her parents (who evidently kept her in good order) to obtain this or that article of dress, more especially the white "Paduasoy." He cared nothing how she was dressed; she was always lovely enough for him, as he took pains to assure her, when she begged him to express in his answers a predilection for particular pieces of finery, in order that she might show what he said to her parents. But at length he seemed to find out that she would not be married till she had a "trousseau" to her mind; and then he sent her a letter, which had evidently accompanied a whole box full of finery, and in which he requested that she might be dressed in everything her heart desired. This was the first letter, ticketed in a frail, delicate hand, "From my dearest John." Shortly afterwards they were married, I suppose, from the intermission in their correspondence.

"We must burn them, I think," said Miss Matty, looking doubtfully at me. "No one will care for them when I am gone." And one by one she dropped them into the middle of the fire, watching each blaze up, die out, and rise away, in faint, white, ghostly semblance, up the chimney, before she gave another to the same fate. The room was light enough now; but I, like her, was fascinated into watching the destruction of those letters, into which the honest warmth of a manly heart had been poured forth.

The next letter, likewise docketed by Miss Jenkyns, was endorsed, "Letter of pious congratulation and exhortation from my venerable grandfather to my beloved mother, on occasion of my own birth. Also some practical remarks on the desirability of keeping warm the extremities of infants, from my excellent grand-mother."

The first part was, indeed, a severe and forcible picture of the responsibilities of mothers, and a warning against the evils that were in the world, and lying in ghastly wait for the little baby of two days old. His wife did not write, said the old gentleman, because he had forbidden it, she being indisposed with a sprained ankle, which (he said) quite incapacitated her from holding a pen. However, at the foot of the page was a small "T.O.," and on turning it over, sure enough, there was a letter to "my dear, dearest Molly," begging her, when she left her room, whatever she did, to go *up* stairs before going *down*: and telling her to wrap her baby's feet up in flannel, and keep it warm by the fire, although it was summer, for babies were so tender.

It was pretty to see from the letters, which were evidently exchanged with some frequency between the young mother and the grandmother, how the girlish vanity was being weeded out of her heart by love for her baby. The white "Padu-asoy" figured again in the letters, with almost as much vigour as before. In one, it was being made into a christening cloak for the baby. It decked it when it went with its parents to spend a day or two at Arley Hall. It added to its charms, when it was "the prettiest little baby that ever was seen. Dear mother, I wish you could see her! Without any pershality, I do think she will grow up a regular bewty!" I thought of Miss Jenkyns, grey, withered, and wrinkled, and I wondered if her mother had known her in the courts of heaven: and then I knew that she had, and that they stood there in angelic guise.

There was a great gap before any of the rector's letters appeared. And then his wife had changed her mode of her endorsement. It was no longer from, "My dearest John;" it was from "My Honoured Husband." The letters were written on occasion of the publication of the same sermon which was represented in the picture. The preaching before "My Lord Judge," and the "publishing by request," was evidently the culminating point—the event of his life. It had been necessary for him to go up to London to superintend it through the press. Many friends had to be called upon and consulted before he could decide on any printer fit for so onerous a task; and at length it was arranged that J. and J. Rivingtons were to have the honourable responsibility. The worthy rector seemed to be strung up by the occasion to a high literary pitch, for he could hardly write a letter to his wife without cropping out into Latin. I remember the end of one of his letters ran thus: "I shall ever hold the virtuous qualities of my Molly in remembrance, *dum memor ipse mei, dum spiritus regit artus*," which, considering that the English of his correspondent was sometimes at fault in grammar, and often in spelling, might be taken as a proof of how much he "idealised his Molly;" and, as Miss Jenkyns used to say, "People talk a great deal about idealising now-a-days, whatever that may mean." But this was nothing to a fit of writing classical poetry which soon seized him, in which his Molly figured away as "Maria." The letter containing the *carmen* was endorsed by her, "Hebrew verses sent me by my honoured husband. I thowt to have had a letter about killing the pig, but must wait. Mem., to send the poetry to Sir Peter Arley, as my husband desires." And in a post-scriptum note in his handwriting it was stated that the Ode had appeared in the *Gentleman's Magazine*, December 1782.

Her letters back to her husband (treasured as fondly by him as if they had been *M. T. Ciceronis Epistolæ*) were more satisfactory to an absent husband and father than his could ever have been to her. She told him how Deborah sewed her seam very neatly every day, and read to her in the books he had set her; how she was a very "forrard," good child, but would ask questions her mother could not answer, but how she did not let herself down by saying she did not know, but took to stirring the fire, or sending the "forrard" child on an errand. Matty was now the mother's darling, and promised (like her sister at her age), to be a great beauty. I was reading this aloud to Miss Matty, who smiled and sighed a little at the hope, so fondly expressed, that "little Matty might not be vain, even if she were a bewty."

"I had very pretty hair, my dear," said Miss Matilda; "and not a bad mouth." And I saw her soon afterwards adjust her cap and draw herself up.

But to return to Mrs Jenkyns's letters. She told her husband about the poor in the parish; what homely domestic medicines she had administered; what kitchen physic she had sent. She had evidently held his displeasure as a rod in pickle over the heads of all the ne'er-do-wells. She asked for his directions about the cows and pigs; and did not always obtain them, as I have shown before.

The kind old grandmother was dead when a little boy was born, soon after the publication of the sermon; but there was another letter of exhortation from the grandfather, more stringent and admonitory than ever, now that there was a boy to be guarded from the snares of the world. He described all the various sins into which men might fall, until I wondered how any man ever came to a natural death. The gallows seemed as if it must have been the termination of the lives of most of the grandfather's friends and acquaintance; and I was not surprised at the way in which he spoke of this life being "a vale of tears."

It seemed curious that I should never have heard of this brother before; but I concluded that he had died young, or else surely his name would have been alluded to by his sisters.

By-and-by we came to packets of Miss Jenkyns's letters. These Miss Matty did regret to burn. She said all the others had been only interesting to those who loved the writers, and that it seemed as if it would have hurt her to allow them to fall into the hands of strangers, who had not known her dear mother, and how good she was, although she did not always spell, quite in the modern fashion; but Deborah's letters were so very superior! Any one might profit by reading them. It was a long time since she had read Mrs Chapone, but she knew she used to think that Deborah could have said the same things quite as well; and as for Mrs Carter! people thought a deal of her letters, just because she had written "Epictetus," but she was quite sure Deborah would never have made use of such a common expression as "I canna be fashed!"

Miss Matty did grudge burning these letters, it was evident. She would not let them be carelessly passed over with any quiet reading, and skipping, to myself. She took them from me, and even lighted the second candle in order to read them aloud with a proper emphasis, and without stumbling over the big words. Oh dear! how I wanted facts instead of reflections, before those letters were concluded! They lasted us two nights; and I won't deny that I made use of the time to think of many other things, and yet I was always at my post at the end of each sentence.

The rector's letters, and those of his wife and mother-in-law, had all been tolerably short and pithy, written in a straight hand, with the lines very close together. Sometimes the whole letter was contained on a mere scrap of paper. The paper was very yellow, and the ink very brown; some of the sheets were (as Miss Matty made me observe) the old original post, with the stamp in the corner representing a post-boy riding for life and twanging his horn. The letters of Mrs Jenkyns and her mother were fastened with a great round red wafer; for it was before Miss Edgeworth's "patronage" had banished wafers from polite society. It was evident, from the tenor of what was said, that franks were in great request, and were even used as a means of paying debts by needy members of Parliament. The rector sealed his epistles with an immense coat of arms, and showed by the care with which he had performed this ceremony that he expected they should be cut open, not broken by any thoughtless or impatient hand. Now, Miss Jenkyns's letters were of a later date in form and writing. She wrote on the square sheet which we have learned to call old-fashioned. Her hand was admirably calculated, together with her use of many-syllabled words, to fill up a sheet, and then came the pride and delight of crossing. Poor Miss Matty got sadly puzzled with this, for the words gathered size like snowballs, and towards the end of her letter Miss Jenkyns used to become quite sesquipedalian. In one to her father, slightly theological and controversial in its tone, she had spoken of Herod, Tetrarch of Idumea. Miss Matty read it "Herod Petrarch of Etruria," and was just as well pleased as if she had been right.

I can't quite remember the date, but I think it was in 1805 that Miss Jenkyns wrote the longest series of letters—on occasion of her absence on a visit to some friends near Newcastle-upon-Tyne. These friends were intimate with the commandant of the garrison there, and heard from him of all the preparations that were being made to repel the invasion of Buonaparte, which some people imagined might take place at the mouth of the Tyne. Miss Jenkyns was evidently very much alarmed; and the first part of her letters was often written in pretty intelligible English, conveying particulars of the preparations which were made in the family with whom she was residing against the dreaded event; the bundles of clothes that were packed up ready for a flight to Alston Moor (a wild hilly piece of ground between Northumberland and Cumberland); the signal that was to be given for this flight, and for the simultaneous turning out of the volunteers under arms—which said signal was to consist (if I remember rightly) in ringing the church bells in a particular and ominous manner. One day, when Miss Jenkyns and her hosts were at a dinner-party in Newcastle, this warning summons was actually given (not a very wise proceeding, if there be any truth in the moral attached to the fable of the Boy and the Wolf; but so it was), and Miss Jenkyns, hardly recovered from her fright, wrote the next day to describe the sound, the breathless shock, the hurry and alarm; and then, taking breath, she added, "How trivial, my dear father, do all our apprehensions of the last evening appear, at the present moment, to calm and enquiring minds!" And here Miss Matty broke in with—

"But, indeed, my dear, they were not at all trivial or trifling at the time. I know I used to wake up in the night many a time and think I heard the tramp of the French entering Cranford. Many people talked of hiding themselves in the salt mines—and meat would have kept capitally down there, only perhaps we should have been thirsty. And my father preached a whole set of sermons on the occasion; one set in the mornings, all about David and Goliath, to spirit up the people to fighting with spades or bricks, if need were; and the other set in the afternoons, proving that Napoleon (that was another name for Bony, as we used to call him) was all the same as an Apollyon and Abaddon. I remember my father rather thought he should be asked to print this last set; but the parish had, perhaps, had enough of them with hearing."

Peter Marmaduke Arley Jenkyns ("poor Peter!" as Miss Matty began to call him) was at school at Shrewsbury by this time. The rector took up his pen, and rubbed up his Latin once more, to correspond with his boy. It was very clear that the lad's were what are called show letters. They were of a highly mental description, giving an account of his studies, and his intellectual hopes of various kinds, with an occasional quotation from the classics; but, now and then, the animal nature broke out in such a little sentence as this, evidently written in a trembling hurry, after the letter had been inspected: "Mother dear, do send me a cake, and put plenty of citron in." The "mother dear" probably answered her boy in the form of cakes and "goody," for there were none of her letters among this set; but a whole collection of the rector's, to whom the Latin in his boy's letters was like a trumpet to the old war-horse. I do not know much about Latin, certainly, and it is, perhaps, an ornamental language, but not very useful, I think—at least to judge from the bits I remember out of the rector's letters. One was, "You have not got that town in your map of Ireland; but *Bonus Bernardus non videt omnia*, as the Proverbia say." Presently it became very evident that "poor Peter" got himself into many scrapes. There were letters of stilted penitence to his father, for some wrong-doing; and among them all was a badly-written, badly-sealed, badly-directed, blotted note:—"My dear, dear, dear, dearest mother, I will be a better boy; I will, indeed; but don't, please, be ill for me; I am not worth it; but I will be good, darling mother."

Miss Matty could not speak for crying, after she had read this note. She gave it to me in silence, and then got up and took it to her sacred recesses in her own room, for fear, by any chance, it might get burnt. "Poor Peter!" she said; "he was always in scrapes; he was too easy. They led him wrong, and then left him in the lurch. But he was too fond of mischief. He could never resist a joke. Poor Peter!"

CHAPTER VI - POOR PETER

POOR Peter's career lay before him rather pleasantly mapped out by kind friends, but *Bonus Bernardus non videt omnia,* in this map too. He was to win honours at the Shrewsbury School, and carry them thick to Cambridge, and after that, a living awaited him, the gift of his godfather, Sir Peter Arley. Poor Peter! his lot in life was very different to what his friends had hoped and planned. Miss Matty told me all about it, and I think it was a relief when she had done so.

He was the darling of his mother, who seemed to dote on all her children, though she was, perhaps, a little afraid of Deborah's superior acquirements. Deborah was the favourite of her father, and when Peter disappointed him, she became his pride. The sole honour Peter brought away from Shrewsbury was the reputation of being the best good fellow that ever was, and of being the captain of the school in the art of practical joking. His father was disappointed, but set about remedying the matter in a manly way. He could not afford to send Peter to read with any tutor, but he could read with him himself; and Miss Matty told me much of the awful preparations in the way of dictionaries and lexicons that were made in her father's study the morning Peter began.

"My poor mother!" said she. "I remember how she used to stand in the hall, just near enough the study-door, to catch the tone of my father's voice. I could tell in a moment if all was going right, by her face. And it did go right for a long time."

"What went wrong at last?" said I. "That tiresome Latin, I dare say."

"No! it was not the Latin. Peter was in high favour with my father, for he worked up well for him. But he seemed to think that the Cranford people might be joked about, and made fun of, and they did not like it; nobody does. He was always hoaxing them; 'hoaxing' is not a pretty word, my dear, and I hope you won't tell your father I used it, for I should not like him to think that I was not choice in my language, after living with such a woman as Deborah. And be sure you never use it yourself. I don't know how it slipped out of my mouth, except it was that I was thinking of poor Peter and it was always his expression. But he was a very gentlemanly boy in many things. He was like dear Captain Brown in always being ready to help any old person or a child. Still, he did like joking and making fun; and he seemed to think the old ladies in Cranford would believe anything. There were many old ladies living here then; we are principally ladies now, I know, but we are not so old as the ladies used to be when I was a girl. I could laugh to think of some of Peter's jokes. No, my dear, I won't tell you of them, because they might not shock you as they ought to do, and they were very shocking. He even took in my father once, by dressing himself up as a lady that was passing through the town and wished to see the Rector of Cranford, 'who had published that admirable Assize Sermon.' Peter said he was awfully frightened himself when he saw how my father took it all in, and even offered to copy out all his Napoleon Buonaparte sermons for her—him, I mean—no, her, for Peter was a lady then. He told me he was more terrified than he ever was before, all the time my father was speaking. He did not think my father would have believed him; and yet if he had not, it would have been a sad thing for Peter. As it was, he was none so glad of it, for my father kept him hard at work copying out all those twelve Buonaparte sermons for the lady—that was for Peter himself, you know. He was the lady. And once when he wanted to go fishing, Peter said, 'Confound the woman!'—very bad language, my dear, but Peter was not always so guarded as he should have been; my father was so angry with him, it nearly frightened me out of my wits: and yet I could hardly keep from laughing at the little curtseys Peter kept making, quite slyly, whenever my father spoke of the lady's excellent taste and sound discrimination."

"Did Miss Jenkyns know of these tricks?" said I.

"Oh, no! Deborah would have been too much shocked. No, no one knew but me. I wish I had always known of Peter's plans; but sometimes he did not tell me. He used to say the old ladies in the town wanted something to talk about; but I don't think they did. They had the *St James's Chronicle* three times a week, just as we have now, and we have plenty to say; and I remember the clacking noise there always was when some of the ladies got together. But, probably, school-boys talk more than ladies. At last there was a terrible, sad thing happened." Miss Matty got up, went to the door, and opened it; no one was there. She rang the bell for Martha, and when Martha came, her mistress told her to go for eggs to a farm at the other end of the town.

"I will lock the door after you, Martha. You are not afraid to go, are you?"

"No, ma'am, not at all; Jem Hearn will be only too proud to go with me."

Miss Matty drew herself up, and as soon as we were alone, she wished that Martha had more maidenly reserve.

"We'll put out the candle, my dear. We can talk just as well by firelight, you know. There! Well, you see, Deborah had gone from home for a fortnight or so; it was a very still, quiet day, I remember, overhead; and the lilacs were all in flower, so I suppose it was spring. My father had gone out to see some sick people in the parish; I recollect seeing him leave the house with his wig and shovel-hat and cane. What possessed our poor Peter I don't know; he had the sweetest temper, and yet he always seemed to like to plague Deborah. She never laughed at his jokes, and thought him ungenteel, and not careful enough about improving his mind; and that vexed him.

"Well! he went to her room, it seems, and dressed himself in her old gown, and shawl, and bonnet; just the things she used to wear in Cranford, and was known by everywhere; and he made the pillow into a little—you are sure you locked the door, my dear, for I should not like anyone to hear—into—into a little baby, with white long clothes. It was only, as he told me afterwards, to make something to talk about in the town; he never thought of it as affecting Deborah. And he went and walked up and down in the Filbert walk—just half-hidden by the rails, and half-seen; and he cuddled his pillow, just like a baby, and talked to it all the nonsense people do. Oh dear! and my father came stepping stately up the street, as he always did; and what should he see but a little black crowd of people—I daresay as many as twenty—all peeping through his garden rails. So he thought, at first, they were only looking at a new rhododendron that was in full bloom, and that he was very proud of; and he walked slower, that they might have more time to admire. And he wondered if he could make out a sermon from the occasion, and thought, perhaps, there was some relation between the rhododendrons and the lilies of the field. My poor father! When he came nearer, he began to wonder that they did not see him; but their heads were all so close together, peeping and peeping! My father was amongst them, meaning, he said, to ask them to walk into the garden with him, and admire the beautiful vegetable production, when—oh, my dear, I tremble to think of it—he looked through the rails himself, and saw—I don't know what he thought he saw, but old Clare told me his face went quite grey-white with anger, and his eyes blazed out under his frowning black brows; and he spoke out—oh, so terribly!—and bade them all stop where they were—not one of them to go, not one of them to stir a step; and, swift as light, he was in at the garden door, and down the Filbert walk, and seized hold of poor Peter, and tore his clothes off his back—bonnet, shawl, gown, and all—and threw the pillow among the people over the railings: and then he was very, very angry indeed, and before all the people he lifted up his cane and flogged Peter!

"My dear, that boy's trick, on that sunny day, when all seemed going straight and well, broke my mother's heart, and changed my father for life. It did, indeed. Old Clare said, Peter looked as white as my father; and stood as still as a statue to be flogged; and my father struck hard! When my father stopped to take breath, Peter said, 'Have you done enough, sir?' quite hoarsely, and still standing quite quiet. I don't know what my father said—or if he said anything. But old Clare said, Peter turned to where the people outside the railing were, and made them a low bow, as grand and as grave as any gentleman; and then walked slowly into the house. I was in the store-room helping my mother to make cowslip wine. I cannot abide the wine now, nor the scent of the flowers; they turn me sick and faint, as they did that day, when Peter came in, looking as haughty as any man—indeed, looking like a man, not like a boy. 'Mother!' he said, 'I am come to say, God bless you for ever.' I saw his lips quiver as he spoke; and I think he durst not say anything more loving, for the purpose that was in his heart. She looked at him rather frightened, and wondering, and asked him what was to do. He did not smile or speak, but put his arms round her and kissed her as if he did not know how to leave off; and before she could speak again, he was gone. We talked it over, and could not understand it, and she bade me go and seek my father, and ask what it was all about. I found him walking up and down, looking very highly displeased.

"'Tell your mother I have flogged Peter, and that he richly deserved it.'

"I durst not ask any more questions. When I told my mother, she sat down, quite faint, for a minute. I remember, a few days after, I saw the poor, withered cowslip flowers thrown out to the leaf heap, to decay and die there. There was no making of cowslip wine that year at the rectory—nor, indeed, ever after.

"Presently my mother went to my father. I know I thought of Queen Esther and King Ahasuerus; for my mother was very pretty and delicate-looking, and my father looked as terrible as King Ahasuerus. Some time after they came out together; and then my mother told me what had happened, and that she was going up to Peter's room at my father's desire—though she was not to tell Peter this—to talk the matter over with him. But no Peter was there. We looked over the house; no Peter was there! Even my father, who had not liked to join in the search at first, helped us before long. The rectory was a very old house—steps up into a room, steps down into a room, all through. At first, my mother went calling low and soft, as if to reassure the poor boy, 'Peter! Peter, dear! it's only me;' but, by-and-by, as the servants came back from the errands my father had sent them, in different directions, to find where Peter was—as we found he was not in the garden, nor the hayloft, nor anywhere about—my mother's cry grew louder and wilder, Peter! Peter, my darling! where are you?' for then she felt and understood that that long kiss meant some sad kind of 'good-bye.' The afternoon went on—my mother never resting, but seeking again and again in every possible place that had been looked into twenty times before, nay, that she had looked into over and over again herself. My father sat with his head in his hands, not speaking except when his messengers came in, bringing no tidings; then he lifted up his face, so strong and sad, and told them to go again in some new direction. My mother kept passing from room to room, in and out of the house, moving noiselessly, but never ceasing. Neither she nor my father durst leave the house, which was the meeting-place for all the messengers. At last (and it was nearly dark), my father rose up. He took hold of my mother's arm as she came with wild, sad pace through one door, and quickly towards another. She started at the touch of his hand, for she had forgotten all in the world but Peter.

"'Molly!' said he, 'I did not think all this would happen.' He looked into her face for comfort—her poor face all wild and white; for neither she nor my father had dared to acknowledge—much less act upon—the terror that was in their hearts, lest Peter should have made away with himself. My father saw no conscious look in his wife's hot, dreary eyes, and he missed the sympathy that she had always been ready to give him—strong man as he was, and at the dumb despair in her face his tears began to flow. But when she saw this, a gentle sorrow came over her countenance, and she said, 'Dearest John! don't cry; come with me, and we'll find him,' almost as cheerfully as if she knew where he was. And she took my father's great hand in her little soft one, and led him along, the tears dropping as he walked on that same unceasing, weary walk, from room to room, through house and garden.

"Oh, how I wished for Deborah! I had no time for crying, for now all seemed to depend on me. I wrote for Deborah to come home. I sent a message privately to that same Mr Holbrook's house—poor Mr Holbrook;—you know who I mean. I don't mean I sent a message to him, but I sent one that I could trust to know if Peter was at his house. For at one time Mr Holbrook was an occasional visitor at the rectory—you know he was Miss Pole's cousin—and he had been very kind to Peter, and taught him how to fish—he was very kind to everybody, and I thought Peter might have gone off there. But Mr Holbrook was from home, and Peter had never been seen. It was night now; but the doors were all wide open, and my father and mother walked on and on; it was more than an hour since he had joined her, and I don't believe they had ever spoken all that time. I was getting the parlour fire lighted, and one of the servants was preparing tea, for I wanted them to have something to eat and drink and warm them, when old Clare asked to speak to me.

"'I have borrowed the nets from the weir, Miss Matty. Shall we drag the ponds to-night, or wait for the morning?'

"I remember staring in his face to gather his meaning; and when I did, I laughed out loud. The horror of that new thought—our bright, darling Peter, cold, and stark, and dead! I remember the ring of my own laugh now.

"The next day Deborah was at home before I was myself again. She would not have been so weak as to give way as I had done; but my screams (my horrible laughter had ended in crying) had roused my sweet dear mother, whose poor wandering wits were called back and collected as soon as a child needed her care. She and Deborah sat by my bedside; I knew by the looks of each that there had been no news of Peter—no awful, ghastly news, which was what I most had dreaded in my dull state between sleeping and waking.

"The same result of all the searching had brought something of the same relief to my mother, to whom, I am sure, the thought that Peter might even then be hanging dead in some of the familiar home places had caused that never-ending walk of yesterday. Her soft eyes never were the same again after that; they had always a restless, craving look, as if seeking for what they could not find. Oh! it was an awful time; coming down like a thunder-bolt on the still sunny day when the lilacs were all in bloom."

"Where was Mr Peter?" said I.

"He had made his way to Liverpool; and there was war then; and some of the king's ships lay off the mouth of the Mersey; and they were only too glad to have a fine likely boy such as him (five foot nine he was), come to offer himself. The captain wrote to my father, and Peter wrote to my mother. Stay! those letters will be somewhere here."

We lighted the candle, and found the captain's letter and Peter's too. And we also found a little simple begging letter from Mrs Jenkyns to Peter, addressed to him at the house of an old schoolfellow whither she fancied he might have gone. They had returned it unopened; and unopened it had remained ever since, having been inadvertently put by among the other letters of that time. This is it:—

> "MY DEAREST PETER,—You did not think we should be so sorry as we are, I know, or you would never have gone away. You are too good. Your father sits and sighs till my heart aches to hear him. He cannot hold up his head for grief; and yet he only did what he thought was right. Perhaps he has been too severe, and perhaps I have not been kind enough; but God knows how we love you, my dear only boy. Don looks so sorry you are gone. Come back, and make us happy, who love you so much. I know you will come back."

But Peter did not come back. That spring day was the last time he ever saw his mother's face. The writer of the letter—the last—the only person who had ever seen what was written in it, was dead long ago; and I, a stranger, not born at the time when this occurrence took place, was the one to open it.

The captain's letter summoned the father and mother to Liverpool instantly, if they wished to see their boy; and, by some of the wild chances of life, the captain's letter had been detained somewhere, somehow.

Miss Matty went on, "And it was racetime, and all the post-horses at Cranford were gone to the races; but my father and mother set off in our own gig—and oh! my dear, they were too late—the ship was gone! And now read Peter's letter to my mother!"

It was full of love, and sorrow, and pride in his new profession, and a sore sense of his disgrace in the eyes of the people at Cranford; but ending with a passionate entreaty that she would come and see him before he left the Mersey: "Mother; we may go into battle. I hope we shall, and lick those French: but I must see you again before that time."

"And she was too late," said Miss Matty; "too late!"

We sat in silence, pondering on the full meaning of those sad, sad words. At length I asked Miss Matty to tell me how her mother bore it.

"Oh!" she said, "she was patience itself. She had never been strong, and this weakened her terribly. My father used to sit looking at her: far more sad than she was. He seemed as if he could look at nothing else when she was by; and he was so humble—so very gentle now. He would, perhaps, speak in his old way—laying down the law, as it were—and then, in a minute or two, he would come round and put his hand on our shoulders, and ask us in a low voice, if he had said anything to hurt us. I did not wonder at his speaking so to Deborah, for she was so clever; but I could not bear to hear him talking so to me.

"But, you see, he saw what we did not—that it was killing my mother. Yes! killing her (put out the candle, my dear; I can talk better in the dark), for she was but a frail woman, and ill-fitted to stand the fright and shock she had gone through; and she would smile at him and comfort him, not in words, but in her looks and tones, which were always cheerful when he was there. And she would speak of how she thought Peter stood a good chance of being admiral very soon—he was so brave and clever; and how she thought of seeing him in his navy uniform, and what sort of hats admirals wore; and how much more fit he was to be a sailor than a clergyman; and all in that way, just to make my father think she was quite glad of what came of that unlucky morning's work, and the flogging which was always in his mind, as we all knew. But oh, my dear! the bitter, bitter crying she had when she was alone; and at last, as she grew weaker, she could not keep her tears in when Deborah or me was by, and would give us message after message for Peter (his ship had gone to the Mediterranean, or somewhere down there, and then he was ordered off to India, and there was no overland route then); but she still said that no one knew where their death lay in wait, and that we were not to think hers was near. We did not think it, but we knew it, as we saw her fading away.

"Well, my dear, it's very foolish of me, I know, when in all likelihood I am so near seeing her again.

"And only think, love! the very day after her death—for she did not live quite a twelvemonth after Peter went away—the very day after—came a parcel for her from India—from her poor boy. It was a large, soft, white Indian shawl, with just a little narrow border all round; just what my mother would have liked.

"We thought it might rouse my father, for he had sat with her hand in his all night long; so Deborah took it in to him, and Peter's letter to her, and all. At first, he took no notice; and we tried to make a kind of light careless talk about the shawl, opening it out and admiring it. Then, suddenly, he got up, and spoke: 'She shall be buried in it,' he said; 'Peter shall have that comfort; and she would have liked it.'

"Well, perhaps it was not reasonable, but what could we do or say? One gives people in grief their own way. He took it up and felt it: 'It is just such a shawl as she wished for when she was married, and her mother did not give it her. I did not know of it till after, or she should have had it—she should; but she shall have it now.'

"My mother looked so lovely in her death! She was always pretty, and now she looked fair, and waxen, and young—younger than Deborah, as she stood trembling and shivering by her. We decked her in the long soft folds; she lay smiling, as if pleased; and people came—all Cranford came—to beg to see her, for they had loved her dearly, as well they might; and the countrywomen brought posies; old Clare's wife brought some white violets and begged they might lie on her breast.

"Deborah said to me, the day of my mother's funeral, that if she had a hundred offers she never would marry and leave my father. It was not very likely she would have so many—I don't know that she had one; but it was not less to her credit to say so. She was such a daughter to my father as I think there never was before or since. His eyes failed him, and she read book after book, and wrote, and copied, and was always at his service in any parish business. She could do many more things than my poor mother could; she even once wrote a letter to the bishop for my father. But he missed my mother sorely; the whole parish noticed it. Not that he was less active; I think he was more so, and more patient in helping every one. I did all I could to set Deborah at liberty to be with him; for I knew I was good for little, and that my best work in the world was to do odd jobs quietly, and set others at liberty. But my father was a changed man."

"Did Mr Peter ever come home?"

"Yes, once. He came home a lieutenant; he did not get to be admiral. And he and my father were such friends! My father took him into every house in the parish, he was so proud of him. He never walked out without Peter's arm to lean upon. Deborah used to smile (I don't think we ever laughed again after my mother's death), and say she was quite put in a corner. Not but what my father always wanted her when there was letter-writing or reading to be done, or anything to be settled."

"And then?" said I, after a pause.

"Then Peter went to sea again; and, by-and-by, my father died, blessing us both, and thanking Deborah for all she had been to him; and, of course, our circumstances were changed; and, instead of living at the rectory, and keeping three maids and a man, we had to come to this small house, and be content with a servant-of-all-work; but, as Deborah used to say, we have always lived genteelly, even if circumstances have compelled us to simplicity. Poor Deborah!"

"And Mr Peter?" asked I.

"Oh, there was some great war in India—I forget what they call it—and we have never heard of Peter since then. I believe he is dead myself; and it sometimes fidgets me that we have never put on mourning for him. And then again, when I sit by myself, and all the house is still, I think I hear his step coming up the street, and my heart begins to flutter and beat; but the sound always goes past—and Peter never comes.

"That's Martha back? No! *I'll* go, my dear; I can always find my way in the dark, you know. And a blow of fresh air at the door will do my head good, and it's rather got a trick of aching."

So she pattered off. I had lighted the candle, to give the room a cheerful appearance against her return.

"Was it Martha?" asked I.

"Yes. And I am rather uncomfortable, for I heard such a strange noise, just as I was opening the door."

"Where?' I asked, for her eyes were round with affright.

"In the street—just outside—it sounded like"—

"Talking?" I put in, as she hesitated a little.

"No! kissing"—

CHAPTER VII - VISITING

ONE morning, as Miss Matty and I sat at our work—it was before twelve o'clock, and Miss Matty had not changed the cap with yellow ribbons that had been Miss Jenkyns's best, and which Miss Matty was now wearing out in private, putting on the one made in imitation of Mrs Jamieson's at all times when she expected to be seen—Martha came up, and asked if Miss Betty Barker might speak to her mistress. Miss Matty assented, and quickly disappeared to change the yellow ribbons, while Miss Barker came upstairs; but, as she had forgotten her spectacles, and was rather flurried by the unusual time of the visit, I was not surprised to see her return with one cap on the top of the other. She was quite unconscious of it herself, and looked at us, with bland satisfaction. Nor do I think Miss Barker perceived it; for, putting aside the little circumstance that she was not so young as she had been, she was very much absorbed in her errand, which she delivered herself of with an oppressive modesty that found vent in endless apologies.

Miss Betty Barker was the daughter of the old clerk at Cranford who had officiated in Mr Jenkyns's time. She and her sister had had pretty good situations as ladies' maids, and had saved money enough to set up a milliner's shop, which had been patronised by the ladies in the neighbourhood. Lady Arley, for instance, would occasionally give Miss Barkers the pattern of an old cap of hers, which they immediately copied and circulated among the *élite* of Cranford. I say the *élite*, for Miss Barkers had caught the trick of the place, and piqued themselves upon their "aristocratic connection." They would not sell their caps and ribbons to anyone without a pedigree. Many a farmer's wife or daughter turned away huffed from Miss Barkers' select millinery, and went rather to the universal shop, where the profits of brown soap and moist sugar enabled the proprietor to go straight to (Paris, he said, until he found his customers too patriotic and John Bullish to wear what the Mounseers wore) London, where, as he often told his customers, Queen Adelaide had appeared, only the very week before, in a cap exactly like the one he showed them, trimmed with yellow and blue ribbons, and had been complimented by King William on the becoming nature of her head-dress.

Miss Barkers, who confined themselves to truth, and did not approve of miscellaneous customers, throve notwithstanding. They were self-denying, good people. Many a time have I seen the eldest of them (she that had been maid to Mrs Jamieson) carrying out some delicate mess to a poor person. They only aped their betters in having "nothing to do" with the class immediately below theirs. And when Miss Barker died, their profits and income were found to be such that Miss Betty was justified in shutting up shop and retiring from business. She also (as I think I have before said) set up her cow; a mark of respectability in Cranford almost as decided as setting up a gig is among some people. She dressed finer than any lady in Cranford; and we did not wonder at it; for it was understood that she was wearing out all the bonnets and caps and outrageous ribbons which had once formed her stock-in-trade. It was five or six years since she had given up shop, so in any other place than Cranford her dress might have been considered *passée*.

And now Miss Betty Barker had called to invite Miss Matty to tea at her house on the following Tuesday. She gave me also an impromptu invitation, as I happened to be a visitor—though I could see she had a little fear lest, since my father had gone to live in Drumble, he might have engaged in that "horrid cotton trade," and so dragged his family down out of "aristocratic society." She prefaced this invitation with so many apologies that she quite excited my curiosity. "Her presumption" was to be excused. What had she been doing? She seemed so overpowered by it I could only think that she had been writing to Queen Adelaide to ask for a receipt for washing lace; but the act which she so characterised was only an invitation she had carried to her sister's former mistress, Mrs Jamieson. "Her former occupation considered, could Miss Matty excuse the liberty?" Ah! thought I, she has found out that double cap, and is going to rectify Miss Matty's head-dress. No! it was simply to extend her invitation to Miss Matty and to me. Miss Matty bowed acceptance; and I wondered that, in the graceful action, she did not feel the unusual weight and extraordinary height of her head-dress. But I do not think she did, for she recovered her balance, and went on talking to Miss Betty in a kind, condescending manner, very different from the fidgety way she would have had if she had suspected how singular her appearance was. "Mrs Jamieson is coming, I think you said?" asked Miss Matty.

"Yes. Mrs Jamieson most kindly and condescendingly said she would be happy to come. One little stipulation she made, that she should bring Carlo. I told her that if I had a weakness, it was for dogs."

"And Miss Pole?" questioned Miss Matty, who was thinking of her pool at Preference, in which Carlo would not be available as a partner.

"I am going to ask Miss Pole. Of course, I could not think of asking her until I had asked you, madam—the rector's daughter, madam. Believe me, I do not forget the situation my father held under yours."

"And Mrs Forrester, of course?"

"And Mrs Forrester. I thought, in fact, of going to her before I went to Miss Pole. Although her circumstances are changed, madam, she was born at Tyrrell, and we can never forget her alliance to the Bigges, of Bigelow Hall."

Miss Matty cared much more for the little circumstance of her being a very good card-player.

"Mrs Fitz-Adam—I suppose"—

"No, madam. I must draw a line somewhere. Mrs Jamieson would not, I think, like to meet Mrs Fitz-Adam. I have the greatest respect for Mrs Fitz-Adam—but I cannot think her fit society for such ladies as Mrs Jamieson and Miss Matilda Jenkyns."

Miss Betty Barker bowed low to Miss Matty, and pursed up her mouth. She looked at me with sidelong dignity, as much as to say, although a retired milliner, she was no democrat, and understood the difference of ranks.

"May I beg you to come as near half-past six to my little dwelling, as possible, Miss Matilda? Mrs Jamieson dines at five, but has kindly promised not to delay her visit beyond that time—half-past six." And with a swimming curtsey Miss Betty Barker took her leave.

My prophetic soul foretold a visit that afternoon from Miss Pole, who usually came to call on Miss Matilda after any event—or indeed in sight of any event—to talk it over with her.

"Miss Betty told me it was to be a choice and select few," said Miss Pole, as she and Miss Matty compared notes.

"Yes, so she said. Not even Mrs Fitz-Adam."

Now Mrs Fitz-Adam was the widowed sister of the Cranford surgeon, whom I have named before. Their parents were respectable farmers, content with their station. The name of these good people was Hoggins. Mr Hoggins was the Cranford doctor now; we disliked the name and considered it coarse; but, as Miss Jenkyns said, if he changed it to Piggins it would not be much better. We had hoped to discover a relationship between him and that Marchioness of Exeter whose name was Molly Hoggins; but the man, careless of his own interests, utterly ignored and denied any such relationship, although, as dear Miss Jenkyns had said, he had a sister called Mary, and the same Christian names were very apt to run in families.

Soon after Miss Mary Hoggins married Mr Fitz-Adam, she disappeared from the neighbourhood for many years. She did not move in a sphere in Cranford society sufficiently high to make any of us care to know what Mr Fitz-Adam was. He died and was gathered to his fathers without our ever having thought about him at all. And then Mrs Fitz-Adam reappeared in Cranford ("as bold as a lion," Miss Pole said), a well-to-do widow, dressed in rustling black silk, so soon after her husband's death that poor Miss Jenkyns was justified in the remark she made, that "bombazine would have shown a deeper sense of her loss."

I remember the convocation of ladies who assembled to decide whether or not Mrs Fitz-Adam should be called upon by the old blue-blooded inhabitants of Cranford. She had taken a large rambling house, which had been usually considered to confer a patent of gentility upon its tenant, because, once upon a time, seventy or eighty years before, the spinster daughter of an earl had resided in it. I am not sure if the inhabiting this house was not also believed to convey some unusual power of intellect; for the earl's daughter, Lady Jane, had a sister, Lady Anne, who had married a general officer in the time of the American war, and this general officer had written one or two comedies, which were still acted on the London boards, and which, when we saw them advertised, made us all draw up, and feel that Drury Lane was paying a very pretty compliment to Cranford. Still, it was not at all a settled thing that Mrs Fitz-Adam was to be visited, when dear Miss Jenkyns died; and, with her, something of the clear knowledge of the strict code of gentility went out too. As Miss Pole observed, "As most of the ladies of good family in Cranford were elderly spinsters, or widows without children, if we did not relax a little, and become less exclusive, by-and-by we should have no society at all."

Mrs Forrester continued on the same side.

"She had always understood that Fitz meant something aristocratic; there was Fitz-Roy—she thought that some of the King's children had been called Fitz-Roy; and there was Fitz-Clarence, now—they were the children of dear good King William the Fourth. Fitz-Adam!—it was a pretty name, and she thought it very probably meant 'Child of Adam.' No one, who had not some good blood in their veins, would dare to be called Fitz; there was a deal in a name—she had had a cousin who spelt his name with two little ffs—ffoulkes—and he always looked down upon capital letters and said they belonged to lately-invented families. She had been afraid he would die a bachelor, he was so very choice. When he met with a Mrs ffarringdon, at a watering-place, he took to her immediately; and a very pretty genteel woman she was—a widow, with a very good fortune; and 'my cousin,' Mr ffoulkes, married her; and it was all owing to her two little ffs."

Mrs Fitz-Adam did not stand a chance of meeting with a Mr Fitz-anything in Cranford, so that could not have been her motive for settling there. Miss Matty thought it might have been the hope of being admitted into the society of the place, which would certainly be a very agreeable rise for *ci-devant* Miss Hoggins; and if this had been her hope it would be cruel to disappoint her.

So everybody called upon Mrs Fitz-Adam—everybody but Mrs Jamieson, who used to show how honourable she was by never seeing Mrs Fitz-Adam when they met at the Cranford parties. There would be only eight or ten ladies in the room, and Mrs Fitz-Adam was the largest of all, and she invariably used to stand up when Mrs Jamieson came in, and curtsey very low to her whenever she turned in her direction—so low, in fact, that I think Mrs Jamieson must have looked at the wall above her, for she never moved a muscle of her face, no more than if she had not seen her. Still Mrs Fitz-Adam persevered.

The spring evenings were getting bright and long when three or four ladies in calashes met at Miss Barker's door. Do you know what a calash is? It is a covering worn over caps, not unlike the heads fastened on old-fashioned gigs; but sometimes it is not quite so large. This kind of head-gear always made an awful impression on the children in Cranford; and now two or three left off their play in the quiet sunny little street, and gathered in wondering silence round Miss Pole, Miss Matty, and myself. We were silent too, so that we could hear loud, suppressed whispers inside Miss Barker's house: "Wait, Peggy! wait till I've run upstairs and washed my hands. When I cough, open the door; I'll not be a minute."

And, true enough it was not a minute before we heard a noise, between a sneeze and a crow; on which the door flew open. Behind it stood a round-eyed maiden, all aghast at the honourable company of calashes, who marched in without a word. She recovered presence of mind enough to usher us into a small room, which had been the shop, but was now converted into a temporary dressing-room. There we unpinned and shook ourselves, and arranged our features before the glass into a sweet and gracious company-face; and then, bowing backwards with "After you, ma'am," we allowed Mrs Forrester to take precedence up the narrow staircase that led to Miss Barker's drawing-room. There she sat, as stately and composed as though we had never heard that odd-sounding cough, from which her throat must have been even then sore and rough. Kind, gentle, shabbily-dressed Mrs Forrester was immediately conducted to the second place of honour—a seat arranged something like Prince Albert's near the Queen's—good, but not so good. The place of pre-eminence was, of course, reserved for the Honourable Mrs Jamieson, who presently came panting up the stairs—Carlo rushing round her on her progress, as if he meant to trip her up.

And now Miss Betty Barker was a proud and happy woman! She stirred the fire, and shut the door, and sat as near to it as she could, quite on the edge of her chair. When Peggy came in, tottering under the weight of the tea-tray, I noticed that Miss Barker was sadly afraid lest Peggy should not keep her distance sufficiently. She and her mistress were on very familiar terms in their every-day intercourse, and Peggy wanted now to make several little confidences to her, which Miss Barker was on thorns to hear, but which she thought it her duty, as a lady, to repress. So she turned away from all Peggy's asides and signs; but she made one or two very malapropos answers to what was said; and at last, seized with a bright idea, she exclaimed, "Poor, sweet Carlo! I'm forgetting him. Come downstairs with me, poor ittie doggie, and it shall have its tea, it shall!"

In a few minutes she returned, bland and benignant as before; but I thought she had forgotten to give the "poor ittie doggie" anything to eat, judging by the avidity with which he swallowed down chance pieces of cake. The tea-tray was abundantly loaded—I was pleased to see it, I was so hungry; but I was afraid the ladies present might think it vulgarly heaped up. I know they would have done at their own houses; but somehow the heaps disappeared here. I saw Mrs Jamieson eating seed-cake, slowly and considerately, as she did everything; and I was rather surprised, for I knew she had told us, on the occasion of her last party, that she never had it in her house, it reminded her so much of scented soap. She always gave us Savoy biscuits. However, Mrs Jamieson was kindly indulgent to Miss Barker's want of knowledge of the customs of high life; and, to spare her feelings, ate three large pieces of seed-cake, with a placid, ruminating expression of countenance, not unlike a cow's.

After tea there was some little demur and difficulty. We were six in number; four could play at Preference, and for the other two there was Cribbage. But all, except myself (I was rather afraid of the Cranford ladies at cards, for it was the most earnest and serious business they ever engaged in), were anxious to be of the "pool." Even Miss Barker, while declaring she did not know Spadille from Manille, was evidently hankering to take a hand. The dilemma was soon put an end to by a singular kind of noise. If a baron's daughter-in-law could ever be supposed to snore, I should have said Mrs Jamieson did so then; for, overcome by the heat of the room, and inclined to doze by nature, the temptation of that very comfortable arm-chair had been too much for her, and Mrs Jamieson was nodding. Once or twice she opened her eyes with an effort, and calmly but unconsciously smiled upon us; but by-and-by, even her benevolence was not equal to this exertion, and she was sound asleep.

"It is very gratifying to me," whispered Miss Barker at the card-table to her three opponents, whom, notwithstanding her ignorance of the game, she was "basting" most unmercifully—"very gratifying indeed, to see how completely Mrs Jamieson feels at home in my poor little dwelling; she could not have paid me a greater compliment."

Miss Barker provided me with some literature in the shape of three or four handsomely-bound fashion-books ten or twelve years old, observing, as she put a little table and a candle for my especial benefit, that she knew young people liked to look at pictures. Carlo lay and snorted, and started at his mistress's feet. He, too, was quite at home.

The card-table was an animated scene to watch; four ladies' heads, with niddle-noddling caps, all nearly meeting over the middle of the table in their eagerness to whisper quick enough and loud enough: and every now and then came Miss Barker's "Hush, ladies! if you please, hush! Mrs Jamieson is asleep."

It was very difficult to steer clear between Mrs Forrester's deafness and Mrs Jamieson's sleepiness. But Miss Barker managed her arduous task well. She repeated the whisper to Mrs Forrester, distorting her face considerably, in order to show, by the motions of her lips, what was said; and then she smiled kindly all round at us, and murmured to herself, "Very gratifying, indeed; I wish my poor sister had been alive to see this day."

Presently the door was thrown wide open; Carlo started to his feet, with a loud snapping bark, and Mrs Jamieson awoke: or, perhaps, she had not been asleep—as she said almost directly, the room had been so light she had been glad to keep her eyes shut, but had been listening with great interest to all our amusing and agreeable conversation. Peggy came in once more, red with importance. Another tray! "Oh, gentility!" thought I, "can yon endure this last shock?" For Miss Barker had ordered (nay, I doubt not, prepared, although she did say, "Why, Peggy, what have you brought us?" and looked pleasantly surprised at the unexpected pleasure) all sorts of good things for supper—scalloped oysters, potted lobsters, jelly, a dish called "little Cupids" (which was in great favour with the Cranford ladies, although too expensive to be given, except on solemn and state occasions—macaroons sopped in brandy, I should have called it, if I had not known its more refined and classical name). In short, we were evidently to be feasted with all that was sweetest and best; and we thought it better to submit graciously, even at the cost of our gentility—which never ate suppers in general, but which, like most non-supper-eaters, was particularly hungry on all special occasions.

Miss Barker, in her former sphere, had, I daresay, been made acquainted with the beverage they call cherry-brandy. We none of us had ever seen such a thing, and rather shrank back when she proffered it us—"just a little, leetle glass, ladies; after the oysters and lobsters, you know. Shell-fish are sometimes thought not very wholesome." We all shook our heads like female mandarins; but, at last, Mrs Jamieson suffered herself to be persuaded, and we followed her lead. It was not exactly unpalatable, though so hot and so strong that we thought ourselves bound to give evidence that we were not accustomed to such things by coughing terribly—almost as strangely as Miss Barker had done, before we were admitted by Peggy.

"It's very strong," said Miss Pole, as she put down her empty glass; "I do believe there's spirit in it."

"Only a little drop—just necessary to make it keep," said Miss Barker. "You know we put brandy-pepper over our preserves to make them keep. I often feel tipsy myself from eating damson tart."

I question whether damson tart would have opened Mrs Jamieson's heart as the cherry-brandy did; but she told us of a coming event, respecting which she had been quite silent till that moment.

"My sister-in-law, Lady Glenmire, is coming to stay with me."

There was a chorus of "Indeed!" and then a pause. Each one rapidly reviewed her wardrobe, as to its fitness to appear in the presence of a baron's widow; for, of course, a series of small festivals were always held in Cranford on the arrival of a visitor at any of our friends' houses. We felt very pleasantly excited on the present occasion.

Not long after this the maids and the lanterns were announced. Mrs Jamieson had the sedan-chair, which had squeezed itself into Miss Barker's narrow lobby with some difficulty, and most literally "stopped the way." It required some skilful manoeuvring on the part of the old chairmen (shoemakers by day, but when summoned to carry the sedan dressed up in a strange old livery—long great-coats, with small capes, coeval with the sedan, and similar to the dress of the class in Hogarth's pictures) to edge, and back, and try at it again, and finally to succeed in carrying their burden out of Miss Barker's front door. Then we heard their quick pit-a-pat along the quiet little street as we put on our calashes and pinned up our gowns; Miss Barker hovering about us with offers of help, which, if she had not remembered her former occupation, and wished us to forget it, would have been much more pressing.

CHAPTER VIII - "YOUR LADYSHIP"

EARLY the next morning—directly after twelve—Miss Pole made her appearance at Miss Matty's. Some very trifling piece of business was alleged as a reason for the call; but there was evidently something behind. At last out it came.

"By the way, you'll think I'm strangely ignorant; but, do you really know, I am puzzled how we ought to address Lady Glenmire. Do you say, 'Your Ladyship,' where you would say 'you' to a common person? I have been puzzling all morning; and are we to say 'My Lady,' instead of 'Ma'am?' Now you knew Lady Arley—will you kindly tell me the most correct way of speaking to the peerage?"

Poor Miss Matty! she took off her spectacles and she put them on again—but how Lady Arley was addressed, she could not remember.

"It is so long ago," she said. "Dear! dear! how stupid I am! I don't think I ever saw her more than twice. I know we used to call Sir Peter, 'Sir Peter'—but he came much oftener to see us than Lady Arley did. Deborah would have known in a minute. 'My lady'—'your ladyship.' It sounds very strange, and as if it was not natural. I never thought of it before; but, now you have named it, I am all in a puzzle."

It was very certain Miss Pole would obtain no wise decision from Miss Matty, who got more bewildered every moment, and more perplexed as to etiquettes of address.

"Well, I really think," said Miss Pole, "I had better just go and tell Mrs Forrester about our little difficulty. One sometimes grows nervous; and yet one would not have Lady Glenmire think we were quite ignorant of the etiquettes of high life in Cranford."

"And will you just step in here, dear Miss Pole, as you come back, please, and tell me what you decide upon? Whatever you and Mrs Forrester fix upon, will be quite right, I'm sure. 'Lady Arley,' 'Sir Peter,'" said Miss Matty to herself, trying to recall the old forms of words.

"Who is Lady Glenmire?" asked I.

"Oh, she's the widow of Mr Jamieson—that's Mrs Jamieson's late husband, you know—widow of his eldest brother. Mrs Jamieson was a Miss Walker, daughter of Governor Walker. 'Your ladyship.' My dear, if they fix on that way of speaking, you must just let me practice a little on you first, for I shall feel so foolish and hot saying it the first time to Lady Glenmire."

It was really a relief to Miss Matty when Mrs Jamieson came on a very unpolite errand. I notice that apathetic people have more quiet impertinence than others; and Mrs Jamieson came now to insinuate pretty plainly that she did not particularly wish that the Cranford ladies should call upon her sister-in-law. I can hardly say how she made this clear; for I grew very indignant and warm, while with slow deliberation she was explaining her wishes to Miss Matty, who, a true lady herself, could hardly understand the feeling which made Mrs Jamieson wish to appear to her noble sister-in-law as if she only visited "county" families. Miss Matty remained puzzled and perplexed long after I had found out the object of Mrs Jamieson's visit.

When she did understand the drift of the honourable lady's call, it was pretty to see with what quiet dignity she received the intimation thus uncourteously given. She was not in the least hurt—she was of too gentle a spirit for that; nor was she exactly conscious of disapproving of Mrs Jamieson's conduct; but there was something of this feeling in her mind, I am sure, which made her pass from the subject to others in a less flurried and more composed manner than usual. Mrs Jamieson was, indeed, the more flurried of the two, and I could see she was glad to take her leave.

A little while afterwards Miss Pole returned, red and indignant. "Well! to be sure! You've had Mrs Jamieson here, I find from Martha; and we are not to call on Lady Glenmire. Yes! I met Mrs Jamieson, half-way between here and Mrs Forrester's, and she told me; she took me so by surprise, I had nothing to say. I wish I had thought of something very sharp and sarcastic; I dare say I shall to-night. And Lady Glenmire is but the widow of a Scotch baron after all! I went on to look at Mrs Forrester's Peerage, to see who this lady was, that is to be kept under a glass case: widow of a Scotch peer—never sat in the House of Lords—and as poor as Job, I dare say; and she—fifth daughter of some Mr Campbell or other. You are the daughter of a rector, at any rate, and related to the Arleys; and Sir Peter might have been Viscount Arley, every one says."

Miss Matty tried to soothe Miss Pole, but in vain. That lady, usually so kind and good-humoured, was now in a full flow of anger.

"And I went and ordered a cap this morning, to be quite ready," said she at last, letting out the secret which gave sting to Mrs Jamieson's intimation. "Mrs Jamieson shall see if it is so easy to get me to make fourth at a pool when she has none of her fine Scotch relations with her!"

In coming out of church, the first Sunday on which Lady Glenmire appeared in Cranford, we sedulously talked together, and turned our backs on Mrs Jamieson and her guest. If we might not call on her, we would not even look at her, though we were dying with curiosity to know what she was like. We had the comfort of questioning Martha in the afternoon. Martha did not belong to a sphere of society whose observation could be an implied compliment to Lady Glenmire, and Martha had made good use of her eyes.

"Well, ma'am! is it the little lady with Mrs Jamieson, you mean? I thought you would like more to know how young Mrs Smith was dressed; her being a bride." (Mrs Smith was the butcher's wife).

Miss Pole said, "Good gracious me! as if we cared about a Mrs Smith;" but was silent as Martha resumed her speech.

"The little lady in Mrs Jamieson's pew had on, ma'am, rather an old black silk, and a shepherd's plaid cloak, ma'am, and very bright black eyes she had, ma'am, and a pleasant, sharp face; not over young, ma'am, but yet, I should guess, younger than Mrs Jamieson herself. She looked up and down the church, like a bird, and nipped up her petticoats, when she came out, as quick and sharp as ever I see. I'll tell you what, ma'am, she's more like Mrs Deacon, at the 'Coach and Horses,' nor any one."

"Hush, Martha!" said Miss Matty, "that's not respectful."

"Isn't it, ma'am? I beg pardon, I'm sure; but Jem Hearn said so as well. He said, she was just such a sharp, stirring sort of a body"—

"Lady," said Miss Pole.

"Lady—as Mrs Deacon."

Another Sunday passed away, and we still averted our eyes from Mrs Jamieson and her guest, and made remarks to ourselves that we thought were very severe—almost too much so. Miss Matty was evidently uneasy at our sarcastic manner of speaking.

Perhaps by this time Lady Glenmire had found out that Mrs Jamieson's was not the gayest, liveliest house in the world; perhaps Mrs Jamieson had found out that most of the county families were in London, and that those who remained in the country were not so alive as they might have been to the circumstance of Lady Glenmire being in their neighbourhood. Great events spring out of small causes; so I will not pretend to say what induced Mrs Jamieson to alter her determination of excluding the Cranford ladies, and send notes of invitation all round for a small party on the following Tuesday. Mr Mulliner himself brought them round. He *would* always ignore the fact of there being a back-door to any house, and gave a louder rat-tat than his mistress, Mrs Jamieson. He had three little notes, which he carried in a large basket, in order to impress his mistress with an idea of their great weight, though they might easily have gone into his waistcoat pocket.

Miss Matty and I quietly decided that we would have a previous engagement at home: it was the evening on which Miss Matty usually made candle-lighters of all the notes and letters of the week; for on Mondays her accounts were always made straight—not a penny owing from the week before; so, by a natural arrangement, making candle-lighters fell upon a Tuesday evening, and gave us a legitimate excuse for declining Mrs Jamieson's invitation. But before our answer was written, in came Miss Pole, with an open note in her hand.

"So!" she said. "Ah! I see you have got your note, too. Better late than never. I could have told my Lady Glenmire she would be glad enough of our society before a fortnight was over."

"Yes," said Miss Matty, "we're asked for Tuesday evening. And perhaps you would just kindly bring your work across and drink tea with us that night. It is my usual regular time for looking over the last week's bills, and notes, and letters, and making candle-lighters of them; but that does not seem quite reason enough for saying I have a previous engagement at home, though I meant to make it do. Now, if you would come, my conscience would be quite at ease, and luckily the note is not written yet."

I saw Miss Pole's countenance change while Miss Matty was speaking.

"Don't you mean to go then?" asked she.

"Oh, no!" said, Miss Matty quietly. "You don't either, I suppose?"

"I don't know," replied Miss Pole. "Yes, I think I do," said she, rather briskly; and on seeing Miss Matty look surprised, she added, "You see, one would not like Mrs Jamieson to think that anything she could do, or say, was of consequence enough to give offence; it would be a kind of letting down of ourselves, that I, for one, should not like. It would be too flattering to Mrs Jamieson if we allowed her to suppose that what she had said affected us a week, nay ten days afterwards."

"Well! I suppose it is wrong to be hurt and annoyed so long about anything; and, perhaps, after all, she did not mean to vex us. But I must say, I could not have brought myself to say the things Mrs Jamieson did about our not calling. I really don't think I shall go."

"Oh, come! Miss Matty, you must go; you know our friend Mrs Jamieson is much more phlegmatic than most people, and does not enter into the little delicacies of feeling which you possess in so remarkable a degree."

"I thought you possessed them, too, that day Mrs Jamieson called to tell us not to go," said Miss Matty innocently.

But Miss Pole, in addition to her delicacies of feeling, possessed a very smart cap, which she was anxious to show to an admiring world; and so she seemed to forget all her angry words uttered not a fortnight before, and to be ready to act on what she called the great Christian principle of "Forgive and forget"; and she lectured dear Miss Matty so long on this head that she absolutely ended by assuring her it was her duty, as a deceased rector's daughter, to buy a new cap and go to the party at Mrs Jamieson's. So "we were most happy to accept," instead of "regretting that we were obliged to decline."

The expenditure on dress in Cranford was principally in that one article referred to. If the heads were buried in smart new caps, the ladies were like ostriches, and cared not what became of their bodies. Old gowns, white and venerable collars, any number of brooches, up and down and everywhere (some with dogs' eyes painted in them; some that were like small picture-frames with mausoleums and weeping-willows neatly executed in hair inside; some, again, with miniatures of ladies and gentlemen sweetly smiling out of a nest of stiff muslin), old brooches for a permanent ornament, and new caps to suit the fashion of the day—the ladies of Cranford always dressed with chaste elegance and propriety, as Miss Barker once prettily expressed it.

And with three new caps, and a greater array of brooches than had ever been seen together at one time since Cranford was a town, did Mrs Forrester, and Miss Matty, and Miss Pole appear on that memorable Tuesday evening. I counted seven brooches myself on Miss Pole's dress. Two were fixed negligently in her cap (one was a butterfly made of Scotch pebbles, which a vivid imagination might believe to be the real insect); one fastened her net neckerchief; one her collar; one ornamented the front of her gown, midway between her throat and waist; and another adorned the point of her stomacher. Where the seventh was I have forgotten, but it was somewhere about her, I am sure.

But I am getting on too fast, in describing the dresses of the company. I should first relate the gathering on the way to Mrs Jamieson's. That lady lived in a large house just outside the town. A road which had known what it was to be a street ran right before the house, which opened out upon it without any intervening garden or court. Whatever the sun was about, he never shone on the front of that house. To be sure, the living-rooms were at the back, looking on to a pleasant garden; the front windows only belonged to kitchens and housekeepers' rooms, and pantries, and in one of them Mr Mulliner was reported to sit. Indeed, looking askance, we often saw the back of a head covered with hair powder, which also extended itself over his coat-collar down to his very waist; and this imposing back was always engaged in reading the *St James's Chronicle*, opened wide, which, in some degree, accounted for the length of time the said newspaper was in reaching us—equal subscribers with Mrs Jamieson, though, in right of her honourableness, she always had the reading of it first. This very Tuesday, the delay in forwarding the last number had been particularly aggravating; just when both Miss Pole and Miss Matty, the former more especially, had been wanting to see it, in order to coach up the Court news ready for the evening's interview with aristocracy. Miss Pole told us she had absolutely taken time by the forelock, and been dressed by five o'clock, in order to be ready if the *St James's Chronicle* should come in at the last moment—the very *St James's Chronicle* which the powdered head was tranquilly and composedly reading as we passed the accustomed window this evening.

"The impudence of the man!" said Miss Pole, in a low indignant whisper. "I should like to ask him whether his mistress pays her quarter-share for his exclusive use."

We looked at her in admiration of the courage of her thought; for Mr Mulliner was an object of great awe to all of us. He seemed never to have forgotten his condescension in coming to live at Cranford. Miss Jenkyns, at times, had stood forth as the undaunted champion of her sex, and spoken to him on terms of equality; but even Miss Jenkyns could get no higher. In his pleasantest and most gracious moods he looked like a sulky cockatoo. He did not speak except in gruff monosyllables. He would wait in the hall when we begged him not to wait, and then look deeply offended because we had kept him there, while, with trembling, hasty hands we prepared ourselves for appearing in company.

Miss Pole ventured on a small joke as we went upstairs, intended, though addressed to us, to afford Mr Mulliner some slight amusement. We all smiled, in order to seem as if we felt at our ease, and timidly looked for Mr Mulliner's sympathy. Not a muscle of that wooden face had relaxed; and we were grave in an instant.

Mrs Jamieson's drawing-room was cheerful; the evening sun came streaming into it, and the large square window was clustered round with flowers. The furniture was white and gold; not the later style, Louis Quatorze, I think they call it, all shells and twirls; no, Mrs Jamieson's chairs and tables had not a curve or bend about them. The chair and table legs diminished as they neared the ground, and were straight and square in all their corners. The chairs were all a-row against the walls, with the exception of four or five which stood in a circle round the fire. They were railed with white bars across the back and knobbed with gold; neither the railings nor the knobs invited to ease. There was a japanned table devoted to literature, on which lay a Bible, a Peerage, and a Prayer-Book. There was another square Pembroke table dedicated to the Fine Arts, on which were a kaleidoscope, conversation-cards, puzzle-cards (tied together to an interminable length with faded pink satin ribbon), and a box painted in fond imitation of the drawings which decorate tea-chests. Carlo lay on the worsted-worked rug, and ungraciously barked at us as we entered. Mrs Jamieson stood up, giving us each a torpid smile of welcome, and looking helplessly beyond us at Mr Mulliner, as if she hoped he would place us in chairs, for, if he did not, she never could. I suppose he thought we could find our way to the circle round the fire, which reminded me of Stonehenge, I don't know why. Lady Glenmire came to the rescue of our hostess, and, somehow or other, we found ourselves for the first time placed agreeably, and not formally, in Mrs Jamieson's house. Lady Glenmire, now we had time to look at her, proved to be a bright little woman of middle age, who had been very pretty in the days of her youth, and who was even yet very pleasant-looking. I saw Miss Pole appraising her dress in the first five minutes, and I take her word when she said the next day—

"My dear! ten pounds would have purchased every stitch she had on—lace and all."

It was pleasant to suspect that a peeress could be poor, and partly reconciled us to the fact that her husband had never sat in the House of Lords; which, when we first heard of it, seemed a kind of swindling us out of our prospects on false pretences; a sort of "A Lord and No Lord" business.

We were all very silent at first. We were thinking what we could talk about, that should be high enough to interest My Lady. There had been a rise in the price of sugar, which, as preserving-time was near, was a piece of intelligence to all our house-keeping hearts, and would have been the natural topic if Lady Glenmire had not been by. But we were not sure if the peerage ate preserves—much less knew how they were made. At last, Miss Pole, who had always a great deal of courage and *savoir faire*, spoke to Lady Glenmire, who on her part had seemed just as much puzzled to know how to break the silence as we were.

"Has your ladyship been to Court lately?" asked she; and then gave a little glance round at us, half timid and half triumphant, as much as to say, "See how judiciously I have chosen a subject befitting the rank of the stranger."

"I never was there in my life," said Lady Glenmire, with a broad Scotch accent, but in a very sweet voice. And then, as if she had been too abrupt, she added: "We very seldom went to London—only twice, in fact, during all my married life; and before I was married my father had far too large a family" (fifth daughter of Mr Campbell was in all our minds, I am sure) "to take us often from our home, even to Edinburgh. Ye'll have been in Edinburgh, maybe?" said she, suddenly brightening up with the hope of a common interest. We had none of us been there; but Miss Pole had an uncle who once had passed a night there, which was very pleasant.

Mrs Jamieson, meanwhile, was absorbed in wonder why Mr Mulliner did not bring the tea; and at length the wonder oozed out of her mouth.

"I had better ring the bell, my dear, had not I?" said Lady Glenmire briskly.

"No—I think not—Mulliner does not like to be hurried."

We should have liked our tea, for we dined at an earlier hour than Mrs Jamieson. I suspect Mr Mulliner had to finish the *St James's Chronicle* before he chose to trouble himself about tea. His mistress fidgeted and fidgeted, and kept saying, "I can't think why Mulliner does not bring tea. I can't think what he can be about." And Lady Glenmire at last grew quite impatient, but it was a pretty kind of impatience after all; and she rang the bell rather sharply, on receiving a half-permission from her sister-in-law to do so. Mr Mulliner appeared in dignified surprise. "Oh!" said Mrs Jamieson, "Lady Glenmire rang the bell; I believe it was for tea."

In a few minutes tea was brought. Very delicate was the china, very old the plate, very thin the bread and butter, and very small the lumps of sugar. Sugar was evidently Mrs Jamieson's favourite economy. I question if the little filigree sugar-tongs, made something like scissors, could have opened themselves wide enough to take up an honest, vulgar good-sized piece; and when I tried to seize two little minnikin pieces at once, so as not to be detected in too many returns to the sugar-basin, they absolutely dropped one, with a little sharp clatter, quite in a malicious and unnatural manner. But before this happened we had had a slight disappointment. In the little silver jug was cream, in the larger one was milk. As soon as Mr Mulliner came in, Carlo began to beg, which was a thing our manners forebade us to do, though I am sure we were just as hungry; and Mrs Jamieson said she was certain we would excuse her if she gave her poor dumb Carlo his tea first. She accordingly mixed a saucerful for him, and put it down for him to lap; and then she told us how intelligent and sensible the dear little fellow was; he knew cream quite well, and constantly refused tea with only milk in it: so the milk was left for us; but we silently thought we were quite as intelligent and sensible as Carlo, and felt as if insult were added to injury when we were called upon to admire the gratitude evinced by his wagging his tail for the cream which should have been ours.

After tea we thawed down into common-life subjects. We were thankful to Lady Glenmire for having proposed some more bread and butter, and this mutual want made us better acquainted with her than we should ever have been with talking about the Court, though Miss Pole did say she had hoped to know how the dear Queen was from some one who had seen her.

The friendship begun over bread and butter extended on to cards. Lady Glenmire played Preference to admiration, and was a complete authority as to Ombre and Quadrille. Even Miss Pole quite forgot to say "my lady," and "your ladyship," and said "Basto! ma'am"; "you have Spadille, I believe," just as quietly as if we had never held the great Cranford Parliament on the subject of the proper mode of addressing a peeress.

As a proof of how thoroughly we had forgotten that we were in the presence of one who might have sat down to tea with a coronet, instead of a cap, on her head, Mrs Forrester related a curious little fact to Lady Glenmire—an anecdote known to the circle of her intimate friends, but of which even Mrs Jamieson was not aware. It related to some fine old lace, the sole relic of better days, which Lady Glenmire was admiring on Mrs Forrester's collar.

"Yes," said that lady, "such lace cannot be got now for either love or money; made by the nuns abroad, they tell me. They say that they can't make it now even there. But perhaps they can, now they've passed the Catholic Emancipation Bill. I should not wonder. But, in the meantime, I treasure up my lace very much. I daren't even trust the washing of it to my maid" (the little charity school-girl I have named before, but who sounded well as "my maid"). "I always wash it myself. And once it had a narrow escape. Of course, your ladyship knows that such lace must never be starched or ironed. Some people wash it in sugar and water, and some in coffee, to make it the right yellow colour; but I myself have a very good receipt for washing it in milk, which stiffens it enough, and gives it a very good creamy colour. Well, ma'am, I had tacked it together (and the beauty of this fine lace is that, when it is wet, it goes into a very little space), and put it to soak in milk, when, unfortunately, I left the room; on my return, I found pussy on the table, looking very like a thief, but gulping very uncomfortably, as if she was half-chocked with something she wanted to swallow and could not. And, would you believe it? At first I pitied her, and said 'Poor pussy! poor pussy!' till, all at once, I looked and saw the cup of milk empty—cleaned out! 'You naughty cat!' said I, and I believe I was provoked enough to give her a slap, which did no good, but only helped the lace down—just as one slaps a choking child on the back. I could have cried, I was so vexed; but I determined I would not give the lace up without a struggle for it. I hoped the lace might disagree with her, at any rate; but it would have been too much for Job, if he had seen, as I did, that cat come in, quite placid and purring, not a quarter of an hour after, and almost expecting to be stroked. 'No, pussy!' said I, 'if you have any conscience you ought not to expect that!' And then a thought struck me; and I rang the bell for my maid, and sent her to Mr Hoggins, with my compliments, and would he be kind enough to lend me one of his top-boots for an hour? I did not think there was anything odd in the message; but Jenny said the young men in the surgery laughed as if they would be ill at my wanting a top-boot. When it came, Jenny and I put pussy in, with her forefeet straight down, so that they were fastened, and could not scratch, and we gave her a teaspoonful of current-jelly in which (your ladyship must excuse me) I had mixed some tartar emetic. I shall never forget how anxious I was for the next half-hour. I took pussy to my own room, and spread a clean towel on the floor. I could have kissed her when she returned the lace to sight, very much as it had gone down. Jenny had boiling water ready, and we soaked it and soaked it, and spread it on a lavender-bush in the sun before I could touch it again, even to put it in milk. But now your ladyship would never guess that it had been in pussy's inside."

We found out, in the course of the evening, that Lady Glenmire was going to pay Mrs Jamieson a long visit, as she had given up her apartments in Edinburgh, and had no ties to take her back there in a hurry. On the whole, we were rather glad to hear this, for she had made a pleasant impression upon us; and it was also very comfortable to find, from things which dropped out in the course of conversation, that, in addition to many other genteel qualities, she was far removed from the "vulgarity of wealth."

"Don't you find it very unpleasant walking?" asked Mrs Jamieson, as our respective servants were announced. It was a pretty regular question from Mrs Jamieson, who had her own carriage in the coach-house, and always went out in a sedan-chair to the very shortest distances. The answers were nearly as much a matter of course.

"Oh dear, no! it is so pleasant and still at night!" "Such a refreshment after the excitement of a party!" "The stars are so beautiful!" This last was from Miss Matty.

"Are you fond of astronomy?" Lady Glenmire asked.

"Not very," replied Miss Matty, rather confused at the moment to remember which was astronomy and which was astrology—but the answer was true under either circumstance, for she read, and was slightly alarmed at Francis Moore's astrological predictions; and, as to astronomy, in a private and confidential conversation, she had told me she never could believe that the earth was moving constantly, and that she would not believe it if she could, it made her feel so tired and dizzy whenever she thought about it.

In our pattens we picked our way home with extra care that night, so refined and delicate were our perceptions after drinking tea with "my lady."

CHAPTER IX - SIGNOR BRUNONI

SOON after the events of which I gave an account in my last paper, I was summoned home by my father's illness; and for a time I forgot, in anxiety about him, to wonder how my dear friends at Cranford were getting on, or how Lady Glenmire could reconcile herself to the dulness of the long visit which she was still paying to her sister-in-law, Mrs Jamieson. When my father grew a little stronger I accompanied him to the seaside, so that altogether I seemed banished from Cranford, and was deprived of the opportunity of hearing any chance intelligence of the dear little town for the greater part of that year.

Late in November—when we had returned home again, and my father was once more in good health—I received a letter from Miss Matty; and a very mysterious letter it was. She began many sentences without ending them, running them one into another, in much the same confused sort of way in which written words run together on blotting-paper. All I could make out was that, if my father was better (which she hoped he was), and would take warning and wear a great-coat from Michaelmas to Lady-day, if turbans were in fashion, could I tell her? Such a piece of gaiety was going to happen as had not been seen or known of since Wombwell's lions came, when one of them ate a little child's arm; and she was, perhaps, too old to care about dress, but a new cap she must have; and, having heard that turbans were worn, and some of the county families likely to come, she would like to look tidy, if I would bring her a cap from the milliner I employed; and oh, dear! how careless of her to forget that she wrote to beg I would come and pay her a visit next Tuesday; when she hoped to have something to offer me in the way of amusement, which she would not now more particularly describe, only sea-green was her favourite colour. So she ended her letter; but in a P.S. she added, she thought she might as well tell me what was the peculiar attraction to Cranford just now; Signor Brunoni was going to exhibit his wonderful magic in the Cranford Assembly Rooms on Wednesday and Friday evening in the following week.

I was very glad to accept the invitation from my dear Miss Matty, independently of the conjuror, and most particularly anxious to prevent her from disfiguring her small, gentle, mousey face with a great Saracen's head turban; and accordingly, I bought her a pretty, neat, middle-aged cap, which, however, was rather a disappointment to her when, on my arrival, she followed me into my bedroom, ostensibly to poke the fire, but in reality, I do believe, to see if the sea-green turban was not inside the cap-box with which I had travelled. It was in vain that I twirled the cap round on my hand to exhibit back and side fronts: her heart had been set upon a turban, and all she could do was to say, with resignation in her look and voice—

"I am sure you did your best, my dear. It is just like the caps all the ladies in Cranford are wearing, and they have had theirs for a year, I dare say. I should have liked something newer, I confess—something more like the turbans Miss Betty Barker tells me Queen Adelaide wears; but it is very pretty, my dear. And I dare say lavender will wear better than sea-green. Well, after all, what is dress, that we should care anything about it? You'll tell me if you want anything, my dear. Here is the bell. I suppose turbans have not got down to Drumble yet?"

So saying, the dear old lady gently bemoaned herself out of the room, leaving me to dress for the evening, when, as she informed me, she expected Miss Pole and Mrs Forrester, and she hoped I should not feel myself too much tired to join the party. Of course I should not; and I made some haste to unpack and arrange my dress; but, with all my speed, I heard the arrivals and the buzz of conversation in the next room before I was ready. Just as I opened the door, I caught the words, "I was foolish to expect anything very genteel out of the Drumble shops; poor girl! she did her best, I've no doubt." But, for all that, I had rather that she blamed Drumble and me than disfigured herself with a turban.

Miss Pole was always the person, in the trio of Cranford ladies now assembled, to have had adventures. She was in the habit of spending the morning in rambling from shop to shop, not to purchase anything (except an occasional reel of cotton or a piece of tape), but to see the new articles and report upon them, and to collect all the stray pieces of intelligence in the town. She had a way, too, of demurely popping hither and thither into all sorts of places to gratify her curiosity on any point—a way which, if she had not looked so very genteel and prim, might have been considered impertinent. And now, by the expressive way in which she cleared her throat, and waited for all minor subjects (such as caps and turbans) to be cleared off the course, we knew she had something very particular to relate, when the due pause came—and I defy any people possessed of common modesty to keep up a conversation long, where one among them sits up aloft in silence, looking down upon all the things they chance to say as trivial and contemptible compared to what they could disclose, if properly entreated. Miss Pole began—

"As I was stepping out of Gordon's shop to-day, I chanced to go into the 'George' (my Betty has a second-cousin who is chambermaid there, and I thought Betty would like to hear how she was), and, not seeing anyone about, I strolled up the staircase, and found myself in the passage leading to the Assembly Room (you and I remember the Assembly Room, I am sure, Miss Matty! and the minuets de la cour!); so I went on, not thinking of what I was about, when, all at once, I perceived that I was in the middle of the preparations for to-morrow night—the room being divided with great clothes-maids, over which Crosby's men were tacking red flannel; very dark and odd it seemed; it quite bewildered me, and I was going on behind the screens, in my absence of mind, when a gentleman (quite the gentleman, I can assure you) stepped forwards and asked if I had any business he could arrange for me. He spoke such pretty broken English, I could not help thinking of Thaddeus of Warsaw, and the Hungarian Brothers, and Santo Sebastiani; and while I was busy picturing his past life to myself, he had bowed me out of the room. But wait a minute! You have not heard half my story yet! I was going downstairs, when who should I meet but Betty's second-cousin. So, of course, I stopped to speak to her for Betty's sake; and she told me that I had really seen the conjuror—the gentleman who spoke broken English was Signor Brunoni himself. Just at this moment he passed us on the stairs, making such a graceful bow! in reply to which I dropped a curtsey—all foreigners have such polite manners, one catches something of it. But when he had gone downstairs, I bethought me that I had dropped my glove in the Assembly Room (it was safe in my muff all the time, but I never found it till afterwards); so I went back, and, just as I was creeping up the passage left on one side of the great screen that goes nearly across the room, who should I see but the very same gentleman that had met me before, and passed me on the stairs, coming now forwards from the inner part of the room, to which there is no entrance—you remember, Miss Matty—and just repeating, in his pretty broken English, the inquiry if I had any business there—I don't mean that he put it quite so bluntly, but he seemed very determined that I should not pass the screen—so, of course, I explained about my glove, which, curiously enough, I found at that very moment."

Miss Pole, then, had seen the conjuror—the real, live conjuror! and numerous were the questions we all asked her. "Had he a beard?" "Was he young, or old?" "Fair, or dark?" "Did he look"—(unable to shape my question prudently, I put it in another form)—"How did he look?" In short, Miss Pole was the heroine of the evening, owing to her morning's encounter. If she was not the rose (that is to say the conjuror) she had been near it.

Conjuration, sleight of hand, magic, witchcraft, were the subjects of the evening. Miss Pole was slightly sceptical, and inclined to think there might be a scientific solution found for even the proceedings of the Witch of Endor. Mrs Forrester believed everything, from ghosts to death-watches. Miss Matty ranged between the two—always convinced by the last speaker. I think she was naturally more inclined to Mrs Forrester's side, but a desire of proving herself a worthy sister to Miss Jenkyns kept her equally balanced—Miss Jenkyns, who would never allow a servant to call the little rolls of tallow that formed themselves round candles "winding-sheets," but insisted on their being spoken of as "roley-poleys!" A sister of hers to be superstitious! It would never do.

After tea, I was despatched downstairs into the dining-parlour for that volume of the old Encyclopædia which contained the nouns beginning with C, in order that Miss Pole might prime herself with scientific explanations for the tricks of the following evening. It spoilt the pool at Preference which Miss Matty and Mrs Forrester had been looking forward to, for Miss Pole became so much absorbed in her subject, and the plates by which it was illustrated, that we felt it would be cruel to disturb her otherwise than by one or two well-timed yawns, which I threw in now and then, for I was really touched by the meek way in which the two ladies were bearing their disappointment. But Miss Pole only read the more zealously, imparting to us no more information than this—

"Ah! I see; I comprehend perfectly. A represents the ball. Put A between B and D—no! between C and F, and turn the second joint of the third finger of your left hand over the wrist of your right H. Very clear indeed! My dear Mrs Forrester, conjuring and witchcraft is a mere affair of the alphabet. Do let me read you this one passage?"

Mrs Forrester implored Miss Pole to spare her, saying, from a child upwards, she never could understand being read aloud to; and I dropped the pack of cards, which I had been shuffling very audibly, and by this discreet movement I obliged Miss Pole to perceive that Preference was to have been the order of the evening, and to propose, rather unwillingly, that the pool should commence. The pleasant brightness that stole over the other two ladies' faces on this! Miss Matty had one or two twinges of self-reproach for having interrupted Miss Pole in her studies: and did not remember her cards well, or give her full attention to the game, until she had soothed her conscience by offering to lend the volume of the Encyclopædia to Miss Pole, who accepted it thankfully, and said Betty should take it home when she came with the lantern.

The next evening we were all in a little gentle flutter at the idea of the gaiety before us. Miss Matty went up to dress betimes, and hurried me until I was ready, when we found we had an hour-and-a-half to wait before the "doors opened at seven precisely." And we had only twenty yards to go! However, as Miss Matty said, it would not do to get too much absorbed in anything, and forget the time; so she thought we had better sit quietly, without lighting the candles, till five minutes to seven. So Miss Matty dozed, and I knitted.

At length we set off; and at the door under the carriage-way at the "George," we met Mrs Forrester and Miss Pole: the latter was discussing the subject of the evening with more vehemence than ever, and throwing X's and B's at our heads like hailstones. She had even copied one or two of the "receipts"—as she called them—for the different tricks, on backs of letters, ready to explain and to detect Signor Brunoni's arts.

We went into the cloak-room adjoining the Assembly Room; Miss Matty gave a sigh or two to her departed youth, and the remembrance of the last time she had been there, as she adjusted her pretty new cap before the strange, quaint old mirror in the cloak-room. The Assembly Room had been added to the inn, about a hundred years before, by the different county families, who met together there once a month during the winter to dance and play at cards. Many a county beauty had first swung through the minuet that she afterwards danced before Queen Charlotte in this very room. It was said that one of the Gunnings had graced the apartment with her beauty; it was certain that a rich and beautiful widow, Lady Williams, had here been smitten with the noble figure of a young artist, who was staying with some family in the neighbourhood for professional purposes, and accompanied his patrons to the Cranford Assembly. And a pretty bargain poor Lady Williams had of her handsome husband, if all tales were true. Now, no beauty blushed and dimpled along the sides of the Cranford Assembly Room; no handsome artist won hearts by his bow, *chapeau bras* in hand; the old room was dingy; the salmon-coloured paint had faded into a drab; great pieces of plaster had chipped off from the fine wreaths and festoons on its walls; but still a mouldy odour of aristocracy lingered about the place, and a dusty recollection of the days that were gone made Miss Matty and Mrs Forrester bridle up as they entered, and walk mincingly up the room, as if there were a number of genteel observers, instead of two little boys with a stick of toffee between them with which to beguile the time.

We stopped short at the second front row; I could hardly understand why, until I heard Miss Pole ask a stray waiter if any of the county families were expected; and when he shook his head, and believed not, Mrs Forrester and Miss Matty moved forwards, and our party represented a conversational square. The front row was soon augmented and enriched by Lady Glenmire and Mrs Jamieson. We six occupied the two front rows, and our aristocratic seclusion was respected by the groups of shop-keepers who strayed in from time to time and huddled together on the back benches. At least I conjectured so, from the noise they made, and the sonorous bumps they gave in sitting down; but when, in weariness of the obstinate green curtain that would not draw up, but would stare at me with two odd eyes, seen through holes, as in the old tapestry story, I would fain have looked round at the merry chattering people behind me, Miss Pole clutched my arm, and begged me not to turn, for "it was not the thing." What "the thing" was, I never could find out, but it must have been something eminently dull and tiresome. However, we all sat eyes right, square front, gazing at the tantalising curtain, and hardly speaking intelligibly, we were so afraid of being caught in the vulgarity of making any noise in a place of public amusement. Mrs Jamieson was the most fortunate, for she fell asleep.

At length the eyes disappeared—the curtain quivered—one side went up before the other, which stuck fast; it was dropped again, and, with a fresh effort, and a vigorous pull from some unseen hand, it flew up, revealing to our sight a magnificent gentleman in the Turkish costume, seated before a little table, gazing at us (I should have said with the same eyes that I had last seen through the hole in the curtain) with calm and condescending dignity, "like a being of another sphere," as I heard a sentimental voice ejaculate behind me.

"That's not Signor Brunoni!" said Miss Pole decidedly; and so audibly that I am sure he heard, for he glanced down over his flowing beard at our party with an air of mute reproach. "Signor Brunoni had no beard—but perhaps he'll come soon." So she lulled herself into patience. Meanwhile, Miss Matty had reconnoitred through her eye-glass, wiped it, and looked again. Then she turned round, and said to me, in a kind, mild, sorrowful tone—

"You see, my dear, turbans *are* worn."

But we had no time for more conversation. The Grand Turk, as Miss Pole chose to call him, arose and announced himself as Signor Brunoni.

"I don't believe him!" exclaimed Miss Pole, in a defiant manner. He looked at her again, with the same dignified upbraiding in his countenance. "I don't!" she repeated more positively than ever. "Signor Brunoni had not got that muffy sort of thing about his chin, but looked like a close-shaved Christian gentleman."

Miss Pole's energetic speeches had the good effect of wakening up Mrs Jamieson, who opened her eyes wide, in sign of the deepest attention—a proceeding which silenced Miss Pole and encouraged the Grand Turk to proceed, which he did in very broken English—so broken that there was no cohesion between the parts of his sentences; a fact which he himself perceived at last, and so left off speaking and proceeded to action.

Now we *were* astonished. How he did his tricks I could not imagine; no, not even when Miss Pole pulled out her pieces of paper and began reading aloud—or at least in a very audible whisper—the separate "receipts" for the most common of his tricks. If ever I saw a man frown and look enraged, I saw the Grand Turk frown at Miss Pole; but, as she said, what could be expected but unchristian looks from a Mussulman? If Miss Pole were sceptical, and more engrossed with her receipts and diagrams than with his tricks, Miss Matty and Mrs Forrester were mystified and perplexed to the highest degree. Mrs Jamieson kept taking her spectacles off and wiping them, as if she thought it was something defective in them which made the legerdemain; and Lady Glenmire, who had seen many curious sights in Edinburgh, was very much struck with the tricks, and would not at all agree with Miss Pole, who declared that anybody could do them with a little practice, and that she would, herself, undertake to do all he did, with two hours given to study the Encyclopædia and make her third finger flexible.

At last Miss Matty and Mrs Forrester became perfectly awestricken. They whispered together. I sat just behind them, so I could not help hearing what they were saying. Miss Matty asked Mrs Forrester "if she thought it was quite right to have come to see such things? She could not help fearing they were lending encouragement to something that was not quite"— A little shake of the head filled up the blank. Mrs Forrester replied, that the same thought had crossed her mind; she too was feeling very uncomfortable, it was so very strange. She was quite certain that it was her pocket-handkerchief which was in that loaf just now; and it had been in her own hand not five minutes before. She wondered who had furnished the bread? She was sure it could not be Dakin, because he was the churchwarden. Suddenly Miss Matty half-turned towards me—

"Will you look, my dear—you are a stranger in the town, and it won't give rise to unpleasant reports—will you just look round and see if the rector is here? If he is, I think we may conclude that this wonderful man is sanctioned by the Church, and that will be a great relief to my mind."

I looked, and I saw the tall, thin, dry, dusty rector, sitting surrounded by National School boys, guarded by troops of his own sex from any approach of the many Cranford spinsters. His kind face was all agape with broad smiles, and the boys around him were in chinks of laughing. I told Miss Matty that the Church was smiling approval, which set her mind at ease.

I have never named Mr Hayter, the rector, because I, as a well-to-do and happy young woman, never came in contact with him. He was an old bachelor, but as afraid of matrimonial reports getting abroad about him as any girl of eighteen: and he would rush into a shop or dive down an entry, sooner than encounter any of the Cranford ladies in the street; and, as for the Preference parties, I did not wonder at his not accepting invitations to them. To tell the truth, I always suspected Miss Pole of having given very vigorous chase to Mr Hayter when he first came to Cranford; and not the less, because now she appeared to share so vividly in his dread lest her name should ever be coupled with his. He found all his interests among the poor and helpless; he had treated the National School boys this very night to the performance; and virtue was for once its own reward, for they guarded him right and left, and clung round him as if he had been the queen-bee and they the swarm. He felt so safe in their environment that he could even afford to give our party a bow as we filed out. Miss Pole ignored his presence, and pretended to be absorbed in convincing us that we had been cheated, and had not seen Signor Brunoni after all.

CHAPTER X - THE PANIC

I THINK a series of circumstances dated from Signor Brunoni's visit to Cranford, which seemed at the time connected in our minds with him, though I don't know that he had anything really to do with them. All at once all sorts of uncomfortable rumours got afloat in the town. There were one or two robberies—real *bonâ fide* robberies; men had up before the magistrates and committed for trial—and that seemed to make us all afraid of being robbed; and for a long time, at Miss Matty's, I know, we used to make a regular expedition all round the kitchens and cellars every night, Miss Matty leading the way, armed with the poker, I following with the hearth-brush, and Martha carrying the shovel and fire-irons with which to sound the alarm; and by the accidental hitting together of them she often frightened us so much that we bolted ourselves up, all three together, in the back-kitchen, or store-room, or wherever we happened to be, till, when our affright was over, we recollected ourselves and set out afresh with double valiance. By day we heard strange stories from the shopkeepers and cottagers, of carts that went about in the dead of night, drawn by horses shod with felt, and guarded by men in dark clothes, going round the town, no doubt in search of some unwatched house or some unfastened door.

Miss Pole, who affected great bravery herself, was the principal person to collect and arrange these reports so as to make them assume their most fearful aspect. But we discovered that she had begged one of Mr Hoggins's worn-out hats to hang up in her lobby, and we (at least I) had doubts as to whether she really would enjoy the little adventure of having her house broken into, as she protested she should. Miss Matty made no secret of being an arrant coward, but she went regularly through her housekeeper's duty of inspection—only the hour for this became earlier and earlier, till at last we went the rounds at half-past six, and Miss Matty adjourned to bed soon after seven, "in order to get the night over the sooner."

Cranford had so long piqued itself on being an honest and moral town that it had grown to fancy itself too genteel and well-bred to be otherwise, and felt the stain upon its character at this time doubly. But we comforted ourselves with the assurance which we gave to each other that the robberies could never have been committed by any Cranford person; it must have been a stranger or strangers who brought this disgrace upon the town, and occasioned as many precautions as if we were living among the Red Indians or the French.

This last comparison of our nightly state of defence and fortification was made by Mrs Forrester, whose father had served under General Burgoyne in the American war, and whose husband had fought the French in Spain. She indeed inclined to the idea that, in some way, the French were connected with the small thefts, which were ascertained facts, and the burglaries and highway robberies, which were rumours. She had been deeply impressed with the idea of French spies at some time in her life; and the notion could never be fairly eradicated, but sprang up again from time to time. And now her theory was this:—The Cranford people respected themselves too much, and were too grateful to the aristocracy who were so kind as to live near the town, ever to disgrace their bringing up by being dishonest or immoral; therefore, we must believe that the robbers were strangers—if strangers, why not foreigners?—if foreigners, who so likely as the French? Signor Brunoni spoke broken English like a Frenchman; and, though he wore a turban like a Turk, Mrs Forrester had seen a print of Madame de Staël with a turban on, and another of Mr Denon in just such a dress as that in which the conjuror had made his appearance, showing clearly that the French, as well as the Turks, wore turbans. There could be no doubt Signor Brunoni was a Frenchman—a French spy come to discover the weak and undefended places of England, and doubtless he had his accomplices. For her part, she, Mrs Forrester, had always had her own opinion of Miss Pole's adventure at the "George Inn"—seeing two men where only one was believed to be. French people had ways and means which, she was thankful to say, the English knew nothing about; and she had never felt quite easy in her mind about going to see that conjuror—it was rather too much like a forbidden thing, though the rector was there. In short, Mrs Forrester grew more excited than we had ever known her before, and, being an officer's daughter and widow, we looked up to her opinion, of course.

Really I do not know how much was true or false in the reports which flew about like wildfire just at this time; but it seemed to me then that there was every reason to believe that at Mardon (a small town about eight miles from Cranford) houses and shops were entered by holes made in the walls, the bricks being silently carried away in the dead of the night, and all done so quietly that no sound was heard either in or out of the house. Miss Matty gave it up in despair when she heard of this. "What was the use," said she, "of locks and bolts, and bells to the windows, and going round the house every night? That last trick was fit for a conjuror. Now she did believe that Signor Brunoni was at the bottom of it."

One afternoon, about five o'clock, we were startled by a hasty knock at the door. Miss Matty bade me run and tell Martha on no account to open the door till she (Miss Matty) had reconnoitred through the window; and she armed herself with a footstool to drop down on the head of the visitor, in case he should show a face covered with black crape, as he looked up in answer to her inquiry of who was there. But it was nobody but Miss Pole and Betty. The former came upstairs, carrying a little hand-basket, and she was evidently in a state of great agitation.

"Take care of that!" said she to me, as I offered to relieve her of her basket. "It's my plate. I am sure there is a plan to rob my house to-night. I am come to throw myself on your hospitality, Miss Matty. Betty is going to sleep with her cousin at the 'George.' I can sit up here all night if you will allow me; but my house is so far from any neighbours, and I don't believe we could be heard if we screamed ever so!"

"But," said Miss Matty, "what has alarmed you so much? Have you seen any men lurking about the house?"

"Oh, yes!" answered Miss Pole. "Two very bad-looking men have gone three times past the house, very slowly; and an Irish beggar-woman came not half-an-hour ago, and all but forced herself in past Betty, saying her children were starving, and she must speak to the mistress. You see, she said 'mistress,' though there was a hat hanging up in the hall, and it would have been more natural to have said 'master.' But Betty shut the door in her face, and came up to me, and we got the spoons together, and sat in the parlour-window watching till we saw Thomas Jones going from his work, when we called to him and asked him to take care of us into the town."

We might have triumphed over Miss Pole, who had professed such bravery until she was frightened; but we were too glad to perceive that she shared in the weaknesses of humanity to exult over her; and I gave up my room to her very willingly, and shared Miss Matty's bed for the night. But before we retired, the two ladies rummaged up, out of the recesses of their memory, such horrid stories of robbery and murder that I quite quaked in my shoes. Miss Pole was evidently anxious to prove that such terrible events had occurred within her experience that she was justified in her sudden panic; and Miss Matty did not like to be outdone, and capped every story with one yet more horrible, till it reminded me oddly enough, of an old story I had read somewhere, of a nightingale and a musician, who strove one against the other which could produce the most admirable music, till poor Philomel dropped down dead.

One of the stories that haunted me for a long time afterwards was of a girl who was left in charge of a great house in Cumberland on some particular fair-day, when the other servants all went off to the gaieties. The family were away in London, and a pedlar came by, and asked to leave his large and heavy pack in the kitchen, saying he would call for it again at night; and the girl (a gamekeeper's daughter), roaming about in search of amusement, chanced to hit upon a gun hanging up in the hall, and took it down to look at the chasing; and it went off through the open kitchen door, hit the pack, and a slow dark thread of blood came oozing out. (How Miss Pole enjoyed this part of the story, dwelling on each word as if she loved it!) She rather hurried over the further account of the girl's bravery, and I have but a confused idea that, somehow, she baffled the robbers with Italian irons, heated red-hot, and then restored to blackness by being dipped in grease.

We parted for the night with an awe-stricken wonder as to what we should hear of in the morning—and, on my part, with a vehement desire for the night to be over and gone: I was so afraid lest the robbers should have seen, from some dark lurking-place, that Miss Pole had carried off her plate, and thus have a double motive for attacking our house.

But until Lady Glenmire came to call next day we heard of nothing unusual. The kitchen fire-irons were in exactly the same position against the back door as when Martha and I had skilfully piled them up, like spillikins, ready to fall with an awful clatter if only a cat had touched the outside panels. I had wondered what we should all do if thus awakened and alarmed, and had proposed to Miss Matty that we should cover up our faces under the bedclothes so that there should be no danger of the robbers thinking that we could identify them; but Miss Matty, who was trembling very much, scouted this idea, and said we owed it to society to apprehend them, and that she should certainly do her best to lay hold of them and lock them up in the garret till morning.

When Lady Glenmire came, we almost felt jealous of her. Mrs Jamieson's house had really been attacked; at least there were men's footsteps to be seen on the flower borders, underneath the kitchen windows, "where nae men should be;" and Carlo had barked all through the night as if strangers were abroad. Mrs Jamieson had been awakened by Lady Glenmire, and they had rung the bell which communicated with Mr Mulliner's room in the third storey, and when his night-capped head had appeared over the bannisters, in answer to the summons, they had told him of their alarm, and the reasons for it; whereupon he retreated into his bedroom, and locked the door (for fear of draughts, as he informed them in the morning), and opened the window, and called out valiantly to say, if the supposed robbers would come to him he would fight them; but, as Lady Glenmire observed, that was but poor comfort, since they would have to pass by Mrs Jamieson's room and her own before they could reach him, and must be of a very pugnacious disposition indeed if they neglected the opportunities of robbery presented by the unguarded lower storeys, to go up to a garret, and there force a door in order to get at the champion of the house. Lady Glenmire, after waiting and listening for some time in the drawing-room, had proposed to Mrs Jamieson that they should go to bed; but that lady said she should not feel comfortable unless she sat up and watched; and, accordingly, she packed herself warmly up on the sofa, where she was found by the housemaid, when she came into the room at six o'clock, fast asleep; but Lady Glenmire went to bed, and kept awake all night.

When Miss Pole heard of this, she nodded her head in great satisfaction. She had been sure we should hear of something happening in Cranford that night; and we had heard. It was clear enough they had first proposed to attack her house; but when they saw that she and Betty were on their guard, and had carried off the plate, they had changed their tactics and gone to Mrs Jamieson's, and no one knew what might have happened if Carlo had not barked, like a good dog as he was!

Poor Carlo! his barking days were nearly over. Whether the gang who infested the neighbourhood were afraid of him, or whether they were revengeful enough, for the way in which he had baffled them on the night in question, to poison him; or whether, as some among the more uneducated people thought, he died of apoplexy, brought on by too much feeding and too little exercise; at any rate, it is certain that, two days after this eventful night, Carlo was found dead, with his poor legs stretched out stiff in the attitude of running, as if by such unusual exertion he could escape the sure pursuer, Death.

We were all sorry for Carlo, the old familiar friend who had snapped at us for so many years; and the mysterious mode of his death made us very uncomfortable. Could Signor Brunoni be at the bottom of this? He had apparently killed a canary with only a word of command; his will seemed of deadly force; who knew but what he might yet be lingering in the neighbourhood willing all sorts of awful things!

We whispered these fancies among ourselves in the evenings; but in the mornings our courage came back with the daylight, and in a week's time we had got over the shock of Carlo's death; all but Mrs Jamieson. She, poor thing, felt it as she had felt no event since her husband's death; indeed, Miss Pole said, that as the Honourable Mr Jamieson drank a good deal, and occasioned her much uneasiness, it was possible that Carlo's death might be the greater affliction. But there was always a tinge of cynicism in Miss Pole's remarks. However, one thing was clear and certain—it was necessary for Mrs Jamieson to have some change of scene; and Mr Mulliner was very impressive on this point, shaking his head whenever we inquired after his mistress, and speaking of her loss of appetite and bad nights very ominously; and with justice too, for if she had two characteristics in her natural state of health they were a facility of eating and sleeping. If she could neither eat nor sleep, she must be indeed out of spirits and out of health.

Lady Glenmire (who had evidently taken very kindly to Cranford) did not like the idea of Mrs Jamieson's going to Cheltenham, and more than once insinuated pretty plainly that it was Mr Mulliner's doing, who had been much alarmed on the occasion of the house being attacked, and since had said, more than once, that he felt it a very responsible charge to have to defend so many women. Be that as it might, Mrs Jamieson went to Cheltenham, escorted by Mr Mulliner; and Lady Glenmire remained in possession of the house, her ostensible office being to take care that the maid-servants did not pick up followers. She made a very pleasant-looking dragon; and, as soon as it was arranged for her stay in Cranford, she found out that Mrs Jamieson's visit to Cheltenham was just the best thing in the world. She had let her house in Edinburgh, and was for the time house-less, so the charge of her sister-in-law's comfortable abode was very convenient and acceptable.

Miss Pole was very much inclined to instal herself as a heroine, because of the decided steps she had taken in flying from the two men and one woman, whom she entitled "that murderous gang." She described their appearance in glowing colours, and I noticed that every time she went over the story some fresh trait of villainy was added to their appearance. One was tall—he grew to be gigantic in height before we had done with him; he of course had black hair—and by-and-by it hung in elf-locks over his forehead and down his back. The other was short and broad—and a hump sprouted out on his shoulder before we heard the last of him; he had red hair—which deepened into carroty; and she was almost sure he had a cast in the eye—a decided squint. As for the woman, her eyes glared, and she was masculine-looking—a perfect virago; most probably a man dressed in woman's clothes; afterwards, we heard of a beard on her chin, and a manly voice and a stride.

If Miss Pole was delighted to recount the events of that afternoon to all inquirers, others were not so proud of their adventures in the robbery line. Mr Hoggins, the surgeon, had been attacked at his own door by two ruffians, who were concealed in the shadow of the porch, and so effectually silenced him that he was robbed in the interval between ringing his bell and the servant's answering it. Miss Pole was sure it would turn out that this robbery had been committed by "her men," and went the very day she heard the report to have her teeth examined, and to question Mr Hoggins. She came to us afterwards; so we heard what she had heard, straight and direct from the source, while we were yet in the excitement and flutter of the agitation caused by the first intelligence; for the event had only occurred the night before.

"Well!" said Miss Pole, sitting down with the decision of a person who has made up her mind as to the nature of life and the world (and such people never tread lightly, or seat themselves without a bump), "well, Miss Matty! men will be men. Every mother's son of them wishes to be considered Samson and Solomon rolled into one—too strong ever to be beaten or discomfited—too wise ever to be outwitted. If you will notice, they have always foreseen events, though they never tell one for one's warning before the events happen. My father was a man, and I know the sex pretty well."

She had talked herself out of breath, and we should have been very glad to fill up the necessary pause as chorus, but we did not exactly know what to say, or which man had suggested this diatribe against the sex; so we only joined in generally, with a grave shake of the head, and a soft murmur of "They are very incomprehensible, certainly!"

"Now, only think," said she. "There, I have undergone the risk of having one of my remaining teeth drawn (for one is terribly at the mercy of any surgeon-dentist; and I, for one, always speak them fair till I have got my mouth out of their clutches), and, after all, Mr Hoggins is too much of a man to own that he was robbed last night."

"Not robbed!" exclaimed the chorus.

"Don't tell me!" Miss Pole exclaimed, angry that we could be for a moment imposed upon. "I believe he was robbed, just as Betty told me, and he is ashamed to own it; and, to be sure, it was very silly of him to be robbed just at his own door; I daresay he feels that such a thing won't raise him in the eyes of Cranford society, and is anxious to conceal it—but he need not have tried to impose upon me, by saying I must have heard an exaggerated account of some petty theft of a neck of mutton, which, it seems, was stolen out of the safe in his yard last week; he had the impertinence to add, he believed that that was taken by the cat. I have no doubt, if I could get at the bottom of it, it was that Irishman dressed up in woman's clothes, who came spying about my house, with the story about the starving children."

After we had duly condemned the want of candour which Mr Hoggins had evinced, and abused men in general, taking him for the representative and type, we got round to the subject about which we had been talking when Miss Pole came in; namely, how far, in the present disturbed state of the country, we could venture to accept an invitation which Miss Matty had just received from Mrs Forrester, to come as usual and keep the anniversary of her wedding-day by drinking tea with her at five o'clock, and playing a quiet pool afterwards. Mrs Forrester had said that she asked us with some diffidence, because the roads were, she feared, very unsafe. But she suggested that perhaps one of us would not object to take the sedan, and that the others, by walking briskly, might keep up with the long trot of the chairmen, and so we might all arrive safely at Over Place, a suburb of the town. (No; that is too large an expression: a small cluster of houses separated from Cranford by about two hundred yards of a dark and lonely lane.) There was no doubt but that a similar note was awaiting Miss Pole at home; so her call was a very fortunate affair, as it enabled us to consult together. We would all much rather have declined this invitation; but we felt that it would not be quite kind to Mrs Forrester, who would otherwise be left to a solitary retrospect of her not very happy or fortunate life. Miss Matty and Miss Pole had been visitors on this occasion for many years, and now they gallantly determined to nail their colours to the mast, and to go through Darkness Lane rather than fail in loyalty to their friend.

But when the evening came, Miss Matty (for it was she who was voted into the chair, as she had a cold), before being shut down in the sedan, like jack-in-a-box, implored the chairmen, whatever might befall, not to run away and leave her fastened up there, to be murdered; and even after they had promised, I saw her tighten her features into the stern determination of a martyr, and she gave me a melancholy and ominous shake of the head through the glass. However, we got there safely, only rather out of breath, for it was who could trot hardest through Darkness Lane, and I am afraid poor Miss Matty was sadly jolted.

Mrs Forrester had made extra preparations, in acknowledgment of our exertion in coming to see her through such dangers. The usual forms of genteel ignorance as to what her servants might send up were all gone through; and harmony and Preference seemed likely to be the order of the evening, but for an interesting conversation that began I don't know how, but which had relation, of course, to the robbers who infested the neighbourhood of Cranford.

Having braved the dangers of Darkness Lane, and thus having a little stock of reputation for courage to fall back upon; and also, I daresay, desirous of proving ourselves superior to men (*videlicet* Mr Hoggins) in the article of candour, we began to relate our individual fears, and the private precautions we each of us took. I owned that my pet apprehension was eyes—eyes looking at me, and watching me, glittering out from some dull, flat, wooden surface; and that if I dared to go up to my looking-glass when I was panic-stricken, I should certainly turn it round, with its back towards me, for fear of seeing eyes behind me looking out of the darkness. I saw Miss Matty nerving herself up for a confession; and at last out it came. She owned that, ever since she had been a girl, she had dreaded being caught by her last leg, just as she was getting into bed, by some one concealed under it. She said, when she was younger and more active, she used to take a flying leap from a distance, and so bring both her legs up safely into bed at once; but that this had always annoyed Deborah, who piqued herself upon getting into bed gracefully, and she had given it up in consequence. But now the old terror would often come over her, especially since Miss Pole's house had been attacked (we had got quite to believe in the fact of the attack having taken place), and yet it was very unpleasant to think of looking under a bed, and seeing a man concealed, with a great, fierce face staring out at you; so she had bethought herself of something—perhaps I had noticed that she had told Martha to buy her a penny ball, such as children play with—and now she rolled this ball under the bed every night: if it came out on the other side, well and good; if not she always took care to have her hand on the bell-rope, and meant to call out John and Harry, just as if she expected men-servants to answer her ring.

We all applauded this ingenious contrivance, and Miss Matty sank back into satisfied silence, with a look at Mrs Forrester as if to ask for *her* private weakness.

Mrs Forrester looked askance at Miss Pole, and tried to change the subject a little by telling us that she had borrowed a boy from one of the neighbouring cottages and promised his parents a hundredweight of coals at Christmas, and his supper every evening, for the loan of him at nights. She had instructed him in his possible duties when he first came; and, finding him sensible, she had given him the Major's sword (the Major was her late husband), and desired him to put it very carefully behind his pillow at night, turning the edge towards the head of the pillow. He was a sharp lad, she was sure; for, spying out the Major's cocked hat, he had said, if he might have that to wear, he was sure he could frighten two Englishmen, or four Frenchmen any day. But she had impressed upon him anew that he was to lose no time in putting on hats or anything else; but, if he heard any noise, he was to run at it with his drawn sword. On my suggesting that some accident might occur from such slaughterous and indiscriminate directions, and that he might rush on Jenny getting up to wash, and have spitted her before he had discovered that she was not a Frenchman, Mrs Forrester said she did not think that that was likely, for he was a very sound sleeper, and generally had to be well shaken or cold-pigged in a morning before they could rouse him. She sometimes thought such dead sleep must be owing to the hearty suppers the poor lad ate, for he was half-starved at home, and she told Jenny to see that he got a good meal at night.

Still this was no confession of Mrs Forrester's peculiar timidity, and we urged her to tell us what she thought would frighten her more than anything. She paused, and stirred the fire, and snuffed the candles, and then she said, in a sounding whisper—

"Ghosts!"

She looked at Miss Pole, as much as to say, she had declared it, and would stand by it. Such a look was a challenge in itself. Miss Pole came down upon her with indigestion, spectral illusions, optical delusions, and a great deal out of Dr Ferrier and Dr Hibbert besides. Miss Matty had rather a leaning to ghosts, as I have mentioned before, and what little she did say was all on Mrs Forrester's side, who, emboldened by sympathy, protested that ghosts were a part of her religion; that surely she, the widow of a major in the army, knew what to be frightened at, and what not; in short, I never saw Mrs Forrester so warm either before or since, for she was a gentle, meek, enduring old lady in most things. Not all the elder-wine that ever was mulled could this night wash out the remembrance of this difference between Miss Pole and her hostess. Indeed, when the elder-wine was brought in, it gave rise to a new burst of discussion; for Jenny, the little maiden who staggered under the tray, had to give evidence of having seen a ghost with her own eyes, not so many nights ago, in Darkness Lane, the very lane we were to go through on our way home.

In spite of the uncomfortable feeling which this last consideration gave me, I could not help being amused at Jenny's position, which was exceedingly like that of a witness being examined and cross-examined by two counsel who are not at all scrupulous about asking leading questions. The conclusion I arrived at was, that Jenny had certainly seen something beyond what a fit of indigestion would have caused. A lady all in white, and without her head, was what she deposed and adhered to, supported by a consciousness of the secret sympathy of her mistress under the withering scorn with which Miss Pole regarded her. And not only she, but many others, had seen this headless lady, who sat by the roadside wringing her hands as in deep grief. Mrs Forrester looked at us from time to time with an air of conscious triumph; but then she had not to pass through Darkness Lane before she could bury herself beneath her own familiar bed-clothes.

We preserved a discreet silence as to the headless lady while we were putting on our things to go home, for there was no knowing how near the ghostly head and ears might be, or what spiritual connection they might be keeping up with the unhappy body in Darkness Lane; and, therefore, even Miss Pole felt that it was as well not to speak lightly on such subjects, for fear of vexing or insulting that woebegone trunk. At least, so I conjecture; for, instead of the busy clatter usual in the operation, we tied on our cloaks as sadly as mutes at a funeral. Miss Matty drew the curtains round the windows of the chair to shut out disagreeable sights, and the men (either because they were in spirits that their labours were so nearly ended, or because they were going down hill), set off at such a round and merry pace, that it was all Miss Pole and I could do to keep up with them. She had breath for nothing beyond an imploring "Don't leave me!" uttered as she clutched my arm so tightly that I could not have quitted her, ghost or no ghost. What a relief it was when the men, weary of their burden and their quick trot, stopped just where Headingley Causeway branches off from Darkness Lane! Miss Pole unloosed me and caught at one of the men—

"Could not you—could not you take Miss Matty round by Headingley Causeway?—the pavement in Darkness Lane jolts so, and she is not very strong."

A smothered voice was heard from the inside of the chair—

"Oh! pray go on! What is the matter? What is the matter? I will give you sixpence more to go on very fast; pray don't stop here."

"And I'll give you a shilling," said Miss Pole, with tremulous dignity, "if you'll go by Headingley Causeway."

The two men grunted acquiescence and took up the chair, and went along the causeway, which certainly answered Miss Pole's kind purpose of saving Miss Matty's bones; for it was covered with soft, thick mud, and even a fall there would have been easy till the getting-up came, when there might have been some difficulty in extrication.

CHAPTER XI - SAMUEL BROWN

THE next morning I met Lady Glenmire and Miss Pole setting out on a long walk to find some old woman who was famous in the neighbourhood for her skill in knitting woollen stockings. Miss Pole said to me, with a smile half-kindly and half-contemptuous upon her countenance, "I have been just telling Lady Glenmire of our poor friend Mrs Forrester, and her terror of ghosts. It comes from living so much alone, and listening to the bug-a-boo stories of that Jenny of hers." She was so calm and so much above superstitious fears herself that I was almost ashamed to say how glad I had been of her Headingley Causeway proposition the night before, and turned off the conversation to something else.

In the afternoon Miss Pole called on Miss Matty to tell her of the adventure—the real adventure they had met with on their morning's walk. They had been perplexed about the exact path which they were to take across the fields in order to find the knitting old woman, and had stopped to inquire at a little wayside public-house, standing on the high road to London, about three miles from Cranford. The good woman had asked them to sit down and rest themselves while she fetched her husband, who could direct them better than she could; and, while they were sitting in the sanded parlour, a little girl came in. They thought that she belonged to the landlady, and began some trifling conversation with her; but, on Mrs Roberts's return, she told them that the little thing was the only child of a couple who were staying in the house. And then she began a long story, out of which Lady Glenmire and Miss Pole could only gather one or two decided facts, which were that, about six weeks ago, a light spring-cart had broken down just before their door, in which there were two men, one woman, and this child. One of the men was seriously hurt—no bones broken, only "shaken," the landlady called it; but he had probably sustained some severe internal injury, for he had languished in their house ever since, attended by his wife, the mother of this little girl. Miss Pole had asked what he was, what he looked like. And Mrs Roberts had made answer that he was not like a gentleman, nor yet like a common person; if it had not been that he and his wife were such decent, quiet people, she could almost have thought he was a mountebank, or something of that kind, for they had a great box in the cart, full of she did not know what. She had helped to unpack it, and take out their linen and clothes, when the other man—his twin-brother, she believed he was—had gone off with the horse and cart.

Miss Pole had begun to have her suspicions at this point, and expressed her idea that it was rather strange that the box and cart and horse and all should have disappeared; but good Mrs Roberts seemed to have become quite indignant at Miss Pole's implied suggestion; in fact, Miss Pole said she was as angry as if Miss Pole had told her that she herself was a swindler. As the best way of convincing the ladies, she bethought her of begging them to see the wife; and, as Miss Pole said, there was no doubting the honest, worn, bronzed face of the woman, who at the first tender word from Lady Glenmire, burst into tears, which she was too weak to check until some word from the landlady made her swallow down her sobs, in order that she might testify to the Christian kindness shown by Mr and Mrs Roberts. Miss Pole came round with a swing to as vehement a belief in the sorrowful tale as she had been sceptical before; and, as a proof of this, her energy in the poor sufferer's behalf was nothing daunted when she found out that he, and no other, was our Signor Brunoni, to whom all Cranford had been attributing all manner of evil this six weeks past! Yes! his wife said his proper name was Samuel Brown—"Sam," she called him—but to the last we preferred calling him "the Signor"; it sounded so much better.

The end of their conversation with the Signora Brunoni was that it was agreed that he should be placed under medical advice, and for any expense incurred in procuring this Lady Glenmire promised to hold herself responsible, and had accordingly gone to Mr Hoggins to beg him to ride over to the "Rising Sun" that very afternoon, and examine into the signor's real state; and, as Miss Pole said, if it was desirable to remove him to Cranford to be more immediately under Mr Hoggins's eye, she would undertake to see for lodgings and arrange about the rent. Mrs Roberts had been as kind as could be all throughout, but it was evident that their long residence there had been a slight inconvenience.

Before Miss Pole left us, Miss Matty and I were as full of the morning's adventure as she was. We talked about it all the evening, turning it in every possible light, and we went to bed anxious for the morning, when we should surely hear from someone what Mr Hoggins thought and recommended; for, as Miss Matty observed, though Mr Hoggins did say "Jack's up," "a fig for his heels," and called Preference "Pref." she believed he was a very worthy man and a very clever surgeon. Indeed, we were rather proud of our doctor at Cranford, as a doctor. We often wished, when we heard of Queen Adelaide or the Duke of Wellington being ill, that they would send for Mr Hoggins; but, on consideration, we were rather glad they did not, for, if we were ailing, what should we do if Mr Hoggins had been appointed physician-in-ordinary to the Royal Family? As a surgeon we were proud of him; but as a man—or rather, I should say, as a gentleman—we could only shake our heads over his name and himself, and wished that he had read Lord Chesterfield's Letters in the days when his manners were susceptible of improvement. Nevertheless, we all regarded his dictum in the signor's case as infallible, and when he said that with care and attention he might rally, we had no more fear for him.

But, although we had no more fear, everybody did as much as if there was great cause for anxiety—as indeed there was until Mr Hoggins took charge of him. Miss Pole looked out clean and comfortable, if homely, lodgings; Miss Matty sent the sedan-chair for him, and Martha and I aired it well before it left Cranford by holding a warming-pan full of red-hot coals in it, and then shutting it up close, smoke and all, until the time when he should get into it at the "Rising Sun." Lady Glenmire undertook the medical department under Mr Hoggins's directions, and rummaged up all Mrs Jamieson's medicine glasses, and spoons, and bed-tables, in a free-and-easy way, that made Miss Matty feel a little anxious as to what that lady and Mr Mulliner might say, if they knew. Mrs Forrester made some of the bread-jelly, for which she was so famous, to have ready as a refreshment in the lodgings when he should arrive. A present of this bread-jelly was the highest mark of favour dear Mrs Forrester could confer. Miss Pole had once asked her for the receipt, but she had met with a very decided rebuff; that lady told her that she could not part with it to any one during her life, and that after her death it was bequeathed, as her executors would find, to Miss Matty. What Miss Matty, or, as Mrs Forrester called her (remembering the clause in her will and the dignity of the occasion), Miss Matilda Jenkyns—might choose to do with the receipt when it came into her possession—whether to make it public, or to hand it down as an heirloom—she did not know, nor would she dictate. And a mould of this admirable, digestible, unique bread-jelly was sent by Mrs Forrester to our poor sick conjuror. Who says that the aristocracy are proud? Here was a lady by birth a Tyrrell, and descended from the great Sir Walter that shot King Rufus, and in whose veins ran the blood of him who murdered the little princes in the Tower, going every day to see what dainty dishes she could prepare for Samuel Brown, a mountebank! But, indeed, it was wonderful to see what kind feelings were called out by this poor man's coming amongst us. And also wonderful to see how the great Cranford panic, which had been occasioned by his first coming in his Turkish dress, melted away into thin air on his second coming—pale and feeble, and with his heavy, filmy eyes, that only brightened a very little when they fell upon the countenance of his faithful wife, or their pale and sorrowful little girl.

Somehow we all forgot to be afraid. I daresay it was that finding out that he, who had first excited our love of the marvellous by his unprecedented arts, had not sufficient every-day gifts to manage a shying horse, made us feel as if we were ourselves again. Miss Pole came with her little basket at all hours of the evening, as if her lonely house and the unfrequented road to it had never been infested by that "murderous gang"; Mrs Forrester said she thought that neither Jenny nor she need mind the headless lady who wept and wailed in Darkness Lane, for surely the power was never given to such beings to harm those who went about to try to do what little good was in their power, to which Jenny tremblingly assented; but the mistress's theory had little effect on the maid's practice until she had sewn two pieces of red flannel in the shape of a cross on her inner garment.

I found Miss Matty covering her penny ball—the ball that she used to roll under her bed—with gay-coloured worsted in rainbow stripes.

"My dear," said she, "my heart is sad for that little careworn child. Although her father is a conjuror, she looks as if she had never had a good game of play in her life. I used to make very pretty balls in this way when I was a girl, and I thought I would try if I could not make this one smart and take it to Phoebe this afternoon. I think 'the gang' must have left the neighbourhood, for one does not hear any more of their violence and robbery now."

We were all of us far too full of the signor's precarious state to talk either about robbers or ghosts. Indeed, Lady Glenmire said she never had heard of any actual robberies, except that two little boys had stolen some apples from Farmer Benson's orchard, and that some eggs had been missed on a market-day off Widow Hayward's stall. But that was expecting too much of us; we could not acknowledge that we had only had this small foundation for all our panic. Miss Pole drew herself up at this remark of Lady Glenmire's, and said "that she wished she could agree with her as to the very small reason we had had for alarm, but with the recollection of a man disguised as a woman who had endeavoured to force himself into her house while his confederates waited outside; with the knowledge gained from Lady Glenmire herself, of the footprints seen on Mrs Jamieson's flower borders; with the fact before her of the audacious robbery committed on Mr Hoggins at his own door"—But here Lady Glenmire broke in with a very strong expression of doubt as to whether this last story was not an entire fabrication founded upon the theft of a cat; she grew so red while she was saying all this that I was not surprised at Miss Pole's manner of bridling up, and I am certain, if Lady Glenmire had not been "her ladyship," we should have had a more emphatic contradiction than the "Well, to be sure!" and similar fragmentary ejaculations, which were all that she ventured upon in my lady's presence. But when she was gone Miss Pole began a long congratulation to Miss Matty that so far they had escaped marriage, which she noticed always made people credulous to the last degree; indeed, she thought it argued great natural credulity in a woman if she could not keep herself from being married; and in what Lady Glenmire had said about Mr Hoggins's robbery we had a specimen of what people came to if they gave way to such a weakness; evidently Lady Glenmire would swallow anything if she could believe the poor vamped-up story about a neck of mutton and a pussy with which he had tried to impose on Miss Pole, only she had always been on her guard against believing too much of what men said.

We were thankful, as Miss Pole desired us to be, that we had never been married; but I think, of the two, we were even more thankful that the robbers had left Cranford; at least I judge so from a speech of Miss Matty's that evening, as we sat over the fire, in which she evidently looked upon a husband as a great protector against thieves, burglars, and ghosts; and said that she did not think that she should dare to be always warning young people against matrimony, as Miss Pole did continually; to be sure, marriage was a risk, as she saw, now she had had some experience; but she remembered the time when she had looked forward to being married as much as any one.

"Not to any particular person, my dear," said she, hastily checking herself up, as if she were afraid of having admitted too much; "only the old story, you know, of ladies always saying, '*When* I marry,' and gentlemen, '*If* I marry.'" It was a joke spoken in rather a sad tone, and I doubt if either of us smiled; but I could not see Miss Matty's face by the flickering fire-light. In a little while she continued—

"But, after all, I have not told you the truth. It is so long ago, and no one ever knew how much I thought of it at the time, unless, indeed, my dear mother guessed; but I may say that there was a time when I did not think I should have been only Miss Matty Jenkyns all my life; for even if I did meet with any one who wished to marry me now (and, as Miss Pole says, one is never too safe), I could not take him—I hope he would not take it too much to heart, but I could *not* take him—or any one but the person I once thought I should be married to; and he is dead and gone, and he never knew how it all came about that I said 'No,' when I had thought many and many a time—Well, it's no matter what I thought. God ordains it all, and I am very happy, my dear. No one has such kind friends as I," continued she, taking my hand and holding it in hers.

If I had never known of Mr Holbrook, I could have said something in this pause, but as I had, I could not think of anything that would come in naturally, and so we both kept silence for a little time.

"My father once made us," she began, "keep a diary, in two columns; on one side we were to put down in the morning what we thought would be the course and events of the coming day, and at night we were to put down on the other side what really had happened. It would be to some people rather a sad way of telling their lives," (a tear dropped upon my hand at these words)—"I don't mean that mine has been sad, only so very different to what I expected. I remember, one winter's evening, sitting over our bedroom fire with Deborah—I remember it as if it were yesterday—and we were planning our future lives, both of us were planning, though only she talked about it. She said she should like to marry an archdeacon, and write his charges; and you know, my dear, she never was married, and, for aught I know, she never spoke to an unmarried archdeacon in her life. I never was ambitious, nor could I have written charges, but I thought I could manage a house (my mother used to call me her right hand), and I was always so fond of little children—the shyest babies would stretch out their little arms to come to me; when I was a girl, I was half my leisure time nursing in the neighbouring cottages; but I don't know how it was, when I grew sad and grave—which I did a year or two after this time—the little things drew back from me, and I am afraid I lost the knack, though I am just as fond of children as ever, and have a strange yearning at my heart whenever I see a mother with her baby in her arms. Nay, my dear" (and by a sudden blaze which sprang up from a fall of the unstirred coals, I saw that her eyes were full of tears—gazing intently on some vision of what might have been), "do you know I dream sometimes that I have a little child—always the same—a little girl of about two years old; she never grows older, though I have dreamt about her for many years. I don't think I ever dream of any words or sound she makes; she is very noiseless and still, but she comes to me when she is very sorry or very glad, and I have wakened with the clasp of her dear little arms round my neck. Only last night—perhaps because I had gone to sleep thinking of this ball for Phoebe—my little darling came in my dream, and put up her mouth to be kissed, just as I have seen real babies do to real mothers before going to bed. But all this is nonsense, dear! only don't be frightened by Miss Pole from being married. I can fancy it may be a very happy state, and a little credulity helps one on through life very smoothly—better than always doubting and doubting and seeing difficulties and disagreeables in everything."

If I had been inclined to be daunted from matrimony, it would not have been Miss Pole to do it; it would have been the lot of poor Signor Brunoni and his wife. And yet again, it was an encouragement to see how, through all their cares and sorrows, they thought of each other and not of themselves; and how keen were their joys, if they only passed through each other, or through the little Phoebe.

The signora told me, one day, a good deal about their lives up to this period. It began by my asking her whether Miss Pole's story of the twin-brothers were true; it sounded so wonderful a likeness, that I should have had my doubts, if Miss Pole had not been unmarried. But the signora, or (as we found out she preferred to be called) Mrs Brown, said it was quite true; that her brother-in-law was by many taken for her husband, which was of great assistance to them in their profession; "though," she continued, "how people can mistake Thomas for the real Signor Brunoni, I can't conceive; but he says they do; so I suppose I must believe him. Not but what he is a very good man; I am sure I don't know how we should have paid our bill at the 'Rising Sun' but for the money he sends; but people must know very little about art if they can take him for my husband. Why, Miss, in the ball trick, where my husband spreads his fingers wide, and throws out his little finger with quite an air and a grace, Thomas just clumps up his hand like a fist, and might have ever so many balls hidden in it. Besides, he has never been in India, and knows nothing of the proper sit of a turban."

"Have you been in India?" said I, rather astonished.

"Oh, yes! many a year, ma'am. Sam was a sergeant in the 31st; and when the regiment was ordered to India, I drew a lot to go, and I was more thankful than I can tell; for it seemed as if it would only be a slow death to me to part from my husband. But, indeed, ma'am, if I had known all, I don't know whether I would not rather have died there and then than gone through what I have done since. To be sure, I've been able to comfort Sam, and to be with him; but, ma'am, I've lost six children," said she, looking up at me with those strange eyes that I've never noticed but in mothers of dead children—with a kind of wild look in them, as if seeking for what they never more might find. "Yes! Six children died off, like little buds nipped untimely, in that cruel India. I thought, as each died, I never could—I never would—love a child again; and when the next came, it had not only its own love, but the deeper love that came from the thoughts of its little dead brothers and sisters. And when Phoebe was coming, I said to my husband, 'Sam, when the child is born, and I am strong, I shall leave you; it will cut my heart cruel; but if this baby dies too, I shall go mad; the madness is in me now; but if you let me go down to Calcutta, carrying my baby step by step, it will, maybe, work itself off; and I will save, and I will hoard, and I will beg—and I will die, to get a passage home to England, where our baby may live?' God bless him! he said I might go; and he saved up his pay, and I saved every pice I could get for washing or any way; and when Phoebe came, and I grew strong again, I set off. It was very lonely; through the thick forests, dark again with their heavy trees—along by the river's side (but I had been brought up near the Avon in Warwickshire, so that flowing noise sounded like home)—from station to station, from Indian village to village, I went along, carrying my child. I had seen one of the officer's ladies with a little picture, ma'am—done by a Catholic foreigner, ma'am—of the Virgin and the little Saviour, ma'am. She had him on her arm, and her form was softly curled round him, and their cheeks touched. Well, when I went to bid good-bye to this lady, for whom I had washed, she cried sadly; for she, too, had lost her children, but she had not another to save, like me; and I was bold enough to ask her would she give me that print. And she cried the more, and said her children were with that little blessed Jesus; and gave it me, and told me that she had heard it had been painted on the bottom of a cask, which made it have that round shape. And when my body was very weary, and my heart was sick (for there were times when I misdoubted if I could ever reach my home, and there were times when I thought of my husband, and one time when I thought my baby was dying), I took out that picture and looked at it, till I could have thought the mother spoke to me, and comforted me. And the natives were very kind. We could not understand one another; but they saw my baby on my breast, and they came out to me, and brought me rice and milk, and sometimes flowers—I have got some of the flowers dried. Then, the next morning, I was so tired; and they wanted me to stay with them—I could tell that—and tried to frighten me from going into the deep woods, which, indeed, looked very strange and dark; but it seemed to me as if Death was following me to take my baby away from me; and as if I must go on, and on—and I thought how God had cared for mothers ever since the world was made, and would care for me; so I bade them good-bye, and set off afresh. And once when my baby was ill, and both she and I needed rest, He led me to a place where I found a kind Englishman lived, right in the midst of the natives."

"And you reached Calcutta safely at last?"

"Yes, safely! Oh! when I knew I had only two days' journey more before me, I could not help it, ma'am—it might be idolatry, I cannot tell—but I was near one of the native temples, and I went into it with my baby to thank God for His great mercy; for it seemed to me that where others had prayed before to their God, in their joy or in their agony, was of itself a sacred place. And I got as servant to an invalid lady, who grew quite fond of my baby aboard-ship; and, in two years' time, Sam earned his discharge, and came home to me, and to our child. Then he had to fix on a trade; but he knew of none; and once, once upon a time, he had learnt some tricks from an Indian juggler; so he set up conjuring, and it answered so well that he took Thomas to help him—as his man, you know, not as another conjuror, though Thomas has set it up now on his own hook. But it has been a great help to us that likeness between the twins, and made a good many tricks go off well that they made up together. And Thomas is a good brother, only he has not the fine carriage of my husband, so that I can't think how he can be taken for Signor Brunoni himself, as he says he is."

"Poor little Phoebe!" said I, my thoughts going back to the baby she carried all those hundred miles.

"Ah! you may say so! I never thought I should have reared her, though, when she fell ill at Chunderabaddad; but that good, kind Aga Jenkyns took us in, which I believe was the very saving of her."

"Jenkyns!" said I.

"Yes, Jenkyns. I shall think all people of that name are kind; for here is that nice old lady who comes every day to take Phoebe a walk!"

But an idea had flashed through my head; could the Aga Jenkyns be the lost Peter? True he was reported by many to be dead. But, equally true, some had said that he had arrived at the dignity of Great Lama of Thibet. Miss Matty thought he was alive. I would make further inquiry.

CHAPTER XII - ENGAGED TO BE MARRIED

WAS the "poor Peter" of Cranford the Aga Jenkyns of Chunderabaddad, or was he not? As somebody says, that was the question.

In my own home, whenever people had nothing else to do, they blamed me for want of discretion. Indiscretion was my bug-bear fault. Everybody has a bug-bear fault, a sort of standing characteristic—a *pièce de résistance* for their friends to cut at; and in general they cut and come again. I was tired of being called indiscreet and incautious; and I determined for once to prove myself a model of prudence and wisdom. I would not even hint my suspicions respecting the Aga. I would collect evidence and carry it home to lay before my father, as the family friend of the two Miss Jenkynses.

In my search after facts, I was often reminded of a description my father had once given of a ladies' committee that he had had to preside over. He said he could not help thinking of a passage in Dickens, which spoke of a chorus in which every man took the tune he knew best, and sang it to his own satisfaction. So, at this charitable committee, every lady took the subject uppermost in her mind, and talked about it to her own great contentment, but not much to the advancement of the subject they had met to discuss. But even that committee could have been nothing to the Cranford ladies when I attempted to gain some clear and definite information as to poor Peter's height, appearance, and when and where he was seen and heard of last. For instance, I remember asking Miss Pole (and I thought the question was very opportune, for I put it when I met her at a call at Mrs Forrester's, and both the ladies had known Peter, and I imagined that they might refresh each other's memories)—I asked Miss Pole what was the very last thing they had ever heard about him; and then she named the absurd report to which I have alluded, about his having been elected Great Lama of Thibet; and this was a signal for each lady to go off on her separate idea. Mrs Forrester's start was made on the veiled prophet in Lalla Rookh—whether I thought he was meant for the Great Lama, though Peter was not so ugly, indeed rather handsome, if he had not been freckled. I was thankful to see her double upon Peter; but, in a moment, the delusive lady was off upon Rowland's Kalydor, and the merits of cosmetics and hair oils in general, and holding forth so fluently that I turned to listen to Miss Pole, who (through the llamas, the beasts of burden) had got to Peruvian bonds, and the share market, and her poor opinion of joint-stock banks in general, and of that one in particular in which Miss Matty's money was invested. In vain I put in "When was it—in what year was it that you heard that Mr Peter was the Great Lama?" They only joined issue to dispute whether llamas were carnivorous animals or not; in which dispute they were not quite on fair grounds, as Mrs Forrester (after they had grown warm and cool again) acknowledged that she always confused carnivorous and graminivorous together, just as she did horizontal and perpendicular; but then she apologised for it very prettily, by saying that in her day the only use people made of four-syllabled words was to teach how they should be spelt.

The only fact I gained from this conversation was that certainly Peter had last been heard of in India, "or that neighbourhood"; and that this scanty intelligence of his whereabouts had reached Cranford in the year when Miss Pole had brought her Indian muslin gown, long since worn out (we washed it and mended it, and traced its decline and fall into a window-blind before we could go on); and in a year when Wombwell came to Cranford, because Miss Matty had wanted to see an elephant in order that she might the better imagine Peter riding on one; and had seen a boa-constrictor too, which was more than she wished to imagine in her fancy-pictures of Peter's locality; and in a year when Miss Jenkyns had learnt some piece of poetry off by heart, and used to say, at all the Cranford parties, how Peter was "surveying mankind from China to Peru," which everybody had thought very grand, and rather appropriate, because India was between China and Peru, if you took care to turn the globe to the left instead of the right.

I suppose all these inquiries of mine, and the consequent curiosity excited in the minds of my friends, made us blind and deaf to what was going on around us. It seemed to me as if the sun rose and shone, and as if the rain rained on Cranford, just as usual, and I did not notice any sign of the times that could be considered as a prognostic of any uncommon event; and, to the best of my belief, not only Miss Matty and Mrs Forrester, but even Miss Pole herself, whom we looked upon as a kind of prophetess, from the knack she had of foreseeing things before they came to pass—although she did not like to disturb her friends by telling them her foreknowledge—even Miss Pole herself was breathless with astonishment when she came to tell us of the astounding piece of news. But I must recover myself; the contemplation of it, even at this distance of time, has taken away my breath and my grammar, and unless I subdue my emotion, my spelling will go too.

We were sitting—Miss Matty and I—much as usual, she in the blue chintz easy-chair, with her back to the light, and her knitting in her hand, I reading aloud the *St James's Chronicle*. A few minutes more, and we should have gone to make the little alterations in dress usual before calling-time (twelve o'clock) in Cranford. I remember the scene and the date well. We had been talking of the signor's rapid recovery since the warmer weather had set in, and praising Mr Hoggins's skill, and lamenting his want of refinement and manner (it seems a curious coincidence that this should have been our subject, but so it was), when a knock was heard—a caller's knock—three distinct taps—and we were flying (that is to say, Miss Matty could not walk very fast, having had a touch of rheumatism) to our rooms, to change cap and collars, when Miss Pole arrested us by calling out, as she came up the stairs, "Don't go—I can't wait—it is not twelve, I know—but never mind your dress—I must speak to you." We did our best to look as if it was not we who had made the hurried movement, the sound of which she had heard; for, of course, we did not like to have it supposed that we had any old clothes that it was convenient to wear out in the "sanctuary of home," as Miss Jenkyns once prettily called the back parlour, where she was tying up preserves. So we threw our gentility with double force into our manners, and very genteel we were for two minutes while Miss Pole recovered breath, and excited our curiosity strongly by lifting up her hands in amazement, and bringing them down in silence, as if what she had to say was too big for words, and could only be expressed by pantomime.

"What do you think, Miss Matty? What *do* you think? Lady Glenmire is to marry—is to be married, I mean—Lady Glenmire—Mr Hoggins—Mr Hoggins is going to marry Lady Glenmire!"

"Marry!" said we. "Marry! Madness!"

"Marry!" said Miss Pole, with the decision that belonged to her character. "*I* said marry! as you do; and I also said, 'What a fool my lady is going to make of herself!' I could have said 'Madness!' but I controlled myself, for it was in a public shop that I heard of it. Where feminine delicacy is gone to, I don't know! You and I, Miss Matty, would have been ashamed to have known that our marriage was spoken of in a grocer's shop, in the hearing of shopmen!"

"But," said Miss Matty, sighing as one recovering from a blow, "perhaps it is not true. Perhaps we are doing her injustice."

"No," said Miss Pole. "I have taken care to ascertain that. I went straight to Mrs Fitz-Adam, to borrow a cookery-book which I knew she had; and I introduced my congratulations *à propos* of the difficulty gentlemen must have in house-keeping; and Mrs Fitz-Adam bridled up, and said that she believed it was true, though how and where I could have heard it she did not know. She said her brother and Lady Glenmire had come to an understanding at last. 'Understanding!' such a coarse word! But my lady will have to come down to many a want of refinement. I have reason to believe Mr Hoggins sups on bread-and-cheese and beer every night.

"Marry!" said Miss Matty once again. "Well! I never thought of it. Two people that we know going to be married. It's coming very near!"

"So near that my heart stopped beating when I heard of it, while you might have counted twelve," said Miss Pole.

"One does not know whose turn may come next. Here, in Cranford, poor Lady Glenmire might have thought herself safe," said Miss Matty, with a gentle pity in her tones.

"Bah!" said Miss Pole, with a toss of her head. "Don't you remember poor dear Captain Brown's song 'Tibbie Fowler,' and the line—

'Set her on the Tintock tap,
The wind will blaw a man till her.'"

"That was because 'Tibbie Fowler' was rich, I think."

"Well! there was a kind of attraction about Lady Glenmire that I, for one, should be ashamed to have."

I put in my wonder. "But how can she have fancied Mr Hoggins? I am not surprised that Mr Hoggins has liked her."

"Oh! I don't know. Mr Hoggins is rich, and very pleasant-looking," said Miss Matty, "and very good-tempered and kind-hearted."

"She has married for an establishment, that's it. I suppose she takes the surgery with it," said Miss Pole, with a little dry laugh at her own joke. But, like many people who think they have made a severe and sarcastic speech, which yet is clever of its kind, she began to relax in her grimness from the moment when she made this allusion to the surgery; and we turned to speculate on the way in which Mrs Jamieson would receive the news. The person whom she had left in charge of her house to keep off followers from her maids to set up a follower of her own! And that follower a man whom Mrs Jamieson had tabooed as vulgar, and inadmissible to Cranford society, not merely on account of his name, but because of his voice, his complexion, his boots, smelling of the stable, and himself, smelling of drugs. Had he ever been to see Lady Glenmire at Mrs Jamieson's? Chloride of lime would not purify the house in its owner's estimation if he had. Or had their interviews been confined to the occasional meetings in the chamber of the poor sick conjuror, to whom, with all our sense of the *mésalliance*, we could not help allowing that they had both been exceedingly kind? And now it turned out that a servant of Mrs Jamieson's had been ill, and Mr Hoggins had been attending her for some weeks. So the wolf had got into the fold, and now he was carrying off the shepherdess. What would Mrs Jamieson say? We looked into the darkness of futurity as a child gazes after a rocket up in the cloudy sky, full of wondering expectation of the rattle, the discharge, and the brilliant shower of sparks and light. Then we brought ourselves down to earth and the present time by questioning each other (being all equally ignorant, and all equally without the slightest data to build any conclusions upon) as to when IT would take place? Where? How much a year Mr Hoggins had? Whether she would drop her title? And how Martha and the other correct servants in Cranford would ever be brought to announce a married couple as Lady Glenmire and Mr Hoggins? But would they be visited? Would Mrs Jamieson let us? Or must we choose between the Honourable Mrs Jamieson and the degraded Lady Glenmire? We all liked Lady Glenmire the best. She was bright, and kind, and sociable, and agreeable; and Mrs Jamieson was dull, and inert, and pompous, and tiresome. But we had acknowledged the sway of the latter so long, that it seemed like a kind of disloyalty now even to meditate disobedience to the prohibition we anticipated.

Mrs Forrester surprised us in our darned caps and patched collars; and we forgot all about them in our eagerness to see how she would bear the information, which we honourably left to Miss Pole, to impart, although, if we had been inclined to take unfair advantage, we might have rushed in ourselves, for she had a most out-of-place fit of coughing for five minutes after Mrs Forrester entered the room. I shall never forget the imploring expression of her eyes, as she looked at us over her pocket-handkerchief. They said, as plain as words could speak, "Don't let Nature deprive me of the treasure which is mine, although for a time I can make no use of it." And we did not.

Mrs Forrester's surprise was equal to ours; and her sense of injury rather greater, because she had to feel for her Order, and saw more fully than we could do how such conduct brought stains on the aristocracy.

When she and Miss Pole left us we endeavoured to subside into calmness; but Miss Matty was really upset by the intelligence she had heard. She reckoned it up, and it was more than fifteen years since she had heard of any of her acquaintance going to be married, with the one exception of Miss Jessie Brown; and, as she said, it gave her quite a shock, and made her feel as if she could not think what would happen next.

I don't know whether it is a fancy of mine, or a real fact, but I have noticed that, just after the announcement of an engagement in any set, the unmarried ladies in that set flutter out in an unusual gaiety and newness of dress, as much as to say, in a tacit and unconscious manner, "We also are spinsters." Miss Matty and Miss Pole talked and thought more about bonnets, gowns, caps, and shawls, during the fortnight that succeeded this call, than I had known them do for years before. But it might be the spring weather, for it was a warm and pleasant March; and merinoes and beavers, and woollen materials of all sorts were but ungracious receptacles of the bright sun's glancing rays. It had not been Lady Glenmire's dress that had won Mr Hoggins's heart, for she went about on her errands of kindness more shabby than ever. Although in the hurried glimpses I caught of her at church or elsewhere she appeared rather to shun meeting any of her friends, her face seemed to have almost something of the flush of youth in it; her lips looked redder and more trembling full than in their old compressed state, and her eyes dwelt on all things with a lingering light, as if she was learning to love Cranford and its belongings. Mr Hoggins looked broad and radiant, and creaked up the middle aisle at church in a brand-new pair of top-boots—an audible, as well as visible, sign of his purposed change of state; for the tradition went, that the boots he had worn till now were the identical pair in which he first set out on his rounds in Cranford twenty-five years ago; only they had been new-pieced, high and low, top and bottom, heel and sole, black leather and brown leather, more times than any one could tell.

None of the ladies in Cranford chose to sanction the marriage by congratulating either of the parties. We wished to ignore the whole affair until our liege lady, Mrs Jamieson, returned. Till she came back to give us our cue, we felt that it would be better to consider the engagement in the same light as the Queen of Spain's legs—facts which certainly existed, but the less said about the better. This restraint upon our tongues—for you see if we did not speak about it to any of the parties concerned, how could we get answers to the questions that we longed to ask?—was beginning to be irksome, and our idea of the dignity of silence was paling before our curiosity, when another direction was given to our thoughts, by an announcement on the part of the principal shopkeeper of Cranford, who ranged the trades from grocer and cheesemonger to man-milliner, as occasion required, that the spring fashions were arrived, and would be exhibited on the following Tuesday at his rooms in High Street. Now Miss Matty had been only waiting for this before buying herself a new silk gown. I had offered, it is true, to send to Drumble for patterns, but she had rejected my proposal, gently implying that she had not forgotten her disappointment about the sea-green turban. I was thankful that I was on the spot now, to counteract the dazzling fascination of any yellow or scarlet silk.

I must say a word or two here about myself. I have spoken of my father's old friendship for the Jenkyns family; indeed, I am not sure if there was not some distant relationship. He had willingly allowed me to remain all the winter at Cranford, in consideration of a letter which Miss Matty had written to him about the time of the panic, in which I suspect she had exaggerated my powers and my bravery as a defender of the house. But now that the days were longer and more cheerful, he was beginning to urge the necessity of my return; and I only delayed in a sort of odd forlorn hope that if I could obtain any clear information, I might make the account given by the signora of the Aga Jenkyns tally with that of "poor Peter," his appearance and disappearance, which I had winnowed out of the conversation of Miss Pole and Mrs Forrester.

CHAPTER XIII - STOPPED PAYMENT

THE very Tuesday morning on which Mr Johnson was going to show the fashions, the post-woman brought two letters to the house. I say the post-woman, but I should say the postman's wife. He was a lame shoemaker, a very clean, honest man, much respected in the town; but he never brought the letters round except on unusual occasions, such as Christmas Day or Good Friday; and on those days the letters, which should have been delivered at eight in the morning, did not make their appearance until two or three in the afternoon, for every one liked poor Thomas, and gave him a welcome on these festive occasions. He used to say, "He was welly stawed wi' eating, for there were three or four houses where nowt would serve 'em but he must share in their breakfast;" and by the time he had done his last breakfast, he came to some other friend who was beginning dinner; but come what might in the way of temptation, Tom was always sober, civil, and smiling; and, as Miss Jenkyns used to say, it was a lesson in patience, that she doubted not would call out that precious quality in some minds, where, but for Thomas, it might have lain dormant and undiscovered. Patience was certainly very dormant in Miss Jenkyns's mind. She was always expecting letters, and always drumming on the table till the post-woman had called or gone past. On Christmas Day and Good Friday she drummed from breakfast till church, from church-time till two o'clock—unless when the fire wanted stirring, when she invariably knocked down the fire-irons, and scolded Miss Matty for it. But equally certain was the hearty welcome and the good dinner for Thomas; Miss Jenkyns standing over him like a bold dragoon, questioning him as to his children—what they were doing—what school they went to; upbraiding him if another was likely to make its appearance, but sending even the little babies the shilling and the mince-pie which was her gift to all the children, with half-a-crown in addition for both father and mother. The post was not half of so much consequence to dear Miss Matty; but not for the world would she have diminished Thomas's welcome and his dole, though I could see that she felt rather shy over the ceremony, which had been regarded by Miss Jenkyns as a glorious opportunity for giving advice and benefiting her fellow-creatures. Miss Matty would steal the money all in a lump into his hand, as if she were ashamed of herself. Miss Jenkyns gave him each individual coin separate, with a "There! that's for yourself; that's for Jenny," etc. Miss Matty would even beckon Martha out of the kitchen while he ate his food: and once, to my knowledge, winked at its rapid disappearance into a blue cotton pocket-handkerchief. Miss Jenkyns almost scolded him if he did not leave a clean plate, however heaped it might have been, and gave an injunction with every mouthful.

I have wandered a long way from the two letters that awaited us on the breakfast-table that Tuesday morning. Mine was from my father. Miss Matty's was printed. My father's was just a man's letter; I mean it was very dull, and gave no information beyond that he was well, that they had had a good deal of rain, that trade was very stagnant, and there were many disagreeable rumours afloat. He then asked me if I knew whether Miss Matty still retained her shares in the Town and County Bank, as there were very unpleasant reports about it; though nothing more than he had always foreseen, and had prophesied to Miss Jenkyns years ago, when she would invest their little property in it—the only unwise step that clever woman had ever taken, to his knowledge (the only time she ever acted against his advice, I knew). However, if anything had gone wrong, of course I was not to think of leaving Miss Matty while I could be of any use, etc.

"Who is your letter from, my dear? Mine is a very civil invitation, signed 'Edwin Wilson,' asking me to attend an important meeting of the shareholders of the Town and County Bank, to be held in Drumble, on Thursday the twenty-first. I am sure, it is very attentive of them to remember me."

I did not like to hear of this "important meeting," for, though I did not know much about business, I feared it confirmed what my father said: however, I thought, ill news always came fast enough, so I resolved to say nothing about my alarm, and merely told her that my father was well, and sent his kind regards to her. She kept turning over and admiring her letter. At last she spoke—

"I remember their sending one to Deborah just like this; but that I did not wonder at, for everybody knew she was so clear-headed. I am afraid I could not help them much; indeed, if they came to accounts, I should be quite in the way, for I never could do sums in my head. Deborah, I know, rather wished to go, and went so far as to order a new bonnet for the occasion: but when the time came she had a bad cold; so they sent her a very polite account of what they had done. Chosen a director, I think it was. Do you think they want me to help them to choose a director? I am sure I should choose your father at once!'

"My father has no shares in the bank," said I.

"Oh, no! I remember. He objected very much to Deborah's buying any, I believe. But she was quite the woman of business, and always judged for herself; and here, you see, they have paid eight per cent. all these years."

It was a very uncomfortable subject to me, with my half-knowledge; so I thought I would change the conversation, and I asked at what time she thought we had better go and see the fashions. "Well, my dear," she said, "the thing is this: it is not etiquette to go till after twelve; but then, you see, all Cranford will be there, and one does not like to be too curious about dress and trimmings and caps with all the world looking on. It is never genteel to be over-curious on these occasions. Deborah had the knack of always looking as if the latest fashion was nothing new to her; a manner she had caught from Lady Arley, who did see all the new modes in London, you know. So I thought we would just slip down—for I do want this morning, soon after breakfast half-a-pound of tea—and then we could go up and examine the things at our leisure, and see exactly how my new silk gown must be made; and then, after twelve, we could go with our minds disengaged, and free from thoughts of dress."

We began to talk of Miss Matty's new silk gown. I discovered that it would be really the first time in her life that she had had to choose anything of consequence for herself: for Miss Jenkyns had always been the more decided character, whatever her taste might have been; and it is astonishing how such people carry the world before them by the mere force of will. Miss Matty anticipated the sight of the glossy folds with as much delight as if the five sovereigns, set apart for the purchase, could buy all the silks in the shop; and (remembering my own loss of two hours in a toyshop before I could tell on what wonder to spend a silver threepence) I was very glad that we were going early, that dear Miss Matty might have leisure for the delights of perplexity.

If a happy sea-green could be met with, the gown was to be sea-green: if not, she inclined to maize, and I to silver gray; and we discussed the requisite number of breadths until we arrived at the shop-door. We were to buy the tea, select the silk, and then clamber up the iron corkscrew stairs that led into what was once a loft, though now a fashion show-room.

The young men at Mr Johnson's had on their best looks; and their best cravats, and pivoted themselves over the counter with surprising activity. They wanted to show us upstairs at once; but on the principle of business first and pleasure afterwards, we stayed to purchase the tea. Here Miss Matty's absence of mind betrayed itself. If she was made aware that she had been drinking green tea at any time, she always thought it her duty to lie awake half through the night afterward (I have known her take it in ignorance many a time without such effects), and consequently green tea was prohibited the house; yet to-day she herself asked for the obnoxious article, under the impression that she was talking about the silk. However, the mistake was soon rectified; and then the silks were unrolled in good truth. By this time the shop was pretty well filled, for it was Cranford market-day, and many of the farmers and country people from the neighbourhood round came in, sleeking down their hair, and glancing shyly about, from under their eyelids, as anxious to take back some notion of the unusual gaiety to the mistress or the lasses at home, and yet feeling that they were out of place among the smart shopmen and gay shawls and summer prints. One honest-looking man, however, made his way up to the counter at which we stood, and boldly asked to look at a shawl or two. The other country folk confined themselves to the grocery side; but our neighbour was evidently too full of some kind intention towards mistress, wife or daughter, to be shy; and it soon became a question with me, whether he or Miss Matty would keep their shopmen the longest time. He thought each shawl more beautiful than the last; and, as for Miss Matty, she smiled and sighed over each fresh bale that was brought out; one colour set off another, and the heap together would, as she said, make even the rainbow look poor.

"I am afraid," said she, hesitating, "Whichever I choose I shall wish I had taken another. Look at this lovely crimson! it would be so warm in winter. But spring is coming on, you know. I wish I could have a gown for every season," said she, dropping her voice—as we all did in Cranford whenever we talked of anything we wished for but could not afford. "However," she continued in a louder and more cheerful tone, "it would give me a great deal of trouble to take care of them if I had them; so, I think, I'll only take one. But which must it be, my dear?"

And now she hovered over a lilac with yellow spots, while I pulled out a quiet sage-green that had faded into insignificance under the more brilliant colours, but which was nevertheless a good silk in its humble way. Our attention was called off to our neighbour. He had chosen a shawl of about thirty shillings' value; and his face looked broadly happy, under the anticipation, no doubt, of the pleasant surprise he would give to some Molly or Jenny at home; he had tugged a leathern purse out of his breeches-pocket, and had offered a five-pound note in payment for the shawl, and for some parcels which had been brought round to him from the grocery counter; and it was just at this point that he attracted our notice. The shopman was examining the note with a puzzled, doubtful air.

"Town and County Bank! I am not sure, sir, but I believe we have received a warning against notes issued by this bank only this morning. I will just step and ask Mr Johnson, sir; but I'm afraid I must trouble you for payment in cash, or in a note of a different bank."

I never saw a man's countenance fall so suddenly into dismay and bewilderment. It was almost piteous to see the rapid change.

"Dang it!" said he, striking his fist down on the table, as if to try which was the harder, "the chap talks as if notes and gold were to be had for the picking up."

Miss Matty had forgotten her silk gown in her interest for the man. I don't think she had caught the name of the bank, and in my nervous cowardice I was anxious that she should not; and so I began admiring the yellow-spotted lilac gown that I had been utterly condemning only a minute before. But it was of no use.

"What bank was it? I mean, what bank did your note belong to?"

"Town and County Bank."

"Let me see it," said she quietly to the shopman, gently taking it out of his hand, as he brought it back to return it to the farmer.

Mr Johnson was very sorry, but, from information he had received, the notes issued by that bank were little better than waste paper.

"I don't understand it," said Miss Matty to me in a low voice. "That is our bank, is it not?—the Town and County Bank?"

"Yes," said I. "This lilac silk will just match the ribbons in your new cap, I believe," I continued, holding up the folds so as to catch the light, and wishing that the man would make haste and be gone, and yet having a new wonder, that had only just sprung up, how far it was wise or right in me to allow Miss Matty to make this expensive purchase, if the affairs of the bank were really so bad as the refusal of the note implied.

But Miss Matty put on the soft dignified manner, peculiar to her, rarely used, and yet which became her so well, and laying her hand gently on mine, she said—

"Never mind the silks for a few minutes, dear. I don't understand you, sir," turning now to the shopman, who had been attending to the farmer. "Is this a forged note?"

"Oh, no, ma'am. It is a true note of its kind; but you see, ma'am, it is a joint-stock bank, and there are reports out that it is likely to break. Mr Johnson is only doing his duty, ma'am, as I am sure Mr Dobson knows."

But Mr Dobson could not respond to the appealing bow by any answering smile. He was turning the note absently over in his fingers, looking gloomily enough at the parcel containing the lately-chosen shawl.

"It's hard upon a poor man," said he, "as earns every farthing with the sweat of his brow. However, there's no help for it. You must take back your shawl, my man; Lizzle must go on with her cloak for a while. And yon figs for the little ones—I promised them to 'em—I'll take them; but the 'bacco, and the other things"—

"I will give you five sovereigns for your note, my good man," said Miss Matty. "I think there is some great mistake about it, for I am one of the shareholders, and I'm sure they would have told me if things had not been going on right."

The shopman whispered a word or two across the table to Miss Matty. She looked at him with a dubious air.

"Perhaps so," said she. "But I don't pretend to understand business; I only know that if it is going to fail, and if honest people are to lose their money because they have taken our notes—I can't explain myself," said she, suddenly becoming aware that she had got into a long sentence with four people for audience; "only I would rather exchange my gold for the note, if you please," turning to the farmer, "and then you can take your wife the shawl. It is only going without my gown a few days longer," she continued, speaking to me. "Then, I have no doubt, everything will be cleared up."

"But if it is cleared up the wrong way?" said I.

"Why, then it will only have been common honesty in me, as a shareholder, to have given this good man the money. I am quite clear about it in my own mind; but, you know, I can never speak quite as comprehensibly as others can, only you must give me your note, Mr Dobson, if you please, and go on with your purchases with these sovereigns."

The man looked at her with silent gratitude—too awkward to put his thanks into words; but he hung back for a minute or two, fumbling with his note.

"I'm loth to make another one lose instead of me, if it is a loss; but, you see, five pounds is a deal of money to a man with a family; and, as you say, ten to one in a day or two the note will be as good as gold again."

"No hope of that, my friend," said the shopman.

"The more reason why I should take it," said Miss Matty quietly. She pushed her sovereigns towards the man, who slowly laid his note down in exchange. "Thank you. I will wait a day or two before I purchase any of these silks; perhaps you will then have a greater choice. My dear, will you come upstairs?"

We inspected the fashions with as minute and curious an interest as if the gown to be made after them had been bought. I could not see that the little event in the shop below had in the least damped Miss Matty's curiosity as to the make of sleeves or the sit of skirts. She once or twice exchanged congratulations with me on our private and leisurely view of the bonnets and shawls; but I was, all the time, not so sure that our examination was so utterly private, for I caught glimpses of a figure dodging behind the cloaks and mantles; and, by a dexterous move, I came face to face with Miss Pole, also in morning costume (the principal feature of which was her being without teeth, and wearing a veil to conceal the deficiency), come on the same errand as ourselves. But she quickly took her departure, because, as she said, she had a bad headache, and did not feel herself up to conversation.

As we came down through the shop, the civil Mr Johnson was awaiting us; he had been informed of the exchange of the note for gold, and with much good feeling and real kindness, but with a little want of tact, he wished to condole with Miss Matty, and impress upon her the true state of the case. I could only hope that he had heard an exaggerated rumour for he said that her shares were worse than nothing, and that the bank could not pay a shilling in the pound. I was glad that Miss Matty seemed still a little incredulous; but I could not tell how much of this was real or assumed, with that self-control which seemed habitual to ladies of Miss Matty's standing in Cranford, who would have thought their dignity compromised by the slightest expression of surprise, dismay, or any similar feeling to an inferior in station, or in a public shop. However, we walked home very silently. I am ashamed to say, I believe I was rather vexed and annoyed at Miss Matty's conduct in taking the note to herself so decidedly. I had so set my heart upon her having a new silk gown, which she wanted sadly; in general she was so undecided anybody might turn her round; in this case I had felt that it was no use attempting it, but I was not the less put out at the result.

Somehow, after twelve o'clock, we both acknowledged to a sated curiosity about the fashions, and to a certain fatigue of body (which was, in fact, depression of mind) that indisposed us to go out again. But still we never spoke of the note; till, all at once, something possessed me to ask Miss Matty if she would think it her duty to offer sovereigns for all the notes of the Town and County Bank she met with? I could have bitten my tongue out the minute I had said it. She looked up rather sadly, and as if I had thrown a new perplexity into her already distressed mind; and for a minute or two she did not speak. Then she said—my own dear Miss Matty—without a shade of reproach in her voice—

"My dear, I never feel as if my mind was what people call very strong; and it's often hard enough work for me to settle what I ought to do with the case right before me. I was very thankful to—I was very thankful, that I saw my duty this morning, with the poor man standing by me; but its rather a strain upon me to keep thinking and thinking what I should do if such and such a thing happened; and, I believe, I had rather wait and see what really does come; and I don't doubt I shall be helped then if I don't fidget myself, and get too anxious beforehand. You know, love, I'm not like Deborah. If Deborah had lived, I've no doubt she would have seen after them, before they had got themselves into this state."

We had neither of us much appetite for dinner, though we tried to talk cheerfully about indifferent things. When we returned into the drawing-room, Miss Matty unlocked her desk and began to look over her account-books. I was so penitent for what I had said in the morning, that I did not choose to take upon myself the presumption to suppose that I could assist her; I rather left her alone, as, with puzzled brow, her eye followed her pen up and down the ruled page. By-and-by she shut the book, locked the desk, and came and drew a chair to mine, where I sat in moody sorrow over the fire. I stole my hand into hers; she clasped it, but did not speak a word. At last she said, with forced composure in her voice, "If that bank goes wrong, I shall lose one hundred and forty-nine pounds thirteen shillings and fourpence a year; I shall only have thirteen pounds a year left." I squeezed her hand hard and tight. I did not know what to say. Presently (it was too dark to see her face) I felt her fingers work convulsively in my grasp; and I knew she was going to speak again. I heard the sobs in her voice as she said, "I hope it's not wrong—not wicked—but, oh! I am so glad poor Deborah is spared this. She could not have borne to come down in the world—she had such a noble, lofty spirit."

This was all she said about the sister who had insisted upon investing their little property in that unlucky bank. We were later in lighting the candle than usual that night, and until that light shamed us into speaking, we sat together very silently and sadly.

However, we took to our work after tea with a kind of forced cheerfulness (which soon became real as far as it went), talking of that never-ending wonder, Lady Glenmire's engagement. Miss Matty was almost coming round to think it a good thing.

"I don't mean to deny that men are troublesome in a house. I don't judge from my own experience, for my father was neatness itself, and wiped his shoes on coming in as carefully as any woman; but still a man has a sort of knowledge of what should be done in difficulties, that it is very pleasant to have one at hand ready to lean upon. Now, Lady Glenmire, instead of being tossed about, and wondering where she is to settle, will be certain of a home among pleasant and kind people, such as our good Miss Pole and Mrs Forrester. And Mr Hoggins is really a very personable man; and as for his manners, why, if they are not very polished, I have known people with very good hearts and very clever minds too, who were not what some people reckoned refined, but who were both true and tender."

She fell off into a soft reverie about Mr Holbrook, and I did not interrupt her, I was so busy maturing a plan I had had in my mind for some days, but which this threatened failure of the bank had brought to a crisis. That night, after Miss Matty went to bed, I treacherously lighted the candle again, and sat down in the drawing-room to compose a letter to the Aga Jenkyns, a letter which should affect him if he were Peter, and yet seem a mere statement of dry facts if he were a stranger. The church clock pealed out two before I had done.

The next morning news came, both official and otherwise, that the Town and County Bank had stopped payment. Miss Matty was ruined.

She tried to speak quietly to me; but when she came to the actual fact that she would have but about five shillings a week to live upon, she could not restrain a few tears.

"I am not crying for myself, dear," said she, wiping them away; "I believe I am crying for the very silly thought of how my mother would grieve if she could know; she always cared for us so much more than for herself. But many a poor person has less, and I am not very extravagant, and, thank God, when the neck of mutton, and Martha's wages, and the rent are paid, I have not a farthing owing. Poor Martha! I think she'll be sorry to leave me."

Miss Matty smiled at me through her tears, and she would fain have had me see only the smile, not the tears.

CHAPTER XIV - FRIENDS IN NEED

IT was an example to me, and I fancy it might be to many others, to see how immediately Miss Matty set about the retrenchment which she knew to be right under her altered circumstances. While she went down to speak to Martha, and break the intelligence to her, I stole out with my letter to the Aga Jenkyns, and went to the signor's lodgings to obtain the exact address. I bound the signora to secrecy; and indeed her military manners had a degree of shortness and reserve in them which made her always say as little as possible, except when under the pressure of strong excitement. Moreover (which made my secret doubly sure), the signor was now so far recovered as to be looking forward to travelling and conjuring again in the space of a few days, when he, his wife, and little Phoebe would leave Cranford. Indeed, I found him looking over a great black and red placard, in which the Signor Brunoni's accomplishments were set forth, and to which only the name of the town where he would next display them was wanting. He and his wife were so much absorbed in deciding where the red letters would come in with most effect (it might have been the Rubric for that matter), that it was some time before I could get my question asked privately, and not before I had given several decisions, the which I questioned afterwards with equal wisdom of sincerity as soon as the signor threw in his doubts and reasons on the important subject. At last I got the address, spelt by sound, and very queer it looked. I dropped it in the post on my way home, and then for a minute I stood looking at the wooden pane with a gaping slit which divided me from the letter but a moment ago in my hand. It was gone from me like life, never to be recalled. It would get tossed about on the sea, and stained with sea-waves perhaps, and be carried among palm-trees, and scented with all tropical fragrance; the little piece of paper, but an hour ago so familiar and commonplace, had set out on its race to the strange wild countries beyond the Ganges! But I could not afford to lose much time on this speculation. I hastened home, that Miss Matty might not miss me. Martha opened the door to me, her face swollen with crying. As soon as she saw me she burst out afresh, and taking hold of my arm she pulled me in, and banged the door to, in order to ask me if indeed it was all true that Miss Matty had been saying.

"I'll never leave her! No; I won't. I telled her so, and said I could not think how she could find in her heart to give me warning. I could not have had the face to do it, if I'd been her. I might ha' been just as good for nothing as Mrs Fitz-

Adam's Rosy, who struck for wages after living seven years and a half in one place. I said I was not one to go and serve Mammon at that rate; that I knew when I'd got a good missus, if she didn't know when she'd got a good servant"—

"But, Martha," said I, cutting in while she wiped her eyes.

"Don't, 'but Martha' me," she replied to my deprecatory tone.

"Listen to reason"—

"I'll not listen to reason," she said, now in full possession of her voice, which had been rather choked with sobbing. "Reason always means what someone else has got to say. Now I think what I've got to say is good enough reason; but reason or not, I'll say it, and I'll stick to it. I've money in the Savings Bank, and I've a good stock of clothes, and I'm not going to leave Miss Matty. No, not if she gives me warning every hour in the day!"

She put her arms akimbo, as much as to say she defied me; and, indeed, I could hardly tell how to begin to remonstrate with her, so much did I feel that Miss Matty, in her increasing infirmity, needed the attendance of this kind and faithful woman.

"Well"—said I at last.

"I'm thankful you begin with 'well!' If you'd have begun with 'but,' as you did afore, I'd not ha' listened to you. Now you may go on."

"I know you would be a great loss to Miss Matty, Martha"—

"I telled her so. A loss she'd never cease to be sorry for," broke in Martha triumphantly.

"Still, she will have so little—so very little—to live upon, that I don't see just now how she could find you food—she will even be pressed for her own. I tell you this, Martha, because I feel you are like a friend to dear Miss Matty, but you know she might not like to have it spoken about."

Apparently this was even a blacker view of the subject than Miss Matty had presented to her, for Martha just sat down on the first chair that came to hand, and cried out loud (we had been standing in the kitchen).

At last she put her apron down, and looking me earnestly in the face, asked, "Was that the reason Miss Matty wouldn't order a pudding to-day? She said she had no great fancy for sweet things, and you and she would just have a mutton chop. But I'll be up to her. Never you tell, but I'll make her a pudding, and a pudding she'll like, too, and I'll pay for it myself; so mind you see she eats it. Many a one has been comforted in their sorrow by seeing a good dish come upon the table."

I was rather glad that Martha's energy had taken the immediate and practical direction of pudding-making, for it staved off the quarrelsome discussion as to whether she should or should not leave Miss Matty's service. She began to tie on a clean apron, and otherwise prepare herself for going to the shop for the butter, eggs, and what else she might require. She would not use a scrap of the articles already in the house for her cookery, but went to an old tea-pot in which her private store of money was deposited, and took out what she wanted.

I found Miss Matty very quiet, and not a little sad; but by-and-by she tried to smile for my sake. It was settled that I was to write to my father, and ask him to come over and hold a consultation, and as soon as this letter was despatched we began to talk over future plans. Miss Matty's idea was to take a single room, and retain as much of her furniture as would be necessary to fit up this, and sell the rest, and there to quietly exist upon what would remain after paying the rent. For my part, I was more ambitious and less contented. I thought of all the things by which a woman, past middle age, and with the education common to ladies fifty years ago, could earn or add to a living without materially losing caste; but at length I put even this last clause on one side, and wondered what in the world Miss Matty could do.

Teaching was, of course, the first thing that suggested itself. If Miss Matty could teach children anything, it would throw her among the little elves in whom her soul delighted. I ran over her accomplishments. Once upon a time I had heard her say she could play "Ah! vous dirai-je, maman?" on the piano, but that was long, long ago; that faint shadow of musical acquirement had died out years before. She had also once been able to trace out patterns very nicely for muslin embroidery, by dint of placing a piece of silver paper over the design to be copied, and holding both against the window-pane while she marked the scollop and eyelet-holes. But that was her nearest approach to the accomplishment of drawing, and I did not think it would go very far. Then again, as to the branches of a solid English education—fancy work and the use of the globes—such as the mistress of the Ladies' Seminary, to which all the tradespeople in Cranford sent their daughters, professed to teach. Miss Matty's eyes were failing her, and I doubted if she could discover the number of threads in a worsted-work pattern, or rightly appreciate the different shades required for Queen Adelaide's face in the loyal wool-work now fashionable in Cranford. As for the use of the globes, I had never been able to find it out myself, so perhaps I was not a good judge of Miss Matty's capability of instructing in this branch of education; but it struck me that equators and tropics, and such mystical circles, were very imaginary lines indeed to her, and that she looked upon the signs of the Zodiac as so many remnants of the Black Art.

What she piqued herself upon, as arts in which she excelled, was making candle-lighters, or "spills" (as she preferred calling them), of coloured paper, cut so as to resemble feathers, and knitting garters in a variety of dainty stitches. I had once said, on receiving a present of an elaborate pair, that I should feel quite tempted to drop one of them in the street, in order to have it admired; but I found this little joke (and it was a very little one) was such a distress to her sense of propriety, and was taken with such anxious, earnest alarm, lest the temptation might some day prove too strong for me, that I quite regretted having ventured upon it. A present of these delicately-wrought garters, a bunch of gay "spills," or a set of cards on which sewing-silk was wound in a mystical manner, were the well-known tokens of Miss Matty's favour. But would any one pay to have their children taught these arts? or, indeed, would Miss Matty sell, for filthy lucre, the knack and the skill with which she made trifles of value to those who loved her?

I had to come down to reading, writing, and arithmetic; and, in reading the chapter every morning, she always coughed before coming to long words. I doubted her power of getting through a genealogical chapter, with any number of coughs. Writing she did well and delicately—but spelling! She seemed to think that the more out-of-the-way this was, and the more trouble it cost her, the greater the compliment she paid to her correspondent; and words that she would spell quite correctly in her letters to me became perfect enigmas when she wrote to my father.

No! there was nothing she could teach to the rising generation of Cranford, unless they had been quick learners and ready imitators of her patience, her humility, her sweetness, her quiet contentment with all that she could not do. I pondered and pondered until dinner was announced by Martha, with a face all blubbered and swollen with crying.

Miss Matty had a few little peculiarities which Martha was apt to regard as whims below her attention, and appeared to consider as childish fancies of which an old lady of fifty-eight should try and cure herself. But to-day everything was attended to with the most careful regard. The bread was cut to the imaginary pattern of excellence that existed in Miss Matty's mind, as being the way which her mother had preferred, the curtain was drawn so as to exclude the dead brick wall of a neighbour's stable, and yet left so as to show every tender leaf of the poplar which was bursting into spring beauty. Martha's tone to Miss Matty was just such as that good, rough-spoken servant usually kept sacred for little children, and which I had never heard her use to any grown-up person.

I had forgotten to tell Miss Matty about the pudding, and I was afraid she might not do justice to it, for she had evidently very little appetite this day; so I seized the opportunity of letting her into the secret while Martha took away the meat. Miss Matty's eyes filled with tears, and she could not speak, either to express surprise or delight, when Martha returned bearing it aloft, made in the most wonderful representation of a lion *couchant* that ever was moulded. Martha's face gleamed with triumph as she set it down before Miss Matty with an exultant "There!" Miss Matty wanted to speak her thanks, but could not; so she took Martha's hand and shook it warmly, which set Martha off crying, and I myself could hardly keep up the necessary composure. Martha burst out of the room, and Miss Matty had to clear her voice once or twice before she could speak. At last she said, "I should like to keep this pudding under a glass shade, my dear!" and the notion of the lion *couchant*, with his currant eyes, being hoisted up to the place of honour on a mantelpiece, tickled my hysterical fancy, and I began to laugh, which rather surprised Miss Matty.

"I am sure, dear, I have seen uglier things under a glass shade before now," said she.

So had I, many a time and oft, and I accordingly composed my countenance (and now I could hardly keep from crying), and we both fell to upon the pudding, which was indeed excellent—only every morsel seemed to choke us, our hearts were so full.

We had too much to think about to talk much that afternoon. It passed over very tranquilly. But when the tea-urn was brought in a new thought came into my head. Why should not Miss Matty sell tea—be an agent to the East India Tea Company which then existed? I could see no objections to this plan, while the advantages were many—always supposing that Miss Matty could get over the degradation of condescending to anything like trade. Tea was neither greasy nor sticky—grease and stickiness being two of the qualities which Miss Matty could not endure. No shop-window would be required. A small, genteel notification of her being licensed to sell tea would, it is true, be necessary, but I hoped that it could be placed where no one would see it. Neither was tea a heavy article, so as to tax Miss Matty's fragile strength. The only thing against my plan was the buying and selling involved.

While I was giving but absent answers to the questions Miss Matty was putting—almost as absently—we heard a clumping sound on the stairs, and a whispering outside the door, which indeed once opened and shut as if by some invisible agency. After a little while Martha came in, dragging after her a great tall young man, all crimson with shyness, and finding his only relief in perpetually sleeking down his hair.

"Please, ma'am, he's only Jem Hearn," said Martha, by way of an introduction; and so out of breath was she that I imagine she had had some bodily struggle before she could overcome his reluctance to be presented on the courtly scene of Miss Matilda Jenkyns's drawing-room.

"And please, ma'am, he wants to marry me off-hand. And please, ma'am, we want to take a lodger—just one quiet lodger, to make our two ends meet; and we'd take any house conformable; and, oh dear Miss Matty, if I may be so bold, would you have any objections to lodging with us? Jem wants it as much as I do." [To Jem]—"You great oaf! why can't you back me!—But he does want it all the same, very bad—don't you, Jem?—only, you see, he's dazed at being called on to speak before quality."

"It's not that," broke in Jem. "It's that you've taken me all on a sudden, and I didn't think for to get married so soon—and such quick words does flabbergast a man. It's not that I'm against it, ma'am" (addressing Miss Matty), "only Martha has such quick ways with her when once she takes a thing into her head; and marriage, ma'am—marriage nails a man, as one may say. I dare say I shan't mind it after it's once over."

"Please, ma'am," said Martha—who had plucked at his sleeve, and nudged him with her elbow, and otherwise tried to interrupt him all the time he had been speaking—"don't mind him, he'll come to; 'twas only last night he was an-axing me, and an-axing me, and all the more because I said I could not think of it for years to come, and now he's only taken aback with the suddenness of the joy; but you know, Jem, you are just as full as me about wanting a lodger." (Another great nudge.)

"Ay! if Miss Matty would lodge with us—otherwise I've no mind to be cumbered with strange folk in the house," said Jem, with a want of tact which I could see enraged Martha, who was trying to represent a lodger as the great object they wished to obtain, and that, in fact, Miss Matty would be smoothing their path and conferring a favour, if she would only come and live with them.

Miss Matty herself was bewildered by the pair; their, or rather Martha's sudden resolution in favour of matrimony staggered her, and stood between her and the contemplation of the plan which Martha had at heart. Miss Matty began—

"Marriage is a very solemn thing, Martha."

"It is indeed, ma'am," quoth Jem. "Not that I've no objections to Martha."

"You've never let me a-be for asking me for to fix when I would be married," said Martha—her face all a-fire, and ready to cry with vexation—"and now you're shaming me before my missus and all."

"Nay, now! Martha don't ee! don't ee! only a man likes to have breathing-time," said Jem, trying to possess himself of her hand, but in vain. Then seeing that she was more seriously hurt than he had imagined, he seemed to try to rally his scattered faculties, and with more straightforward dignity than, ten minutes before, I should have thought it possible for him to assume, he turned to Miss Matty, and said, "I hope, ma'am, you know that I am bound to respect every one who has been kind to Martha. I always looked on her as to be my wife—some time; and she has often and often spoken of you as the kindest lady that ever was; and though the plain truth is, I would not like to be troubled with lodgers of the common run, yet if, ma'am, you'd honour us by living with us, I'm sure Martha would do her best to make you comfortable; and I'd keep out of your way as much as I could, which I reckon would be the best kindness such an awkward chap as me could do."

Miss Matty had been very busy with taking off her spectacles, wiping them, and replacing them; but all she could say was, "Don't let any thought of me hurry you into marriage: pray don't. Marriage is such a very solemn thing!"

"But Miss Matilda will think of your plan, Martha," said I, struck with the advantages that it offered, and unwilling to lose the opportunity of considering about it. "And I'm sure neither she nor I can ever forget your kindness; nor your's either, Jem."

"Why, yes, ma'am! I'm sure I mean kindly, though I'm a bit fluttered by being pushed straight ahead into matrimony, as it were, and mayn't express myself conformable. But I'm sure I'm willing enough, and give me time to get accustomed; so, Martha, wench, what's the use of crying so, and slapping me if I come near?"

This last was *sotto voce*, and had the effect of making Martha bounce out of the room, to be followed and soothed by her lover. Whereupon Miss Matty sat down and cried very heartily, and accounted for it by saying that the thought of Martha being married so soon gave her quite a shock, and that she should never forgive herself if she thought she was hurrying the poor creature. I think my pity was more for Jem, of the two; but both Miss Matty and I appreciated to the full the kindness of the honest couple, although we said little about this, and a good deal about the chances and dangers of matrimony.

The next morning, very early, I received a note from Miss Pole, so mysteriously wrapped up, and with so many seals on it to secure secrecy, that I had to tear the paper before I could unfold it. And when I came to the writing I could hardly understand the meaning, it was so involved and oracular. I made out, however, that I was to go to Miss Pole's at eleven o'clock; the number *eleven* being written in full length as well as in numerals, and *A.M.* twice dashed under, as if I were very likely to come at eleven at night, when all Cranford was usually a-bed and asleep by ten. There was no signature except Miss Pole's initials reversed, P.E.; but as Martha had given me the note, "with Miss Pole's kind regards," it needed no wizard to find out who sent it; and if the writer's name was to be kept secret, it was very well that I was alone when Martha delivered it.

I went as requested to Miss Pole's. The door was opened to me by her little maid Lizzy in Sunday trim, as if some grand event was impending over this workday. And the drawing-room upstairs was arranged in accordance with this idea. The table was set out with the best green card-cloth, and writing materials upon it. On the little chiffonier was a tray with a newly-decanted bottle of cowslip wine, and some ladies'-finger biscuits. Miss Pole herself was in solemn array, as if to receive visitors, although it was only eleven o'clock. Mrs Forrester was there, crying quietly and sadly, and my arrival seemed only to call forth fresh tears. Before we had finished our greetings, performed with lugubrious mystery of demeanour, there was another rat-tat-tat, and Mrs Fitz-Adam appeared, crimson with walking and excitement. It seemed as if this was all the company expected; for now Miss Pole made several demonstrations of being about to open the business of the meeting, by stirring the fire, opening and shutting the door, and coughing and blowing her nose. Then she arranged us all round the table, taking care to place me opposite to her; and last of all, she inquired of me if the sad report was true, as she feared it was, that Miss Matty had lost all her fortune?

Of course, I had but one answer to make; and I never saw more unaffected sorrow depicted on any countenances than I did there on the three before me.

"I wish Mrs Jamieson was here!" said Mrs Forrester at last; but to judge from Mrs Fitz-Adam's face, she could not second the wish.

"But without Mrs Jamieson," said Miss Pole, with just a sound of offended merit in her voice, "we, the ladies of Cranford, in my drawing-room assembled, can resolve upon something. I imagine we are none of us what may be called rich, though we all possess a genteel competency, sufficient for tastes that are elegant and refined, and would not, if they could, be vulgarly ostentatious." (Here I observed Miss Pole refer to a small card concealed in her hand, on which I imagine she had put down a few notes.)

"Miss Smith," she continued, addressing me (familiarly known as "Mary" to all the company assembled, but this was a state occasion), "I have conversed in private—I made it my business to do so yesterday afternoon—with these ladies on the misfortune which has happened to our friend, and one and all of us have agreed that while we have a superfluity, it is not only a duty, but a pleasure—a true pleasure, Mary!"—her voice was rather choked just here, and she had to wipe her spectacles before she could go on—"to give what we can to assist her—Miss Matilda Jenkyns. Only in consideration of the feelings of delicate independence existing in the mind of every refined female"—I was sure she had got back to the card now—"we wish to contribute our mites in a secret and concealed manner, so as not to hurt the feelings I have referred to. And our object in requesting you to meet us this morning is that, believing you are the daughter—that your father is, in fact, her confidential adviser, in all pecuniary matters, we imagined that, by consulting with him, you might devise some mode in which our contribution could be made to appear the legal due which Miss Matilda Jenkyns ought to receive from— Probably your father, knowing her investments, can fill up the blank."

Miss Pole concluded her address, and looked round for approval and agreement.

"I have expressed your meaning, ladies, have I not? And while Miss Smith considers what reply to make, allow me to offer you some little refreshment."

I had no great reply to make: I had more thankfulness at my heart for their kind thoughts than I cared to put into words; and so I only mumbled out something to the effect "that I would name what Miss Pole had said to my father, and that if anything could be arranged for dear Miss Matty,"—and here I broke down utterly, and had to be refreshed with a glass of cowslip wine before I could check the crying which had been repressed for the last two or three days. The worst was, all the ladies cried in concert. Even Miss Pole cried, who had said a hundred times that to betray emotion before any one was a sign of weakness and want of self-control. She recovered herself into a slight degree of impatient anger, directed against me, as having set them all off; and, moreover, I think she was vexed that I could not make a speech back in return for hers; and if I had known beforehand what was to be said, and had a card on which to express the probable feelings that would rise in my heart, I would have tried to gratify her. As it was, Mrs Forrester was the person to speak when we had recovered our composure.

"I don't mind, among friends, stating that I—no! I'm not poor exactly, but I don't think I'm what you may call rich; I wish I were, for dear Miss Matty's sake—but, if you please, I'll write down in a sealed paper what I can give. I only wish it was more; my dear Mary, I do indeed."

Now I saw why paper, pens, and ink were provided. Every lady wrote down the sum she could give annually, signed the paper, and sealed it mysteriously. If their proposal was acceded to, my father was to be allowed to open the papers, under pledge of secrecy. If not, they were to be returned to their writers.

When the ceremony had been gone through, I rose to depart; but each lady seemed to wish to have a private conference with me. Miss Pole kept me in the drawing-room to explain why, in Mrs Jamieson's absence, she had taken the lead in this "movement," as she was pleased to call it, and also to inform me that she had heard from good sources that Mrs Jamieson was coming home directly in a state of high displeasure against her sister-in-law, who was forthwith to leave her house, and was, she believed, to return to Edinburgh that very afternoon. Of course this piece of intelligence could not be communicated before Mrs Fitz-Adam, more especially as Miss Pole was inclined to think that Lady Glenmire's engagement to Mr Hoggins could not possibly hold against the blaze of Mrs Jamieson's displeasure. A few hearty inquiries after Miss Matty's health concluded my interview with Miss Pole.

On coming downstairs I found Mrs Forrester waiting for me at the entrance to the dining-parlour; she drew me in, and when the door was shut, she tried two or three times to begin on some subject, which was so unapproachable apparently, that I began to despair of our ever getting to a clear understanding. At last out it came; the poor old lady trembling all the time as if it were a great crime which she was exposing to daylight, in telling me how very, very little she had to live upon; a confession which she was brought to make from a dread lest we should think that the small contribution named in her paper bore any proportion to her love and regard for Miss Matty. And yet that sum which she so eagerly relinquished was, in truth, more than a twentieth part of what she had to live upon, and keep house, and a little serving-maid, all as became one born a Tyrrell. And when the whole income does not nearly amount to a hundred pounds, to give up a twentieth of it will necessitate many careful economies, and many pieces of self-denial, small and insignificant in the world's account, but bearing a different value in another account-book that I have heard of. She did so wish she was rich, she said, and this wish she kept repeating, with no thought of herself in it, only with a longing, yearning desire to be able to heap up Miss Matty's measure of comforts.

It was some time before I could console her enough to leave her; and then, on quitting the house, I was waylaid by Mrs Fitz-Adam, who had also her confidence to make of pretty nearly the opposite description. She had not liked to put down all that she could afford and was ready to give. She told me she thought she never could look Miss Matty in the face again if she presumed to be giving her so much as she should like to do. "Miss Matty!" continued she, "that I thought was such a fine young lady when I was nothing but a country girl, coming to market with eggs and butter and such like things. For my father, though well-to-do, would always make me go on as my mother had done before me, and I had to come into Cranford every Saturday, and see after sales, and prices, and what not. And one day, I remember, I met Miss Matty in the lane that leads to Combehurst; she was walking on the footpath, which, you know, is raised a good way above the road, and a gentleman rode beside her, and was talking to her, and she was looking down at some primroses she had gathered, and pulling them all to pieces, and I do believe she was crying. But after she had passed, she turned round and ran after me to ask—oh, so kindly—about my poor mother, who lay on her death-bed; and when I cried she took hold of my hand to comfort me—and the gentleman waiting for her all the time—and her poor heart very full of something, I am sure; and I thought it such an honour to be spoken to in that pretty way by the rector's daughter, who visited at Arley Hall. I have loved her ever since, though perhaps I'd no right to do it; but if you can think of any way in which I might be allowed to give a little more without any one knowing it, I should be so much obliged to you, my dear. And my brother would be delighted to doctor her for nothing—medicines, leeches, and all. I know that he and her ladyship (my dear, I little thought in the days I was telling you of that I should ever come to be sister-in-law to a ladyship!) would do anything for her. We all would."

I told her I was quite sure of it, and promised all sorts of things in my anxiety to get home to Miss Matty, who might well be wondering what had become of me—absent from her two hours without being able to account for it. She had taken very little note of time, however, as she had been occupied in numberless little arrangements preparatory to the great step of giving up her house. It was evidently a relief to her to be doing something in the way of retrenchment, for, as she said, whenever she paused to think, the recollection of the poor fellow with his bad five-pound note came over her, and she felt quite dishonest; only if it made her so uncomfortable, what must it not be doing to the directors of the bank, who must know so much more of the misery consequent upon this failure? She almost made me angry by dividing her sympathy between these directors (whom she imagined overwhelmed by self-reproach for the mismanagement of other people's affairs) and those who were suffering like her. Indeed, of the two, she seemed to think poverty a lighter burden than self-reproach; but I privately doubted if the directors would agree with her.

Old hoards were taken out and examined as to their money value which luckily was small, or else I don't know how Miss Matty would have prevailed upon herself to part with such things as her mother's wedding-ring, the strange, uncouth brooch with which her father had disfigured his shirt-frill, &c. However, we arranged things a little in order as to their pecuniary estimation, and were all ready for my father when he came the next morning.

I am not going to weary you with the details of all the business we went through; and one reason for not telling about them is, that I did not understand what we were doing at the time, and cannot recollect it now. Miss Matty and I sat assenting to accounts, and schemes, and reports, and documents, of which I do not believe we either of us understood a word; for my father was clear-headed and decisive, and a capital man of business, and if we made the slightest inquiry, or expressed the slightest want of comprehension, he had a sharp way of saying, "Eh? eh? it's as clear as daylight. What's your objection?" And as we had not comprehended anything of what he had proposed, we found it rather difficult to shape our objections; in fact, we never were sure if we had any. So presently Miss Matty got into a nervously acquiescent state, and said "Yes," and "Certainly," at every pause, whether required or not; but when I once joined in as chorus to a "Decidedly," pronounced by Miss Matty in a tremblingly dubious tone, my father fired round at me and asked me "What there was to decide?" And I am sure to this day I have never known. But, in justice to him, I must say he had come over from Drumble to help Miss Matty when he could ill spare the time, and when his own affairs were in a very anxious state.

While Miss Matty was out of the room giving orders for luncheon—and sadly perplexed between her desire of honouring my father by a delicate, dainty meal, and her conviction that she had no right, now that all her money was gone, to indulge this desire—I told him of the meeting of the Cranford ladies at Miss Pole's the day before. He kept brushing his hand before his eyes as I spoke—and when I went back to Martha's offer the evening before, of receiving Miss Matty as a lodger, he fairly walked away from me to the window, and began drumming with his fingers upon it. Then he turned abruptly round, and said, "See, Mary, how a good, innocent life makes friends all around. Confound it! I could make a good lesson out of it if I were a parson; but, as it is, I can't get a tail to my sentences—only I'm sure you feel what I want to say. You and I will have a walk after lunch and talk a bit more about these plans."

The lunch—a hot savoury mutton-chop, and a little of the cold loin sliced and fried—was now brought in. Every morsel of this last dish was finished, to Martha's great gratification. Then my father bluntly told Miss Matty he wanted to talk to me alone, and that he would stroll out and see some of the old places, and then I could tell her what plan we thought desirable. Just before we went out, she called me back and said, "Remember, dear, I'm the only one left—I mean, there's no one to be hurt by what I do. I'm willing to do anything that's right and honest; and I don't think, if Deborah knows where she is, she'll care so very much if I'm not genteel; because, you see, she'll know all, dear. Only let me see what I can do, and pay the poor people as far as I'm able."

I gave her a hearty kiss, and ran after my father. The result of our conversation was this. If all parties were agreeable, Martha and Jem were to be married with as little delay as possible, and they were to live on in Miss Matty's present abode; the sum which the Cranford ladies had agreed to contribute annually being sufficient to meet the greater part of the rent, and leaving Martha free to appropriate what Miss Matty should pay for her lodgings to any little extra comforts required. About the sale, my father was dubious at first. He said the old rectory furniture, however carefully used and reverently treated, would fetch very little; and that little would be but as a drop in the sea of the debts of the Town and County Bank. But when I represented how Miss Matty's tender conscience would be soothed by feeling that she had done what she could, he gave way; especially after I had told him the five-pound note adventure, and he had scolded me well for allowing it. I then alluded to my idea that she might add to her small income by selling tea; and, to my surprise (for I had nearly given up the plan), my father grasped at it with all the energy of a tradesman. I think he reckoned his chickens before they were hatched, for he immediately ran up the profits of the sales that she could effect in Cranford to more than twenty pounds a year. The small dining-parlour was to be converted into a shop, without any of its degrading characteristics; a table was to be the counter; one window was to be retained unaltered, and the other changed into a glass door. I evidently rose in his estimation for having made this bright suggestion. I only hoped we should not both fall in Miss Matty's.

But she was patient and content with all our arrangements. She knew, she said, that we should do the best we could for her; and she only hoped, only stipulated, that she should pay every farthing that she could be said to owe, for her father's sake, who had been so respected in Cranford. My father and I had agreed to say as little as possible about the bank, indeed never to mention it again, if it could be helped. Some of the plans were evidently a little perplexing to her; but she had seen me sufficiently snubbed in the morning for want of comprehension to venture on too many inquiries now; and all passed over well with a hope on her part that no one would be hurried into marriage on her account. When we came to the proposal that she should sell tea, I could see it was rather a shock to her; not on account of any personal loss of gentility involved, but only because she distrusted her own powers of action in a new line of life, and would timidly have preferred a little more privation to any exertion for which she feared she was unfitted. However, when she saw my father was bent upon it, she sighed, and said she would try; and if she did not do well, of course she might give it up. One good thing about it was, she did not think men ever bought tea; and it was of men particularly she was afraid. They had such sharp loud ways with them; and did up accounts, and counted their change so quickly! Now, if she might only sell comfits to children, she was sure she could please them!

CHAPTER XV - A HAPPY RETURN

BEFORE I left Miss Matty at Cranford everything had been comfortably arranged for her. Even Mrs Jamieson's approval of her selling tea had been gained. That oracle had taken a few days to consider whether by so doing Miss Matty would forfeit her right to the privileges of society in Cranford. I think she had some little idea of mortifying Lady Glenmire by the decision she gave at last; which was to this effect: that whereas a married woman takes her husband's rank by the strict laws of precedence, an unmarried woman retains the station her father occupied. So Cranford was allowed to visit Miss Matty; and, whether allowed or not, it intended to visit Lady Glenmire.

But what was our surprise—our dismay—when we learnt that Mr and *Mrs Hoggins* were returning on the following Tuesday! Mrs Hoggins! Had she absolutely dropped her title, and so, in a spirit of bravado, cut the aristocracy to become a Hoggins! She, who might have been called Lady Glenmire to her dying day! Mrs Jamieson was pleased. She said it only convinced her of what she had known from the first, that the creature had a low taste. But "the creature" looked very happy on Sunday at church; nor did we see it necessary to keep our veils down on that side of our bonnets on which Mr and Mrs Hoggins sat, as Mrs Jamieson did; thereby missing all the smiling glory of his face, and all the becoming blushes of hers. I am not sure if Martha and Jem looked more radiant in the afternoon, when they, too, made their first appearance. Mrs Jamieson soothed the turbulence of her soul by having the blinds of her windows drawn down, as if for a funeral, on the day when Mr and Mrs Hoggins received callers; and it was with some difficulty that she was prevailed upon to continue the *St James's Chronicle*, so indignant was she with its having inserted the announcement of the marriage.

Miss Matty's sale went off famously. She retained the furniture of her sitting-room and bedroom; the former of which she was to occupy till Martha could meet with a lodger who might wish to take it; and into this sitting-room and bedroom she had to cram all sorts of things, which were (the auctioneer assured her) bought in for her at the sale by an unknown friend. I always suspected Mrs Fitz-Adam of this; but she must have had an accessory, who knew what articles were particularly regarded by Miss Matty on account of their associations with her early days. The rest of the house looked rather bare, to be sure; all except one tiny bedroom, of which my father allowed me to purchase the furniture for my occasional use in case of Miss Matty's illness.

I had expended my own small store in buying all manner of comfits and lozenges, in order to tempt the little people whom Miss Matty loved so much to come about her. Tea in bright green canisters, and comfits in tumblers—Miss Matty and I felt quite proud as we looked round us on the evening before the shop was to be opened. Martha had scoured the boarded floor to a white cleanness, and it was adorned with a brilliant piece of oil-cloth, on which customers were to stand before the table-counter. The wholesome smell of plaster and whitewash pervaded the apartment. A very small "Matilda Jenkyns, licensed to sell tea," was hidden under the lintel of the new door, and two boxes of tea, with cabalistic inscriptions all over them, stood ready to disgorge their contents into the canisters.

Miss Matty, as I ought to have mentioned before, had had some scruples of conscience at selling tea when there was already Mr Johnson in the town, who included it among his numerous commodities; and, before she could quite reconcile herself to the adoption of her new business, she had trotted down to his shop, unknown to me, to tell him of the project that was entertained, and to inquire if it was likely to injure his business. My father called this idea of hers "great nonsense," and "wondered how tradespeople were to get on if there was to be a continual consulting of each other's interests, which would put a stop to all competition directly." And, perhaps, it would not have done in Drumble, but in Cranford it answered very well; for not only did Mr Johnson kindly put at rest all Miss Matty's scruples and fear of injuring his business, but I have reason to know he repeatedly sent customers to her, saying that the teas he kept were of a common kind, but that Miss Jenkyns had all the choice sorts. And expensive tea is a very favourite luxury with well-to-do tradespeople and rich farmers' wives, who turn up their noses at the Congou and Souchong prevalent at many tables of gentility, and will have nothing else than Gunpowder and Pekoe for themselves.

But to return to Miss Matty. It was really very pleasant to see how her unselfishness and simple sense of justice called out the same good qualities in others. She never seemed to think any one would impose upon her, because she should be so grieved to do it to them. I have heard her put a stop to the asseverations of the man who brought her coals by quietly saying, "I am sure you would be sorry to bring me wrong weight;" and if the coals were short measure that time, I don't believe they ever were again. People would have felt as much ashamed of presuming on her good faith as they would have done on that of a child. But my father says "such simplicity might be very well in Cranford, but would never do in the world." And I fancy the world must be very bad, for with all my father's suspicion of every one with whom he has dealings, and in spite of all his many precautions, he lost upwards of a thousand pounds by roguery only last year.

I just stayed long enough to establish Miss Matty in her new mode of life, and to pack up the library, which the rector had purchased. He had written a very kind letter to Miss Matty, saying "how glad he should be to take a library, so well selected as he knew that the late Mr Jenkyns's must have been, at any valuation put upon them." And when she agreed to this, with a touch of sorrowful gladness that they would go back to the rectory and be arranged on the accustomed walls once more, he sent word that he feared that he had not room for them all, and perhaps Miss Matty would kindly allow him to leave some volumes on her shelves. But Miss Matty said that she had her Bible and "Johnson's Dictionary," and should not have much time for reading, she was afraid; still, I retained a few books out of consideration for the rector's kindness.

The money which he had paid, and that produced by the sale, was partly expended in the stock of tea, and part of it was invested against a rainy day—*i.e.* old age or illness. It was but a small sum, it is true; and it occasioned a few evasions of truth and white lies (all of which I think very wrong indeed—in theory—and would rather not put them in practice), for we knew Miss Matty would be perplexed as to her duty if she were aware of any little reserve-fund being made for her while the debts of the bank remained unpaid. Moreover, she had never been told of the way in which her friends were contributing to pay the rent. I should have liked to tell her this, but the mystery of the affair gave a piquancy to their deed of kindness which the ladies were unwilling to give up; and at first Martha had to shirk many a perplexed question as to her ways and means of living in such a house, but by-and-by Miss Matty's prudent uneasiness sank down into acquiescence with the existing arrangement.

I left Miss Matty with a good heart. Her sales of tea during the first two days had surpassed my most sanguine expectations. The whole country round seemed to be all out of tea at once. The only alteration I could have desired in Miss Matty's way of doing business was, that she should not have so plaintively entreated some of her customers not to buy green tea—running it down as a slow poison, sure to destroy the nerves, and produce all manner of evil. Their pertinacity in taking it, in spite of all her warnings, distressed her so much that I really thought she would relinquish the sale of it, and so lose half her custom; and I was driven to my wits' end for instances of longevity entirely attributable to a persevering use of green tea. But the final argument, which settled the question, was a happy reference of mine to the train-oil and tallow candles which the Esquimaux not only enjoy but digest. After that she acknowledged that "one man's meat might be another man's poison," and contented herself thence-forward with an occasional remonstrance when she thought the purchaser was too young and innocent to be acquainted with the evil effects green tea produced on some constitutions, and an habitual sigh when people old enough to choose more wisely would prefer it.

I went over from Drumble once a quarter at least to settle the accounts, and see after the necessary business letters. And, speaking of letters, I began to be very much ashamed of remembering my letter to the Aga Jenkyns, and very glad I had never named my writing to any one. I only hoped the letter was lost. No answer came. No sign was made.

About a year after Miss Matty set up shop, I received one of Martha's hieroglyphics, begging me to come to Cranford very soon. I was afraid that Miss

Matty was ill, and went off that very afternoon, and took Martha by surprise when she saw me on opening the door. We went into the kitchen as usual, to have our confidential conference, and then Martha told me she was expecting her confinement very soon—in a week or two; and she did not think Miss Matty was aware of it, and she wanted me to break the news to her, "for indeed, miss," continued Martha, crying hysterically, "I'm afraid she won't approve of it, and I'm sure I don't know who is to take care of her as she should be taken care of when I am laid up."

I comforted Martha by telling her I would remain till she was about again, and only wished she had told me her reason for this sudden summons, as then I would have brought the requisite stock of clothes. But Martha was so tearful and tender-spirited, and unlike her usual self, that I said as little as possible about myself, and endeavoured rather to comfort Martha under all the probable and possible misfortunes which came crowding upon her imagination.

I then stole out of the house-door, and made my appearance as if I were a customer in the shop, just to take Miss Matty by surprise, and gain an idea of how she looked in her new situation. It was warm May weather, so only the little half-door was closed; and Miss Matty sat behind the counter, knitting an elaborate pair of garters; elaborate they seemed to me, but the difficult stitch was no weight upon her mind, for she was singing in a low voice to herself as her needles went rapidly in and out. I call it singing, but I dare say a musician would not use that word to the tuneless yet sweet humming of the low worn voice. I found out from the words, far more than from the attempt at the tune, that it was the Old Hundredth she was crooning to herself; but the quiet continuous sound told of content, and gave me a pleasant feeling, as I stood in the street just outside the door, quite in harmony with that soft May morning. I went in. At first she did not catch who it was, and stood up as if to serve me; but in another minute watchful pussy had clutched her knitting, which was dropped in eager joy at seeing me. I found, after we had had a little conversation, that it was as Martha said, and that Miss Matty had no idea of the approaching household event. So I thought I would let things take their course, secure that when I went to her with the baby in my arms, I should obtain that forgiveness for Martha which she was needlessly frightening herself into believing that Miss Matty would withhold, under some notion that the new claimant would require attentions from its mother that it would be faithless treason to Miss Matty to render.

But I was right. I think that must be an hereditary quality, for my father says he is scarcely ever wrong. One morning, within a week after I arrived, I went to call Miss Matty, with a little bundle of flannel in my arms. She was very much awe-struck when I showed her what it was, and asked for her spectacles off the dressing-table, and looked at it curiously, with a sort of tender wonder at its small perfection of parts. She could not banish the thought of the surprise all day, but went about on tiptoe, and was very silent. But she stole up to see Martha and they both cried with joy, and she got into a complimentary speech to Jem, and did not know how to get out of it again, and was only extricated from her dilemma by the sound of the shop-bell, which was an equal relief to the shy, proud, honest Jem, who shook my hand so vigorously when I congratulated him, that I think I feel the pain of it yet.

I had a busy life while Martha was laid up. I attended on Miss Matty, and prepared her meals; I cast up her accounts, and examined into the state of her canisters and tumblers. I helped her, too, occasionally, in the shop; and it gave me no small amusement, and sometimes a little uneasiness, to watch her ways there. If a little child came in to ask for an ounce of almond-comfits (and four of the large kind which Miss Matty sold weighed that much), she always added one more by "way of make-weight," as she called it, although the scale was handsomely turned before; and when I remonstrated against this, her reply was, "The little things like it so much!" There was no use in telling her that the fifth comfit weighed a quarter of an ounce, and made every sale into a loss to her pocket. So I remembered the green tea, and winged my shaft with a feather out of her own plumage. I told her how unwholesome almond-comfits were, and how ill excess in them might make the little children. This argument produced some effect; for, henceforward, instead of the fifth comfit, she always told them to hold out their tiny palms, into which she shook either peppermint or ginger lozenges, as a preventive to the dangers that might arise from the previous sale. Altogether the lozenge trade, conducted on these principles, did not promise to be remunerative; but I was happy to find she had made more than twenty pounds during the last year by her sales of tea; and, moreover, that now she was accustomed to it, she did not dislike the employment, which brought her into kindly intercourse with many of the people round about. If she gave them good weight, they, in their turn, brought many a little country present to the "old rector's daughter"; a cream cheese, a few new-laid eggs, a little fresh ripe fruit, a bunch of flowers. The counter was quite loaded with these offerings sometimes, as she told me.

As for Cranford in general, it was going on much as usual. The Jamieson and Hoggins feud still raged, if a feud it could be called, when only one side cared much about it. Mr and Mrs Hoggins were very happy together, and, like most very happy people, quite ready to be friendly; indeed, Mrs Hoggins was really desirous to be restored to Mrs Jamieson's good graces, because of the former intimacy. But Mrs Jamieson considered their very happiness an insult to the Glenmire family, to which she had still the honour to belong, and she doggedly refused and rejected every advance. Mr Mulliner, like a faithful clansman, espoused his mistress' side with ardour. If he saw either Mr or Mrs Hoggins, he would cross the street, and appear absorbed in the contemplation of life in general, and his own path in particular, until he had passed them by. Miss Pole used to amuse herself with wondering what in the world Mrs Jamieson would do, if either she, or Mr Mulliner, or any other member of her household was taken ill; she could hardly have the face to call in Mr Hoggins after the way she had behaved to them. Miss Pole grew quite impatient for some indisposition or accident to befall Mrs Jamieson or her dependents, in order that Cranford might see how she would act under the perplexing circumstances.

Martha was beginning to go about again, and I had already fixed a limit, not very far distant, to my visit, when one afternoon, as I was sitting in the shop-parlour with Miss Matty—I remember the weather was colder now than it had been in May, three weeks before, and we had a fire and kept the door fully closed—we saw a gentleman go slowly past the window, and then stand opposite to the door, as if looking out for the name which we had so carefully hidden. He took out a double eyeglass and peered about for some time before he could discover it. Then he came in. And, all on a sudden, it flashed across me that it was the Aga himself! For his clothes had an out-of-the-way foreign cut about them, and his face was deep brown, as if tanned and re-tanned by the sun. His complexion contrasted oddly with his plentiful snow-white hair, his eyes were dark and piercing, and he had an odd way of contracting them and puckering up his cheeks into innumerable wrinkles when he looked earnestly at objects. He did so to Miss Matty when he first came in. His glance had first caught and lingered a little upon me, but then turned, with the peculiar searching look I have described, to Miss Matty. She was a little fluttered and nervous, but no more so than she always was when any man came into her shop. She thought that he would probably have a note, or a sovereign at least, for which she would have to give change, which was an operation she very much disliked to perform. But the present customer stood opposite to her, without asking for anything, only looking fixedly at her as he drummed upon the table with his fingers, just for all the world as Miss Jenkyns used to do. Miss Matty was on the point of asking him what he wanted (as she told me afterwards), when he turned sharp to me: "Is your name Mary Smith?"

"Yes!" said I.

All my doubts as to his identity were set at rest, and I only wondered what he would say or do next, and how Miss Matty would stand the joyful shock of what he had to reveal. Apparently he was at a loss how to announce himself, for he looked round at last in search of something to buy, so as to gain time, and, as it happened, his eye caught on the almond-comfits, and he boldly asked for a pound of "those things." I doubt if Miss Matty had a whole pound in the shop, and, besides the unusual magnitude of the order, she was distressed with the idea of the indigestion they would produce, taken in such unlimited quantities. She looked up to remonstrate. Something of tender relaxation in his face struck home to her heart. She said, "It is—oh, sir! can you be Peter?" and trembled from head to foot. In a moment he was round the table and had her in his arms, sobbing the tearless cries of old age. I brought her a glass of wine, for indeed her colour had changed so as to alarm me and Mr Peter too. He kept saying, "I have been too sudden for you, Matty—I have, my little girl."

I proposed that she should go at once up into the drawing-room and lie down on the sofa there. She looked wistfully at her brother, whose hand she had held tight, even when nearly fainting; but on his assuring her that he would not leave her, she allowed him to carry her upstairs.

I thought that the best I could do was to run and put the kettle on the fire for early tea, and then to attend to the shop, leaving the brother and sister to exchange some of the many thousand things they must have to say. I had also to break the news to Martha, who received it with a burst of tears which nearly infected me. She kept recovering herself to ask if I was sure it was indeed Miss Matty's brother, for I had mentioned that he had grey hair, and she had always heard that he was a very handsome young man. Something of the same kind perplexed Miss Matty at tea-time, when she was installed in the great easy-chair opposite to Mr Jenkyns in order to gaze her fill. She could hardly drink for looking at him, and as for eating, that was out of the question.

"I suppose hot climates age people very quickly," said she, almost to herself. "When you left Cranford you had not a grey hair in your head."

"But how many years ago is that?" said Mr Peter, smiling.

"Ah, true! yes, I suppose you and I are getting old. But still I did not think we were so very old! But white hair is very becoming to you, Peter," she continued—a little afraid lest she had hurt him by revealing how his appearance had impressed her.

"I suppose I forgot dates too, Matty, for what do you think I have brought for you from India? I have an Indian muslin gown and a pearl necklace for you somewhere in my chest at Portsmouth." He smiled as if amused at the idea of the incongruity of his presents with the appearance of his sister; but this did not strike her all at once, while the elegance of the articles did. I could see that for a moment her imagination dwelt complacently on the idea of herself thus attired; and instinctively she put her hand up to her throat—that little delicate throat which (as Miss Pole had told me) had been one of her youthful charms; but the hand met the touch of folds of soft muslin in which she was always swathed up to her chin, and the sensation recalled a sense of the unsuitableness of a pearl necklace to her age. She said, "I'm afraid I'm too old; but it was very kind of you to think of it. They are just what I should have liked years ago—when I was young."

"So I thought, my little Matty. I remembered your tastes; they were so like my dear mother's." At the mention of that name the brother and sister clasped each other's hands yet more fondly, and, although they were perfectly silent, I fancied they might have something to say if they were unchecked by my presence, and I got up to arrange my room for Mr Peter's occupation that night, intending myself to share Miss Matty's bed. But at my movement, he started up. "I must go and settle about a room at the 'George.' My carpet-bag is there too."

"No!" said Miss Matty, in great distress—"you must not go; please, dear Peter—pray, Mary—oh! you must not go!"

She was so much agitated that we both promised everything she wished. Peter sat down again and gave her his hand, which for better security she held in both of hers, and I left the room to accomplish my arrangements.

Long, long into the night, far, far into the morning, did Miss Matty and I talk. She had much to tell me of her brother's life and adventures, which he had communicated to her as they had sat alone. She said all was thoroughly clear to her; but I never quite understood the whole story; and when in after days I lost my awe of Mr Peter enough to question him myself, he laughed at my curiosity, and told me stories that sounded so very much like Baron Munchausen's, that I was sure he was making fun of me. What I heard from Miss Matty was that he had been a volunteer at the siege of Rangoon; had been taken prisoner by the Burmese; and somehow obtained favour and eventual freedom from knowing how to bleed the chief of the small tribe in some case of dangerous illness; that on his release from years of captivity he had had his letters returned from England with the ominous word "Dead" marked upon them; and, believing himself to be the last of his race, he had settled down as an indigo planter, and had proposed to spend the remainder of his life in the country to whose inhabitants and modes of life he had become habituated, when my letter had reached him; and, with the odd vehemence which characterised him in age as it had done in youth, he had sold his land and all his possessions to the first purchaser, and come home to the poor old sister, who was more glad and rich than any princess when she looked at him. She talked me to sleep at last, and then I was awakened by a slight sound at the door, for which she begged my pardon as she crept penitently into bed; but it seems that when I could no longer confirm her belief that the long-lost was really here—under the same roof—she had begun to fear lest it was only a waking dream of hers; that there never had been a Peter sitting by her all that blessed evening—but that the real Peter lay dead far away beneath some wild sea-wave, or under some strange eastern tree. And so strong had this nervous feeling of hers become, that she was fain to get up and go and convince herself that he was really there by listening through the door to his even, regular breathing—I don't like to call it snoring, but I heard it myself through two closed doors—and by-and-by it soothed Miss Matty to sleep.

I don't believe Mr Peter came home from India as rich as a nabob; he even considered himself poor, but neither he nor Miss Matty cared much about that. At any rate, he had enough to live upon "very genteelly" at Cranford; he and Miss Matty together. And a day or two after his arrival, the shop was closed, while troops of little urchins gleefully awaited the shower of comfits and lozenges that came from time to time down upon their faces as they stood up-gazing at Miss Matty's drawing-room windows. Occasionally Miss Matty would say to them (half-hidden behind the curtains), "My dear children, don't make yourselves ill;" but a strong arm pulled her back, and a more rattling shower than ever succeeded. A part of the tea was sent in presents to the Cranford ladies; and some of it was distributed among the old people who remembered Mr Peter in the days of his frolicsome youth. The Indian muslin gown was reserved for darling Flora Gordon (Miss Jessie Brown's daughter). The Gordons had been on the Continent for the last few years, but were now expected to return very soon; and Miss Matty, in her sisterly pride, anticipated great delight in the joy of showing them Mr Peter. The pearl necklace disappeared; and about that time many handsome and useful presents made their appearance in the households of Miss Pole and Mrs Forrester; and some rare and delicate Indian ornaments graced the drawing-rooms of Mrs Jamieson and Mrs Fitz-Adam. I myself was not forgotten. Among other things, I had the handsomest-bound and best edition of Dr Johnson's works that could be procured; and dear Miss Matty, with tears in her eyes, begged me to consider it as a present from her sister as well as herself. In short, no one was forgotten; and, what was more, every one, however insignificant, who had shown kindness to Miss Matty at any time, was sure of Mr Peter's cordial regard.

CHAPTER XVI - PEACE TO CRANFORD

IT was not surprising that Mr Peter became such a favourite at Cranford. The ladies vied with each other who should admire him most; and no wonder, for their quiet lives were astonishingly stirred up by the arrival from India—especially as the person arrived told more wonderful stories than Sindbad the Sailor; and, as Miss Pole said, was quite as good as an Arabian Night any evening. For my own part, I had vibrated all my life between Drumble and Cranford, and I thought it was quite possible that all Mr Peter's stories might be true, although wonderful; but when I found that, if we swallowed an anecdote of tolerable magnitude one week, we had the dose considerably increased the next, I began to have my doubts; especially as I noticed that when his sister was present the accounts of Indian life were comparatively tame; not that she knew more than we did, perhaps less. I noticed also that when the rector came to call, Mr Peter talked in a different way about the countries he had been in. But I don't think the ladies in Cranford would have considered him such a wonderful traveller if they had only heard him talk in the quiet way he did to him. They liked him the better, indeed, for being what they called "so very Oriental."

One day, at a select party in his honour, which Miss Pole gave, and from which, as Mrs Jamieson honoured it with her presence, and had even offered to send Mr Mulliner to wait, Mr and Mrs Hoggins and Mrs Fitz-Adam were necessarily excluded—one day at Miss Pole's, Mr Peter said he was tired of sitting upright against the hard-backed uneasy chairs, and asked if he might not indulge himself in sitting cross-legged. Miss Pole's consent was eagerly given, and down he went with the utmost gravity. But when Miss Pole asked me, in an audible whisper, "if he did not remind me of the Father of the Faithful?" I could not help thinking of poor Simon Jones, the lame tailor, and while Mrs Jamieson slowly commented on the elegance and convenience of the attitude, I remembered how we had all followed that lady's lead in condemning Mr Hoggins for vulgarity because he simply crossed his legs as he sat still on his chair. Many of Mr Peter's ways of eating were a little strange amongst such ladies as Miss Pole, and Miss Matty, and Mrs Jamieson, especially when I recollected the untasted green peas and two-pronged forks at poor Mr Holbrook's dinner.

The mention of that gentleman's name recalls to my mind a conversation between Mr Peter and Miss Matty one evening in the summer after he returned to

Cranford. The day had been very hot, and Miss Matty had been much oppressed by the weather, in the heat of which her brother revelled. I remember that she had been unable to nurse Martha's baby, which had become her favourite employment of late, and which was as much at home in her arms as in its mother's, as long as it remained a light-weight, portable by one so fragile as Miss Matty. This day to which I refer, Miss Matty had seemed more than usually feeble and languid, and only revived when the sun went down, and her sofa was wheeled to the open window, through which, although it looked into the principal street of Cranford, the fragrant smell of the neighbouring hayfields came in every now and then, borne by the soft breezes that stirred the dull air of the summer twilight, and then died away. The silence of the sultry atmosphere was lost in the murmuring noises which came in from many an open window and door; even the children were abroad in the street, late as it was (between ten and eleven), enjoying the game of play for which they had not had spirits during the heat of the day. It was a source of satisfaction to Miss Matty to see how few candles were lighted, even in the apartments of those houses from which issued the greatest signs of life. Mr Peter, Miss Matty, and I had all been quiet, each with a separate reverie, for some little time, when Mr Peter broke in—

"Do you know, little Matty, I could have sworn you were on the high road to matrimony when I left England that last time! If anybody had told me you would have lived and died an old maid then, I should have laughed in their faces."

Miss Matty made no reply, and I tried in vain to think of some subject which should effectually turn the conversation; but I was very stupid; and before I spoke he went on—

"It was Holbrook, that fine manly fellow who lived at Woodley, that I used to think would carry off my little Matty. You would not think it now, I dare say, Mary; but this sister of mine was once a very pretty girl—at least, I thought so, and so I've a notion did poor Holbrook. What business had he to die before I came home to thank him for all his kindness to a good-for-nothing cub as I was? It was that that made me first think he cared for you; for in all our fishing expeditions it was Matty, Matty, we talked about. Poor Deborah! What a lecture she read me on having asked him home to lunch one day, when she had seen the Arley carriage in the town, and thought that my lady might call. Well, that's long years ago; more than half a life-time, and yet it seems like yesterday! I don't know a fellow I should have liked better as a brother-in-law. You must have played your cards badly, my little Matty, somehow or another—wanted your brother to be a good go-between, eh, little one?" said he, putting out his hand to take hold of hers as she lay on the sofa. "Why, what's this? you're shivering and shaking, Matty, with that confounded open window. Shut it, Mary, this minute!"

I did so, and then stooped down to kiss Miss Matty, and see if she really were chilled. She caught at my hand, and gave it a hard squeeze—but unconsciously, I think—for in a minute or two she spoke to us quite in her usual voice, and smiled our uneasiness away, although she patiently submitted to the prescriptions we enforced of a warm bed and a glass of weak negus. I was to leave Cranford the next day, and before I went I saw that all the effects of the open window had quite vanished. I had superintended most of the alterations necessary in the house and household during the latter weeks of my stay. The shop was once more a parlour: the empty resounding rooms again furnished up to the very garrets.

There had been some talk of establishing Martha and Jem in another house, but Miss Matty would not hear of this. Indeed, I never saw her so much roused as when Miss Pole had assumed it to be the most desirable arrangement. As long as Martha would remain with Miss Matty, Miss Matty was only too thankful to have her about her; yes, and Jem too, who was a very pleasant man to have in the house, for she never saw him from week's end to week's end. And as for the probable children, if they would all turn out such little darlings as her god-daughter, Matilda, she should not mind the number, if Martha didn't. Besides, the next was to be called Deborah—a point which Miss Matty had reluctantly yielded to Martha's stubborn determination that her first-born was to be Matilda. So Miss Pole had to lower her colours, and even her voice, as she said to me that, as Mr and Mrs Hearn were still to go on living in the same house with Miss Matty, we had certainly done a wise thing in hiring Martha's niece as an auxiliary.

I left Miss Matty and Mr Peter most comfortable and contented; the only subject for regret to the tender heart of the one, and the social friendly nature of the other, being the unfortunate quarrel between Mrs Jamieson and the plebeian Hogginses and their following. In joke, I prophesied one day that this would only last until Mrs Jamieson or Mr Mulliner were ill, in which case they would only be too glad to be friends with Mr Hoggins; but Miss Matty did not like my looking forward to anything like illness in so light a manner, and before the year was out all had come round in a far more satisfactory way.

I received two Cranford letters on one auspicious October morning. Both Miss Pole and Miss Matty wrote to ask me to come over and meet the Gordons, who had returned to England alive and well with their two children, now almost grown up. Dear Jessie Brown had kept her old kind nature, although she had changed her name and station; and she wrote to say that she and Major Gordon expected to be in Cranford on the fourteenth, and she hoped and begged to be remembered to Mrs Jamieson (named first, as became her honourable station), Miss Pole and Miss Matty—could she ever forget their kindness to her poor father and sister?—Mrs Forrester, Mr Hoggins (and here again came in an allusion to kindness shown to the dead long ago), his new wife, who as such must allow Mrs Gordon to desire to make her acquaintance, and who was, moreover, an old Scotch friend of her husband's. In short, every one was named, from the rector—who had been appointed to Cranford in the interim between Captain Brown's death and Miss Jessie's marriage, and was now associated with the latter event—down to Miss Betty Barker. All were asked to the luncheon; all except Mrs Fitz-Adam, who had come to live in Cranford since Miss Jessie Brown's days, and whom I found rather moping on account of the omission. People wondered at Miss Betty Barker's being included in the honourable list; but, then, as Miss Pole said, we must remember the disregard of the genteel proprieties of life in which the poor captain had educated his girls, and for his sake we swallowed our pride. Indeed, Mrs Jamieson rather took it as a compliment, as putting Miss Betty (formerly *her* maid) on a level with "those Hogginses."

But when I arrived in Cranford, nothing was as yet ascertained of Mrs Jamieson's own intentions; would the honourable lady go, or would she not? Mr Peter declared that she should and she would; Miss Pole shook her head and desponded. But Mr Peter was a man of resources. In the first place, he persuaded Miss Matty to write to Mrs Gordon, and to tell her of Mrs Fitz-Adam's existence, and to beg that one so kind, and cordial, and generous, might be included in the pleasant invitation. An answer came back by return of post, with a pretty little note for Mrs Fitz-Adam, and a request that Miss Matty would deliver it herself and explain the previous omission. Mrs Fitz-Adam was as pleased as could be, and thanked Miss Matty over and over again. Mr Peter had said, "Leave Mrs Jamieson to me;" so we did; especially as we knew nothing that we could do to alter her determination if once formed.

I did not know, nor did Miss Matty, how things were going on, until Miss Pole asked me, just the day before Mrs Gordon came, if I thought there was anything between Mr Peter and Mrs Jamieson in the matrimonial line, for that Mrs Jamieson was really going to the lunch at the "George." She had sent Mr Mulliner down to desire that there might be a footstool put to the warmest seat in the room, as she meant to come, and knew that their chairs were very high. Miss Pole had picked this piece of news up, and from it she conjectured all sorts of things, and bemoaned yet more. "If Peter should marry, what would become of poor dear Miss Matty? And Mrs Jamieson, of all people!" Miss Pole seemed to think there were other ladies in Cranford who would have done more credit to his choice, and I think she must have had someone who was unmarried in her head, for she kept saying, "It was so wanting in delicacy in a widow to think of such a thing."

When I got back to Miss Matty's I really did begin to think that Mr Peter might be thinking of Mrs Jamieson for a wife, and I was as unhappy as Miss Pole about it. He had the proof sheet of a great placard in his hand. "Signor Brunoni, Magician to the King of Delhi, the Rajah of Oude, and the great Lama of Thibet," &c. &c., was going to "perform in Cranford for one night only," the very next night; and Miss Matty, exultant, showed me a letter from the Gordons, promising to remain over this gaiety, which Miss Matty said was entirely Peter's doing. He had written to ask the signor to come, and was to be at all the expenses of the affair. Tickets were to be sent gratis to as many as the room would hold. In short, Miss Matty was charmed with the plan, and said that to-morrow Cranford would remind her of the Preston Guild, to which she had been in her youth—a luncheon at the "George," with the dear Gordons, and the signor in the Assembly Room in the evening. But I—I looked only at the fatal words:—

"*Under the Patronage of the* HONOURABLE MRS JAMIESON."

She, then, was chosen to preside over this entertainment of Mr Peter's; she was perhaps going to displace my dear Miss Matty in his heart, and make her life lonely once more! I could not look forward to the morrow with any pleasure; and every innocent anticipation of Miss Matty's only served to add to my annoyance.

So, angry and irritated, and exaggerating every little incident which could add to my irritation, I went on till we were all assembled in the great parlour at the "George." Major and Mrs Gordon and pretty Flora and Mr Ludovic were all as bright and handsome and friendly as could be; but I could hardly attend to them for watching Mr Peter, and I saw that Miss Pole was equally busy. I had never seen Mrs Jamieson so roused and animated before; her face looked full of interest in what Mr Peter was saying. I drew near to listen. My relief was great when I caught that his words were not words of love, but that, for all his grave face, he was at his old tricks. He was telling her of his travels in India, and describing the wonderful height of the Himalaya mountains: one touch after another added to their size, and each exceeded the former in absurdity; but Mrs Jamieson really enjoyed all in perfect good faith. I suppose she required strong stimulants to excite her to come out of her apathy. Mr Peter wound up his account by saying that, of course, at that altitude there were none of the animals to be found that existed in the lower regions; the game,—everything was different. Firing one day at some flying creature, he was very much dismayed when it fell, to find that he had shot a cherubim! Mr Peter caught my eye at this moment, and gave me such a funny twinkle, that I felt sure he had no thoughts of Mrs Jamieson as a wife from that time. She looked uncomfortably amazed—

"But, Mr Peter, shooting a cherubim—don't you think—I am afraid that was sacrilege!"

Mr Peter composed his countenance in a moment, and appeared shocked at the idea, which, as he said truly enough, was now presented to him for the first time; but then Mrs Jamieson must remember that he had been living for a long time among savages—all of whom were heathens—some of them, he was afraid, were downright Dissenters. Then, seeing Miss Matty draw near, he hastily changed the conversation, and after a little while, turning to me, he said, "Don't be shocked, prim little Mary, at all my wonderful stories. I consider Mrs Jamieson fair game, and besides I am bent on propitiating her, and the first step towards it is keeping her well awake. I bribed her here by asking her to let me have her name as patroness for my poor conjuror this evening; and I don't want to give her time enough to get up her rancour against the Hogginses, who are just coming in. I want everybody to be friends, for it harasses Matty so much to hear of these quarrels. I shall go at it again by-and-by, so you need not look shocked. I intend to enter the Assembly Room to-night with Mrs Jamieson on one side, and my lady, Mrs Hoggins, on the other. You see if I don't."

Somehow or another he did; and fairly got them into conversation together. Major and Mrs Gordon helped at the good work with their perfect ignorance of any existing coolness between any of the inhabitants of Cranford.

Ever since that day there has been the old friendly sociability in Cranford society; which I am thankful for, because of my dear Miss Matty's love of peace and kindliness. We all love Miss Matty, and I somehow think we are all of us better when she is near us.

RUTH

Drop, drop, slow tears!
   And bathe those beauteous feet,
Which brought from heaven
   The news and Prince of peace.
Cease not, wet eyes,
   For mercy to entreat:
To cry for vengeance
   Sin doth never cease.
In your deep floods
   Drown all my faults and fears;
Nor let His eye
   See sin, but through my tears.

Phineas Fletcher

CHAPTER I - THE DRESSMAKER'S APPRENTICE AT WORK

There is an assize-town in one of the eastern counties which was much distinguished by the Tudor sovereigns, and, in consequence of their favour and protection, attained a degree of importance that surprises the modern traveller.

A hundred years ago its appearance was that of picturesque grandeur. The old houses, which were the temporary residences of such of the county-families as contented themselves with the gaieties of a provincial town, crowded the streets and gave them the irregular but noble appearance yet to be seen in the cities of Belgium. The sides of the streets had a quaint richness, from the effect of the gables, and the stacks of chimneys which cut against the blue sky above; while, if the eye fell lower down, the attention was arrested by all kinds of projections in the shape of balcony and oriel; and it was amusing to see the infinite variety of windows that had been crammed into the walls long before Mr Pitt's days of taxation. The streets below suffered from all these projections and advanced stories above; they were dark, and ill-paved with large, round, jolting pebbles, and with no side-path protected by kerb-stones; there were no lamp-posts for long winter nights; and no regard was paid to the wants of the middle class, who neither drove about in coaches of their own, nor were carried by their own men in their own sedans into the very halls of their friends. The professional men and their wives, the shopkeepers and their spouses, and all such people, walked about at considerable peril both night and day. The broad unwieldy carriages hemmed them up against the houses in the narrow streets. The inhospitable houses projected their flights of steps almost into the carriage-way, forcing pedestrians again into the danger they had avoided for twenty or thirty paces. Then, at night, the only light was derived from the glaring, flaring oil-lamps hung above the doors of the more aristocratic mansions; just allowing space for the passers-by to become visible, before they again disappeared into the darkness, where it was no uncommon thing for robbers to be in waiting for their prey.

The traditions of those bygone times, even to the smallest social particular, enable one to understand more clearly the circumstances which contributed to the formation of character. The daily life into which people are born, and into which they are absorbed before they are well aware, forms chains which only one in a hundred has moral strength enough to despise, and to break when the right time comes—when an inward necessity for independent individual action arises, which is superior to all outward conventionalities. Therefore it is well to know what were the chains of daily domestic habit which were the natural leading-strings of our forefathers before they learnt to go alone.

The picturesqueness of those ancient streets has departed now. The Astleys, the Dunstans, the Waverhams—names of power in that district—go up duly to London in the season, and have sold their residences in the county-town fifty years ago, or more. And when the county-town lost its attraction for the Astleys, the Dunstans, the Waverhams, how could it be supposed that the Domvilles, the Bextons, and the Wildes would continue to go and winter there in their second-rate houses, and with their increased expenditure? So the grand old houses stood empty awhile; and then speculators ventured to purchase, and to turn the deserted mansions into many smaller dwellings, fitted for professional men, or even (bend your ear lower, lest the shade of Marmaduke, first Baron Waverham, hear) into shops!

Even that was not so very bad, compared with the next innovation on the old glories. The shopkeepers found out that the once fashionable street was dark, and that the dingy light did not show off their goods to advantage; the surgeon could not see to draw his patient's teeth; the lawyer had to ring for candles an hour earlier than he was accustomed to do when living in a more plebeian street. In short, by mutual consent, the whole front of one side of the street was pulled down, and rebuilt in the flat, mean, unrelieved style of George the Third. The body of the houses was too solidly grand to submit to alteration; so people were occasionally surprised, after passing through a commonplace-looking shop, to find themselves at the foot of a grand carved oaken staircase, lighted by a window of stained glass, storied all over with armorial bearings.

Up such a stair—past such a window (through which the moonlight fell on her with a glory of many colours)—Ruth Hilton passed wearily one January night, now many years ago. I call it night; but, strictly speaking, it was morning. Two o'clock in the morning chimed forth the old bells of St Saviour's. And yet more than a dozen girls still sat in the room into which Ruth entered, stitching away as if for very life, not daring to gape, or show any outward manifestation of sleepiness. They only sighed a little when Ruth told Mrs Mason the hour of the night, as the result of her errand; for they knew that, stay up as late as they might, the work-hours of the next day must begin at eight, and their young limbs were very weary.

Mrs Mason worked away as hard as any of them; but she was older and tougher; and, besides, the gains were hers. But even she perceived that some rest was needed. "Young ladies! there will be an interval allowed of half an hour. Ring the bell, Miss Sutton. Martha shall bring you up some bread and cheese and beer. You will be so good as to eat it standing—away from the dresses—and to have your hands washed ready for work when I return. In half an hour," said she once more, very distinctly; and then she left the room.

It was curious to watch the young girls as they instantaneously availed themselves of Mrs Mason's absence. One fat, particularly heavy-looking damsel laid her head on her folded arms and was asleep in a moment; refusing to be wakened for her share in the frugal supper, but springing up with a frightened look at the sound of Mrs Mason's returning footstep, even while it was still far off on the echoing stairs. Two or three others huddled over the scanty fireplace, which, with every possible economy of space, and no attempt whatever at anything of grace or ornament, was inserted in the slight, flat-looking wall, that had been run up by the present owner of the property to portion off this division of the grand old drawing-room of the mansion. Some employed the time in eating their bread and cheese, with as measured and incessant a motion of the jaws (and almost as stupidly placid an expression of countenance), as you may see in cows ruminating in the first meadow you happen to pass.

Some held up admiringly the beautiful ball-dress in progress, while others examined the effect, backing from the object to be criticised in the true artistic manner. Others stretched themselves into all sorts of postures to relieve the weary muscles; one or two gave vent to all the yawns, coughs, and sneezes that had been pent up so long in the presence of Mrs Mason. But Ruth Hilton sprang to the large old window, and pressed against it as a bird presses against the bars of its cage. She put back the blind, and gazed into the quiet moonlight night. It was doubly light—almost as much so as day—for everything was covered with the deep snow which had been falling silently ever since the evening before. The window was in a square recess; the old strange little panes of glass had been replaced by those which gave more light. A little distance off, the feathery branches of a larch waved softly to and fro in the scarcely perceptible night-breeze. Poor old larch! the time had been when it had stood in a pleasant lawn, with the tender grass creeping caressingly up to its very trunk; but now the lawn was divided into yards and squalid back premises, and the larch was pent up and girded about with flagstones. The snow lay thick on its boughs, and now and then fell noiselessly down. The old stables had been added to, and altered into a dismal street of mean-looking houses, back to back with the ancient mansions. And over all these changes from grandeur to squalor, bent down the purple heavens with their unchanging splendour!

Ruth pressed her hot forehead against the cold glass, and strained her aching eyes in gazing out on the lovely sky of a winter's night. The impulse was strong upon her to snatch up a shawl, and wrapping it round her head, to sally forth and enjoy the glory; and time was when that impulse would have been instantly followed; but now, Ruth's eyes filled with tears, and she stood quite still, dreaming of the days that were gone. Some one touched her shoulder while her thoughts were far away, remembering past January nights, which had resembled this, and were yet so different.

"Ruth, love," whispered a girl who had unwillingly distinguished herself by a long hard fit of coughing, "come and have some supper. You don't know yet how it helps one through the night."

"One run—one blow of the fresh air would do me more good," said Ruth.

"Not such a night as this," replied the other, shivering at the very thought.

"And why not such a night as this, Jenny?" answered Ruth. "Oh! at home I have many a time run up the lane all the way to the mill, just to see the icicles hang on the great wheel; and when I was once out, I could hardly find in my heart to come in, even to mother, sitting by the fire;—even to mother," she added, in a low, melancholy tone, which had something of inexpressible sadness in it. "Why, Jenny!" said she, rousing herself, but not before her eyes were swimming with tears, "own, now, that you never saw those dismal, hateful, tumble-down old houses there look half so—what shall I call them? almost beautiful—as they do now, with that soft, pure, exquisite covering; and if they are so improved, think of what trees, and grass, and ivy must be on such a night as this."

Jenny could not be persuaded into admiring the winter's night, which to her came only as a cold and dismal time, when her cough was more troublesome, and the pain in her side worse than usual. But she put her arm round Ruth's neck, and stood by her, glad that the orphan apprentice, who was not yet inured to the hardship of a dressmaker's workroom, should find so much to give her pleasure in such a common occurrence as a frosty night.

They remained deep in separate trains of thought till Mrs Mason's step was heard, when each returned, supperless but refreshed, to her seat.

Ruth's place was the coldest and the darkest in the room, although she liked it the best; she had instinctively chosen it for the sake of the wall opposite to her, on which was a remnant of the beauty of the old drawing-room, which must once have been magnificent, to judge from the faded specimen left. It was divided into panels of pale sea-green, picked out with white and gold; and on these panels were painted—were thrown with the careless, triumphant hand of a master—the most lovely wreaths of flowers, profuse and luxuriant beyond description, and so real-looking, that you could almost fancy you smelt their fragrance, and heard the south wind go softly rustling in and out among the crimson roses—the branches of purple and white lilac—the floating golden-tressed laburnum boughs. Besides these, there were stately white lilies, sacred to the Virgin—hollyhocks, fraxinella, monk's-hood, pansies, primroses; every flower which blooms profusely in charming old-fashioned country gardens was there, depicted among its graceful foliage, but not in the wild disorder in which I have enumerated them. At the bottom of the panel lay a holly-branch, whose stiff straightness was ornamented by a twining drapery of English ivy and mistletoe and winter aconite; while down either side hung pendant garlands of spring and autumn flowers; and, crowning all, came gorgeous summer with the sweet musk-roses, and the rich-coloured flowers of June and July.

Surely Monnoyer, or whoever the dead and gone artist might be, would have been gratified to know the pleasure his handiwork, even in its wane, had power to give to the heavy heart of a young girl; for they conjured up visions of other sister-flowers that grew, and blossomed, and withered away in her early home.

Mrs Mason was particularly desirous that her workwomen should exert themselves to-night, for, on the next, the annual hunt-ball was to take place. It was the one gaiety of the town since the assize-balls had been discontinued. Many were the dresses she had promised should be sent home "without fail" the next morning; she had not let one slip through her fingers, for fear, if it did, it might fall into the hands of the rival dressmaker, who had just established herself in the very same street.

She determined to administer a gentle stimulant to the flagging spirits, and with a little preliminary cough to attract attention, she began:

"I may as well inform you, young ladies, that I have been requested this year, as on previous occasions, to allow some of my young people to attend in the ante-chamber of the assembly-room with sandal ribbon, pins, and such little matters, and to be ready to repair any accidental injury to the ladies' dresses. I shall send four—of the most diligent." She laid a marked emphasis on the last words, but without much effect; they were too sleepy to care for any of the pomps and vanities, or, indeed, for any of the comforts of this world, excepting one sole thing—their beds.

Mrs Mason was a very worthy woman, but, like many other worthy women, she had her foibles; and one (very natural to her calling) was to pay an extreme regard to appearances. Accordingly, she had already selected in her own mind the four girls who were most likely to do credit to the "establishment;" and these were secretly determined upon, although it was very well to promise the reward to the most diligent. She was really not aware of the falseness of this conduct; being an adept in that species of sophistry with which people persuade themselves that what they wish to do is right.

At last there was no resisting the evidence of weariness. They were told to go to bed; but even that welcome command was languidly obeyed. Slowly they folded up their work, heavily they moved about, until at length all was put away, and they trooped up the wide, dark staircase.

"Oh! how shall I get through five years of these terrible nights! in that close room! and in that oppressive stillness! which lets every sound of the thread be heard as it goes eternally backwards and forwards," sobbed out Ruth, as she threw herself on her bed, without even undressing herself.

"Nay, Ruth, you know it won't be always as it has been to-night. We often get to bed by ten o'clock; and by-and-by you won't mind the closeness of the room. You're worn out to-night, or you would not have minded the sound of the needle; I never hear it. Come, let me unfasten you," said Jenny.

"What is the use of undressing? We must be up again and at work in three hours."

"And in those three hours you may get a great deal of rest, if you will but undress yourself and fairly go to bed. Come, love."

Jenny's advice was not resisted; but before Ruth went to sleep, she said:

"Oh! I wish I was not so cross and impatient. I don't think I used to be."

"No, I am sure not. Most new girls get impatient at first; but it goes off, and they don't care much for anything after awhile. Poor child! she's asleep already," said Jenny to herself.

She could not sleep or rest. The tightness at her side was worse than usual. She almost thought she ought to mention it in her letters home; but then she remembered the premium her father had struggled hard to pay, and the large family, younger than herself, that had to be cared for, and she determined to bear on, and trust that when the warm weather came both the pain and the cough would go away. She would be prudent about herself.

What was the matter with Ruth? She was crying in her sleep as if her heart would break. Such agitated slumber could be no rest; so Jenny wakened her.

"Ruth! Ruth!"

"Oh, Jenny!" said Ruth, sitting up in bed, and pushing back the masses of hair that were heating her forehead, "I thought I saw mamma by the side of the bed, coming, as she used to do, to see if I were asleep and comfortable; and when I tried to take hold of her, she went away and left me alone—I don't know where; so strange!"

"It was only a dream; you know you'd been talking about her to me, and you're feverish with sitting up late. Go to sleep again, and I'll watch, and waken you if you seem uneasy."

"But you'll be so tired. Oh, dear! dear!" Ruth was asleep again, even while she sighed.

Morning came, and though their rest had been short, the girls arose refreshed.

"Miss Sutton, Miss Jennings, Miss Booth, and Miss Hilton, you will see that you are ready to accompany me to the shire-hall by eight o'clock."

One or two of the girls looked astonished, but the majority, having anticipated the selection, and knowing from experience the unexpressed rule by which it was made, received it with the sullen indifference which had become their feeling with regard to most events—a deadened sense of life, consequent upon their unnatural mode of existence, their sedentary days, and their frequent nights of late watching.

But to Ruth it was inexplicable. She had yawned, and loitered, and looked off at the beautiful panel, and lost herself in thoughts of home, until she fully expected the reprimand which at any other time she would have been sure to receive, and now, to her surprise, she was singled out as one of the most diligent!

Much as she longed for the delight of seeing the noble shire-hall—the boast of the county—and of catching glimpses of the dancers, and hearing the band; much as she longed for some variety to the dull, monotonous life she was leading, she could not feel happy to accept a privilege, granted, as she believed, in ignorance of the real state of the case; so she startled her companions by rising abruptly and going up to Mrs Mason, who was finishing a dress which ought to have been sent home two hours before:

"If you please, Mrs Mason, I was not one of the most diligent; I am afraid—I believe—I was not diligent at all. I was very tired; and I could not help thinking, and when I think, I can't attend to my work." She stopped, believing she had sufficiently explained her meaning; but Mrs Mason would not understand, and did not wish for any further elucidation.

"Well, my dear, you must learn to think and work too; or, if you can't do both, you must leave off thinking. Your guardian, you know, expects you to make great progress in your business, and I am sure you won't disappoint him."

But that was not to the point. Ruth stood still an instant, although Mrs Mason resumed her employment in a manner which any one but a "new girl" would have known to be intelligible enough, that she did not wish for any more conversation just then.

"But as I was not diligent I ought not to go, ma'am. Miss Wood was far more industrious than I, and many of the others."

"Tiresome girl!" muttered Mrs Mason; "I've half a mind to keep her at home for plaguing me so." But, looking up, she was struck afresh with the remarkable beauty which Ruth possessed; such a credit to the house, with her waving outline of figure, her striking face, with dark eyebrows and dark lashes, combined with auburn hair and a fair complexion. No! diligent or idle, Ruth Hilton must appear to-night.

"Miss Hilton," said Mrs Mason, with stiff dignity, "I am not accustomed (as these young ladies can tell you) to have my decisions questioned. What I say, I mean; and I have my reasons. So sit down, if you please, and take care and be ready by eight. Not a word more," as she fancied she saw Ruth again about to speak.

"Jenny! you ought to have gone, not me," said Ruth, in no low voice to Miss Wood, as she sat down by her.

"Hush! Ruth. I could not go if I might, because of my cough. I would rather give it up to you than any one, if it were mine to give. And suppose it is, and take the pleasure as my present, and tell me every bit about it when you come home to-night."

"Well! I shall take it in that way, and not as if I'd earned it, which I haven't. So thank you. You can't think how I shall enjoy it now. I did work diligently for five minutes last night, after I heard of it, I wanted to go so much. But I could not keep it up. Oh, dear! and I shall really hear a band! and see the inside of that beautiful shire-hall!"

CHAPTER II - RUTH GOES TO THE SHIRE-HALL

In due time that evening, Mrs Mason collected "her young ladies" for an inspection of their appearance before proceeding to the shire-hall. Her eager, important, hurried manner of summoning them was not unlike that of a hen clucking her chickens together; and to judge from the close investigation they had to undergo, it might have been thought that their part in the evening's performance was to be far more important than that of temporary ladies'-maids.

"Is that your best frock, Miss Hilton?" asked Mrs Mason, in a half-dissatisfied tone, turning Ruth about; for it was only her Sunday black silk, and was somewhat worn and shabby.

"Yes, ma'am," answered Ruth, quietly.

"Oh! indeed. Then it will do" (still the half-satisfied tone). "Dress, young ladies, you know, is a very secondary consideration. Conduct is everything. Still, Miss Hilton, I think you should write and ask your guardian to send you money for another gown. I am sorry I did not think of it before."

"I do not think he would send any if I wrote," answered Ruth, in a low voice. "He was angry when I wanted a shawl, when the cold weather set in."

Mrs Mason gave her a little push of dismissal, and Ruth fell into the ranks by her friend, Miss Wood.

"Never mind, Ruthie; you're prettier than any of them," said a merry, good-natured girl, whose plainness excluded her from any of the envy of rivalry.

"Yes! I know I am pretty," said Ruth, sadly, "but I am sorry I have no better gown, for this is very shabby. I am ashamed of it myself, and I can see Mrs Mason is twice as much ashamed. I wish I need not go. I did not know we should have to think about our own dress at all, or I should not have wished to go."

"Never mind, Ruth," said Jenny, "you've been looked at now, and Mrs Mason will soon be too busy to think about you and your gown."

"Did you hear Ruth Hilton say she knew she was pretty?" whispered one girl to another, so loudly that Ruth caught the words.

"I could not help knowing," answered she, simply, "for many people have told me so."

At length these preliminaries were over, and they were walking briskly through the frosty air; the free motion was so inspiriting that Ruth almost danced along, and quite forgot all about shabby gowns and grumbling guardians. The shire-hall was even more striking than she had expected. The sides of the staircase were painted with figures that showed ghostly in the dim light, for only their faces looked out of the dark, dingy canvas, with a strange fixed stare of expression.

The young milliners had to arrange their wares on tables in the ante-room, and make all ready before they could venture to peep into the ball-room, where the musicians were already tuning their instruments, and where one or two char-women (strange contrast! with their dirty, loose attire, and their incessant chatter, to the grand echoes of the vaulted room) were completing the dusting of benches and chairs.

They quitted the place as Ruth and her companions entered. They had talked lightly and merrily in the ante-room, but now their voices were hushed, awed by the old magnificence of the vast apartment. It was so large, that objects showed dim at the further end, as through a mist. Full-length figures of county worthies hung around, in all varieties of costume, from the days of Holbein to the present time. The lofty roof was indistinct, for the lamps were not fully lighted yet; while through the richly-painted Gothic window at one end the moonbeams fell, many-tinted, on the floor, and mocked with their vividness the struggles of the artificial light to illuminate its little sphere.

High above sounded the musicians, fitfully trying some strain of which they were not certain. Then they stopped playing and talked, and their voices sounded goblin-like in their dark recess, where candles were carried about in an uncertain wavering manner, reminding Ruth of the flickering zigzag motion of the will-o'-the-wisp.

Suddenly the room sprang into the full blaze of light, and Ruth felt less impressed with its appearance, and more willing to obey Mrs Mason's sharp summons to her wandering flock, than she had been when it was dim and mysterious. They had presently enough to do in rendering offices of assistance to the ladies who thronged in, and whose voices drowned all the muffled sound of the band Ruth had longed so much to hear. Still, if one pleasure was less, another was greater than she had anticipated.

"On condition" of such a number of little observances that Ruth thought Mrs Mason would never have ended enumerating them, they were allowed during the dances to stand at a side-door and watch. And what a beautiful sight it was! Floating away to that bounding music—now far away, like garlands of fairies, now near, and showing as lovely women, with every ornament of graceful dress—the elite of the county danced on, little caring whose eyes gazed and were dazzled. Outside all was cold, and colourless, and uniform, one coating of snow over all. But inside it was warm, and glowing, and vivid; flowers scented the air, and wreathed the head, and rested on the bosom, as if it were midsummer. Bright colours flashed on the eye and were gone, and succeeded by others as lovely in the rapid movement of the dance. Smiles dimpled every face, and low tones of happiness murmured indistinctly through the room in every pause of the music.

Ruth did not care to separate the figures that formed a joyous and brilliant whole; it was enough to gaze, and dream of the happy smoothness of the lives in which such music, and such profusion of flowers, of jewels, elegance of every description, and beauty of all shapes and hues, were everyday things. She did not want to know who the people were; although to hear a catalogue of names seemed to be the great delight of most of her companions.

In fact, the enumeration rather disturbed her; and to avoid the shock of too rapid a descent into the commonplace world of Miss Smiths and Mr Thomsons, she returned to her post in the ante-room. There she stood thinking, or dreaming. She was startled back to actual life by a voice close to her. One of the dancing young ladies had met with a misfortune. Her dress, of some gossamer material, had been looped up by nosegays of flowers, and one of these had fallen off in the dance, leaving her gown to trail. To repair this, she had begged her partner to bring her to the room where the assistants should have been. None were there but Ruth.

"Shall I leave you?" asked the gentleman. "Is my absence necessary?"

"Oh, no!" replied the lady. "A few stitches will set all to rights. Besides, I dare not enter that room by myself." So far she spoke sweetly and prettily. But now she addressed Ruth. "Make haste. Don't keep me an hour." And her voice became cold and authoritative.

She was very pretty, with long dark ringlets and sparkling black eyes. These had struck Ruth in the hasty glance she had taken, before she knelt down to her task. She also saw that the gentleman was young and elegant.

"Oh, that lovely galop! How I long to dance to it! Will it never be done? What a frightful time you are taking; and I'm dying to return in time for this galop!"

By way of showing a pretty, childlike impatience, she began to beat time with her feet to the spirited air the band was playing. Ruth could not darn the rent in her dress with this continual motion, and she looked up to remonstrate. As she threw her head back for this purpose, she caught the eye of the gentleman who was standing by; it was so expressive of amusement at the airs and graces of his pretty partner, that Ruth was infected by the feeling, and had to bend her face down to conceal the smile that mantled there. But not before he had seen it, and not before his attention had been thereby drawn to consider the kneeling figure, that, habited in black up to the throat, with the noble head bent down to the occupation in which she was engaged, formed such a contrast to the flippant, bright, artificial girl who sat to be served with an air as haughty as a queen on her throne.

"Oh, Mr Bellingham! I'm ashamed to detain you so long. I had no idea any one could have spent so much time over a little tear. No wonder Mrs Mason charges so much for dress-making, if her work-women are so slow."

It was meant to be witty, but Mr Bellingham looked grave. He saw the scarlet colour of annoyance flush to that beautiful cheek which was partially presented to him. He took a candle from the table, and held it so that Ruth had more light. She did not look up to thank him, for she felt ashamed that he should have seen the smile which she had caught from him.

"I am sorry I have been so long, ma'am," said she, gently, as she finished her work. "I was afraid it might tear out again if I did not do it carefully." She rose.

"I would rather have had it torn than have missed that charming galop," said the young lady, shaking out her dress as a bird shakes its plumage. "Shall we go, Mr Bellingham?" looking up at him.

He was surprised that she gave no word or sign of thanks to the assistant. He took up a camellia that some one had left on the table.

"Allow me, Miss Duncombe, to give this in your name to this young lady, as thanks for her dexterous help."

"Oh—of course," said she.

Ruth received the flower silently, but with a grave, modest motion of her head. They had gone, and she was once more alone. Presently, her companions returned.

"What was the matter with Miss Duncombe? Did she come here?" asked they.

"Only her lace dress was torn, and I mended it," answered Ruth, quietly.

"Did Mr Bellingham come with her? They say he's going to be married to her; did he come, Ruth?"

"Yes," said Ruth, and relapsed into silence.

Mr Bellingham danced on gaily and merrily through the night, and flirted with Miss Duncombe, as he thought good. But he looked often to the side-door where the milliner's apprentices stood; and once he recognised the tall, slight figure, and the rich auburn hair of the girl in black; and then his eye sought for the camellia. It was there, snowy white in her bosom. And he danced on more gaily than ever.

The cold grey dawn was drearily lighting up the streets when Mrs Mason and her company returned home. The lamps were extinguished, yet the shutters of the shops and dwelling-houses were not opened. All sounds had an echo unheard by day. One or two houseless beggars sat on doorsteps, and, shivering, slept, with heads bowed on their knees, or resting against the cold hard support afforded by the wall.

Ruth felt as if a dream had melted away, and she were once more in the actual world. How long it would be, even in the most favourable chance, before she should again enter the shire-hall! or hear a band of music! or even see again those bright, happy people—as much without any semblance of care or woe as if they belonged to another race of beings. Had they ever to deny themselves a wish, much less a want? Literally and figuratively, their lives seemed to wander through flowery pleasure-paths. Here was cold, biting mid-winter for her, and such as her—for those poor beggars almost a season of death; but to Miss Duncombe and her companions, a happy, merry time, when flowers still bloomed, and fires crackled, and comforts and luxuries were piled around them like fairy gifts. What did they know of the meaning of the word, so terrific to the poor? What was winter to them? But Ruth fancied that Mr Bellingham looked as if he could understand the feelings of those removed from him by circumstance and station. He had drawn up the windows of his carriage, it is true, with a shudder.

Ruth, then, had been watching him.

Yet she had no idea that any association made her camellia precious to her. She believed it was solely on account of its exquisite beauty that she tended it so carefully. She told Jenny every particular of its presentation, with open, straight-looking eye, and without the deepening of a shade of colour.

"Was it not kind of him? You can't think how nicely he did it, just when I was a little bit mortified by her ungracious ways."

"It was very nice, indeed," replied Jenny. "Such a beautiful flower! I wish it had some scent."

"I wish it to be exactly as it is; it is perfect. So pure!" said Ruth, almost clasping her treasure as she placed it in water. "Who is Mr Bellingham?"

"He is son to that Mrs Bellingham of the Priory, for whom we made the grey satin pelisse," answered Jenny, sleepily.

"That was before my time," said Ruth. But there was no answer. Jenny was asleep.

It was long before Ruth followed her example. Even on a winter day, it was clear morning light that fell upon her face as she smiled in her slumber. Jenny would not waken her, but watched her face with admiration; it was so lovely in its happiness.

"She is dreaming of last night," thought Jenny.

It was true she was; but one figure flitted more than all the rest through her visions. He presented flower after flower to her in that baseless morning dream, which was all too quickly ended. The night before, she had seen her dead mother in her sleep, and she wakened, weeping. And now she dreamed of Mr Bellingham, and smiled.

And yet, was this a more evil dream than the other?

The realities of life seemed to cut more sharply against her heart than usual that morning. The late hours of the preceding nights, and perhaps the excitement of the evening before, had indisposed her to bear calmly the rubs and crosses which beset all Mrs Mason's young ladies at times.

For Mrs Mason, though the first dressmaker in the county, was human after all; and suffered, like her apprentices, from the same causes that affected them. This morning she was disposed to find fault with everything, and everybody. She seemed to have risen with the determination of putting the world and all that it contained (her world, at least) to rights before night; and abuses and negligences, which had long passed unreproved, or winked at, were to-day to be dragged to light, and sharply reprimanded. Nothing less than perfection would satisfy Mrs Mason at such times.

She had her ideas of justice, too; but they were not divinely beautiful and true ideas; they were something more resembling a grocer's, or tea-dealer's ideas of equal right. A little over-indulgence last night was to be balanced by a good deal of over-severity to-day; and this manner of rectifying previous errors fully satisfied her conscience.

Ruth was not inclined for, or capable of, much extra exertion; and it would have tasked all her powers to have pleased her superior. The work-room seemed filled with sharp calls. "Miss Hilton! where have you put the blue Persian? Whenever things are mislaid, I know it has been Miss Hilton's evening for siding away!"

"Miss Hilton was going out last night, so I offered to clear the workroom for her. I will find it directly, ma'am," answered one of the girls.

"Oh, I am well aware of Miss Hilton's custom of shuffling off her duties upon any one who can be induced to relieve her," replied Mrs Mason.

Ruth reddened, and tears sprang to her eyes; but she was so conscious of the falsity of the accusation, that she rebuked herself for being moved by it, and, raising her head, gave a proud look round, as if in appeal to her companions.

"Where is the skirt of Lady Farnham's dress? The flounces not put on! I am surprised. May I ask to whom this work was entrusted yesterday?" inquired Mrs Mason, fixing her eyes on Ruth.

"I was to have done it, but I made a mistake, and had to undo it. I am very sorry."

"I might have guessed, certainly. There is little difficulty, to be sure, in discovering, when work has been neglected or spoilt, into whose hands it has fallen."

Such were the speeches which fell to Ruth's share on this day of all days, when she was least fitted to bear them with equanimity.

In the afternoon it was necessary for Mrs Mason to go a few miles into the country. She left injunctions, and orders, and directions, and prohibitions without end; but at last she was gone, and in the relief of her absence, Ruth laid her arms on the table, and, burying her head, began to cry aloud, with weak, unchecked sobs.

"Don't cry, Miss Hilton,"—"Ruthie, never mind the old dragon,"—"How will you bear on for five years, if you don't spirit yourself up not to care a straw for what she says?"—were some of the modes of comfort and sympathy administered by the young workwomen.

Jenny, with a wiser insight into the grievance and its remedy, said:

"Suppose Ruth goes out instead of you, Fanny Barton, to do the errands. The fresh air will do her good; and you know you dislike the cold east winds, while Ruth says she enjoys frost and snow, and all kinds of shivery weather."

Fanny Barton was a great sleepy-looking girl, huddling over the fire. No one so willing as she to relinquish the walk on this bleak afternoon, when the east wind blew keenly down the street, drying up the very snow itself. There was no temptation to come abroad, for those who were not absolutely obliged to leave their warm rooms; indeed, the dusk hour showed that it was the usual tea-time for the humble inhabitants of that part of the town through which Ruth had to pass on her shopping expedition. As she came to the high ground just above the river, where the street sloped rapidly down to the bridge, she saw the flat country beyond all covered with snow, making the black dome of the cloud-laden sky appear yet blacker; as if the winter's night had never fairly gone away, but had hovered on the edge of the world all through the short bleak day. Down by the bridge (where there was a little shelving bank, used as a landing-place for any pleasure-boats that could float on that shallow stream) some children were playing, and defying the cold; one of them had got a large washing-tub, and with the use of a broken oar kept steering and pushing himself hither and thither in the little creek, much to the admiration of his companions, who stood gravely looking on, immovable in their attentive observation of the hero, although their faces were blue with cold, and their hands crammed deep into their pockets with some faint hope of finding warmth there. Perhaps they feared that, if they unpacked themselves from their lumpy attitudes and began to move about, the cruel wind would find its way into every cranny of their tattered dress. They were all huddled up, and still; with eyes intent on the embryo sailor. At last, one little man, envious of the reputation that his playfellow was acquiring by his daring, called out:

"I'll set thee a craddy, Tom! Thou dar'n't go over yon black line in the water, out into the real river."

Of course the challenge was not to be refused, and Tom paddled away towards the dark line, beyond which the river swept with smooth, steady current. Ruth (a child in years herself) stood at the top of the declivity watching the adventurer, but as unconscious of any danger as the group of children below. At their playfellow's success, they broke through the calm gravity of observation into boisterous marks of applause, clapping their hands, and stamping their impatient little feet, and shouting, "Well done, Tom; thou hast done it rarely!"

Tom stood in childish dignity for a moment, facing his admirers; then, in an instant, his washing-tub boat was whirled round, and he lost his balance, and fell out; and both he and his boat were carried away slowly, but surely, by the strong full river which eternally moved onwards to the sea.

The children shrieked aloud with terror; and Ruth flew down to the little bay, and far into its shallow waters, before she felt how useless such an action was, and that the sensible plan would have been to seek for efficient help. Hardly had this thought struck her, when, louder and sharper than the sullen roar of the stream that was ceaselessly and unrelentingly flowing on, came the splash of a horse galloping through the water in which she was standing. Past her like lightning—down in the stream, swimming along with the current—a stooping rider—an outstretched, grasping arm—a little life redeemed, and a child saved to those who loved it! Ruth stood dizzy and sick with emotion while all this took place; and when the rider turned his swimming horse, and slowly breasted up the river to the landing-place, she recognised him as the Mr Bellingham of the night before. He carried the unconscious child across his horse; the body hung in so lifeless a manner that Ruth believed it was dead, and her eyes were suddenly blinded with tears. She waded back to the beach, to the point towards which Mr Bellingham was directing his horse.

"Is he dead?" asked she, stretching out her arms to receive the little fellow; for she instinctively felt that the position in which he hung was not the most conducive to returning consciousness, if, indeed, it would ever return.

"I think not," answered Mr Bellingham, as he gave the child to her, before springing off his horse. "Is he your brother? Do you know who he is?"

"Look!" said Ruth, who had sat down upon the ground, the better to prop the poor lad, "his hand twitches! he lives! oh, sir, he lives! Whose boy is he?" (to the people, who came hurrying and gathering to the spot at the rumour of an accident).

"He's old Nelly Brownson's," said they. "Her grandson."

"We must take him into a house directly," said she. "Is his home far off?"

"No, no; it's just close by."

"One of you go for a doctor at once," said Mr Bellingham, authoritatively, "and bring him to the old woman's without delay. You must not hold him any longer," he continued, speaking to Ruth, and remembering her face now for the first time; "your dress is dripping wet already. Here! you fellow, take him up, d'ye see!"

But the child's hand had nervously clenched Ruth's dress, and she would not have him disturbed. She carried her heavy burden very tenderly towards a mean little cottage indicated by the neighbours; an old crippled woman was coming out of the door, shaking all over with agitation.

"Dear heart!" said she, "he's the last of 'em all, and he's gone afore me."

"Nonsense," said Mr Bellingham, "the boy is alive, and likely to live."

But the old woman was helpless and hopeless, and insisted on believing that her grandson was dead; and dead he would have been if it had not been for Ruth, and one or two of the more sensible neighbours, who, under Mr Bellingham's directions, bustled about, and did all that was necessary until animation was restored.

"What a confounded time these people are in fetching the doctor," said Mr Bellingham to Ruth, between whom and himself a sort of silent understanding had sprung up from the circumstance of their having been the only two (besides mere children) who had witnessed the accident, and also the only two to whom a certain degree of cultivation had given the power of understanding each other's thoughts and even each other's words.

"It takes so much to knock an idea into such stupid people's heads. They stood gaping and asking which doctor they were to go for, as if it signified whether it was Brown or Smith, so long as he had his wits about him. I have no more time to waste here, either; I was on the gallop when I caught sight of the lad; and, now he has fairly sobbed and opened his eyes, I see no use in my staying in this stifling atmosphere. May I trouble you with one thing? Will you be so good as to see that the little fellow has all that he wants? If you'll allow me, I'll leave you my purse," continued he, giving it to Ruth, who was only too glad to have this power entrusted to her of procuring one or two requisites which she had perceived to be wanted. But she saw some gold between the net-work; she did not like the charge of such riches.

"I shall not want so much, really, sir. One sovereign will be plenty—more than enough. May I take that out, and I will give you back what is left of it when I see you again? or, perhaps I had better send it to you, sir?"

"I think you had better keep it all at present. Oh! what a horrid dirty place this is; insufferable two minutes longer. You must not stay here; you'll be poisoned with this abominable air. Come towards the door, I beg. Well, if you think one sovereign will be enough, I will take my purse; only, remember you apply to me if you think they want more."

They were standing at the door, where some one was holding Mr Bellingham's horse. Ruth was looking at him with her earnest eyes (Mrs Mason and her errands quite forgotten in the interest of the afternoon's event), her whole thoughts bent upon rightly understanding and following out his wishes for the little boy's welfare; and until now this had been the first object in his own mind. But at this moment the strong perception of Ruth's exceeding beauty came again upon him. He almost lost the sense of what he was saying, he was so startled into admiration. The night before, he had not seen her eyes; and now they looked straight and innocently full at him, grave, earnest, and deep. But when she instinctively read the change in the expression of his countenance, she dropped her large white veiling lids; and he thought her face was lovelier still.

The irresistible impulse seized him to arrange matters so that he might see her again before long.

"No!" said he. "I see it would be better that you should keep the purse. Many things may be wanted for the lad which we cannot calculate upon now. If I remember rightly, there are three sovereigns and some loose change; I shall, perhaps, see you again in a few days, when, if there be any money left in the purse, you can restore it to me."

"Oh, yes, sir," said Ruth, alive to the magnitude of the wants to which she might have to administer, and yet rather afraid of the responsibility implied in the possession of so much money.

"Is there any chance of my meeting you again in this house?" asked he.

"I hope to come whenever I can, sir; but I must run in errand-times, and I don't know when my turn may be."

"Oh"—he did not fully understand this answer—"I should like to know how you think the boy is going on, if it is not giving you too much trouble; do you ever take walks?"

"Not for walking's sake, sir."

"Well!" said he, "you go to church, I suppose? Mrs Mason does not keep you at work on Sundays, I trust?"

"Oh, no, sir. I go to church regularly."

"Then, perhaps, you will be so good as to tell me what church you go to, and I will meet you there next Sunday afternoon?"

"I go to St Nicholas', sir. I will take care and bring you word how the boy is, and what doctor they get; and I will keep an account of the money I spend."

"Very well; thank you. Remember, I trust to you."

He meant that he relied on her promise to meet him; but Ruth thought that he was referring to the responsibility of doing the best she could for the child. He was going away, when a fresh thought struck him, and he turned back into the cottage once more, and addressed Ruth, with a half smile on his countenance:

"It seems rather strange, but we have no one to introduce us; my name is Bellingham—yours is—?"

"Ruth Hilton, sir," she answered, in a low voice, for, now that the conversation no longer related to the boy, she felt shy and restrained.

He held out his hand to shake hers, and just as she gave it to him, the old grandmother came tottering up to ask some question. The interruption jarred upon him, and made him once more keenly alive to the closeness of the air, and the squalor and dirt by which he was surrounded.

"My good woman," said he to Nelly Brownson, "could you not keep your place a little neater and cleaner? It is more fit for pigs than human beings. The air in this room is quite offensive, and the dirt and filth is really disgraceful."

By this time he was mounted, and, bowing to Ruth, he rode away.

Then the old woman's wrath broke out.

"Who may you be, that knows no better manners than to come into a poor woman's house to abuse it?—fit for pigs, indeed! What d'ye call yon fellow?"

"He is Mr Bellingham," said Ruth, shocked at the old woman's apparent ingratitude. "It was he that rode into the water to save your grandson. He would have been drowned but for Mr Bellingham. I thought once they would both have been swept away by the current, it was so strong."

"The river is none so deep, either," the old woman said, anxious to diminish as much as possible the obligation she was under to one who had offended her. "Some one else would have saved him, if this fine young spark had never been near. He's an orphan, and God watches over orphans, they say. I'd rather it had been any one else as had picked him out, than one who comes into a poor body's house only to abuse it."

"He did not come in only to abuse it," said Ruth, gently. "He came with little Tom; he only said it was not quite so clean as it might be."

"What! you're taking up the cry, are you? Wait till you are an old woman like me, crippled with rheumatiz, and a lad to see after like Tom, who is always in mud when he isn't in water; and his food and mine to scrape together (God knows we're often short, and do the best I can), and water to fetch up that steep brow."

She stopped to cough; and Ruth judiciously changed the subject, and began to consult the old woman as to the wants of her grandson, in which consultation they were soon assisted by the medical man.

When Ruth had made one or two arrangements with a neighbour, whom she asked to procure the most necessary things, and had heard from the doctor that all would be right in a day or two, she began to quake at the recollection of the length of time she had spent at Nelly Brownson's, and to remember, with some affright, the strict watch kept by Mrs Mason over her apprentices' out-goings and incomings on working days. She hurried off to the shops, and tried to recall her wandering thoughts to the respective merits of pink and blue as a match to lilac, found she had lost her patterns, and went home with ill-chosen things, and in a fit of despair at her own stupidity.

The truth was, that the afternoon's adventure filled her mind; only, the figure of Tom (who was now safe, and likely to do well) was receding into the background, and that of Mr Bellingham becoming more prominent than it had been. His spirited and natural action of galloping into the water to save the child, was magnified by Ruth into the most heroic deed of daring; his interest about the boy was tender, thoughtful benevolence in her eyes, and his careless liberality of money was fine generosity; for she forgot that generosity implies some degree of self-denial. She was gratified, too, by the power of dispensing comfort he had entrusted to her, and was busy with Alnaschar visions of wise expenditure, when the necessity of opening Mrs Mason's house-door summoned her back into actual present life, and the dread of an immediate scolding.

For this time, however, she was spared; but spared for such a reason that she would have been thankful for some blame in preference to her impunity. During her absence, Jenny's difficulty of breathing had suddenly become worse, and the girls had, on their own responsibility, put her to bed, and were standing round her in dismay, when Mrs Mason's return home (only a few minutes before Ruth arrived) fluttered them back into the workroom.

And now, all was confusion and hurry; a doctor to be sent for; a mind to be unburdened of directions for a dress to a forewoman, who was too ill to understand; scoldings to be scattered with no illiberal hand amongst a group of frightened girls, hardly sparing the poor invalid herself for her inopportune illness. In the middle of all this turmoil, Ruth crept quietly to her place, with a heavy saddened heart at the indisposition of the gentle forewoman. She would gladly have nursed Jenny herself, and often longed to do it, but she could not be spared. Hands, unskilful in fine and delicate work, would be well enough qualified to tend the sick, until the mother arrived from home. Meanwhile, extra diligence was required in the workroom; and Ruth found no opportunity of going to see little Tom, or to fulfil the plans for making him and his grandmother more comfortable, which she had proposed to herself. She regretted her rash promise to Mr Bellingham, of attending to the little boy's welfare; all that she could do was done by means of Mrs Mason's servant, through whom she made inquiries, and sent the necessary help.

The subject of Jenny's illness was the prominent one in the house. Ruth told of her own adventure, to be sure; but when she was at the very crisis of the boy's fall into the river, the more fresh and vivid interest of some tidings of Jenny was brought into the room, and Ruth ceased, almost blaming herself for caring for anything besides the question of life or death to be decided in that very house.

Then a pale, gentle-looking woman was seen moving softly about; and it was whispered that this was the mother come to nurse her child. Everybody liked her, she was so sweet-looking, and gave so little trouble, and seemed so patient, and so thankful for any inquiries about her daughter, whose illness, it was understood, although its severity was mitigated, was likely to be long and tedious. While all the feelings and thoughts relating to Jenny were predominant, Sunday arrived. Mrs Mason went the accustomed visit to her father's, making some little show of apology to Mrs Wood for leaving her and her daughter; the apprentices dispersed to the various friends with whom they were in the habit of spending the day; and Ruth went to St Nicholas', with a sorrowful heart, depressed on account of Jenny, and self-reproachful at having rashly undertaken what she had been unable to perform.

As she came out of church, she was joined by Mr Bellingham. She had half hoped that he might have forgotten the arrangement, and yet she wished to relieve herself of her responsibility. She knew his step behind her, and the contending feelings made her heart beat hard, and she longed to run away.

"Miss Hilton, I believe," said he, overtaking her, and bowing forward, so as to catch a sight of her rose-red face. "How is our little sailor going on? Well, I trust, from the symptoms the other day."

"I believe, sir, he is quite well now. I am very sorry, but I have not been able to go and see him. I am so sorry—I could not help it. But I have got one or two things through another person. I have put them down on this slip of paper; and here is your purse, sir, for I am afraid I can do nothing more for him. We have illness in the house, and it makes us very busy."

Ruth had been so much accustomed to blame of late, that she almost anticipated some remonstrance or reproach now, for not having fulfilled her promise better. She little guessed that Mr Bellingham was far more busy trying to devise some excuse for meeting her again, during the silence that succeeded her speech, than displeased with her for not bringing a more particular account of the little boy, in whom he had ceased to feel any interest.

She repeated, after a minute's pause:

"I am very sorry I have done so little, sir."

"Oh, yes, I am sure you have done all you could. It was thoughtless in me to add to your engagements."

"He is displeased with me," thought Ruth, "for what he believes to have been neglect of the boy, whose life he risked his own to save. If I told all, he would see that I could not do more; but I cannot tell him all the sorrows and worries that have taken up my time."

"And yet I am tempted to give you another little commission, if it is not taking up too much of your time, and presuming too much on your good-nature," said he, a bright idea having just struck him. "Mrs Mason lives in Heneage Place, does not she? My mother's ancestors lived there; and once, when the house was being repaired, she took me in to show me the old place. There was an old hunting-piece painted on a panel over one of the chimney-pieces; the figures were portraits of my ancestors. I have often thought I should like to purchase it, if it still remained there. Can you ascertain this for me, and bring me word next Sunday?"

"Oh, yes, sir," said Ruth, glad that this commission was completely within her power to execute, and anxious to make up for her previous seeming neglect. "I'll look directly I get home, and ask Mrs Mason to write and let you know."

"Thank you," said he, only half satisfied; "I think perhaps, however, it might be as well not to trouble Mrs Mason about it; you see, it would compromise me, and I am not quite determined to purchase the picture; if you would ascertain whether the painting is there, and tell me, I would take a little time to reflect, and afterwards I could apply to Mrs Mason myself."

"Very well, sir; I will see about it." So they parted.

Before the next Sunday, Mrs Wood had taken her daughter to her distant home, to recruit in that quiet place. Ruth watched her down the street from an upper window, and, sighing deep and long, returned to the workroom, whence the warning voice and the gentle wisdom had departed.

CHAPTER III - SUNDAY AT MRS MASON'S

Mr Bellingham attended afternoon service at St Nicholas' church the next Sunday. His thoughts had been far more occupied by Ruth than hers by him, although his appearance upon the scene of her life was more an event to her than it was to him. He was puzzled by the impression she had produced on him, though he did not in general analyse the nature of his feelings, but simply enjoyed them with the delight which youth takes in experiencing new and strong emotion.

He was old compared to Ruth, but young as a man; hardly three-and-twenty. The fact of his being an only child had given him, as it does to many, a sort of inequality in those parts of the character which are usually formed by the number of years that a person has lived.

The unevenness of discipline to which only children are subjected; the thwarting, resulting from over-anxiety; the indiscreet indulgence, arising from a love centred all in one object; had been exaggerated in his education, probably from the circumstance that his mother (his only surviving parent) had been similarly situated to himself.

He was already in possession of the comparatively small property he inherited from his father. The estate on which his mother lived was her own; and her income gave her the means of indulging or controlling him, after he had grown to man's estate, as her wayward disposition and her love of power prompted her.

Had he been double-dealing in his conduct towards her, had he condescended to humour her in the least, her passionate love for him would have induced her to strip herself of all her possessions to add to his dignity or happiness. But although he felt the warmest affection for her, the regardlessness which she had taught him (by example, perhaps, more than by precept) of the feelings of others, was continually prompting him to do things that she, for the time being, resented as mortal affronts. He would mimic the clergyman she specially esteemed, even to his very face; he would refuse to visit her schools for months and months; and, when wearied into going at last, revenge himself by puzzling the children with the most ridiculous questions (gravely put) that he could imagine.

All these boyish tricks annoyed and irritated her far more than the accounts which reached her of more serious misdoings at college and in town. Of these grave offences she never spoke; of the smaller misdeeds she hardly ever ceased speaking.

Still, at times, she had great influence over him, and nothing delighted her more than to exercise it. The submission of his will to hers was sure to be liberally rewarded; for it gave her great happiness to extort, from his indifference or his affection, the concessions which she never sought by force of reason, or by appeals to principle—concessions which he frequently withheld, solely for the sake of asserting his independence of her control.

She was anxious for him to marry Miss Duncombe. He cared little or nothing about it—it was time enough to be married ten years hence; and so he was dawdling through some months of his life—sometimes flirting with the nothing-loath Miss Duncombe, sometimes plaguing, and sometimes delighting his mother, at all times taking care to please himself—when he first saw Ruth Hilton, and a new, passionate, hearty feeling shot through his whole being. He did not know why he was so fascinated by her. She was very beautiful, but he had seen others equally beautiful, and with many more *agaceries* calculated to set off the effect of their charms.

There was, perhaps, something bewitching in the union of the grace and loveliness of womanhood with the *naïveté*, simplicity, and innocence of an intelligent child. There was a spell in the shyness, which made her avoid and shun all admiring approaches to acquaintance. It would be an exquisite delight to attract and tame her wildness, just as he had often allured and tamed the timid fawns in his mother's park.

By no over-bold admiration, or rash, passionate word, would he startle her; and, surely, in time she might be induced to look upon him as a friend, if not something nearer and dearer still.

In accordance with this determination, he resisted the strong temptation of walking by her side the whole distance home after church. He only received the intelligence she brought respecting the panel with thanks, spoke a few words about the weather, bowed, and was gone. Ruth believed she should never see him again; and, in spite of sundry self-upbraidings for her folly, she could not help feeling as if a shadow were drawn over her existence for several days to come.

Mrs Mason was a widow, and had to struggle for the sake of the six or seven children left dependent on her exertions; thus there was some reason, and great excuse, for the pinching economy which regulated her household affairs.

On Sundays she chose to conclude that all her apprentices had friends who would be glad to see them to dinner, and give them a welcome reception for the remainder of the day; while she, and those of her children who were not at school, went to spend the day at her father's house, several miles out of the town. Accordingly, no dinner was cooked on Sundays for the young workwomen; no fires were lighted in any rooms to which they had access. On this morning they breakfasted in Mrs Mason's own parlour, after which the room was closed against them through the day by some understood, though unspoken prohibition.

What became of such as Ruth, who had no home and no friends in that large, populous, desolate town? She had hitherto commissioned the servant, who went to market on Saturdays for the family, to buy her a bun or biscuit, whereon she made her fasting dinner in the deserted workroom, sitting in her walking-dress to keep off the cold, which clung to her in spite of shawl and bonnet. Then she would sit at the window, looking out on the dreary prospect till her eyes were often blinded by tears; and, partly to shake off thoughts and recollections, the indulgence in which she felt to be productive of no good, and partly to have some ideas to dwell upon during the coming week beyond those suggested by the constant view of the same room, she would carry her Bible, and place herself in the window-seat on the wide landing, which commanded the street in front of the house. From thence she could see the irregular grandeur of the place; she caught a view of the grey church-tower, rising hoary and massive into mid-air; she saw one or two figures loiter along on the sunny side of the street, in all the enjoyment of their fine clothes and Sunday leisure; and she imagined histories for them, and tried to picture to herself their homes and their daily doings.

And before long, the bells swung heavily in the church-tower, and struck out with musical clang the first summons to afternoon church.

After church was over, she used to return home to the same window-seat, and watch till the winter twilight was over and gone, and the stars came out over the black masses of houses. And then she would steal down to ask for a candle, as a companion to her in the deserted workroom. Occasionally the servant would bring her up some tea; but of late Ruth had declined taking any, as she had discovered she was robbing the kind-hearted creature of part of the small provision left out for her by Mrs Mason. She sat on, hungry and cold, trying to read her Bible, and to think the old holy thoughts which had been her childish meditations at her mother's knee, until one after another the apprentices returned, weary with their day's enjoyment, and their week's late watching; too weary to make her in any way a partaker of their pleasure by entering into details of the manner in which they had spent their day.

And last of all, Mrs Mason returned; and, summoning her "young people" once more into the parlour, she read a prayer before dismissing them to bed. She always expected to find them all in the house when she came home, but asked no questions as to their proceedings through the day; perhaps because she dreaded to hear that one or two had occasionally nowhere to go, and that it would be sometimes necessary to order a Sunday's dinner, and leave a lighted fire on that day.

For five months Ruth had been an inmate at Mrs Mason's, and such had been the regular order of the Sundays. While the forewoman stayed there, it is true, she was ever ready to give Ruth the little variety of hearing of recreations in which she was no partaker; and however tired Jenny might be at night, she had ever some sympathy to bestow on Ruth for the dull length of day she had passed. After her departure, the monotonous idleness of the Sunday seemed worse to bear than the incessant labour of the work-days; until the time came when it seemed to be a recognised hope in her mind, that on Sunday afternoons she should see Mr Bellingham, and hear a few words from him, as from a friend who took an interest in her thoughts and proceedings during the past week.

Ruth's mother had been the daughter of a poor curate in Norfolk, and, early left without parents or home, she was thankful to marry a respectable farmer a good deal older than herself. After their marriage, however, everything seemed to go wrong. Mrs Hilton fell into a delicate state of health, and was unable to bestow the ever-watchful attention to domestic affairs so requisite in a farmer's wife. Her husband had a series of misfortunes—of a more important kind than the death of a whole brood of turkeys from getting among the nettles, or the year of bad cheeses spoilt by a careless dairymaid—which were the consequences (so the neighbours said) of Mr Hilton's mistake in marrying a delicate, fine lady. His crops failed; his horses died; his barn took fire; in short, if he had been in any way a remarkable character, one might have supposed him to be the object of an avenging fate, so successive were the evils which pursued him; but as he was only a somewhat commonplace farmer, I believe we must attribute his calamities to some want in his character of the one quality required to act as keystone to many excellences. While his wife lived, all worldly misfortunes seemed as nothing to him; her strong sense and lively faculty of hope upheld him from despair; her sympathy was always ready, and the invalid's room had an atmosphere of peace and encouragement, which affected all who entered it. But when Ruth was about twelve, one morning in the busy hay-time, Mrs Hilton was left alone for some hours. This had often happened before, nor had she seemed weaker than usual when they had gone forth to the field; but on their return, with merry voices, to fetch the dinner prepared for the haymakers, they found an unusual silence brooding over the house; no low voice called out gently to welcome them, and ask after the day's progress; and, on entering the little parlour, which was called Mrs Hilton's, and was sacred to her, they found her lying dead on her accustomed sofa. Quite calm and peaceful she lay; there had been no struggle at last; the struggle was for the survivors, and one sank under it. Her husband did not make much ado at first—at least, not in outward show; her memory seemed to keep in check all external violence of grief; but, day by day, dating from his wife's death, his mental powers decreased. He was still a hale-looking elderly man, and his bodily health appeared as good as ever; but he sat for hours in his easy-chair, looking into the fire, not moving, nor speaking, unless when it was absolutely necessary to answer repeated questions. If Ruth, with coaxings and draggings, induced him to come out with her, he went with measured steps around his fields, his head bent to the ground with the same abstracted, unseeing look; never smiling—never changing the expression of his face, not even to one of deeper sadness, when anything occurred which might be supposed to remind him of his dead wife. But in this abstraction from all outward things, his worldly affairs went ever lower down. He paid money away, or received it, as if it had been so much water; the gold mines of Potosi could not have touched the deep grief of his soul; but God in His mercy knew the sure balm, and sent the Beautiful Messenger to take the weary one home.

After his death, the creditors were the chief people who appeared to take any interest in the affairs; and it seemed strange to Ruth to see people, whom she scarcely knew, examining and touching all that she had been accustomed to consider as precious and sacred. Her father had made his will at her birth. With the pride of newly and late-acquired paternity, he had considered the office of guardian to his little darling as one which would have been an additional honour to the lord-lieutenant of the county; but as he had not the pleasure of his lordship's acquaintance, he selected the person of most consequence amongst those whom he did know; not any very ambitious appointment, in those days of comparative prosperity; but certainly the flourishing maltster of Skelton was a little surprised, when, fifteen years later, he learnt that he was executor to a will bequeathing many vanished hundreds of pounds, and guardian to a young girl whom he could not remember ever to have seen.

He was a sensible, hard-headed man of the world; having a very fair proportion of conscience as consciences go; indeed, perhaps more than many people; for he had some ideas of duty extending to the circle beyond his own family; and did not, as some would have done, decline acting altogether, but speedily summoned the creditors, examined into the accounts, sold up the farming-stock, and discharged all the debts; paid about £80 into the Skelton bank for a week, while he inquired for a situation or apprenticeship of some kind for poor heart-broken Ruth; heard of Mrs Mason's; arranged all with her in two short conversations; drove over for Ruth in his gig; waited while she and the old servant packed up her clothes; and grew very impatient while she ran, with her eyes streaming with tears, round the garden, tearing off in a passion of love whole boughs of favourite China and damask roses, late flowering against the casement-window of what had been her mother's room. When she took her seat in the gig, she was little able, even if she had been inclined, to profit by her guardian's lectures on economy and self-reliance; but she was quiet and silent, looking forward with longing to the night-time, when, in her bedroom, she might give way to all her passionate sorrow at being wrenched from the home where she had lived with her parents, in that utter absence of any anticipation of change, which is either the blessing or the curse of childhood. But at night there were four other girls in her room, and she could not cry before them. She watched and waited till, one by one, they dropped off to sleep, and then she buried her face in the pillow, and shook with sobbing grief; and then she paused to conjure up, with fond luxuriance, every recollection of the happy days, so little valued in their uneventful peace while they lasted, so passionately regretted when once gone for ever; to remember every look and word of the dear mother, and to moan afresh over the change caused by her death;—the first clouding in of Ruth's day of life. It was Jenny's sympathy on this first night, when awakened by Ruth's irrepressible agony, that had made the bond between them. But Ruth's loving disposition, continually sending forth fibres in search of nutriment, found no other object for regard among those of her daily life to compensate for the want of natural ties.

But, almost insensibly, Jenny's place in Ruth's heart was filled up; there was some one who listened with tender interest to all her little revelations; who questioned her about her early days of happiness, and, in return, spoke of his own childhood—not so golden in reality as Ruth's, but more dazzling, when recounted with stories of the beautiful cream-coloured Arabian pony, and the old picture-gallery in the house, and avenues, and terraces, and fountains in the garden, for Ruth to paint, with all the vividness of imagination, as scenery and background for the figure which was growing by slow degrees most prominent in her thoughts.

It must not be supposed that this was effected all at once, though the intermediate stages have been passed over. On Sunday, Mr Bellingham only spoke to her to receive the information about the panel; nor did he come to St Nicholas' the next, nor yet the following Sunday. But the third he walked by her side a little way, and, seeing her annoyance, he left her; and then she wished for him back again, and found the day very dreary, and wondered why a strange undefined feeling had made her imagine she was doing wrong in walking alongside of one so kind and good as Mr Bellingham; it had been very foolish of her to be self-conscious all the time, and if ever he spoke to her again she would not think of what people might say, but enjoy the pleasure which his kind words and evident interest in her might give. Then she thought it was very likely he never would notice her again, for she knew she had been very rude with her short answers; it was very provoking that she had behaved so rudely. She should be sixteen in another month, and she was still childish and awkward. Thus she lectured herself, after parting with Mr Bellingham; and the consequence was, that on the following Sunday she was ten times as blushing and conscious, and (Mr Bellingham thought) ten times more beautiful than ever. He suggested, that instead of going straight home through High-street, she should take the round by the Leasowes; at first she declined, but then, suddenly wondering and questioning herself why she refused a thing which was, as far as reason and knowledge (*her* knowledge) went, so innocent, and which was certainly so tempting and pleasant, she agreed to go the round; and when she was once in the meadows that skirted the town, she forgot all doubt and awkwardness—nay, almost forgot the presence of Mr Bellingham—in her delight at the new tender beauty of an early spring day in February. Among the last year's brown ruins, heaped together by the wind in the hedgerows, she found the fresh green crinkled leaves and pale star-like flowers of the primroses. Here and there a golden celandine made brilliant the sides of the little brook that (full of water in "February fill-dyke") bubbled along by the side of the path; the sun was low in the horizon, and once, when they came to a higher part of the Leasowes, Ruth burst into an exclamation of delight at the evening glory of mellow light which was in the sky behind the purple distance, while the brown leafless woods in the foreground derived an almost metallic lustre from the golden mist and haze of the sunset. It was but three-quarters of a mile round by the meadows, but somehow it took them an hour to walk it. Ruth turned to thank Mr Bellingham for his kindness in taking her home by this beautiful way, but his look of admiration at her glowing, animated face, made her suddenly silent; and, hardly wishing him good-bye, she quickly entered the house with a beating, happy, agitated heart.

"How strange it is," she thought that evening, "that I should feel as if this charming afternoon's walk were, somehow, not exactly wrong, but yet as if it were not right. Why can it be? I am not defrauding Mrs Mason of any of her time; that I know would be wrong; I am left to go where I like on Sundays. I have been to church, so it can't be because I have missed doing my duty. If I had gone this walk with Jenny, I wonder whether I should have felt as I do now. There must be something wrong in me, myself, to feel so guilty when I have done nothing which is not right; and yet I can thank God for the happiness I have had in this charming spring walk, which dear mamma used to say was a sign when pleasures were innocent and good for us."

She was not conscious, as yet, that Mr Bellingham's presence had added any charm to the ramble; and when she might have become aware of this, as, week after week, Sunday after Sunday, loitering ramble after loitering ramble succeeded each other, she was too much absorbed with one set of thoughts to have much inclination for self-questioning.

"Tell me everything, Ruth, as you would to a brother; let me help you, if I can, in your difficulties," he said to her one afternoon. And he really did try to understand, and to realise, how an insignificant and paltry person like Mason the dressmaker could be an object of dread, and regarded as a person having authority, by Ruth. He flamed up with indignation when, by way of impressing him with Mrs Mason's power and consequence, Ruth spoke of some instance of the effects of her employer's displeasure. He declared his mother should never have a gown made again by such a tyrant—such a Mrs Brownrigg; that he would prevent all his acquaintances from going to such a cruel dressmaker; till Ruth was alarmed at the threatened consequences of her one-sided account, and pleaded for Mrs Mason as earnestly as if a young man's menace of this description were likely to be literally fulfilled.

"Indeed, sir, I have been very wrong; if you please, sir, don't be so angry. She is often very good to us; it is only sometimes she goes into a passion; and we are very provoking, I dare say. I know I am for one. I have often to undo my work, and you can't think how it spoils anything (particularly silk) to be unpicked; and Mrs Mason has to bear all the blame. Oh! I am sorry I said anything about it. Don't speak to your mother about it, pray, sir. Mrs Mason thinks so much of Mrs Bellingham's custom."

"Well, I won't this time"—recollecting that there might be some awkwardness in accounting to his mother for the means by which he had obtained his very correct information as to what passed in Mrs Mason's workroom—"but if ever she does so again, I'll not answer for myself."

"I will take care and not tell again, sir," said Ruth, in a low voice.

"Nay, Ruth, you are not going to have secrets from me, are you? Don't you remember your promise to consider me as a brother? Go on telling me everything that happens to you, pray; you cannot think how much interest I take in all your interests. I can quite fancy that charming home at Milham you told me about last

Sunday. I can almost fancy Mrs Mason's workroom; and that, surely, is a proof either of the strength of my imagination, or of your powers of description."

Ruth smiled. "It is, indeed, sir. Our workroom must be so different to anything you ever saw. I think you must have passed through Milham often on your way to Lowford."

"Then you don't think it is any stretch of fancy to have so clear an idea as I have of Milham Grange? On the left hand of the road, is it, Ruth?"

"Yes, sir, just over the bridge, and up the hill where the elm-trees meet overhead and make a green shade; and then comes the dear old Grange, that I shall never see again."

"Never! Nonsense, Ruthie; it is only six miles off; you may see it any day. It is not an hour's ride."

"Perhaps I may see it again when I am grown old; I did not think exactly what 'never' meant; it is so very long since I was there, and I don't see any chance of my going for years and years, at any rate."

"Why, Ruth, you—we may go next Sunday afternoon, if you like."

She looked up at him with a lovely light of pleasure in her face at the idea. "How, sir? Can I walk it between afternoon service and the time Mrs Mason comes home? I would go for only one glimpse; but if I could get into the house—oh, sir! if I could just see mamma's room again!"

He was revolving plans in his head for giving her this pleasure, and he had also his own in view. If they went in any of his carriages, the loitering charm of the walk would be lost; and they must, to a certain degree, be encumbered by, and exposed to, the notice of servants.

"Are you a good walker, Ruth? Do you think you can manage six miles? If we set off at two o'clock, we shall be there by four, without hurrying; or say half-past four. Then we might stay two hours, and you could show me all the old walks and old places you love, and we could still come leisurely home. Oh, it's all arranged directly!"

"But do you think it would be right, sir? It seems as if it would be such a great pleasure, that it must be in some way wrong."

"Why, you little goose, what can be wrong in it?"

"In the first place, I miss going to church by setting out at two," said Ruth, a little gravely.

"Only for once. Surely you don't see any harm in missing church for once? You will go in the morning, you know."

"I wonder if Mrs Mason would think it right—if she would allow it?"

"No, I dare say not. But you don't mean to be governed by Mrs Mason's notions of right and wrong. She thought it right to treat that poor girl Palmer in the way you told me about. You would think that wrong, you know, and so would every one of sense and feeling. Come, Ruth, don't pin your faith on any one, but judge for yourself. The pleasure is perfectly innocent; it is not a selfish pleasure either, for I shall enjoy it to the full as much as you will. I shall like to see the places where you spent your childhood; I shall almost love them as much as you do." He had dropped his voice; and spoke in low, persuasive tones. Ruth hung down her head, and blushed with exceeding happiness; but she could not speak, even to urge her doubts afresh. Thus it was in a manner settled.

How delightfully happy the plan made her through the coming week! She was too young when her mother died to have received any cautions or words of advice respecting *the* subject of a woman's life—if, indeed, wise parents ever directly speak of what, in its depth and power, cannot be put into words—which is a brooding spirit with no definite form or shape that men should know it, but which is there, and present before we have recognised and realised its existence. Ruth was innocent and snow-pure. She had heard of falling in love, but did not know the signs and symptoms thereof; nor, indeed, had she troubled her head much about them. Sorrow had filled up her days, to the exclusion of all lighter thoughts than the consideration of present duties, and the remembrance of the happy time which had been. But the interval of blank, after the loss of her mother and during her father's life-in-death, had made her all the more ready to value and cling to sympathy—first from Jenny, and now from Mr Bellingham. To see her home again, and to see it with him; to show him (secure of his interest) the haunts of former times, each with its little tale of the past—of dead and gone events!—No coming shadow threw its gloom over this week's dream of happiness—a dream which was too bright to be spoken about to common and indifferent ears.

CHAPTER IV - TREADING IN PERILOUS PLACES

Sunday came, as brilliant as if there were no sorrow, or death, or guilt in the world; a day or two of rain had made the earth fresh and brave as the blue heavens above. Ruth thought it was too strong a realisation of her hopes, and looked for an over-clouding at noon; but the glory endured, and at two o'clock she was in the Leasowes, with a beating heart full of joy, longing to stop the hours, which would pass too quickly through the afternoon.

They sauntered through the fragrant lanes, as if their loitering would prolong the time, and check the fiery-footed steeds galloping apace towards the close of the happy day. It was past five o'clock before they came to the great mill-wheel, which stood in Sabbath idleness, motionless in a brown mass of shade, and still wet with yesterday's immersion in the deep transparent water beneath. They clambered the little hill, not yet fully shaded by the overarching elms; and then Ruth checked Mr Bellingham, by a slight motion of the hand which lay within his arm, and glanced up into his face to see what that face should express as it looked on Milham Grange, now lying still and peaceful in its afternoon shadows. It was a house of after-thoughts; building materials were plentiful in the neighbourhood, and every successive owner had found a necessity for some addition or projection, till it was a picturesque mass of irregularity—of broken light and shadow—which, as a whole, gave a full and complete idea of a "Home." All its gables and nooks were blended and held together by the tender green of the climbing roses and young creepers. An old couple were living in the house until it should be let, but they dwelt in the back part, and never used the front door; so the little birds had grown tame and familiar, and perched upon the window-sills and porch, and on the old stone cistern which caught the water from the roof.

They went silently through the untrimmed garden, full of the pale-coloured flowers of spring. A spider had spread her web over the front door. The sight of this conveyed a sense of desolation to Ruth's heart; she thought it was possible the state entrance had never been used since her father's dead body had been borne forth, and, without speaking a word, she turned abruptly away, and went round the house to another door. Mr Bellingham followed without questioning, little understanding her feelings, but full of admiration for the varying expression called out upon her face.

The old woman had not yet returned from church, or from the weekly gossip or neighbourly tea which succeeded. The husband sat in the kitchen, spelling the psalms for the day in his Prayer-book, and reading the words out aloud—a habit he had acquired from the double solitude of his life, for he was deaf. He did not hear the quiet entrance of the pair, and they were struck with the sort of ghostly echo which seems to haunt half-furnished and uninhabited houses. The verses he was reading were the following:

> Why art thou so vexed, O my soul: and why art thou so disquieted within me?
> O put thy trust in God: for I will yet thank him, which is the help of my countenance, and my God.

And when he had finished he shut the book, and sighed with the satisfaction of having done his duty. The words of holy trust, though perhaps they were not fully understood, carried a faithful peace down into the depths of his soul. As he looked up, he saw the young couple standing on the middle of the floor. He pushed his iron-rimmed spectacles on to his forehead, and rose to greet the daughter of his old master and ever-honoured mistress.

"God bless thee, lass; God bless thee! My old eyes are glad to see thee again."

Ruth sprang forward to shake the horny hand stretched forward in the action of blessing. She pressed it between both of hers, as she rapidly poured out questions. Mr Bellingham was not altogether comfortable at seeing one whom he had already begun to appropriate as his own, so tenderly familiar with a hard-featured, meanly-dressed day-labourer. He sauntered to the window, and looked out into the grass-grown farm-yard; but he could not help overhearing some of the conversation, which seemed to him carried on too much in the tone of equality. "And who's yon?" asked the old labourer at last. "Is he your sweetheart? Your missis's son, I reckon. He's a spruce young chap, anyhow."

Mr Bellingham's "blood of all the Howards" rose and tingled about his ears, so that he could not hear Ruth's answer. It began by "Hush, Thomas; pray hush!" but how it went on he did not catch. The idea of his being Mrs Mason's son! It was really too ridiculous; but, like most things which are "too ridiculous," it made him very angry. He was hardly himself again when Ruth shyly came to the window-recess and asked him if he would like to see the house-place, into which the front door entered; many people thought it very pretty, she said, half timidly, for his face had unconsciously assumed a hard and haughty expression, which he could not instantly soften down. He followed her, however; but before he left the kitchen he saw the old man standing, looking at Ruth's companion with a strange, grave air of dissatisfaction.

They went along one or two zigzag, damp-smelling stone passages, and then entered the house-place, or common sitting-room for a farmer's family in that part of the country. The front door opened into it, and several other apartments issued out of it, such as the dairy, the state bedroom (which was half-parlour as well), and a small room which had been appropriated to the late Mrs Hilton, where she sat, or more frequently lay, commanding through the open door the comings and goings of her household. In those days the house-place had been a cheerful room, full of life, with the passing to and fro of husband, child, and servants; with a great merry wood fire crackling and blazing away every evening, and hardly let out in the very heat of summer; for with the thick stone walls, and the deep window-seats, and the drapery of vine-leaves and ivy, that room, with its flag-floor, seemed always to want the sparkle and cheery warmth of a fire. But now the green shadows from without seemed to have become black in the uninhabited desolation. The oaken shovel-board, the heavy dresser, and the carved cupboards, were now dull and damp, which were formerly polished up to the brightness of a looking-glass where the fire-blaze was for ever glinting; they only added to the oppressive gloom; the flag-floor was wet with heavy moisture. Ruth stood gazing into the room, seeing nothing of what was present. She saw a vision of former days—an evening in the days of her childhood; her father sitting in the "master's corner" near the fire, sedately smoking his pipe, while he dreamily watched his wife and child; her mother reading to her, as she sat on a little stool at her feet. It was gone—all gone into the land of shadows; but for the moment it seemed so present in the old room, that Ruth believed her actual life to be the dream. Then, still silent, she went on into her mother's parlour. But there, the bleak look of what had once been full of peace and mother's love, struck cold on her heart. She uttered a cry, and threw herself down by the sofa, hiding her face in her hands, while her frame quivered with her repressed sobs.

"Dearest Ruth, don't give way so. It can do no good; it cannot bring back the dead," said Mr Bellingham, distressed at witnessing her distress.

"I know it cannot," murmured Ruth; "and that is why I cry. I cry because nothing will ever bring them back again." She sobbed afresh, but more gently, for his kind words soothed her, and softened, if they could not take away, her sense of desolation.

"Come away; I cannot have you stay here, full of painful associations as these rooms must be. Come"—raising her with gentle violence—"show me your little garden you have often told me about. Near the window of this very room, is it not? See how well I remember everything you tell me."

He led her round through the back part of the house into the pretty old-fashioned garden. There was a sunny border just under the windows, and clipped box and yew-trees by the grass-plat, further away from the house; and she prattled again of her childish adventures and solitary plays. When they turned round they saw the old man, who had hobbled out with the help of his stick, and was looking at them with the same grave, sad look of anxiety.

Mr Bellingham spoke rather sharply:

"Why does that old man follow us about in that way? It is excessively impertinent of him, I think."

"Oh, don't call old Thomas impertinent. He is so good and kind, he is like a father to me. I remember sitting on his knee many and many a time when I was a child, whilst he told me stories out of the 'Pilgrim's Progress.' He taught me to suck up milk through a straw. Mamma was very fond of him too. He used to sit with us always in the evenings when papa was away at market, for mamma was rather afraid of having no man in the house, and used to beg old Thomas to stay; and he would take me on his knee, and listen just as attentively as I did while mamma read aloud."

"You don't mean to say you have sat upon that old fellow's knee?"

"Oh, yes! many and many a time."

Mr Bellingham looked graver than he had done while witnessing Ruth's passionate emotion in her mother's room. But he lost his sense of indignity in admiration of his companion as she wandered among the flowers, seeking for favourite bushes or plants, to which some history or remembrance was attached. She wound in and out in natural, graceful, wavy lines between the luxuriant and overgrown shrubs, which were fragrant with a leafy smell of spring growth; she went on, careless of watching eyes, indeed unconscious, for the time, of their existence. Once she stopped to take hold of a spray of jessamine, and softly kiss it; it had been her mother's favourite flower.

Old Thomas was standing by the horse-mount, and was also an observer of all her goings-on. But, while Mr Bellingham's feeling was that of passionate admiration mingled with a selfish kind of love, the old man gazed with tender anxiety, and his lips moved in words of blessing:

"She's a pretty creature, with a glint of her mother about her; and she's the same kind lass as ever. Not a bit set up with yon fine manty-maker's shop she's in. I misdoubt that young fellow though, for all she called him a real gentleman, and checked me when I asked if he was her sweetheart. If his are not sweetheart's looks, I've forgotten all my young days. Here! they're going, I suppose. Look! he wants her to go without a word to the old man; but she is none so changed as that, I reckon."

Not Ruth, indeed! She never perceived the dissatisfied expression of Mr Bellingham's countenance, visible to the old man's keen eye; but came running up to Thomas to send her love to his wife, and to shake him many times by the hand.

"Tell Mary I'll make her such a fine gown, as soon as ever I set up for myself; it shall be all in the fashion, big gigot sleeves, that she shall not know herself in them! Mind you tell her that, Thomas, will you?"

"Aye, that I will, lass; and I reckon she'll be pleased to hear thou hast not forgotten thy old merry ways. The Lord bless thee—the Lord lift up the light of His countenance upon thee."

Ruth was half-way towards the impatient Mr Bellingham when her old friend called her back. He longed to give her a warning of the danger that he thought she was in, and yet he did not know how. When she came up, all he could think of to say was a text; indeed, the language of the Bible was the language in which he thought, whenever his ideas went beyond practical everyday life into expressions of emotion or feeling. "My dear, remember the devil goeth about as a roaring lion, seeking whom he may devour; remember that, Ruth."

The words fell on her ear, but gave no definite idea. The utmost they suggested was the remembrance of the dread she felt as a child when this verse came into her mind, and how she used to imagine a lion's head with glaring eyes peering out of the bushes in a dark shady part of the wood, which, for this reason, she had always avoided, and even now could hardly think of without a shudder. She never imagined that the grim warning related to the handsome young man who awaited her with a countenance beaming with love, and tenderly drew her hand within his arm.

The old man sighed as he watched them away. "The Lord may help her to guide her steps aright. He may. But I'm afeard she's treading in perilous places. I'll put my missis up to going to the town and getting speech of her, and telling her a bit of her danger. An old motherly woman like our Mary will set about it better nor a stupid fellow like me."

The poor old labourer prayed long and earnestly that night for Ruth. He called it "wrestling for her soul;" and I think his prayers were heard, for "God judgeth not as man judgeth."

Ruth went on her way, all unconscious of the dark phantoms of the future that were gathering around her; her melancholy turned, with the pliancy of childish years, at sixteen not yet lost, into a softened manner which was infinitely charming. By-and-by she cleared up into sunny happiness. The evening was still and full of mellow light, and the new-born summer was so delicious that, in common with all young creatures, she shared its influence and was glad.

They stood together at the top of a steep ascent, "the hill" of the hundred. At the summit there was a level space, sixty or seventy yards square, of unenclosed and broken ground, over which the golden bloom of the gorse cast a rich hue, while its delicious scent perfumed the fresh and nimble air. On one side of this common, the ground sloped down to a clear bright pond, in which were mirrored the rough sand-cliffs that rose abrupt on the opposite bank; hundreds of martens found a home there, and were now wheeling over the transparent water, and dipping in their wings in their evening sport. Indeed, all sorts of birds seemed to haunt the lonely pool; the water-wagtails were scattered around its margin, the linnets perched on the topmost sprays of the gorse-bushes, and other hidden warblers sang their vespers on the uneven ground beyond. On the far side of the green waste, close by the road, and well placed for the requirements of horses or their riders who might be weary with the ascent of the hill, there was a public-house, which was more of a farm than an inn. It was a long, low building, rich in dormer-windows on the weather side, which were necessary in such an exposed situation, and with odd projections and unlooked-for gables on every side; there was a deep porch in front, on whose hospitable benches a dozen persons might sit and enjoy the balmy air. A noble sycamore grew right before the house, with seats all round it ("such tents the patriarchs loved"); and a nondescript sign hung from a branch on the side next to the road, which, being wisely furnished with an interpretation, was found to mean King Charles in the oak.

Near this comfortable, quiet, unfrequented inn, there was another pond, for household and farm-yard purposes, from which the cattle were drinking, before returning to the fields after they had been milked. Their very motions were so lazy and slow, that they served to fill up the mind with the sensation of dreamy rest. Ruth and Mr Bellingham plunged through the broken ground to regain the road near the wayside inn. Hand-in-hand, now pricked by the far-spreading gorse, now ankle-deep in sand; now pressing the soft, thick heath, which should make so brave an autumn show; and now over wild thyme and other fragrant herbs, they made their way, with many a merry laugh. Once on the road, at the summit, Ruth stood silent, in breathless delight at the view before her. The hill fell suddenly down into the plain, extending for a dozen miles or more. There was a clump of dark Scotch firs close to them, which cut clear against the western sky, and threw back the nearest levels into distance. The plain below them was richly wooded, and was tinted by the young tender hues of the earliest summer, for all the trees of the wood had donned their leaves except the cautious ash, which here and there gave a soft, pleasant greyness to the landscape. Far away in the champaign were spires, and towers, and stacks of chimneys belonging to some distant hidden farm-house, which were traced downwards through the golden air by the thin columns of blue smoke sent up from the evening fires. The view was bounded by some rising ground in deep purple shadow against the sunset sky.

When first they stopped, silent with sighing pleasure, the air seemed full of pleasant noises; distant church-bells made harmonious music with the little singing-birds near at hand; nor were the lowings of the cattle, nor the calls of the farm-servants discordant, for the voices seemed to be hushed by the brooding consciousness of the Sabbath. They stood loitering before the house, quietly enjoying the view. The clock in the little inn struck eight, and it sounded clear and sharp in the stillness.

"Can it be so late?" asked Ruth.

"I should not have thought it possible," answered Mr Bellingham. "But, never mind, you will be at home long before nine. Stay, there is a shorter road, I know, through the fields; just wait a moment, while I go in and ask the exact way." He dropped Ruth's arm, and went into the public-house.

A gig had been slowly toiling up the sandy hill behind, unperceived by the young couple, and now it reached the table-land, and was close upon them as they separated. Ruth turned round, when the sound of the horse's footsteps came distinctly as he reached the level. She faced Mrs Mason!

They were not ten—no, not five yards apart. At the same moment they recognised each other, and, what was worse, Mrs Mason had clearly seen, with her sharp, needle-like eyes, the attitude in which Ruth had stood with the young man who had just quitted her. Ruth's hand had been lying in his arm, and fondly held there by his other hand.

Mrs Mason was careless about the circumstances of temptation into which the girls entrusted to her as apprentices were thrown, but severely intolerant if their conduct was in any degree influenced by the force of these temptations. She called this intolerance "keeping up the character of her establishment." It would have been a better and more Christian thing, if she had kept up the character of her girls by tender vigilance and maternal care.

This evening, too, she was in an irritated state of temper. Her brother had undertaken to drive her round by Henbury, in order to give her the unpleasant information of the misbehaviour of her eldest son, who was an assistant in a draper's shop in a neighbouring town. She was full of indignation against want of steadiness, though not willing to direct her indignation against the right object—her ne'er-do-well darling. While she was thus charged with anger (for her brother justly defended her son's master and companions from her attacks), she saw Ruth standing with a lover, far away from home, at such a time in the evening, and she boiled over with intemperate displeasure.

"Come here directly, Miss Hilton," she exclaimed, sharply. Then, dropping her voice to low, bitter tones of concentrated wrath, she said to the trembling, guilty Ruth:

"Don't attempt to show your face at my house again after this conduct. I saw you, and your spark, too. I'll have no slurs on the character of my apprentices. Don't say a word. I saw enough. I shall write and tell your guardian to-morrow."

The horse started away, for he was impatient to be off, and Ruth was left standing there, stony, sick, and pale, as if the lightning had torn up the ground beneath her feet. She could not go on standing, she was so sick and faint; she staggered back to the broken sand-bank, and sank down, and covered her face with her hands.

"My dearest Ruth! are you ill? Speak, darling! My love, my love, do speak to me!"

What tender words after such harsh ones! They loosened the fountain of Ruth's tears, and she cried bitterly.

"Oh! did you see her—did you hear what she said?"

"She! Who, my darling? Don't sob so, Ruth; tell me what it is. Who has been near you?—who has been speaking to you to make you cry so?"

"Oh, Mrs Mason." And there was a fresh burst of sorrow.

"You don't say so! are you sure? I was not away five minutes."

"Oh, yes, sir, I'm quite sure. She was so angry; she said I must never show my face there again. Oh, dear! what shall I do?"

It seemed to the poor child as if Mrs Mason's words were irrevocable, and, that being so, she was shut out from every house. She saw how much she had done that was deserving of blame, now when it was too late to undo it. She knew with what severity and taunts Mrs Mason had often treated her for involuntary failings, of which she had been quite unconscious; and now she had really done wrong, and shrank with terror from the consequences. Her eyes were so blinded by the fast-falling tears, she did not see (nor had she seen would she have been able to interpret) the change in Mr Bellingham's countenance, as he stood silently watching her. He was silent so long, that even in her sorrow she began to wonder that he did not speak, and to wish to hear his soothing words once more.

"It is very unfortunate," he began, at last; and then he stopped; then he began again: "It is very unfortunate; for, you see, I did not like to name it to you before, but, I believe—I have business, in fact, which obliges me to go to town to-morrow—to London, I mean; and I don't know when I shall be able to return."

"To London!" cried Ruth; "are you going away? Oh, Mr Bellingham!" She wept afresh, giving herself up to the desolate feeling of sorrow, which absorbed all the terror she had been experiencing at the idea of Mrs Mason's anger. It seemed to her at this moment as though she could have borne everything but his departure; but she did not speak again; and after two or three minutes had elapsed, he spoke—not in his natural careless voice, but in a sort of constrained, agitated tone.

"I can hardly bear the idea of leaving you, my own Ruth. In such distress, too; for where you can go I do not know at all. From all you have told me of Mrs Mason, I don't think she is likely to mitigate her severity in your case."

No answer, but tears quietly, incessantly flowing. Mrs Mason's displeasure seemed a distant thing; his going away was the present distress. He went on:

"Ruth, would you go with me to London? My darling, I cannot leave you here without a home; the thought of leaving you at all is pain enough, but in these circumstances—so friendless, so homeless—it is impossible. You must come with me, love, and trust to me."

Still she did not speak. Remember how young, and innocent, and motherless she was! It seemed to her as if it would be happiness enough to be with him; and as for the future, he would arrange and decide for that. The future lay wrapped in a golden mist, which she did not care to penetrate; but if he, her sun, was out of sight and gone, the golden mist became dark heavy gloom, through which no hope could come. He took her hand.

"Will you not come with me? Do you not love me enough to trust me? Oh, Ruth," (reproachfully), "can you not trust me?"

She had stopped crying, but was sobbing sadly.

"I cannot bear this, love. Your sorrow is absolute pain to me; but it is worse to feel how indifferent you are—how little you care about our separation."

He dropped her hand. She burst into a fresh fit of crying.

"I may have to join my mother in Paris; I don't know when I shall see you again. Oh, Ruth!" said he, vehemently, "do you love me at all?"

She said something in a very low voice; he could not hear it, though he bent down his head—but he took her hand again.

"What was it you said, love? Was it not that you did love me? My darling, you do! I can tell it by the trembling of this little hand; then you will not suffer me to go away alone and unhappy, most anxious about you? There is no other course open to you; my poor girl has no friends to receive her. I will go home directly, and return in an hour with a carriage. You make me too happy by your silence, Ruth."

"Oh, what can I do!" exclaimed Ruth. "Mr Bellingham, you should help me, and instead of that you only bewilder me."

"How, my dearest Ruth? Bewilder you! It seems so clear to me. Look at the case fairly! Here you are, an orphan, with only one person to love you, poor child!—thrown off, for no fault of yours, by the only creature on whom you have a claim, that creature a tyrannical, inflexible woman; what is more natural (and, being natural, more right) than that you should throw yourself upon the care of the one who loves you dearly—who would go through fire and water for you—who would shelter you from all harm? Unless, indeed, as I suspect, you do not care for him. If so, Ruth! if you do not care for me, we had better part—I will leave you at once; it will be better for me to go, if you do not care for me."

He said this very sadly (it seemed so to Ruth, at least), and made as though he would have drawn his hand from hers, but now she held it with soft force.

"Don't leave me, please, sir. It is very true I have no friend but you. Don't leave me, please. But, oh! do tell me what I must do!"

"Will you do it if I tell you? If you will trust me, I will do my very best for you. I will give you my best advice. You see your position. Mrs Mason writes and gives her own exaggerated account to your guardian; he is bound by no great love to you, from what I have heard you say, and throws you off; I, who might be able to befriend you—through my mother, perhaps—I, who could at least comfort you a little (could not I, Ruth?), am away, far away, for an indefinite time; that is your position at present. Now, what I advise is this. Come with me into this little inn; I will order tea for you—(I am sure you require it sadly)—and I will leave you there, and go home for the carriage. I will return in an hour at the latest. Then we are together, come what may; that is enough for me; is it not for you, Ruth? Say, yes—say it ever so low, but give me the delight of hearing it. Ruth, say yes."

Low and soft, with much hesitation, came the "Yes;" the fatal word of which she so little imagined the infinite consequences. The thought of being with him was all and everything.

"How you tremble, my darling! You are cold, love! Come into the house, and I'll order tea directly and be off."

She rose, and, leaning on his arm, went into the house. She was shaking and dizzy with the agitation of the last hour. He spoke to the civil farmer-landlord, who conducted them into a neat parlour, with windows opening into the garden at the back of the house. They had admitted much of the evening's fragrance through their open casements, before they were hastily closed by the attentive host.

"Tea, directly, for this lady!" The landlord vanished.

"Dearest Ruth, I must go; there is not an instant to be lost; promise me to take some tea, for you are shivering all over, and deadly pale with the fright that abominable woman has given you. I must go; I shall be back in half an hour—and then no more partings, darling."

He kissed her pale cold face, and went away. The room whirled round before Ruth; it was a dream—a strange, varying, shifting dream—with the old home of her childhood for one scene, with the terror of Mrs Mason's unexpected appearance for another; and then, strangest, dizziest, happiest of all, there was the consciousness of his love, who was all the world to her; and the remembrance of the tender words, which still kept up their low soft echo in her heart.

Her head ached so much that she could hardly see; even the dusky twilight was a dazzling glare to her poor eyes; and when the daughter of the house brought in the sharp light of the candles, preparatory for tea, Ruth hid her face in the sofa pillows with a low exclamation of pain.

"Does your head ache, miss?" asked the girl, in a gentle, sympathising voice. "Let me make you some tea, miss, it will do you good. Many's the time poor mother's headaches were cured by good strong tea."

Ruth murmured acquiescence; the young girl (about Ruth's own age, but who was the mistress of the little establishment, owing to her mother's death) made tea, and brought Ruth a cup to the sofa where she lay. Ruth was feverish and thirsty, and eagerly drank it off, although she could not touch the bread and butter which the girl offered her. She felt better and fresher, though she was still faint and weak.

"Thank you," said Ruth. "Don't let me keep you; perhaps you are busy. You have been very kind, and the tea has done me a great deal of good."

The girl left the room. Ruth became as hot as she had previously been cold, and went and opened the window, and leant out into the still, sweet, evening air. The bush of sweetbrier, underneath the window, scented the place, and the delicious fragrance reminded her of her old home. I think scents affect and quicken the memory more than either sights or sounds; for Ruth had instantly before her eyes the little garden beneath the window of her mother's room, with the old man leaning on his stick, watching her, just as he had done, not three hours before, on that very afternoon.

"Dear old Thomas! He and Mary would take me in, I think; they would love me all the more if I were cast off. And Mr Bellingham would, perhaps, not be so very long away; and he would know where to find me if I stayed at Milham Grange. Oh, would it not be better to go to them? I wonder if he would be very sorry! I could not bear to make him sorry, so kind as he has been to me; but I do believe it would be better to go to them, and ask their advice, at any rate. He would follow me there; and I could talk over what I had better do, with the three best friends I have in the world—the only friends I have."

She put on her bonnet, and opened the parlour-door; but then she saw the square figure of the landlord standing at the open house-door, smoking his evening pipe, and looming large and distinct against the dark air and landscape beyond. Ruth remembered the cup of tea that she had drank; it must be paid for, and she had no money with her. She feared that he would not let her quit the house without paying. She thought that she would leave a note for Mr Bellingham, saying where she was gone, and how she had left the house in debt, for (like a child) all dilemmas appeared of equal magnitude to her; and the difficulty of passing the landlord while he stood there, and of giving him an explanation of the circumstances (as far as such explanation was due to him), appeared insuperable, and as awkward, and fraught with inconvenience, as far more serious situations.

She kept peeping out of her room, after she had written her little pencil-note, to see if the outer door was still obstructed. There he stood, motionless, enjoying his pipe, and looking out into the darkness which gathered thick with the coming night. The fumes of the tobacco were carried by the air into the house, and brought back Ruth's sick headache. Her energy left her; she became stupid and languid, and incapable of spirited exertion; she modified her plan of action, to the determination of asking Mr Bellingham to take her to Milham Grange, to the care of her humble friends, instead of to London. And she thought, in her simplicity, that he would instantly consent when he had heard her reasons.

She started up. A carriage dashed up to the door. She hushed her beating heart, and tried to stop her throbbing head to listen. She heard him speaking to the landlord, though she could not distinguish what he said; heard the jingling of money, and, in another moment, he was in the room, and had taken her arm to lead her to the carriage.

"Oh, sir! I want you to take me to Milham Grange," said she, holding back. "Old Thomas would give me a home."

"Well, dearest, we'll talk of all that in the carriage; I am sure you will listen to reason. Nay, if you will go to Milham you must go in the carriage," said he, hurriedly. She was little accustomed to oppose the wishes of any one—obedient and docile by nature, and unsuspicious and innocent of any harmful consequences. She entered the carriage, and drove towards London.

CHAPTER V - IN NORTH WALES

The June of 18— had been glorious and sunny, and full of flowers; but July came in with pouring rain, and it was a gloomy time for travellers and for weather-bound tourists, who lounged away the days in touching up sketches, dressing flies, and reading over again for the twentieth time the few volumes they had brought with them. A number of the *Times*, five days old, had been in constant demand in all the sitting-rooms of a certain inn in a little mountain village of North Wales, through a long July morning. The valleys around were filled with thick cold mist, which had crept up the hillsides till the hamlet itself was folded in its white dense curtain, and from the inn-windows nothing was seen of the beautiful scenery around. The tourists who thronged the rooms might as well have been "wi' their dear little bairnies at hame;" and so some of them seemed to think, as they stood, with their faces flattened against the window-panes, looking abroad in search of an event to fill up the dreary time. How many dinners were hastened that day, by way of getting through the morning, let the poor Welsh kitchen-maid say! The very village children kept indoors; or if one or two more adventurous stole out into the land of temptation and puddles, they were soon clutched back by angry and busy mothers.

It was only four o'clock, but most of the inmates of the inn thought it must be between six and seven, the morning had seemed so long—so many hours had passed since dinner—when a Welsh car, drawn by two horses, rattled briskly up to the door. Every window of the ark was crowded with faces at the sound; the leathern curtains were undrawn to their curious eyes, and out sprang a gentleman, who carefully assisted a well-cloaked-up lady into the little inn, despite the landlady's assurances of not having a room to spare.

The gentleman (it was Mr Bellingham) paid no attention to the speeches of the hostess, but quietly superintended the unpacking of the carriage, and paid the postillion; then, turning round with his face to the light, he spoke to the landlady, whose voice had been rising during the last five minutes:

"Nay, Jenny, you're strangely altered, if you can turn out an old friend on such an evening as this. If I remember right, Pen trê Voelas is twenty miles across the bleakest mountain road I ever saw."

"Indeed, sir, and I did not know you; Mr Bellingham, I believe. Indeed, sir, Pen trê Voelas is not above eighteen miles—we only charge for eighteen; it may not be much above seventeen; and we're quite full, indeed, more's the pity."

"Well, but Jenny, to oblige me, an old friend, you can find lodgings out for some of your people—the house across, for instance."

"Indeed, sir, and it's at liberty; perhaps you would not mind lodging there yourself; I could get you the best rooms, and send over a trifle or so of furniture, if they wern't as you'd wish them to be."

"No, Jenny! here I stay. You'll not induce me to venture over into those rooms, whose dirt I know of old. Can't you persuade some one who is not an old friend to move across? Say, if you like, that I had written beforehand to bespeak the rooms. Oh! I know you can manage it—I know your good-natured ways."

"Indeed, sir—well! I'll see, if you and the lady will just step into the back parlour, sir—there's no one there just now; the lady is keeping her bed to-day for a cold, and the gentleman is having a rubber at whist in number three. I'll see what I can do."

"Thank you, thank you. Is there a fire? if not, one must be lighted. Come, Ruthie, come."

He led the way into a large, bow-windowed room, which looked gloomy enough that afternoon, but which I have seen bright and buoyant with youth and hope within, and sunny lights creeping down the purple mountain slope, and stealing over the green, soft meadows, till they reached the little garden, full of roses and lavender-bushes, lying close under the window. I have seen—but I shall see no more.

"I did not know you had been here before," said Ruth, as Mr Bellingham helped her off with her cloak.

"Oh, yes; three years ago I was here on a reading party. We were here above two months, attracted by Jenny's kind heart and oddities; but driven away finally by the insufferable dirt. However, for a week or two it won't much signify."

"But can she take us in, sir? I thought I heard her saying her house was full."

"Oh, yes—I dare say it is; but I shall pay her well; she can easily make excuses to some poor devil, and send him over to the other side; and, for a day or two, so that we have shelter, it does not much signify."

"Could not we go to the house on the other side, sir?"

"And have our meals carried across to us in a half-warm state, to say nothing of having no one to scold for bad cooking! You don't know these out-of-the-way Welsh inns yet, Ruthie."

"No! I only thought it seemed rather unfair—" said Ruth, gently; but she did not end her sentence, for Mr Bellingham formed his lips into a whistle, and walked to the window to survey the rain.

The remembrance of his former good payment prompted many little lies of which Mrs Morgan was guilty that afternoon, before she succeeded in turning out a gentleman and lady, who were only planning to remain till the ensuing Saturday at the outside, so, if they did fulfil their threat, and leave on the next day, she would be no very great loser.

These household arrangements complete, she solaced herself with tea in her own little parlour, and shrewdly reviewed the circumstances of Mr Bellingham's arrival.

"Indeed! and she's not his wife," thought Jenny, "that's clear as day. His wife would have brought her maid, and given herself twice as many airs about the sitting-rooms; while this poor miss never spoke, but kept as still as a mouse. Indeed, and young men will be young men; and, as long as their fathers and mothers shut their eyes, it's none of my business to go about asking questions."

In this manner they settled down to a week's enjoyment of that Alpine country. It was most true enjoyment to Ruth. It was opening a new sense; vast ideas of beauty and grandeur filled her mind at the sight of the mountains now first beheld in full majesty. She was almost overpowered by the vague and solemn delight; but by-and-by her love for them equalled her awe, and in the night-time she would softly rise, and steal to the window to see the white moonlight, which gave a new aspect to the everlasting hills that girdle the mountain village.

Their breakfast-hour was late, in accordance with Mr Bellingham's tastes and habits; but Ruth was up betimes, and out and away, brushing the dew-drops from the short crisp grass; the lark sung high above her head, and she knew not if she moved or stood still, for the grandeur of this beautiful earth absorbed all idea of separate and individual existence. Even rain was a pleasure to her. She sat in the window-seat of their parlour (she would have gone out gladly, but that such a proceeding annoyed Mr Bellingham, who usually at such times lounged away the listless hours on a sofa, and relieved himself by abusing the weather); she saw the swift-fleeting showers come athwart the sunlight like a rush of silver arrows; she watched the purple darkness on the heathery mountain-side, and then the pale golden gleam which succeeded. There was no change or alteration of nature that had not its own peculiar beauty in the eyes of Ruth; but if she had complained of the changeable climate, she would have pleased Mr Bellingham more; her admiration and her content made him angry, until her pretty motions and loving eyes soothed down his impatience.

"Really, Ruth," he exclaimed one day, when they had been imprisoned by rain a whole morning, "one would think you had never seen a shower of rain before; it quite wearies me to see you sitting there watching this detestable weather with such a placid countenance; and for the last two hours you have said nothing more amusing or interesting than—'Oh, how beautiful!' or, 'There's another cloud coming across Moel Wynn.'"

Ruth left her seat very gently, and took up her work. She wished she had the gift of being amusing; it must be dull for a man accustomed to all kinds of active employments to be shut up in the house. She was recalled from her absolute self-forgetfulness. What could she say to interest Mr Bellingham? While she thought, he spoke again:

"I remember when we were reading here three years ago, we had a week of just such weather as this; but Howard and Johnson were capital whist players, and Wilbraham not bad, so we got through the days famously. Can you play *écarté*, Ruth, or picquet?"

"No, sir; I have sometimes played at beggar-my-neighbour," answered Ruth, humbly, regretting her own deficiencies.

He murmured impatiently, and there was silence for another half-hour. Then he sprang up, and rung the bell violently. "Ask Mrs Morgan for a pack of cards. Ruthie, I'll teach you *écarté*," said he.

But Ruth was stupid, not so good as a dummy, he said; and it was no fun betting against himself. So the cards were flung across the table—on the floor—anywhere. Ruth picked them up. As she rose, she sighed a little with the depression of spirits consequent upon her own want of power to amuse and occupy him she loved.

"You're pale, love!" said he, half repenting of his anger at her blunders over the cards. "Go out before dinner; you know you don't mind this cursed weather; and see that you come home full of adventures to relate. Come, little blockhead! give me a kiss, and begone."

She left the room with a feeling of relief; for if he were dull without her, she should not feel responsible, and unhappy at her own stupidity. The open air, that kind soothing balm which gentle mother Nature offers to us all in our seasons of depression, relieved her. The rain had ceased, though every leaf and blade was loaded with trembling glittering drops. Ruth went down to the circular dale, into which the brown-foaming mountain river fell and made a deep pool, and, after resting there for a while, ran on between broken rocks down to the valley below. The waterfall was magnificent, as she had anticipated; she longed to extend her walk to the other side of the stream, so she sought the stepping-stones, the usual crossing-place, which were over-shadowed by trees, a few yards from the pool. The waters ran high and rapidly, as busy as life, between the pieces of grey rock; but Ruth had no fear, and went lightly and steadily on. About the middle, however, there was a great gap; either one of the stones was so covered with water as to be invisible, or it had been washed lower down; at any rate, the spring from stone to stone was long, and Ruth hesitated for a moment before taking it. The sound of rushing waters was in her ears to the exclusion of every other noise; her eyes were on the current running swiftly below her feet; and thus she was startled to see a figure close before her on one of the stones, and to hear a voice offering help.

She looked up and saw a man, who was apparently long past middle life, and of the stature of a dwarf; a second glance accounted for the low height of the speaker, for then she saw he was deformed. As the consciousness of this infirmity came into her mind, it must have told itself in her softened eyes, for a faint flush of colour came into the pale face of the deformed gentleman, as he repeated his words:

"The water is very rapid; will you take my hand? Perhaps I can help you."

Ruth accepted the offer, and with this assistance she was across in a moment. He made way for her to precede him in the narrow wood path, and then silently followed her up the glen.

When they had passed out of the wood into the pasture-land beyond, Ruth once more turned to mark him. She was struck afresh with the mild beauty of the face, though there was something in the countenance which told of the body's deformity, something more and beyond the pallor of habitual ill-health, something of a quick spiritual light in the deep set-eyes, a sensibility about the mouth; but altogether, though a peculiar, it was a most attractive face.

"Will you allow me to accompany you if you are going the round by Cwm Dhu, as I imagine you are? The hand-rail is blown away from the little wooden bridge by the storm last night, and the rush of waters below may make you dizzy; and it is really dangerous to fall there, the stream is so deep."

They walked on without much speech. She wondered who her companion might be. She should have known him, if she had seen him among the strangers at the inn; and yet he spoke English too well to be a Welshman; he knew the country and the paths so perfectly, he must be a resident; and so she tossed him from England to Wales and back again in her imagination.

"I only came here yesterday," said he, as a widening in the path permitted them to walk abreast. "Last night I went to the higher waterfalls; they are most splendid."

"Did you go out in all that rain?" asked Ruth, timidly.

"Oh, yes. Rain never hinders me from walking. Indeed, it gives a new beauty to such a country as this. Besides, my time for my excursion is so short, I cannot afford to waste a day."

"Then, you do not live here?" asked Ruth.

"No! my home is in a very different place. I live in a busy town, where at times it is difficult to feel the truth that

There are in this loud stunning tide
   Of human care and crime,
With whom the melodies abide
   Of th' everlasting chime;
Who carry music in their heart
Through dusky lane and crowded mart,
Plying their task with busier feet,
Because their secret souls a holy strain repeat.

I have an annual holiday, which I generally spend in Wales; and often in this immediate neighbourhood."

"I do not wonder at your choice," replied Ruth. "It is a beautiful country."

"It is, indeed; and I have been inoculated by an old innkeeper at Conway with a love for its people, and history, and traditions. I have picked up enough of the language to understand many of their legends; and some are very fine and awe-inspiring, others very poetic and fanciful."

Ruth was too shy to keep up the conversation by any remark of her own, although his gentle, pensive manner was very winning.

"For instance," said he, touching a long bud-laden stem of fox-glove in the hedge-side, at the bottom of which one or two crimson-speckled flowers were bursting from their green sheaths, "I dare say, you don't know what makes this fox-glove bend and sway so gracefully. You think it is blown by the wind, don't you?" He looked at her with a grave smile, which did not enliven his thoughtful eyes, but gave an inexpressible sweetness to his face.

"I always thought it was the wind. What is it?" asked Ruth, innocently.

"Oh, the Welsh tell you that this flower is sacred to the fairies, and that it has the power of recognising them, and all spiritual beings who pass by, and that it bows in deference to them as they waft along. Its Welsh name is Maneg Ellyllyn—the good people's glove; and hence, I imagine, our folk's-glove or fox-glove."

"It's a very pretty fancy," said Ruth, much interested, and wishing that he would go on, without expecting her to reply.

But they were already at the wooden bridge; he led her across, and then, bowing his adieu, he had taken a different path even before Ruth had thanked him for his attention.

It was an adventure to tell Mr Bellingham, however; and it roused and amused him till dinner-time came, after which he sauntered forth with a cigar.

"Ruth," said he, when he returned, "I've seen your little hunchback. He looks like Riquet-with-the-Tuft. He's not a gentleman, though. If it had not been for his deformity, I should not have made him out from your description; you called him a gentleman."

"And don't you, sir?" asked Ruth, surprised.

"Oh, no! he's regularly shabby and seedy in his appearance; lodging, too, the ostler told me, over that horrible candle and cheese shop, the smell of which is insufferable twenty yards off—no gentleman could endure it; he must be a traveller or artist, or something of that kind."

"Did you see his face, sir?" asked Ruth.

"No; but a man's back—his *tout ensemble* has character enough in it to decide his rank."

"His face was very singular; quite beautiful!" said she, softly; but the subject did not interest Mr Bellingham, and he let it drop.

CHAPTER VI - TROUBLES GATHER ABOUT RUTH

The next day the weather was brave and glorious; a perfect "bridal of the earth and sky;" and every one turned out of the inn to enjoy the fresh beauty of nature. Ruth was quite unconscious of being the object of remark, and, in her light, rapid passings to and fro, had never looked at the doors and windows, where many watchers stood observing her, and commenting upon her situation or her appearance.

"She's a very lovely creature," said one gentleman, rising from the breakfast-table to catch a glimpse of her as she entered from her morning's ramble. "Not above sixteen, I should think. Very modest and innocent-looking in her white gown!"

His wife, busy administering to the wants of a fine little boy, could only say (without seeing the young girl's modest ways, and gentle, downcast countenance):

"Well! I do think it's a shame such people should be allowed to come here. To think of such wickedness under the same roof! Do come away, my dear, and don't flatter her by such notice."

The husband returned to the breakfast-table; he smelt the broiled ham and eggs, and he heard his wife's commands. Whether smelling or hearing had most to do in causing his obedience, I cannot tell; perhaps you can.

"Now, Harry, go and see if nurse and baby are ready to go out with you. You must lose no time this beautiful morning."

Ruth found Mr Bellingham was not yet come down; so she sallied out for an additional half-hour's ramble. Flitting about through the village, trying to catch all the beautiful sunny peeps at the scenery between the cold stone houses, which threw the radiant distance into aërial perspective far away, she passed by the little shop; and, just issuing from it, came the nurse and baby, and little boy. The baby sat in placid dignity in her nurse's arms, with a face of queenly calm. Her fresh, soft, peachy complexion was really tempting; and Ruth, who was always fond of children, went up to coo and to smile at the little thing, and, after some "peep-boing," she was about to snatch a kiss, when Harry, whose face had been reddening ever since the play began, lifted up his sturdy little right arm and hit Ruth a great blow on the face.

"Oh, for shame, sir!" said the nurse, snatching back his hand; "how dare you do that to the lady who is so kind as to speak to Sissy."

"She's not a lady!" said he, indignantly. "She's a bad naughty girl—mamma said so, she did; and she shan't kiss our baby."

The nurse reddened in her turn. She knew what he must have heard; but it was awkward to bring it out, standing face to face with the elegant young lady.

"Children pick up such notions, ma'am," said she at last, apologetically, to Ruth, who stood, white and still, with a new idea running through her mind.

"It's no notion; it's true, nurse; and I heard you say it yourself. Go away, naughty woman!" said the boy, in infantile vehemence of passion to Ruth.

To the nurse's infinite relief, Ruth turned away, humbly and meekly, with bent head, and slow, uncertain steps. But as she turned, she saw the mild sad face of the deformed gentleman, who was sitting at the open window above the shop; he looked sadder and graver than ever; and his eyes met her glance with an expression of deep sorrow. And so, condemned alike by youth and age, she stole with timid step into the house. Mr Bellingham was awaiting her coming in the sitting-room. The glorious day restored all his buoyancy of spirits. He talked gaily away, without pausing for a reply; while Ruth made tea, and tried to calm her heart, which was yet beating with the agitation of the new ideas she had received from the occurrence of the morning. Luckily for her, the only answers required for some time were mono-syllables; but those few words were uttered in so depressed and mournful a tone, that at last they struck Mr Bellingham with surprise and displeasure, as the condition of mind they unconsciously implied did not harmonise with his own.

"Ruth, what is the matter this morning? You really are very provoking. Yesterday, when everything was gloomy, and you might have been aware that I was out of spirits, I heard nothing but expressions of delight; to-day, when every creature under heaven is rejoicing, you look most deplorable and woe-begone. You really should learn to have a little sympathy."

The tears fell quickly down Ruth's cheeks, but she did not speak. She could not put into words the sense she was just beginning to entertain of the estimation in which she was henceforward to be held. She thought he would be as much grieved as she was at what had taken place that morning; she fancied she should sink in his opinion if she told him how others regarded her; besides, it seemed ungenerous to dilate upon the suffering of which he was the cause.

"I will not," thought she, "embitter his life; I will try and be cheerful. I must not think of myself so much. If I can but make him happy, what need I care for chance speeches?"

Accordingly, she made every effort possible to be as light-hearted as he was; but, somehow, the moment she relaxed, thoughts would intrude, and wonders would force themselves upon her mind; so that altogether she was not the gay and bewitching companion Mr Bellingham had previously found her.

They sauntered out for a walk. The path they chose led to a wood on the side of a hill, and they entered, glad of the shade of the trees. At first, it appeared like any common grove, but they soon came to a deep descent, on the summit of which they stood, looking down on the tree-tops, which were softly waving far beneath their feet. There was a path leading sharp down, and they followed it; the ledge of rock made it almost like going down steps, and their walk grew into a bounding, and their bounding into a run, before they reached the lowest plane. A green gloom reigned there; it was the still hour of noon; the little birds were quiet in some leafy shade. They went on a few yards, and then they came to a circular pool overshadowed by the trees, whose highest boughs had been beneath their feet a few minutes before. The pond was hardly below the surface of the ground, and there was nothing like a bank on any side. A heron was standing there motionless, but when he saw them he flapped his wings and slowly rose, and soared above the green heights of the wood up into the very sky itself, for at that depth the trees appeared to touch the round white clouds which brooded over the earth. The speed-well grew in the shallowest water of the pool, and all around its margin, but the flowers were hardly seen at first, so deep was the green shadow cast by the trees. In the very middle of the pond the sky was mirrored clear and dark, a blue which looked as if a black void lay behind.

"Oh, there are water-lilies," said Ruth, her eye catching on the farther side. "I must go and get some."

"No; I will get them for you. The ground is spongy all round there. Sit still, Ruth; this heap of grass will make a capital seat."

He went round, and she waited quietly for his return. When he came back he took off her bonnet, without speaking, and began to place his flowers in her hair. She was quite still while he arranged her coronet, looking up in his face with loving eyes, with a peaceful composure. She knew that he was pleased from his manner, which had the joyousness of a child playing with a new toy, and she did not think twice of his occupation. It was pleasant to forget everything except his pleasure. When he had decked her out, he said:

"There, Ruth! now you'll do. Come and look at yourself in the pond. Here, where there are no weeds. Come."

She obeyed, and could not help seeing her own loveliness; it gave her a sense of satisfaction for an instant, as the sight of any other beautiful object would have done, but she never thought of associating it with herself. She knew that she was beautiful; but that seemed abstract, and removed from herself. Her existence was in feeling, and thinking, and loving.

Down in that green hollow they were quite in harmony. Her beauty was all that Mr Bellingham cared for, and it was supreme. It was all he recognised of her, and he was proud of it. She stood in her white dress against the trees which grew around; her face was flushed into a brilliancy of colour which resembled that of a rose in June; the great heavy white flowers drooped on either side of her beautiful head, and if her brown hair was a little disordered, the very disorder only seemed to add a grace. She pleased him more by looking so lovely than by all her tender endeavours to fall in with his varying humour.

But when they left the wood, and Ruth had taken out her flowers, and resumed her bonnet, as they came near the inn, the simple thought of giving him pleasure was not enough to secure Ruth's peace. She became pensive and sad, and could not rally into gaiety.

"Really, Ruth," said he, that evening, "you must not encourage yourself in this habit of falling into melancholy reveries without any cause. You have been sighing twenty times during the last half-hour. Do be a little cheerful. Remember, I have no companion but you in this out-of-the-way place."

"I am very sorry, sir," said Ruth, her eyes filling with tears; and then she remembered that it was very dull for him to be alone with her, heavy-hearted as she had been all day. She said in a sweet, penitent tone:

"Would you be so kind as to teach me one of those games at cards you were speaking about yesterday, sir? I would do my best to learn."

Her soft, murmuring voice won its way. They rang for the cards, and he soon forgot that there was such a thing as depression or gloom in the world, in the pleasure of teaching such a beautiful ignoramus the mysteries of card-playing.

"There!" said he, at last, "that's enough for one lesson. Do you know, little goose, your blunders have made me laugh myself into one of the worst headaches I have had for years."

He threw himself on the sofa, and in an instant she was by his side.

"Let me put my cool hands on your forehead," she begged; "that used to do mamma good."

He lay still, his face away from the light, and not speaking. Presently he fell asleep. Ruth put out the candles, and sat patiently by him for a long time, fancying he would awaken refreshed. The room grew cool in the night air; but Ruth dared not rouse him from what appeared to be sound, restoring slumber. She covered him with her shawl, which she had thrown over a chair on coming in from their twilight ramble. She had ample time to think; but she tried to banish thought. At last, his breathing became quick and oppressed, and, after listening to it for some minutes with increasing affright, Ruth ventured to waken him. He seemed stupified and shivery. Ruth became more and more terrified; all the household were asleep except one servant-girl, who was wearied out of what little English she had knowledge of in more waking hours, and she could only answer, "Iss, indeed, ma'am," to any question put to her by Ruth.

She sat by the bedside all night long. He moaned and tossed, but never spoke sensibly. It was a new form of illness to the miserable Ruth. Her yesterday's suffering went into the black distance of long-past years. The present was all-in-all. When she heard people stirring, she went in search of Mrs Morgan, whose shrewd, sharp manners, unsoftened by inward respect for the poor girl, had awed Ruth even when Mr Bellingham was by to protect her.

"Mrs Morgan," said she, sitting down in the little parlour appropriated to the landlady, for she felt her strength suddenly desert her—"Mrs Morgan, I'm afraid Mr Bellingham is very ill;"—here she burst into tears, but instantly checking herself, "Oh, what must I do?" continued she; "I don't think he has known anything all through the night, and he looks so strange and wild this morning."

She gazed up into Mrs Morgan's face, as if reading an oracle.

"Indeed, miss, ma'am, and it's a very awkward thing. But don't cry, that can do no good, 'deed it can't. I'll go and see the poor young man myself, and then I can judge if a doctor is wanting."

Ruth followed Mrs Morgan upstairs. When they entered the sick-room Mr Bellingham was sitting up in bed, looking wildly about him, and as he saw them, he exclaimed:

"Ruth! Ruth! come here; I won't be left alone!" and then he fell down exhausted on the pillow. Mrs Morgan went up and spoke to him, but he did not answer or take any notice.

"I'll send for Mr Jones, my dear, 'deed and I will; we'll have him here in a couple of hours, please God."

"Oh, can't he come sooner?" asked Ruth, wild with terror.

"'Deed no; he lives at Llanglâs when he's at home, and that's seven mile away, and he may be gone a round eight or nine mile on the other side Llanglâs; but I'll send a boy on the pony directly."

Saying this, Mrs Morgan left Ruth alone. There was nothing to be done, for Mr Bellingham had again fallen into a heavy sleep. Sounds of daily life began, bells rang, breakfast-services clattered up and down the passages, and Ruth sat on shivering by the bedside in that darkened room. Mrs Morgan sent her breakfast upstairs by a chambermaid, but Ruth motioned it away in her sick agony, and the girl had no right to urge her to partake of it. That alone broke the monotony of the long morning. She heard the sound of merry parties setting out on excursions, on horseback or in carriages; and once, stiff and wearied, she stole to the window, and looked out on one side of the blind; but the day looked bright and discordant to her aching, anxious heart. The gloom of the darkened room was better and more befitting.

It was some hours after he was summoned before the doctor made his appearance. He questioned his patient, and, receiving no coherent answers, he asked Ruth concerning the symptoms; but when she questioned him in turn he only shook his head and looked grave. He made a sign to Mrs Morgan to follow him out of the room, and they went down to her parlour, leaving Ruth in a depth of despair, lower than she could have thought it possible there remained for her to experience, an hour before.

"I am afraid this is a bad case," said Mr Jones to Mrs Morgan in Welsh. "A brain-fever has evidently set in."

"Poor young gentleman! poor young man! He looked the very picture of health!"

"That very appearance of robustness will, in all probability, make his disorder more violent. However, we must hope for the best, Mrs Morgan. Who is to attend upon him? He will require careful nursing. Is that young lady his sister? She looks too young to be his wife?"

"No, indeed! Gentlemen like you must know, Mr Jones, that we can't always look too closely into the ways of young men who come to our houses. Not but what I'm sorry for her, for she's an innocent, inoffensive young creature. I always think it right, for my own morals, to put a little scorn into my manners when such as her come to stay here; but, indeed, she's so gentle, I've found it hard work to show the proper contempt."

She would have gone on to her inattentive listener if she had not heard a low tap at the door, which recalled her from her morality, and Mr Jones from his consideration of the necessary prescriptions.

"Come in!" said Mrs Morgan, sharply. And Ruth came in. She was white and trembling; but she stood in that dignity which strong feeling, kept down by self-command, always imparts.

"I wish you, sir, to be so kind as to tell me, clearly and distinctly, what I must do for Mr Bellingham. Every direction you give me shall be most carefully attended to. You spoke about leeches—I can put them on, and see about them. Tell me everything, sir, that you wish to have done!"

Her manner was calm and serious, and her countenance and deportment showed that the occasion was calling out strength sufficient to meet it. Mr Jones spoke with a deference which he had not thought of using upstairs, even while he supposed her to be the sister of the invalid. Ruth listened gravely; she repeated some of the injunctions, in order that she might be sure that she fully comprehended them, and then, bowing, left the room.

"She is no common person," said Mr Jones. "Still she is too young to have the responsibility of such a serious case. Have you any idea where his friends live, Mrs Morgan?"

"Indeed and I have. His mother, as haughty a lady as you would wish to see, came travelling through Wales last year; she stopped here, and, I warrant you, nothing was good enough for her; she was real quality. She left some clothes and books behind her (for the maid was almost as fine as the mistress, and little thought of seeing after her lady's clothes, having a taste for going to see scenery along with the man-servant), and we had several letters from her. I have them locked in the drawers in the bar, where I keep such things."

"Well! I should recommend your writing to the lady, and telling her her son's state."

"It would be a favour, Mr Jones, if you would just write it yourself. English writing comes so strange to my pen."

The letter was written, and, in order to save time, Mr Jones took it to the Llanglâs post-office.

CHAPTER VII - THE CRISIS—WATCHING AND WAITING

Ruth put away every thought of the past or future; everything that could unfit her for the duties of the present. Exceeding love supplied the place of experience. She never left the room after the first day; she forced herself to eat, because his service needed her strength. She did not indulge in any tears, because the weeping she longed for would make her less able to attend upon him. She watched, and waited, and prayed: prayed with an utter forgetfulness of self, only with a consciousness that God was all-powerful, and that he, whom she loved so much, needed the aid of the Mighty One.

Day and night, the summer night, seemed merged into one. She lost count of time in the hushed and darkened room. One morning Mrs Morgan beckoned her out; and she stole on tiptoe into the dazzling gallery, on one side of which the bedrooms opened.

"She's come," whispered Mrs Morgan, looking very much excited, and forgetting that Ruth had never heard that Mrs Bellingham had been summoned.

"Who is come?" asked Ruth. The idea of Mrs Mason flashed through her mind—but with a more terrible, because a more vague dread, she heard that it was his mother; the mother of whom he had always spoken as a person whose opinion was to be regarded more than that of any other individual.

"What must I do? Will she be angry with me?" said she, relapsing into her child-like dependence on others; and feeling that even Mrs Morgan was some one to stand between her and Mrs Bellingham.

Mrs Morgan herself was a little perplexed. Her morality was rather shocked at the idea of a proper real lady like Mrs Bellingham discovering that she had winked at the connexion between her son and Ruth. She was quite inclined to encourage Ruth in her inclination to shrink out of Mrs Bellingham's observation, an inclination which arose from no definite consciousness of having done wrong, but principally from the representations she had always heard of the lady's awfulness. Mrs Bellingham swept into her son's room as if she were unconscious what poor young creature had lately haunted it; while Ruth hurried into some unoccupied bedroom, and, alone there, she felt her self-restraint suddenly give way, and burst into the saddest, most utterly wretched weeping she had ever known. She was worn out with watching, and exhausted by passionate crying, and she lay down on the bed and fell asleep. The day passed on; she slumbered unnoticed and unregarded; she awoke late in the evening with a sense of having done wrong in sleeping so long; the strain upon her responsibility had not yet left her. Twilight was closing fast around; she waited until it had become night, and then she stole down to Mrs Morgan's parlour.

"If you please, may I come in?" asked she.

Jenny Morgan was doing up the hieroglyphics which she called her accounts; she answered sharply enough, but it was a permission to enter, and Ruth was thankful for it.

"Will you tell me how he is? Do you think I may go back to him?"

"No, indeed, that you may not. Nest, who has made his room tidy these many days, is not fit to go in now. Mrs Bellingham has brought her own maid, and the family nurse, and Mr Bellingham's man; such a tribe of servants and no end to packages; water-beds coming by the carrier, and a doctor from London coming down to-morrow, as if feather-beds and Mr Jones was not good enough. Why, she won't let a soul of us into the room; there's no chance for you!"

Ruth sighed. "How is he?" she inquired, after a pause.

"How can I tell indeed, when I'm not allowed to go near him? Mr Jones said to-night was a turning point; but I doubt it, for it is four days since he was taken ill, and who ever heard of a sick person taking a turn on an even number of days; it's always on the third, or the fifth, or seventh, or so on. He'll not turn till to-morrow night, take my word for it, and their fine London doctor will get all the credit, and honest Mr Jones will be thrown aside. I don't think he will get better myself, though—Gelert does not howl for nothing. My patience! what's the matter with the girl?—lord, child, you're never going to faint, and be ill on my hands?" Her sharp voice recalled Ruth from the sick unconsciousness that had been creeping over her as she listened to the latter part of this speech. She sat down and could not speak—the room whirled round and round—her white feebleness touched Mrs Morgan's heart.

"You've had no tea, I guess. Indeed, and the girls are very careless." She rang the bell with energy, and seconded her pull by going to the door and shouting out sharp directions, in Welsh, to Nest and Gwen, and three or four other rough, kind, slatternly servants.

They brought her tea, which was comfortable, according to the idea of comfort prevalent in that rude, hospitable place; there was plenty to eat, too much, indeed, for it revolted the appetite it was intended to provoke. But the heartiness with which the kind, rosy waiter pressed her to eat, and the scolding Mrs Morgan gave her when she found the buttered toast untouched (toast on which she had herself desired that the butter might not be spared), did Ruth more good than the tea. She began to hope, and to long for the morning when hope might have become certainty. It was all in vain that she was told that the room she had been in all day was at her service; she did not say a word, but she was not going to bed that night, of all nights in the year, when life or death hung trembling in the balance. She went into the bedroom till the bustling house was still, and heard busy feet passing to and fro in the room she might not enter; and voices, imperious, though hushed down to a whisper, ask for innumerable things. Then there was silence; and when she thought that all were dead asleep, except the watchers, she stole out into the gallery. On the other side were two windows, cut into the thick stone wall, and flower pots were placed on the shelves thus formed, where great, untrimmed, straggling geraniums grew, and strove to reach the light. The window near Mr Bellingham's door was open; the soft, warm-scented night air came sighing in in faint gusts, and then was still. It was summer; there was no black darkness in the twenty-four hours; only the light grew dusky, and colour disappeared from objects, of which the shape and form remained distinct. A soft grey oblong of barred light fell on the flat wall opposite to the windows, and deeper grey shadows marked out the tracery of the plants, more graceful thus than in reality. Ruth crouched where no light fell. She sat on the ground close by the door; her whole existence was absorbed in listening; all was still; it was only her heart beating with the strong, heavy, regular sound of a hammer. She wished she could stop its rushing, incessant clang. She heard a rustle of a silken gown, and knew it ought not to have been worn in a sick-room; for her senses seemed to have passed into the keeping of the invalid, and to feel only as he felt. The noise was probably occasioned by some change of posture in the watcher inside, for it was once more dead-still. The soft wind outside sank with a low, long, distant moan among the windings of the hills, and lost itself there, and came no more again. But Ruth's heart beat loud. She rose with as little noise as if she were a vision, and crept to the open window to try and lose the nervous listening for the ever-recurring sound. Out beyond, under the calm sky, veiled with a mist rather than with a cloud, rose the high, dark outlines of the mountains, shutting in that village as if it lay in a nest. They stood, like giants, solemnly watching for the end of Earth and Time. Here and there a black round shadow reminded Ruth of some "Cwm," or hollow, where she and her lover had rambled in sun and in gladness. She then thought the land enchanted into everlasting brightness and happiness; she fancied, then, that into a region so lovely no bale or woe could enter, but would be charmed away and disappear before the sight of the glorious guardian mountains. Now she knew the truth, that earth has no barrier which avails against agony. It comes lightning-like down from heaven, into the mountain house and the town garret; into the palace and into the cottage. The garden lay close under the house; a bright spot enough by day; for in that soil, whatever was planted grew and blossomed in spite of neglect. The white roses glimmered out in the dusk all the night through; the red were lost in shadow. Between the low boundary of the garden and the hills swept one or two green meadows; Ruth looked into the grey darkness till she traced each separate wave of outline. Then she heard a little restless bird chirp out its wakefulness from a nest in the ivy round the walls of the house. But the mother-bird spread her soft feathers, and hushed it into silence. Presently, however, many little birds began to scent the coming dawn, and rustled among the leaves, and chirruped loud and clear. Just above the horizon, too, the mist became a silvery grey cloud hanging on the edge of the world; presently it turned shimmering white; and then, in an instant, it flushed into rose, and the mountain-tops sprang into heaven, and bathed in the presence of the shadow of God. With a bound, the sun of a molten fiery red came above the horizon, and immediately thousands of little birds sang out for joy, and a soft chorus of mysterious, glad murmurs came forth from the earth; the low whispering wind left its hiding-place among the clefts and hollows of the hills, and wandered among the rustling herbs and trees, waking the flower-buds to the life of another day. Ruth gave a sigh of relief that the night was over and gone; for she knew that soon suspense would be ended, and the verdict known, whether for life or for death. She grew faint and sick with anxiety; it almost seemed as if she must go into the room and learn the truth. Then she heard movements, but they were not sharp or rapid, as if prompted by any emergency; then, again, it was still. She sat curled up upon the floor, with her head thrown back against the wall, and her hands clasped round her knees. She had yet to wait. Meanwhile, the invalid was slowly rousing himself from a long, deep, sound, health-giving sleep. His mother had sat by him the night through, and was now daring to change her position for the first time; she was even venturing to give directions in a low voice to the old nurse, who had dozed away in an arm-chair, ready to obey any summons of her mistress. Mrs Bellingham went on tiptoe towards the door, and chiding herself because her stiff, weary limbs made some slight noise. She had an irrepressible longing for a few minutes' change of scene after her night of watching. She felt that the crisis was over; and the relief to her mind made her conscious of every bodily feeling and irritation, which had passed unheeded as long as she had been in suspense.

She slowly opened the door. Ruth sprang upright at the first sound of the creaking handle. Her very lips were stiff and unpliable with the force of the blood which rushed to her head. It seemed as if she could not form words. She stood right before Mrs Bellingham. "How is he, madam?"

Mrs Bellingham was for a moment surprised at the white apparition which seemed to rise out of the ground. But her quick, proud mind understood it all in an instant. This was the girl, then, whose profligacy had led her son astray; had raised up barriers in the way of her favourite scheme of his marriage with Miss Duncombe; nay, this was the real cause of his illness, his mortal danger at this present time, and of her bitter, keen anxiety. If, under any circumstances, Mrs Bellingham could have been guilty of the ill-breeding of not answering a question, it was now; and for a moment she was tempted to pass on in silence. Ruth could not wait; she spoke again:

"For the love of God, madam, speak! How is he? Will he live?"

If she did not answer her, she thought the creature was desperate enough to force her way into his room. So she spoke.

"He has slept well: he is better."

"Oh! my God, I thank Thee," murmured Ruth, sinking back against the wall.

It was too much to hear this wretched girl thanking God for her son's life; as if, in fact, she had any lot or part in him, and to dare to speak to the Almighty on her son's behalf! Mrs Bellingham looked at her with cold, contemptuous eyes, whose glances were like ice-bolts, and made Ruth shiver up away from them.

"Young woman, if you have any propriety or decency left, I trust that you will not dare to force yourself into his room."

She stood for a moment as if awaiting an answer, and half expecting it to be a defiance. But she did not understand Ruth. She did not imagine the faithful trustfulness of her heart. Ruth believed that if Mr Bellingham was alive and likely to live, all was well. When he wanted her, he would send for her, ask for her, yearn for her, till every one would yield before his steadfast will. At present she imagined that he was probably too weak to care or know who was about him; and though it would have been an infinite delight to her to hover and brood around him, yet it was of him she thought and not of herself. She gently drew herself on one side to make way for Mrs Bellingham to pass.

By-and-by Mrs Morgan came up. Ruth was still near the door, from which it seemed as if she could not tear herself away.

"Indeed, miss, and you must not hang about the door in this way; it is not pretty manners. Mrs Bellingham has been speaking very sharp and cross about it, and I shall lose the character of my inn if people take to talking as she does. Did not I give you a room last night to keep in, and never be seen or heard of; and did I not tell you what a particular lady Mrs Bellingham was, but you must come out here right in her way? Indeed, it was not pretty, nor grateful to me, Jenny Morgan, and that I must say."

Ruth turned away like a chidden child. Mrs Morgan followed her to her room, scolding as she went; and then, having cleared her heart after her wont by uttering hasty words, her real kindness made her add, in a softened tone:

"You stop up here like a good girl. I'll send you your breakfast by-and-by, and let you know from time to time how he is; and you can go out for a walk, you know; but if you do, I'll take it as a favour if you'll go out by the side door. It will, maybe, save scandal."

All that day long, Ruth kept herself close prisoner in the room to which Mrs Morgan accorded her; all that day, and many succeeding days. But at nights, when the house was still, and even the little brown mice had gathered up the crumbs, and darted again to their holes, Ruth stole out, and crept to his door to catch, if she could, the sound of his beloved voice. She could tell by its tones how he felt, and how he was getting on, as well as any of the watchers in the room. She yearned and pined to see him once more; but she had reasoned herself down into something like patience. When he was well enough to leave his room, when he had not always one of the nurses with him, then he would send for her, and she would tell him how very patient she had been for his dear sake. But it was long to wait even with this thought of the manner in which the waiting would end. Poor Ruth! her faith was only building up vain castles in the air; they towered up into heaven, it is true, but, after all, they were but visions.

CHAPTER VIII - MRS BELLINGHAM "DOES THE THING HANDSOMELY"

If Mr Bellingham did not get rapidly well, it was more owing to the morbid querulous fancy attendant on great weakness than from any unfavourable medical symptom. But he turned away with peevish loathing from the very sight of food, prepared in the slovenly manner which had almost disgusted him when he was well. It was of no use telling him that Simpson, his mother's maid, had superintended the preparation at every point. He offended her by detecting something offensive and to be avoided in her daintiest messes, and made Mrs Morgan mutter many a hasty speech, which, however, Mrs Bellingham thought it better not to hear until her son should be strong enough to travel.

"I think you are better to-day," said she, as his man wheeled his sofa to the bedroom window. "We shall get you downstairs to-morrow."

"If it were to get away from this abominable place, I could go down to-day; but I believe I'm to be kept prisoner here for ever. I shall never get well here, I'm sure."

He sank back on his sofa in impatient despair. The surgeon was announced, and eagerly questioned by Mrs Bellingham as to the possibility of her son's removal; and he, having heard the same anxiety for the same end expressed by Mrs Morgan in the regions below, threw no great obstacles in the way. After the doctor had taken his departure, Mrs Bellingham cleared her throat several times. Mr Bellingham knew the prelude of old, and winced with nervous annoyance.

"Henry, there is something I must speak to you about; an unpleasant subject, certainly, but one which has been forced upon me by the very girl herself; you must be aware to what I refer without giving me the pain of explaining myself."

Mr Bellingham turned himself sharply round to the wall, and prepared himself for a lecture by concealing his face from her notice; but she herself was in too nervous a state to be capable of observation.

"Of course," she continued, "it was my wish to be as blind to the whole affair as possible, though you can't imagine how Mrs Mason has blazoned it abroad; all Fordham rings with it; but of course it could not be pleasant, or, indeed, I may say correct, for me to be aware that a person of such improper character was under the same—I beg your pardon, dear Henry, what do you say?"

"Ruth is no improper character, mother; you do her injustice!"

"My dear boy, you don't mean to uphold her as a paragon of virtue!"

"No, mother, but I led her wrong; I—"

"We will let all discussions into the cause or duration of her present character drop, if you please," said Mrs Bellingham, with the sort of dignified authority which retained a certain power over her son—a power which originated in childhood, and which he only defied when he was roused into passion. He was too weak in body to oppose himself to her, and fight the ground inch by inch. "As I have implied, I do not wish to ascertain your share of blame; from what I saw of her one morning, I am convinced of her forward, intrusive manners, utterly without shame, or even common modesty."

"What are you referring to?" asked Mr Bellingham, sharply.

"Why, when you were at the worst, and I had been watching you all night, and had just gone out in the morning for a breath of fresh air, this girl pushed herself before me, and insisted upon speaking to me. I really had to send Mrs Morgan to her before I could return to your room. A more impudent, hardened manner, I never saw."

"Ruth was neither impudent nor hardened; she was ignorant enough, and might offend from knowing no better."

He was getting weary of the discussion, and wished it had never been begun. From the time he had become conscious of his mother's presence, he had felt the dilemma he was in in regard to Ruth, and various plans had directly crossed his brain; but it had been so troublesome to weigh and consider them all properly, that they had been put aside to be settled when he grew stronger. But this difficulty in which he was placed by his connexion with Ruth, associated the idea of her in his mind with annoyance and angry regret at the whole affair. He wished, in the languid way in which he wished and felt everything not immediately relating to his daily comfort, that he had never seen her. It was a most awkward, a most unfortunate affair. Notwithstanding this annoyance connected with and arising out of Ruth, he would not submit to hear her abused; and something in his manner impressed this on his mother, for she immediately changed her mode of attack.

"We may as well drop all dispute as to the young woman's manners; but I suppose you do not mean to defend your connexion with her; I suppose you are not so lost to all sense of propriety as to imagine it fit or desirable that your mother and this degraded girl should remain under the same roof, liable to meet at any hour of the day?" She waited for an answer, but no answer came.

"I ask you a simple question; is it, or is it not desirable?"

"I suppose it is not," he replied, gloomily.

"And *I* suppose, from your manner, that you think the difficulty would be best solved by my taking my departure, and leaving you with your vicious companion?"

Again no answer, but inward and increasing annoyance, of which Mr Bellingham considered Ruth the cause. At length he spoke.

"Mother, you are not helping me in my difficulty. I have no desire to banish you, nor to hurt you, after all your care for me. Ruth has not been so much to blame as you imagine, that I must say; but I do not wish to see her again, if you can tell me how to arrange it otherwise, without behaving unhandsomely. Only spare me all this worry while I am so weak. I put myself in your hands. Dismiss her, as you wish it; but let it be done handsomely, and let me hear no more about it; I cannot bear it; let me have a quiet life, without being lectured while I am pent up here, and unable to shake off unpleasant thoughts."

"My dear Henry, rely upon me."

"No more, mother; it's a bad business, and I can hardly avoid blaming myself in the matter; I don't want to dwell upon it."

"Don't be too severe in your self-reproaches while you are so feeble, dear Henry; it is right to repent, but I have no doubt in my own mind she led you wrong with her artifices. But, as you say, everything should be done handsomely. I confess I was deeply grieved when I first heard of the affair, but since I have seen the girl— Well! I'll say no more about her, since I see it displeases you; but I am thankful to God that you see the error of your ways."

She sat silent, thinking for a little while, and then sent for her writing-case, and began to write. Her son became restless, and nervously irritated.

"Mother," he said, "this affair worries me to death. I cannot shake off the thoughts of it."

"Leave it to me, I'll arrange it satisfactorily."

"Could we not leave to-night? I should not be so haunted by this annoyance in another place. I dread seeing her again, because I fear a scene; and yet I believe I ought to see her, in order to explain."

"You must not think of such a thing, Henry," said she, alarmed at the very idea. "Sooner than that, we will leave in half an hour, and try to get to Pen trê Voelas to-night. It is not yet three, and the evenings are very long. Simpson should stay and finish the packing; she could go straight to London and meet us there. Macdonald and nurse could go with us. Could you bear twenty miles, do you think?"

Anything to get rid of his uneasiness. He felt that he was not behaving as he should do, to Ruth, though the really right never entered his head. But it would extricate him from his present dilemma, and save him many lectures; he knew that his mother, always liberal where money was concerned, would "do the thing handsomely," and it would always be easy to write and give Ruth what explanation he felt inclined, in a day or two; so he consented, and soon lost some of his uneasiness in watching the bustle of the preparation for their departure.

All this time Ruth was quietly spending in her room, beguiling the waiting, weary hours, with pictures of the meeting at the end. Her room looked to the back, and was in a side-wing away from the principal state apartments, consequently she was not roused to suspicion by any of the commotion; but, indeed, if she had heard the banging of doors, the sharp directions, the carriage-wheels, she would still not have suspected the truth; her own love was too faithful.

It was four o'clock and past, when some one knocked at her door, and, on entering, gave her a note, which Mrs Bellingham had left. That lady had found some difficulty in wording it, so as to satisfy herself, but it was as follows:

> My son, on recovering from his illness, is, I thank God, happily conscious of the sinful way in which he has been living with you. By his earnest desire, and in order to avoid seeing you again, we are on the point of leaving this place; but before I go, I wish to exhort you to repentance, and to remind you that you will not have your own guilt alone upon your head, but that of any young man whom you may succeed in entrapping into vice. I shall pray that you may turn to an honest life, and I strongly recommend you, if indeed you are not 'dead in trespasses and sins,' to enter some penitentiary. In accordance with my son's wishes, I forward you in this envelope a bank-note of fifty pounds.
>
> MARGARET BELLINGHAM.

Was this the end of all? Had he, indeed, gone? She started up, and asked this last question of the servant, who, half guessing at the purport of the note, had lingered about the room, curious to see the effect produced.

"Iss, indeed, miss; the carriage drove from the door as I came upstairs. You'll see it now on the Yspytty road, if you'll please to come to the window of No. 24."

Ruth started up, and followed the chambermaid. Aye, there it was, slowly winding up the steep white road, on which it seemed to move at a snail's pace.

She might overtake him—she might—she might speak one farewell word to him, print his face on her heart with a last look—nay, when he saw her he might retract, and not utterly, for ever, leave her. Thus she thought; and she flew back to her room, and snatching up her bonnet, ran, tying the strings with her trembling hands as she went down the stairs, out at the nearest door, little heeding the angry words of Mrs Morgan; for the hostess, more irritated at Mrs Bellingham's severe upbraiding at parting, than mollified by her ample payment, was offended by the circumstance of Ruth, in her wild haste, passing through the prohibited front door.

But Ruth was away before Mrs Morgan had finished her speech, out and away, scudding along the road, thought-lost in the breathless rapidity of her motion. Though her heart and head beat almost to bursting, what did it signify if she could but overtake the carriage? It was a nightmare, constantly evading the most passionate wishes and endeavours, and constantly gaining ground. Every time it was visible it was in fact more distant, but Ruth would not believe it. If she could but gain the summit of that weary, everlasting hill, she believed that she could run again, and would soon be nigh upon the carriage. As she ran, she prayed with wild eagerness; she prayed that she might see his face once more, even if she died on the spot before him. It was one of those prayers which God is too merciful to grant; but despairing and wild as it was, Ruth put her soul into it, and prayed it again, and yet again.

Wave above wave of the ever-rising hills were gained, were crossed, and at last Ruth struggled up to the very top and stood on the bare table of moor, brown and purple, stretching far away till it was lost in the haze of the summer afternoon; and the white road was all flat before her, but the carriage she sought and the figure she sought had disappeared. There was no human being there; a few wild, black-faced mountain sheep quietly grazing near the road, as if it were long since they had been disturbed by the passing of any vehicle, was all the life she saw on the bleak moorland.

She threw herself down on the ling by the side of the road in despair. Her only hope was to die, and she believed she was dying. She could not think; she could believe anything. Surely life was a horrible dream, and God would mercifully awaken her from it. She had no penitence, no consciousness of error or offence; no knowledge of any one circumstance but that he was gone. Yet afterwards, long afterwards, she remembered the exact motion of a bright green beetle busily meandering among the wild thyme near her, and she recalled the musical, balanced, wavering drop of a skylark into her nest near the heather-bed where she lay. The sun was sinking low, the hot air had ceased to quiver near the hotter earth, when she bethought her once more of the note which she had impatiently thrown down before half mastering its contents. "Oh, perhaps," she thought, "I have been too hasty. There may be some words of explanation from him on the other side of the page, to which, in my blind anguish, I never turned. I will go and find it."

She lifted herself heavily and stiffly from the crushed heather. She stood dizzy and confused with her change of posture; and was so unable to move at first, that her walk was but slow and tottering; but, by-and-by, she was tasked and goaded by thoughts which forced her into rapid motion, as if, by it, she could escape from her agony. She came down on the level ground, just as many gay or peaceful groups were sauntering leisurely home with hearts at ease; with low laughs and quiet smiles, and many an exclamation at the beauty of the summer evening.

Ever since her adventure with the little boy and his sister, Ruth had habitually avoided encountering these happy—innocents, may I call them?—these happy fellow-mortals! And even now, the habit grounded on sorrowful humiliation had power over her; she paused, and then, on looking back, she saw more people who had come into the main road from a side path. She opened a gate into a pasture-field, and crept up to the hedge-bank until all should have passed by, and she could steal into the inn unseen. She sat down on the sloping turf by the roots of an old hawthorn-tree which grew in the hedge; she was still tearless with hot burning eyes; she heard the merry walkers pass by; she heard the footsteps of the village children as they ran along to their evening play; she saw the small black cows come into the fields after being milked; and life seemed yet abroad. When would the world be still and dark, and fit for such a deserted, desolate creature as she was? Even in her hiding-place she was not long at peace. The little children, with their curious eyes peering here and there, had peeped through the hedge, and through the gate, and now they gathered from all the four corners of the hamlet, and crowded round the gate; and one more adventurous than the rest had run into the field to cry, "Gi' me a halfpenny," which set the example to every little one, emulous of his boldness; and there, where she sat, low on the ground, and longing for the sure hiding-place earth gives to the weary, the children kept running in, and pushing one another forwards, and laughing. Poor things; their time had not come for understanding what sorrow is. Ruth would have begged them to leave her alone, and not madden her utterly; but they knew no English save the one eternal "Gi' me a halfpenny." She felt in her heart that there was no pity anywhere. Suddenly, while she thus doubted God, a shadow fell across her garments, on which her miserable eyes were bent. She looked up. The deformed gentleman she had twice before seen, stood there. He had been attracted by the noisy little crowd, and had questioned them in Welsh, but not understanding enough of the language to comprehend their answers, he had obeyed their signs, and entered the gate to which they pointed. There he saw the young girl whom he had noticed at first for her innocent beauty, and the second time for the idea he had gained respecting her situation; there he saw her, crouched up like some hunted creature, with a wild, scared look of despair, which almost made her lovely face seem fierce; he saw her dress soiled and dim, her bonnet crushed and battered with her tossings to and fro on the moorland bed; he saw the poor, lost wanderer, and when he saw her, he had compassion on her.

There was some look of heavenly pity in his eyes, as gravely and sadly they met her upturned gaze, which touched her stony heart. Still looking at him, as if drawing some good influence from him, she said low and mournfully, "He has left me, sir!—sir, he has indeed—he has gone and left me!"

Before he could speak a word to comfort her, she had burst into the wildest, dreariest crying ever mortal cried. The settled form of the event, when put into words, went sharp to her heart; her moans and sobs wrung his soul; but as no speech of his could be heard, if he had been able to decide what best to say, he stood by her in apparent calmness, while she, wretched, wailed and uttered her woe. But when she lay worn out, and stupefied into silence, she heard him say to himself, in a low voice:

"Oh, my God! for Christ's sake, pity her!"

Ruth lifted up her eyes, and looked at him with a dim perception of the meaning of his words. She regarded him fixedly in a dreamy way, as if they struck some chord in her heart, and she were listening to its echo; and so it was. His pitiful look, or his words, reminded her of the childish days when she knelt at her mother's knee, and she was only conscious of a straining, longing desire to recall it all.

He let her take her time, partly because he was powerfully affected himself by all the circumstances, and by the sad pale face upturned to his; and partly by an instinctive consciousness that the softest patience was required. But suddenly she startled him, as she herself was startled into a keen sense of the suffering agony of the present; she sprang up and pushed him aside, and went rapidly towards the gate of the field. He could not move as quickly as most men, but he put forth his utmost speed. He followed across the road, on to the rocky common; but as he went along, with his uncertain gait, in the dusk gloaming, he stumbled, and fell over some sharp projecting stone. The acute pain which shot up his back forced a short cry from him; and, when bird and beast are hushed into rest and the stillness of the night is over all, a high-pitched sound, like the voice of pain, is carried far in the quiet air. Ruth, speeding on in her despair, heard the sharp utterance, and stopped suddenly short. It did what no remonstrance could have done; it called her out of herself. The tender nature was in her still, in that hour when all good angels seemed to have abandoned her. In the old days she could never bear to hear or see bodily suffering in any of God's meanest creatures, without trying to succour them; and now, in her rush to the awful death of the suicide, she stayed her wild steps, and turned to find from whom that sharp sound of anguish had issued.

He lay among the white stones, too faint with pain to move, but with an agony in his mind far keener than any bodily pain, as he thought that by his unfortunate fall he had lost all chance of saving her. He was almost overpowered by his intense thankfulness when he saw her white figure pause, and stand listening, and turn again with slow footsteps, as if searching for some lost thing. He could hardly speak, but he made a sound which, though his heart was inexpressibly glad, was like a groan. She came quickly towards him.

"I am hurt," said he; "do not leave me;" his disabled and tender frame was overcome by the accident and the previous emotions, and he fainted away. Ruth flew to the little mountain stream, the dashing sound of whose waters had been tempting her, but a moment before, to seek forgetfulness in the deep pool into which they fell. She made a basin of her joined hands, and carried enough of the cold fresh water back to dash into his face and restore him to consciousness. While he still kept silence, uncertain what to say best fitted to induce her to listen to him, she said softly:

"Are you better, sir?—are you very much hurt?"

"Not very much; I am better. Any quick movement is apt to cause me a sudden loss of power in my back, and I believe I stumbled over some of these projecting stones. It will soon go off, and you will help me to go home, I am sure."

"Oh, yes! Can you go now? I am afraid of your lying too long on this heather; there is a heavy dew."

He was so anxious to comply with her wish, and not weary out her thought for him, and so turn her back upon herself, that he tried to rise. The pain was acute, and this she saw.

"Don't hurry yourself, sir; I can wait."

Then came across her mind the recollection of the business that was thus deferred; but the few homely words which had been exchanged between them seemed to have awakened her from her madness. She sat down by him, and, covering her face with her hands, cried mournfully and unceasingly. She forgot his presence, and yet she had a consciousness that some one looked for her kind offices, that she was wanted in the world, and must not rush hastily out of it. The consciousness did not take this definite form, it did not become a thought, but it kept her still, and it was gradually soothing her.

"Can you help me to rise now?" said he, after a while. She did not speak, but she helped him up, and then he took her arm, and she led him tenderly through all the little velvet paths, where the turf grew short and soft between the rugged stones. Once more on the highway, they slowly passed along in the moonlight. He guided her by a slight motion of the arm, through the more unfrequented lanes, to his lodgings at the shop; for he thought for her, and conceived the pain she would have in seeing the lighted windows of the inn. He leant more heavily on her arm, as they awaited the opening of the door.

"Come in," said he, not relaxing his hold, and yet dreading to tighten it, lest she should defy restraint, and once more rush away.

They went slowly into the little parlour behind the shop. The bonny-looking hostess, Mrs Hughes by name, made haste to light the candle, and then they saw each other, face to face. The deformed gentleman looked very pale, but Ruth looked as if the shadow of death was upon her.

CHAPTER IX - THE STORM-SPIRIT SUBDUED

Mrs Hughes bustled about with many a sympathetic exclamation, now in pretty broken English, now in more fluent Welsh, which sounded as soft as Russian or Italian, in her musical voice. Mr Benson, for that was the name of the hunchback, lay on the sofa, thinking; while the tender Mrs Hughes made every arrangement for his relief from pain. He had lodged with her for three successive years, and she knew and loved him.

Ruth stood in the little bow-window, looking out. Across the moon, and over the deep blue heavens, large, torn, irregular-shaped clouds went hurrying, as if summoned by some storm-spirit. The work they were commanded to do was not here; the mighty gathering-place lay eastward, immeasurable leagues, and on they went, chasing each other over the silent earth, now black, now silver-white at one transparent edge, now with the moon shining like Hope through their darkest centre, now again with a silver lining; and now, utterly black, they sailed lower in the lift, and disappeared behind the immovable mountains; they were rushing in the very direction in which Ruth had striven and struggled to go that afternoon; they, in their wild career, would soon pass over the very spot where he (her world's he) was lying sleeping, or perhaps not sleeping, perhaps thinking of her. The storm was in her mind, and rent and tore her purposes into forms as wild and irregular as the heavenly shapes she was looking at. If, like them, she could pass the barrier horizon in the night, she might overtake him.

Mr Benson saw her look, and read it partially. He saw her longing gaze outwards upon the free, broad world, and thought that the syren waters, whose deadly music yet rang in her ears, were again tempting her. He called her to him, praying that his feeble voice might have power.

"My dear young lady, I have much to say to you; and God has taken my strength from me now when I most need it.—Oh, I sin to speak so—but, for His sake, I implore you to be patient here, if only till to-morrow morning." He looked at her, but her face was immovable, and she did not speak. She could not give up her hope, her chance, her liberty till to-morrow.

"God help me," said he, mournfully, "my words do not touch her;" and, still holding her hand, he sank back on the pillows. Indeed, it was true that his words did not vibrate in her atmosphere. The storm-spirit raged there, and filled her heart with the thought that she was an outcast; and the holy words, "for His sake," were answered by the demon, who held possession, with a blasphemous defiance of the merciful God:

"What have I to do with Thee?"

He thought of every softening influence of religion which over his own disciplined heart had power, but put them aside as useless. Then the still small voice whispered, and he spake:

"In your mother's name, whether she be dead or alive, I command you to stay here until I am able to speak to you."

She knelt down at the foot of the sofa, and shook it with her sobs. Her heart was touched, and he hardly dared to speak again. At length he said:

"I know you will not go—you could not—for her sake. You will not, will you?"

"No," whispered Ruth; and then there was a great blank in her heart. She had given up her chance. She was calm, in the utter absence of all hope.

"And now you will do what I tell you," said he, gently, but, unconsciously to himself, in the tone of one who has found the hidden spell by which to rule spirits.

She slowly said, "Yes." But she was subdued.

He called Mrs Hughes. She came from her adjoining shop.

"You have a bedroom within yours, where your daughter used to sleep, I think? I am sure you will oblige me, and I shall consider it as a great favour, if you will allow this young lady to sleep there to-night. Will you take her there now? Go, my dear. I have full trust in your promise not to leave until I can speak to you." His voice died away to silence; but as Ruth rose from her knees at his bidding, she looked at his face through her tears. His lips were moving in earnest, unspoken prayer, and she knew it was for her.

That night, although his pain was relieved by rest, he could not sleep; and, as in fever, the coming events kept unrolling themselves before him in every changing and fantastic form. He met Ruth in all possible places and ways, and addressed her in every manner he could imagine most calculated to move and affect her to penitence and virtue. Towards morning he fell asleep, but the same thoughts haunted his dreams; he spoke, but his voice refused to utter aloud; and she fled, relentless, to the deep, black pool.

But God works in His own way.

The visions melted into deep, unconscious sleep. He was awakened by a knock at the door, which seemed a repetition of what he had heard in his last sleeping moments.

It was Mrs Hughes. She stood at the first word of permission within the room.

"Please, sir, I think the young lady is very ill indeed, sir; perhaps you would please to come to her."

"How is she ill?" said he, much alarmed.

"Quite quiet-like, sir; but I think she is dying, that's all, indeed, sir!"

"Go away, I will be with you directly!" he replied, his heart sinking within him.

In a very short time he was standing with Mrs Hughes by Ruth's bedside. She lay as still as if she were dead, her eyes shut, her wan face numbed into a fixed anguish of expression. She did not speak when they spoke, though after a while they thought she strove to do so. But all power of motion and utterance had left her. She was dressed in everything, except her bonnet, as she had been the day before; although sweet, thoughtful Mrs Hughes had provided her with nightgear, which lay on the little chest of drawers that served as a dressing-table. Mr Benson lifted up her arm to feel her feeble, fluttering pulse; and when he let go her hand, it fell upon the bed in a dull, heavy way, as if she were already dead.

"You gave her some food?" said he, anxiously, to Mrs Hughes.

"Indeed, and I offered her the best in the house, but she shook her poor pretty head, and only asked if I would please to get her a cup of water. I brought her some milk though, and 'deed, I think she'd rather have had the water; but not to seem sour and cross, she took some milk." By this time Mrs Hughes was fairly crying.

"When does the doctor come up here?"

"Indeed, sir, and he's up nearly every day now, the inn is so full."

"I'll go for him. And can you manage to undress her and lay her in bed? Open the window too, and let in the air; if her feet are cold, put bottles of hot water to them."

It was a proof of the true love, which was the nature of both, that it never crossed their minds to regret that this poor young creature had been thus thrown upon their hands. On the contrary, Mrs Hughes called it "a blessing."

"It blesseth him that gives, and him that takes."

CHAPTER X - A NOTE AND THE ANSWER

At the inn everything was life and bustle. Mr Benson had to wait long in Mrs Morgan's little parlour before she could come to him, and he kept growing more and more impatient. At last she made her appearance and heard his story.

People may talk as they will about the little respect that is paid to virtue, unaccompanied by the outward accidents of wealth or station; but I rather think it will be found that, in the long run, true and simple virtue always has its proportionate reward in the respect and reverence of every one whose esteem is worth having. To be sure, it is not rewarded after the way of the world as mere worldly possessions are, with low obeisance and lip-service; but all the better and more noble qualities in the hearts of others make ready and go forth to meet it on its approach, provided only it be pure, simple, and unconscious of its own existence.

Mr Benson had little thought for outward tokens of respect just then, nor had Mrs Morgan much time to spare; but she smoothed her ruffled brow, and calmed her bustling manner, as soon as ever she saw who it was that awaited her; for Mr Benson was well known in the village where he had taken up his summer holiday among the mountains year after year, always a resident at the shop, and seldom spending a shilling at the inn.

Mrs Morgan listened patiently—for her.

"Mr Jones will come this afternoon. But it is a shame you should be troubled with such as her. I had but little time yesterday, but I guessed there was something wrong, and Gwen has just been telling me her bed has not been slept in. They were in a pretty hurry to be gone yesterday, for all that the gentleman was not fit to travel, to my way of thinking; indeed, William Wynn, the post-boy, said he was weary enough before he got to the end of that Yspytty road; and he thought they would have to rest there a day or two before they could go further than Pen trê Voelas. Indeed, and anyhow, the servant is to follow them with the baggage this very morning; and now I remember, William Wynn said they would wait for her. You'd better write a note, Mr Benson, and tell them her state."

It was good, though unpalatable advice. It came from one accustomed to bring excellent, if unrefined sense, to bear quickly upon any emergency, and to decide rapidly. She was, in truth, so little accustomed to have her authority questioned, that before Mr Benson had made up his mind, she had produced paper, pens, and ink from the drawer in her bureau, placed them before him, and was going to leave the room.

"Leave the note on this shelf, and trust me that it goes by the maid. The boy that drives her there in the car shall bring you an answer back."

She was gone before he could rally his scattered senses enough to remember that he had not the least idea of the name of the party to whom he was to write. The quiet leisure and peace of his little study at home favoured his habit of reverie and long deliberation, just as her position as mistress of an inn obliged her to quick, decisive ways.

Her advice, though good in some points, was unpalatable in others. It was true that Ruth's condition ought to be known by those who were her friends; but were these people to whom he was now going to write, friends? He knew there was a rich mother, and a handsome, elegant son; and he had also some idea of the circumstances which might a little extenuate their mode of quitting Ruth. He had wide enough sympathy to understand that it must have been a most painful position in which the mother had been placed, on finding herself under the same roof with a girl who was living with her son, as Ruth was. And yet he did not like to apply to her; to write to the son was still more out of the question, as it seemed like asking him to return. But through one or the other lay the only clue to her friends, who certainly ought to be made acquainted with her position. At length he wrote:

> MADAM,—I write to tell you of the condition of the poor young woman—[here came a long pause of deliberation]—who accompanied your son on his arrival here, and who was left behind on your departure yesterday. She is lying (as it appears to me) in a very dangerous state at my lodgings; and, if I may suggest, it would be kind to allow your maid to return and attend upon her until she is sufficiently recovered to be restored to her friends, if, indeed, they could not come to take charge of her themselves.
>
> I remain, madam,
Your obedient servant,
THURSTAN BENSON.

The note was very unsatisfactory after all his consideration, but it was the best he could do. He made inquiry of a passing servant as to the lady's name, directed the note, and placed it on the indicated shelf. He then returned to his lodgings, to await the doctor's coming and the post-boy's return. There was no alteration in Ruth; she was as one stunned into unconsciousness; she did not move her posture, she hardly breathed. From time to time Mrs Hughes wetted her mouth with some liquid, and there was a little mechanical motion of the lips; that was the only sign of life she gave. The doctor came and shook his head,—"a thorough prostration of strength, occasioned by some great shock on the nerves,"—and prescribed care and quiet, and mysterious medicines, but acknowledged that the result was doubtful, very doubtful. After his departure, Mr Benson took his Welsh grammar and tried again to master the ever-puzzling rules for the mutations of letters; but it was of no use, for his thoughts were absorbed by the life-in-death condition of the young creature, who was lately bounding and joyous.

The maid and the luggage, the car and the driver, had arrived before noon at their journey's end, and the note had been delivered. It annoyed Mrs Bellingham exceedingly. It was the worst of these kind of connexions, there was no calculating the consequences; they were never-ending. All sorts of claims seemed to be established, and all sorts of people to step in to their settlement. The idea of sending her maid! Why, Simpson would not go if she asked her. She soliloquised thus while reading the letter; and then, suddenly turning round to the favourite attendant, who had been listening to her mistress's remarks with no inattentive ear, she asked:

"Simpson, would you go and nurse this creature, as this—" she looked at the signature—"Mr Benson, whoever he is, proposes?"

"Me! no, indeed, ma'am," said the maid, drawing herself up, stiff in her virtue. "I'm sure, ma'am, you would not expect it of me; I could never have the face to dress a lady of character again."

"Well, well! don't be alarmed; I cannot spare you; by the way, just attend to the strings on my dress; the chambermaid here pulled them into knots, and broke them terribly, last night. It is awkward though, very," said she, relapsing into a musing fit over the condition of Ruth.

"If you'll allow me, ma'am, I think I might say something that would alter the case. I believe, ma'am, you put a bank-note into the letter to the young woman yesterday?"

Mrs Bellingham bowed acquiescence, and the maid went on:

"Because, ma'am, when the little deformed man wrote that note (he's Mr Benson, ma'am), I have reason to believe neither he nor Mrs Morgan knew of any provision being made for the young woman. Me and the chambermaid found your letter and the bank-note lying quite promiscuous, like waste paper, on the floor of her room; for I believe she rushed out like mad after you left."

"That, as you say, alters the case. This letter, then, is principally a sort of delicate hint that some provision ought to have been made, which is true enough, only it has been attended to already; what became of the money?"

"Law, ma'am! do you ask? Of course, as soon as I saw it, I picked it up and took it to Mrs Morgan, in trust for the young person."

"Oh, that's right. What friends has she? Did you ever hear from Mason?—perhaps they ought to know where she is."

"Mrs Mason did tell me, ma'am, she was an orphan; with a guardian who was no-ways akin, and who washed his hands of her when she ran off; but Mrs Mason was sadly put out, and went into hysterics, for fear you would think she had not seen after her enough, and that she might lose your custom; she said it was no fault of hers, for the girl was always a forward creature, boasting of her beauty, and saying how pretty she was, and striving to get where her good looks could be seen and admired,—one night in particular, ma'am, at a county ball; and how Mrs Mason had found out she used to meet Mr Bellingham at an old woman's house, who was a regular old witch, ma'am, and lives in the lowest part of the town, where all the bad characters haunt."

"There! that's enough," said Mrs Bellingham, sharply, for the maid's chattering had outrun her tact; and in her anxiety to vindicate the character of her friend Mrs Mason by blackening that of Ruth, she had forgotten that she a little implicated her mistress's son, whom his proud mother did not like to imagine as ever passing through a low and degraded part of the town.

"If she has no friends, and is the creature you describe (which is confirmed by my own observation), the best place for her is, as I said before, the Penitentiary. Her fifty pounds will keep her for a week or so, if she is really unable to travel, and pay for her journey; and if on her return to Fordham she will let me know, I will undertake to obtain her admission immediately."

"I'm sure it's well for her she has to do with a lady who will take any interest in her, after what has happened."

Mrs Bellingham called for her writing-desk, and wrote a few hasty lines to be sent back by the post-boy, who was on the point of starting:

> Mrs Bellingham presents her compliments to her unknown correspondent, Mr Benson, and begs to inform him of a circumstance of which she believes he was ignorant when he wrote the letter with which she has been favoured; namely, that provision to the amount of £50 was left for the unfortunate young person who is the subject of Mr Benson's letter. This sum is in the hands of Mrs Morgan, as well as a note from Mrs Bellingham to the miserable girl, in which she proposes to procure her admission into the Fordham Penitentiary, the best place for such a character, as by this profligate action she has forfeited the only friend remaining to her in the world. This proposition, Mrs Bellingham repeats; and they are the young woman's best friends who most urge her to comply with the course now pointed out.

"Take care Mr Bellingham hears nothing of this Mr Benson's note," said Mrs Bellingham, as she delivered the answer to her maid; "he is so sensitive just now that it would annoy him sadly, I am sure."

CHAPTER XI - THURSTAN AND FAITH BENSON

You have now seen the note which was delivered into Mr Benson's hands, as the cool shades of evening stole over the glowing summer sky. When he had read it, he again prepared to write a few hasty lines before the post went out. The post-boy was even now sounding his horn through the village as a signal for letters to be ready; and it was well that Mr Benson, in his long morning's meditation, had decided upon the course to be pursued, in case of such an answer as that which he had received from Mrs Bellingham. His present note was as follows:

> DEAR FAITH,—You must come to this place directly, where I earnestly desire you and your advice. I am well myself, so do not be alarmed. I have no time for explanation, but I am sure you will not refuse me; let me trust that I shall see you on Saturday at the latest. You know the mode by which I came; it is the best for expedition and cheapness. Dear Faith, do not fail me.
>
> Your affectionate brother,
>
> THURSTAN BENSON.
>
> P.S.—I am afraid the money I left may be running short. Do not let this stop you. Take my Facciolati to Johnson's, he will advance upon it; it is the third row, bottom shelf. Only come.

When this letter was despatched he had done all he could; and the next two days passed like a long monotonous dream of watching, thought, and care, undisturbed by any event, hardly by the change from day to night, which, now the harvest moon was at her full, was scarcely perceptible. On Saturday morning the answer came.

> DEAREST THURSTAN,—Your incomprehensible summons has just reached me, and I obey, thereby proving my right to my name of Faith. I shall be with you almost as soon as this letter. I cannot help feeling anxious, as well as curious. I have money enough, and it is well I have; for Sally, who guards your room like a dragon, would rather see me walk the whole way, than have any of your things disturbed.

Your affectionate sister,
FAITH BENSON.

It was a great relief to Mr Benson to think that his sister would so soon be with him. He had been accustomed from childhood to rely on her prompt judgment and excellent sense; and to her care he felt that Ruth ought to be consigned, as it was too much to go on taxing good Mrs Hughes with night watching and sick nursing, with all her other claims on her time. He asked her once more to sit by Ruth, while he went to meet his sister.

The coach passed by the foot of the steep ascent which led up to Llan-dhu. He took a boy to carry his sister's luggage when she arrived; they were too soon at the bottom of the hill, and the boy began to make ducks and drakes in the shallowest part of the stream, which there flowed glassy and smooth, while Mr Benson sat down on a great stone, under the shadow of an alder bush which grew where the green, flat meadow skirted the water. It was delightful to be once more in the open air, and away from the scenes and thoughts which had been pressing on him for the last three days. There was new beauty in everything: from the blue mountains which glimmered in the distant sunlight, down to the flat, rich, peaceful vale, with its calm round shadows, where he sat. The very margin of white pebbles which lay on the banks of the stream had a sort of cleanly beauty about it. He felt calmer and more at ease than he had done for some days; and yet, when he began to think, it was rather a strange story which he had to tell his sister, in order to account for his urgent summons. Here was he, sole friend and guardian of a poor sick girl, whose very name he did not know; about whom all that he did know was, that she had been the mistress of a man who had deserted her, and that he feared—he believed—she had contemplated suicide. The offence, too, was one for which his sister, good and kind as she was, had little compassion. Well, he must appeal to her love for him, which was a very unsatisfactory mode of proceeding, as he would far rather have had her interest in the girl founded on reason, or some less personal basis than showing it merely because her brother wished it.

The coach came slowly rumbling over the stony road. His sister was outside, but got down in a brisk active way, and greeted her brother heartily and affectionately. She was considerably taller than he was, and must have been very handsome; her black hair was parted plainly over her forehead, and her dark, expressive eyes and straight nose still retained the beauty of her youth. I do not know whether she was older than her brother, but, probably owing to his infirmity requiring her care, she had something of a mother's manner towards him.

"Thurstan, you are looking pale! I do not believe you are well, whatever you may say. Have you had the old pain in your back?"

"No—a little—never mind that, dearest Faith. Sit down here, while I send the boy up with your box." And then, with some little desire to show his sister how well he was acquainted with the language, he blundered out his directions in very grammatical Welsh; so grammatical, in fact, and so badly pronounced, that the boy, scratching his head, made answer,

"Dim Saesoneg."

So he had to repeat it in English.

"Well now, Thurstan, here I sit as you bid me. But don't try me too long; tell me why you sent for me."

Now came the difficulty, and oh! for a seraph's tongue, and a seraph's powers of representation! but there was no seraph at hand, only the soft running waters singing a quiet tune, and predisposing Miss Benson to listen with a soothed spirit to any tale, not immediately involving her brother's welfare, which had been the cause of her seeing that lovely vale.

"It is an awkward story to tell, Faith, but there is a young woman lying ill at my lodgings whom I wanted you to nurse."

He thought he saw a shadow on his sister's face, and detected a slight change in her voice as she spoke.

"Nothing very romantic, I hope, Thurstan. Remember, I cannot stand much romance; I always distrust it."

"I don't know what you mean by romance. The story is real enough, and not out of the common way, I'm afraid."

He paused; he did not get over the difficulty.

"Well, tell it me at once, Thurstan. I am afraid you have let some one, or perhaps only your own imagination, impose upon you; but don't try my patience too much; you know I've no great stock."

"Then I'll tell you. The young girl was brought to the inn here by a gentleman, who has left her; she is very ill, and has no one to see after her."

Miss Benson had some masculine tricks, and one was whistling a long, low whistle when surprised or displeased. She had often found it a useful vent for feelings, and she whistled now. Her brother would rather she had spoken.

"Have you sent for her friends?" she asked at last.

"She has none."

Another pause and another whistle, but rather softer and more wavering than the last.

"How is she ill?"

"Pretty nearly as quiet as if she were dead. She does not speak, or move, or even sigh."

"It would be better for her to die at once, I think."

"Faith!"

That one word put them right. It was spoken in the tone which had authority over her; it was so full of grieved surprise and mournful upbraiding. She was accustomed to exercise a sway over him, owing to her greater decision of character, and, probably, if everything were traced to its cause, to her superior vigour of constitution; but at times she was humbled before his pure, childlike nature, and felt where she was inferior. She was too good and true to conceal this feeling, or to resent its being forced upon her. After a time she said,

"Thurstan, dear, let us go to her."

She helped him with tender care, and gave him her arm up the long and tedious hill; but when they approached the village, without speaking a word on the subject, they changed their position, and she leant (apparently) on him. He stretched himself up into as vigorous a gait as he could, when they drew near to the abodes of men.

On the way they had spoken but little. He had asked after various members of his congregation, for he was a Dissenting minister in a country town, and she had answered; but they neither of them spoke of Ruth, though their minds were full of her.

Mrs Hughes had tea ready for the traveller on her arrival. Mr Benson chafed a little internally at the leisurely way in which his sister sipped and sipped, and paused to tell him some trifling particular respecting home affairs, which she had forgotten before.

"Mr Bradshaw has refused to let the children associate with the Dixons any longer, because one evening they played at acting charades."

"Indeed;—a little more bread and butter, Faith?"

"Thank you. This Welsh air does make one hungry. Mrs Bradshaw is paying poor old Maggie's rent, to save her from being sent into the workhouse."

"That's right. Won't you have another cup of tea?"

"I have had two. However, I think I'll take another."

Mr Benson could not refrain from a little sigh as he poured it out. He thought he had never seen his sister so deliberately hungry and thirsty before. He did not guess that she was feeling the meal rather a respite from a distasteful interview, which she was aware was awaiting her at its conclusion. But all things come to an end, and so did Miss Benson's tea.

"Now, will you go and see her?"

"Yes."

And so they went. Mrs Hughes had pinned up a piece of green calico, by way of a Venetian blind, to shut out the afternoon sun; and in the light thus shaded lay Ruth, still, and wan, and white. Even with her brother's account of Ruth's state, such death-like quietness startled Miss Benson—startled her into pity for the poor lovely creature who lay thus stricken and felled. When she saw her, she could no longer imagine her to be an impostor, or a hardened sinner; such prostration of woe belonged to neither. Mr Benson looked more at his sister's face than at Ruth's; he read her countenance as a book.

Mrs Hughes stood by, crying.

Mr Benson touched his sister, and they left the room together.

"Do you think she will live?" asked he.

"I cannot tell," said Miss Benson, in a softened voice. "But how young she looks! Quite a child, poor creature! When will the doctor come, Thurstan? Tell me all about her; you have never told me the particulars."

Mr Benson might have said, she had never cared to hear them before, and had rather avoided the subject; but he was too happy to see this awakening of interest in his sister's warm heart to say anything in the least reproachful. He told her the story as well as he could; and, as he felt it deeply, he told it with heart's eloquence; and, as he ended and looked at her, there were tears in the eyes of both.

"And what does the doctor say?" asked she, after a pause.

"He insists upon quiet; he orders medicines and strong broth. I cannot tell you all; Mrs Hughes can. She has been so truly good. 'Doing good, hoping for nothing again.'"

"She looks very sweet and gentle. I shall sit up to-night and watch her myself; and I shall send you and Mrs Hughes early to bed, for you have both a worn look about you I don't like. Are you sure the effect of that fall has gone off? Do you feel anything of it in your back still? After all, I owe her something for turning back to your help. Are you sure she was going to drown herself?"

"I cannot be sure, for I have not questioned her. She has not been in a state to be questioned; but I have no doubt whatever about it. But you must not think of sitting up after your journey, Faith."

"Answer me, Thurstan. Do you feel any bad effect from that fall?"

"No, hardly any. Don't sit up, Faith, to-night!"

"Thurstan, it's no use talking, for I shall; and, if you go on opposing me, I dare say I shall attack your back, and put a blister on it. Do tell me what that 'hardly any' means. Besides, to set you quite at ease, you know I have never seen mountains before, and they fill me and oppress me so much that I could not sleep; I must keep awake this first night, and see that they don't fall on the earth and overwhelm it. And now answer my questions about yourself."

Miss Benson had the power, which some people have, of carrying her wishes through to their fulfilment; her will was strong, her sense was excellent, and people yielded to her—they did not know why. Before ten o'clock she reigned sole power and potentate in Ruth's little chamber. Nothing could have been better devised for giving her an interest in the invalid. The very dependence of one so helpless upon her care inclined her heart towards her. She thought she perceived a slight improvement in the symptoms during the night, and she was a little pleased that this progress should have been made while she reigned monarch of the sick-room. Yes, certainly there was an improvement. There was more consciousness in the look of the eyes, although the whole countenance still retained its painful traces of acute suffering, manifested in an anxious, startled, uneasy aspect. It was broad morning light, though barely five o'clock, when Miss Benson caught the sight of Ruth's lips moving, as if in speech. Miss Benson stooped down to listen.

"Who are you?" asked Ruth, in the faintest of whispers.

"Miss Benson—Mr Benson's sister," she replied.

The words conveyed no knowledge to Ruth; on the contrary, weak as a babe in mind and body as she was, her lips began to quiver, and her eyes to show a terror similar to that of any little child who wakens in the presence of a stranger, and sees no dear, familiar face of mother or nurse to reassure its trembling heart.

Miss Benson took her hand in hers, and began to stroke it caressingly.

"Don't be afraid, dear; I'm a friend come to take care of you. Would you like some tea now, my love?"

The very utterance of these gentle words was unlocking Miss Benson's heart. Her brother was surprised to see her so full of interest, when he came to inquire later on in the morning. It required Mrs Hughes's persuasions, as well as his own, to induce her to go to bed for an hour or two after breakfast; and, before she went, she made them promise that she should be called when the doctor came. He did not come until late in the afternoon. The invalid was rallying fast, though rallying to a consciousness of sorrow, as was evinced by the tears which came slowly rolling down her pale sad cheeks—tears which she had not the power to wipe away.

Mr Benson had remained in the house all day to hear the doctor's opinion; and now that he was relieved from the charge of Ruth by his sister's presence, he had the more time to dwell upon the circumstances of her case—so far as they were known to him. He remembered his first sight of her; her little figure swaying to and fro as she balanced herself on the slippery stones, half smiling at her own dilemma, with a bright, happy light in the eyes that seemed like a reflection from the glancing waters sparkling below. Then he recalled the changed, affrighted look of those eyes as they met his, after the child's rebuff of her advances;—how that little incident filled up the tale at which Mrs Hughes had hinted, in a kind of sorrowful way, as if loath (as a Christian should be) to believe evil. Then that fearful evening, when he had only just saved her from committing suicide, and that nightmare sleep! And now, lost, forsaken, and but just delivered from the jaws of death, she lay dependent for everything on his sister and him,—utter strangers a few weeks ago. Where was her lover? Could he be easy and happy? Could he grow into perfect health, with these great sins pressing on his conscience with a strong and hard pain? Or had he a conscience?

Into whole labyrinths of social ethics Mr Benson's thoughts wandered, when his sister entered suddenly and abruptly.

"What does the doctor say? Is she better?"

"Oh, yes! she's better," answered Miss Benson, sharp and short. Her brother looked at her in dismay. She bumped down into a chair in a cross, disconcerted manner. They were both silent for a few minutes; only Miss Benson whistled and clucked alternately.

"What is the matter, Faith? You say she is better."

"Why, Thurstan, there is something so shocking the matter, that I cannot tell you."

Mr Benson changed colour with affright. All things possible and impossible crossed his mind but the right one. I said, "all things possible;" I made a mistake. He never believed Ruth to be more guilty than she seemed.

"Faith, I wish you would tell me, and not bewilder me with those noises of yours," said he, nervously.

"I beg your pardon; but something so shocking has just been discovered—I don't know how to word it—She will have a child. The doctor says so."

She was allowed to make noises unnoticed for a few minutes. Her brother did not speak. At last she wanted his sympathy.

"Isn't it shocking, Thurstan? You might have knocked me down with a straw when he told me."

"Does she know?"

"Yes; and I am not sure that that isn't the worst part of all."

"How?—what do you mean?"

"Oh! I was just beginning to have a good opinion of her, but I'm afraid she is very depraved. After the doctor was gone, she pulled the bed-curtain aside, and looked as if she wanted to speak to me. (I can't think how she heard, for we were close to the window, and spoke very low.) Well, I went to her, though I really had taken quite a turn against her. And she whispered, quite eagerly, 'Did he say I should have a baby?' Of course, I could not keep it from her; but I thought it my duty to look as cold and severe as I could. She did not seem to understand how it ought to be viewed, but took it just as if she had a right to have a baby. She said, 'Oh, my God, I thank Thee! Oh! I will be so good!' I had no patience with her then, so I left the room."

"Who is with her?"

"Mrs Hughes. She is not seeing the thing in a moral light, as I should have expected."

Mr Benson was silent again. After some time he began:

"Faith, I don't see this affair quite as you do. I believe I am right."

"You surprise me, brother! I don't understand you."

"Wait awhile! I want to make my feelings very clear to you, but I don't know where to begin, or how to express myself."

"It is, indeed, an extraordinary subject for us to have to talk about; but if once I get clear of this girl, I'll wash my hands of all such cases again."

Her brother was not attending to her; he was reducing his own ideas to form.

"Faith, do you know I rejoice in this child's advent?"

"May God forgive you, Thurstan!—if you know what you are saying. But, surely, it is a temptation, dear Thurstan."

"I do not think it is a delusion. The sin appears to me to be quite distinct from its consequences."

"Sophistry—and a temptation," said Miss Benson, decidedly.

"No, it is not," said her brother, with equal decision. "In the eye of God, she is exactly the same as if the life she has led had left no trace behind. We knew her errors before, Faith."

"Yes, but not this disgrace—this badge of her shame!"

"Faith, Faith! let me beg of you not to speak so of the little innocent babe, who may be God's messenger to lead her back to Him. Think again of her first words—the burst of nature from her heart! Did she not turn to God, and enter into a covenant with Him—'I will be so good?' Why, it draws her out of herself! If her life has hitherto been self-seeking, and wickedly thoughtless, here is the very instrument to make her forget herself, and be thoughtful for another. Teach her (and God will teach her, if man does not come between) to reverence her child; and this reverence will shut out sin,—will be purification."

He was very much excited; he was even surprised at his own excitement; but his thoughts and meditations through the long afternoon had prepared his mind for this manner of viewing the subject.

"These are quite new ideas to me," said Miss Benson, coldly. "I think you, Thurstan, are the first person I ever heard rejoicing over the birth of an illegitimate child. It appears to me, I must own, rather questionable morality."

"I do not rejoice. I have been all this afternoon mourning over the sin which has blighted this young creature; I have been dreading lest, as she recovered consciousness, there should be a return of her despair. I have been thinking of every holy word, every promise to the penitent—of the tenderness which led the Magdalen aright. I have been feeling, severely and reproachfully, the timidity which has hitherto made me blink all encounter with evils of this particular kind. Oh, Faith! once for all, do not accuse me of questionable morality, when I am trying more than ever I did in my life to act as my blessed Lord would have done."

He was very much agitated. His sister hesitated, and then she spoke more softly than before.

"But, Thurstan, everything might have been done to 'lead her right' (as you call it), without this child, this miserable offspring of sin."

"The world has, indeed, made such children miserable, innocent as they are; but I doubt if this be according to the will of God, unless it be His punishment for the parents' guilt; and even then the world's way of treatment is too apt to harden the mother's natural love into something like hatred. Shame, and the terror of friends' displeasure, turn her mad—defile her holiest instincts; and, as for the fathers—God forgive them! I cannot—at least, not just now."

Miss Benson thought on what her brother said. At length she asked, "Thurstan (remember I'm not convinced), how would you have this girl treated according to your theory?"

"It will require some time, and much Christian love, to find out the best way. I know I'm not very wise; but the way I think it would be right to act in, would be this—" He thought for some time before he spoke, and then said:

"She has incurred a responsibility—that we both acknowledge. She is about to become a mother, and have the direction and guidance of a little tender life. I fancy such a responsibility must be serious and solemn enough, without making it into a heavy and oppressive burden, so that human nature recoils from bearing it. While we do all we can to strengthen her sense of responsibility, I would likewise do all we can to make her feel that it is responsibility for what may become a blessing."

"Whether the children are legitimate or illegitimate?" asked Miss Benson, drily.

"Yes!" said her brother, firmly. "The more I think, the more I believe I am right. No one," said he, blushing faintly as he spoke, "can have a greater recoil from profligacy than I have. You yourself have not greater sorrow over this young creature's sin than I have: the difference is this, you confuse the consequences with the sin."

"I don't understand metaphysics."

"I am not aware that I am talking metaphysics. I can imagine that if the present occasion be taken rightly, and used well, all that is good in her may be raised to a height unmeasured but by God; while all that is evil and dark may, by His blessing, fade and disappear in the pure light of her child's presence. Oh, Father! listen to my prayer, that her redemption may date from this time. Help us to speak to her in the loving spirit of thy Holy Son!"

The tears were full in his eyes; he almost trembled in his earnestness. He was faint with the strong power of his own conviction, and with his inability to move his sister. But she was shaken. She sat very still for a quarter of an hour or more, while he leaned back, exhausted by his own feelings.

"The poor child!" said she, at length—"the poor, poor child! what it will have to struggle through and endure! Do you remember Thomas Wilkins, and the way he threw the registry of his birth and baptism back in your face? Why, he would not have the situation; he went to sea and was drowned, rather than present the record of his shame."

"I do remember it all. It has often haunted me. She must strengthen her child to look to God, rather than to man's opinion. It will be the discipline, the penance, she has incurred. She must teach it to be (humanly speaking) self-dependent."

"But after all," said Miss Benson (for she had known and esteemed poor Thomas Wilkins, and had mourned over his untimely death, and the recollection thereof softened her)—"after all, it might be concealed. The very child need never know its illegitimacy."

"How?" asked her brother.

"Why—we know so little about her yet; but in that letter, it said she had no friends;—now, could she not go into quite a fresh place, and be passed off as a widow?"

Ah, tempter! unconscious tempter! Here was a way of evading the trials for the poor little unborn child, of which Mr Benson had never thought. It was the decision—the pivot, on which the fate of years moved; and he turned it the wrong way. But it was not for his own sake. For himself, he was brave enough to tell the truth; for the little helpless baby, about to enter a cruel, biting world, he was tempted to evade the difficulty. He forgot what he had just said, of the discipline and penance to the mother consisting in strengthening her child to meet, trustfully and bravely, the consequences of her own weakness. He remembered more clearly the wild fierceness, the Cain-like look, of Thomas Wilkins, as the obnoxious word in the baptismal registry told him that he must go forth branded into the world, with his hand against every man's, and every man's against him.

"How could it be managed, Faith?"

"Nay, I must know much more, which she alone can tell us, before I can see how it is to be managed. It is certainly the best plan."

"Perhaps it is," said her brother, thoughtfully, but no longer clearly or decidedly; and so the conversation dropped.

Ruth moved the bed-curtain aside, in her soft manner, when Miss Benson re-entered the room; she did not speak, but she looked at her as if she wished her to come near. Miss Benson went and stood by her. Ruth took her hand in hers and kissed it; then, as if fatigued even by this slight movement, she fell asleep.

Miss Benson took up her work, and thought over her brother's speeches. She was not convinced, but she was softened and bewildered.

CHAPTER XII - LOSING SIGHT OF THE WELSH MOUNTAINS

Miss Benson continued in an undecided state of mind for the two next days; but on the third, as they sat at breakfast, she began to speak to her brother.

"That young creature's name is Ruth Hilton."

"Indeed! how did you find it out?"

"From herself, of course. She is much stronger. I slept with her last night, and I was aware she was awake long before I liked to speak, but at last I began. I don't know what I said, or how it went on, but I think it was a little relief to her to tell me something about herself. She sobbed and cried herself to sleep; I think she is asleep now."

"Tell me what she said about herself."

"Oh, it was really very little; it was evidently a most painful subject. She is an orphan, without brother or sister, and with a guardian, whom, I think she said, she never saw but once. He apprenticed her (after her father's death) to a dressmaker. This Mr Bellingham got acquainted with her, and they used to meet on Sunday afternoons. One day they were late, lingering on the road, when the dressmaker came up by accident. She seems to have been very angry, and not unnaturally so. The girl took fright at her threats, and the lover persuaded her to go off with him to London, there and then. Last May, I think it was. That's all."

"Did she express any sorrow for her error?"

"No, not in words, but her voice was broken with sobs, though she tried to make it steady. After a while she began to talk about her baby, but shyly, and with much hesitation. She asked me how much I thought she could earn as a dressmaker, by working very, very hard; and that brought us round to her child. I thought of what you had said, Thurstan, and I tried to speak to her as you wished me. I am not sure if it was right; I am doubtful in my own mind still."

"Don't be doubtful, Faith! Dear Faith, I thank you for your kindness."

"There is really nothing to thank me for. It is almost impossible to help being kind to her; there is something so meek and gentle about her, so patient, and so grateful!"

"What does she think of doing?"

"Poor child! she thinks of taking lodgings—very cheap ones, she says; there she means to work night and day to earn enough for her child. For, she said to me, with such pretty earnestness, 'It must never know want, whatever I do. I have deserved suffering, but it will be such a little innocent darling!' Her utmost earnings would not be more than seven or eight shillings a week, I'm afraid; and then she is so young and so pretty!"

"There is that fifty pounds Mrs Morgan brought me, and those two letters. Does she know about them yet?"

"No; I did not like to tell her till she is a little stronger. Oh, Thurstan! I wish there was not this prospect of a child. I cannot help it. I do—I could see a way in which we might help her, if it were not for that."

"How do you mean?"

"Oh, it's no use thinking of it, as it is! Or else we might have taken her home with us, and kept her till she had got a little dress-making in the congregation, but for this meddlesome child; that spoils everything. You must let me grumble to you, Thurstan. I was very good to her, and spoke as tenderly and respectfully of the little thing as if it were the Queen's, and born in lawful matrimony."

"That's right, my dear Faith! Grumble away to me, if you like. I'll forgive you, for the kind thought of taking her home with us. But do you think her situation is an insuperable objection?"

"Why, Thurstan!—it's so insuperable, it puts it quite out of the question."

"How?—that's only repeating your objection. Why is it out of the question?"

"If there had been no child coming, we might have called her by her right name—Miss Hilton; that's one thing. Then, another is, the baby in our house. Why, Sally would go distraught!"

"Never mind Sally. If she were an orphan relation of our own, left widowed," said he, pausing, as if in doubt. "You yourself suggested she should be considered as a widow, for the child's sake. I'm only taking up your ideas, dear Faith. I respect you for thinking of taking her home; it is just what we ought to do. Thank you for reminding me of my duty."

"Nay, it was only a passing thought. Think of Mr Bradshaw. Oh! I tremble at the thought of his grim displeasure."

"We must think of a higher than Mr Bradshaw. I own I should be a very coward, if he knew. He is so severe, so inflexible. But after all he sees so little of us; he never comes to tea, you know, but is always engaged when Mrs Bradshaw comes. I don't think he knows of what our household consists."

"Not know Sally? Oh yes, but he does. He asked Mrs Bradshaw one day, if she knew what wages we gave her, and said we might get a far more efficient and younger servant for the money. And, speaking about money, think what our expenses would be if we took her home for the next six months."

That consideration was a puzzling one; and both sat silent and perplexed for a time. Miss Benson was as sorrowful as her brother, for she was becoming as anxious as he was to find it possible that her plan could be carried out.

"There's the fifty pounds," said he, with a sigh of reluctance at the idea.

"Yes, there's the fifty pounds," echoed his sister, with the same sadness in her tone. "I suppose it is hers."

"I suppose it is; and being so, we must not think who gave it to her. It will defray her expenses. I am very sorry, but I think we must take it."

"It would never do to apply to him under the present circumstances," said Miss Benson, in a hesitating manner.

"No, that we won't," said her brother, decisively. "If she consents to let us take care of her, we will never let her stoop to request anything from him, even for his child. She can live on bread and water. We can all live on bread and water rather than that."

"Then I will speak to her and propose the plan. Oh, Thurstan! from a child you could persuade me to anything! I hope I am doing right. However much I oppose you at first, I am sure to yield soon; almost in proportion to my violence at first. I think I am very weak."

"No, not in this instance. We are both right: I, in the way in which the child ought to be viewed; you, dear good Faith, for thinking of taking her home with us. God bless you, dear, for it!"

When Ruth began to sit up (and the strange, new, delicious prospect of becoming a mother seemed to give her some mysterious source of strength, so that her recovery was rapid and swift from that time), Miss Benson brought her the letters and the bank-note.

"Do you recollect receiving this letter, Ruth?" asked she, with grave gentleness. Ruth changed colour, and took it and read it again without making any reply to Miss Benson. Then she sighed, and thought a while; and then took up and read the second note—the note which Mrs Bellingham had sent to Mr Benson in answer to his. After that she took up the bank-note and turned it round and round, but not as if she saw it. Miss Benson noticed that her fingers trembled sadly, and that her lips were quivering for some time before she spoke.

"If you please, Miss Benson, I should like to return this money."

"Why, my dear?"

"I have a strong feeling against taking it. While he," said she, deeply blushing, and letting her large white lids drop down and veil her eyes, "loved me, he gave me many things—my watch—oh, many things; and I took them from him gladly and thankfully because he loved me—for I would have given him anything—and I thought of them as signs of love. But this money pains my heart. He has left off loving me, and has gone away. This money seems—oh, Miss Benson—it seems as if he could comfort me, for being forsaken, by money." And at that word the tears, so long kept back and repressed, forced their way like rain.

She checked herself, however, in the violence of her emotion, for she thought of her child.

"So, will you take the trouble of sending it back to Mrs Bellingham?"

"That I will, my dear. I am glad of it, that I am! They don't deserve to have the power of giving: they don't deserve that you should take it."

Miss Benson went and enclosed it up, there and then; simply writing these words in the envelope, "From Ruth Hilton."

"And now we wash our hands of these Bellinghams," said she, triumphantly. But Ruth looked tearful and sad; not about returning the note, but from the conviction that the reason she had given for the ground of her determination was true—he no longer loved her.

To cheer her, Miss Benson began to speak of the future. Miss Benson was one of those people who, the more she spoke of a plan in its details, and the more she realised it in her own mind, the more firmly she became a partisan of the project. Thus she grew warm and happy in the idea of taking Ruth home; but Ruth remained depressed and languid under the conviction that he no longer loved her. No home, no future, but the thought of her child, could wean her from this sorrow. Miss Benson was a little piqued; and this pique showed itself afterwards in talking to her brother of the morning's proceedings in the sick-chamber.

"I admired her at the time for sending away her fifty pounds so proudly; but I think she has a cold heart: she hardly thanked me at all for my proposal of taking her home with us."

"Her thoughts are full of other things just now; and people have such different ways of showing feeling: some by silence, some by words. At any rate, it is unwise to expect gratitude."

"What do you expect—not indifference or ingratitude?"

"It is better not to expect or calculate consequences. The longer I live, the more fully I see that. Let us try simply to do right actions, without thinking of the feelings they are to call out in others. We know that no holy or self-denying effort can fall to the ground vain and useless; but the sweep of eternity is large, and God alone knows when the effect is to be produced. We are trying to do right now, and to feel right; don't let us perplex ourselves with endeavouring to map out how she should feel, or how she should show her feelings."

"That's all very fine, and I dare say very true," said Miss Benson, a little chagrined. "But 'a bird in the hand is worth two in the bush;' and I would rather have had one good, hearty 'Thank you,' now, for all I have been planning to do for her, than the grand effects you promise me in the 'sweep of eternity.' Don't be grave and sorrowful, Thurstan, or I'll go out of the room. I can stand Sally's scoldings, but I can't bear your look of quiet depression whenever I am a little hasty or impatient. I had rather you would give me a good box on the ear."

"And I would often rather you would speak, if ever so hastily, instead of whistling. So, if I box your ears when I am vexed with you, will you promise to scold me when you are put out of the way, instead of whistling?"

"Very well! that's a bargain. You box, and I scold. But, seriously, I began to calculate our money when she so cavalierly sent off the fifty-pound note (I can't help admiring her for it), and I am very much afraid we shall not have enough to pay the doctor's bill, and take her home with us."

"She must go inside the coach whatever we do," said Mr Benson, decidedly. "Who's there? Come in! Oh! Mrs Hughes! Sit down."

"Indeed, sir, and I cannot stay; but the young lady has just made me find up her watch for her, and asked me to get it sold to pay the doctor, and the little things she has had since she came; and please, sir, indeed, I don't know where to sell it nearer than Carnarvon."

"That is good of her," said Miss Benson, her sense of justice satisfied; and, remembering the way in which Ruth had spoken of the watch, she felt what a sacrifice it must have been to resolve to part with it.

"And her goodness just helps us out of our dilemma," said her brother, who was unaware of the feelings with which Ruth regarded her watch, or, perhaps, he might have parted with his Facciolati.

Mrs Hughes patiently awaited their leisure for answering her practical question. Where could the watch be sold? Suddenly her face brightened.

"Mr Jones, the doctor, is going to be married, perhaps he would like nothing better than to give this pretty watch to his bride; indeed, and I think it's very likely; and he'll pay money for it as well as letting alone his bill. I'll ask him, sir, at any rate."

Mr Jones was only too glad to obtain possession of so elegant a present at so cheap a rate. He even, as Mrs Hughes had foretold, "paid money for it;" more than was required to defray the expenses of Ruth's accommodation; as the most of the articles of food she had were paid for at the time by Mr or Miss Benson, but they strictly forbade Mrs Hughes to tell Ruth of this.

"Would you object to my buying you a black gown?" said Miss Benson to her the day after the sale of the watch. She hesitated a little, and then went on:

"My brother and I think it would be better to call you—as if in fact you were—a widow. It will save much awkwardness, and it will spare your child much—" Mortification she was going to have added, but that word did not exactly do. But, at the mention of her child, Ruth started and turned ruby-red; as she always did when allusion was made to it.

"Oh, yes! certainly. Thank you much for thinking of it. Indeed," said she, very low, as if to herself, "I don't know how to thank you for all you are doing; but I do love you, and will pray for you, if I may."

"If you may, Ruth!" repeated Miss Benson, in a tone of surprise.

"Yes, if I may. If you will let me pray for you."

"Certainly, my dear. My dear Ruth, you don't know how often I sin; I do so wrong, with my few temptations. We are both of us great sinners in the eyes of the Most Holy; let us pray for each other. Don't speak so again, my dear; at least, not to me!"

Miss Benson was actually crying. She had always looked upon herself as so inferior to her brother in real goodness; had seen such heights above her, that she was distressed by Ruth's humility. After a short time she resumed the subject.

"Then I may get you a black gown?—and we may call you Mrs Hilton?"

"No; not Mrs Hilton!" said Ruth, hastily.

Miss Benson, who had hitherto kept her eyes averted from Ruth's face from a motive of kindly delicacy, now looked at her with surprise.

"Why not?" asked she.

"It was my mother's name," said Ruth, in a low voice. "I had better not be called by it."

"Then, let us call you by my mother's name," said Miss Benson, tenderly. "She would have— But I'll talk to you about my mother some other time. Let me call you Mrs Denbigh. It will do very well, too. People will think you are a distant relation."

When she told Mr Benson this choice of name, he was rather sorry; it was like his sister's impulsive kindness—impulsive in everything—and he could imagine how Ruth's humility had touched her. He was sorry, but he said nothing.

And now the letter was written home, announcing the probable arrival of the brother and sister on a certain day, "with a distant relation, early left a widow," as Miss Benson expressed it. She desired the spare room might be prepared, and made every provision she could think of for Ruth's comfort; for Ruth still remained feeble and weak.

When the black gown, at which she had stitched away incessantly, was finished—when nothing remained but to rest for the next day's journey—Ruth could not sit still. She wandered from window to window, learning off each rock and tree by heart. Each had its tale, which it was agony to remember; but which it would have been worse agony to forget. The sound of running waters she heard that quiet evening, was in her ears as she lay on her death-bed; so well had she learnt their tune.

And now all was over. She had driven in to Llan-dhu, sitting by her lover's side, living in the bright present, and strangely forgetful of the past or the future; she had dreamed out her dream, and she had awakened from the vision of love. She walked slowly and sadly down the long hill, her tears fast falling, but as quickly wiped away; while she strove to make steady the low quivering voice which was often called upon to answer some remark of Miss Benson's.

They had to wait for the coach. Ruth buried her face in some flowers which Mrs Hughes had given her on parting; and was startled when the mail drew up with a sudden pull, which almost threw the horses on their haunches. She was placed inside, and the coach had set off again, before she was fully aware that Mr and Miss Benson were travelling on the outside; but it was a relief to feel she might now cry without exciting their notice. The shadow of a heavy thunder-cloud was on the valley, but the little upland village church (that showed the spot in which so much of her life had passed) stood out clear in the sunshine. She grudged the tears that blinded her as she gazed. There was one passenger, who tried after a while to comfort her.

"Don't cry, miss," said the kind-hearted woman. "You're parting from friends, maybe? Well, that's bad enough, but when you come to my age, you'll think none of it. Why, I've three sons, and they're soldiers and sailors, all of them—here, there, and everywhere. One is in America, beyond seas; another is in China, making tea; and another is at Gibraltar, three miles from Spain; and yet, you see, I can laugh and eat and enjoy myself. I sometimes think I'll try and fret a bit, just to make myself a better figure; but, Lord! it's no use, it's against my nature; so I laugh and grow fat again. I'd be quite thankful for a fit of anxiety as would make me feel easy in my clothes, which them manty-makers will make so tight I'm fairly throttled."

Ruth durst cry no more; it was no relief, now she was watched and noticed, and plied with a sandwich or a gingerbread each time she looked sad. She lay back with her eyes shut, as if asleep, and went on, and on, the sun never seeming to move from his high place in the sky, nor the bright hot day to show the least sign of waning. Every now and then, Miss Benson scrambled down, and made kind inquiries of the pale, weary Ruth; and once they changed coaches, and the fat old lady left her with a hearty shake of the hand.

"It is not much further now," said Miss Benson, apologetically, to Ruth. "See! we are losing sight of the Welsh mountains. We have about eighteen miles of plain, and then we come to the moors and the rising ground, amidst which Eccleston lies. I wish we were there, for my brother is sadly tired."

The first wonder in Ruth's mind was, why then, if Mr Benson were so tired, did they not stop where they were for the night; for she knew little of the expenses of a night at an inn. The next thought was, to beg that Mr Benson would take her place inside the coach, and allow her to mount up by Miss Benson. She proposed this, and Miss Benson was evidently pleased.

"Well, if you're not tired, it would make a rest and a change for him, to be sure; and if you were by me I could show you the first sight of Eccleston, if we reach there before it is quite dark."

So Mr Benson got down, and changed places with Ruth.

She hardly yet understood the numerous small economies which he and his sister had to practise—the little daily self-denials,—all endured so cheerfully, and simply, that they had almost ceased to require an effort, and it had become natural to them to think of others before themselves. Ruth had not understood that it was for economy that their places had been taken on the outside of the coach, while hers, as an invalid requiring rest, was to be the inside; and that the biscuits which supplied the place of a dinner were, in fact, chosen because the difference in price between the two would go a little way towards fulfilling their plan for receiving her as an inmate. Her thought about money had been hitherto a child's thought; the subject had never touched her; but afterwards, when she had lived a little with the Bensons, her eyes were opened, and she remembered their simple kindness on the journey, and treasured the remembrance of it in her heart.

A low grey cloud was the first sign of Eccleston; it was the smoke of the town hanging over the plain. Beyond the place where she was expected to believe it existed, arose round, waving uplands; nothing to the fine outlines of the Welsh mountains, but still going up nearer to heaven than the rest of the flat world into which she had now entered. Rumbling stones, lamp-posts, a sudden stop, and they were in the town of Eccleston; and a strange, uncouth voice, on the dark side of the coach, was heard to say,

"Be ye there, measter?"

"Yes, yes!" said Miss Benson, quickly. "Did Sally send you, Ben? Get the ostler's lantern, and look out the luggage."

CHAPTER XIII - THE DISSENTING MINISTER'S HOUSEHOLD

Miss Benson had resumed every morsel of the briskness which she had rather lost in the middle of the day; her foot was on her native stones, and a very rough set they were, and she was near her home and among known people. Even Mr Benson spoke very cheerfully to Ben, and made many inquiries of him respecting people whose names were strange to Ruth. She was cold, and utterly weary. She took Miss Benson's offered arm, and could hardly drag herself as far as the little quiet street in which Mr Benson's house was situated. The street was so quiet that their footsteps sounded like a loud disturbance, and announced their approach as effectually as the "trumpet's lordly blare" did the coming of Abdallah. A door flew open, and a lighted passage stood before them. As soon as they had entered, a stout, elderly servant emerged from behind the door, her face radiant with welcome.

"Eh, bless ye! are ye back again? I thought I should ha' been lost without ye."

She gave Mr Benson a hearty shake of the hand, and kissed Miss Benson warmly; then, turning to Ruth, she said, in a loud whisper,

"Who's yon?"

Mr Benson was silent, and walked a step onwards. Miss Benson said boldly out,

"The lady I named in my note, Sally—Mrs Denbigh, a distant relation."

"Aye, but you said hoo was a widow. Is this chit a widow?"

"Yes, this is Mrs Denbigh," answered Miss Benson.

"If I'd been her mother, I'd ha' given her a lollypop instead of a husband. Hoo looks fitter for it."

"Hush! Sally, Sally! Look, there's your master trying to move that heavy box." Miss Benson calculated well when she called Sally's attention to her master; for it was well believed by every one, and by Sally herself, that his deformity was owing to a fall he had had when he was scarcely more than a baby, and entrusted to her care—a little nurse-girl, as she then was, not many years older than himself. For years the poor girl had cried herself to sleep on her pallet-bed, moaning over the blight her carelessness had brought upon her darling; nor was this self-reproach diminished by the forgiveness of the gentle mother, from whom

Thurstan Benson derived so much of his character. The way in which comfort stole into Sally's heart was in the gradually-formed resolution that she would never leave him nor forsake him, but serve him faithfully all her life long; and she had kept to her word. She loved Miss Benson, but she almost worshipped the brother. The reverence for him was in her heart, however, and did not always show itself in her manners. But if she scolded him herself, she allowed no one else that privilege. If Miss Benson differed from her brother, and ventured to think his sayings or doings might have been improved, Sally came down upon her like a thunder-clap.

"My goodness gracious, Master Thurstan, when will you learn to leave off meddling with other folks' business! Here, Ben! help me up with these trunks."

The little narrow passage was cleared, and Miss Benson took Ruth into the sitting-room. There were only two sitting-rooms on the ground-floor, one behind the other. Out of the back room the kitchen opened, and for this reason the back parlour was used as the family sitting-room; or else, being, with its garden aspect, so much the pleasanter of the two, both Sally and Miss Benson would have appropriated it for Mr Benson's study. As it was, the front room, which looked to the street, was his room; and many a person coming for help—help of which giving money was the lowest kind—was admitted, and let forth by Mr Benson, unknown to any one else in the house. To make amends for his having the least cheerful room on the ground-floor, he had the garden bedroom, while his sister slept over his study. There were two more rooms again over these, with sloping ceilings, though otherwise large and airy. The attic looking into the garden was the spare bedroom; while the front belonged to Sally. There was no room over the kitchen, which was, in fact, a supplement to the house. The sitting-room was called by the pretty, old-fashioned name of the parlour, while Mr Benson's room was styled the study.

The curtains were drawn in the parlour; there was a bright fire and a clean hearth; indeed, exquisite cleanliness seemed the very spirit of the household, for the door which was open to the kitchen showed a delicately-white and spotless floor, and bright glittering tins, on which the ruddy firelight danced.

From the place in which Ruth sat she could see all Sally's movements; and though she was not conscious of close or minute observation at the time (her body being weary, and her mind full of other thoughts), yet it was curious how faithfully that scene remained depicted on her memory in after years. The warm light filled every corner of the kitchen, in strong distinction to the faint illumination of the one candle in the parlour, whose radiance was confined, and was lost in the dead folds of window-curtains, carpet, and furniture. The square, stout, bustling figure, neat and clean in every respect, but dressed in the peculiar, old-fashioned costume of the county, namely, a dark-striped linsey-woolsey petticoat, made very short, displaying sturdy legs in woollen stockings beneath; a loose kind of jacket called there a "bedgown," made of pink print; a snow-white apron and cap, both of linen, and the latter made in the shape of a "mutch;"—these articles completed Sally's costume, and were painted on Ruth's memory. Whilst Sally was busied in preparing tea, Miss Benson took off Ruth's things; and the latter instinctively felt that Sally, in the midst of her movements, was watching their proceedings. Occasionally she also put in a word in the conversation, and these little sentences were uttered quite in the tone of an equal, if not of a superior. She had dropped the more formal "you," with which at first she had addressed Miss Benson, and thou'd her quietly and habitually.

All these particulars sank unconsciously into Ruth's mind; but they did not rise to the surface, and become perceptible, for a length of time. She was weary, and much depressed. Even the very kindness that ministered to her was overpowering. But over the dark, misty moor a little light shone,—a beacon; and on that she fixed her eyes, and struggled out of her present deep dejection—the little child that was coming to her!

Mr Benson was as languid and weary as Ruth, and was silent during all this bustle and preparation. His silence was more grateful to Ruth than Miss Benson's many words, although she felt their kindness. After tea, Miss Benson took her upstairs to her room. The white dimity bed, and the walls, stained green, had something of the colouring and purity of effect of a snowdrop; while the floor, rubbed with a mixture that turned it into a rich dark brown, suggested the idea of the garden-mould out of which the snowdrop grows. As Miss Benson helped the pale Ruth to undress, her voice became less full-toned and hurried; the hush of approaching night subdued her into a softened, solemn kind of tenderness, and the murmured blessing sounded like granted prayer.

When Miss Benson came downstairs, she found her brother reading some letters which had been received during his absence. She went and softly shut the door of communication between the parlour and the kitchen; and then, fetching a grey worsted stocking which she was knitting, sat down near him, her eyes not looking at her work but fixed on the fire; while the eternal rapid click of the knitting-needles broke the silence of the room, with a sound as monotonous and incessant as the noise of a hand-loom. She expected him to speak, but he did not. She enjoyed an examination into, and discussion of, her feelings; it was an interest and amusement to her, while he dreaded and avoided all such conversation. There were times when his feelings, which were always earnest, and sometimes morbid, burst forth, and defied control, and overwhelmed him; when a force was upon him compelling him to speak. But he, in general, strove to preserve his composure, from a fear of the compelling pain of such times, and the consequent exhaustion. His heart had been very full of Ruth all day long, and he was afraid of his sister beginning the subject; so he read on, or seemed to do so, though he hardly saw the letter he held before him. It was a great relief to him when Sally threw open the middle door with a bang, which did not indicate either calmness of mind or sweetness of temper.

"Is yon young woman going to stay any length o' time with us?" asked she of Miss Benson.

Mr Benson put his hand gently on his sister's arm, to check her from making any reply, while he said,

"We cannot exactly tell, Sally. She will remain until after her confinement."

"Lord bless us and save us!—a baby in the house! Nay, then my time's come, and I'll pack up and begone. I never could abide them things. I'd sooner have rats in the house."

Sally really did look alarmed.

"Why, Sally!" said Mr Benson, smiling, "I was not much more than a baby when you came to take care of me."

"Yes, you were, Master Thurstan; you were a fine bouncing lad of three year old and better."

Then she remembered the change she had wrought in the "fine bouncing lad," and her eyes filled with tears, which she was too proud to wipe away with her apron; for, as she sometimes said to herself, "she could not abide crying before folk."

"Well, it's no use talking, Sally," said Miss Benson, too anxious to speak to be any longer repressed. "We've promised to keep her, and we must do it; you'll have none of the trouble, Sally, so don't be afraid."

"Well, I never! as if I minded trouble! You might ha' known me better nor that. I've scoured master's room twice over, just to make the boards look white, though the carpet is to cover them, and now you go and cast up about me minding my trouble. If them's the fashions you've learnt in Wales, I'm thankful I've never been there."

Sally looked red, indignant, and really hurt. Mr Benson came in with his musical voice and soft words of healing.

"Faith knows you don't care for trouble, Sally; she is only anxious about this poor young woman, who has no friends but ourselves. We know there will be more trouble in consequence of her coming to stay with us; and I think, though we never spoke about it, that in making our plans we reckoned on your kind help, Sally, which has never failed us yet when we needed it."

"You've twice the sense of your sister, Master Thurstan, that you have. Boys always has. It's truth there will be more trouble, and I shall have my share on't, I reckon. I can face it if I'm told out and out, but I cannot abide the way some folk has of denying there's trouble or pain to be met; just as if their saying there was none, would do away with it. Some folk treats one like a babby, and I don't like it. I'm not meaning *you*, Master Thurstan."

"No, Sally, you need not say that. I know well enough who you mean when you say 'some folk.' However, I admit I was wrong in speaking as if you minded trouble, for there never was a creature minded it less. But I want you to like Mrs Denbigh," said Miss Benson.

"I dare say I should, if you'd let me alone. I did na like her sitting down in master's chair. Set her up, indeed, in an arm-chair wi' cushions! Wenches in my day were glad enough of stools."

"She was tired to-night," said Mr Benson. "We are all tired; so if you have done your work, Sally, come in to reading."

The three quiet people knelt down side by side, and two of them prayed earnestly for "them that had gone astray." Before ten o'clock, the household were in bed.

Ruth, sleepless, weary, restless with the oppression of a sorrow which she dared not face and contemplate bravely, kept awake all the early part of the night. Many a time did she rise, and go to the long casement window, and look abroad over the still and quiet town—over the grey stone walls, and chimneys, and old high-pointed roofs—on to the far-away hilly line of the horizon, lying calm under the bright moonshine. It was late in the morning when she woke from her long-deferred slumbers; and when she went downstairs, she found Mr and Miss Benson awaiting her in the parlour. That homely, pretty, old-fashioned little room! How bright and still and clean it looked! The window (all the windows at the back of the house were casements) was open, to let in the sweet morning air, and streaming eastern sunshine. The long jessamine sprays, with their white-scented stars, forced themselves almost into the room. The little square garden beyond, with grey stone walls all round, was rich and mellow in its autumnal colouring, running from deep crimson hollyhocks up to amber and gold nasturtiums, and all toned down by the clear and delicate air. It was so still, that the gossamer-webs, laden with dew, did not tremble or quiver in the least; but the sun was drawing to himself the sweet incense of many flowers, and the parlour was scented with the odours of mignonette and stocks. Miss Benson was arranging a bunch of China and damask roses in an old-fashioned jar; they lay, all dewy and fresh, on the white breakfast-cloth when Ruth entered. Mr Benson was reading in some large folio. With gentle morning speech they greeted her; but the quiet repose of the scene was instantly broken by Sally popping in from the kitchen, and glancing at Ruth with sharp reproach. She said:

"I reckon I may bring in breakfast, now?" with a strong emphasis on the last word.

"I am afraid I am very late," said Ruth.

"Oh, never mind," said Mr Benson, gently. "It was our fault for not telling you our breakfast hour. We always have prayers at half-past seven; and, for Sally's sake, we never vary from that time; for she can so arrange her work, if she knows the hour of prayers, as to have her mind calm and untroubled."

"Ahem!" said Miss Benson, rather inclined to "testify" against the invariable calmness of Sally's mind at any hour of the day; but her brother went on as if he did not hear her.

"But the breakfast does not signify being delayed a little; and I am sure you were sadly tired with your long day yesterday."

Sally came slapping in, and put down some withered, tough, dry toast, with—

"It's not my doing if it is like leather;" but as no one appeared to hear her, she withdrew to her kitchen, leaving Ruth's cheeks like crimson at the annoyance she had caused.

All day long, she had that feeling common to those who go to stay at a fresh house among comparative strangers: a feeling of the necessity that she should become accustomed to the new atmosphere in which she was placed, before she could move and act freely; it was, indeed, a purer ether, a diviner air, which she was breathing in now, than what she had been accustomed to for long months. The gentle, blessed mother, who had made her childhood's home holy ground, was in her very nature so far removed from any of earth's stains and temptations, that she seemed truly one of those

> Who ask not if Thine eye
> Be on them; who, in love and truth,
> Where no misgiving is, rely
> Upon the genial sense of youth.

In the Bensons' house there was the same unconsciousness of individual merit, the same absence of introspection and analysis of motive, as there had been in her mother; but it seemed that their lives were pure and good, not merely from a lovely and beautiful nature, but from some law, the obedience to which was, of itself, harmonious peace, and which governed them almost implicitly, and with as little questioning on their part, as the glorious stars which haste not, rest not, in their eternal obedience. This household had many failings: they were but human, and, with all their loving desire to bring their lives into harmony with the will of God, they often erred and fell short; but, somehow, the very errors and faults of one individual served to call out higher excellences in another, and so they reacted upon each other, and the result of short discords was exceeding harmony and peace. But they had themselves no idea of the real state of things; they did not trouble themselves with marking their progress by self-examination; if Mr Benson did sometimes, in hours of sick incapacity for exertion, turn inwards, it was to cry aloud with almost morbid despair, "God be merciful to me a sinner!" But he strove to leave his life in the hands of God, and to forget himself.

Ruth sat still and quiet through the long first day. She was languid and weary from her journey; she was uncertain what help she might offer to give in the household duties, and what she might not. And, in her languor and in her uncertainty, it was pleasant to watch the new ways of the people among whom she was placed. After breakfast, Mr Benson withdrew to his study, Miss Benson took away the cups and saucers, and, leaving the kitchen door open, talked sometimes to Ruth, sometimes to Sally, while she washed them up. Sally had upstairs duties to perform, for which Ruth was thankful, as she kept receiving rather angry glances for her unpunctuality as long as Sally remained downstairs. Miss Benson assisted in the preparation for the early dinner, and brought some kidney-beans to shred into a basin of bright, pure spring-water, which caught and danced in the sunbeams as she sat near the open casement of the parlour, talking to Ruth of things and people which as yet the latter did not understand, and could not arrange and comprehend. She was like a child who gets a few pieces of a dissected map, and is confused until a glimpse of the whole unity is shown him. Mr and Mrs Bradshaw were the centre pieces in Ruth's map; their children, their servants, were the accessories; and one or two other names were occasionally mentioned. Ruth wondered and almost wearied at Miss Benson's perseverance in talking to her about people whom she did not know; but, in truth, Miss Benson heard the long-drawn, quivering sighs which came from the poor heavy heart, when it was left to silence, and had leisure to review the past; and her quick accustomed ear caught also the low mutterings of the thunder in the distance, in the shape of Sally's soliloquies, which, like the asides at a theatre, were intended to be heard. Suddenly, Miss Benson called Ruth out of the room, upstairs into her own bed-chamber, and then began rummaging in little old-fashioned boxes, drawn out of an equally old-fashioned bureau, half desk, half table, and wholly drawers.

"My dear, I've been very stupid and thoughtless. Oh! I'm so glad I thought of it before Mrs Bradshaw came to call. Here it is!" and she pulled out an old wedding-ring, and hurried it on Ruth's finger. Ruth hung down her head, and reddened deep with shame; her eyes smarted with the hot tears that filled them. Miss Benson talked on, in a nervous hurried way:

"It was my grandmother's; it's very broad; they made them so then, to hold a posy inside: there's one in that;

> Thine own sweetheart
> Till death doth part,

I think it is. There, there! Run away, and look as if you'd always worn it."

Ruth went up to her room, and threw herself down on her knees by the bed-side, and cried as if her heart would break; and then, as if a light had come down into her soul, she calmed herself and prayed—no words can tell how humbly, and with what earnest feeling. When she came down, she was tear-stained and wretchedly pale; but even Sally looked at her with new eyes, because of the dignity with which she was invested by an earnestness of purpose which had her child for its object. She sat and thought, but she no longer heaved those bitter sighs which had wrung Miss Benson's heart in the morning. In this way the day wore on; early dinner, early tea, seemed to make it preternaturally long to Ruth; the only event was some unexplained absence of Sally's, who had disappeared out of the house in the evening, much to Miss Benson's surprise, and somewhat to her indignation.

At night, after Ruth had gone up to her room, this absence was explained to her at least. She had let down her long waving glossy hair, and was standing absorbed in thought in the middle of the room, when she heard a round clumping knock at her door, different from that given by the small knuckles of delicate fingers, and in walked Sally, with a judge-like severity of demeanour, holding in her hand two widow's caps of commonest make and coarsest texture. Queen Eleanor herself, when she presented the bowl to Fair Rosamond, had not a more relentless purpose stamped on her demeanour than had Sally at this moment. She walked up to the beautiful, astonished Ruth, where she stood in her long, soft, white dressing-gown, with all her luxuriant brown hair hanging dishevelled down her figure, and thus Sally spoke:

"Missus—or miss, as the case may be—I've my doubts as to you. I'm not going to have my master and Miss Faith put upon, or shame come near them. Widows wears these sort o' caps, and has their hair cut off; and whether widows wears wedding-rings or not, they shall have their hair cut off—they shall. I'll have no half work in this house. I've lived with the family forty-nine year come Michaelmas, and I'll not see it disgraced by any one's fine long curls. Sit down and let me snip off your hair, and let me see you sham decently in a widow's cap to-morrow, or I'll leave the house. Whatten's come over Miss Faith, as used to be as mim a lady as ever was, to be taken by such as you, I dunnot know. Here! sit down with ye, and let me crop you."

She laid no light hand on Ruth's shoulder; and the latter, partly intimidated by the old servant, who had hitherto only turned her vixen lining to observation, and partly because she was broken-spirited enough to be indifferent to the measure proposed, quietly sat down. Sally produced the formidable pair of scissors that always hung at her side, and began to cut in a merciless manner. She expected some remonstrance or some opposition, and had a torrent of words ready to flow forth at the least sign of rebellion; but Ruth was still and silent, with meekly-bowed head, under the strange hands that were shearing her beautiful hair into the clipped shortness of a boy's. Long before she had finished, Sally had some slight misgivings as to the fancied necessity of her task; but it was too late, for half the curls were gone, and the rest must now come off. When she had done, she lifted up Ruth's face by placing her hand under the round white chin. She gazed into the countenance, expecting to read some anger there, though it had not come out in words; but she only met the large, quiet eyes, that looked at her with sad gentleness out of their finely-hollowed orbits. Ruth's soft, yet dignified submission, touched Sally with compunction, though she did not choose to show the change in her feelings. She tried to hide it, indeed, by stooping to pick up the long bright tresses; and, holding them up admiringly, and letting them drop down and float on the air (like the pendant branches of the weeping birch), she said: "I thought we should ha' had some crying—I did. They're pretty curls enough; you've not been so bad to let them be cut off neither. You see, Master Thurstan is no wiser than a babby in some things; and Miss Faith just lets him have his own way; so it's all left to me to keep him out of scrapes. I'll wish you a very good night. I've heard many a one say as long hair was not wholesome. Good night."

But in a minute she popped her head into Ruth's room once more:

"You'll put on them caps to-morrow morning. I'll make you a present on them."

Sally had carried away the beautiful curls, and she could not find it in her heart to throw such lovely chestnut tresses away, so she folded them up carefully in paper, and placed them in a safe corner of her drawer.

CHAPTER XIV - RUTH'S FIRST SUNDAY AT ECCLESTON

Ruth felt very shy when she came down (at half-past seven) the next morning, in her widow's cap. Her smooth, pale face, with its oval untouched by time, looked more young and childlike than ever, when contrasted with the head-gear usually associated with ideas of age. She blushed very deeply as Mr and Miss Benson showed the astonishment, which they could not conceal, in their looks. She said in a low voice to Miss Benson,

"Sally thought I had better wear it."

Miss Benson made no reply; but was startled at the intelligence, which she thought was conveyed in this speech, of Sally's acquaintance with Ruth's real situation. She noticed Sally's looks particularly this morning. The manner in which the old servant treated Ruth had in it far more of respect than there had been the day before; but there was a kind of satisfied way of braving out Miss Benson's glances which made the latter uncertain and uncomfortable.

She followed her brother into his study.

"Do you know, Thurstan, I am almost certain Sally suspects."

Mr Benson sighed. The deception grieved him, and yet he thought he saw its necessity.

"What makes you think so?" asked he.

"Oh! many little things. It was her odd way of ducking her head about, as if to catch a good view of Ruth's left hand, that made me think of the wedding-ring; and once, yesterday, when I thought I had made up quite a natural speech, and was saying how sad it was for so young a creature to be left a widow, she broke in with 'widow be farred!' in a very strange, contemptuous kind of manner."

"If she suspects, we had far better tell her the truth at once. She will never rest till she finds it out, so we must make a virtue of necessity."

"Well, brother, you shall tell her then, for I am sure I daren't. I don't mind doing the thing, since you talked to me that day, and since I've got to know Ruth; but I do mind all the clatter people will make about it."

"But Sally is not 'people.'"

"Oh, I see it must be done; she'll talk as much as all the other persons put together, so that's the reason I call her 'people.' Shall I call her?" (For the house was too homely and primitive to have bells.)

Sally came, fully aware of what was now going to be told her, and determined not to help them out in telling their awkward secret, by understanding the nature of it before it was put into the plainest language. In every pause, when they hoped she had caught the meaning they were hinting at, she persisted in looking stupid and perplexed, and in saying, "Well," as if quite unenlightened as to the end of the story. When it was all complete and plain before her, she said, honestly enough,

"It's just as I thought it was; and I think you may thank me for having had the sense to put her into widow's caps, and clip off that bonny brown hair that was fitter for a bride in lawful matrimony than for such as her. She took it very well, though. She was as quiet as a lamb, and I clipped her pretty roughly at first. I must say, though, if I'd ha' known who your visitor was, I'd ha' packed up my things and cleared myself out of the house before such as her came into it. As it's done, I suppose I must stand by you, and help you through with it; I only hope I shan't lose my character,—and me a parish clerk's daughter."

"Oh, Sally! people know you too well to think any ill of you," said Miss Benson, who was pleased to find the difficulty so easily got over; for, in truth, Sally had been much softened by the unresisting gentleness with which Ruth had submitted to the "clipping" of the night before.

"If I'd been with you, Master Thurstan, I'd ha' seen sharp after you, for you're always picking up some one or another as nobody else would touch with a pair of tongs. Why, there was that Nelly Brandon's child as was left at our door, if I hadn't gone to th' overseer we should have had that Irish tramp's babby saddled on us for life; but I went off and told th' overseer, and th' mother was caught."

"Yes," said Mr Benson, sadly, "and I often lie awake and wonder what is the fate of that poor little thing, forced back on the mother who tried to get quit of it. I often doubt whether I did right; but it's no use thinking about it now."

"I'm thankful it isn't," said Sally; "and now, if we've talked doctrine long enough, I'll go make th' beds. Yon girl's secret is safe enough for me."

Saying this she left the room, and Miss Benson followed. She found Ruth busy washing the breakfast things; and they were done in so quiet and orderly a manner, that neither Miss Benson nor Sally, both particular enough, had any of their little fancies or prejudices annoyed. She seemed to have an instinctive knowledge of the exact period when her help was likely to become a hindrance, and withdrew from the busy kitchen just at the right time.

That afternoon, as Miss Benson and Ruth sat at their work, Mrs and Miss Bradshaw called. Miss Benson was so nervous as to surprise Ruth, who did not understand the probable and possible questions which might be asked respecting any visitor at the minister's house. Ruth went on sewing, absorbed in her own thoughts, and glad that the conversation between the two elder ladies and the silence of the younger one, who sat at some distance from her, gave her an opportunity of retreating into the haunts of memory; and soon the work fell from her hands, and her eyes were fixed on the little garden beyond, but she did not see its flowers or its walls; she saw the mountains which girdled Llan-dhu, and saw the sun rise from behind their iron outline, just as it had done—how long ago? was it months or was it years?—since she had watched the night through, crouched up at *his* door. Which was the dream and which the reality? that distant life, or this? His moans rang more clearly in her ears than the buzzing of the conversation between Mrs Bradshaw and Miss Benson.

At length the subdued, scared-looking little lady and her bright-eyed silent daughter rose to take leave; Ruth started into the present, and stood up and curtseyed, and turned sick at heart with sudden recollection.

Miss Benson accompanied Mrs Bradshaw to the door; and in the passage gave her a long explanation of Ruth's (fictitious) history. Mrs Bradshaw looked so much interested and pleased, that Miss Benson enlarged a little more than was necessary, and rounded off her invention with one or two imaginary details, which, she was quite unconscious, were overheard by her brother through the half-open study door.

She was rather dismayed when he called her into his room after Mrs Bradshaw's departure, and asked her what she had been saying about Ruth?

"Oh! I thought it was better to explain it thoroughly—I mean, to tell the story we wished to have believed once for all—you know we agreed about that, Thurstan?" deprecatingly.

"Yes; but I heard you saying you believed her husband had been a young surgeon, did I not?"

"Well, Thurstan, you know he must have been something; and young surgeons are so in the way of dying, it seemed very natural. Besides," said she, with sudden boldness, "I do think I've a talent for fiction, it is so pleasant to invent, and make the incidents dovetail together; and after all, if we are to tell a lie, we may as well do it thoroughly, or else it's of no use. A bungling lie would be worse than useless. And, Thurstan—it may be very wrong—but I believe—I am afraid I enjoy not being fettered by truth. Don't look so grave. You know it is necessary, if ever it was, to tell falsehoods now; and don't be angry with me because I do it well."

He was shading his eyes with his hand, and did not speak for some time. At last he said:

"If it were not for the child, I would tell all; but the world is so cruel. You don't know how this apparent necessity for falsehood pains me, Faith, or you would not invent all these details, which are so many additional lies."

"Well, well! I will restrain myself if I have to talk about Ruth again. But Mrs Bradshaw will tell every one who need to know. You don't wish me to contradict it, Thurstan, surely—it was such a pretty, probable story."

"Faith! I hope God will forgive us if we are doing wrong; and pray, dear, don't add one unnecessary word that is not true."

Another day elapsed, and then it was Sunday; and the house seemed filled with a deep peace. Even Sally's movements were less hasty and abrupt. Mr Benson seemed invested with a new dignity, which made his bodily deformity be forgotten in his calm, grave composure of spirit. Every trace of week-day occupation was put away; the night before, a bright new handsome tablecloth had been smoothed down over the table, and the jars had been freshly filled with flowers. Sunday was a festival and a holy day in the house. After the very early breakfast, little feet pattered into Mr Benson's study, for he had a class for boys—a sort of domestic Sunday-school, only that there was more talking between teacher and pupils, than dry, absolute lessons going on. Miss Benson, too, had her little, neat-tippeted maidens sitting with her in the parlour; and she was far more particular in keeping them to their reading and spelling, than her brother was with his boys. Sally, too, put in her word of instruction from the kitchen, helping, as she fancied, though her assistance was often rather *malapropos*; for instance, she called out, to a little fat, stupid, roly-poly girl, to whom Miss Benson was busy explaining the meaning of the word quadruped,

"Quadruped, a thing wi' four legs, Jenny; a chair is a quadruped, child!"

But Miss Benson had a deaf manner sometimes when her patience was not too severely tried, and she put it on now. Ruth sat on a low hassock, and coaxed the least of the little creatures to her, and showed it pictures till it fell asleep in her arms, and sent a thrill through her, at the thought of the tiny darling who would lie on her breast before long, and whom she would have to cherish and to shelter from the storms of the world.

And then she remembered, that she was once white and sinless as the wee lassie who lay in her arms; and she knew that she had gone astray. By-and-by the children trooped away, and Miss Benson summoned her to put on her things for chapel.

The chapel was up a narrow street, or rather *cul-de-sac*, close by. It stood on the outskirts of the town, almost in fields. It was built about the time of Matthew and Philip Henry, when the Dissenters were afraid of attracting attention or observation, and hid their places of worship in obscure and out-of-the-way parts of the towns in which they were built. Accordingly, it often happened, as in the present case, that the buildings immediately surrounding, as well as the chapels themselves, looked as if they carried you back to a period a hundred and fifty years ago. The chapel had a picturesque and old-world look, for luckily the congregation had been too poor to rebuild it, or new-face it, in George the Third's time. The staircases which led to the galleries were outside, at each end of the building, and the irregular roof and worn stone steps looked grey and stained by time and weather. The grassy hillocks, each with a little upright headstone, were shaded by a grand old wych-elm. A lilac-bush or two, a white rose-tree, and a few laburnums, all old and gnarled enough, were planted round the chapel yard; and the casement windows of the chapel were made of heavy-leaded, diamond-shaped panes, almost covered with ivy, producing a green gloom, not without its solemnity, within. This ivy was the home of an infinite number of little birds, which twittered and warbled, till it might have been thought that they were emulous of the power of praise possessed by the human creatures within, with such earnest, long-drawn strains did this crowd of winged songsters rejoice and be glad in their beautiful gift of life. The interior of the building was plain and simple as plain and simple could be. When it was fitted up, oak-timber was much cheaper than it is now, so the wood-work was all of that description; but roughly hewed, for the early builders had not much wealth to spare. The walls were whitewashed, and were recipients of the shadows of the beauty without; on their "white plains" the tracery of the ivy might be seen, now still, now stirred by the sudden flight of some little bird. The congregation consisted of here and there a farmer with his labourers, who came down from the uplands beyond the town to worship where their fathers worshipped, and who loved the place because they knew how much those fathers had suffered for it, although they never troubled themselves with the reason why they left the parish church; of a few shopkeepers, far more thoughtful and reasoning, who were Dissenters from conviction, unmixed with old ancestral association; and of one or two families of still higher worldly station. With many poor, who were drawn there by love for Mr Benson's character, and by a feeling that the faith which made him what he was could not be far wrong, for the base of the pyramid, and with Mr Bradshaw for its apex, the congregation stood complete.

The country people came in sleeking down their hair, and treading with earnest attempts at noiseless lightness of step over the floor of the aisle; and by-and-by, when all were assembled, Mr Benson followed, unmarshalled and unattended. When he had closed the pulpit-door, and knelt in prayer for an instant or two, he gave out a psalm from the dear old Scottish paraphrase, with its primitive inversion of the simple perfect Bible words; and a kind of precentor stood up, and, having sounded the note on a pitch-pipe, sang a couple of lines by way of indicating the tune; then all the congregation stood up, and sang aloud, Mr Bradshaw's great bass voice being half a note in advance of the others, in accordance with his place of precedence as principal member of the congregation. His powerful voice was like an organ very badly played, and very much out of tune; but as he had no ear, and no diffidence, it pleased him very much to hear the fine loud sound. He was a tall, large-boned, iron man; stern, powerful, and authoritative in appearance; dressed in clothes of the finest broadcloth, and scrupulously ill-made, as if to show that he was indifferent to all outward things. His wife was sweet and gentle-looking, but as if she was thoroughly broken into submission.

Ruth did not see this, or hear aught but the words which were reverently—oh, how reverently!—spoken by Mr Benson. He had had Ruth present in his thoughts all the time he had been preparing for his Sunday duty; and he had tried carefully to eschew everything which she might feel as an allusion to her own case. He remembered how the Good Shepherd, in Poussin's beautiful picture, tenderly carried the lambs which had wearied themselves by going astray, and felt how like tenderness was required towards poor Ruth. But where is the chapter which does not contain something which a broken and contrite spirit may not apply to itself? And so it fell out that, as he read, Ruth's heart was smitten, and she sank down, and down, till she was kneeling on the floor of the pew, and speaking to God in the spirit, if not in the words, of the Prodigal Son: "Father! I have sinned against Heaven and before Thee, and am no more worthy to be called Thy child!" Miss Benson was thankful (although she loved Ruth the better for this self-abandonment) that the minister's seat was far in the shade of the gallery. She tried to look most attentive to her brother, in order that Mr Bradshaw might not suspect anything unusual, while she stealthily took hold of Ruth's passive hand, as it lay helpless on the cushion, and pressed it softly and tenderly. But Ruth sat on the ground, bowed down and crushed in her sorrow, till all was ended.

Miss Benson loitered in her seat, divided between the consciousness that she, as *locum tenens* for the minister's wife, was expected to be at the door to receive the kind greetings of many after her absence from home, and her unwillingness to disturb Ruth, who was evidently praying, and, by her quiet breathing, receiving grave and solemn influences into her soul. At length she rose up, calm and composed even to dignity. The chapel was still and empty; but Miss Benson heard the buzz of voices in the chapel-yard without. They were probably those of people waiting for her; and she summoned courage, and taking Ruth's arm in hers, and holding her hand affectionately, they went out into the broad daylight. As they issued forth, Miss Benson heard Mr Bradshaw's strong bass voice speaking to her brother, and winced, as she knew he would be wincing, under the broad praise, which is impertinence, however little it may be intended or esteemed as such.

"Oh, yes!—my wife told me yesterday about her—her husband was a surgeon; my father was a surgeon too, as I think you have heard. Very much to your credit, I must say, Mr Benson, with your limited means, to burden yourself with a poor relation. Very creditable indeed."

Miss Benson glanced at Ruth; she either did not hear or did not understand, but passed on into the awful sphere of Mr Bradshaw's observation unmoved. He was in a bland and condescending humour of universal approval, and when he saw Ruth, he nodded his head in token of satisfaction. That ordeal was over, Miss Benson thought, and in the thought rejoiced.

"After dinner, you must go and lie down, my dear," said she, untying Ruth's bonnet-strings, and kissing her. "Sally goes to church again, but you won't mind staying alone in the house. I am sorry we have so many people to dinner, but my brother will always have enough on Sundays for any old or weak people, who may have come from a distance, to stay and dine with us; and to-day they all seem to have come, because it is his first Sabbath at home."

In this way Ruth's first Sabbath passed over.

CHAPTER XV - MOTHER AND CHILD

"Here is a parcel for you, Ruth!" said Miss Benson on the Tuesday morning.

"For me!" said Ruth, all sorts of rushing thoughts and hopes filling her mind, and turning her dizzy with expectation. If it had been from "him," the new-born resolutions would have had a hard struggle for existence.

"It is directed 'Mrs Denbigh,'" said Miss Benson, before giving it up. "It is in Mrs Bradshaw's handwriting;" and, far more curious than Ruth, she awaited the untying of the close-knotted string. When the paper was opened, it displayed a whole piece of delicate cambric-muslin; and there was a short note from Mrs Bradshaw to Ruth, saying her husband had wished her to send this muslin in aid of any preparations Mrs Denbigh might have to make. Ruth said nothing, but coloured up, and sat down again to her employment.

"Very fine muslin indeed," said Miss Benson, feeling it, and holding it up against the light, with the air of a connoisseur; yet all the time she was glancing at Ruth's grave face. The latter kept silence, and showed no wish to inspect her present further. At last she said, in a low voice,

"I suppose I may send it back again?"

"My dear child! send it back to Mr Bradshaw! You'd offend him for life. You may depend upon it, he means it as a mark of high favour!"

"What right had he to send it me?" asked Ruth, still in her quiet voice.

"What right? Mr Bradshaw thinks— I don't know exactly what you mean by 'right.'"

Ruth was silent for a moment, and then said:

"There are people to whom I love to feel that I owe gratitude—gratitude which I cannot express, and had better not talk about—but I cannot see why a person whom I do not know should lay me under an obligation. Oh! don't say I must take this muslin, please, Miss Benson!"

What Miss Benson might have said if her brother had not just then entered the room, neither he nor any other person could tell; but she felt his presence was most opportune, and called him in as umpire. He had come hastily, for he had much to do; but he no sooner heard the case than he sat down, and tried to draw some more explicit declaration of her feeling from Ruth, who had remained silent during Miss Benson's explanation.

"You would rather send this present back?" said he.

"Yes," she answered, softly. "Is it wrong?"

"Why do you want to return it?"

"Because I feel as if Mr Bradshaw had no right to offer it me."

Mr Benson was silent.

"It's beautifully fine," said Miss Benson, still examining the piece.

"You think that it is a right which must be earned?"

"Yes," said she, after a minute's pause. "Don't you?"

"I understand what you mean. It is a delight to have gifts made to you by those whom you esteem and love, because then such gifts are merely to be considered as fringes to the garment—as inconsiderable additions to the mighty treasure of their affection, adding a grace, but no additional value, to what before was precious, and proceeding as naturally out of that as leaves burgeon out upon the trees; but you feel it to be different when there is no regard for the giver to idealise the gift—when it simply takes its stand among your property as so much money's value. Is this it, Ruth?"

"I think it is. I never reasoned why I felt as I did; I only knew that Mr Bradshaw's giving me a present hurt me, instead of making me glad."

"Well, but there is another side of the case we have not looked at yet—we must think of that, too. You know who said, 'Do unto others as ye would that they should do unto you'? Mr Bradshaw may not have had that in his mind when he desired his wife to send you this; he may have been self-seeking, and only anxious to gratify his love of patronising—that is the worst motive we can give him; and that would be no excuse for your thinking only of yourself, and returning his present."

"But you would not have me pretend to be obliged?" asked Ruth.

"No, I would not. I have often been similarly situated to you, Ruth; Mr Bradshaw has frequently opposed me on the points on which I feel the warmest—am the most earnestly convinced. He, no doubt, thinks me Quixotic, and often speaks of me, and to me, with great contempt when he is angry. I suppose he has a little fit of penitence afterwards, or perhaps he thinks he can pay for ungracious speeches by a present; so, formerly, he invariably sent me something after these occasions. It was a time, of all others, to feel as you are doing now; but I became convinced it would be right to accept them, giving only the very cool thanks which I felt. This omission of all show of much gratitude had the best effect—the presents have much diminished; but if the gifts have lessened, the unjustifiable speeches have decreased in still greater proportion, and I am sure we respect each other more. Take this muslin, Ruth, for the reason I named; and thank him as your feelings prompt you. Overstrained expressions of gratitude always seem like an endeavour to place the receiver of these expressions in the position of debtor for future favours. But you won't fall into this error."

Ruth listened to Mr Benson; but she had not yet fallen sufficiently into the tone of his mind to understand him fully. She only felt that he comprehended her better than Miss Benson, who once more tried to reconcile her to her present, by calling her attention to the length and breadth thereof.

"I will do what you wish me," she said, after a little pause of thoughtfulness. "May we talk of something else?"

Mr Benson saw that his sister's frame of mind was not particularly congenial with Ruth's, any more than Ruth's was with Miss Benson's; and, putting aside all thought of returning to the business which had appeared to him so important when he came into the room (but which principally related to himself), he remained above an hour in the parlour, interesting them on subjects far removed from the present, and left them at the end of that time soothed and calm.

But the present gave a new current to Ruth's ideas. Her heart was as yet too sore to speak, but her mind was crowded with plans. She asked Sally to buy her (with the money produced by the sale of a ring or two) the coarsest linen, the homeliest dark blue print, and similar materials; on which she set busily to work to make clothes for herself; and as they were made, she put them on; and as she put them on, she gave a grace to each, which such homely material and simple shaping had never had before. Then the fine linen and delicate soft white muslin, which she had chosen in preference to more expensive articles of dress when Mr Bellingham had given her *carte blanche* in London, were cut into small garments, most daintily stitched and made ready for the little creature, for whom in its white purity of soul nothing could be too precious.

The love which dictated this extreme simplicity and coarseness of attire, was taken for stiff, hard economy by Mr Bradshaw, when he deigned to observe it. And economy by itself, without any soul or spirit in it to make it living and holy, was a great merit in his eyes. Indeed, Ruth altogether found favour with him. Her quiet manner, subdued by an internal consciousness of a deeper cause for sorrow than he was aware of, he interpreted into a very proper and becoming awe of him. He looked off from his own prayers to observe how well she attended to hers at chapel; when he came to any verse in the hymn relating to immortality or a future life, he sang it unusually loud, thinking he should thus comfort her in her sorrow for her deceased husband. He desired Mrs Bradshaw to pay her every attention she could; and even once remarked, that he thought her so respectable a young person that he should not object to her being asked to tea the next time Mr and Miss Benson came. He added, that he thought, indeed, Benson had looked last Sunday as if he rather hoped to get an invitation; and it was right to encourage the ministers, and to show them respect, even though their salaries were small. The only thing against this Mrs Denbigh was the circumstance of her having married too early, and without any provision for a family. Though Ruth pleaded delicacy of health, and declined accompanying Mr and Miss Benson on their visit to Mr Bradshaw, she still preserved her place in his esteem; and Miss Benson had to call a little upon her "talent for fiction" to spare Ruth from the infliction of further presents, in making which his love of patronising delighted.

The yellow and crimson leaves came floating down on the still October air; November followed, bleak and dreary; it was more cheerful when the earth put on her beautiful robe of white, which covered up all the grey naked stems, and loaded the leaves of the hollies and evergreens each with its burden of feathery snow.

When Ruth sank down to languor and sadness, Miss Benson trotted upstairs, and rummaged up every article of spare or worn-out clothing, and bringing down a variety of strange materials, she tried to interest Ruth in making them up into garments for the poor. But though Ruth's fingers flew through the work, she still sighed with thought and remembrance. Miss Benson was at first disappointed, and then she was angry. When she heard the low, long sigh, and saw the dreamy eyes filling with glittering tears, she would say, "What is the matter, Ruth?" in a half-reproachful tone, for the sight of suffering was painful to her; she had done all in her power to remedy it; and, though she acknowledged a cause beyond her reach for Ruth's deep sorrow, and, in fact, loved and respected her all the more for these manifestations of grief, yet at the time they irritated her. Then Ruth would snatch up the dropped work, and stitch away with drooping eyes, from which the hot tears fell fast; and Miss Benson was then angry with herself, yet not at all inclined to agree with Sally when she asked her mistress "why she kept 'mithering' the poor lass with asking her for ever what was the matter, as if she did not know well enough." Some element of harmony was wanting—some little angel of peace, in loving whom all hearts and natures should be drawn together, and their discords hushed.

The earth was still "hiding her guilty front with innocent snow," when a little baby was laid by the side of the pale white mother. It was a boy; beforehand she had wished for a girl, as being less likely to feel the want of a father—as being what a mother, worse than widowed, could most effectually shelter. But now she did not think or remember this. What it was, she would not have exchanged for a wilderness of girls. It was her own, her darling, her individual baby, already, though not an hour old, separate and sole in her heart, strangely filling up its measure with love and peace, and even hope. For here was a new, pure, beautiful, innocent life, which she fondly imagined, in that early passion of maternal love, she could guard from every touch of corrupting sin by ever watchful and most tender care. And *her* mother had thought the same, most probably; and thousands of others think the same, and pray to God to purify and cleanse their souls, that they may be fit guardians for their little children. Oh, how Ruth prayed, even while she was yet too weak to speak; and how she felt the beauty and significance of the words, "Our Father!"

She was roused from this holy abstraction by the sound of Miss Benson's voice. It was very much as if she had been crying.

"Look, Ruth!" it said, softly, "my brother sends you these. They are the first snowdrops in the garden." And she put them on the pillow by Ruth; the baby lay on the opposite side.

"Won't you look at him?" said Ruth; "he is so pretty!"

Miss Benson had a strange reluctance to see him. To Ruth, in spite of all that had come and gone, she was reconciled—nay, more, she was deeply attached; but over the baby there hung a cloud of shame and disgrace. Poor little creature! her heart was closed against it—firmly, as she thought. But she could not resist Ruth's low faint voice, nor her pleading eyes, and she went round to peep at him as he lay in his mother's arm, as yet his shield and guard.

"Sally says he will have black hair, she thinks," said Ruth. "His little hand is quite a man's, already. Just feel how firmly he closes it;" and with her own weak fingers she opened his little red fist, and taking Miss Benson's reluctant hand, placed one of her fingers in his grasp. That baby-touch called out her love; the doors of her heart were thrown open wide for the little infant to go in and take possession.

"Ah, my darling!" said Ruth, falling back weak and weary. "If God will but spare you to me, never mother did more than I will. I have done you a grievous wrong—but, if I may but live, I will spend my life in serving you!"

"And in serving God!" said Miss Benson, with tears in her eyes. "You must not make him into an idol, or God will, perhaps, punish you through him."

A pang of affright shot through Ruth's heart at these words; had she already sinned and made her child into an idol, and was there punishment already in store for her through him? But then the internal voice whispered that God was "Our Father," and that He knew our frame, and knew how natural was the first outburst of a mother's love; so, although she treasured up the warning, she ceased to affright herself for what had already gushed forth.

"Now go to sleep, Ruth," said Miss Benson, kissing her, and darkening the room. But Ruth could not sleep; if her heavy eyes closed, she opened them again with a start, for sleep seemed to be an enemy stealing from her the consciousness of being a mother. That one thought excluded all remembrance and all anticipation, in those first hours of delight.

But soon remembrance and anticipation came. There was the natural want of the person, who alone could take an interest similar in kind, though not in amount, to the mother's. And sadness grew like a giant in the still watches of the night, when she remembered that there would be no father to guide and strengthen the child, and place him in a favourable position for fighting the hard "Battle of Life." She hoped and believed that no one would know the sin of his parents, and that that struggle might be spared to him. But a father's powerful care and mighty guidance would never be his; and then, in those hours of spiritual purification, came the wonder and the doubt of how far the real father would be the one to whom, with her desire of heaven for her child, whatever might become of herself, she would wish to entrust him. Slight speeches, telling of a selfish, worldly nature, unnoticed at the time, came back upon her ear, having a new significance. They told of a low standard, of impatient self-indulgence, of no acknowledgment of things spiritual and heavenly. Even while this examination was forced upon her, by the new spirit of maternity that had entered into her, and made her child's welfare supreme, she hated and reproached herself for the necessity there seemed upon her of examining and judging the absent father of her child. And so the compelling presence that had taken possession of her wearied her into a kind of feverish slumber; in which she dreamt that the innocent babe that lay by her side in soft ruddy slumber had started up into man's growth, and, instead of the pure and noble being whom she had prayed to present as her child to "Our Father in heaven," he was a repetition of his father; and, like him, lured some maiden (who in her dream seemed strangely like herself, only more utterly sad and desolate even than she) into sin, and left her there to even a worse fate than that of suicide. For Ruth believed there was a worse. She dreamt she saw the girl, wandering, lost; and that she saw her son in high places, prosperous—but with more than blood on his soul. She saw her son dragged down by the clinging girl into some pit of horrors into which she dared not look, but from whence his father's voice was heard, crying aloud, that in his day and generation he had not remembered the words of God, and that now he was "tormented in this flame." Then she started in sick terror, and saw, by the dim rushlight, Sally, nodding in an arm-chair by the fire; and felt her little soft warm babe, nestled up against her breast, rocked by her heart, which yet beat hard from the effects of the evil dream. She dared not go to sleep again, but prayed. And every time she prayed, she asked with a more complete wisdom, and a more utter and self-forgetting faith. Little child! thy angel was with God, and drew her nearer and nearer to Him, whose face is continually beheld by the angels of little children.

CHAPTER XVI - SALLY TELLS OF HER SWEETHEARTS, AND DISCOURSES ON THE DUTIES OF LIFE

Sally and Miss Benson took it in turns to sit up, or rather, they took it in turns to nod by the fire; for if Ruth was awake she lay very still in the moonlight calm of her sick bed. That time resembled a beautiful August evening, such as I have seen. The white, snowy rolling mist covers up under its great sheet all trees and meadows, and tokens of earth; but it cannot rise high enough to shut out the heavens, which on such nights seem bending very near, and to be the only real and present objects; and so near, so real and present, did heaven, and eternity, and God seem to Ruth, as she lay encircling her mysterious holy child.

One night Sally found out she was not asleep.

"I'm a rare hand at talking folks to sleep," said she. "I'll try on thee, for thou must get strength by sleeping and eating. What must I talk to thee about, I wonder. Shall I tell thee a love story or a fairy story, such as I've telled Master Thurstan many a time and many a time, for all his father set his face again fairies, and called it vain talking; or shall I tell you the dinner I once cooked, when Mr Harding, as was Miss Faith's sweetheart, came unlooked for, and we'd nought in the house but a neck of mutton, out of which I made seven dishes, all with a different name?"

"Who was Mr Harding?" asked Ruth.

"Oh, he was a grand gentleman from Lunnon, as had seen Miss Faith, and been struck by her pretty looks when she was out on a visit, and came here to ask her to marry him. She said, 'No, she would never leave Master Thurstan, as could never marry;' but she pined a deal at after he went away. She kept up afore Master Thurstan, but I seed her fretting, though I never let on that I did, for I thought she'd soonest get over it and be thankful at after she'd the strength to do right. However, I've no business to be talking of Miss Benson's concerns. I'll tell you of my own sweethearts and welcome, or I'll tell you of the dinner, which was the grandest thing I ever did in my life, but I thought a Lunnoner should never think country folks knew nothing; and, my word! I puzzled him with his dinner. I'm doubting whether to this day he knows whether what he was eating was fish, flesh, or fowl. Shall I tell you how I managed?"

But Ruth said she would rather hear about Sally's sweethearts, much to the disappointment of the latter, who considered the dinner by far the greatest achievement.

"Well, you see, I don't know as I should call them sweethearts; for excepting John Rawson, who was shut up in the mad-house the next week, I never had what you may call a downright offer of marriage but once. But I had once; and so I may say I had a sweetheart. I was beginning to be afeard though, for one likes to be axed; that's but civility; and I remember, after I had turned forty, and afore Jeremiah Dixon had spoken, I began to think John Rawson had perhaps not been so very mad, and that I'd done ill to lightly his offer, as a madman's, if it was to be the only one I was ever to have; I don't mean as I'd have had him, but I thought, if it was to come o'er again, I'd speak respectful of him to folk, and say it were only his way to go about on all fours, but that he was a sensible man in most things. However, I'd had my laugh, and so had others, at my crazy lover, and it was late now to set him up as a Solomon. However, I thought it would be no bad thing to be tried again; but I little thought the trial would come when it did. You see, Saturday night is a leisure night in counting-houses and such-like places, while it's the busiest of all for servants. Well! it was a Saturday night, and I'd my baize apron on, and the tails of my bed-gown pinned together behind, down on my knees, pipeclaying the kitchen, when a knock comes to the back door. 'Come in!' says I; but it knocked again, as if it were too stately to open the door for itself; so I got up, rather cross, and opened the door; and there stood Jerry Dixon, Mr Holt's head clerk; only he was not head clerk then. So I stood, stopping up the door, fancying he wanted to speak to master; but he kind of pushed past me, and telling me summut about the weather (as if I could not see it for myself), he took a chair, and sat down by the oven. 'Cool and easy!' thought I; meaning hisself, not his place, which I knew must be pretty hot. Well! it seemed no use standing waiting for my gentleman to go; not that he had much to say either; but he kept twirling his hat round and round, and smoothing the nap on't with the back of his hand. So at last I squatted down to my work, and thinks I, I shall be on my knees all ready if he puts up a prayer, for I knew he was a Methodee by bringing-up, and had only lately turned to master's way of thinking; and them Methodees are terrible hands at unexpected prayers when one least looks for 'em. I can't say I like their way of taking one by surprise, as it were; but then I'm a parish clerk's daughter, and could never demean myself to dissenting fashions, always save and except Master Thurstan's, bless him. However, I'd been caught once or twice unawares, so this time I thought I'd be up to it, and I moved a dry duster wherever I went, to kneel upon in case he began when I were in a wet place. By-and-by I thought, if the man would pray it would be a blessing, for it would prevent his sending his eyes after me wherever I went; for when they takes to praying they shuts their eyes, and quivers th' lids in a queer kind o' way—them Dissenters does. I can speak pretty plain to you, for you're bred in the Church like mysel', and must find it as out o' the way as I do to be among dissenting folk. God forbid I should speak disrespectful of Master Thurstan and Miss Faith, though; I never think on them as

Church or Dissenters, but just as Christians. But to come back to Jerry. First, I tried always to be cleaning at his back; but when he wheeled round, so as always to face me, I thought I'd try a different game. So, says I, 'Master Dixon, I ax your pardon, but I must pipeclay under your chair. Will you please to move?' Well, he moved; and by-and-by I was at him again with the same words; and at after that, again and again, till he were always moving about wi' his chair behind him, like a snail as carries its house on its back. And the great gaupus never seed that I were pipeclaying the same places twice over. At last I got desperate cross, he were so in my way; so I made two big crosses on the tails of his brown coat; for you see, whenever he went, up or down, he drew out the tails of his coat from under him, and stuck them through the bars of the chair; and flesh and blood could not resist pipeclaying them for him; and a pretty brushing he'd have, I reckon, to get it off again. Well! at length he clears his throat uncommon loud; so I spreads my duster, and shuts my eyes all ready; but when nought comed of it, I opened my eyes a little bit to see what he were about. My word! if there he wasn't down on his knees right facing me, staring as hard as he could. Well! I thought it would be hard work to stand that, if he made a long ado; so I shut my eyes again, and tried to think serious, as became what I fancied were coming; but, forgive me! but I thought why couldn't the fellow go in and pray wi' Master Thurstan, as had always a calm spirit ready for prayer, instead o' me, who had my dresser to scour, let alone an apron to iron. At last he says, says he, 'Sally! will you oblige me with your hand?' So I thought it were, maybe, Methodee fashion to pray hand in hand; and I'll not deny but I wished I'd washed it better after black-leading the kitchen fire. I thought I'd better tell him it were not so clean as I could wish, so says I, 'Master Dixon, you shall have it, and welcome, if I may just go and wash 'em first.' But, says he, 'My dear Sally, dirty or clean it's all the same to me, seeing I'm only speaking in a figuring way. What I'm asking on my bended knees is, that you'd please to be so kind as to be my wedded wife; week after next will suit me, if it's agreeable to you!' My word! I were up on my feet in an instant! It were odd now, weren't it? I never thought of taking the fellow, and getting married; for all, I'll not deny, I had been thinking it would be agreeable to be axed. But all at once, I couldn't abide the chap. 'Sir,' says I, trying to look shame-faced as became the occasion, but for all that, feeling a twittering round my mouth that I were afeard might end in a laugh—'Master Dixon, I'm obleeged to you for the compliment, and thank ye all the same, but I think I'd prefer a single life.' He looked mighty taken aback; but in a minute he cleared up, and was as sweet as ever. He still kept on his knees, and I wished he'd take himself up; but, I reckon, he thought it would give force to his words; says he, 'Think again, my dear Sally. I've a four-roomed house, and furniture conformable; and eighty pound a year. You may never have such a chance again.' There were truth enough in that, but it was not pretty in the man to say it; and it put me up a bit. 'As for that, neither you nor I can tell, Master Dixon. You're not the first chap as I've had down on his knees afore me, axing me to marry him (you see I were thinking of John Rawson, only I thought there were no need to say he were on all fours—it were truth he were on his knees, you know), and maybe you'll not be the last. Anyhow, I've no wish to change my condition just now.' 'I'll wait till Christmas,' says he. 'I've a pig as will be ready for killing then, so I must get married before that.' Well now! would you believe it? the pig were a temptation. I'd a receipt for curing hams, as Miss Faith would never let me try, saying the old way were good enough. However, I resisted. Says I, very stern, because I felt I'd been wavering, 'Master Dixon, once for all, pig or no pig, I'll not marry you. And if you'll take my advice, you'll get up off your knees. The flags is but damp yet, and it would be an awkward thing to have rheumatiz just before winter.' With that he got up, stiff enough. He looked as sulky a chap as ever I clapped eyes on. And as he were so black and cross, I thought I'd done well (whatever came of the pig) to say 'No' to him. 'You may live to repent this,' says he, very red. 'But I'll not be too hard upon ye, I'll give you another chance. I'll let you have the night to think about it, and I'll just call in to hear your second thoughts, after chapel to-morrow.' Well now! did ever you hear the like? But that is the way with all of them men, thinking so much of theirselves, and that it's but ask and have. They've never had me, though; and I shall be sixty-one next Martinmas, so there's not much time left for them to try me, I reckon. Well! when Jeremiah said that, he put me up more than ever, and I says, 'My first thoughts, second thoughts, and third thoughts is all one and the same; you've but tempted me once, and that was when you spoke of your pig. But of yoursel' you're nothing to boast on, and so I'll bid you good night, and I'll keep my manners, or else, if I told the truth, I should say it had been a great loss of time listening to you. But I'll be civil—so good night.' He never said a word, but went off as black as thunder, slamming the door after him. The master called me in to prayers, but I can't say I could put my mind to them, for my heart was beating so. However, it was a comfort to have had an offer of holy matrimony; and though it flustered me, it made me think more of myself. In the night, I began to wonder if I'd not been cruel and hard to him. You see, I were feverish-like; and the old song of Barbary Allen would keep running in my head, and I thought I were Barbary, and he were young Jemmy Gray, and that maybe he'd die for love of me; and I pictured him to mysel', lying on his death-bed, with his face turned to the wall, 'wi' deadly sorrow sighing,' and I could ha' pinched mysel' for having been so like cruel Barbary Allen. And when I got up next day, I found it hard to think on the real Jerry Dixon I had seen the night before, apart from the sad and sorrowful Jerry I thought on a-dying, when I were between sleeping and waking. And for many a day I turned sick, when I heard the passing bell, for I thought it were the bell loud-knelling which were to break my heart wi' a sense of what I'd missed in saying 'No' to Jerry, and so killing him with cruelty. But in less than a three week, I heard parish bells a-ringing merrily for a wedding; and in the course of a morning, some one says to me, 'Hark! how the bells is ringing for Jerry Dixon's wedding!' And, all on a sudden, he changed back again from a heart-broken young fellow, like Jemmy Gray, into a stout, middle-aged man, ruddy-complexioned, with a wart on his left cheek like life!"

Sally waited for some exclamation at the conclusion of her tale; but receiving none, she stepped softly to the bedside, and there lay Ruth, peaceful as death, with her baby on her breast.

"I thought I'd lost some of my gifts if I could not talk a body to sleep," said Sally, in a satisfied and self-complacent tone.

Youth is strong and powerful, and makes a hard battle against sorrow. So Ruth strove and strengthened, and her baby flourished accordingly; and before the little celandines were out on the hedge-banks, or the white violets had sent forth their fragrance from the border under the south wall of Miss Benson's small garden, Ruth was able to carry her baby into that sheltered place on sunny days.

She often wished to thank Mr Benson and his sister, but she did not know how to tell the deep gratitude she felt, and therefore she was silent. But they understood her silence well. One day, as she watched her sleeping child, she spoke to Miss Benson, with whom she happened to be alone.

"Do you know of any cottage where the people are clean, and where they would not mind taking me in?" asked she.

"Taking you in! What do you mean?" said Miss Benson, dropping her knitting, in order to observe Ruth more closely.

"I mean," said Ruth, "where I might lodge with my baby—any very poor place would do, only it must be clean, or he might be ill."

"And what in the world do you want to go and lodge in a cottage for?" said Miss Benson, indignantly.

Ruth did not lift up her eyes, but she spoke with a firmness which showed that she had considered the subject.

"I think I could make dresses. I know I did not learn as much as I might, but perhaps I might do for servants, and people who are not particular."

"Servants are as particular as any one," said Miss Benson, glad to lay hold of the first objection that she could.

"Well! somebody who would be patient with me," said Ruth.

"Nobody is patient over an ill-fitting gown," put in Miss Benson. "There's the stuff spoilt, and what not!"

"Perhaps I could find plain work to do," said Ruth, very meekly. "That I can do very well; mamma taught me, and I liked to learn from her. If you would be so good, Miss Benson, you might tell people I could do plain work very neatly, and punctually, and cheaply."

"You'd get sixpence a day, perhaps," said Miss Benson, "and who would take care of baby, I should like to know? Prettily he'd be neglected, would not he? Why, he'd have the croup and the typhus fever in no time, and be burnt to ashes after."

"I have thought of all. Look how he sleeps! Hush, darling;" for just at this point he began to cry, and to show his determination to be awake, as if in contradiction to his mother's words. Ruth took him up, and carried him about the room while she went on speaking.

"Yes, just now I know he will not sleep; but very often he will, and in the night he always does."

"And so you'd work in the night and kill yourself, and leave your poor baby an orphan. Ruth! I'm ashamed of you. Now, brother" (Mr Benson had just come in), "is not this too bad of Ruth; here she is planning to go away and leave us, just as we—as I, at least, have grown so fond of baby, and he's beginning to know me."

"Where were you thinking of going to, Ruth?" interrupted Mr Benson, with mild surprise.

"Anywhere to be near you and Miss Benson; in any poor cottage where I might lodge very cheaply, and earn my livelihood by taking in plain sewing, and perhaps a little dressmaking; and where I could come and see you and dear Miss Benson sometimes and bring baby."

"If he was not dead before then of some fever, or burn, or scald, poor neglected child; or you had not worked yourself to death with never sleeping," said Miss Benson.

Mr Benson thought a minute or two, and then he spoke to Ruth.

"Whatever you may do when this little fellow is a year old, and able to dispense with some of a mother's care, let me beg you, Ruth, as a favour to me—as a still greater favour to my sister, is it not, Faith?"

"Yes; you may put it so if you like."

"To stay with us," continued he, "till then. When baby is twelve months old, we'll talk about it again, and very likely before then some opening may be shown us. Never fear leading an idle life, Ruth. We'll treat you as a daughter, and set you all the household tasks; and it is not for your sake that we ask you to stay, but for this little dumb helpless child's; and it is not for our sake that you must stay, but for his."

Ruth was sobbing.

"I do not deserve your kindness," said she, in a broken voice; "I do not deserve it."

Her tears fell fast and soft like summer rain, but no further word was spoken. Mr Benson quietly passed on to make the inquiry for which he had entered the room.

But when there was nothing to decide upon, and no necessity for entering upon any new course of action, Ruth's mind relaxed from its strung-up state. She fell into trains of reverie, and mournful regretful recollections which rendered her languid and tearful. This was noticed both by Miss Benson and Sally, and as each had keen sympathies, and felt depressed when they saw any one near them depressed, and as each, without much reasoning on the cause or reason for such depression, felt irritated at the uncomfortable state into which they themselves were thrown, they both resolved to speak to Ruth on the next fitting occasion.

Accordingly, one afternoon—the morning of that day had been spent by Ruth in housework, for she had insisted on Mr Benson's words, and had taken Miss Benson's share of the more active and fatiguing household duties, but she went through them heavily, and as if her heart was far away—in the afternoon when she was nursing her child, Sally, on coming into the back parlour, found her there alone, and easily detected the fact that she had been crying.

"Where's Miss Benson?" said Sally, gruffly.

"Gone out with Mr Benson," answered Ruth, with an absent sadness in her voice and manner. Her tears, scarce checked while she spoke, began to fall afresh; and as Sally stood and gazed she saw the babe look back in his mother's face, and his little lip begin to quiver, and his open blue eye to grow over-clouded, as with some mysterious sympathy with the sorrowful face bent over him. Sally took him briskly from his mother's arms; Ruth looked up in grave surprise, for in truth she had forgotten Sally's presence, and the suddenness of the motion startled her.

"My bonny boy! are they letting the salt tears drop on thy sweet face before thou'rt weaned! Little somebody knows how to be a mother—I could make a better myself. 'Dance, thumbkin, dance—dance, ye merry men every one.' Aye, that's it! smile, my pretty. Any one but a child like thee," continued she, turning to Ruth, "would have known better than to bring ill-luck on thy babby by letting tears fall on its face before it was weaned. But thou'rt not fit to have a babby, and so I've said many a time. I've a great mind to buy thee a doll, and take thy babby mysel'."

Sally did not look at Ruth, for she was too much engaged in amusing the baby with the tassel of the string to the window-blind, or else she would have seen the dignity which the mother's soul put into Ruth at that moment. Sally was quelled into silence by the gentle composure, the self-command over her passionate sorrow, which gave to Ruth an unconscious grandeur of demeanour as she came up to the old servant.

"Give him back to me, please. I did not know it brought ill-luck, or if my heart broke I would not have let a tear drop on his face—I never will again. Thank you, Sally," as the servant relinquished him to her who came in the name of a mother. Sally watched Ruth's grave, sweet smile, as she followed up Sally's play with the tassel, and imitated, with all the docility inspired by love, every movement and sound which had amused her babe.

"Thou'lt be a mother, after all," said Sally, with a kind of admiration of the control which Ruth was exercising over herself. "But why talk of thy heart breaking? I don't question thee about what's past and gone; but now thou'rt wanting for nothing, nor thy child either; the time to come is the Lord's, and in His hands; and yet thou goest about a-sighing and a-moaning in a way that I can't stand or thole."

"What do I do wrong?" said Ruth; "I try to do all I can."

"Yes, in a way," said Sally, puzzled to know how to describe her meaning. "Thou dost it—but there's a right and a wrong way of setting about everything—and to my thinking, the right way is to take a thing up heartily, if it is only making a bed. Why! dear ah me, making a bed may be done after a Christian fashion, I take it, or else what's to come of such as me in heaven, who've had little enough time on earth for clapping ourselves down on our knees for set prayers? When I was a girl, and wretched enough about Master Thurstan, and the crook on his back which came of the fall I gave him, I took to praying and sighing, and giving up the world; and I thought it were wicked to care for the flesh, so I made heavy puddings, and was careless about dinner and the rooms, and thought I was doing my duty, though I did call myself a miserable sinner. But one night, the old missus (Master Thurstan's mother) came in, and sat down by me, as I was a-scolding myself, without thinking of what I was saying; and, says she, 'Sally! what are you blaming yourself about, and groaning over? We hear you in the parlour every night, and it makes my heart ache.' 'Oh, ma'am,' says I, 'I'm a miserable sinner, and I'm travailing in the new birth.' 'Was that the reason,' says she, 'why the pudding was so heavy to-day?' 'Oh, ma'am, ma'am,' said I, 'if you would not think of the things of the flesh, but trouble yourself about your immortal soul.' And I sat a-shaking my head to think about her soul. 'But,' says she, in her sweet-dropping voice, 'I do try to think of my soul every hour of the day, if by that you mean trying to do the will of God, but we'll talk now about the pudding; Master Thurstan could not eat it, and I know you'll be sorry for that.' Well! I was sorry, but I didn't choose to say so, as she seemed to expect me; so says I, 'It's a pity to see children brought up to care for things of the flesh;' and then I could have bitten my tongue out, for the missus looked so grave, and I thought of my darling little lad pining for want of his food. At last, says she, 'Sally, do you think God has put us into the world just to be selfish, and do nothing but see after our own souls? or to help one another with heart and hand, as Christ did to all who wanted help?' I was silent, for, you see, she puzzled me. So she went on, 'What is that beautiful answer in your Church catechism, Sally?' I were pleased to hear a Dissenter, as I did not think would have done it, speak so knowledgeably about the catechism, and she went on: '"to do my duty in that station of life unto which it shall please God to call me;" well, your station is a servant, and it is as honourable as a king's, if you look at it right; you are to help and serve others in one way, just as a king is to help others in another. Now what way are you to help and serve, or to do your duty, in that station of life unto which it has pleased God to call you? Did it answer God's purpose, and serve Him, when the food was unfit for a child to eat, and unwholesome for any one?' Well! I would not give it up, I was so pig-headed about my soul; so says I, 'I wish folks would be content with locusts and wild honey, and leave other folks in peace to work out their salvation;' and I groaned out pretty loud to think of missus's soul. I often think since she smiled a bit at me; but she said, 'Well, Sally, to-morrow, you shall have time to work out your salvation; but as we have no locusts in England, and I don't think they'd agree with Master Thurstan if we had, I will come and make the pudding; but I shall try and do it well, not only for him to like it, but because everything may be done in a right way or a wrong; the right way is to do it as well as we can, as in God's sight; the wrong is to do it in a self-seeking spirit, which either leads us to neglect it to follow out some device of our own for our own ends, or to give up too much time and thought to it both before and after the doing.' Well! I thought of all old missus's words this morning, when I saw you making the beds. You sighed so, you could not half shake the pillows; your heart was not in your work; and yet it was the duty God had set you, I reckon; I know it's not the work parsons preach about;

though I don't think they go so far off the mark when they read, 'whatsoever thy hand findeth to do, that do with all thy might.' Just try for a day to think of all the odd jobs as has to be done well and truly as in God's sight, not just slurred over anyhow, and you'll go through them twice as cheerfully, and have no thought to spare for sighing or crying."

Sally bustled off to set on the kettle for tea, and felt half ashamed, in the quiet of the kitchen, to think of the oration she had made in the parlour. But she saw with much satisfaction, that henceforward Ruth nursed her boy with a vigour and cheerfulness that were reflected back from him; and the household work was no longer performed with a languid indifference, as if life and duty were distasteful. Miss Benson had her share in this improvement, though Sally placidly took all the credit to herself. One day as she and Ruth sat together, Miss Benson spoke of the child, and thence went on to talk about her own childhood. By degrees they spoke of education, and the book-learning that forms one part of it; and the result was that Ruth determined to get up early all through the bright summer mornings, to acquire the knowledge hereafter to be given to her child. Her mind was uncultivated, her reading scant; beyond the mere mechanical arts of education she knew nothing; but she had a refined taste, and excellent sense and judgment to separate the true from the false. With these qualities, she set to work under Mr Benson's directions. She read in the early morning the books that he marked out; she trained herself with strict perseverance to do all thoroughly; she did not attempt to acquire any foreign language, although her ambition was to learn Latin, in order to teach it to her boy. Those summer mornings were happy, for she was learning neither to look backwards nor forwards, but to live faithfully and earnestly in the present. She rose while the hedge-sparrow was yet singing his *réveillé* to his mate; she dressed and opened her window, shading the soft-blowing air and the sunny eastern light from her baby. If she grew tired, she went and looked at him, and all her thoughts were holy prayers for him. Then she would gaze awhile out of the high upper window on to the moorlands, that swelled in waves one behind the other, in the grey, cool morning light. These were her occasional relaxations, and after them she returned with strength to her work.

CHAPTER XVII - LEONARD'S CHRISTENING

In that body of Dissenters to which Mr Benson belonged, it is not considered necessary to baptize infants as early as the ceremony can be performed; and many circumstances concurred to cause the solemn thanksgiving and dedication of the child (for so these Dissenters look upon christenings) to be deferred until it was probably somewhere about six months old. There had been many conversations in the little sitting-room between the brother and sister and their *protegée*, which had consisted more of questions betraying a thoughtful wondering kind of ignorance on the part of Ruth, and answers more suggestive than explanatory from Mr Benson; while Miss Benson kept up a kind of running commentary, always simple and often quaint, but with that intuition into the very heart of all things truly religious which is often the gift of those who seem, at first sight, to be only affectionate and sensible. When Mr Benson had explained his own views of what a christening ought to be considered, and, by calling out Ruth's latent feelings into pious earnestness, brought her into a right frame of mind, he felt that he had done what he could to make the ceremony more than a mere form, and to invest it, quiet, humble, and obscure as it must necessarily be in outward shape—mournful and anxious as much of its antecedents had rendered it—with the severe grandeur of an act done in faith and truth.

It was not far to carry the little one, for, as I said, the chapel almost adjoined the minister's house. The whole procession was to have consisted of Mr and Miss Benson, Ruth carrying her baby, and Sally, who felt herself, as a Church-of-England woman, to be condescending and kind in requesting leave to attend a baptism among "them Dissenters;" but unless she had asked permission, she would not have been desired to attend, so careful was the habit of her master and mistress that she should be allowed that freedom which they claimed for themselves. But they were glad she wished to go; they liked the feeling that all were of one household, and that the interests of one were the interests of all. It produced a consequence, however, which they did not anticipate. Sally was full of the event which her presence was to sanction, and, as it were, to redeem from the character of being utterly schismatic; she spoke about it with an air of patronage to three or four, and among them to some of the servants at Mr Bradshaw's.

Miss Benson was rather surprised to receive a call from Jemima Bradshaw, on the very morning of the day on which little Leonard was to be baptized; Miss

Bradshaw was rosy and breathless with eagerness. Although the second in the family, she had been at school when her younger sisters had been christened, and she was now come, in the full warmth of a girl's fancy, to ask if she might be present at the afternoon's service. She had been struck with Mrs Denbigh's grace and beauty at the very first sight, when she had accompanied her mother to call upon the Bensons on their return from Wales; and had kept up an enthusiastic interest in thc widow only a little older than herself, whose very reserve and retirement but added to her unconscious power of enchantment.

"Oh, Miss Benson! I never saw a christening; papa says I may go, if you think Mr Benson and Mrs Denbigh would not dislike it; and I will be quite quiet, and sit up behind the door, or anywhere; and that sweet little baby! I should so like to see him christened; is he to be called Leonard, did you say? After Mr Denbigh, is it?"

"No—not exactly," said Miss Benson, rather discomfited.

"Was not Mr Denbigh's name Leonard, then? Mamma thought it would be sure to be called after him, and so did I. But I may come to the christening, may I not, dear Miss Benson?"

Miss Benson gave her consent with a little inward reluctance. Both her brother and Ruth shared in this feeling, although no one expressed it; and it was presently forgotten.

Jemima stood grave and quiet in the old-fashioned vestry adjoining the chapel, as they entered with steps subdued to slowness. She thought Ruth looked so pale and awed because she was left a solitary parent; but Ruth came to the presence of God, as one who had gone astray, and doubted her own worthiness to be called His child; she came as a mother who had incurred a heavy responsibility, and who entreated His almighty aid to enable her to discharge it; full of passionate, yearning love which craved for more faith in God, to still her distrust and fear of the future that might hang over her darling. When she thought of her boy, she sickened and trembled; but when she heard of God's loving-kindness, far beyond all tender mother's love, she was hushed into peace and prayer. There she stood, her fair pale cheek resting on her baby's head, as he slumbered on her bosom; her eyes went slanting down under their half-closed white lids; but their gaze was not on the primitive cottage-like room, it was earnestly fixed on a dim mist, through which she fain would have seen the life that lay before her child; but the mist was still and dense, too thick a veil for anxious human love to penetrate. The future was hid with God.

Mr Benson stood right under the casement window that was placed high up in the room; he was almost in shade, except for one or two marked lights which fell on hair already silvery white; his voice was always low and musical when he spoke to few; it was too weak to speak so as to be heard by many without becoming harsh and strange; but now it filled the little room with a loving sound, like the stock-dove's brooding murmur over her young. He and Ruth forgot all in their earnestness of thought; and when he said "Let us pray," and the little congregation knelt down, you might have heard the baby's faint breathing, scarcely sighing out upon the stillness, so absorbed were all in the solemnity. But the prayer was long;

thought followed thought, and fear crowded upon fear, and all were to be laid bare before God, and His aid and counsel asked. Before the end Sally had shuffled quietly out of the vestry into the green chapel-yard, upon which the door opened. Miss Benson was alive to this movement, and so full of curiosity as to what it might mean that she could no longer attend to her brother, and felt inclined to rush off and question Sally the moment all was ended. Miss Bradshaw hung about the babe and Ruth, and begged to be allowed to carry the child home, but Ruth pressed him to her, as if there was no safe harbour for him but in his mother's breast. Mr Benson saw her feeling, and caught Miss Bradshaw's look of disappointment.

"Come home with us," said he, "and stay to tea. You have never drank tea with us since you went to school."

"I wish I might," said Miss Bradshaw, colouring with pleasure. "But I must ask papa. May I run home and ask?"

"To be sure, my dear!"

Jemima flew off; and fortunately her father was at home; for her mother's permission would have been deemed insufficient. She received many directions about her behaviour.

"Take no sugar in your tea, Jemima. I am sure the Bensons ought not to be able to afford sugar, with their means. And do not eat much; you can have plenty at home on your return; remember Mrs Denbigh's keep must cost them a great deal."

So Jemima returned considerably sobered, and very much afraid of her hunger leading her to forget Mr Benson's poverty. Meanwhile Miss Benson and Sally, acquainted with Mr Benson's invitation to Jemima, set about making some capital tea-cakes on which they piqued themselves. They both enjoyed the offices of hospitality; and were glad to place some home-made tempting dainty before their guests.

"What made ye leave the chapel-vestry before my brother had ended?" inquired Miss Benson.

"Indeed, ma'am, I thought master had prayed so long he'd be drouthy. So I just slipped out to put on the kettle for tea."

Miss Benson was on the point of reprimanding her for thinking of anything besides the object of the prayer, when she remembered how she herself had been unable to attend after Sally's departure for wondering what had become of her; so she was silent.

It was a disappointment to Miss Benson's kind and hospitable expectation when Jemima, as hungry as a hound, confined herself to one piece of the cake which her hostess had had such pleasure in making. And Jemima wished she had not a prophetic feeling all tea-time of the manner in which her father would inquire into the particulars of the meal, elevating his eyebrows at every viand named beyond plain bread-and-butter, and winding up with some such sentence as this: "Well, I marvel how, with Benson's salary, he can afford to keep such a table." Sally could have told of self-denial when no one was by, when the left hand did not know what the right hand did, on the part of both her master and mistress, practised without thinking even to themselves that it was either a sacrifice or a virtue, in order to enable them to help those who were in need, or even to gratify Miss Benson's kind, old-fashioned feelings on such occasions as the present, when a stranger came to the house. Her homely, affectionate pleasure in making others comfortable, might have shown that such little occasional extravagances were not waste, but a good work; and were not to be gauged by the standard of money-spending. This evening her spirits were damped by Jemima's refusal to eat. Poor Jemima! the cakes were so good, and she was so hungry; but still she refused.

While Sally was clearing away the tea-things, Miss Benson and Jemima accompanied Ruth upstairs, when she went to put little Leonard to bed.

"A christening is a very solemn service," said Miss Bradshaw; "I had no idea it was so solemn. Mr Benson seemed to speak as if he had a weight of care on his heart that God alone could relieve or lighten."

"My brother feels these things very much," said Miss Benson, rather wishing to cut short the conversation, for she had been aware of several parts in the prayer which she knew were suggested by the peculiarity and sadness of the case before him.

"I could not quite follow him all through," continued Jemima; "what did he mean by saying, 'This child, rebuked by the world and bidden to stand apart, Thou wilt not rebuke, but wilt suffer it to come to Thee and be blessed with Thine almighty blessing'? Why is this little darling to be rebuked? I do not think I remember the exact words, but he said something like that."

"My dear! your gown is dripping wet! it must have dipped into the tub; let me wring it out."

"Oh, thank you! Never mind my gown!" said Jemima, hastily, and wanting to return to her question; but just then she caught the sight of tears falling fast down the cheeks of the silent Ruth as she bent over her child, crowing and splashing away in his tub. With a sudden consciousness that unwittingly she had touched on some painful chord, Jemima rushed into another subject, and was eagerly seconded by Miss Benson. The circumstance seemed to die away, and leave no trace; but in after-years it rose, vivid and significant, before Jemima's memory. At present it was enough for her, if Mrs Denbigh would let her serve her in every possible way. Her admiration for beauty was keen, and little indulged at home; and Ruth was very beautiful in her quiet mournfulness; her mean and homely dress left herself only the more open to admiration, for she gave it a charm by her unconscious wearing of it that made it seem like the drapery of an old Greek statue—subordinate to the figure it covered, yet imbued by it with an unspeakable grace. Then the pretended circumstances of her life were such as to catch the imagination of a young romantic girl. Altogether, Jemima could have kissed her hand and professed herself Ruth's slave. She moved away all the articles used at this little *coucher*; she folded up Leonard's day-clothes; she felt only too much honoured when Ruth trusted him to her for a few minutes—only too amply rewarded when

Ruth thanked her with a grave, sweet smile, and a grateful look of her loving eyes.

When Jemima had gone away with the servant who was sent to fetch her, there was a little chorus of praise.

"She's a warm-hearted girl," said Miss Benson. "She remembers all the old days before she went to school. She is worth two of Mr Richard. They're each of them just the same as they were when they were children, when they broke that window in the chapel, and he ran away home, and she came knocking at our door, with a single knock, just like a beggar's, and I went to see who it was, and was quite startled to see her round, brown, honest face looking up at me, half-frightened, and telling me what she had done, and offering me the money in her savings bank to pay for it. We never should have heard of Master Richard's share in the business if it had not been for Sally."

"But remember," said Mr Benson, "how strict Mr Bradshaw has always been with his children. It is no wonder if poor Richard was a coward in those days."

"He is now, or I'm much mistaken," answered Miss Benson. "And Mr Bradshaw was just as strict with Jemima, and she's no coward. But I've no faith in Richard. He has a look about him that I don't like. And when Mr Bradshaw was away on business in Holland last year, for those months my young gentleman did not come half as regularly to chapel, and I always believe that story of his being seen out with the hounds at Smithiles."

"Those are neither of them great offences in a young man of twenty," said Mr Benson, smiling.

"No! I don't mind them in themselves; but when he could change back so easily to being regular and mim when his father came home, I don't like that."

"Leonard shall never be afraid of me," said Ruth, following her own train of thought. "I will be his friend from the very first; and I will try and learn how to be a wise friend, and you will teach me, won't you, sir?"

"What made you wish to call him Leonard, Ruth?" asked Miss Benson.

"It was my mother's father's name; and she used to tell me about him and his goodness, and I thought if Leonard could be like him—"

"Do you remember the discussion there was about Miss Bradshaw's name, Thurstan? Her father wanting her to be called Hepzibah, but insisting that she was to have a Scripture name at any rate; and Mrs Bradshaw wanting her to be Juliana, after some novel she had read not long before; and at last Jemima was fixed upon, because it would do either for a Scripture name or a name for a heroine out of a book."

"I did not know Jemima was a Scripture name," said Ruth.

"Oh yes, it is. One of Job's daughters; Jemima, Kezia, and Keren-Happuch. There are a good many Jemimas in the world, and some Kezias, but I never heard of a Keren-Happuch; and yet we know just as much of one as of another. People really like a pretty name, whether in Scripture or out of it."

"When there is no particular association with the name," said Mr Benson.

"Now, I was called Faith after the cardinal virtue; and I like my name, though many people would think it too Puritan; that was according to our gentle mother's pious desire. And Thurstan was called by his name because my father wished it; for, although he was what people called a radical and a democrat in his ways of talking and thinking, he was very proud in his heart of being descended from some old Sir Thurstan, who figured away in the French wars."

"The difference between theory and practice, thinking and being," put in Mr Benson, who was in a mood for allowing himself a little social enjoyment. He leant back in his chair, with his eyes looking at, but not seeing the ceiling. Miss Benson was clicking away with her eternal knitting-needles, looking at her brother, and seeing him, too. Ruth was arranging her child's clothes against the morrow. It was but their usual way of spending an evening; the variety was given by the different tone which the conversation assumed on the different nights. Yet, somehow, the peacefulness of the time, the window open into the little garden, the scents that came stealing in, and the clear summer heaven above, made the time be remembered as a happy festival by Ruth. Even Sally seemed more placid than usual when she came in to prayers; and she and Miss Benson followed Ruth to her bedroom, to look at the beautiful sleeping Leonard.

"God bless him!" said Miss Benson, stooping down to kiss his little dimpled hand, which lay outside the coverlet, tossed abroad in the heat of the evening.

"Now, don't get up too early, Ruth! Injuring your health will be short-sighted wisdom and poor economy. Good night!"

"Good night, dear Miss Benson. Good night, Sally." When Ruth had shut her door, she went again to the bed, and looked at her boy till her eyes filled with tears.

"God bless thee, darling! I only ask to be one of His instruments, and not thrown aside as useless—or worse than useless."

So ended the day of Leonard's christening.

Mr Benson had sometimes taught the children of different people as an especial favour, when requested by them. But then his pupils were only children, and by their progress he was little prepared for Ruth's. She had had early teaching, of that kind which need never be unlearnt, from her mother; enough to unfold many of her powers; they had remained inactive now for several years, but had grown strong in the dark and quiet time. Her tutor was surprised at the bounds by which she surmounted obstacles, the quick perception and ready adaptation of truths and first principles, and her immediate sense of the fitness of things. Her delight in what was strong and beautiful called out her master's sympathy; but, most of all, he admired the complete unconsciousness of uncommon power, or unusual progress. It was less of a wonder than he considered it to be, it is true, for she never thought of comparing what she was now with her former self, much less with another. Indeed, she did not think of herself at all, but of her boy, and what she must learn in order to teach him to be and to do as suited her hope and her prayer. If any one's devotion could have flattered her into self-consciousness, it was Jemima's. Mr Bradshaw never dreamed that his daughter could feel herself inferior to the minister's *protegée*, but so it was; and no knight-errant of old could consider himself more honoured by his ladye's commands than did Jemima, if Ruth allowed her to do anything for her or for her boy. Ruth loved her heartily, even while she was rather annoyed at the open expressions Jemima used of admiration.

"Please, I really would rather not be told if people do think me pretty."

"But it was not merely beautiful; it was sweet-looking and good, Mrs Postlethwaite called you," replied Jemima.

"All the more I would rather not hear it. I may be pretty, but I know I am not good. Besides, I don't think we ought to hear what is said of us behind our backs."

Ruth spoke so gravely, that Jemima feared lest she was displeased.

"Dear Mrs Denbigh, I never will admire or praise you again. Only let me love you."

"And let me love you!" said Ruth, with a tender kiss.

Jemima would not have been allowed to come so frequently if Mr Bradshaw had not been possessed with the idea of patronising Ruth. If the latter had chosen, she might have gone dressed from head to foot in the presents which he wished to make her, but she refused them constantly; occasionally to Miss Benson's great annoyance. But if he could not load her with gifts, he could show his approbation by asking her to his house; and after some deliberation, she consented to accompany Mr and Miss Benson there. The house was square and massy-looking, with a great deal of drab-colour about the furniture. Mrs Bradshaw, in her lackadaisical, sweet-tempered way, seconded her husband in his desire of being kind to Ruth; and as she cherished privately a great taste for what was beautiful or interesting, as opposed to her husband's love of the purely useful, this taste of hers had rarely had so healthy and true a mode of gratification as when she watched Ruth's movements about the room, which seemed in its unobtrusiveness and poverty of colour to receive the requisite ornament of light and splendour from Ruth's presence. Mrs Bradshaw sighed, and wished she had a daughter as lovely, about whom to weave a romance; for castle-building, after the manner of the Minerva press, was the outlet by which she escaped from the pressure of her prosaic life, as Mr Bradshaw's wife. Her perception was only of external beauty, and she was not always alive to that, or she might have seen how a warm, affectionate, ardent nature, free from all envy or carking care of self, gave an unspeakable charm to her plain, bright-faced daughter Jemima, whose dark eyes kept challenging admiration for her friend. The first evening spent at Mr Bradshaw's passed like many succeeding visits there. There was tea, the equipage for which was as handsome and as ugly as money could purchase. Then the ladies produced their sewing, while Mr Bradshaw stood before the fire, and gave the assembled party the benefit of his opinions on many subjects. The opinions were as good and excellent as the opinions of any man can be who sees one side of a case very strongly, and almost ignores the other. They coincided in many points with those held by Mr Benson, but he once or twice interposed with a plea for those who might differ; and then he was heard by Mr Bradshaw with a kind of evident and indulgent pity, such as one feels for a child who unwittingly talks nonsense. By-and-by, Mrs

Bradshaw and Miss Benson fell into one *tête à tête*, and Ruth and Jemima into another. Two well-behaved but unnaturally quiet children were sent to bed early in the evening, in an authoritative voice, by their father, because one of them had spoken too loud while he was enlarging on an alteration in the tariff. Just before the supper-tray was brought in, a gentleman was announced whom Ruth had never previously seen, but who appeared well known to the rest of the party. It was Mr Farquhar, Mr Bradshaw's partner; he had been on the Continent for the last year, and had only recently returned. He seemed perfectly at home, but spoke little. He leaned back in his chair, screwed up his eyes, and watched everybody; yet there was nothing unpleasant or impertinent in his keenness of observation. Ruth wondered to hear him contradict Mr Bradshaw, and almost expected some rebuff; but Mr Bradshaw, if he did not yield the point, admitted, for the first time that evening, that it was possible something might be said on the other side. Mr Farquhar differed also from Mr Benson, but it was in a more respectful manner than Mr Bradshaw had done. For these reasons, although Mr Farquhar had never spoken to Ruth, she came away with the impression that he was a man to be respected, and perhaps liked.

Sally would have thought herself mightily aggrieved if, on their return, she had not heard some account of the evening. As soon as Miss Benson came in, the old servant began:

"Well, and who was there? and what did they give you for supper?"

"Only Mr Farquhar besides ourselves; and sandwiches, sponge-cake, and wine; there was no occasion for anything more," replied Miss Benson, who was tired and preparing to go upstairs.

"Mr Farquhar! Why they do say he's thinking of Miss Jemima!"

"Nonsense, Sally! why he's old enough to be her father!" said Miss Benson, half way up the first flight.

"There's no need for it to be called nonsense, though he may be ten year older," muttered Sally, retreating towards the kitchen. "Bradshaw's Betsy knows what she's about, and wouldn't have said it for nothing."

Ruth wondered a little about it. She loved Jemima well enough to be interested in what related to her; but, after thinking for a few minutes, she decided that such a marriage was, and would ever be, very unlikely.

CHAPTER XVIII - RUTH BECOMES A GOVERNESS IN MR BRADSHAW'S FAMILY

One afternoon, not long after this, Mr and Miss Benson set off to call upon a farmer, who attended the chapel, but lived at some distance from the town. They intended to stay to tea if they were invited, and Ruth and Sally were left to spend a long afternoon together. At first, Sally was busy in her kitchen, and Ruth employed herself in carrying her baby out into the garden. It was now nearly a year since she came to the Bensons'; it seemed like yesterday, and yet as if a lifetime had gone between. The flowers were budding now, that were all in bloom when she came down, on the first autumnal morning, into the sunny parlour. The yellow jessamine, that was then a tender plant, had now taken firm root in the soil, and was sending out strong shoots; the wall-flowers, which Miss Benson had sown on the wall a day or two after her arrival, were scenting the air with their fragrant flowers. Ruth knew every plant now; it seemed as though she had always lived here, and always known the inhabitants of the house. She heard Sally singing her accustomed song in the kitchen, a song she never varied over her afternoon's work. It began,

> As I was going to Derby, sir,
> Upon a market-day.

And if music is a necessary element in a song, perhaps I had better call it by some other name.

But the strange change was in Ruth herself. She was conscious of it though she could not define it, and did not dwell upon it. Life had become significant and full of duty to her. She delighted in the exercise of her intellectual powers, and liked the idea of the infinite amount of which she was ignorant; for it was a grand pleasure to learn—to crave, and be satisfied. She strove to forget what had gone before this last twelve months. She shuddered up from contemplating it; it was like a bad, unholy dream. And yet, there was a strange yearning kind of love for the father of the child whom she pressed to her heart, which came, and she could not bid it begone as sinful, it was so pure and natural, even when thinking of it, as in the sight of God. Little Leonard cooed to the flowers, and stretched after their bright colours; and Ruth laid him on the dry turf, and pelted him with the gay petals. He chinked and crowed with laughing delight, and clutched at her cap, and pulled it off. Her short rich curls were golden-brown in the slanting sunlight, and by their very shortness made her look more child-like. She hardly seemed as if she could be the mother of the noble babe over whom she knelt, now snatching kisses, now matching his cheek with rose-leaves. All at once, the bells of the old church struck the hour; and far away, high up in the air, began slowly to play the old tune of "Life let us cherish;" they had played it for years—for the life of man—and it always sounded fresh and strange and aërial. Ruth was still in a moment, she knew not why; and the tears came into her eyes as she listened. When it was ended, she kissed her baby, and bade God bless him.

Just then Sally came out, dressed for the evening, with a leisurely look about her. She had done her work, and she and Ruth were to drink tea together in the exquisitely clean kitchen; but while the kettle was boiling, she came out to enjoy the flowers. She gathered a piece of southern-wood, and stuffed it up her nose, by way of smelling it.

"Whatten you call this in your country?" asked she.

"Old-man," replied Ruth.

"We call it here lad's-love. It and peppermint-drops always remind me of going to church in the country. Here! I'll get you a black-currant leaf to put in the teapot. It gives it a flavour. We had bees once against this wall; but when missus died, we forgot to tell 'em, and put 'em in mourning, and, in course, they swarmed away without our knowing, and the next winter came a hard frost, and they died. Now, I dare say, the water will be boiling; and it's time for little master there to come in, for the dew is falling. See, all the daisies is shutting themselves up."

Sally was most gracious as a hostess. She quite put on her company manners to receive Ruth in the kitchen. They laid Leonard to sleep on the sofa in the parlour, that they might hear him the more easily, and then they sat quietly down to their sewing by the bright kitchen fire. Sally was, as usual, the talker; and, as usual, the subject was the family of whom for so many years she had formed a part.

"Aye! things was different when I was a girl," quoth she. "Eggs was thirty for a shilling, and butter only sixpence a pound. My wage when I came here was but three pound, and I did on it, and was always clean and tidy, which is more than many a lass can say now who gets her seven and eight pound a year; and tea was kept for an afternoon drink, and pudding was eaten afore meat in them days, and the upshot was, people paid their debts better; aye, aye! we'n gone backwards, and we thinken we'n gone forrards."

After shaking her head a little over the degeneracy of the times, Sally returned to a part of the subject on which she thought she had given Ruth a wrong idea.

"You'll not go for to think now that I've not more than three pound a year. I've a deal above that now. First of all, old missus gave me four pound, for she said I were worth it, and I thought in my heart that I were; so I took it without more ado; but after her death, Master Thurstan and Miss Faith took a fit of spending, and says they to me, one day as I carried tea in, 'Sally, we think your wages ought to be raised.' 'What matter what you think!' said I, pretty sharp, for I thought they'd ha' shown more respect to missus if they'd let things stand as they were in her time; and they'd gone and moved the sofa away from the wall to where it stands now, already that very day. So I speaks up sharp, and, says I, 'As long as I'm content, I think it's no business of yours to be meddling wi' me and my money matters.' 'But,' says Miss Faith (she's always the one to speak first if you'll notice, though it's master that comes in and clinches the matter with some reason she'd never ha' thought of—he were always a sensible lad), 'Sally, all the servants in the town have six pound and better, and you have as hard a place as any of 'em.' 'Did you ever hear me grumble about my work that you talk about it in that way? wait till I grumble,' says I, 'but don't meddle wi' me till then.' So I flung off in a huff; but in the course of the evening, Master Thurstan came in and sat down in the kitchen, and he's such winning ways he wiles one over to anything; and besides, a notion had come into my head—now, you'll not tell," said she, glancing round the room, and hitching her chair nearer to Ruth in a confidential manner; Ruth promised, and Sally went on:

"I thought I should like to be an heiress wi' money, and leave it all to Master and Miss Faith; and I thought if I'd six pound a year I could, maybe, get to be an heiress; all I was feared on was that some chap or other might marry me for my money, but I've managed to keep the fellows off; so I looks mim and grateful, and I thanks Master Thurstan for his offer, and I takes the wages; and what do you think I've done?" asked Sally, with an exultant air.

"What have you done?" asked Ruth.

"Why," replied Sally, slowly and emphatically, "I've saved thirty pound! but that's not it. I've getten a lawyer to make me a will; that's it, wench!" said she, slapping Ruth on the back.

"How did you manage it?" asked Ruth.

"Aye, that was it," said Sally; "I thowt about it many a night before I hit on the right way. I was afeard the money might be thrown into Chancery, if I didn't make it all safe, and yet I could na' ask Master Thurstan. At last and at length, John Jackson, the grocer, had a nephew come to stay a week with him, as was 'prentice to a lawyer in Liverpool; so now was my time, and here was my lawyer. Wait a minute! I could tell you my story better if I had my will in my hand; and I'll scomfish you if ever you go for to tell."

She held up her hand, and threatened Ruth as she left the kitchen to fetch the will.

When she came back, she brought a parcel tied up in a blue pocket-handkerchief; she sat down, squared her knees, untied the handkerchief, and displayed a small piece of parchment.

"Now, do you know what this is?" said she, holding it up. "It's parchment, and it's the right stuff to make wills on. People gets into Chancery if they don't make them o' this stuff, and I reckon Tom Jackson thowt he'd have a fresh job on it if he could get it into Chancery; for the rascal went and wrote it on a piece of paper at first, and came and read it me out loud off a piece of paper no better than what one writes letters upon. I were up to him; and, thinks I, Come, come, my lad, I'm not a fool, though you may think so; I know a paper will won't stand, but I'll let you run your rig. So I sits and I listens. And would you belie' me, he read it out as if it were as clear a business as your giving me that thimble—no more ado, though it were thirty pound! I could understand it mysel'—that were no law for me. I wanted summat to consider about, and for th' meaning to be wrapped up as I wrap up my best gown. So says I, 'Tom! it's not on parchment. I mun have it on parchment.' 'This 'ill do as well,' says he. 'We'll get it witnessed, and it will stand good.' Well! I liked the notion of having it witnessed, and for a while that soothed me; but after a bit, I felt I should like it done according to law, and not plain out as anybody might ha' done it; I mysel', if I could have written. So says I, 'Tom! I mun have it on parchment.' 'Parchment costs money,' says he, very grave. 'Oh, oh, my lad! are ye there?' thinks I. 'That's the reason I'm clipped of law.' So says I, 'Tom! I mun have it on parchment. I'll pay the money and welcome. It's thirty pound, and what I can lay to it. I'll make it safe. It shall be on parchment, and I'll tell thee what, lad! I'll gie ye sixpence for every good law-word you put in it, sounding like, and not to be caught up as a person runs. Your master had need to be ashamed of you as a 'prentice if you can't do a thing more tradesman-like than this!' Well! he laughed above a bit, but I were firm, and stood to it. So he made it out on parchment. Now, woman, try and read it!" said she, giving it to Ruth.

Ruth smiled, and began to read; Sally listening with rapt attention. When Ruth came to the word "testatrix," Sally stopped her.

"That was the first sixpence," said she. "I thowt he was going to fob me off again wi' plain language; but when that word came, I out wi' my sixpence, and gave it to him on the spot. Now go on."

Presently Ruth read, "accruing."

"That was the second sixpence. Four sixpences it were in all, besides six-and-eightpence as we bargained at first, and three-and-fourpence parchment. There! that's what I call a will; witnessed according to law, and all. Master Thurstan will be prettily taken in when I die, and he finds all his extra wage left back to him. But it will teach him it's not so easy as he thinks for, to make a woman give up her way."

The time was now drawing near when little Leonard might be weaned—the time appointed by all three for Ruth to endeavour to support herself in some way more or less independent of Mr and Miss Benson. This prospect dwelt much in all of their minds, and was in each shaded with some degree of perplexity; but they none of them spoke of it for fear of accelerating the event. If they had felt clear and determined as to the best course to be pursued, they were none of them deficient in courage to commence upon that course at once. Miss Benson would, perhaps, have objected the most to any alteration in their present daily mode of life; but that was because she had the habit of speaking out her thoughts as they arose, and she particularly disliked and dreaded change. Besides this, she had felt her heart open out, and warm towards the little helpless child, in a strong and powerful manner. Nature had intended her warm instincts to find vent in a mother's duties; her heart had yearned after children, and made her restless in her childless state, without her well knowing why; but now, the delight she experienced in tending, nursing, and contriving for the little boy—even contriving to the point of sacrificing many of her cherished whims—made her happy and satisfied and peaceful. It was more difficult to sacrifice her whims than her comforts; but all had been given up when and where required by the sweet lordly baby, who reigned paramount in his very helplessness.

From some cause or other, an exchange of ministers for one Sunday was to be effected with a neighbouring congregation, and Mr Benson went on a short absence from home. When he returned on Monday, he was met at the house-door by his sister, who had evidently been looking out for him for some time. She stepped out to greet him.

"Don't hurry yourself, Thurstan! all's well; only I wanted to tell you something. Don't fidget yourself—baby is quite well, bless him! It's only good news. Come into your room, and let me talk a little quietly with you."

She drew him into his study, which was near the outer door, and then she took off his coat, and put his carpet-bag in a corner, and wheeled a chair to the fire, before she would begin.

"Well, now! to think how often things fall out just as we want them, Thurstan! Have not you often wondered what was to be done with Ruth when the time came at which we promised her she should earn her living? I am sure you have, because I have so often thought about it myself. And yet I never dared to speak out my fear, because that seemed giving it a shape. And now Mr Bradshaw has put all to rights. He invited Mr Jackson to dinner yesterday, just as we were going into chapel; and then he turned to me and asked me if I would come to tea—straight from afternoon chapel, because Mrs Bradshaw wanted to speak to me. He made it very clear I was not to bring Ruth; and, indeed, she was only too happy to stay at home with baby. And so I went; and Mrs Bradshaw took me into her bedroom, and shut the doors, and said Mr Bradshaw had told her, that he did not like Jemima being so much confined with the younger ones while they were at their lessons, and that he wanted some one above a nursemaid to sit with them while their masters were there—some one who would see about their learning their lessons, and who would walk out with them; a sort of nursery governess, I think she meant, though she did not say so; and Mr Bradshaw (for, of course, I saw his thoughts and words constantly peeping out, though he had told her to speak to me) believed that our Ruth would be the very person. Now, Thurstan, don't look so surprised, as if she had never come into your head! I am sure I saw what Mrs Bradshaw was driving at, long before she came to the point; and I could scarcely keep from smiling, and saying, 'We'd jump at the proposal'—long before I ought to have known anything about it."

"Oh, I wonder what we ought to do!" said Mr Benson. "Or rather, I believe I see what we ought to do, if I durst but do it."

"Why, what ought we to do?" asked his sister, in surprise.

"I ought to go and tell Mr Bradshaw the whole story—"

"And get Ruth turned out of our house," said Miss Benson, indignantly.

"They can't make us do that," said her brother. "I do not think they would try."

"Yes, Mr Bradshaw would try; and he would blazon out poor Ruth's sin, and there would not be a chance for her left. I know him well, Thurstan; and why should he be told now, more than a year ago?"

"A year ago he did not want to put her in a situation of trust about his children."

"And you think she'll abuse that trust, do you? You've lived a twelvemonth in the house with Ruth, and the end of it is, you think she will do his children harm! Besides, who encouraged Jemima to come to the house so much to see Ruth? Did you not say it would do them both good to see something of each other?"

Mr Benson sat thinking.

"If you had not known Ruth as well as you do—if during her stay with us you had marked anything wrong, or forward, or deceitful, or immodest, I would say at once, 'Don't allow Mr Bradshaw to take her into his house;' but still I would say, 'Don't tell of her sin and her sorrow to so severe a man—so unpitiful a judge.' But here I ask you, Thurstan, can you, or I, or Sally (quick-eyed as she is), say, that in any one thing we have had true, just occasion to find fault with Ruth? I don't mean that she is perfect—she acts without thinking, her temper is sometimes warm and hasty; but have we any right to go and injure her prospects for life, by telling Mr Bradshaw all we know of her errors—only sixteen when she did so wrong, and never to escape from it all her many years to come—to have the despair which would arise from its being known, clutching her back into worse sin? What harm do you think she can do? What is the risk to which you think you are exposing Mr Bradshaw's children?" She paused, out of breath, her eyes glittering with tears of indignation, and impatient for an answer, that she might knock it to pieces.

"I do not see any danger that can arise," said he at length, and with slow difficulty, as if not fully convinced. "I have watched Ruth, and I believe she is pure and truthful; and the very sorrow and penitence she has felt—the very suffering she has gone through—has given her a thoughtful conscientiousness beyond her age."

"That and the care of her baby," said Miss Benson, secretly delighted at the tone of her brother's thoughts.

"Ah, Faith! that baby you so much dreaded once, is turning out a blessing, you see," said Thurstan, with a faint, quiet smile.

"Yes! any one might be thankful, and better too, for Leonard; but how could I tell that it would be like him?"

"But to return to Ruth and Mr Bradshaw. What did you say?"

"Oh! with my feelings, of course, I was only too glad to accept the proposal, and so I told Mrs Bradshaw then; and I afterwards repeated it to Mr Bradshaw, when he asked me if his wife had mentioned their plans. They would understand that I must consult you and Ruth, before it could be considered as finally settled."

"And have you named it to her?"

"Yes," answered Miss Benson, half afraid lest he should think she had been too precipitate.

"And what did she say?" asked he, after a little pause of grave silence.

"At first she seemed very glad, and fell into my mood of planning how it should all be managed; how Sally and I should take care of the baby the hours that she was away at Mr Bradshaw's; but by-and-by she became silent and thoughtful, and knelt down by me and hid her face in my lap, and shook a little as if she was crying; and then I heard her speak in a very low smothered voice, for her head was still bent down—quite hanging down, indeed, so that I could not see her face, so I stooped to listen, and I heard her say, 'Do you think I should be good enough to teach little girls, Miss Benson?' She said it so humbly and fearfully that all I thought of was how to cheer her, and I answered and asked her if she did not hope to be good enough to bring up her own darling to be a brave Christian man? And she lifted up her head, and I saw her eyes looking wild and wet and earnest, and she said, 'With God's help, that will I try to make my child.' And I said then, 'Ruth, as you strive and as you pray for your own child, so you must strive and pray to make Mary and Elizabeth good, if you are trusted with them.' And she said out quite clear, though her face was hidden from me once more, 'I will strive, and I will pray.' You would not have had any fears, Thurstan, if you could have heard and seen her last night."

"I have no fear," said he, decidedly. "Let the plan go on." After a minute, he added, "But I am glad it was so far arranged before I heard of it. My indecision about right and wrong—my perplexity as to how far we are to calculate consequences—grows upon me, I fear."

"You look tired and weary, dear. You should blame your body rather than your conscience at these times."

"A very dangerous doctrine."

The scroll of Fate was closed, and they could not foresee the Future; and yet, if they could have seen it, though they might have shrunk fearfully at first, they would have smiled and thanked God when all was done and said.

CHAPTER XIX - AFTER FIVE YEARS

The quiet days grew into weeks and months, and even years, without any event to startle the little circle into the consciousness of the lapse of time. One who had known them at the date of Ruth's becoming a governess in Mr Bradshaw's family, and had been absent until the time of which I am now going to tell you, would have noted some changes which had imperceptibly come over all; but he, too, would have thought, that the life which had brought so little of turmoil and vicissitude must have been calm and tranquil, and in accordance with the bygone activity of the town in which their existence passed away.

The alterations that he would have perceived were those caused by the natural progress of time. The Benson home was brightened into vividness by the presence of the little Leonard, now a noble boy of six, large and grand in limb and stature, and with a face of marked beauty and intelligence. Indeed, he might have been considered by many as too intelligent for his years; and often the living with old and thoughtful people gave him, beyond most children, the appearance of pondering over the mysteries which meet the young on the threshold of life, but which fade away as advancing years bring us more into contact with the practical and tangible—fade away and vanish, until it seems to require the agitation of some great storm of the soul before we can again realise spiritual things.

But, at times, Leonard seemed oppressed and bewildered, after listening intent, with grave and wondering eyes, to the conversation around him; at others, the bright animal life shone forth radiant, and no three-months' kitten—no foal, suddenly tossing up its heels by the side of its sedate dam, and careering around the pasture in pure mad enjoyment—no young creature of any kind, could show more merriment and gladness of heart.

"For ever in mischief," was Sally's account of him at such times; but it was not intentional mischief; and Sally herself would have been the first to scold any one else who had used the same words in reference to her darling. Indeed, she was once nearly giving warning, because she thought the boy was being ill-used. The occasion was this: Leonard had for some time shown a strange, odd disregard of truth; he invented stories, and told them with so grave a face, that unless there was some internal evidence of their incorrectness (such as describing a cow with a bonnet on), he was generally believed, and his statements, which were given with the full appearance of relating a real occurrence, had once or twice led to awkward results. All the three, whose hearts were pained by this apparent unconsciousness of the difference between truth and falsehood, were unaccustomed to children, or they would have recognised this as a stage through which most infants, who have lively imaginations, pass; and, accordingly, there was a consultation in Mr Benson's study one morning. Ruth was there, quiet, very pale, and with compressed lips, sick at heart as she heard Miss Benson's arguments for the necessity of whipping, in order to cure Leonard of his story-telling. Mr Benson looked unhappy and uncomfortable. Education was but a series of experiments to them all, and they all had a secret dread of spoiling the noble boy, who was the darling of their hearts. And, perhaps, this very intensity of love begot an impatient, unnecessary anxiety, and made them resolve on sterner measures than the parent of a large family (where love was more spread abroad) would have dared to use. At any rate, the vote for whipping carried the day; and even Ruth, trembling and cold, agreed that it must be done; only she asked, in a meek, sad voice, if she need be present (Mr Benson was to be the executioner—the scene, the study); and being instantly told that she had better not, she went slowly and languidly up to her room, and kneeling down, she closed her ears, and prayed.

Miss Benson, having carried her point, was very sorry for the child, and would have begged him off; but Mr Benson had listened more to her arguments than now to her pleadings, and only answered, "If it is right, it shall be done!" He went into the garden, and deliberately, almost as if he wished to gain time, chose and cut off a little switch from the laburnum-tree. Then he returned through the kitchen, and gravely taking the awed and wondering little fellow by the hand, he led him silently into the study, and placing him before him, began an admonition on the importance of truthfulness, meaning to conclude with what he believed to be the moral of all punishment: "As you cannot remember this of yourself, I must give you a little pain to make you remember it. I am very sorry it is necessary, and that you cannot recollect without my doing so."

But before he had reached this very proper and desirable conclusion, and while he was yet working his way, his heart aching with the terrified look of the child at the solemnly sad face and words of upbraiding, Sally burst in:

"And what may ye be going to do with that fine switch I saw ye gathering, Master Thurstan?" asked she, her eyes gleaming with anger at the answer she knew must come, if answer she had at all.

"Go away, Sally," said Mr Benson, annoyed at the fresh difficulty in his path.

"I'll not stir never a step till you give me that switch, as you've got for some mischief, I'll be bound."

"Sally! remember where it is said, 'He that spareth the rod, spoileth the child,'" said Mr Benson, austerely.

"Aye, I remember; and I remember a bit more than you want me to remember, I reckon. It were King Solomon as spoke them words, and it were King Solomon's son that were King Rehoboam, and no great shakes either. I can remember what is said on him, 2 Chronicles, xii. chapter, 14th verse: 'And he,' that's King Rehoboam, the lad that tasted the rod, 'did evil, because he prepared not his heart to seek the Lord.' I've not been reading my chapters every night for fifty year to be caught napping by a Dissenter, neither!" said she, triumphantly. "Come along, Leonard." She stretched out her hand to the child, thinking that she had conquered.

But Leonard did not stir. He looked wistfully at Mr Benson. "Come!" said she, impatiently. The boy's mouth quivered.

"If you want to whip me, uncle, you may do it. I don't much mind."

Put in this form, it was impossible to carry out his intentions; and so Mr Benson told the lad he might go—that he would speak to him another time. Leonard went away, more subdued in spirit than if he had been whipped. Sally lingered a moment. She stopped to add: "I think it's for them without sin to throw stones at a poor child, and cut up good laburnum-branches to whip him. I only do as my betters do, when I call Leonard's mother Mrs Denbigh." The moment she had said this she was sorry; it was an ungenerous advantage after the enemy had acknowledged himself defeated. Mr Benson dropped his head upon his hands, and hid his face, and sighed deeply.

Leonard flew in search of his mother, as in search of a refuge. If he had found her calm, he would have burst into a passion of crying after his agitation; as it was, he came upon her kneeling and sobbing, and he stood quite still. Then he threw his arms round her neck, and said: "Mamma! mamma! I will be good—I make a promise; I will speak true—I make a promise." And he kept his word.

Miss Benson piqued herself upon being less carried away by her love for this child than any one else in the house; she talked severely, and had capital theories; but her severity ended in talk, and her theories would not work. However, she read several books on education, knitting socks for Leonard all the while; and, upon the whole, I think, the hands were more usefully employed than the head, and the good honest heart better than either. She looked older than when we first knew her, but it was a ripe, kindly age that was coming over her. Her excellent practical sense, perhaps, made her a more masculine character than her brother. He was often so much perplexed by the problems of life, that he let the time for action go by; but she kept him in check by her clear, pithy talk, which brought back his wandering thoughts to the duty that lay straight before him, waiting for action; and then he remembered that it was the faithful part to "wait patiently upon God," and leave the ends in His hands, who alone knows why Evil exists in this world, and why it ever hovers on either side of Good. In this respect, Miss Benson had more faith than her brother—or so it seemed; for quick, resolute action in the next step of Life was all she required, while he deliberated and trembled, and often did wrong from his very deliberation, when his first instinct would have led him right.

But although decided and prompt as ever, Miss Benson was grown older since the summer afternoon when she dismounted from the coach at the foot of the long Welsh hill that led to Llan-dhu, where her brother awaited her to consult her about Ruth. Though her eye was as bright and straight-looking as ever, quick and brave in its glances, her hair had become almost snowy white; and it was on this point she consulted Sally, soon after the date of Leonard's last untruth. The two were arranging Miss Benson's room one morning, when, after dusting the looking-glass, she suddenly stopped in her operation, and after a close inspection of herself, startled Sally by this speech:

"Sally! I'm looking a great deal older than I used to do!"

Sally, who was busy dilating on the increased price of flour, considered this remark of Miss Benson's as strangely irrelevant to the matter in hand, and only noticed it by a

"To be sure! I suppose we all on us do. But two-and-fourpence a dozen is too much to make us pay for it."

Miss Benson went on with her inspection of herself, and Sally with her economical projects.

"Sally!" said Miss Benson, "my hair is nearly white. The last time I looked it was only pepper-and-salt. What must I do?"

"Do—why, what would the wench do?" asked Sally, contemptuously. "Ye're never going to be taken in, at your time of life, by hair-dyes and such gimcracks, as can only take in young girls whose wisdom-teeth are not cut."

"And who are not very likely to want them," said Miss Benson, quietly. "No! but you see, Sally, it's very awkward having such grey hair, and feeling so young. Do you know, Sally, I've as great a mind for dancing, when I hear a lively tune on the street-organs, as ever; and as great a mind to sing when I'm happy—to sing in my old way, Sally, you know."

"Aye, you had it from a girl," said Sally; "and many a time, when the door's been shut, I did not know if it was you in the parlour, or a big bumble-bee in the kitchen, as was making that drumbling noise. I heard you at it yesterday."

"But an old woman with grey hair ought not to have a fancy for dancing or singing," continued Miss Benson.

"Whatten nonsense are ye talking?" said Sally, roused to indignation. "Calling yoursel' an old woman when you're better than ten years younger than me! and many a girl has grey hair at five-and-twenty."

"But I'm more than five-and-twenty, Sally. I'm fifty-seven next May!"

"More shame for ye, then, not to know better than to talk of dyeing your hair. I cannot abide such vanities!"

"Oh, dear! Sally, when will you understand what I mean? I want to know how I am to keep remembering how old I am, so as to prevent myself from feeling so young? I was quite startled just now to see my hair in the glass, for I can generally tell if my cap is straight by feeling. I'll tell you what I'll do—I'll cut off a piece of my grey hair, and plait it together for a marker in my Bible!" Miss Benson expected applause for this bright idea, but Sally only made answer:

"You'll be taking to painting your cheeks next, now you've once thought of dyeing your hair." So Miss Benson plaited her grey hair in silence and quietness, Leonard holding one end of it while she wove it, and admiring the colour and texture all the time, with a sort of implied dissatisfaction at the auburn colour of his own curls, which was only half-comforted away by Miss Benson's information, that, if he lived long enough, his hair would be like hers.

Mr Benson, who had looked old and frail while he was yet but young, was now stationary as to the date of his appearance. But there was something more of nervous restlessness in his voice and ways than formerly; that was the only change six years had brought to him. And as for Sally, she chose to forget age and the passage of years altogether, and had as much work in her, to use her own expression, as she had at sixteen; nor was her appearance very explicit as to the flight of time. Fifty, sixty, or seventy, she might be—not more than the last, not less than the first—though her usual answer to any circuitous inquiry as to her age was now (what it had been for many years past), "I'm feared I shall never see thirty again."

Then as to the house. It was not one where the sitting-rooms are refurnished every two or three years; not now, even (since Ruth came to share their living) a place where, as an article grew shabby or worn, a new one was purchased. The furniture looked poor, and the carpets almost threadbare; but there was such a dainty spirit of cleanliness abroad, such exquisite neatness of repair, and altogether so bright and cheerful a look about the rooms—everything so above-board—no shifts to conceal poverty under flimsy ornament—that many a splendid drawing-room would give less pleasure to those who could see evidences of character in inanimate things. But whatever poverty there might be in the house, there was full luxuriance in the little square wall-encircled garden, on two sides of which the parlour and kitchen looked. The laburnum-tree, which when Ruth came was like a twig stuck into the ground, was now a golden glory in spring, and a pleasant shade in summer. The wild hop, that Mr Benson had brought home from one of his country rambles, and planted by the parlour-window, while Leonard was yet a baby in his mother's arms, was now a garland over the casement, hanging down long tendrils, that waved in the breezes, and threw pleasant shadows and traceries, like some Bacchanalian carving, on the parlour-walls, at "morn or dusky eve." The yellow rose had clambered up to the window of Mr Benson's bedroom, and its blossom-laden branches were supported by a jargonelle pear-tree rich in autumnal fruit.

But, perhaps, in Ruth herself there was the greatest external change; for of the change which had gone on in her heart, and mind, and soul, or if there had been any, neither she nor any one around her was conscious; but sometimes Miss Benson did say to Sally, "How very handsome Ruth is grown!" To which Sally made ungracious answer, "Yes! she's well enough. Beauty is deceitful, and favour a snare, and I'm thankful the Lord has spared me from such man-traps and spring-guns." But even Sally could not help secretly admiring Ruth. If her early brilliancy of colour was gone, a clear ivory skin, as smooth as satin, told of complete and perfect health, and was as lovely, if not so striking in effect, as the banished lilies and roses. Her hair had grown darker and deeper, in the shadow that lingered in its masses; her eyes, even if you could have guessed that they had shed bitter tears in their day, had a thoughtful, spiritual look about them, that made you wonder at their depth, and look—and look again. The increase of dignity in her face had been imparted to her form. I do not know if she had grown taller since the birth of her child, but she looked as if she had. And although she had lived in a very humble home, yet there was something about either it or her, or the people amongst whom she had been thrown during the last few years, which had so changed her, that whereas, six or seven years ago, you would have perceived that she was not altogether a lady by birth and education, yet now she might have been placed among the highest in the land, and would have been taken by the most critical judge for their equal, although ignorant of their conventional etiquette—an ignorance which she would have acknowledged in a simple child-like way, being unconscious of any false shame.

Her whole heart was in her boy. She often feared that she loved him too much—more than God Himself—yet she could not bear to pray to have her love for her child lessened. But she would kneel down by his little bed at night—at the deep, still midnight—with the stars that kept watch over Rizpah shining down upon her, and tell God what I have now told you, that she feared she loved her child too much, yet could not, would not, love him less; and speak to Him of her one treasure as she could speak to no earthly friend. And so, unconsciously, her love for her child led her up to love to God, to the All-knowing, who read her heart.

It might be superstition—I dare say it was—but, somehow, she never lay down to rest without saying, as she looked her last on her boy, "Thy will, not mine, be done;" and even while she trembled and shrank with infinite dread from sounding the depths of what that will might be, she felt as if her treasure were more secure to waken up rosy and bright in the morning, as one over whose slumbers God's holy angels had watched, for the very words which she had turned away in sick terror from realising the night before.

Her daily absence at her duties to the Bradshaw children only ministered to her love for Leonard. Everything does minister to love when its foundation lies deep in a true heart, and it was with an exquisite pang of delight that, after a moment of vague fear,

> (Oh, mercy! to myself I said,
> If Lucy should be dead!),

she saw her child's bright face of welcome as he threw open the door every afternoon on her return home. For it was his silently-appointed work to listen for her knock, and rush breathless to let her in. If he were in the garden, or upstairs among the treasures of the lumber-room, either Miss Benson, or her brother, or Sally, would fetch him to his happy little task; no one so sacred as he to the allotted duty. And the joyous meeting was not deadened by custom, to either mother or child.

Ruth gave the Bradshaws the highest satisfaction, as Mr Bradshaw often said both to her and to the Bensons; indeed, she rather winced under his pompous approbation. But his favourite recreation was patronising; and when Ruth saw how quietly and meekly Mr Benson submitted to gifts and praise, when an honest word of affection, or a tacit, implied acknowledgment of equality, would have been worth everything said and done, she tried to be more meek in spirit, and to recognise the good that undoubtedly existed in Mr Bradshaw. He was richer and more prosperous than ever;—a keen, far-seeing man of business, with an undisguised contempt for all who failed in the success which he had achieved. But it was not alone those who were less fortunate in obtaining wealth than himself that he visited with severity of judgment; every moral error or delinquency came under his unsparing comment. Stained by no vice himself, either in his own eyes or in that of any human being who cared to judge him, having nicely and wisely proportioned and adapted his means to his ends, he could afford to speak and act with a severity which was almost sanctimonious in its ostentation of thankfulness as to himself. Not a misfortune or a sin was brought to light but Mr Bradshaw could trace it to its cause in some former mode of action, which he had long ago foretold would lead to shame. If another's son turned out wild or bad, Mr Bradshaw had little sympathy; it might have been prevented by a stricter rule, or more religious life at home; young Richard Bradshaw was quiet and steady, and other fathers might have had sons like him if they had taken the same pains to enforce obedience. Richard was an only son, and yet Mr Bradshaw might venture to say, he had never had his own way in his life. Mrs Bradshaw was, he confessed (Mr Bradshaw did not dislike confessing his wife's errors), rather less firm than he should have liked with the girls; and with some people, he believed, Jemima was rather headstrong; but to his wishes she had always shown herself obedient. All children were obedient, if their parents were decided and authoritative; and every one would turn out well, if properly managed. If they did not prove good, they must take the consequences of their errors.

Mrs Bradshaw murmured faintly at her husband when his back was turned; but if his voice was heard, or his footsteps sounded in the distance, she was mute, and hurried her children into the attitude or action most pleasing to their father. Jemima, it is true, rebelled against this manner of proceeding, which savoured to her a little of deceit; but even she had not, as yet, overcome her awe of her father sufficiently to act independently of him, and according to her own sense of right—or rather, I should say, according to her own warm, passionate impulses. Before him the wilfulness which made her dark eyes blaze out at times was hushed and still; he had no idea of her self-tormenting, no notion of the almost southern jealousy which seemed to belong to her brunette complexion. Jemima was not pretty; the flatness and shortness of her face made her almost plain; yet most people looked twice at her expressive countenance, at the eyes which flamed or melted at every trifle, at the rich colour which came at every expressed emotion into her usually sallow face, at the faultless teeth which made her smile like a sunbeam. But then, again, when she thought she was not kindly treated, when a suspicion crossed her mind, or when she was angry with herself, her lips were tight-pressed together, her colour was wan and almost livid, and a stormy gloom clouded her eyes as with a film. But before her father her words were few, and he did not notice looks or tones.

Her brother Richard had been equally silent before his father in boyhood and early youth; but since he had gone to be clerk in a London house, preparatory to assuming his place as junior partner in Mr Bradshaw's business, he spoke more on his occasional visits at home. And very proper and highly moral was his conversation; set sentences of goodness, which were like the flowers that children stick in the ground, and that have not sprung upwards from roots—deep down in the hidden life and experience of the heart. He was as severe a judge as his father of other people's conduct, but you felt that Mr Bradshaw was sincere in his condemnation of all outward error and vice, and that he would try himself by the same laws as he tried others; somehow, Richard's words were frequently heard with a lurking distrust, and many shook their heads over the pattern son; but then it was those whose sons had gone astray, and been condemned, in no private or tender manner, by Mr Bradshaw, so it might be revenge in them. Still, Jemima felt that all was not right; her heart sympathised in the rebellion against his father's commands, which her brother had confessed to her in an unusual moment of confidence, but her uneasy conscience condemned the deceit which he had practised.

The brother and sister were sitting alone over a blazing Christmas fire, and Jemima held an old newspaper in her hand to shield her face from the hot light. They were talking of family events, when, during a pause, Jemima's eye caught the name of a great actor, who had lately given prominence and life to a character in one of Shakspeare's plays. The criticism in the paper was fine, and warmed Jemima's heart.

"How I should like to see a play!" exclaimed she.

"Should you?" said her brother, listlessly.

"Yes, to be sure! Just hear this!" and she began to read a fine passage of criticism.

"Those newspaper people can make an article out of anything," said he, yawning. "I've seen the man myself, and it was all very well, but nothing to make such a fuss about."

"You! you seen ——! Have you seen a play, Richard? Oh, why did you never tell me before? Tell me all about it! Why did you never name seeing —— in your letters?"

He half smiled, contemptuously enough. "Oh! at first it strikes one rather, but after a while one cares no more for the theatre than one does for mince-pies."

"Oh, I wish I might go to London!" said Jemima, impatiently. "I've a great mind to ask papa to let me go to the George Smiths', and then I could see ——. I would not think him like mince-pies."

"You must not do any such thing!" said Richard, now neither yawning nor contemptuous. "My father would never allow you to go to the theatre; and the George Smiths are such old fogeys—they would be sure to tell."

"How do you go, then? Does my father give you leave?"

"Oh! many things are right for men which are not for girls."

Jemima sat and pondered. Richard wished he had not been so confidential.

"You need not name it," said he, rather anxiously.

"Name what?" said she, startled, for her thoughts had gone far afield.

"Oh, name my going once or twice to the theatre!"

"No, I shan't name it!" said she. "No one here would care to hear it."

But it was with some little surprise, and almost with a feeling of disgust, that she heard Richard join with her father in condemning some one, and add to Mr Bradshaw's list of offences, by alleging that the young man was a playgoer. He did not think his sister heard his words.

Mary and Elizabeth were the two girls whom Ruth had in charge; they resembled Jemima more than their brother in character. The household rules were occasionally a little relaxed in their favour, for Mary, the elder, was nearly eight years younger than Jemima, and three intermediate children had died. They loved Ruth dearly, made a great pet of Leonard, and had many profound secrets together, most of which related to their wonders if Jemima and Mr Farquhar would ever be married. They watched their sister closely; and every day had some fresh confidence to make to each other, confirming or discouraging to their hopes.

Ruth rose early, and shared the household work with Sally and Miss Benson till seven; and then she helped Leonard to dress, and had a quiet time alone with him till prayers and breakfast. At nine she was to be at Mr Bradshaw's house. She sat in the room with Mary and Elizabeth during the Latin, the writing, and arithmetic lessons, which they received from masters; then she read, and walked with them, they clinging to her as to an elder sister; she dined with her pupils at the family lunch, and reached home by four. That happy home—those quiet days!

And so the peaceful days passed on into weeks, and months, and years, and Ruth and Leonard grew and strengthened into the riper beauty of their respective ages; while as yet no touch of decay had come on the quaint, primitive elders of the household.

CHAPTER XX - JEMIMA REFUSES TO BE MANAGED

It was no wonder that the lookers-on were perplexed as to the state of affairs between Jemima and Mr Farquhar, for they too were sorely puzzled themselves at the sort of relationship between them. Was it love, or was it not? that was the question in Mr Farquhar's mind. He hoped it was not; he believed it was not; and yet he felt as if it were. There was something preposterous, he thought, in a man nearly forty years of age being in love with a girl of twenty. He had gone on reasoning through all the days of his manhood on the idea of a staid, noble-minded wife, grave and sedate, the fit companion in experience of her husband. He had spoken with admiration of reticent characters, full of self-control and dignity; and he hoped—he trusted, that all this time he had not been allowing himself unconsciously to fall in love with a wild-hearted, impetuous girl, who knew nothing of life beyond her father's house, and who chafed under the strict discipline enforced there. For it was rather a suspicious symptom of the state of Mr Farquhar's affections, that he had discovered the silent rebellion which continued in Jemima's heart, unperceived by any of her own family, against the severe laws and opinions of her father. Mr Farquhar shared in these opinions; but in him they were modified, and took a milder form. Still, he approved of much that Mr Bradshaw did and said; and this made it all the more strange that he should wince so for Jemima, whenever anything took place which he instinctively knew that she would dislike. After an evening at Mr Bradshaw's, when Jemima had gone to the very verge of questioning or disputing some of her father's severe judgments, Mr Farquhar went home in a dissatisfied, restless state of mind, which he was almost afraid to analyse. He admired the inflexible integrity—and almost the pomp of principle—evinced by Mr Bradshaw on every occasion; he wondered how it was that Jemima could not see how grand a life might be, whose every action was shaped in obedience to some eternal law; instead of which, he was afraid she rebelled against every law, and was only guided by impulse. Mr Farquhar had been taught to dread impulses as promptings of the devil. Sometimes, if he tried to present her father's opinions before her in another form, so as to bring himself and her rather more into that state of agreement he longed for, she flashed out upon him with the indignation of difference that she dared not show to, or before, her father, as if she had some diviner instinct which taught her more truly than they knew, with all their experience; at least, in her first expressions there seemed something good and fine; but opposition made her angry and irritable, and the arguments which he was constantly provoking (whenever he was with her in her father's absence) frequently ended in some vehemence of expression on her part that offended Mr Farquhar, who did not see how she expiated her anger in tears and self-reproaches when alone in her chamber. Then he would lecture himself severely on the interest he could not help feeling in a wilful girl; he would determine not to interfere with her opinions in future, and yet, the very next time they differed, he strove to argue her into harmony with himself, in spite of all resolutions to the contrary.

Mr Bradshaw saw just enough of this interest which Jemima had excited in his partner's mind, to determine him in considering their future marriage as a settled affair. The fitness of the thing had long ago struck him; her father's partner—so the fortune he meant to give her might continue in the business; a man of such steadiness of character, and such a capital eye for a desirable speculation as Mr Farquhar—just the right age to unite the paternal with the conjugal affection, and consequently the very man for Jemima, who had something unruly in her, which might break out under a *régime* less wisely adjusted to the circumstances than was Mr Bradshaw's (in his own opinion)—a house ready-furnished, at a convenient distance from her home—no near relations on Mr Farquhar's side, who might be inclined to consider his residence as their own for an indefinite time, and so add to the household expenses—in short, what could be more suitable in every way? Mr Bradshaw respected the very self-restraint he thought he saw in Mr Farquhar's demeanour, attributing it to a wise desire to wait until trade should be rather more slack, and the man of business more at leisure to become the lover.

As for Jemima, at times she thought she almost hated Mr Farquhar.

"What business has he," she would think, "to lecture me? Often I can hardly bear it from papa, and I will not bear it from him. He treats me just like a child, and as if I should lose all my present opinions when I know more of the world. I am sure I should like never to know the world, if it was to make me think as he does, hard man that he is! I wonder what made him take Jem Brown on as gardener again, if he does not believe that above one criminal in a thousand is restored to goodness. I'll ask him, some day, if that was not acting on impulse rather than principle. Poor impulse! how you do get abused. But I will tell Mr Farquhar I will not let him interfere with me. If I do what papa bids me, no one has a right to notice whether I do it willingly or not."

So then she tried to defy Mr Farquhar, by doing and saying things that she knew he would disapprove. She went so far that he was seriously grieved, and did not even remonstrate and "lecture," and then she was disappointed and irritated; for, somehow, with all her indignation at interference, she liked to be lectured by him; not that she was aware of this liking of hers, but still it would have been more pleasant to be scolded than so quietly passed over. Her two little sisters, with their wide-awake eyes, had long ago put things together, and conjectured.

Every day they had some fresh mystery together, to be imparted in garden walks and whispered talks.

"Lizzie, did you see how the tears came into Mimie's eyes when Mr Farquhar looked so displeased when she said good people were always dull? I think she's in love." Mary said the last words with grave emphasis, and felt like an oracle of twelve years of age.

"I don't," said Lizzie. "I know I cry often enough when papa is cross, and I'm not in love with him."

"Yes! but you don't look as Mimie did."

"Don't call her Mimie—you know papa does not like it."

"Yes; but there are so many things papa does not like I can never remember them all. Never mind about that; but listen to something I've got to tell you, if you'll never, never tell."

"No, indeed I won't, Mary. What is it?"

"Not to Mrs Denbigh?"

"No, not even to Mrs Denbigh."

"Well, then, the other day—last Friday, Mimie—"

"Jemima!" interrupted the more conscientious Elizabeth.

"Jemima, if it must be so," jerked out Mary, "sent me to her desk for an envelope, and what do you think I saw?"

"What?" asked Elizabeth, expecting nothing less than a red-hot Valentine, signed Walter Farquhar, *pro* Bradshaw, Farquhar, and Co., in full.

"Why, a piece of paper, with dull-looking lines upon it, just like the scientific dialogues; and I remembered all about it. It was once when Mr Farquhar had been telling us that a bullet does not go in a straight line, but in a something curve, and he drew some lines on a piece of paper; and Mimie—"

"Jemima," put in Elizabeth.

"Well, well! she had treasured it up, and written in a corner, 'W. F., April 3rd.' Now, that's rather like love, is not it? For Jemima hates useful information just as much as I do, and that's saying a great deal; and yet she had kept this paper, and dated it."

"If that's all, I know Dick keeps a paper with Miss Benson's name written on it, and yet he's not in love with her; and perhaps Jemima may like Mr Farquhar, and he may not like her. It seems such a little while since her hair was turned up, and he has always been a grave middle-aged man ever since I can recollect; and then, have you never noticed how often he finds fault with her—almost lectures her?"

"To be sure," said Mary; "but he may be in love, for all that. Just think how often papa lectures mamma; and yet, of course, they're in love with each other."

"Well! we shall see," said Elizabeth.

Poor Jemima little thought of the four sharp eyes that watched her daily course while she sat alone, as she fancied, with her secret in her own room. For, in a passionate fit of grieving, at the impatient, hasty temper which had made her so seriously displease Mr Farquhar that he had gone away without remonstrance, without more leave-taking than a distant bow, she had begun to suspect that rather than not be noticed at all by him, rather than be an object of indifference to him—oh! far rather would she be an object of anger and upbraiding; and the thoughts that followed this confession to herself, stunned and bewildered her; and for once that they made her dizzy with hope, ten times they made her sick with fear. For an instant she planned to become and to be all he could wish her; to change her very nature for him. And then a great gush of pride came over her, and she set her teeth tight together, and determined that he should either love her as she was, or not at all. Unless he could take her with all her faults, she would not care for his regard; "love" was too noble a word to call such cold, calculating feeling as his must be, who went about with a pattern idea in his mind, trying to find a wife to match. Besides, there was something degrading, Jemima thought, in trying to alter herself to gain the love of any human creature. And yet, if he did not care for her, if this late indifference were to last, what a great shroud was drawn over life! Could she bear it?

From the agony she dared not look at, but which she was going to risk encountering, she was aroused by the presence of her mother.

"Jemima! your father wants to speak to you in the dining-room."

"What for?" asked the girl.

"Oh! he is fidgeted by something Mr Farquhar said to me, and which I repeated. I am sure I thought there was no harm in it, and your father always likes me to tell him what everybody says in his absence."

Jemima went with a heavy heart into her father's presence.

He was walking up and down the room, and did not see her at first.

"Oh, Jemima! is that you? Has your mother told you what I want to speak to you about?"

"No!" said Jemima. "Not exactly."

"She has been telling me what proves to me how very seriously you must have displeased and offended Mr Farquhar, before he could have expressed himself to her as he did, when he left the house. You know what he said?"

"No!" said Jemima, her heart swelling within her. "He has no right to say anything about me." She was desperate, or she durst not have said this before her father.

"No right!—what do you mean, Jemima?" said Mr Bradshaw, turning sharp round. "Surely you must know that I hope he may one day be your husband; that is to say, if you prove yourself worthy of the excellent training I have given you. I cannot suppose Mr Farquhar would take any undisciplined girl as a wife."

Jemima held tight by a chair near which she was standing. She did not speak; her father was pleased by her silence—it was the way in which he liked his projects to be received.

"But you cannot suppose," he continued, "that Mr Farquhar will consent to marry you—"

"Consent to marry me!" repeated Jemima, in a low tone of brooding indignation; were those the terms upon which her rich woman's heart was to be given, with a calm consent of acquiescent acceptance, but a little above resignation on the part of the receiver?

—"if you give way to a temper which, although you have never dared to show it to me, I am well aware exists, although I hoped the habits of self-examination I had instilled had done much to cure you of manifesting it. At one time, Richard promised to be the more headstrong of the two; now, I must desire you to take pattern by him. Yes," he continued, falling into his old train of thought, "it would be a most fortunate connexion for you in every way. I should have you under my own eye, and could still assist you in the formation of your character, and I should be at hand to strengthen and confirm your principles. Mr Farquhar's connexion with the firm would be convenient and agreeable to me in a pecuniary point of view. He—" Mr Bradshaw was going on in his enumeration of the advantages which he in particular, and Jemima in the second place, would derive from this marriage, when his daughter spoke, at first so low that he could not hear her, as he walked up and down the room with his creaking boots, and he had to stop to listen.

"Has Mr Farquhar ever spoken to you about it?" Jemima's cheek was flushed as she asked the question; she wished that she might have been the person to whom he had first addressed himself.

Mr Bradshaw answered,

"No, not spoken. It has been implied between us for some time. At least, I have been so aware of his intentions that I have made several allusions, in the course of business, to it, as a thing that might take place. He can hardly have misunderstood; he must have seen that I perceived his design, and approved of it," said Mr Bradshaw, rather doubtfully; as he remembered how very little, in fact, passed between him and his partner which could have reference to the subject, to any but a mind prepared to receive it. Perhaps Mr Farquhar had not really thought of it; but then again, that would imply that his own penetration had been mistaken, a thing not impossible certainly, but quite beyond the range of probability. So he reassured himself, and (as he thought) his daughter, by saying,

"The whole thing is so suitable—the advantages arising from the connexion are so obvious; besides which, I am quite aware, from many little speeches of Mr Farquhar's, that he contemplates marriage at no very distant time; and he seldom leaves Eccleston, and visits few families besides our own—certainly, none that can compare with ours in the advantages you have all received in moral and religious training." But then Mr Bradshaw was checked in his implied praises of himself (and only himself could be his martingale when he once set out on such a career) by a recollection that Jemima must not feel too secure, as she might become if he dwelt too much on the advantages of her being her father's daughter. Accordingly, he said: "But you must be aware, Jemima, that you do very little credit to the education I have given you, when you make such an impression as you must have done to-day, before Mr Farquhar could have said what he did of you!"

"What did he say?" asked Jemima, still in the low, husky tone of suppressed anger.

"Your mother says he remarked to her, 'What a pity it is, that Jemima cannot maintain her opinions without going into a passion; and what a pity it is, that her opinions are such as to sanction, rather than curb, these fits of rudeness and anger!'"

"Did he say that?" said Jemima, in a still lower tone, not questioning her father, but speaking rather to herself.

"I have no doubt he did," replied her father, gravely. "Your mother is in the habit of repeating accurately to me what takes place in my absence; besides which, the whole speech is not one of hers; she has not altered a word in the repetition, I am convinced. I have trained her to habits of accuracy very unusual in a woman."

At another time, Jemima might have been inclined to rebel against this system of carrying constant intelligence to headquarters, which she had long ago felt as an insurmountable obstacle to any free communication with her mother; but now, her father's means of acquiring knowledge faded into insignificance before the nature of the information he imparted. She stood quite still, grasping the chair-back, longing to be dismissed.

"I have said enough now, I hope, to make you behave in a becoming manner to Mr Farquhar; if your temper is too unruly to be always under your own control, at least have respect to my injunctions, and take some pains to curb it before him."

"May I go?" asked Jemima, chafing more and more.

"You may," said her father. When she left the room he gently rubbed his hands together, satisfied with the effect he had produced, and wondering how it was, that one so well brought up as his daughter could ever say or do anything to provoke such a remark from Mr Farquhar as that which he had heard repeated.

"Nothing can be more gentle and docile than she is when spoken to in the proper manner. I must give Farquhar a hint," said Mr Bradshaw to himself.

Jemima rushed upstairs, and locked herself into her room. She began pacing up and down at first, without shedding a tear; but then she suddenly stopped, and burst out crying with passionate indignation.

"So! I am to behave well, not because it is right—not because it is right—but to show off before Mr Farquhar. Oh, Mr Farquhar!" said she, suddenly changing to a sort of upbraiding tone of voice, "I did not think so of you an hour ago. I did not think you could choose a wife in that cold-hearted way, though you did profess to act by rule and line; but you think to have me, do you? because it is fitting and suitable, and you want to be married, and can't spare time for wooing" (she was lashing herself up by an exaggeration of all her father had said). "And how often I have thought you were too grand for me! but now I know better. Now I can believe that all you do is done from calculation; you are good because it adds to your business credit—you talk in that high strain about principle because it sounds well, and is respectable—and even these things are better than your cold way of looking out for a wife, just as you would do for a carpet, to add to your comforts, and settle you respectably. But I won't be that wife. You shall see something of me which shall make you not acquiesce so quietly in the arrangements of the firm." She cried too vehemently to go on thinking or speaking. Then she stopped, and said:

"Only an hour ago I was hoping—I don't know what I was hoping—but I thought—oh! how I was deceived!—I thought he had a true, deep, loving, manly heart, which God might let me win; but now I know he has only a calm, calculating head—"

If Jemima had been vehement and passionate before this conversation with her father, it was better than the sullen reserve she assumed now whenever Mr Farquhar came to the house. He felt it deeply; no reasoning with himself took off the pain he experienced. He tried to speak on the subjects she liked, in the manner she liked, until he despised himself for the unsuccessful efforts.

He stood between her and her father once or twice, in obvious inconsistency with his own previously expressed opinions; and Mr Bradshaw piqued himself upon his admirable management, in making Jemima feel that she owed his indulgence or forbearance to Mr Farquhar's interference; but Jemima—perverse, miserable Jemima—thought that she hated Mr Farquhar all the more. She respected her father inflexible, much more than her father pompously giving up to Mr Farquhar's subdued remonstrances on her behalf. Even Mr Bradshaw was perplexed, and shut himself up to consider how Jemima was to be made more fully to understand his wishes and her own interests. But there was nothing to take hold of as a ground for any further conversation with her. Her actions were so submissive that they were spiritless; she did all her father desired; she did it with a nervous quickness and haste, if she thought that otherwise Mr Farquhar would interfere in any way. She wished evidently to owe nothing to him. She had begun by leaving the room when he came in, after the conversation she had had with her father; but at Mr Bradshaw's first expression of his wish that she should remain, she remained—silent, indifferent, inattentive to all that was going on; at least there was this appearance of inattention. She would work away at her sewing as if she were to earn her livelihood by it; the light was gone out of her eyes as she lifted them up heavily before replying to any question, and the eyelids were often swollen with crying.

But in all this there was no positive fault. Mr Bradshaw could not have told her not to do this, or to do that, without her doing it; for she had become much more docile of late.

It was a wonderful proof of the influence Ruth had gained in the family, that Mr Bradshaw, after much deliberation, congratulated himself on the wise determination he had made of requesting her to speak to Jemima, and find out what feeling was at the bottom of all this change in her ways of going on.

He rang the bell.

"Is Mrs Denbigh here?" he inquired of the servant who answered it.

"Yes, sir; she is just come."

"Beg her to come to me in this room as soon as she can leave the young ladies."

Ruth came.

"Sit down, Mrs Denbigh; sit down. I want to have a little conversation with you; not about your pupils, they are going on well under your care, I am sure; and I often congratulate myself on the choice I made—I assure you I do. But now I want to speak to you about Jemima. She is very fond of you, and perhaps you could take some opportunity of observing to her—in short, of saying to her, that she is behaving very foolishly—in fact, disgusting Mr Farquhar (who was, I know, inclined to like her) by the sullen, sulky way she behaves in, when he is by."

He paused for the ready acquiescence he expected. But Ruth did not quite comprehend what was required of her, and disliked the glimpse she had gained of the task very much.

"I hardly understand, sir. You are displeased with Miss Bradshaw's manners to Mr Farquhar."

"Well, well! not quite that; I am displeased with her manners—they are sulky and abrupt, particularly when he is by—and I want you (of whom she is so fond) to speak to her about it."

"But I have never had the opportunity of noticing them. Whenever I have seen her, she has been most gentle and affectionate."

"But I think you do not hesitate to believe me, when I say that I have noticed the reverse," said Mr Bradshaw, drawing himself up.

"No, sir. I beg your pardon if I have expressed myself so badly as to seem to doubt. But am I to tell Miss Bradshaw that you have spoken of her faults to me?" asked Ruth, a little astonished, and shrinking more than ever from the proposed task.

"If you would allow me to finish what I have got to say, without interruption, I could then tell you what I do wish."

"I beg your pardon, sir," said Ruth, gently.

"I wish you to join our circle occasionally in an evening; Mrs Bradshaw shall send you an invitation when Mr Farquhar is likely to be here. Warned by me, and, consequently, with your observation quickened, you can hardly fail to notice instances of what I have pointed out; and then I will trust to your own good sense" (Mr Bradshaw bowed to her at this part of his sentence) "to find an opportunity to remonstrate with her."

Ruth was beginning to speak, but he waved his hand for another minute of silence.

"Only a minute, Mrs Denbigh. I am quite aware that, in requesting your presence occasionally in the evening, I shall be trespassing upon the time which is, in fact, your money; you may be assured that I shall not forget this little circumstance, and you can explain what I have said on this head to Benson and his sister."

"I am afraid I cannot do it," Ruth began; but while she was choosing words delicate enough to express her reluctance to act as he wished, he had almost bowed her out of the room; and thinking that she was modest in her estimate of her qualifications for remonstrating with his daughter, he added, blandly,

"No one so able, Mrs Denbigh. I have observed many qualities in you—observed when, perhaps, you have little thought it."

If he had observed Ruth that morning, he would have seen an absence of mind, and depression of spirits, not much to her credit as a teacher; for she could not bring herself to feel that she had any right to go into the family purposely to watch over and find fault with any one member of it. If she had seen anything wrong in Jemima, Ruth loved her so much that she would have told her of it in private; and with many doubts, how far she was the one to pull out the mote from any one's eye, even in the most tender manner;—she would have had to conquer reluctance before she could have done even this; but there was something undefinably repugnant to her in the manner of acting which Mr Bradshaw had proposed, and she determined not to accept the invitations which were to place her in so false a position.

But as she was leaving the house, after the end of the lessons, while she stood in the hall tying on her bonnet, and listening to the last small confidences of her two pupils, she saw Jemima coming in through the garden-door, and was struck by the change in her looks. The large eyes, so brilliant once, were dim and clouded; the complexion sallow and colourless; a lowering expression was on the dark brow, and the corners of her mouth drooped as with sorrowful thoughts. She looked up, and her eyes met Ruth's.

"Oh! you beautiful creature!" thought Jemima, "with your still, calm, heavenly face, what are you to know of earth's trials! You have lost your beloved by death—but that is a blessed sorrow; the sorrow I have pulls me down and down, and makes me despise and hate every one—not you, though." And, her face changing to a soft, tender look, she went up to Ruth, and kissed her fondly; as if it were a relief to be near some one on whose true, pure heart she relied. Ruth returned the caress; and even while she did so, she suddenly rescinded her resolution to keep clear of what Mr Bradshaw had desired her to do. On her way home she resolved, if she could, to find out what were Jemima's secret feelings; and if (as, from some previous knowledge, she suspected) they were morbid and exaggerated in any way, to try and help her right with all the wisdom which true love gives. It was time that some one should come to still the storm in Jemima's turbulent heart, which was daily and hourly knowing less and less of peace. The irritating difficulty was to separate the two characters, which at two different times she had attributed to Mr Farquhar—the old one, which she had formerly believed to be true, that he was a man acting up to a high standard of lofty principle, and acting up without a struggle (and this last had been the circumstance which had made her rebellious and irritable once); the new one, which her father had excited in her suspicious mind, that Mr Farquhar was cold and calculating in all he did, and that she was to be transferred by the former, and accepted by the

latter, as a sort of stock-in-trade—these were the two Mr Farquhars who clashed together in her mind. And in this state of irritation and prejudice, she could not bear the way in which he gave up his opinions to please her; that was not the way to win her; she liked him far better when he inflexibly and rigidly adhered to his idea of right and wrong, not even allowing any force to temptation, and hardly any grace to repentance, compared with that beauty of holiness which had never yielded to sin. He had been her idol in those days, as she found out now, however much at the time she had opposed him with violence.

As for Mr Farquhar, he was almost weary of himself; no reasoning, even no principle, seemed to have influence over him, for he saw that Jemima was not at all what he approved of in woman. He saw her uncurbed and passionate, affecting to despise the rules of life he held most sacred, and indifferent to, if not positively disliking him; and yet he loved her dearly. But he resolved to make a great effort of will, and break loose from these trammels of sense. And while he resolved, some old recollection would bring her up, hanging on his arm, in all the confidence of early girlhood, looking up in his face with her soft, dark eyes, and questioning him upon the mysterious subjects which had so much interest for both of them at that time, although they had become only matter for dissension in these later days.

It was also true, as Mr Bradshaw had said, Mr Farquhar wished to marry, and had not much choice in the small town of Eccleston. He never put this so plainly before himself, as a reason for choosing Jemima, as her father had done to her; but it was an unconscious motive all the same. However, now he had lectured himself into the resolution to make a pretty long absence from Eccleston, and see if, amongst his distant friends, there was no woman more in accordance with his ideal, who could put the naughty, wilful, plaguing Jemima Bradshaw out of his head, if he did not soon perceive some change in her for the better.

A few days after Ruth's conversation with Mr Bradshaw, the invitation she had been expecting, yet dreading, came. It was to her alone. Mr and Miss Benson were pleased at the compliment to her, and urged her acceptance of it. She wished that they had been included; she had not thought it right, or kind to Jemima, to tell them why she was going, and she feared now lest they should feel a little hurt that they were not asked too. But she need not have been afraid. They were glad and proud of the attention to her, and never thought of themselves.

"Ruthie, what gown shall you wear to-night? your dark grey one, I suppose?" asked Miss Benson.

"Yes, I suppose so. I never thought of it; but that is my best."

"Well; then, I shall quill up a ruff for you. You know I am a famous quiller of net."

Ruth came downstairs with a little flush on her cheeks when she was ready to go. She held her bonnet and shawl in her hand, for she knew Miss Benson and Sally would want to see her dressed.

"Is not mamma pretty?" asked Leonard, with a child's pride.

"She looks very nice and tidy," said Miss Benson, who had an idea that children should not talk or think about beauty.

"I think my ruff looks so nice," said Ruth, with gentle pleasure. And indeed it did look nice, and set off the pretty round throat most becomingly. Her hair, now grown long and thick, was smoothed as close to her head as its waving nature would allow, and plaited up in a great rich knot low down behind. The grey gown was as plain as plain could be.

"You should have light gloves, Ruth," said Miss Benson. She went upstairs, and brought down a delicate pair of Limerick ones, which had been long treasured up in a walnut-shell.

"They say them gloves is made of chickens'-skins," said Sally, examining them curiously. "I wonder how they set about skinning 'em."

"Here, Ruth," said Mr Benson, coming in from the garden, "here's a rose or two for you. I am sorry there are no more; I hoped I should have had my yellow rose out by this time, but the damask and the white are in a warmer corner, and have got the start."

Miss Benson and Leonard stood at the door, and watched her down the little passage-street till she was out of sight.

She had hardly touched the bell at Mr Bradshaw's door, when Mary and Elizabeth opened it with boisterous glee.

"We saw you coming—we've been watching for you—we want you to come round the garden before tea; papa is not come in yet. Do come!"

She went round the garden with a little girl clinging to each arm. It was full of sunshine and flowers, and this made the contrast between it and the usual large family room (which fronted the north-east, and therefore had no evening sun to light up its cold, drab furniture) more striking than usual. It looked very gloomy. There was the great dining-table, heavy and square; the range of chairs, straight and square; the work-boxes, useful and square; the colouring of walls, and carpet, and curtains, all of the coldest description; everything was handsome, and everything was ugly. Mrs Bradshaw was asleep in her easy-chair when they came in. Jemima had just put down her work, and, lost in thought, she leant her cheek on her hand. When she saw Ruth she brightened a little, and went to her and kissed her. Mrs Bradshaw jumped up at the sound of their entrance, and was wide awake in a moment.

"Oh! I thought your father was here," said she, evidently relieved to find that he had not come in and caught her sleeping.

"Thank you, Mrs Denbigh, for coming to us to-night," said she, in the quiet tone in which she generally spoke in her husband's absence. When he was there, a sort of constant terror of displeasing him made her voice sharp and nervous; the children knew that many a thing passed over by their mother when their father was away, was sure to be noticed by her when he was present; and noticed, too, in a cross and querulous manner, for she was so much afraid of the blame which on any occasion of their misbehaviour fell upon her. And yet she looked up to her husband with a reverence and regard, and a faithfulness of love, which his deci-

sion of character was likely to produce on a weak and anxious mind. He was a rest and a support to her, on whom she cast all her responsibilities; she was an obedient, unremonstrating wife to him; no stronger affection had ever brought her duty to him into conflict with any desire of her heart. She loved her children dearly, though they all perplexed her very frequently. Her son was her especial darling, because he very seldom brought her into any scrapes with his father; he was so cautious and prudent, and had the art of "keeping a calm sough" about any difficulty he might be in. With all her dutiful sense of the obligation, which her husband enforced upon her, to notice and tell him everything that was going wrong in the household, and especially among his children, Mrs Bradshaw, somehow, contrived to be honestly blind to a good deal that was not praiseworthy in Master Richard.

Mr Bradshaw came in before long, bringing with him Mr Farquhar. Jemima had been talking to Ruth with some interest before then; but, on seeing Mr Farquhar, she bent her head down over her work, went a little paler, and turned obstinately silent. Mr Bradshaw longed to command her to speak; but even he had a suspicion that what she might say, when so commanded, might be rather worse in its effect than her gloomy silence; so he held his peace, and a discontented, angry kind of peace it was. Mrs Bradshaw saw that something was wrong, but could not tell what; only she became every moment more trembling, and nervous, and irritable, and sent Mary and Elizabeth off on all sorts of contradictory errands to the servants, and made the tea twice as strong, and sweetened it twice as much as usual, in hopes of pacifying her husband with good things.

Mr Farquhar had gone for the last time, or so he thought. He had resolved (for the fifth time) that he would go and watch Jemima once more, and if her temper got the better of her, and she showed the old sullenness again, and gave the old proofs of indifference to his good opinion, he would give her up altogether, and seek a wife elsewhere. He sat watching her with folded arms, and in silence. Altogether they were a pleasant family party!

Jemima wanted to wind a skein of wool. Mr Farquhar saw it, and came to her, anxious to do her this little service. She turned away pettishly, and asked Ruth to hold it for her.

Ruth was hurt for Mr Farquhar, and looked sorrowfully at Jemima; but Jemima would not see her glance of upbraiding, as Ruth, hoping that she would relent, delayed a little to comply with her request. Mr Farquhar did; and went back to his seat to watch them both. He saw Jemima turbulent and stormy in look; he saw Ruth, to all appearance heavenly calm as the angels, or with only that little tinge of sorrow which her friend's behaviour had called forth. He saw the unusual beauty of her face and form, which he had never noticed before; and he saw Jemima, with all the brilliancy she once possessed in eyes and complexion, dimmed and faded. He watched Ruth, speaking low and soft to the little girls, who seemed to come to her in every difficulty; and he remarked her gentle firmness when their bedtime came, and they pleaded to stay up longer (their father was absent in his counting-house, or they would not have dared to do so). He liked Ruth's soft, dis-

tinct, unwavering "No! you must go. You must keep to what is right," far better than the good-natured yielding to entreaty he had formerly admired in Jemima. He was wandering off into this comparison, while Ruth, with delicate and unconscious tact, was trying to lead Jemima into some subject which should take her away from the thoughts, whatever they were, that made her so ungracious and rude.

Jemima was ashamed of herself before Ruth, in a way which she had never been before any one else. She valued Ruth's good opinion so highly, that she dreaded lest her friend should perceive her faults. She put a check upon herself—a check at first; but after a little time she had forgotten something of her trouble, and listened to Ruth, and questioned her about Leonard, and smiled at his little witticisms; and only the sighs, that would come up from the very force of habit, brought back the consciousness of her unhappiness. Before the end of the evening, Jemima had allowed herself to speak to Mr Farquhar in the old way—questioning, differing, disputing. She was recalled to the remembrance of that miserable conversation by the entrance of her father. After that she was silent. But he had seen her face more animated, and bright with a smile, as she spoke to Mr Farquhar; and although he regretted the loss of her complexion (for she was still very pale), he was highly pleased with the success of his project. He never doubted but that Ruth had given her some sort of private exhortation to behave better. He could not have understood the pretty art with which, by simply banishing unpleasant subjects, and throwing a wholesome natural sunlit tone over others, Ruth had insensibly drawn Jemima out of her gloom. He resolved to buy Mrs Denbigh a handsome silk gown the very next day. He did not believe she had a silk gown, poor creature! He had noticed that dark grey stuff, this long, long time, as her Sunday dress. He liked the colour; the silk one should be just the same tinge. Then he thought that it would, perhaps, be better to choose a lighter shade, one which might be noticed as different to the old gown. For he had no doubt she would like to have it remarked, and, perhaps, would not object to tell people, that it was a present from Mr Bradshaw—a token of his approbation. He smiled a little to himself as he thought of this additional source of pleasure to Ruth. She, in the meantime, was getting up to go home. While Jemima was lighting the bed-candle at the lamp, Ruth came round to bid good night. Mr Bradshaw could not allow her to remain till the morrow, uncertain whether he was satisfied or not.

"Good night, Mrs Denbigh," said he. "Good night. Thank you. I am obliged to you—I am exceedingly obliged to you."

He laid emphasis on these words, for he was pleased to see Mr Farquhar step forward to help Jemima in her little office.

Mr Farquhar offered to accompany Ruth home; but the streets that intervened between Mr Bradshaw's and the Chapel-house were so quiet that he desisted, when he learnt from Ruth's manner how much she disliked his proposal. Mr Bradshaw, too, instantly observed:

"Oh! Mrs Denbigh need not trouble you, Farquhar. I have servants at liberty at any moment to attend on her, if she wishes it."

In fact, he wanted to make hay while the sun shone, and to detain Mr Farquhar a little longer, now that Jemima was so gracious. She went upstairs with Ruth to help her to put on her things.

"Dear Jemima!" said Ruth, "I am so glad to see you looking better to-night! You quite frightened me this morning, you looked so ill."

"Did I?" replied Jemima. "Oh, Ruth! I have been so unhappy lately. I want you to come and put me to rights," she continued, half smiling. "You know I'm a sort of out-pupil of yours, though we are so nearly of an age. You ought to lecture me, and make me good."

"Should I, dear?" said Ruth. "I don't think I'm the one to do it."

"Oh, yes! you are—you've done me good to-night."

"Well, if I can do anything for you, tell me what it is?" asked Ruth, tenderly.

"Oh, not now—not now," replied Jemima. "I could not tell you here. It's a long story, and I don't know that I can tell you at all. Mamma might come up at any moment, and papa would be sure to ask what we had been talking about so long."

"Take your own time, love," said Ruth; "only remember, as far as I can, how glad I am to help you."

"You're too good, my darling!" said Jemima, fondly.

"Don't say so," replied Ruth, earnestly, almost as if she were afraid. "God knows I am not."

"Well! we're none of us too good," answered Jemima; "I know that. But you *are* very good. Nay, I won't call you so, if it makes you look so miserable. But come away downstairs."

With the fragrance of Ruth's sweetness lingering about her, Jemima was her best self during the next half-hour. Mr Bradshaw was more and more pleased, and raised the price of the silk, which he was going to give Ruth, sixpence a yard during the time. Mr Farquhar went home through the garden-way, happier than he had been this long time. He even caught himself humming the old refrain:

On revient, on revient toujours,
A ses premiers amours.

But as soon as he was aware of what he was doing, he cleared away the remnants of the song into a cough, which was sonorous, if not perfectly real.

CHAPTER XXI - MR FARQUHAR'S ATTENTIONS TRANSFERRED

The next morning, as Jemima and her mother sat at their work, it came into the head of the former to remember her father's very marked way of thanking Ruth the evening before.

"What a favourite Mrs Denbigh is with papa," said she. "I am sure I don't wonder at it. Did you notice, mamma, how he thanked her for coming here last night?"

"Yes, dear; but I don't think it was all—" Mrs Bradshaw stopped short. She was never certain if it was right or wrong to say anything.

"Not all what?" asked Jemima, when she saw her mother was not going to finish the sentence.

"Not all because Mrs Denbigh came to tea here," replied Mrs Bradshaw.

"Why, what else could he be thanking her for? What has she done?" asked Jemima, stimulated to curiosity by her mother's hesitating manner.

"I don't know if I ought to tell you," said Mrs Bradshaw.

"Oh, very well!" said Jemima, rather annoyed.

"Nay, dear! your papa never said I was not to tell; perhaps I may."

"Never mind! I don't want to hear," in a piqued tone.

There was silence for a little while. Jemima was trying to think of something else, but her thoughts would revert to the wonder what Mrs Denbigh could have done for her father.

"I think I may tell you, though," said Mrs Bradshaw, half questioning.

Jemima had the honour not to urge any confidence, but she was too curious to take any active step towards repressing it.

Mrs Bradshaw went on. "I think you deserve to know. It is partly your doing that papa is so pleased with Mrs Denbigh. He is going to buy her a silk gown this morning, and I think you ought to know why."

"Why?" asked Jemima.

"Because papa is so pleased to find that you mind what she says."

"I mind what she says! To be sure I do, and always did. But why should papa give her a gown for that? I think he ought to give it me rather," said Jemima, half laughing.

"I am sure he would, dear; he will give you one, I am certain, if you want one. He was so pleased to see you like your old self to Mr Farquhar last night. We neither of us could think what had come over you this last month; but now all seems right."

A dark cloud came over Jemima's face. She did not like this close observation and constant comment upon her manners; and what had Ruth to do with it?

"I am glad you were pleased," said she, very coldly. Then, after a pause, she added, "But you have not told me what Mrs Denbigh had to do with my good behaviour."

"Did not she speak to you about it?" asked Mrs Bradshaw, looking up.

"No; why should she? She has no right to criticise what I do. She would not be so impertinent," said Jemima, feeling very uncomfortable and suspicious.

"Yes, love! she would have had a right, for papa had desired her to do it."

"Papa desired her! What do you mean, mamma?"

"Oh, dear! I dare say I should not have told you," said Mrs Bradshaw, perceiving, from Jemima's tone of voice, that something had gone wrong. "Only you spoke as if it would be impertinent in Mrs Denbigh, and I am sure she would not do anything that was impertinent. You know, it would be but right for her to do what papa told her; and he said a great deal to her, the other day, about finding out why you were so cross, and bringing you right. And you are right now, dear!" said Mrs Bradshaw, soothingly, thinking that Jemima was annoyed (like a good child) at the recollection of how naughty she had been.

"Then papa is going to give Mrs Denbigh a gown because I was civil to Mr Farquhar last night?"

"Yes, dear!" said Mrs Bradshaw, more and more frightened at Jemima's angry manner of speaking—low-toned, but very indignant.

Jemima remembered, with smouldered anger, Ruth's pleading way of wiling her from her sullenness the night before. Management everywhere! but in this case it was peculiarly revolting; so much so, that she could hardly bear to believe that the seemingly-transparent Ruth had lent herself to it.

"Are you sure, mamma, that papa asked Mrs Denbigh to make me behave differently? It seems so strange."

"I am quite sure. He spoke to her last Friday morning in the study. I remember it was Friday, because Mrs Dean was working here."

Jemima remembered now that she had gone into the school-room on the Friday, and found her sisters lounging about, and wondering what papa could possibly want with Mrs Denbigh.

After this conversation, Jemima repulsed all Ruth's timid efforts to ascertain the cause of her disturbance, and to help her if she could. Ruth's tender, sympathising manner, as she saw Jemima daily looking more wretched, was distasteful to the latter in the highest degree. She could not say that Mrs Denbigh's conduct was positively wrong—it might even be quite right; but it was inexpressibly repugnant to her to think of her father consulting with a stranger (a week ago she almost considered Ruth as a sister) how to manage his daughter, so as to obtain the end he wished for; yes, even if that end was for her own good.

She was thankful and glad to see a brown paper parcel lying on the hall-table, with a note in Ruth's handwriting, addressed to her father. She *knew* what it was, the grey silk dress. That she was sure Ruth would never accept.

No one henceforward could induce Jemima to enter into conversation with Mr Farquhar. She suspected manœuvring in the simplest actions, and was miserable in this constant state of suspicion. She would not allow herself to like Mr Farquhar, even when he said things the most after her own heart. She heard him, one evening, talking with her father about the principles of trade. Her father stood out for the keenest, sharpest work, consistent with honesty; if he had not been her father she would, perhaps, have thought some of his sayings inconsistent with true Christian honesty. He was for driving hard bargains, exacting interest and payment of just bills to a day. That was (he said) the only way in which trade could be conducted. Once allow a margin of uncertainty, or where feelings, instead of maxims, were to be the guide, and all hope of there ever being any good men of business was ended.

"Suppose a delay of a month in requiring payment might save a man's credit—prevent his becoming a bankrupt?" put in Mr Farquhar.

"I would not give it him. I would let him have money to set up again as soon as he had passed the Bankruptcy Court; if he never passed, I might, in some cases, make him an allowance; but I would always keep my justice and my charity separate."

"And yet charity (in your sense of the word) degrades; justice, tempered with mercy and consideration, elevates."

"That is not justice—justice is certain and inflexible. No! Mr Farquhar, you must not allow any Quixotic notions to mingle with your conduct as a tradesman."

And so they went on; Jemima's face glowing with sympathy in all Mr Farquhar said; till once, on looking up suddenly with sparkling eyes, she saw a glance of her father's which told her, as plain as words could say, that he was watching the effect of Mr Farquhar's speeches upon his daughter. She was chilled thenceforward; she thought her father prolonged the argument, in order to call out those sentiments which he knew would most recommend his partner to his daughter. She would so fain have let herself love Mr Farquhar; but this constant manœuvring, in which she did not feel clear that he did not take a passive part, made her sick at heart. She even wished that they might not go through the form of pretending to try to gain her consent to the marriage, if it involved all this premeditated action and speech-making—such moving about of every one into their right places, like pieces at chess. She felt as if she would rather be bought openly, like an Oriental daughter, where no one is degraded in their own eyes by being parties to such a contract. The consequences of all this "admirable management" of Mr Bradshaw's would have been very unfortunate to Mr Farquhar (who was innocent of all connivance in any of the plots—indeed, would have been as much annoyed at them as Jemima, had he been aware of them), but that the impression made upon him by Ruth on the evening I have so lately described, was deepened by the contrast which her behaviour made to Miss Bradshaw's on one or two more recent occasions.

There was no use, he thought, in continuing attentions so evidently distasteful to Jemima. To her, a young girl hardly out of the schoolroom, he probably appeared like an old man; and he might even lose the friendship with which she used to regard him, and which was, and ever would be, very dear to him, if he persevered in trying to be considered as a lover. He should always feel affectionately towards her; her very faults gave her an interest in his eyes, for which he had blamed himself most conscientiously and most uselessly when he was looking upon her as his future wife, but which the said conscience would learn to approve of when she sank down to the place of a young friend, over whom he might exercise a good and salutary interest. Mrs Denbigh, if not many months older in years, had known sorrow and cares so early that she was much older in character. Besides, her shy reserve, and her quiet daily walk within the lines of duty, were much in accordance with Mr Farquhar's notion of what a wife should be. Still, it was a wrench to take his affections away from Jemima. If she had not helped him to do so by every means in her power, he could never have accomplished it.

Yes! by every means in her power had Jemima alienated her lover, her beloved—for so he was in fact. And now her quick-sighted eyes saw he was gone for ever—past recall; for did not her jealous, sore heart feel, even before he himself was conscious of the fact, that he was drawn towards sweet, lovely, composed, and dignified Ruth—one who always thought before she spoke (as Mr Farquhar used to bid Jemima do)—who never was tempted by sudden impulse, but walked the world calm and self-governed. What now availed Jemima's reproaches, as she remembered the days when he had watched her with earnest, attentive eyes, as he now watched Ruth; and the times since, when, led astray by her morbid fancy, she had turned away from all his advances!

"It was only in March—last March, he called me 'dear Jemima.' Ah, don't I remember it well? The pretty nosegay of green-house flowers that he gave me in exchange for the wild daffodils—and how he seemed to care for the flowers I gave him—and how he looked at me, and thanked me—that is all gone and over now."

Her sisters came in bright and glowing.

"Oh, Jemima, how nice and cool you are, sitting in this shady room!" (She had felt it even chilly.) "We have been such a long walk! We are so tired. It is so hot."

"Why did you go, then?" said she.

"Oh! we wanted to go. We would not have stayed at home on any account. It has been so pleasant," said Mary.

"We've been to Scaurside Wood, to gather wild strawberries," said Elizabeth. "Such a quantity! We've left a whole basketful in the dairy. Mr Farquhar says he'll teach us how to dress them in the way he learnt in Germany, if we can get him some hock. Do you think papa will let us have some?"

"Was Mr Farquhar with you?" asked Jemima, a dull light coming into her eyes.

"Yes; we told him this morning that mamma wanted us to take some old linen to the lame man at Scaurside Farm, and that we meant to coax Mrs Denbigh to let us go into the wood and gather strawberries," said Elizabeth.

"I thought he would make some excuse and come," said the quick-witted Mary, as eager and thoughtless an observer of one love-affair as of another, and quite forgetting that, not many weeks ago, she had fancied an attachment between him and Jemima.

"Did you? I did not," replied Elizabeth. "At least I never thought about it. I was quite startled when I heard his horse's feet behind us on the road."

"He said he was going to the farm, and could take our basket. Was not it kind of him?" Jemima did not answer, so Mary continued:

"You know it's a great pull up to the farm, and we were so hot already. The road was quite white and baked; it hurt my eyes terribly. I was so glad when Mrs Denbigh said we might turn into the wood. The light was quite green there, the branches are so thick overhead."

"And there are whole beds of wild strawberries," said Elizabeth, taking up the tale now Mary was out of breath. Mary fanned herself with her bonnet, while Elizabeth went on:

"You know where the grey rock crops out, don't you, Jemima? Well, there was a complete carpet of strawberry runners. So pretty! And we could hardly step without treading the little bright scarlet berries under foot."

"We did so wish for Leonard," put in Mary.

"Yes! but Mrs Denbigh gathered a great many for him. And Mr Farquhar gave her all his."

"I thought you said he had gone on to Dawson's farm," said Jemima.

"Oh, yes! he just went up there; and then he left his horse there, like a wise man, and came to us in the pretty, cool, green wood. Oh, Jemima, it was so pretty—little flecks of light coming down here and there through the leaves, and quivering on the ground. You must go with us to-morrow."

"Yes," said Mary, "we're going again to-morrow. We could not gather nearly all the strawberries."

"And Leonard is to go too, to-morrow."

"Yes! we thought of such a capital plan. That's to say, Mr Farquhar thought of it—we wanted to carry Leonard up the hill in a king's cushion, but Mrs Denbigh would not hear of it."

"She said it would tire us so; and yet she wanted him to gather strawberries!"

"And so," interrupted Mary, for by this time the two girls were almost speaking together, "Mr Farquhar is to bring him up before him on his horse."

"You'll go with us, won't you, dear Jemima?" asked Elizabeth; "it will be at—"

"No! I can't go!" said Jemima, abruptly. "Don't ask me—I can't."

The little girls were hushed into silence by her manner; for whatever she might be to those above her in age and position, to those below her Jemima was almost invariably gentle. She felt that they were wondering at her.

"Go upstairs and take off your things. You know papa does not like you to come into this room in the shoes in which you have been out."

She was glad to cut her sisters short in the details which they were so mercilessly inflicting—details which she must harden herself to, before she could hear them quietly and unmoved. She saw that she had lost her place as the first object in Mr Farquhar's eyes—a position she had hardly cared for while she was secure in the enjoyment of it; but the charm of it now was redoubled, in her acute sense of how she had forfeited it by her own doing, and her own fault. For if he were the cold, calculating man her father had believed him to be, and had represented him as being to her, would he care for a portionless widow in humble circumstances like Mrs Denbigh; no money, no connexion, encumbered with her boy? The very action which proved Mr Farquhar to be lost to Jemima reinstated him on his throne in her fancy. And she must go on in hushed quietness, quivering with every fresh token of his preference for another! That other, too, one so infinitely more worthy of him than herself; so that she could not have even the poor comfort of thinking that he had no discrimination, and was throwing himself away on a common or worthless person. Ruth was beautiful, gentle, good, and conscientious. The hot colour flushed up into Jemima's sallow face as she became aware that, even while she acknowledged these excellences on Mrs Denbigh's part, she hated her. The recollection of her marble face wearied her even to sickness; the tones of her low voice were irritating from their very softness. Her goodness, undoubted as it was, was more distasteful than many faults which had more savour of human struggle in them.

"What was this terrible demon in her heart?" asked Jemima's better angel. "Was she, indeed, given up to possession? Was not this the old stinging hatred which had prompted so many crimes? The hatred of all sweet virtues which might win the love denied to us? The old anger that wrought in the elder brother's heart, till it ended in the murder of the gentle Abel, while yet the world was young?"

"Oh, God! help me! I did not know I was so wicked," cried Jemima aloud in her agony. It had been a terrible glimpse into the dark, lurid gulf—the capability for evil, in her heart. She wrestled with the demon, but he would not depart; it was to be a struggle whether or not she was to be given up to him, in this her time of sore temptation.

All the next day long she sat and pictured the happy strawberry gathering going on, even then, in pleasant Scaurside Wood. Every touch of fancy which could heighten her idea of their enjoyment, and of Mr Farquhar's attention to the blushing, conscious Ruth—every such touch which would add a pang to her self-reproach and keen jealousy, was added by her imagination. She got up and walked about, to try and stop her over-busy fancy by bodily exercise. But she had eaten little all day, and was weak and faint in the intense heat of the sunny garden. Even the long grass-walk under the filbert-hedge, was parched and dry in the glowing August sun. Yet her sisters found her there when they returned, walking quickly up and down, as if to warm herself on some winter's day. They were very weary; and not half so communicative as on the day before, now that Jemima was craving for every detail to add to her agony.

"Yes! Leonard came up before Mr Farquhar. Oh! how hot it is, Jemima; do sit down, and I'll tell you about it, but I can't if you keep walking so!"

"I can't sit still to-day," said Jemima, springing up from the turf as soon as she had sat down. "Tell me! I can hear you while I walk about."

"Oh! but I can't shout; I can hardly speak I am so tired. Mr Farquhar brought Leonard—"

"You've told me that before," said Jemima, sharply.

"Well! I don't know what else to tell. Somebody had been since yesterday, and gathered nearly all the strawberries off the grey rock. Jemima! Jemima!" said Elizabeth, faintly, "I am so dizzy—I think I am ill."

The next minute the tired girl lay swooning on the grass. It was an outlet for Jemima's fierce energy. With a strength she had never again, and never had known before, she lifted up her fainting sister, and bidding Mary run and clear the way, she carried her in through the open garden-door, up the wide old-fashioned stairs, and laid her on the bed in her own room, where the breeze from the window came softly and pleasantly through the green shade of the vine-leaves and jessamine.

"Give me the water. Run for mamma, Mary," said Jemima, as she saw that the fainting-fit did not yield to the usual remedy of a horizontal position and the water sprinkling.

"Dear! dear Lizzie!" said Jemima, kissing the pale, unconscious face. "I think you loved me, darling."

The long walk on the hot day had been too much for the delicate Elizabeth, who was fast outgrowing her strength. It was many days before she regained any portion of her spirit and vigour. After that fainting-fit, she lay listless and weary, without appetite or interest, through the long sunny autumn weather, on the bed or on the couch in Jemima's room, whither she had been carried at first. It was a comfort to Mrs Bradshaw to be able at once to discover what it was that had knocked up Elizabeth; she did not rest easily until she had settled upon a cause for every ailment or illness in the family. It was a stern consolation to Mr Bradshaw, during his time of anxiety respecting his daughter, to be able to blame somebody. He could not, like his wife, have taken comfort from an inanimate fact; he wanted the satisfaction of feeling that some one had been in fault, or else this never could have happened. Poor Ruth did not need his implied reproaches. When she saw her gentle Elizabeth lying feeble and languid, her heart blamed her for thoughtlessness so severely as to make her take all Mr Bradshaw's words and hints as too light censure for the careless way in which, to please her own child, she had allowed her two pupils to fatigue themselves with such long walks. She begged hard to take her share of nursing. Every spare moment she went to Mr Bradshaw's, and asked, with earnest humility, to be allowed to pass them with

Elizabeth; and, as it was often a relief to have her assistance, Mrs Bradshaw received these entreaties very kindly, and desired her to go upstairs, where Elizabeth's pale countenance brightened when she saw her, but where Jemima sat in silent annoyance that her own room was now become open ground for one, whom her heart rose up against, to enter in and be welcomed. Whether it was that Ruth, who was not an inmate of the house, brought with her a fresher air, more change of thought to the invalid, I do not know, but Elizabeth always gave her a peculiarly tender greeting; and if she had sunk down into languid fatigue, in spite of all Jemima's endeavours to interest her, she roused up into animation when Ruth came in with a flower, a book, or a brown and ruddy pear, sending out the warm fragrance it retained from the sunny garden-wall at Chapel-house.

The jealous dislike which Jemima was allowing to grow up in her heart against Ruth was, as she thought, never shown in word or deed. She was cold in manner, because she could not be hypocritical; but her words were polite and kind in purport; and she took pains to make her actions the same as formerly. But rule and line may measure out the figure of a man; it is the soul that gives it life; and there was no soul, no inner meaning, breathing out in Jemima's actions. Ruth felt the change acutely. She suffered from it some time before she ventured to ask what had occasioned it. But, one day, she took Miss Bradshaw by surprise, when they were alone together for a few minutes, by asking her if she had vexed her in any way, she was so changed? It is sad when friendship has cooled so far as to render such a question necessary. Jemima went rather paler than usual, and then made answer:

"Changed! How do you mean? How am I changed? What do I say or do different from what I used to do?"

But the tone was so constrained and cold, that Ruth's heart sank within her. She knew now, as well as words could have told her, that not only had the old feeling of love passed away from Jemima, but that it had gone unregretted, and no attempt had been made to recall it. Love was very precious to Ruth now, as of old time. It was one of the faults of her nature to be ready to make any sacrifices for those who loved her, and to value affection almost above its price. She had yet to learn the lesson, that it is more blessed to love than to be beloved; and lonely as the impressible years of her youth had been—without parents, without brother or sister—it was, perhaps, no wonder that she clung tenaciously to every symptom of regard, and could not relinquish the love of any one without a pang.

The doctor who was called in to Elizabeth prescribed sea-air as the best means of recruiting her strength. Mr Bradshaw, who liked to spend money ostentatiously, went down straight to Abermouth, and engaged a house for the remainder of the autumn; for, as he told the medical man, money was no object to him in comparison with his children's health; and the doctor cared too little about the mode in which his remedy was administered, to tell Mr Bradshaw that lodgings would have done as well, or better, than the complete house he had seen fit to take. For it was now necessary to engage servants, and take much trouble, which might have been obviated, and Elizabeth's removal effected more quietly and speedily, if she had gone into lodgings. As it was, she was weary of hearing all the planning and talking, and deciding and un-deciding, and re-deciding, before it was possible for her to go. Her only comfort was in the thought that dear Mrs Denbigh was to go with her.

It had not been entirely by way of pompously spending his money that Mr Bradshaw had engaged this seaside house. He was glad to get his little girls and their governess out of the way; for a busy time was impending, when he should want his head clear for electioneering purposes, and his house clear for electioneering hospitality. He was the mover of a project for bringing forward a man on the Liberal and Dissenting interest, to contest the election with the old Tory member, who had on several successive occasions walked over the course, as he and his family owned half the town, and votes and rent were paid alike to the landlord.

Kings of Eccleston had Mr Cranworth and his ancestors been this many a long year; their right was so little disputed that they never thought of acknowledging the allegiance so readily paid to them. The old feudal feeling between land-owner and tenant did not quake prophetically at the introduction of manufactures; the Cranworth family ignored the growing power of the manufacturers, more especially as the principal person engaged in the trade was a Dissenter. But notwithstanding this lack of patronage from the one great family in the neighbourhood, the business flourished, increased, and spread wide; and the Dissenting head thereof looked around, about the time of which I speak, and felt himself powerful enough to defy the great Cranworth interest even in their hereditary stronghold, and, by so doing, avenge the slights of many years—slights which rankled in Mr Bradshaw's mind as much as if he did not go to chapel twice every Sunday, and pay the largest pew-rent of any member of Mr Benson's congregation.

Accordingly, Mr Bradshaw had applied to one of the Liberal parliamentary agents in London—a man whose only principle was to do wrong on the Liberal side; he would not act, right or wrong, for a Tory, but for a Whig the latitude of his conscience had never yet been discovered. It was possible Mr Bradshaw was not aware of the character of this agent; at any rate, he knew he was the man for his purpose, which was to hear of some one who would come forward as a candidate for the representation of Eccleston on the Dissenting interest.

"There are in round numbers about six hundred voters," said he; "two hundred are decidedly in the Cranworth interest—dare not offend Mr Cranworth, poor souls! Two hundred more we may calculate upon as pretty certain—factory hands, or people connected with our trade in some way or another—who are indignant at the stubborn way in which Cranworth has contested the right of water; two hundred are doubtful."

"Don't much care either way," said the parliamentary agent. "Of course, we must make them care."

Mr Bradshaw rather shrunk from the knowing look with which this was said. He hoped that Mr Pilson did not mean to allude to bribery; but he did not express this hope, because he thought it would deter the agent from using this means, and it was possible it might prove to be the only way. And if he (Mr Bradshaw) once embarked on such an enterprise, there must be no failure. By some expedient or another, success must be certain, or he could have nothing to do with it.

The parliamentary agent was well accustomed to deal with all kinds and shades of scruples. He was most at home with men who had none; but still he could allow for human weakness; and he perfectly understood Mr Bradshaw.

"I have a notion I know of a man who will just suit your purpose. Plenty of money—does not know what to do with it, in fact—tired of yachting, travelling; wants something new. I heard, through some of the means of intelligence I employ, that not very long ago he was wishing for a seat in Parliament."

"A Liberal?" said Mr Bradshaw.

"Decidedly. Belongs to a family who were in the Long Parliament in their day."

Mr Bradshaw rubbed his hands.

"Dissenter?" asked he.

"No, no! Not so far as that. But very lax Church."

"What is his name?" asked Mr Bradshaw, eagerly.

"Excuse me. Until I am certain that he would like to come forward for Eccleston, I think I had better not mention his name."

The anonymous gentleman did like to come forward, and his name proved to be Donne. He and Mr Bradshaw had been in correspondence during all the time of Mr Ralph Cranworth's illness; and when he died, everything was arranged ready for a start, even before the Cranworths had determined who should keep the seat warm till the eldest son came of age, for the father was already member for the county. Mr Donne was to come down to canvass in person, and was to take up his abode at Mr Bradshaw's; and therefore it was that the seaside house, within twenty miles' distance of Eccleston, was found to be so convenient as an infirmary and nursery for those members of his family who were likely to be useless, if not positive encumbrances, during the forthcoming election.

CHAPTER XXII - THE LIBERAL CANDIDATE AND HIS PRECURSOR

Jemima did not know whether she wished to go to Abermouth or not. She longed for change. She wearied of the sights and sounds of home. But yet she could not bear to leave the neighbourhood of Mr Farquhar; especially as, if she went to Abermouth, Ruth would in all probability be left to take her holiday at home.

When Mr Bradshaw decided that she was to go, Ruth tried to feel glad that he gave her the means of repairing her fault towards Elizabeth; and she resolved to watch over the two girls most faithfully and carefully, and to do all in her power to restore the invalid to health. But a tremor came over her whenever she thought of leaving Leonard; she had never quitted him for a day, and it seemed to her as if her brooding, constant care was his natural and necessary shelter from all evils—from very death itself. She would not go to sleep at nights, in order to enjoy the blessed consciousness of having him near her; when she was away from him teaching her pupils, she kept trying to remember his face, and print it deep on her heart, against the time when days and days would elapse without her seeing that little darling countenance. Miss Benson would wonder to her brother that Mr Bradshaw did not propose that Leonard should accompany his mother; he only begged her not to put such an idea into Ruth's head, as he was sure Mr Bradshaw had no thoughts of doing any such thing, yet to Ruth it might be a hope, and then a disappointment. His sister scolded him for being so cold-hearted; but he was full of sympathy, although he did not express it, and made some quiet little sacrifices in order to set himself at liberty to take Leonard a long walking expedition on the day when his mother left Eccleston.

Ruth cried until she could cry no longer, and felt very much ashamed of herself as she saw the grave and wondering looks of her pupils, whose only feeling on leaving home was delight at the idea of Abermouth, and into whose minds the possibility of death to any of their beloved ones never entered. Ruth dried her eyes, and spoke cheerfully as soon as she caught the perplexed expression of their faces; and by the time they arrived at Abermouth, she was as much delighted with all the new scenery as they were, and found it hard work to resist their entreaties to go rambling out on the seashore at once; but Elizabeth had undergone more fatigue that day than she had had before for many weeks, and Ruth was determined to be prudent.

Meanwhile, the Bradshaws' house at Eccleston was being rapidly adapted for electioneering hospitality. The partition-wall between the unused drawing-room and the school-room was broken down, in order to admit of folding doors; the "ingenious" upholsterer of the town (and what town does not boast of the upholsterer full of contrivances and resources, in opposition to the upholsterer of steady capital and no imagination, who looks down with uneasy contempt on ingenuity?) had come in to give his opinion, that "nothing could be easier than to convert a bathroom into a bedroom, by the assistance of a little drapery to conceal the shower-bath," the string of which was to be carefully concealed, for fear that the unconscious occupier of the bath-bed might innocently take it for a bell-rope. The professional cook of the town had been already engaged to take up her abode for a month at Mr Bradshaw's, much to the indignation of Betsy, who became a vehement partisan of Mr Cranworth, as soon as ever she heard of the plan of her deposition from sovereign authority in the kitchen, in which she had reigned supreme for fourteen years. Mrs Bradshaw sighed and bemoaned herself in all her leisure moments, which were not many, and wondered why their house was to be turned into an inn for this Mr Donne, when everybody knew that the George was good enough for the Cranworths, who never thought of asking the electors to the Hall;—and they had lived at Cranworth ever since Julius Caesar's time, and if that was not being an old family, she did not know what was. The excitement soothed Jemima. There was something to do. It was she who planned with the upholsterer; it was she who soothed Betsy into angry silence; it was she who persuaded her mother to lie down and rest, while she herself went out to buy the heterogeneous things required to make the family and house presentable to Mr Donne and his precursor—the friend of the parliamentary agent. This latter gentleman never appeared himself on the scene of action, but pulled all the strings notwithstanding. The friend was a Mr Hickson, a lawyer—a briefless barrister, some people called him; but he himself professed a great disgust to the law, as a "great sham," which involved an immensity of underhand action, and truckling, and time-serving, and was perfectly encumbered by useless forms and ceremonies, and dead obsolete words. So, instead of putting his shoulder to the wheel to reform the law, he talked eloquently against it, in such a high-priest style, that it was occasionally a matter of surprise how he could ever have made a friend of the parliamentary agent before mentioned. But, as Mr Hickson himself said, it was the very corruptness of the law which he was fighting against, in doing all he could to effect the return of certain members to Parliament; these certain members being pledged to effect a reform in the law, according to Mr Hickson. And, as he once observed confidentially, "If you had to destroy a hydra-headed monster, would you measure swords with the demon as if he were a gentleman? Would you not rather seize the first weapon that came to hand? And so do I. My great object in life, sir, is to reform the law of England, sir. Once get a majority of Liberal members into the House, and the thing is done. And I consider myself justified, for so high—for, I may say, so holy—an end, in using men's weaknesses to work out my purpose. Of course, if men were angels, or even immaculate—men invulnerable to bribes, we would not bribe."

"Could you?" asked Jemima, for the conversation took place at Mr Bradshaw's dinner-table, where a few friends were gathered together to meet Mr Hickson; and among them was Mr Benson.

"We neither would nor could," said the ardent barrister, disregarding in his vehemence the point of the question, and floating on over the bar of argument into the wide ocean of his own eloquence: "As it is—as the world stands, they who would succeed even in good deeds must come down to the level of expediency; and therefore, I say once more, if Mr Donne is the man for your purpose, and your purpose is a good one, a lofty one, a holy one" (for Mr Hickson remembered the Dissenting character of his little audience, and privately considered the introduction of the word "holy" a most happy hit), "then, I say, we must put all the squeamish scruples which might befit Utopia, or some such place, on one side, and treat men as they are. If they are avaricious, it is not we who have made them so; but as we have to do with them, we must consider their failings in dealing with them; if they have been careless or extravagant, or have had their little peccadillos, we must administer the screw. The glorious reform of the law will justify, in my idea, all means to obtain the end—that law, from the profession of which I have withdrawn myself from perhaps a too scrupulous conscience!" he concluded softly to himself.

"We are not to do evil that good may come," said Mr Benson. He was startled at the deep sound of his own voice as he uttered these words; but he had not been speaking for some time, and his voice came forth strong and unmodulated.

"True, sir; most true," said Mr Hickson, bowing. "I honour you for the observation." And he profited by it, insomuch that he confined his further remarks on elections to the end of the table, where he sat near Mr Bradshaw, and one or two equally eager, though not equally influential partisans of Mr Donne's. Meanwhile, Mr Farquhar took up Mr Benson's quotation, at the end where he and Jemima sat near to Mrs Bradshaw and him.

"But in the present state of the world, as Mr Hickson says, it is rather difficult to act upon that precept."

"Oh, Mr Farquhar!" said Jemima, indignantly, the tears springing to her eyes with a feeling of disappointment. For she had been chafing under all that Mr Hickson had been saying, perhaps the more for one or two attempts on his part at a flirtation with the daughter of his wealthy host, which she resented with all the loathing of a pre-occupied heart; and she had longed to be a man, to speak out her wrath at this paltering with right and wrong. She had felt grateful to Mr Benson for his one clear, short precept, coming down with a divine force against which there was no appeal; and now to have Mr Farquhar taking the side of expediency! It was too bad.

"Nay, Jemima!" said Mr Farquhar, touched, and secretly flattered by the visible pain his speech had given. "Don't be indignant with me till I have explained myself a little more. I don't understand myself yet; and it is a very intricate question, or so it appears to me, which I was going to put, really, earnestly, and humbly, for Mr Benson's opinion. Now, Mr Benson, may I ask, if you always find it practicable to act strictly in accordance with that principle? For if you do not, I am sure no man living can! Are there not occasions when it is absolutely necessary to wade through evil to good? I am not speaking in the careless, presumptuous way of that man yonder," said he, lowering his voice, and addressing himself to Jemima more exclusively; "I am really anxious to hear what Mr Benson will say on the subject, for I know no one to whose candid opinion I should attach more weight."

But Mr Benson was silent. He did not see Mrs Bradshaw and Jemima leave the room. He was really, as Mr Farquhar supposed him, completely absent, questioning himself as to how far his practice tallied with his principle. By degrees he came to himself; he found the conversation still turned on the election; and Mr Hickson, who felt that he had jarred against the little minister's principles, and yet knew, from the *carte du pays* which the scouts of the parliamentary agent had given him, that Mr Benson was a person to be conciliated, on account of his influence over many of the working people, began to ask him questions with an air of deferring to superior knowledge, that almost surprised Mr Bradshaw, who had been accustomed to treat "Benson" in a very different fashion, of civil condescending indulgence, just as one listens to a child who can have had no opportunities of knowing better.

At the end of a conversation that Mr Hickson held with Mr Benson, on a subject in which the latter was really interested, and on which he had expressed himself at some length, the young barrister turned to Mr Bradshaw, and said very audibly,

"I wish Donne had been here. This conversation during the last half-hour would have interested him almost as much as it has done me."

Mr Bradshaw little guessed the truth, that Mr Donne was, at that very moment, coaching up the various subjects of public interest in Eccleston, and privately cursing the particular subject on which Mr Benson had been holding forth, as being an unintelligible piece of Quixotism; or the leading Dissenter of the town need not have experienced a pang of jealousy at the possible future admiration his minister might excite in the possible future member for Eccleston. And if Mr Benson had been clairvoyant, he need not have made an especial subject of gratitude out of the likelihood that he might have an opportunity of so far interesting Mr Donne in the condition of the people of Eccleston as to induce him to set his face against any attempts at bribery.

Mr Benson thought of this half the night through; and ended by determining to write a sermon on the Christian view of political duties, which might be good for all, both electors and member, to hear on the eve of an election. For Mr Donne was expected at Mr Bradshaw's before the next Sunday; and, of course, as Mr and Miss Benson had settled it, he would appear at the chapel with them on that day. But the stinging conscience refused to be quieted. No present plan of usefulness allayed the aching remembrance of the evil he had done that good might come. Not even the look of Leonard, as the early dawn fell on him, and Mr Benson's sleepless eyes saw the rosy glow on his firm round cheeks; his open mouth, through which the soft, long-drawn breath came gently quivering; and his eyes not fully shut, but closed to outward sight—not even the aspect of the quiet, innocent child could soothe the troubled spirit.

Leonard and his mother dreamt of each other that night. Her dream of him was one of undefined terror—terror so great that it wakened her up, and she strove not to sleep again, for fear that ominous ghastly dream should return. He, on the contrary, dreamt of her sitting watching and smiling by his bedside, as her gentle self had been many a morning; and when she saw him awake (so it fell out in the dream), she smiled still more sweetly, and bending down she kissed him, and then spread out large, soft, white-feathered wings (which in no way surprised her child—he seemed to have known they were there all along), and sailed away through the open window far into the blue sky of a summer's day. Leonard wakened up then, and remembered how far away she really was—far more distant and inaccessible than the beautiful blue sky to which she had betaken herself in his dream—and cried himself to sleep again.

In spite of her absence from her child, which made one great and abiding sorrow, Ruth enjoyed her seaside visit exceedingly. In the first place, there was the delight of seeing Elizabeth's daily and almost hourly improvement. Then, at the doctor's express orders, there were so few lessons to be done, that there was time for the long exploring rambles, which all three delighted in. And when the rain came and the storms blew, the house, with its wild sea-views, was equally delightful.

It was a large house, built on the summit of a rock, which nearly overhung the shore below; there were, to be sure, a series of zigzag tacking paths down the face of this rock, but from the house they could not be seen. Old or delicate people would have considered the situation bleak and exposed; indeed, the present proprietor wanted to dispose of it on this very account; but by its present inhabitants, this exposure and bleakness were called by other names, and considered as charms. From every part of the rooms they saw the grey storms gather on the sea-horizon, and put themselves in marching array; and soon the march became a sweep, and the great dome of the heavens was covered with the lurid clouds, between which and the vivid green earth below there seemed to come a purple atmosphere, making the very threatening beautiful; and by-and-by the house was wrapped in sheets of rain shutting out sky, and sea, and inland view; till, of a sudden, the storm was gone by, and the heavy rain-drops glistened in the sun as they hung on leaf and grass, and the "little birds sang east, and the little birds sang west," and there was a pleasant sound of running waters all abroad.

"Oh! if papa would but buy this house!" exclaimed Elizabeth, after one such storm, which she had watched silently from the very beginning of the "little cloud no bigger than a man's hand."

"Mamma would never like it, I am afraid," said Mary. "She would call our delicious gushes of air, draughts, and think we should catch cold."

"Jemima would be on our side. But how long Mrs Denbigh is! I hope she was near enough the post-office when the rain came on!"

Ruth had gone to "the shop" in the little village, about half-a-mile distant, where all letters were left till fetched. She only expected one, but that one was to tell her of Leonard. She, however, received two; the unexpected one was from Mr Bradshaw, and the news it contained was, if possible, a greater surprise than the letter itself. Mr Bradshaw informed her, that he planned arriving by dinner-time the following Saturday at Eagle's Crag; and more, that he intended bringing Mr Donne and one or two other gentlemen with him, to spend the Sunday there! The letter went on to give every possible direction regarding the household preparations. The dinner-hour was fixed to be at six; but, of course, Ruth and the girls would have dined long before. The (professional) cook would arrive the day before, laden with all the provisions that could not be obtained on the spot. Ruth was to engage a waiter from the inn, and this it was that detained her so long. While she sat in the little parlour, awaiting the coming of the landlady, she could not help wondering why Mr Bradshaw was bringing this strange gentleman to spend two days at Abermouth, and thus giving himself so much trouble and fuss of preparation.

There were so many small reasons that went to make up the large one which had convinced Mr Bradshaw of the desirableness of this step, that it was not likely that Ruth should guess at one half of them. In the first place, Miss Benson, in the pride and fulness of her heart, had told Mrs Bradshaw what her brother had told her; how he meant to preach upon the Christian view of the duties involved in political rights; and as, of course, Mrs Bradshaw had told Mr Bradshaw, he began to dislike the idea of attending chapel on that Sunday at all; for he had an uncomfortable idea that by the Christian standard—that divine test of the true and pure—bribery would not be altogether approved of; and yet he was tacitly coming round to the understanding that "packets" would be required, for what purpose both he and Mr Donne were to be supposed to remain ignorant. But it would be very awkward, so near to the time, if he were to be clearly convinced that bribery, however disguised by names and words, was in plain terms a sin. And yet he knew Mr Benson had once or twice convinced him against his will of certain things, which he had thenceforward found it impossible to do, without such great uneasiness of mind, that he had left off doing them, which was sadly against his interest. And if Mr Donne (whom he had intended to take with him to chapel, as fair Dissenting prey) should also become convinced, why, the Cranworths would win the day, and he should be the laughing-stock of Eccleston. No! in this one case bribery must be allowed—was allowable; but it was a great pity human nature was so corrupt, and if his member succeeded, he would double his subscription to the schools, in order that the next generation might be taught better. There were various other reasons, which strengthened Mr Bradshaw in the bright idea of going down to Abermouth for the Sunday; some connected with the out-of-door politics, and some with the domestic. For instance, it had been the plan of the house to have a cold dinner on the Sundays—Mr Bradshaw had piqued himself on this strictness—and yet he had an instinctive feeling that Mr Donne was not quite the man to partake of cold meat for conscience' sake with cheerful indifference to his fare.

Mr Donne had, in fact, taken the Bradshaw household a little by surprise. Before he came, Mr Bradshaw had pleased himself with thinking, that more unlikely things had happened than the espousal of his daughter with the member of a small borough. But this pretty airy bubble burst as soon as he saw Mr Donne; and its very existence was forgotten in less than half an hour, when he felt the quiet but incontestible difference of rank and standard that there was, in every respect, between his guest and his own family. It was not through any circumstance so palpable, and possibly accidental, as the bringing down a servant, whom Mr Donne seemed to consider as much a matter of course as a carpet-bag (though the smart gentleman's arrival "fluttered the Volscians in Corioli" considerably more than his gentle-spoken master's). It was nothing like this; it was something indescribable—a quiet being at ease, and expecting every one else to be so—an attention to women, which was so habitual as to be unconsciously exercised to those subordinate persons in Mr Bradshaw's family—a happy choice of simple and expressive words, some of which it must be confessed were slang, but fashionable slang, and that makes all the difference—a measured, graceful way of utterance, with a style of pronunciation quite different to that of Eccleston. All these put together make but a part of the indescribable whole which unconsciously affected Mr Bradshaw, and established Mr Donne in his estimation as a creature quite different to any he had seen before, and as most unfit to mate with Jemima. Mr Hickson, who had appeared as a model of gentlemanly ease before Mr Donne's arrival, now became vulgar and coarse in Mr Bradshaw's eyes. And yet, such was the charm of that languid, high-bred manner, that Mr Bradshaw "cottoned" (as he expressed it to Mr Farquhar) to his new candidate at once. He was only afraid lest Mr Donne was too indifferent to all things under the sun to care whether he gained or lost the election; but he was reassured after the first conversation they had together on the subject. Mr Donne's eye lightened with an eagerness that was almost fierce, though his tones were as musical, and nearly as slow, as ever; and when Mr Bradshaw alluded distantly to "probable expenses" and "packets," Mr Donne replied,

"Oh, of course! disagreeable necessity! Better speak as little about such things as possible; other people can be found to arrange all the dirty work. Neither you nor I would like to soil our fingers by it, I am sure. Four thousand pounds are in Mr Pilson's hands, and I shall never inquire what becomes of them; they may, very probably, be absorbed in the law expenses, you know. I shall let it be clearly understood from the hustings, that I most decidedly disapprove of bribery, and leave the rest to Hickson's management. He is accustomed to these sort of things. I am not."

Mr Bradshaw was rather perplexed by this want of bustling energy on the part of the new candidate; and if it had not been for the four thousand pounds aforesaid, would have doubted whether Mr Donne cared sufficiently for the result of the election. Jemima thought differently. She watched her father's visitor attentively, with something like the curious observation which a naturalist bestows on a new species of animal.

"Do you know what Mr Donne reminds me of, mamma?" said she, one day, as the two sat at work, while the gentlemen were absent canvassing.

"No! he is not like anybody I ever saw. He quite frightens me, by being so ready to open the door for me if I am going out of the room, and by giving me a chair when I come in. I never saw any one like him. Who is it, Jemima?"

"Not any person—not any human being, mamma," said Jemima, half smiling. "Do you remember our stopping at Wakefield once, on our way to Scarborough, and there were horse-races going on somewhere, and some of the racers were in the stables at the inn where we dined?"

"Yes! I remember it; but what about that?"

"Why, Richard, somehow, knew one of the jockeys, and, as we were coming in from our ramble through the town, this man, or boy, asked us to look at one of the racers he had the charge of."

"Well, my dear!"

"Well, mamma! Mr Donne is like that horse!"

"Nonsense, Jemima; you must not say so. I don't know what your father would say, if he heard you likening Mr Donne to a brute."

"Brutes are sometimes very beautiful, mamma. I am sure I should think it a compliment to be likened to a race-horse, such as the one we saw. But the thing in which they are alike, is the sort of repressed eagerness in both."

"Eager! Why, I should say there never was any one cooler than Mr Donne. Think of the trouble your papa has had this month past, and then remember the slow way in which Mr Donne moves when he is going out to canvass, and the low, drawling voice in which he questions the people who bring him intelligence. I can see your papa standing by, ready to shake them to get out their news."

"But Mr Donne's questions are always to the point, and force out the grain without the chaff. And look at him, if any one tells him ill news about the election! Have you never seen a dull red light come into his eyes? That is like my race-horse. Her flesh quivered all over, at certain sounds and noises which had some meaning to her; but she stood quite still, pretty creature! Now, Mr Donne is just as eager as she was, though he may be too proud to show it. Though he seems so gentle, I almost think he is very headstrong in following out his own will."

"Well! don't call him like a horse again, for I am sure papa would not like it. Do you know, I thought you were going to say he was like little Leonard, when you asked me who he was like."

"Leonard! Oh, mamma, he is not in the least like Leonard. He is twenty times more like my race-horse.

"Now, my dear Jemima, do be quiet. Your father thinks racing so wrong, that I am sure he would be very seriously displeased if he were to hear you."

To return to Mr Bradshaw, and to give one more of his various reasons for wishing to take Mr Donne to Abermouth. The wealthy Eccleston manufacturer was uncomfortably impressed with an indefinable sense of inferiority to his visitor. It was not in education, for Mr Bradshaw was a well-educated man; it was not in power, for, if he chose, the present object of Mr Donne's life might be utterly defeated; it did not arise from anything overbearing in manner, for Mr Donne was habitually polite and courteous, and was just now anxious to propitiate his host, whom he looked upon as a very useful man. Whatever this sense of inferiority arose from, Mr Bradshaw was anxious to relieve himself of it, and imagined that if he could make more display of his wealth his object would be obtained. Now his house in Eccleston was old-fashioned, and ill-calculated to exhibit money's worth. His mode of living, though strained to a high pitch just at this time, he became aware was no more than Mr Donne was accustomed to every day of his life. The first day at dessert, some remark (some opportune remark, as Mr Bradshaw in his innocence had thought) was made regarding the price of pine-apples, which was rather exorbitant that year, and Mr Donne asked Mrs Bradshaw, with quiet surprise, if they had no pinery, as if to be without a pinery were indeed a depth of pitiable destitution. In fact, Mr Donne had been born and cradled in all that wealth could purchase, and so had his ancestors before him for so many generations, that refinement and luxury seemed the natural condition of man, and they that dwelt without were in the position of monsters. The absence was noticed; but not the presence.

Now, Mr Bradshaw knew that the house and grounds of Eagle's Crag were exorbitantly dear, and yet he really thought of purchasing them. And as one means of exhibiting his wealth, and so raising himself up to the level of Mr Donne, he thought that if he could take the latter down to Abermouth, and show him the place for which, "because his little girls had taken a fancy to it," he was willing to give the fancy-price of fourteen thousand pounds, he should at last make those half-shut dreamy eyes open wide, and their owner confess that, in wealth at least, the Eccleston manufacturer stood on a par with him.

All these mingled motives caused the determination which made Ruth sit in the little inn-parlour at Abermouth during the wild storm's passage.

She wondered if she had fulfilled all Mr Bradshaw's directions. She looked at the letter. Yes! everything was done. And now home with her news, through the wet lane, where the little pools by the roadside reflected the deep blue sky and the round white clouds with even deeper blue and clearer white; and the rain-drops hung so thick on the trees, that even a little bird's flight was enough to shake them down in a bright shower as of rain. When she told the news, Mary exclaimed,

"Oh, how charming! Then we shall see this new member after all!" while Elizabeth added,

"Yes! I shall like to do that. But where must we be? Papa will want the dining-room and this room, and where must we sit?"

"Oh!" said Ruth, "in the dressing-room next to my room. All that your papa wants always, is that you are quiet and out of the way."

CHAPTER XXIII - RECOGNITION

Saturday came. Torn, ragged clouds were driven across the sky. It was not a becoming day for the scenery, and the little girls regretted it much. First they hoped for a change at twelve o'clock, and then at the afternoon tide-turning. But at neither time did the sun show his face.

"Papa will never buy this dear place," said Elizabeth, sadly, as she watched the weather. "The sun is everything to it. The sea looks quite leaden to-day, and there is no sparkle on it. And the sands, that were so yellow and sun-speckled on Thursday, are all one dull brown now."

"Never mind! to-morrow may be better," said Ruth, cheerily.

"I wonder what time they will come at?" inquired Mary.

"Your papa said they would be at the station at five o'clock. And the landlady at the Swan said it would take them half an hour to get here."

"And they are to dine at six?" asked Elizabeth.

"Yes," answered Ruth. "And I think if we had our tea half an hour earlier, at half-past four, and then went out for a walk, we should be nicely out of the way just during the bustle of the arrival and dinner; and we could be in the drawing-room ready against your papa came in after dinner."

"Oh! that would be nice," said they; and tea was ordered accordingly.

The south-westerly wind had dropped, and the clouds were stationary, when they went out on the sands. They dug little holes near the in-coming tide, and made canals to them from the water, and blew the light sea-foam against each other; and then stole on tiptoe near to the groups of grey and white sea-gulls, which despised their caution, flying softly and slowly away to a little distance as soon as they drew near. And in all this Ruth was as great a child as any. Only she longed for Leonard with a mother's longing, as indeed she did every day, and all hours of the day. By-and-by the clouds thickened yet more, and one or two drops of rain were felt. It was very little, but Ruth feared a shower for her delicate Elizabeth, and besides, the September evening was fast closing in the dark and sunless day. As they turned homewards in the rapidly increasing dusk, they saw three figures on the sand near the rocks, coming in their direction.

"Papa and Mr Donne!" exclaimed Mary. "Now we shall see him!"

"Which do you make out is him?" asked Elizabeth.

"Oh! the tall one, to be sure. Don't you see how papa always turns to him, as if he was speaking to him and not to the other?"

"Who is the other?" asked Elizabeth.

"Mr Bradshaw said that Mr Farquhar and Mr Hickson would come with him. But that is not Mr Farquhar, I am sure," said Ruth.

The girls looked at each other, as they always did, when Ruth mentioned Mr Farquhar's name; but she was perfectly unconscious both of the look and of the conjectures which gave rise to it.

As soon as the two parties drew near, Mr Bradshaw called out in his strong voice,

"Well, my dears! we found there was an hour before dinner, so we came down upon the sands, and here you are."

The tone of his voice assured them that he was in a bland and indulgent mood, and the two little girls ran towards him. He kissed them, and shook hands with Ruth; told his companions that these were the little girls who were tempting him to this extravagance of purchasing Eagle's Crag; and then, rather doubtfully, and because he saw that Mr Donne expected it, he introduced "My daughters' governess, Mrs Denbigh."

It was growing darker every moment, and it was time they should hasten back to the rocks, which were even now indistinct in the grey haze. Mr Bradshaw held a hand of each of his daughters, and Ruth walked alongside, the two strange gentlemen being on the outskirts of the party.

Mr Bradshaw began to give his little girls some home news. He told them that Mr Farquhar was ill, and could not accompany them; but Jemima and their mamma were quite well.

The gentleman nearest to Ruth spoke to her.

"Are you fond of the sea?" asked he. There was no answer, so he repeated his question in a different form.

"Do you enjoy staying by the seaside? I should rather ask."

The reply was "Yes," rather breathed out in a deep inspiration than spoken in a sound. The sands heaved and trembled beneath Ruth. The figures near her vanished into strange nothingness; the sounds of their voices were as distant sounds in a dream, while the echo of one voice thrilled through and through. She could have caught at his arm for support, in the awful dizziness which wrapped her up, body and soul. That voice! No! if name, and face, and figure were all changed, that voice was the same which had touched her girlish heart, which had spoken most tender words of love, which had won, and wrecked her, and which she had last heard in the low mutterings of fever. She dared not look round to see the figure of him who spoke, dark as it was. She knew he was there—she heard him speak in the manner in which he used to address strangers years ago; perhaps she answered him, perhaps she did not—God knew. It seemed as if weights were tied to her feet—as if the steadfast rocks receded—as if time stood still;—it was so long, so terrible, that path across the reeling sand.

At the foot of the rocks they separated. Mr Bradshaw, afraid lest dinner should cool, preferred the shorter way for himself and his friends. On Elizabeth's account, the girls were to take the longer and easier path, which wound upwards through a rocky field, where larks' nests abounded, and where wild thyme and heather were now throwing out their sweets to the soft night air.

The little girls spoke in eager discussion of the strangers. They appealed to Ruth, but Ruth did not answer, and they were too impatient to convince each other to repeat the question. The first little ascent from the sands to the field surmounted, Ruth sat down suddenly and covered her face with her hands. This was so unusual—their wishes, their good, was so invariably the rule of motion or of rest in their walks—that the girls, suddenly checked, stood silent and affrighted in surprise. They were still more startled when Ruth wailed aloud some inarticulate words.

"Are you not well, dear Mrs Denbigh?" asked Elizabeth, gently, kneeling down on the grass by Ruth.

She sat facing the west. The low watery twilight was on her face as she took her hands away. So pale, so haggard, so wild and wandering a look the girls had never seen on human countenance before.

"Well! what are you doing here with me? You should not be with me," said she, shaking her head slowly.

They looked at each other.

"You are sadly tired," said Elizabeth, soothingly. "Come home, and let me help you to bed. I will tell papa you are ill, and ask him to send for a doctor."

Ruth looked at her as if she did not understand the meaning of her words. No more she did at first. But by-and-by the dulled brain began to think most vividly and rapidly, and she spoke in a sharp way which deceived the girls into a belief that nothing had been the matter.

"Yes! I was tired. I am tired. Those sands—oh! those sands, those weary, dreadful sands! But that is all over now. Only my heart aches still. Feel how it flutters and beats," said she, taking Elizabeth's hand, and holding it to her side. "I am quite well, though," she continued, reading pity in the child's looks, as she felt the trembling, quivering beat. "We will go straight to the dressing-room, and read a chapter; that will still my heart; and then I'll go to bed, and Mr Bradshaw will excuse me, I know, this one night. I only ask for one night. Put on your right frocks, dears, and do all you ought to do. But I know you will," said she, bending down to kiss Elizabeth, and then, before she had done so, raising her head abruptly. "You are good and dear girls—God keep you so!"

By a strong effort at self-command, she went onwards at an even pace, neither rushing nor pausing to sob and think. The very regularity of motion calmed her. The front and back doors of the house were on two sides, at right angles with each other. They all shrunk a little from the idea of going in at the front door, now that the strange gentlemen were about, and, accordingly, they went through the quiet farm-yard right into the bright, ruddy kitchen, where the servants were dashing about with the dinner things. It was a contrast in more than colour to the lonely, dusky field, which even the little girls perceived; and the noise, the warmth, the very bustle of the servants, were a positive relief to Ruth, and for the time lifted off the heavy press of pent-up passion. A silent house, with moonlit rooms, or with a faint gloom brooding over the apartments, would have been more to be dreaded. Then, she must have given way, and cried out. As it was, she went up the old awkward back stairs, and into the room they were to sit in. There was no candle. Mary volunteered to go down for one; and when she returned she was full of the wonders of preparation in the drawing-room, and ready and eager to dress, so as to take her place there before the gentlemen had finished dinner. But she was struck by the strange paleness of Ruth's face, now that the light fell upon it.

"Stay up here, dear Mrs Denbigh! We'll tell papa you are tired, and are gone to bed."

Another time Ruth would have dreaded Mr Bradshaw's displeasure; for it was an understood thing that no one was to be ill or tired in his household without leave asked, and cause given and assigned. But she never thought of that now. Her great desire was to hold quiet till she was alone. Quietness it was not—it was rigidity; but she succeeded in being rigid in look and movement, and went through her duties to Elizabeth (who preferred remaining with her upstairs) with wooden precision. But her heart felt at times like ice, at times like burning fire; always a heavy, heavy weight within her. At last Elizabeth went to bed. Still Ruth dared not think. Mary would come upstairs soon; and with a strange, sick, shrinking yearning, Ruth awaited her—and the crumbs of intelligence she might drop out about *him*. Ruth's sense of hearing was quickened to miserable intensity as she stood before the chimney-piece, grasping it tight with both hands—gazing into the dying fire, but seeing—not the dead grey embers, or the little sparks of vivid light that ran hither and thither among the wood-ashes—but an old farm-house, and climbing, winding road, and a little golden breezy common, with a rural inn on the hill-top, far, far away. And through the thoughts of the past came the sharp sounds of the present—of three voices, one of which was almost silence, it was so hushed. Indifferent people would only have guessed that Mr Donne was speaking by the quietness in which the others listened; but Ruth heard the voice and many of the words, though they conveyed no idea to her mind. She was too much stunned even to feel curious to know to what they related. *He* spoke. That was her one fact.

Presently up came Mary, bounding, exultant. Papa had let her stay up one quarter of an hour longer, because Mr Hickson had asked. Mr Hickson was so clever! She did not know what to make of Mr Donne, he seemed such a dawdle. But he was very handsome. Had Ruth seen him? Oh, no! She could not, it was so dark on those stupid sands. Well, never mind, she would see him to-morrow. She *must* be well to-morrow. Papa seemed a good deal put out that neither she nor Elizabeth were in the drawing-room to-night; and his last words were, "Tell Mrs Denbigh I hope" (and papa's "hopes" always meant "expect") "she will be able to make breakfast at nine o'clock;" and then she would see Mr Donne.

That was all Ruth heard about him. She went with Mary into her bedroom, helped her to undress, and put the candle out. At length she was alone in her own room! At length!

But the tension did not give way immediately. She fastened her door, and threw open the window, cold and threatening as was the night. She tore off her gown; she put her hair back from her heated face. It seemed now as if she could not think—as if thought and emotion had been repressed so sternly that they would not come to relieve her stupified brain. Till all at once, like a flash of lightning, her life, past and present, was revealed to her in its minutest detail. And when she saw her very present "Now," the strange confusion of agony was too great to be bornc, and she cried aloud. Then she was quite dead, and listened as to the sound of galloping armies.

"If I might see him! If I might see him! If I might just ask him why he left me; if I had vexed him in any way; it was so strange—so cruel! It was not him; it was his mother," said she, almost fiercely, as if answering herself. "Oh, God! but he might have found me out before this," she continued, sadly. "He did not care for me, as I did for him. He did not care for me at all," she went on wildly and sharply. "He did me cruel harm. I can never again lift up my face in innocence. They think I have forgotten all, because I do not speak. Oh, darling love! am I talking against you?" asked she, tenderly. "I am so torn and perplexed! You, who are the father of my child!"

But that very circumstance, full of such tender meaning in many cases, threw a new light into her mind. It changed her from the woman into the mother—the stern guardian of her child. She was still for a time, thinking. Then she began again, but in a low, deep voice,

"He left me. He might have been hurried off, but he might have inquired—he might have learnt, and explained. He left me to bear the burden and the shame; and never cared to learn, as he might have done, of Leonard's birth. He has no love for his child, and I will have no love for him."

She raised her voice while uttering this determination, and then, feeling her own weakness, she moaned out, "Alas! alas!"

And then she started up, for all this time she had been rocking herself backwards and forwards as she sat on the ground, and began to pace the room with hurried steps.

"What am I thinking of? Where am I? I who have been praying these years and years to be worthy to be Leonard's mother. My God! what a depth of sin is in my heart! Why, the old time would be as white as snow to what it would be now, if I sought him out, and prayed for the explanation, which should re-establish him in my heart. I who have striven (or made a mock of trying) to learn God's holy will, in order to bring up Leonard into the full strength of a Christian—I who have taught his sweet innocent lips to pray, 'Lead us not into temptation, but deliver us from evil;' and yet, somehow, I've been longing to give him to his father, who is—who is—" she almost choked, till at last she cried sharp out, "Oh, my God! I do believe Leonard's father is a bad man, and yet, oh! pitiful God, I love him; I cannot forget—I cannot!"

She threw her body half out of the window into the cold night air. The wind was rising, and came in great gusts. The rain beat down on her. It did her good. A still, calm night would not have soothed her as this did. The wild tattered clouds, hurrying past the moon, gave her a foolish kind of pleasure that almost made her smile a vacant smile. The blast-driven rain came on her again, and drenched her hair through and through. The words "stormy wind fulfilling His word" came into her mind.

She sat down on the floor. This time her hands were clasped round her knees. The uneasy rocking motion was stilled.

"I wonder if my darling is frightened with this blustering, noisy wind. I wonder if he is awake."

And then her thoughts went back to the various times of old, when, affrighted by the weather—sounds so mysterious in the night—he had crept into her bed and clung to her, and she had soothed him, and sweetly awed him into stillness and childlike faith, by telling him of the goodness and power of God.

Of a sudden she crept to a chair, and there knelt as in the very presence of God, hiding her face, at first not speaking a word (for did He not know her heart), but by-and-by moaning out, amid her sobs and tears (and now for the first time she wept),

"Oh, my God, help me, for I am very weak. My God! I pray Thee be my rock and my strong fortress, for I of myself am nothing. If I ask in His name, Thou wilt give it me. In the name of Jesus Christ I pray for strength to do Thy will!"

She could not think, or, indeed, remember anything but that she was weak, and God was strong, and "a very present help in time of trouble;" and the wind rose yet higher, and the house shook and vibrated as, in measured time, the great and terrible gusts came from the four quarters of the heavens and blew around it, dying away in the distance with loud and unearthly wails, which were not utterly still before the sound of the coming blast was heard like the trumpets of the vanguard of the Prince of Air.

There was a knock at the bedroom door—a little, gentle knock, and a soft child's voice.

"Mrs Denbigh, may I come in, please? I am so frightened!"

It was Elizabeth. Ruth calmed her passionate breathing by one hasty draught of water, and opened the door to the timid girl.

"Oh, Mrs Denbigh! did you ever hear such a night? I am so frightened! and Mary sleeps so sound."

Ruth was too much shaken to be able to speak all at once; but she took Elizabeth in her arms to reassure her. Elizabeth stood back.

"Why, how wet you are, Mrs Denbigh! and there's the window open, I do believe! Oh, how cold it is!" said she, shivering.

"Get into my bed, dear!" said Ruth.

"But do come too! The candle gives such a strange light with that long wick, and, somehow, your face does not look like you. Please, put the candle out, and come to bed. I am so frightened, and it seems as if I should be safer if you were by me."

Ruth shut the window, and went to bed. Elizabeth was all shivering and quaking. To soothe her, Ruth made a great effort; and spoke of Leonard and his fears, and, in a low hesitating voice, she spoke of God's tender mercy, but very humbly, for she feared lest Elizabeth should think her better and holier than she was. The little girl was soon asleep, her fears forgotten; and Ruth, worn out by passionate emotion, and obliged to be still for fear of awaking her bedfellow, went off into a short slumber, through the depths of which the echoes of her waking sobs quivered up.

When she awoke the grey light of autumnal dawn was in the room. Elizabeth slept on; but Ruth heard the servants about, and the early farmyard sounds. After she had recovered from the shock of consciousness and recollection, she collected her thoughts with a stern calmness. He was here. In a few hours she must meet him. There was no escape, except through subterfuges and contrivances that were both false and cowardly. How it would all turn out she could not say, or even guess. But of one thing she was clear, and to one thing she would hold fast: that was, that, come what might, she would obey God's law, and, be the end of all what it might, she would say, "Thy will be done!" She only asked for strength enough to do this when the time came. How the time would come—what speech or action would be requisite on her part, she did not know—she did not even try to conjecture. She left that in His hands.

She was icy cold, but very calm, when the breakfast-bell rang. She went down immediately; because she felt that there was less chance of a recognition if she were already at her place beside the tea-urn, and busied with the cups, than if she came in after all were settled. Her heart seemed to stand still, but she felt almost a strange exultant sense of power over herself. She felt, rather than saw, that he was not there. Mr Bradshaw and Mr Hickson were, and so busy talking election-politics that they did not interrupt their conversation even when they bowed to her. Her pupils sat one on each side of her. Before they were quite settled, and while the other two gentlemen yet hung over the fire, Mr Donne came in. Ruth felt as if that moment was like death. She had a kind of desire to make some sharp sound, to relieve a choking sensation, but it was over in an instant, and she sat on very composed and silent—to all outward appearance the very model of a governess who knew her place. And by-and-by she felt strangely at ease in her sense of power. She could even listen to what was being said. She had never dared as yet to look at Mr Donne, though her heart burnt to see him once again. He sounded changed. The voice had lost its fresh and youthful eagerness of tone, though in peculiarity of modulation it was the same. It could never be mistaken for the voice of another person. There was a good deal said at that breakfast, for none seemed inclined to hurry, although it was Sunday morning. Ruth was compelled to sit there, and it was good for her that she did. That half-hour seemed to separate the present Mr Donne very effectively from her imagination of what Mr Bellingham had been. She was no analyser; she hardly even had learnt to notice character; but she felt there was some strange difference between the people she had lived with lately and the man who now leant back in his chair, listening in a careless manner to the conversation, but never joining in, or expressing any interest in it, unless it somewhere, or somehow, touched himself. Now, Mr Bradshaw always threw himself into a subject; it might be in a pompous, dogmatic sort of way, but he did do it, whether it related to himself or not; and it was part of Mr Hickson's trade to assume an interest if he felt it not. But Mr Donne did neither the one nor the other. When the other two were talking of many of the topics of the day, he put his glass in his eye, the better to examine into the exact nature of a cold game-pie at the other side of the table. Suddenly Ruth felt that his attention was caught by her. Until now, seeing his short-sightedness, she had believed herself safe; now her face flushed with a painful, miserable blush. But in an instant she was strong and quiet. She looked up straight at his face; and, as if this action took him aback, he dropped his glass, and began eating away with great diligence. She had seen him. He was changed, she knew not how. In fact, the expression, which had been only occasional formerly, when his worse self predominated, had become permanent. He looked restless and dissatisfied. But he was very handsome still; and her quick eye had recognised, with a sort of strange pride, that the eyes and mouth were like Leonard's. Although perplexed by the straightforward, brave look she had sent right at him, he was not entirely baffled. He thought this Mrs Denbigh was certainly like poor Ruth; but this woman was far handsomer. Her face was positively Greek; and then such a proud, superb turn of her head; quite queenly! A governess in Mr Bradshaw's family! Why, she might be a Percy or a Howard for the grandeur of her grace! Poor Ruth! This woman's hair was darker, though; and she had less colour; altogether a more refined-looking person. Poor Ruth! and, for the first time for several years, he wondered what had become of her; though, of course, there was but one thing that could have happened, and perhaps it was as well he did not know her end, for most likely it would have made him very uncomfortable. He leant back in his chair, and, unobserved (for he would not have thought it gentlemanly to look so fixedly at her if she or any one noticed him), he put up his glass again. She was speaking to one of her pupils, and did not see him.

By Jove! it must be she, though! There were little dimples came out about the mouth as she spoke, just like those he used to admire so much in Ruth, and which he had never seen in any one else—the sunshine without the positive movement of a smile. The longer he looked the more he was convinced; and it was with a jerk that he recovered himself enough to answer Mr Bradshaw's question, whether he wished to go to church or not.

"Church? how far—a mile? No; I think I shall perform my devotions at home to-day."

He absolutely felt jealous when Mr Hickson sprang up to open the door as Ruth and her pupils left the room. He was pleased to feel jealous again. He had been really afraid he was too much "used-up" for such sensations. But Hickson must keep his place. What he was paid for was doing the talking to the electors, not paying attention to the ladies in their families. Mr Donne had noticed that Mr Hickson had tried to be gallant to Miss Bradshaw; let him, if he liked; but let him beware how he behaved to this fair creature, Ruth or no Ruth. It certainly was Ruth; only how the devil had she played her cards so well as to be the governess—the respected governess, in such a family as Mr Bradshaw's?

Mr Donne's movements were evidently to be the guide of Mr Hickson's. Mr Bradshaw always disliked going to church, partly from principle, partly because he never could find the places in the Prayer-book. Mr Donne was in the drawing-room as Mary came down ready equipped; he was turning over the leaves of the large and handsome Biblc. Seeing Mary, he was struck with a new idea.

"How singular it is," said he, "that the name of Ruth is so seldom chosen by those good people who go to the Bible before they christen their children. It is a pretty name, I think."

Mr Bradshaw looked up. "Why, Mary!" said he, "is not that Mrs Denbigh's name?"

"Yes, papa," replied Mary, eagerly; "and I know two other Ruths; there's Ruth Brown here, and Ruth Macartney at Eccleston."

"And I have an aunt called Ruth, Mr Donne! I don't think your observation holds good. Besides my daughters' governess, I know three other Ruths."

"Oh! I have no doubt I was wrong. It was just a speech of which one perceives the folly the moment it is made."

But, secretly, he rejoiced with a fierce joy over the success of his device.

Elizabeth came to summon Mary.

Ruth was glad when she got into the open air, and away from the house. Two hours were gone and over. Two out of a day, a day and a half—for it might be late on Monday morning before the Eccleston party returned.

She felt weak and trembling in body, but strong in power over herself. They had left the house in good time for church, so they needed not to hurry; and they went leisurely along the road, now and then passing some country person whom they knew, and with whom they exchanged a kindly, placid greeting. But presently, to Ruth's dismay, she heard a step behind, coming at a rapid pace, a peculiar clank of rather high-heeled boots, which gave a springy sound to the walk, that she had known well long ago. It was like a nightmare, where the Evil dreaded is never avoided, never completely shunned, but is by one's side at the very moment of triumph in escape. There he was by her side; and there was a quarter of a mile intervening between her and the church; but even yet she trusted that he had not recognised her.

"I have changed my mind, you see," said he, quietly. "I have some curiosity to see the architecture of the church; some of these old country churches have singular bits about them. Mr Bradshaw kindly directed me part of the way, but I was so much puzzled by 'turns to the right,' and 'turns to the left,' that I was quite glad to espy your party."

That speech required no positive answer of any kind; and no answer did it receive. He had not expected a reply. He knew, if she were Ruth, she could not answer any indifferent words of his; and her silence made him more certain of her identity with the lady by his side.

"The scenery here is of a kind new to me; neither grand, wild, nor yet marked by high cultivation; and yet it has great charms. It reminds me of some parts of Wales." He breathed deeply, and then added, "You have been in Wales, I believe?"

He spoke low; almost in a whisper. The little church-bell began to call the lagging people with its quick, sharp summons. Ruth writhed in body and spirit, but struggled on. The church-door would be gained at last; and in that holy place she would find peace.

He repeated in a louder tone, so as to compel an answer in order to conceal her agitation from the girls:

"Have you never been in Wales?" He used "never" instead of "ever," and laid the emphasis on that word, in order to mark his meaning to Ruth, and Ruth only. But he drove her to bay.

"I have been in Wales, sir," she replied, in a calm, grave tone. "I was there many years ago. Events took place there, which contribute to make the recollection of that time most miserable to me. I shall be obliged to you, sir, if you will make no further reference to it."

The little girls wondered how Mrs Denbigh could speak in such a tone of quiet authority to Mr Donne, who was almost a member of Parliament. But they settled that her husband must have died in Wales, and, of course, that would make the recollection of the country "most miserable," as she said.

Mr Donne did not dislike the answer, and he positively admired the dignity with which she spoke. His leaving her as he did must have made her very miserable; and he liked the pride that made her retain her indignation, until he could speak to her in private, and explain away a good deal of what she might complain of with some justice.

The church was reached. They all went up the middle aisle into the Eagle's Crag pew. He followed them in, entered himself, and shut the door. Ruth's heart sank as she saw him there; just opposite to her; coming between her and the clergyman who was to read out the Word of God. It was merciless—it was cruel to haunt her there. She durst not lift her eyes to the bright eastern light—she could not see how peacefully the marble images of the dead lay on their tombs, for he was between her and all Light and Peace. She knew that his look was on her; that he never turned his glance away. She could not join in the prayer for the remission of sins while he was there, for his very presence seemed as a sign that their stain would never be washed out of her life. But, although goaded and chafed by her thoughts and recollections, she kept very still. No sign of emotion, no flush of colour was on her face as he looked at her. Elizabeth could not find her place, and then Ruth breathed once, long and deeply, as she moved up the pew, and out of the straight, burning glance of those eyes of evil meaning. When they sat down for the reading of the first lesson, Ruth turned the corner of the seat so as no longer to be opposite to him. She could not listen. The words seemed to be uttered in some world far away, from which she was exiled and cast out; their sound, and yet more their meaning, was dim and distant. But in this extreme tension of mind to hold in her bewildered agony, it so happened that one of her senses was preternaturally acute. While all the church and the people swam in misty haze, one point in a dark corner grew clearer and clearer till she saw (what at another time she could not have discerned at all) a face—a gargoyle I think they call it—at the end of the arch next to the narrowing of the nave into the chancel, and in the shadow of that contraction. The face was beautiful in feature (the next to it was a grinning monkey), but it was not the features that were the most striking part. There was a half-open mouth, not in any way distorted out of its exquisite beauty by the intense expression of suffering it conveyed. Any distortion of the face by mental agony implies that a struggle with circumstance is going on. But in this face, if such struggle had been, it was over now. Circumstance had conquered; and there was no hope from mortal endeavour, or help from mortal creature to be had. But the eyes looked onward and upward to the "Hills from whence cometh our help." And though the parted lips seemed ready to quiver with agony, yet the expression of the whole face, owing to these strange, stony, and yet spiritual eyes, was high and consoling. If mortal gaze had never sought its meaning before, in the deep shadow where it had been placed long centuries ago, yet Ruth's did now. Who could have imagined such a look? Who could have witnessed—perhaps felt—such infinite sorrow, and yet dared to lift it up by Faith into a peace so pure? Or was it a mere conception? If so, what a soul the unknown carver must have had! for creator and handicraftsman must have been one; no two minds could have been in such perfect harmony. Whatever it was—however it came there—imaginer, carver, sufferer, all were long passed away. Human art was ended—human life done—human suffering over; but this remained; it stilled Ruth's beating heart to look on it. She grew still enough to hear words which have come to many in their time of need, and awed them in the presence of the extremest suffering that the hushed world has ever heard of.

The second lesson for the morning of the 25th of September is the 26th chapter of St Matthew's Gospel.

And when they prayed again, Ruth's tongue was unloosed, and she also could pray, in His name, who underwent the agony in the garden.

As they came out of church, there was a little pause and gathering at the door. It had begun to rain; those who had umbrellas were putting them up; those who had not were regretting, and wondering how long it would last. Standing for a moment, impeded by the people who were thus collected under the porch, Ruth heard a voice close to her say, very low, but very distinctly,

"I have much to say to you—much to explain. I entreat you to give me the opportunity."

Ruth did not reply. She would not acknowledge that she heard; but she trembled nevertheless, for the well-remembered voice was low and soft, and had yet its power to thrill. She earnestly desired to know why and how he had left her. It appeared to her as if that knowledge could alone give her a relief from the restless wondering that distracted her mind, and that one explanation could do no harm.

"*No!*" the higher spirit made answer; "*it must not be.*"

Ruth and the girls had each an umbrella. She turned to Mary, and said,

"Mary, give your umbrella to Mr Donne, and come under mine." Her way of speaking was short and decided; she was compressing her meaning into as few words as possible. The little girl obeyed in silence. As they went first through the churchyard stile, Mr Donne spoke again.

"You are unforgiving," said he. "I only ask you to hear me. I have a right to be heard, Ruth! I won't believe you are so much changed, as not to listen to me when I entreat."

He spoke in a tone of soft complaint. But he himself had done much to destroy the illusion which had hung about his memory for years, whenever Ruth had allowed herself to think of it. Besides which, during the time of her residence in the Benson family, her feeling of what people ought to be had been unconsciously raised and refined; and Mr Donne, even while she had to struggle against the force of past recollections, repelled her so much by what he was at present, that every speech of his, every minute they were together, served to make her path more and more easy to follow. His voice retained something of its former influence. When he spoke, without her seeing him, she could not help remembering former days.

She did not answer this last speech any more than the first. She saw clearly, that, putting aside all thought as to the character of their former relationship, it had been dissolved by his will—his act and deed; and that, therefore, the power to refuse any further intercourse whatsoever remained with her.

It sometimes seems a little strange how, after having earnestly prayed to be delivered from temptation, and having given ourselves with shut eyes into God's hand, from that time every thought, every outward influence, every acknowledged law of life, seems to lead us on from strength to strength. It seems strange sometimes, because we notice the coincidence; but it is the natural, unavoidable consequence of all truth and goodness being one and the same, and therefore carried out in every circumstance, external and internal, of God's creation.

When Mr Donne saw that Ruth would not answer him, he became only the more determined that she should hear what he had to say. What that was he did not exactly know. The whole affair was most mysterious and piquant.

The umbrella protected Ruth from more than the rain on that walk homewards, for under its shelter she could not be spoken to unheard. She had not rightly understood at what time she and the girls were to dine. From the gathering at mealtimes she must not shrink. She must show no sign of weakness. But, oh! the relief, after that walk, to sit in her own room, locked up, so that neither Mary nor Elizabeth could come by surprise, and to let her weary frame (weary with being so long braced up to rigidity and stiff quiet) fall into a chair anyhow—all helpless, nerveless, motionless, as if the very bones had melted out of her!

The peaceful rest which her mind took was in thinking of Leonard. She dared not look before or behind, but she could see him well at present. She brooded over the thought of him, till she dreaded his father more and more. By the light of her child's purity and innocence, she saw evil clearly, and yet more clearly. She thought that, if Leonard ever came to know the nature of his birth, she had nothing for it but to die out of his sight. He could never know—human heart could never know, her ignorant innocence, and all the small circumstances which had impelled her onwards. But God knew. And if Leonard heard of his mother's error, why, nothing remained but death; for she felt, then, as if she had it in her power to die innocently out of such future agony; but that escape is not so easy. Suddenly a fresh thought came, and she prayed that, through whatever suffering, she might be purified. Whatever trials, woes, measureless pangs, God might see fit to chastise her with, she would not shrink, if only at last she might come into His presence in Heaven. Alas! the shrinking from suffering we cannot help. That part of her prayer was vain. And as for the rest, was not the sure justice of His law finding her out even now? His laws once broken, His justice and the very nature of those laws bring the immutable retribution; but if we turn penitently to Him, He enables us to bear our punishment with a meek and docile heart, "for His mercy endureth for ever."

Mr Bradshaw had felt himself rather wanting in proper attention to his guest, inasmuch as he had been unable, all in a minute, to comprehend Mr Donne's rapid change of purpose; and, before it had entered into his mind that, notwithstanding the distance of the church, Mr Donne was going thither, that gentleman was out of the sight, and far out of the reach, of his burly host. But though the latter had so far neglected the duties of hospitality as to allow his visitor to sit in the Eagle's Crag pew with no other guard of honour than the children and the governess, Mr Bradshaw determined to make up for it by extra attention during the remainder of the day. Accordingly he never left Mr Donne. Whatever wish that gentleman expressed, it was the study of his host to gratify. Did he hint at the pleasure which a walk in such beautiful scenery would give him, Mr Bradshaw was willing to accompany him, although at Eccleston it was a principle with him not to take any walks for pleasure on a Sunday. When Mr Donne turned round, and recollected letters which must be written, and which would compel him to stay at home, Mr Bradshaw instantly gave up the walk, and remained at hand, ready to furnish him with any writing-materials which could be wanted, and which were not laid out in the half-furnished house. Nobody knew where Mr Hickson was all this time. He had sauntered out after Mr Donne, when the latter set off for church, and he had never returned. Mr Donne kept wondering if he could have met Ruth—if, in fact, she had gone out with her pupils, now that the afternoon had cleared up. This uneasy wonder, and a few mental imprecations on his host's polite attention, together with the letter-writing pretence, passed away the afternoon—the longest afternoon he had ever spent; and of weariness he had had his share. Lunch was lingering in the dining-room, left there for the truant Mr Hickson; but of the children or Ruth there was no sign. He ventured on a distant inquiry as to their whereabouts.

"They dine early; they are gone to church again. Mrs Denbigh was a member of the Establishment once; and, though she attends chapel at home, she seems glad to have an opportunity of going to church."

Mr Donne was on the point of asking some further questions about "Mrs Denbigh," when Mr Hickson came in, loud-spoken, cheerful, hungry, and as ready to talk about his ramble, and the way in which he had lost and found himself, as he was about everything else. He knew how to dress up the commonest occurrence with a little exaggeration, a few puns, and a happy quotation or two, so as to make it sound very agreeable. He could read faces, and saw that he had been missed; both host and visitor looked moped to death. He determined to devote himself to their amusement during the remainder of the day, for he had really lost himself, and felt that he had been away too long on a dull Sunday, when people were apt to get hypped if not well amused.

"It is really a shame to be indoors in such a place. Rain? yes, it rained some hours ago, but now it is splendid weather. I feel myself quite qualified for guide, I assure you. I can show you all the beauties of the neighbourhood, and throw in a bog and a nest of vipers to boot."

Mr Donne languidly assented to this proposal of going out; and then he became restless until Mr Hickson had eaten a hasty lunch, for he hoped to meet Ruth on the way from church, to be near her, and watch her, though he might not be able to speak to her. To have the slow hours roll away—to know he must leave the next day—and yet, so close to her, not to be seeing her—was more than he could bear. In an impetuous kind of way, he disregarded all Mr Hickson's offers of guidance to lovely views, and turned a deaf ear to Mr Bradshaw's expressed wish of showing him the land belonging to the house ("very little for fourteen thousand pounds"), and set off wilfully on the road leading to the church, from which, he averred, he had seen a view which nothing else about the place could equal.

They met the country people dropping homewards. No Ruth was there. She and her pupils had returned by the field-way, as Mr Bradshaw informed his guests at dinner-time. Mr Donne was very captious all through dinner. He thought it would never be over, and cursed Hickson's interminable stories, which were told on purpose to amuse him. His heart gave a fierce bound when he saw her in the drawing-room with the little girls.

She was reading to them—with how sick and trembling a heart, no words can tell. But she could master and keep down outward signs of her emotion. An hour more to-night (part of which was to be spent in family prayer, and all in the safety of company), another hour in the morning (when all would be engaged in the bustle of departure)—if, during this short space of time, she could not avoid speaking to him, she could at least keep him at such a distance as to make him feel that henceforward her world and his belonged to separate systems, wide as the heavens apart.

By degrees she felt that he was drawing near to where she stood. He was by the table examining the books that lay upon it. Mary and Elizabeth drew off a little space, awe-stricken by the future member for Eccleston. As he bent his head over a book, he said, "I implore you; five minutes alone."

The little girls could not hear; but Ruth, hemmed in so that no escape was possible, did hear.

She took sudden courage, and said, in a clear voice,

"Will you read the whole passage aloud? I do not remember it."

Mr Hickson, hovering at no great distance, heard these words, and drew near to second Mrs Denbigh's request. Mr Bradshaw, who was very sleepy after his unusually late dinner, and longing for bedtime, joined in the request, for it would save the necessity for making talk, and he might, perhaps, get in a nap, undisturbed and unnoticed, before the servants came in to prayers.

Mr Donne was caught; he was obliged to read aloud, although he did not know what he was reading. In the middle of some sentence the door opened, a rush of servants came in, and Mr Bradshaw became particularly wide awake in an instant, and read them a long sermon with great emphasis and unction, winding up with a prayer almost as long.

Ruth sat with her head drooping, more from exhaustion after a season of effort than because she shunned Mr Donne's looks. He had so lost his power over her—his power, which had stirred her so deeply the night before—that, except as one knowing her error and her shame, and making a cruel use of such knowledge, she had quite separated him from the idol of her youth. And yet, for the sake of that first and only love, she would gladly have known what explanation he could offer to account for leaving her. It would have been something gained to her own self-respect, if she had learnt that he was not then, as she felt him to be now, cold and egotistical, caring for no one and nothing but what related to himself.

Home, and Leonard—how strangely peaceful the two seemed! Oh, for the rest that a dream about Leonard would bring!

Mary and Elizabeth went to bed immediately after prayers, and Ruth accompanied them. It was planned that the gentlemen should leave early the next morning. They were to breakfast half an hour sooner, to catch the railway train; and this by Mr Donne's own arrangement, who had been as eager about his canvassing, the week before, as it was possible for him to be, but who now wished Eccleston and the Dissenting interest therein very fervently at the devil.

Just as the carriage came round, Mr Bradshaw turned to Ruth: "Any message for Leonard beyond love, which is a matter of course?"

Ruth gasped—for she saw Mr Donne catch at the name; she did not guess the sudden sharp jealousy called out by the idea that Leonard was a grown-up man.

"Who is Leonard?" said he to the little girl standing by him; he did not know which she was.

"Mrs Denbigh's little boy," answered Mary.

Under some pretence or other, he drew near to Ruth; and in that low voice, which she had learnt to loathe, he said,

"Our child!"

By the white misery that turned her face to stone—by the wild terror in her imploring eyes—by the gasping breath which came out as the carriage drove away—he knew that he had seized the spell to make her listen at last.

CHAPTER XXIV - THE MEETING ON THE SANDS

"He will take him away from me! He will take the child from me!"

These words rang like a tolling bell through Ruth's head. It seemed to her that her doom was certain. Leonard would be taken from her! She had a firm conviction—not the less firm because she knew not on what it was based—that a child, whether legitimate or not, belonged of legal right to the father. And Leonard, of all children, was the prince and monarch. Every man's heart would long to call Leonard "Child!" She had been too strongly taxed to have much power left her to reason coolly and dispassionately, just then, even if she had been with any one who could furnish her with information from which to draw correct conclusions. The one thought haunted her night and day—"He will take my child away from me!" In her dreams she saw Leonard borne away into some dim land, to which she could not follow. Sometimes he sat in a swiftly-moving carriage, at his father's side, and smiled on her as he passed by, as if going to promised pleasure. At another time he was struggling to return to her; stretching out his little arms, and crying to her for the help she could not give. How she got through the days, she did not know; her body moved about and habitually acted, but her spirit was with her child. She thought often of writing and warning Mr Benson of Leonard's danger; but then she shrank from recurring to circumstances, all mention of which had ceased years ago; the very recollection of which seemed buried deep for ever. Besides, she feared occasioning discord or commotion in the quiet circle in which she lived. Mr Benson's deep anger against her betrayer had been shown too clearly in the old time to allow her to think that he would keep it down without expression now. He would cease to do anything to forward his election; he would oppose him as much as he could; and Mr Bradshaw would be angry, and a storm would arise, from the bare thought of which Ruth shrank with the cowardliness of a person thoroughly worn out with late contest. She was bodily wearied with her spiritual buffeting.

One morning, three or four days after their departure, she received a letter from Miss Benson. She could not open it at first, and put it on one side, clenching her hand over it all the time. At last she tore it open. Leonard was safe as yet. There were a few lines in his great round hand, speaking of events no larger than the loss of a beautiful "alley." There was a sheet from Miss Benson. She always wrote letters in the manner of a diary. "Monday we did so-and-so; Tuesday, so-and-so, &c." Ruth glanced rapidly down the page. Yes, here it was! Sick, fluttering heart, be still!

"In the middle of the damsons, when they were just on the fire, there was a knock at the door. My brother was out, and Sally was washing up, and I was stirring the preserve with my great apron and bib on; so I bade Leonard come in from the garden and open the door. But I would have washed his face first, if I had known who it was! It was Mr Bradshaw and the Mr Donne that they hope to send up to the House of Commons, as member of Parliament for Eccleston, and another gentleman, whose name I never heard. They had come canvassing; and when they found my brother was out, they asked Leonard if they could see me. The child said, 'Yes! if I could leave the damsons;' and straightway came to call me, leaving them standing in the passage. I whipped off my apron, and took Leonard by the hand, for I fancied I should feel less awkward if he was with me; and then I went and asked them all into the study, for I thought I should like them to see how many books Thurstan had got. Then they began talking politics at me in a very polite manner, only I could not make head or tail of what they meant; and Mr Donne took a deal of notice of Leonard, and called him to him; and I am sure he noticed what a noble, handsome boy he was, though his face was very brown and red, and hot with digging, and his curls all tangled. Leonard talked back as if he had known him all his life, till, I think, Mr Bradshaw thought he was making too much noise, and bid him remember he ought to be seen, not heard. So he stood as still and stiff as a soldier, close to Mr Donne; and as I could not help looking at the two, and thinking how handsome they both were in their different ways, I could not tell Thurstan half the messages the gentlemen left for him. But there was one thing more I must tell you, though I said I would not. When Mr Donne was talking to Leonard, he took off his watch and chain and put it round the boy's neck, who was pleased enough, you may be sure. I bade him give it back to the gentleman, when they were all going away; and I was quite surprised, and very uncomfortable, when Mr Donne said he had given it to Leonard, and that he was to keep it for his own. I could see Mr Bradshaw was annoyed, and he and the other gentleman spoke to Mr Donne, and I heard them say, 'too barefaced;' and I shall never forget Mr Donne's proud, stubborn look back at them, nor his way of saying, 'I allow no one to interfere with what I choose to do with my own.' And he looked so haughty and displeased, I durst say nothing at the time. But when I told Thurstan, he was very grieved and angry; and said he had heard that our party were bribing, but that he never could have thought they would have tried to do it at his house. Thurstan is very much out of spirits about this election altogether; and, indeed, it does make sad work up and down the town. However, he sent back the watch with a letter to Mr Bradshaw; and Leonard was very good about it, so I gave him a taste of the new damson-preserve on his bread for supper."

Although a stranger might have considered this letter wearisome from the multiplicity of the details, Ruth craved greedily after more. What had Mr Donne said to Leonard? Had Leonard liked his new acquaintance? Were they likely to meet again? After wondering and wondering over these points, Ruth composed herself by the hope that in a day or two she should hear again; and to secure this end, she answered the letters by return of post. That was on Thursday. On Friday she had another letter, in a strange hand. It was from Mr Donne. No name, no initials were given. If it had fallen into another person's hands, they could not have recognised the writer, nor guessed to whom it was sent. It contained simply these words:

"For our child's sake, and in his name, I summon you to appoint a place where I can speak, and you can listen, undisturbed. The time must be on Sunday; the limit of distance may be the circumference of your power of walking. My words may be commands, but my fond heart entreats. More I shall not say now, but, remember! your boy's welfare depends on your acceding to this request. Address B. D., Post-Office, Eccleston."

Ruth did not attempt to answer this letter till the last five minutes before the post went out. She could not decide until forced to it. Either way she dreaded. She was very nearly leaving the letter altogether unanswered. But suddenly she resolved she would know all, the best, the worst. No cowardly dread of herself, or of others, should make her neglect aught that came to her in her child's name. She took up a pen and wrote:

"The sands below the rocks, where we met you the other night. Time, afternoon church."

Sunday came.

"I shall not go to church this afternoon. You know the way, of course; and I can trust you to go steadily by yourselves."

When they came to kiss her before leaving her, according to their fond wont, they were struck by the coldness of her face and lips.

"Are you not well, dear Mrs Denbigh? How cold you are!"

"Yes, darling! I am well;" and tears sprang into her eyes as she looked at their anxious little faces. "Go now, dears. Five o'clock will soon be here, and then we will have tea."

"And that will warm you!" said they, leaving the room.

"And then it will be over," she murmured—"over."

It never came into her head to watch the girls as they disappeared down the lane on their way to church. She knew them too well to distrust their doing what they were told. She sat still, her head bowed on her arms for a few minutes, and then rose up and went to put on her walking things. Some thoughts impelled her to sudden haste. She crossed the field by the side of the house, ran down the steep and rocky path, and was carried by the impetus of her descent far out on the level sands—but not far enough for her intent. Without looking to the right hand or to the left, where comers might be seen, she went forwards to the black posts, which, rising above the heaving waters, marked where the fishermen's nets were laid. She went straight towards this place, and hardly stinted her pace even where the wet sands were glittering with the receding waves. Once there, she turned round, and in a darting glance, saw that as yet no one was near. She was perhaps half-a-mile or more from the grey, silvery rocks, which sloped away into brown moorland, interspersed with a field here and there of golden, waving corn. Behind were purple hills, with sharp, clear outlines, touching the sky. A little on one side from where she stood, she saw the white cottages and houses which formed the village of Abermouth, scattered up and down, and, on a windy hill, about a mile inland, she saw the little grey church, where even now many were worshipping in peace.

"Pray for me!" she sighed out, as this object caught her eye.

And now, close under the heathery fields, where they fell softly down and touched the sands, she saw a figure moving in the direction of the great shadow made by the rocks—going towards the very point where the path from Eagle's Crag came down to the shore.

"It is he!" said she to herself. And she turned round and looked seaward. The tide had turned; the waves were slowly receding, as if loath to lose the hold they had, so lately, and with such swift bounds, gained on the yellow sands. The eternal moan they have made since the world began filled the ear, broken only by the skirl of the grey sea-birds as they alighted in groups on the edge of the waters, or as they rose up with their measured, balancing motion, and the sunlight caught their white breasts. There was no sign of human life to be seen; no boat, or distant sail, or near shrimper. The black posts there were all that spoke of men's work or labour. Beyond a stretch of the waters, a few pale grey hills showed like films; their summits clear, though faint, their bases lost in a vapoury mist.

On the hard, echoing sands, and distinct from the ceaseless murmur of the salt sea waves, came footsteps—nearer—nearer. Very near they were when Ruth, unwilling to show the fear that rioted in her heart, turned round, and faced Mr Donne.

He came forward, with both hands extended.

"This is kind! my own Ruth," said he. Ruth's arms hung down motionless at her sides.

"What! Ruth, have you no word for me?"

"I have nothing to say," said Ruth.

"Why, you little revengeful creature! And so I am to explain all before you will even treat me with decent civility."

"I do not want explanations," said Ruth, in a trembling tone. "We must not speak of the past. You asked me to come in Leonard's—in my child's name, and to hear what you had to say about him."

"But what I have to say about him relates to you even more. And how can we talk about him without recurring to the past? That past, which you try to ignore—I know you cannot do it in your heart—is full of happy recollections to me. Were you not happy in Wales?" he said, in his tenderest tone.

But there was no answer; not even one faint sigh, though he listened intently.

"You dare not speak; you dare not answer me. Your heart will not allow you to prevaricate, and you know you were happy."

Suddenly Ruth's beautiful eyes were raised to him, full of lucid splendour, but grave and serious in their expression; and her cheeks, heretofore so faintly tinged with the tenderest blush, flashed into a ruddy glow.

"I was happy. I do not deny it. Whatever comes, I will not blench from the truth. I have answered you."

"And yet," replied he, secretly exulting in her admission, and not perceiving the inner strength of which she must have been conscious before she would have dared to make it—"and yet, Ruth, we are not to recur to the past! Why not? If it was happy at the time, is the recollection of it so miserable to you?"

He tried once more to take her hand, but she quietly stepped back.

"I came to hear what you had to say about my child," said she, beginning to feel very weary.

"*Our* child, Ruth."

She drew herself up, and her face went very pale.

"What have you to say about him?" asked she, coldly.

"Much," exclaimed he—"much that may affect his whole life. But it all depends upon whether you will hear me or not."

"I listen."

"Good Heavens! Ruth, you will drive me mad. Oh! what a changed person you are from the sweet, loving creature you were! I wish you were not so beautiful." She did not reply, but he caught a deep, involuntary sigh.

"Will you hear me if I speak, though I may not begin all at once to talk of this boy—a boy of whom any mother—any parent, might be proud? I could see that, Ruth. I have seen him; he looked like a prince in that cramped, miserable house, and with no earthly advantages. It is a shame he should not have every kind of opportunity laid open before him."

There was no sign of maternal ambition on the motionless face, though there might be some little spring in her heart, as it beat quick and strong at the idea of the proposal she imagined he was going to make of taking her boy away to give him the careful education she had often craved for him. She should refuse it, as she would everything else which seemed to imply that she acknowledged a claim over Leonard; but yet sometimes, for her boy's sake, she had longed for a larger opening—a more extended sphere.

"Ruth! you acknowledge we were happy once;—there were circumstances which, if I could tell you them all in detail, would show you how in my weak, convalescent state I was almost passive in the hands of others. Ah, Ruth! I have not forgotten the tender nurse who soothed me in my delirium. When I am feverish, I dream that I am again at Llan-dhu, in the little old bed-chamber, and you, in white—which you always wore then, you know—flitting about me."

The tears dropped, large and round, from Ruth's eyes—she could not help it—how could she?

"We were happy then," continued he, gaining confidence from the sight of her melted mood, and recurring once more to the admission which he considered so much in his favour. "Can such happiness never return?" Thus he went on, quickly, anxious to lay before her all he had to offer, before she should fully understand his meaning.

"If you would consent, Leonard should be always with you—educated where and how you liked—money to any amount you might choose to name should be secured to you and him—if only, Ruth—if only those happy days might return."

Ruth spoke.

"I said that I was happy, because I had asked God to protect and help me—and I dared not tell a lie. I was happy. Oh! what is happiness or misery that we should talk about them now?"

Mr Donne looked at her, as she uttered these words, to see if she was wandering in her mind, they seemed to him so utterly strange and incoherent.

"I dare not think of happiness—I must not look forward to sorrow. God did not put me here to consider either of these things."

"My dear Ruth, compose yourself! There is no hurry in answering the question I asked."

"What was it?" said Ruth.

"I love you so, I cannot live without you. I offer you my heart, my life—I offer to place Leonard wherever you would have him placed. I have the power and the means to advance him in any path of life you choose. All who have shown kindness to you shall be rewarded by me, with a gratitude even surpassing your own. If there is anything else I can do that you can suggest, I will do it."

"Listen to me!" said Ruth, now that the idea of what he proposed had entered her mind. "When I said that I was happy with you long ago, I was choked with shame as I said it. And yet it may be a vain, false excuse that I make for myself. I was very young; I did not know how such a life was against God's pure and holy will—at least, not as I know it now; and I tell you truth—all the days of my years since I have gone about with a stain on my hidden soul—a stain which made me loathe myself, and envy those who stood spotless and undefiled; which made me shrink from my child—from Mr Benson, from his sister, from the innocent girls whom I teach—nay, even I have cowered away from God Himself; and what I did wrong then, I did blindly to what I should do now if I listened to you."

She was so strongly agitated that she put her hands over her face, and sobbed without restraint. Then, taking them away, she looked at him with a glowing face, and beautiful, honest, wet eyes, and tried to speak calmly, as she asked if she needed to stay longer (she would have gone away at once but that she thought of Leonard, and wished to hear all that his father might have to say). He was so struck anew by her beauty, and understood her so little, that he believed that she only required a little more urging to consent to what he wished; for in all she had said there was no trace of the anger and resentment for his desertion of her, which he had expected would be a prominent feature—the greatest obstacle he had to encounter. The deep sense of penitence she expressed, he mistook for earthly shame; which he imagined he could soon soothe away.

"Yes, I have much more to say. I have not said half. I cannot tell you how fondly I will—how fondly I do love you—how my life shall be spent in ministering to your wishes. Money, I see—I know, you despise—"

"Mr Bellingham! I will not stay to hear you speak to me so again. I have been sinful, but it is not you who should—" She could not speak, she was so choking with passionate sorrow.

He wanted to calm her, as he saw her shaken with repressed sobs. He put his hand on her arm. She shook it off impatiently, and moved away in an instant.

"Ruth!" said he, nettled by her action of repugnance, "I begin to think you never loved me."

"I! —I never loved you! Do you dare to say so?"

Her eyes flamed on him as she spoke. Her red, round lip curled into beautiful contempt.

"Why do you shrink so from me?" said he, in his turn getting impatient.

"I did not come here to be spoken to in this way," said she. "I came, if by any chance I could do Leonard good. I would submit to many humiliations for his sake—but to no more from you."

"Are not you afraid to brave me so?" said he. "Don't you know how much you are in my power?"

She was silent. She longed to go away, but dreaded lest he should follow her, where she might be less subject to interruption than she was here—near the fisherman's nets, which the receding tide was leaving every moment barer and more bare, and the posts they were fastened to more blackly uprising above the waters.

Mr Donne put his hands on her arms as they hung down before her—her hands tightly clasped together.

"Ask me to let you go," said he. "I will, if you will ask me." He looked very fierce and passionate and determined. The vehemence of his action took Ruth by surprise, and the painful tightness of the grasp almost made her exclaim. But she was quite still and mute.

"Ask me," said he, giving her a little shake. She did not speak. Her eyes, fixed on the distant shore, were slowly filling with tears. Suddenly a light came through the mist that obscured them, and the shut lips parted. She saw some distant object that gave her hope.

"It is Stephen Bromley," said she. "He is coming to his nets. They say he is a very desperate, violent man, but he will protect me."

"You obstinate, wilful creature!" said Mr Donne, releasing his grasp. "You forget that one word of mine could undeceive all these good people at Eccleston; and that if I spoke out ever so little, they would throw you off in an instant. Now!" he continued, "do you understand how much you are in my power?"

"Mr and Miss Benson know all—they have not thrown me off," Ruth gasped out. "Oh! for Leonard's sake! you would not be so cruel."

"Then do not you be cruel to him—to me. Think once more!"

"I think once more;" she spoke solemnly. "To save Leonard from the shame and agony of knowing my disgrace, I would lie down and die. Oh! perhaps it would be best for him—for me, if I might; my death would be a stingless grief—but to go back into sin would be the real cruelty to him. The errors of my youth may be washed away by my tears—it was so once when the gentle, blessed Christ was upon earth; but now, if I went into wilful guilt, as you would have me, how could I teach Leonard God's holy will? I should not mind his knowing my past sin, compared to the awful corruption it would be if he knew me living now, as you would have me, lost to all fear of God—" Her speech was broken by sobs. "Whatever may be my doom—God is just—I leave myself in His hands. I will save Leonard from evil. Evil would it be for him if I lived with you. I will let him die first!" She lifted her eyes to heaven, and clasped and wreathed her hands together tight. Then she said: "You have humbled me enough, sir. I shall leave you now."

She turned away resolutely. The dark, grey fisherman was at hand. Mr Donne folded his arms, and set his teeth, and looked after her.

"What a stately step she has! How majestic and graceful all her attitudes were! She thinks she has baffled me now. We will try something more, and bid a higher price." He unfolded his arms, and began to follow her. He gained upon her, for her beautiful walk was now wavering and unsteady. The works which had kept her in motion were running down fast.

"Ruth!" said he, overtaking her. "You shall hear me once more. Aye, look round! Your fisherman is near. He may hear me, if he chooses—hear your triumph. I am come to offer to marry you, Ruth; come what may, I will have you. Nay—I will make you hear me. I will hold this hand till you have heard me. Tomorrow I will speak to any one in Eccleston you like—to Mr Bradshaw; Mr ——, the little minister, I mean. We can make it worth while for him to keep our secret, and no one else need know but what you are really Mrs Denbigh. Leonard shall still bear this name, but in all things else he shall be treated as my son. He and you would grace any situation. I will take care the highest paths are open to him!"

He looked to see the lovely face brighten into sudden joy; on the contrary, the head was still hung down with a heavy droop.

"I cannot," said she; her voice was very faint and low.

"It is sudden for you, my dearest. But be calm. It will all be easily managed. Leave it to me."

"I cannot," repeated she, more distinct and clear, though still very low.

"Why! what on earth makes you say that?" asked he, in a mood to be irritated by any repetition of such words.

"I do not love you. I did once. Don't say I did not love you then; but I do not now. I could never love you again. All you have said and done since you came with Mr Bradshaw to Abermouth first, has only made me wonder how I ever could have loved you. We are very far apart. The time that has pressed down my life like brands of hot iron, and scarred me for ever, has been nothing to you. You have talked of it with no sound of moaning in your voice—no shadow over the brightness of your face; it has left no sense of sin on your conscience, while me it haunts and haunts; and yet I might plead that I was an ignorant child—only I will not plead anything, for God knows all— But this is only one piece of our great difference—"

"You mean that I am no saint," he said, impatient at her speech. "Granted. But people who are no saints have made very good husbands before now. Come, don't let any morbid, overstrained conscientiousness interfere with substantial happiness—happiness both to you and to me—for I am sure I can make you happy—aye! and make you love me, too, in spite of your pretty defiance. I love you so dearly I must win love back. And here are advantages for Leonard, to be gained by you quite in a holy and legitimate way."

She stood very erect.

"If there was one thing needed to confirm me, you have named it. You shall have nothing to do with my boy, by my consent, much less by my agency. I would rather see him working on the roadside than leading such a life—being such a one as you are. You have heard my mind now, Mr Bellingham. You have humbled me—you have baited me; and if at last I have spoken out too harshly, and too much in a spirit of judgment, the fault is yours. If there were no other reason to prevent our marriage but the one fact that it would bring Leonard into contact with you, that would be enough."

"It is enough!" said he, making her a low bow. "Neither you nor your child shall ever more be annoyed by me. I wish you a good evening."

They walked apart—he back to the inn, to set off instantly, while the blood was hot within him, from the place where he had been so mortified—she to steady herself along till she reached the little path, more like a rude staircase than anything else, by which she had to climb to the house.

She did not turn round for some time after she was fairly lost to the sight of any one on the shore; she clambered on, almost stunned by the rapid beating of her heart. Her eyes were hot and dry; and at last became as if she were suddenly blind. Unable to go on, she tottered into the tangled underwood which grew among the stones, filling every niche and crevice, and little shelving space, with green and delicate tracery. She sank down behind a great overhanging rock, which hid her from any one coming up the path. An ash-tree was rooted in this rock, slanting away from the sea-breezes that were prevalent in most weathers; but this was a still, autumnal Sabbath evening. As Ruth's limbs fell, so they lay. She had no strength, no power of volition to move a finger. She could not think or remember. She was literally stunned. The first sharp sensation which roused her from her torpor was a quick desire to see him once more; up she sprang, and climbed to an out-jutting dizzy point of rock, but a little above her sheltered nook, yet commanding a wide view over the bare, naked sands;—far away below, touching the rippling water-line, was Stephen Bromley, busily gathering in his nets; besides him there was no living creature visible. Ruth shaded her eyes, as if she thought they might have deceived her; but no, there was no one there. She went slowly down to her old place, crying sadly as she went.

"Oh! if I had not spoken so angrily to him—the last things I said were so bitter—so reproachful!—and I shall never, never see him again!"

She could not take in the general view and scope of their conversation—the event was too near her for that; but her heart felt sore at the echo of her last words, just and true as their severity was. Her struggle, her constant flowing tears, which fell from very weakness, made her experience a sensation of intense bodily fatigue; and her soul had lost the power of throwing itself forward, or contemplating anything beyond the dreary present, when the expanse of grey, wild, bleak moors, stretching wide away below a sunless sky, seemed only an outward sign of the waste world within her heart, for which she could claim no sympathy;—for she could not even define what its woes were; and if she could, no one would understand how the present time was haunted by the terrible ghost of the former love.

"I am so weary! I am so weary!" she moaned aloud at last. "I wonder if I might stop here, and just die away."

She shut her eyes, until through the closed lids came a ruddy blaze of light. The clouds had parted away, and the sun was going down in a crimson glory behind the distant purple hills. The whole western sky was one flame of fire. Ruth forgot herself in looking at the gorgeous sight. She sat up gazing, and, as she gazed, the tears dried on her cheeks; and, somehow, all human care and sorrow were swallowed up in the unconscious sense of God's infinity. The sunset calmed her more than any words, however wise and tender, could have done. It even seemed to give her strength and courage; she did not know how or why, but so it was.

She rose, and went slowly towards home. Her limbs were very stiff, and every now and then she had to choke down an unbidden sob. Her pupils had been long returned from church, and had busied themselves in preparing tea—an occupation which had probably made them feel the time less long.

If they had ever seen a sleep-walker, they might have likened Ruth to one for the next few days, so slow and measured did her movements seem—so far away was her intelligence from all that was passing around her—so hushed and strange were the tones of her voice. They had letters from home announcing the triumphant return of Mr Donne as M.P. for Eccleston. Mrs Denbigh heard the news without a word, and was too languid to join in the search after purple and yellow flowers with which to deck the sitting-room at Eagle's Crag.

A letter from Jemima came the next day, summoning them home. Mr Donne and his friends had left the place, and quiet was restored in the Bradshaw household; so it was time that Mary's and Elizabeth's holiday should cease. Mrs Denbigh had also a letter—a letter from Miss Benson, saying that Leonard was not quite well. There was so much pains taken to disguise anxiety, that it was very evident much anxiety was felt; and the girls were almost alarmed by Ruth's sudden change from taciturn langour to eager, vehement energy. Body and mind seemed strained to exertion. Every plan that could facilitate packing and winding-up affairs at Abermouth, every errand and arrangement that could expedite their departure by one minute, was done by Ruth with stern promptitude. She spared herself in nothing. She made them rest, made them lie down, while she herself lifted weights and transacted business with feverish power, never resting, and trying never to have time to think.

For in remembrance of the Past there was Remorse,—how had she forgotten Leonard these last few days!—how had she repined and been dull of heart to her blessing! And in anticipation of the Future there was one sharp point of red light in the darkness which pierced her brain with agony, and which she would not see or recognise—and saw and recognised all the more for such mad determination—which is not the true shield against the bitterness of the arrows of Death.

When the seaside party arrived in Eccleston, they were met by Mrs and Miss Bradshaw and Mr Benson. By a firm resolution, Ruth kept from shaping the question, "Is he alive?" as if by giving shape to her fears she made their realisation more imminent. She said merely, "How is he?" but she said it with drawn, tight, bloodless lips, and in her eyes Mr Benson read her anguish of anxiety.

"He is very ill, but we hope he will soon be better. It is what every child has to go through."

CHAPTER XXV - JEMIMA MAKES A DISCOVERY

Mr Bradshaw had been successful in carrying his point. His member had been returned; his proud opponents mortified. So the public thought he ought to be well pleased; but the public were disappointed to see that he did not show any of the gratification they supposed him to feel.

The truth was, that he had met with so many small mortifications during the progress of the election, that the pleasure which he would otherwise have felt in the final success of his scheme was much diminished.

He had more than tacitly sanctioned bribery; and now that the excitement was over, he regretted it; not entirely from conscientious motives, though he was uneasy from a slight sense of wrong-doing; but he was more pained, after all, to think that, in the eyes of some of his townsmen, his hitherto spotless character had received a blemish. He, who had been so stern and severe a censor on the undue influence exercised by the opposite party in all preceding elections, could not expect to be spared by their adherents now, when there were rumours that the hands of the scrupulous Dissenters were not clean. Before, it had been his boast that neither friend nor enemy could say one word against him; now, he was constantly afraid of an indictment for bribery, and of being compelled to appear before a Committee to swear to his own share in the business.

His uneasy, fearful consciousness made him stricter and sterner than ever; as if he would quench all wondering, slanderous talk about him in the town by a renewed austerity of uprightness; that the slack-principled Mr Bradshaw of one month of ferment and excitement might not be confounded with the highly-conscientious and deeply-religious Mr Bradshaw, who went to chapel twice a day, and gave a hundred pounds a-piece to every charity in the town, as a sort of thank-offering that his end was gained.

But he was secretly dissatisfied with Mr Donne. In general, that gentleman had been rather too willing to act in accordance with any one's advice, no matter whose; as if he had thought it too much trouble to weigh the wisdom of his friends, in which case Mr Bradshaw's would have, doubtless, proved the most valuable. But now and then he unexpectedly, and utterly without reason, took the conduct of affairs into his own hands, as when he had been absent without leave only just before the day of nomination. No one guessed whither he had gone; but the fact of his being gone was enough to chagrin Mr Bradshaw, who was quite ready to pick a quarrel on this very head, if the election had not terminated favourably. As it was, he had a feeling of proprietorship in Mr Donne which was not disagreeable. He had given the new M.P. his seat; his resolution, his promptitude, his energy, had made Mr Donne "our member;" and Mr Bradshaw began to feel proud of him accordingly. But there had been no one circumstance during this period to bind Jemima and Mr Farquhar together. They were still misunderstanding each other with all their power. The difference in the result was this: Jemima loved him all the more, in spite of quarrels and coolness. He was growing utterly weary of thc pctulant temper uf which he was never certain; of the reception which varied day after day, according to the mood she was in and the thoughts that were uppermost; and he was almost startled to find how very glad he was that the little girls and Mrs Denbigh were coming home. His was a character to bask in peace; and lovely, quiet Ruth, with her low tones and quiet replies, her delicate waving movements, appeared to him the very type of what a woman should be—a calm, serene soul, fashioning the body to angelic grace.

It was, therefore, with no slight interest that Mr Farquhar inquired daily after the health of little Leonard. He asked at the Bensons' house; and Sally answered him, with swollen and tearful eyes, that the child was very bad—very bad indeed. He asked at the doctor's; and the doctor told him, in a few short words, that "it was only a bad kind of measles, and that the lad might have a struggle for it, but he thought he would get through. Vigorous children carried their force into everything; never did things by halves; if they were ill, they were sure to be in a high fever directly; if they were well, there was no peace in the house for their rioting. For his part," continued the doctor, "he thought he was glad he had had no children; as far as he could judge, they were pretty much all plague and no profit." But as he ended his speech he sighed; and Mr Farquhar was none the less convinced that common report was true, which represented the clever, prosperous surgeon of Eccleston as bitterly disappointed at his failure of offspring.

While these various interests and feelings had their course outside the Chapel-house, within there was but one thought which possessed all the inmates. When Sally was not cooking for the little invalid, she was crying; for she had had a dream about green rushes, not three months ago, which, by some queer process of oneiromancy she interpreted to mean the death of a child; and all Miss Benson's endeavours were directed to making her keep silence to Ruth about this dream. Sally thought that the mother ought to be told; what were dreams sent for but for warnings? But it was just like a pack of Dissenters, who would not believe anything like other folks. Miss Benson was too much accustomed to Sally's contempt for Dissenters, as viewed from the pinnacle of the Establishment, to pay much attention to all this grumbling; especially as Sally was willing to take as much trouble about Leonard as if she believed he was going to live, and that his recovery depended upon her care. Miss Benson's great object was to keep her from having any confidential talks with Ruth; as if any repetition of the dream could have deepened the conviction in Ruth's mind that the child would die.

It seemed to her that his death would only be the fitting punishment for the state of indifference towards him—towards life and death—towards all things earthly or divine, into which she had suffered herself to fall since her last interview with Mr Donne. She did not understand that such exhaustion is but the natural consequence of violent agitation and severe tension of feeling. The only relief she experienced was in constantly serving Leonard; she had almost an animal's jealousy lest any one should come between her and her young. Mr Benson saw this jealous suspicion, although he could hardly understand it; but he calmed his sister's wonder and officious kindness, so that the two patiently and quietly provided all that Ruth might want, but did not interfere with her right to nurse Leonard. But when he was recovering, Mr Benson, with the slight tone of authority he knew how to assume when need was, bade Ruth lie down and take some rest, while his sister watched. Ruth did not answer, but obeyed in a dull, weary kind of surprise at being so commanded. She lay down by her child, gazing her fill at his calm slumber; and as she gazed, her large white eyelids were softly pressed down as with a gentle irresistible weight, and she fell asleep.

She dreamed that she was once more on the lonely shore, striving to carry Leonard away from some pursuer—some human pursuer—she knew he was human, and she knew who he was, although she dared not say his name even to herself, he seemed so close and present, gaining on her flying footsteps, rushing after her as with the sound of the roaring tide. Her feet seemed heavy weights fixed to the ground; they would not move. All at once, just near the shore, a great black whirlwind of waves clutched her back to her pursuer; she threw Leonard on to land, which was safety; but whether he reached it or no, or was swept back like her into a mysterious something too dreadful to be borne, she did not know, for the terror awakened her. At first the dream seemed yet a reality, and she thought that the pursuer was couched even there, in that very room, and the great boom of the sea was still in her ears. But as full consciousness returned, she saw herself safe in the dear old room—the haven of rest—the shelter from storms. A bright fire was glowing in the little old-fashioned, cup-shaped grate, niched into a corner of the wall, and guarded on either side by whitewashed bricks, which rested on hobs. On one of these the kettle hummed and buzzed, within two points of boiling whenever she or Leonard required tea. In her dream that home-like sound had been the roaring of the relentless sea, creeping swiftly on to seize its prey. Miss Benson sat by the fire, motionless and still; it was too dark to read any longer without a candle; but yet on the ceiling and upper part of the walls the golden light of the setting sun was slowly moving—so slow, and yet a motion gives the feeling of rest to the weary yet more than perfect stillness. The old clock on the staircase told its monotonous click-clack, in that soothing way which more marked the quiet of the house than disturbed with any sense of sound. Leonard still slept that renovating slumber, almost in her arms, far from that fatal pursuing sea, with its human form of cruelty. The dream was a vision; the reality which prompted the dream was over and past—Leonard was safe—she was safe; all this loosened the frozen springs, and they gushed forth in her heart, and her lips moved in accordance with her thoughts.

"What were you saying, my darling?" said Miss Benson, who caught sight of the motion, and fancied she was asking for something. Miss Benson bent over the side of the bed on which Ruth lay, to catch the low tones of her voice.

"I only said," replied Ruth, timidly, "thank God! I have so much to thank Him for, you don't know."

"My dear, I am sure we have all of us cause to be thankful that our boy is spared. See! he is wakening up; and we will have a cup of tea together."

Leonard strode on to perfect health; but he was made older in character and looks by his severe illness. He grew tall and thin, and the lovely child was lost in the handsome boy. He began to wonder, and to question. Ruth mourned a little over the vanished babyhood, when she was all in all, and over the childhood, whose petals had fallen away; it seemed as though two of her children were gone—the one an infant, the other a bright, thoughtless darling; and she wished that they could have remained quick in her memory for ever, instead of being absorbed in loving pride for the present boy. But these were only fanciful regrets, flitting like shadows across a mirror. Peace and thankfulness were once more the atmosphere of her mind; nor was her unconsciousness disturbed by any suspicion of Mr Farquhar's increasing approbation and admiration, which he was diligently nursing up into love for her. She knew that he had sent—she did not know how often he had brought—fruit for the convalescent Leonard. She heard, on her return from her daily employment, that Mr Farquhar had brought a little gentle pony on which Leonard, weak as he was, might ride. To confess the truth, her maternal pride was such that she thought that all kindness shown to such a boy as Leonard was but natural; she believed him to be

A child whom all that looked on, loved.

As in truth he was; and the proof of this was daily shown in many kind inquiries, and many thoughtful little offerings, besides Mr Farquhar's. The poor (warm and kind of heart to all sorrow common to humanity) were touched with pity for the young widow, whose only child lay ill, and nigh unto death. They brought what they could—a fresh egg, when eggs were scarce—a few ripe pears that grew on the sunniest side of the humblest cottage, where the fruit was regarded as a source of income—a call of inquiry, and a prayer that God would spare the child, from an old crippled woman, who could scarcely drag herself so far as the Chapel-house, yet felt her worn and weary heart stirred with a sharp pang of sympathy, and a very present remembrance of the time when she too was young, and saw the life-breath quiver out of her child, now an angel in that heaven which felt more like home to the desolate old creature than this empty earth. To all such, when Leonard was better, Ruth went, and thanked them from her heart. She and the old cripple sat hand in hand over the scanty fire on the hearth of the latter, while she told in solemn, broken, homely words, how her child sickened and died. Tears fell like rain down Ruth's cheeks; but those of the old woman were dry. All tears had been wept out of her long ago, and now she sat patient and quiet, waiting for death. But after this, Ruth "clave unto her," and the two were henceforward a pair of friends. Mr Farquhar was only included in the general gratitude which she felt towards all who had been kind to her boy.

The winter passed away in deep peace after the storms of the autumn, yet every now and then a feeling of insecurity made Ruth shake for an instant. Those wild autumnal storms had torn aside the quiet flowers and herbage that had gathered over the wreck of her early life, and shown her that all deeds, however hidden and long passed by, have their eternal consequences. She turned sick and faint whenever Mr Donne's name was casually mentioned. No one saw it; but she felt the miserable stop in her heart's beating, and wished that she could prevent it by any exercise of self-command. She had never named his identity with Mr Bellingham, nor had she spoken about the seaside interview. Deep shame made her silent and reserved on all her life before Leonard's birth; from that time she rose again in her self-respect, and spoke as openly as a child (when need was) of all occurrences which had taken place since then; except that she could not, and would not, tell of this mocking echo, this haunting phantom, this past, that would not rest in its grave. The very circumstance that it was stalking abroad in the world, and might reappear at any moment, made her a coward: she trembled away from contemplating what the reality had been; only she clung more faithfully than before to the thought of the great God, who was a rock in the dreary land, where no shadow was.

Autumn and winter, with their lowering skies, were less dreary than the woeful, desolate feelings that shed a gloom on Jemima. She found too late that she had considered Mr Farquhar so securely her own for so long a time, that her heart refused to recognise him as lost to her, unless her reason went through the same weary, convincing, miserable evidence day after day, and hour after hour. He never spoke to her now, except from common civility. He never cared for her contradictions; he never tried, with patient perseverance, to bring her over to his opinions; he never used the wonted wiles (so tenderly remembered now they had no existence but in memory) to bring her round out of some wilful mood—and such moods were common enough now! Frequently she was sullenly indifferent to the feelings of others—not from any unkindness, but because her heart seemed numb and stony, and incapable of sympathy. Then afterwards her self-reproach was terrible—in the dead of night, when no one saw it. With a strange perversity, the only intelligence she cared to hear, the only sights she cared to see, were the circumstances which gave confirmation to the idea that Mr Farquhar was thinking of Ruth for a wife. She craved with stinging curiosity to hear something of their affairs every day; partly because the torture which such intelligence gave was almost a relief from the deadness of her heart to all other interests.

And so spring (*gioventu dell'anno*) came back to her, bringing all the contrasts which spring alone can bring to add to the heaviness of the soul. The little winged creatures filled the air with bursts of joy; the vegetation came bright and hopefully onwards, without any check of nipping frost. The ash-trees in the Bradshaws' garden were out in leaf by the middle of May, which that year wore more the aspect of summer than most Junes do. The sunny weather mocked Jemima, and the unusual warmth oppressed her physical powers. She felt very weak and languid; she was acutely sensible that no one else noticed her want of strength; father, mother, all seemed too full of other things to care if, as she believed, her life was waning. She herself felt glad that it was so. But her delicacy was not unnoticed by all. Her mother often anxiously asked her husband if he did not think Jemima was looking ill; nor did his affirmation to the contrary satisfy her, as most of his affirmations did. She thought every morning, before she got up, how she could tempt Jemima to eat, by ordering some favourite dainty for dinner; in many other little ways she tried to minister to her child; but the poor girl's own abrupt irritability of temper had made her mother afraid of openly speaking to her about her health.

Ruth, too, saw that Jemima was not looking well. How she had become an object of dislike to her former friend she did not know; but she was sensible that Miss Bradshaw disliked her now. She was not aware that this feeling was growing and strengthening almost into repugnance, for she seldom saw Jemima out of school-hours, and then only for a minute or two. But the evil element of a fellow-creature's dislike oppressed the atmosphere of her life. That fellow-creature was one who had once loved her so fondly, and whom she still loved, although she had learnt to fear her, as we fear those whose faces cloud over when we come in sight—who cast unloving glances at us, of which we, though not seeing, are conscious, as of some occult influence; and the cause of whose dislike is unknown to us, though every word and action seems to increase it. I believe that this sort of dislike is only shown by the jealous, and that it renders the disliker even more miserable, because more continually conscious than the object; but the growing evidence of Jemima's feeling made Ruth very unhappy at times. This very May, too, an idea had come into her mind, which she had tried to repress—namely, that Mr Farquhar was in love with her. It annoyed her extremely; it made her reproach herself that she ever should think such a thing possible. She tried to strangle the notion, to drown it, to starve it out by neglect—its existence caused her such pain and distress.

The worst was, he had won Leonard's heart, who was constantly seeking him out; or, when absent, talking about him. The best was some journey connected with business, which would take him to the Continent for several weeks; and, during that time, surely this disagreeable fancy of his would die away, if untrue; and if true, some way would be opened by which she might put a stop to all increase of predilection on his part, and yet retain him as a friend for Leonard—that darling for whom she was far-seeing and covetous, and miserly of every scrap of love and kindly regard.

Mr Farquhar would not have been flattered if he had known how much his departure contributed to Ruth's rest of mind on the Saturday afternoon on which he set out on his journey. It was a beautiful day; the sky of that intense quivering blue which seemed as though you could look through it for ever, yet not reach the black, infinite space which is suggested as lying beyond. Now and then a thin, torn, vaporous cloud floated slowly within the vaulted depth; but the soft air that gently wafted it was not perceptible among the leaves on the trees, which did not even tremble. Ruth sat at her work in the shadow formed by the old grey garden wall; Miss Benson and Sally—the one in the parlour window-seat mending stockings, the other hard at work in her kitchen—were both within talking distance, for it was weather for open doors and windows; but none of the three kept up any continued conversation; and in the intervals Ruth sang low a brooding song, such as she remembered her mother singing long ago. Now and then she stopped to look at Leonard, who was labouring away with vehement energy at digging over a small plot of ground, where he meant to prick out some celery plants that had been given to him. Ruth's heart warmed at the earnest, spirited way in which he thrust his large spade deep down into the brown soil, his ruddy face glowing, his curly hair wet with the exertion; and yet she sighed to think that the days were over when her deeds of skill could give him pleasure. Now, his delight was in acting himself; last year, not fourteen months ago, he had watched her making a daisy-chain for him, as if he could not admire her cleverness enough; this year—this week, when she had been devoting every spare hour to the simple tailoring which she performed for her boy (she had always made every article he wore, and felt almost jealous of the employment), he had come to her with a wistful look, and asked when he might begin to have clothes made by a man?

Ever since the Wednesday when she had accompanied Mary and Elizabeth, at Mrs Bradshaw's desire, to be measured for spring clothes by the new Eccleston dressmaker, she had been looking forward to this Saturday afternoon's pleasure of making summer trousers for Leonard; but the satisfaction of the employment was a little taken away by Leonard's speech. It was a sign, however, that her life was very quiet and peaceful, that she had leisure to think upon the thing at all; and often she forgot it entirely in her low, chanting song, or in listening to the thrush warbling out his afternoon ditty to his patient mate in the holly-bush below.

The distant rumble of carts through the busy streets (it was market-day) not only formed a low rolling bass to the nearer and pleasanter sounds, but enhanced the sense of peace by the suggestion of the contrast afforded to the repose of the garden by the bustle not far off.

But besides physical din and bustle, there is mental strife and turmoil.

That afternoon, as Jemima was restlessly wandering about the house, her mother desired her to go on an errand to Mrs Pearson's, the new dressmaker, in order to give some directions about her sisters' new frocks. Jemima went, rather than have the trouble of resisting; or else she would have preferred staying at home, moving or being outwardly quiet according to her own fitful will. Mrs Bradshaw, who, as I have said, had been aware for some time that something was wrong with her daughter, and was very anxious to set it to rights if she only knew how, had rather planned this errand with a view to dispel Jemima's melancholy.

"And, Mimie, dear," said her mother, "when you are there, look out for a new bonnet for yourself; she has got some very pretty ones, and your old one is so shabby."

"It does for me, mother," said Jemima, heavily. "I don't want a new bonnet."

"But I want you to have one, my lassie. I want my girl to look well and nice."

There was something of homely tenderness in Mrs Bradshaw's tone that touched Jemima's heart. She went to her mother, and kissed her with more of affection than she had shown to any one for weeks before; and the kiss was returned with warm fondness.

"I think you love me, mother," said Jemima.

"We all love you, dear, if you would but think so. And if you want anything, or wish for anything, only tell me, and with a little patience I can get your father to give it you, I know. Only be happy, there's a good girl."

"Be happy! as if one could by an effort of will!" thought Jemima, as she went along the street, too absorbed in herself to notice the bows of acquaintances and friends, but instinctively guiding herself right among the throng and press of carts, and gigs, and market people in High Street.

But her mother's tones and looks, with their comforting power, remained longer in her recollection than the inconsistency of any words spoken. When she had completed her errand about the frocks, she asked to look at some bonnets, in order to show her recognition of her mother's kind thought.

Mrs Pearson was a smart, clever-looking woman of five or six and thirty. She had all the variety of small-talk at her finger-ends that was formerly needed by barbers to amuse the people who came to be shaved. She had admired the town till Jemima was weary of its praises, sick and oppressed by its sameness, as she had been these many weeks.

"Here are some bonnets, ma'am, that will be just the thing for you—elegant and tasty, yet quite of the simple style, suitable to young ladies. Oblige me by trying on this white silk!"

Jemima looked at herself in the glass; she was obliged to own it was very becoming, and perhaps not the less so for the flush of modest shame which came into her cheeks as she heard Mrs Pearson's open praises of the "rich, beautiful hair," and the "Oriental eyes" of the wearer.

"I induced the young lady who accompanied your sisters the other day—the governess, is she, ma'am?"

"Yes—Mrs Denbigh is her name," said Jemima, clouding over.

"Thank you, ma'am. Well, I persuaded Mrs Denbigh to try on that bonnet, and you can't think how charming she looked in it; and yet I don't think it became her as much as it does you."

"Mrs Denbigh is very beautiful," said Jemima, taking off the bonnet, and not much inclined to try on any other.

"Very, ma'am. Quite a peculiar style of beauty. If I might be allowed, I should say that hers was a Grecian style of loveliness, while yours was Oriental. She reminded me of a young person I once knew in Fordham." Mrs Pearson sighed an audible sigh.

"In Fordham!" said Jemima, remembering that Ruth had once spoken of the place as one in which she had spent some time, while the county in which it was situated was the same in which Ruth was born. "In Fordham! Why, I think Mrs Denbigh comes from that neighbourhood."

"Oh, ma'am! she cannot be the young person I mean—I am sure, ma'am—holding the position she does in your establishment. I should hardly say I knew her myself; for I only saw her two or three times at my sister's house; but she was so remarked for her beauty, that I remember her face quite well—the more so, on account of her vicious conduct afterwards."

"Her vicious conduct!" repeated Jemima, convinced by these words that there could be no identity between Ruth and the "young person" alluded to. "Then it could not have been our Mrs Denbigh."

"Oh, no, ma'am! I am sure I should be sorry to be understood to have suggested anything of the kind. I beg your pardon if I did so. All I meant to say—and perhaps that was a liberty I ought not to have taken, considering what Ruth Hilton was—"

"Ruth Hilton!" said Jemima, turning suddenly round, and facing Mrs Pearson.

"Yes, ma'am, that was the name of the young person I allude to."

"Tell me about her—what did she do?" asked Jemima, subduing her eagerness of tone and look as best she might, but trembling as on the verge of some strange discovery.

"I don't know whether I ought to tell you, ma'am—it is hardly a fit story for a young lady; but this Ruth Hilton was an apprentice to my sister-in-law, who had a first-rate business in Fordham, which brought her a good deal of patronage from the county families; and this young creature was very artful and bold, and thought sadly too much of her beauty; and, somehow, she beguiled a young gentleman, who took her into keeping (I am sure, ma'am, I ought to apologise for polluting your ears—)"

"Go on," said Jemima, breathlessly.

"I don't know much more. His mother followed him into Wales. She was a lady of a great deal of religion, and of a very old family, and was much shocked at her son's misfortune in being captivated by such a person; but she led him to repentance, and took him to Paris, where, I think, she died; but I am not sure, for, owing to family differences, I have not been on terms for some years with my sister-in-law, who was my informant."

"Who died?" interrupted Jemima—"the young man's mother, or—or Ruth Hilton?"

"Oh dear, ma'am! pray don't confuse the two. It was the mother, Mrs— I forget the name—something like Billington. It was the lady who died."

"And what became of the other?" asked Jemima, unable, as her dark suspicion seemed thickening, to speak the name.

"The girl? Why, ma'am, what could become of her? Not that I know exactly—only one knows they can but go from bad to worse, poor creatures! God forgive me, if I am speaking too transiently of such degraded women, who, after all, are a disgrace to our sex."

"Then you know nothing more about her?" asked Jemima.

"I did hear that she had gone off with another gentleman that she met with in Wales, but I'm sure I can't tell who told me."

There was a little pause. Jemima was pondering on all she had heard. Suddenly she felt that Mrs Pearson's eyes were upon her, watching her; not with curiosity, but with a newly-awakened intelligence;—and yet she must ask one more question; but she tried to ask it in an indifferent, careless tone, handling the bonnet while she spoke.

"How long is it since all this—all you have been telling me about—happened?" (Leonard was eight years old.)

"Why—let me see. It was before I was married, and I was married three years, and poor dear Pearson has been deceased five—I should say going on for nine years this summer. Blush roses would become your complexion, perhaps, better than these lilacs," said she, as with superficial observation she watched Jemima turning the bonnet round and round on her hand—the bonnet that her dizzy eyes did not see.

"Thank you. It is very pretty. But I don't want a bonnet. I beg your pardon for taking up your time." And with an abrupt bow to the discomfited Mrs Pearson, she was out and away in the open air, threading her way with instinctive energy along the crowded street. Suddenly she turned round, and went back to Mrs Pearson's with even more rapidity than she had been walking away from the house.

"I have changed my mind," said she, as she came, breathless, up into the show-room. "I will take the bonnet. How much is it?"

"Allow me to change the flowers; it can be done in an instant, and then you can see if you would not prefer the roses; but with either foliage it is a lovely little bonnet," said Mrs Pearson, holding it up admiringly on her hand.

"Oh! never mind the flowers—yes! change them to roses." And she stood by, agitated (Mrs Pearson thought with impatience), all the time the milliner was making the alteration with skilful, busy haste.

"By the way," said Jemima, when she saw the last touches were being given, and that she must not delay executing the purpose which was the real cause of her return—"Papa, I am sure, would not like your connecting Mrs Denbigh's name with such a—story as you have been telling me."

"Oh dear! ma'am, I have too much respect for you all to think of doing such a thing! Of course I know, ma'am, that it is not to be cast up to any lady that she is like anybody disreputable."

"But I would rather you did not name the likeness to any one," said Jemima; "not to any one. Don't tell any one the story you have told me this morning."

"Indeed, ma'am, I should never think of such a thing! My poor husband could have borne witness that I am as close as the grave where there is anything to conceal."

"Oh dear!" said Jemima, "Mrs Pearson, there is nothing to conceal; only you must not speak about it."

"I certainly shall not do it, ma'am; you may rest assured of me."

This time Jemima did not go towards home, but in the direction of the outskirts of the town, on the hilly side. She had some dim recollection of hearing her sisters ask if they might not go and invite Leonard and his mother to tea; and how could she face Ruth, after the conviction had taken possession of her heart that she, and the sinful creature she had just heard of, were one and the same?

It was yet only the middle of the afternoon; the hours were early in the old-fashioned town of Eccleston. Soft white clouds had come slowly sailing up out of the west; the plain was flecked with thin floating shadows, gently borne along by the westerly wind that was waving the long grass in the hay-fields into alternate light and shade. Jemima went into one of these fields, lying by the side of the up-land road. She was stunned by the shock she had received. The diver, leaving the green sward, smooth and known, where his friends stand with their familiar smiling faces, admiring his glad bravery—the diver, down in an instant in the horrid depths of the sea, close to some strange, ghastly, lidless-eyed monster, can hardly more feel his blood curdle at the near terror than did Jemima now. Two hours ago—but a point of time on her mind's dial—she had never imagined that she should ever come in contact with any one who had committed open sin; she had never shaped her conviction into words and sentences, but still it was *there*, that all the respectable, all the family and religious circumstances of her life, would hedge her in, and guard her from ever encountering the great shock of coming face to face with vice. Without being pharisaical in her estimation of herself, she had all a Pharisee's dread of publicans and sinners, and all a child's cowardliness—that cowardliness which prompts it to shut its eyes against the object of terror, rather than acknowledge its existence with brave faith. Her father's often reiterated speeches had not been without their effect. He drew a clear line of partition, which separated mankind into two great groups, to one of which, by the grace of God, he and his belonged; while the other was composed of those whom it was his duty to try and reform, and bring the whole force of his morality to bear upon, with lectures, admonitions, and exhortations—a duty to be performed, because it was a duty—but with very little of that Hope and Faith which is the Spirit that maketh alive. Jemima had rebelled against these hard doctrines of her father's, but their frequent repetition had had its effect, and led her to look upon those who had gone astray with shrinking, shuddering recoil, instead of with a pity so Christ-like as to have both wisdom and tenderness in it.

And now she saw among her own familiar associates one, almost her housefellow, who had been stained with that evil most repugnant to her womanly modesty, that would fain have ignored its existence altogether. She loathed the thought of meeting Ruth again. She wished that she could take her up, and put her down at a distance somewhere—anywhere—where she might never see or hear of her more; never be reminded, as she must be whenever she saw her, that such things were in this sunny, bright, lark-singing earth, over which the blue dome of heaven bent softly down as Jemima sat in the hayfield that June afternoon; her cheeks flushed and red, but her lips pale and compressed, and her eyes full of a heavy, angry sorrow. It was Saturday, and the people in that part of the country left their work an hour earlier on that day. By this, Jemima knew it must be growing time for her to be at home. She had had so much of conflict in her own mind of late, that she had grown to dislike struggle, or speech, or explanation; and so strove to conform to times and hours much more than she had done in happier days. But oh! how full of hate her heart was growing against the world! And oh! how she sickened at the thought of seeing Ruth! Who was to be trusted more, if Ruth—calm, modest, delicate, dignified Ruth—had a memory blackened by sin?

As she went heavily along, the thought of Mr Farquhar came into her mind. It showed how terrible had been the stun, that he had been forgotten until now. With the thought of him came in her first merciful feeling towards Ruth. This would never have been, had therc been the least latent suspicion in Jemima's jealous mind that Ruth had purposely done aught—looked a look—uttered a word—modulated a tone—for the sake of attracting. As Jemima recalled all the passages of their intercourse, she slowly confessed to herself how pure and simple had been all Ruth's ways in relation to Mr Farquhar. It was not merely that there had been no coquetting, but there had been simple unconsciousness on Ruth's part, for so long a time after Jemima had discovered Mr Farquhar's inclination for her; and when at length she had slowly awakened to some perception of the state of his feelings, there had been a modest, shrinking dignity of manner, not startled, or emotional, or even timid, but pure, grave, and quiet; and this conduct of Ruth's, Jemima instinctively acknowledged to be of necessity transparent and sincere. Now, and here, there was no hypocrisy; but some time, somewhere, on the part of somebody, what hypocrisy, what lies must have been acted, if not absolutely spoken, before Ruth could have been received by them all as the sweet, gentle, girlish widow, which she remembered they had all believed Mrs Denbigh to be when first she came among them! Could Mr and Miss Benson know? Could they be a party to the deceit? Not sufficiently acquainted with the world to understand how strong had been the temptation to play the part they did, if they wished to give Ruth a chance, Jemima could not believe them guilty of such deceit as the knowledge of Mrs Denbigh's previous conduct would imply; and yet how it darkened the latter into a treacherous hypocrite, with a black secret shut up in her soul for years—living in apparent confidence, and daily household familiarity with the Bensons for years, yet never telling the remorse that ought to be corroding her heart! Who was true? Who was not? Who was good and pure? Who was not? The very foundations of Jemima's belief in her mind were shaken.

Could it be false? Could there be two Ruth Hiltons? She went over every morsel of evidence. It could not be. She knew that Mrs Denbigh's former name had been Hilton. She had heard her speak casually, but charily, of having lived in Fordham. She knew she had been in Wales but a short time before she made her appearance in Eccleston. There was no doubt of the identity. Into the middle of Jemima's pain and horror at the afternoon's discovery, there came a sense of the power which the knowledge of this secret gave her over Ruth; but this was no relief, only an aggravation of the regret with which Jemima looked back on her state of ignorance. It was no wonder that when she arrived at home, she was so oppressed with headache that she had to go to bed directly.

"Quiet, mother! quiet, dear, dear mother" (for she clung to the known and tried goodness of her mother more than ever now), "that is all I want." And she was left to the stillness of her darkened room, the blinds idly flapping to and fro in the soft evening breeze, and letting in the rustling sound of the branches which waved close to her window, and the thrush's gurgling warble, and the distant hum of the busy town.

Her jealousy was gone—she knew not how or where. She might shun and recoil from Ruth, but she now thought that she could never more be jealous of her. In her pride of innocence, she felt almost ashamed that such a feeling could have had existence. Could Mr Farquhar hesitate between her own self and one who— No! she could not name what Ruth had been, even in thought. And yet he might never know, so fair a seeming did her rival wear. Oh! for one ray of God's holy light to know what was seeming, and what was truth, in this traitorous hollow earth! It might be—she used to think such things possible, before sorrow had embittered her—that Ruth had worked her way through the deep purgatory of repentance up to something like purity again; God only knew! If her present goodness was real—if, after having striven back thus far on the heights, a fellow-woman was to throw her down into some terrible depth with her unkind, incontinent tongue, that would be too cruel! And yet, if—there was such woeful uncertainty and deceit somewhere—if Ruth— No! that Jemima, with noble candour, admitted was impossible. Whatever Ruth had been, she was good, and to be respected as such, now. It did not follow that Jemima was to preserve the secret always; she doubted her own power to do so, if Mr Farquhar came home again, and were still constant in his admiration of Mrs Denbigh, and if Mrs Denbigh gave him any—the least encouragement. But this last she thought, from what she knew of Ruth's character, was impossible. Only, what was impossible after this afternoon's discovery? At any rate, she would watch and wait. Come what might, Ruth was in her power. And, strange to say, this last certainty gave Jemima a kind of protecting, almost pitying, feeling for Ruth. Her horror at the wrong was not diminished; but the more she thought of the struggles that the wrong-doer must have made to extricate herself, the more she felt how cruel it would be to baffle all by revealing what had been. But for her sisters' sake she had a duty to perform; she must watch Ruth. For her love's sake she could not have helped watching; but she was too much stunned to recognise the force of her love, while duty seemed the only stable thing to cling to. For the present she would neither meddle nor mar in Ruth's course of life.

CHAPTER XXVI - MR BRADSHAW'S VIRTUOUS INDIGNATION

So it was that Jemima no longer avoided Ruth, nor manifested by word or look the dislike which for a long time she had been scarce concealing. Ruth could not help noticing that Jemima always sought to be in her presence while she was at Mr Bradshaw's house; either when daily teaching Mary and Elizabeth, or when she came as an occasional visitor with Mr and Miss Benson, or by herself. Up to this time Jemima had used no gentle skill to conceal the abruptness with which she would leave the room rather than that Ruth and she should be brought into contact—rather than that it should fall to her lot to entertain Ruth during any part of the evening. It was months since Jemima had left off sitting in the schoolroom, as had been her wont during the first few years of Ruth's governess-ship. Now, each morning Miss Bradshaw seated herself at a little round table in the window, at her work, or at her writing; but whether she sewed, or wrote, or read, Ruth felt that she was always watching—watching. At first Ruth had welcomed all these changes in habit and behaviour, as giving her a chance, she thought, by some patient waiting or some opportune show of enduring, constant love, to regain her lost friend's regard; but by-and-by the icy chillness, immovable and grey, struck more to her heart than many sudden words of unkindness could have done. They might be attributed to the hot impulses of a hasty temper—to the vehement anger of an accuser; but this measured manner was the conscious result of some deep-seated feeling; this cold sternness befitted the calm implacability of some severe judge. The watching, which Ruth felt was ever upon her, made her unconsciously shiver, as you would if you saw that the passionless eyes of the dead were visibly gazing upon you. Her very being shrivelled and parched up in Jemima's presence, as if blown upon by a bitter, keen, east wind.

Jemima bent every power she possessed upon the one object of ascertaining what Ruth really was. Sometimes the strain was very painful; the constant tension made her soul weary; and she moaned aloud, and upbraided circumstance (she dared not go higher—to the Maker of circumstance) for having deprived her of her unsuspicious happy ignorance.

Things were in this state when Mr Richard Bradshaw came on his annual home visit. He was to remain another year in London, and then to return and be admitted into the firm. After he had been a week at home, he grew tired of the monotonous regularity of his father's household, and began to complain of it to Jemima.

"I wish Farquhar were at home. Though he is such a stiff, quiet old fellow, his coming in in the evenings makes a change. What has become of the Millses? They used to drink tea with us sometimes, formerly."

"Oh! papa and Mr Mills took opposite sides at the election, and we have never visited since. I don't think they are any great loss."

"Anybody is a loss—the stupidest bore that ever was would be a blessing, if he only would come in sometimes."

"Mr and Miss Benson have drank tea here twice since you came."

"Come, that's capital! Apropos of stupid bores, you talk of the Bensons. I did not think you had so much discrimination, my little sister."

Jemima looked up in surprise; and then reddened angrily.

"I never meant to say a word against Mr or Miss Benson, and that you know quite well, Dick."

"Never mind! I won't tell tales. They are stupid old fogeys, but they are better than nobody, especially as that handsome governess of the girls always comes with them to be looked at."

There was a little pause; Richard broke it by saying:

"Do you know, Mimie, I've a notion, if she plays her cards well, she may hook Farquhar!"

"Who?" asked Jemima, shortly, though she knew quite well.

"Mrs Denbigh, to be sure. We were talking of her, you know. Farquhar asked me to dine with him at his hotel as he passed through town, and—I'd my own reasons for going and trying to creep up his sleeve—I wanted him to tip me, as he used to do."

"For shame! Dick," burst in Jemima.

"Well! well! not tip me exactly, but lend me some money. The governor keeps me so deucedly short."

"Why! it was only yesterday, when my father was speaking about your expenses, and your allowance, I heard you say that you'd more than you knew how to spend."

"Don't you see that was the perfection of art? If my father had thought me extravagant, he would have kept me in with a tight rein; as it is, I'm in great hopes of a handsome addition, and I can tell you it's needed. If my father had given me what I ought to have had at first, I should not have been driven to the speculations and messes I've got into."

"What speculations? What messes?" asked Jemima, with anxious eagerness.

"Oh! messes was not the right word. Speculations hardly was; for they are sure to turn out well, and then I shall surprise my father with my riches." He saw that he had gone a little too far in his confidence, and was trying to draw in.

"But, what do you mean? Do explain it to me."

"Never you trouble your head about my business, my dear. Women can't understand the share-market, and such things. Don't think I've forgotten the awful blunders you made when you tried to read the state of the money-market aloud to my father, that night when he had lost his spectacles. What were we talking of? Oh! of Farquhar and pretty Mrs Denbigh. Yes! I soon found out that was the subject my gentleman liked me to dwell on. He did not talk about her much himself, but his eyes sparkled when I told him what enthusiastic letters Polly and Elizabeth wrote about her. How old d'ye think she is?"

"I know!" said Jemima. "At least, I heard her age spoken about, amongst other things, when first she came. She will be five-and-twenty this autumn."

"And Farquhar is forty, if he is a day. She's young, too, to have such a boy as Leonard; younger-looking, or full as young-looking as she is! I tell you what, Mimie, she looks younger than you. How old are you? Three-and-twenty, ain't it?"

"Last March," replied Jemima.

"You'll have to make haste and pick up somebody, if you're losing your good looks at this rate. Why, Jemima, I thought you had a good chance of Farquhar a year or two ago. How come you to have lost him? I'd far rather you'd had him than that proud, haughty Mrs Denbigh, who flashes her great grey eyes upon me if ever I dare to pay her a compliment. She ought to think it an honour that I take that much notice of her. Besides, Farquhar is rich, and it's keeping the business of the firm in one's own family; and if he marries Mrs Denbigh she will be sure to be wanting Leonard in when he's of age, and I won't have that. Have a try for Farquhar, Mimie! Ten to one it's not too late. I wish I'd brought you a pink bonnet down. You go about so dowdy—so careless of how you look."

"If Mr Farquhar has not liked me as I am," said Jemima, choking, "I don't want to owe him to a pink bonnet."

"Nonsense! I don't like to have my sisters' governess stealing a march on my sister. I tell you Farquhar is worth trying for. If you'll wear the pink bonnet I'll give it you, and I'll back you against Mrs Denbigh. I think you might have done something with 'our member,' as my father calls him, when you had him so long in the house. But, altogether, I should like Farquhar best for a brother-in-law. By the way, have you heard down here that Donne is going to be married? I heard of it in town, just before I left, from a man that was good authority. Some Sir Thomas Campbell's seventh daughter: a girl without a penny; father ruined himself by gambling, and obliged to live abroad. But Donne is not a man to care for any obstacle, from all accounts, when once he has taken a fancy. It was love at first sight, they say. I believe he did not know of her existence a month ago."

"No! we have not heard of it," replied Jemima. "My father will like to know; tell it him;" continued she, as she was leaving the room, to be alone, in order to still her habitual agitation whenever she heard Mr Farquhar and Ruth coupled together.

Mr Farquhar came home the day before Richard Bradshaw left for town. He dropped in after tea at the Bradshaws'; he was evidently disappointed to see none but the family there, and looked round whenever the door opened.

"Look! look!" said Dick to his sister. "I wanted to make sure of his coming in to-night, to save me my father's parting exhortations against the temptations of the world (as if I did not know much more of the world than he does!), so I used a spell I thought would prove efficacious; I told him that we should be by ourselves, with the exception of Mrs Denbigh, and look how he is expecting her to come in!"

Jemima did see; did understand. She understood, too, why certain packets were put carefully on one side, apart from the rest of the purchases of Swiss toys and jewellery, by which Mr Farquhar proved that none of Mr Bradshaw's family had been forgotten by him during his absence. Before the end of the evening, she was very conscious that her sore heart had not forgotten how to be jealous. Her brother did not allow a word, a look, or an incident, which might be supposed on Mr Farquhar's side to refer to Ruth, to pass unnoticed; he pointed out all to his sister, never dreaming of the torture he was inflicting, only anxious to prove his own extreme penetration. At length Jemima could stand it no longer, and left the room. She went into the schoolroom, where the shutters were not closed, as it only looked into the garden. She opened the window, to let the cool night air blow in on her hot cheeks. The clouds were hurrying over the moon's face in a tempestuous and unstable manner, making all things seem unreal; now clear out in its bright light, now trembling and quivering in shadow. The pain at her heart seemed to make Jemima's brain grow dull; she laid her head on her arms, which rested on the window-sill, and grew dizzy with the sick weary notion that the earth was wandering lawless and aimless through the heavens, where all seemed one tossed and whirling wrack of clouds. It was a waking nightmare, from the uneasy heaviness of which she was thankful to be roused by Dick's entrance.

"What, you are here, are you? I have been looking everywhere for you. I wanted to ask you if you have any spare money you could lend me for a few weeks?"

"How much do you want?" asked Jemima, in a dull, hopeless voice.

"Oh! the more the better. But I should be glad of any trifle, I am kept so confoundedly short."

When Jemima returned with her little store, even her careless, selfish brother was struck by the wanness of her face, lighted by the bed-candle she carried.

"Come, Mimie, don't give it up. If I were you, I would have a good try against Mrs Denbigh. I'll send you the bonnet as soon as ever I get back to town, and you pluck up a spirit, and I'll back you against her even yet."

It seemed to Jemima strange—and yet only a fitting part of this strange, chaotic world—to find that her brother, who was the last person to whom she could have given her confidence in her own family, and almost the last person of her acquaintance to whom she could look for real help and sympathy, should have been the only one to hit upon the secret of her love. And the idea passed away from his mind as quickly as all ideas not bearing upon his own self-interests did.

The night, the sleepless night, was so crowded and haunted by miserable images, that she longed for day; and when day came, with its stinging realities, she wearied and grew sick for the solitude of night. For the next week, she seemed to see and hear nothing but what confirmed the idea of Mr Farquhar's decided attachment to Ruth. Even her mother spoke of it as a thing which was impending, and which she wondered how Mr Bradshaw would like; for his approval or disapproval was the standard by which she measured all things.

"Oh! merciful God," prayed Jemima, in the dead silence of the night, "the strain is too great—I cannot bear it longer—my life—my love—the very essence of me, which is myself through time and eternity; and on the other side there is all-pitying Charity. If she had not been what she is—if she had shown any sign of triumph—any knowledge of her prize—if she had made any effort to gain his dear heart, I must have given way long ago, and taunted her, even if I did not tell others—taunted her, even though I sank down to the pit the next moment.

"The temptation is too strong for me. Oh Lord! where is Thy peace that I believed in, in my childhood?—that I hear people speaking of now, as if it hushed up the troubles of life, and had not to be sought for—sought for, as with tears of blood!"

There was no sound nor sight in answer to this wild imploring cry, which Jemima half thought must force out a sign from Heaven. But there was a dawn stealing on through the darkness of her night.

It was glorious weather for the end of August. The nights were as full of light as the days—everywhere, save in the low dusky meadows by the river-side, where the mists rose and blended the pale sky with the lands below. Unknowing of the care and trouble around them, Mary and Elizabeth exulted in the weather, and saw some new glory in every touch of the year's decay. They were clamorous for an expedition to the hills, before the calm stillness of the autumn should be disturbed by storms. They gained permission to go on the next Wednesday—the next half-holiday. They had won their mother over to consent to a full holiday, but their father would not hear of it. Mrs Bradshaw had proposed an early dinner, but the idea was scouted at by the girls. What would the expedition be worth if they did not carry their dinners with them in baskets? Anything out of a basket, and eaten in the open air, was worth twenty times as much as the most sumptuous meal in the house. So the baskets were packed up, while Mrs Bradshaw wailed over probable colds to be caught from sitting on the damp ground. Ruth and Leonard were to go; they four. Jemima had refused all invitations to make one of the party; and yet she had a half-sympathy with her sisters' joy—a sort of longing, lingering look back to the time when she too would have revelled in the prospect that lay before them. They, too, would grow up, and suffer; though now they played, regardless of their doom.

The morning was bright and glorious; just cloud enough, as some one said, to make the distant plain look beautiful from the hills, with its floating shadows passing over the golden corn-fields. Leonard was to join them at twelve, when his lessons with Mr Benson, and the girls' with their masters, should be over. Ruth took off her bonnet, and folded her shawl with her usual dainty, careful neatness, and laid them aside in a corner of the room to be in readiness. She tried to forget the pleasure she always anticipated from a long walk towards the hills, while the morning's work went on; but she showed enough of sympathy to make the girls cling round her with many a caress of joyous love. Everything was beautiful in their eyes; from the shadows of the quivering leaves on the wall to the glittering beads of dew, not yet absorbed by the sun, which decked the gossamer web in the vine outside the window. Eleven o'clock struck. The Latin master went away, wondering much at the radiant faces of his pupils, and thinking that it was only very young people who could take such pleasure in the "Delectus." Ruth said, "Now, do let us try to be very steady this next hour," and Mary pulled back Ruth's head, and gave the pretty budding mouth a kiss. They sat down to work, while Mrs Denbigh read aloud. A fresh sun-gleam burst into the room, and they looked at each other with glad, anticipating eyes.

Jemima came in, ostensibly to seek for a book, but really from that sort of restless weariness of any one place or employment, which had taken possession of her since Mr Farquhar's return. She stood before the bookcase in the recess, languidly passing over the titles in search of the one she wanted. Ruth's voice lost a tone or two of its peacefulness, and her eyes looked more dim and anxious at Jemima's presence. She wondered in her heart if she dared to ask Miss Bradshaw to accompany them in their expedition. Eighteen months ago she would have urged it on her friend with soft, loving entreaty; now she was afraid even to propose it as a hard possibility; everything she did or said was taken so wrongly—seemed to add to the old dislike, or the later stony contempt with which Miss Bradshaw had regarded her. While they were in this way Mr Bradshaw came into the room. His entrance—his being at home at all at this time—was so unusual a thing, that the reading was instantly stopped; and all four involuntarily looked at him, as if expecting some explanation of his unusual proceeding.

His face was almost purple with suppressed agitation.

"Mary and Elizabeth, leave the room. Don't stay to pack up your books. Leave the room, I say!" He spoke with trembling anger, and the frightened girls obeyed without a word. A cloud passing over the sun cast a cold gloom into the room which was late so bright and beaming; but, by equalising the light, it took away the dark shadow from the place where Jemima had been standing, and her figure caught her father's eye.

"Leave the room, Jemima," said he.

"Why, father?" replied she, in an opposition that was strange even to herself, but which was prompted by the sullen passion which seethed below the stagnant surface of her life, and which sought a vent in defiance. She maintained her ground, facing round upon her father, and Ruth—Ruth, who had risen, and stood trembling, shaking, a lightning-fear having shown her the precipice on which she stood. It was of no use; no quiet, innocent life—no profound silence, even to her own heart, as to the Past; the old offence could never be drowned in the Deep; but thus, when all was calm on the great, broad, sunny sea, it rose to the surface, and faced her with its unclosed eyes and its ghastly countenance. The blood bubbled up to her brain, and made such a sound there, as of boiling waters, that she did not hear the words which Mr Bradshaw first spoke; indeed, his speech was broken and disjointed by intense passion. But she needed not to hear; she knew. As she rose up at first, so she stood now—numb and helpless. When her ears heard again (as if the sounds were drawing nearer, and becoming more distinct, from some faint, vague distance of space), Mr Bradshaw was saying, "If there be one sin I hate—I utterly loathe—more than all others, it is wantonness. It includes all other sins. It is but of a piece that you should have come with your sickly, hypocritical face, imposing upon us all. I trust Benson did not know of it—for his own sake, I trust not. Before God, if he got you into my house on false pretences, he shall find his charity at other men's expense shall cost him dear—you—the common talk of Eccleston for your profligacy—" He was absolutely choked by his boiling indignation. Ruth stood speechless, motionless. Her head drooped a little forward, her eyes were more than half veiled by the large quivering lids, her arms hung down straight and heavy. At last she heaved the weight off her heart enough to say, in a faint, moaning voice, speaking with infinite difficulty:

"I was so young."

"The more depraved, the more disgusting you," Mr Bradshaw exclaimed, almost glad that the woman, unresisting so long, should now begin to resist. But to his surprise (for in his anger he had forgotten her presence) Jemima moved forwards, and said, "Father!"

"You hold your tongue, Jemima. You have grown more and more insolent—more and more disobedient every day. I now know who to thank for it. When such a woman came into my family there is no wonder at any corruption—any evil—any defilement—"

"Father!"

"Not a word! If, in your disobedience, you choose to stay and hear what no modest young woman would put herself in the way of hearing, you shall be silent when I bid you. The only good you can gain is in the way of warning. Look at that woman" (indicating Ruth, who moved her drooping head a little on one side, as if by such motion she could avert the pitiless pointing—her face growing whiter and whiter still every instant)—"look at that woman, I say—corrupt long before she was your age—hypocrite for years! If ever you, or any child of mine, cared for her, shake her off from you, as St Paul shook off the viper—even into the fire." He stopped for very want of breath. Jemima, all flushed and panting, went up and stood side by side with wan Ruth. She took the cold, dead hand which hung next to her in her warm convulsive grasp, and holding it so tight that it was blue and discoloured for days, she spoke out beyond all power of restraint from her father.

"Father, I will speak. I will not keep silence. I will bear witness to Ruth. I have hated her—so keenly, may God forgive me! but you may know, from that, that my witness is true. I have hated her, and my hatred was only quenched into contempt—not contempt now, dear Ruth—dear Ruth"—(this was spoken with infinite softness and tenderness, and in spite of her father's fierce eyes and passionate gesture)—"I heard what you have learnt now, father, weeks and weeks ago—a year it may be, all time of late has been so long; and I shuddered up from her and from her sin; and I might have spoken of it, and told it there and then, if I had not been afraid that it was from no good motive I should act in so doing, but to gain a way to the desire of my own jealous heart. Yes, father, to show you what a witness I am for Ruth, I will own that I was stabbed to the heart with jealousy; some one—some one cared for Ruth that—oh, father! spare me saying all." Her face was double-dyed with crimson blushes, and she paused for one moment—no more.

"I watched her, and I watched her with my wild-beast eyes. If I had seen one paltering with duty—if I had witnessed one flickering shadow of untruth in word or action—if, more than all things, my woman's instinct had ever been conscious of the faintest speck of impurity in thought, or word, or look, my old hate would have flamed out with the flame of hell! my contempt would have turned to loathing disgust, instead of my being full of pity, and the stirrings of new-awakened love, and most true respect. Father, I have borne my witness!"

"And I will tell you how much your witness is worth," said her father, beginning low, that his pent-up wrath might have room to swell out. "It only convinces me more and more how deep is the corruption this wanton has spread in my family. She has come amongst us with her innocent seeming, and spread her nets well and skilfully. She has turned right into wrong, and wrong into right, and taught you all to be uncertain whether there be any such thing as Vice in the world, or whether it ought not to be looked upon as Virtue. She has led you to the brink of the deep pit, ready for the first chance circumstance to push you in. And I trusted her—I trusted her—I welcomed her."

"I have done very wrong," murmured Ruth, but so low, that perhaps he did not hear her, for he went on, lashing himself up.

"I welcomed her. I was duped into allowing her bastard—(I sicken at the thought of it)—"

At the mention of Leonard, Ruth lifted up her eyes for the first time since the conversation began, the pupils dilating, as if she were just becoming aware of some new agony in store for her. I have seen such a look of terror on a poor dumb animal's countenance, and once or twice on human faces. I pray I may never see it again on either! Jemima felt the hand she held in her strong grasp writhe itself free. Ruth spread her arms before her, clasping and lacing her fingers together, her head thrown a little back, as if in intensest suffering.

Mr Bradshaw went on:

"That very child and heir of shame to associate with my own innocent children! I trust they are not contaminated."

"I cannot bear it—I cannot bear it!" were the words wrung out of Ruth.

"Cannot bear it! cannot bear it!" he repeated. "You must bear it, madam. Do you suppose your child is to be exempt from the penalties of his birth? Do you suppose that he alone is to be saved from the upbraiding scoff? Do you suppose that he is ever to rank with other boys, who are not stained and marked with sin from their birth? Every creature in Eccleston may know what he is; do you think they will spare him their scorn? 'Cannot bear it,' indeed! Before you went into your sin, you should have thought whether you could bear the consequences or not—have had some idea how far your offspring would be degraded and scouted, till the best thing that could happen to him would be for him to be lost to all sense of shame, dead to all knowledge of guilt, for his mother's sake."

Ruth spoke out. She stood like a wild creature at bay, past fear now. "I appeal to God against such a doom for my child. I appeal to God to help me. I am a mother, and as such I cry to God for help—for help to keep my boy in His pitying sight, and to bring him up in His holy fear. Let the shame fall on me! I have deserved it, but he—he is so innocent and good."

Ruth had caught up her shawl, and was tying on her bonnet with her trembling hands. What if Leonard was hearing of her shame from common report? What would be the mysterious shock of the intelligence? She must face him, and see the look in his eyes, before she knew whether he recoiled from her; he might have his heart turned to hate her, by their cruel jeers.

Jemima stood by, dumb and pitying. Her sorrow was past her power. She helped in arranging the dress, with one or two gentle touches, which were hardly felt by Ruth, but which called out all Mr Bradshaw's ire afresh; he absolutely took her by the shoulders and turned her by force out of the room. In the hall, and along the stairs, her passionate woeful crying was heard. The sound only concentrated Mr Bradshaw's anger on Ruth. He held the street-door open wide, and said, between his teeth, "If ever you, or your bastard, darken this door again, I will have you both turned out by the police!"

He need not have added this, if he had seen Ruth's face.

CHAPTER XXVII - PREPARING TO STAND ON THE TRUTH

As Ruth went along the accustomed streets, every sight and every sound seemed to bear a new meaning, and each and all to have some reference to her boy's disgrace. She held her head down, and scudded along dizzy with fear, lest some word should have told him what she had been, and what he was, before she could reach him. It was a wild, unreasoning fear, but it took hold of her as strongly as if it had been well founded. And, indeed, the secret whispered by Mrs Pearson, whose curiosity and suspicion had been excited by Jemima's manner, and confirmed since by many a little corroborating circumstance, had spread abroad, and was known to most of the gossips in Eccleston before it reached Mr Bradshaw's ears.

As Ruth came up to the door of the Chapel-house, it was opened, and Leonard came out, bright and hopeful as the morning, his face radiant at the prospect of the happy day before him. He was dressed in the clothes it had been such a pleasant pride to her to make for him. He had the dark blue ribbon tied round his neck that she had left out for him that very morning, with a smiling thought of how it would set off his brown, handsome face. She caught him by the hand as they met, and turned him, with his face homewards, without a word. Her looks, her rushing movement, her silence, awed him; and although he wondered, he did not stay to ask why she did so. The door was on the latch; she opened it, and only said, "Upstairs," in a hoarse whisper. Up they went into her own room. She drew him in, and bolted the door; and then, sitting down, she placed him (she had never let go of him) before her, holding him with her hands on each of his shoulders, and gazing into his face with a woeful look of the agony that could not find vent in words. At last she tried to speak; she tried with strong bodily effort, almost amounting to convulsion. But the words would not come; it was not till she saw the absolute terror depicted on his face that she found utterance; and then the sight of that terror changed the words from what she meant them to have been. She drew him to her, and laid her head upon his shoulder; hiding her face even there.

"My poor, poor boy! my poor, poor darling! Oh! would that I had died—I had died, in my innocent girlhood!"

"Mother! mother!" sobbed Leonard. "What is the matter? Why do you look so wild and ill? Why do you call me your 'poor boy'? Are we not going to Scaurside-hill? I don't much mind it, mother; only please don't gasp and quiver so. Dearest mother, are you ill? Let me call Aunt Faith!"

Ruth lifted herself up, and put away the hair that had fallen over and was blinding her eyes. She looked at him with intense wistfulness.

"Kiss me, Leonard!" said she—"kiss me, my darling, once more in the old way!" Leonard threw himself into her arms and hugged her with all his force, and their lips clung together as in the kiss given to the dying.

"Leonard!" said she at length, holding him away from her, and nerving herself up to tell him all by one spasmodic effort—"listen to me." The boy stood breathless and still, gazing at her. On her impetuous transit from Mr Bradshaw's to the Chapel-house, her wild, desperate thought had been that she would call herself by every violent, coarse name which the world might give her—that Leonard should hear those words applied to his mother first from her own lips; but the influence of his presence—for he was a holy and sacred creature in her eyes, and this point remained steadfast, though all the rest were upheaved—subdued her; and now it seemed as if she could not find words fine enough, and pure enough, to convey the truth that he must learn, and should learn from no tongue but hers.

"Leonard—when I was very young I did very wrong. I think God, who knows all, will judge me more tenderly than men—but I did wrong in a way which you cannot understand yet" (she saw the red flush come into his cheek, and it stung her as the first token of that shame which was to be his portion through life)—"in a way people never forget, never forgive. You will hear me called the hardest names that ever can be thrown at women—I have been, to-day; and, my child, you must bear it patiently, because they will be partly true. Never get confused, by your love for me, into thinking that what I did was right.—Where was I?" said she, suddenly faltering, and forgetting all she had said and all she had got to say; and then, seeing Leonard's face of wonder, and burning shame and indignation, she went on more rapidly, as fearing lest her strength should fail before she had ended.

"And, Leonard," continued she, in a trembling, sad voice, "this is not all. The punishment of punishments lies awaiting me still. It is to see you suffer for my wrongdoing. Yes, darling! they will speak shameful things of you, poor innocent child! as well as of me, who am guilty. They will throw it in your teeth through life, that your mother was never married—was not married when you were born—"

"Were not you married? Are not you a widow?" asked he abruptly, for the first time getting anything like a clear idea of the real state of the case.

"No! May God forgive me, and help me!" exclaimed she, as she saw a strange look of repugnance cloud over the boy's face, and felt a slight motion on his part to extricate himself from her hold. It was as slight, as transient as it could be—over in an instant. But she had taken her hands away, and covered up her face with them as quickly—covered up her face in shame before her child; and in the bitterness of her heart she was wailing out, "Oh, would to God I had died—that I had died as a baby—that I had died as a little baby hanging at my mother's breast!"

"Mother," said Leonard, timidly putting his hand on her arm; but she shrunk from him, and continued her low, passionate wailing. "Mother," said he, after a pause, coming nearer, though she saw it not—"mammy darling," said he, using the caressing name, which he had been trying to drop as not sufficiently manly, "mammy, my own, own dear, dear, darling mother, I don't believe them—I don't, I don't, I don't, I don't!" He broke out into a wild burst of crying as he said this. In a moment her arms were round the poor boy, and she was hushing him up like a baby on her bosom. "Hush, Leonard! Leonard, be still, my child! I have been too sudden with you!—I have done you harm—oh! I have done you nothing but harm," cried she, in a tone of bitter self-reproach.

"No, mother," said he, stopping his tears, and his eyes blazing out with earnestness; "there never was such a mother as you have been to me, and I won't believe any one who says it. I won't; and I'll knock them down if they say it again, I will!" He clenched his fist, with a fierce, defiant look on his face.

"You forget, my child," said Ruth, in the sweetest, saddest tone that ever was heard, "I said it of myself; I said it because it was true." Leonard threw his arms tight round her, and hid his face against her bosom. She felt him pant there like some hunted creature. She had no soothing comfort to give him. "Oh, that she and he lay dead!"

At last, exhausted, he lay so still and motionless, that she feared to look. She wanted him to speak, yet dreaded his first words. She kissed his hair, his head, his very clothes, murmuring low, inarticulate, moaning sounds.

"Leonard," said she, "Leonard, look up at me! Leonard, look up!" But he only clung the closer, and hid his face the more.

"My boy!" said she, "what can I do or say? If I tell you never to mind it—that it is nothing—I tell you false. It is a bitter shame and a sorrow that I have drawn down upon you. A shame, Leonard, because of me, your mother; but, Leonard, it is no disgrace or lowering of you in the eyes of God." She spoke now as if she had found the clue which might lead him to rest and strength at last. "Remember that, always. Remember that, when the time of trial comes—and it seems a hard and cruel thing that you should be called reproachful names by men, and all for what was no fault of yours—remember God's pity and God's justice; and though my sin shall have made you an outcast in the world—oh, my child, my child!"—(she felt him kiss her, as if mutely trying to comfort her—it gave her strength to go on)—"remember, darling of my heart, it is only your own sin that can make you an outcast from God."

She grew so faint that her hold of him relaxed. He looked up affrighted. He brought her water—he threw it over her; in his terror at the notion that she was going to die and leave him, he called her by every fond name, imploring her to open her eyes.

When she partially recovered, he helped her to the bed, on which she lay still, wan and death-like. She almost hoped the swoon that hung around her might be Death, and in that imagination she opened her eyes to take a last look at her boy. She saw him pale and terror-stricken; and pity for his affright roused her, and made her forget herself in the wish that he should not see her death, if she were indeed dying.

"Go to Aunt Faith!" whispered she; "I am weary, and want sleep."

Leonard arose slowly and reluctantly. She tried to smile upon him, that what she thought would be her last look might dwell in his remembrance as tender and strong; she watched him to the door; she saw him hesitate, and return to her. He came back to her, and said in a timid, apprehensive tone:

"Mother—will *they* speak to me about—it?"

Ruth closed her eyes, that they might not express the agony she felt, like a sharp knife, at this question. Leonard had asked it with a child's desire of avoiding painful and mysterious topics,—from no personal sense of shame as she understood it, shame beginning thus early, thus instantaneously.

"No," she replied. "You may be sure they will not."

So he went. But now she would have been thankful for the unconsciousness of fainting; that one little speech bore so much meaning to her hot, irritable brain. Mr and Miss Benson, all in their house, would never speak to the boy—but in his home alone would he be safe from what he had already learnt to dread. Every form in which shame and opprobrium could overwhelm her darling, haunted her. She had been exercising strong self-control for his sake ever since she had met him at the house-door; there was now a reaction. His presence had kept her mind on its perfect balance. When that was withdrawn, the effect of the strain of power was felt. And athwart the fever-mists that arose to obscure her judgment, all sorts of will-o'-the-wisp plans flittered before her; tempting her to this and that course of action—to anything rather than patient endurance—to relieve her present state of misery by some sudden spasmodic effort, that took the semblance of being wise and right. Gradually all her desires, all her longing, settled themselves on one point. What had she done—what could she do, to Leonard, but evil? If she were away, and gone no one knew where—lost in mystery, as if she were dead—perhaps the cruel hearts might relent, and show pity on Leonard; while her perpetual presence would but call up the remembrance of his birth. Thus she reasoned in her hot, dull brain; and shaped her plans in accordance.

Leonard stole downstairs noiselessly. He listened to find some quiet place where he could hide himself. The house was very still. Miss Benson thought the purposed expedition had taken place, and never dreamed but that Ruth and Leonard were on distant, sunny Scaurside-hill; and after a very early dinner, she had set out to drink tea with a farmer's wife who lived in the country two or three miles off. Mr Benson meant to have gone with her; but while they were at dinner, he had received an unusually authoritative note from Mr Bradshaw desiring to speak with him, so he went to that gentleman's house instead. Sally was busy in her kitchen, making a great noise (not unlike a groom rubbing down a horse) over her cleaning. Leonard stole into the sitting-room, and crouched behind the large old-fashioned sofa to ease his sore, aching heart, by crying with all the prodigal waste and abandonment of childhood.

Mr Benson was shown into Mr Bradshaw's own particular room. The latter gentleman was walking up and down, and it was easy to perceive that something had occurred to chafe him to great anger.

"Sit down, sir!" said he to Mr Benson, nodding to a chair.

Mr Benson sat down. But Mr Bradshaw continued his walk for a few minutes longer without speaking. Then he stopped abruptly, right in front of Mr Benson; and in a voice which he tried to render calm, but which trembled with passion—with a face glowing purple as he thought of his wrongs (and real wrongs they were), he began:

"Mr Benson, I have sent for you to ask—I am almost too indignant at the bare suspicion to speak as becomes me—but did you—I really shall be obliged to beg your pardon, if you are as much in the dark as I was yesterday as to the character of that woman who lives under your roof?"

There was no answer from Mr Benson. Mr Bradshaw looked at him very earnestly. His eyes were fixed on the ground—he made no inquiry—he uttered no expression of wonder or dismay. Mr Bradshaw ground his foot on the floor with gathering rage; but just as he was about to speak, Mr Benson rose up—a poor deformed old man—before the stern and portly figure that was swelling and panting with passion.

"Hear me, sir!" (stretching out his hand as if to avert the words which were impending). "Nothing you can say, can upbraid me like my own conscience; no degradation you can inflict, by word or deed, can come up to the degradation I have suffered for years, at being a party to a deceit, even for a good end—"

"For a good end!—Nay! what next?"

The taunting contempt with which Mr Bradshaw spoke these words almost surprised himself by what he imagined must be its successful power of withering; but in spite of it, Mr Benson lifted his grave eyes to Mr Bradshaw's countenance, and repeated:

"For a good end. The end was not, as perhaps you consider it to have been, to obtain her admission into your family—nor yet to put her in the way of gaining her livelihood; my sister and I would willingly have shared what we have with her; it was our intention to do so at first, if not for any length of time, at least as long as her health might require it. Why I advised (perhaps I only yielded to advice) a change of name—an assumption of a false state of widowhood—was because I earnestly desired to place her in circumstances in which she might work out her self-redemption; and you, sir, know how terribly the world goes against all such as have sinned as Ruth did. She was so young, too."

"You mistake, sir; my acquaintance has not lain so much among that class of sinners as to give me much experience of the way in which they are treated. But, judging from what I have seen, I should say they meet with full as much leniency as they deserve; and supposing they do not—I know there are plenty of sickly sentimentalists just now who reserve all their interest and regard for criminals—why not pick out one of these to help you in your task of washing the blackamoor white? Why choose me to be imposed upon—my household into which to intrude your protégée? Why were my innocent children to be exposed to corruption? I say," said Mr Bradshaw, stamping his foot, "how dared you come into this house, where you were looked upon as a minister of religion, with a lie in your mouth? How dared you single me out, of all people, to be gulled and deceived, and pointed at through the town as the person who had taken an abandoned woman into his house to teach his daughters?"

"I own my deceit was wrong and faithless."

"Yes! you can own it, now it is found out! There is small merit in that, I think!"

"Sir! I claim no merit. I take shame to myself. I did not single you out. You applied to me with your proposal that Ruth should be your children's governess."

"Pah!"

"And the temptation was too great— No! I will not say that—but the temptation was greater than I could stand—it seemed to open out a path of usefulness."

"Now, don't let me hear you speak so," said Mr Bradshaw, blazing up. "I can't stand it. It is too much to talk in that way when the usefulness was to consist in contaminating my innocent girls."

"God knows that if I had believed there had been any danger of such contamination—God knows how I would have died sooner than have allowed her to enter your family. Mr Bradshaw, you believe me, don't you?" asked Mr Benson, earnestly.

"I really must be allowed the privilege of doubting what you say in future," said Mr Bradshaw, in a cold, contemptuous manner.

"I have deserved this," Mr Benson replied. "But," continued he, after a moment's pause, "I will not speak of myself, but of Ruth. Surely, sir, the end I aimed at (the means I took to obtain it were wrong; you cannot feel that more than I do) was a right one; and you will not—you cannot say, that your children have suffered from associating with her. I had her in my family, under the watchful eyes of three anxious persons for a year or more; we saw faults—no human being is without them—and poor Ruth's were but slight venial errors; but we saw no sign of a corrupt mind—no glimpse of boldness or forwardness—no token of want of conscientiousness; she seemed, and was, a young and gentle girl, who had been led astray before she fairly knew what life was."

"I suppose most depraved women have been innocent in their time," said Mr Bradshaw, with bitter contempt.

"Oh, Mr Bradshaw! Ruth was not depraved, and you know it. You cannot have seen her—have known her daily, all these years, without acknowledging that!" Mr Benson was almost breathless, awaiting Mr Bradshaw's answer. The quiet self-control which he had maintained so long, was gone now.

"I saw her daily—I did *not* know her. If I had known her, I should have known she was fallen and depraved, and consequently not fit to come into my house, nor to associate with my pure children."

"Now I wish God would give me power to speak out convincingly what I believe to be His truth, that not every woman who has fallen is depraved; that many—how many the Great Judgment Day will reveal to those who have shaken off the poor, sore, penitent hearts on earth—many, many crave and hunger after a chance for virtue—the help which no man gives to them—help—that gentle, tender help which Jesus gave once to Mary Magdalen." Mr Benson was almost choked by his own feelings.

"Come, come, Mr Benson, let us have no more of this morbid way of talking. The world has decided how such women are to be treated; and, you may depend upon it, there is so much practical wisdom in the world that its way of acting is right in the long run, and that no one can fly in its face with impunity, unless, indeed, they stoop to deceit and imposition."

"I take my stand with Christ against the world," said Mr Benson, solemnly, disregarding the covert allusion to himself. "What have the world's ways ended in? Can we be much worse than we are?"

"Speak for yourself, if you please."

"Is it not time to change some of our ways of thinking and acting? I declare before God, that if I believe in any one human truth, it is this—that to every woman who, like Ruth, has sinned, should be given a chance of self-redemption—and that such a chance should be given in no supercilious or contemptuous manner, but in the spirit of the holy Christ."

"Such as getting her into a friend's house under false colours."

"I do not argue on Ruth's case. In that I have acknowledged my error. I do not argue on any case. I state my firm belief, that it is God's will that we should not dare to trample any of His creatures down to the hopeless dust; that it is God's will that the women who have fallen should be numbered among those who have broken hearts to be bound up, not cast aside as lost beyond recall. If this be God's will, as a thing of God it will stand; and He will open a way."

"I should have attached much more importance to all your exhortation on this point if I could have respected your conduct in other matters. As it is, when I see a man who has deluded himself into considering falsehood right, I am disinclined to take his opinion on subjects connected with morality; and I can no longer regard him as a fitting exponent of the will of God. You perhaps understand what I mean, Mr Benson. I can no longer attend your chapel."

If Mr Benson had felt any hope of making Mr Bradshaw's obstinate mind receive the truth, that he acknowledged and repented of his connivance at the falsehood by means of which Ruth had been received into the Bradshaw family, this last sentence prevented his making the attempt. He simply bowed and took his leave—Mr Bradshaw attending him to the door with formal ceremony.

He felt acutely the severance of the tie which Mr Bradshaw had just announced to him. He had experienced many mortifications in his intercourse with that gentleman, but they had fallen off from his meek spirit like drops of water from a bird's plumage; and now he only remembered the acts of substantial kindness rendered (the ostentation all forgotten)—many happy hours and pleasant evenings—the children whom he had loved dearer than he thought till now—the young people about whom he had cared, and whom he had striven to lead aright. He was but a young man when Mr Bradshaw first came to his chapel; they had grown old together; he had never recognised Mr Bradshaw as an old familiar friend so completely as now when they were severed.

It was with a heavy heart that he opened his own door. He went to his study immediately; he sat down to steady himself into his position.

How long he was there—silent and alone—reviewing his life—confessing his sins—he did not know; but he heard some unusual sound in the house that disturbed him—roused him to present life. A slow, languid step came along the passage to the front door—the breathing was broken by many sighs.

Ruth's hand was on the latch when Mr Benson came out. Her face was very white, except two red spots on each cheek—her eyes were deep-sunk and hollow, but glittered with feverish lustre. "Ruth!" exclaimed he. She moved her lips, but her throat and mouth were too dry for her to speak.

"Where are you going?" asked he; for she had all her walking things on, yet trembled so, even as she stood, that it was evident she could not walk far without falling.

She hesitated—she looked up at him, still with the same dry glittering eyes. At last she whispered (for she could only speak in a whisper), "To Helmsby—I am going to Helmsby."

"Helmsby! my poor girl—may God have mercy upon you!" for he saw she hardly knew what she was saying. "Where is Helmsby?"

"I don't know. In Lincolnshire, I think."

"But why are you going there?"

"Hush! he's asleep," said she, as Mr Benson had unconsciously raised his voice.

"Who is asleep?" asked Mr Benson.

"That poor little boy," said she, beginning to quiver and cry.

"Come here!" said he, authoritatively, drawing her into the study.

"Sit down in that chair. I will come back directly."

He went in search of his sister, but she had not returned. Then he had recourse to Sally, who was as busy as ever about her cleaning.

"How long has Ruth been at home?" asked he.

"Ruth! She has never been at home sin' morning. She and Leonard were to be off for the day somewhere or other with them Bradshaw girls."

"Then she has had no dinner?"

"Not here, at any rate. I can't answer for what she may have done at other places."

"And Leonard—where is he?"

"How should I know? With his mother, I suppose. Leastways, that was what was fixed on. I've enough to do of my own, without routing after other folks."

She went on scouring in no very good temper. Mr Benson stood silent for a moment.

"Sally," he said, "I want a cup of tea. Will you make it as soon as you can; and some dry toast too? I'll come for it in ten minutes."

Struck by something in his voice, she looked up at him for the first time.

"What ha' ye been doing to yourself, to look so grim and grey? Tiring yourself all to tatters, looking after some naught, I'll be bound! Well! well! I mun make ye your tea, I reckon; but I did hope as you grew older you'd ha' grown wiser!"

Mr Benson made no reply, but went to look for Leonard, hoping that the child's presence might bring back to his mother the power of self-control. He opened the parlour-door, and looked in, but saw no one. Just as he was shutting it, however, he heard a deep, broken, sobbing sigh; and, guided by the sound, he found the boy lying on the floor, fast asleep, but with his features all swollen and disfigured by passionate crying.

"Poor child! This was what she meant, then," thought Mr Benson. "He has begun his share of the sorrows too," he continued, pitifully. "No! I will not waken him back to consciousness." So he returned alone into the study. Ruth sat where he had placed her, her head bent back, and her eyes shut. But when he came in she started up.

"I must be going," she said, in a hurried way.

"Nay, Ruth, you must not go. You must not leave us. We cannot do without you. We love you too much."

"Love me!" said she, looking at him wistfully. As she looked, her eyes filled slowly with tears. It was a good sign, and Mr Benson took heart to go on.

"Yes! Ruth. You know we do. You may have other things to fill up your mind just now, but you know we love you; and nothing can alter our love for you. You ought not to have thought of leaving us. You would not, if you had been quite well."

"Do you know what has happened?" she asked, in a low, hoarse voice.

"Yes. I know all," he answered. "It makes no difference to us. Why should it?"

"Oh! Mr Benson, don't you know that my shame is discovered?" she replied, bursting into tears—"and I must leave you, and leave Leonard, that you may not share in my disgrace."

"You must do no such thing. Leave Leonard! You have no right to leave Leonard. Where could you go to?"

"To Helmsby," she said, humbly. "It would break my heart to go, but I think I ought, for Leonard's sake. I know I ought." She was crying sadly by this time, but Mr Benson knew the flow of tears would ease her brain. "It will break my heart to go, but I know I must."

"Sit still here at present," said he, in a decided tone of command. He went for the cup of tea. He brought it to her without Sally's being aware for whom it was intended.

"Drink this!" He spoke as you would do to a child, if desiring it to take medicine. "Eat some toast." She took the tea, and drank it feverishly; but when she tried to eat, the food seemed to choke her. Still she was docile, and she tried.

"I cannot," said she at last, putting down the piece of toast. There was a return to something of her usual tone in the words. She spoke gently and softly; no longer in the shrill, hoarse voice she had used at first. Mr Benson sat down by her.

"Now, Ruth, we must talk a little together. I want to understand what your plan was. Where is Helmsby? Why did you fix to go there?"

"It is where my mother lived," she answered. "Before she was married she lived there; and wherever she lived, the people all loved her dearly; and I thought—I think, that for her sake some one would give me work. I meant to tell them the truth," said she, dropping her eyes; "but still they would, perhaps, give me some employment—I don't care what—for her sake. I could do many things," said she, suddenly looking up. "I am sure I could weed—I could in gardens—if they did not like to have me in their houses. But perhaps some one, for my mother's sake—oh! my dear, dear mother!—do you know where and what I am?" she cried out, sobbing afresh.

Mr Benson's heart was very sore, though he spoke authoritatively, and almost sternly.

"Ruth! you must be still and quiet. I cannot have this. I want you to listen to me. Your thought of Helmsby would be a good one, if it was right for you to leave Eccleston; but I do not think it is. I am certain of this, that it would be a great sin in you to separate yourself from Leonard. You have no right to sever the tie by which God has bound you together."

"But if I am here they will all know and remember the shame of his birth; and if I go away they may forget—"

"And they may not. And if you go away, he may be unhappy or ill; and you, who above all others have—and have from God—remember *that*, Ruth!—the power to comfort him, the tender patience to nurse him, have left him to the care of strangers. Yes; I know! But we ourselves are as strangers, dearly as we love him, compared to a mother. He may turn to sin, and want the long forbearance, the serene authority of a parent; and where are you? No dread of shame, either for yourself, or even for him, can ever make it right for you to shake off your responsibility." All this time he was watching her narrowly, and saw her slowly yield herself up to the force of what he was saying.

"Besides, Ruth," he continued, "we have gone on falsely hitherto. It has been my doing, my mistake, my sin. I ought to have known better. Now, let us stand firm on the truth. You have no new fault to repent of. Be brave and faithful. It is to God you answer, not to men. The shame of having your sin known to the world, should be as nothing to the shame you felt at having sinned. We have dreaded men too much, and God too little, in the course we have taken. But now be of good cheer. Perhaps you will have to find your work in the world very low—not quite working in the fields," said he, with a gentle smile, to which she, downcast and miserable, could give no response. "Nay, perhaps, Ruth," he went on, "you may have to stand and wait for some time; no one may be willing to use the services you would gladly render; all may turn aside from you, and may speak very harshly of you. Can you accept all this treatment meekly, as but the reasonable and just penance God has laid upon you—feeling no anger against those who slight you, no impatience for the time to come (and come it surely will—I speak as having the word of God for what I say) when He, having purified you, even as by fire, will make a straight path for your feet? My child, it is Christ the Lord who has told us of this infinite mercy of God. Have you faith enough in it to be brave, and bear on, and do rightly in patience and in tribulation?"

Ruth had been hushed and very still until now, when the pleading earnestness of his question urged her to answer:

"Yes!" said she. "I hope—I believe I can be faithful for myself, for I have sinned and done wrong. But Leonard—" She looked up at him.

"But Leonard," he echoed. "Ah! there it is hard, Ruth. I own the world is hard and persecuting to such as he." He paused to think of the true comfort for this sting. He went on. "The world is not everything, Ruth; nor is the want of men's good opinion and esteem the highest need which man has. Teach Leonard this. You would not wish his life to be one summer's day. You dared not make it so, if you had the power. Teach him to bid a noble, Christian welcome to the trials which God sends—and this is one of them. Teach him not to look on a life of struggle, and perhaps of disappointment and incompleteness, as a sad and mournful end, but as the means permitted to the heroes and warriors in the army of Christ, by which to show their faithful following. Tell him of the hard and thorny path which was trodden once by the bleeding feet of One. Ruth! think of the Saviour's life and cruel death, and of His divine faithfulness. Oh, Ruth!" exclaimed he, "when I look and see what you may be—what you *must* be to that boy, I cannot think how you could be coward enough, for a moment, to shrink from your work! But we have all been cowards hitherto," he added, in bitter self-accusation. "God help us to be so no longer!"

Ruth sat very quiet. Her eyes were fixed on the ground, and she seemed lost in thought. At length she rose up.

"Mr Benson!" said she, standing before him, and propping herself by the table, as she was trembling sadly from weakness, "I mean to try very, very hard, to do my duty to Leonard—and to God," she added, reverently. "I am only afraid my faith may sometimes fail about Leonard—"

"Ask, and it shall be given unto you. That is no vain or untried promise, Ruth!"

She sat down again, unable longer to stand. There was another long silence.

"I must never go to Mr Bradshaw's again," she said at last, as if thinking aloud.

"No, Ruth, you shall not," he answered.

"But I shall earn no money!" added she, quickly, for she thought that he did not perceive the difficulty that was troubling her.

"You surely know, Ruth, that while Faith and I have a roof to shelter us, or bread to eat, you and Leonard share it with us."

"I know—I know your most tender goodness," said she, "but it ought not to be."

"It must be at present," he said, in a decided manner. "Perhaps before long you may have some employment; perhaps it may be some time before an opportunity occurs."

"Hush," said Ruth; "Leonard is moving about in the parlour. I must go to him."

But when she stood up, she turned so dizzy, and tottered so much, that she was glad to sit down again immediately.

"You must rest here. I will go to him," said Mr Benson. He left her; and when he was gone, she leaned her head on the back of the chair, and cried quietly and incessantly; but there was a more patient, hopeful, resolved feeling in her heart, which all along, through all the tears she shed, bore her onwards to higher thoughts, until at last she rose to prayers.

Mr Benson caught the new look of shrinking shame in Leonard's eye, as it first sought, then shunned, meeting his. He was pained, too, by the sight of the little sorrowful, anxious face, on which, until now, hope and joy had been predominant. The constrained voice, the few words the boy spoke, when formerly there would have been a glad and free utterance—all this grieved Mr Benson inexpressibly, as but the beginning of an unwonted mortification, which must last for years. He himself made no allusion to any unusual occurrence; he spoke of Ruth as sitting, overcome by headache, in the study for quietness: he hurried on the preparations for tea, while Leonard sat by in the great arm-chair, and looked on with sad, dreamy eyes. He strove to lessen the shock which he knew Leonard had received, by every mixture of tenderness and cheerfulness that Mr Benson's gentle heart prompted; and now and then a languid smile stole over the boy's face. When his bedtime came, Mr Benson told him of the hour, although he feared that Leonard would have but another sorrowful crying of himself to sleep; but he was anxious to accustom the boy to cheerful movement within the limits of domestic law, and by no disobedience to it to weaken the power of glad submission to the Supreme; to begin the new life that lay before him, where strength to look up to God as the Law-giver and Ruler of events would be pre-eminently required. When Leonard had gone upstairs, Mr Benson went immediately to Ruth, and said,

"Ruth! Leonard is just gone up to bed," secure in the instinct which made her silently rise, and go up to the boy—certain, too, that they would each be the other's best comforter, and that God would strengthen each through the other.

Now, for the first time, he had leisure to think of himself; and to go over all the events of the day. The half-hour of solitude in his study, that he had before his sister's return, was of inestimable value; he had leisure to put events in their true places, as to importance and eternal significance.

Miss Faith came in laden with farm produce. Her kind entertainers had brought her in their shandry to the opening of the court in which the Chapel-house stood; but she was so heavily burdened with eggs, mushrooms, and plums, that when her brother opened the door she was almost breathless.

"Oh, Thurstan! take this basket—it is such a weight! Oh, Sally, is that you? Here are some magnum-bonums which we must preserve to-morrow. There are guinea-fowl eggs in that basket."

Mr Benson let her unburden her body, and her mind too, by giving charges to Sally respecting her housekeeping treasures, before he said a word; but when she returned into the study, to tell him the small pieces of intelligence respecting her day at the farm, she stood aghast.

"Why, Thurstan, dear! What's the matter? Is your back hurting you?"

He smiled to reassure her; but it was a sickly and forced smile.

"No, Faith! I am quite well, only rather out of spirits, and wanting to talk to you to cheer me."

Miss Faith sat down, straight, sitting bolt-upright to listen the better.

"I don't know how, but the real story about Ruth is found out."

"Oh, Thurstan!" exclaimed Miss Benson, turning quite white.

For a moment, neither of them said another word. Then she went on.

"Does Mr Bradshaw know?"

"Yes! He sent for me, and told me."

"Does Ruth know that it has all come out?"

"Yes. And Leonard knows."

"How? Who told him?"

"I do not know. I have asked no questions. But of course it was his mother."

"She was very foolish and cruel, then," said Miss Benson, her eyes blazing, and her lips trembling, at the thought of the suffering her darling boy must have gone through.

"I think she was wise. I am sure it was not cruel. He must have soon known that there was some mystery, and it was better that it should be told him openly and quietly by his mother than by a stranger."

"How could she tell him quietly?" asked Miss Benson, still indignant.

"Well! perhaps I used the wrong word—of course no one was by—and I don't suppose even they themselves could now tell how it was told, or in what spirit it was borne."

Miss Benson was silent again.

"Was Mr Bradshaw very angry?"

"Yes, very; and justly so. I did very wrong in making that false statement at first."

"No! I am sure you did not," said Miss Faith. "Ruth has had some years of peace, in which to grow stronger and wiser, so that she can bear her shame now in a way she never could have done at first."

"All the same it was wrong in me to do what I did."

"I did it too, as much or more than you. And I don't think it wrong. I'm certain it was quite right, and I would do just the same again."

"Perhaps it has not done you the harm it has done me."

"Nonsense! Thurstan. Don't be morbid. I'm sure you are as good—and better than ever you were."

"No, I am not. I have got what you call morbid just in consequence of the sophistry by which I persuaded myself that wrong could be right. I torment myself. I have lost my clear instincts of conscience. Formerly, if I believed that such or such an action was according to the will of God, I went and did it, or at least I tried to do it, without thinking of consequences. Now, I reason and weigh what will happen if I do so and so—I grope where formerly I saw. Oh, Faith! it is such a relief to me to have the truth known, that I am afraid I have not been sufficiently sympathising with Ruth."

"Poor Ruth!" said Miss Benson. "But at any rate our telling a lie has been the saving of her. There is no fear of her going wrong now."

"God's omnipotence did not need our sin."

They did not speak for some time.

"You have not told me what Mr Bradshaw said."

"One can't remember the exact words that are spoken on either side in moments of such strong excitement. He was very angry, and said some things about me that were very just, and some about Ruth that were very hard. His last words were that he should give up coming to chapel."

"Oh, Thurstan! did it come to that?"

"Yes."

"Does Ruth know all he said?"

"No! Why should she? I don't know if she knows he has spoken to me at all. Poor creature! she had enough to craze her almost without that! She was for going away and leaving us, that we might not share in her disgrace. I was afraid of her being quite delirious. I did so want you, Faith! However, I did the best I could; I spoke to her very coldly, and almost sternly, all the while my heart was bleeding for her. I dared not give her sympathy; I tried to give her strength. But I did so want you, Faith."

"And I was so full of enjoyment, I am ashamed to think of it. But the Dawsons are so kind—and the day was so fine— Where is Ruth now?"

"With Leonard. He is her great earthly motive—I thought that being with him would be best. But he must be in bed and asleep now."

"I will go up to her," said Miss Faith.

She found Ruth keeping watch by Leonard's troubled sleep; but when she saw Miss Faith she rose up, and threw herself on her neck and clung to her, without speaking. After a while Miss Benson said:

"You must go to bed, Ruth!" So, after she had kissed the sleeping boy, Miss Benson led her away, and helped to undress her, and brought her up a cup of soothing violet tea—not so soothing as tender actions and soft loving tones.

CHAPTER XXVIII - AN UNDERSTANDING BETWEEN LOVERS

It was well they had so early and so truly strengthened the spirit to bear, for the events which had to be endured soon came thick and threefold.

Every evening Mr and Miss Benson thought the worst must be over; and every day brought some fresh occurrence to touch upon the raw place. They could not be certain, until they had seen all their acquaintances, what difference it would make in the cordiality of their reception: in some cases it made much; and Miss Benson was proportionably indignant. She felt this change in behaviour more than her brother. His great pain arose from the coolness of the Bradshaws. With all the faults which had at times grated on his sensitive nature (but which he now forgot, and remembered only their kindness), they were his old familiar friends—his kind, if ostentatious, patrons—his great personal interest, out of his own family; and he could not get over the suffering he experienced from seeing their large square pew empty on Sundays—from perceiving how Mr Bradshaw, though he bowed in a distant manner when he and Mr Benson met face to face, shunned him as often as he possibly could. All that happened in the household, which once was as patent to him as his own, was now a sealed book; he heard of its doings by chance, if he heard at all. Just at the time when he was feeling the most depressed from this cause, he met Jemima at a sudden turn of the street. He was uncertain for a moment how to accost her, but she saved him all doubt; in an instant she had his hand in both of hers, her face flushed with honest delight.

"Oh, Mr Benson, I am so glad to see you! I have so wanted to know all about you! How is poor Ruth? dear Ruth! I wonder if she has forgiven me my cruelty to her? And I may not go to her now, when I should be so glad and thankful to make up for it."

"I never heard you had been cruel to her. I am sure she does not think so."

"She ought; she must. What is she doing? Oh! I have so much to ask, I can never hear enough; and papa says"—she hesitated a moment, afraid of giving pain, and then, believing that they would understand the state of affairs, and the reason for her behaviour better if she told the truth, she went on: "Papa says I must not go to your house—I suppose it's right to obey him?"

"Certainly, my dear. It is your clear duty. We know how you feel towards us."

"Oh! but if I could do any good—if I could be of any use or comfort to any of you—especially to Ruth, I should come, duty or not. I believe it would be my duty," said she, hurrying on to try and stop any decided prohibition from Mr Benson. "No! don't be afraid; I won't come till I know I can do some good. I hear bits about you through Sally every now and then, or I could not have waited so long. Mr Benson," continued she, reddening very much, "I think you did quite right about poor Ruth."

"Not in the falsehood, my dear."

"No! not perhaps in that. I was not thinking of that. But I have been thinking a great deal about poor Ruth's—you know I could not help it when everybody was talking about it—and it made me think of myself, and what I am. With a father and mother, and home and careful friends, I am not likely to be tempted like Ruth; but oh! Mr Benson," said she, lifting her eyes, which were full of tears, to his face, for the first time since she began to speak, "if you knew all I have been thinking and feeling this last year, you would see how I have yielded to every temptation that was able to come to me; and, seeing how I have no goodness or strength in me, and how I might just have been like Ruth, or rather, worse than she ever was, because I am more headstrong and passionate by nature, I do so thank you and love you for what you did for her! And will you tell me really and truly now if I can ever do anything for Ruth? If you'll promise me that, I won't rebel unnecessarily against papa; but if you don't, I will, and come and see you all this very afternoon. Remember! I trust you!" said she, breaking away. Then turning back, she came to ask after Leonard.

"He must know something of it," said she. "Does he feel it much?"

"Very much," said Mr Benson. Jemima shook her head sadly.

"It is hard upon him," said she.

"It is," Mr Benson replied.

For in truth, Leonard was their greatest anxiety indoors. His health seemed shaken, he spoke half sentences in his sleep, which showed that in his dreams he was battling on his mother's behalf against an unkind and angry world. And then he would wail to himself, and utter sad words of shame, which they never thought had reached his ears. By day, he was in general grave and quiet; but his appetite varied, and he was evidently afraid of going into the streets, dreading to be pointed at as an object of remark. Each separately in their hearts longed to give him change of scene, but they were all silent, for where was the requisite money to come from?

His temper became fitful and variable. At times he would be most sullen against his mother; and then give way to a passionate remorse. When Mr Benson caught Ruth's look of agony at her child's rebuffs, his patience failed; or rather, I should say, he believed that a stronger, severer hand than hers was required for the management of the lad. But, when she heard Mr Benson say so, she pleaded with him.

"Have patience with Leonard," she said. "I have deserved the anger that is fretting in his heart. It is only I who can reinstate myself in his love and respect. I have no fear. When he sees me really striving hard and long to do what is right, he must love me. I am not afraid."

Even while she spoke, her lips quivered, and her colour went and came with eager anxiety. So Mr Benson held his peace, and let her take her course. It was beautiful to see the intuition by which she divined what was passing in every fold of her child's heart, so as to be always ready with the right words to soothe or to strengthen him. Her watchfulness was unwearied, and with no thought of self-tainting in it, or else she might have often paused to turn aside and weep at the clouds of shame which came over Leonard's love for her, and hid it from all but her faithful heart; she believed and knew that he was yet her own affectionate boy, although he might be gloomily silent, or apparently hard and cold. And in all this, Mr Benson could not choose but admire the way in which she was insensibly teaching Leonard to conform to the law of right, to recognise Duty in the mode in which every action was performed. When Mr Benson saw this, he knew that all goodness would follow, and that the claims which his mother's infinite love had on the boy's heart would be acknowledged at last, and all the more fully because she herself never urged them, but silently admitted the force of the reason that caused them to be for a time forgotten. By-and-by Leonard's remorse at his ungracious and sullen ways to his mother—ways that alternated with passionate, fitful bursts of clinging love—assumed more the character of repentance; he tried to do so no more. But still his health was delicate; he was averse to going out-of-doors; he was much graver and sadder than became his age. It was what must be, an inevitable consequence of what had been; and Ruth had to be patient, and pray in secret, and with many tears, for the strength she needed.

She knew what it was to dread the going out into the streets after her story had become known. For days and days she had silently shrunk from this effort. But one evening towards dusk, Miss Benson was busy, and asked her to go an errand for her; and Ruth got up and silently obeyed her. That silence as to inward suffering was only one part of her peculiar and exquisite sweetness of nature; part of the patience with which she "accepted her penance." Her true instincts told her that it was not right to disturb others with many expressions of her remorse; that the holiest repentance consisted in a quiet and daily sacrifice. Still there were times when she wearied pitifully of her inaction. She was so willing to serve and work, and every one despised her services. Her mind, as I have said before, had been well cultivated during these last few years; so now she used all the knowledge she had gained in teaching Leonard, which was an employment that Mr Benson relinquished willingly, because he felt that it would give her some of the occupation that she needed. She endeavoured to make herself useful in the house in every way she could; but the waters of housekeeping had closed over her place during the time of her absence at Mr Bradshaw's—and, besides, now that they were trying to restrict every unnecessary expense, it was sometimes difficult to find work for three women. Many and many a time Ruth turned over in her mind every possible chance of obtaining employment for her leisure hours, and nowhere could she find it. Now and then Sally, who was her confidante in this wish, procured her some needlework, but it was of a coarse and common kind, soon done, lightly paid for. But whatever it was, Ruth took it, and was thankful, although it added but a few pence to the household purse. I do not mean that there was any great need of money; but a new adjustment of expenditure was required—a reduction of wants which had never been very extravagant.

Ruth's salary of forty pounds was gone, while more of her "keep," as Sally called it, was thrown upon the Bensons. Mr Benson received about eighty pounds a year for his salary as minister. Of this, he knew that twenty pounds came from Mr Bradshaw; and when the old man appointed to collect the pew-rents brought him the quarterly amount, and he found no diminution in them, he inquired how it was, and learnt that, although Mr Bradshaw had expressed to the collector his determination never to come to chapel again, he had added, that of course his pew-rent should be paid all the same. But this Mr Benson could not suffer; and the old man was commissioned to return the money to Mr Bradshaw, as being what his deserted minister could not receive.

Mr and Miss Benson had about thirty or forty pounds coming in annually from a sum which, in happier days, Mr Bradshaw had invested in Canal shares for them. Altogether their income did not fall much short of a hundred a year, and they lived in the Chapel-house free of rent. So Ruth's small earnings were but very little in actual hard commercial account, though in another sense they were much; and Miss Benson always received them with quiet simplicity. By degrees, Mr Benson absorbed some of Ruth's time in a gracious and natural way. He employed her mind in all the kind offices he was accustomed to render to the poor around him. And as much of the peace and ornament of life as they gained now, was gained on a firm basis of truth. If Ruth began low down to find her place in the world, at any rate there was no flaw in the foundation.

Leonard was still their great anxiety. At times the question seemed to be, could he live through all this trial of the elasticity of childhood? And then they knew how precious a blessing—how true a pillar of fire, he was to his mother; and how black the night, and how dreary the wilderness would be, when he was not. The child and the mother were each messengers of God—angels to each other.

They had long gaps between the pieces of intelligence respecting the Bradshaws. Mr Bradshaw had at length purchased the house at Abermouth, and they were much there. The way in which the Bensons heard most frequently of the family of their former friends, was through Mr Farquhar. He called on Mr Benson about a month after the latter had met Jemima in the street. Mr Farquhar was not in the habit of paying calls on any one; and though he had always entertained and evinced the most kind and friendly feeling towards Mr Benson, he had rarely been in the Chapel-house. Mr Benson received him courteously, but he rather expected that there would be some especial reason alleged, before the conclusion of the visit, for its occurrence; more particularly as Mr Farquhar sat talking on the topics of the day in a somewhat absent manner, as if they were not the subjects most present to his mind. The truth was, he could not help recurring to the last time when he was in that room, waiting to take Leonard a ride, and his heart beating rather more quickly than usual at the idea that Ruth might bring the boy in when he was equipped. He was very full now of the remembrance of Ruth; and yet he was also most thankful, most self-gratulatory, that he had gone no further in his admiration of her—that he had never expressed his regard in words—that no one, as he believed, was cognisant of the incipient love which had grown partly out of his admiration, and partly out of his reason. He was thankful to be spared any implication in the nine-days' wonder which her story had made in Eccleston. And yet his feeling for her had been of so strong a character, that he winced, as with extreme pain, at every application of censure to her name. These censures were often exaggerated, it is true; but when they were just in their judgment of the outward circumstances of the case, they were not the less painful and distressing to him. His first rebound to Jemima was occasioned by Mrs Bradshaw's account of how severely her husband was displeased at her daughter's having taken part with Ruth; and he could have thanked and almost blessed Jemima when she dropped in (she dared do no more) her pleading excuses and charitable explanations on Ruth's behalf. Jemima had learnt some humility from the discovery which had been to her so great a shock; standing, she had learnt to take heed lest she fell; and when she had once been aroused to a perception of the violence of the hatred which she had indulged against Ruth, she was more reticent and measured in the expression of all her opinions. It showed how much her character had been purified from pride, that now she felt aware that what in her was again attracting Mr Farquhar was her faithful advocacy of her rival, wherever such advocacy was wise or practicable. He was quite unaware that Jemima had been conscious of his great admiration for Ruth; he did not know that she had ever cared enough for him to be jealous. But the unacknowledged bond between them now was their grief, and sympathy, and pity for Ruth; only in Jemima these feelings were ardent, and would fain have become active; while in Mr Farquhar they were strongly mingled with thankfulness that he had escaped a disagreeable position, and a painful notoriety. His natural caution induced him to make a resolution never to think of any woman as a wife until he had ascertained all her antecedents, from her birth upwards; and the same spirit of caution, directed inwardly, made him afraid of giving too much pity to Ruth, for fear of the conclusions to which such a feeling might lead him. But still his old regard for her, for Leonard, and his esteem and respect for the Bensons, induced him to lend a willing ear to Jemima's earnest entreaty that he would go and call on Mr Benson, in order that she might learn something about the family in general, and Ruth in particular. It was thus that he came to sit by Mr Benson's study fire, and to talk, in an absent way, to that gentleman. How they got on the subject he did not know, more than one-half of his attention being distracted; but they were speaking about politics, when Mr Farquhar learned that Mr Benson took in no newspaper.

"Will you allow me to send you over my *Times*? I have generally done with it before twelve o'clock, and after that it is really waste-paper in my house. You will oblige me by making use of it."

"I am sure I am very much obliged to you for thinking of it. But do not trouble yourself to send it; Leonard can fetch it."

"How is Leonard now?" asked Mr Farquhar, and he tried to speak indifferently; but a grave look of intelligence clouded his eyes as he looked for Mr Benson's answer. "I have not met him lately."

"No!" said Mr Benson, with an expression of pain in his countenance, though he, too, strove to speak in his usual tone.

"Leonard is not strong, and we find it difficult to induce him to go much out-of-doors."

There was a little silence for a minute or two, during which Mr Farquhar had to check an unbidden sigh. But, suddenly rousing himself into a determination to change the subject, he said:

"You will find rather a lengthened account of the exposure of Sir Thomas Campbell's conduct at Baden. He seems to be a complete blackleg, in spite of his baronetcy. I fancy the papers are glad to get hold of anything just now."

"Who is Sir Thomas Campbell?" asked Mr Benson.

"Oh, I thought you might have heard the report—a true one, I believe—of Mr Donne's engagement to his daughter. He must be glad she jilted him now, I fancy, after this public exposure of her father's conduct." (That was an awkward speech, as Mr Farquhar felt; and he hastened to cover it, by going on without much connexion:)

"Dick Bradshaw is my informant about all these projected marriages in high life—they are not much in my way; but since he has come down from London to take his share in the business, I think I have heard more of the news and the scandal of what, I suppose, would be considered high life, than ever I did before; and Mr Donne's proceedings seem to be an especial object of interest to him."

"And Mr Donne is engaged to a Miss Campbell, is he?"

"Was engaged; if I understood right, she broke off the engagement to marry some Russian prince or other—a better match, Dick Bradshaw told me. I assure you," continued Mr Farquhar, smiling, "I am a very passive recipient of all such intelligence, and might very probably have forgotten all about it, if the *Times* of this morning had not been so full of the disgrace of the young lady's father."

"Richard Bradshaw has quite left London, has he?" asked Mr Benson, who felt far more interest in his old patron's family than in all the Campbells that ever were or ever would be.

"Yes. He has come to settle down here. I hope he may do well, and not disappoint his father, who has formed very high expectations from him; I am not sure if they are not too high for any young man to realise." Mr Farquhar could have said more, but Dick Bradshaw was Jemima's brother, and an object of anxiety to her.

"I am sure, I trust such a mortification—such a grief as any disappointment in Richard, may not befall his father," replied Mr Benson.

"Jemima—Miss Bradshaw," said Mr Farquhar, hesitating, "was most anxious to hear of you all. I hope I may tell her you are all well" (with an emphasis on *all*); "that—"

"Thank you. Thank her for us. We are all well; all except Leonard, who is not strong, as I said before. But we must be patient. Time, and such devoted, tender love as he has from his mother, must do much."

Mr Farquhar was silent.

"Send him to my house for the papers. It will be a little necessity for him to have some regular exercise, and to face the world. He must do it, sooner or later."

The two gentlemen shook hands with each other on parting; but no further allusion was made to either Ruth or Leonard.

So Leonard went for the papers. Stealing along by back streets—running with his head bent down—his little heart panting with dread of being pointed out as his mother's child—so he used to come back, and run trembling to Sally, who would hush him up to her breast with many a rough-spoken word of pity and sympathy.

Mr Farquhar tried to catch him to speak to him, and tame him as it were; and, by-and-by, he contrived to interest him sufficiently to induce the boy to stay a little while in the house, or stables, or garden. But the race through the streets was always to be dreaded as the end of ever so pleasant a visit.

Mr Farquhar kept up the intercourse with the Bensons which he had thus begun. He persevered in paying calls—quiet visits, where not much was said, political or local news talked about, and the same inquiries always made and answered as to the welfare of the two families, who were estranged from each other. Mr Farquhar's reports were so little varied that Jemima grew anxious to know more particulars.

"Oh, Mr Farquhar!" said she; "do you think they tell you the truth? I wonder what Ruth can be doing to support herself and Leonard? Nothing that you can hear of, you say; and, of course, one must not ask the downright question. And yet I am sure they must be pinched in some way. Do you think Leonard is stronger?"

"I am not sure. He is growing fast; and such a blow as he has had will be certain to make him more thoughtful and full of care than most boys of his age; both these circumstances may make him thin and pale, which he certainly is."

"Oh! how I wish I might go and see them all! I could tell in a twinkling the real state of things." She spoke with a tinge of her old impatience.

"I will go again, and pay particular attention to anything you wish me to observe. You see, of course, I feel a delicacy about asking any direct questions, or even alluding in any way to these late occurrences."

"And you never see Ruth by any chance?"

"Never!"

They did not look at each other while this last question was asked and answered.

"I will take the paper to-morrow myself; it will be an excuse for calling again, and I will try to be very penetrating; but I have not much hope of success."

"Oh, thank you. It is giving you a great deal of trouble; but you are very kind."

"Kind, Jemima!" he repeated, in a tone which made her go very red and hot; "must I tell you how you can reward me?—Will you call me Walter?—say, thank you, Walter—just for once."

Jemima felt herself yielding to the voice and tone in which this was spoken; but her very consciousness of the depth of her love made her afraid of giving way, and anxious to be wooed, that she might be reinstated in her self-esteem.

"No!" said she, "I don't think I can call you so. You are too old. It would not be respectful." She meant it half in joke, and had no idea he would take the allusion to his age so seriously as he did. He rose up, and coldly, as a matter of form, in a changed voice, wished her "Good-bye." Her heart sank; yet the old pride was there. But as he was at the very door, some sudden impulse made her speak:

"I have not vexed you, have I, Walter?"

He turned round, glowing with a thrill of delight. She was as red as any rose; her looks dropped down to the ground.

They were not raised when, half an hour afterwards, she said, "You won't forbid my going to see Ruth, will you? because if you do, I give you notice I shall disobey you." The arm around her waist clasped her yet more fondly at the idea, suggested by this speech, of the control which he should have a right to exercise over her actions at some future day.

"Tell me," said he, "how much of your goodness to me, this last happy hour, has been owing to the desire of having more freedom as a wife than as a daughter?"

She was almost glad that he should think she needed any additional motive to her love for him before she could have accepted him. She was afraid that she had betrayed the deep, passionate regard with which she had long looked upon him. She was lost in delight at her own happiness. She was silent for a time. At length she said:

"I don't think you know how faithful I have been to you ever since the days when you first brought me pistachio-candy from London—when I was quite a little girl."

"Not more faithful than I have been to you," for in truth, the recollection of his love for Ruth had utterly faded away, and he thought himself a model of constancy; "and you have tried me pretty well. What a vixen you have been!"

Jemima sighed; smitten with the consciousness of how little she had deserved her present happiness; humble with the recollection of the evil thoughts that had raged in her heart during the time (which she remembered well, though he might have forgotten it) when Ruth had had the affection which her jealous rival coveted.

"I may speak to your father, may not I, Jemima?"

No! for some reason or fancy which she could not define, and could not be persuaded out of, she wished to keep their mutual understanding a secret. She had a natural desire to avoid the congratulations she expected from her family. She dreaded her father's consideration of the whole affair as a satisfactory disposal of his daughter to a worthy man, who, being his partner, would not require any abstraction of capital from the concern, and Richard's more noisy delight at his sister's having "hooked" so good a match. It was only her simple-hearted mother that she longed to tell. She knew that her mother's congratulations would not jar upon her, though they might not sound the full organ-peal of her love. But all that her mother knew passed onwards to her father; so for the present, at any rate, she determined to realise her secret position alone. Somehow, the sympathy of all others that she most longed for was Ruth's; but the first communication of such an event was due to her parents. She imposed very strict regulations on Mr Farquhar's behaviour; and quarrelled and differed from him more than ever, but with a secret joyful understanding with him in her heart, even while they disagreed with each other—for similarity of opinion is not always—I think not often—needed for fulness and perfection of love.

After Ruth's "detection," as Mr Bradshaw used to call it, he said he could never trust another governess again; so Mary and Elizabeth had been sent to school the following Christmas, and their place in the family was but poorly supplied by the return of Mr Richard Bradshaw, who had left London, and been received as a partner.

CHAPTER XXIX - SALLY TAKES HER MONEY OUT OF THE BANK

The conversation narrated in the last chapter as taking place between Mr Farquhar and Jemima, occurred about a year after Ruth's dismissal from her situation. That year, full of small events, and change of place to the Bradshaws, had been monotonous and long in its course to the other household. There had been no want of peace and tranquillity; there had, perhaps, been more of them than in the preceding years, when, though unacknowledged by any, all must have occasionally felt the oppression of the falsehood—and a slight glancing dread must have flashed across their most prosperous state, lest, somehow or another, the mystery should be disclosed. But now, as the shepherd-boy in John Bunyan sweetly sang, "He that is low need fear no fall."

Still, their peace was as the stillness of a grey autumnal day, when no sun is to be seen above, and when a quiet film seems drawn before both sky and earth, as if to rest the wearied eyes after the summer's glare. Few events broke the monotony of their lives, and those events were of a depressing kind. They consisted in Ruth's futile endeavours to obtain some employment, however humble; in Leonard's fluctuations of spirits and health; in Sally's increasing deafness; in the final and unmendable wearing-out of the parlour carpet, which there was no spare money to replace, and so they cheerfully supplied its want by a large hearth-rug that Ruth made out of ends of list; and, what was more a subject of unceasing regret to Mr Benson than all, the defection of some of the members of his congregation, who followed Mr Bradshaw's lead. Their places, to be sure, were more than filled up by the poor, who thronged to his chapel; but still it was a disappointment to find that people about whom he had been earnestly thinking—to whom he had laboured to do good—should dissolve the connexion without a word of farewell or explanation. Mr Benson did not wonder that they should go; nay, he even felt it right that they should seek that spiritual help from another, which he, by his error, had forfeited his power to offer; he only wished they had spoken of their intention to him in an open and manly way. But not the less did he labour on among those to whom God permitted him to be of use. He felt age stealing upon him apace, although he said nothing about it, and no one seemed to be aware of it; and he worked the more diligently while "it was yet day." It was not the number of his years that made him feel old, for he was only sixty, and many men are hale and strong at that time of life; in all probability, it was that early injury to his spine which affected the constitution of his mind as well as his body, and predisposed him, in the opinion of some at least, to a feminine morbidness of conscience. He had shaken off somewhat of this since the affair with Mr Bradshaw; he was simpler and more dignified than he had been for several years before, during which time he had been anxious and uncertain in his manner, and more given to thought than to action.

The one happy bright spot in this grey year was owing to Sally. As she said of herself, she believed she grew more "nattered" as she grew older; but that she was conscious of her "natteredness" was a new thing, and a great gain to the comfort of the house, for it made her very grateful for forbearance, and more aware of kindness than she had ever been before. She had become very deaf; yet she was uneasy and jealous if she were not informed of all the family thoughts, plans, and proceedings, which often had (however private in their details) to be shouted to her at the full pitch of the voice. But she always heard Leonard perfectly. His clear and bell-like voice, which was similar to his mother's, till sorrow had taken the ring out of it, was sure to be heard by the old servant, though every one else had failed. Sometimes, however, she "got her hearing sudden," as she phrased it, and was alive to every word and noise, more particularly when they did not want her to hear; and at such times she resented their continuance of the habit of speaking loud as a mortal offence. One day, her indignation at being thought deaf called out one of the rare smiles on Leonard's face; she saw it, and said, "Bless thee, lad! if it but amuses thee, they may shout through a ram's horn to me, and I'll never let on I'm not deaf. It's as good a use as I can be of," she continued to herself, "if I can make that poor lad smile a bit."

If she expected to be everybody's confidante, she made Leonard hers. "There!" said she, when she came home from her marketing one Saturday night, "look here, lad! Here's forty-two pound, seven shillings, and twopence! It's a mint of money, isn't it? I took it all in sovereigns for fear of fire."

"What is it all for, Sally?" said he.

"Aye, lad! that's asking. It's Mr Benson's money," said she, mysteriously, "that I've been keeping for him. Is he in the study, think ye?"

"Yes! I think so. Where have you been keeping it?"

"Never you mind!" She went towards the study, but thinking she might have been hard on her darling in refusing to gratify his curiosity, she turned back, and said:

"I say—if thou wilt, thou mayst do me a job of work some day. I'm wanting a frame made for a piece of writing."

And then she returned to go into the study, carrying her sovereigns in her apron.

"Here, Master Thurstan," said she, pouring them out on the table before her astonished master. "Take it, it's all yours."

"All mine! What can you mean?" asked he, bewildered.

She did not hear him, and went on:

"Lock it up safe, out o' the way. Dunnot go and leave it about to tempt folks. I'll not answer for myself if money's left about. I may be cribbing a sovereign."

"But where does it come from?" said he.

"Come from!" she replied. "Where does all money come from, but the bank, to be sure? I thought any one could tell that."

"I have no money in the bank!" said he, more and more perplexed.

"No! I knowed that; but I had. Dunnot ye remember how you would raise my wage, last Martinmas eighteen year? You and Faith were very headstrong, but I was too deep for you. See thee! I went and put it i' th' bank. I was never going to touch it; and if I had died it would have been all right, for I'd a will made, all regular and tight—made by a lawyer (leastways he would have been a lawyer, if he hadn't got transported first). And now, thinks I, I think I'll just go and get it out and give it 'em. Banks is not always safe."

"I'll take care of it for you with the greatest pleasure. Still, you know, banks allow interest."

"D'ye suppose I don't know all about interest, and compound interest too, by this time? I tell ye I want ye to spend it. It's your own. It's not mine. It always was yours. Now you're not going to fret me by saying you think it mine."

Mr Benson held out his hand to her, for he could not speak. She bent forward to him as he sat there, and kissed him.

"Eh, bless ye, lad! It's the first kiss I've had of ye sin' ye were a little lad, and it's a great refreshment. Now don't you and Faith go and bother me with talking about it. It's just yours, and make no more ado."

She went back into the kitchen, and brought out her will, and gave Leonard directions how to make a frame for it; for the boy was a very tolerable joiner, and had a box of tools which Mr Bradshaw had given him some years ago.

"It's a pity to lose such fine writing," said she; "though I can't say as I can read it. Perhaps you'd just read it for me, Leonard." She sat open-mouthed with admiration at all the long words.

The frame was made, and the will hung up opposite to her bed, unknown to any one but Leonard; and, by dint of his repeated reading it over to her, she learnt all the words, except "testatrix," which she would always call "testy tricks." Mr Benson had been too much gratified and touched, by her unconditional gift of all she had in the world, to reject it; but he only held it in his hands as a deposit until he could find a safe investment befitting so small a sum. The little rearrangements of the household expenditure had not touched him as they had done the women. He was aware that meat dinners were not now every-day occurrences; but he preferred puddings and vegetables, and was glad of the exchange. He observed, too, that they all sat together in the kitchen in the evenings; but the kitchen, with the well-scoured dresser, the shining saucepans, the well-blacked grate and whitened hearth, and the warmth which seemed to rise up from the very flags, and ruddily cheer the most distant corners, appeared a very cozy and charming sitting-room; and, besides, it appeared but right that Sally, in her old age, should have the companionship of those with whom she had lived in love and faithfulness for so many years. He only wished he could more frequently leave the solitary comfort of his study, and join the kitchen party, where Sally sat as mistress in the chimney-corner, knitting by fire-light, and Miss Benson and Ruth, with the candle between them, stitched away at their work; while Leonard strewed the ample dresser with his slate and books. He did not mope and pine over his lessons; they were the one thing that took him out of himself. As yet his mother could teach him, though in some respects it was becoming a strain upon her acquirements and powers. Mr Benson saw this, but reserved his offers of help as long as he could, hoping that before his assistance became absolutely necessary, some mode of employment beyond that of occasional plain-work might be laid open to Ruth.

In spite of the communication they occasionally had with Mr Farquhar, when he gave them the intelligence of his engagement to Jemima, it seemed like a glimpse into a world from which they were shut out. They wondered—Miss Benson and Ruth did at least—much about the details. Ruth sat over her sewing, fancying how all had taken place; and as soon as she had arranged the events which were going on among people and places once so familiar to her, she found some discrepancy, and set-to afresh to picture the declaration of love, and the yielding, blushing acceptance; for Mr Farquhar had told little beyond the mere fact that there was an engagement between himself and Jemima which had existed for some time, but which had been kept secret until now, when it was acknowledged, sanctioned, and to be fulfilled as soon as he returned from an arrangement of family affairs in Scotland. This intelligence had been enough for Mr Benson, who was the only person Mr Farquhar saw; as Ruth always shrank from the post of opening the door, and Mr Benson was apt at recognising individual knocks, and always prompt to welcome Mr Farquhar.

Miss Benson occasionally thought—and what she thought she was in the habit of saying—that Jemima might have come herself to announce such an event to old friends; but Mr Benson decidedly vindicated her from any charge of neglect, by expressing his strong conviction that to her they owed Mr Farquhar's calls—his all but outspoken offers of service—his quiet, steady interest in Leonard; and, moreover (repeating the conversation he had had with her in the street, the first time they met after the disclosure), Mr Benson told his sister how glad he was to find that, with all the warmth of her impetuous disposition hurrying her on to rebellion against her father, she was now attaining to that just self-control which can distinguish between mere wishes and true reasons—that she could abstain from coming to see Ruth while she could do but little good, reserving herself for some great occasion or strong emergency.

Ruth said nothing, but she yearned all the more in silence to see Jemima. In her recollection of that fearful interview with Mr Bradshaw, which haunted her yet, sleeping or waking, she was painfully conscious that she had not thanked Jemima for her generous, loving advocacy; it had passed unregarded at the time in intensity of agony—but now she recollected that by no word, or tone, or touch, had she given any sign of gratitude. Mr Benson had never told her of his meeting with Jemima; so it seemed as if there were no hope of any future opportunity: for it is strange how two households, rent apart by some dissension, can go through life, their parallel existences running side by side, yet never touching each other, near neighbours as they are, habitual and familiar guests as they may have been.

Ruth's only point of hope was Leonard. She was weary of looking for work and employment, which everywhere seemed held above her reach. She was not impatient of this, but she was very, very sorry. She felt within her such capability, and all ignored her, and passed her by on the other side. But she saw some progress in Leonard. Not that he could continue to have the happy development, and genial ripening, which other boys have; leaping from childhood to boyhood, and thence to youth, with glad bounds, and unconsciously enjoying every age. At present there was no harmony in Leonard's character; he was as full of thought and self-consciousness as many men, planning his actions long beforehand, so as to avoid what he dreaded, and what she could not yet give him strength to face, coward as she was herself, and shrinking from hard remarks. Yet Leonard was regaining some of his lost tenderness towards his mother; when they were alone he would throw himself on her neck and smother her with kisses, without any apparent cause for such a passionate impulse. If any one was by, his manner was cold and reserved. The hopeful parts of his character were the determination evident in him to be a "law unto himself," and the serious thought which he gave to the formation of this law. There was an inclination in him to reason, especially and principally with Mr Benson, on the great questions of ethics which the majority of the world have settled long ago. But I do not think he ever so argued with his mother. Her lovely patience, and her humility, was earning its reward; and from her quiet piety, bearing sweetly the denial of her wishes—the refusal of her begging—the disgrace in which she lay, while others, less worthy, were employed—this, which perplexed him, and almost angered him at first, called out his reverence at last, and what she said he took for his law with proud humility; and thus softly, she was leading him up to God. His health was not strong; it was not likely to be. He moaned and talked in his sleep, and his appetite was still variable, part of which might be owing to his preference of the hardest lessons to any outdoor exercise. But this last unnatural symptom was vanishing before the assiduous kindness of Mr Farquhar, and the quiet but firm desire of his mother. Next to Ruth, Sally had perhaps the most influence over him; but he dearly loved both Mr and Miss Benson; although he was reserved on this, as on every point not purely intellectual. His was a hard childhood, and his mother felt that it was so. Children bear any moderate degree of poverty and privation cheerfully; but, in addition to a good deal of this, Leonard had to bear a sense of disgrace attaching to him and to the creature he loved best; this it was that took out of him the buoyancy and natural gladness of youth, in a way which no scantiness of food or clothing, or want of any outward comfort, could ever have done.

Two years had passed away—two long, eventless years. Something was now going to happen, which touched their hearts very nearly, though out of their sight and hearing. Jemima was going to be married this August, and by-and-by the very day was fixed. It was to be on the 14th. On the evening of the 13th, Ruth was sitting alone in the parlour, idly gazing out on the darkening shadows in the little garden; her eyes kept filling with quiet tears, that rose, not for her own isolation from all that was going on of bustle and preparation for the morrow's event, but because she had seen how Miss Benson had felt that she and her brother were left out from the gathering of old friends in the Bradshaw family. As Ruth sat, suddenly she was aware of a figure by her; she started up, and in the gloom of the apartment she recognised Jemima. In an instant they were in each other's arms—a long, fast embrace.

"Can you forgive me?" whispered Jemima in Ruth's ear.

"Forgive you! What do you mean? What have I to forgive? The question is, can I ever thank you as I long to do, if I could find words?"

"Oh, Ruth, how I hated you once!"

"It was all the more noble in you to stand by me as you did. You must have hated me when you knew how I was deceiving you all!"

"No, that was not it that made me hate you. It was before that. Oh, Ruth, I did hate you!"

They were silent for some time, still holding each other's hands. Ruth spoke first.

"And you are going to be married to-morrow!"

"Yes," said Jemima. "To-morrow, at nine o'clock. But I don't think I could have been married without coming to wish Mr Benson and Miss Faith good-bye."

"I will go for them," said Ruth.

"No, not just yet. I want to ask you one or two questions first. Nothing very particular; only it seems as if there had been such a strange, long separation between us. Ruth," said she, dropping her voice, "is Leonard stronger than he was? I was so sorry to hear about him from Walter. But he is better?" asked she, anxiously.

"Yes, he is better. Not what a boy of his age should be," replied his mother, in a tone of quiet but deep mournfulness. "Oh, Jemima!" continued she, "my sharpest punishment comes through him. To think what he might have been, and what he is!"

"But Walter says he is both stronger in health, and not so—nervous and shy." Jemima added the last words in a hesitating and doubtful manner, as if she did not know how to express her full meaning without hurting Ruth.

"He does not show that he feels his disgrace so much. I cannot talk about it, Jemima, my heart aches so about him. But he is better," she continued, feeling that Jemima's kind anxiety required an answer at any cost of pain to herself. "He is only studying too closely now; he takes to his lessons evidently as a relief from thought. He is very clever, and I hope and trust, yet I tremble to say it, I believe he is very good."

"You must let him come and see us very often when we come back. We shall be two months away. We are going to Germany, partly on Walter's business.

Ruth, I have been talking to papa to-night, very seriously and quietly, and it has made me love him so much more, and understand him so much better."

"Does he know of your coming here? I hope he does," said Ruth.

"Yes. Not that he liked my doing it at all. But, somehow, I can always do things against a person's wishes more easily when I am on good terms with them—that's not exactly what I meant; but now to-night, after papa had been showing me that he really loved me more than I ever thought he had done (for I always fancied he was so absorbed in Dick, he did not care much for us girls), I felt brave enough to say that I intended to come here and bid you all good-bye. He was silent for a minute, and then said I might do it, but I must remember he did not approve of it, and was not to be compromised by my coming; still I can tell that, at the bottom of his heart, there is some of the old kindly feeling to Mr and Miss Benson, and I don't despair of its all being made up, though, perhaps, I ought to say that mamma does."

"Mr and Miss Benson won't hear of my going away," said Ruth, sadly.

"They are quite right."

"But I am earning nothing. I cannot get any employment. I am only a burden and an expense."

"Are you not also a pleasure? And Leonard, is he not a dear object of love? It is easy for me to talk, I know, who am so impatient. Oh, I never deserved to be so happy as I am! You don't know how good Walter is. I used to think him so cold and cautious. But now, Ruth, will you tell Mr and Miss Benson that I am here? There is signing of papers, and I don't know what to be done at home. And when I come back, I hope to see you often, if you'll let me."

Mr and Miss Benson gave her a warm greeting. Sally was called in, and would bring a candle with her, to have a close inspection of her, in order to see if she was changed—she had not seen her for so long a time, she said; and Jemima stood laughing and blushing in the middle of the room, while Sally studied her all over, and would not be convinced that the old gown which she was wearing for the last time was not one of the new wedding ones. The consequence of which misunderstanding was, that Sally, in her short petticoats and bedgown, turned up her nose at the old-fashioned way in which Miss Bradshaw's gown was made. But Jemima knew the old woman, and rather enjoyed the contempt for her dress. At last she kissed them all, and ran away to her impatient Mr Farquhar, who was awaiting her.

Not many weeks after this, the poor old woman whom I have named as having become a friend of Ruth's, during Leonard's illness three years ago, fell down and broke her hip-bone. It was a serious—probably a fatal injury, for one so old; and as soon as Ruth heard of it she devoted all her leisure time to old Ann Fleming. Leonard had now outstript his mother's powers of teaching, and Mr Benson gave him his lessons; so Ruth was a great deal at the cottage both night and day.

There Jemima found her one November evening, the second after their return from their prolonged stay on the Continent. She and Mr Farquhar had been to the Bensons, and had sat there some time; and now Jemima had come on just to see

Ruth for five minutes, before the evening was too dark for her to return alone. She found Ruth sitting on a stool before the fire, which was composed of a few sticks on the hearth. The blaze they gave was, however, enough to enable her to read; and she was deep in study of the Bible, in which she had read aloud to the poor old woman, until the latter had fallen asleep. Jemima beckoned her out, and they stood on the green just before the open door, so that Ruth could see if Ann awoke.

"I have not many minutes to stay, only I felt as if I must see you. And we want Leonard to come to us to see all our German purchases, and hear all our German adventures. May he come to-morrow?"

"Yes; thank you. Oh! Jemima, I have heard something—I have got a plan that makes me so happy! I have not told any one yet. But Mr Wynne (the parish doctor, you know) has asked me if I would go out as a sick nurse—he thinks he could find me employment."

"You, a sick nurse!" said Jemima, involuntarily glancing over the beautiful lithe figure, and the lovely refinement of Ruth's face as the light of the rising moon fell upon it. "My dear Ruth, I don't think you are fitted for it!"

"Don't you?" said Ruth, a little disappointed. "I think I am; at least, that I should be very soon. I like being about sick and helpless people; I always feel so sorry for them; and then I think I have the gift of a very delicate touch, which is such a comfort in many cases. And I should try to be very watchful and patient. Mr Wynne proposed it himself."

"It was not in that way I meant you were not fitted for it. I meant that you were fitted for something better. Why, Ruth, you are better educated than I am!"

"But if nobody will allow me to teach?—for that is what I suppose you mean. Besides, I feel as if all my education would be needed to make me a good sick nurse."

"Your knowledge of Latin, for instance," said Jemima, hitting, in her vexation at the plan, on the first acquirement of Ruth she could think of.

"Well!" said Ruth, "that won't come amiss; I can read the prescriptions."

"Which the doctors would rather you did not do."

"Still, you can't say that any knowledge of any kind will be in my way, or will unfit me for my work."

"Perhaps not. But all your taste and refinement will be in your way, and will unfit you."

"You have not thought about this so much as I have, or you would not say so. Any fastidiousness I shall have to get rid of, and I shall be better without; but any true refinement I am sure I shall find of use; for don't you think that every power we have may be made to help us in any right work, whatever that is? Would you not rather be nursed by a person who spoke gently and moved quietly about than by a loud bustling woman?"

"Yes, to be sure; but a person unfit for anything else may move quietly, and speak gently, and give medicine when the doctor orders it, and keep awake at night; and those are the best qualities I ever heard of in a sick nurse."

Ruth was quite silent for some time. At last she said: "At any rate it is work, and as such I am thankful for it. You cannot discourage me—and perhaps you know too little of what my life has been—how set apart in idleness I have been—to sympathise with me fully."

"And I wanted you to come to see us—me in my new home. Walter and I had planned that we would persuade you to come to us very often" (she had planned, and Mr Farquhar had consented); "and now you will have to be fastened up in a sick-room."

"I could not have come," said Ruth quickly. "Dear Jemima! it is like you to have thought of it—but I could not come to your house. It is not a thing to reason about. It is just feeling. But I do feel as if I could not go. Dear Jemima! if you are ill or sorrowful, and want me, I will come—"

"So you would and must to any one, if you take up that calling."

"But I should come to you, love, in quite a different way; I should go to you with my heart full of love—so full that I am afraid I should be too anxious."

"I almost wish I were ill, that I might make you come at once."

"And I am almost ashamed to think how I should like you to be in some position in which I could show you how well I remember that day—that terrible day in the school-room. God bless you for it, Jemima!"

CHAPTER XXX - THE FORGED DEED

Mr Wynne, the parish surgeon, was right. He could and did obtain employment for Ruth as a sick nurse. Her home was with the Bensons; every spare moment was given to Leonard and to them; but she was at the call of all the invalids in the town. At first her work lay exclusively among the paupers. At first, too, there was a recoil from many circumstances, which impressed upon her the most fully the physical sufferings of those whom she tended. But she tried to lose the sense of these—or rather to lessen them, and make them take their appointed places—in thinking of the individuals themselves, as separate from their decaying frames; and all along she had enough self-command to control herself from expressing any sign of repugnance. She allowed herself no nervous haste of movement or touch that should hurt the feelings of the poorest, most friendless creature, who ever lay a victim to disease. There was no rough getting over of all the disagreeable and painful work of her employment. When it was a lessening of pain to have the touch careful and delicate, and the ministration performed with gradual skill, Ruth thought of her charge, and not of herself. As she had foretold, she found a use for all her powers. The poor patients themselves were unconsciously gratified and soothed by her harmony and refinement of manner, voice, and gesture. If this harmony and refinement had been merely superficial, it would not have had this balmy effect. That arose from its being the true expression of a kind, modest, and humble spirit. By degrees her reputation as a nurse spread upwards, and many sought her good offices who could well afford to pay for them. Whatever remuneration was offered to her, she took it simply and without comment; for she felt that it was not hers to refuse; that it was, in fact, owing to the Bensons for her and her child's subsistence. She went wherever her services were first called for. If the poor bricklayer, who broke both his legs in a fall from the scaffolding, sent for her when she was disengaged, she went and remained with him until he could spare her, let who would be the next claimant. From the happy and prosperous in all but health, she would occasionally beg off, when some one less happy and more friendless wished for her; and sometimes she would ask for a little money from Mr Benson to give to such in their time of need. But it was astonishing how much she was able to do without money.

Her ways were very quiet; she never spoke much. Any one who has been oppressed with the weight of a vital secret for years, and much more any one the character of whose life has been stamped by one event, and that producing sorrow and shame, is naturally reserved. And yet Ruth's silence was not like reserve; it was too gentle and tender for that. It had more the effect of a hush of all loud or disturbing emotions, and out of the deep calm the words that came forth had a beautiful power. She did not talk much about religion; but those who noticed her knew that it was the unseen banner which she was following. The low-breathed sentences which she spoke into the ear of the sufferer and the dying carried them upwards to God.

She gradually became known and respected among the roughest boys of the rough populace of the town. They would make way for her when she passed along the streets with more deference than they used to most; for all knew something of the tender care with which she had attended this or that sick person, and, besides, she was so often in connexion with Death that something of the superstitious awe with which the dead were regarded by those rough boys in the midst of their strong life, surrounded her.

She herself did not feel changed. She felt just as faulty—as far from being what she wanted to be, as ever. She best knew how many of her good actions were incomplete, and marred with evil. She did not feel much changed from the earliest Ruth she could remember. Everything seemed to change but herself. Mr and Miss Benson grew old, and Sally grew deaf, and Leonard was shooting up, and Jemima was a mother. She and the distant hills that she saw from her chamber window, seemed the only things which were the same as when she first came to Eccleston. As she sat looking out, and taking her fill of solitude, which sometimes was her most thorough rest—as she sat at the attic window looking abroad—she saw their next-door neighbour carried out to sun himself in his garden. When she first came to Eccleston, this neighbour and his daughter were often seen taking long and regular walks; by-and-by his walks became shorter, and the attentive daughter would convoy him home, and set out afresh to finish her own. Of late years he had only gone out in the garden behind his house; but at first he had walked pretty briskly there by his daughter's help—now he was carried, and placed in a large, cushioned easy-chair, his head remaining where it was placed against the pillow, and hardly moving when his kind daughter, who was now middle-aged, brought him the first roses of the summer. This told Ruth of the lapse of life and time.

Mr and Mrs Farquhar were constant in their attentions; but there was no sign of Mr Bradshaw ever forgiving the imposition which had been practised upon him, and Mr Benson ceased to hope for any renewal of their intercourse. Still, he thought that he must know of all the kind attentions which Jemima paid to them, and of the fond regard which both she and her husband bestowed on Leonard. This latter feeling even went so far that Mr Farquhar called one day, and with much diffidence begged Mr Benson to urge Ruth to let him be sent to school at his (Mr Farquhar's) expense.

Mr Benson was taken by surprise, and hesitated. "I do not know. It would be a great advantage in some respects; and yet I doubt whether it would in others. His mother's influence over him is thoroughly good, and I should fear that any thoughtless allusions to his peculiar position might touch the raw spot in his mind."

"But he is so unusually clever, it seems a shame not to give him all the advantages he can have. Besides, does he see much of his mother now?"

"Hardly a day passes without her coming home to be an hour or so with him, even at her busiest times; she says it is her best refreshment. And often, you know, she is disengaged for a week or two, except the occasional services which she is always rendering to those who need her. Your offer is very tempting, but there is so decidedly another view of the question to be considered, that I believe we must refer it to her."

"With all my heart. Don't hurry her to a decision. Let her weigh it well. I think she will find the advantages preponderate."

"I wonder if I might trouble you with a little business, Mr Farquhar, as you are here?"

"Certainly; I am only too glad to be of any use to you."

"Why, I see from the report of the Star Life Assurance Company in the *Times*, which you are so good as to send me, that they have declared a bonus on the shares; now it seems strange that I have received no notification of it, and I thought that perhaps it might be lying at your office, as Mr Bradshaw was the purchaser of the shares, and I have always received the dividends through your firm."

Mr Farquhar took the newspaper, and ran his eye over the report.

"I've no doubt that's the way of it," said he. "Some of our clerks have been careless about it; or it may be Richard himself. He is not always the most punctual and exact of mortals; but I'll see about it. Perhaps after all it mayn't come for a day or two; they have always such numbers of these circulars to send out."

"Oh! I'm in no hurry about it. I only want to receive it some time before I incur any expenses, which the promise of this bonus may tempt me to indulge in."

Mr Farquhar took his leave. That evening there was a long conference, for, as it happened, Ruth was at home. She was strenuously against the school plan. She could see no advantages that would counterbalance the evil which she dreaded from any school for Leonard; namely, that the good opinion and regard of the world would assume too high an importance in his eyes. The very idea seemed to produce in her so much shrinking affright, that by mutual consent the subject was dropped; to be taken up again, or not, according to circumstances.

Mr Farquhar wrote the next morning, on Mr Benson's behalf, to the Insurance Company, to inquire about the bonus. Although he wrote in the usual formal way, he did not think it necessary to tell Mr Bradshaw what he had done; for Mr Benson's name was rarely mentioned between the partners; each had been made fully aware of the views which the other entertained on the subject that had caused the estrangement; and Mr Farquhar felt that no external argument could affect Mr Bradshaw's resolved disapproval and avoidance of his former minister.

As it happened, the answer from the Insurance Company (directed to the firm) was given to Mr Bradshaw along with the other business letters. It was to the effect that Mr Benson's shares had been sold and transferred above a twelvemonth ago, which sufficiently accounted for the circumstance that no notification of the bonus had been sent to him.

Mr Bradshaw tossed the letter on one side, not displeased to have a good reason for feeling a little contempt at the unbusiness-like forgetfulness of Mr Benson, at whose instance some one had evidently been writing to the Insurance Company. On Mr Farquhar's entrance he expressed this feeling to him.

"Really," he said, "these Dissenting ministers have no more notion of exactitude in their affairs than a child! The idea of forgetting that he has sold his shares, and applying for the bonus, when it seems he has transferred them only a year ago!"

Mr Farquhar was reading the letter while Mr Bradshaw spoke.

"I don't quite understand it," said he. "Mr Benson was quite clear about it. He could not have received his half-yearly dividends unless he had been possessed of these shares; and I don't suppose Dissenting ministers, with all their ignorance of business, are unlike other men in knowing whether or not they receive the money that they believe to be owing to them."

"I should not wonder if they were—if Benson was, at any rate. Why, I never knew his watch to be right in all my life—it was always too fast or too slow; it must have been a daily discomfort to him. It ought to have been. Depend upon it, his money matters are just in the same irregular state; no accounts kept, I'll be bound."

"I don't see that that follows," said Mr Farquhar, half amused. "That watch of his is a very curious one—belonged to his father and grandfather, I don't know how far back."

"And the sentimental feelings which he is guided by prompt him to keep it, to the inconvenience of himself and every one else."

Mr Farquhar gave up the subject of the watch as hopeless.

"But about this letter. I wrote, at Mr Benson's desire, to the Insurance Office, and I am not satisfied with this answer. All the transaction has passed through our hands. I do not think it is likely Mr Benson would write and sell the shares without, at any rate, informing us at the time, even though he forgot all about it afterwards."

"Probably he told Richard, or Mr Watson."

"We can ask Mr Watson at once. I am afraid we must wait till Richard comes home, for I don't know where a letter would catch him."

Mr Bradshaw pulled the bell that rang into the head-clerk's room, saying as he did so,

"You may depend upon it, Farquhar, the blunder lies with Benson himself. He is just the man to muddle away his money in indiscriminate charity, and then to wonder what has become of it."

Mr Farquhar was discreet enough to hold his tongue.

"Mr Watson," said Mr Bradshaw, as the old clerk made his appearance, "here is some mistake about those Insurance shares we purchased for Benson ten or a dozen years ago. He spoke to Mr Farquhar about some bonus they are paying to the shareholders, it seems; and, in reply to Mr Farquhar's letter, the Insurance Company say the shares were sold twelve months since. Have you any knowledge of the transaction? Has the transfer passed through your hands? By the way" (turning to Mr Farquhar), "who kept the certificates? Did Benson or we?"

"I really don't know," said Mr Farquhar. "Perhaps Mr Watson can tell us."

Mr Watson meanwhile was studying the letter. When he had ended it, he took off his spectacles, wiped them, and replacing them, he read it again.

"It seems very strange, sir," he said at length, with his trembling, aged voice, "for I paid Mr Benson the account of the dividends myself last June, and got a receipt in form, and that is since the date of the alleged transfer."

"Pretty nearly twelve months after it took place," said Mr Farquhar.

"How did you receive the dividends? An order on the Bank, along with old Mrs Cranmer's?" asked Mr Bradshaw, sharply.

"I don't know how they came. Mr Richard gave me the money, and desired me to get the receipt."

"It's unlucky Richard is from home," said Mr Bradshaw. "He could have cleared up this mystery for us."

Mr Farquhar was silent.

"Do you know where the certificates were kept, Mr Watson?" said he.

"I'll not be sure, but I think they were with Mrs Cranmer's papers and deeds in box A, 24."

"I wish old Cranmer would have made any other man his executor. She, too, is always coming with some unreasonable request or other."

"Mr Benson's inquiry about his bonus is perfectly reasonable, at any rate."

Mr Watson, who was dwelling in the slow fashion of age on what had been said before, now spoke:

"I'll not be sure, but I am almost certain, Mr Benson said, when I paid him last June, that he thought he ought to give the receipt on a stamp, and had spoken about it to Mr Richard the time before, but that Mr Richard said it was of no consequence. Yes," continued he, gathering up his memory as he went on, "he did—I remember now—and I thought to myself that Mr Richard was but a young man. Mr Richard will know all about it."

"Yes," said Mr Farquhar, gravely.

"I shan't wait till Richard's return," said Mr Bradshaw. "We can soon see if the certificates are in the box Watson points out; if they are there, the Insurance people are no more fit to manage their concern than that cat, and I shall tell them so. If they are not there (as I suspect will prove to be the case), it is just forgetfulness on Benson's part, as I have said from the first."

"You forget the payment of the dividends," said Mr Farquhar, in a low voice.

"Well, sir! what then?" said Mr Bradshaw, abruptly. While he spoke—while his eye met Mr Farquhar's—the hinted meaning of the latter flashed through his mind; but he was only made angry to find that such a suspicion could pass through any one's imagination.

"I suppose I may go, sir," said Watson, respectfully, an uneasy consciousness of what was in Mr Farquhar's thoughts troubling the faithful old clerk.

"Yes. Go. What do you mean about the dividends?" asked Mr Bradshaw, impetuously of Mr Farquhar.

"Simply, that I think there can have been no forgetfulness—no mistake on Mr Benson's part," said Mr Farquhar, unwilling to put his dim suspicion into words.

"Then of course it is some blunder of that confounded Insurance Company. I will write to them to-day, and make them a little brisker and more correct in their statements."

"Don't you think it would be better to wait till Richard's return? He may be able to explain it."

"No, sir!" said Mr Bradshaw, sharply. "I do not think it would be better. It has not been my way of doing business to spare any one, or any company, the consequences of their own carelessness; nor to obtain information second-hand when I could have it direct from the source. I shall write to the Insurance Office by the next post."

Mr Farquhar saw that any further remonstrance on his part would only aggravate his partner's obstinacy; and, besides, it was but a suspicion—an uncomfortable suspicion. It was possible that some of the clerks at the Insurance Office might have made a mistake. Watson was not sure, after all, that the certificates had been deposited in box A, 24; and when he and Mr Farquhar could not find them there, the old man drew more and yet more back from his first assertion of belief that they had been placed there.

Mr Bradshaw wrote an angry and indignant reproach of carelessness to the Insurance Company. By the next mail one of their clerks came down to Eccleston; and having leisurely refreshed himself at the inn, and ordered his dinner with care, he walked up to the great warehouse of Bradshaw and Co., and sent in his card, with a pencil notification, "On the part of the Star Insurance Company," to Mr Bradshaw himself.

Mr Bradshaw held the card in his hand for a minute or two without raising his eyes. Then he spoke out loud and firm:

"Desire the gentleman to walk up. Stay! I will ring my bell in a minute or two, and then show him upstairs."

When the errand-boy had closed the door, Mr Bradshaw went to a cupboard where he usually kept a glass and a bottle of wine (of which he very seldom partook, for he was an abstemious man). He intended now to take a glass, but the bottle was empty; and though there was plenty more to be had for ringing, or even simply going into another room, he would not allow himself to do this. He stood and lectured himself in thought.

"After all, I am a fool for once in my life. If the certificates are in no box which I have yet examined, that does not imply they may not be in some one which I have not had time to search. Farquhar would stay so late last night! And even if they are in none of the boxes here, that does not prove—" He gave the bell a jerking ring, and it was yet sounding when Mr Smith, the insurance clerk, entered.

The manager of the Insurance Company had been considerably nettled at the tone of Mr Bradshaw's letter; and had instructed the clerk to assume some dignity at first in vindicating (as it was well in his power to do) the character of the proceedings of the Company, but at the same time he was not to go too far, for the firm of Bradshaw and Co. was daily looming larger in the commercial world, and if any reasonable explanation could be given it was to be received, and bygones be bygones.

"Sit down, sir!" said Mr Bradshaw.

"You are aware, sir, I presume, that I come on the part of Mr Dennison, the manager of the Star Insurance Company, to reply in person to a letter of yours, of the 29th, addressed to him?"

Mr Bradshaw bowed. "A very careless piece of business," he said, stiffly.

"Mr Dennison does not think you will consider it as such when you have seen the deed of transfer, which I am commissioned to show you."

Mr Bradshaw took the deed with a steady hand. He wiped his spectacles quietly, without delay, and without hurry, and adjusted them on his nose. It is possible that he was rather long in looking over the document—at least, the clerk had just begun to wonder if he was reading through the whole of it, instead of merely looking at the signature, when Mr Bradshaw said: "It is possible that it may be—of

course, you will allow me to take this paper to Mr Benson, to—to inquire if this be his signature?"

"There can be no doubt of it, I think, sir," said the clerk, calmly smiling, for he knew Mr Benson's signature well.

"I don't know, sir—I don't know." (He was speaking as if the pronunciation of every word required a separate effort of will, like a man who has received a slight paralytic stroke.)

"You have heard, sir, of such a thing as forgery—forgery, sir?" said he, repeating the last word very distinctly; for he feared that the first time he had said it, it was rather slurred over.

"Oh, sir! there is no room for imagining such a thing, I assure you. In our affairs we become aware of curious forgetfulness on the part of those who are not of business habits."

"Still I should like to show it Mr Benson, to prove to him his forgetfulness, you know. I believe, on my soul, it is some of his careless forgetfulness—I do, sir," said he. Now he spoke very quickly. "It must have been. Allow me to convince myself. You shall have it back to-night, or the first thing in the morning."

The clerk did not quite like to relinquish the deed, nor yet did he like to refuse Mr Bradshaw. If that very uncomfortable idea of forgery should have any foundation in truth—and he had given up the writing! There were a thousand chances to one against its being anything but a stupid blunder; the risk was more imminent of offending one of the directors.

As he hesitated, Mr Bradshaw spoke, very calmly, and almost with a smile on his face. He had regained his self-command. "You are afraid, I see. I assure you, you may trust me. If there has been any fraud—if I have the slightest suspicion of the truth of the surmise I threw out just now,"—he could not quite speak the bare naked word that was chilling his heart—"I will not fail to aid the ends of justice, even though the culprit should be my own son."

He ended, as he began, with a smile—such a smile!—the stiff lips refused to relax and cover the teeth. But all the time he kept saying to himself:

"I don't believe it—I don't believe it. I'm convinced it's a blunder of that old fool Benson."

But when he had dismissed the clerk, and secured the piece of paper, he went and locked the door, and laid his head on his desk, and moaned aloud.

He had lingered in the office for the two previous nights; at first, occupying himself in searching for the certificates of the Insurance shares; but, when all the boxes and other repositories for papers had been ransacked, the thought took hold of him that they might be in Richard's private desk; and, with the determination which overlooks the means to get at the end, he had first tried all his own keys on the complicated lock, and then broken it open with two decided blows of a poker, the instrument nearest at hand. He did not find the certificates. Richard had always considered himself careful in destroying any dangerous or tell-tale papers; but the stern father found enough, in what remained, to convince him that his pattern son—more even than his pattern son, his beloved pride—was far other than what he seemed.

Mr Bradshaw did not skip or miss a word. He did not shrink while he read. He folded up letter by letter; he snuffed the candle just when its light began to wane, and no sooner; but he did not miss or omit one paper—he read every word. Then, leaving the letters in a heap upon the table, and the broken desk to tell its own tale, he locked the door of the room which was appropriated to his son as junior partner, and carried the key away with him.

There was a faint hope, even after this discovery of many circumstances of Richard's life which shocked and dismayed his father—there was still a faint hope that he might not be guilty of forgery—that it might be no forgery after all—only a blunder—an omission—a stupendous piece of forgetfulness. That hope was the one straw that Mr Bradshaw clung to.

Late that night Mr Benson sat in his study. Every one else in the house had gone to bed; but he was expecting a summons to someone who was dangerously ill. He was not startled, therefore, at the knock which came to the front door about twelve; but he was rather surprised at the character of the knock, so slow and loud, with a pause between each rap. His study-door was but a step from that which led into the street. He opened it, and there stood—Mr Bradshaw; his large, portly figure not to be mistaken even in the dusky night.

He said, "That is right. It was you I wanted to see." And he walked straight into the study. Mr Benson followed, and shut the door. Mr Bradshaw was standing by the table, fumbling in his pocket. He pulled out the deed; and opening it, after a pause, in which you might have counted five, he held it out to Mr Benson.

"Read it!" said he. He spoke not another word until time had been allowed for its perusal. Then he added:

"That is your signature?" The words were an assertion, but the tone was that of question.

"No, it is not," said Mr Benson, decidedly. "It is very like my writing. I could almost say it was mine, but I know it is not."

"Recollect yourself a little. The date is August the third of last year, fourteen months ago. You may have forgotten it." The tone of the voice had a kind of eager entreaty in it, which Mr Benson did not notice,—he was so startled at the fetch of his own writing.

"It is most singularly like mine; but I could not have signed away these shares—all the property I have—without the slightest remembrance of it."

"Stranger things have happened. For the love of Heaven, think if you did not sign it. It's a deed of transfer for those Insurance shares, you see. You don't remember it? You did not write this name—these words?" He looked at Mr Benson with craving wistfulness for one particular answer. Mr Benson was struck at last by the whole proceeding, and glanced anxiously at Mr Bradshaw, whose manner, gait, and voice were so different from usual that he might well excite attention. But as soon as the latter was aware of this momentary inspection, he changed his tone all at once.

"Don't imagine, sir, I wish to force any invention upon you as a remembrance. If you did not write this name, I know who did. Once more I ask you,—does no glimmering recollection of—having needed money, we'll say—I never wanted you to refuse my subscription to the chapel, God knows!—of having sold these accursed shares?—Oh! I see by your face you did not write it; you need not speak to me—I know."

He sank down into a chair near him. His whole figure drooped. In a moment he was up, and standing straight as an arrow, confronting Mr Benson, who could find no clue to this stern man's agitation.

"You say you did not write these words?" pointing to the signature, with an untrembling finger. "I believe you; Richard Bradshaw did write them."

"My dear sir—my dear old friend!" exclaimed Mr Benson, "you are rushing to a conclusion for which, I am convinced, there is no foundation; there is no reason to suppose that because—"

"There is reason, sir. Do not distress yourself—I am perfectly calm." His stony eyes and immovable face did indeed look rigid. "What we have now to do is to punish the offence. I have not one standard for myself and those I love—(and, Mr Benson, I did love him)—and another for the rest of the world. If a stranger had forged my name, I should have known it was my duty to prosecute him. You must prosecute Richard."

"I will not," said Mr Benson.

"You think, perhaps, that I shall feel it acutely. You are mistaken. He is no longer as my son to me. I have always resolved to disown any child of mine who was guilty of sin. I disown Richard. He is as a stranger to me. I shall feel no more at his exposure—his punishment—" He could not go on, for his voice was choking. "Of course, you understand that I must feel shame at our connexion; it is that that is troubling me; that is but consistent with a man who has always prided himself on the integrity of his name; but as for that boy, who has been brought up all his life as I have brought up my children, it must be some innate wickedness! Sir, I can cut him off, though he has been as my right hand—beloved. Let me be no hindrance to the course of justice, I beg. He has forged your name—he has defrauded you of money—of your all, I think you said."

"Someone has forged my name. I am not convinced that it was your son. Until I know all the circumstances, I decline to prosecute."

"What circumstances?" asked Mr Bradshaw, in an authoritative manner, which would have shown irritation but for his self-command.

"The force of the temptation—the previous habits of the person—"

"Of Richard. He is the person," Mr Bradshaw put in.

Mr Benson went on, without taking any notice. "I should think it right to prosecute, if I found out that this offence against me was only one of a series committed, with premeditation, against society. I should then feel, as a protector of others more helpless than myself—"

"It was your all," said Mr Bradshaw.

"It was all my money; it was not my all," replied Mr Benson; and then he went on as if the interruption had never been: "Against an habitual offender. I shall not prosecute Richard. Not because he is your son—do not imagine that! I should decline taking such a step against any young man without first ascertaining the particulars about him, which I know already about Richard, and which determine me against doing what would blast his character for life—would destroy every good quality he has."

"What good quality remains to him?" asked Mr Bradshaw. "He has deceived me—he has offended God."

"Have we not all offended Him?" Mr Benson said, in a low tone.

"Not consciously. I never do wrong consciously. But Richard—Richard." The remembrance of the undeceiving letters—the forgery—filled up his heart so completely that he could not speak for a minute or two. Yet when he saw Mr Benson on the point of saying something, he broke in:

"It is no use talking, sir. You and I cannot agree on these subjects. Once more, I desire you to prosecute that boy, who is no longer a child of mine."

"Mr Bradshaw, I shall not prosecute him. I have said it once for all. To-morrow you will be glad that I do not listen to you. I should only do harm by saying more at present."

There is always something aggravating in being told, that the mood in which we are now viewing things strongly will not be our mood at some other time. It implies that our present feelings are blinding us, and that some more clear-sighted spectator is able to distinguish our future better than we do ourselves. The most shallow person dislikes to be told that any one can gauge his depth. Mr Bradshaw was not soothed by this last remark of Mr Benson's. He stooped down to take up his hat and be gone. Mr Benson saw his dizzy way of groping, and gave him what he sought for; but he received no word of thanks. Mr Bradshaw went silently towards the door, but, just as he got there, he turned round, and said:

"If there were more people like me, and fewer like you, there would be less evil in the world, sir. It's your sentimentalists that nurse up sin."

Although Mr Benson had been very calm during this interview, he had been much shocked by what had been let out respecting Richard's forgery; not by the fact itself so much as by what it was a sign of. Still, he had known the young man from childhood, and had seen, and often regretted, that his want of moral courage had rendered him peculiarly liable to all the bad effects arising from his father's severe and arbitrary mode of treatment. Dick would never have had "pluck" enough to be a hardened villain, under any circumstances; but, unless some good influence, some strength, was brought to bear upon him, he might easily sink into the sneaking scoundrel. Mr Benson determined to go to Mr Farquhar's the first thing in the morning, and consult him as a calm, clear-headed family friend—partner in the business, as well as son and brother-in-law to the people concerned.

CHAPTER XXXI - AN ACCIDENT TO THE DOVER COACH

While Mr Benson lay awake for fear of oversleeping himself, and so being late at Mr Farquhar's (it was somewhere about six o'clock—dark as an October morning is at that time), Sally came to his door and knocked. She was always an early riser; and if she had not been gone to bed long before Mr Bradshaw's visit last night, Mr Benson might safely have trusted to her calling him.

"Here's a woman down below as must see you directly. She'll be upstairs after me if you're not down quick."

"Is it any one from Clarke's?"

"No, no! not it, master," said she, through the keyhole; "I reckon it's Mrs Bradshaw, for all she's muffled up."

He needed no other word. When he went down, Mrs Bradshaw sat in his easy-chair, swaying her body to and fro, and crying without restraint. Mr Benson came up to her, before she was aware that he was there.

"Oh! sir," said she, getting up and taking hold of both his hands, "you won't be so cruel, will you? I have got some money somewhere—some money my father settled on me, sir; I don't know how much, but I think it's more than two thousand pounds, and you shall have it all. If I can't give it you now, I'll make a will, sir. Only be merciful to poor Dick—don't go and prosecute him, sir."

"My dear Mrs Bradshaw, don't agitate yourself in this way. I never meant to prosecute him."

"But Mr Bradshaw says that you must."

"I shall not, indeed. I have told Mr Bradshaw so."

"Has he been here? Oh! is not he cruel? I don't care. I've been a good wife till now. I know I have. I have done all he bid me, ever since we were married. But now I will speak my mind, and say to everybody how cruel he is—how hard to his own flesh and blood! If he puts poor Dick in prison, I will go too. If I'm to choose between my husband and my son, I choose my son; for he will have no friends, unless I am with him."

"Mr Bradshaw will think better of it. You will see that, when his first anger and disappointment are over, he will not be hard or cruel."

"You don't know Mr Bradshaw," said she, mournfully, "if you think he'll change. I might beg and beg—I have done many a time, when we had little children, and I wanted to save them a whipping—but no begging ever did any good. At last I left it off. He'll not change."

"Perhaps not for human entreaty. Mrs Bradshaw, is there nothing more powerful?"

The tone of his voice suggested what he did not say.

"If you mean that God may soften his heart," replied she, humbly, "I'm not going to deny God's power—I have need to think of Him," she continued, bursting into fresh tears, "for I am a very miserable woman. Only think! he cast it up against me last night, and said, if I had not spoilt Dick this never would have happened."

"He hardly knew what he was saying last night. I will go to Mr Farquhar's directly, and see him; and you had better go home, my dear Mrs Bradshaw; you may rely upon our doing all that we can."

With some difficulty he persuaded her not to accompany him to Mr Farquhar's; but he had, indeed, to take her to her own door before he could convince her that, at present, she could do nothing but wait the result of the consultation of others.

It was before breakfast, and Mr Farquhar was alone; so Mr Benson had a quiet opportunity of telling the whole story to the husband before the wife came down. Mr Farquhar was not much surprised, though greatly distressed. The general opinion he had always entertained of Richard's character had predisposed him to fear, even before the inquiry respecting the Insurance shares. But it was still a shock when it came, however much it might have been anticipated.

"What can we do?" said Mr Benson, as Mr Farquhar sat gloomily silent.

"That is just what I was asking myself. I think I must see Mr Bradshaw, and try and bring him a little out of this unmerciful frame of mind. That must be the first thing. Will you object to accompany me at once? It seems of particular consequence that we should subdue his obduracy before the affair gets wind."

"I will go with you willingly. But I believe I rather serve to irritate Mr Bradshaw; he is reminded of things he has said to me formerly, and which he thinks he is bound to act up to. However, I can walk with you to the door, and wait for you (if you'll allow me) in the street. I want to know how he is to-day, both bodily and mentally; for indeed, Mr Farquhar, I should not have been surprised last night if he had dropped down dead, so terrible was his strain upon himself."

Mr Benson was left at the door as he had desired, while Mr Farquhar went in.

"Oh, Mr Farquhar, what is the matter?" exclaimed the girls, running to him. "Mamma sits crying in the old nursery. We believe she has been there all night. She will not tell us what it is, nor let us be with her; and papa is locked up in his room, and won't even answer us when we speak, though we know he is up and awake, for we heard him tramping about all night."

"Let me go up to him," said Mr Farquhar.

"He won't let you in. It will be of no use." But in spite of what they said, he went up; and to their surprise, after hearing who it was, their father opened the door, and admitted their brother-in-law. He remained with Mr Bradshaw about half an hour, and then came into the dining-room, where the two girls stood huddled over the fire, regardless of the untasted breakfast behind them; and, writing a few lines, he desired them to take his note up to their mother, saying it would comfort her a little, and that he should send Jemima, in two or three hours, with the baby—perhaps to remain some days with them. He had no time to tell them more; Jemima would.

He left them, and rejoined Mr Benson. "Come home and breakfast with me. I am off to London in an hour or two, and must speak with you first."

On reaching his house, he ran upstairs to ask Jemima to breakfast alone in her dressing-room, and returned in five minutes or less.

"Now I can tell you about it," said he. "I see my way clearly to a certain point. We must prevent Dick and his father meeting just now, or all hope of Dick's reformation is gone for ever. His father is as hard as the nether mill-stone. He has forbidden me his house."

"Forbidden you!"

"Yes; because I would not give up Dick as utterly lost and bad; and because I said I should return to London with the clerk, and fairly tell Dennison (he's a Scotchman, and a man of sense and feeling) the real state of the case. By the way, we must not say a word to the clerk; otherwise he will expect an answer, and make out all sorts of inferences for himself, from the unsatisfactory reply he must have. Dennison will be upon honour—will see every side of the case—will know you refuse to prosecute; the Company of which he is manager are no losers. Well! when I said what I thought wise, of all this—when I spoke as if my course were a settled and decided thing, the grim old man asked me if he was to be an automaton in his own house. He assured me he had no feeling for Dick—all the time he was shaking like an aspen; in short, repeated much the same things he must have said to you last night. However, I defied him; and the consequence is, I'm forbidden the house, and, what is more, he says he will not come to the office while I remain a partner."

"What shall you do?"

"Send Jemima and the baby. There's nothing like a young child for bringing people round to a healthy state of feeling; and you don't know what Jemima is, Mr Benson! No! though you've known her from her birth. If she can't comfort her mother, and if the baby can't steal into her grandfather's heart, why—I don't know what you may do to me. I shall tell Jemima all, and trust to her wit and wisdom to work at this end, while I do my best at the other."

"Richard is abroad, is not he?"

"He will be in England to-morrow. I must catch him somewhere; but that I can easily do. The difficult point will be, what to do with him—what to say to him, when I find him. He must give up his partnership, that's clear. I did not tell his father so, but I am resolved upon it. There shall be no tampering with the honour of the firm to which I belong."

"But what will become of him?" asked Mr Benson, anxiously.

"I do not yet know. But, for Jemima's sake—for his dear old father's sake—I will not leave him adrift. I will find him some occupation as clear from temptation as I can. I will do all in my power. And he will do much better, if he has any good in him, as a freer agent, not cowed by his father into a want of individuality and self-respect. I believe I must dismiss you, Mr Benson," said he, looking at his watch; "I have to explain all to my wife, and to go to that clerk. You shall hear from me in a day or two."

Mr Benson half envied the younger man's elasticity of mind, and power of acting promptly. He himself felt as if he wanted to sit down in his quiet study, and think over the revelations and events of the last twenty-four hours. It made him dizzy even to follow Mr Farquhar's plans, as he had briefly detailed them; and some solitude and consideration would be required before Mr Benson could decide upon their justice and wisdom. He had been much shocked by the discovery of the overt act of guilt which Richard had perpetrated, low as his opinion of that young man had been for some time; and the consequence was, that he felt depressed, and unable to rally for the next few days. He had not even the comfort of his sister's sympathy, as he felt bound in honour not to tell her anything; and she was luckily so much absorbed in some household contest with Sally that she did not notice her brother's quiet languor.

Mr Benson felt that he had no right at this time to intrude into the house which he had been once tacitly forbidden. If he went now to Mr Bradshaw's without being asked, or sent for, he thought it would seem like presuming on his knowledge of the hidden disgrace of one of the family. Yet he longed to go: he knew that Mr Farquhar must be writing almost daily to Jemima, and he wanted to hear what he was doing. The fourth day after her husband's departure she came, within half an hour of the post-delivery, and asked to speak to Mr Benson alone.

She was in a state of great agitation, and had evidently been crying very much.

"Oh, Mr Benson!" said she, "will you come with me, and tell papa this sad news about Dick? Walter has written me a letter at last to say he has found him—he could not at first; but now it seems that, the day before yesterday, he heard of an accident which had happened to the Dover coach; it was overturned—two passengers killed, and several badly hurt. Walter says we ought to be thankful, as he is, that Dick was not killed. He says it was such a relief to him on going to the place—the little inn nearest to where the coach was overturned—to find that Dick was only severely injured; not one of those who was killed. But it is a terrible shock to us all. We had had no more dreadful fear to lessen the shock; mamma is quite unfit for anything, and we none of us dare to tell papa." Jemima had hard work to keep down her sobs thus far, and now they overmastered her.

"How is your father? I have wanted to hear every day," asked Mr Benson, tenderly.

"It was careless of me not to come and tell you; but, indeed, I have had so much to do. Mamma would not go near him. He has said something which she seems as if she could not forgive. Because he came to meals, she would not. She has almost lived in the nursery; taking out all Dick's old playthings, and what clothes of his were left, and turning them over, and crying over them."

"Then Mr Bradshaw has joined you again; I was afraid, from what Mr Farquhar said, he was going to isolate himself from you all?"

"I wish he had," said Jemima, crying afresh. "It would have been more natural than the way he has gone on; the only difference from his usual habits is, that he has never gone near the office, or else he has come to meals just as usual, and talked just as usual; and even done what I never knew him do before, tried to make jokes—all in order to show us how little he cares."

"Does he not go out at all?"

"Only in the garden. I am sure he does care after all; he must care; he cannot shake off a child in this way, though he thinks he can; and that makes me so afraid of telling him of this accident. Will you come, Mr Benson?"

He needed no other word. He went with her, as she rapidly threaded her way through the by-streets. When they reached the house, she went in without knocking, and putting her husband's letter into Mr Benson's hand, she opened the door of her father's room, and saying—"Papa, here is Mr Benson," left them alone.

Mr Benson felt nervously incapable of knowing what to do, or to say. He had surprised Mr Bradshaw sitting idly over the fire—gazing dreamily into the embers. But he had started up, and drawn his chair to the table, on seeing his visitor; and, after the first necessary words of politeness were over, he seemed to expect him to open the conversation.

"Mrs Farquhar has asked me," said Mr Benson, plunging into the subject with a trembling heart, "to tell you about a letter she has received from her husband;" he stopped for an instant, for he felt that he did not get nearer the real difficulty, and yet could not tell the best way of approaching it.

"She need not have given you that trouble. I am aware of the reason of Mr Farquhar's absence. I entirely disapprove of his conduct. He is regardless of my wishes; and disobedient to the commands which, as my son-in-law, I thought he would have felt bound to respect. If there is any more agreeable subject that you can introduce, I shall be glad to hear you, sir."

"Neither you, nor I, must think of what we like to hear or to say. You must hear what concerns your son."

"I have disowned the young man who was my son," replied he, coldly.

"The Dover coach has been overturned," said Mr Benson, stimulated into abruptness by the icy sternness of the father. But, in a flash, he saw what lay below that terrible assumption of indifference. Mr Bradshaw glanced up in his face one look of agony—and then went grey-pale; so livid that Mr Benson got up to ring the bell in affright, but Mr Bradshaw motioned to him to sit still.

"Oh! I have been too sudden, sir—he is alive, he is alive!" he exclaimed, as he saw the ashy face working in a vain attempt to speak; but the poor lips (so wooden, not a minute ago) went working on and on, as if Mr Benson's words did not sink down into the mind, or reach the understanding. Mr Benson went hastily for Mrs Farquhar.

"Oh, Jemima!" said he, "I have done it so badly—I have been so cruel—he is very ill, I fear—bring water, brandy—" and he returned with all speed into the room. Mr Bradshaw—the great, strong, iron man—lay back in his chair in a swoon, a fit.

"Fetch my mother, Mary. Send for the doctor, Elizabeth," said Jemima, rushing to her father. She and Mr Benson did all in their power to restore him. Mrs Bradshaw forgot all her vows of estrangement from the dead-like husband, who might never speak to her, or hear her again, and bitterly accused herself for every angry word she had spoken against him during these last few miserable days.

Before the doctor came, Mr Bradshaw had opened his eyes and partially rallied, although he either did not, or could not speak. He looked struck down into old age. His eyes were sensible in their expression, but had the dim glaze of many years of life upon them. His lower jaw fell from his upper one, giving a look of melancholy depression to the face, although the lips hid the unclosed teeth. But he answered correctly (in monosyllables, it is true) all the questions which the doctor chose to ask. And the medical man was not so much impressed with the serious character of the seizure as the family, who knew all the hidden mystery behind, and had seen their father lie for the first time with the precursor aspect of death upon his face. Rest, watching, and a little medicine were what the doctor prescribed; it was so slight a prescription, for what had appeared to Mr Benson so serious an attack, that he wished to follow the medical man out of the room to make further inquiries, and learn the real opinion which he thought must lurk behind. But as he was following the doctor, he—they all—were aware of the effort Mr Bradshaw was making to rise, in order to arrest Mr Benson's departure. He did stand up, supporting himself with one hand on the table, for his legs shook under him. Mr Benson came back instantly to the spot where he was. For a moment it seemed as if he had not the right command of his voice: but at last he said, with a tone of humble, wistful entreaty, which was very touching:

"He is alive, sir; is he not?"

"Yes, sir—indeed he is; he is only hurt. He is sure to do well. Mr Farquhar is with him," said Mr Benson, almost unable to speak for tears.

Mr Bradshaw did not remove his eyes from Mr Benson's face for more than a minute after his question had been answered. He seemed as though he would read his very soul, and there see if he spoke the truth. Satisfied at last, he sank slowly into his chair; and they were silent for a little space, waiting to perceive if he would wish for any further information just then. At length he put his hands slowly together in the clasped attitude of prayer, and said—"Thank God!"

CHAPTER XXXII - THE BRADSHAW PEW AGAIN OCCUPIED

If Jemima allowed herself now and then to imagine that one good would result from the discovery of Richard's delinquency, in the return of her father and Mr Benson to something of their old understanding and their old intercourse—if this hope fluttered through her mind, it was doomed to disappointment. Mr Benson would have been most happy to go, if Mr Bradshaw had sent for him; he was on the watch for what might be even the shadow of such an invitation—but none came. Mr Bradshaw, on his part, would have been thoroughly glad if the wilful seclusion of his present life could have been broken by the occasional visits of the old friend whom he had once forbidden the house; but this prohibition having passed his lips, he stubbornly refused to do anything which might be construed into unsaying it. Jemima was for some time in despair of his ever returning to the office, or resuming his old habits of business. He had evidently threatened as much to her husband. All that Jemima could do was to turn a deaf ear to every allusion to this menace, which he threw out from time to time, evidently with a view to see if it had struck deep enough into her husband's mind for him to have repeated it to his wife. If Mr Farquhar had named it—if it was known only to two or three to have been, but for one half-hour even, his resolution—Mr Bradshaw could have adhered to it, without any other reason than the maintenance of what he called consistency, but which was in fact doggedness. Jemima was often thankful that her mother was absent, and gone to nurse her son. If she had been at home, she would have entreated and implored her husband to fall back into his usual habits, and would have shown such a dread of his being as good as his word, that he would have been compelled to adhere to it by the very consequence affixed to it. Mr Farquhar had hard work, as it was, in passing rapidly enough between the two places—attending to his business at Eccleston; and deciding, comforting, and earnestly talking, in Richard's sick-room. During an absence of his, it was necessary to apply to one of the partners on some matter of importance; and accordingly, to Jemima's secret joy, Mr Watson came up and asked if her father was well enough to see him on business? Jemima carried in this inquiry literally; and the hesitating answer which her father gave was in the affirmative. It was not long before she saw him leave the house, accompanied by the faithful old clerk; and when he met her at dinner, he made no allusion to his morning visitor, or to his subsequent going out. But from that time forwards he went regularly to the office. He received all the information about Dick's accident, and his progress towards recovery, in perfect silence, and in as indifferent a manner as he could assume; but yet he lingered about the family sitting-room every morning until the post had come in which brought all letters from the south.

When Mr Farquhar at last returned to bring the news of Dick's perfect convalescence, he resolved to tell Mr Bradshaw all that he had done and arranged for his son's future career; but, as Mr Farquhar told Mr Benson afterwards, he could not really say if Mr Bradshaw had attended to one word that he said.

"Rely upon it," said Mr Benson, "he has not only attended to it, but treasured up every expression you have used."

"Well, I tried to get some opinion, or sign of emotion, out of him. I had not much hope of the latter, I must own; but I thought he would have said whether I had done wisely or not in procuring that Glasgow situation for Dick—that he would, perhaps, have been indignant at my ousting him from the partnership so entirely on my own responsibility."

"How did Richard take it?"

"Oh, nothing could exceed his penitence. If one had never heard of the proverb, 'When the devil was sick, the devil a monk would be,' I should have had greater faith in him; or if he had had more strength of character to begin with, or more reality and less outward appearance of good principle instilled into him. However, this Glasgow situation is the very thing; clear, defined duties, no great trust reposed in him, a kind and watchful head, and introductions to a better class of associates than I fancy he has ever been thrown amongst before. For, you know, Mr Bradshaw dreaded all intimacies for his son, and wanted him to eschew all society beyond his own family—would never allow him to ask a friend home. Really, when I think of the unnatural life Mr Bradshaw expected him to lead, I get into charity with him, and have hopes. By the way, have you ever succeeded in persuading his mother to send Leonard to school? He may run the same risk from isolation as Dick: not be able to choose his companions wisely when he grows up, but be too much overcome by the excitement of society to be very discreet as to who are his associates. Have you spoken to her about my plan?"

"Yes! but to no purpose. I cannot say that she would even admit an argument on the subject. She seemed to have an invincible repugnance to the idea of exposing him to the remarks of other boys on his peculiar position."

"They need never know of it. Besides, sooner or later, he must step out of his narrow circle, and encounter remark and scorn."

"True," said Mr Benson, mournfully. "And you may depend upon it, if it really is the best for Leonard, she will come round to it by-and-by. It is almost extraordinary to see the way in which her earnest and most unselfish devotion to this boy's real welfare leads her to right and wise conclusions."

"I wish I could tame her so as to let me meet her as a friend. Since the baby was born, she comes to see Jemima. My wife tells me, that she sits and holds it soft in her arms, and talks to it as if her whole soul went out to the little infant. But if she hears a strange footstep on the stair, what Jemima calls the 'wild-animal look' comes back into her eyes, and she steals away like some frightened creature. With all that she has done to redeem her character, she should not be so timid of observation."

"You may well say 'with all that she has done!' We of her own household hear little or nothing of what she does. If she wants help, she simply tells us how and why; but if not—perhaps because it is some relief to her to forget for a time the scenes of suffering in which she has been acting the part of comforter, and perhaps because there always was a shy, sweet reticence about her—we never should know what she is and what she does, except from the poor people themselves, who would bless her in words if the very thought of her did not choke them with tears. Yet, I do assure you, she passes out of all this gloom, and makes sunlight in our house. We are never so cheerful as when she is at home. She always had the art of diffusing peace, but now it is positive cheerfulness. And about Leonard; I doubt if the wisest and most thoughtful schoolmaster could teach half as much directly, as his mother does unconsciously and indirectly every hour that he is with her. Her noble, humble, pious endurance of the consequences of what was wrong in her early life, seems expressly fitted to act upon him, whose position is (unjustly, for he has done no harm) so similar to hers."

"Well! I suppose we must leave it alone for the present. You will think me a hard practical man when I own to you, that all I expect from Leonard's remaining a home-bird is that, with such a mother, it will do him no harm. At any rate, remember my offer is the same for a year—two years hence, as now. What does she look forward to making him into, finally?"

"I don't know. The wonder comes into my mind sometimes; but never into hers, I think. It is part of her character—part perhaps of that which made her what she was—that she never looks forward, and seldom back. The present is enough for her."

And so the conversation ended. When Mr Benson repeated the substance of it to his sister, she mused awhile, breaking out into an occasional whistle (although she had cured herself of this habit in a great measure), and at last she said:

"Now, do you know, I never liked poor Dick; and yet I'm angry with Mr Farquhar for getting him out of the partnership in such a summary way. I can't get over it, even though he has offered to send Leonard to school. And here he's reigning lord-paramount at the office! As if you, Thurstan, weren't as well able to teach him as any schoolmaster in England! But I should not mind that affront, if I were not sorry to think of Dick (though I never could abide him) labouring away in Glasgow for a petty salary of nobody knows how little, while Mr Farquhar is taking halves, instead of thirds, of the profits here!"

But her brother could not tell her—and even Jemima did not know, till long afterwards—that the portion of income which would have been Dick's as a junior partner, if he had remained in the business, was carefully laid aside for him by Mr

Farquhar; to be delivered up, with all its accumulated interest, when the prodigal should have proved his penitence by his conduct.

When Ruth had no call upon her time, it was indeed a holiday at Chapel-house. She threw off as much as she could of the care and the sadness in which she had been sharing; and returned fresh and helpful, ready to go about in her soft, quiet way, and fill up every measure of service, and heap it with the fragrance of her own sweet nature. The delicate mending, that the elder women could no longer see to do, was put by for Ruth's swift and nimble fingers. The occasional copying, or patient writing to dictation, that gave rest to Mr Benson's weary spine, was done by her with sunny alacrity. But, most of all, Leonard's heart rejoiced when his mother came home. Then came the quiet confidences, the tender exchange of love, the happy walks from which he returned stronger and stronger—going from strength to strength as his mother led the way. It was well, as they saw now, that the great shock of the disclosure had taken place when it did. She, for her part, wondered at her own cowardliness in having even striven to keep back the truth from her child—the truth that was so certain to be made clear, sooner or later, and which it was only owing to God's mercy that she was alive to encounter with him, and, by so encountering, shield and give him good courage. Moreover, in her secret heart, she was thankful that all occurred while he was yet too young to have much curiosity as to his father. If an unsatisfied feeling of this kind occasionally stole into his mind, at any rate she never heard any expression of it; for the past was a sealed book between them. And so, in the bright strength of good endeavour, the days went on, and grew again to months and years.

Perhaps one little circumstance which occurred during this time had scarcely external importance enough to be called an event; but in Mr Benson's mind it took rank as such. One day, about a year after Richard Bradshaw had ceased to be a partner in his father's house, Mr Benson encountered Mr Farquhar in the street, and heard from him of the creditable and respectable manner in which Richard was conducting himself in Glasgow, where Mr Farquhar had lately been on business.

"I am determined to tell his father of this," said he; "I think his family are far too obedient to his tacit prohibition of all mention of Richard's name."

"Tacit prohibition?" inquired Mr Benson.

"Oh! I dare say I use the words in a wrong sense for the correctness of a scholar; but what I mean is, that he made a point of immediately leaving the room if Richard's name was mentioned; and did it in so marked a manner, that by degrees they understood that it was their father's desire that he should never be alluded to; which was all very well as long as there was nothing pleasant to be said about him; but to-night I am going there, and shall take good care he does not escape me before I have told him all I have heard and observed about Richard. He will never be a hero of virtue, for his education has drained him of all moral courage; but with care, and the absence of all strong temptation for a time, he will do very well; nothing to gratify paternal pride, but certainly nothing to be ashamed of."

It was on the Sunday after this that the little circumstance to which I have alluded took place.

During the afternoon service, Mr Benson became aware that the large Bradshaw pew was no longer unoccupied. In a dark corner Mr Bradshaw's white head was to be seen, bowed down low in prayer. When last he had worshipped there, the hair on that head was iron-grey, and even in prayer he had stood erect, with an air of conscious righteousness sufficient for all his wants, and even some to spare with which to judge others. Now, that white and hoary head was never uplifted; part of his unobtrusiveness might, it is true, be attributed to the uncomfortable feeling which was sure to attend any open withdrawal of the declaration he had once made, never to enter the chapel in which Mr Benson was minister again; and as such a feeling was natural to all men, and especially to such a one as Mr Bradshaw, Mr Benson instinctively respected it, and passed out of the chapel with his household, without ever directing his regards to the obscure place where Mr Bradshaw still remained immovable.

From this day Mr Benson felt sure that the old friendly feeling existed once more between them, although some time might elapse before any circumstance gave the signal for a renewal of their intercourse.

CHAPTER XXXIII - A MOTHER TO BE PROUD OF

Old people tell of certain years when typhus fever swept over the country like a pestilence; years that bring back the remembrance of deep sorrow—refusing to be comforted—to many a household; and which those whose beloved passed through the fiery time unscathed, shrink from recalling: for great and tremulous was the anxiety—miserable the constant watching for evil symptoms; and beyond the threshold of home a dense cloud of depression hung over society at large. It seemed as if the alarm was proportionate to the previous light-heartedness of fancied security—and indeed it was so; for, since the days of King Belshazzar, the solemn decrees of Doom have ever seemed most terrible when they awe into silence the merry revellers of life. So it was this year to which I come in the progress of my story.

The summer had been unusually gorgeous. Some had complained of the steaming heat, but others had pointed to the lush vegetation, which was profuse and luxuriant. The early autumn was wet and cold, but people did not regard it, in contemplation of some proud rejoicing of the nation, which filled every newspaper and gave food to every tongue. In Eccleston these rejoicings were greater than in most places; for, by the national triumph of arms, it was supposed that a new market for the staple manufacture of the place would be opened; and so the trade, which had for a year or two been languishing, would now revive with redoubled vigour. Besides these legitimate causes of good spirits, there was the rank excitement of a coming election, in consequence of Mr Donne having accepted a Government office, procured for him by one of his influential relations. This time, the Cranworths roused themselves from their magnificent torpor of security in good season, and were going through a series of pompous and ponderous hospitalities, in order to bring back the Eccleston voters to their allegiance.

While the town was full of these subjects by turns—now thinking and speaking of the great revival of trade—now of the chances of the election, as yet some weeks distant—now of the balls at Cranworth Court, in which Mr Cranworth had danced with all the belles of the shopocracy of Eccleston—there came creeping, creeping, in hidden, slimy courses, the terrible fever—that fever which is never utterly banished from the sad haunts of vice and misery, but lives in such darkness, like a wild beast in the recesses of his den. It had begun in the low Irish lodging-houses; but there it was so common it excited little attention. The poor creatures died almost without the attendance of the unwarned medical men, who received their first notice of the spreading plague from the Roman Catholic priests.

Before the medical men of Eccleston had had time to meet together and consult, and compare the knowledge of the fever which they had severally gained, it had, like the blaze of a fire which had long smouldered, burst forth in many places at once—not merely among the loose-living and vicious, but among the decently poor—nay, even among the well-to-do and respectable. And to add to the horror, like all similar pestilences, its course was most rapid at first, and was fatal in the great majority of cases—hopeless from the beginning. There was a cry, and then a deep silence, and then rose the long wail of the survivors.

A portion of the Infirmary of the town was added to that already set apart for a fever-ward; the smitten were carried thither at once, whenever it was possible, in order to prevent the spread of infection; and on that lazar-house was concentrated all the medical skill and force of the place.

But when one of the physicians had died, in consequence of his attendance—when the customary staff of matrons and nurses had been swept off in two days—and the nurses belonging to the Infirmary had shrunk from being drafted into the pestilential fever-ward—when high wages had failed to tempt any to what, in their panic, they considered as certain death—when the doctors stood aghast at the swift mortality among the untended sufferers, who were dependent only on the care of the most ignorant hirelings, too brutal to recognise the solemnity of Death (all this had happened within a week from the first acknowledgment of the presence of the plague)—Ruth came one day, with a quieter step than usual, into Mr Benson's study, and told him she wanted to speak to him for a few minutes.

"To be sure, my dear! Sit down," said he; for she was standing and leaning her head against the chimney-piece, idly gazing into the fire. She went on standing there, as if she had not heard his words; and it was a few moments before she began to speak. Then she said:

"I want to tell you, that I have been this morning and offered myself as matron to the fever-ward while it is so full. They have accepted me; and I am going this evening."

"Oh, Ruth! I feared this; I saw your look this morning as we spoke of this terrible illness."

"Why do you say 'fear,' Mr Benson? You yourself have been with John Harrison, and old Betty, and many others, I dare say, of whom we have not heard."

"But this is so different! in such poisoned air! among such malignant cases! Have you thought and weighed it enough, Ruth?"

She was quite still for a moment, but her eyes grew full of tears. At last she said, very softly, with a kind of still solemnity:

"Yes! I have thought, and I have weighed. But through the very midst of all my fears and thoughts I have felt that I must go."

The remembrance of Leonard was present in both their minds; but for a few moments longer they neither of them spoke. Then Ruth said:

"I believe I have no fear. That is a great preservative, they say. At any rate, if I have a little natural shrinking, it is quite gone when I remember that I am in God's hands! Oh, Mr Benson," continued she, breaking out into the irrepressible tears—"Leonard, Leonard!"

And now it was his turn to speak out the brave words of faith.

"Poor, poor mother!" said he. "Be of good heart. He, too, is in God's hands. Think what a flash of time only will separate you from him, if you should die in this work!"

"But he—but he—it will be long to him, Mr Benson! He will be alone!"

"No, Ruth, he will not. God and all good men will watch over him. But if you cannot still this agony of fear as to what will become of him, you ought not to go. Such tremulous passion will predispose you to take the fever."

"I will not be afraid," she replied, lifting up her face, over which a bright light shone, as of God's radiance. "I am not afraid for myself. I will not be so for my darling."

After a little pause, they began to arrange the manner of her going, and to speak of the length of time that she might be absent on her temporary duties. In talking of her return, they assumed it to be certain, although the exact time when was to them unknown, and would be dependent entirely on the duration of the fever; but not the less, in their secret hearts, did they feel where alone the issue lay. Ruth was to communicate with Leonard and Miss Faith through Mr Benson alone, who insisted on his determination to go every evening to the Hospital to learn the proceedings of the day, and the state of Ruth's health.

"It is not alone on your account, my dear! There may be many sick people of whom, if I can give no other comfort, I can take intelligence to their friends."

All was settled with grave composure; yet still Ruth lingered, as if nerving herself up for some effort. At length she said, with a faint smile upon her pale face:

"I believe I am a great coward. I stand here talking because I dread to tell Leonard."

"You must not think of it," exclaimed he. "Leave it to me. It is sure to unnerve you."

"I must think of it. I shall have self-control enough in a minute to do it calmly—to speak hopefully. For only think," continued she, smiling through the tears that would gather in her eyes, "what a comfort the remembrance of the last few words may be to the poor fellow, if—" The words were choked, but she smiled bravely on. "No!" said she, "that must be done; but perhaps you will spare me one thing—will you tell Aunt Faith? I suppose I am very weak, but, knowing that I must go, and not knowing what may be the end, I feel as if I could not bear to resist her entreaties just at last. Will you tell her, sir, while I go to Leonard?"

Silently he consented, and the two rose up and came forth, calm and serene. And calmly and gently did Ruth tell her boy of her purpose; not daring even to use any unaccustomed tenderness of voice or gesture, lest, by so doing, she should alarm him unnecessarily as to the result. She spoke hopefully, and bade him be of good courage; and he caught her bravery, though his, poor boy, had root rather in his ignorance of the actual imminent danger than in her deep faith.

When he had gone down, Ruth began to arrange her dress. When she came downstairs she went into the old familiar garden and gathered a nosegay of the last lingering autumn flowers—a few roses and the like.

Mr Benson had tutored his sister well; and although Miss Faith's face was swollen with crying, she spoke with almost exaggerated cheerfulness to Ruth. Indeed, as they all stood at the front door, making-believe to have careless nothings to say, just as at an ordinary leave-taking, you would not have guessed the strained chords of feeling there were in each heart. They lingered on, the last rays of the setting sun falling on the group. Ruth once or twice had roused herself to the pitch of saying "Good-bye," but when her eye fell on Leonard she was forced to hide the quivering of her lips, and conceal her trembling mouth amid the bunch of roses.

"They won't let you have your flowers, I'm afraid," said Miss Benson. "Doctors so often object to the smell."

"No; perhaps not," said Ruth, hurriedly. "I did not think of it. I will only keep this one rose. Here, Leonard, darling!" She gave the rest to him. It was her farewell; for having now no veil to hide her emotion, she summoned all her bravery for one parting smile, and, smiling, turned away. But she gave one look back from the street, just from the last point at which the door could be seen, and catching a glimpse of Leonard standing foremost on the step, she ran back, and he met her half-way, and mother and child spoke never a word in that close embrace.

"Now, Leonard," said Miss Faith, "be a brave boy. I feel sure she will come back to us before very long."

But she was very near crying herself; and she would have given way, I believe, if she had not found the wholesome outlet of scolding Sally, for expressing just the same opinion respecting Ruth's proceedings as she herself had done not two hours before. Taking what her brother had said to her as a text, she delivered such a lecture to Sally on want of faith that she was astonished at herself, and so much affected by what she had said that she had to shut the door of communication between the kitchen and the parlour pretty hastily, in order to prevent Sally's threatened reply from weakening her belief in the righteousness of what Ruth had done. Her words had gone beyond her conviction.

Evening after evening Mr Benson went forth to gain news of Ruth; and night after night he returned with good tidings. The fever, it is true, raged; but no plague came nigh her. He said her face was ever calm and bright, except when clouded by sorrow as she gave the accounts of the deaths which occurred in spite of every care. He said he had never seen her face so fair and gentle as it was now, when she was living in the midst of disease and woe.

One evening Leonard (for they had grown bolder as to the infection) accompanied him to the street on which the hospital abutted. Mr Benson left him there, and told him to return home; but the boy lingered, attracted by the crowd that had gathered, and were gazing up intently towards the lighted windows of the hospital. There was nothing beyond to be seen; but the greater part of these poor people had friends or relations in that palace of Death.

Leonard stood and listened. At first their talk consisted of vague and exaggerated accounts (if such could be exaggerated) of the horrors of the fever. Then they spoke of Ruth—of his mother; and Leonard held his breath to hear.

"They say she has been a great sinner, and that this is her penance," quoth one. And as Leonard gasped, before rushing forward to give the speaker straight the lie, an old man spoke:

"Such a one as her has never been a great sinner; nor does she do her work as a penance, but for the love of God, and of the blessed Jesus. She will be in the light of God's countenance when you and I will be standing afar off. I tell you, man, when my poor wench died, as no one would come near, her head lay at that hour on this woman's sweet breast. I could fell you," the old man went on, lifting his shaking arm, "for calling that woman a great sinner. The blessing of them who were ready to perish is upon her."

Immediately there arose a clamour of tongues, each with some tale of his mother's gentle doings, till Leonard grew dizzy with the beatings of his glad, proud heart. Few were aware how much Ruth had done; she never spoke of it, shrinking with sweet shyness from over-much allusion to her own work at all times. Her left hand truly knew not what her right hand did; and Leonard was overwhelmed now to hear of the love and the reverence with which the poor and outcast had surrounded her. It was irrepressible. He stepped forward with a proud bearing, and touching the old man's arm who had first spoken, Leonard tried to speak; but for an instant he could not, his heart was too full: tears came before words, but at length he managed to say:

"Sir, I am her son!"

"Thou! thou her bairn! God bless you, lad," said an old woman, pushing through the crowd. "It was but last night she kept my child quiet with singing psalms the night through. Low and sweet, low and sweet, they tell me—till many poor things were hushed, though they were out of their minds, and had not heard psalms this many a year. God in heaven bless you, lad!"

Many other wild, woe-begone creatures pressed forward with blessings on Ruth's son, while he could only repeat:

"She is my mother."

From that day forward Leonard walked erect in the streets of Eccleston, where "many arose and called her blessed."

After some weeks the virulence of the fever abated; and the general panic subsided—indeed, a kind of fool-hardiness succeeded. To be sure, in some instances the panic still held possession of individuals to an exaggerated extent. But the number of patients in the hospital was rapidly diminishing, and, for money, those were to be found who could supply Ruth's place. But to her it was owing that the overwrought fear of the town was subdued; it was she who had gone voluntarily, and, with no thought of greed or gain, right into the very jaws of the fierce disease. She bade the inmates of the hospital farewell, and after carefully submitting herself to the purification recommended by Mr Davis, the principal surgeon of the place, who had always attended Leonard, she returned to Mr Benson's just at gloaming time.

They each vied with the other in the tenderest cares. They hastened tea; they wheeled the sofa to the fire; they made her lie down; and to all she submitted with the docility of a child; and when the candles came, even Mr Benson's anxious eye could see no change in her looks, but that she seemed a little paler. The eyes were as full of spiritual light, the gently parted lips as rosy, and the smile, if more rare, yet as sweet as ever.

CHAPTER XXXIV - "I MUST GO AND NURSE MR BELLINGHAM"

The next morning, Miss Benson would insist upon making Ruth lie down on the sofa. Ruth longed to do many things; to be much more active; but she submitted, when she found that it would gratify Miss Faith if she remained as quiet as if she were really an invalid.

Leonard sat by her holding her hand. Every now and then he looked up from his book, as if to make sure that she indeed was restored to him. He had brought her down the flowers which she had given him the day of her departure, and which he had kept in water as long as they had any greenness or fragrance, and then had carefully dried and put by. She too, smiling, had produced the one rose which she had carried away to the hospital. Never had the bond between her and her boy been drawn so firm and strong.

Many visitors came this day to the quiet Chapel-house. First of all Mrs Farquhar appeared. She looked very different from the Jemima Bradshaw of three years ago. Happiness had called out beauty; the colouring of her face was lovely, and vivid as that of an autumn day; her berry-red lips scarce closed over the short white teeth for her smiles; and her large dark eyes glowed and sparkled with daily happiness. They were softened by a mist of tears as she looked upon Ruth.

"Lie still! Don't move! You must be content to-day to be waited upon, and nursed! I have just seen Miss Benson in the lobby, and had charge upon charge not to fatigue you. Oh, Ruth! how we all love you, now we have you back again! Do you know, I taught Rosa to say her prayers as soon as ever you were gone to that horrid place, just on purpose that her little innocent lips might pray for you—I wish you could hear her say it—'Please, dear God, keep Ruth safe.' Oh, Leonard! are not you proud of your mother?"

Leonard said "Yes," rather shortly, as if he were annoyed that any one else should know, or even have a right to imagine, how proud he was. Jemima went on:

"Now, Ruth! I have got a plan for you. Walter and I have partly made it; and partly it's papa's doing. Yes, dear! papa has been quite anxious to show his respect for you. We all want you to go to the dear Eagle's Crag for this next month, and get strong, and have some change in that fine air at Abermouth. I am going to take little Rosa there. Papa has lent it to us. And the weather is often very beautiful in November."

"Thank you very much. It is very tempting; for I have been almost longing for some such change. I cannot tell all at once whether I can go; but I will see about it, if you will let me leave it open a little."

"Oh! as long as you like, so that you will but go at last. And, Master Leonard! you are to come too. Now, I know I have you on my side."

Ruth thought of the place. Her only reluctance arose from the remembrance of that one interview on the sands. That walk she could never go again; but how much remained! How much that would be a charming balm and refreshment to her!

"What happy evenings we shall have together! Do you know, I think Mary and Elizabeth may perhaps come."

A bright gleam of sunshine came into the room. "Look! how bright and propitious for our plans. Dear Ruth, it seems like an omen for the future!"

Almost while she spoke, Miss Benson entered, bringing with her Mr Grey, the rector of Eccleston. He was an elderly man, short and stoutly-built, with something very formal in his manner; but any one might feel sure of his steady benevolence who noticed the expression of his face, and especially of the kindly black eyes that gleamed beneath his grey and shaggy eyebrows. Ruth had seen him at the hospital once or twice, and Mrs Farquhar had met him pretty frequently in general society.

"Go and tell your uncle," said Miss Benson to Leonard.

"Stop, my boy! I have just met Mr Benson in the street, and my errand now is to your mother. I should like you to remain and hear what it is; and I am sure that my business will give these ladies"—bowing to Miss Benson and Jemima—"so much pleasure, that I need not apologise for entering upon it in their presence."

He pulled out his double eye-glass, saying, with a grave smile:

"You ran away from us yesterday so quietly and cunningly, Mrs Denbigh, that you were, perhaps, not aware that the Board was sitting at that very time, and trying to form a vote sufficiently expressive of our gratitude to you. As Chairman, they requested me to present you with this letter, which I shall have the pleasure of reading."

With all due emphasis he read aloud a formal letter from the Secretary to the Infirmary, conveying a vote of thanks to Ruth.

The good rector did not spare her one word, from date to signature; and then, folding the letter up, he gave it to Leonard, saying:

"There, sir! when you are an old man, you may read that testimony to your mother's noble conduct with pride and pleasure. For, indeed," continued he, turning to Jemima, "no words can express the relief it was to us. I speak of the gentlemen composing the Board of the Infirmary. When Mrs Denbigh came forward, the panic was at its height, and the alarm of course aggravated the disorder. The poor creatures died rapidly; there was hardly time to remove the dead bodies before others were brought in to occupy the beds, so little help was to be procured on account of the universal terror; and the morning when Mrs Denbigh offered us her services, we seemed at the very worst. I shall never forget the sensation of relief in my mind when she told us what she proposed to do; but we thought it right to warn her to the full extent—

"Nay, madam," said he, catching a glimpse of Ruth's changing colour, "I will spare you any more praises. I will only say, if I can be a friend to you, or a friend to your child, you may command my poor powers to the utmost."

He got up, and bowing formally, he took his leave. Jemima came and kissed Ruth. Leonard went upstairs to put the precious letter away. Miss Benson sat crying heartily in a corner of the room. Ruth went to her and threw her arms round her neck, and said:

"I could not tell him just then. I durst not speak for fear of breaking down; but if I have done right, it was all owing to you and Mr Benson. Oh! I wish I had said how the thought first came into my head from seeing the things Mr Benson has done so quietly ever since the fever first came amongst us. I could not speak; and it seemed as if I was taking those praises to myself, when all the time I was feeling how little I deserved them—how it was all owing to you."

"Under God, Ruth," said Miss Benson, speaking through her tears.

"Oh! I think there is nothing humbles one so much as undue praise. While he was reading that letter, I could not help feeling how many things I have done wrong! Could he know of—of what I have been?" asked she, dropping her voice very low.

"Yes!" said Jemima, "he knew—everybody in Eccleston did know—but the remembrance of those days is swept away. Miss Benson," she continued, for she was anxious to turn the subject, "you must be on my side, and persuade Ruth to come to Abermouth for a few weeks. I want her and Leonard both to come."

"I'm afraid my brother will think that Leonard is missing his lessons sadly. Just of late we could not wonder that the poor child's heart was so full; but he must make haste, and get on all the more for his idleness." Miss Benson piqued herself on being a disciplinarian.

"Oh, as for lessons, Walter is so very anxious that you should give way to his superior wisdom, Ruth, and let Leonard go to school. He will send him to any school you fix upon, according to the mode of life you plan for him."

"I have no plan," said Ruth. "I have no means of planning. All I can do is to try and make him ready for anything."

"Well," said Jemima, "we must talk it over at Abermouth; for I am sure you won't refuse to come, dearest, dear Ruth! Think of the quiet, sunny days, and the still evenings, that we shall have together, with little Rosa to tumble about among the fallen leaves; and there's Leonard to have his first sight of the sea."

"I do think of it," said Ruth, smiling at the happy picture Jemima drew. And both smiling at the hopeful prospect before them, they parted—never to meet again in life.

No sooner had Mrs Farquhar gone than Sally burst in.

"Oh! dear, dear!" said she, looking around her. "If I had but known that the rector was coming to call, I'd ha' put on the best covers, and the Sunday table-cloth! You're well enough," continued she, surveying Ruth from head to foot; "you're always trim and dainty in your gowns, though I reckon they cost but tuppence a yard, and you've a face to set 'em off; but as for you" (as she turned to Miss Benson), "I think you might ha' had something better on than that old stuff, if it had only been to do credit to a parishioner like me, whom he has known ever sin' my father was his clerk."

"You forget, Sally, I have been making jelly all the morning. How could I tell it was Mr Grey when there was a knock at the door?" Miss Benson replied.

"You might ha' letten me do the jelly; I'se warrant I could ha' pleased Ruth as well as you. If I had but known he was coming, I'd ha' slipped round the corner and bought ye a neck-ribbon, or summut to lighten ye up. I'se loath he should think I'm living with Dissenters, that don't know how to keep themselves trig and smart."

"Never mind, Sally; he never thought of me. What he came for, was to see Ruth; and, as you say, she's always neat and dainty."

"Well! I reckon it cannot be helped now; but if I buy ye a ribbon, will you promise to wear it when church-folks come? for I cannot abide the way they have of scoffing at the Dissenters about their dress."

"Very well! we'll make that bargain," said Miss Benson; "and now, Ruth, I'll go and fetch you a cup of warm jelly."

"Oh! indeed, Aunt Faith," said Ruth, "I am very sorry to balk you; but if you're going to treat me as an invalid, I am afraid I shall rebel."

But when she found that Aunt Faith's heart was set upon it, she submitted very graciously, only dimpling up a little, as she found that she must consent to lie on the sofa, and be fed, when, in truth, she felt full of health, with a luxurious sensation of languor stealing over her now and then, just enough to make it very pleasant to think of the salt breezes, and the sea beauty which awaited her at Abermouth.

Mr Davis called in the afternoon, and his visit was also to Ruth. Mr and Miss Benson were sitting with her in the parlour, and watching her with contented love, as she employed herself in household sewing, and hopefully spoke about the Abermouth plan.

"Well! so you had our worthy rector here to-day; I am come on something of the same kind of errand; only I shall spare you the reading of my letter, which, I'll answer for it, he did not. Please to take notice," said he, putting down a sealed letter, "that I have delivered you a vote of thanks from my medical brothers; and open and read it at your leisure; only not just now, for I want to have a little talk with you on my own behoof. I want to ask you a favour, Mrs Denbigh."

"A favour!" exclaimed Ruth; "what can I do for you? I think I may say I will do it, without hearing what it is."

"Then you're a very imprudent woman," replied he; "however, I'll take you at your word. I want you to give me your boy."

"Leonard!"

"Aye! there it is, you see, Mr Benson. One minute she is as ready as can be, and the next, she looks at me as if I was an ogre!"

"Perhaps we don't understand what you mean," said Mr Benson.

"The thing is this. You know I've no children; and I can't say I've ever fretted over it much; but my wife has; and whether it is that she has infected me, or that I grieve over my good practice going to a stranger, when I ought to have had a son to take it after me, I don't know; but, of late, I've got to look with covetous eyes on all healthy boys, and at last I've settled down my wishes on this Leonard of yours, Mrs Denbigh."

Ruth could not speak; for, even yet, she did not understand what he meant. He went on:

"Now, how old is the lad?" He asked Ruth, but Miss Benson replied:

"He'll be twelve next February."

"Umph! only twelve! He's tall and old-looking for his age. You look young enough, it is true." He said this last sentence as if to himself, but seeing Ruth crimson up, he abruptly changed his tone.

"Twelve, is he! Well, I take him from now. I don't mean that I really take him away from you," said he, softening all at once, and becoming grave and considerate. "His being your son—the son of one whom I have seen—as I have seen you, Mrs Denbigh (out and out the best nurse I ever met with, Miss Benson; and good nurses are things we doctors know how to value)—his being your son is his great recommendation to me; not but what the lad himself is a noble boy. I shall be glad to leave him with you as long and as much as we can; he could not be tied to your apron-strings all his life, you know. Only I provide for his education, subject to your consent and good pleasure, and he is bound apprentice to me. I, his guardian, bind him to myself, the first surgeon in Eccleston, be the other who he may; and in process of time he becomes partner, and some day or other succeeds me. Now, Mrs Denbigh, what have you got to say against this plan? My wife is just as full of it as me. Come! begin with your objections. You're not a woman if you have not a whole bag-full of them ready to turn out against any reasonable proposal."

"I don't know," faltered Ruth. "It is so sudden—"

"It is very, very kind of you, Mr Davis," said Miss Benson, a little scandalised at Ruth's non-expression of gratitude.

"Pooh! pooh! I'll answer for it, in the long run, I am taking good care of my own interests. Come, Mrs Denbigh, is it a bargain?"

Now Mr Benson spoke.

"Mr Davis, it is rather sudden, as she says. As far as I can see, it is the best as well as the kindest proposal that could have been made; but I think we must give her a little time to think about it."

"Well, twenty-four hours! Will that do?"

Ruth lifted up her head. "Mr Davis, I am not ungrateful because I can't thank you" (she was crying while she spoke); "let me have a fortnight to consider about it. In a fortnight I will make up my mind. Oh, how good you all are!"

"Very well. Then this day fortnight—Thursday the 28th—you will let me know your decision. Mind! if it's against me, I shan't consider it a decision, for I'm determined to carry my point. I'm not going to make Mrs Denbigh blush, Mr Benson, by telling you, in her presence, of all I have observed about her this last three weeks, that has made me sure of the good qualities I shall find in this boy of hers. I was watching her when she little thought it. Do you remember that night when Hector O'Brien was so furiously delirious, Mrs Denbigh?"

Ruth went very white at the remembrance.

"Why now, look there! how pale she is at the very thought of it. And yet, I assure you, she was the one to go up and take the piece of glass from him which he had broken out of the window for the sole purpose of cutting his throat, or the throat of any one else, for that matter. I wish we had some others as brave as she is."

"I thought the great panic was passed away!" said Mr Benson.

"Aye! the general feeling of alarm is much weaker; but, here and there, there are as great fools as ever. Why, when I leave here, I am going to see our precious member, Mr Donne—"

"Mr Donne?" said Ruth.

"Mr Donne, who lies ill at the Queen's—came last week, with the intention of canvassing, but was too much alarmed by what he heard of the fever to set to work; and, in spite of all his precautions, he has taken it; and you should see the terror they are in at the hotel; landlord, landlady, waiters, servants—all; there's not a creature will go near him, if they can help it; and there's only his groom—a lad he saved from drowning, I'm told—to do anything for him. I must get him a proper nurse, somehow or somewhere, for all my being a Cranworth man. Ah, Mr Benson! you don't know the temptations we medical men have. Think, if I allowed your member to die now, as he might very well, if he had no nurse—how famously Mr Cranworth would walk over the course!—Where's Mrs Denbigh gone to? I hope I've not frightened her away by reminding her of Hector O'Brien, and that awful night, when I do assure you she behaved like a heroine!"

As Mr Benson was showing Mr Davis out, Ruth opened the study-door, and said, in a very calm, low voice:

"Mr Benson! will you allow me to speak to Mr Davis alone?"

Mr Benson immediately consented, thinking that, in all probability, she wished to ask some further questions about Leonard; but as Mr Davis came into the room, and shut the door, he was struck by her pale, stern face of determination, and awaited her speaking first.

"Mr Davis! I must go and nurse Mr Bellingham," said she at last, clenching her hands tight together, but no other part of her body moving from its intense stillness.

"Mr Bellingham?" asked he, astonished at the name.

"Mr Donne, I mean," said she, hurriedly. "His name was Bellingham."

"Oh! I remember hearing he had changed his name for some property. But you must not think of any more such work just now. You are not fit for it. You are looking as white as ashes."

"I must go," she repeated.

"Nonsense! Here's a man who can pay for the care of the first hospital nurses in London—and I doubt if his life is worth the risk of one of theirs even, much more of yours."

"We have no right to weigh human lives against each other."

"No! I know we have not. But it's a way we doctors are apt to get into; and, at any rate, it's ridiculous of you to think of such a thing. Just listen to reason."

"I can't! I can't!" cried she, with sharp pain in her voice. "You must let me go, dear Mr Davis!" said she, now speaking with soft entreaty.

"No!" said he, shaking his head authoritatively. "I'll do no such thing."

"Listen," said she, dropping her voice, and going all over the deepest scarlet; "he is Leonard's father! Now! you will let me go!"

Mr Davis was indeed staggered by what she said, and for a moment he did not speak. So she went on:

"You will not tell! You must not tell! No one knows, not even Mr Benson, who it was. And now—it might do him so much harm to have it known. You will not tell!"

"No! I will not tell," replied he. "But, Mrs Denbigh, you must answer me this one question, which I ask you in all true respect, but which I must ask, in order to guide both myself and you aright—of course I knew Leonard was illegitimate—in fact, I will give you secret for secret: it was being so myself that first made me sympathise with him, and desire to adopt him. I knew that much of your history; but tell me, do you now care for this man? Answer me truly—do you love him?"

For a moment or two she did not speak; her head was bent down; then she raised it up, and looked with clear and honest eyes into his face.

"I have been thinking—but I do not know—I cannot tell—I don't think I should love him, if he were well and happy—but you said he was ill—and alone—how can I help caring for him?—how can I help caring for him?" repeated she, covering her face with her hands, and the quick hot tears stealing through her fingers. "He is Leonard's father," continued she, looking up at Mr Davis suddenly. "He need not know—he shall not—that I have ever been near him. If he is like the others, he must be delirious—I will leave him before he comes to himself—but now let me go—I must go."

"I wish my tongue had been bitten out before I had named him to you. He would do well enough without you; and, I dare say, if he recognises you, he will only be annoyed."

"It is very likely," said Ruth, heavily.

"Annoyed,—why! he may curse you for your unasked-for care of him. I have heard my poor mother—and she was as pretty and delicate a creature as you are—cursed for showing tenderness when it was not wanted. Now, be persuaded by an old man like me, who has seen enough of life to make his heart ache—leave this fine gentleman to his fate. I'll promise you to get him as good a nurse as can be had for money."

"No!" said Ruth, with dull persistency—as if she had not attended to his dissuasions; "I must go. I will leave him before he recognises me."

"Why, then," said the old surgeon, "if you're so bent upon it, I suppose I must let you. It is but what my mother would have done—poor, heart-broken thing! However, come along, and let us make the best of it. It saves me a deal of trouble, I know; for, if I have you for a right hand, I need not worry myself continually with wondering how he is taken care of. Go! get your bonnet, you tender-hearted fool of a woman! Let us get you out of the house without any more scenes or explanations; I'll make all straight with the Bensons."

"You will not tell my secret, Mr Davis," she said, abruptly.

"No! not I! Does the woman think I had never to keep a secret of the kind before? I only hope he'll lose his election, and never come near the place again. After all," continued he, sighing, "I suppose it is but human nature!" He began recalling the circumstances of his own early life, and dreamily picturing scenes in the grey dying embers of the fire; and he was almost startled when she stood before him, ready equipped, grave, pale, and quiet.

"Come along!" said he. "If you're to do any good at all, it must be in these next three days. After that, I'll ensure his life for this bout; and mind! I shall send you home then; for he might know you, and I'll have no excitement to throw him back again, and no sobbing and crying from you. But now every moment your care is precious to him. I shall tell my own story to the Bensons, as soon as I have installed you."

Mr Donne lay in the best room of the Queen's Hotel—no one with him but his faithful, ignorant servant, who was as much afraid of the fever as any one else could be, but who, nevertheless, would not leave his master—his master who had saved his life as a child, and afterwards put him in the stables at Bellingham Hall, where he learnt all that he knew. He stood in a farther corner of the room, watching his delirious master with affrighted eyes, not daring to come near him, nor yet willing to leave him.

"Oh! if that doctor would but come! He'll kill himself or me—and them stupid servants won't stir a step over the threshold; how shall I get over the night? Blessings on him—here's the old doctor back again! I hear him creaking and scolding up the stairs!"

The door opened, and Mr Davis entered, followed by Ruth.

"Here's the nurse, my good man—such a nurse as there is not in the three counties. Now, all you'll have to do is to mind what she says."

"Oh, sir! he's mortal bad! won't you stay with us through the night, sir?"

"Look there!" whispered Mr Davis to the man, "see how she knows how to manage him! Why, I could not do it better myself!"

She had gone up to the wild, raging figure, and with soft authority had made him lie down: and then, placing a basin of cold water by the bedside, she had dipped in it her pretty hands, and was laying their cool dampness on his hot brow, speaking in a low soothing voice all the time, in a way that acted like a charm in hushing his mad talk.

"But I will stay," said the doctor, after he had examined his patient; "as much on her account as his! and partly to quieten the fears of this poor, faithful fellow."

CHAPTER XXXV - OUT OF DARKNESS INTO LIGHT

The third night after this was to be the crisis—the turning-point between Life and Death. Mr Davis came again to pass it by the bedside of the sufferer. Ruth was there, constant and still, intent upon watching the symptoms, and acting according to them, in obedience to Mr Davis's directions. She had never left the room. Every sense had been strained in watching—every power of thought or judgment had been kept on the full stretch. Now that Mr Davis came and took her place, and that the room was quiet for the night, she became oppressed with heaviness, which yet did not tend to sleep. She could not remember the present time, or where she was. All times of her earliest youth—the days of her childhood—were in her memory with a minuteness and fulness of detail which was miserable; for all along she felt that she had no real grasp on the scenes that were passing through her mind—that, somehow, they were long gone by, and gone by for ever—and yet she could not remember who she was now, nor where she was, and whether she had now any interests in life to take the place of those which she was conscious had passed away, although their remembrance filled her mind with painful acuteness. Her head lay on her arms, and they rested on the table. Every now and then she opened her eyes, and saw the large room, handsomely furnished with articles that were each one incongruous with the other, as if bought at sales. She saw the flickering night-light—she heard the ticking of the watch, and the two breathings, each going on at a separate rate—one hurried, abruptly stopping, and then panting violently, as if to make up for lost time; and the other slow, steady, and regular, as if the breather was asleep; but this supposition was contradicted by an occasional repressed sound of yawning. The sky through the uncurtained window looked dark and black—would this night never have an end? Had the sun gone down for ever, and would the world at last awaken to a general sense of everlasting night?

Then she felt as if she ought to get up, and go and see how the troubled sleeper in yonder bed was struggling through his illness; but she could not remember who the sleeper was, and she shrunk from seeing some phantom-face on the pillow, such as now began to haunt the dark corners of the room, and look at her, jibbering and mowing as they looked. So she covered her face again, and sank into a whirling stupor of sense and feeling. By-and-by she heard her fellow-watcher stirring, and a dull wonder stole over her as to what he was doing; but the heavy languor pressed her down, and kept her still. At last she heard the words, "Come here," and listlessly obeyed the command. She had to steady herself in the rocking chamber before she could walk to the bed by which Mr Davis stood; but the effort to do so roused her, and, although conscious of an oppressive headache, she viewed with sudden and clear vision all the circumstances of her present position. Mr Davis was near the head of the bed, holding the night-lamp high, and shading it with his hand, that it might not disturb the sick person, who lay with his face towards them, in feeble exhaustion, but with every sign that the violence of the fever had left him. It so happened that the rays of the lamp fell bright and full upon Ruth's countenance, as she stood with her crimson lips parted with the hurrying breath, and the fever-flush brilliant on her cheeks. Her eyes were wide open, and their pupils distended. She looked on the invalid in silence, and hardly understood why Mr Davis had summoned her there.

"Don't you see the change? He is better!—the crisis is past!"

But she did not speak; her looks were riveted on his softly-unclosing eyes, which met hers as they opened languidly. She could not stir or speak. She was held fast by that gaze of his, in which a faint recognition dawned, and grew to strength.

He murmured some words. They strained their sense to hear. He repeated them even lower than before; but this time they caught what he was saying.

"Where are the water-lilies? Where are the lilies in her hair?"

Mr Davis drew Ruth away.

"He is still rambling," said he, "but the fever has left him."

The grey dawn was now filling the room with its cold light; was it that made Ruth's cheek so deadly pale? Could that call out the wild entreaty of her look, as if imploring help against some cruel foe that held her fast, and was wrestling with her Spirit of Life? She held Mr Davis's arm. If she had let it go, she would have fallen.

"Take me home," she said, and fainted dead away.

Mr Davis carried her out of the chamber, and sent the groom to keep watch by his master. He ordered a fly to convey her to Mr Benson's, and lifted her in when it came, for she was still half unconscious. It was he who carried her upstairs to her room, where Miss Benson and Sally undressed and laid her in her bed.

He awaited their proceedings in Mr Benson's study. When Mr Benson came in, Mr Davis said:

"Don't blame me. Don't add to my self-reproach. I have killed her. I was a cruel fool to let her go. Don't speak to me."

"It may not be so bad," said Mr Benson, himself needing comfort in that shock. "She may recover. She surely will recover. I believe she will."

"No, no! she won't. But by —— she shall, if I can save her." Mr Davis looked defiantly at Mr Benson, as if he were Fate. "I tell you she shall recover, or else I am a murderer. What business had I to take her to nurse him—"

He was cut short by Sally's entrance and announcement that Ruth was now prepared to see him.

From that time forward Mr Davis devoted all his leisure, his skill, his energy, to save her. He called on the rival surgeon to beg him to undertake the management of Mr Donne's recovery, saying, with his usual self-mockery, "I could not answer it to Mr Cranworth if I had brought his opponent round, you know, when I had had such a fine opportunity in my power. Now, with your patients, and general Radical interest, it will be rather a feather in your cap; for he may want a good deal of care yet, though he is getting on famously—so rapidly, in fact, that it's a strong temptation to me to throw him back—a relapse, you know."

The other surgeon bowed gravely, apparently taking Mr Davis in earnest, but certainly very glad of the job thus opportunely thrown in his way. In spite of Mr Davis's real and deep anxiety about Ruth, he could not help chuckling over his rival's literal interpretation of all he had said.

"To be sure, what fools men are! I don't know why one should watch and strive to keep them in the world. I have given this fellow something to talk about confidentially to all his patients; I wonder how much stronger a dose the man would have swallowed! I must begin to take care of my practice for that lad yonder. Well-a-day! well-a-day! What was this sick fine gentleman sent here for, that she should run a chance of her life for him? or why was he sent into the world at all, for that matter?"

Indeed, however much Mr Davis might labour with all his professional skill—however much they might all watch—and pray—and weep—it was but too evident that Ruth "home must go, and take her wages." Poor, poor Ruth!

It might be that, utterly exhausted by watching and nursing, first in the hospital, and then by the bedside of her former lover, the power of her constitution was worn out; or, it might be, her gentle, pliant sweetness, but she displayed no outrage or discord even in her delirium. There she lay in the attic-room in which her baby had been born, her watch over him kept, her confession to him made; and now she was stretched on the bed in utter helplessness, softly gazing at vacancy with her open, unconscious eyes, from which all the depth of their meaning had fled, and all they told was of a sweet, child-like insanity within. The watchers could not touch her with their sympathy, or come near her in her dim world;—so, mutely, but looking at each other from time to time with tearful eyes, they took a poor comfort from the one evident fact that, though lost and gone astray, she was happy and at peace. They had never heard her sing; indeed, the simple art which her mother had taught her, had died, with her early joyousness, at that dear mother's death. But now she sang continually, very soft and low. She went from one childish ditty to another without let or pause, keeping a strange sort of time with her pretty fingers, as they closed and unclosed themselves upon the counterpane. She never looked at any one with the slightest glimpse of memory or intelligence in her face; no, not even at Leonard.

Her strength faded day by day; but she knew it not. Her sweet lips were parted to sing, even after the breath and the power to do so had left her, and her fingers fell idly on the bed. Two days she lingered thus—all but gone from them, and yet still there.

They stood around her bedside, not speaking, or sighing, or moaning; they were too much awed by the exquisite peacefulness of her look for that. Suddenly she opened wide her eyes, and gazed intently forwards, as if she saw some happy vision, which called out a lovely, rapturous, breathless smile. They held their very breaths.

"I see the Light coming," said she. "The Light is coming," she said. And, raising herself slowly, she stretched out her arms, and then fell back, very still for evermore.

They did not speak. Mr Davis was the first to utter a word.

"It is over!" said he. "She is dead!"

Out rang through the room the cry of Leonard:

"Mother! mother! mother! You have not left me alone! You will not leave me alone! You are not dead! Mother! Mother!"

They had pent in his agony of apprehension till then, that no wail of her child might disturb her ineffable calm. But now there was a cry heard through the house, of one refusing to be comforted: "Mother! Mother!"

But Ruth lay dead.

CHAPTER XXXVI - THE END

A stupor of grief succeeded to Leonard's passionate cries. He became so much depressed, physically as well as mentally, before the end of the day, that Mr Davis was seriously alarmed for the consequences. He hailed with gladness a proposal made by the Farquhars, that the boy should be removed to their house, and placed under the fond care of his mother's friend, who sent her own child to Abermouth the better to devote herself to Leonard.

When they told him of this arrangement, he at first refused to go and leave *her*; but when Mr Benson said:

"*She* would have wished it, Leonard! Do it for her sake!" he went away very quietly; not speaking a word, after Mr Benson had made the voluntary promise that he should see her once again. He neither spoke nor cried for many hours; and all Jemima's delicate wiles were called forth, before his heavy heart could find the relief of tears. And then he was so weak, and his pulse so low, that all who loved him feared for his life.

Anxiety about him made a sad distraction from the sorrow for the dead. The three old people, who now formed the household in the Chapel-house, went about slowly and dreamily, each with a dull wonder at their hearts why they, the infirm and worn-out, were left, while she was taken in her lovely prime.

The third day after Ruth's death, a gentleman came to the door and asked to speak to Mr Benson. He was very much wrapped up in furs and cloaks, and the upper, exposed part of his face was sunk and hollow, like that of one but partially recovered from illness. Mr and Miss Benson were at Mr Farquhar's, gone to see Leonard, and poor old Sally had been having a hearty cry over the kitchen fire before answering the door-knock. Her heart was tenderly inclined just then towards any one who had the aspect of suffering; so, although her master was out, and she was usually chary of admitting strangers, she proposed to Mr Donne (for it was he) that he should come in and await Mr Benson's return in the study. He was glad enough to avail himself of her offer; for he was feeble and nervous, and come on a piece of business which he exceedingly disliked, and about which he felt very awkward. The fire was nearly, if not quite, out; nor did Sally's vigorous blows do much good, although she left the room with an assurance that it would soon burn up. He leant against the chimney-piece, thinking over events, and with a sensation of discomfort, both external and internal, growing and gathering upon him. He almost wondered whether the proposal he meant to make with regard to Leonard could not be better arranged by letter than by an interview. He became very shivery, and impatient of the state of indecision to which his bodily weakness had reduced him.

Sally opened the door and came in. "Would you like to walk upstairs, sir?" asked she, in a trembling voice, for she had learnt who the visitor was from the driver of the fly, who had run up to the house to inquire what was detaining the gentleman that he had brought from the Queen's Hotel; and, knowing that Ruth had caught the fatal fever from her attendance on Mr Donne, Sally imagined that it was but a piece of sad civility to invite him upstairs to see the poor dead body, which she had laid out and decked for the grave, with such fond care that she had grown strangely proud of its marble beauty.

Mr Donne was glad enough of any proposal of a change from the cold and comfortless room where he had thought uneasy, remorseful thoughts. He fancied that a change of place would banish the train of reflection that was troubling him; but the change he anticipated was to a well-warmed, cheerful sitting-room, with signs of life, and a bright fire therein; and he was on the last flight of stairs,—at the door of the room where Ruth lay—before he understood whither Sally was conducting him. He shrank back for an instant, and then a strange sting of curiosity impelled him on. He stood in the humble low-roofed attic, the window open, and the tops of the distant snow-covered hills filling up the whiteness of the general aspect. He muffled himself up in his cloak, and shuddered, while Sally reverently drew down the sheet, and showed the beautiful, calm, still face, on which the last rapturous smile still lingered, giving an ineffable look of bright serenity. Her arms were crossed over her breast; the wimple-like cap marked the perfect oval of her face, while two braids of the waving auburn hair peeped out of the narrow border, and lay on the delicate cheeks.

He was awed into admiration by the wonderful beauty of that dead woman.

"How beautiful she is!" said he, beneath his breath. "Do all dead people look so peaceful—so happy?"

"Not all," replied Sally, crying. "Few has been as good and as gentle as she was in their lives." She quite shook with her sobbing.

Mr Donne was disturbed by her distress.

"Come, my good woman! we must all die—" he did not know what to say, and was becoming infected by her sorrow. "I am sure you loved her very much, and were very kind to her in her lifetime; you must take this from me to buy yourself some remembrance of her." He had pulled out a sovereign, and really had a kindly desire to console her, and reward her, in offering it to her.

But she took her apron from her eyes, as soon as she became aware of what he was doing, and, still holding it midway in her hands, she looked at him indignantly, before she burst out:

"And who are you, that think to pay for my kindness to her by money? And I was not kind to you, my darling," said she, passionately addressing the motionless, serene body—"I was not kind to you. I frabbed you, and plagued you from the first, my lamb! I came and cut off your pretty locks in this very room—I did—and you said never an angry word to me;—no! not then, nor many a time after, when I was very sharp and cross to you.—No! I never was kind to you, and I dunnot think the world was kind to you, my darling,—but you are gone where the angels are very tender to such as you—you are, my poor wench!" She bent down and kissed the lips, from whose marble, unyielding touch Mr Donne recoiled, even in thought.

Just then, Mr Benson entered the room. He had returned home before his sister, and come upstairs in search of Sally, to whom he wanted to speak on some subject relating to the funeral. He bowed in recognition of Mr Donne, whom he knew as the member for the town, and whose presence impressed him painfully, as his illness had been the proximate cause of Ruth's death. But he tried to check this feeling, as it was no fault of Mr Donne's. Sally stole out of the room, to cry at leisure in her kitchen.

"I must apologise for being here," said Mr Donne. "I was hardly conscious where your servant was leading me to, when she expressed her wish that I should walk upstairs."

"It is a very common idea in this town, that it is a gratification to be asked to take a last look at the dead," replied Mr Benson.

"And in this case I am glad to have seen her once more," said Mr Donne. "Poor Ruth!"

Mr Benson glanced up at him at the last word. How did he know her name? To him she had only been Mrs Denbigh. But Mr Donne had no idea that he was talking to one unaware of the connexion that had formerly existed between them; and, though he would have preferred carrying on the conversation in a warmer room, yet, as Mr Benson was still gazing at her with sad, lingering love, he went on:

"I did not recognise her when she came to nurse me; I believe I was delirious. My servant, who had known her long ago, in Fordham, told me who she was. I cannot tell how I regret that she should have died in consequence of her love of me."

Mr Benson looked up at him again, a stern light filling his eyes as he did so. He waited impatiently to hear more, either to quench or confirm his suspicions. If she had not been lying there, very still and calm, he would have forced the words out of Mr Donne, by some abrupt question. As it was, he listened silently, his heart quick-beating.

"I know that money is but a poor compensation,—is no remedy for this event, or for my youthful folly."

Mr Benson set his teeth hard together, to keep in words little short of a curse.

"Indeed, I offered her money to almost any amount before;—do me justice, sir," catching the gleam of indignation on Mr Benson's face; "I offered to marry her, and provide for the boy as if he had been legitimate. It's of no use recurring to that time," said he, his voice faltering; "what is done cannot be undone. But I came now to say, that I should be glad to leave the boy still under your charge, and that every expense you think it right to incur in his education I will defray;—

and place a sum of money in trust for him—say, two thousand pounds—or more: fix what you will. Of course, if you decline retaining him, I must find some one else; but the provision for him shall be the same, for my poor Ruth's sake."

Mr Benson did not speak. He could not, till he had gathered some peace from looking at the ineffable repose of the Dead.

Then, before he answered, he covered up her face; and in his voice there was the stillness of ice.

"Leonard is not unprovided for. Those that honoured his mother will take care of him. He shall never touch a penny of your money. Every offer of service you have made, I reject in his name,—and in her presence," said he, bending towards the Dead. "Men may call such actions as yours, youthful follies! There is another name for them with God. Sir! I will follow you downstairs."

All the way down, Mr Benson heard Mr Donne's voice urging and entreating, but the words he could not recognise for the thoughts that filled his brain—the rapid putting together of events that was going on there. And when Mr Donne turned at the door, to speak again, and repeat his offers of service to Leonard, Mr Benson made answer, without well knowing whether the answer fitted the question or not:

"I thank God, you have no right, legal or otherwise, over the child. And for her sake, I will spare him the shame of ever hearing your name as his father."

He shut the door in Mr Donne's face.

"An ill-bred, puritanical old fellow! He may have the boy, I am sure, for aught I care. I have done my duty, and will get out of this abominable place as soon as I can. I wish my last remembrance of my beautiful Ruth was not mixed up with all these people."

Mr Benson was bitterly oppressed with this interview; it disturbed the peace with which he was beginning to contemplate events. His anger ruffled him, although such anger had been just, and such indignation well deserved, and both had been unconsciously present in his heart for years against the unknown seducer, whom he met face to face by the death-bed of Ruth.

It gave him a shock which he did not recover from for many days. He was nervously afraid lest Mr Donne should appear at the funeral; and not all the reasons he alleged to himself against this apprehension, put it utterly away from him. Before then, however, he heard casually (for he would allow himself no inquiries) that he had left the town. No! Ruth's funeral passed over in calm and simple solemnity. Her child, her own household, her friend, and Mr Farquhar, quietly walked after the bier, which was borne by some of the poor to whom she had been very kind in her lifetime. And many others stood aloof in the little burying-ground, sadly watching that last ceremony.

They slowly dispersed; Mr Benson leading Leonard by the hand, and secretly wondering at his self-restraint. Almost as soon as they had let themselves into the Chapel-house, a messenger brought a note from Mrs Bradshaw, with a pot of quince marmalade, which, she said to Miss Benson, she thought that Leonard might fancy, and if he did, they were to be sure and let her know, as she had plenty more; or, was there anything else that he would like? She would gladly make him whatever he fancied.

Poor Leonard! he lay stretched on the sofa, white and tearless, beyond the power of any such comfort, however kindly offered; but this was only one of the many homely, simple attentions, which all came round him to offer, from Mr Grey, the rector, down to the nameless poor who called at the back door to inquire how it fared with *her* child.

Mr Benson was anxious, according to Dissenting custom, to preach an appropriate funeral sermon. It was the last office he could render to her; it should be done well and carefully. Moreover, it was possible that the circumstances of her life, which were known to all, might be made effective in this manner to work conviction of many truths. Accordingly, he made great preparation of thought and paper; he laboured hard, destroying sheet after sheet—his eyes filling with tears between-whiles, as he remembered some fresh proof of the humility and sweetness of her life. Oh, that he could do her justice! but words seemed hard and inflexible, and refused to fit themselves to his ideas. He sat late on Saturday, writing; he watched through the night till Sunday morning was far advanced. He had never taken such pains with any sermon, and he was only half satisfied with it after all.

Mrs Farquhar had comforted the bitterness of Sally's grief by giving her very handsome mourning. At any rate, she felt oddly proud and exulting when she thought of her new black gown; but when she remembered why she wore it, she scolded herself pretty sharply for her satisfaction, and took to crying afresh with redoubled vigour. She spent the Sunday morning in alternately smoothing down her skirts and adjusting her broad hemmed collar, or bemoaning the occasion with tearful earnestness. But the sorrow overcame the little quaint vanity of her heart, as she saw troop after troop of humbly-dressed mourners pass by into the old chapel. They were very poor—but each had mounted some rusty piece of crape, or some faded black ribbon. The old came halting and slow—the mothers carried their quiet, awe-struck babes.

And not only these were there—but others—equally unaccustomed to nonconformist worship: Mr Davis, for instance, to whom Sally acted as chaperone; for he sat in the minister's pew, as a stranger; and, as she afterwards said, she had a fellow-feeling with him, being a Church-woman herself, and Dissenters had such awkward ways; however, she had been there before, so she could set him to rights about their fashions.

From the pulpit, Mr Benson saw one and all—the well-filled Bradshaw pew—all in deep mourning, Mr Bradshaw conspicuously so (he would have attended the funeral gladly if they would have asked him)—the Farquhars—the many strangers—the still more numerous poor—one or two wild-looking outcasts, who stood afar off, but wept silently and continually. Mr Benson's heart grew very full.

His voice trembled as he read and prayed. But he steadied it as he opened his sermon—his great, last effort in her honour—the labour that he had prayed God to bless to the hearts of many. For an instant the old man looked on all the upturned faces, listening, with wet eyes, to hear what he could say to interpret that which was in their hearts, dumb and unshaped, of God's doings as shown in her life. He looked, and, as he gazed, a mist came before him, and he could not see his sermon, nor his hearers, but only Ruth, as she had been—stricken low, and crouching from sight, in the upland field by Llan-dhu—like a woeful, hunted creature. And now her life was over! her struggle ended! Sermon and all was forgotten. He sat down, and hid his face in his hands for a minute or so. Then he arose, pale and serene. He put the sermon away, and opened the Bible, and read the seventh chapter of Revelations, beginning at the ninth verse.

Before it was finished, most of his hearers were in tears. It came home to them as more appropriate than any sermon could have been. Even Sally, though full of anxiety as to what her fellow-Churchman would think of such proceedings, let the sobs come freely as she heard the words:

> And he said to me, These are they which came out of great tribulation, and have washed their robes, and made them white in the blood of the Lamb.
>
> Therefore are they before the throne of God, and serve him day and night in his temple; and he that sitteth on the throne shall dwell among them.
>
> They shall hunger no more, neither thirst any more; neither shall the sun light on them, nor any heat.
>
> For the Lamb which is in the midst of the throne shall feed them, and shall lead them unto living fountains of waters, and God shall wipe away all tears from their eyes.

"He preaches sermons sometimes," said Sally, nudging Mr Davis, as they rose from their knees at last. "I make no doubt there was as grand a sermon in yon paper-book as ever we hear in church. I've heard him pray uncommon fine—quite beyond any but learned folk."

Mr Bradshaw had been anxious to do something to testify his respect for the woman, who, if all had entertained his opinions, would have been driven into hopeless sin. Accordingly, he ordered the first stonemason of the town to meet him in the chapel-yard on Monday morning, to take measurement and receive directions for a tombstone. They threaded their way among the grassy heaps to where Ruth was buried, in the south corner, beneath the great Wych-elm. When they got there, Leonard raised himself up from the new-stirred turf. His face was swollen with weeping; but when he saw Mr Bradshaw he calmed himself, and checked his sobs, and, as an explanation of being where he was when thus surprised, he could find nothing to say but the simple words:

"My mother is dead, sir."

His eyes sought those of Mr Bradshaw with a wild look of agony, as if to find comfort for that great loss in human sympathy; and at the first word—the first touch of Mr Bradshaw's hand on his shoulder—he burst out afresh.

"Come, come! my boy!—Mr Francis, I will see you about this to-morrow—I will call at your house.—Let me take you home, my poor fellow. Come, my lad, come!"

The first time, for years, that he had entered Mr Benson's house, he came leading and comforting her son—and, for a moment, he could not speak to his old friend, for the sympathy which choked up his voice, and filled his eyes with tears.

NORTH AND SOUTH

First published in serial form in *Household Words* in 1854-1855 and in volume form in 1855.

On its appearance in 'Household Words,' this tale was obliged to conform to the conditions imposed by the requirements of a weekly publication, and likewise to confine itself within certain advertised limits, in order that faith might be kept with the public. Although these conditions were made as light as they well could be, the author found it impossible to develope the story in the manner originally intended, and, more especially, was compelled to hurry on events with an improbable rapidity towards the close. In some degree to remedy this obvious defect, various short passages have been inserted, and several new chapters added. With this brief explanation, the tale is commended to the kindness of the reader;

'Beseking hym lowly, of mercy and pite,
Of its rude makyng to have compassion.'

CHAPTER I - 'HASTE TO THE WEDDING'

'Wooed and married and a'.'

'Edith!' said Margaret, gently, 'Edith!'

But, as Margaret half suspected, Edith had fallen asleep. She lay curled up on the sofa in the back drawing-room in Harley Street, looking very lovely in her white muslin and blue ribbons. If Titania had ever been dressed in white muslin and blue ribbons, and had fallen asleep on a crimson damask sofa in a back drawing-room, Edith might have been taken for her. Margaret was struck afresh by her cousin's beauty. They had grown up together from childhood, and all along Edith had been remarked upon by every one, except Margaret, for her prettiness; but Margaret had never thought about it until the last few days, when the prospect of soon losing her companion seemed to give force to every sweet quality and charm which Edith possessed. They had been talking about wedding dresses, and wedding ceremonies; and Captain Lennox, and what he had told Edith about her future life at Corfu, where his regiment was stationed; and the difficulty of keeping a piano in good tune (a difficulty which Edith seemed to consider as one of the most formidable that could befall her in her married life), and what gowns she should want in the visits to Scotland, which would immediately succeed her marriage; but the whispered tone had latterly become more drowsy; and Margaret, after a pause of a few minutes, found, as she fancied, that in spite of the buzz in the next room, Edith had rolled herself up into a soft ball of muslin and ribbon, and silken curls, and gone off into a peaceful little after-dinner nap.

Margaret had been on the point of telling her cousin of some of the plans and visions which she entertained as to her future life in the country parsonage, where her father and mother lived; and where her bright holidays had always been passed, though for the last ten years her aunt Shaw's house had been considered as her home. But in default of a listener, she had to brood over the change in her life silently as heretofore. It was a happy brooding, although tinged with regret at being separated for an indefinite time from her gentle aunt and dear cousin. As she thought of the delight of filling the important post of only daughter in Helstone parsonage, pieces of the conversation out of the next room came upon her ears. Her aunt Shaw was talking to the five or six ladies who had been dining there, and whose husbands were still in the dining-room. They were the familiar acquaintances of the house; neighbours whom Mrs. Shaw called friends, because she happened to dine with them more frequently than with any other people, and because if she or Edith wanted anything from them, or they from her, they did not scruple to make a call at each other's houses before luncheon. These ladies and their husbands were invited, in their capacity of friends, to eat a farewell dinner in honour of Edith's approaching marriage. Edith had rather objected to this arrangement, for Captain Lennox was expected to arrive by a late train this very evening; but, although she was a spoiled child, she was too careless and idle to have a very strong will of her own, and gave way when she found that her mother had absolutely ordered those extra delicacies of the season which are always supposed to be efficacious against immoderate grief at farewell dinners. She contented herself by leaning back in her chair, merely playing with the food on her plate, and looking grave and absent; while all around her were enjoying the mots of Mr. Grey, the gentleman who always took the bottom of the table at Mrs. Shaw's dinner parties, and asked Edith to give them some music in the drawing-room. Mr. Grey was particularly agreeable over this farewell dinner, and the gentlemen staid down stairs longer than usual. It was very well they did—to judge from the fragments of conversation which Margaret overheard.

'I suffered too much myself; not that I was not extremely happy with the poor dear General, but still disparity of age is a drawback; one that I was resolved Edith should not have to encounter. Of course, without any maternal partiality, I foresaw that the dear child was likely to marry early; indeed, I had often said that I was sure she would be married before she was nineteen. I had quite a prophetic feeling when Captain Lennox'—and here the voice dropped into a whisper, but Margaret could easily supply the blank. The course of true love in Edith's case had run remarkably smooth. Mrs. Shaw had given way to the presentiment, as she expressed it; and had rather urged on the marriage, although it was below the expectations which many of Edith's acquaintances had formed for her, a young and pretty heiress. But Mrs. Shaw said that her only child should marry for love,—and sighed emphatically, as if love had not been her motive for marrying the General. Mrs. Shaw enjoyed the romance of the present engagement rather more than her daughter. Not but that Edith was very thoroughly and properly in love; still she would certainly have preferred a good house in Belgravia, to all the picturesqueness of the life which Captain Lennox described at Corfu. The very parts which made Margaret glow as she listened, Edith pretended to shiver and shudder at; partly for the pleasure she had in being coaxed out of her dislike by her fond lover, and partly because anything of a gipsy or make-shift life was really distasteful to her. Yet had any one come with a fine house, and a fine estate, and a fine title to boot, Edith would still have clung to Captain Lennox while the temptation lasted; when it was over, it is possible she might have had little qualms of ill-concealed regret that Captain Lennox could not have united in his person everything that was desirable. In this she was but her mother's child; who, after deliberately marrying General Shaw with no warmer feeling than respect for his character and establishment, was constantly, though quietly, bemoaning her hard lot in being united to one whom she could not love.

'I have spared no expense in her trousseau,' were the next words Margaret heard.

'She has all the beautiful Indian shawls and scarfs the General gave to me, but which I shall never wear again.'

'She is a lucky girl,' replied another voice, which Margaret knew to be that of Mrs. Gibson, a lady who was taking a double interest in the conversation, from the fact of one of her daughters having been married within the last few weeks.

'Helen had set her heart upon an Indian shawl, but really when I found what an extravagant price was asked, I was obliged to refuse her. She will be quite envious when she hears of Edith having Indian shawls. What kind are they? Delhi? with the lovely little borders?'

Margaret heard her aunt's voice again, but this time it was as if she had raised herself up from her half-recumbent position, and were looking into the more dimly lighted back drawing-room. 'Edith! Edith!' cried she; and then she sank as if wearied by the exertion. Margaret stepped forward.

'Edith is asleep, Aunt Shaw. Is it anything I can do?'

All the ladies said 'Poor child!' on receiving this distressing intelligence about Edith; and the minute lap-dog in Mrs. Shaw's arms began to bark, as if excited by the burst of pity.

'Hush, Tiny! you naughty little girl! you will waken your mistress. It was only to ask Edith if she would tell Newton to bring down her shawls: perhaps you would go, Margaret dear?'

Margaret went up into the old nursery at the very top of the house, where Newton was busy getting up some laces which were required for the wedding. While Newton went (not without a muttered grumbling) to undo the shawls, which had already been exhibited four or five times that day, Margaret looked round upon the nursery; the first room in that house with which she had become familiar nine years ago, when she was brought, all untamed from the forest, to share the home, the play, and the lessons of her cousin Edith. She remembered the dark, dim look of the London nursery, presided over by an austere and ceremonious nurse, who was terribly particular about clean hands and torn frocks. She recollected the first tea up there—separate from her father and aunt, who were dining somewhere down below an infinite depth of stairs; for unless she were up in the sky (the child thought), they must be deep down in the bowels of the earth. At home—before she came to live in Harley Street—her mother's dressing-room had been her nursery; and, as they kept early hours in the country parsonage, Margaret had always had her meals with her father and mother. Oh! well did the tall stately girl of eighteen remember the tears shed with such wild passion of grief by the little girl of nine, as she hid her face under the bed-clothes, in that first night; and how she was bidden not to cry by the nurse, because it would disturb Miss Edith; and how she had cried as bitterly, but more quietly, till her newly-seen, grand, pretty aunt had come softly upstairs with Mr. Hale to show him his little sleeping daughter. Then the little Margaret had hushed her sobs, and tried to lie quiet as if asleep, for fear of making her father unhappy by her grief, which she dared not express before her aunt, and which she rather thought it was wrong to feel at all after the long hoping, and planning, and contriving they had gone through at home, before her wardrobe could be arranged so as to suit her grander circumstances, and before papa could leave his parish to come up to London, even for a few days.

Now she had got to love the old nursery, though it was but a dismantled place; and she looked all round, with a kind of cat-like regret, at the idea of leaving it for ever in three days.

'Ah Newton!' said she, 'I think we shall all be sorry to leave this dear old room.'

'Indeed, miss, I shan't for one. My eyes are not so good as they were, and the light here is so bad that I can't see to mend laces except just at the window, where there's always a shocking draught—enough to give one one's death of cold.'

Well, I dare say you will have both good light and plenty of warmth at Naples. You must keep as much of your darning as you can till then. Thank you, Newton, I can take them down—you're busy.'

So Margaret went down laden with shawls, and snuffing up their spicy Eastern smell. Her aunt asked her to stand as a sort of lay figure on which to display them, as Edith was still asleep. No one thought about it; but Margaret's tall, finely made figure, in the black silk dress which she was wearing as mourning for some distant relative of her father's, set off the long beautiful folds of the gorgeous shawls that would have half-smothered Edith. Margaret stood right under the chandelier, quite silent and passive, while her aunt adjusted the draperies. Occasionally, as she was turned round, she caught a glimpse of herself in the mirror over the chimney-piece, and smiled at her own appearance there—the familiar features in the usual garb of a princess. She touched the shawls gently as they hung around her, and took a pleasure in their soft feel and their brilliant colours, and rather liked to be dressed in such splendour—enjoying it much as a child would do, with a quiet pleased smile on her lips. Just then the door opened, and Mr. Henry Lennox was suddenly announced. Some of the ladies started back, as if half-ashamed of their feminine interest in dress. Mrs. Shaw held out her hand to the new-comer; Margaret stood perfectly still, thinking she might be yet wanted as a sort of block for the shawls; but looking at Mr. Lennox with a bright, amused face, as if sure of his sympathy in her sense of the ludicrousness at being thus surprised.

Her aunt was so much absorbed in asking Mr. Henry Lennox—who had not been able to come to dinner—all sorts of questions about his brother the bridegroom, his sister the bridesmaid (coming with the Captain from Scotland for the occasion), and various other members of the Lennox family, that Margaret saw she was no more wanted as shawl-bearer, and devoted herself to the amusement of the other visitors, whom her aunt had for the moment forgotten. Almost immediately, Edith came in from the back drawing-room, winking and blinking her eyes at the stronger light, shaking back her slightly-ruffled curls, and altogether looking like the Sleeping Beauty just startled from her dreams. Even in her slumber she had instinctively felt that a Lennox was worth rousing herself for; and she had a multitude of questions to ask about dear Janet, the future, unseen sister-in-law, for whom she professed so much affection, that if Margaret had not been very proud she might have almost felt jealous of the mushroom rival. As Margaret sank rather more into the background on her aunt's joining the conversation, she saw Henry Lennox directing his look towards a vacant seat near her; and she knew perfectly well that as soon as Edith released him from her questioning, he would take possession of that chair. She had not been quite sure, from her aunt's rather confused account of his engagements, whether he would come that night; it was almost a surprise to see him; and now she was sure of a pleasant evening. He liked and disliked pretty nearly the same things that she did. Margaret's face was lightened up into an honest, open brightness. By-and-by he came. She received him with a smile which had not a tinge of shyness or self-consciousness in it.

'Well, I suppose you are all in the depths of business—ladies' business, I mean. Very different to my business, which is the real true law business. Playing with shawls is very different work to drawing up settlements.

'Ah, I knew how you would be amused to find us all so occupied in admiring finery. But really Indian shawls are very perfect things of their kind.'

'I have no doubt they are. Their prices are very perfect, too. Nothing wanting.' The gentlemen came dropping in one by one, and the buzz and noise deepened in tone.

'This is your last dinner-party, is it not? There are no more before Thursday?'

'No. I think after this evening we shall feel at rest, which I am sure I have not done for many weeks; at least, that kind of rest when the hands have nothing more to do, and all the arrangements are complete for an event which must occupy one's head and heart. I shall be glad to have time to think, and I am sure Edith will.'

'I am not so sure about her; but I can fancy that you will. Whenever I have seen you lately, you have been carried away by a whirlwind of some other person's making.'

'Yes,' said Margaret, rather sadly, remembering the never-ending commotion about trifles that had been going on for more than a month past: 'I wonder if a marriage must always be preceded by what you call a whirlwind, or whether in some cases there might not rather be a calm and peaceful time just before it.'

'Cinderella's godmother ordering the trousseau, the wedding-breakfast, writing the notes of invitation, for instance,' said Mr. Lennox, laughing.

'But are all these quite necessary troubles?' asked Margaret, looking up straight at him for an answer. A sense of indescribable weariness of all the arrangements for a pretty effect, in which Edith had been busied as supreme authority for the last six weeks, oppressed her just now; and she really wanted some one to help her to a few pleasant, quiet ideas connected with a marriage.

'Oh, of course,' he replied with a change to gravity in his tone. 'There are forms and ceremonies to be gone through, not so much to satisfy oneself, as to stop the world's mouth, without which stoppage there would be very little satisfaction in life. But how would you have a wedding arranged?'

'Oh, I have never thought much about it; only I should like it to be a very fine summer morning; and I should like to walk to church through the shade of trees; and not to have so many bridesmaids, and to have no wedding-breakfast. I dare say I am resolving against the very things that have given me the most trouble just now.'

'No, I don't think you are. The idea of stately simplicity accords well with your character.'

Margaret did not quite like this speech; she winced away from it more, from remembering former occasions on which he had tried to lead her into a discussion (in which he took the complimentary part) about her own character and ways of going on. She cut his speech rather short by saying:

'It is natural for me to think of Helstone church, and the walk to it, rather than of driving up to a London church in the middle of a paved street.'

'Tell me about Helstone. You have never described it to me. I should like to have some idea of the place you will be living in, when ninety-six Harley Street will be looking dingy and dirty, and dull, and shut up. Is Helstone a village, or a town, in the first place?'

'Oh, only a hamlet; I don't think I could call it a village at all. There is the church and a few houses near it on the green—cottages, rather—with roses growing all over them.'

'And flowering all the year round, especially at Christmas—make your picture complete,' said he.

'No,' replied Margaret, somewhat annoyed, 'I am not making a picture. I am trying to describe Helstone as it really is. You should not have said that.'

'I am penitent,' he answered. 'Only it really sounded like a village in a tale rather than in real life.'

'And so it is,' replied Margaret, eagerly. 'All the other places in England that I have seen seem so hard and prosaic-looking, after the New Forest. Helstone is like a village in a poem—in one of Tennyson's poems. But I won't try and describe it any more. You would only laugh at me if I told you what I think of it—what it really is.'

'Indeed, I would not. But I see you are going to be very resolved. Well, then, tell me that which I should like still better to know what the parsonage is like.'

'Oh, I can't describe my home. It is home, and I can't put its charm into words.'

'I submit. You are rather severe to-night, Margaret.

'How?' said she, turning her large soft eyes round full upon him. 'I did not know I was.'

'Why, because I made an unlucky remark, you will neither tell me what Helstone is like, nor will you say anything about your home, though I have told you how much I want to hear about both, the latter especially.'

'But indeed I cannot tell you about my own home. I don't quite think it is a thing to be talked about, unless you knew it.'

'Well, then'—pausing for a moment—'tell me what you do there. Here you read, or have lessons, or otherwise improve your mind, till the middle of the day; take a walk before lunch, go a drive with your aunt after, and have some kind of engagement in the evening. There, now fill up your day at Helstone. Shall you ride, drive, or walk?'

'Walk, decidedly. We have no horse, not even for papa. He walks to the very extremity of his parish. The walks are so beautiful, it would be a shame to drive—almost a shame to ride.'

'Shall you garden much? That, I believe, is a proper employment for young ladies in the country.'

'I don't know. I am afraid I shan't like such hard work.'

'Archery parties—pic-nics—race-balls—hunt-balls?'

'Oh no!' said she, laughing. 'Papa's living is very small; and even if we were near such things, I doubt if I should go to them.'

'I see, you won't tell me anything. You will only tell me that you are not going to do this and that. Before the vacation ends, I think I shall pay you a call, and see what you really do employ yourself in.'

'I hope you will. Then you will see for yourself how beautiful Helstone is. Now I must go. Edith is sitting down to play, and I just know enough of music to turn over the leaves for her; and besides, Aunt Shaw won't like us to talk.' Edith played brilliantly. In the middle of the piece the door half-opened, and Edith saw Captain Lennox hesitating whether to come in. She threw down her music, and rushed out of the room, leaving Margaret standing confused and blushing to explain to the astonished guests what vision had shown itself to cause Edith's sudden flight. Captain Lennox had come earlier than was expected; or was it really so late? They looked at their watches, were duly shocked, and took their leave.

Then Edith came back, glowing with pleasure, half-shyly, half-proudly leading in her tall handsome Captain. His brother shook hands with him, and Mrs. Shaw welcomed him in her gentle kindly way, which had always something plaintive in it, arising from the long habit of considering herself a victim to an uncongenial marriage. Now that, the General being gone, she had every good of life, with as few drawbacks as possible, she had been rather perplexed to find an anxiety, if not a sorrow. She had, however, of late settled upon her own health as a source of apprehension; she had a nervous little cough whenever she thought about it; and some complaisant doctor ordered her just what she desired,—a winter in Italy. Mrs. Shaw had as strong wishes as most people, but she never liked to do anything from the open and acknowledged motive of her own good will and pleasure; she preferred being compelled to gratify herself by some other person's command or desire. She really did persuade herself that she was submitting to some hard external necessity; and thus she was able to moan and complain in her soft manner, all the time she was in reality doing just what she liked.

It was in this way she began to speak of her own journey to Captain Lennox, who assented, as in duty bound, to all his future mother-in-law said, while his eyes sought Edith, who was busying herself in rearranging the tea-table, and ordering up all sorts of good things, in spite of his assurances that he had dined within the last two hours.

Mr. Henry Lennox stood leaning against the chimney-piece, amused with the family scene. He was close by his handsome brother; he was the plain one in a singularly good-looking family; but his face was intelligent, keen, and mobile; and now and then Margaret wondered what it was that he could be thinking about, while he kept silence, but was evidently observing, with an interest that was slightly sarcastic, all that Edith and she were doing. The sarcastic feeling was called out by Mrs. Shaw's conversation with his brother; it was separate from the interest which was excited by what he saw. He thought it a pretty sight to see the two cousins so busy in their little arrangements about the table. Edith chose to do most herself. She was in a humour to enjoy showing her lover how well she could behave as a soldier's wife. She found out that the water in the urn was cold, and ordered up the great kitchen tea-kettle; the only consequence of which was that when she met it at the door, and tried to carry it in, it was too heavy for her, and she came in pouting, with a black mark on her muslin gown, and a little round white hand indented by the handle, which she took to show to Captain Lennox, just like a hurt child, and, of course, the remedy was the same in both cases. Margaret's quickly-adjusted spirit-lamp was the most efficacious contrivance, though not so like the gypsy-encampment which Edith, in some of her moods, chose to consider the nearest resemblance to a barrack-life. After this evening all was bustle till the wedding was over.

CHAPTER II - ROSES AND THORNS

'By the soft green light in the woody glade,
On the banks of moss where thy childhood played;
By the household tree, thro' which thine eye
First looked in love to the summer sky.'
MRS. HEMANS.

Margaret was once more in her morning dress, travelling quietly home with her father, who had come up to assist at the wedding. Her mother had been detained at home by a multitude of half-reasons, none of which anybody fully understood, except Mr. Hale, who was perfectly aware that all his arguments in favour of a grey satin gown, which was midway between oldness and newness, had proved unavailing; and that, as he had not the money to equip his wife afresh, from top to toe, she would not show herself at her only sister's only child's wedding. If Mrs. Shaw had guessed at the real reason why Mrs. Hale did not accompany her husband, she would have showered down gowns upon her; but it was nearly twenty years since Mrs. Shaw had been the poor, pretty Miss Beresford, and she had really forgotten all grievances except that of the unhappiness arising from disparity of age in married life, on which she could descant by the half-hour. Dearest Maria had married the man of her heart, only eight years older than herself, with the sweetest temper, and that blue-black hair one so seldom sees. Mr. Hale was one of the most delightful preachers she had ever heard, and a perfect model of a parish priest. Perhaps it was not quite a logical deduction from all these premises, but it was still Mrs. Shaw's characteristic conclusion, as she thought over her sister's lot: 'Married for love, what can dearest Maria have to wish for in this world?' Mrs. Hale, if she spoke truth, might have answered with a ready-made list, 'a silver-grey glace silk, a white chip bonnet, oh! dozens of things for the wedding, and hundreds of things for the house.' Margaret only knew that her mother had not found it convenient to come, and she was not sorry to think that their meeting and greeting would take place at Helstone parsonage, rather than, during the confusion of the last two or three days, in the house in Harley Street, where she herself had had to play the part of Figaro, and was wanted everywhere at one and the same time. Her mind and body ached now with the recollection of all she had done and said within the last forty-eight hours. The farewells so hurriedly taken, amongst all the other good-byes, of those she had lived with so long, oppressed her now with a sad regret for the times that were no more; it did not signify what those times had been, they were gone never to return. Margaret's heart felt more heavy than she could ever have thought it possible in going to her own dear home, the place and the life she had longed for for years—at that time of all times for yearning and longing, just before the sharp senses lose their outlines in sleep. She took her mind away with a wrench from the recollection of the past to the bright serene contemplation of the hopeful future. Her eyes began to see, not visions of what had been, but the sight actually before her; her dear father leaning back asleep in the railway carriage. His blue-black hair was grey now, and lay thinly over his brows. The bones of his face were plainly to be seen—too plainly for beauty, if his features had been less finely cut; as it was, they had a grace if not a comeliness of their own. The face was in repose; but it was rather rest after weariness, than the serene calm of the countenance of one who led a placid, contented life. Margaret was painfully struck by the worn, anxious expression; and she went back over the open and avowed circumstances of her father's life, to find the cause for the lines that spoke so plainly of habitual distress and depression.

'Poor Frederick!' thought she, sighing. 'Oh! if Frederick had but been a clergyman, instead of going into the navy, and being lost to us all! I wish I knew all about it. I never understood it from Aunt Shaw; I only knew he could not come back to England because of that terrible affair. Poor dear papa! how sad he looks! I am so glad I am going home, to be at hand to comfort him and mamma.

She was ready with a bright smile, in which there was not a trace of fatigue, to greet her father when he awakened. He smiled back again, but faintly, as if it were an unusual exertion. His face returned into its lines of habitual anxiety. He had a trick of half-opening his mouth as if to speak, which constantly unsettled the form of the lips, and gave the face an undecided expression. But he had the same large, soft eyes as his daughter,—eyes which moved slowly and almost grandly round in their orbits, and were well veiled by their transparent white eyelids. Margaret was more like him than like her mother. Sometimes people wondered that parents so handsome should have a daughter who was so far from regularly beautiful; not beautiful at all, was occasionally said. Her mouth was wide; no rosebud that could only open just enough to let out a 'yes' and 'no,' and 'an't please you, sir.' But the wide mouth was one soft curve of rich red lips; and the skin, if not white and fair, was of an ivory smoothness and delicacy. If the look on her face was, in general, too dignified and reserved for one so young, now, talking to her father, it was bright as the morning,—full of dimples, and glances that spoke of childish gladness, and boundless hope in the future.

It was the latter part of July when Margaret returned home. The forest trees were all one dark, full, dusky green; the fern below them caught all the slanting sunbeams; the weather was sultry and broodingly still. Margaret used to tramp along by her father's side, crushing down the fern with a cruel glee, as she felt it yield under her light foot, and send up the fragrance peculiar to it,—out on the broad commons into the warm scented light, seeing multitudes of wild, free, living creatures, revelling in the sunshine, and the herbs and flowers it called forth. This life—at least these walks—realised all Margaret's anticipations. She took a pride in her forest. Its people were her people. She made hearty friends with them; learned and delighted in using their peculiar words; took up her freedom amongst them; nursed their babies; talked or read with slow distinctness to their old people; carried dainty messes to their sick; resolved before long to teach at the school, where her father went every day as to an appointed task, but she was continually tempted off to go and see some individual friend—man, woman, or child—in some cottage in the green shade of the forest. Her out-of-doors life was perfect. Her in-doors life had its drawbacks. With the healthy shame of a child, she blamed herself for her keenness of sight, in perceiving that all was not as it should be there. Her mother—her mother always so kind and tender towards her—seemed now and then so much discontented with their situation; thought that the bishop strangely neglected his episcopal duties, in not giving Mr. Hale a better living; and almost reproached her husband because he could not bring himself to say that he wished to leave the parish, and undertake the charge of a larger. He would sigh aloud as he answered, that if he could do what he ought in little Helstone, he should be thankful; but every day he was more overpowered; the world became more bewildering. At each repeated urgency of his wife, that he would put himself in the way of seeking some preferment, Margaret saw that her father shrank more and more; and she strove at such times to reconcile her mother to Helstone. Mrs. Hale said that the near neighbourhood of so many trees affected her health; and Margaret would try to tempt her forth on to the beautiful, broad, upland, sun-streaked, cloud-shadowed common; for she was sure that her mother had accustomed herself too much to an in-doors life, seldom extending her walks beyond the church, the school, and the neighbouring cottages. This did good for a time; but when the autumn drew on, and the weather became more changeable, her mother's idea of the unhealthiness of the place increased; and she repined even more frequently that her husband, who was more learned than Mr. Hume, a better parish priest than Mr. Houldsworth, should not have met with the preferment that these two former neighbours of theirs had done.

This marring of the peace of home, by long hours of discontent, was what Margaret was unprepared for. She knew, and had rather revelled in the idea, that she should have to give up many luxuries, which had only been troubles and trammels to her freedom in Harley Street. Her keen enjoyment of every sensuous pleasure, was balanced finely, if not overbalanced, by her conscious pride in being able to do without them all, if need were. But the cloud never comes in that quarter of the horizon from which we watch for it. There had been slight complaints and passing regrets on her mother's part, over some trifle connected with Helstone, and her father's position there, when Margaret had been spending her holidays at home before; but in the general happiness of the recollection of those times, she had forgotten the small details which were not so pleasant. In the latter half of September, the autumnal rains and storms came on, and Margaret was obliged to remain more in the house than she had hitherto done. Helstone was at some distance from any neighbours of their own standard of cultivation.

'It is undoubtedly one of the most out-of-the-way places in England,' said Mrs. Hale, in one of her plaintive moods. 'I can't help regretting constantly that papa has really no one to associate with here; he is so thrown away; seeing no one but farmers and labourers from week's end to week's end. If we only lived at the other side of the parish, it would be something; there we should be almost within walking distance of the Stansfields; certainly the Gormans would be within a walk.'

'Gormans,' said Margaret. 'Are those the Gormans who made their fortunes in trade at Southampton? Oh! I'm glad we don't visit them. I don't like shoppy people. I think we are far better off, knowing only cottagers and labourers, and people without pretence.'

'You must not be so fastidious, Margaret, dear!' said her mother, secretly thinking of a young and handsome Mr. Gorman whom she had once met at Mr. Hume's.

'No! I call mine a very comprehensive taste; I like all people whose occupations have to do with land; I like soldiers and sailors, and the three learned professions, as they call them. I'm sure you don't want me to admire butchers and bakers, and candlestick-makers, do you, mamma?'

'But the Gormans were neither butchers nor bakers, but very respectable coach-builders.'

'Very well. Coach-building is a trade all the same, and I think a much more useless one than that of butchers or bakers. Oh! how tired I used to be of the drives every day in Aunt Shaw's carriage, and how I longed to walk!'

And walk Margaret did, in spite of the weather. She was so happy out of doors, at her father's side, that she almost danced; and with the soft violence of the west wind behind her, as she crossed some heath, she seemed to be borne onwards, as lightly and easily as the fallen leaf that was wafted along by the autumnal breeze. But the evenings were rather difficult to fill up agreeably. Immediately after tea her father withdrew into his small library, and she and her mother were left alone. Mrs. Hale had never cared much for books, and had discouraged her husband, very early in their married life, in his desire of reading aloud to her, while she worked. At one time they had tried backgammon as a resource; but as Mr. Hale grew to take an increasing interest in his school and his parishioners, he found that the interruptions which arose out of these duties were regarded as hardships by his wife, not to be accepted as the natural conditions of his profession, but to be regretted and struggled against by her as they severally arose. So he withdrew, while the children were yet young, into his library, to spend his evenings (if he were at home), in reading the speculative and metaphysical books which were his delight.

When Margaret had been here before, she had brought down with her a great box of books, recommended by masters or governess, and had found the summer's day all too short to get through the reading she had to do before her return to town. Now there were only the well-bound little-read English Classics, which were weeded out of her father's library to fill up the small book-shelves in the drawing-room. Thomson's Seasons, Hayley's Cowper, Middleton's Cicero, were by far the lightest, newest, and most amusing. The book-shelves did not afford much resource. Margaret told her mother every particular of her London life, to all of which Mrs. Hale listened with interest, sometimes amused and questioning, at others a little inclined to compare her sister's circumstances of ease and comfort with the narrower means at Helstone vicarage. On such evenings Margaret was apt to stop talking rather abruptly, and listen to the drip-drip of the rain upon the leads of the little bow-window. Once or twice Margaret found herself mechanically counting the repetition of the monotonous sound, while she wondered if she might venture to put a question on a subject very near to her heart, and ask where Frederick was now; what he was doing; how long it was since they had heard from him. But a consciousness that her mother's delicate health, and positive dislike to Helstone, all dated from the time of the mutiny in which Frederick had been engaged,—the full account of which Margaret had never heard, and which now seemed doomed to be buried in sad oblivion,—made her pause and turn away from the subject each time she approached it. When she was with her mother, her father seemed the best person to apply to for information; and when with him, she thought that she could speak more easily to her mother. Probably there was nothing much to be heard that was new. In one of the letters she had received before leaving Harley Street, her father had told her that they had heard from Frederick; he was still at Rio, and very well in health, and sent his best love to her; which was dry bones, but not the living intelligence she longed for. Frederick was always spoken of, in the rare times when his name was mentioned, as 'Poor Frederick.' His room was kept exactly as he had left it; and was regularly dusted, and put into order by Dixon, Mrs. Hale's maid, who touched no other part of the household work, but always remembered the day when she had been engaged by Lady Beresford as ladies' maid to Sir John's wards, the pretty Miss Beresfords, the belles of Rutlandshire. Dixon had always considered Mr. Hale as the blight which had fallen upon her young lady's prospects in life. If Miss Beresford had not been in such a hurry to marry a poor country clergyman, there was no knowing what she might not have become. But Dixon was too loyal to desert her in her affliction and downfall (alias her married life). She remained with her, and was devoted to her interests; always considering herself as the good and protecting fairy, whose duty it was to baffle the malignant giant, Mr. Hale. Master Frederick had been her favorite and pride; and it was with a little softening of her dignified look and manner, that she went in weekly to arrange the chamber as carefully as if he might be coming home that very evening. Margaret could not help believing that there had been some late intelligence of Frederick, unknown to her mother, which was making her father anxious and uneasy. Mrs. Hale did not seem to perceive any alteration in her husband's looks or ways. His spirits were always tender and gentle, readily affected by any small piece of intelligence concerning the welfare of others. He would be depressed for many days after witnessing a death-bed, or hearing of any crime. But now Margaret noticed an absence of mind, as if his thoughts were pre-occupied by some subject, the oppression of which could not be relieved by any daily action, such as comforting the survivors, or teaching at the school in hope of lessening the evils in the generation to come. Mr. Hale did not go out among his parishioners as much as usual; he was more shut up in his study; was anxious for the village postman, whose summons to the house-hold was a rap on the back-kitchen window-shutter—a signal which at one time had often to be repeated before any one was sufficiently alive to the hour of the day to understand what it was, and attend to him. Now Mr. Hale loitered about the garden if the morning was fine, and if not, stood dreamily by the study window until the postman had called, or gone down the lane, giving a half-respectful, half-confidential shake of the head to the parson, who watched him away beyond the sweet-briar hedge, and past the great arbutus, before he turned into the room to begin his day's work, with all the signs of a heavy heart and an occupied mind.

But Margaret was at an age when any apprehension, not absolutely based on a knowledge of facts, is easily banished for a time by a bright sunny day, or some happy outward circumstance. And when the brilliant fourteen fine days of October came on, her cares were all blown away as lightly as thistledown, and she thought of nothing but the glories of the forest. The fern-harvest was over, and now that the rain was gone, many a deep glade was accessible, into which Margaret had only peeped in July and August weather. She had learnt drawing with Edith; and she had sufficiently regretted, during the gloom of the bad weather, her idle revelling in the beauty of the woodlands while it had yet been fine, to make her determined to sketch what she could before winter fairly set in. Accordingly, she was busy preparing her board one morning, when Sarah, the housemaid, threw wide open the drawing-room door and announced, 'Mr. Henry Lennox.'

CHAPTER III - 'THE MORE HASTE THE WORSE SPEED'

'Learn to win a lady's faith
 Nobly, as the thing is high;
 Bravely, as for life and death—
 With a loyal gravity.

Lead her from the festive boards,
Point her to the starry skies,
Guard her, by your truthful words,
Pure from courtship's flatteries.'

MRS. BROWNING.

'Mr. Henry Lennox.' Margaret had been thinking of him only a moment before, and remembering his inquiry into her probable occupations at home. It was 'parler du soleil et l'on en voit les rayons;' and the brightness of the sun came over Margaret's face as she put down her board, and went forward to shake hands with him. 'Tell mamma, Sarah,' said she. 'Mamma and I want to ask you so many questions about Edith; I am so much obliged to you for coming.'

'Did not I say that I should?' asked he, in a lower tone than that in which she had spoken.

'But I heard of you so far away in the Highlands that I never thought Hampshire could come in.

'Oh!' said he, more lightly, 'our young couple were playing such foolish pranks, running all sorts of risks, climbing this mountain, sailing on that lake, that I really thought they needed a Mentor to take care of them. And indeed they did; they were quite beyond my uncle's management, and kept the old gentleman in a panic for sixteen hours out of the twenty-four. Indeed, when I once saw how unfit they were to be trusted alone, I thought it my duty not to leave them till I had seen them safely embarked at Plymouth.'

'Have you been at Plymouth? Oh! Edith never named that. To be sure, she has written in such a hurry lately. Did they really sail on Tuesday?'

'Really sailed, and relieved me from many responsibilities. Edith gave me all sorts of messages for you. I believe I have a little diminutive note somewhere; yes, here it is.'

'Oh! thank you,' exclaimed Margaret; and then, half wishing to read it alone and unwatched, she made the excuse of going to tell her mother again (Sarah surely had made some mistake) that Mr. Lennox was there.

When she had left the room, he began in his scrutinising way to look about him. The little drawing-room was looking its best in the streaming light of the morning sun. The middle window in the bow was opened, and clustering roses and the scarlet honeysuckle came peeping round the corner; the small lawn was gorgeous with verbenas and geraniums of all bright colours. But the very brightness outside made the colours within seem poor and faded. The carpet was far from new; the chintz had been often washed; the whole apartment was smaller and shabbier than he had expected, as back-ground and frame-work for Margaret, herself so queenly. He took up one of the books lying on the table; it was the Paradiso of Dante, in the proper old Italian binding of white vellum and gold; by it lay a dictionary, and some words copied out in Margaret's hand-writing. They were a dull list of words, but somehow he liked looking at them. He put them down with a sigh.

'The living is evidently as small as she said. It seems strange, for the Beresfords belong to a good family.'

Margaret meanwhile had found her mother. It was one of Mrs. Hale's fitful days, when everything was a difficulty and a hardship; and Mr. Lennox's appearance took this shape, although secretly she felt complimented by his thinking it worth while to call.

'It is most unfortunate! We are dining early to-day, and having nothing but cold meat, in order that the servants may get on with their ironing; and yet, of course, we must ask him to dinner—Edith's brother-in-law and all. And your papa is in such low spirits this morning about something—I don't know what. I went into the study just now, and he had his face on the table, covering it with his hands. I told him I was sure Helstone air did not agree with him any more than with me, and he suddenly lifted up his head, and begged me not to speak a word more against Helstone, he could not bear it; if there was one place he loved on earth it was Helstone. But I am sure, for all that, it is the damp and relaxing air.'

Margaret felt as if a thin cold cloud had come between her and the sun. She had listened patiently, in hopes that it might be some relief to her mother to unburden herself; but now it was time to draw her back to Mr. Lennox.

'Papa likes Mr. Lennox; they got on together famously at the wedding breakfast. I dare say his coming will do papa good. And never mind the dinner, dear mamma. Cold meat will do capitally for a lunch, which is the light in which Mr. Lennox will most likely look upon a two o'clock dinner.'

'But what are we to do with him till then? It is only half-past ten now.'

'I'll ask him to go out sketching with me. I know he draws, and that will take him out of your way, mamma. Only do come in now; he will think it so strange if you don't.'

Mrs. Hale took off her black silk apron, and smoothed her face. She looked a very pretty lady-like woman, as she greeted Mr. Lennox with the cordiality due to one who was almost a relation. He evidently expected to be asked to spend the day, and accepted the invitation with a glad readiness that made Mrs. Hale wish she could add something to the cold beef. He was pleased with everything; delighted with Margaret's idea of going out sketching together; would not have Mr. Hale disturbed for the world, with the prospect of so soon meeting him at dinner. Margaret brought out her drawing materials for him to choose from; and after the paper and brushes had been duly selected, the two set out in the merriest spirits in the world.

'Now, please, just stop here for a minute or two, said Margaret. 'These are the cottages that haunted me so during the rainy fortnight, reproaching me for not having sketched them.'

'Before they tumbled down and were no more seen. Truly, if they are to be sketched—and they are very picturesque—we had better not put it off till next year. But where shall we sit?'

'Oh! You might have come straight from chambers in the Temple,' instead of having been two months in the Highlands! Look at this beautiful trunk of a tree, which the wood-cutters have left just in the right place for the light. I will put my plaid over it, and it will be a regular forest throne.'

'With your feet in that puddle for a regal footstool! Stay, I will move, and then you can come nearer this way. Who lives in these cottages?'

'They were built by squatters fifty or sixty years ago. One is uninhabited; the foresters are going to take it down, as soon as the old man who lives in the other is dead, poor old fellow! Look—there he is I must go and speak to him. He is so deaf you will hear all our secrets.'

The old man stood bareheaded in the sun, leaning on his stick at the front of his cottage. His stiff features relaxed into a slow smile as Margaret went up and spoke to him. Mr. Lennox hastily introduced the two figures into his sketch, and finished up the landscape with a subordinate reference to them—as Margaret perceived, when the time came for getting up, putting away water, and scraps of paper, and exhibiting to each other their sketches. She laughed and blushed: Mr. Lennox watched her countenance.

'Now, I call that treacherous,' said she. 'I little thought you were making old Isaac and me into subjects, when you told me to ask him the history of these cottages.'

'It was irresistible. You can't know how strong a temptation it was. I hardly dare tell you how much I shall like this sketch.'

He was not quite sure whether she heard this latter sentence before she went to the brook to wash her palette. She came back rather flushed, but looking perfectly innocent and unconscious. He was glad of it, for the speech had slipped from him unawares—a rare thing in the case of a man who premeditated his actions so much as Henry Lennox.

The aspect of home was all right and bright when they reached it. The clouds on her mother's brow had cleared off under the propitious influence of a brace of carp, most opportunely presented by a neighbour. Mr. Hale had returned from his morning's round, and was awaiting his visitor just outside the wicket gate that led into the garden. He looked a complete gentleman in his rather threadbare coat and well-worn hat.

Margaret was proud of her father; she had always a fresh and tender pride in seeing how favourably he impressed every stranger; still her quick eye sought over his face and found there traces of some unusual disturbance, which was only put aside, not cleared away.

Mr. Hale asked to look at their sketches.

'I think you have made the tints on the thatch too dark, have you not?' as he returned Margaret's to her, and held out his hand for Mr. Lennox's, which was withheld from him one moment, no more.

'No, papa! I don't think I have. The house-leek and stone-crop have grown so much darker in the rain. Is it not like, papa?' said she, peeping over his shoulder, as he looked at the figures in Mr. Lennox's drawing.

'Yes, very like. Your figure and way of holding yourself is capital. And it is just poor old Isaac's stiff way of stooping his long rheumatic back. What is this hanging from the branch of the tree? Not a bird's nest, surely.'

'Oh no! that is my bonnet. I never can draw with my bonnet on; it makes my head so hot. I wonder if I could manage figures. There are so many people about here whom I should like to sketch.'

'I should say that a likeness you very much wish to take you would always succeed in,' said Mr. Lennox. 'I have great faith in the power of will. I think myself I have succeeded pretty well in yours.' Mr. Hale had preceded them into the house, while Margaret was lingering to pluck some roses, with which to adorn her morning gown for dinner.

'A regular London girl would understand the implied meaning of that speech,' thought Mr. Lennox. 'She would be up to looking through every speech that a young man made her for the *arriere-pensée* of a compliment. But I don't believe Margaret,—Stay!' exclaimed he, 'Let me help you;' and he gathered for her some velvety cramoisy roses that were above her reach, and then dividing the spoil he placed two in his button-hole, and sent her in, pleased and happy, to arrange her flowers.

The conversation at dinner flowed on quietly and agreeably. There were plenty of questions to be asked on both sides—the latest intelligence which each could give of Mrs. Shaw's movements in Italy to be exchanged; and in the interest of what was said, the unpretending simplicity of the parsonage-ways—above all, in the neighbourhood of Margaret, Mr. Lennox forgot the little feeling of disappointment with which he had at first perceived that she had spoken but the simple truth when she had described her father's living as very small.

'Margaret, my child, you might have gathered us some pears for our dessert,' said Mr. Hale, as the hospitable luxury of a freshly-decanted bottle of wine was placed on the table.

Mrs. Hale was hurried. It seemed as if desserts were impromptu and unusual things at the parsonage; whereas, if Mr. Hale would only have looked behind him, he would have seen biscuits and marmalade, and what not, all arranged in formal order on the sideboard. But the idea of pears had taken possession of Mr. Hale's mind, and was not to be got rid of.

'There are a few brown beurres against the south wall which are worth all foreign fruits and preserves. Run, Margaret, and gather us some.'

'I propose that we adjourn into the garden, and eat them there' said Mr. Lennox.

'Nothing is so delicious as to set one's teeth into the crisp, juicy fruit, warm and scented by the sun. The worst is, the wasps are impudent enough to dispute it with one, even at the very crisis and summit of enjoyment.

He rose, as if to follow Margaret, who had disappeared through the window he only awaited Mrs. Hale's permission. She would rather have wound up the dinner in the proper way, and with all the ceremonies which had gone on so smoothly hitherto, especially as she and Dixon had got out the finger-glasses from the store-room on purpose to be as correct as became General Shaw's widow's sister, but as Mr. Hale got up directly, and prepared to accompany his guest, she could only submit.

'I shall arm myself with a knife,' said Mr. Hale: 'the days of eating fruit so primitively as you describe are over with me. I must pare it and quarter it before I can enjoy it.'

Margaret made a plate for the pears out of a beetroot leaf, which threw up their brown gold colour admirably. Mr. Lennox looked more at her than at the pears; but her father, inclined to cull fastidiously the very zest and perfection of the hour he had stolen from his anxiety, chose daintily the ripest fruit, and sat down on the garden bench to enjoy it at his leisure. Margaret and Mr. Lennox strolled along the little terrace-walk under the south wall, where the bees still hummed and worked busily in their hives.

'What a perfect life you seem to live here! I have always felt rather contemptuously towards the poets before, with their wishes, "Mine be a cot beside a hill," and that sort of thing: but now I am afraid that the truth is, I have been nothing better than a cockney. Just now I feel as if twenty years' hard study of law would be amply rewarded by one year of such an exquisite serene life as this—such skies!' looking up—'such crimson and amber foliage, so perfectly motionless as that!' pointing to some of the great forest trees which shut in the garden as if it were a nest.

'You must please to remember that our skies are not always as deep a blue as they are now. We have rain, and our leaves do fall, and get sodden: though I think Helstone is about as perfect a place as any in the world. Recollect how you rather scorned my description of it one evening in Harley Street: "a village in a tale."'

'Scorned, Margaret! That is rather a hard word.'

'Perhaps it is. Only I know I should have liked to have talked to you of what I was very full at the time, and you—what must I call it, then?—spoke disrespectfully of Helstone as a mere village in a tale.'

'I will never do so again,' said he, warmly. They turned the corner of the walk.

'I could almost wish, Margaret—— ' he stopped and hesitated. It was so unusual for the fluent lawyer to hesitate that Margaret looked up at him, in a little state of questioning wonder; but in an instant—from what about him she could not tell—she wished herself back with her mother—her father—anywhere away from him, for she was sure he was going to say something to which she should not know what to reply. In another moment the strong pride that was in her came to conquer her sudden agitation, which she hoped he had not perceived. Of course she could answer, and answer the right thing; and it was poor and despicable of her to shrink from hearing any speech, as if she had not power to put an end to it with her high maidenly dignity.

'Margaret,' said he, taking her by surprise, and getting sudden possession of her hand, so that she was forced to stand still and listen, despising herself for the fluttering at her heart all the time; 'Margaret, I wish you did not like Helstone so much—did not seem so perfectly calm and happy here. I have been hoping for these three months past to find you regretting London—and London friends, a little—enough to make you listen more kindly' (for she was quietly, but firmly, striving to extricate her hand from his grasp) 'to one who has not much to offer, it is true—nothing but prospects in the future—but who does love you, Margaret, almost in spite of himself. Margaret, have I startled you too much? Speak!' For he saw her lips quivering almost as if she were going to cry. She made a strong effort to be calm; she would not speak till she had succeeded in mastering her voice, and then she said:

'I was startled. I did not know that you cared for me in that way. I have always thought of you as a friend; and, please, I would rather go on thinking of you so. I don't like to be spoken to as you have been doing. I cannot answer you as you want me to do, and yet I should feel so sorry if I vexed you.'

'Margaret,' said he, looking into her eyes, which met his with their open, straight look, expressive of the utmost good faith and reluctance to give pain.

'Do you'—he was going to say—'love any one else?' But it seemed as if this question would be an insult to the pure serenity of those eyes. 'Forgive me I have been too abrupt. I am punished. Only let me hope. Give me the poor comfort of telling me you have never seen any one whom you could—— ' Again a pause. He could not end his sentence. Margaret reproached herself acutely as the cause of his distress.

'Ah! if you had but never got this fancy into your head! It was such a pleasure to think of you as a friend.'

'But I may hope, may I not, Margaret, that some time you will think of me as a lover? Not yet, I see—there is no hurry—but some time—— ' She was silent for a minute or two, trying to discover the truth as it was in her own heart, before replying; then she said:

'I have never thought of—you, but as a friend. I like to think of you so; but I am sure I could never think of you as anything else. Pray, let us both forget that all this' ('disagreeable,' she was going to say, but stopped short) 'conversation has taken place.'

He paused before he replied. Then, in his habitual coldness of tone, he answered:

'Of course, as your feelings are so decided, and as this conversation has been so evidently unpleasant to you, it had better not be remembered. That is all very fine in theory, that plan of forgetting whatever is painful, but it will be somewhat difficult for me, at least, to carry it into execution.'

'You are vexed,' said she, sadly; 'yet how can I help it?'

She looked so truly grieved as she said this, that he struggled for a moment with his real disappointment, and then answered more cheerfully, but still with a little hardness in his tone:

'You should make allowances for the mortification, not only of a lover, Margaret, but of a man not given to romance in general—prudent, worldly, as some people call me—who has been carried out of his usual habits by the force of a passion—well, we will say no more of that; but in the one outlet which he has formed for the deeper and better feelings of his nature, he meets with rejection and repulse. I shall have to console myself with scorning my own folly. A struggling barrister to think of matrimony!'

Margaret could not answer this. The whole tone of it annoyed her. It seemed to touch on and call out all the points of difference which had often repelled her in him; while yet he was the pleasantest man, the most sympathising friend, the person of all others who understood her best in Harley Street. She felt a tinge of contempt mingle itself with her pain at having refused him. Her beautiful lip curled in a slight disdain. It was well that, having made the round of the garden, they came suddenly upon Mr. Hale, whose whereabouts had been quite forgotten by them. He had not yet finished the pear, which he had delicately peeled in one long strip of silver-paper thinness, and which he was enjoying in a deliberate manner. It was like the story of the eastern king, who dipped his head into a basin of water, at the magician's command, and ere he instantly took it out went through the experience of a lifetime. Margaret felt stunned, and unable to recover her self-possession enough to join in the trivial conversation that ensued between her father and Mr. Lennox. She was grave, and little disposed to speak; full of wonder when Mr. Lennox would go, and allow her to relax into thought on the events of the last quarter of an hour. He was almost as anxious to take his departure as she was for him to leave; but a few minutes light and careless talking, carried on at whatever effort, was a sacrifice which he owed to his mortified vanity, or his self-respect. He glanced from time to time at her sad and pensive face.

'I am not so indifferent to her as she believes,' thought he to himself. 'I do not give up hope.'

Before a quarter of an hour was over, he had fallen into a way of conversing with quiet sarcasm; speaking of life in London and life in the country, as if he were conscious of his second mocking self, and afraid of his own satire. Mr. Hale was puzzled. His visitor was a different man to what he had seen him before at the wedding-breakfast, and at dinner to-day; a lighter, cleverer, more worldly man, and, as such, dissonant to Mr. Hale. It was a relief to all three when Mr. Lennox said that he must go directly if he meant to catch the five o'clock train. They proceeded to the house to find Mrs. Hale, and wish her good-bye. At the last moment, Henry Lennox's real self broke through the crust.

'Margaret, don't despise me; I have a heart, notwithstanding all this good-for-nothing way of talking. As a proof of it, I believe I love you more than ever—if I do not hate you—for the disdain with which you have listened to me during this last half-hour. Good-bye, Margaret—Margaret!'

CHAPTER IV - DOUBTS AND DIFFICULTIES

'Cast me upon some naked shore,
Where I may tracke
Only the print of some sad wracke,
If thou be there, though the seas roare,
I shall no gentler calm implore.'
HABINGTON.

He was gone. The house was shut up for the evening. No more deep blue skies or crimson and amber tints. Margaret went up to dress for the early tea, finding Dixon in a pretty temper from the interruption which a visitor had naturally occasioned on a busy day. She showed it by brushing away viciously at Margaret's hair, under pretence of being in a great hurry to go to Mrs. Hale. Yet, after all, Margaret had to wait a long time in the drawing-room before her mother came down. She sat by herself at the fire, with unlighted candles on the table behind her, thinking over the day, the happy walk, happy sketching, cheerful pleasant dinner, and the uncomfortable, miserable walk in the garden.

How different men were to women! Here was she disturbed and unhappy, because her instinct had made anything but a refusal impossible; while he, not many minutes after he had met with a rejection of what ought to have been the deepest, holiest proposal of his life, could speak as if briefs, success, and all its superficial consequences of a good house, clever and agreeable society, were the sole avowed objects of his desires. Oh dear! how she could have loved him if he had but been different, with a difference which she felt, on reflection, to be one that went low—deep down. Then she took it into her head that, after all, his lightness might be but assumed, to cover a bitterness of disappointment which would have been stamped on her own heart if she had loved and been rejected.

Her mother came into the room before this whirl of thoughts was adjusted into anything like order. Margaret had to shake off the recollections of what had been done and said through the day, and turn a sympathising listener to the account of how Dixon had complained that the ironing-blanket had been burnt again; and how Susan Lightfoot had been seen with artificial flowers in her bonnet, thereby giving evidence of a vain and giddy character. Mr. Hale sipped his tea in abstracted silence; Margaret had the responses all to herself. She wondered how her father and mother could be so forgetful, so regardless of their companion through the day, as never to mention his name. She forgot that he had not made them an offer.

After tea Mr. Hale got up, and stood with his elbow on the chimney-piece, leaning his head on his hand, musing over something, and from time to time sighing deeply. Mrs. Hale went out to consult with Dixon about some winter clothing for the poor. Margaret was preparing her mother's worsted work, and rather shrinking from the thought of the long evening, and wishing bed-time were come that she might go over the events of the day again.

'Margaret!' said Mr. Hale, at last, in a sort of sudden desperate way, that made her start. 'Is that tapestry thing of immediate consequence? I mean, can you leave it and come into my study? I want to speak to you about something very serious to us all.'

'Very serious to us all.' Mr. Lennox had never had the opportunity of having any private conversation with her father after her refusal, or else that would indeed be a very serious affair. In the first place, Margaret felt guilty and ashamed of having grown so much into a woman as to be thought of in marriage; and secondly, she did not know if her father might not be displeased that she had taken upon herself to decline Mr. Lennox's proposal. But she soon felt it was not about anything, which having only lately and suddenly occurred, could have given rise to any complicated thoughts, that her father wished to speak to her. He made her take a chair by him; he stirred the fire, snuffed the candles, and sighed once or twice before he could make up his mind to say—and it came out with a jerk after all—'Margaret! I am going to leave Helstone.'

'Leave Helstone, papa! But why?'

Mr. Hale did not answer for a minute or two. He played with some papers on the table in a nervous and confused manner, opening his lips to speak several times, but closing them again without having the courage to utter a word. Margaret could not bear the sight of the suspense, which was even more distressing to her father than to herself.

'But why, dear papa? Do tell me!'

He looked up at her suddenly, and then said with a slow and enforced calmness:

'Because I must no longer be a minister in the Church of England.'

Margaret had imagined nothing less than that some of the preferments which her mother so much desired had befallen her father at last—something that would force him to leave beautiful, beloved Helstone, and perhaps compel him to go and live in some of the stately and silent Closes which Margaret had seen from time to time in cathedral towns. They were grand and imposing places, but if, to go there, it was necessary to leave Helstone as a home for ever, that would have been a sad, long, lingering pain. But nothing to the shock she received from Mr. Hale's last speech. What could he mean? It was all the worse for being so mysterious. The aspect of piteous distress on his face, almost as imploring a merciful and kind judgment from his child, gave her a sudden sickening. Could he have become implicated in anything Frederick had done? Frederick was an outlaw. Had her father, out of a natural love for his son, connived at any—

'Oh! what is it? do speak, papa! tell me all! Why can you no longer be a clergyman? Surely, if the bishop were told all we know about Frederick, and the hard, unjust—'

'It is nothing about Frederick; the bishop would have nothing to do with that. It is all myself. Margaret, I will tell you about it. I will answer any questions this once, but after to-night let us never speak of it again. I can meet the consequences of my painful, miserable doubts; but it is an effort beyond me to speak of what has caused me so much suffering.'

'Doubts, papa! Doubts as to religion?' asked Margaret, more shocked than ever.

'No! not doubts as to religion; not the slightest injury to that.' He paused. Margaret sighed, as if standing on the verge of some new horror. He began again, speaking rapidly, as if to get over a set task:

'You could not understand it all, if I told you—my anxiety, for years past, to know whether I had any right to hold my living—my efforts to quench my smouldering doubts by the authority of the Church. Oh! Margaret, how I love the holy Church from which I am to be shut out!' He could not go on for a moment or two. Margaret could not tell what to say; it seemed to her as terribly mysterious as if her father were about to turn Mahometan.

'I have been reading to-day of the two thousand who were ejected from their churches,'—continued Mr. Hale, smiling faintly,—'trying to steal some of their bravery; but it is of no use—no use—I cannot help feeling it acutely.'

'But, papa, have you well considered? Oh! it seems so terrible, so shocking,' said Margaret, suddenly bursting into tears. The one staid foundation of her home, of her idea of her beloved father, seemed reeling and rocking. What could she say? What was to be done? The sight of her distress made Mr. Hale nerve himself, in order to try and comfort her. He swallowed down the dry choking sobs which had been heaving up from his heart hitherto, and going to his bookcase he took down a volume, which he had often been reading lately, and from which he thought he had derived strength to enter upon the course in which he was now embarked.

'Listen, dear Margaret,' said he, putting one arm round her waist. She took his hand in hers and grasped it tight, but she could not lift up her head; nor indeed could she attend to what he read, so great was her internal agitation.

'This is the soliloquy of one who was once a clergyman in a country parish, like me; it was written by a Mr. Oldfield, minister of Carsington, in Derbyshire, a hundred and sixty years ago, or more. His trials are over. He fought the good fight.' These last two sentences he spoke low, as if to himself. Then he read aloud,—

'When thou canst no longer continue in thy work without dishonour to God, discredit to religion, foregoing thy integrity, wounding conscience, spoiling thy peace, and hazarding the loss of thy salvation; in a word, when the conditions upon which thou must continue (if thou wilt continue) in thy employments are sinful, and unwarranted by the word of God, thou mayest, yea, thou must believe that God will turn thy very silence, suspension, deprivation, and laying aside, to His glory, and the advancement of the Gospel's interest. When God will not use thee in one kind, yet He will in another. A soul that desires to serve and honour Him shall never want opportunity to do it; nor must thou so limit the Holy One of Israel as to think He hath but one way in which He can glorify Himself by thee. He can do it by thy silence as well as by thy preaching; thy laying aside as well as thy continuance in thy work. It is not pretence of doing God the greatest service, or performing the weightiest duty, that will excuse the least sin, though that sin capacitated or gave us the opportunity for doing that duty. Thou wilt have little thanks, O my soul! if, when thou art charged with corrupting God's worship, falsifying thy vows, thou pretendest a necessity for it in order to a continuance in the ministry. As he read this, and glanced at much more which he did not read, he gained resolution for himself, and felt as if he too could be brave and firm in doing what he believed to be right; but as he ceased he heard Margaret's low convulsive sob; and his courage sank down under the keen sense of suffering.

'Margaret, dear!' said he, drawing her closer, 'think of the early martyrs; think of the thousands who have suffered.'

'But, father,' said she, suddenly lifting up her flushed, tear-wet face, 'the early martyrs suffered for the truth, while you—oh! dear, dear papa!'

'I suffer for conscience' sake, my child,' said he, with a dignity that was only tremulous from the acute sensitiveness of his character; 'I must do what my conscience bids. I have borne long with self-reproach that would have roused any mind less torpid and cowardly than mine.' He shook his head as he went on. 'Your poor mother's fond wish, gratified at last in the mocking way in which over-fond wishes are too often fulfilled—Sodom apples as they are—has brought on this crisis, for which I ought to be, and I hope I am thankful. It is not a month since the bishop offered me another living; if I had accepted it, I should have had to make a fresh declaration of conformity to the Liturgy at my institution. Margaret, I tried to do it; I tried to content myself with simply refusing the additional preferment, and stopping quietly here,—strangling my conscience now, as I had strained it before. God forgive me!'

He rose and walked up and down the room, speaking low words of self-reproach and humiliation, of which Margaret was thankful to hear but few. At last he said,

'Margaret, I return to the old sad burden we must leave Helstone.'

'Yes! I see. But when?'

'I have written to the bishop—I dare say I have told you so, but I forget things just now,' said Mr. Hale, collapsing into his depressed manner as soon as he came to talk of hard matter-of-fact details, 'informing him of my intention to resign this vicarage. He has been most kind; he has used arguments and expostulations, all in vain—in vain. They are but what I have tried upon myself, without avail. I shall have to take my deed of resignation, and wait upon the bishop myself, to bid him farewell. That will be a trial, but worse, far worse, will be the parting from my dear people. There is a curate appointed to read prayers—a Mr. Brown. He will come to stay with us to-morrow. Next Sunday I preach my farewell sermon.'

Was it to be so sudden then? thought Margaret; and yet perhaps it was as well. Lingering would only add stings to the pain; it was better to be stunned into numbness by hearing of all these arrangements, which seemed to be nearly completed before she had been told. 'What does mamma say?' asked she, with a deep sigh.

To her surprise, her father began to walk about again before he answered. At length he stopped and replied:

'Margaret, I am a poor coward after all. I cannot bear to give pain. I know so well your mother's married life has not been all she hoped—all she had a right to expect—and this will be such a blow to her, that I have never had the heart, the power to tell her. She must be told though, now,' said he, looking wistfully at his daughter. Margaret was almost overpowered with the idea that her mother knew nothing of it all, and yet the affair was so far advanced!

'Yes, indeed she must,' said Margaret. 'Perhaps, after all, she may not—Oh yes! she will, she must be shocked'—as the force of the blow returned upon herself in trying to realise how another would take it. 'Where are we to go to?' said she at last, struck with a fresh wonder as to their future plans, if plans indeed her father had.

'To Milton-Northern,' he answered, with a dull indifference, for he had perceived that, although his daughter's love had made her cling to him, and for a moment strive to soothe him with her love, yet the keenness of the pain was as fresh as ever in her mind.

'Milton-Northern! The manufacturing town in Darkshire?'

'Yes,' said he, in the same despondent, indifferent way.

'Why there, papa?' asked she.

'Because there I can earn bread for my family. Because I know no one there, and no one knows Helstone, or can ever talk to me about it.'

'Bread for your family! I thought you and mamma had'—and then she stopped, checking her natural interest regarding their future life, as she saw the gathering gloom on her father's brow. But he, with his quick intuitive sympathy, read in her face, as in a mirror, the reflections of his own moody depression, and turned it off with an effort.

'You shall be told all, Margaret. Only help me to tell your mother. I think I could do anything but that: the idea of her distress turns me sick with dread. If I tell you all, perhaps you could break it to her to-morrow. I am going out for the day, to bid Farmer Dobson and the poor people on Bracy Common good-bye. Would you dislike breaking it to her very much, Margaret?'

Margaret did dislike it, did shrink from it more than from anything she had ever had to do in her life before. She could not speak, all at once. Her father said,

'You dislike it very much, don't you, Margaret?' Then she conquered herself, and said, with a bright strong look on her face:

'It is a painful thing, but it must be done, and I will do it as well as ever I can. You must have many painful things to do.'

Mr. Hale shook his head despondingly: he pressed her hand in token of gratitude. Margaret was nearly upset again into a burst of crying. To turn her thoughts, she said: 'Now tell me, papa, what our plans are. You and mamma have some money, independent of the income from the living, have not you? Aunt Shaw has, I know.'

'Yes. I suppose we have about a hundred and seventy pounds a year of our own. Seventy of that has always gone to Frederick, since he has been abroad. I don't know if he wants it all,' he continued in a hesitating manner. 'He must have some pay for serving with the Spanish army.'

'Frederick must not suffer,' said Margaret, decidedly; 'in a foreign country; so unjustly treated by his own. A hundred is left. Could not you, and I, and mamma live on a hundred a year in some very cheap—very quiet part of England? Oh! I think we could.'

'No!' said Mr. Hale. 'That would not answer. I must do something. I must make myself busy, to keep off morbid thoughts. Besides, in a country parish I should be so painfully reminded of Helstone, and my duties here. I could not bear it, Margaret. And a hundred a year would go a very little way, after the necessary wants of housekeeping are met, towards providing your mother with all the comforts she has been accustomed to, and ought to have. No: we must go to Milton. That is settled. I can always decide better by myself, and not influenced by those whom I love,' said he, as a half apology for having arranged so much before he had told any one of his family of his intentions. 'I cannot stand objections. They make me so undecided.'

Margaret resolved to keep silence. After all, what did it signify where they went, compared to the one terrible change?

Mr. Hale continued: 'A few months ago, when my misery of doubt became more than I could bear without speaking, I wrote to Mr. Bell—you remember Mr. Bell, Margaret?'

'No; I never saw him, I think. But I know who he is. Frederick's godfather—your old tutor at Oxford, don't you mean?'

'Yes. He is a Fellow of Plymouth College there. He is a native of Milton-Northern, I believe. At any rate, he has property there, which has very much increased in value since Milton has become such a large manufacturing town. Well, I had reason to suspect—to imagine—I had better say nothing about it, however. But I felt sure of sympathy from Mr. Bell. I don't know that he gave me much strength. He has lived an easy life in his college all his days. But he has been as kind as can be. And it is owing to him we are going to Milton.'

'How?' said Margaret.

'Why he has tenants, and houses, and mills there; so, though he dislikes the place—too bustling for one of his habits—he is obliged to keep up some sort of connection; and he tells me that he hears there is a good opening for a private tutor there.'

'A private tutor!' said Margaret, looking scornful: 'What in the world do manufacturers want with the classics, or literature, or the accomplishments of a gentleman?'

'Oh,' said her father, 'some of them really seem to be fine fellows, conscious of their own deficiencies, which is more than many a man at Oxford is. Some want resolutely to learn, though they have come to man's estate. Some want their children to be better instructed than they themselves have been. At any rate, there is an opening, as I have said, for a private tutor. Mr. Bell has recommended me to a Mr. Thornton, a tenant of his, and a very intelligent man, as far as I can judge from his letters. And in Milton, Margaret, I shall find a busy life, if not a happy one, and people and scenes so different that I shall never be reminded of Helstone.'

There was the secret motive, as Margaret knew from her own feelings. It would be different. Discordant as it was—with almost a detestation for all she had ever heard of the North of England, the manufacturers, the people, the wild and bleak country—there was this one recommendation—it would be different from Helstone, and could never remind them of that beloved place.

'When do we go?' asked Margaret, after a short silence.

'I do not know exactly. I wanted to talk it over with you. You see, your mother knows nothing about it yet: but I think, in a fortnight;—after my deed of resignation is sent in, I shall have no right to remain.

Margaret was almost stunned.

'In a fortnight!'

'No—no, not exactly to a day. Nothing is fixed,' said her father, with anxious hesitation, as he noticed the filmy sorrow that came over her eyes, and the sudden change in her complexion. But she recovered herself immediately.

'Yes, papa, it had better be fixed soon and decidedly, as you say. Only mamma to know nothing about it! It is that that is the great perplexity.'

'Poor Maria!' replied Mr. Hale, tenderly. 'Poor, poor Maria! Oh, if I were not married—if I were but myself in the world, how easy it would be! As it is—Margaret, I dare not tell her!'

'No,' said Margaret, sadly, 'I will do it. Give me till to-morrow evening to choose my time Oh, papa,' cried she, with sudden passionate entreaty, 'say—tell me it is a night-mare—a horrid dream—not the real waking truth! You cannot mean that you are really going to leave the Church—to give up Helstone—to be for ever separate from me, from mamma—led away by some delusion—some temptation! You do not really mean it!'

Mr. Hale sat in rigid stillness while she spoke.

Then he looked her in the face, and said in a slow, hoarse, measured way—'I do mean it, Margaret. You must not deceive yourself into doubting the reality of my words—my fixed intention and resolve.' He looked at her in the same steady, stony manner, for some moments after he had done speaking. She, too, gazed back with pleading eyes before she would believe that it was irrevocable. Then she arose and went, without another word or look, towards the door. As her fingers were on the handle he called her back. He was standing by the fireplace, shrunk and stooping; but as she came near he drew himself up to his full height, and, placing his hands on her head, he said, solemnly:

'The blessing of God be upon thee, my child!'

'And may He restore you to His Church,' responded she, out of the fulness of her heart. The next moment she feared lest this answer to his blessing might be irreverent, wrong—might hurt him as coming from his daughter, and she threw her arms round his neck. He held her to him for a minute or two. She heard him murmur to himself, 'The martyrs and confessors had even more pain to bear—I will not shrink.'

They were startled by hearing Mrs. Hale inquiring for her daughter. They started asunder in the full consciousness of all that was before them. Mr. Hale hurriedly said—'Go, Margaret, go. I shall be out all to-morrow. Before night you will have told your mother.'

'Yes,' she replied, and she returned to the drawing-room in a stunned and dizzy state.

CHAPTER V - DECISION

'I ask Thee for a thoughtful love,
 Through constant watching wise,
 To meet the glad with joyful smiles,
 And to wipe the weeping eyes;
 And a heart at leisure from itself
  To soothe and sympathise.'
   ANON.

Margaret made a good listener to all her mother's little plans for adding some small comforts to the lot of the poorer parishioners. She could not help listening, though each new project was a stab to her heart. By the time the frost had set in, they should be far away from Helstone. Old Simon's rheumatism might be bad and his eyesight worse; there would be no one to go and read to him, and comfort him with little porringers of broth and good red flannel: or if there was, it would be a stranger, and the old man would watch in vain for her. Mary Domville's little crippled boy would crawl in vain to the door and look for her coming through the forest. These poor friends would never understand why she had forsaken them; and there were many others besides. 'Papa has always spent the income he derived from his living in the parish. I am, perhaps, encroaching upon the next dues, but the winter is likely to be severe, and our poor old people must be helped.'

'Oh, mamma, let us do all we can,' said Margaret eagerly, not seeing the prudential side of the question, only grasping at the idea that they were rendering such help for the last time; 'we may not be here long.'

'Do you feel ill, my darling?' asked Mrs. Hale, anxiously, misunderstanding Margaret's hint of the uncertainty of their stay at Helstone. 'You look pale and tired. It is this soft, damp, unhealthy air.'

'No—no, mamma, it is not that: it is delicious air. It smells of the freshest, purest fragrance, after the smokiness of Harley Street. But I am tired: it surely must be near bedtime.'

'Not far off—it is half-past nine. You had better go to bed at once dear. Ask Dixon for some gruel. I will come and see you as soon as you are in bed. I am afraid you have taken cold; or the bad air from some of the stagnant ponds—'

'Oh, mamma,' said Margaret, faintly smiling as she kissed her mother, 'I am quite well—don't alarm yourself about me; I am only tired.'

Margaret went upstairs. To soothe her mother's anxiety she submitted to a basin of gruel. She was lying languidly in bed when Mrs. Hale came up to make some last inquiries and kiss her before going to her own room for the night. But the instant she heard her mother's door locked, she sprang out of bed, and throwing her dressing-gown on, she began to pace up and down the room, until the creaking of one of the boards reminded her that she must make no noise. She went and curled herself up on the window-seat in the small, deeply-recessed window. That morning when she had looked out, her heart had danced at seeing the bright clear lights on the church tower, which foretold a fine and sunny day. This evening—sixteen hours at most had past by—she sat down, too full of sorrow to cry, but with a dull cold pain, which seemed to have pressed the youth and buoyancy out of her heart, never to return. Mr. Henry Lennox's visit—his offer—was like a dream, a thing beside her actual life. The hard reality was, that her father had so admitted tempting doubts into his mind as to become a schismatic—an outcast; all the changes consequent upon this grouped themselves around that one great blighting fact.

She looked out upon the dark-gray lines of the church tower, square and straight in the centre of the view, cutting against the deep blue transparent depths beyond, into which she gazed, and felt that she might gaze for ever, seeing at every moment some farther distance, and yet no sign of God! It seemed to her at the moment, as if the earth was more utterly desolate than if girt in by an iron dome, behind which there might be the ineffaceable peace and glory of the Almighty: those never-ending depths of space, in their still serenity, were more mocking to her than any material bounds could be—shutting in the cries of earth's sufferers, which now might ascend into that infinite splendour of vastness and be lost—lost for ever, before they reached His throne. In this mood her father came in unheard. The moonlight was strong enough to let him see his daughter in her unusual place and attitude. He came to her and touched her shoulder before she was aware that he was there.

'Margaret, I heard you were up. I could not help coming in to ask you to pray with me—to say the Lord's Prayer; that will do good to both of us.'

Mr. Hale and Margaret knelt by the window-seat—he looking up, she bowed down in humble shame. God was there, close around them, hearing her father's whispered words. Her father might be a heretic; but had not she, in her despairing doubts not five minutes before, shown herself a far more utter sceptic? She spoke not a word, but stole to bed after her father had left her, like a child ashamed of its fault. If the world was full of perplexing problems she would trust, and only ask to see the one step needful for the hour. Mr. Lennox—his visit, his proposal—the remembrance of which had been so rudely pushed aside by the subsequent events of the day—haunted her dreams that night. He was climbing up some tree of fabulous height to reach the branch whereon was slung her bonnet: he was falling, and she was struggling to save him, but held back by some invisible powerful hand.

He was dead. And yet, with a shifting of the scene, she was once more in the Harley Street drawing-room, talking to him as of old, and still with a consciousness all the time that she had seen him killed by that terrible fall.

Miserable, unresting night! Ill preparation for the coming day! She awoke with a start, unrefreshed, and conscious of some reality worse even than her feverish dreams. It all came back upon her; not merely the sorrow, but the terrible discord in the sorrow. Where, to what distance apart, had her father wandered, led by doubts which were to her temptations of the Evil One? She longed to ask, and yet would not have heard for all the world.

The fine crisp morning made her mother feel particularly well and happy at breakfast-time. She talked on, planning village kindnesses, unheeding the silence of her husband and the monosyllabic answers of Margaret. Before the things were cleared away, Mr. Hale got up; he leaned one hand on the table, as if to support himself:

'I shall not be at home till evening. I am going to Bracy Common, and will ask Farmer Dobson to give me something for dinner. I shall be back to tea at seven.' He did not look at either of them, but Margaret knew what he meant. By seven the announcement must be made to her mother. Mr. Hale would have delayed making it till half-past six, but Margaret was of different stuff. She could not bear the impending weight on her mind all the day long: better get the worst over; the day would be too short to comfort her mother. But while she stood by the window, thinking how to begin, and waiting for the servant to have left the room, her mother had gone up-stairs to put on her things to go to the school. She came down ready equipped, in a brisker mood than usual.

'Mother, come round the garden with me this morning; just one turn,' said Margaret, putting her arm round Mrs. Hale's waist.

They passed through the open window. Mrs. Hale spoke—said something—Margaret could not tell what. Her eye caught on a bee entering a deep-belled flower: when that bee flew forth with his spoil she would begin—that should be the sign. Out he came.

'Mamma! Papa is going to leave Helstone!' she blurted forth. 'He's going to leave the Church, and live in Milton-Northern.' There were the three hard facts hardly spoken.

'What makes you say so?' asked Mrs. Hale, in a surprised incredulous voice. 'Who has been telling you such nonsense?'

'Papa himself,' said Margaret, longing to say something gentle and consoling, but literally not knowing how. They were close to a garden-bench. Mrs. Hale sat down, and began to cry.

'I don't understand you,' she said. 'Either you have made some great mistake, or I don't quite understand you.'

'No, mother, I have made no mistake. Papa has written to the bishop, saying that he has such doubts that he cannot conscientiously remain a priest of the Church of England, and that he must give up Helstone. He has also consulted Mr. Bell—Frederick's godfather, you know, mamma; and it is arranged that we go to live in Milton-Northern.' Mrs. Hale looked up in Margaret's face all the time she was speaking these words: the shadow on her countenance told that she, at least, believed in the truth of what she said.

'I don't think it can be true,' said Mrs. Hale, at length. 'He would surely have told me before it came to this.'

It came strongly upon Margaret's mind that her mother ought to have been told: that whatever her faults of discontent and repining might have been, it was an error in her father to have left her to learn his change of opinion, and his approaching change of life, from her better-informed child. Margaret sat down by her mother, and took her unresisting head on her breast, bending her own soft cheeks down caressingly to touch her face.

'Dear, darling mamma! we were so afraid of giving you pain. Papa felt so acutely—you know you are not strong, and there must have been such terrible suspense to go through.'

'When did he tell you, Margaret?'

'Yesterday, only yesterday,' replied Margaret, detecting the jealousy which prompted the inquiry. 'Poor papa!'—trying to divert her mother's thoughts into compassionate sympathy for all her father had gone through. Mrs. Hale raised her head.

'What does he mean by having doubts?' she asked. 'Surely, he does not mean that he thinks differently—that he knows better than the Church.' Margaret shook her head, and the tears came into her eyes, as her mother touched the bare nerve of her own regret.

'Can't the bishop set him right?' asked Mrs. Hale, half impatiently.

'I'm afraid not,' said Margaret. 'But I did not ask. I could not bear to hear what he might answer. It is all settled at any rate. He is going to leave Helstone in a fortnight. I am not sure if he did not say he had sent in his deed of resignation.'

'In a fortnight!' exclaimed Mrs. Hale, 'I do think this is very strange—not at all right. I call it very unfeeling,' said she, beginning to take relief in tears. 'He has doubts, you say, and gives up his living, and all without consulting me. I dare say, if he had told me his doubts at the first I could have nipped them in the bud.'

Mistaken as Margaret felt her father's conduct to have been, she could not bear to hear it blamed by her mother. She knew that his very reserve had originated in a tenderness for her, which might be cowardly, but was not unfeeling.

'I almost hoped you might have been glad to leave Helstone, mamma,' said she, after a pause. 'You have never been well in this air, you know.'

'You can't think the smoky air of a manufacturing town, all chimneys and dirt like Milton-Northern, would be better than this air, which is pure and sweet, if it is too soft and relaxing. Fancy living in the middle of factories, and factory people! Though, of course, if your father leaves the Church, we shall not be admitted into society anywhere. It will be such a disgrace to us! Poor dear Sir John! It is well he is not alive to see what your father has come to! Every day after dinner, when I was a girl, living with your aunt Shaw, at Beresford Court, Sir John used to give for the first toast—"Church and King, and down with the Rump."'

Margaret was glad that her mother's thoughts were turned away from the fact of her husband's silence to her on the point which must have been so near his heart. Next to the serious vital anxiety as to the nature of her father's doubts, this was the one circumstance of the case that gave Margaret the most pain.

'You know, we have very little society here, mamma. The Gormans, who are our nearest neighbours (to call society—and we hardly ever see them), have been in trade just as much as these Milton-Northern people.'

'Yes,' said Mrs. Hale, almost indignantly, 'but, at any rate, the Gormans made carriages for half the gentry of the county, and were brought into some kind of intercourse with them; but these factory people, who on earth wears cotton that can afford linen?'

'Well, mamma, I give up the cotton-spinners; I am not standing up for them, any more than for any other trades-people. Only we shall have little enough to do with them.'

'Why on earth has your father fixed on Milton-Northern to live in?'

'Partly,' said Margaret, sighing, 'because it is so very different from Helstone—partly because Mr. Bell says there is an opening there for a private tutor.'

'Private tutor in Milton! Why can't he go to Oxford, and be a tutor to gentlemen?'

'You forget, mamma! He is leaving the Church on account of his opinions—his doubts would do him no good at Oxford.'

Mrs. Hale was silent for some time, quietly crying. At last she said:—

'And the furniture—How in the world are we to manage the removal? I never removed in my life, and only a fortnight to think about it!'

Margaret was inexpressibly relieved to find that her mother's anxiety and distress was lowered to this point, so insignificant to herself, and on which she could do so much to help. She planned and promised, and led her mother on to arrange fully as much as could be fixed before they knew somewhat more definitively what Mr. Hale intended to do. Throughout the day Margaret never left her mother; bending her whole soul to sympathise in all the various turns her feelings took; towards evening especially, as she became more and more anxious that her father should find a soothing welcome home awaiting him, after his return from his day of fatigue and distress. She dwelt upon what he must have borne in secret for long; her mother only replied coldly that he ought to have told her, and that then at any rate he would have had an adviser to give him counsel; and Margaret turned faint at heart when she heard her father's step in the hall. She dared not go to meet him, and tell him what she had done all day, for fear of her mother's jealous annoyance. She heard him linger, as if awaiting her, or some sign of her; and she dared not stir; she saw by her mother's twitching lips, and changing colour, that she too was aware that her husband had returned. Presently he opened the room-door, and stood there uncertain whether to come in. His face was gray and pale; he had a timid, fearful look in his eyes; something almost pitiful to see in a man's face; but that look of despondent uncertainty, of mental and bodily languor, touched his wife's heart. She went to him, and threw herself on his breast, crying out—

'Oh! Richard, Richard, you should have told me sooner!'

And then, in tears, Margaret left her, as she rushed up-stairs to throw herself on her bed, and hide her face in the pillows to stifle the hysteric sobs that would force their way at last, after the rigid self-control of the whole day. How long she lay thus she could not tell. She heard no noise, though the housemaid came in to arrange the room. The affrighted girl stole out again on tip-toe, and went and told Mrs. Dixon that Miss Hale was crying as if her heart would break: she was sure she would make herself deadly ill if she went on at that rate. In consequence of this, Margaret felt herself touched, and started up into a sitting posture; she saw the accustomed room, the figure of Dixon in shadow, as the latter stood holding the candle a little behind her, for fear of the effect on Miss Hale's startled eyes, swollen and blinded as they were.

'Oh, Dixon! I did not hear you come into the room!' said Margaret, resuming her trembling self-restraint. 'Is it very late?' continued she, lifting herself languidly off the bed, yet letting her feet touch the ground without fairly standing down, as she shaded her wet ruffled hair off her face, and tried to look as though nothing were the matter; as if she had only been asleep.

'I hardly can tell what time it is,' replied Dixon, in an aggrieved tone of voice. 'Since your mamma told me this terrible news, when I dressed her for tea, I've lost all count of time. I'm sure I don't know what is to become of us all. When Charlotte told me just now you were sobbing, Miss Hale, I thought, no wonder, poor thing! And master thinking of turning Dissenter at his time of life, when, if it is not to be said he's done well in the Church, he's not done badly after all. I had a cousin, miss, who turned Methodist preacher after he was fifty years of age, and a tailor all his life; but then he had never been able to make a pair of trousers to fit, for as long as he had been in the trade, so it was no wonder; but for master! as I said to missus, "What would poor Sir John have said? he never liked your marrying Mr. Hale, but if he could have known it would have come to this, he would have sworn worse oaths than ever, if that was possible!"'

Dixon had been so much accustomed to comment upon Mr. Hale's proceedings to her mistress (who listened to her, or not, as she was in the humour), that she never noticed Margaret's flashing eye and dilating nostril. To hear her father talked of in this way by a servant to her face!

'Dixon,' she said, in the low tone she always used when much excited, which had a sound in it as of some distant turmoil, or threatening storm breaking far away. 'Dixon! you forget to whom you are speaking.' She stood upright and firm on her feet now, confronting the waiting-maid, and fixing her with her steady discerning eye. 'I am Mr. Hale's daughter. Go! You have made a strange mistake, and one that I am sure your own good feeling will make you sorry for when you think about it.'

Dixon hung irresolutely about the room for a minute or two. Margaret repeated, 'You may leave me, Dixon. I wish you to go.' Dixon did not know whether to resent these decided words or to cry; either course would have done with her mistress: but, as she said to herself, 'Miss Margaret has a touch of the old gentleman about her, as well as poor Master Frederick; I wonder where they get it from?' and she, who would have resented such words from any one less haughty and determined in manner, was subdued enough to say, in a half humble, half injured tone:

'Mayn't I unfasten your gown, miss, and do your hair?'

'No! not to-night, thank you.' And Margaret gravely lighted her out of the room, and bolted the door. From henceforth Dixon obeyed and admired Margaret. She said it was because she was so like poor Master Frederick; but the truth was, that Dixon, as do many others, liked to feel herself ruled by a powerful and decided nature.

Margaret needed all Dixon's help in action, and silence in words; for, for some time, the latter thought it her duty to show her sense of affront by saying as little as possible to her young lady; so the energy came out in doing rather than in speaking. A fortnight was a very short time to make arrangements for so serious a removal; as Dixon said, 'Any one but a gentleman—indeed almost any other gentleman—' but catching a look at Margaret's straight, stern brow just here, she coughed the remainder of the sentence away, and meekly took the horehound drop that Margaret offered her, to stop the 'little tickling at my chest, miss.' But almost any one but Mr. Hale would have had practical knowledge enough to see, that in so short a time it would be difficult to fix on any house in Milton-Northern, or indeed elsewhere, to which they could remove the furniture that had of necessity to be taken out of Helstone vicarage. Mrs. Hale, overpowered by all the troubles and necessities for immediate household decisions that seemed to come upon her at once, became really ill, and Margaret almost felt it as a relief when her mother fairly took to her bed, and left the management of affairs to her. Dixon, true to her post of body-guard, attended most faithfully to her mistress, and only emerged from Mrs. Hale's bed-room to shake her head, and murmur to herself in a manner which Margaret did not choose to hear. For, the one thing clear and straight before her, was the necessity for leaving Helstone. Mr. Hale's successor in the living was appointed; and, at any rate, after her father's decision; there must be no lingering now, for his sake, as well as from every other consideration. For he came home every evening more and more depressed, after the necessary leave-taking which he had resolved to have with every individual parishioner. Margaret, inexperienced as she was in all the necessary matter-of-fact business to be got through, did not know to whom to apply for advice. The cook and Charlotte worked away with willing arms and stout hearts at all the moving and packing; and as far as that went, Margaret's admirable sense enabled her to see what was best, and to direct how it should be done. But where were they to go to? In a week they must be gone. Straight to Milton, or where? So many arrangements depended on this decision that Margaret resolved to ask her father one evening, in spite of his evident fatigue and low spirits. He answered:

'My dear! I have really had too much to think about to settle this. What does your mother say? What does she wish? Poor Maria!'

He met with an echo even louder than his sigh. Dixon had just come into the room for another cup of tea for Mrs. Hale, and catching Mr. Hale's last words, and protected by his presence from Margaret's upbraiding eyes, made bold to say, 'My poor mistress!'

'You don't think her worse to-day,' said Mr. Hale, turning hastily.

'I'm sure I can't say, sir. It's not for me to judge. The illness seems so much more on the mind than on the body.'

Mr. Hale looked infinitely distressed.

'You had better take mamma her tea while it is hot, Dixon,' said Margaret, in a tone of quiet authority.

'Oh! I beg your pardon, miss! My thoughts was otherwise occupied in thinking of my poor—— of Mrs. Hale.'

'Papa!' said Margaret, 'it is this suspense that is bad for you both. Of course, mamma must feel your change of opinions: we can't help that,' she continued, softly; 'but now the course is clear, at least to a certain point. And I think, papa, that I could get mamma to help me in planning, if you could tell me what to plan for. She has never expressed any wish in any way, and only thinks of what can't be helped. Are we to go straight to Milton? Have you taken a house there?'

'No,' he replied. 'I suppose we must go into lodgings, and look about for a house.

'And pack up the furniture so that it can be left at the railway station, till we have met with one?'

'I suppose so. Do what you think best. Only remember, we shall have much less money to spend.'

They had never had much superfluity, as Margaret knew. She felt that it was a great weight suddenly thrown upon her shoulders. Four months ago, all the decisions she needed to make were what dress she would wear for dinner, and to help Edith to draw out the lists of who should take down whom in the dinner parties at home. Nor was the household in which she lived one that called for much decision. Except in the one grand case of Captain Lennox's offer, everything went on with the regularity of clockwork. Once a year, there was a long discussion between her aunt and Edith as to whether they should go to the Isle of Wight, abroad, or to Scotland; but at such times Margaret herself was secure of drifting, without any exertion of her own, into the quiet harbour of home. Now, since that day when Mr. Lennox came, and startled her into a decision, every day brought some question, momentous to her, and to those whom she loved, to be settled.

Her father went up after tea to sit with his wife. Margaret remained alone in the drawing-room. Suddenly she took a candle and went into her father's study for a great atlas, and lugging it back into the drawing-room, she began to pore over the map of England. She was ready to look up brightly when her father came down stairs.

'I have hit upon such a beautiful plan. Look here—in Darkshire, hardly the breadth of my finger from Milton, is Heston, which I have often heard of from people living in the north as such a pleasant little bathing-place. Now, don't you think we could get mamma there with Dixon, while you and I go and look at houses, and get one all ready for her in Milton? She would get a breath of sea air to set her up for the winter, and be spared all the fatigue, and Dixon would enjoy taking care of her.'

'Is Dixon to go with us?' asked Mr. Hale, in a kind of helpless dismay.

'Oh, yes!' said Margaret. 'Dixon quite intends it, and I don't know what mamma would do without her.'

'But we shall have to put up with a very different way of living, I am afraid. Everything is so much dearer in a town. I doubt if Dixon can make herself comfortable. To tell you the truth Margaret, I sometimes feel as if that woman gave herself airs.'

'To be sure she does, papa,' replied Margaret; 'and if she has to put up with a different style of living, we shall have to put up with her airs, which will be worse. But she really loves us all, and would be miserable to leave us, I am sure—especially in this change; so, for mamma's sake, and for the sake of her faithfulness, I do think she must go.'

'Very well, my dear. Go on. I am resigned. How far is Heston from Milton? The breadth of one of your fingers does not give me a very clear idea of distance.'

'Well, then, I suppose it is thirty miles; that is not much!'

'Not in distance, but in—. Never mind! If you really think it will do your mother good, let it be fixed so.'

This was a great step. Now Margaret could work, and act, and plan in good earnest. And now Mrs. Hale could rouse herself from her languor, and forget her real suffering in thinking of the pleasure and the delight of going to the sea-side. Her only regret was that Mr. Hale could not be with her all the fortnight she was to be there, as he had been for a whole fortnight once, when they were engaged, and she was staying with Sir John and Lady Beresford at Torquay.

CHAPTER VI - FAREWELL

'Unwatch'd the garden bough shall sway,
The tender blossom flutter down,
Unloved that beech will gather brown,
The maple burn itself away;

Unloved, the sun-flower, shining fair,
Ray round with flames her disk of seed,
And many a rose-carnation feed
With summer spice the humming air;

* * * * * *

Till from the garden and the wild
A fresh association blow,
And year by year the landscape grow
Familiar to the stranger's child;

As year by year the labourer tills
His wonted glebe, or lops the glades;
And year by year our memory fades
From all the circle of the hills.'

TENNYSON.

The last day came; the house was full of packing-cases, which were being carted off at the front door, to the nearest railway station. Even the pretty lawn at the side of the house was made unsightly and untidy by the straw that had been wafted upon it through the open door and windows. The rooms had a strange echoing sound in them,—and the light came harshly and strongly in through the uncurtained windows,—seeming already unfamiliar and strange. Mrs. Hale's dressing-room was left untouched to the last; and there she and Dixon were packing up clothes, and interrupting each other every now and then to exclaim at, and turn over with fond regard, some forgotten treasure, in the shape of some relic of the children while they were yet little. They did not make much progress with their work. Down-stairs, Margaret stood calm and collected, ready to counsel or advise the men who had been called in to help the cook and Charlotte. These two last, crying between whiles, wondered how the young lady could keep up so this last day, and settled it between them that she was not likely to care much for Helstone, having been so long in London. There she stood, very pale and quiet, with her large grave eyes observing everything,—up to every present circumstance, however small. They could not understand how her heart was aching all the time, with a heavy pressure that no sighs could lift off or relieve, and how constant exertion for her perceptive faculties was the only way to keep herself from crying out with pain. Moreover, if she gave way, who was to act? Her father was examining papers, books, registers, what not, in the vestry with the clerk; and when he came in, there were his own books to pack up, which no one but himself could do to his satisfaction. Besides, was Margaret one to give way before strange men, or even household friends like the cook and Charlotte! Not she. But at last the four packers went into the kitchen to their tea; and Margaret moved stiffly and slowly away from the place in the hall where she had been standing so long, out through the bare echoing drawing-room, into the twilight of an early November evening. There was a filmy veil of soft dull mist obscuring, but not hiding, all objects, giving them a lilac hue, for the sun had not yet fully set; a robin was singing,—perhaps, Margaret thought, the very robin that her father had so often talked of as his winter pet, and for which he had made, with his own hands, a kind of robin-house by his study-window. The leaves were more gorgeous than ever; the first touch of frost would lay them all low on the ground. Already one or two kept constantly floating down, amber and golden in the low slanting sun-rays.

Margaret went along the walk under the pear-tree wall. She had never been along it since she paced it at Henry Lennox's side. Here, at this bed of thyme, he began to speak of what she must not think of now. Her eyes were on that late-blowing rose as she was trying to answer; and she had caught the idea of the vivid beauty of the feathery leaves of the carrots in the very middle of his last sentence. Only a fortnight ago! And all so changed! Where was he now? In London,—going through the old round; dining with the old Harley Street set, or with gayer young friends of his own. Even now, while she walked sadly through that damp and drear garden in the dusk, with everything falling and fading, and turning to decay around her, he might be gladly putting away his law-books after a day of satisfactory toil, and freshening himself up, as he had told her he often did, by a run in the Temple Gardens, taking in the while the grand inarticulate mighty roar of tens of thousands of busy men, nigh at hand, but not seen, and catching ever, at his quick turns, glimpses of the lights of the city coming up out of the depths of the river. He had often spoken to Margaret of these hasty walks, snatched in the intervals between study and dinner. At his best times and in his best moods had he spoken of them; and the thought of them had struck upon her fancy. Here there was no sound. The robin had gone away into the vast stillness of night. Now and then, a cottage door in the distance was opened and shut, as if to admit the tired labourer to his home; but that sounded very far away. A stealthy, creeping, cranching sound among the crisp fallen leaves of the forest, beyond the garden, seemed almost close at hand. Margaret knew it was some poacher. Sitting up in her bed-room this past autumn, with the light of her candle extinguished, and purely revelling in the solemn beauty of the heavens and the earth, she had many a time seen the light noiseless leap of the poachers over the garden-fence, their quick tramp across the dewy moonlit lawn, their disappearance in the black still shadow beyond. The wild adventurous freedom of their life had taken her fancy; she felt inclined to wish them success; she had no fear of them. But to-night she was afraid, she knew not why. She heard Charlotte shutting the windows, and fastening up for the night, unconscious that any one had gone out into the garden. A small branch—it might be of rotten wood, or it might be broken by force—came heavily down in the nearest part of the forest, Margaret ran, swift as Camilla, down to the window, and rapped at it with a hurried tremulousness which startled Charlotte within.

'Let me in! Let me in! It is only me, Charlotte!' Her heart did not still its fluttering till she was safe in the drawing-room, with the windows fastened and bolted, and the familiar walls hemming her round, and shutting her in. She had sate down upon a packing case; cheerless, Chill was the dreary and dismantled room—no fire nor other light, but Charlotte's long unsnuffed candle. Charlotte looked at Margaret with surprise; and Margaret, feeling it rather than seeing it, rose up.

'I was afraid you were shutting me out altogether, Charlotte,' said she, half-smiling. 'And then you would never have heard me in the kitchen, and the doors into the lane and churchyard are locked long ago.'

'Oh, miss, I should have been sure to have missed you soon. The men would have wanted you to tell them how to go on. And I have put tea in master's study, as being the most comfortable room, so to speak.'

'Thank you, Charlotte. You are a kind girl. I shall be sorry to leave you. You must try and write to me, if I can ever give you any little help or good advice. I shall always be glad to get a letter from Helstone, you know. I shall be sure and send you my address when I know it.'

The study was all ready for tea. There was a good blazing fire, and unlighted candles on the table. Margaret sat down on the rug, partly to warm herself, for the dampness of the evening hung about her dress, and over-fatigue had made her chilly. She kept herself balanced by clasping her hands together round her knees; her head dropped a little towards her chest; the attitude was one of despondency, whatever her frame of mind might be. But when she heard her father's step on the gravel outside, she started up, and hastily shaking her heavy black hair back, and wiping a few tears away that had come on her cheeks she knew not how, she went out to open the door for him. He showed far more depression than she did. She could hardly get him to talk, although she tried to speak on subjects that would interest him, at the cost of an effort every time which she thought would be her last.

'Have you been a very long walk to-day?' asked she, on seeing his refusal to touch food of any kind.

'As far as Fordham Beeches. I went to see Widow Maltby; she is sadly grieved at not having wished you good-bye. She says little Susan has kept watch down the lane for days past.—Nay, Margaret, what is the matter, dear?' The thought of the little child watching for her, and continually disappointed—from no forgetfulness on her part, but from sheer inability to leave home—was the last drop in poor Margaret's cup, and she was sobbing away as if her heart would break. Mr. Hale was distressingly perplexed. He rose, and walked nervously up and down the room. Margaret tried to check herself, but would not speak until she could do so with firmness. She heard him talking, as if to himself.

'I cannot bear it. I cannot bear to see the sufferings of others. I think I could go through my own with patience. Oh, is there no going back?'

'No, father,' said Margaret, looking straight at him, and speaking low and steadily. 'It is bad to believe you in error. It would be infinitely worse to have known you a hypocrite.' She dropped her voice at the last few words, as if entertaining the idea of hypocrisy for a moment in connection with her father savoured of irreverence.

'Besides,' she went on, 'it is only that I am tired to-night; don't think that I am suffering from what you have done, dear papa. We can't either of us talk about it to-night, I believe,' said she, finding that tears and sobs would come in spite of herself. 'I had better go and take mamma up this cup of tea. She had hers very early, when I was too busy to go to her, and I am sure she will be glad of another now.'

Railroad time inexorably wrenched them away from lovely, beloved Helstone, the next morning. They were gone; they had seen the last of the long low parsonage home, half-covered with China-roses and pyracanthus—more homelike than ever in the morning sun that glittered on its windows, each belonging to some well-loved room. Almost before they had settled themselves into the car, sent from Southampton to fetch them to the station, they were gone away to return no more. A sting at Margaret's heart made her strive to look out to catch the last glimpse of the old church tower at the turn where she knew it might be seen above a wave of the forest trees; but her father remembered this too, and she silently acknowledged his greater right to the one window from which it could be seen. She leant back and shut her eyes, and the tears welled forth, and hung glittering for an instant on the shadowing eye-lashes before rolling slowly down her cheeks, and dropping, unheeded, on her dress.

They were to stop in London all night at some quiet hotel. Poor Mrs. Hale had cried in her way nearly all day long; and Dixon showed her sorrow by extreme crossness, and a continual irritable attempt to keep her petticoats from even touching the unconscious Mr. Hale, whom she regarded as the origin of all this suffering.

They went through the well-known streets, past houses which they had often visited, past shops in which she had lounged, impatient, by her aunt's side, while that lady was making some important and interminable decision-nay, absolutely past acquaintances in the streets; for though the morning had been of an incalculable length to them, and they felt as if it ought long ago to have closed in for the repose of darkness, it was the very busiest time of a London afternoon in November when they arrived there. It was long since Mrs. Hale had been in London; and she roused up, almost like a child, to look about her at the different streets, and to gaze after and exclaim at the shops and carriages.

'Oh, there's Harrison's, where I bought so many of my wedding-things. Dear! how altered! They've got immense plate-glass windows, larger than Crawford's in Southampton. Oh, and there, I declare—no, it is not—yes, it is—Margaret, we have just passed Mr. Henry Lennox. Where can he be going, among all these shops?'

Margaret started forwards, and as quickly fell back, half-smiling at herself for the sudden motion. They were a hundred yards away by this time; but he seemed like a relic of Helstone—he was associated with a bright morning, an eventful day, and she should have liked to have seen him, without his seeing her,—without the chance of their speaking.

The evening, without employment, passed in a room high up in an hotel, was long and heavy. Mr. Hale went out to his bookseller's, and to call on a friend or two. Every one they saw, either in the house or out in the streets, appeared hurrying to some appointment, expected by, or expecting somebody. They alone seemed strange and friendless, and desolate. Yet within a mile, Margaret knew of house after house, where she for her own sake, and her mother for her aunt Shaw's, would be welcomed, if they came in gladness, or even in peace of mind. If they came sorrowing, and wanting sympathy in a complicated trouble like the present, then they would be felt as a shadow in all these houses of intimate acquaintances, not friends. London life is too whirling and full to admit of even an hour of that deep silence of feeling which the friends of Job showed, when 'they sat with him on the ground seven days and seven nights, and none spake a word unto him; for they saw that his grief was very great.'

CHAPTER VII - NEW SCENES AND FACES

'Mist clogs the sunshine,
Smoky dwarf houses
Have we round on every side.'
MATTHEW ARNOLD.

The next afternoon, about twenty miles from Milton-Northern, they entered on the little branch railway that led to Heston. Heston itself was one long straggling street, running parallel to the seashore. It had a character of its own, as different from the little bathing-places in the south of England as they again from those of the continent. To use a Scotch word, every thing looked more 'purposelike.' The country carts had more iron, and less wood and leather about the horse-gear; the people in the streets, although on pleasure bent, had yet a busy mind. The colours looked grayer—more enduring, not so gay and pretty. There were no smock-frocks, even among the country folk; they retarded motion, and were apt to catch on machinery, and so the habit of wearing them had died out. In such towns in the south of England, Margaret had seen the shopmen, when not employed in their business, lounging a little at their doors, enjoying the fresh air, and the look up and down the street. Here, if they had any leisure from customers, they made themselves business in the shop—even, Margaret fancied, to the unnecessary un-rolling and rerolling of ribbons. All these differences struck upon her mind, as she and her mother went out next morning to look for lodgings.

Their two nights at hotels had cost more than Mr. Hale had anticipated, and they were glad to take the first clean, cheerful rooms they met with that were at liberty to receive them. There, for the first time for many days, did Margaret feel at rest. There was a dreaminess in the rest, too, which made it still more perfect and luxurious to repose in. The distant sea, lapping the sandy shore with measured sound; the nearer cries of the donkey-boys; the unusual scenes moving before her like pictures, which she cared not in her laziness to have fully explained before they passed away; the stroll down to the beach to breathe the sea-air, soft and warm on that sandy shore even to the end of November; the great long misty sea-line touching the tender-coloured sky; the white sail of a distant boat turning silver in some pale sunbeam:—it seemed as if she could dream her life away in such luxury of pensiveness, in which she made her present all in all, from not daring to think of the past, or wishing to contemplate the future.

But the future must be met, however stern and iron it be. One evening it was arranged that Margaret and her father should go the next day to Milton-Northern, and look out for a house. Mr. Hale had received several letters from Mr. Bell, and one or two from Mr. Thornton, and he was anxious to ascertain at once a good many particulars respecting his position and chances of success there, which he could only do by an interview with the latter gentleman. Margaret knew that they ought to be removing; but she had a repugnance to the idea of a manufacturing town, and believed that her mother was receiving benefit from Heston air, so she would willingly have deferred the expedition to Milton.

For several miles before they reached Milton, they saw a deep lead-coloured cloud hanging over the horizon in the direction in which it lay. It was all the darker from contrast with the pale gray-blue of the wintry sky; for in Heston there had been the earliest signs of frost. Nearer to the town, the air had a faint taste and smell of smoke; perhaps, after all, more a loss of the fragrance of grass and herbage than any positive taste or smell. Quick they were whirled over long, straight, hopeless streets of regularly-built houses, all small and of brick. Here and there a great oblong many-windowed factory stood up, like a hen among her chickens, puffing out black 'unparliamentary' smoke, and sufficiently accounting for the cloud which Margaret had taken to foretell rain. As they drove through the larger and wider streets, from the station to the hotel, they had to stop constantly; great loaded lorries blocked up the not over-wide thoroughfares. Margaret had now and then been into the city in her drives with her aunt. But there the heavy lumbering vehicles seemed various in their purposes and intent; here every van, every waggon and truck, bore cotton, either in the raw shape in bags, or the woven shape in bales of calico. People thronged the footpaths, most of them well-dressed as regarded the material, but with a slovenly looseness which struck Margaret as different from the shabby, threadbare smartness of a similar class in London.

'New Street,' said Mr. Hale. 'This, I believe, is the principal street in Milton. Bell has often spoken to me about it. It was the opening of this street from a lane into a great thoroughfare, thirty years ago, which has caused his property to rise so much in value. Mr. Thornton's mill must be somewhere not very far off, for he is Mr. Bell's tenant. But I fancy he dates from his warehouse.'

'Where is our hotel, papa?'

'Close to the end of this street, I believe. Shall we have lunch before or after we have looked at the houses we marked in the Milton Times?'

'Oh, let us get our work done first.'

'Very well. Then I will only see if there is any note or letter for me from Mr. Thornton, who said he would let me know anything he might hear about these houses, and then we will set off. We will keep the cab; it will be safer than losing ourselves, and being too late for the train this afternoon.'

There were no letters awaiting him. They set out on their house-hunting. Thirty pounds a-year was all they could afford to give, but in Hampshire they could have met with a roomy house and pleasant garden for the money. Here, even the necessary accommodation of two sitting-rooms and four bed-rooms seemed unattainable. They went through their list, rejecting each as they visited it. Then they looked at each other in dismay.

'We must go back to the second, I think. That one,—in Crampton, don't they call the suburb? There were three sitting-rooms; don't you remember how we laughed at the number compared with the three bed-rooms? But I have planned it all. The front room down-stairs is to be your study and our dining-room (poor papa!), for, you know, we settled mamma is to have as cheerful a sitting-room as we can get; and that front room up-stairs, with the atrocious blue and pink paper and heavy cornice, had really a pretty view over the plain, with a great bend of river, or canal, or whatever it is, down below. Then I could have the little bed-room behind, in that projection at the head of the first flight of stairs—over the kitchen, you know—and you and mamma the room behind the drawing-room, and that closet in the roof will make you a splendid dressing-room.'

'But Dixon, and the girl we are to have to help?'

'Oh, wait a minute. I am overpowered by the discovery of my own genius for management. Dixon is to have—let me see, I had it once—the back sitting-room. I think she will like that. She grumbles so much about the stairs at Heston; and the girl is to have that sloping attic over your room and mamma's. Won't that do?'

'I dare say it will. But the papers. What taste! And the overloading such a house with colour and such heavy cornices!'

'Never mind, papa! Surely, you can charm the landlord into re-papering one or two of the rooms—the drawing-room and your bed-room—for mamma will come most in contact with them; and your book-shelves will hide a great deal of that gaudy pattern in the dining-room.'

'Then you think it the best? If so, I had better go at once and call on this Mr. Donkin, to whom the advertisement refers me. I will take you back to the hotel, where you can order lunch, and rest, and by the time it is ready, I shall be with you. I hope I shall be able to get new papers.'

Margaret hoped so too, though she said nothing. She had never come fairly in contact with the taste that loves ornament, however bad, more than the plainness and simplicity which are of themselves the framework of elegance. Her father took her through the entrance of the hotel, and leaving her at the foot of the staircase, went to the address of the landlord of the house they had fixed upon. Just as Margaret had her hand on the door of their sitting-room, she was followed by a quick-stepping waiter:

'I beg your pardon, ma'am. The gentleman was gone so quickly, I had no time to tell him. Mr. Thornton called almost directly after you left; and, as I understood from what the gentleman said, you would be back in an hour, I told him so, and he came again about five minutes ago, and said he would wait for Mr. Hale. He is in your room now, ma'am.'

'Thank you. My father will return soon, and then you can tell him.' Margaret opened the door and went in with the straight, fearless, dignified presence habitual to her. She felt no awkwardness; she had too much the habits of society for that. Here was a person come on business to her father; and, as he was one who had shown himself obliging, she was disposed to treat him with a full measure of civility. Mr. Thornton was a good deal more surprised and discomfited than she. Instead of a quiet, middle-aged clergyman, a young lady came forward with frank dignity,—a young lady of a different type to most of those he was in the habit of seeing. Her dress was very plain: a close straw bonnet of the best material and shape, trimmed with white ribbon; a dark silk gown, without any trimming or flounce; a large Indian shawl, which hung about her in long heavy folds, and which she wore as an empress wears her drapery. He did not understand who she was, as he caught the simple, straight, unabashed look, which showed that his being there was of no concern to the beautiful countenance, and called up no flush of surprise to the pale ivory of the complexion. He had heard that Mr. Hale had a daughter, but he had imagined that she was a little girl.

'Mr. Thornton, I believe!' said Margaret, after a half-instant's pause, during which his unready words would not come. 'Will you sit down. My father brought me to the door, not a minute ago, but unfortunately he was not told that you were here, and he has gone away on some business. But he will come back almost directly. I am sorry you have had the trouble of calling twice.'

Mr. Thornton was in habits of authority himself, but she seemed to assume some kind of rule over him at once. He had been getting impatient at the loss of his time on a market-day, the moment before she appeared, yet now he calmly took a seat at her bidding.

'Do you know where it is that Mr. Hale has gone to? Perhaps I might be able to find him.'

'He has gone to a Mr. Donkin's in Canute Street. He is the land-lord of the house my father wishes to take in Crampton.'

Mr. Thornton knew the house. He had seen the advertisement, and been to look at it, in compliance with a request of Mr. Bell's that he would assist Mr. Hale to the best of his power: and also instigated by his own interest in the case of a clergyman who had given up his living under circumstances such as those of Mr. Hale. Mr. Thornton had thought that the house in Crampton was really just the thing; but now that he saw Margaret, with her superb ways of moving and looking, he began to feel ashamed of having imagined that it would do very well for the Hales, in spite of a certain vulgarity in it which had struck him at the time of his looking it over.

Margaret could not help her looks; but the short curled upper lip, the round, massive up-turned chin, the manner of carrying her head, her movements, full of a soft feminine defiance, always gave strangers the impression of haughtiness. She was tired now, and would rather have remained silent, and taken the rest her father had planned for her; but, of course, she owed it to herself to be a gentlewoman, and to speak courteously from time to time to this stranger; not over-brushed, nor over-polished, it must be confessed, after his rough encounter with Milton streets and crowds. She wished that he would go, as he had once spoken of doing, instead of sitting there, answering with curt sentences all the remarks she made. She had taken off her shawl, and hung it over the back of her chair. She sat facing him and facing the light; her full beauty met his eye; her round white flexile throat rising out of the full, yet lithe figure; her lips, moving so slightly as she spoke, not breaking the cold serene look of her face with any variation from the one lovely haughty curve; her eyes, with their soft gloom, meeting his with quiet maiden freedom. He almost said to himself that he did not like her, before their conversation ended; he tried so to compensate himself for the mortified feeling, that while he looked upon her with an admiration he could not repress, she looked at him with proud indifference, taking him, he thought, for what, in his irritation, he told himself he was—a great rough fellow, with not a grace or a refinement about him. Her quiet coldness of demeanour he interpreted into contemptuousness, and resented it in his heart to the pitch of almost inclining him to get up and go away, and have nothing more to do with these Hales, and their superciliousness.

Just as Margaret had exhausted her last subject of conversation—and yet conversation that could hardly be called which consisted of so few and such short speeches—her father came in, and with his pleasant gentlemanly courteousness of apology, reinstated his name and family in Mr. Thornton's good opinion.

Mr. Hale and his visitor had a good deal to say respecting their mutual friend, Mr. Bell; and Margaret, glad that her part of entertaining the visitor was over, went to the window to try and make herself more familiar with the strange aspect of the street. She got so much absorbed in watching what was going on outside that she hardly heard her father when he spoke to her, and he had to repeat what he said:

'Margaret! the landlord will persist in admiring that hideous paper, and I am afraid we must let it remain.'

'Oh dear! I am sorry!' she replied, and began to turn over in her mind the possibility of hiding part of it, at least, by some of her sketches, but gave up the idea at last, as likely only to make bad worse. Her father, meanwhile, with his kindly country hospitality, was pressing Mr. Thornton to stay to luncheon with them. It would have been very inconvenient to him to do so, yet he felt that he should have yielded, if Margaret by word or look had seconded her father's invitation; he was glad she did not, and yet he was irritated at her for not doing it. She gave him a low, grave bow when he left, and he felt more awkward and self-conscious in every limb than he had ever done in all his life before.

'Well, Margaret, now to luncheon, as fast we can. Have you ordered it?'

'No, papa; that man was here when I came home, and I have never had an opportunity.'

'Then we must take anything we can get. He must have been waiting a long time, I'm afraid.'

'It seemed exceedingly long to me. I was just at the last gasp when you came in. He never went on with any subject, but gave little, short, abrupt answers.'

'Very much to the point though, I should think. He is a clearheaded fellow. He said (did you hear?) that Crampton is on gravelly soil, and by far the most healthy suburb in the neighbourhood of Milton.'

When they returned to Heston, there was the day's account to be given to Mrs. Hale, who was full of questions which they answered in the intervals of tea-drinking.

'And what is your correspondent, Mr. Thornton, like?'

'Ask Margaret,' said her husband. 'She and he had a long attempt at conversation, while I was away speaking to the landlord.'

'Oh! I hardly know what he is like,' said Margaret, lazily; too tired to tax her powers of description much. And then rousing herself, she said, 'He is a tall, broad-shouldered man, about—how old, papa?'

'I should guess about thirty.'

'About thirty—with a face that is neither exactly plain, nor yet handsome, nothing remarkable—not quite a gentleman; but that was hardly to be expected.'

'Not vulgar, or common though,' put in her father, rather jealous of any disparagement of the sole friend he had in Milton.

'Oh no!' said Margaret. 'With such an expression of resolution and power, no face, however plain in feature, could be either vulgar or common. I should not like to have to bargain with him; he looks very inflexible. Altogether a man who seems made for his niche, mamma; sagacious, and strong, as becomes a great tradesman.'

'Don't call the Milton manufacturers tradesmen, Margaret,' said her father.

'They are very different.'

'Are they? I apply the word to all who have something tangible to sell; but if you think the term is not correct, papa, I won't use it. But, oh mamma! speaking of vulgarity and commonness, you must prepare yourself for our drawing-room paper. Pink and blue roses, with yellow leaves! And such a heavy cornice round the room!'

But when they removed to their new house in Milton, the obnoxious papers were gone. The landlord received their thanks very composedly; and let them think, if they liked, that he had relented from his expressed determination not to repaper. There was no particular need to tell them, that what he did not care to do for a Reverend Mr. Hale, unknown in Milton, he was only too glad to do at the one short sharp remonstrance of Mr. Thornton, the wealthy manufacturer.

CHAPTER VIII - HOME SICKNESS

'And it's hame, hame; hame,
  Hame fain wad I be.'

It needed the pretty light papering of the rooms to reconcile them to Milton. It needed more—more that could not be had. The thick yellow November fogs had come on; and the view of the plain in the valley, made by the sweeping bend of the river, was all shut out when Mrs. Hale arrived at her new home.

Margaret and Dixon had been at work for two days, unpacking and arranging, but everything inside the house still looked in disorder; and outside a thick fog crept up to the very windows, and was driven in to every open door in choking white wreaths of unwholesome mist.

'Oh, Margaret! are we to live here?' asked Mrs. Hale in blank dismay. Margaret's heart echoed the dreariness of the tone in which this question was put. She could scarcely command herself enough to say, 'Oh, the fogs in London are sometimes far worse!'

'But then you knew that London itself, and friends lay behind it. Here—well! we are desolate. Oh Dixon, what a place this is!'

'Indeed, ma'am, I'm sure it will be your death before long, and then I know who'll—stay! Miss Hale, that's far too heavy for you to lift.'

'Not at all, thank you, Dixon,' replied Margaret, coldly. 'The best thing we can do for mamma is to get her room quite ready for her to go to bed, while I go and bring her a cup of coffee.'

Mr. Hale was equally out of spirits, and equally came upon Margaret for sympathy.

'Margaret, I do believe this is an unhealthy place. Only suppose that your mother's health or yours should suffer. I wish I had gone into some country place in Wales; this is really terrible,' said he, going up to the window. There was no comfort to be given. They were settled in Milton, and must endure smoke and fogs for a season; indeed, all other life seemed shut out from them by as thick a fog of circumstance. Only the day before, Mr. Hale had been reckoning up with dismay how much their removal and fortnight at Heston had cost, and he found it had absorbed nearly all his little stock of ready money. No! here they were, and here they must remain.

At night when Margaret realised this, she felt inclined to sit down in a stupor of despair. The heavy smoky air hung about her bedroom, which occupied the long narrow projection at the back of the house. The window, placed at the side of the oblong, looked to the blank wall of a similar projection, not above ten feet distant. It loomed through the fog like a great barrier to hope. Inside the room everything was in confusion. All their efforts had been directed to make her mother's room comfortable. Margaret sat down on a box, the direction card upon which struck her as having been written at Helstone—beautiful, beloved Helstone! She lost herself in dismal thought: but at last she determined to take her mind away from the present; and suddenly remembered that she had a letter from Edith which she had only half read in the bustle of the morning. It was to tell of their arrival at Corfu; their voyage along the Mediterranean—their music, and dancing on board ship; the gay new life opening upon her; her house with its trellised balcony, and its views over white cliffs and deep blue sea. Edith wrote fluently and well, if not graphically. She could not only seize the salient and characteristic points of a scene, but she could enumerate enough of indiscriminate particulars for Margaret to make it out for herself. Captain Lennox and another lately married officer shared a villa, high up on the beautiful precipitous rocks overhanging the sea. Their days, late as it was in the year, seemed spent in boating or land pic-nics; all out-of-doors, pleasure-seeking and glad, Edith's life seemed like the deep vault of blue sky above her, free—utterly free from fleck or cloud. Her husband had to attend drill, and she, the most musical officer's wife there, had to copy the new and popular tunes out of the most recent English music, for the benefit of the bandmaster; those seemed their most severe and arduous duties. She expressed an affectionate hope that, if the regiment stopped another year at Corfu, Margaret might come out and pay her a long visit. She asked Margaret if she remembered the day twelve-month on which she, Edith, wrote—how it rained all day long in Harley Street; and how she would not put on her new gown to go to a stupid dinner, and get it all wet and splashed in going to the carriage; and how at that very dinner they had first met Captain Lennox.

Yes! Margaret remembered it well. Edith and Mrs. Shaw had gone to dinner. Margaret had joined the party in the evening. The recollection of the plentiful luxury of all the arrangements, the stately handsomeness of the furniture, the size of the house, the peaceful, untroubled ease of the visitors—all came vividly before her, in strange contrast to the present time. The smooth sea of that old life closed up, without a mark left to tell where they had all been. The habitual dinners, the calls, the shopping, the dancing evenings, were all going on, going on for ever, though her Aunt Shaw and Edith were no longer there; and she, of course, was even less missed. She doubted if any one of that old set ever thought of her, except Henry Lennox. He too, she knew, would strive to forget her, because of the pain she had caused him. She had heard him often boast of his power of putting any disagreeable thought far away from him. Then she penetrated farther into what might have been. If she had cared for him as a lover, and had accepted him, and this change in her father's opinions and consequent station had taken place, she could not doubt but that it would have been impatiently received by Mr. Lennox. It was a bitter mortification to her in one sense; but she could bear it patiently, because she knew her father's purity of purpose, and that strengthened her to endure his errors, grave and serious though in her estimation they were. But the fact of the world esteeming her father degraded, in its rough wholesale judgment, would have oppressed and irritated Mr. Lennox. As she realised what might have been, she grew to be thankful for what was. They were at the lowest now; they could not be worse. Edith's astonishment and her aunt Shaw's dismay would have to be met bravely, when their letters came. So Margaret rose up and began slowly to undress herself, feeling the full luxury of acting leisurely, late as it was, after all the past hurry of the day. She fell asleep, hoping for some brightness, either internal or external. But if she had known how long it would be before the brightness came, her heart would have sunk low down. The time of the year was most unpropitious to health as well as to spirits. Her mother caught a severe cold, and Dixon herself was evidently not well, although Margaret could not insult her more than by trying to save her, or by taking any care of her. They could hear of no girl to assist her; all were at work in the factories; at least, those who applied were well scolded by Dixon, for thinking that such as they could ever be trusted to work in a gentleman's house. So they had to keep a charwoman in almost constant employ. Margaret longed to send for Charlotte; but besides the objection of her being a better servant than they could now afford to keep, the distance was too great.

Mr. Hale met with several pupils, recommended to him by Mr. Bell, or by the more immediate influence of Mr. Thornton. They were mostly of the age when many boys would be still at school, but, according to the prevalent, and apparently well-founded notions of Milton, to make a lad into a good tradesman he must be caught young, and acclimated to the life of the mill, or office, or warehouse. If he were sent to even the Scotch Universities, he came back unsettled for commercial pursuits; how much more so if he went to Oxford or Cambridge, where he could not be entered till he was eighteen? So most of the manufacturers placed their sons in sucking situations' at fourteen or fifteen years of age, unsparingly cutting away all off-shoots in the direction of literature or high mental cultivation, in hopes of throwing the whole strength and vigour of the plant into commerce. Still there were some wiser parents; and some young men, who had sense enough to perceive their own deficiencies, and strive to remedy them. Nay, there were a few no longer youths, but men in the prime of life, who had the stern wisdom to acknowledge their own ignorance, and to learn late what they should have learnt early. Mr. Thornton was perhaps the oldest of Mr. Hale's pupils. He was certainly the favourite. Mr. Hale got into the habit of quoting his opinions so frequently, and with such regard, that it became a little domestic joke to wonder what time, during the hour appointed for instruction, could be given to absolute learning, so much of it appeared to have been spent in conversation.

Margaret rather encouraged this light, merry way of viewing her father's acquaintance with Mr. Thornton, because she felt that her mother was inclined to look upon this new friendship of her husband's with jealous eyes. As long as his time had been solely occupied with his books and his parishioners, as at Helstone, she had appeared to care little whether she saw much of him or not; but now that he looked eagerly forward to each renewal of his intercourse with Mr. Thornton, she seemed hurt and annoyed, as if he were slighting her companionship for the first time. Mr. Hale's over-praise had the usual effect of over-praise upon his auditors; they were a little inclined to rebel against Aristides being always called the Just.

After a quiet life in a country parsonage for more than twenty years, there was something dazzling to Mr. Hale in the energy which conquered immense difficulties with ease; the power of the machinery of Milton, the power of the men of Milton, impressed him with a sense of grandeur, which he yielded to without caring to inquire into the details of its exercise. But Margaret went less abroad, among machinery and men; saw less of power in its public effect, and, as it happened, she was thrown with one or two of those who, in all measures affecting masses of people, must be acute sufferers for the good of many. The question always is, has everything been done to make the sufferings of these exceptions as small as possible? Or, in the triumph of the crowded procession, have the helpless been trampled on, instead of being gently lifted aside out of the roadway of the conqueror, whom they have no power to accompany on his march?

It fell to Margaret's share to have to look out for a servant to assist Dixon, who had at first undertaken to find just the person she wanted to do all the rough work of the house. But Dixon's ideas of helpful girls were founded on the recollection of tidy elder scholars at Helstone school, who were only too proud to be allowed to come to the parsonage on a busy day, and treated Mrs. Dixon with all the respect, and a good deal more of fright, which they paid to Mr. and Mrs. Hale. Dixon was not unconscious of this awed reverence which was given to her; nor did she dislike it; it flattered her much as Louis the Fourteenth was flattered by his courtiers shading their eyes from the dazzling light of his presence. But nothing short of her faithful love for Mrs. Hale could have made her endure the rough independent way in which all the Milton girls, who made application for the servant's place, replied to her inquiries respecting their qualifications. They even went the length of questioning her back again; having doubts and fears of their own, as to the solvency of a family who lived in a house of thirty pounds a-year, and yet gave themselves airs, and kept two servants, one of them so very high and mighty. Mr. Hale was no longer looked upon as Vicar of Helstone, but as a man who only spent at a certain rate. Margaret was weary and impatient of the accounts which Dixon perpetually brought to Mrs. Hale of the behaviour of these would-be servants. Not but what Margaret was repelled by the rough uncourteous manners of these people; not but what she shrunk with fastidious pride from their hail-fellow accost and severely resented their unconcealed curiosity as to the means and position of any family who lived in Milton, and yet were not engaged in trade of some kind. But the more Margaret felt impertinence, the more likely she was to be silent on the subject; and, at any rate, if she took upon herself to make inquiry for a servant, she could spare her mother the recital of all her disappointments and fancied or real insults.

Margaret accordingly went up and down to butchers and grocers, seeking for a nonpareil of a girl; and lowering her hopes and expectations every week, as she found the difficulty of meeting with any one in a manufacturing town who did not prefer the better wages and greater independence of working in a mill. It was something of a trial to Margaret to go out by herself in this busy bustling place. Mrs. Shaw's ideas of propriety and her own helpless dependence on others, had always made her insist that a footman should accompany Edith and Margaret, if they went beyond Harley Street or the immediate neighbourhood. The limits by which this rule of her aunt's had circumscribed Margaret's independence had been silently rebelled against at the time: and she had doubly enjoyed the free walks and rambles of her forest life, from the contrast which they presented. She went along there with a bounding fearless step, that occasionally broke out into a run, if she were in a hurry, and occasionally was stilled into perfect repose, as she stood listening to, or watching any of the wild creatures who sang in the leafy courts, or glanced out with their keen bright eyes from the low brushwood or tangled furze. It was a trial to come down from such motion or such stillness, only guided by her own sweet will, to the even and decorous pace necessary in streets. But she could have laughed at herself for minding this change, if it had not been accompanied by what was a more serious annoyance. The side of the town on which Crampton lay was especially a thoroughfare for the factory people. In the back streets around them there were many mills, out of which poured streams of men and women two or three times a day. Until Margaret had learnt the times of their ingress and egress, she was very unfortunate in constantly falling in with them. They came rushing along, with bold, fearless faces, and loud laughs and jests, particularly aimed at all those who appeared to be above them in rank or station. The tones of their unrestrained voices, and their carelessness of all common rules of street politeness, frightened Margaret a little at first. The girls, with their rough, but not unfriendly freedom, would comment on her dress, even touch her shawl or gown to ascertain the exact material; nay, once or twice she was asked questions relative to some article which they particularly admired. There was such a simple reliance on her womanly sympathy with their love of dress, and on her kindliness, that she gladly replied to these inquiries, as soon as she understood them; and half smiled back at their remarks. She did not mind meeting any number of girls, loud spoken and boisterous though they might be. But she alternately dreaded and fired up against the workmen, who commented not on her dress, but on her looks, in the same open fearless manner. She, who had hitherto felt that even the most refined remark on her personal appearance was an impertinence, had to endure undisguised admiration from these outspoken men. But the very out-spokenness marked their innocence of any intention to hurt her delicacy, as she would have perceived if she had been less frightened by the disorderly tumult. Out of her fright came a flash of indignation which made her face scarlet, and her dark eyes gather flame, as she heard some of their speeches. Yet there were other sayings of theirs, which, when she reached the quiet safety of home, amused her even while they irritated her.

For instance, one day, after she had passed a number of men, several of whom had paid her the not unusual compliment of wishing she was their sweetheart, one of the lingerers added, 'Your bonny face, my lass, makes the day look brighter.' And another day, as she was unconsciously smiling at some passing thought, she was addressed by a poorly-dressed, middle-aged workman, with 'You may well smile, my lass; many a one would smile to have such a bonny face.' This man looked so careworn that Margaret could not help giving him an answering smile, glad to think that her looks, such as they were, should have had the power to call up a pleasant thought. He seemed to understand her acknowledging glance, and a silent recognition was established between them whenever the chances of the day brought them across each other's paths. They had never exchanged a word; nothing had been said but that first compliment; yet somehow Margaret looked upon this man with more interest than upon any one else in Milton. Once or twice, on Sundays, she saw him walking with a girl, evidently his daughter, and, if possible, still more unhealthy than he was himself.

One day Margaret and her father had been as far as the fields that lay around the town; it was early spring, and she had gathered some of the hedge and ditch flowers, dog-violets, lesser celandines, and the like, with an unspoken lament in her heart for the sweet profusion of the South. Her father had left her to go into Milton upon some business; and on the road home she met her humble friends. The girl looked wistfully at the flowers, and, acting on a sudden impulse, Margaret offered them to her. Her pale blue eyes lightened up as she took them, and her father spoke for her.

'Thank yo, Miss. Bessy'll think a deal o' them flowers; that hoo will; and I shall think a deal o' yor kindness. Yo're not of this country, I reckon?'

'No!' said Margaret, half sighing. 'I come from the South—from Hampshire,' she continued, a little afraid of wounding his consciousness of ignorance, if she used a name which he did not understand.

'That's beyond London, I reckon? And I come fro' Burnley-ways, and forty mile to th' North. And yet, yo see, North and South has both met and made kind o' friends in this big smoky place.'

Margaret had slackened her pace to walk alongside of the man and his daughter, whose steps were regulated by the feebleness of the latter. She now spoke to the girl, and there was a sound of tender pity in the tone of her voice as she did so that went right to the heart of the father.

'I'm afraid you are not very strong.'

'No,' said the girl, 'nor never will be.'

'Spring is coming,' said Margaret, as if to suggest pleasant, hopeful thoughts.

'Spring nor summer will do me good,' said the girl quietly.

Margaret looked up at the man, almost expecting some contradiction from him, or at least some remark that would modify his daughter's utter hopelessness. But, instead, he added—

'I'm afeared hoo speaks truth. I'm afeared hoo's too far gone in a waste.'

'I shall have a spring where I'm boun to, and flowers, and amaranths, and shining robes besides.'

'Poor lass, poor lass!' said her father in a low tone. 'I'm none so sure o' that; but it's a comfort to thee, poor lass, poor lass. Poor father! it'll be soon.'

Margaret was shocked by his words—shocked but not repelled; rather attracted and interested.

'Where do you live? I think we must be neighbours, we meet so often on this road.'

'We put up at nine Frances Street, second turn to th' left at after yo've past th' Goulden Dragon.'

'And your name? I must not forget that.'

'I'm none ashamed o' my name. It's Nicholas Higgins. Hoo's called Bessy Higgins. Whatten yo' asking for?'

Margaret was surprised at this last question, for at Helstone it would have been an understood thing, after the inquiries she had made, that she intended to come and call upon any poor neighbour whose name and habitation she had asked for.

'I thought—I meant to come and see you.' She suddenly felt rather shy of offering the visit, without having any reason to give for her wish to make it, beyond a kindly interest in a stranger. It seemed all at once to take the shape of an impertinence on her part; she read this meaning too in the man's eyes.

'I'm none so fond of having strange folk in my house.' But then relenting, as he saw her heightened colour, he added, 'Yo're a foreigner, as one may say, and maybe don't know many folk here, and yo've given my wench here flowers out of yo'r own hand;—yo may come if yo like.'

Margaret was half-amused, half-nettled at this answer. She was not sure if she would go where permission was given so like a favour conferred. But when they came to the town into Frances Street, the girl stopped a minute, and said,

'Yo'll not forget yo're to come and see us.'

'Aye, aye,' said the father, impatiently, 'hoo'll come. Hoo's a bit set up now, because hoo thinks I might ha' spoken more civilly; but hoo'll think better on it, and come. I can read her proud bonny face like a book. Come along, Bess; there's the mill bell ringing.'

Margaret went home, wondering at her new friends, and smiling at the man's insight into what had been passing in her mind. From that day Milton became a brighter place to her. It was not the long, bleak sunny days of spring, nor yet was it that time was reconciling her to the town of her habitation. It was that in it she had found a human interest.

CHAPTER IX - DRESSING FOR TEA

'Let China's earth, enrich'd with colour'd stains,
Pencil'd with gold, and streak'd with azure veins,
The grateful flavour of the Indian leaf,
Or Mocho's sunburnt berry glad receive.'
MRS. BARBAULD.

The day after this meeting with Higgins and his daughter, Mr. Hale came upstairs into the little drawing-room at an unusual hour. He went up to different objects in the room, as if examining them, but Margaret saw that it was merely a nervous trick—a way of putting off something he wished, yet feared to say. Out it came at last—

'My dear! I've asked Mr. Thornton to come to tea to-night.'

Mrs. Hale was leaning back in her easy chair, with her eyes shut, and an expression of pain on her face which had become habitual to her of late. But she roused up into querulousness at this speech of her husband's.

'Mr. Thornton!—and to-night! What in the world does the man want to come here for? And Dixon is washing my muslins and laces, and there is no soft water with these horrid east winds, which I suppose we shall have all the year round in Milton.'

'The wind is veering round, my dear,' said Mr. Hale, looking out at the smoke, which drifted right from the east, only he did not yet understand the points of the compass, and rather arranged them ad libitum, according to circumstances.

'Don't tell me!' said Mrs. Hale, shuddering up, and wrapping her shawl about her still more closely. 'But, east or west wind, I suppose this man comes.'

'Oh, mamma, that shows you never saw Mr. Thornton. He looks like a person who would enjoy battling with every adverse thing he could meet with—enemies, winds, or circumstances. The more it rains and blows, the more certain we are to have him. But I'll go and help Dixon. I'm getting to be a famous clear-starcher. And he won't want any amusement beyond talking to papa. Papa, I am really longing to see the Pythias to your Damon. You know I never saw him but once, and then we were so puzzled to know what to say to each other that we did not get on particularly well.'

'I don't know that you would ever like him, or think him agreeable, Margaret. He is not a lady's man.'

Margaret wreathed her throat in a scornful curve.

'I don't particularly admire ladies' men, papa. But Mr. Thornton comes here as your friend—as one who has appreciated you'—

'The only person in Milton,' said Mrs. Hale.

'So we will give him a welcome, and some cocoa-nut cakes. Dixon will be flattered if we ask her to make some; and I will undertake to iron your caps, mamma.'

Many a time that morning did Margaret wish Mr. Thornton far enough away. She had planned other employments for herself: a letter to Edith, a good piece of Dante, a visit to the Higginses. But, instead, she ironed away, listening to Dixon's complaints, and only hoping that by an excess of sympathy she might prevent her from carrying the recital of her sorrows to Mrs. Hale. Every now and then, Margaret had to remind herself of her father's regard for Mr. Thornton, to subdue the irritation of weariness that was stealing over her, and bringing on one of the bad headaches to which she had lately become liable. She could hardly speak when she sat down at last, and told her mother that she was no longer Peggy the laundry-maid, but Margaret Hale the lady. She meant this speech for a little joke, and was vexed enough with her busy tongue when she found her mother taking it seriously.

'Yes! if any one had told me, when I was Miss Beresford, and one of the belles of the county, that a child of mine would have to stand half a day, in a little poky kitchen, working away like any servant, that we might prepare properly for the reception of a tradesman, and that this tradesman should be the only'—'Oh, mamma!' said Margaret, lifting herself up, 'don't punish me so for a careless speech. I don't mind ironing, or any kind of work, for you and papa. I am myself a born and bred lady through it all, even though it comes to scouring a floor, or washing dishes. I am tired now, just for a little while; but in half an hour I shall be ready to do the same over again. And as to Mr. Thornton's being in trade, why he can't help that now, poor fellow. I don't suppose his education would fit him for much else.' Margaret lifted herself slowly up, and went to her own room; for just now she could not bear much more.

In Mr. Thornton's house, at this very same time, a similar, yet different, scene was going on. A large-boned lady, long past middle age, sat at work in a grim handsomely-furnished dining-room. Her features, like her frame, were strong and massive, rather than heavy. Her face moved slowly from one decided expression to another equally decided. There was no great variety in her countenance; but those who looked at it once, generally looked at it again; even the passers-by in the street, half-turned their heads to gaze an instant longer at the firm, severe, dignified woman, who never gave way in street-courtesy, or paused in her straightonward course to the clearly-defined end which she proposed to herself. She was handsomely dressed in stout black silk, of which not a thread was worn or discoloured. She was mending a large long table-cloth of the finest texture, holding it up against the light occasionally to discover thin places, which required her delicate care. There was not a book about in the room, with the exception of Matthew Henry's Bible Commentaries, six volumes of which lay in the centre of the massive side-board, flanked by a tea-urn on one side, and a lamp on the other. In some remote apartment, there was exercise upon the piano going on. Some one was practising up a morceau de salon, playing it very rapidly; every third note, on an average, being either indistinct, or wholly missed out, and the loud chords at the end being half of them false, but not the less satisfactory to the performer. Mrs. Thornton heard a step, like her own in its decisive character, pass the dining-room door.

'John! Is that you?'

Her son opened the door and showed himself.

'What has brought you home so early? I thought you were going to tea with that friend of Mr. Bell's; that Mr. Hale.'

'So I am, mother; I am come home to dress!'

'Dress! humph! When I was a girl, young men were satisfied with dressing once in a day. Why should you dress to go and take a cup of tea with an old parson?'

'Mr. Hale is a gentleman, and his wife and daughter are ladies.'

'Wife and daughter! Do they teach too? What do they do? You have never mentioned them.'

'No! mother, because I have never seen Mrs. Hale; I have only seen Miss Hale for half an hour.'

'Take care you don't get caught by a penniless girl, John.'

'I am not easily caught, mother, as I think you know. But I must not have Miss Hale spoken of in that way, which, you know, is offensive to me. I never was aware of any young lady trying to catch me yet, nor do I believe that any one has ever given themselves that useless trouble.'

Mrs. Thornton did not choose to yield the point to her son; or else she had, in general, pride enough for her sex.

'Well! I only say, take care. Perhaps our Milton girls have too much spirit and good feeling to go angling after husbands; but this Miss Hale comes out of the aristocratic counties, where, if all tales be true, rich husbands are reckoned prizes.'

Mr. Thornton's brow contracted, and he came a step forward into the room.

'Mother' (with a short scornful laugh), 'you will make me confess. The only time I saw Miss Hale, she treated me with a haughty civility which had a strong flavour of contempt in it. She held herself aloof from me as if she had been a queen, and I her humble, unwashed vassal. Be easy, mother.'

'No! I am not easy, nor content either. What business had she, a renegade clergyman's daughter, to turn up her nose at you! I would dress for none of them—a saucy set! if I were you.' As he was leaving the room, he said:—

'Mr. Hale is good, and gentle, and learned. He is not saucy. As for Mrs. Hale, I will tell you what she is like to-night, if you care to hear.' He shut the door and was gone.

'Despise my son! treat him as her vassal, indeed! Humph! I should like to know where she could find such another! Boy and man, he's the noblest, stoutest heart I ever knew. I don't care if I am his mother; I can see what's what, and not be blind. I know what Fanny is; and I know what John is. Despise him! I hate her!'

CHAPTER X - WROUGHT IRON AND GOLD

'We are the trees whom shaking fastens more.'
GEORGE HERBERT.

Mr. Thornton left the house without coming into the dining-room again. He was rather late, and walked rapidly out to Crampton. He was anxious not to slight his new friend by any disrespectful unpunctuality. The church-clock struck half-past seven as he stood at the door awaiting Dixon's slow movements; always doubly tardy when she had to degrade herself by answering the door-bell. He was ushered into the little drawing-room, and kindly greeted by Mr. Hale, who led him up to his wife, whose pale face, and shawl-draped figure made a silent excuse for the cold languor of her greeting. Margaret was lighting the lamp when he entered, for the darkness was coming on. The lamp threw a pretty light into the centre of the dusky room, from which, with country habits, they did not exclude the night-skies, and the outer darkness of air. Somehow, that room contrasted itself with the one he had lately left; handsome, ponderous, with no sign of feminine habitation, except in the one spot where his mother sate, and no convenience for any other employment than eating and drinking. To be sure, it was a dining-room; his mother preferred to sit in it; and her will was a household law. But the drawing-room was not like this. It was twice—twenty times as fine; not one quarter as comfortable. Here were no mirrors, not even a scrap of glass to reflect the light, and answer the same purpose as water in a landscape; no gilding; a warm, sober breadth of colouring, well relieved by the dear old Helstone chintz-curtains and chair covers. An open davenport stood in the window opposite the door; in the other there was a stand, with a tall white china vase, from which drooped wreaths of English ivy, pale-green birch, and copper-coloured beech-leaves. Pretty baskets of work stood about in different places: and books, not cared for on account of their binding solely, lay on one table, as if recently put down. Behind the door was another table, decked out for tea, with a white table-cloth, on which flourished the cocoa-nut cakes, and a basket piled with oranges and ruddy American apples, heaped on leaves.

It appeared to Mr. Thornton that all these graceful cares were habitual to the family; and especially of a piece with Margaret. She stood by the tea-table in a light-coloured muslin gown, which had a good deal of pink about it. She looked as if she was not attending to the conversation, but solely busy with the tea-cups, among which her round ivory hands moved with pretty, noiseless, daintiness. She had a bracelet on one taper arm, which would fall down over her round wrist. Mr. Thornton watched the replacing of this troublesome ornament with far more attention than he listened to her father. It seemed as if it fascinated him to see her push it up impatiently, until it tightened her soft flesh; and then to mark the loosening—the fall. He could almost have exclaimed—'There it goes, again!' There was so little left to be done after he arrived at the preparation for tea, that he was almost sorry the obligation of eating and drinking came so soon to prevent his watching Margaret. She handed him his cup of tea with the proud air of an unwilling slave; but her eye caught the moment when he was ready for another cup; and he almost longed to ask her to do for him what he saw her compelled to do for her father, who took her little finger and thumb in his masculine hand, and made them serve as sugar-tongs. Mr. Thornton saw her beautiful eyes lifted to her father, full of light, half-laughter and half-love, as this bit of pantomime went on between the two, unobserved, as they fancied, by any. Margaret's head still ached, as the paleness of her complexion, and her silence might have testified; but she was resolved to throw herself into the breach, if there was any long untoward pause, rather than that her father's friend, pupil, and guest should have cause to think himself in any way neglected. But the conversation went on; and Margaret drew into a corner, near her mother, with her work, after the tea-things were taken away; and felt that she might let her thoughts roam, without fear of being suddenly wanted to fill up a gap.

Mr. Thornton and Mr. Hale were both absorbed in the continuation of some subject which had been started at their last meeting. Margaret was recalled to a sense of the present by some trivial, low-spoken remark of her mother's; and on suddenly looking up from her work, her eye was caught by the difference of outward appearance between her father and Mr. Thornton, as betokening such distinctly opposite natures. Her father was of slight figure, which made him appear taller than he really was, when not contrasted, as at this time, with the tall, massive frame of another. The lines in her father's face were soft and waving, with a frequent undulating kind of trembling movement passing over them, showing every fluctuating emotion; the eyelids were large and arched, giving to the eyes a peculiar languid beauty which was almost feminine. The brows were finely arched, but were, by the very size of the dreamy lids, raised to a considerable distance from the eyes. Now, in Mr. Thornton's face the straight brows fell low over the clear, deep-set earnest eyes, which, without being unpleasantly sharp, seemed intent enough to penetrate into the very heart and core of what he was looking at. The lines in the face were few but firm, as if they were carved in marble, and lay principally about the lips, which were slightly compressed over a set of teeth so faultless and beautiful as to give the effect of sudden sunlight when the rare bright smile, coming in an instant and shining out of the eyes, changed the whole look from the severe and resolved expression of a man ready to do and dare everything, to the keen honest enjoyment of the moment, which is seldom shown so fearlessly and instantaneously except by children. Margaret liked this smile; it was the first thing she had admired in this new friend of her father's; and the opposition of character, shown in all these details of appearance she had just been noticing, seemed to explain the attraction they evidently felt towards each other.

She rearranged her mother's worsted-work, and fell back into her own thoughts—as completely forgotten by Mr. Thornton as if she had not been in the room, so thoroughly was he occupied in explaining to Mr. Hale the magnificent power, yet delicate adjustment of the might of the steam-hammer, which was recalling to Mr. Hale some of the wonderful stories of subservient genii in the Arabian Nights—one moment stretching from earth to sky and filling all the width of the horizon, at the next obediently compressed into a vase small enough to be borne in the hand of a child.

'And this imagination of power, this practical realisation of a gigantic thought, came out of one man's brain in our good town. That very man has it within him to mount, step by step, on each wonder he achieves to higher marvels still. And I'll be bound to say, we have many among us who, if he were gone, could spring into the breach and carry on the war which compels, and shall compel, all material power to yield to science.'

'Your boast reminds me of the old lines—

"I've a hundred
captains in England," he said,
"As good as ever was he."'

At her father's quotation Margaret looked suddenly up, with inquiring wonder in her eyes. How in the world had they got from cog-wheels to Chevy Chace?

'It is no boast of mine,' replied Mr. Thornton; 'it is plain matter-of-fact. I won't deny that I am proud of belonging to a town—or perhaps I should rather say a district—the necessities of which give birth to such grandeur of conception. I would rather be a man toiling, suffering—nay, failing and successless—here, than lead a dull prosperous life in the old worn grooves of what you call more aristocratic society down in the South, with their slow days of careless ease. One may be clogged with honey and unable to rise and fly.'

'You are mistaken,' said Margaret, roused by the aspersion on her beloved South to a fond vehemence of defence, that brought the colour into her cheeks and the angry tears into her eyes. 'You do not know anything about the South. If there is less adventure or less progress—I suppose I must not say less excitement—from the gambling spirit of trade, which seems requisite to force out these wonderful inventions, there is less suffering also. I see men here going about in the streets who look ground down by some pinching sorrow or care—who are not only sufferers but haters. Now, in the South we have our poor, but there is not that terrible expression in their countenances of a sullen sense of injustice which I see here. You do not know the South, Mr. Thornton,' she concluded, collapsing into a determined silence, and angry with herself for having said so much.

'And may I say you do not know the North?' asked he, with an inexpressible gentleness in his tone, as he saw that he had really hurt her. She continued resolutely silent; yearning after the lovely haunts she had left far away in Hampshire, with a passionate longing that made her feel her voice would be unsteady and trembling if she spoke.

'At any rate, Mr. Thornton,' said Mrs. Hale, 'you will allow that Milton is a much more smoky, dirty town than you will ever meet with in the South.'

'I'm afraid I must give up its cleanliness,' said Mr. Thornton, with the quick gleaming smile. 'But we are bidden by parliament to burn our own smoke; so I suppose, like good little children, we shall do as we are bid—some time.'

'But I think you told me you had altered your chimneys so as to consume the smoke, did you not?' asked Mr. Hale.

'Mine were altered by my own will, before parliament meddled with the affair. It was an immediate outlay, but it repays me in the saving of coal. I'm not sure whether I should have done it, if I had waited until the act was passed. At any rate, I should have waited to be informed against and fined, and given all the trouble in yielding that I legally could. But all laws which depend for their enforcement upon informers and fines, become inert from the odiousness of the machinery. I doubt if there has been a chimney in Milton informed against for five years past, although some are constantly sending out one-third of their coal in what is called here unparliamentary smoke.'

'I only know it is impossible to keep the muslin blinds clean here above a week together; and at Helstone we have had them up for a month or more, and they have not looked dirty at the end of that time. And as for hands—Margaret, how many times did you say you had washed your hands this morning before twelve o'clock? Three times, was it not?'

'Yes, mamma.'

'You seem to have a strong objection to acts of parliament and all legislation affecting your mode of management down here at Milton,' said Mr. Hale.

'Yes, I have; and many others have as well. And with justice, I think. The whole machinery—I don't mean the wood and iron machinery now—of the cotton trade is so new that it is no wonder if it does not work well in every part all at once. Seventy years ago what was it? And now what is it not? Raw, crude materials came together; men of the same level, as regarded education and station, took suddenly the different positions of masters and men, owing to the motherwit, as regarded opportunities and probabilities, which distinguished some, and made them far-seeing as to what great future lay concealed in that rude model of Sir Richard Arkwright's. The rapid development of what might be called a new trade, gave those early masters enormous power of wealth and command. I don't mean merely over the workmen; I mean over purchasers—over the whole world's market. Why, I may give you, as an instance, an advertisement, inserted not fifty years ago in a Milton paper, that so-and-so (one of the half-dozen calico-printers of the time) would close his warehouse at noon each day; therefore, that all purchasers must come before that hour. Fancy a man dictating in this manner the time when he would sell and when he would not sell. Now, I believe, if a good customer chose to come at midnight, I should get up, and stand hat in hand to receive his orders.'

Margaret's lip curled, but somehow she was compelled to listen; she could no longer abstract herself in her own thoughts.

'I only name such things to show what almost unlimited power the manufacturers had about the beginning of this century. The men were rendered dizzy by it. Because a man was successful in his ventures, there was no reason that in all other things his mind should be well-balanced. On the contrary, his sense of justice, and his simplicity, were often utterly smothered under the glut of wealth that came down upon him; and they tell strange tales of the wild extravagance of living indulged in on gala-days by those early cotton-lords. There can be no doubt, too, of the tyranny they exercised over their work-people. You know the proverb, Mr. Hale, "Set a beggar on horseback, and he'll ride to the devil,"—well, some of these early manufacturers did ride to the devil in a magnificent style—crushing human bone and flesh under their horses' hoofs without remorse. But by-and-by came a re-action, there were more factories, more masters; more men were wanted. The power of masters and men became more evenly balanced; and now the battle is pretty fairly waged between us. We will hardly submit to the decision of an umpire, much less to the interference of a meddler with only a smattering of the knowledge of the real facts of the case, even though that meddler be called the High Court of Parliament.

'Is there necessity for calling it a battle between the two classes?' asked Mr. Hale. 'I know, from your using the term, it is one which gives a true idea of the real state of things to your mind.'

'It is true; and I believe it to be as much a necessity as that prudent wisdom and good conduct are always opposed to, and doing battle with ignorance and improvidence. It is one of the great beauties of our system, that a working-man may raise himself into the power and position of a master by his own exertions and behaviour; that, in fact, every one who rules himself to decency and sobriety of conduct, and attention to his duties, comes over to our ranks; it may not be always as a master, but as an over-looker, a cashier, a book-keeper, a clerk, one on the side of authority and order.'

'You consider all who are unsuccessful in raising themselves in the world, from whatever cause, as your enemies, then, if I under-stand you rightly,' said Margaret in a clear, cold voice.

'As their own enemies, certainly,' said he, quickly, not a little piqued by the haughty disapproval her form of expression and tone of speaking implied. But, in a moment, his straightforward honesty made him feel that his words were but a poor and quibbling answer to what she had said; and, be she as scornful as she liked, it was a duty he owed to himself to explain, as truly as he could, what he did mean. Yet it was very difficult to separate her interpretation, and keep it distinct from his meaning. He could best have illustrated what he wanted to say by telling them something of his own life; but was it not too personal a subject to speak about to strangers? Still, it was the simple straightforward way of explaining his meaning; so, putting aside the touch of shyness that brought a momentary flush of colour into his dark cheek, he said:

'I am not speaking without book. Sixteen years ago, my father died under very miserable circumstances. I was taken from school, and had to become a man (as well as I could) in a few days. I had such a mother as few are blest with; a woman of strong power, and firm resolve. We went into a small country town, where living was cheaper than in Milton, and where I got employment in a draper's shop (a capital place, by the way, for obtaining a knowledge of goods). Week by week our income came to fifteen shillings, out of which three people had to be kept. My mother managed so that I put by three out of these fifteen shillings regularly. This made the beginning; this taught me self-denial. Now that I am able to afford my mother such comforts as her age, rather than her own wish, requires, I thank her silently on each occasion for the early training she gave me. Now when I feel that in my own case it is no good luck, nor merit, nor talent,—but simply the habits of life which taught me to despise indulgences not thoroughly earned,—indeed, never to think twice about them,—I believe that this suffering, which Miss Hale says is impressed on the countenances of the people of Milton, is but the natural punishment of dishonestly-enjoyed pleasure, at some former period of their lives. I do not look on self-indulgent, sensual people as worthy of my hatred; I simply look upon them with contempt for their poorness of character.'

'But you have had the rudiments of a good education,' remarked Mr. Hale. 'The quick zest with which you are now reading Homer, shows me that you do not come to it as an unknown book; you have read it before, and are only recalling your old knowledge.'

'That is true,—I had blundered along it at school; I dare say, I was even considered a pretty fair classic in those days, though my Latin and Greek have slipt away from me since. But I ask you, what preparation they were for such a life as I had to lead? None at all. Utterly none at all. On the point of education, any man who can read and write starts fair with me in the amount of really useful knowledge that I had at that time.'

'Well! I don't agree with you. But there I am perhaps somewhat of a pedant. Did not the recollection of the heroic simplicity of the Homeric life nerve you up?'

'Not one bit!' exclaimed Mr. Thornton, laughing. 'I was too busy to think about any dead people, with the living pressing alongside of me, neck to neck, in the struggle for bread. Now that I have my mother safe in the quiet peace that becomes her age, and duly rewards her former exertions, I can turn to all that old narration and thoroughly enjoy it.'

'I dare say, my remark came from the professional feeling of there being nothing like leather,' replied Mr. Hale.

When Mr. Thornton rose up to go away, after shaking hands with Mr. and Mrs. Hale, he made an advance to Margaret to wish her good-bye in a similar manner. It was the frank familiar custom of the place; but Margaret was not prepared for it. She simply bowed her farewell; although the instant she saw the hand, half put out, quickly drawn back, she was sorry she had not been aware of the intention. Mr. Thornton, however, knew nothing of her sorrow, and, drawing himself up to his full height, walked off, muttering as he left the house—

'A more proud, disagreeable girl I never saw. Even her great beauty is blotted out of one's memory by her scornful ways.'

CHAPTER XI - FIRST IMPRESSIONS

'There's iron, they say, in all our blood,
And a grain or two perhaps is good;
But his, he makes me harshly feel,
Has got a little too much of steel.'
ANON.

'Margaret!' said Mr. Hale, as he returned from showing his guest downstairs; 'I could not help watching your face with some anxiety, when Mr. Thornton made his confession of having been a shop-boy. I knew it all along from Mr. Bell; so I was aware of what was coming; but I half expected to see you get up and leave the room.'

'Oh, papa! you don't mean that you thought me so silly? I really liked that account of himself better than anything else he said. Everything else revolted me, from its hardness; but he spoke about himself so simply—with so little of the pretence that makes the vulgarity of shop-people, and with such tender respect for his mother, that I was less likely to leave the room then than when he was boasting about Milton, as if there was not such another place in the world; or quietly professing to despise people for careless, wasteful improvidence, without ever seeming to think it his duty to try to make them different,—to give them anything of the training which his mother gave him, and to which he evidently owes his position, whatever that may be. No! his statement of having been a shop-boy was the thing I liked best of all.'

'I am surprised at you, Margaret,' said her mother. 'You who were always accusing people of being shoppy at Helstone! I don't think, Mr. Hale, you have done quite right in introducing such a person to us without telling us what he had been. I really was very much afraid of showing him how much shocked I was at some parts of what he said. His father "dying in miserable circumstances." Why it might have been in the workhouse.'

'I am not sure if it was not worse than being in the workhouse,' replied her husband. 'I heard a good deal of his previous life from Mr. Bell before we came here; and as he has told you a part, I will fill up what he left out. His father speculated wildly, failed, and then killed himself, because he could not bear the disgrace. All his former friends shrunk from the disclosures that had to be made of his dishonest gambling—wild, hopeless struggles, made with other people's money, to regain his own moderate portion of wealth. No one came forwards to help the mother and this boy. There was another child, I believe, a girl; too young to earn money, but of course she had to be kept. At least, no friend came forwards immediately, and Mrs. Thornton is not one, I fancy, to wait till tardy kindness comes to find her out. So they left Milton. I knew he had gone into a shop, and that his earnings, with some fragment of property secured to his mother, had been made to keep them for a long time. Mr. Bell said they absolutely lived upon water-porridge for years—how, he did not know; but long after the creditors had given up hope of any payment of old Mr. Thornton's debts (if, indeed, they ever had hoped at all about it, after his suicide,) this young man returned to Milton, and went quietly round to each creditor, paying him the first instalment of the money owing to him. No noise—no gathering together of creditors—it was done very silently and quietly, but all was paid at last; helped on materially by the circumstance of one of the creditors, a crabbed old fellow (Mr. Bell says), taking in Mr. Thornton as a kind of partner.'

'That really is fine,' said Margaret. 'What a pity such a nature should be tainted by his position as a Milton manufacturer.'

'How tainted?' asked her father.

'Oh, papa, by that testing everything by the standard of wealth. When he spoke of the mechanical powers, he evidently looked upon them only as new ways of extending trade and making money. And the poor men around him—they were poor because they were vicious—out of the pale of his sympathies because they had not his iron nature, and the capabilities that it gives him for being rich.'

'Not vicious; he never said that. Improvident and self-indulgent were his words.'

Margaret was collecting her mother's working materials, and preparing to go to bed. Just as she was leaving the room, she hesitated—she was inclined to make an acknowledgment which she thought would please her father, but which to be full and true must include a little annoyance. However, out it came.

'Papa, I do think Mr. Thornton a very remarkable man; but personally I don't like him at all.'

'And I do!' said her father laughing. 'Personally, as you call it, and all. I don't set him up for a hero, or anything of that kind. But good night, child. Your mother looks sadly tired to-night, Margaret.'

Margaret had noticed her mother's jaded appearance with anxiety for some time past, and this remark of her father's sent her up to bed with a dim fear lying like a weight on her heart. The life in Milton was so different from what Mrs. Hale had been accustomed to live in Helstone, in and out perpetually into the fresh and open air; the air itself was so different, deprived of all revivifying principle as it seemed to be here; the domestic worries pressed so very closely, and in so new and sordid a form, upon all the women in the family, that there was good reason to fear that her mother's health might be becoming seriously affected.

There were several other signs of something wrong about Mrs. Hale. She and Dixon held mysterious consultations in her bedroom, from which Dixon would come out crying and cross, as was her custom when any distress of her mistress called upon her sympathy. Once Margaret had gone into the chamber soon after Dixon left it, and found her mother on her knees, and as Margaret stole out she caught a few words, which were evidently a prayer for strength and patience to endure severe bodily suffering. Margaret yearned to re-unite the bond of intimate confidence which had been broken by her long residence at her aunt Shaw's, and strove by gentle caresses and softened words to creep into the warmest place in her mother's heart. But though she received caresses and fond words back again, in such profusion as would have gladdened her formerly, yet she felt that there was a secret withheld from her, and she believed it bore serious reference to her mother's health. She lay awake very long this night, planning how to lessen the evil influence of their Milton life on her mother. A servant to give Dixon permanent assistance should be got, if she gave up her whole time to the search; and then, at any rate, her mother might have all the personal attention she required, and had been accustomed to her whole life. Visiting register offices, seeing all manner of unlikely people, and very few in the least likely, absorbed Margaret's time and thoughts for several days. One afternoon she met Bessy Higgins in the street, and stopped to speak to her.

'Well, Bessy, how are you? Better, I hope, now the wind has changed.'

'Better and not better, if yo' know what that means.'

'Not exactly,' replied Margaret, smiling.

'I'm better in not being torn to pieces by coughing o'nights, but I'm weary and tired o' Milton, and longing to get away to the land o' Beulah; and when I think I'm farther and farther off, my heart sinks, and I'm no better; I'm worse.' Margaret turned round to walk alongside of the girl in her feeble progress homeward. But for a minute or two she did not speak. At last she said in a low voice,

'Bessy, do you wish to die?' For she shrank from death herself, with all the clinging to life so natural to the young and healthy.

Bessy was silent in her turn for a minute or two. Then she replied,

'If yo'd led the life I have, and getten as weary of it as I have, and thought at times, "maybe it'll last for fifty or sixty years—it does wi' some,"—and got dizzy and dazed, and sick, as each of them sixty years seemed to spin about me, and mock me with its length of hours and minutes, and endless bits o' time—oh, wench! I tell thee thou'd been glad enough when th' doctor said he feared thou'd never see another winter.'

'Why, Bessy, what kind of a life has yours been?'

'Nought worse than many others, I reckon. Only I fretted again it, and they didn't.'

'But what was it? You know, I'm a stranger here, so perhaps I'm not so quick at understanding what you mean as if I'd lived all my life at Milton.'

'If yo'd ha' come to our house when yo' said yo' would, I could maybe ha' told you. But father says yo're just like th' rest on 'em; it's out o' sight out o' mind wi' you.'

'I don't know who the rest are; and I've been very busy; and, to tell the truth, I had forgotten my promise—'

'Yo' offered it! we asked none of it.'

'I had forgotten what I said for the time,' continued Margaret quietly. 'I should have thought of it again when I was less busy. May I go with you now?' Bessy gave a quick glance at Margaret's face, to see if the wish expressed was really felt. The sharpness in her eye turned to a wistful longing as she met Margaret's soft and friendly gaze.

'I ha' none so many to care for me; if yo' care yo' may come.

So they walked on together in silence. As they turned up into a small court, opening out of a squalid street, Bessy said,

'Yo'll not be daunted if father's at home, and speaks a bit gruffish at first. He took a mind to ye, yo' see, and he thought a deal o' your coming to see us; and just because he liked yo' he were vexed and put about.'

'Don't fear, Bessy.'

But Nicholas was not at home when they entered. A great slatternly girl, not so old as Bessy, but taller and stronger, was busy at the wash-tub, knocking about the furniture in a rough capable way, but altogether making so much noise that Margaret shrunk, out of sympathy with poor Bessy, who had sat down on the first chair, as if completely tired out with her walk. Margaret asked the sister for a cup of water, and while she ran to fetch it (knocking down the fire-irons, and tumbling over a chair in her way), she unloosed Bessy's bonnet strings, to relieve her catching breath.

'Do you think such life as this is worth caring for?' gasped Bessy, at last. Margaret did not speak, but held the water to her lips. Bessy took a long and feverish draught, and then fell back and shut her eyes. Margaret heard her murmur to herself: 'They shall hunger no more, neither thirst any more; neither shall the sun light on them, nor any heat.'

Margaret bent over and said, 'Bessy, don't be impatient with your life, whatever it is—or may have been. Remember who gave it you, and made it what it is!' She was startled by hearing Nicholas speak behind her; he had come in without her noticing him.

'Now, I'll not have my wench preached to. She's bad enough as it is, with her dreams and her methodee fancies, and her visions of cities with goulden gates and precious stones. But if it amuses her I let it a be, but I'm none going to have more stuff poured into her.'

'But surely,' said Margaret, facing round, 'you believe in what I said, that God gave her life, and ordered what kind of life it was to be?'

'I believe what I see, and no more. That's what I believe, young woman. I don't believe all I hear—no! not by a big deal. I did hear a young lass make an ado about knowing where we lived, and coming to see us. And my wench here thought a deal about it, and flushed up many a time, when hoo little knew as I was looking at her, at the sound of a strange step. But hoo's come at last,—and hoo's welcome, as long as hoo'll keep from preaching on what hoo knows nought about.' Bessy had been watching Margaret's face; she half sate up to speak now, laying her hand on Margaret's arm with a gesture of entreaty. 'Don't be vexed wi' him—there's many a one thinks like him; many and many a one here. If yo' could hear them speak, yo'd not be shocked at him; he's a rare good man, is father—but oh!' said she, falling back in despair, 'what he says at times makes me long to die more than ever, for I want to know so many things, and am so tossed about wi' wonder.'

'Poor wench—poor old wench,—I'm loth to vex thee, I am; but a man mun speak out for the truth, and when I see the world going all wrong at this time o' day, bothering itself wi' things it knows nought about, and leaving undone all the things that lie in disorder close at its hand—why, I say, leave a' this talk about religion alone, and set to work on what yo' see and know. That's my creed. It's simple, and not far to fetch, nor hard to work.'

But the girl only pleaded the more with Margaret.

'Don't think hardly on him—he's a good man, he is. I sometimes think I shall be moped wi' sorrow even in the City of God, if father is not there.' The feverish colour came into her cheek, and the feverish flame into her eye. 'But you will be there, father! you shall! Oh! my heart!' She put her hand to it, and became ghastly pale.

Margaret held her in her arms, and put the weary head to rest upon her bosom. She lifted the thin soft hair from off the temples, and bathed them with water. Nicholas understood all her signs for different articles with the quickness of love, and even the round-eyed sister moved with laborious gentleness at Margaret's 'hush!' Presently the spasm that foreshadowed death had passed away, and Bessy roused herself and said,—

'I'll go to bed,—it's best place; but,' catching at Margaret's gown, 'yo'll come again,—I know yo' will—but just say it!'

'I will come to-morrow, said Margaret.

Bessy leant back against her father, who prepared to carry her upstairs; but as Margaret rose to go, he struggled to say something: 'I could wish there were a God, if it were only to ask Him to bless thee.'

Margaret went away very sad and thoughtful.

She was late for tea at home. At Helstone unpunctuality at meal-times was a great fault in her mother's eyes; but now this, as well as many other little irregularities, seemed to have lost their power of irritation, and Margaret almost longed for the old complainings.

'Have you met with a servant, dear?'

'No, mamma; that Anne Buckley would never have done.'

'Suppose I try,' said Mr. Hale. 'Everybody else has had their turn at this great difficulty. Now let me try. I may be the Cinderella to put on the slipper after all.'

Margaret could hardly smile at this little joke, so oppressed was she by her visit to the Higginses.

'What would you do, papa? How would you set about it?'

'Why, I would apply to some good house-mother to recommend me one known to herself or her servants.'

'Very good. But we must first catch our house-mother.'

'You have caught her. Or rather she is coming into the snare, and you will catch her to-morrow, if you're skilful.'

'What do you mean, Mr. Hale?' asked his wife, her curiosity aroused.

'Why, my paragon pupil (as Margaret calls him), has told me that his mother intends to call on Mrs. and Miss Hale to-morrow.'

'Mrs. Thornton!' exclaimed Mrs. Hale.

'The mother of whom he spoke to us?' said Margaret.

'Mrs. Thornton; the only mother he has, I believe,' said Mr. Hale quietly.

'I shall like to see her. She must be an uncommon person,' her mother added.

'Perhaps she may have a relation who might suit us, and be glad of our place. She sounded to be such a careful economical person, that I should like any one out of the same family.'

'My dear,' said Mr. Hale alarmed. 'Pray don't go off on that idea. I fancy Mrs. Thornton is as haughty and proud in her way, as our little Margaret here is in hers, and that she completely ignores that old time of trial, and poverty, and economy, of which he speaks so openly. I am sure, at any rate, she would not like strangers to know anything about It.'

'Take notice that is not my kind of haughtiness, papa, if I have any at all; which I don't agree to, though you're always accusing me of it.'

'I don't know positively that it is hers either; but from little things I have gathered from him, I fancy so.'

They cared too little to ask in what manner her son had spoken about her. Margaret only wanted to know if she must stay in to receive this call, as it would prevent her going to see how Bessy was, until late in the day, since the early morning was always occupied in household affairs; and then she recollected that her mother must not be left to have the whole weight of entertaining her visitor.

CHAPTER XII - MORNING CALLS

'Well—I suppose we must.'
FRIENDS IN COUNCIL.

Mr. Thornton had had some difficulty in working up his mother to the desired point of civility. She did not often make calls; and when she did, it was in heavy state that she went through her duties. Her son had given her a carriage; but she refused to let him keep horses for it; they were hired for the solemn occasions, when she paid morning or evening visits. She had had horses for three days, not a fortnight before, and had comfortably 'killed off' all her acquaintances, who might now put themselves to trouble and expense in their turn. Yet Crampton was too far off for her to walk; and she had repeatedly questioned her son as to whether his wish that she should call on the Hales was strong enough to bear the expense of cab-hire. She would have been thankful if it had not; for, as she said, 'she saw no use in making up friendships and intimacies with all the teachers and masters in Milton; why, he would be wanting her to call on Fanny's dancing-master's wife, the next thing!'

'And so I would, mother, if Mr. Mason and his wife were friendless in a strange place, like the Hales.'

'Oh! you need not speak so hastily. I am going to-morrow. I only wanted you exactly to understand about it.'

'If you are going to-morrow, I shall order horses.'

'Nonsense, John. One would think you were made of money.'

'Not quite, yet. But about the horses I'm determined. The last time you were out in a cab, you came home with a headache from the jolting.'

'I never complained of it, I'm sure.'

'No. My mother is not given to complaints,' said he, a little proudly. 'But so much the more I have to watch over you. Now as for Fanny there, a little hardship would do her good.'

'She is not made of the same stuff as you are, John. She could not bear it.' Mrs. Thornton was silent after this; for her last words bore relation to a subject which mortified her. She had an unconscious contempt for a weak character; and Fanny was weak in the very points in which her mother and brother were strong. Mrs.

Thornton was not a woman much given to reasoning; her quick judgment and firm resolution served her in good stead of any long arguments and discussions with herself; she felt instinctively that nothing could strengthen Fanny to endure hardships patiently, or face difficulties bravely; and though she winced as she made this acknowledgment to herself about her daughter, it only gave her a kind of pitying tenderness of manner towards her; much of the same description of demeanour with which mothers are wont to treat their weak and sickly children. A stranger, a careless observer might have considered that Mrs. Thornton's manner to her children betokened far more love to Fanny than to John. But such a one would have been deeply mistaken. The very daringness with which mother and son spoke out unpalatable truths, the one to the other, showed a reliance on the firm centre of each other's souls, which the uneasy tenderness of Mrs. Thornton's manner to her daughter, the shame with which she thought to hide the poverty of her child in all the grand qualities which she herself possessed unconsciously, and which she set so high a value upon in others—this shame, I say, betrayed the want of a secure resting-place for her affection. She never called her son by any name but John; 'love,' and 'dear,' and such like terms, were reserved for Fanny. But her heart gave thanks for him day and night; and she walked proudly among women for his sake.

'Fanny dear I shall have horses to the carriage to-day, to go and call on these Hales. Should not you go and see nurse? It's in the same direction, and she's always so glad to see you. You could go on there while I am at Mrs. Hale's.'

'Oh! mamma, it's such a long way, and I am so tired.'

'With what?' asked Mrs. Thornton, her brow slightly contracting.

'I don't know—the weather, I think. It is so relaxing. Couldn't you bring nurse here, mamma? The carriage could fetch her, and she could spend the rest of the day here, which I know she would like.'

Mrs. Thornton did not speak; but she laid her work on the table, and seemed to think.

'It will be a long way for her to walk back at night!' she remarked, at last.

'Oh, but I will send her home in a cab. I never thought of her walking.' At this point, Mr. Thornton came in, just before going to the mill.

'Mother! I need hardly say, that if there is any little thing that could serve Mrs. Hale as an invalid, you will offer it, I'm sure.'

'If I can find it out, I will. But I have never been ill myself, so I am not much up to invalids' fancies.'

'Well! here is Fanny then, who is seldom without an ailment. She will be able to suggest something, perhaps—won't you, Fan?'

'I have not always an ailment,' said Fanny, pettishly; 'and I am not going with mamma. I have a headache to-day, and I shan't go out.'

Mr. Thornton looked annoyed. His mother's eyes were bent on her work, at which she was now stitching away busily.

'Fanny! I wish you to go,' said he, authoritatively. 'It will do you good, instead of harm. You will oblige me by going, without my saying anything more about it.'

He went abruptly out of the room after saying this.

If he had staid a minute longer, Fanny would have cried at his tone of command, even when he used the words, 'You will oblige me.' As it was, she grumbled.

'John always speaks as if I fancied I was ill, and I am sure I never do fancy any such thing. Who are these Hales that he makes such a fuss about?'

'Fanny, don't speak so of your brother. He has good reasons of some kind or other, or he would not wish us to go. Make haste and put your things on.'

But the little altercation between her son and her daughter did not incline Mrs. Thornton more favourably towards 'these Hales.' Her jealous heart repeated her daughter's question, 'Who are they, that he is so anxious we should pay them all this attention?' It came up like a burden to a song, long after Fanny had forgotten all about it in the pleasant excitement of seeing the effect of a new bonnet in the looking-glass.

Mrs. Thornton was shy. It was only of late years that she had had leisure enough in her life to go into society; and as society she did not enjoy it. As dinner-giving, and as criticising other people's dinners, she took satisfaction in it. But this going to make acquaintance with strangers was a very different thing. She was ill at ease, and looked more than usually stern and forbidding as she entered the Hales' little drawing-room.

Margaret was busy embroidering a small piece of cambric for some little article of dress for Edith's expected baby—'Flimsy, useless work,' as Mrs. Thornton observed to herself. She liked Mrs. Hale's double knitting far better; that was sensible of its kind. The room altogether was full of knick-knacks, which must take a long time to dust; and time to people of limited income was money. She made all these reflections as she was talking in her stately way to Mrs. Hale, and uttering all the stereotyped commonplaces that most people can find to say with their senses blindfolded. Mrs. Hale was making rather more exertion in her answers, captivated by some real old lace which Mrs. Thornton wore; 'lace,' as she afterwards observed to Dixon, 'of that old English point which has not been made for this seventy years, and which cannot be bought. It must have been an heir-loom, and shows that she had ancestors.' So the owner of the ancestral lace became worthy of something more than the languid exertion to be agreeable to a visitor, by which Mrs. Hale's efforts at conversation would have been otherwise bounded. And presently, Margaret, racking her brain to talk to Fanny, heard her mother and Mrs. Thornton plunge into the interminable subject of servants.

'I suppose you are not musical,' said Fanny, 'as I see no piano.'

'I am fond of hearing good music; I cannot play well myself; and papa and mamma don't care much about it; so we sold our old piano when we came here.'

'I wonder how you can exist without one. It almost seems to me a necessary of life.'

'Fifteen shillings a week, and three saved out of them!' thought Margaret to herself 'But she must have been very young. She probably has forgotten her own personal experience. But she must know of those days.' Margaret's manner had an extra tinge of coldness in it when she next spoke.

'You have good concerts here, I believe.'

'Oh, yes! Delicious! Too crowded, that is the worst. The directors admit so indiscriminately. But one is sure to hear the newest music there. I always have a large order to give to Johnson's, the day after a concert.'

'Do you like new music simply for its newness, then?'

'Oh; one knows it is the fashion in London, or else the singers would not bring it down here. You have been in London, of course.'

'Yes,' said Margaret, 'I have lived there for several years.'

'Oh! London and the Alhambra are the two places I long to see!'

'London and the Alhambra!'

'Yes! ever since I read the Tales of the Alhambra. Don't you know them?'

'I don't think I do. But surely, it is a very easy journey to London.'

'Yes; but somehow,' said Fanny, lowering her voice, 'mamma has never been to London herself, and can't understand my longing. She is very proud of Milton; dirty, smoky place, as I feel it to be. I believe she admires it the more for those very qualities.'

'If it has been Mrs. Thornton's home for some years, I can well understand her loving it,' said Margaret, in her clear bell-like voice.

'What are you saying about me, Miss Hale? May I inquire?'

Margaret had not the words ready for an answer to this question, which took her a little by surprise, so Miss Thornton replied:

'Oh, mamma! we are only trying to account for your being so fond of Milton.'

'Thank you,' said Mrs. Thornton. 'I do not feel that my very natural liking for the place where I was born and brought up,—and which has since been my residence for some years, requires any accounting for.'

Margaret was vexed. As Fanny had put it, it did seem as if they had been impertinently discussing Mrs. Thornton's feelings; but she also rose up against that lady's manner of showing that she was offended.

Mrs. Thornton went on after a moment's pause:

'Do you know anything of Milton, Miss Hale? Have you seen any of our factories? our magnificent warehouses?'

'No!' said Margaret. 'I have not seen anything of that description as yet.' Then she felt that, by concealing her utter indifference to all such places, she was hardly speaking with truth; so she went on:

'I dare say, papa would have taken me before now if I had cared. But I really do not find much pleasure in going over manufactories.'

'They are very curious places,' said Mrs. Hale, 'but there is so much noise and dirt always. I remember once going in a lilac silk to see candles made, and my gown was utterly ruined.'

'Very probably,' said Mrs. Thornton, in a short displeased manner. 'I merely thought, that as strangers newly come to reside in a town which has risen to eminence in the country, from the character and progress of its peculiar business, you might have cared to visit some of the places where it is carried on; places unique in the kingdom, I am informed. If Miss Hale changes her mind and condescends to be curious as to the manufactures of Milton, I can only say I shall be glad to procure her admission to print-works, or reed-making, or the more simple operations of spinning carried on in my son's mill. Every improvement of machinery is, I believe, to be seen there, in its highest perfection.'

'I am so glad you don't like mills and manufactories, and all those kind of things,' said Fanny, in a half-whisper, as she rose to accompany her mother, who was taking leave of Mrs. Hale with rustling dignity.

'I think I should like to know all about them, if I were you,' replied Margaret quietly.

'Fanny!' said her mother, as they drove away, 'we will be civil to these Hales: but don't form one of your hasty friendships with the daughter. She will do you no good, I see. The mother looks very ill, and seems a nice, quiet kind of person.'

'I don't want to form any friendship with Miss Hale, mamma,' said Fanny, pouting. 'I thought I was doing my duty by talking to her, and trying to amuse her.'

'Well! at any rate John must be satisfied now.'

CHAPTER XIII - A SOFT BREEZE IN A SULTRY PLACE

'That doubt and trouble, fear and pain,
And anguish, all, are shadows vain,
That death itself shall not remain;

That weary deserts we may tread,
A dreary labyrinth may thread,
Thro' dark ways underground be led;

Yet, if we will one Guide obey,
The dreariest path, the darkest way
Shall issue out in heavenly day;

And we, on divers shores now cast,
Shall meet, our perilous voyage past,
All in our Father's house at last!'
R. C. TRENCH.

Margaret flew upstairs as soon as their visitors were gone, and put on her bonnet and shawl, to run and inquire how Bessy Higgins was, and sit with her as long as she could before dinner. As she went along the crowded narrow streets, she felt how much of interest they had gained by the simple fact of her having learnt to care for a dweller in them.

Mary Higgins, the slatternly younger sister, had endeavoured as well as she could to tidy up the house for the expected visit. There had been rough-stoning done in the middle of the floor, while the flags under the chairs and table and round the walls retained their dark unwashed appearance. Although the day was hot, there burnt a large fire in the grate, making the whole place feel like an oven. Margaret did not understand that the lavishness of coals was a sign of hospitable welcome to her on Mary's part, and thought that perhaps the oppressive heat was necessary for Bessy. Bessy herself lay on a squab, or short sofa, placed under the window. She was very much more feeble than on the previous day, and tired with raising herself at every step to look out and see if it was Margaret coming. And now that Margaret was there, and had taken a chair by her, Bessy lay back silent, and content to look at Margaret's face, and touch her articles of dress, with a childish admiration of their fineness of texture.

'I never knew why folk in the Bible cared for soft raiment afore. But it must be nice to go dressed as yo' do. It's different fro' common. Most fine folk tire my eyes out wi' their colours; but some how yours rest me. Where did ye get this frock?'

'In London,' said Margaret, much amused.

'London! Have yo' been in London?'

'Yes! I lived there for some years. But my home was in a forest; in the country.

'Tell me about it,' said Bessy. 'I like to hear speak of the country and trees, and such like things.' She leant back, and shut her eye and crossed her hands over her breast, lying at perfect rest, as if to receive all the ideas Margaret could suggest.

Margaret had never spoken of Helstone since she left it, except just naming the place incidentally. She saw it in dreams more vivid than life, and as she fell away to slumber at nights her memory wandered in all its pleasant places. But her heart was opened to this girl; 'Oh, Bessy, I loved the home we have left so dearly! I wish you could see it. I cannot tell you half its beauty. There are great trees standing all about it, with their branches stretching long and level, and making a deep shade of rest even at noonday. And yet, though every leaf may seem still, there is a continual rushing sound of movement all around—not close at hand. Then sometimes the turf is as soft and fine as velvet; and sometimes quite lush with the perpetual moisture of a little, hidden, tinkling brook near at hand. And then in other parts there are billowy ferns—whole stretches of fern; some in the green shadow; some with long streaks of golden sunlight lying on them—just like the sea.'

'I have never seen the sea,' murmured Bessy. 'But go on.'

'Then, here and there, there are wide commons, high up as if above the very tops of the trees—'

'I'm glad of that. I felt smothered like down below. When I have gone for an out, I've always wanted to get high up and see far away, and take a deep breath o' fulness in that air. I get smothered enough in Milton, and I think the sound yo' speak of among the trees, going on for ever and ever, would send me dazed; it's that made my head ache so in the mill. Now on these commons I reckon there is but little noise?'

'No,' said Margaret; 'nothing but here and there a lark high in the air. Sometimes I used to hear a farmer speaking sharp and loud to his servants; but it was so far away that it only reminded me pleasantly that other people were hard at work in some distant place, while I just sat on the heather and did nothing.'

'I used to think once that if I could have a day of doing nothing, to rest me—a day in some quiet place like that yo' speak on—it would maybe set me up. But now I've had many days o' idleness, and I'm just as weary o' them as I was o' my work. Sometimes I'm so tired out I think I cannot enjoy heaven without a piece of rest first. I'm rather afeard o' going straight there without getting a good sleep in the grave to set me up.'

'Don't be afraid, Bessy,' said Margaret, laying her hand on the girl's; 'God can give you more perfect rest than even idleness on earth, or the dead sleep of the grave can do.'

Bessy moved uneasily; then she said:

'I wish father would not speak as he does. He means well, as I telled yo' yesterday, and tell yo' again and again. But yo' see, though I don't believe him a bit by day, yet by night—when I'm in a fever, half-asleep and half-awake—it comes back upon me—oh! so bad! And I think, if this should be th' end of all, and if all I've been born for is just to work my heart and my life away, and to sicken i' this dree place, wi' them mill-noises in my ears for ever, until I could scream out for them to stop, and let me have a little piece o' quiet—and wi' the fluff filling my lungs, until I thirst to death for one long deep breath o' the clear air yo' speak on—and my mother gone, and I never able to tell her again how I loved her, and o' all my troubles—I think if this life is th' end, and that there's no God to wipe away all tears from all eyes—yo' wench, yo'!' said she, sitting up, and clutching violently, almost fiercely, at Margaret's hand, 'I could go mad, and kill yo', I could.' She fell back completely worn out with her passion. Margaret knelt down by her.

'Bessy—we have a Father in Heaven.'

'I know it! I know it,' moaned she, turning her head uneasily from side to side.

'I'm very wicked. I've spoken very wickedly. Oh! don't be frightened by me and never come again. I would not harm a hair of your head. And,' opening her eyes, and looking earnestly at Margaret, 'I believe, perhaps, more than yo' do o' what's to come. I read the book o' Revelations until I know it off by heart, and I never doubt when I'm waking, and in my senses, of all the glory I'm to come to.'

'Don't let us talk of what fancies come into your head when you are feverish. I would rather hear something about what you used to do when you were well.'

'I think I was well when mother died, but I have never been rightly strong sin' somewhere about that time. I began to work in a carding-room soon after, and the fluff got into my lungs and poisoned me.'

'Fluff?' said Margaret, inquiringly.

'Fluff,' repeated Bessy. 'Little bits, as fly off fro' the cotton, when they're carding it, and fill the air till it looks all fine white dust. They say it winds round the lungs, and tightens them up. Anyhow, there's many a one as works in a carding-room, that falls into a waste, coughing and spitting blood, because they're just poisoned by the fluff.'

'But can't it be helped?' asked Margaret.

'I dunno. Some folk have a great wheel at one end o' their carding-rooms to make a draught, and carry off th' dust; but that wheel costs a deal o' money—five or six hundred pound, maybe, and brings in no profit; so it's but a few of th' masters as will put 'em up; and I've heard tell o' men who didn't like working places where there was a wheel, because they said as how it mad 'em hungry, at after they'd been long used to swallowing fluff, to go without it, and that their wage ought to be raised if they were to work in such places. So between masters and men th' wheels fall through. I know I wish there'd been a wheel in our place, though.'

'Did not your father know about it?' asked Margaret.

'Yes! And he were sorry. But our factory were a good one on the whole; and a steady likely set o' people; and father was afeard of letting me go to a strange place, for though yo' would na think it now, many a one then used to call me a gradely lass enough. And I did na like to be reckoned nesh and soft, and Mary's schooling were to be kept up, mother said, and father he were always liking to buy books, and go to lectures o' one kind or another—all which took money—so I just worked on till I shall ne'er get the whirr out o' my ears, or the fluff out o' my throat i' this world. That's all.'

'How old are you?' asked Margaret.

'Nineteen, come July.'

'And I too am nineteen.' She thought, more sorrowfully than Bessy did, of the contrast between them. She could not speak for a moment or two for the emotion she was trying to keep down.

'About Mary,' said Bessy. 'I wanted to ask yo' to be a friend to her. She's seventeen, but she's th' last on us. And I don't want her to go to th' mill, and yet I dunno what she's fit for.'

'She could not do'—Margaret glanced unconsciously at the uncleaned corners of the room—'She could hardly undertake a servant's place, could she? We have an old faithful servant, almost a friend, who wants help, but who is very particular; and it would not be right to plague her with giving her any assistance that would really be an annoyance and an irritation.'

'No, I see. I reckon yo're right. Our Mary's a good wench; but who has she had to teach her what to do about a house? No mother, and me at the mill till I were good for nothing but scolding her for doing badly what I didn't know how to do a bit. But I wish she could ha' lived wi' yo', for all that.'

'But even though she may not be exactly fitted to come and live with us as a servant—and I don't know about that—I will always try and be a friend to her for your sake, Bessy. And now I must go. I will come again as soon as I can; but if it should not be to-morrow, or the next day, or even a week or a fortnight hence, don't think I've forgotten you. I may be busy.'

'I'll know yo' won't forget me again. I'll not mistrust yo' no more. But remember, in a week or a fortnight I may be dead and buried!'

'I'll come as soon as I can, Bessy,' said Margaret, squeezing her hand tight.

'But you'll let me know if you are worse.

'Ay, that will I,' said Bessy, returning the pressure.

From that day forwards Mrs. Hale became more and more of a suffering invalid. It was now drawing near to the anniversary of Edith's marriage, and looking back upon the year's accumulated heap of troubles, Margaret wondered how they had been borne. If she could have anticipated them, how she would have shrunk away and hid herself from the coming time! And yet day by day had, of itself, and by itself, been very endurable—small, keen, bright little spots of positive enjoyment having come sparkling into the very middle of sorrows. A year ago, or when she first went to Helstone, and first became silently conscious of the querulousness in her mother's temper, she would have groaned bitterly over the idea of a long illness to be borne in a strange, desolate, noisy, busy place, with diminished comforts on every side of the home life. But with the increase of serious and just ground of complaint, a new kind of patience had sprung up in her mother's mind. She was gentle and quiet in intense bodily suffering, almost in proportion as she had been restless and depressed when there had been no real cause for grief. Mr. Hale was in exactly that stage of apprehension which, in men of his stamp, takes the shape of wilful blindness. He was more irritated than Margaret had ever known him at his daughter's expressed anxiety.

'Indeed, Margaret, you are growing fanciful! God knows I should be the first to take the alarm if your mother were really ill; we always saw when she had her headaches at Helstone, even without her telling us. She looks quite pale and white when she is ill; and now she has a bright healthy colour in her cheeks, just as she used to have when I first knew her.'

'But, papa,' said Margaret, with hesitation, 'do you know, I think that is the flush of pain.'

'Nonsense, Margaret. I tell you, you are too fanciful. You are the person not well, I think. Send for the doctor to-morrow for yourself; and then, if it will make your mind easier, he can see your mother.'

'Thank you, dear papa. It will make me happier, indeed.' And she went up to him to kiss him. But he pushed her away—gently enough, but still as if she had suggested unpleasant ideas, which he should be glad to get rid of as readily as he could of her presence. He walked uneasily up and down the room.

'Poor Maria!' said he, half soliloquising, 'I wish one could do right without sacrificing others. I shall hate this town, and myself too, if she—— Pray, Margaret, does your mother often talk to you of the old places of Helstone, I mean?'

'No, papa,' said Margaret, sadly.

'Then, you see, she can't be fretting after them, eh? It has always been a comfort to me to think that your mother was so simple and open that I knew every little grievance she had. She never would conceal anything seriously affecting her health from me: would she, eh, Margaret? I am quite sure she would not. So don't let me hear of these foolish morbid ideas. Come, give me a kiss, and run off to bed.'

But she heard him pacing about (racooning, as she and Edith used to call it) long after her slow and languid undressing was finished—long after she began to listen as she lay in bed.

CHAPTER XIV - THE MUTINY

'I was used
  To sleep at nights as sweetly as a child,—
  Now if the wind blew rough, it made me start,
  And think of my poor boy tossing about
  Upon the roaring seas. And then I seemed
  To feel that it was hard to take him from me
  For such a little fault.'
          SOUTHEY.

It was a comfort to Margaret about this time, to find that her mother drew more tenderly and intimately towards her than she had ever done since the days of her childhood. She took her to her heart as a confidential friend—the post Margaret had always longed to fill, and had envied Dixon for being preferred to. Margaret took pains to respond to every call made upon her for sympathy—and they were many—even when they bore relation to trifles, which she would no more have noticed or regarded herself than the elephant would perceive the little pin at his feet, which yet he lifts carefully up at the bidding of his keeper. All unconsciously Margaret drew near to a reward.

One evening, Mr. Hale being absent, her mother began to talk to her about her brother Frederick, the very subject on which Margaret had longed to ask questions, and almost the only one on which her timidity overcame her natural openness. The more she wanted to hear about him, the less likely she was to speak.

'Oh, Margaret, it was so windy last night! It came howling down the chimney in our room! I could not sleep. I never can when there is such a terrible wind. I got into a wakeful habit when poor Frederick was at sea; and now, even if I don't waken all at once, I dream of him in some stormy sea, with great, clear, glass-green walls of waves on either side his ship, but far higher than her very masts, curling over her with that cruel, terrible white foam, like some gigantic crested serpent. It is an old dream, but it always comes back on windy nights, till I am thankful to waken, sitting straight and stiff up in bed with my terror. Poor Frederick! He is on land now, so wind can do him no harm. Though I did think it might shake down some of those tall chimneys.'

'Where is Frederick now, mamma? Our letters are directed to the care of Messrs. Barbour, at Cadiz, I know; but where is he himself?'

'I can't remember the name of the place, but he is not called Hale; you must remember that, Margaret. Notice the F. D. in every corner of the letters. He has taken the name of Dickenson. I wanted him to have been called Beresford, to which he had a kind of right, but your father thought he had better not. He might be recognised, you know, if he were called by my name.'

'Mamma,' said Margaret, 'I was at Aunt Shaw's when it all happened; and I suppose I was not old enough to be told plainly about it. But I should like to know now, if I may—if it does not give you too much pain to speak about it.'

'Pain! No,' replied Mrs. Hale, her cheek flushing. 'Yet it is pain to think that perhaps I may never see my darling boy again. Or else he did right, Margaret. They may say what they like, but I have his own letters to show, and I'll believe him, though he is my son, sooner than any court-martial on earth. Go to my little japan cabinet, dear, and in the second left-hand drawer you will find a packet of letters.'

Margaret went. There were the yellow, sea-stained letters, with the peculiar fragrance which ocean letters have: Margaret carried them back to her mother, who untied the silken string with trembling fingers, and, examining their dates, she gave them to Margaret to read, making her hurried, anxious remarks on their contents, almost before her daughter could have understood what they were.

'You see, Margaret, how from the very first he disliked Captain Reid. He was second lieutenant in the ship—the *Orion*—in which Frederick sailed the very first time. Poor little fellow, how well he looked in his midshipman's dress, with his dirk in his hand, cutting open all the newspapers with it as if it were a paper-knife! But this Mr. Reid, as he was then, seemed to take a dislike to Frederick from the very beginning. And then—stay! these are the letters he wrote on board the *Russell*. When he was appointed to her, and found his old enemy Captain Reid in command, he did mean to bear all his tyranny patiently. Look! this is the letter. Just read it, Margaret. Where is it he says—Stop—'my father may rely upon me, that I will bear with all proper patience everything that one officer and gentleman can take from another. But from my former knowledge of my present captain, I confess I look forward with apprehension to a long course of tyranny on board the *Russell*.' You see, he promises to bear patiently, and I am sure he did, for he was the sweetest-tempered boy, when he was not vexed, that could possibly be. Is that the letter in which he speaks of Captain Reid's impatience with the men, for not going through the ship's manœuvres as quickly as the *Avenger*? You see, he says that they had many new hands on board the *Russell*, while the *Avenger* had been nearly three years on the station, with nothing to do but to keep slavers off, and work her men, till they ran up and down the rigging like rats or monkeys.'

Margaret slowly read the letter, half illegible through the fading of the ink. It might be—it probably was—a statement of Captain Reid's imperiousness in trifles, very much exaggerated by the narrator, who had written it while fresh and warm from the scene of altercation. Some sailors being aloft in the main-topsail rigging, the captain had ordered them to race down, threatening the hindmost with the cat-of-nine-tails. He who was the farthest on the spar, feeling the impossibility of passing his companions, and yet passionately dreading the disgrace of the flogging, threw himself desperately down to catch a rope considerably lower, failed, and fell senseless on deck. He only survived for a few hours afterwards, and the indignation of the ship's crew was at boiling point when young Hale wrote.

'But we did not receive this letter till long, long after we heard of the mutiny. Poor Fred! I dare say it was a comfort to him to write it even though he could not have known how to send it, poor fellow! And then we saw a report in the papers—that's to say, long before Fred's letter reached us—of an atrocious mutiny having broken out on board the *Russell*, and that the mutineers had remained in possession of the ship, which had gone off, it was supposed, to be a pirate; and that Captain Reid was sent adrift in a boat with some men—officers or something—whose names were all given, for they were picked up by a West-Indian steamer. Oh, Margaret! how your father and I turned sick over that list, when there was no name of Frederick Hale. We thought it must be some mistake; for poor Fred was such a fine fellow, only perhaps rather too passionate; and we hoped that the name of Carr, which was in the list, was a misprint for that of Hale—newspapers are so careless. And towards post-time the next day, papa set off to walk to Southampton to get the papers; and I could not stop at home, so I went to meet him. He was very late—much later than I thought he would have been; and I sat down under the hedge to wait for him. He came at last, his arms hanging loose down, his head sunk, and walking heavily along, as if every step was a labour and a trouble. Margaret, I see him now.'

'Don't go on, mamma. I can understand it all,' said Margaret, leaning up caressingly against her mother's side, and kissing her hand.

'No, you can't, Margaret. No one can who did not see him then. I could hardly lift myself up to go and meet him—everything seemed so to reel around me all at once. And when I got to him, he did not speak, or seem surprised to see me there, more than three miles from home, beside the Oldham beech-tree; but he put my arm in his, and kept stroking my hand, as if he wanted to soothe me to be very quiet under some great heavy blow; and when I trembled so all over that I could not speak, he took me in his arms, and stooped down his head on mine, and began to shake and to cry in a strange muffled, groaning voice, till I, for very fright, stood quite still, and only begged him to tell me what he had heard. And then, with his hand jerking, as if some one else moved it against his will, he gave me a wicked newspaper to read, calling our Frederick a "traitor of the blackest dye," "a base, ungrateful disgrace to his profession." Oh! I cannot tell what bad words they did not use. I took the paper in my hands as soon as I had read it—I tore it up to little bits—I tore it—oh! I believe Margaret, I tore it with my teeth. I did not cry. I could not. My cheeks were as hot as fire, and my very eyes burnt in my head. I saw your father looking grave at me. I said it was a lie, and so it was. Months after, this letter came, and you see what provocation Frederick had. It was not for himself, or his own injuries, he rebelled; but he would speak his mind to Captain Reid, and so it went on from bad to worse; and you see, most of the sailors stuck by Frederick.

'I think, Margaret,' she continued, after a pause, in a weak, trembling, exhausted voice, 'I am glad of it—I am prouder of Frederick standing up against injustice, than if he had been simply a good officer.'

'I am sure I am,' said Margaret, in a firm, decided tone. 'Loyalty and obedience to wisdom and justice are fine; but it is still finer to defy arbitrary power, unjustly and cruelly used-not on behalf of ourselves, but on behalf of others more helpless.'

'For all that, I wish I could see Frederick once more—just once. He was my first baby, Margaret.' Mrs. Hale spoke wistfully, and almost as if apologising for the yearning, craving wish, as though it were a depreciation of her remaining child. But such an idea never crossed Margaret's mind. She was thinking how her mother's desire could be fulfilled.

'It is six or seven years ago—would they still prosecute him, mother? If he came and stood his trial, what would be the punishment? Surely, he might bring evidence of his great provocation.'

'It would do no good,' replied Mrs. Hale. 'Some of the sailors who accompanied Frederick were taken, and there was a court-martial held on them on board the Amicia; I believed all they said in their defence, poor fellows, because it just agreed with Frederick's story—but it was of no use,—' and for the first time during the conversation Mrs. Hale began to cry; yet something possessed Margaret to force the information she foresaw, yet dreaded, from her mother.

'What happened to them, mamma?' asked she.

'They were hung at the yard-arm,' said Mrs. Hale, solemnly. 'And the worst was that the court, in condemning them to death, said they had suffered themselves to be led astray from their duty by their superior officers.'

They were silent for a long time.

'And Frederick was in South America for several years, was he not?'

'Yes. And now he is in Spain. At Cadiz, or somewhere near it. If he comes to England he will be hung. I shall never see his face again—for if he comes to England he will be hung.'

There was no comfort to be given. Mrs. Hale turned her face to the wall, and lay perfectly still in her mother's despair. Nothing could be said to console her. She took her hand out of Margaret's with a little impatient movement, as if she would fain be left alone with the recollection of her son. When Mr. Hale came in, Margaret went out, oppressed with gloom, and seeing no promise of brightness on any side of the horizon.

CHAPTER XV - MASTERS AND MEN

'Thought fights with thought;
out springs a spark of truth
From the collision of the sword and shield.'
W. S. LANDOR.

'Margaret,' said her father, the next day, 'we must return Mrs. Thornton's call. Your mother is not very well, and thinks she cannot walk so far; but you and I will go this afternoon.'

As they went, Mr. Hale began about his wife's health, with a kind of veiled anxiety, which Margaret was glad to see awakened at last.

'Did you consult the doctor, Margaret? Did you send for him?'

'No, papa, you spoke of his coming to see me. Now I was well. But if I only knew of some good doctor, I would go this afternoon, and ask him to come, for I am sure mamma is seriously indisposed.'

She put the truth thus plainly and strongly because her father had so completely shut his mind against the idea, when she had last named her fears. But now the case was changed. He answered in a despondent tone:

'Do you think she has any hidden complaint? Do you think she is really very ill? Has Dixon said anything? Oh, Margaret! I am haunted by the fear that our coming to Milton has killed her. My poor Maria!'

'Oh, papa! don't imagine such things,' said Margaret, shocked. 'She is not well, that is all. Many a one is not well for a time; and with good advice gets better and stronger than ever.'

'But has Dixon said anything about her?'

'No! You know Dixon enjoys making a mystery out of trifles; and she has been a little mysterious about mamma's health, which has alarmed me rather, that is all. Without any reason, I dare say. You know, papa, you said the other day I was getting fanciful.'

'I hope and trust you are. But don't think of what I said then. I like you to be fanciful about your mother's health. Don't be afraid of telling me your fancies. I like to hear them, though, I dare say, I spoke as if I was annoyed. But we will ask Mrs. Thornton if she can tell us of a good doctor. We won't throw away our money on any but some one first-rate. Stay, we turn up this street.' The street did not look as if it could contain any house large enough for Mrs. Thornton's habitation. Her son's presence never gave any impression as to the kind of house he lived in; but, unconsciously, Margaret had imagined that tall, massive, handsomely dressed Mrs. Thornton must live in a house of the same character as herself. Now Marlborough Street consisted of long rows of small houses, with a blank wall here and there; at least that was all they could see from the point at which they entered it.

'He told me he lived in Marlborough Street, I'm sure,' said Mr. Hale, with a much perplexed air.

'Perhaps it is one of the economies he still practises, to live in a very small house. But here are plenty of people about; let me ask.'

She accordingly inquired of a passer-by, and was informed that Mr. Thornton lived close to the mill, and had the factory lodge-door pointed out to her, at the end of the long dead wall they had noticed.

The lodge-door was like a common garden-door; on one side of it were great closed gates for the ingress and egress of lorries and wagons. The lodge-keeper admitted them into a great oblong yard, on one side of which were offices for the transaction of business; on the opposite, an immense many-windowed mill, whence proceeded the continual clank of machinery and the long groaning roar of the steam-engine, enough to deafen those who lived within the enclosure. Opposite to the wall, along which the street ran, on one of the narrow sides of the oblong, was a handsome stone-coped house,—blackened, to be sure, by the smoke, but with paint, windows, and steps kept scrupulously clean. It was evidently a house which had been built some fifty or sixty years. The stone facings—the long, narrow windows, and the number of them—the flights of steps up to the front door, ascending from either side, and guarded by railing—all witnessed to its age. Margaret only wondered why people who could afford to live in so good a house, and keep it in such perfect order, did not prefer a much smaller dwelling in the country, or even some suburb; not in the continual whirl and din of the factory. Her unaccustomed ears could hardly catch her father's voice, as they stood on the steps awaiting the opening of the door. The yard, too, with the great doors in the dead wall as a boundary, was but a dismal look-out for the sitting-rooms of the house—as Margaret found when they had mounted the old-fashioned stairs, and been ushered into the drawing-room, the three windows of which went over the front door and the room on the right-hand side of the entrance. There was no one in the drawing-room. It seemed as though no one had been in it since the day when the furniture was bagged up with as much care as if the house was to be overwhelmed with lava, and discovered a thousand years hence. The walls were pink and gold; the pattern on the carpet represented bunches of flowers on a light ground, but it was carefully covered up in the centre by a linen drugget, glazed and colourless. The window-curtains were lace; each chair and sofa had its own particular veil of netting, or knitting. Great alabaster groups occupied every flat surface, safe from dust under their glass shades. In the middle of the room, right under the bagged-up chandelier, was a large circular table, with smartly-bound books arranged at regular intervals round the circumference of its polished surface, like gaily-coloured spokes of a wheel. Everything reflected light, nothing absorbed it. The whole room had a painfully spotted, spangled, speckled look about it, which impressed Margaret so unpleasantly that she was hardly conscious of the peculiar cleanliness required to keep everything so white and pure in such an atmosphere, or of the trouble that must be willingly expended to secure that effect of icy, snowy discomfort. Wherever she looked there was evidence of care and labour, but not care and labour to procure ease, to help on habits of tranquil home employment; solely to ornament, and then to preserve ornament from dirt or destruction.

They had leisure to observe, and to speak to each other in low voices, before Mrs. Thornton appeared. They were talking of what all the world might hear; but it is a common effect of such a room as this to make people speak low, as if unwilling to awaken the unused echoes.

At last Mrs. Thornton came in, rustling in handsome black silk, as was her wont; her muslins and laces rivalling, not excelling, the pure whiteness of the muslins and netting of the room. Margaret explained how it was that her mother could not accompany them to return Mrs. Thornton's call; but in her anxiety not to bring back her father's fears too vividly, she gave but a bungling account, and left the impression on Mrs. Thornton's mind that Mrs. Hale's was some temporary or fanciful fine-ladyish indisposition, which might have been put aside had there been a strong enough motive; or that if it was too severe to allow her to come out that day, the call might have been deferred. Remembering, too, the horses to her carriage, hired for her own visit to the Hales, and how Fanny had been ordered to go by Mr. Thornton, in order to pay every respect to them, Mrs. Thornton drew up slightly offended, and gave Margaret no sympathy—indeed, hardly any credit for the statement of her mother's indisposition.

'How is Mr. Thornton?' asked Mr. Hale. 'I was afraid he was not well, from his hurried note yesterday.'

'My son is rarely ill; and when he is, he never speaks about it, or makes it an excuse for not doing anything. He told me he could not get leisure to read with you last night, sir. He regretted it, I am sure; he values the hours spent with you.'

'I am sure they are equally agreeable to me,' said Mr. Hale. 'It makes me feel young again to see his enjoyment and appreciation of all that is fine in classical literature.'

'I have no doubt the classics are very desirable for people who have leisure. But, I confess, it was against my judgment that my son renewed his study of them. The time and place in which he lives, seem to me to require all his energy and attention. Classics may do very well for men who loiter away their lives in the country or in colleges; but Milton men ought to have their thoughts and powers absorbed in the work of to-day. At least, that is my opinion.' This last clause she gave out with 'the pride that apes humility.'

'But, surely, if the mind is too long directed to one object only, it will get stiff and rigid, and unable to take in many interests,' said Margaret.

'I do not quite understand what you mean by a mind getting stiff and rigid. Nor do I admire those whirligig characters that are full of this thing to-day, to be utterly forgetful of it in their new interest to-morrow. Having many interests does not suit the life of a Milton manufacturer. It is, or ought to be, enough for him to have one great desire, and to bring all the purposes of his life to bear on the fulfilment of that.'

'And that is—?' asked Mr. Hale.

Her sallow cheek flushed, and her eye lightened, as she answered:

'To hold and maintain a high, honourable place among the merchants of his country—the men of his town. Such a place my son has earned for himself. Go where you will—I don't say in England only, but in Europe—the name of John Thornton of Milton is known and respected amongst all men of business. Of course, it is unknown in the fashionable circles,' she continued, scornfully.

'Idle gentlemen and ladies are not likely to know much of a Milton manufacturer, unless he gets into parliament, or marries a lord's daughter.' Both Mr. Hale and Margaret had an uneasy, ludicrous consciousness that they had never heard of this great name, until Mr. Bell had written them word that Mr. Thornton would be a good friend to have in Milton. The proud mother's world was not their world of Harley Street gentilities on the one hand, or country clergymen and Hampshire squires on the other. Margaret's face, in spite of all her endeavours to keep it simply listening in its expression told the sensitive Mrs. Thornton this feeling of hers.

'You think you never heard of this wonderful son of mine, Miss Hale. You think I'm an old woman whose ideas are bounded by Milton, and whose own crow is the whitest ever seen.'

'No,' said Margaret, with some spirit. 'It may be true, that I was thinking I had hardly heard Mr. Thornton's name before I came to Milton. But since I have come here, I have heard enough to make me respect and admire him, and to feel how much justice and truth there is in what you have said of him.'

'Who spoke to you of him?' asked Mrs. Thornton, a little mollified, yet jealous lest any one else's words should not have done him full justice. Margaret hesitated before she replied. She did not like this authoritative questioning. Mr. Hale came in, as he thought, to the rescue.

'It was what Mr. Thornton said himself, that made us know the kind of man he was. Was it not, Margaret?'

Mrs. Thornton drew herself up, and said—

'My son is not the one to tell of his own doings. May I again ask you, Miss Hale, from whose account you formed your favourable opinion of him? A mother is curious and greedy of commendation of her children, you know.'

Margaret replied, 'It was as much from what Mr. Thornton withheld of that which we had been told of his previous life by Mr. Bell,—it was more that than what he said, that made us all feel what reason you have to be proud of him.'

'Mr. Bell! What can he know of John? He, living a lazy life in a drowsy college. But I'm obliged to you, Miss Hale. Many a missy young lady would have shrunk from giving an old woman the pleasure of hearing that her son was well spoken of.'

'Why?' asked Margaret, looking straight at Mrs. Thornton, in bewilderment.

'Why! because I suppose they might have consciences that told them how surely they were making the old mother into an advocate for them, in case they had any plans on the son's heart.'

She smiled a grim smile, for she had been pleased by Margaret's frankness; and perhaps she felt that she had been asking questions too much as if she had a right to catechise. Margaret laughed outright at the notion presented to her; laughed so merrily that it grated on Mrs. Thornton's ear, as if the words that called forth that laugh, must have been utterly and entirely ludicrous. Margaret stopped her merriment as soon as she saw Mrs. Thornton's annoyed look.

'I beg your pardon, madam. But I really am very much obliged to you for exonerating me from making any plans on Mr. Thornton's heart.'

'Young ladies have, before now,' said Mrs. Thornton, stiffly.

'I hope Miss Thornton is well,' put in Mr. Hale, desirous of changing the current of the conversation.

'She is as well as she ever is. She is not strong,' replied Mrs. Thornton, shortly.

'And Mr. Thornton? I suppose I may hope to see him on Thursday?'

'I cannot answer for my son's engagements. There is some uncomfortable work going on in the town; a threatening of a strike. If so, his experience and judgment will make him much consulted by his friends. But I should think he could come on Thursday. At any rate, I am sure he will let you know if he cannot.'

'A strike!' asked Margaret. 'What for? What are they going to strike for?'

'For the mastership and ownership of other people's property,' said Mrs. Thornton, with a fierce snort. 'That is what they always strike for. If my son's work-people strike, I will only say they are a pack of ungrateful hounds. But I have no doubt they will.'

'They are wanting higher wages, I suppose?' asked Mr. Hale.

'That is the face of the thing. But the truth is, they want to be masters, and make the masters into slaves on their own ground. They are always trying at it; they always have it in their minds and every five or six years, there comes a struggle between masters and men. They'll find themselves mistaken this time, I fancy,—a little out of their reckoning. If they turn out, they mayn't find it so easy to go in again. I believe, the masters have a thing or two in their heads which will teach the men not to strike again in a hurry, if they try it this time.'

'Does it not make the town very rough?' asked Margaret.

'Of course it does. But surely you are not a coward, are you? Milton is not the place for cowards. I have known the time when I have had to thread my way through a crowd of white, angry men, all swearing they would have Makinson's blood as soon as he ventured to show his nose out of his factory; and he, knowing nothing of it, some one had to go and tell him, or he was a dead man, and it needed to be a woman,—so I went. And when I had got in, I could not get out. It was as much as my life was worth. So I went up to the roof, where there were stones piled ready to drop on the heads of the crowd, if they tried to force the factory doors. And I would have lifted those heavy stones, and dropped them with as good an aim as the best man there, but that I fainted with the heat I had gone through. If you live in Milton, you must learn to have a brave heart, Miss Hale.'

'I would do my best,' said Margaret rather pale. 'I do not know whether I am brave or not till I am tried; but I am afraid I should be a coward.'

'South country people are often frightened by what our Darkshire men and women only call living and struggling. But when you've been ten years among a people who are always owing their betters a grudge, and only waiting for an opportunity to pay it off, you'll know whether you are a coward or not, take my word for it.'

Mr. Thornton came that evening to Mr. Hale's. He was shown up into the drawing-room, where Mr. Hale was reading aloud to his wife and daughter.

'I am come partly to bring you a note from my mother, and partly to apologise for not keeping to my time yesterday. The note contains the address you asked for; Dr. Donaldson.'

'Thank you!' said Margaret, hastily, holding out her hand to take the note, for she did not wish her mother to hear that they had been making any inquiry about a doctor. She was pleased that Mr. Thornton seemed immediately to understand her feeling; he gave her the note without another word of explanation. Mr. Hale began to talk about the strike. Mr. Thornton's face assumed a likeness to his mother's worst expression, which immediately repelled the watching Margaret.

'Yes; the fools will have a strike. Let them. It suits us well enough. But we gave them a chance. They think trade is flourishing as it was last year. We see the storm on the horizon and draw in our sails. But because we don't explain our reasons, they won't believe we're acting reasonably. We must give them line and letter for the way we choose to spend or save our money. Henderson tried a dodge with his men, out at Ashley, and failed. He rather wanted a strike; it would have suited his book well enough. So when the men came to ask for the five per cent. they are claiming, he told 'em he'd think about it, and give them his answer on the pay day; knowing all the while what his answer would be, of course, but thinking he'd strengthen their conceit of their own way. However, they were too deep for him, and heard something about the bad prospects of trade. So in they came on the Friday, and drew back their claim, and now he's obliged to go on working. But we Milton masters have to-day sent in our decision. We won't advance a penny. We tell them we may have to lower wages; but can't afford to raise. So here we stand, waiting for their next attack.'

'And what will that be?' asked Mr. Hale.

'I conjecture, a simultaneous strike. You will see Milton without smoke in a few days, I imagine, Miss Hale.'

'But why,' asked she, 'could you not explain what good reason you have for expecting a bad trade? I don't know whether I use the right words, but you will understand what I mean.'

'Do you give your servants reasons for your expenditure, or your economy in the use of your own money? We, the owners of capital, have a right to choose what we will do with it.'

'A human right,' said Margaret, very low.

'I beg your pardon, I did not hear what you said.'

'I would rather not repeat it,' said she; 'it related to a feeling which I do not think you would share.'

'Won't you try me?' pleaded he; his thoughts suddenly bent upon learning what she had said. She was displeased with his pertinacity, but did not choose to affix too much importance to her words.

'I said you had a human right. I meant that there seemed no reason but religious ones, why you should not do what you like with your own.

'I know we differ in our religious opinions; but don't you give me credit for having some, though not the same as yours?'

He was speaking in a subdued voice, as if to her alone. She did not wish to be so exclusively addressed. She replied out in her usual tone:

'I do not think that I have any occasion to consider your special religious opinions in the affair. All I meant to say is, that there is no human law to prevent the employers from utterly wasting or throwing away all their money, if they choose; but that there are passages in the Bible which would rather imply—to me at least—that they neglected their duty as stewards if they did so. However I know so little about strikes, and rate of wages, and capital, and labour, that I had better not talk to a political economist like you.'

'Nay, the more reason,' said he, eagerly. 'I shall only be too glad to explain to you all that may seem anomalous or mysterious to a stranger; especially at a time like this, when our doings are sure to be canvassed by every scribbler who can hold a pen.'

'Thank you,' she answered, coldly. 'Of course, I shall apply to my father in the first instance for any information he can give me, if I get puzzled with living here amongst this strange society.'

'You think it strange. Why?'

'I don't know—I suppose because, on the very face of it, I see two classes dependent on each other in every possible way, yet each evidently regarding the interests of the other as opposed to their own; I never lived in a place before where there were two sets of people always running each other down.'

'Who have you heard running the masters down? I don't ask who you have heard abusing the men; for I see you persist in misunderstanding what I said the other day. But who have you heard abusing the masters?'

Margaret reddened; then smiled as she said,

'I am not fond of being catechised. I refuse to answer your question. Besides, it has nothing to do with the fact. You must take my word for it, that I have heard some people, or, it may be, only someone of the workpeople, speak as though it were the interest of the employers to keep them from acquiring money—that it would make them too independent if they had a sum in the savings' bank.'

'I dare say it was that man Higgins who told you all this,' said Mrs Hale. Mr. Thornton did not appear to hear what Margaret evidently did not wish him to know. But he caught it, nevertheless.

'I heard, moreover, that it was considered to the advantage of the masters to have ignorant workmen—not hedge-lawyers, as Captain Lennox used to call those men in his company who questioned and would know the reason for every order.' This latter part of her sentence she addressed rather to her father than to Mr. Thornton. Who is Captain Lennox? asked Mr. Thornton of himself, with a strange kind of displeasure, that prevented him for the moment from replying to her! Her father took up the conversation.

'You never were fond of schools, Margaret, or you would have seen and known before this, how much is being done for education in Milton.'

'No!' said she, with sudden meekness. 'I know I do not care enough about schools. But the knowledge and the ignorance of which I was speaking, did not relate to reading and writing,—the teaching or information one can give to a child. I am sure, that what was meant was ignorance of the wisdom that shall guide men and women. I hardly know what that is. But he—that is, my informant—spoke as if the masters would like their hands to be merely tall, large children—living in the present moment—with a blind unreasoning kind of obedience.'

'In short, Miss Hale, it is very evident that your informant found a pretty ready listener to all the slander he chose to utter against the masters,' said Mr. Thornton, in an offended tone.

Margaret did not reply. She was displeased at the personal character Mr. Thornton affixed to what she had said.

Mr. Hale spoke next:

'I must confess that, although I have not become so intimately acquainted with any workmen as Margaret has, I am very much struck by the antagonism between the employer and the employed, on the very surface of things. I even gather this impression from what you yourself have from time to time said.'

Mr. Thornton paused awhile before he spoke. Margaret had just left the room, and he was vexed at the state of feeling between himself and her. However, the little annoyance, by making him cooler and more thoughtful, gave a greater dignity to what he said:

'My theory is, that my interests are identical with those of my workpeople and vice-versa. Miss Hale, I know, does not like to hear men called 'hands,' so I won't use that word, though it comes most readily to my lips as the technical term, whose origin, whatever it was, dates before my time. On some future day—in some millennium—in Utopia, this unity may be brought into practice—just as I can fancy a republic the most perfect form of government.'

'We will read Plato's Republic as soon as we have finished Homer.'

'Well, in the Platonic year, it may fall out that we are all—men women, and children—fit for a republic: but give me a constitutional monarchy in our present state of morals and intelligence. In our infancy we require a wise despotism to govern us. Indeed, long past infancy, children and young people are the happiest under the unfailing laws of a discreet, firm authority. I agree with Miss Hale so far as to consider our people in the condition of children, while I deny that we, the masters, have anything to do with the making or keeping them so. I maintain that despotism is the best kind of government for them; so that in the hours in which I come in contact with them I must necessarily be an autocrat. I will use my best discretion—from no humbug or philanthropic feeling, of which we have had rather too much in the North—to make wise laws and come to just decisions in the conduct of my business—laws and decisions which work for my own good in the first instance—for theirs in the second; but I will neither be forced to give my reasons, nor flinch from what I have once declared to be my resolution. Let them turn out! I shall suffer as well as they: but at the end they will find I have not bated nor altered one jot.'

Margaret had re-entered the room and was sitting at her work; but she did not speak. Mr. Hale answered—

'I dare say I am talking in great ignorance; but from the little I know, I should say that the masses were already passing rapidly into the troublesome stage which intervenes between childhood and manhood, in the life of the multitude as well as that of the individual. Now, the error which many parents commit in the treatment of the individual at this time is, insisting on the same unreasoning obedience as when all he had to do in the way of duty was, to obey the simple laws of "Come when you're called" and "Do as you're bid!" But a wise parent humours the desire for independent action, so as to become the friend and adviser when his absolute rule shall cease. If I get wrong in my reasoning, recollect, it is you who adopted the analogy.'

'Very lately,' said Margaret, 'I heard a story of what happened in Nuremberg only three or four years ago. A rich man there lived alone in one of the immense mansions which were formerly both dwellings and warehouses. It was reported that he had a child, but no one knew of it for certain. For forty years this rumour kept rising and falling—never utterly dying away. After his death it was found to be true. He had a son—an overgrown man with the unexercised intellect of a child, whom he had kept up in that strange way, in order to save him from temptation and error. But, of course, when this great old child was turned loose into the world, every bad counsellor had power over him. He did not know good from evil. His father had made the blunder of bringing him up in ignorance and taking it for innocence; and after fourteen months of riotous living, the city authorities had to take charge of him, in order to save him from starvation. He could not even use words effectively enough to be a successful beggar.'

'I used the comparison (suggested by Miss Hale) of the position of the master to that of a parent; so I ought not to complain of your turning the simile into a weapon against me. But, Mr. Hale, when you were setting up a wise parent as a model for us, you said he humoured his children in their desire for independent action. Now certainly, the time is not come for the hands to have any independent action during business hours; I hardly know what you would mean by it then. And

I say, that the masters would be trenching on the independence of their hands, in a way that I, for one, should not feel justified in doing, if we interfered too much with the life they lead out of the mills. Because they labour ten hours a-day for us, I do not see that we have any right to impose leading-strings upon them for the rest of their time. I value my own independence so highly that I can fancy no degradation greater than that of having another man perpetually directing and advising and lecturing me, or even planning too closely in any way about my actions. He might be the wisest of men, or the most powerful—I should equally rebel and resent his interference I imagine this is a stronger feeling in the North of England that in the South.'

'I beg your pardon, but is not that because there has been none of the equality of friendship between the adviser and advised classes? Because every man has had to stand in an unchristian and isolated position, apart from and jealous of his brother-man: constantly afraid of his rights being trenched upon?'

'I only state the fact. I am sorry to say, I have an appointment at eight o'clock, and I must just take facts as I find them to-night, without trying to account for them; which, indeed, would make no difference in determining how to act as things stand—the facts must be granted.'

'But,' said Margaret in a low voice, 'it seems to me that it makes all the difference in the world—.' Her father made a sign to her to be silent, and allow Mr. Thornton to finish what he had to say. He was already standing up and preparing to go.

'You must grant me this one point. Given a strong feeling of independence in every Darkshire man, have I any right to obtrude my views, of the manner in which he shall act, upon another (hating it as I should do most vehemently myself), merely because he has labour to sell and I capital to buy?'

'Not in the least,' said Margaret, determined just to say this one thing; 'not in the least because of your labour and capital positions, whatever they are, but because you are a man, dealing with a set of men over whom you have, whether you reject the use of it or not, immense power, just because your lives and your welfare are so constantly and intimately interwoven. God has made us so that we must be mutually dependent. We may ignore our own dependence, or refuse to acknowledge that others depend upon us in more respects than the payment of weekly wages; but the thing must be, nevertheless. Neither you nor any other master can help yourselves. The most proudly independent man depends on those around him for their insensible influence on his character—his life. And the most isolated of all your Darkshire Egos has dependants clinging to him on all sides; he cannot shake them off, any more than the great rock he resembles can shake off—'

'Pray don't go into similes, Margaret; you have led us off once already,' said her father, smiling, yet uneasy at the thought that they were detaining Mr. Thornton against his will, which was a mistake; for he rather liked it, as long as Margaret would talk, although what she said only irritated him.

'Just tell me, Miss Hale, are you yourself ever influenced—no, that is not a fair way of putting it;—but if you are ever conscious of being influenced by others, and not by circumstances, have those others been working directly or indirectly? Have they been labouring to exhort, to enjoin, to act rightly for the sake of example, or have they been simple, true men, taking up their duty, and doing it unflinchingly, without a thought of how their actions were to make this man industrious, that man saving? Why, if I were a workman, I should be twenty times more impressed by the knowledge that my master was honest, punctual, quick, resolute in all his doings (and hands are keener spies even than valets), than by any amount of interference, however kindly meant, with my ways of going on out of work-hours. I do not choose to think too closely on what I am myself; but, I believe, I rely on the straightforward honesty of my hands, and the open nature of their opposition, in contra-distinction to the way in which the turnout will be managed in some mills, just because they know I scorn to take a single dishonourable advantage, or do an underhand thing myself. It goes farther than a whole course of lectures on "Honesty is the Best Policy"—life diluted into words. No, no! What the master is, that will the men be, without over-much taking thought on his part.'

'That is a great admission,' said Margaret, laughing. 'When I see men violent and obstinate in pursuit of their rights, I may safely infer that the master is the same that he is a little ignorant of that spirit which suffereth long, and is kind, and seeketh not her own.'

'You are just like all strangers who don't understand the working of our system, Miss Hale,' said he, hastily. 'You suppose that our men are puppets of dough, ready to be moulded into any amiable form we please. You forget we have only to do with them for less than a third of their lives; and you seem not to perceive that the duties of a manufacturer are far larger and wider than those merely of an employer of labour: we have a wide commercial character to maintain, which makes us into the great pioneers of civilisation.'

'It strikes me,' said Mr. Hale, smiling, 'that you might pioneer a little at home. They are a rough, heathenish set of fellows, these Milton men of yours.'

'They are that,' replied Mr. Thornton. 'Rosewater surgery won't do for them. Cromwell would have made a capital mill-owner, Miss Hale. I wish we had him to put down this strike for us.'

'Cromwell is no hero of mine,' said she, coldly. 'But I am trying to reconcile your admiration of despotism with your respect for other men's independence of character.'

He reddened at her tone. 'I choose to be the unquestioned and irresponsible master of my hands, during the hours that they labour for me. But those hours past, our relation ceases; and then comes in the same respect for their independence that I myself exact.'

He did not speak again for a minute, he was too much vexed. But he shook it off, and bade Mr. and Mrs. Hale good night. Then, drawing near to Margaret, he said in a lower voice—

'I spoke hastily to you once this evening, and I am afraid, rather rudely. But you know I am but an uncouth Milton manufacturer; will you forgive me?'

'Certainly,' said she, smiling up in his face, the expression of which was somewhat anxious and oppressed, and hardly cleared away as he met her sweet sunny countenance, out of which all the north-wind effect of their discussion had entirely vanished. But she did not put out her hand to him, and again he felt the omission, and set it down to pride.

CHAPTER XVI - THE SHADOW OF DEATH

'Trust in that veiled hand, which leads
None by the path that he would go;
And always be for change prepared,
For the world's law is ebb and flow.'
FROM THE ARABIC.

The next afternoon Dr. Donaldson came to pay his first visit to Mrs. Hale. The mystery that Margaret hoped their late habits of intimacy had broken through, was resumed. She was excluded from the room, while Dixon was admitted. Margaret was not a ready lover, but where she loved she loved passionately, and with no small degree of jealousy.

She went into her mother's bed-room, just behind the drawing-room, and paced it up and down, while awaiting the doctor's coming out. Every now and then she stopped to listen; she fancied she heard a moan. She clenched her hands tight, and held her breath. She was sure she heard a moan. Then all was still for a few minutes more; and then there was the moving of chairs, the raised voices, all the little disturbances of leave-taking.

When she heard the door open, she went quickly out of the bed-room.

'My father is from home, Dr. Donaldson; he has to attend a pupil at this hour. May I trouble you to come into his room down stairs?'

She saw, and triumphed over all the obstacles which Dixon threw in her way; assuming her rightful position as daughter of the house in something of the spirit of the Elder Brother, which quelled the old servant's officiousness very effectually. Margaret's conscious assumption of this unusual dignity of demeanour towards Dixon, gave her an instant's amusement in the midst of her anxiety. She knew, from the surprised expression on Dixon's face, how ridiculously grand she herself must be looking; and the idea carried her down stairs into the room; it gave her that length of oblivion from the keen sharpness of the recollection of the actual business in hand. Now, that came back, and seemed to take away her breath. It was a moment or two before she could utter a word.

But she spoke with an air of command, as she asked:—'

'What is the matter with mamma? You will oblige me by telling the simple truth.' Then, seeing a slight hesitation on the doctor's part, she added—

'I am the only child she has—here, I mean. My father is not sufficiently alarmed, I fear; and, therefore, if there is any serious apprehension, it must be broken to him gently. I can do this. I can nurse my mother. Pray, speak, sir; to see your face, and not be able to read it, gives me a worse dread than I trust any words of yours will justify.'

'My dear young lady, your mother seems to have a most attentive and efficient servant, who is more like her friend—'

'I am her daughter, sir.'

'But when I tell you she expressly desired that you might not be told—'

'I am not good or patient enough to submit to the prohibition. Besides, I am sure you are too wise—too experienced to have promised to keep the secret.'

'Well,' said he, half-smiling, though sadly enough, 'there you are right. I did not promise. In fact, I fear, the secret will be known soon enough without my revealing it.'

He paused. Margaret went very white, and compressed her lips a little more. Otherwise not a feature moved. With the quick insight into character, without which no medical man can rise to the eminence of Dr. Donaldson, he saw that she would exact the full truth; that she would know if one iota was withheld; and that the withholding would be torture more acute than the knowledge of it. He spoke two short sentences in a low voice, watching her all the time; for the pupils of her eyes dilated into a black horror and the whiteness of her complexion became livid. He ceased speaking. He waited for that look to go off,—for her gasping breath to come. Then she said:—

'I thank you most truly, sir, for your confidence. That dread has haunted me for many weeks. It is a true, real agony. My poor, poor mother!' her lips began to quiver, and he let her have the relief of tears, sure of her power of self-control to check them.

A few tears—those were all she shed, before she recollected the many questions she longed to ask.

'Will there be much suffering?'

He shook his head. 'That we cannot tell. It depends on constitution; on a thousand things. But the late discoveries of medical science have given us large power of alleviation.'

'My father!' said Margaret, trembling all over.

'I do not know Mr. Hale. I mean, it is difficult to give advice. But I should say, bear on, with the knowledge you have forced me to give you so abruptly, till the fact which I could not with-hold has become in some degree familiar to you, so that you may, without too great an effort, be able to give what comfort you can to your father. Before then,—my visits, which, of course, I shall repeat from time to time, although I fear I can do nothing but alleviate,—a thousand little circumstances will have occurred to awaken his alarm, to deepen it—so that he will be all the better prepared.—Nay, my dear young lady—nay, my dear—I saw Mr.

Thornton, and I honour your father for the sacrifice he has made, however mistaken I may believe him to be.—Well, this once, if it will please you, my dear. Only remember, when I come again, I come as a friend. And you must learn to look upon me as such, because seeing each other—getting to know each other at such times as these, is worth years of morning calls.' Margaret could not speak for crying: but she wrung his hand at parting.

'That's what I call a fine girl!' thought Dr. Donaldson, when he was seated in his carriage, and had time to examine his ringed hand, which had slightly suffered from her pressure. 'Who would have thought that little hand could have given such a squeeze? But the bones were well put together, and that gives immense power. What a queen she is! With her head thrown back at first, to force me into speaking the truth; and then bent so eagerly forward to listen. Poor thing! I must see she does not overstrain herself. Though it's astonishing how much those thorough-bred creatures can do and suffer. That girl's game to the back-bone. Another, who had gone that deadly colour, could never have come round without either fainting or hysterics. But she wouldn't do either—not she! And the very force of her will brought her round. Such a girl as that would win my heart, if I were thirty years younger. It's too late now. Ah! here we are at the Archers'.' So out he jumped, with thought, wisdom, experience, sympathy, and ready to attend to the calls made upon them by this family, just as if there were none other in the world.

Meanwhile, Margaret had returned into her father's study for a moment, to recover strength before going upstairs into her mother's presence.

'Oh, my God, my God! but this is terrible. How shall I bear it? Such a deadly disease! no hope! Oh, mamma, mamma, I wish I had never gone to aunt Shaw's, and been all those precious years away from you! Poor mamma! how much she must have borne! Oh, I pray thee, my God, that her sufferings may not be too acute, too dreadful. How shall I bear to see them? How can I bear papa's agony? He must not be told yet; not all at once. It would kill him. But I won't lose another moment of my own dear, precious mother.'

She ran upstairs. Dixon was not in the room. Mrs. Hale lay back in an easy chair, with a soft white shawl wrapped around her, and a becoming cap put on, in expectation of the doctor's visit. Her face had a little faint colour in it, and the very exhaustion after the examination gave it a peaceful look. Margaret was surprised to see her look so calm.

'Why, Margaret, how strange you look! What is the matter?' And then, as the idea stole into her mind of what was indeed the real state of the case, she added, as if a little displeased: 'you have not been seeing Dr. Donaldson, and asking him any questions—have you, child?' Margaret did not reply—only looked wistfully towards her. Mrs. Hale became more displeased. 'He would not, surely, break his word to me, and'—

'Oh yes, mamma, he did. I made him. It was I—blame me.' She knelt down by her mother's side, and caught her hand—she would not let it go, though Mrs. Hale tried to pull it away. She kept kissing it, and the hot tears she shed bathed it.

'Margaret, it was very wrong of you. You knew I did not wish you to know.' But, as if tired with the contest, she left her hand in Margaret's clasp, and by-and-by she returned the pressure faintly. That encouraged Margaret to speak.

'Oh, mamma! let me be your nurse. I will learn anything Dixon can teach me. But you know I am your child, and I do think I have a right to do everything for you.'

'You don't know what you are asking,' said Mrs. Hale, with a shudder.

'Yes, I do. I know a great deal more than you are aware of. Let me be your nurse. Let me try, at any rate. No one has ever, shall ever try so hard as I will do. It will be such a comfort, mamma.'

'My poor child! Well, you shall try. Do you know, Margaret, Dixon and I thought you would quite shrink from me if you knew—'

'Dixon thought!' said Margaret, her lip curling. 'Dixon could not give me credit for enough true love—for as much as herself! She thought, I suppose, that I was one of those poor sickly women who like to lie on rose leaves, and be fanned all day. Don't let Dixon's fancies come any more between you and me, mamma. Don't, please!' implored she.

'Don't be angry with Dixon,' said Mrs. Hale, anxiously. Margaret recovered herself.

'No! I won't. I will try and be humble, and learn her ways, if you will only let me do all I can for you. Let me be in the first place, mother—I am greedy of that. I used to fancy you would forget me while I was away at aunt Shaw's, and cry myself to sleep at nights with that notion in my head.'

'And I used to think, how will Margaret bear our makeshift poverty after the thorough comfort and luxury in Harley Street, till I have many a time been more ashamed of your seeing our contrivances at Helstone than of any stranger finding them out.'

'Oh, mamma! and I did so enjoy them. They were so much more amusing than all the jog-trot Harley Street ways. The wardrobe shelf with handles, that served as a supper-tray on grand occasions! And the old tea-chests stuffed and covered for ottomans! I think what you call the makeshift contrivances at dear Helstone were a charming part of the life there.'

'I shall never see Helstone again, Margaret,' said Mrs. Hale, the tears welling up into her eyes. Margaret could not reply. Mrs. Hale went on. 'While I was there, I was for ever wanting to leave it. Every place seemed pleasanter. And now I shall die far away from it. I am rightly punished.'

'You must not talk so,' said Margaret, impatiently. 'He said you might live for years. Oh, mother! we will have you back at Helstone yet.'

'No never! That I must take as a just penance. But, Margaret—Frederick!' At the mention of that one word, she suddenly cried out loud, as in some sharp agony. It seemed as if the thought of him upset all her composure, destroyed the calm, overcame the exhaustion. Wild passionate cry succeeded to cry—'Frederick! Frederick! Come to me. I am dying. Little first-born child, come to me once again!'

She was in violent hysterics. Margaret went and called Dixon in terror. Dixon came in a huff, and accused Margaret of having over-excited her mother. Margaret bore all meekly, only trusting that her father might not return. In spite of her alarm, which was even greater than the occasion warranted, she obeyed all Dixon's directions promptly and well, without a word of self-justification. By so doing she mollified her accuser. They put her mother to bed, and Margaret sate by her till she fell asleep, and afterwards till Dixon beckoned her out of the room, and, with a sour face, as if doing something against the grain, she bade her drink a cup of coffee which she had prepared for her in the drawing-room, and stood over her in a commanding attitude as she did so.

'You shouldn't have been so curious, Miss, and then you wouldn't have needed to fret before your time. It would have come soon enough. And now, I suppose, you'll tell master, and a pretty household I shall have of you!'

'No, Dixon,' said Margaret, sorrowfully, 'I will not tell papa. He could not bear it as I can.' And by way of proving how well she bore it, she burst into tears.

'Ay! I knew how it would be. Now you'll waken your mamma, just after she's gone to sleep so quietly. Miss Margaret my dear, I've had to keep it down this many a week; and though I don't pretend I can love her as you do, yet I loved her better than any other man, woman, or child—no one but Master Frederick ever came near her in my mind. Ever since Lady Beresford's maid first took me in to see her dressed out in white crape, and corn-ears, and scarlet poppies, and I ran a needle down into my finger, and broke it in, and she tore up her worked pocket-handkerchief, after they'd cut it out, and came in to wet the bandages again with lotion when she returned from the ball—where she'd been the prettiest young lady of all—I've never loved any one like her. I little thought then that I should live to see her brought so low. I don't mean no reproach to nobody. Many a one calls you pretty and handsome, and what not. Even in this smoky place, enough to blind one's eyes, the owls can see that. But you'll never be like your mother for beauty—never; not if you live to be a hundred.'

'Mamma is very pretty still. Poor mamma!'

'Now don't ye set off again, or I shall give way at last' (whimpering). 'You'll never stand master's coming home, and questioning, at this rate. Go out and take a walk, and come in something like. Many's the time I've longed to walk it off—the thought of what was the matter with her, and how it must all end.'

'Oh, Dixon!' said Margaret, 'how often I've been cross with you, not knowing what a terrible secret you had to bear!'

'Bless you, child! I like to see you showing a bit of a spirit. It's the good old Beresford blood. Why, the last Sir John but two shot his steward down, there where he stood, for just telling him that he'd racked the tenants, and he'd racked the tenants till he could get no more money off them than he could get skin off a flint.'

'Well, Dixon, I won't shoot you, and I'll try not to be cross again.'

'You never have. If I've said it at times, it has always been to myself, just in private, by way of making a little agreeable conversation, for there's no one here fit to talk to. And when you fire up, you're the very image of Master Frederick. I could find in my heart to put you in a passion any day, just to see his stormy look coming like a great cloud over your face. But now you go out, Miss. I'll watch over missus; and as for master, his books are company enough for him, if he should come in.'

'I will go,' said Margaret. She hung about Dixon for a minute or so, as if afraid and irresolute; then suddenly kissing her, she went quickly out of the room.

'Bless her!' said Dixon. 'She's as sweet as a nut. There are three people I love: it's missus, Master Frederick, and her. Just them three. That's all. The rest be hanged, for I don't know what they're in the world for. Master was born, I suppose, for to marry missus. If I thought he loved her properly, I might get to love him in time. But he should ha' made a deal more on her, and not been always reading, reading, thinking, thinking. See what it has brought him to! Many a one who never reads nor thinks either, gets to be Rector, and Dean, and what not; and I dare say master might, if he'd just minded missus, and let the weary reading and thinking alone.—There she goes' (looking out of the window as she heard the front door shut). 'Poor young lady! her clothes look shabby to what they did when she came to Helstone a year ago. Then she hadn't so much as a darned stocking or a cleaned pair of gloves in all her wardrobe. And now—!'

CHAPTER XVII - WHAT IS A STRIKE?

'There are briars besetting every path,
Which call for patient care;
There is a cross in every lot,
And an earnest need for prayer.'
ANON.

Margaret went out heavily and unwillingly enough. But the length of a street—yes, the air of a Milton Street—cheered her young blood before she reached her first turning. Her step grew lighter, her lip redder. She began to take notice, instead of having her thoughts turned so exclusively inward. She saw unusual loiterers in the streets: men with their hands in their pockets sauntering along; loud-laughing and loud-spoken girls clustered together, apparently excited to high spirits, and a boisterous independence of temper and behaviour. The more ill-looking of the men—the discreditable minority—hung about on the steps of the beer-houses and gin-shops, smoking, and commenting pretty freely on every passer-by. Margaret disliked the prospect of the long walk through these streets, before she came to the fields which she had planned to reach. Instead, she would go and see Bessy Higgins. It would not be so refreshing as a quiet country walk, but still it would perhaps be doing the kinder thing.

Nicholas Higgins was sitting by the fire smoking, as she went in. Bessy was rocking herself on the other side.

Nicholas took the pipe out of his mouth, and standing up, pushed his chair towards Margaret; he leant against the chimney piece in a lounging attitude, while she asked Bessy how she was.

'Hoo's rather down i' th' mouth in regard to spirits, but hoo's better in health. Hoo doesn't like this strike. Hoo's a deal too much set on peace and quietness at any price.'

'This is th' third strike I've seen,' said she, sighing, as if that was answer and explanation enough.

'Well, third time pays for all. See if we don't dang th' masters this time. See if they don't come, and beg us to come back at our own price. That's all. We've missed it afore time, I grant yo'; but this time we'n laid our plans desperate deep.'

'Why do you strike?' asked Margaret. 'Striking is leaving off work till you get your own rate of wages, is it not? You must not wonder at my ignorance; where I come from I never heard of a strike.'

'I wish I were there,' said Bessy, wearily. 'But it's not for me to get sick and tired o' strikes. This is the last I'll see. Before it's ended I shall be in the Great City—the Holy Jerusalem.'

'Hoo's so full of th' life to come, hoo cannot think of th' present. Now I, yo' see, am bound to do the best I can here. I think a bird i' th' hand is worth two i' th' bush. So them's the different views we take on th' strike question.'

'But,' said Margaret, 'if the people struck, as you call it, where I come from, as they are mostly all field labourers, the seed would not be sown, the hay got in, the corn reaped.'

'Well?' said he. He had resumed his pipe, and put his 'well' in the form of an interrogation.

'Why,' she went on, 'what would become of the farmers.'

He puffed away. 'I reckon they'd have either to give up their farms, or to give fair rate of wage.'

'Suppose they could not, or would not do the last; they could not give up their farms all in a minute, however much they might wish to do so; but they would have no hay, nor corn to sell that year; and where would the money come from to pay the labourers' wages the next?'

Still puffing away. At last he said:

'I know nought of your ways down South. I have heerd they're a pack of spiritless, down-trodden men; welly clemmed to death; too much dazed wi' clemming to know when they're put upon. Now, it's not so here. We known when we're put upon; and we'en too much blood in us to stand it. We just take our hands fro' our looms, and say, "Yo' may clem us, but yo'll not put upon us, my masters!" And be danged to 'em, they shan't this time!'

'I wish I lived down South,' said Bessy.

'There's a deal to bear there,' said Margaret. 'There are sorrows to bear everywhere. There is very hard bodily labour to be gone through, with very little food to give strength.'

'But it's out of doors,' said Bessy. 'And away from the endless, endless noise, and sickening heat.'

'It's sometimes in heavy rain, and sometimes in bitter cold. A young person can stand it; but an old man gets racked with rheumatism, and bent and withered before his time; yet he must just work on the same, or else go to the workhouse.'

'I thought yo' were so taken wi' the ways of the South country.'

'So I am,' said Margaret, smiling a little, as she found herself thus caught. 'I only mean, Bessy, there's good and bad in everything in this world; and as you felt the bad up here, I thought it was but fair you should know the bad down there.'

'And yo' say they never strike down there?' asked Nicholas, abruptly.

'No!' said Margaret; 'I think they have too much sense.'

'An' I think,' replied he, dashing the ashes out of his pipe with so much vehemence that it broke, 'it's not that they've too much sense, but that they've too little spirit.'

'O, father!' said Bessy, 'what have ye gained by striking? Think of that first strike when mother died—how we all had to clem—you the worst of all; and yet many a one went in every week at the same wage, till all were gone in that there was work for; and some went beggars all their lives at after.'

'Ay,' said he. 'That there strike was badly managed. Folk got into th' management of it, as were either fools or not true men. Yo'll see, it'll be different this time.'

'But all this time you've not told me what you're striking for,' said Margaret, again.

'Why, yo' see, there's five or six masters who have set themselves again paying the wages they've been paying these two years past, and flourishing upon, and getting richer upon. And now they come to us, and say we're to take less. And we won't. We'll just clem them to death first; and see who'll work for 'em then. They'll have killed the goose that laid 'em the golden eggs, I reckon.'

'And so you plan dying, in order to be revenged upon them!'

'No,' said he, 'I dunnot. I just look forward to the chance of dying at my post sooner than yield. That's what folk call fine and honourable in a soldier, and why not in a poor weaver-chap?'

'But,' said Margaret, 'a soldier dies in the cause of the Nation—in the cause of others.'

He laughed grimly. 'My lass,' said he, 'yo're but a young wench, but don't yo' think I can keep three people—that's Bessy, and Mary, and me—on sixteen shilling a week? Dun yo' think it's for mysel' I'm striking work at this time? It's just as much in the cause of others as yon soldier—only m'appen, the cause he dies for is just that of somebody he never clapt eyes on, nor heerd on all his born days, while I take up John Boucher's cause, as lives next door but one, wi' a sickly wife, and eight childer, none on 'em factory age; and I don't take up his cause only, though he's a poor good-for-nought, as can only manage two looms at a time, but I take up th' cause o' justice. Why are we to have less wage now, I ask, than two year ago?'

'Don't ask me,' said Margaret; 'I am very ignorant. Ask some of your masters. Surely they will give you a reason for it. It is not merely an arbitrary decision of theirs, come to without reason.'

'Yo're just a foreigner, and nothing more,' said he, contemptuously. 'Much yo' know about it. Ask th' masters! They'd tell us to mind our own business, and they'd mind theirs. Our business being, yo' understand, to take the bated' wage, and be thankful, and their business to bate us down to clemming point, to swell their profits. That's what it is.'

'But said Margaret, determined not to give way, although she saw she was irritating him, 'the state of trade may be such as not to enable them to give you the same remuneration.

'State o' trade! That's just a piece o' masters' humbug. It's rate o' wages I was talking of. Th' masters keep th' state o' trade in their own hands; and just walk it forward like a black bug-a-boo, to frighten naughty children with into being good. I'll tell yo' it's their part,—their cue, as some folks call it,—to beat us down, to swell their fortunes; and it's ours to stand up and fight hard,—not for ourselves alone, but for them round about us—for justice and fair play. We help to make their profits, and we ought to help spend 'em. It's not that we want their brass so much this time, as we've done many a time afore. We'n getten money laid by; and we're resolved to stand and fall together; not a man on us will go in for less wage than th' Union says is our due. So I say, "hooray for the strike," and let Thornton, and Slickson, and Hamper, and their set look to it!'

'Thornton!' said Margaret. 'Mr. Thornton of Marlborough Street?'

'Aye! Thornton o' Marlborough Mill, as we call him.'

'He is one of the masters you are striving with, is he not? What sort of a master is he?'

'Did yo' ever see a bulldog? Set a bulldog on hind legs, and dress him up in coat and breeches, and yo'n just getten John Thornton.'

'Nay,' said Margaret, laughing, 'I deny that. Mr. Thornton is plain enough, but he's not like a bulldog, with its short broad nose, and snarling upper lip.'

'No! not in look, I grant yo'. But let John Thornton get hold on a notion, and he'll stick to it like a bulldog; yo' might pull him away wi' a pitch-fork ere he'd leave go. He's worth fighting wi', is John Thornton. As for Slickson, I take it, some o' these days he'll wheedle his men back wi' fair promises; that they'll just get cheated out of as soon as they're in his power again. He'll work his fines well out on 'em, I'll warrant. He's as slippery as an eel, he is. He's like a cat,—as sleek, and cunning, and fierce. It'll never be an honest up and down fight wi' him, as it will be wi' Thornton. Thornton's as dour as a door-nail; an obstinate chap, every inch on him,—th' oud bulldog!'

'Poor Bessy!' said Margaret, turning round to her. 'You sigh over it all. You don't like struggling and fighting as your father does, do you?'

'No!' said she, heavily. 'I'm sick on it. I could have wished to have had other talk about me in my latter days, than just the clashing and clanging and clattering that has wearied a' my life long, about work and wages, and masters, and hands, and knobsticks.'

'Poor wench! latter days be farred! Thou'rt looking a sight better already for a little stir and change. Beside, I shall be a deal here to make it more lively for thee.'

'Tobacco-smoke chokes me!' said she, querulously.

'Then I'll never smoke no more i' th' house!' he replied, tenderly. 'But why didst thou not tell me afore, thou foolish wench?'

She did not speak for a while, and then so low that only Margaret heard her:

'I reckon, he'll want a' the comfort he can get out o' either pipe or drink afore he's done.'

Her father went out of doors, evidently to finish his pipe.

Bessy said passionately,

'Now am not I a fool,—am I not, Miss?—there, I knew I ought for to keep father at home, and away fro' the folk that are always ready for to tempt a man, in time o' strike, to go drink,—and there my tongue must needs quarrel with this pipe o' his'n,—and he'll go off, I know he will,—as often as he wants to smoke—and nobody knows where it'll end. I wish I'd letten myself be choked first.'

'But does your father drink?' asked Margaret.

'No—not to say drink,' replied she, still in the same wild excited tone. 'But what win ye have? There are days wi' you, as wi' other folk, I suppose, when yo' get up and go through th' hours, just longing for a bit of a change—a bit of a fillip, as it were. I know I ha' gone and bought a four-pounder out o' another baker's shop to common on such days, just because I sickened at the thought of going on for ever wi' the same sight in my eyes, and the same sound in my ears, and the same taste i' my mouth, and the same thought (or no thought, for that matter) in my head, day after day, for ever. I've longed for to be a man to go spreeing, even it were only a tramp to some new place in search o' work. And father—all men—have it stronger in 'em than me to get tired o' sameness and work for ever. And what is 'em to do? It's little blame to them if they do go into th' gin-shop for to make their blood flow quicker, and more lively, and see things they never see at no other time—pictures, and looking-glass, and such like. But father never was a drunkard, though maybe, he's got worse for drink, now and then. Only yo' see,' and now her voice took a mournful, pleading tone, 'at times o' strike there's much to knock a man down, for all they start so hopefully; and where's the comfort to come fro'? He'll get angry and mad—they all do—and then they get tired out wi' being angry and mad, and maybe ha' done things in their passion they'd be glad to forget. Bless yo'r sweet pitiful face! but yo' dunnot know what a strike is yet.'

'Come, Bessy,' said Margaret, 'I won't say you're exaggerating, because I don't know enough about it: but, perhaps, as you're not well, you're only looking on one side, and there is another and a brighter to be looked to.'

'It's all well enough for yo' to say so, who have lived in pleasant green places all your life long, and never known want or care, or wickedness either, for that matter.'

'Take care,' said Margaret, her cheek flushing, and her eye lightening, 'how you judge, Bessy. I shall go home to my mother, who is so ill—so ill, Bessy, that there's no outlet but death for her out of the prison of her great suffering; and yet I must speak cheerfully to my father, who has no notion of her real state, and to whom the knowledge must come gradually. The only person—the only one who could sympathise with me and help me—whose presence could comfort my mother more than any other earthly thing—is falsely accused—would run the risk of death if he came to see his dying mother. This I tell you—only you, Bessy. You must not mention it. No other person in Milton—hardly any other person in England knows. Have I not care? Do I not know anxiety, though I go about well-dressed, and have food enough? Oh, Bessy, God is just, and our lots are well portioned out by Him, although none but He knows the bitterness of our souls.'

'I ask your pardon,' replied Bessy, humbly. 'Sometimes, when I've thought o' my life, and the little pleasure I've had in it, I've believed that, maybe, I was one of those doomed to die by the falling of a star from heaven; "And the name of the star is called Wormwood;" and the third part of the waters became wormwood; and men died of the waters, because they were made bitter." One can bear pain and sorrow better if one thinks it has been prophesied long before for one: somehow, then it seems as if my pain was needed for the fulfilment; otherways it seems all sent for nothing.'

'Nay, Bessy—think!' said Margaret. 'God does not willingly afflict. Don't dwell so much on the prophecies, but read the clearer parts of the Bible.'

'I dare say it would be wiser; but where would I hear such grand words of promise—hear tell o' anything so far different fro' this dreary world, and this town above a', as in Revelations? Many's the time I've repeated the verses in the seventh chapter to myself, just for the sound. It's as good as an organ, and as different from every day, too. No, I cannot give up Revelations. It gives me more comfort than any other book i' the Bible.'

'Let me come and read you some of my favourite chapters.'

'Ay,' said she, greedily, 'come. Father will maybe hear yo'. He's deaved wi' my talking; he says it's all nought to do with the things o' to-day, and that's his business.'

'Where is your sister?'

'Gone fustian-cutting. I were loth to let her go; but somehow we must live; and th' Union can't afford us much.'

'Now I must go. You have done me good, Bessy.'

'I done you good!'

'Yes. I came here very sad, and rather too apt to think my own cause for grief was the only one in the world. And now I hear how you have had to bear for years, and that makes me stronger.'

'Bless yo'! I thought a' the good-doing was on the side of gentle folk. I shall get proud if I think I can do good to yo'.'

'You won't do it if you think about it. But you'll only puzzle yourself if you do, that's one comfort.'

'Yo're not like no one I ever seed. I dunno what to make of yo'.'

'Nor I of myself. Good-bye!'

Bessy stilled her rocking to gaze after her.

'I wonder if there are many folk like her down South. She's like a breath of country air, somehow. She freshens me up above a bit. Who'd ha' thought that face—as bright and as strong as the angel I dream of—could have known the sorrow she speaks on? I wonder how she'll sin. All on us must sin. I think a deal on her, for sure. But father does the like, I see. And Mary even. It's not often hoo's stirred up to notice much.'

CHAPTER XVIII - LIKES AND DISLIKES

'My heart revolts within me, and two voices
Make themselves audible within my bosom.'
WALLENSTEIN.

On Margaret's return home she found two letters on the table: one was a note for her mother,—the other, which had come by the post, was evidently from her Aunt Shaw—covered with foreign post-marks—thin, silvery, and rustling. She took up the other, and was examining it, when her father came in suddenly:

'So your mother is tired, and gone to bed early! I'm afraid, such a thundery day was not the best in the world for the doctor to see her. What did he say? Dixon tells me he spoke to you about her.'

Margaret hesitated. Her father's looks became more grave and anxious:

'He does not think her seriously ill?'

'Not at present; she needs care, he says; he was very kind, and said he would call again, and see how his medicines worked.'

'Only care—he did not recommend change of air?—he did not say this smoky town was doing her any harm, did he, Margaret?'

'No! not a word,' she replied, gravely. 'He was anxious, I think.'

'Doctors have that anxious manner; it's professional,' said he.

Margaret saw, in her father's nervous ways, that the first impression of possible danger was made upon his mind, in spite of all his making light of what she told him. He could not forget the subject,—could not pass from it to other things; he kept recurring to it through the evening, with an unwillingness to receive even the slightest unfavourable idea, which made Margaret inexpressibly sad.

'This letter is from Aunt Shaw, papa. She has got to Naples, and finds it too hot, so she has taken apartments at Sorrento. But I don't think she likes Italy.'

'He did not say anything about diet, did he?'

'It was to be nourishing, and digestible. Mamma's appetite is pretty good, I think.'

'Yes! and that makes it all the more strange he should have thought of speaking about diet.'

'I asked him, papa.' Another pause. Then Margaret went on: 'Aunt Shaw says, she has sent me some coral ornaments, papa; but,' added Margaret, half smiling, 'she's afraid the Milton Dissenters won't appreciate them. She has got all her ideas of Dissenters from the Quakers, has not she?'

'If ever you hear or notice that your mother wishes for anything, be sure you let me know. I am so afraid she does not tell me always what she would like. Pray, see after that girl Mrs. Thornton named. If we had a good, efficient house-servant, Dixon could be constantly with her, and I'd answer for it we'd soon set her up amongst us, if care will do it. She's been very much tired of late, with the hot weather, and the difficulty of getting a servant. A little rest will put her quite to rights—eh, Margaret?'

'I hope so,' said Margaret,—but so sadly, that her father took notice of it. He pinched her cheek.

'Come; if you look so pale as this, I must rouge you up a little. Take care of yourself, child, or you'll be wanting the doctor next.'

But he could not settle to anything that evening. He was continually going backwards and forwards, on laborious tiptoe, to see if his wife was still asleep. Margaret's heart ached at his restlessness—his trying to stifle and strangle the hideous fear that was looming out of the dark places of his heart. He came back at last, somewhat comforted.

'She's awake now, Margaret. She quite smiled as she saw me standing by her. Just her old smile. And she says she feels refreshed, and ready for tea. Where's the note for her? She wants to see it. I'll read it to her while you make tea.'

The note proved to be a formal invitation from Mrs. Thornton, to Mr., Mrs., and Miss Hale to dinner, on the twenty-first instant. Margaret was surprised to find an acceptance contemplated, after all she had learnt of sad probabilities during the day. But so it was. The idea of her husband's and daughter's going to this dinner had quite captivated Mrs. Hale's fancy, even before Margaret had heard the contents of the note. It was an event to diversify the monotony of the invalid's life; and she clung to the idea of their going, with even fretful pertinacity when Margaret objected.

'Nay, Margaret? if she wishes it, I'm sure we'll both go willingly. She never would wish it unless she felt herself really stronger—really better than we thought she was, eh, Margaret?' said Mr. Hale, anxiously, as she prepared to write the note of acceptance, the next day.

'Eh! Margaret?' questioned he, with a nervous motion of his hands. It seemed cruel to refuse him the comfort he craved for. And besides, his passionate refusal to admit the existence of fear, almost inspired Margaret herself with hope.

'I do think she is better since last night,' said she. 'Her eyes look brighter, and her complexion clearer.'

'God bless you,' said her father, earnestly. 'But is it true? Yesterday was so sultry every one felt ill. It was a most unlucky day for Mr. Donaldson to see her on.'

So he went away to his day's duties, now increased by the preparation of some lectures he had promised to deliver to the working people at a neighbouring Lyceum. He had chosen Ecclesiastical Architecture as his subject, rather more in accordance with his own taste and knowledge than as falling in with the character of the place or the desire for particular kinds of information among those to whom he was to lecture. And the institution itself, being in debt, was only too glad to get a gratis course from an educated and accomplished man like Mr. Hale, let the subject be what it might.

'Well, mother,' asked Mr. Thornton that night, 'who have accepted your invitations for the twenty-first?'

'Fanny, where are the notes? The Slicksons accept, Collingbrooks accept, Stephenses accept, Browns decline. Hales—father and daughter come,—mother too great an invalid—Macphersons come, and Mr. Horsfall, and Mr. Young. I was thinking of asking the Porters, as the Browns can't come.'

'Very good. Do you know, I'm really afraid Mrs. Hale is very far from well, from what Dr. Donaldson says.'

'It's strange of them to accept a dinner-invitation if she's very ill,' said Fanny.

'I didn't say very ill,' said her brother, rather sharply. 'I only said very far from well. They may not know it either.' And then he suddenly remembered that, from what Dr. Donaldson had told him, Margaret, at any rate, must be aware of the exact state of the case.

'Very probably they are quite aware of what you said yesterday, John—of the great advantage it would be to them—to Mr. Hale, I mean, to be introduced to such people as the Stephenses and the Collingbrooks.'

'I'm sure that motive would not influence them. No! I think I understand how it is.'

'John!' said Fanny, laughing in her little, weak, nervous way. 'How you profess to understand these Hales, and how you never will allow that we can know anything about them. Are they really so very different to most people one meets with?'

She did not mean to vex him; but if she had intended it, she could not have done it more thoroughly. He chafed in silence, however, not deigning to reply to her question.

'They do not seem to me out of the common way,' said Mrs. Thornton. 'He appears a worthy kind of man enough; rather too simple for trade—so it's perhaps as well he should have been a clergyman first, and now a teacher. She's a bit of a fine lady, with her invalidism; and as for the girl—she's the only one who puzzles me when I think about her,—which I don't often do. She seems to have a great notion of giving herself airs; and I can't make out why. I could almost fancy she thinks herself too good for her company at times. And yet they're not rich, from all I can hear they never have been.'

'And she's not accomplished, mamma. She can't play.'

'Go on, Fanny. What else does she want to bring her up to your standard?'

'Nay! John,' said his mother, 'that speech of Fanny's did no harm. I myself heard Miss Hale say she could not play. If you would let us alone, we could perhaps like her, and see her merits.'

'I'm sure I never could!' murmured Fanny, protected by her mother. Mr. Thornton heard, but did not care to reply. He was walking up and down the dining-room, wishing that his mother would order candles, and allow him to set to work at either reading or writing, and so put a stop to the conversation. But he never thought of interfering in any of the small domestic regulations that Mrs. Thornton observed, in habitual remembrance of her old economies.

'Mother,' said he, stopping, and bravely speaking out the truth, 'I wish you would like Miss Hale.'

'Why?' asked she, startled by his earnest, yet tender manner. 'You're never thinking of marrying her?—a girl without a penny.'

'She would never have me,' said he, with a short laugh.

'No, I don't think she would,' answered his mother. 'She laughed in my face, when I praised her for speaking out something Mr. Bell had said in your favour. I liked the girl for doing it so frankly, for it made me sure she had no thought of you; and the next minute she vexed me so by seeming to think—— Well, never mind! Only you're right in saying she's too good an opinion of herself to think of you. The saucy jade! I should like to know where she'd find a better!' If these words hurt her son, the dusky light prevented him from betraying any emotion. In a minute he came up quite cheerfully to his mother, and putting one hand lightly on her shoulder, said:

'Well, as I'm just as much convinced of the truth of what you have been saying as you can be; and as I have no thought or expectation of ever asking her to be my wife, you'll believe me for the future that I'm quite disinterested in speaking about her. I foresee trouble for that girl—perhaps want of motherly care—and I only wish you to be ready to be a friend to her, in case she needs one. Now, Fanny,' said he, 'I trust you have delicacy enough to understand, that it is as great an injury to Miss Hale as to me—in fact, she would think it a greater—to suppose that I have any reason, more than I now give, for begging you and my mother to show her every kindly attention.'

'I cannot forgive her her pride,' said his mother; 'I will befriend her, if there is need, for your asking, John. I would befriend Jezebel herself if you asked me. But this girl, who turns up her nose at us all—who turns up her nose at you—— '

'Nay, mother; I have never yet put myself, and I mean never to put myself, within reach of her contempt.'

'Contempt, indeed!'—(One of Mrs. Thornton's expressive snorts.)—'Don't go on speaking of Miss Hale, John, if I've to be kind to her. When I'm with her, I don't know if I like or dislike her most; but when I think of her, and hear you talk of her, I hate her. I can see she's given herself airs to you as well as if you'd told me out.'

'And if she has,' said he—and then he paused for a moment—then went on: 'I'm not a lad, to be cowed by a proud look from a woman, or to care for her misunderstanding me and my position. I can laugh at it!'

'To be sure! and at her too, with her fine notions and haughty tosses!'

'I only wonder why you talk so much about her, then,' said Fanny. 'I'm sure, I'm tired enough of the subject.'

'Well!' said her brother, with a shade of bitterness. 'Suppose we find some more agreeable subject. What do you say to a strike, by way of something pleasant to talk about?'

'Have the hands actually turned out?' asked Mrs. Thornton, with vivid interest.

'Hamper's men are actually out. Mine are working out their week, through fear of being prosecuted for breach of contract. I'd have had every one of them up and punished for it, that left his work before his time was out.'

'The law expenses would have been more than the hands them selves were worth—a set of ungrateful naughts!' said his mother.

'To be sure. But I'd have shown them how I keep my word, and how I mean them to keep theirs. They know me by this time. Slickson's men are off—pretty certain he won't spend money in getting them punished. We're in for a turn-out, mother.'

'I hope there are not many orders in hand?'

'Of course there are. They know that well enough. But they don't quite understand all, though they think they do.'

'What do you mean, John?'

Candles had been brought, and Fanny had taken up her interminable piece of worsted-work, over which she was yawning; throwing herself back in her chair, from time to time, to gaze at vacancy, and think of nothing at her ease.

'Why,' said he, 'the Americans are getting their yarns so into the general market, that our only chance is producing them at a lower rate. If we can't, we may shut up shop at once, and hands and masters go alike on tramp. Yet these fools go back to the prices paid three years ago—nay, some of their leaders quote Dickinson's prices now—though they know as well as we do that, what with fines pressed out of their wages as no honourable man would extort them, and other ways which I for one would scorn to use, the real rate of wage paid at Dickinson's is less than at ours. Upon my word, mother, I wish the old combination-laws were in force. It is too bad to find out that fools—ignorant wayward men like these—just by uniting their weak silly heads, are to rule over the fortunes of those who bring all the wisdom that knowledge and experience, and often painful thought and anxiety, can give. The next thing will be—indeed, we're all but come to it now—that we shall have to go and ask—stand hat in hand—and humbly ask the secretary of the Spinner' Union to be so kind as to furnish us with labour at their own price. That's what they want—they, who haven't the sense to see that, if we don't get a fair share of the profits to compensate us for our wear and tear here in England, we can move off to some other country; and that, what with home and foreign competition, we are none of us likely to make above a fair share, and may be thankful enough if we can get that, in an average number of years.'

'Can't you get hands from Ireland? I wouldn't keep these fellows a day. I'd teach them that I was master, and could employ what servants I liked.'

'Yes! to be sure, I can; and I will, too, if they go on long. It will be trouble and expense, and I fear there will be some danger; but I will do it, rather than give in.'

'If there is to be all this extra expense, I'm sorry we're giving a dinner just now.'

'So am I,—not because of the expense, but because I shall have much to think about, and many unexpected calls on my time. But we must have had Mr. Horsfall, and he does not stay in Milton long. And as for the others, we owe them dinners, and it's all one trouble.'

He kept on with his restless walk—not speaking any more, but drawing a deep breath from time to time, as if endeavouring to throw off some annoying thought. Fanny asked her mother numerous small questions, all having nothing to do with the subject, which a wiser person would have perceived was occupying her attention. Consequently, she received many short answers. She was not sorry when, at ten o'clock, the servants filed in to prayers. These her mother always read,—first reading a chapter. They were now working steadily through the Old Testament. When prayers were ended, and his mother had wished him goodnight, with that long steady look of hers which conveyed no expression of the tenderness that was in her heart, but yet had the intensity of a blessing, Mr. Thornton continued his walk. All his business plans had received a check, a sudden pull-up, from this approaching turn-out. The forethought of many anxious hours was thrown away, utterly wasted by their insane folly, which would injure themselves even more than him, though no one could set any limit to the mischief they were doing. And these were the men who thought themselves fitted to direct the masters in the disposal of their capital! Hamper had said, only this very day, that if he were ruined by the strike, he would start life again, comforted by the conviction that those who brought it on were in a worse predicament than he himself,—for he had head as well as hands, while they had only hands; and if they drove away their market, they could not follow it, nor turn to anything else. But this thought was no consolation to Mr. Thornton. It might be that revenge gave him no pleasure; it might be that he valued the position he had earned with the sweat of his brow, so much that he keenly felt its being endangered by the ignorance or folly of others,—so keenly that he had no thoughts to spare for what would be the consequences of their conduct to themselves. He paced up and down, setting his teeth a little now and then. At last it struck two. The candles were flickering in their sockets. He lighted his own, muttering to himself:

'Once for all, they shall know whom they have got to deal with. I can give them a fortnight,—no more. If they don't see their madness before the end of that time, I must have hands from Ireland. I believe it's Slickson's doing,—confound him and his dodges! He thought he was overstocked; so he seemed to yield at first, when the deputation came to him,—and of course, he only confirmed them in their folly, as he meant to do. That's where it spread from.'

CHAPTER XIX - ANGEL VISITS

'As angels in some brighter dreams
  Call to the soul when man doth sleep,
  So some strange thoughts transcend our wonted themes,
  And into glory peep.'
        HENRY VAUGHAN.

Mrs. Hale was curiously amused and interested by the idea of the Thornton dinner party. She kept wondering about the details, with something of the simplicity of a little child, who wants to have all its anticipated pleasures described beforehand. But the monotonous life led by invalids often makes them like children, inasmuch as they have neither of them any sense of proportion in events, and seem each to believe that the walls and curtains which shut in their world, and shut out everything else, must of necessity be larger than anything hidden beyond. Besides, Mrs. Hale had had her vanities as a girl; had perhaps unduly felt their mortification when she became a poor clergyman's wife;—they had been smothered and kept down; but they were not extinct; and she liked to think of seeing Margaret dressed for a party, and discussed what she should wear, with an unsettled anxiety that amused Margaret, who had been more accustomed to society in her one in Harley Street than her mother in five and twenty years of Helstone.

'Then you think you shall wear your white silk. Are you sure it will fit? It's nearly a year since Edith was married!'

'Oh yes, mamma! Mrs. Murray made it, and it's sure to be right; it may be a straw's breadth shorter or longer-waisted, according to my having grown fat or thin. But I don't think I've altered in the least.'

'Hadn't you better let Dixon see it? It may have gone yellow with lying by.'

'If you like, mamma. But if the worst comes to the worst, I've a very nice pink gauze which aunt Shaw gave me, only two or three months before Edith was married. That can't have gone yellow.'

'No! but it may have faded.'

'Well! then I've a green silk. I feel more as if it was the embarrassment of riches.'

'I wish I knew what you ought to wear,' said Mrs. Hale, nervously. Margaret's manner changed instantly. 'Shall I go and put them on one after another, mamma, and then you could see which you liked best?'

'But—yes! perhaps that will be best.'

So off Margaret went. She was very much inclined to play some pranks when she was dressed up at such an unusual hour; to make her rich white silk balloon out into a cheese, to retreat backwards from her mother as if she were the queen; but when she found that these freaks of hers were regarded as interruptions to the serious business, and as such annoyed her mother, she became grave and sedate. What had possessed the world (her world) to fidget so about her dress, she could not understand; but that very after noon, on naming her engagement to Bessy Higgins (apropos of the servant that Mrs. Thornton had promised to inquire about), Bessy quite roused up at the intelligence.

'Dear! and are you going to dine at Thornton's at Marlborough Mills?'

'Yes, Bessy. Why are you so surprised?'

'Oh, I dunno. But they visit wi' a' th' first folk in Milton.'

'And you don't think we're quite the first folk in Milton, eh, Bessy?' Bessy's cheeks flushed a little at her thought being thus easily read.

'Well,' said she, 'yo' see, they thinken a deal o' money here and I reckon yo've not getten much.'

'No,' said Margaret, 'that's very true. But we are educated people, and have lived amongst educated people. Is there anything so wonderful, in our being asked out to dinner by a man who owns himself inferior to my father by coming to him to be instructed? I don't mean to blame Mr. Thornton. Few drapers' assistants, as he was once, could have made themselves what he is.'

'But can yo' give dinners back, in yo'r small house? Thornton's house is three times as big.'

'Well, I think we could manage to give Mr. Thornton a dinner back, as you call it. Perhaps not in such a large room, nor with so many people. But I don't think we've thought about it at all in that way.'

'I never thought yo'd be dining with Thorntons,' repeated I Bessy. 'Why, the mayor hissel' dines there; and the members of Parliament and all.'

'I think I could support the honour of meeting the mayor of Milton.

'But them ladies dress so grand!' said Bessy, with an anxious look at Margaret's print gown, which her Milton eyes appraised at sevenpence a yard. Margaret's face dimpled up into a merry laugh. 'Thank You, Bessy, for thinking so kindly about my looking nice among all the smart people. But I've plenty of grand gowns,—a week ago, I should have said they were far too grand for anything I should ever want again. But as I'm to dine at Mr. Thornton's, and perhaps to meet the mayor, I shall put on my very best gown, you may be sure.'

'What win yo' wear?' asked Bessy, somewhat relieved.

'White silk,' said Margaret. 'A gown I had for a cousin's wedding, a year ago.

'That'll do!' said Bessy, falling back in her chair. 'I should be loth to have yo' looked down upon.

'Oh! I'll be fine enough, if that will save me from being looked down upon in Milton.'

'I wish I could see you dressed up,' said Bessy. 'I reckon, yo're not what folk would ca' pretty; yo've not red and white enough for that. But dun yo' know, I ha' dreamt of yo', long afore ever I seed yo'.'

'Nonsense, Bessy!'

'Ay, but I did. Yo'r very face,—looking wi' yo'r clear steadfast eyes out o' th' darkness, wi' yo'r hair blown off from yo'r brow, and going out like rays round yo'r forehead, which was just as smooth and as straight as it is now,—and yo' always came to give me strength, which I seemed to gather out o' yo'r deep comforting eyes,—and yo' were drest in shining raiment—just as yo'r going to be drest. So, yo' see, it was yo'!'

'Nay, Bessy,' said Margaret, gently, 'it was but a dream.'

'And why might na I dream a dream in my affliction as well as others? Did not many a one i' the Bible? Ay, and see visions too! Why, even my father thinks a deal o' dreams! I tell yo' again, I saw yo' as plainly, coming swiftly towards me, wi' yo'r hair blown back wi' the very swiftness o' the motion, just like the way it grows, a little standing off like; and the white shining dress on yo've getten to wear. Let me come and see yo' in it. I want to see yo' and touch yo' as in very deed yo' were in my dream.'

'My dear Bessy, it is quite a fancy of yours.'

'Fancy or no fancy,—yo've come, as I knew yo' would, when I saw yo'r movement in my dream,—and when yo're here about me, I reckon I feel easier in my mind, and comforted, just as a fire comforts one on a dree day. Yo' said it were on th' twenty-first; please God, I'll come and see yo'.'

'Oh Bessy! you may come and welcome; but don't talk so—it really makes me sorry. It does indeed.'

'Then I'll keep it to mysel', if I bite my tongue out. Not but what it's true for all that.'

Margaret was silent. At last she said,

'Let us talk about it sometimes, if you think it true. But not now. Tell me, has your father turned out?'

'Ay!' said Bessy, heavily—in a manner very different from that she had spoken in but a minute or two before. 'He and many another,—all Hamper's men,—and many a one besides. Th' women are as bad as th' men, in their savageness, this time. Food is high,—and they mun have food for their childer, I reckon. Suppose Thorntons sent 'em their dinner out,—th' same money, spent on potatoes and meal, would keep many a crying babby quiet, and hush up its mother's heart for a bit!'

'Don't speak so!' said Margaret. 'You'll make me feel wicked and guilty in going to this dinner.'

'No!' said Bessy. 'Some's pre-elected to sumptuous feasts, and purple and fine linen,—may be yo're one on 'em. Others toil and moil all their lives long—and the very dogs are not pitiful in our days, as they were in the days of Lazarus. But if yo' ask me to cool yo'r tongue wi' th' tip of my finger, I'll come across the great gulf to yo' just for th' thought o' what yo've been to me here.'

'Bessy! you're very feverish! I can tell it in the touch of your hand, as well as in what you're saying. It won't be division enough, in that awful day, that some of us have been beggars here, and some of us have been rich,—we shall not be judged by that poor accident, but by our faithful following of Christ.' Margaret got up, and found some water and soaking her pocket-handkerchief in it, she laid the cool wetness on Bessy's forehead, and began to chafe the stone-cold feet. Bessy shut her eyes, and allowed herself to be soothed. At last she said,

'Yo'd ha' been deaved out o' yo'r five wits, as well as me, if yo'd had one body after another coming in to ask for father, and staying to tell me each one their tale. Some spoke o' deadly hatred, and made my blood run cold wi' the terrible things they said o' th' masters,—but more, being women, kept plaining, plaining (wi' the tears running down their cheeks, and never wiped away, nor heeded), of the price o' meat, and how their childer could na sleep at nights for th' hunger.'

'And do they think the strike will mend this?' asked Margaret.

'They say so,' replied Bessy. 'They do say trade has been good for long, and the masters has made no end o' money; how much father doesn't know, but, in course, th' Union does; and, as is natural, they wanten their share o' th' profits, now that food is getting dear; and th' Union says they'll not be doing their duty if they don't make the masters give 'em their share. But masters has getten th' upper hand somehow; and I'm feared they'll keep it now and evermore. It's like th' great battle o' Armageddon, the way they keep on, grinning and fighting at each other, till even while they fight, they are picked off into the pit.' Just then, Nicholas Higgins came in. He caught his daughter's last words.

'Ay! and I'll fight on too; and I'll get it this time. It'll not take long for to make 'em give in, for they've getten a pretty lot of orders, all under contract; and they'll soon find out they'd better give us our five per cent than lose the profit they'll gain; let alone the fine for not fulfilling the contract. Aha, my masters! I know who'll win.'

Margaret fancied from his manner that he must have been drinking, not so much from what he said, as from the excited way in which he spoke; and she was rather confirmed in this idea by the evident anxiety Bessy showed to hasten her departure. Bessy said to her,—

'The twenty-first—that's Thursday week. I may come and see yo' dressed for Thornton's, I reckon. What time is yo'r dinner?'

Before Margaret could answer, Higgins broke out,

'Thornton's! Ar' t' going to dine at Thornton's? Ask him to give yo' a bumper to the success of his orders. By th' twenty-first, I reckon, he'll be pottered in his brains how to get 'em done in time. Tell him, there's seven hundred'll come marching into Marlborough Mills, the morning after he gives the five per cent, and will help him through his contract in no time. You'll have 'em all there. My master, Hamper. He's one o' th' oud-fashioned sort. Ne'er meets a man bout an oath or a curse; I should think he were going to die if he spoke me civil; but arter all, his bark's waur than his bite, and yo' may tell him one o' his turn-outs said so, if yo' like. Eh! but yo'll have a lot of prize mill-owners at Thornton's! I should like to get speech o' them, when they're a bit inclined to sit still after dinner, and could na run for the life on 'em. I'd tell 'em my mind. I'd speak up again th' hard way they're driving on us!'

'Good-bye!' said Margaret, hastily. 'Good-bye, Bessy! I shall look to see you on the twenty-first, if you're well enough.'

The medicines and treatment which Dr. Donaldson had ordered for Mrs. Hale, did her so much good at first that not only she herself, but Margaret, began to hope that he might have been mistaken, and that she could recover permanently. As for Mr. Hale, although he had never had an idea of the serious nature of their apprehensions, he triumphed over their fears with an evident relief, which proved how much his glimpse into the nature of them had affected him. Only Dixon croaked for ever into Margaret's ear. However, Margaret defied the raven, and would hope.

They needed this gleam of brightness in-doors, for out-of-doors, even to their uninstructed eyes, there was a gloomy brooding appearance of discontent. Mr. Hale had his own acquaintances among the working men, and was depressed with their earnestly told tales of suffering and long-endurance. They would have scorned to speak of what they had to bear to any one who might, from his position, have understood it without their words. But here was this man, from a distant county, who was perplexed by the workings of the system into the midst of which he was thrown, and each was eager to make him a judge, and to bring witness of his own causes for irritation. Then Mr. Hale brought all his budget of grievances, and laid it before Mr. Thornton, for him, with his experience as a master, to arrange them, and explain their origin; which he always did, on sound economical principles; showing that, as trade was conducted, there must always be a waxing and waning of commercial prosperity; and that in the waning a certain number of masters, as well as of men, must go down into ruin, and be no more seen among the ranks of the happy and prosperous. He spoke as if this consequence were so entirely logical, that neither employers nor employed had any right to complain if it became their fate: the employer to turn aside from the race he could no longer run, with a bitter sense of incompetency and failure—wounded in the struggle—trampled down by his fellows in their haste to get rich—slighted where he once was honoured—humbly asking for, instead of bestowing, employment with a lordly hand. Of course, speaking so of the fate that, as a master, might be his own in the fluctuations of commerce, he was not likely to have more sympathy with that of the workmen, who were passed by in the swift merciless improvement or alteration who would fain lie down and quietly die out of the world that needed them not, but felt as if they could never rest in their graves for the clinging cries of the beloved and helpless they would leave behind; who envied the power of the wild bird, that can feed her young with her very heart's blood. Margaret's whole soul rose up against him while he reasoned in this way—as if commerce were everything and humanity nothing. She could hardly, thank him for the individual kindness, which brought him that very evening to offer her—for the delicacy which made him understand that he must offer her privately—every convenience for illness that his own wealth or his mother's foresight had caused them to accumulate in their household, and which, as he learnt from Dr. Donaldson, Mrs. Hale might possibly require. His presence, after the way he had spoken—his bringing before her the doom, which she was vainly trying to persuade herself might yet be averted from her mother—all conspired to set Margaret's teeth on edge, as she looked at him, and listened to him. What business had he to be the only person, except Dr. Donaldson and Dixon, admitted to the awful secret, which she held shut up in the most dark and sacred recess of her heart—not daring to look at it, unless she invoked heavenly strength to bear the sight—that, some day soon, she should cry aloud for her mother, and no answer would come out of the blank, dumb darkness? Yet he knew all. She saw it in his pitying eyes. She heard it in his grave and tremulous voice. How reconcile those eyes, that voice, with the hard-reasoning, dry, merciless way in which he laid down axioms of trade, and serenely followed them out to their full consequences? The discord jarred upon her inexpressibly. The more because of the gathering woe of which she heard from Bessy. To be sure, Nicholas Higgins, the father, spoke differently. He had been appointed a committee-man, and said that he knew secrets of which the exoteric knew nothing. He said this more expressly and particularly, on the very day before Mrs. Thornton's dinner-party, when Margaret, going in to speak to Bessy, found him arguing the point with Boucher, the neighbour of whom she had frequently heard mention, as by turns exciting Higgins's compassion, as an unskilful workman with a large family depending upon him for support, and at other times enraging his more energetic and sanguine neighbour by his want of what the latter called spirit. It was very evident that Higgins was in a passion when Margaret entered. Boucher stood, with both hands on the rather high mantel-piece, swaying himself a little on the support which his arms, thus placed, gave him, and looking wildly into the fire, with a kind of despair that irritated Higgins, even while it went to his heart. Bessy was rocking herself violently backwards and forwards, as was her wont (Margaret knew by this time) when she was agitated. Her sister Mary was tying on her bonnet (in great clumsy bows, as suited her great clumsy fingers), to go to her fustian-cutting, blubbering out loud the while, and evidently longing to be away from a scene that distressed her. Margaret came in upon this scene. She stood for a moment at the door—then, her finger on her lips, she stole to a seat on the squab near Bessy. Nicholas saw her come in, and greeted her with a gruff, but not unfriendly nod. Mary hurried out of the house catching gladly at the open door, and crying aloud when she got away from her father's presence. It was only John Boucher that took no notice whatever who came in and who went out.

'It's no use, Higgins. Hoo cannot live long a' this'n. Hoo's just sinking away—not for want o' meat hersel'—but because hoo cannot stand th' sight o' the little ones clemming. Ay, clemming! Five shilling a week may do well enough for thee, wi' but two mouths to fill, and one on 'em a wench who can welly earn her own meat. But it's clemming to us. An' I tell thee plain—if hoo dies as I'm 'feard hoo will afore we've getten th' five per cent, I'll fling th' money back i' th' master's face, and say, "Be domned to yo'; be domned to th' whole cruel world o' yo'; that could na leave me th' best wife that ever bore childer to a man!" An' look thee, lad, I'll hate thee, and th' whole pack o' th' Union. Ay, an' chase yo' through heaven wi' my hatred,—I will, lad! I will,—if yo're leading me astray i' this matter. Thou saidst, Nicholas, on Wednesday sennight—and it's now Tuesday i' th' second week—that afore a fortnight we'd ha' the masters coming a-begging to us to take back our' work, at our own wage—and time's nearly up,—and there's our lile Jack lying a-bed, too weak to cry, but just every now and then sobbing up his heart for want o' food,—our lile Jack, I tell thee, lad! Hoo's never looked up sin' he were born, and hoo loves him as if he were her very life,—as he is,—for I reckon he'll ha' cost me that precious price,—our lile Jack, who wakened me each morn wi' putting his sweet little lips to my great rough fou' face, a-seeking a smooth place to kiss,—an' he lies clemming.' Here the deep sobs choked the poor man, and Nicholas looked up, with eyes brimful of tears, to Margaret, before he could gain courage to speak.

'Hou'd up, man. Thy lile Jack shall na' clem. I ha' getten brass, and we'll go buy the chap a sup o' milk an' a good four-pounder this very minute. What's mine's thine, sure enough, i' thou'st i' want. Only, dunnot lose heart, man!' continued he, as he fumbled in a tea-pot for what money he had. 'I lay yo' my heart and soul we'll win for a' this: it's but bearing on one more week, and yo just see th' way th' masters 'll come round, praying on us to come back to our mills. An' th' Union,—that's to say, I—will take care yo've enough for th' childer and th' missus. So dunnot turn faint-heart, and go to th' tyrants a-seeking work.'

The man turned round at these words,—turned round a face so white, and gaunt, and tear-furrowed, and hopeless, that its very calm forced Margaret to weep. 'Yo' know well, that a worser tyrant than e'er th' masters were says "Clem to death, and see 'em a' clem to death, ere yo' dare go again th' Union." Yo' know it well, Nicholas, for a' yo're one on 'em. Yo' may be kind hearts, each separate; but once banded together, yo've no more pity for a man than a wild hunger-maddened wolf.'

Nicholas had his hand on the lock of the door—he stopped and turned round on Boucher, close following:

'So help me God! man alive—if I think not I'm doing best for thee, and for all on us. If I'm going wrong when I think I'm going right, it's their sin, who ha' left me where I am, in my ignorance. I ha' thought till my brains ached,—Beli' me, John, I have. An' I say again, there's no help for us but having faith i' th' Union. They'll win the day, see if they dunnot!'

Not one word had Margaret or Bessy spoken. They had hardly uttered the sighing, that the eyes of each called to the other to bring up from the depths of her heart. At last Bessy said,

'I never thought to hear father call on God again. But yo' heard him say, "So help me God!"'

'Yes!' said Margaret. 'Let me bring you what money I can spare,—let me bring you a little food for that poor man's children. Don't let them know it comes from any one but your father. It will be but little.'

Bessy lay back without taking any notice of what Margaret said. She did not cry—she only quivered up her breath,

'My heart's drained dry o' tears,' she said. 'Boucher's been in these days past, a telling me of his fears and his troubles. He's but a weak kind o' chap, I know, but he's a man for a' that; and tho' I've been angry, many a time afore now, wi' him an' his wife, as knew no more nor him how to manage, yet, yo' see, all folks isn't wise, yet God lets 'em live—ay, an' gives 'em some one to love, and be loved by, just as good as Solomon. An', if sorrow comes to them they love, it hurts 'em as sore as e'er it did Solomon. I can't make it out. Perhaps it's as well such a one as Boucher has th' Union to see after him. But I'd just like for to see th' mean as make th' Union, and put 'em one by one face to face wi' Boucher. I reckon, if they heard him, they'd tell him (if I cotched 'em one by one), he might go back and get what he could for his work, even if it weren't so much as they ordered.'

Margaret sat utterly silent. How was she ever to go away into comfort and forget that man's voice, with the tone of unutterable agony, telling more by far than his words of what he had to suffer? She took out her purse; she had not much in it of what she could call her own, but what she had she put into Bessy's hand without speaking.

'Thank yo'. There's many on 'em gets no more, and is not so bad off,—leastways does not show it as he does. But father won't let 'em want, now he knows. Yo' see, Boucher's been pulled down wi' his childer,—and her being so cranky, and a' they could pawn has gone this last twelvemonth. Yo're not to think we'd ha' letten 'em clem, for all we're a bit pressed oursel'; if neighbours doesn't see after neighbours, I dunno who will.' Bessy seemed almost afraid lest Margaret should think they had not the will, and, to a certain degree, the power of helping one whom she evidently regarded as having a claim upon them. 'Besides,' she went on, 'father is sure and positive the masters must give in within these next few days,—that they canna hould on much longer. But I thank yo' all the same,—I thank yo' for mysel', as much as for Boucher, for it just makes my heart warm to yo' more and more.'

Bessy seemed much quieter to-day, but fearfully languid and exhausted. As she finished speaking, she looked so faint and weary that Margaret became alarmed.

'It's nout,' said Bessy. 'It's not death yet. I had a fearfu' night wi' dreams—or somewhat like dreams, for I were wide awake—and I'm all in a swounding daze to-day,—only yon poor chap made me alive again. No! it's not death yet, but death is not far off. Ay! Cover me up, and I'll may be sleep, if th' cough will let me. Good night—good afternoon, m'appen I should say—but th' light is dim an' misty to-day.'

CHAPTER XX - MEN AND GENTLEMEN

'Old and young, boy, let 'em all eat, I have it;
Let 'em have ten tire of teeth a-piece, I care not.'
ROLLO, DUKE OF NORMANDY.

Margaret went home so painfully occupied with what she had heard and seen that she hardly knew how to rouse herself up to the duties which awaited her; the necessity for keeping up a constant flow of cheerful conversation for her mother, who, now that she was unable to go out, always looked to Margaret's return from the shortest walk as bringing in some news.

'And can your factory friend come on Thursday to see you dressed?'

'She was so ill I never thought of asking her,' said Margaret, dolefully.

'Dear! Everybody is ill now, I think,' said Mrs. Hale, with a little of the jealousy which one invalid is apt to feel of another. 'But it must be very sad to be ill in one of those little back streets.' (Her kindly nature prevailing, and the old Helstone habits of thought returning.) 'It's bad enough here. What could you do for her, Margaret? Mr. Thornton has sent me some of his old port wine since you went out. Would a bottle of that do her good, think you?'

'No, mamma! I don't believe they are very poor,—at least, they don't speak as if they were; and, at any rate, Bessy's illness is consumption—she won't want wine. Perhaps, I might take her a little preserve, made of our dear Helstone fruit. No! there's another family to whom I should like to give—Oh mamma, mamma! how am I to dress up in my finery, and go off and away to smart parties, after the sorrow I have seen to-day?' exclaimed Margaret, bursting the bounds she had preordained for herself before she came in, and telling her mother of what she had seen and heard at Higgins's cottage.

It distressed Mrs. Hale excessively. It made her restlessly irritated till she could do something. She directed Margaret to pack up a basket in the very drawing-room, to be sent there and then to the family; and was almost angry with her for saying, that it would not signify if it did not go till morning, as she knew Higgins had provided for their immediate wants, and she herself had left money with Bessy. Mrs. Hale called her unfeeling for saying this; and never gave herself breathing-time till the basket was sent out of the house. Then she said:

'After all, we may have been doing wrong. It was only the last time Mr. Thornton was here that he said, those were no true friends who helped to prolong the struggle by assisting the turn outs. And this Boucher-man was a turn-out, was he not?'

The question was referred to Mr. Hale by his wife, when he came up-stairs, fresh from giving a lesson to Mr. Thornton, which had ended in conversation, as was their wont. Margaret did not care if their gifts had prolonged the strike; she did not think far enough for that, in her present excited state.

Mr. Hale listened, and tried to be as calm as a judge; he recalled all that had seemed so clear not half-an-hour before, as it came out of Mr. Thornton's lips; and then he made an unsatisfactory compromise. His wife and daughter had not only done quite right in this instance, but he did not see for a moment how they could have done otherwise. Nevertheless, as a general rule, it was very true what Mr. Thornton said, that as the strike, if prolonged, must end in the masters' bringing hands from a distance (if, indeed, the final result were not, as it had often been before, the invention of some machine which would diminish the need of hands at all), why, it was clear enough that the kindest thing was to refuse all help which might bolster them up in their folly. But, as to this Boucher, he would go and see him the first thing in the morning, and try and find out what could be done for him.

Mr. Hale went the next morning, as he proposed. He did not find Boucher at home, but he had a long talk with his wife; promised to ask for an Infirmary order for her; and, seeing the plenty provided by Mrs. Hale, and somewhat lavishly used by the children, who were masters down-stairs in their father's absence, he came back with a more consoling and cheerful account than Margaret had dared to hope for; indeed, what she had said the night before had prepared her father for so much worse a state of things that, by a reaction of his imagination, he described all as better than it really was.

'But I will go again, and see the man himself,' said Mr. Hale. 'I hardly know as yet how to compare one of these houses with our Helstone cottages. I see furniture here which our labourers would never have thought of buying, and food commonly used which they would consider luxuries; yet for these very families there seems no other resource, now that their weekly wages are stopped, but the pawn-shop. One had need to learn a different language, and measure by a different standard, up here in Milton.'

Bessy, too, was rather better this day. Still she was so weak that she seemed to have entirely forgotten her wish to see Margaret dressed—if, indeed, that had not been the feverish desire of a half-delirious state.

Margaret could not help comparing this strange dressing of hers, to go where she did not care to be—her heart heavy with various anxieties—with the old, merry, girlish toilettes that she and Edith had performed scarcely more than a year ago. Her only pleasure now in decking herself out was in thinking that her mother would take delight in seeing her dressed. She blushed when Dixon, throwing the drawing-room door open, made an appeal for admiration.

'Miss Hale looks well, ma'am,—doesn't she? Mrs. Shaw's coral couldn't have come in better. It just gives the right touch of colour, ma'am. Otherwise, Miss Margaret, you would have been too pale.'

Margaret's black hair was too thick to be plaited; it needed rather to be twisted round and round, and have its fine silkiness compressed into massive coils, that encircled her head like a crown, and then were gathered into a large spiral knot behind. She kept its weight together by two large coral pins, like small arrows for length. Her white silk sleeves were looped up with strings of the same material, and on her neck, just below the base of her curved and milk-white throat, there lay heavy coral beads.

'Oh, Margaret! how I should like to be going with you to one of the old Barrington assemblies,—taking you as Lady Beresford used to take me.' Margaret kissed her mother for this little burst of maternal vanity; but she could hardly smile at it, she felt so much out of spirits.

'I would rather stay at home with you,—much rather, mamma.'

'Nonsense, darling! Be sure you notice the dinner well. I shall like to hear how they manage these things in Milton. Particularly the second course, dear. Look what they have instead of game.'

Mrs. Hale would have been more than interested,—she would have been astonished, if she had seen the sumptuousness of the dinner-table and its appointments. Margaret, with her London cultivated taste, felt the number of delicacies to be oppressive one half of the quantity would have been enough, and the effect lighter and more elegant. But it was one of Mrs. Thornton's rigorous laws of hospitality, that of each separate dainty enough should be provided for all the guests to partake, if they felt inclined. Careless to abstemiousness in her daily habits, it was part of her pride to set a feast before such of her guests as cared for it. Her son shared this feeling. He had never known—though he might have imagined, and had the capability to relish any kind of society but that which depended on an exchange of superb meals and even now, though he was denying himself the personal expenditure of an unnecessary sixpence, and had more than once regretted that the invitations for this dinner had been sent out, still, as it was to be, he was glad to see the old magnificence of preparation. Margaret and her father were the first to arrive. Mr. Hale was anxiously punctual to the time specified. There was no one up-stairs in the drawing-room but Mrs. Thornton and Fanny. Every cover was taken off, and the apartment blazed forth in yellow silk damask and a brilliantly-flowered carpet. Every corner seemed filled up with ornament, until it became a weariness to the eye, and presented a strange contrast to the bald ugliness of the look-out into the great mill-yard, where wide folding gates were thrown open for the admission of carriages. The mill loomed high on the left-hand side of the windows, casting a shadow down from its many stories, which darkened the summer evening before its time.

'My son was engaged up to the last moment on business. He will be here directly, Mr. Hale. May I beg you to take a seat?'

Mr. Hale was standing at one of the windows as Mrs. Thornton spoke. He turned away, saying,

'Don't you find such close neighbourhood to the mill rather unpleasant at times?'

She drew herself up:

'Never. I am not become so fine as to desire to forget the source of my son's wealth and power. Besides, there is not such another factory in Milton. One room alone is two hundred and twenty square yards.'

'I meant that the smoke and the noise—the constant going out and coming in of the work-people, might be annoying!'

'I agree with you, Mr. Hale!' said Fanny. 'There is a continual smell of steam, and oily machinery—and the noise is perfectly deafening.'

'I have heard noise that was called music far more deafening. The engine-room is at the street-end of the factory; we hardly hear it, except in summer weather, when all the windows are open; and as for the continual murmur of the work-people, it disturbs me no more than the humming of a hive of bees. If I think of it at all, I connect it with my son, and feel how all belongs to him, and that his is the head that directs it. Just now, there are no sounds to come from the mill; the hands have been ungrateful enough to turn out, as perhaps you have heard. But the very business (of which I spoke, when you entered), had reference to the steps he is going to take to make them learn their place.' The expression on her face, always stern, deepened into dark anger, as she said this. Nor did it clear away when Mr. Thornton entered the room; for she saw, in an instant, the weight of care and anxiety which he could not shake off, although his guests received from him a greeting that appeared both cheerful and cordial. He shook hands with Margaret. He knew it was the first time their hands had met, though she was perfectly unconscious of the fact. He inquired after Mrs. Hale, and heard Mr. Hale's sanguine, hopeful account; and glancing at Margaret, to understand how far she agreed with her father, he saw that no dissenting shadow crossed her face. And as he looked with this intention, he was struck anew with her great beauty. He had never seen her in such dress before and yet now it appeared as if such elegance of attire was so befitting her noble figure and lofty serenity of countenance, that she ought to go always thus apparelled. She was talking to Fanny; about what, he could not hear; but he saw his sister's restless way of continually arranging some part of her gown, her wandering eyes, now glancing here, now there, but without any purpose in her observation; and he contrasted them uneasily with the large soft eyes that looked forth steadily at one object, as if from out their light beamed some gentle influence of repose: the curving lines of the red lips, just parted in the interest of listening to what her companion said—the head a little bent forwards, so as to make a long sweeping line from the summit, where the light caught on the glossy raven hair, to the smooth ivory tip of the shoulder; the round white arms, and taper hands, laid lightly across each other, but perfectly motionless in their pretty attitude. Mr. Thornton sighed as he took in all this with one of his sudden comprehensive glances. And then he turned his back to the young ladies, and threw himself, with an effort, but with all his heart and soul, into a conversation with Mr. Hale.

More people came—more and more. Fanny left Margaret's side, and helped her mother to receive her guests. Mr. Thornton felt that in this influx no one was speaking to Margaret, and was restless under this apparent neglect. But he never went near her himself; he did not look at her. Only, he knew what she was doing—or not doing—better than he knew the movements of any one else in the room. Margaret was so unconscious of herself, and so much amused by watching other people, that she never thought whether she was left unnoticed or not. Somebody took her down to dinner; she did not catch the name; nor did he seem much inclined to talk to her. There was a very animated conversation going on among the gentlemen; the ladies, for the most part, were silent, employing themselves in taking notes of the dinner and criticising each other's dresses. Margaret caught the clue to the general conversation, grew interested and listened attentively. Mr. Horsfall, the stranger, whose visit to the town was the original germ of the party, was asking questions relative to the trade and manufactures of the place; and the rest of the gentlemen—all Milton men,—were giving him answers and explanations. Some dispute arose, which was warmly contested; it was referred to Mr. Thornton, who had hardly spoken before; but who now gave an opinion, the grounds of which were so clearly stated that even the opponents yielded. Margaret's attention was thus called to her host; his whole manner as master of the house, and entertainer of his friends, was so straightforward, yet simple and modest, as to be thoroughly dignified. Margaret thought she had never seen him to so much advantage. When he had come to their house, there had been always something, either of over-eagerness or of that kind of vexed annoyance which seemed ready to pre-suppose that he was unjustly judged, and yet felt too proud to try and make himself better understood. But now, among his fellows, there was no uncertainty as to his position. He was regarded by them as a man of great force of character; of power in many ways. There was no need to struggle for their respect. He had it, and he knew it; and the security of this gave a fine grand quietness to his voice and ways, which Margaret had missed before.

He was not in the habit of talking to ladies; and what he did say was a little formal. To Margaret herself he hardly spoke at all. She was surprised to think how much she enjoyed this dinner. She knew enough now to understand many local interests—nay, even some of the technical words employed by the eager mill-owners. She silently took a very decided part in the question they were discussing. At any rate, they talked in desperate earnest,—not in the used-up style that wearied her so in the old London parties. She wondered that with all this dwelling on the manufactures and trade of the place, no allusion was made to the strike then pending. She did not yet know how coolly such things were taken by the masters, as having only one possible end. To be sure, the men were cutting their own throats, as they had done many a time before; but if they would be fools, and put themselves into the hands of a rascally set of paid delegates, they must take the consequence. One or two thought Thornton looked out of spirits;

and, of course, he must lose by this turn-out. But it was an accident that might happen to themselves any day; and Thornton was as good to manage a strike as any one; for he was as iron a chap as any in Milton. The hands had mistaken their man in trying that dodge on him. And they chuckled inwardly at the idea of the workmen's discomfiture and defeat, in their attempt to alter one iota of what Thornton had decreed. It was rather dull for Margaret after dinner. She was glad when the gentlemen came, not merely because she caught her father's eye to brighten her sleepiness up; but because she could listen to something larger and grander than the petty interests which the ladies had been talking about. She liked the exultation in the sense of power which these Milton men had. It might be rather rampant in its display, and savour of boasting; but still they seemed to defy the old limits of possibility, in a kind of fine intoxication, caused by the recollection of what had been achieved, and what yet should be. If in her cooler moments she might not approve of their spirit in all things, still there was much to admire in their forgetfulness of themselves and the present, in their anticipated triumphs over all inanimate matter at some future time which none of them should live to see. She was rather startled when Mr. Thornton spoke to her, close at her elbow:

'I could see you were on our side in our discussion at dinner,—were you not, Miss Hale?'

'Certainly. But then I know so little about it. I was surprised, however, to find from what Mr. Horsfall said, that there were others who thought in so diametrically opposite a manner, as the Mr. Morison he spoke about. He cannot be a gentleman—is he?'

'I am not quite the person to decide on another's gentlemanliness, Miss Hale. I mean, I don't quite understand your application of the word. But I should say that this Morison is no true man. I don't know who he is; I merely judge him from Mr. Horsfall's account.'

'I suspect my "gentleman" includes your "true man."'

'And a great deal more, you would imply. I differ from you. A man is to me a higher and a completer being than a gentleman.'

'What do you mean?' asked Margaret. 'We must understand the words differently.'

'I take it that "gentleman" is a term that only describes a person in his relation to others; but when we speak of him as "a man," we consider him not merely with regard to his fellow-men, but in relation to himself,—to life—to time—to eternity. A cast-away lonely as Robinson Crusoe—a prisoner immured in a dungeon for life—nay, even a saint in Patmos, has his endurance, his strength, his faith, best described by being spoken of as "a man." I am rather weary of this word "gentlemanly," which seems to me to be often inappropriately used, and often, too, with such exaggerated distortion of meaning, while the full simplicity of the noun "man," and the adjective "manly" are unacknowledged—that I am induced to class it with the cant of the day.'

Margaret thought a moment,—but before she could speak her slow conviction, he was called away by some of the eager manufacturers, whose speeches she could not hear, though she could guess at their import by the short clear answers Mr. Thornton gave, which came steady and firm as the boom of a distant minute gun. They were evidently talking of the turn-out, and suggesting what course had best be pursued. She heard Mr. Thornton say:

'That has been done.' Then came a hurried murmur, in which two or three joined.

'All those arrangements have been made.'

Some doubts were implied, some difficulties named by Mr. Slickson, who took hold of Mr. Thornton's arm, the better to impress his words. Mr. Thornton moved slightly away, lifted his eyebrows a very little, and then replied:

'I take the risk. You need not join in it unless you choose.' Still some more fears were urged.

'I'm not afraid of anything so dastardly as incendiarism. We are open enemies; and I can protect myself from any violence that I apprehend. And I will assuredly protect all others who come to me for work. They know my determination by this time, as well and as fully as you do.'

Mr. Horsfall took him a little on one side, as Margaret conjectured, to ask him some other question about the strike; but, in truth, it was to inquire who she herself was—so quiet, so stately, and so beautiful.

'A Milton lady?' asked he, as the name was given.

'No! from the south of England—Hampshire, I believe,' was the cold, indifferent answer.

Mrs. Slickson was catechising Fanny on the same subject.

'Who is that fine distinguished-looking girl? a sister of Mr. Horsfall's?'

'Oh dear, no! That is Mr. Hale, her father, talking now to Mr. Stephens. He gives lessons; that is to say, he reads with young men. My brother John goes to him twice a week, and so he begged mamma to ask them here, in hopes of getting him known. I believe, we have some of their prospectuses, if you would like to have one.'

'Mr. Thornton! Does he really find time to read with a tutor, in the midst of all his business,—and this abominable strike in hand as well?'

Fanny was not sure, from Mrs. Slickson's manner, whether she ought to be proud or ashamed of her brother's conduct; and, like all people who try and take other people's 'ought' for the rule of their feelings, she was inclined to blush for any singularity of action. Her shame was interrupted by the dispersion of the guests.

CHAPTER XXI - THE DARK NIGHT

'On earth is known to none
  The smile that is not sister to a tear.'
    ELLIOTT.

Margaret and her father walked home. The night was fine, the streets clean, and with her pretty white silk, like Leezie Lindsay's gown o' green satin, in the ballad, 'kilted up to her knee,' she was off with her father—ready to dance along with the excitement of the cool, fresh night air.

'I rather think Thornton is not quite easy in his mind about this strike. He seemed very anxious to-night.'

'I should wonder if he were not. But he spoke with his usual coolness to the others, when they suggested different things, just before we came away.'

'So he did after dinner as well. It would take a good deal to stir him from his cool manner of speaking; but his face strikes me as anxious.'

'I should be, if I were he. He must know of the growing anger and hardly smothered hatred of his workpeople, who all look upon him as what the Bible calls a "hard man,"—not so much unjust as unfeeling; clear in judgment, standing upon his "rights" as no human being ought to stand, considering what we and all our petty rights are in the sight of the Almighty. I am glad you think he looks anxious. When I remember Boucher's half mad words and ways, I cannot bear to think how coolly Mr. Thornton spoke.'

'In the first place, I am not so convinced as you are about that man Boucher's utter distress; for the moment, he was badly off, I don't doubt. But there is always a mysterious supply of money from these Unions; and, from what you said, it was evident the man was of a passionate, demonstrative nature, and gave strong expression to all he felt.'

'Oh, papa!'

'Well! I only want you to do justice to Mr. Thornton, who is, I suspect, of an exactly opposite nature,—a man who is far too proud to show his feelings. Just the character I should have thought beforehand, you would have admired, Margaret.'

'So I do,—so I should; but I don't feel quite so sure as you do of the existence of those feelings. He is a man of great strength of character,—of unusual intellect, considering the few advantages he has had.'

'Not so few. He has led a practical life from a very early age; has been called upon to exercise judgment and self-control. All that developes one part of the intellect. To be sure, he needs some of the knowledge of the past, which gives the truest basis for conjecture as to the future; but he knows this need,—he perceives it, and that is something. You are quite prejudiced against Mr. Thornton, Margaret.'

'He is the first specimen of a manufacturer—of a person engaged in trade—that I had ever the opportunity of studying, papa. He is my first olive: let me make a face while I swallow it. I know he is good of his kind, and by and by I shall like the kind. I rather think I am already beginning to do so. I was very much interested by what the gentlemen were talking about, although I did not understand half of it. I was quite sorry when Miss Thornton came to take me to the other end of the room, saying she was sure I should be uncomfortable at being the only lady among so many gentlemen. I had never thought about it, I was so busy listening; and the ladies were so dull, papa—oh, so dull! Yet I think it was clever too. It reminded me of our old game of having each so many nouns to introduce into a sentence.'

'What do you mean, child?' asked Mr. Hale.

'Why, they took nouns that were signs of things which gave evidence of wealth,—housekeepers, under-gardeners, extent of glass, valuable lace, diamonds, and all such things; and each one formed her speech so as to bring them all in, in the prettiest accidental manner possible.'

'You will be as proud of your one servant when you get her, if all is true about her that Mrs. Thornton says.'

'To be sure, I shall. I felt like a great hypocrite to-night, sitting there in my white silk gown, with my idle hands before me, when I remembered all the good, thorough, house-work they had done to-day. They took me for a fine lady, I'm sure.'

'Even I was mistaken enough to think you looked like a lady my dear,' said Mr. Hale, quietly smiling.

But smiles were changed to white and trembling looks, when they saw Dixon's face, as she opened the door.

'Oh, master!—Oh, Miss Margaret! Thank God you are come! Dr. Donaldson is here. The servant next door went for him, for the charwoman is gone home. She's better now; but, oh, sir! I thought she'd have died an hour ago.'

Mr. Hale caught Margaret's arm to steady himself from falling. He looked at her face, and saw an expression upon it of surprise and extremest sorrow, but not the agony of terror that contracted his own unprepared heart. She knew more than he did, and yet she listened with that hopeless expression of awed apprehension.

'Oh! I should not have left her—wicked daughter that I am!' moaned forth Margaret, as she supported her trembling father's hasty steps up-stairs. Dr. Donaldson met them on the landing.

'She is better now,' he whispered. 'The opiate has taken effect. The spasms were very bad: no wonder they frightened your maid; but she'll rally this time.'

'This time! Let me go to her!' Half an hour ago, Mr. Hale was a middle-aged man; now his sight was dim, his senses wavering, his walk tottering, as if he were seventy years of age.

Dr. Donaldson took his arm, and led him into the bedroom. Margaret followed close. There lay her mother, with an unmistakable look on her face. She might be better now; she was sleeping, but Death had signed her for his own, and it was clear that ere long he would return to take possession. Mr. Hale looked at her for some time without a word. Then he began to shake all over, and, turning away from Dr. Donaldson's anxious care, he groped to find the door; he could not see it, although several candles, brought in the sudden affright, were burning and flaring there. He staggered into the drawing-room, and felt about for a chair. Dr. Donaldson wheeled one to him, and placed him in it. He felt his pulse.

'Speak to him, Miss Hale. We must rouse him.'

'Papa!' said Margaret, with a crying voice that was wild with pain. 'Papa! Speak to me!' The speculation came again into his eyes, and he made a great effort.

'Margaret, did you know of this? Oh, it was cruel of you!'

'No, sir, it was not cruel!' replied Dr. Donaldson, with quick decision. 'Miss Hale acted under my directions. There may have been a mistake, but it was not cruel. Your wife will be a different creature to-morrow, I trust. She has had spasms, as I anticipated, though I did not tell Miss Hale of my apprehensions. She has taken the opiate I brought with me; she will have a good long sleep; and to-morrow, that look which has alarmed you so much will have passed away.'

'But not the disease?'

Dr. Donaldson glanced at Margaret. Her bent head, her face raised with no appeal for a temporary reprieve, showed that quick observer of human nature that she thought it better that the whole truth should be told.

'Not the disease. We cannot touch the disease, with all our poor vaunted skill. We can only delay its progress—alleviate the pain it causes. Be a man, sir—a Christian. Have faith in the immortality of the soul, which no pain, no mortal disease, can assail or touch!'

But all the reply he got, was in the choked words, 'You have never been married, Dr. Donaldson; you do not know what it is,' and in the deep, manly sobs, which went through the stillness of the night like heavy pulses of agony. Margaret knelt by him, caressing him with tearful caresses. No one, not even Dr. Donaldson, knew how the time went by. Mr. Hale was the first to dare to speak of the necessities of the present moment.

'What must we do?' asked he. 'Tell us both. Margaret is my staff—my right hand.'

Dr. Donaldson gave his clear, sensible directions. No fear for to-night—nay, even peace for to-morrow, and for many days yet. But no enduring hope of recovery. He advised Mr. Hale to go to bed, and leave only one to watch the slumber, which he hoped would be undisturbed. He promised to come again early in the morning. And with a warm and kindly shake of the hand, he left them. They spoke but few words; they were too much exhausted by their terror to do more than decide upon the immediate course of action. Mr. Hale was resolved to sit up through the night, and all that Margaret could do was to prevail upon him to rest on the drawing-room sofa. Dixon stoutly and bluntly refused to go to bed; and, as for Margaret, it was simply impossible that she should leave her mother, let all the doctors in the world speak of 'husbanding resources,' and 'one watcher only being required.' So, Dixon sat, and stared, and winked, and drooped, and picked herself up again with a jerk, and finally gave up the battle, and fairly snored. Margaret had taken off her gown and tossed it aside with a sort of impatient disgust, and put on her dressing-gown. She felt as if she never could sleep again; as if her whole senses were acutely vital, and all endued with double keenness, for the purposes of watching. Every sight and sound—nay, even every thought, touched some nerve to the very quick. For more than two hours, she heard her father's restless movements in the next room. He came perpetually to the door of her mother's chamber, pausing there to listen, till she, not hearing his close unseen presence, went and opened it to tell him how all went on, in reply to the questions his baked lips could hardly form. At last he, too, fell asleep, and all the house was still. Margaret sate behind the curtain thinking. Far away in time, far away in space, seemed all the interests of past days. Not more than thirty-six hours ago, she cared for Bessy Higgins and her father, and her heart was wrung for Boucher; now, that was all like a dreaming memory of some former life;—everything that had passed out of doors seemed dissevered from her mother, and therefore unreal. Even Harley Street appeared more distinct; there she remembered, as if it were yesterday, how she had pleased herself with tracing out her mother's features in her Aunt Shaw's face,—and how letters had come, making her dwell on the thoughts of home with all the longing of love. Helstone, itself, was in the dim past. The dull gray days of the preceding winter and spring, so uneventless and monotonous, seemed more associated with what she cared for now above all price. She would fain have caught at the skirts of that departing time, and prayed it to return, and give her back what she had too little valued while it was yet in her possession. What a vain show Life seemed! How unsubstantial, and flickering, and flitting! It was as if from some aerial belfry, high up above the stir and jar of the earth, there was a bell continually tolling, 'All are shadows!—all are passing!—all is past!' And when the morning dawned, cool and gray, like many a happier morning before—when Margaret looked one by one at the sleepers, it seemed as if the terrible night were unreal as a dream; it, too, was a shadow. It, too, was past.

Mrs. Hale herself was not aware when she awoke, how ill she had been the night before. She was rather surprised at Dr. Donaldson's early visit, and perplexed by the anxious faces of husband and child. She consented to remain in bed that day, saying she certainly was tired; but, the next, she insisted on getting up; and Dr. Donaldson gave his consent to her returning into the drawing-room. She was restless and uncomfortable in every position, and before night she became very feverish. Mr. Hale was utterly listless, and incapable of deciding on anything.

'What can we do to spare mamma such another night?' asked Margaret on the third day.

'It is, to a certain degree, the reaction after the powerful opiates I have been obliged to use. It is more painful for you to see than for her to bear, I believe. But, I think, if we could get a water-bed it might be a good thing. Not but what she will be better to-morrow; pretty much like herself as she was before this attack. Still, I should like her to have a water-bed. Mrs. Thornton has one, I know. I'll try and call there this afternoon. Stay,' said he, his eye catching on Margaret's face, blanched with watching in a sick room, 'I'm not sure whether I can go; I've a long round to take. It would do you no harm to have a brisk walk to Marlborough Street, and ask Mrs. Thornton if she can spare it.'

'Certainly,' said Margaret. 'I could go while mamma is asleep this afternoon. I'm sure Mrs. Thornton would lend it to us.'

Dr. Donaldson's experience told them rightly. Mrs. Hale seemed to shake off the consequences of her attack, and looked brighter and better this afternoon than Margaret had ever hoped to see her again. Her daughter left her after dinner, sitting in her easy chair, with her hand lying in her husband's, who looked more worn and suffering than she by far. Still, he could smile now—rather slowly, rather faintly, it is true; but a day or two before, Margaret never thought to see him smile again.

It was about two miles from their house in Crampton Crescent to Marlborough Street. It was too hot to walk very quickly. An August sun beat straight down into the street at three o'clock in the afternoon. Margaret went along, without noticing anything very different from usual in the first mile and a half of her journey; she was absorbed in her own thoughts, and had learnt by this time to thread her way through the irregular stream of human beings that flowed through Milton streets. But, by and by, she was struck with an unusual heaving among the mass of people in the crowded road on which she was entering. They did not appear to be moving on, so much as talking, and listening, and buzzing with excitement, without much stirring from the spot where they might happen to be. Still, as they made way for her, and, wrapt up in the purpose of her errand, and the necessities that suggested it, she was less quick of observation than she might have been, if her mind had been at ease, she had got into Marlborough Street before the full conviction forced itself upon her, that there was a restless, oppressive sense of irritation abroad among the people; a thunderous atmosphere, morally as well as physically, around her. From every narrow lane opening out on Marlborough Street came up a low distant roar, as of myriads of fierce indignant voices. The inhabitants of each poor squalid dwelling were gathered round the doors and windows, if indeed they were not actually standing in the middle of the narrow ways—all with looks intent towards one point. Marlborough Street itself was the focus of all those human eyes, that betrayed intensest interest of various kinds; some fierce with anger, some lowering with relentless threats, some dilated with fear, or imploring entreaty; and, as Margaret reached the small side-entrance by the folding doors, in the great dead wall of Marlborough mill-yard and waited the porter's answer to the bell, she looked round and heard the first long far-off roll of the tempest;—saw the first slow-surging wave of the dark crowd come, with its threatening crest, tumble over, and retreat, at the far end of the street, which a moment ago, seemed so full of repressed noise, but which now was ominously still; all these circumstances forced themselves on Margaret's notice, but did not sink down into her pre-occupied heart. She did not know what they meant—what was their deep significance; while she did know, did feel the keen sharp pressure of the knife that was soon to stab her through and through by leaving her motherless. She was trying to realise that, in order that, when it came, she might be ready to comfort her father.

The porter opened the door cautiously, not nearly wide enough to admit her.

'It's you, is it, ma'am?' said he, drawing a long breath, and widening the entrance, but still not opening it fully. Margaret went in. He hastily bolted it behind her.

'Th' folk are all coming up here I reckon?' asked he.

'I don't know. Something unusual seemed going on; but this street is quite empty, I think.'

She went across the yard and up the steps to the house door. There was no near sound,—no steam-engine at work with beat and pant,—no click of machinery, or mingling and clashing of many sharp voices; but far away, the ominous gathering roar, deep-clamouring.

CHAPTER XXII - A BLOW AND ITS CONSEQUENCES

'But work grew scarce, while bread grew dear,
And wages lessened, too;
For Irish hordes were bidders here,
Our half-paid work to do.'
CORN LAW RHYMES.

Margaret was shown into the drawing-room. It had returned into its normal state of bag and covering. The windows were half open because of the heat, and the Venetian blinds covered the glass,—so that a gray grim light, reflected from the pavement below, threw all the shadows wrong, and combined with the green-tinged upper light to make even Margaret's own face, as she caught it in the mirrors, look ghastly and wan. She sat and waited; no one came. Every now and then, the wind seemed to bear the distant multitudinous sound nearer; and yet there was no wind! It died away into profound stillness between whiles.

Fanny came in at last.

'Mamma will come directly, Miss Hale. She desired me to apologise to you as it is. Perhaps you know my brother has imported hands from Ireland, and it has irritated the Milton people excessively—as if he hadn't a right to get labour where he could; and the stupid wretches here wouldn't work for him; and now they've frightened these poor Irish starvelings so with their threats, that we daren't let them out. You may see them huddled in that top room in the mill,—and they're to sleep there, to keep them safe from those brutes, who will neither work nor let them work. And mamma is seeing about their food, and John is speaking to them, for some of the women are crying to go back. Ah! here's mamma!'

Mrs. Thornton came in with a look of black sternness on her face, which made Margaret feel she had arrived at a bad time to trouble her with her request. However, it was only in compliance with Mrs. Thornton's expressed desire, that she would ask for whatever they might want in the progress of her mother's illness. Mrs. Thornton's brow contracted, and her mouth grew set, while Margaret spoke with gentle modesty of her mother's restlessness, and Dr. Donaldson's wish that she should have the relief of a water-bed. She ceased. Mrs. Thornton did not reply immediately. Then she started up and exclaimed—

'They're at the gates! Call John, Fanny,—call him in from the mill! They're at the gates! They'll batter them in! Call John, I say!'

And simultaneously, the gathering tramp—to which she had been listening, instead of heeding Margaret's words—was heard just right outside the wall, and an increasing din of angry voices raged behind the wooden barrier, which shook as if the unseen maddened crowd made battering-rams of their bodies, and retreated a short space only to come with more united steady impetus against it, till their great beats made the strong gates quiver, like reeds before the wind. The women gathered round the windows, fascinated to look on the scene which terrified them. Mrs. Thornton, the women-servants, Margaret,—all were there. Fanny had returned, screaming up-stairs as if pursued at every step, and had thrown herself in hysterical sobbing on the sofa. Mrs. Thornton watched for her son, who was still in the mill. He came out, looked up at them—the pale cluster of faces—and smiled good courage to them, before he locked the factory-door. Then he called to one of the women to come down and undo his own door, which Fanny had fastened behind her in her mad flight. Mrs. Thornton herself went. And the sound of his well-known and commanding voice, seemed to have been like the taste of blood to the infuriated multitude outside. Hitherto they had been voiceless, wordless, needing all their breath for their hard-labouring efforts to break down the gates. But now, hearing him speak inside, they set up such a fierce unearthly groan, that even Mrs. Thornton was white with fear as she preceded him into the room. He came in a little flushed, but his eyes gleaming, as in answer to the trumpet-call of danger, and with a proud look of defiance on his face, that made him a noble, if not a handsome man. Margaret had always dreaded lest her courage should fail her in any emergency, and she should be proved to be, what she dreaded lest she was—a coward. But now, in this real great time of reasonable fear and nearness of terror, she forgot herself, and felt only an intense sympathy—intense to painfulness—in the interests of the moment.

Mr. Thornton came frankly forwards:

'I'm sorry, Miss Hale, you have visited us at this unfortunate moment, when, I fear, you may be involved in whatever risk we have to bear. Mother! hadn't you better go into the back rooms? I'm not sure whether they may not have made their way from Pinner's Lane into the stable-yard; but if not, you will be safer there than here. Go Jane!' continued he, addressing the upper-servant. And she went, followed by the others.

'I stop here!' said his mother. 'Where you are, there I stay.' And indeed, retreat into the back rooms was of no avail; the crowd had surrounded the outbuildings at the rear, and were sending forth their awful threatening roar behind. The servants retreated into the garrets, with many a cry and shriek. Mr. Thornton smiled scornfully as he heard them. He glanced at Margaret, standing all by herself at the window nearest the factory. Her eyes glittered, her colour was deepened on cheek and lip. As if she felt his look, she turned to him and asked a question that had been for some time in her mind:

'Where are the poor imported work-people? In the factory there?'

'Yes! I left them cowered up in a small room, at the head of a back flight of stairs; bidding them run all risks, and escape down there, if they heard any attack made on the mill-doors. But it is not them—it is me they want.'

'When can the soldiers be here?' asked his mother, in a low but not unsteady voice.

He took out his watch with the same measured composure with which he did everything. He made some little calculation:

'Supposing Williams got straight off when I told him, and hadn't to dodge about amongst them—it must be twenty minutes yet.'

'Twenty minutes!' said his mother, for the first time showing her terror in the tones of her voice.

'Shut down the windows instantly, mother,' exclaimed he: 'the gates won't bear such another shock. Shut down that window, Miss Hale.'

Margaret shut down her window, and then went to assist Mrs. Thornton's trembling fingers.

From some cause or other, there was a pause of several minutes in the unseen street. Mrs. Thornton looked with wild anxiety at her son's countenance, as if to gain the interpretation of the sudden stillness from him. His face was set into rigid lines of contemptuous defiance; neither hope nor fear could be read there.

Fanny raised herself up:

'Are they gone?' asked she, in a whisper.

'Gone!' replied he. 'Listen!'

She did listen; they all could hear the one great straining breath; the creak of wood slowly yielding; the wrench of iron; the mighty fall of the ponderous gates. Fanny stood up tottering—made a step or two towards her mother, and fell forwards into her arms in a fainting fit. Mrs. Thornton lifted her up with a strength that was as much that of the will as of the body, and carried her away.

'Thank God!' said Mr. Thornton, as he watched her out. 'Had you not better go upstairs, Miss Hale?'

Margaret's lips formed a 'No!'—but he could not hear her speak, for the tramp of innumerable steps right under the very wall of the house, and the fierce growl of low deep angry voices that had a ferocious murmur of satisfaction in them, more dreadful than their baffled cries not many minutes before.

'Never mind!' said he, thinking to encourage her. 'I am very sorry you should have been entrapped into all this alarm; but it cannot last long now; a few minutes more, and the soldiers will be here.'

'Oh, God!' cried Margaret, suddenly; 'there is Boucher. I know his face, though he is livid with rage,—he is fighting to get to the front—look! look!'

'Who is Boucher?' asked Mr. Thornton, coolly, and coming close to the window to discover the man in whom Margaret took such an interest. As soon as they saw Mr. Thornton, they set up a yell,—to call it not human is nothing,—it was as the demoniac desire of some terrible wild beast for the food that is withheld from his ravening. Even he drew back for a moment, dismayed at the intensity of hatred he had provoked.

'Let them yell!' said he. 'In five minutes more—. I only hope my poor Irishmen are not terrified out of their wits by such a fiendlike noise. Keep up your courage for five minutes, Miss Hale.'

'Don't be afraid for me,' she said hastily. 'But what in five minutes? Can you do nothing to soothe these poor creatures? It is awful to see them.'

'The soldiers will be here directly, and that will bring them to reason.'

'To reason!' said Margaret, quickly. 'What kind of reason?'

'The only reason that does with men that make themselves into wild beasts. By heaven! they've turned to the mill-door!'

'Mr. Thornton,' said Margaret, shaking all over with her passion, 'go down this instant, if you are not a coward. Go down and face them like a man. Save these poor strangers, whom you have decoyed here. Speak to your workmen as if they were human beings. Speak to them kindly. Don't let the soldiers come in and cut down poor creatures who are driven mad. I see one there who is. If you have any courage or noble quality in you, go out and speak to them, man to man.'

He turned and looked at her while she spoke. A dark cloud came over his face while he listened. He set his teeth as he heard her words.

'I will go. Perhaps I may ask you to accompany me downstairs, and bar the door behind me; my mother and sister will need that protection.'

'Oh! Mr. Thornton! I do not know—I may be wrong—only—'

But he was gone; he was downstairs in the hall; he had unbarred the front door; all she could do, was to follow him quickly, and fasten it behind him, and clamber up the stairs again with a sick heart and a dizzy head. Again she took her place by the farthest window. He was on the steps below; she saw that by the direction of a thousand angry eyes; but she could neither see nor hear anything save the savage satisfaction of the rolling angry murmur. She threw the window wide open. Many in the crowd were mere boys; cruel and thoughtless,—cruel because they were thoughtless; some were men, gaunt as wolves, and mad for prey. She knew how it was; they were like Boucher, with starving children at home—relying on ultimate success in their efforts to get higher wages, and enraged beyond measure at discovering that Irishmen were to be brought in to rob their little ones of bread. Margaret knew it all; she read it in Boucher's face, forlornly desperate and livid with rage. If Mr. Thornton would but say something to them—let them hear his voice only—it seemed as if it would be better than this wild beating and raging against the stony silence that vouchsafed them no word, even of anger or reproach. But perhaps he was speaking now; there was a momentary hush of their noise, inarticulate as that of a troop of animals. She tore her bonnet off; and bent forwards to hear. She could only see; for if Mr. Thornton had indeed made the attempt to speak, the momentary instinct to listen to him was past and gone, and the people were raging worse than ever. He stood with his arms folded; still as a statue; his face pale with repressed excitement. They were trying to intimidate him—to make him flinch; each was urging the other on to some immediate act of personal violence. Margaret felt intuitively, that in an instant all would be uproar; the first touch would cause an explosion, in which, among such hundreds of infuriated men and reckless boys, even Mr. Thornton's life would be unsafe,—that in another instant the stormy passions would have passed their bounds, and swept away all barriers of reason, or apprehension of consequence. Even while she looked, she saw lads in the back-ground stooping to take off their heavy wooden clogs—the readiest missile they could find; she saw it was the spark to the gunpowder, and, with a cry, which no one heard, she rushed out of the room, down stairs,—she had lifted the great iron bar of the door with an imperious force—had thrown the door open wide—and was there, in face of that angry sea of men, her eyes smiting them with flaming arrows of reproach. The clogs were arrested in the hands that held them—the countenances, so fell not a moment before, now looked irresolute, and as if asking what this meant. For she stood between them and their enemy. She could not speak, but held out her arms towards them till she could recover breath.

'Oh, do not use violence! He is one man, and you are many; but her words died away, for there was no tone in her voice; it was but a hoarse whisper. Mr. Thornton stood a little on one side; he had moved away from behind her, as if jealous of anything that should come between him and danger.

'Go!' said she, once more (and now her voice was like a cry). 'The soldiers are sent for—are coming. Go peaceably. Go away. You shall have relief from your complaints, whatever they are.'

'Shall them Irish blackguards be packed back again?' asked one from out the crowd, with fierce threatening in his voice.

'Never, for your bidding!' exclaimed Mr. Thornton. And instantly the storm broke. The hootings rose and filled the air,—but Margaret did not hear them. Her eye was on the group of lads who had armed themselves with their clogs some time before. She saw their gesture—she knew its meaning,—she read their aim. Another moment, and Mr. Thornton might be smitten down,—he whom she had urged and goaded to come to this perilous place. She only thought how she could save him. She threw her arms around him; she made her body into a shield from the fierce people beyond. Still, with his arms folded, he shook her off.

'Go away,' said he, in his deep voice. 'This is no place for you.'

'It is!' said she. 'You did not see what I saw.' If she thought her sex would be a protection,—if, with shrinking eyes she had turned away from the terrible anger of these men, in any hope that ere she looked again they would have paused and reflected, and slunk away, and vanished,—she was wrong. Their reckless passion had carried them too far to stop—at least had carried some of them too far; for it is always the savage lads, with their love of cruel excitement, who head the riot—reckless to what bloodshed it may lead. A clog whizzed through the air. Margaret's fascinated eyes watched its progress; it missed its aim, and she turned sick with affright, but changed not her position, only hid her face on Mr. Thornton s arm. Then she turned and spoke again:'

'For God's sake! do not damage your cause by this violence. You do not know what you are doing.' She strove to make her words distinct.

A sharp pebble flew by her, grazing forehead and cheek, and drawing a blinding sheet of light before her eyes. She lay like one dead on Mr. Thornton's shoulder. Then he unfolded his arms, and held her encircled in one for an instant:

'You do well!' said he. 'You come to oust the innocent stranger. You fall—you hundreds—on one man; and when a woman comes before you, to ask you for your own sakes to be reasonable creatures, your cowardly wrath falls upon her! You do well!' They were silent while he spoke. They were watching, open-eyed and open-mouthed, the thread of dark-red blood which wakened them up from their trance of passion. Those nearest the gate stole out ashamed; there was a movement through all the crowd—a retreating movement. Only one voice cried out:

'Th' stone were meant for thee; but thou wert sheltered behind a woman!'

Mr. Thornton quivered with rage. The blood-flowing had made Margaret conscious—dimly, vaguely conscious. He placed her gently on the door-step, her head leaning against the frame.

'Can you rest there?' he asked. But without waiting for her answer, he went slowly down the steps right into the middle of the crowd. 'Now kill me, if it is your brutal will. There is no woman to shield me here. You may beat me to death—you will never move me from what I have determined upon—not you!' He stood amongst them, with his arms folded, in precisely the same attitude as he had been in on the steps.

But the retrograde movement towards the gate had begun—as unreasoningly, perhaps as blindly, as the simultaneous anger. Or, perhaps, the idea of the approach of the soldiers, and the sight of that pale, upturned face, with closed eyes, still and sad as marble, though the tears welled out of the long entanglement of eyelashes and dropped down; and, heavier, slower plash than even tears, came the drip of blood from her wound. Even the most desperate—Boucher himself—drew back, faltered away, scowled, and finally went off, muttering curses on the master, who stood in his unchanging attitude, looking after their retreat with defiant eyes. The moment that retreat had changed into a flight (as it was sure from its very character to do), he darted up the steps to Margaret. She tried to rise without his help.

'It is nothing,' she said, with a sickly smile. 'The skin is grazed, and I was stunned at the moment. Oh, I am so thankful they are gone!' And she cried without restraint.

He could not sympathise with her. His anger had not abated; it was rather rising the more as his sense of immediate danger was passing away. The distant clank of the soldiers was heard just five minutes too late to make this vanished mob feel the power of authority and order. He hoped they would see the troops, and be quelled by the thought of their narrow escape. While these thoughts crossed his mind, Margaret clung to the doorpost to steady herself: but a film came over her eyes—he was only just in time to catch her. 'Mother—mother!'

cried he; 'Come down—they are gone, and Miss Hale is hurt!' He bore her into the dining-room, and laid her on the sofa there; laid her down softly, and looking on her pure white face, the sense of what she was to him came upon him so keenly that he spoke it out in his pain:

'Oh, my Margaret—my Margaret! no one can tell what you are to me! Dead—cold as you lie there, you are the only woman I ever loved! Oh, Margaret—Margaret!' Inarticulately as he spoke, kneeling by her, and rather moaning than saying the words, he started up, ashamed of himself, as his mother came in. She saw nothing, but her son a little paler, a little sterner than usual.

'Miss Hale is hurt, mother. A stone has grazed her temple. She has lost a good deal of blood, I'm afraid.'

'She looks very seriously hurt,—I could almost fancy her dead,' said Mrs. Thornton, a good deal alarmed.

'It is only a fainting-fit. She has spoken to me since.' But all the blood in his body seemed to rush inwards to his heart as he spoke, and he absolutely trembled.

'Go and call Jane,—she can find me the things I want; and do you go to your Irish people, who are crying and shouting as if they were mad with fright.' He went. He went away as if weights were tied to every limb that bore him from her. He called Jane; he called his sister. She should have all womanly care, all gentle tendance. But every pulse beat in him as he remembered how she had come down and placed herself in foremost danger,—could it be to save him? At the time, he had pushed her aside, and spoken gruffly; he had seen nothing but the unnecessary danger she had placed herself in. He went to his Irish people, with every nerve in his body thrilling at the thought of her, and found it difficult to understand enough of what they were saying to soothe and comfort away their fears. There, they declared, they would not stop; they claimed to be sent back. And so he had to think, and talk, and reason.

Mrs. Thornton bathed Margaret's temples with eau de Cologne. As the spirit touched the wound, which till then neither Mrs. Thornton nor Jane had perceived, Margaret opened her eyes; but it was evident she did not know where she was, nor who they were. The dark circles deepened, the lips quivered and contracted, and she became insensible once more.

'She has had a terrible blow,' said Mrs. Thornton. 'Is there any one who will go for a doctor?'

'Not me, ma'am, if you please,' said Jane, shrinking back. 'Them rabble may be all about; I don't think the cut is so deep, ma'am, as it looks.'

'I will not run the chance. She was hurt in our house. If you are a coward, Jane, I am not. I will go.'

'Pray, ma'am, let me send one of the police. There's ever so many come up, and soldiers too.'

'And yet you're afraid to go! I will not have their time taken up with our errands. They'll have enough to do to catch some of the mob. You will not be afraid to stop in this house,' she asked contemptuously, 'and go on bathing Miss Hale's forehead, shall you? I shall not be ten minutes away.'

'Couldn't Hannah go, ma'am?'

'Why Hannah? Why any but you? No, Jane, if you don't go, I do.'

Mrs. Thornton went first to the room in which she had left Fanny stretched on the bed. She started up as her mother entered.

'Oh, mamma, how you terrified me! I thought you were a man that had got into the house.'

'Nonsense! The men are all gone away. There are soldiers all round the place, seeking for their work now it is too late. Miss Hale is lying on the dining-room sofa badly hurt. I am going for the doctor.'

'Oh! don't, mamma! they'll murder you.' She clung to her mother's gown. Mrs. Thornton wrenched it away with no gentle hand.

'Find me some one else to go but that girl must not bleed to death.'

'Bleed! oh, how horrid! How has she got hurt?'

'I don't know,—I have no time to ask. Go down to her, Fanny, and do try to make yourself of use. Jane is with her; and I trust it looks worse than it is. Jane has refused to leave the house, cowardly woman! And I won't put myself in the way of any more refusals from my servants, so I am going myself.'

'Oh, dear, dear!' said Fanny, crying, and preparing to go down rather than be left alone, with the thought of wounds and bloodshed in the very house.

'Oh, Jane!' said she, creeping into the dining-room, 'what is the matter? How white she looks! How did she get hurt? Did they throw stones into the drawing-room?'

Margaret did indeed look white and wan, although her senses were beginning to return to her. But the sickly daze of the swoon made her still miserably faint. She was conscious of movement around her, and of refreshment from the eau de Cologne, and a craving for the bathing to go on without intermission; but when they stopped to talk, she could no more have opened her eyes, or spoken to ask for more bathing, than the people who lie in death-like trance can move, or utter sound, to arrest the awful preparations for their burial, while they are yet fully aware, not merely of the actions of those around them, but of the idea that is the motive for such actions.

Jane paused in her bathing, to reply to Miss Thornton's question.

'She'd have been safe enough, miss, if she'd stayed in the drawing-room, or come up to us; we were in the front garret, and could see it all, out of harm's way.'

'Where was she, then?' said Fanny, drawing nearer by slow degrees, as she became accustomed to the sight of Margaret's pale face.

'Just before the front door—with master!' said Jane, significantly.

'With John! with my brother! How did she get there?'

'Nay, miss, that's not for me to say,' answered Jane, with a slight toss of her head. 'Sarah did'——

'Sarah what?' said Fanny, with impatient curiosity.

Jane resumed her bathing, as if what Sarah did or said was not exactly the thing she liked to repeat.

'Sarah what?' asked Fanny, sharply. 'Don't speak in these half sentences, or I can't understand you.'

'Well, miss, since you will have it—Sarah, you see, was in the best place for seeing, being at the right-hand window; and she says, and said at the very time too, that she saw Miss Hale with her arms about master's neck, hugging him before all the people.'

'I don't believe it,' said Fanny. 'I know she cares for my brother; any one can see that; and I dare say, she'd give her eyes if he'd marry her,—which he never will, I can tell her. But I don't believe she'd be so bold and forward as to put her arms round his neck.'

'Poor young lady! she's paid for it dearly if she did. It's my belief, that the blow has given her such an ascendency of blood to the head as she'll never get the better from. She looks like a corpse now.'

'Oh, I wish mamma would come!' said Fanny, wringing her hands. 'I never was in the room with a dead person before.'

'Stay, miss! She's not dead: her eye-lids are quivering, and here's wet tears a-coming down her cheeks. Speak to her, Miss Fanny!'

'Are you better now?' asked Fanny, in a quavering voice.

No answer; no sign of recognition; but a faint pink colour returned to her lips, although the rest of her face was ashen pale.

Mrs. Thornton came hurriedly in, with the nearest surgeon she could find. 'How is she? Are you better, my dear?' as Margaret opened her filmy eyes, and gazed dreamily at her. 'Here is Mr. Lowe come to see you.'

Mrs. Thornton spoke loudly and distinctly, as to a deaf person. Margaret tried to rise, and drew her ruffled, luxuriant hair instinctly over the cut. 'I am better now,' said she, in a very low, faint voice. I was a little sick.' She let him take her hand and feel her pulse. The bright colour came for a moment into her face, when he asked to examine the wound in her forehead; and she glanced up at Jane, as if shrinking from her inspection more than from the doctor's.

'It is not much, I think. I am better now. I must go home.'

'Not until I have applied some strips of plaster; and you have rested a little.'

She sat down hastily, without another word, and allowed it to be bound up.

'Now, if you please,' said she, 'I must go. Mamma will not see it, I think. It is under the hair, is it not?'

'Quite; no one could tell.'

'But you must not go,' said Mrs. Thornton, impatiently. 'You are not fit to go.

'I must,' said Margaret, decidedly. 'Think of mamma. If they should hear—— Besides, I must go,' said she, vehemently. 'I cannot stay here. May I ask for a cab?'

'You are quite flushed and feverish,' observed Mr. Lowe.

'It is only with being here, when I do so want to go. The air—getting away, would do me more good than anything,' pleaded she.

'I really believe it is as she says,' Mr. Lowe replied. 'If her mother is so ill as you told me on the way here, it may be very serious if she hears of this riot, and does not see her daughter back at the time she expects. The injury is not deep. I will fetch a cab, if your servants are still afraid to go out.'

'Oh, thank you!' said Margaret. 'It will do me more good than anything. It is the air of this room that makes me feel so miserable.'

She leant back on the sofa, and closed her eyes. Fanny beckoned her mother out of the room, and told her something that made her equally anxious with Margaret for the departure of the latter. Not that she fully believed Fanny's statement; but she credited enough to make her manner to Margaret appear very much constrained, at wishing her good-bye.

Mr. Lowe returned in the cab.

'If you will allow me, I will see you home, Miss Hale. The streets are not very quiet yet.'

Margaret's thoughts were quite alive enough to the present to make her desirous of getting rid of both Mr. Lowe and the cab before she reached Crampton Crescent, for fear of alarming her father and mother. Beyond that one aim she would not look. That ugly dream of insolent words spoken about herself, could never be forgotten—but could be put aside till she was stronger—for, oh! she was very weak; and her mind sought for some present fact to steady itself upon, and keep it from utterly losing consciousness in another hideous, sickly swoon.

CHAPTER XXIII - MISTAKES

'Which when his mother saw, she in her mind
Was troubled sore, ne wist well what to ween.'
SPENSER.

Margaret had not been gone five minutes when Mr. Thornton came in, his face all a-glow.

'I could not come sooner: the superintendent would—— Where is she?' He looked round the dining-room, and then almost fiercely at his mother, who was quietly re-arranging the disturbed furniture, and did not instantly reply. 'Where is Miss Hale?' asked he again.

'Gone home,' said she, rather shortly.

'Gone home!'

'Yes. She was a great deal better. Indeed, I don't believe it was so very much of a hurt; only some people faint at the least thing.'

'I am sorry she is gone home,' said he, walking uneasily about. 'She could not have been fit for it.'

'She said she was; and Mr. Lowe said she was. I went for him myself.'

'Thank you, mother.' He stopped, and partly held out his hand to give her a grateful shake. But she did not notice the movement.

'What have you done with your Irish people?'

'Sent to the Dragon for a good meal for them, poor wretches. And then, luckily, I caught Father Grady, and I've asked him in to speak to them, and dissuade them from going off in a body. How did Miss Hale go home? I'm sure she could not walk.'

'She had a cab. Everything was done properly, even to the paying. Let us talk of something else. She has caused disturbance enough.'

'I don't know where I should have been but for her.'

'Are you become so helpless as to have to be defended by a girl?' asked Mrs. Thornton, scornfully.

He reddened. 'Not many girls would have taken the blows on herself which were meant for me;—meant with right down good-will, too.'

'A girl in love will do a good deal,' replied Mrs. Thornton, shortly.

'Mother!' He made a step forwards; stood still; heaved with passion.

She was a little startled at the evident force he used to keep himself calm. She was not sure of the nature of the emotions she had provoked. It was only their violence that was clear. Was it anger? His eyes glowed, his figure was dilated, his breath came thick and fast. It was a mixture of joy, of anger, of pride, of glad surprise, of panting doubt; but she could not read it. Still it made her uneasy,—as the presence of all strong feeling, of which the cause is not fully understood or sympathised in, always has this effect. She went to the side-board, opened a drawer, and took out a duster, which she kept there for any occasional purpose. She had seen a drop of eau de Cologne on the polished arm of the sofa, and instinctively sought to wipe it off. But she kept her back turned to her son much longer than was necessary; and when she spoke, her voice seemed unusual and constrained.

'You have taken some steps about the rioters, I suppose? You don't apprehend any more violence, do you? Where were the police? Never at hand when they're wanted!'

'On the contrary, I saw three or four of them, when the gates gave way, struggling and beating about in fine fashion; and more came running up just when the yard was clearing. I might have given some of the fellows in charge then, if I had had my wits about me. But there will be no difficulty, plenty of people can identify them.'

'But won't they come back to-night?'

'I'm going to see about a sufficient guard for the premises. I have appointed to meet Captain Hanbury in half an hour at the station.'

'You must have some tea first.'

'Tea! Yes, I suppose I must. It's half-past six, and I may be out for some time. Don't sit up for me, mother.'

'You expect me to go to bed before I have seen you safe, do you?'

'Well, perhaps not.' He hesitated for a moment. 'But if I've time, I shall go round by Crampton, after I've arranged with the police and seen Hamper and Clarkson.' Their eyes met; they looked at each other intently for a minute. Then she asked:

'Why are you going round by Crampton?'

'To ask after Miss Hale.'

'I will send. Williams must take the water-bed she came to ask for. He shall inquire how she is.'

'I must go myself.'

'Not merely to ask how Miss Hale is?'

'No, not merely for that. I want to thank her for the way in which she stood between me and the mob.'

'What made you go down at all? It was putting your head into the lion's mouth!' He glanced sharply at her; saw that she did not know what had passed between him and Margaret in the drawing-room; and replied by another question:

'Shall you be afraid to be left without me, until I can get some of the police; or had we better send Williams for them now, and they could be here by the time we have done tea? There's no time to be lost. I must be off in a quarter of an hour.'

Mrs. Thornton left the room. Her servants wondered at her directions, usually so sharply-cut and decided, now confused and uncertain. Mr. Thornton remained in the dining-room, trying to think of the business he had to do at the police-office, and in reality thinking of Margaret. Everything seemed dim and vague beyond—behind—besides the touch of her arms round his neck—the soft clinging which made the dark colour come and go in his cheek as he thought of it.

The tea would have been very silent, but for Fanny's perpetual description of her own feelings; how she had been alarmed—and then thought they were gone—and then felt sick and faint and trembling in every limb.

'There, that's enough,' said her brother, rising from the table. 'The reality was enough for me.' He was going to leave the room, when his mother stopped him with her hand upon his arm.

'You will come back here before you go to the Hales', said she, in a low, anxious voice.

'I know what I know,' said Fanny to herself.

'Why? Will it be too late to disturb them?'

'John, come back to me for this one evening. It will be late for Mrs. Hale. But that is not it. To-morrow, you will—— Come back to-night, John!' She had seldom pleaded with her son at all—she was too proud for that: but she had never pleaded in vain.

'I will return straight here after I have done my business. You will be sure to inquire after them?—after her?'

Mrs. Thornton was by no means a talkative companion to Fanny, nor yet a good listener while her son was absent. But on his return, her eyes and ears were keen to see and to listen to all the details which he could give, as to the steps he had taken to secure himself, and those whom he chose to employ, from any repetition of the day's outrages. He clearly saw his object. Punishment and suffering, were the natural consequences to those who had taken part in the riot. All that was necessary, in order that property should be protected, and that the will of the proprietor might cut to his end, clean and sharp as a sword.

'Mother! You know what I have got to say to Miss Hale, to-morrow?' The question came upon her suddenly, during a pause in which she, at least, had forgotten Margaret.

She looked up at him.

'Yes! I do. You can hardly do otherwise.'

'Do otherwise! I don't understand you.'

'I mean that, after allowing her feelings so to overcome her, I consider you bound in honour—'

'Bound in honour,' said he, scornfully. 'I'm afraid honour has nothing to do with it. "Her feelings overcome her!" What feelings do you mean?'

'Nay, John, there is no need to be angry. Did she not rush down, and cling to you to save you from danger?'

'She did!' said he. 'But, mother,' continued he, stopping short in his walk right in front of her, 'I dare not hope. I never was fainthearted before; but I cannot believe such a creature cares for me.'

'Don't be foolish, John. Such a creature! Why, she might be a duke's daughter, to hear you speak. And what proof more would you have, I wonder, of her caring for you? I can believe she has had a struggle with her aristocratic way of viewing things; but I like her the better for seeing clearly at last. It is a good deal for me to say,' said Mrs. Thornton, smiling slowly, while the tears stood in her eyes; 'for after to-night, I stand second. It was to have you to myself, all to myself, a few hours longer, that I begged you not to go till to-morrow!'

'Dearest mother!' (Still love is selfish, and in an instant he reverted to his own hopes and fears in a way that drew the cold creeping shadow over Mrs. Thornton's heart.) 'But I know she does not care for me. I shall put myself at her feet—I must. If it were but one chance in a thousand—or a million—I should do it.'

'Don't fear!' said his mother, crushing down her own personal mortification at the little notice he had taken of the rare ebullition of her maternal feelings—of the pang of jealousy that betrayed the intensity of her disregarded love. 'Don't be afraid,' she said, coldly. 'As far as love may go she may be worthy of you. It must have taken a good deal to overcome her pride. Don't be afraid, John,' said she, kissing him, as she wished him good-night. And she went slowly and majestically out of the room. But when she got into her own, she locked the door, and sate down to cry unwonted tears.

Margaret entered the room (where her father and mother still sat, holding low conversation together), looking very pale and white. She came close up to them before she could trust herself to speak.

'Mrs. Thornton will send the water-bed, mamma.'

'Dear, how tired you look! Is it very hot, Margaret?'

'Very hot, and the streets are rather rough with the strike.'

Margaret's colour came back vivid and bright as ever; but it faded away instantly.

'Here has been a message from Bessy Higgins, asking you to go to her,' said Mrs. Hale. 'But I'm sure you look too tired.'

'Yes!' said Margaret. 'I am tired, I cannot go.'

She was very silent and trembling while she made tea. She was thankful to see her father so much occupied with her mother as not to notice her looks. Even after her mother went to bed, he was not content to be absent from her, but undertook to read her to sleep. Margaret was alone.

'Now I will think of it—now I will remember it all. I could not before—I dared not.' She sat still in her chair, her hands clasped on her knees, her lips compressed, her eyes fixed as one who sees a vision. She drew a deep breath.

'I, who hate scenes—I, who have despised people for showing emotion—who have thought them wanting in self-control—I went down and must needs throw myself into the melee, like a romantic fool! Did I do any good? They would have gone away without me I dare say.' But this was over-leaping the rational conclusion,—as in an instant her well-poised judgment felt. 'No, perhaps they would not. I did some good. But what possessed me to defend that man as if he were a helpless child! Ah!' said she, clenching her hands together, 'it is no wonder those people thought I was in love with him, after disgracing myself in that way. I in love—and with him too!' Her pale cheeks suddenly became one flame of fire; and she covered her face with her hands. When she took them away, her palms were wet with scalding tears.

'Oh how low I am fallen that they should say that of me! I could not have been so brave for any one else, just because he was so utterly indifferent to me—if, indeed, I do not positively dislike him. It made me the more anxious that there should be fair play on each side; and I could see what fair play was. It was not fair, said she, vehemently, 'that he should stand there—sheltered, awaiting the soldiers, who might catch those poor maddened creatures as in a trap—without an effort on his part, to bring them to reason. And it was worse than unfair for them to set on him as they threatened. I would do it again, let who will say what they like of me. If I saved one blow, one cruel, angry action that might otherwise have been committed, I did a woman's work. Let them insult my maiden pride as they will—I walk pure before God!'

She looked up, and a noble peace seemed to descend and calm her face, till it was 'stiller than chiselled marble.'

Dixon came in:

'If you please, Miss Margaret, here's the water-bed from Mrs. Thornton's. It's too late for to-night, I'm afraid, for missus is nearly asleep: but it will do nicely for to-morrow.'

'Very,' said Margaret. 'You must send our best thanks.'

Dixon left the room for a moment.

'If you please, Miss Margaret, he says he's to ask particular how you are. I think he must mean missus; but he says his last words were, to ask how Miss Hale was.'

'Me!' said Margaret, drawing herself up. 'I am quite well. Tell him I am perfectly well.' But her complexion was as deadly white as her handkerchief; and her head ached intensely.

Mr. Hale now came in. He had left his sleeping wife; and wanted, as Margaret saw, to be amused and interested by something that she was to tell him. With sweet patience did she bear her pain, without a word of complaint; and rummaged up numberless small subjects for conversation—all except the riot, and that she never named once. It turned her sick to think of it.

'Good-night, Margaret. I have every chance of a good night myself, and you are looking very pale with your watching. I shall call Dixon if your mother needs anything. Do you go to bed and sleep like a top; for I'm sure you need it, poor child!'

'Good-night, papa.'

She let her colour go—the forced smile fade away—the eyes grow dull with heavy pain. She released her strong will from its laborious task. Till morning she might feel ill and weary.

She lay down and never stirred. To move hand or foot, or even so much as one finger, would have been an exertion beyond the powers of either volition or motion. She was so tired, so stunned, that she thought she never slept at all; her feverish thoughts passed and repassed the boundary between sleeping and waking, and kept their own miserable identity. She could not be alone, prostrate, powerless as she was,—a cloud of faces looked up at her, giving her no idea of fierce vivid anger, or of personal danger, but a deep sense of shame that she should thus be the object of universal regard—a sense of shame so acute that it seemed as if she would fain have burrowed into the earth to hide herself, and yet she could not escape out of that unwinking glare of many eyes.

CHAPTER XXIV - MISTAKES CLEARED UP

'Your beauty was the first that won the place,
And scal'd the walls of my undaunted heart,
Which, captive now, pines in a caitive case,
Unkindly met with rigour for desert;—
Yet not the less your servant shall abide,
In spite of rude repulse or silent pride.'
WILLIAM FOWLER.

The next morning, Margaret dragged herself up, thankful that the night was over,—unrefreshed, yet rested. All had gone well through the house; her mother had only wakened once. A little breeze was stirring in the hot air, and though there were no trees to show the playful tossing movement caused by the wind among the leaves, Margaret knew how, somewhere or another, by way-side, in copses, or in thick green woods, there was a pleasant, murmuring, dancing sound,—a rushing and falling noise, the very thought of which was an echo of distant gladness in her heart.

She sat at her work in Mrs. Hale's room. As soon as that forenoon slumber was over, she would help her mother to dress after dinner, she would go and see Bessy Higgins. She would banish all recollection of the Thornton family,—no need to think of them till they absolutely stood before her in flesh and blood. But, of course, the effort not to think of them brought them only the more strongly before her; and from time to time, the hot flush came over her pale face sweeping it into colour, as a sunbeam from between watery clouds comes swiftly moving over the sea.

Dixon opened the door very softly, and stole on tiptoe up to Margaret, sitting by the shaded window.

'Mr. Thornton, Miss Margaret. He is in the drawing-room.'

Margaret dropped her sewing.

'Did he ask for me? Isn't papa come in?'

'He asked for you, miss; and master is out.'

'Very well, I will come,' said Margaret, quietly. But she lingered strangely. Mr. Thornton stood by one of the windows, with his back to the door, apparently absorbed in watching something in the street. But, in truth, he was afraid of himself. His heart beat thick at the thought of her coming. He could not forget the touch of her arms around his neck, impatiently felt as it had been at the time; but now the recollection of her clinging defence of him, seemed to thrill him through and through,—to melt away every resolution, all power of self-control, as if it were wax before a fire. He dreaded lest he should go forwards to meet her, with his arms held out in mute entreaty that she would come and nestle there, as she had done, all unheeded, the day before, but never unheeded again. His heart throbbed loud and quick. Strong man as he was, he trembled at the anticipation of what he had to say, and how it might be received. She might droop, and flush, and flutter to his arms, as to her natural home and resting-place. One moment, he glowed with impatience at the thought that she might do this, the next, he feared a passionate rejection, the very idea of which withered up his future with so deadly a blight that he refused to think of it. He was startled by the sense of the presence of some one else in the room. He turned round. She had come in so gently, that he had never heard her; the street noises had been more distinct to his inattentive ear than her slow movements, in her soft muslin gown.

She stood by the table, not offering to sit down. Her eyelids were dropped half over her eyes; her teeth were shut, not compressed; her lips were just parted over them, allowing the white line to be seen between their curve. Her slow deep breathings dilated her thin and beautiful nostrils; it was the only motion visible on her countenance. The fine-grained skin, the oval cheek, the rich outline of her mouth, its corners deep set in dimples,—were all wan and pale to-day; the loss of their usual natural healthy colour being made more evident by the heavy shadow of the dark hair, brought down upon the temples, to hide all sign of the blow she had received. Her head, for all its drooping eyes, was thrown a little back, in the old proud attitude. Her long arms hung motion-less by her sides. Altogether she looked like some prisoner, falsely accused of a crime that she loathed and despised, and from which she was too indignant to justify herself.

Mr. Thornton made a hasty step or two forwards; recovered himself, and went with quiet firmness to the door (which she had left open), and shut it. Then he came back, and stood opposite to her for a moment, receiving the general impression of her beautiful presence, before he dared to disturb it, perhaps to repel it, by what he had to say.

'Miss Hale, I was very ungrateful yesterday—'

'You had nothing to be grateful for,' said she, raising her eyes, and looking full and straight at him. 'You mean, I suppose, that you believe you ought to thank me for what I did.' In spite of herself—in defiance of her anger—the thick blushes came all over her face, and burnt into her very eyes; which fell not nevertheless from their grave and steady look. 'It was only a natural instinct; any woman would have done just the same. We all feel the sanctity of our sex as a high privilege when we see danger. I ought rather,' said she, hastily, 'to apologise to you, for having said thoughtless words which sent you down into the danger.'

'It was not your words; it was the truth they conveyed, pungently as it was expressed. But you shall not drive me off upon that, and so escape the expression of my deep gratitude, my—' he was on the verge now; he would not speak in the haste of his hot passion; he would weigh each word. He would; and his will was triumphant. He stopped in mid career.

'I do not try to escape from anything,' said she. 'I simply say, that you owe me no gratitude; and I may add, that any expression of it will be painful to me, because I do not feel that I deserve it. Still, if it will relieve you from even a fancied obligation, speak on.'

'I do not want to be relieved from any obligation,' said he, goaded by her calm manner. 'Fancied, or not fancied—I question not myself to know which—I choose to believe that I owe my very life to you—ay—smile, and think it an exaggeration if you will. I believe it, because it adds a value to that life to think—oh, Miss Hale!' continued he, lowering his voice to such a tender intensity of passion that she shivered and trembled before him, 'to think circumstance so wrought, that whenever I exult in existence henceforward, I may say to myself, "All this gladness in life, all honest pride in doing my work in the world, all this keen sense of being, I owe to her!" And it doubles the gladness, it makes the pride glow, it sharpens the sense of existence till I hardly know if it is pain or pleasure, to think that I owe it to one—nay, you must, you shall hear'—said he, stepping forwards with stern determination—'to one whom I love, as I do not believe man ever loved woman before.' He held her hand tight in his. He panted as he listened for what should come. He threw the hand away with indignation, as he heard her icy tone; for icy it was, though the words came faltering out, as if she knew not where to find them.

'Your way of speaking shocks me. It is blasphemous. I cannot help it, if that is my first feeling. It might not be so, I dare say, if I understood the kind of feeling you describe. I do not want to vex you; and besides, we must speak gently, for mamma is asleep; but your whole manner offends me—'

'How!' exclaimed he. 'Offends you! I am indeed most unfortunate.'

'Yes!' said she, with recovered dignity. 'I do feel offended; and, I think, justly. You seem to fancy that my conduct of yesterday'—again the deep carnation blush, but this time with eyes kindling with indignation rather than shame—'was a personal act between you and me; and that you may come and thank me for it, instead of perceiving, as a gentleman would—yes! a gentleman,' she repeated, in allusion to their former conversation about that word, 'that any woman, worthy of the name of woman, would come forward to shield, with her reverenced helplessness, a man in danger from the violence of numbers.'

'And the gentleman thus rescued is forbidden the relief of thanks!' he broke in contemptuously. 'I am a man. I claim the right of expressing my feelings.'

'And I yielded to the right; simply saying that you gave me pain by insisting upon it,' she replied, proudly. 'But you seem to have imagined, that I was not merely guided by womanly instinct, but'—and here the passionate tears (kept down for long—struggled with vehemently) came up into her eyes, and choked her voice—'but that I was prompted by some particular feeling for you—you! Why, there was not a man—not a poor desperate man in all that crowd—for whom I had not more sympathy—for whom I should not have done what little I could more heartily.'

'You may speak on, Miss Hale. I am aware of all these misplaced sympathies of yours. I now believe that it was only your innate sense of oppression—(yes; I, though a master, may be oppressed)—that made you act so nobly as you did. I know you despise me; allow me to say, it is because you do not understand me.'

'I do not care to understand,' she replied, taking hold of the table to steady herself; for she thought him cruel—as, indeed, he was—and she was weak with her indignation.

'No, I see you do not. You are unfair and unjust.'

Margaret compressed her lips. She would not speak in answer to such accusations. But, for all that—for all his savage words, he could have thrown himself at her feet, and kissed the hem of her garment. She did not speak; she did not move. The tears of wounded pride fell hot and fast. He waited awhile, longing for her to say something, even a taunt, to which he might reply. But she was silent. He took up his hat.

'One word more. You look as if you thought it tainted you to be loved by me. You cannot avoid it. Nay, I, if I would, cannot cleanse you from it. But I would not, if I could. I have never loved any woman before: my life has been too busy, my thoughts too much absorbed with other things. Now I love, and will love. But do not be afraid of too much expression on my part.'

'I am not afraid,' she replied, lifting herself straight up. 'No one yet has ever dared to be impertinent to me, and no one ever shall. But, Mr. Thornton, you have been very kind to my father,' said she, changing her whole tone and bearing to a most womanly softness. 'Don't let us go on making each other angry. Pray don't!' He took no notice of her words: he occupied himself in smoothing the nap of his hat with his coat-sleeve, for half a minute or so; and then, rejecting her offered hand, and making as if he did not see her grave look of regret, he turned abruptly away, and left the room. Margaret caught one glance at his face before he went.

When he was gone, she thought she had seen the gleam of unshed tears in his eyes; and that turned her proud dislike into something different and kinder, if nearly as painful—self-reproach for having caused such mortification to any one.

'But how could I help it?' asked she of herself. 'I never liked him. I was civil; but I took no trouble to conceal my indifference. Indeed, I never thought about myself or him, so my manners must have shown the truth. All that yesterday, he might mistake. But that is his fault, not mine. I would do it again, if need were, though it does lead me into all this shame and trouble.'

CHAPTER XXV - FREDERICK

'Revenge may have her own;
Roused discipline aloud proclaims their cause,
And injured navies urge their broken laws.'
BYRON.

Margaret began to wonder whether all offers were as unexpected beforehand,—as distressing at the time of their occurrence, as the two she had had. An involuntary comparison between Mr. Lennox and Mr. Thornton arose in her mind. She had been sorry that an expression of any other feeling than friendship had been lured out by circumstances from Henry Lennox. That regret was the predominant feeling, on the first occasion of her receiving a proposal. She had not felt so stunned—so impressed as she did now, when echoes of Mr. Thornton's voice yet lingered about the room. In Lennox's case, he seemed for a moment to have slid over the boundary between friendship and love; and the instant afterwards, to regret it nearly as much as she did, although for different reasons. In Mr. Thornton's case, as far as Margaret knew, there was no intervening stage of friendship. Their intercourse had been one continued series of opposition. Their opinions clashed; and indeed, she had never perceived that he had cared for her opinions, as belonging to her, the individual. As far as they defied his rock-like power of character, his passion-strength, he seemed to throw them off from him with contempt, until she felt the weariness of the exertion of making useless protests; and now, he had come, in this strange wild passionate way, to make known his love. For, although at first it had struck her, that his offer was forced and goaded out of him by sharp compassion for the exposure she had made of herself,—which he, like others, might misunderstand—yet, even before he left the room,—and certainly, not five minutes after, the clear conviction dawned upon her, shined bright upon her, that he did love her; that he had loved her; that he would love her. And she shrank and shuddered as under the fascination of some great power, repugnant to her whole previous life. She crept away, and hid from his idea. But it was of no use. To parody a line out of Fairfax's Tasso—

'His strong idea wandered through her thought.'

She disliked him the more for having mastered her inner will. How dared he say that he would love her still, even though she shook him off with contempt? She wished she had spoken more—stronger. Sharp, decisive speeches came thronging into her mind, now that it was too late to utter them. The deep impression made by the interview, was like that of a horror in a dream; that will not leave the room although we waken up, and rub our eyes, and force a stiff rigid smile upon our lips. It is there—there, cowering and gibbering, with fixed ghastly eyes, in some corner of the chamber, listening to hear whether we dare to breathe of its presence to any one. And we dare not; poor cowards that we are!

And so she shuddered away from the threat of his enduring love. What did he mean? Had she not the power to daunt him? She would see. It was more daring than became a man to threaten her so. Did he ground it upon the miserable yesterday? If need were, she would do the same to-morrow,—by a crippled beggar, willingly and gladly,—but by him, she would do it, just as bravely, in spite of his deductions, and the cold slime of women's impertinence. She did it because it was right, and simple, and true to save where she could save; even to try to save. *'Fais ce que dois, advienne que pourra.'*

Hitherto she had not stirred from where he had left her; no outward circumstances had roused her out of the trance of thought in which she had been plunged by his last words, and by the look of his deep intent passionate eyes, as their flames had made her own fall before them. She went to the window, and threw it open, to dispel the oppression which hung around her. Then she went and opened the door, with a sort of impetuous wish to shake off the recollection of the past hour in the company of others, or in active exertion. But all was profoundly hushed in the noonday stillness of a house, where an invalid catches the unrefreshing sleep that is denied to the night-hours. Margaret would not be alone. What should she do? 'Go and see Bessy Higgins, of course,' thought she, as the recollection of the message sent the night before flashed into her mind.

And away she went.

When she got there, she found Bessy lying on the settle, moved close to the fire, though the day was sultry and oppressive. She was laid down quite flat, as if resting languidly after some paroxysm of pain. Margaret felt sure she ought to have the greater freedom of breathing which a more sitting posture would procure; and, without a word, she raised her up, and so arranged the pillows, that Bessy was more at ease, though very languid.

'I thought I should na' ha' seen yo' again,' said she, at last, looking wistfully in Margaret's face.

'I'm afraid you're much worse. But I could not have come yesterday, my mother was so ill—for many reasons,' said Margaret, colouring.

'Yo'd m'appen think I went beyond my place in sending Mary for yo'. But the wranglin' and the loud voices had just torn me to pieces, and I thought when father left, oh! if I could just hear her voice, reading me some words o' peace and promise, I could die away into the silence and rest o' God, just as a babby is hushed up to sleep by its mother's lullaby.'

'Shall I read you a chapter, now?'

'Ay, do! M'appen I shan't listen to th' sense, at first; it will seem far away—but when yo' come to words I like—to th' comforting texts—it'll seem close in my ear, and going through me as it were.'

Margaret began. Bessy tossed to and fro. If, by an effort, she attended for one moment, it seemed as though she were convulsed into double restlessness the next. At last, she burst out 'Don't go on reading. It's no use. I'm blaspheming all the time in my mind, wi' thinking angrily on what canna be helped.—Yo'd hear of th' riot, m'appen, yesterday at Marlborough Mills? Thornton's factory, yo' know.'

'Your father was not there, was he?' said Margaret, colouring deep.

'Not he. He'd ha' given his right hand if it had never come to pass. It's that that's fretting me. He's fairly knocked down in his mind by it. It's no use telling him, fools will always break out o' bounds. Yo' never saw a man so down-hearted as he is.'

'But why?' asked Margaret. 'I don't understand.'

'Why yo' see, he's a committee-man on this special strike'. Th' Union appointed him because, though I say it as shouldn't say it, he's reckoned a deep chap, and true to th' back-bone. And he and t' other committee-men laid their plans. They were to hou'd together through thick and thin; what the major part thought, t'oth-ers were to think, whether they would or no. And above all there was to be no going again the law of the land. Folk would go with them if they saw them striv-ing and starving wi' dumb patience; but if there was once any noise o' fighting and struggling—even wi' knobsticks—all was up, as they knew by th' experience of many, and many a time before. They would try and get speech o' th' knobsticks, and coax 'em, and reason wi' 'em, and m'appen warn 'em off; but whatever came, the Committee charged all members o' th' Union to lie down and die, if need were, without striking a blow; and then they reckoned they were sure o' carrying th' public with them. And beside all that, Committee knew they were right in their demand, and they didn't want to have right all mixed up wi' wrong, till folk can't separate it, no more nor I can th' physic-powder from th' jelly yo' gave me to mix it in; jelly is much the biggest, but powder tastes it all through. Well, I've told yo' at length about this'n, but I'm tired out. Yo' just think for yo'rsel, what it mun be for father to have a' his work undone, and by such a fool as Boucher, who must needs go right again the orders of Committee, and ruin th' strike, just as bad as if he meant to be a Judas. Eh! but father giv'd it him last night! He went so far as to say, he'd go and tell police where they might find th' ringleader o' th' riot; he'd give him up to th' mill-owners to do what they would wi' him. He'd show the world that th' real leaders o' the strike were not such as Boucher, but steady thoughtful men; good hands, and good citizens, who were friendly to law and judgment, and would uphold order; who only wanted their right wage, and wouldn't work, even though they starved, till they got 'em; but who would ne'er injure property or life: For,' dropping her voice, 'they do say, that Boucher threw a stone at Thornton's sister, that welly killed her.'

'That's not true,' said Margaret. 'It was not Boucher that threw the stone'—she went first red, then white.

'Yo'd be there then, were yo'?' asked Bessy languidly for indeed, she had spoken with many pauses, as if speech was unusually difficult to her.

'Yes. Never mind. Go on. Only it was not Boucher that threw the stone. But what did he answer to your father?'

'He did na' speak words. He were all in such a tremble wi' spent passion, I could na' bear to look at him. I heard his breath coming quick, and at one time I thought he were sobbing. But when father said he'd give him up to police, he gave a great cry, and struck father on th' face wi' his closed fist, and be off like lightning. Father were stunned wi' the blow at first, for all Boucher were weak wi' passion and wi' clemming. He sat down a bit, and put his hand afore his eyes; and then made for th' door. I dunno' where I got strength, but I threw mysel' off th' settle and clung to him. "Father, father!" said I. "Thou'll never go peach on that poor clemmed man. I'll never leave go on thee, till thou sayst thou wunnot." "Dunnot be a fool," says he, "words come readier than deeds to most men. I never thought o' telling th' police on him; though by G—, he deserves it, and I should na' ha' minded if some one else had done the dirty work, and got him clapped up. But now he has strucken me, I could do it less nor ever, for it would be getting other men to take up my quarrel. But if ever he gets well o'er this clemming, and is in good condition, he and I'll have an up and down fight, purring an' a', and I'll see what I can do for him." And so father shook me off,—for indeed, I was low and faint enough, and his face was all clay white, where it weren't bloody, and turned me sick to look at. And I know not if I slept or waked, or were in a dead swoon, till Mary come in; and I telled her to fetch yo' to me. And now dunnot talk to me, but just read out th' chapter. I'm easier in my mind for having spit it out; but I want some thoughts of the world that's far away to take the weary taste of it out o' my mouth. Read me not a sermon chapter, but a story chapter; they've pictures in them, which I see when my eyes are shut. Read about the New Heavens, and the New Earth; and m'appen I'll forget this.'

Margaret read in her soft low voice. Though Bessy's eyes were shut, she was listening for some time, for the moisture of tears gathered heavy on her eyelashes. At last she slept; with many starts, and muttered pleadings. Margaret covered her up, and left her, for she had an uneasy consciousness that she might be wanted at home, and yet, until now, it seemed cruel to leave the dying girl. Mrs. Hale was in the drawing-room on her daughter's return. It was one of her better days, and she was full of praises of the water-bed. It had been more like the beds at Sir John Beresford's than anything she had slept on since. She did not know how it was, but people seemed to have lost the art of making the same kind of beds as they used to do in her youth. One would think it was easy enough; there was the same kind of feathers to be had, and yet somehow, till this last night she did not know when she had had a good sound resting sleep. Mr. Hale suggested, that something of the merits of the featherbeds of former days might be attributed to the activity of youth, which gave a relish to rest; but this idea was not kindly received by his wife.

'No, indeed, Mr. Hale, it was those beds at Sir John's. Now, Margaret, you're young enough, and go about in the day; are the beds comfortable? I appeal to you. Do they give you a feeling of perfect repose when you lie down upon them; or rather, don't you toss about, and try in vain to find an easy position, and waken in the morning as tired as when you went to bed?'

Margaret laughed. 'To tell the truth, mamma, I've never thought about my bed at all, what kind it is. I'm so sleepy at night, that if I only lie down anywhere, I nap off directly. So I don't think I'm a competent witness. But then, you know, I never had the opportunity of trying Sir John Beresford's beds. I never was at Oxenham.'

'Were not you? Oh, no! to be sure. It was poor darling Fred I took with me, I remember. I only went to Oxenham once after I was married,—to your Aunt Shaw's wedding; and poor little Fred was the baby then. And I know Dixon did not like changing from lady's maid to nurse, and I was afraid that if I took her near her old home, and amongst her own people, she might want to leave me. But poor baby was taken ill at Oxenham, with his teething; and, what with my being a great deal with Anna just before her marriage, and not being very strong myself, Dixon had more of the charge of him than she ever had before; and it made her so fond of him, and she was so proud when he would turn away from every one and cling to her, that I don't believe she ever thought of leaving me again; though it was very different from what she'd been accustomed to. Poor Fred! Everybody loved him. He was born with the gift of winning hearts. It makes me think very badly of Captain Reid when I know that he disliked my own dear boy. I think it a certain proof he had a bad heart. Ah! Your poor father, Margaret. He has left the room. He can't bear to hear Fred spoken of.'

'I love to hear about him, mamma. Tell me all you like; you never can tell me too much. Tell me what he was like as a baby.'

'Why, Margaret, you must not be hurt, but he was much prettier than you were. I remember, when I first saw you in Dixon's arms, I said, "Dear, what an ugly little thing!" And she said, "It's not every child that's like Master Fred, bless him!" Dear! how well I remember it. Then I could have had Fred in my arms every minute of the day, and his cot was close by my bed; and now, now—Margaret—I don't know where my boy is, and sometimes I think I shall never see him again.'

Margaret sat down by her mother's sofa on a little stool, and softly took hold of her hand, caressing it and kissing it, as if to comfort. Mrs. Hale cried without restraint. At last, she sat straight, stiff up on the sofa, and turning round to her daughter, she said with tearful, almost solemn earnestness, 'Margaret, if I can get better,—if God lets me have a chance of recovery, it must be through seeing my son Frederick once more. It will waken up all the poor springs of health left in me.

She paused, and seemed to try and gather strength for something more yet to be said. Her voice was choked as she went on—was quavering as with the contemplation of some strange, yet closely-present idea.

'And, Margaret, if I am to die—if I am one of those appointed to die before many weeks are over—I must see my child first. I cannot think how it must be managed; but I charge you, Margaret, as you yourself hope for comfort in your last illness, bring him to me that I may bless him. Only for five minutes, Margaret. There could be no danger in five minutes. Oh, Margaret, let me see him before I die!'

Margaret did not think of anything that might be utterly unreasonable in this speech: we do not look for reason or logic in the passionate entreaties of those who are sick unto death; we are stung with the recollection of a thousand slighted opportunities of fulfilling the wishes of those who will soon pass away from among us: and do they ask us for the future happiness of our lives, we lay it at their feet, and will it away from us. But this wish of Mrs. Hale's was so natural, so just, so right to both parties, that Margaret felt as if, on Frederick's account as well as on her mother's, she ought to overlook all intermediate chances of danger, and pledge herself to do everything in her power for its realisation. The large, pleading, dilated eyes were fixed upon her wistfully, steady in their gaze, though the poor white lips quivered like those of a child. Margaret gently rose up and stood opposite to her frail mother; so that she might gather the secure fulfilment of her wish from the calm steadiness of her daughter's face.

'Mamma, I will write to-night, and tell Frederick what you say. I am as sure that he will come directly to us, as I am sure of my life. Be easy, mamma, you shall see him as far as anything earthly can be promised.'

'You will write to-night? Oh, Margaret! the post goes out at five—you will write by it, won't you? I have so few hours left—I feel, dear, as if I should not recover, though sometimes your father over-persuades me into hoping; you will write directly, won't you? Don't lose a single post; for just by that very post I may miss him.'

'But, mamma, papa is out.'

'Papa is out! and what then? Do you mean that he would deny me this last wish, Margaret? Why, I should not be ill—be dying—if he had not taken me away from Helstone, to this unhealthy, smoky, sunless place.'

'Oh, mamma!' said Margaret.

'Yes; it is so, indeed. He knows it himself; he has said so many a time. He would do anything for me; you don't mean he would refuse me this last wish—prayer, if you will. And, indeed, Margaret, the longing to see Frederick stands between me and God. I cannot pray till I have this one thing; indeed, I cannot. Don't lose time, dear, dear Margaret. Write by this very next post. Then he may be here—here in twenty-two days! For he is sure to come. No cords or chains can keep him. In twenty-two days I shall see my boy.' She fell back, and for a short time she took no notice of the fact that Margaret sat motionless, her hand shading her eyes.

'You are not writing!' said her mother at last 'Bring me some pens and paper; I will try and write myself.' She sat up, trembling all over with feverish eagerness. Margaret took her hand down and looked at her mother sadly.

'Only wait till papa comes in. Let us ask him how best to do it.'

'You promised, Margaret, not a quarter of an hour ago;—you said he should come.'

'And so he shall, mamma; don't cry, my own dear mother. I'll write here, now,—you shall see me write,—and it shall go by this very post; and if papa thinks fit, he can write again when he comes in,—it is only a day's delay. Oh, mamma, don't cry so pitifully,—it cuts me to the heart.'

Mrs. Hale could not stop her tears; they came hysterically; and, in truth, she made no effort to control them, but rather called up all the pictures of the happy past, and the probable future—painting the scene when she should lie a corpse, with the son she had longed to see in life weeping over her, and she unconscious of his presence—till she was melted by self-pity into a state of sobbing and exhaustion that made Margaret's heart ache. But at last she was calm, and greedily watched her daughter, as she began her letter; wrote it with swift urgent entreaty; sealed it up hurriedly, for fear her mother should ask to see it: and then, to make security most sure, at Mrs. Hale's own bidding, took it herself to the post-office. She was coming home when her father overtook her.

'And where have you been, my pretty maid?' asked he.

'To the post-office,—with a letter; a letter to Frederick. Oh, papa, perhaps I have done wrong: but mamma was seized with such a passionate yearning to see him—she said it would make her well again,—and then she said that she must see him before she died,—I cannot tell you how urgent she was! Did I do wrong?' Mr. Hale did not reply at first. Then he said:

'You should have waited till I came in, Margaret.'

'I tried to persuade her—' and then she was silent.

'I don't know,' said Mr. Hale, after a pause. 'She ought to see him if she wishes it so much, for I believe it would do her much more good than all the doctor's medicine,—and, perhaps, set her up altogether; but the danger to him, I'm afraid, is very great.'

'All these years since the mutiny, papa?'

'Yes; it is necessary, of course, for government to take very stringent measures for the repression of offences against authority, more particularly in the navy, where a commanding officer needs to be surrounded in his men's eyes with a vivid consciousness of all the power there is at home to back him, and take up his cause, and avenge any injuries offered to him, if need be. Ah! it's no matter to them how far their authorities have tyrannised,—galled hasty tempers to madness,—or, if that can be any excuse afterwards, it is never allowed for in the first instance; they spare no expense, they send out ships,—they scour the seas to lay hold of the offenders,—the lapse of years does not wash out the memory of the offence,—it is a fresh and vivid crime on the Admiralty books till it is blotted out by blood.'

'Oh, papa, what have I done! And yet it seemed so right at the time. I'm sure Frederick himself, would run the risk.'

'So he would; so he should! Nay, Margaret, I'm glad it is done, though I durst not have done it myself. I'm thankful it is as it is; I should have hesitated till, perhaps, it might have been too late to do any good. Dear Margaret, you have done what is right about it; and the end is beyond our control.'

It was all very well; but her father's account of the relentless manner in which mutinies were punished made Margaret shiver and creep. If she had decoyed her brother home to blot out the memory of his error by his blood! She saw her father's anxiety lay deeper than the source of his latter cheering words. She took his arm and walked home pensively and wearily by his side.

CHAPTER XXVI - MOTHER AND SON

'I have found that holy place of rest
  Still changeless.'
            MRS. HEMANS.

When Mr. Thornton had left the house that morning he was almost blinded by his baffled passion. He was as dizzy as if Margaret, instead of looking, and speaking, and moving like a tender graceful woman, had been a sturdy fish-wife, and given him a sound blow with her fists. He had positive bodily pain,—a violent headache, and a throbbing intermittent pulse. He could not bear the noise, the garish light, the continued rumble and movement of the street. He called himself a fool for suffering so; and yet he could not, at the moment, recollect the cause of his suffering, and whether it was adequate to the consequences it had produced. It would have been a relief to him, if he could have sat down and cried on a door-step by a little child, who was raging and storming, through his passionate tears, at some injury he had received. He said to himself, that he hated Margaret, but a wild, sharp sensation of love cleft his dull, thunderous feeling like lightning, even as he shaped the words expressive of hatred. His greatest comfort was in hugging his torment; and in feeling, as he had indeed said to her, that though she might despise him, contemn him, treat him with her proud sovereign indifference, he did not change one whit. She could not make him change. He loved her, and would love her; and defy her, and this miserable bodily pain.

He stood still for a moment, to make this resolution firm and clear. There was an omnibus passing—going into the country; the conductor thought he was wishing for a place, and stopped near the pavement. It was too much trouble to apologise and explain; so he mounted upon it, and was borne away,—past long rows of houses—then past detached villas with trim gardens, till they came to real country hedge-rows, and, by-and-by, to a small country town. Then everybody got down; and so did Mr. Thornton, and because they walked away he did so too. He went into the fields, walking briskly, because the sharp motion relieved his mind. He could remember all about it now; the pitiful figure he must have cut; the absurd way in which he had gone and done the very thing he had so often agreed with himself in thinking would be the most foolish thing in the world; and had met with exactly the consequences which, in these wise moods, he had always fore-told were certain to follow, if he ever did make such a fool of himself. Was he bewitched by those beautiful eyes, that soft, half-open, sighing mouth which lay so close upon his shoulder only yesterday? He could not even shake off the recollection that she had been there; that her arms had been round him, once—if never again. He only caught glimpses of her; he did not understand her altogether. At one time she was so brave, and at another so timid; now so tender, and then so haughty and regal-proud. And then he thought over every time he had ever seen her once again, by way of finally forgetting her. He saw her in every dress, in every mood, and did not know which became her best. Even this morning, how magnificent she had looked,—her eyes flashing out upon him at the idea that, because she had shared his danger yesterday, she had cared for him the least!

If Mr. Thornton was a fool in the morning, as he assured himself at least twenty times he was, he did not grow much wiser in the afternoon. All that he gained in return for his sixpenny omnibus ride, was a more vivid conviction that there never was, never could be, any one like Margaret; that she did not love him and never would; but that she—no! nor the whole world—should never hinder him from loving her. And so he returned to the little market-place, and remounted the omnibus to return to Milton.

It was late in the afternoon when he was set down, near his warehouse. The accustomed places brought back the accustomed habits and trains of thought. He knew how much he had to do—more than his usual work, owing to the commotion of the day before. He had to see his brother magistrates; he had to complete the arrangements, only half made in the morning, for the comfort and safety of his newly imported Irish hands; he had to secure them from all chance of communication with the discontented work-people of Milton. Last of all, he had to go home and encounter his mother.

Mrs. Thornton had sat in the dining-room all day, every moment expecting the news of her son's acceptance by Miss Hale. She had braced herself up many and many a time, at some sudden noise in the house; had caught up the half-dropped work, and begun to ply her needle diligently, though through dimmed spectacles, and with an unsteady hand! and many times had the door opened, and some indifferent person entered on some insignificant errand. Then her rigid face unstiffened from its gray frost-bound expression, and the features dropped into the relaxed look of despondency, so unusual to their sternness. She wrenched herself away from the contemplation of all the dreary changes that would be brought about to herself by her son's marriage; she forced her thoughts into the accustomed household grooves. The newly-married couple-to-be would need fresh household stocks of linen; and Mrs. Thornton had clothes-basket upon clothes-basket, full of table-cloths and napkins, brought in, and began to reckon up the store. There was some confusion between what was hers, and consequently marked G. H. T. (for George and Hannah Thornton), and what was her son's—bought with his money, marked with his initials. Some of those marked G. H. T. were Dutch damask of the old kind, exquisitely fine; none were like them now.

Mrs. Thornton stood looking at them long,—they had been her pride when she was first married. Then she knit her brows, and pinched and compressed her lips tight, and carefully unpicked the G. H. She went so far as to search for the Turkey-red marking-thread to put in the new initials; but it was all used,—and she had no heart to send for any more just yet. So she looked fixedly at vacancy; a series of visions passing before her, in all of which her son was the principal, the sole object,—her son, her pride, her property. Still he did not come. Doubtless he was with Miss Hale. The new love was displacing her already from her place as first in his heart. A terrible pain—a pang of vain jealousy—shot through her: she hardly knew whether it was more physical or mental; but it forced her to sit down. In a moment, she was up again as straight as ever,—a grim smile upon her face for the first time that day, ready for the door opening, and the rejoicing triumphant one, who should never know the sore regret his mother felt at his marriage. In all this, there was little thought enough of the future daughter-in-law as an individual. She was to be John's wife. To take Mrs. Thornton's place as mistress of the house, was only one of the rich consequences which decked out the supreme glory; all household plenty and comfort, all purple and fine linen, honour, love, obedience, troops of friends, would all come as naturally as jewels on a king's robe, and be as little thought of for their separate value. To be chosen by John, would separate a kitchen-wench from the rest of the world. And Miss Hale was not so bad. If she had been a Milton lass, Mrs. Thornton would have positively liked her. She was pungent, and had taste, and spirit, and flavour in her. True, she was sadly prejudiced, and very ignorant; but that was to be expected from her southern breeding. A strange sort of mortified comparison of Fanny with her, went on in Mrs. Thornton's mind; and for once she spoke harshly to her daughter; abused her roundly; and then, as if by way of penance, she took up Henry's Commentaries, and tried to fix her attention on it, instead of pursuing the employment she took pride and pleasure in, and continuing her inspection of the table-linen.

His step at last! She heard him, even while she thought she was finishing a sentence; while her eye did pass over it, and her memory could mechanically have repeated it word for word, she heard him come in at the hall-door. Her quickened sense could interpret every sound of motion: now he was at the hat-stand—now at the very room-door. Why did he pause? Let her know the worst.

Yet her head was down over the book; she did not look up. He came close to the table, and stood still there, waiting till she should have finished the paragraph which apparently absorbed her. By an effort she looked up. 'Well, John?'

He knew what that little speech meant. But he had steeled himself. He longed to reply with a jest; the bitterness of his heart could have uttered one, but his mother deserved better of him. He came round behind her, so that she could not see his looks, and, bending back her gray, stony face, he kissed it, murmuring:

'No one loves me,—no one cares for me, but you, mother.'

He turned away and stood leaning his head against the mantel-piece, tears forcing themselves into his manly eyes. She stood up,—she tottered. For the first time in her life, the strong woman tottered. She put her hands on his shoulders; she was a tall woman. She looked into his face; she made him look at her.

'Mother's love is given by God, John. It holds fast for ever and ever. A girl's love is like a puff of smoke,—it changes with every wind. And she would not have you, my own lad, would not she?' She set her teeth; she showed them like a dog for the whole length of her mouth. He shook his head.

'I am not fit for her, mother; I knew I was not.'

She ground out words between her closed teeth. He could not hear what she said; but the look in her eyes interpreted it to be a curse,—if not as coarsely worded, as fell in intent as ever was uttered. And yet her heart leapt up light, to know he was her own again.

'Mother!' said he, hurriedly, 'I cannot hear a word against her. Spare me,—spare me! I am very weak in my sore heart;—I love her yet; I love her more than ever.'

'And I hate her,' said Mrs. Thornton, in a low fierce voice. 'I tried not to hate her, when she stood between you and me, because,—I said to myself,—she will make him happy; and I would give my heart's blood to do that. But now, I hate her for your misery's sake. Yes, John, it's no use hiding up your aching heart from me. I am the mother that bore you, and your sorrow is my agony; and if you don't hate her, I do.'

'Then, mother, you make me love her more. She is unjustly treated by you, and I must make the balance even. But why do we talk of love or hatred? She does not care for me, and that is enough,—too much. Let us never name the subject again. It is the only thing you can do for me in the matter. Let us never name her.'

'With all my heart. I only wish that she, and all belonging to her, were swept back to the place they came from.'

He stood still, gazing into the fire for a minute or two longer. Her dry dim eyes filled with unwonted tears as she looked at him; but she seemed just as grim and quiet as usual when he next spoke.

'Warrants are out against three men for conspiracy, mother. The riot yesterday helped to knock up the strike.'

And Margaret's name was no more mentioned between Mrs. Thornton and her son. They fell back into their usual mode of talk,—about facts, not opinions, far less feelings. Their voices and tones were calm and cold a stranger might have gone away and thought that he had never seen such frigid indifference of demeanour between such near relations.

CHAPTER XXVII - FRUIT-PIECE

'For never any thing can be amiss
  When simpleness and duty tender it.'
MIDSUMMER NIGHT'S DREAM.

Mr. Thornton went straight and clear into all the interests of the following day. There was a slight demand for finished goods; and as it affected his branch of the trade, he took advantage of it, and drove hard bargains. He was sharp to the hour at the meeting of his brother magistrates,—giving them the best assistance of his strong sense, and his power of seeing consequences at a glance, and so coming to a rapid decision. Older men, men of long standing in the town, men of far greater wealth—realised and turned into land, while his was all floating capital, engaged in his trade—looked to him for prompt, ready wisdom. He was the one deputed to see and arrange with the police—to lead in all the requisite steps. And he cared for their unconscious deference no more than for the soft west wind, that scarcely made the smoke from the great tall chimneys swerve in its straight upward course. He was not aware of the silent respect paid to him. If it had been otherwise, he would have felt it as an obstacle in his progress to the object he had in view. As it was, he looked to the speedy accomplishment of that alone. It was his mother's greedy ears that sucked in, from the women-kind of these magistrates and wealthy men, how highly Mr. This or Mr. That thought of Mr. Thornton; that if he had not been there, things would have gone on very differently,—very badly, indeed. He swept off his business right and left that day. It seemed as though his deep mortification of yesterday, and the stunned purposeless course of the hours afterwards, had cleared away all the mists from his intellect. He felt his power and revelled in it. He could almost defy his heart. If he had known it, he could have sang the song of the miller who lived by the river Dee:—

'I care for nobody—
  Nobody cares for me.'

The evidence against Boucher, and other ringleaders of the riot, was taken before him; that against the three others, for conspiracy, failed. But he sternly charged the police to be on the watch; for the swift right arm of the law should be in readiness to strike, as soon as they could prove a fault. And then he left the hot reeking room in the borough court, and went out into the fresher, but still sultry street. It seemed as though he gave way all at once; he was so languid that he could not control his thoughts; they would wander to her; they would bring back the scene,—not of his repulse and rejection the day before but the looks, the actions of the day before that. He went along the crowded streets mechanically, winding in and out among the people, but never seeing them,—almost sick with longing for that one half-hour—that one brief space of time when she clung to him, and her heart beat against his—to come once again.

'Why, Mr. Thornton you're cutting me very coolly, I must say. And how is Mrs. Thornton? Brave weather this! We doctors don't like it, I can tell you!'

'I beg your pardon, Dr. Donaldson. I really didn't see you. My mother's quite well, thank you. It is a fine day, and good for the harvest, I hope. If the wheat is well got in, we shall have a brisk trade next year, whatever you doctors have.'

'Ay, ay. Each man for himself. Your bad weather, and your bad times, are my good ones. When trade is bad, there's more undermining of health, and preparation for death, going on among you Milton men than you're aware of.'

'Not with me, Doctor. I'm made of iron. The news of the worst bad debt I ever had, never made my pulse vary. This strike, which affects me more than any one else in Milton,—more than Hamper,—never comes near my appetite. You must go elsewhere for a patient, Doctor.'

'By the way, you've recommended me a good patient, poor lady! Not to go on talking in this heartless way, I seriously believe that Mrs. Hale—that lady in Crampton, you know—hasn't many weeks to live. I never had any hope of cure, as I think I told you; but I've been seeing her to-day, and I think very badly of her.'

Mr. Thornton was silent. The vaunted steadiness of pulse failed him for an instant.

'Can I do anything, Doctor?' he asked, in an altered voice. 'You know—you would see, that money is not very plentiful; are there any comforts or dainties she ought to have?'

'No,' replied the Doctor, shaking his head. 'She craves for fruit,—she has a constant fever on her; but jargonelle pears will do as well as anything, and there are quantities of them in the market.'

'You will tell me, if there is anything I can do, I'm sure,' replied Mr. Thornton. 'I rely upon you.'

'Oh! never fear! I'll not spare your purse,—I know it's deep enough. I wish you'd give me *carte-blanche* for all my patients, and all their wants.'

But Mr. Thornton had no general benevolence,—no universal philanthropy; few even would have given him credit for strong affections. But he went straight to the first fruit-shop in Milton, and chose out the bunch of purple grapes with the most delicate bloom upon them,—the richest-coloured peaches,—the freshest vine-leaves. They were packed into a basket, and the shopman awaited the answer to his inquiry, 'Where shall we send them to, sir?'

There was no reply. 'To Marlborough Mills, I suppose, sir?'

'No!' Mr. Thornton said. 'Give the basket to me,—I'll take it.'

It took up both his hands to carry it; and he had to pass through the busiest part of the town for feminine shopping. Many a young lady of his acquaintance turned to look after him, and thought it strange to see him occupied just like a porter or an errand-boy.

He was thinking, 'I will not be daunted from doing as I choose by the thought of her. I like to take this fruit to the poor mother, and it is simply right that I should. She shall never scorn me out of doing what I please. A pretty joke, indeed, if, for fear of a haughty girl, I failed in doing a kindness to a man I liked! I do it for Mr. Hale; I do it in defiance of her.'

He went at an unusual pace, and was soon at Crampton. He went upstairs two steps at a time, and entered the drawing-room before Dixon could announce him,—his face flushed, his eyes shining with kindly earnestness. Mrs. Hale lay on the sofa, heated with fever. Mr. Hale was reading aloud. Margaret was working on a low stool by her mother's side. Her heart fluttered, if his did not, at this interview. But he took no notice of her, hardly of Mr. Hale himself; he went up straight with his basket to Mrs. Hale, and said, in that subdued and gentle tone, which is so touching when used by a robust man in full health, speaking to a feeble invalid—

'I met Dr. Donaldson, ma'am, and as he said fruit would be good for you, I have taken the liberty—the great liberty of bringing you some that seemed to me fine.' Mrs. Hale was excessively surprised; excessively pleased; quite in a tremble of eagerness. Mr. Hale with fewer words expressed a deeper gratitude.

'Fetch a plate, Margaret—a basket—anything.' Margaret stood up by the table, half afraid of moving or making any noise to arouse Mr. Thornton into a consciousness of her being in the room. She thought it would be awkward for both to be brought into conscious collision; and fancied that, from her being on a low seat at first, and now standing behind her father, he had overlooked her in his haste. As if he did not feel the consciousness of her presence all over, though his eyes had never rested on her!

'I must go,' said he, 'I cannot stay. If you will forgive this liberty,—my rough ways,—too abrupt, I fear—but I will be more gentle next time. You will allow me the pleasure of bringing you some fruit again, if I should see any that is tempting. Good afternoon, Mr. Hale. Good-bye, ma'am.'

He was gone. Not one word: not one look to Margaret. She believed that he had not seen her. She went for a plate in silence, and lifted the fruit out tenderly, with the points of her delicate taper fingers. It was good of him to bring it; and after yesterday too!

'Oh! it is so delicious!' said Mrs. Hale, in a feeble voice. 'How kind of him to think of me! Margaret love, only taste these grapes! Was it not good of him?'

'Yes!' said Margaret, quietly.

'Margaret!' said Mrs. Hale, rather querulously, 'you won't like anything Mr. Thornton does. I never saw anybody so prejudiced.'

Mr. Hale had been peeling a peach for his wife; and, cutting off a small piece for himself, he said:

'If I had any prejudices, the gift of such delicious fruit as this would melt them all away. I have not tasted such fruit—no! not even in Hampshire—since I was a boy; and to boys, I fancy, all fruit is good. I remember eating sloes and crabs with a relish. Do you remember the matted-up currant bushes, Margaret, at the corner of the west-wall in the garden at home?'

Did she not? Did she not remember every weather-stain on the old stone wall; the gray and yellow lichens that marked it like a map; the little crane's-bill that grew in the crevices? She had been shaken by the events of the last two days; her whole life just now was a strain upon her fortitude; and, somehow, these careless words of her father's, touching on the remembrance of the sunny times of old, made her start up, and, dropping her sewing on the ground, she went hastily out of the room into her own little chamber. She had hardly given way to the first choking sob, when she became aware of Dixon standing at her drawers, and evidently searching for something.

'Bless me, miss! How you startled me! Missus is not worse, is she? Is anything the matter?'

'No, nothing. Only I'm silly, Dixon, and want a glass of water. What are you looking for? I keep my muslins in that drawer.'

Dixon did not speak, but went on rummaging. The scent of lavender came out and perfumed the room.

At last Dixon found what she wanted; what it was Margaret could not see. Dixon faced round, and spoke to her:

'Now I don't like telling you what I wanted, because you've fretting enough to go through, and I know you'll fret about this. I meant to have kept it from you till night, may be, or such times as that.'

'What is the matter? Pray, tell me, Dixon, at once.'

'That young woman you go to see—Higgins, I mean.'

'Well?'

'Well! she died this morning, and her sister is here—come to beg a strange thing. It seems, the young woman who died had a fancy for being buried in something of yours, and so the sister's come to ask for it,—and I was looking for a night-cap that wasn't too good to give away.'

'Oh! let me find one,' said Margaret, in the midst of her tears. 'Poor Bessy! I never thought I should not see her again.'

'Why, that's another thing. This girl down-stairs wanted me to ask you, if you would like to see her.'

'But she's dead!' said Margaret, turning a little pale. 'I never saw a dead person. No! I would rather not.'

'I should never have asked you, if you hadn't come in. I told her you wouldn't.'

'I will go down and speak to her,' said Margaret, afraid lest Dixon's harshness of manner might wound the poor girl. So, taking the cap in her hand, she went to the kitchen. Mary's face was all swollen with crying, and she burst out afresh when she saw Margaret.

'Oh, ma'am, she loved yo', she loved yo', she did indeed!' And for a long time, Margaret could not get her to say anything more than this. At last, her sympathy, and Dixon's scolding, forced out a few facts. Nicholas Higgins had gone out in the morning, leaving Bessy as well as on the day before. But in an hour she was taken worse; some neighbour ran to the room where Mary was working; they did not know where to find her father; Mary had only come in a few minutes before she died.

'It were a day or two ago she axed to be buried in somewhat o' yourn. She were never tired o' talking o' yo'. She used to say yo' were the prettiest thing she'd ever clapped eyes on. She loved yo' dearly. Her last words were, "Give her my affectionate respects; and keep father fro' drink." Yo'll come and see her, ma'am. She would ha' thought it a great compliment, I know.'

Margaret shrank a little from answering.

'Yes, perhaps I may. Yes, I will. I'll come before tea. But where's your father, Mary?'

Mary shook her head, and stood up to be going.

'Miss Hale,' said Dixon, in a low voice, 'where's the use o' your going to see the poor thing laid out? I'd never say a word against it, if it could do the girl any good; and I wouldn't mind a bit going myself, if that would satisfy her. They've just a notion, these common folks, of its being a respect to the departed. Here,' said she, turning sharply round, 'I'll come and see your sister. Miss Hale is busy, and she can't come, or else she would.'

The girl looked wistfully at Margaret. Dixon's coming might be a compliment, but it was not the same thing to the poor sister, who had had her little pangs of jealousy, during Bessy's lifetime, at the intimacy between her and the young lady.

'No, Dixon!' said Margaret with decision. 'I will go. Mary, you shall see me this afternoon.' And for fear of her own cowardice, she went away, in order to take from herself any chance of changing her determination.

CHAPTER XXVIII - COMFORT IN SORROW

'Through cross to crown!—And though thy spirit's life
  Trials untold assail with giant strength,
  Good cheer! good cheer! Soon ends the bitter strife,
  And thou shalt reign in peace with Christ at length.'
            KOSEGARTEN.

'Ay sooth, we feel too strong in weal, to need Thee on that road;
  But woe being come, the soul is dumb, that crieth not on "God."'
            MRS. BROWNING.

That afternoon she walked swiftly to the Higgins's house. Mary was looking out for her, with a half-distrustful face. Margaret smiled into her eyes to re-assure her. They passed quickly through the house-place, upstairs, and into the quiet presence of the dead. Then Margaret was glad that she had come. The face, often so weary with pain, so restless with troublous thoughts, had now the faint soft smile of eternal rest upon it. The slow tears gathered into Margaret's eyes, but a deep calm entered into her soul. And that was death! It looked more peaceful than life. All beautiful scriptures came into her mind. 'They rest from their labours.' 'The weary are at rest.' 'He giveth His beloved sleep.'

Slowly, slowly Margaret turned away from the bed. Mary was humbly sobbing in the back-ground. They went down stairs without a word.

Resting his hand upon the house-table, Nicholas Higgins stood in the midst of the floor; his great eyes startled open by the news he had heard, as he came along the court, from many busy tongues. His eyes were dry and fierce; studying the reality of her death; bringing himself to understand that her place should know her no more. For she had been sickly, dying so long, that he had persuaded himself she would not die; that she would 'pull through.'

Margaret felt as if she had no business to be there, familiarly acquainting herself with the surroundings of death which he, the father, had only just learnt. There had been a pause of an instant on the steep crooked stair, when she first saw him; but now she tried to steal past his abstracted gaze, and to leave him in the solemn circle of his household misery.

Mary sat down on the first chair she came to, and throwing her apron over her head, began to cry.

The noise appeared to rouse him. He took sudden hold of Margaret's arm, and held her till he could gather words to speak seemed dry; they came up thick, and choked, and hoarse:

'Were yo' with her? Did yo' see her die?'

'No!' replied Margaret, standing still with the utmost patience, now she found herself perceived. It was some time before he spoke again, but he kept his hold on her arm.

'All men must die,' said he at last, with a strange sort of gravity, which first suggested to Margaret the idea that he had been drinking—not enough to intoxicate himself, but enough to make his thoughts bewildered. 'But she were younger than me.' Still he pondered over the event, not looking at Margaret, though he grasped her tight. Suddenly, he looked up at her with a wild searching inquiry in his glance. 'Yo're sure and certain she's dead—not in a dwam, a faint?—she's been so before, often.'

'She is dead,' replied Margaret. She felt no fear in speaking to him, though he hurt her arm with his gripe, and wild gleams came across the stupidity of his eyes.

'She is dead!' she said.

He looked at her still with that searching look, which seemed to fade out of his eyes as he gazed. Then he suddenly let go his hold of Margaret, and, throwing his body half across the table, he shook it and every piece of furniture in the room, with his violent sobs. Mary came trembling towards him.

'Get thee gone!—get thee gone!' he cried, striking wildly and blindly at her. 'What do I care for thee?' Margaret took her hand, and held it softly in hers. He tore his hair, he beat his head against the hard wood, then he lay exhausted and stupid. Still his daughter and Margaret did not move. Mary trembled from head to foot.

At last—it might have been a quarter of an hour, it might have been an hour—he lifted himself up. His eyes were swollen and bloodshot, and he seemed to have forgotten that any one was by; he scowled at the watchers when he saw them. He shook himself heavily, gave them one more sullen look, spoke never a word, but made for the door.

'Oh, father, father!' said Mary, throwing herself upon his arm,—'not to-night! Any night but to-night. Oh, help me! he's going out to drink again! Father, I'll not leave yo'. Yo' may strike, but I'll not leave yo'. She told me last of all to keep yo' fro' drink!'

But Margaret stood in the doorway, silent yet commanding. He looked up at her defyingly.

'It's my own house. Stand out o' the way, wench, or I'll make yo'!' He had shaken off Mary with violence; he looked ready to strike Margaret. But she never moved a feature—never took her deep, serious eyes off him. He stared back on her with gloomy fierceness. If she had stirred hand or foot, he would have thrust her aside with even more violence than he had used to his own daughter, whose face was bleeding from her fall against a chair.

'What are yo' looking at me in that way for?' asked he at last, daunted and awed by her severe calm. 'If yo' think for to keep me from going what gait I choose, because she loved yo'—and in my own house, too, where I never asked yo' to come, yo're mista'en. It's very hard upon a man that he can't go to the only comfort left.'

Margaret felt that he acknowledged her power. What could she do next? He had seated himself on a chair, close to the door; half-conquered, half-resenting; intending to go out as soon as she left her position, but unwilling to use the violence he had threatened not five minutes before. Margaret laid her hand on his arm.

'Come with me,' she said. 'Come and see her!'

The voice in which she spoke was very low and solemn; but there was no fear or doubt expressed in it, either of him or of his compliance. He sullenly rose up. He stood uncertain, with dogged irresolution upon his face. She waited him there; quietly and patiently waited for his time to move. He had a strange pleasure in making her wait; but at last he moved towards the stairs.

She and he stood by the corpse.

'Her last words to Mary were, "Keep my father fro' drink."'

'It canna hurt her now,' muttered he. 'Nought can hurt her now.' Then, raising his voice to a wailing cry, he went on: 'We may quarrel and fall out—we may make peace and be friends—we may clem to skin and bone—and nought o' all our griefs will ever touch her more. Hoo's had her portion on 'em. What wi' hard work first, and sickness at last, hoo's led the life of a dog. And to die without knowing one good piece o' rejoicing in all her days! Nay, wench, whatever hoo said, hoo can know nought about it now, and I mun ha' a sup o' drink just to steady me again sorrow.'

'No,' said Margaret, softening with his softened manner. 'You shall not. If her life has been what you say, at any rate she did not fear death as some do. Oh, you should have heard her speak of the life to come—the life hidden with God, that she is now gone to.'

He shook his head, glancing sideways up at Margaret as he did so. His pale, haggard face struck her painfully.

'You are sorely tired. Where have you been all day—not at work?'

'Not at work, sure enough,' said he, with a short, grim laugh. 'Not at what you call work. I were at the Committee, till I were sickened out wi' trying to make fools hear reason. I were fetched to Boucher's wife afore seven this morning. She's bed-fast, but she were raving and raging to know where her dunder-headed brute of a chap was, as if I'd to keep him—as if he were fit to be ruled by me. The d—— d fool, who has put his foot in all our plans! And I've walked my feet sore wi' going about for to see men who wouldn't be seen, now the law is raised again us. And I were sore-hearted, too, which is worse than sore-footed; and if I did see a friend who ossed to treat me, I never knew hoo lay a-dying here. Bess, lass, thou'd believe me, thou wouldst—wouldstn't thou?' turning to the poor dumb form with wild appeal.

'I am sure,' said Margaret, 'I am sure you did not know: it was quite sudden. But now, you see, it would be different; you do know; you do see her lying there; you hear what she said with her last breath. You will not go?'

No answer. In fact, where was he to look for comfort?

'Come home with me,' said she at last, with a bold venture, half trembling at her own proposal as she made it. 'At least you shall have some comfortable food, which I'm sure you need.'

'Yo'r father's a parson?' asked he, with a sudden turn in his ideas.

'He was,' said Margaret, shortly.

'I'll go and take a dish o' tea with him, since yo've asked me. I've many a thing I often wished to say to a parson, and I'm not particular as to whether he's preaching now, or not.'

Margaret was perplexed; his drinking tea with her father, who would be totally unprepared for his visitor—her mother so ill—seemed utterly out of the question; and yet if she drew back now, it would be worse than ever—sure to drive him to the gin-shop. She thought that if she could only get him to their own house, it was so great a step gained that she would trust to the chapter of accidents for the next.

'Goodbye, ou'd wench! We've parted company at last, we have! But thou'st been a blessin' to thy father ever sin' thou wert born. Bless thy white lips, lass,—they've a smile on 'em now! and I'm glad to see it once again, though I'm lone and forlorn for evermore.'

He stooped down and fondly kissed his daughter; covered up her face, and turned to follow Margaret. She had hastily gone down stairs to tell Mary of the arrangement; to say it was the only way she could think of to keep him from the gin-palace; to urge Mary to come too, for her heart smote her at the idea of leaving the poor affectionate girl alone. But Mary had friends among the neighbours, she said, who would come in and sit a bit with her, it was all right; but father—

He was there by them as she would have spoken more. He had shaken off his emotion, as if he was ashamed of having ever given way to it; and had even o'er-leaped himself so much that he assumed a sort of bitter mirth, like the crackling of thorns under a pot.

'I'm going to take my tea wi' her father, I am!'

But he slouched his cap low down over his brow as he went out into the street, and looked neither to the right nor to the left, while he tramped along by Margaret's side; he feared being upset by the words, still more the looks, of sympathising neighbours. So he and Margaret walked in silence.

As he got near the street in which he knew she lived, he looked down at his clothes, his hands, and shoes.

'I should m'appen ha' cleaned mysel', first?'

It certainly would have been desirable, but Margaret assured him he should be allowed to go into the yard, and have soap and towel provided; she could not let him slip out of her hands just then.

While he followed the house-servant along the passage, and through the kitchen, stepping cautiously on every dark mark in the pattern of the oil-cloth, in order to conceal his dirty foot-prints, Margaret ran upstairs. She met Dixon on the landing.

'How is mamma?—where is papa?'

Missus was tired, and gone into her own room. She had wanted to go to bed, but Dixon had persuaded her to lie down on the sofa, and have her tea brought to her there; it would be better than getting restless by being too long in bed.

So far, so good. But where was Mr. Hale? In the drawing-room. Margaret went in half breathless with the hurried story she had to tell. Of course, she told it incompletely; and her father was rather 'taken aback' by the idea of the drunken weaver awaiting him in his quiet study, with whom he was expected to drink tea, and on whose behalf Margaret was anxiously pleading. The meek, kind-hearted Mr. Hale would have readily tried to console him in his grief, but, unluckily, the point Margaret dwelt upon most forcibly was the fact of his having been drinking, and her having brought him home with her as a last expedient to keep him from the gin-shop. One little event had come out of another so naturally that Margaret was hardly conscious of what she had done, till she saw the slight look of repugnance on her father's face.

'Oh, papa! he really is a man you will not dislike—if you won't be shocked to begin with.'

'But, Margaret, to bring a drunken man home—and your mother so ill!'

Margaret's countenance fell. 'I am sorry, papa. He is very quiet—he is not tipsy at all. He was only rather strange at first, but that might be the shock of poor Bessy's death.' Margaret's eyes filled with tears. Mr. Hale took hold of her sweet pleading face in both his hands, and kissed her forehead.

'It is all right, dear. I'll go and make him as comfortable as I can, and do you attend to your mother. Only, if you can come in and make a third in the study, I shall be glad.'

'Oh, yes—thank you.' But as Mr. Hale was leaving the room, she ran after him:

'Papa—you must not wonder at what he says: he's an—— I mean he does not believe in much of what we do.'

'Oh dear! a drunken infidel weaver!' said Mr. Hale to himself, in dismay. But to Margaret he only said, 'If your mother goes to sleep, be sure you come directly.'

Margaret went into her mother's room. Mrs. Hale lifted herself up from a doze.

'When did you write to Frederick, Margaret? Yesterday, or the day before?'

'Yesterday, mamma.'

'Yesterday. And the letter went?'

'Yes. I took it myself'

'Oh, Margaret, I'm so afraid of his coming! If he should be recognised! If he should be taken! If he should be executed, after all these years that he has kept away and lived in safety! I keep falling asleep and dreaming that he is caught and being tried.'

'Oh, mamma, don't be afraid. There will be some risk no doubt; but we will lessen it as much as ever we can. And it is so little! Now, if we were at Helstone, there would be twenty—a hundred times as much. There, everybody would remember him and if there was a stranger known to be in the house, they would be sure to guess it was Frederick; while here, nobody knows or cares for us enough to notice what we do. Dixon will keep the door like a dragon—won't you, Dixon—while he is here?'

'They'll be clever if they come in past me!' said Dixon, showing her teeth at the bare idea.

'And he need not go out, except in the dusk, poor fellow!'

'Poor fellow!' echoed Mrs. Hale. 'But I almost wish you had not written. Would it be too late to stop him if you wrote again, Margaret?'

'I'm afraid it would, mamma,' said Margaret, remembering the urgency with which she had entreated him to come directly, if he wished to see his mother alive.

'I always dislike that doing things in such a hurry,' said Mrs. Hale.

Margaret was silent.

'Come now, ma'am,' said Dixon, with a kind of cheerful authority, 'you know seeing Master Frederick is just the very thing of all others you're longing for. And I'm glad Miss Margaret wrote off straight, without shilly-shallying. I've had a great mind to do it myself. And we'll keep him snug, depend upon it. There's only Martha in the house that would not do a good deal to save him on a pinch; and I've been thinking she might go and see her mother just at that very time. She's been saying once or twice she should like to go, for her mother has had a stroke since she came here, only she didn't like to ask. But I'll see about her being safe off, as soon as we know when he comes, God bless him! So take your tea, ma'am, in comfort, and trust to me.'

Mrs. Hale did trust in Dixon more than in Margaret. Dixon's words quieted her for the time. Margaret poured out the tea in silence, trying to think of something agreeable to say; but her thoughts made answer something like Daniel O'Rourke, when the man-in-the-moon asked him to get off his reaping-hook. 'The more you ax us, the more we won't stir.' The more she tried to think of something anything besides the danger to which Frederick would be exposed—the more closely her imagination clung to the unfortunate idea presented to her. Her mother prattled with Dixon, and seemed to have utterly forgotten the possibility of Frederick being tried and executed—utterly forgotten that at her wish, if by Margaret's deed, he was summoned into this danger. Her mother was one of those who throw out terrible possibilities, miserable probabilities, unfortunate chances of all kinds, as a rocket throws out sparks; but if the sparks light on some combustible matter, they smoulder first, and burst out into a frightful flame at last. Margaret was glad when, her filial duties gently and carefully performed, she could go down into the study. She wondered how her father and Higgins had got on.

In the first place, the decorous, kind-hearted, simple, old-fashioned gentleman, had unconsciously called out, by his own refinement and courteousness of manner, all the latent courtesy in the other.

Mr. Hale treated all his fellow-creatures alike: it never entered into his head to make any difference because of their rank. He placed a chair for Nicholas stood up till he, at Mr. Hale's request, took a seat; and called him, invariably, 'Mr. Higgins,' instead of the curt 'Nicholas' or 'Higgins,' to which the 'drunken infidel weaver' had been accustomed. But Nicholas was neither an habitual drunkard nor a thorough infidel. He drank to drown care, as he would have himself expressed it: and he was infidel so far as he had never yet found any form of faith to which he could attach himself, heart and soul.

Margaret was a little surprised, and very much pleased, when she found her father and Higgins in earnest conversation—each speaking with gentle politeness to the other, however their opinions might clash. Nicholas—clean, tidied (if only at the pump-trough), and quiet spoken—was a new creature to her, who had only seen him in the rough independence of his own hearthstone. He had 'slicked' his hair down with the fresh water; he had adjusted his neck-handkerchief, and borrowed an odd candle-end to polish his clogs with and there he sat, enforcing some opinion on her father, with a strong Darkshire accent, it is true, but with a lowered voice, and a good, earnest composure on his face. Her father, too, was interested in what his companion was saying. He looked round as she came in, smiled, and quietly gave her his chair, and then sat down afresh as quickly as possible, and with a little bow of apology to his guest for the interruption. Higgins nodded to her as a sign of greeting; and she softly adjusted her working materials on the table, and prepared to listen.

'As I was a-sayin, sir, I reckon yo'd not ha' much belief in yo' if yo' lived here,—if yo'd been bred here. I ax your pardon if I use wrong words; but what I mean by belief just now, is a-thinking on sayings and maxims and promises made by folk yo' never saw, about the things and the life, yo' never saw, nor no one else. Now, yo' say these are true things, and true sayings, and a true life. I just say, where's the proof? There's many and many a one wiser, and scores better learned than I am around me,—folk who've had time to think on these things,—while my time has had to be gi'en up to getting my bread. Well, I sees these people. Their lives is pretty much open to me. They're real folk. They don't believe i' the Bible,—not they. They may say they do, for form's sake; but Lord, sir, d'ye think their first cry i' th' morning is, "What shall I do to get hold on eternal life?" or "What shall I do to fill my purse this blessed day? Where shall I go? What bargains shall I strike?" The purse and the gold and the notes is real things; things as can be felt and touched; them's realities; and eternal life is all a talk, very fit for—I ax your pardon, sir; yo'r a parson out o' work, I believe. Well! I'll never speak disrespectful of a man in the same fix as I'm in mysel'. But I'll just ax yo another question, sir, and I dunnot want yo to answer it, only to put in yo'r pipe, and smoke it, afore yo' go for to set down us, who only believe in what we see, as fools and noddies. If salvation, and life to come, and what not, was true—not in men's words, but in men's hearts' core—dun yo' not think they'd din us wi' it as they do wi' political 'conomy? They're mighty anxious to come round us wi' that piece o' wisdom; but t'other would be a greater convarsion, if it were true.'

'But the masters have nothing to do with your religion. All that they are connected with you in is trade,—so they think,—and all that it concerns them, therefore, to rectify your opinions in is the science of trade.'

'I'm glad, sir,' said Higgins, with a curious wink of his eye, 'that yo' put in, "so they think." I'd ha' thought yo' a hypocrite, I'm afeard, if yo' hadn't, for all yo'r a parson, or rayther because yo'r a parson. Yo' see, if yo'd spoken o' religion as a thing that, if it was true, it didn't concern all men to press on all men's attention, above everything else in this 'varsal earth, I should ha' thought yo' a knave for to be a parson; and I'd rather think yo' a fool than a knave. No offence, I hope, sir.'

'None at all. You consider me mistaken, and I consider you far more fatally mistaken. I don't expect to convince you in a day,—not in one conversation; but let us know each other, and speak freely to each other about these things, and the truth will prevail. I should not believe in God if I did not believe that. Mr. Higgins, I trust, whatever else you have given up, you believe'—(Mr. Hale's voice dropped low in reverence)—'you believe in Him.'

Nicholas Higgins suddenly stood straight, stiff up. Margaret started to her feet,—for she thought, by the working of his face, he was going into convulsions. Mr. Hale looked at her dismayed. At last Higgins found words:

'Man! I could fell yo' to the ground for tempting me. Whatten business have yo' to try me wi' your doubts? Think o' her lying theere, after the life hoo's led and think then how yo'd deny me the one sole comfort left—that there is a God, and that He set her her life. I dunnot believe she'll ever live again,' said he, sitting down, and drearily going on, as if to the unsympathising fire. 'I dunnot believe in any other life than this, in which she dreed such trouble, and had such never-ending care; and I cannot bear to think it were all a set o' chances, that might ha' been altered wi' a breath o' wind. There's many a time when I've thought I didna believe in God, but I've never put it fair out before me in words, as many men do. I may ha' laughed at those who did, to brave it out like—but I have looked round at after, to see if He heard me, if so be there was a He; but to-day, when I'm left desolate, I wunnot listen to yo' wi' yo'r questions, and yo'r doubts. There's but one thing steady and quiet i' all this reeling world, and, reason or no reason, I'll cling to that. It's a' very well for happy folk'——

Margaret touched his arm very softly. She had not spoken before, nor had he heard her rise.

'Nicholas, we do not want to reason; you misunderstand my father. We do not reason—we believe; and so do you. It is the one sole comfort in such times.'

He turned round and caught her hand. 'Ay! it is, it is—(brushing away the tears with the back of his hand).—'But yo' know, she's lying dead at home and I'm welly dazed wi' sorrow, and at times I hardly know what I'm saying. It's as if speeches folk ha' made—clever and smart things as I've thought at the time—come up now my heart's welly brossen. Th' strike's failed as well; dun yo' know that, miss? I were coming whoam to ask her, like a beggar as I am, for a bit o' comfort i' that trouble; and I were knocked down by one who telled me she were dead—just dead. That were all; but that were enough for me.

Mr. Hale blew his nose, and got up to snuff the candles in order to conceal his emotion. 'He's not an infidel, Margaret; how could you say so?' muttered he reproachfully 'I've a good mind to read him the fourteenth chapter of Job.'

'Not yet, papa, I think. Perhaps not at all. Let us ask him about the strike, and give him all the sympathy he needs, and hoped to have from poor Bessy.'

So they questioned and listened. The workmen's calculations were based (like too many of the masters') on false premises. They reckoned on their fellow-men as if they possessed the calculable powers of machines, no more, no less; no allowance for human passions getting the better of reason, as in the case of Boucher and the rioters; and believing that the representations of their injuries would have the same effect on strangers far away, as the injuries (fancied or real) had upon themselves. They were consequently surprised and indignant at the poor Irish, who had allowed themselves to be imported and brought over to take their places. This indignation was tempered, in some degree, by contempt for 'them Irishers,' and by pleasure at the idea of the bungling way in which they would set to work, and perplex their new masters with their ignorance and stupidity, strange exaggerated stories of which were already spreading through the town. But the most cruel cut of all was that of the Milton workmen, who had defied and disobeyed the commands of the Union to keep the peace, whatever came; who had originated discord in the camp, and spread the panic of the law being arrayed against them.

'And so the strike is at an end,' said Margaret.

'Ay, miss. It's save as save can. Th' factory doors will need open wide tomorrow to let in all who'll be axing for work; if it's only just to show they'd nought to do wi' a measure, which if we'd been made o' th' right stuff would ha' brought wages up to a point they'n not been at this ten year.'

'You'll get work, shan't you?' asked Margaret. 'You're a famous workman, are not you?'

'Hamper'll let me work at his mill, when he cuts off his right hand—not before, and not after,' said Nicholas, quietly. Margaret was silenced and sad.

'About the wages,' said Mr. Hale. 'You'll not be offended, but I think you make some sad mistakes. I should like to read you some remarks in a book I have.' He got up and went to his book-shelves.

'Yo' needn't trouble yoursel', sir,' said Nicholas. 'Their book-stuff goes in at one ear and out at t'other. I can make nought on't. Afore Hamper and me had this split, th' overlooker telled him I were stirring up the men to ask for higher wages; and Hamper met me one day in th' yard. He'd a thin book i' his hand, and says he, "Higgins, I'm told you're one of those damned fools that think you can get higher wages for asking for 'em; ay, and keep 'em up too, when you've forced 'em up. Now, I'll give yo' a chance and try if yo've any sense in yo'. Here's a book written by a friend o' mine, and if yo'll read it yo'll see how wages find their own level, without either masters or men having aught to do with them; except the men cut their own throats wi' striking, like the confounded noodles they are." Well, now, sir, I put it to yo', being a parson, and having been in th' preaching line, and having had to try and bring folk o'er to what yo' thought was a right way o' thinking—did yo' begin by calling 'em fools and such like, or didn't yo' raything give 'em some kind words at first, to make 'em ready for to listen and be convinced, if they could; and in yo'r preaching, did yo' stop every now and then, and say, half to them and half to yo'rsel', "But yo're such a pack o' fools, that I've a strong notion it's no use my trying to put sense into yo'?" I were not i' th' best state, I'll own, for taking in what Hamper's friend had to say—I were so vexed at the way it were put to me;—but I thought, "Come, I'll see what these chaps has got to say, and try if it's them or me as is th' noodle." So I took th' book and tugged at it; but, Lord bless yo', it went on about capital and labour, and labour and capital, till it fair sent me off to sleep. I ne'er could rightly fix i' my mind which was which; and it spoke on 'em as if they was vartues or vices; and what I wanted for to know were the rights o' men, whether they were rich or poor—so be they only were men.'

'But for all that,' said Mr. Hale, 'and granting to the full the offensiveness, the folly, the unchristianness of Mr. Hamper's way of speaking to you in recommending his friend's book, yet if it told you what he said it did, that wages find their own level, and that the most successful strike can only force them up for a moment, to sink in far greater proportion afterwards, in consequence of that very strike, the book would have told you the truth.'

'Well, sir,' said Higgins, rather doggedly; 'it might, or it might not. There's two opinions go to settling that point. But suppose it was truth double strong, it were no truth to me if I couldna take it in. I daresay there's truth in yon Latin book on your shelves; but it's gibberish and not truth to me, unless I know the meaning o' the words. If yo', sir, or any other knowledgable, patient man come to me, and says he'll larn me what the words mean, and not blow me up if I'm a bit stupid, or forget how one thing hangs on another—why, in time I may get to see the truth of it; or I may not. I'll not be bound to say I shall end in thinking the same as any man. And I'm not one who think truth can be shaped out in words, all neat and clean, as th' men at th' foundry cut out sheet-iron. Same bones won't go down wi' every one. It'll stick here i' this man's throat, and there i' t'other's. Let alone that, when down, it may be too strong for this one, too weak for that. Folk who sets up to doctor th' world wi' their truth, mun suit different for different minds; and be a bit tender in th' way of giving it too, or th' poor sick fools may spit it out i' their faces. Now Hamper first gi'es me a box on my ear, and then he throws his big bolus at me, and says he reckons it'll do me no good, I'm such a fool, but there it is.'

'I wish some of the kindest and wisest of the masters would meet some of you men, and have a good talk on these things; it would, surely, be the best way of getting over your difficulties, which, I do believe, arise from your ignorance—excuse me, Mr. Higgins—on subjects which it is for the mutual interest of both masters and men should be well understood by both. I wonder'—(half to his daughter), 'if Mr. Thornton might not be induced to do such a thing?'

'Remember, papa,' said she in a very low voice, 'what he said one day—about governments, you know.' She was unwilling to make any clearer allusion to the conversation they had held on the mode of governing work-people—by giving men intelligence enough to rule themselves, or by a wise despotism on the part of the master—for she saw that Higgins had caught Mr. Thornton's name, if not the whole of the speech: indeed, he began to speak of him.

'Thornton! He's the chap as wrote off at once for these Irishers; and led to th' riot that ruined th' strike. Even Hamper wi' all his bullying, would ha' waited a while—but it's a word and a blow wi' Thornton. And, now, when th' Union would ha' thanked him for following up th' chase after Boucher, and them chaps as went right again our commands, it's Thornton who steps forrard and coolly says that, as th' strike's at an end, he, as party injured, doesn't want to press the charge again the rioters. I thought he'd had more pluck. I thought he'd ha' carried his point, and had his revenge in an open way; but says he (one in court telled me his very words) "they are well known; they will find the natural punishment of their conduct, in the difficulty they will meet wi' in getting employment. That will be severe enough." I only wish they'd cotched Boucher, and had him up before Hamper. I see th' oud tiger setting on him! would he ha' let him off? Not he!'

'Mr. Thornton was right,' said Margaret. You are angry against Boucher, Nicholas; or else you would be the first to see, that where the natural punishment would be severe enough for the offence, any farther punishment would be something like revenge.

'My daughter is no great friend of Mr. Thornton's,' said Mr. Hale, smiling at Margaret; while she, as red as any carnation, began to work with double diligence, 'but I believe what she says is the truth. I like him for it.'

'Well, sir, this strike has been a weary piece o' business to me; and yo'll not wonder if I'm a bit put out wi' seeing it fail, just for a few men who would na suffer in silence, and hou'd out, brave and firm.'

'You forget!' said Margaret. 'I don't know much of Boucher; but the only time I saw him it was not his own sufferings he spoke of, but those of his sick wife—his little children.'

'True! but he were not made of iron himsel'. He'd ha' cried out for his own sorrows, next. He were not one to bear.'

'How came he into the Union?' asked Margaret innocently. 'You don't seem to have much respect for him; nor gained much good from having him in.'

Higgins's brow clouded. He was silent for a minute or two. Then he said, shortly enough:

'It's not for me to speak o' th' Union. What they does, they does. Them that is of a trade mun hang together; and if they're not willing to take their chance along wi' th' rest, th' Union has ways and means.'

Mr. Hale saw that Higgins was vexed at the turn the conversation had taken, and was silent. Not so Margaret, though she saw Higgins's feeling as clearly as he did. By instinct she felt, that if he could but be brought to express himself in plain words, something clear would be gained on which to argue for the right and the just.

'And what are the Union's ways and means?'

He looked up at her, as if on' the point of dogged resistance to her wish for information. But her calm face, fixed on his, patient and trustful, compelled him to answer.

'Well! If a man doesn't belong to th' Union, them as works next looms has orders not to speak to him—if he's sorry or ill it's a' the same; he's out o' bounds; he's none o' us; he comes among us, he works among us, but he's none o' us. I' some places them's fined who speaks to him. Yo' try that, miss; try living a year or two among them as looks away if yo' look at 'em; try working within two yards o' crowds o' men, who, yo' know, have a grinding grudge at yo' in their hearts—to whom if yo' say yo'r glad, not an eye brightens, nor a lip moves,—to whom if your heart's heavy, yo' can never say nought, because they'll ne'er take notice on your sighs or sad looks (and a man 's no man who'll groan out loud 'bout folk asking him what 's the matter?)—just yo' try that, miss—ten hours for three hundred days, and yo'll know a bit what th' Union is.'

'Why!' said Margaret, 'what tyranny this is! Nay, Higgins, I don't care one straw for your anger. I know you can't be angry with me if you would, and I must tell you the truth: that I never read, in all the history I have read, of a more slow, lingering torture than this. And you belong to the Union! And you talk of the tyranny of the masters!'

'Nay,' said Higgins, 'yo' may say what yo' like! The dead stand between yo and every angry word o' mine. D' ye think I forget who's lying *there*, and how hoo loved yo'? And it's th' masters as has made us sin, if th' Union is a sin. Not this generation maybe, but their fathers. Their fathers ground our fathers to the very dust; ground us to powder! Parson! I reckon, I've heerd my mother read out a text, "The fathers have eaten sour grapes and th' children's teeth are set on edge." It's so wi' them. In those days of sore oppression th' Unions began; it were a necessity. It's a necessity now, according to me. It's a withstanding of injustice, past, present, or to come. It may be like war; along wi' it come crimes; but I think it were a greater crime to let it alone. Our only chance is binding men together in one common interest; and if some are cowards and some are fools, they mun come along and join the great march, whose only strength is in numbers.'

'Oh!' said Mr. Hale, sighing, 'your Union in itself would be beautiful, glorious,—it would be Christianity itself—if it were but for an end which affected the good of all, instead of that of merely one class as opposed to another.'

'I reckon it's time for me to be going, sir,' said Higgins, as the clock struck ten.

'Home?' said Margaret very softly. He understood her, and took her offered hand. 'Home, miss. Yo' may trust me, tho' I am one o' th' Union.'

'I do trust you most thoroughly, Nicholas.'

'Stay!' said Mr. Hale, hurrying to the book-shelves. 'Mr. Higgins! I'm sure you'll join us in family prayer?'

Higgins looked at Margaret, doubtfully. Her grave sweet eyes met his; there was no compulsion, only deep interest in them. He did not speak, but he kept his place.

Margaret the Churchwoman, her father the Dissenter, Higgins the Infidel, knelt down together. It did them no harm.

CHAPTER XXIX - A RAY OF SUNSHINE

'Some wishes crossed my mind and dimly cheered it,
And one or two poor melancholy pleasures,
Each in the pale unwarming light of hope,
Silvering its flimsy wing, flew silent by—
Moths in the moonbeam!'
COLERIDGE.

The next morning brought Margaret a letter from Edith. It was affectionate and inconsequent like the writer. But the affection was charming to Margaret's own affectionate nature; and she had grown up with the inconsequence, so she did not perceive it. It was as follows:—

'Oh, Margaret, it is worth a journey from England to see my boy! He is a superb little fellow, especially in his caps, and most especially in the one you sent him, you good, dainty-fingered, persevering little lady! Having made all the mothers here envious, I want to show him to somebody new, and hear a fresh set of admiring expressions; perhaps, that's all the reason; perhaps it is not—nay, possibly, there is just a little cousinly love mixed with it; but I do want you so much to come here, Margaret! I'm sure it would be the very best thing for Aunt Hale's health; everybody here is young and well, and our skies are always blue, and our sun always shines, and the band plays deliciously from morning till night; and, to come back to the burden of my ditty, my baby always smiles. I am constantly wanting you to draw him for me, Margaret. It does not signify what he is doing; that very thing is prettiest, gracefulest, best. I think I love him a great deal better than my husband, who is getting stout, and grumpy,—what he calls "busy." No! he is not. He has just come in with news of such a charming pic-nic, given by the officers of the Hazard, at anchor in the bay below. Because he has brought in such a pleasant piece of news, I retract all I said just now. Did not somebody burn his hand for having said or done something he was sorry for? Well, I can't burn mine, because it would hurt me, and the scar would be ugly; but I'll retract all I said as fast as I can. Cosmo is quite as great a darling as baby, and not a bit stout, and as un-grumpy as ever husband was; only, sometimes he is very, very busy. I may say that without love—wifely duty—where was I?—I had something very particular to say, I know, once. Oh, it is this—Dearest Margaret!—you must come and see me; it would do Aunt Hale good, as I said before. Get the doctor to order it for her. Tell him that it's the smoke of Milton that does her harm. I have no doubt it is that, really. Three months (you must not come for less) of this delicious climate—all sunshine, and grapes as common as blackberries, would quite cure her. I don't ask my uncle'—(Here the letter became more constrained, and better written; Mr. Hale was in the corner, like a naughty child, for having given up his living.)—'because, I dare say, he disapproves of war, and soldiers, and bands of music; at least, I know that many Dissenters are members of the Peace Society, and I am afraid he would not like to come; but, if he would, dear, pray say that Cosmo and I will do our best to make him happy; and I'll hide up Cosmo's red coat and sword, and make the band play all sorts of grave, solemn things; or, if they do play pomps and vanities, it shall be in double slow time. Dear Margaret, if he would like to accompany you and Aunt Hale, we will try and make it pleasant, though I'm rather afraid of any one who has done something for conscience sake. You never did, I hope. Tell Aunt Hale not to bring many warm clothes, though I'm afraid it will be late in the year before you can come. But you have no idea of the heat here! I tried to wear my great beauty Indian shawl at a pic-nic. I kept myself up with proverbs as long as I could; "Pride must abide,"—and such wholesome pieces of pith; but it was of no use. I was like mamma's little dog Tiny with an elephant's trappings on; smothered, hidden, killed with my finery; so I made it into a capital carpet for us all to sit down upon. Here's this boy of mine, Margaret,—if you don't pack up your things as soon as you get this letter, a come straight off to see him, I shall think you're descended from King Herod!'

Margaret did long for a day of Edith's life—her freedom from care, her cheerful home, her sunny skies. If a wish could have transported her, she would have gone off; just for one day. She yearned for the strength which such a change would give,—even for a few hours to be in the midst of that bright life, and to feel young again. Not yet twenty! and she had had to bear up against such hard pressure that she felt quite old. That was her first feeling after reading Edith's letter. Then she read it again, and, forgetting herself, was amused at its likeness to Edith's self, and was laughing merrily over it when Mrs. Hale came into the drawing-room, leaning on Dixon's arm. Margaret flew to adjust the pillows. Her mother seemed more than usually feeble.

'What were you laughing at, Margaret?' asked she, as soon as she had recovered from the exertion of settling herself on the sofa.

'A letter I have had this morning from Edith. Shall I read it you, mamma?'

She read it aloud, and for a time it seemed to interest her mother, who kept wondering what name Edith had given to her boy, and suggesting all probable names, and all possible reasons why each and all of these names should be given. Into the very midst of these wonders Mr. Thornton came, bringing another offering of fruit for Mrs. Hale. He could not—say rather, he would not—deny himself the chance of the pleasure of seeing Margaret. He had no end in this but the present gratification. It was the sturdy wilfulness of a man usually most reasonable and self-controlled. He entered the room, taking in at a glance the fact of Margaret's presence; but after the first cold distant bow, he never seemed to let his eyes fall on her again. He only stayed to present his peaches—to speak some gentle kindly words—and then his cold offended eyes met Margaret's with a grave farewell, as he left the room. She sat down silent and pale.

'Do you know, Margaret, I really begin quite to like Mr. Thornton.'

No answer at first. Then Margaret forced out an icy 'Do you?'

'Yes! I think he is really getting quite polished in his manners.'

Margaret's voice was more in order now. She replied,

'He is very kind and attentive,—there is no doubt of that.'

'I wonder Mrs. Thornton never calls. She must know I am ill, because of the water-bed.'

'I dare say, she hears how you are from her son.'

'Still, I should like to see her. You have so few friends here, Margaret.'

Margaret felt what was in her mother's thoughts,—a tender craving to bespeak the kindness of some woman towards the daughter that might be so soon left motherless. But she could not speak.

'Do you think,' said Mrs. Hale, after a pause, 'that you could go and ask Mrs. Thornton to come and see me? Only once,—I don't want to be troublesome.'

'I will do anything, if you wish it, mamma,—but if—but when Frederick comes——'

'Ah, to be sure! we must keep our doors shut,—we must let no one in. I hardly know whether I dare wish him to come or not. Sometimes I think I would rather not. Sometimes I have such frightful dreams about him.'

'Oh, mamma! we'll take good care. I will put my arm in the bolt sooner than he should come to the slightest harm. Trust the care of him to me, mamma. I will watch over him like a lioness over her young.'

'When can we hear from him?'

'Not for a week yet, certainly,—perhaps more.'

'We must send Martha away in good time. It would never do to have her here when he comes, and then send her off in a hurry.'

'Dixon is sure to remind us of that. I was thinking that, if we wanted any help in the house while he is here, we could perhaps get Mary Higgins. She is very slack of work, and is a good girl, and would take pains to do her best, I am sure, and would sleep at home, and need never come upstairs, so as to know who is in the house.'

'As you please. As Dixon pleases. But, Margaret, don't get to use these horrid Milton words. "Slack of work:" it is a provincialism. What will your aunt Shaw say, if she hears you use it on her return?'

'Oh, mamma! don't try and make a bugbear of aunt Shaw' said Margaret, laughing. 'Edith picked up all sorts of military slang from Captain Lennox, and aunt Shaw never took any notice of it.'

'But yours is factory slang.'

'And if I live in a factory town, I must speak factory language when I want it. Why, mamma, I could astonish you with a great many words you never heard in your life. I don't believe you know what a knobstick is.'

'Not I, child. I only know it has a very vulgar sound and I don't want to hear you using it.'

'Very well, dearest mother, I won't. Only I shall have to use a whole explanatory sentence instead.'

'I don't like this Milton,' said Mrs. Hale. 'Edith is right enough in saying it's the smoke that has made me so ill.'

Margaret started up as her mother said this. Her father had just entered the room, and she was most anxious that the faint impression she had seen on his mind that the Milton air had injured her mother's health, should not be deepened,—should not receive any confirmation. She could not tell whether he had heard what Mrs. Hale had said or not; but she began speaking hurriedly of other things, unaware that Mr. Thornton was following him.

'Mamma is accusing me of having picked up a great deal of vulgarity since we came to Milton.'

The 'vulgarity' Margaret spoke of, referred purely to the use of local words, and the expression arose out of the conversation they had just been holding. But Mr. Thornton's brow darkened; and Margaret suddenly felt how her speech might be misunderstood by him; so, in the natural sweet desire to avoid giving unnecessary pain, she forced herself to go forwards with a little greeting, and continue what she was saying, addressing herself to him expressly.

'Now, Mr. Thornton, though "knobstick" has not a very pretty sound, is it not expressive? Could I do without it, in speaking of the thing it represents? If using local words is vulgar, I was very vulgar in the Forest,—was I not, mamma?'

It was unusual with Margaret to obtrude her own subject of conversation on others; but, in this case, she was so anxious to prevent Mr. Thornton from feeling annoyance at the words he had accidentally overheard, that it was not until she had done speaking that she coloured all over with consciousness, more especially as Mr. Thornton seemed hardly to understand the exact gist or bearing of what she was saying, but passed her by, with a cold reserve of ceremonious movement, to speak to Mrs. Hale.

The sight of him reminded her of the wish to see his mother, and commend Margaret to her care. Margaret, sitting in burning silence, vexed and ashamed of her difficulty in keeping her right place, and her calm unconsciousness of heart, when Mr. Thornton was by, heard her mother's slow entreaty that Mrs. Thornton would come and see her; see her soon; to-morrow, if it were possible. Mr. Thornton promised that she should—conversed a little, and then took his leave; and Margaret's movements and voice seemed at once released from some invisible chains. He never looked at her; and yet, the careful avoidance of his eyes betokened that in some way he knew exactly where, if they fell by chance, they would rest on her. If she spoke, he gave no sign of attention, and yet his next speech to any one else was modified by what she had said; sometimes there was an express answer to what she had remarked, but given to another person as though unsuggested by her. It was not the bad manners of ignorance; it was the wilful bad manners arising from deep offence. It was wilful at the time, repented of afterwards. But no deep plan, no careful cunning could have stood him in such good stead. Margaret thought about him more than she had ever done before; not with any tinge of what is called love, but with regret that she had wounded him so deeply,—and with a gentle, patient striving to return to their former position of antagonistic friendship; for a friend's position was what she found that he had held in her regard, as well as in that of the rest of the family. There was a pretty humility in her behaviour to him, as if mutely apologising for the over-strong words which were the reaction from the deeds of the day of the riot.

But he resented those words bitterly. They rung in his ears; and he was proud of the sense of justice which made him go on in every kindness he could offer to her parents. He exulted in the power he showed in compelling himself to face her, whenever he could think of any action which might give her father or mother pleasure. He thought that he disliked seeing one who had mortified him so keenly; but he was mistaken. It was a stinging pleasure to be in the room with her, and feel her presence. But he was no great analyser of his own motives, and was mistaken as I have said.

CHAPTER XXX - HOME AT LAST

'The saddest birds a season find to sing.'
SOUTHWELL.

'Never to fold the robe o'er secret pain,
Never, weighed down by memory's clouds again,
To bow thy head! Thou art gone home!'
MRS. HEMANS.

Mrs. Thornton came to see Mrs. Hale the next morning. She was much worse. One of those sudden changes—those great visible strides towards death, had been taken in the night, and her own family were startled by the gray sunken look her features had assumed in that one twelve hours of suffering. Mrs. Thornton—who had not seen her for weeks—was softened all at once. She had come because her son asked it from her as a personal favour, but with all the proud bitter feelings of her nature in arms against that family of which Margaret formed one. She doubted the reality of Mrs. Hale's illness; she doubted any want beyond a momentary fancy on that lady's part, which should take her out of her previously settled course of employment for the day. She told her son that she wished they had never come near the place; that he had never got acquainted with them; that there had been no such useless languages as Latin and Greek ever invented. He bore all this pretty silently; but when she had ended her invective against the dead languages, he quietly returned to the short, curt, decided expression of his wish that she should go and see Mrs. Hale at the time appointed, as most likely to be convenient to the invalid. Mrs. Thornton submitted with as bad a grace as she could to her son's desire, all the time liking him the better for having it; and exaggerating in her own mind the same notion that he had of extraordinary goodness on his part in so perseveringly keeping up with the Hales.

His goodness verging on weakness (as all the softer virtues did in her mind), and her own contempt for Mr. and Mrs. Hale, and positive dislike to Margaret, were the ideas which occupied Mrs. Thornton, till she was struck into nothingness before the dark shadow of the wings of the angel of death. There lay Mrs. Hale—a mother like herself—a much younger woman than she was,—on the bed from which there was no sign of hope that she might ever rise again. No more variety of light and shade for her in that darkened room; no power of action, scarcely change of movement; faint alternations of whispered sound and studious silence; and yet that monotonous life seemed almost too much! When Mrs. Thornton, strong and prosperous with life, came in, Mrs. Hale lay still, although from the look on her face she was evidently conscious of who it was. But she did not even open her eyes for a minute or two. The heavy moisture of tears stood on the eye-lashes before she looked up, then with her hand groping feebly over the bed-clothes, for the touch of Mrs. Thornton's large firm fingers, she said, scarcely above her breath—Mrs. Thornton had to stoop from her erectness to listen,—

'Margaret—you have a daughter—my sister is in Italy. My child will be without a mother;—in a strange place,—if I die—will you'——

And her filmy wandering eyes fixed themselves with an intensity of wistfulness on Mrs. Thornton's face. For a minute, there was no change in its rigidness; it was stern and unmoved;—nay, but that the eyes of the sick woman were growing dim with the slow-gathering tears, she might have seen a dark cloud cross the cold features. And it was no thought of her son, or of her living daughter Fanny, that stirred her heart at last; but a sudden remembrance, suggested by something in the arrangement of the room,—of a little daughter—dead in infancy—long years ago—that, like a sudden sunbeam, melted the icy crust, behind which there was a real tender woman.

'You wish me to be a friend to Miss Hale,' said Mrs. Thornton, in her measured voice, that would not soften with her heart, but came out distinct and clear.

Mrs. Hale, her eyes still fixed on Mrs. Thornton's face, pressed the hand that lay below hers on the coverlet. She could not speak. Mrs. Thornton sighed, 'I will be a true friend, if circumstances require it. Not a tender friend. That I cannot be,'—('to her,' she was on the point of adding, but she relented at the sight of that poor, anxious face.)—'It is not my nature to show affection even where I feel it, nor do I volunteer advice in general. Still, at your request,—if it will be any comfort to you, I will promise you.' Then came a pause. Mrs. Thornton was too conscientious to promise what she did not mean to perform; and to perform anything in the way of kindness on behalf of Margaret, more disliked at this moment than ever, was difficult; almost impossible.

'I promise,' said she, with grave severity; which, after all, inspired the dying woman with faith as in something more stable than life itself,—flickering, flitting, wavering life! 'I promise that in any difficulty in which Miss Hale'——

'Call her Margaret!' gasped Mrs. Hale.

'In which she comes to me for help, I will help her with every power I have, as if she were my own daughter. I also promise that if ever I see her doing what I think is wrong'——

'But Margaret never does wrong—not wilfully wrong,' pleaded Mrs. Hale. Mrs. Thornton went on as before; as if she had not heard:

'If ever I see her doing what I believe to be wrong—such wrong not touching me or mine, in which case I might be supposed to have an interested motive—I will tell her of it, faithfully and plainly, as I should wish my own daughter to be told.'

There was a long pause. Mrs. Hale felt that this promise did not include all; and yet it was much. It had reservations in it which she did not understand; but then she was weak, dizzy, and tired. Mrs. Thornton was reviewing all the probable cases in which she had pledged herself to act. She had a fierce pleasure in the idea of telling Margaret unwelcome truths, in the shape of performance of duty. Mrs. Hale began to speak:

'I thank you. I pray God to bless you. I shall never see you again in this world. But my last words are, I thank you for your promise of kindness to my child.'

'Not kindness!' testified Mrs. Thornton, ungraciously truthful to the last. But having eased her conscience by saying these words, she was not sorry that they were not heard. She pressed Mrs. Hale's soft languid hand; and rose up and went her way out of the house without seeing a creature.

During the time that Mrs. Thornton was having this interview with Mrs. Hale, Margaret and Dixon were laying their heads together, and consulting how they should keep Frederick's coming a profound secret to all out of the house. A letter from him might now be expected any day; and he would assuredly follow quickly on its heels. Martha must be sent away on her holiday; Dixon must keep stern guard on the front door, only admitting the few visitors that ever came to the house into Mr. Hale's room down-stairs—Mrs. Hale's extreme illness giving her a good excuse for this. If Mary Higgins was required as a help to Dixon in the kitchen she was to hear and see as little of Frederick as possible; and he was, if necessary to be spoken of to her under the name of Mr. Dickinson. But her sluggish and incurious nature was the greatest safeguard of all.

They resolved that Martha should leave them that very afternoon for this visit to her mother. Margaret wished that she had been sent away on the previous day, as she fancied it might be thought strange to give a servant a holiday when her mistress's state required so much attendance.

Poor Margaret! All that afternoon she had to act the part of a Roman daughter, and give strength out of her own scanty stock to her father. Mr. Hale would hope, would not despair, between the attacks of his wife's malady; he buoyed himself up in every respite from her pain, and believed that it was the beginning of ultimate recovery. And so, when the paroxysms came on, each more severe than the last, they were fresh agonies, and greater disappointments to him. This afternoon, he sat in the drawing-room, unable to bear the solitude of his study, or to employ himself in any way. He buried his head in his arms, which lay folded on the table. Margaret's heart ached to see him; yet, as he did not speak, she did not like to volunteer any attempt at comfort. Martha was gone. Dixon sat with Mrs. Hale while she slept. The house was very still and quiet, and darkness came on, without any movement to procure candles. Margaret sat at the window, looking out at the lamps and the street, but seeing nothing,—only alive to her father's heavy sighs. She did not like to go down for lights, lest the tacit restraint of her presence being withdrawn, he might give way to more violent emotion, without her being at hand to comfort him. Yet she was just thinking that she ought to go and see after the well-doing of the kitchen fire, which there was nobody but herself to attend to when she heard the muffled door-ring with so violent a pull, that the wires jingled all through the house, though the positive sound was not great. She started up, passed her father, who had never moved at the veiled, dull sound,—returned, and kissed him tenderly. And still he never moved, nor took any notice of her fond embrace. Then she went down softly, through the dark, to the door. Dixon would have put the chain on before she opened it, but Margaret had not a thought of fear in her pre-occupied mind. A man's tall figure stood between her and the luminous street. He was looking away; but at the sound of the latch he turned quickly round.

'Is this Mr. Hale's?' said he, in a clear, full, delicate voice.

Margaret trembled all over; at first she did not answer. In a moment she sighed out,

'Frederick!' and stretched out both her hands to catch his, and draw him in.

'Oh, Margaret!' said he, holding her off by her shoulders, after they had kissed each other, as if even in that darkness he could see her face, and read in its expression a quicker answer to his question than words could give,—

'My mother! is she alive?'

'Yes, she is alive, dear, dear brother! She—as ill as she can be she is; but alive! She is alive!'

'Thank God!' said he.

'Papa is utterly prostrate with this great grief.'

'You expect me, don't you?'

'No, we have had no letter.'

'Then I have come before it. But my mother knows I am coming?'

'Oh! we all knew you would come. But wait a little! Step in here. Give me your hand. What is this? Oh! your carpet-bag. Dixon has shut the shutters; but this is papa's study, and I can take you to a chair to rest yourself for a few minutes; while I go and tell him.'

She groped her way to the taper and the lucifer matches. She suddenly felt shy, when the little feeble light made them visible. All she could see was, that her brother's face was unusually dark in complexion, and she caught the stealthy look of a pair of remarkably long-cut blue eyes, that suddenly twinkled up with a droll consciousness of their mutual purpose of inspecting each other. But though the brother and sister had an instant of sympathy in their reciprocal glances, they did not exchange a word; only, Margaret felt sure that she should like her brother as a companion as much as she already loved him as a near relation. Her heart was wonderfully lighter as she went up-stairs; the sorrow was no less in reality, but it became less oppressive from having some one in precisely the same relation to it as that in which she stood. Not her father's desponding attitude had power to damp her now. He lay across the table, helpless as ever; but she had the spell by which to rouse him. She used it perhaps too violently in her own great relief.

'Papa,' said she, throwing her arms fondly round his neck; pulling his weary head up in fact with her gentle violence, till it rested in her arms, and she could look into his eyes, and let them gain strength and assurance from hers.

'Papa! guess who is here!'

He looked at her; she saw the idea of the truth glimmer into their filmy sadness, and be dismissed thence as a wild imagination.

He threw himself forward, and hid his face once more in his stretched-out arms, resting upon the table as heretofore. She heard him whisper; she bent tenderly down to listen. 'I don't know. Don't tell me it is Frederick—not Frederick. I cannot bear it,—I am too weak. And his mother is dying!' He began to cry and wail like a child. It was so different to all which Margaret had hoped and expected, that she turned sick with disappointment, and was silent for an instant. Then she spoke again—very differently—not so exultingly, far more tenderly and carefully.

'Papa, it is Frederick! Think of mamma, how glad she will be! And oh, for her sake, how glad we ought to be! For his sake, too,—our poor, poor boy!'

Her father did not change his attitude, but he seemed to be trying to understand the fact.

'Where is he?' asked he at last, his face still hidden in his prostrate arms.

'In your study, quite alone. I lighted the taper, and ran up to tell you. He is quite alone, and will be wondering why—'

'I will go to him,' broke in her father; and he lifted himself up and leant on her arm as on that of a guide.

Margaret led him to the study door, but her spirits were so agitated that she felt she could not bear to see the meeting. She turned away, and ran up-stairs, and cried most heartily. It was the first time she had dared to allow herself this relief for days. The strain had been terrible, as she now felt. But Frederick was come! He, the one precious brother, was there, safe, amongst them again! She could hardly believe it. She stopped her crying, and opened her bedroom door. She heard no sound of voices, and almost feared she might have dreamt. She went down-stairs, and listened at the study door. She heard the buzz of voices; and that was enough. She went into the kitchen, and stirred up the fire, and lighted the house, and prepared for the wanderer's refreshment. How fortunate it was that her mother slept! She knew that she did, from the candle-lighter thrust through the keyhole of her bedroom door. The traveller could be refreshed and bright, and the first excitement of the meeting with his father all be over, before her mother became aware of anything unusual.

When all was ready, Margaret opened the study door, and went in like a serving-maiden, with a heavy tray held in her extended arms. She was proud of serving Frederick. But he, when he saw her, sprang up in a minute, and relieved her of her burden. It was a type, a sign, of all the coming relief which his presence would bring. The brother and sister arranged the table together, saying little, but their hands touching, and their eyes speaking the natural language of expression, so intelligible to those of the same blood. The fire had gone out; and Margaret applied herself to light it, for the evenings had begun to be chilly; and yet it was desirable to make all noises as distant as possible from Mrs. Hale's room.

'Dixon says it is a gift to light a fire; not an art to be acquired.'

'Poeta nascitur, non fit,' murmured Mr. Hale; and Margaret was glad to hear a quotation once more, however languidly given.

'Dear old Dixon! How we shall kiss each other!' said Frederick. 'She used to kiss me, and then look in my face to be sure I was the right person, and then set to again! But, Margaret, what a bungler you are! I never saw such a little awkward, good-for-nothing pair of hands. Run away, and wash them, ready to cut bread-and-butter for me, and leave the fire. I'll manage it. Lighting fires is one of my natural accomplishments.'

So Margaret went away; and returned; and passed in and out of the room, in a glad restlessness that could not be satisfied with sitting still. The more wants Frederick had, the better she was pleased; and he understood all this by instinct. It was a joy snatched in the house of mourning, and the zest of it was all the more pungent, because they knew in the depths of their hearts what irremediable sorrow awaited them.

In the middle, they heard Dixon's foot on the stairs. Mr. Hale started from his languid posture in his great armchair, from which he had been watching his children in a dreamy way, as if they were acting some drama of happiness, which it was pretty to look at, but which was distinct from reality, and in which he had no part. He stood up, and faced the door, showing such a strange, sudden anxiety to conceal Frederick from the sight of any person entering, even though it were the faithful Dixon, that a shiver came over Margaret's heart: it reminded her of the new fear in their lives. She caught at Frederick's arm, and clutched it tight, while a stern thought compressed her brows, and caused her to set her teeth. And yet they knew it was only Dixon's measured tread. They heard her walk the length of the passage, into the kitchen. Margaret rose up.

'I will go to her, and tell her. And I shall hear how mamma is.' Mrs. Hale was awake. She rambled at first; but after they had given her some tea she was refreshed, though not disposed to talk. It was better that the night should pass over before she was told of her son's arrival. Dr. Donaldson's appointed visit would bring nervous excitement enough for the evening; and he might tell them how to prepare her for seeing Frederick. He was there, in the house; could be summoned at any moment.

Margaret could not sit still. It was a relief to her to aid Dixon in all her preparations for 'Master Frederick.' It seemed as though she never could be tired again. Each glimpse into the room where he sate by his father, conversing with him, about, she knew not what, nor cared to know,—was increase of strength to her. Her own time for talking and hearing would come at last, and she was too certain of this to feel in a hurry to grasp it now. She took in his appearance and liked it. He had delicate features, redeemed from effeminacy by the swarthiness of his complexion, and his quick intensity of expression. His eyes were generally merry-looking, but at times they and his mouth so suddenly changed, and gave her such an idea of latent passion, that it almost made her afraid. But this look was only for an instant; and had in it no doggedness, no vindictiveness; it was rather the instantaneous ferocity of expression that comes over the countenances of all natives of wild or southern countries—a ferocity which enhances the charm of the childlike softness into which such a look may melt away. Margaret might fear the violence of the impulsive nature thus occasionally betrayed, but there was nothing in it to make her distrust, or recoil in the least, from the new-found brother. On the contrary, all their intercourse was peculiarly charming to her from the very first. She knew then how much responsibility she had had to bear, from the exquisite sensation of relief which she felt in Frederick's presence. He understood his father and mother—their characters and their weaknesses, and went along with a careless freedom, which was yet most delicately careful not to hurt or wound any of their feelings. He seemed to know instinctively when a little of the natural brilliancy of his manner and conversation would not jar on the deep depression of his father, or might relieve his mother's pain. Whenever it would have been out of tune, and out of time, his patient devotion and watchfulness came into play, and made him an admirable nurse. Then Margaret was almost touched into tears by the allusions which he often made to their childish days in the New Forest; he had never forgotten her—or Helstone either—all the time he had been roaming among distant countries and foreign people. She might talk to him of the old spot, and never fear tiring him. She had been afraid of him before he came, even while she had longed for his coming; seven or eight years had, she felt, produced such great changes in herself that, forgetting how much of the original Margaret was left, she had reasoned that if her tastes and feelings had so materially altered, even in her stay-at-home life, his wild career, with which she was but imperfectly acquainted, must have almost substituted another Frederick for the tall stripling in his middy's uniform, whom she remembered looking up to with such admiring awe. But in their absence they had grown nearer to each other in age, as well as in many other things. And so it was that the weight, this sorrowful time, was lightened to Margaret. Other light than that of Frederick's presence she had none. For a few hours, the mother rallied on seeing her son. She sate with his hand in hers; she would not part with it even while she slept; and Margaret had to feed him like a baby, rather than that he should disturb her mother by removing a finger. Mrs. Hale wakened while they were thus engaged; she slowly moved her head round on the pillow, and smiled at her children, as she understood what they were doing, and why it was done.

'I am very selfish,' said she; 'but it will not be for long.' Frederick bent down and kissed the feeble hand that imprisoned his.

This state of tranquillity could not endure for many days, nor perhaps for many hours; so Dr. Donaldson assured Margaret. After the kind doctor had gone away, she stole down to Frederick, who, during the visit, had been adjured to remain quietly concealed in the back parlour, usually Dixon's bedroom, but now given up to him.

Margaret told him what Dr. Donaldson said.

'I don't believe it,' he exclaimed. 'She is very ill; she may be dangerously ill, and in immediate danger, too; but I can't imagine that she could be as she is, if she were on the point of death. Margaret! she should have some other advice—some London doctor. Have you never thought of that?'

'Yes,' said Margaret, 'more than once. But I don't believe it would do any good. And, you know, we have not the money to bring any great London surgeon down, and I am sure Dr. Donaldson is only second in skill to the very best,—if, indeed, he is to them.'

Frederick began to walk up and down the room impatiently.

'I have credit in Cadiz,' said he, 'but none here, owing to this wretched change of name. Why did my father leave Helstone? That was the blunder.'

'It was no blunder,' said Margaret gloomily. 'And above all possible chances, avoid letting papa hear anything like what you have just been saying. I can see that he is tormenting himself already with the idea that mamma would never have been ill if we had stayed at Helstone, and you don't know papa's agonising power of self-reproach!'

Frederick walked away as if he were on the quarter-deck. At last he stopped right opposite to Margaret, and looked at her drooping and desponding attitude for an instant.

'My little Margaret!' said he, caressing her. 'Let us hope as long as we can. Poor little woman! what! is this face all wet with tears? I will hope. I will, in spite of a thousand doctors. Bear up, Margaret, and be brave enough to hope!'

Margaret choked in trying to speak, and when she did it was very low.

'I must try to be meek enough to trust. Oh, Frederick! mamma was getting to love me so! And I was getting to understand her. And now comes death to snap us asunder!'

'Come, come, come! Let us go up-stairs, and do something, rather than waste time that may be so precious. Thinking has, many a time, made me sad, darling; but doing never did in all my life. My theory is a sort of parody on the maxim of "Get money, my son, honestly if you can; but get money." My precept is, "Do something, my sister, do good if you can; but, at any rate, do something."'

'Not excluding mischief,' said Margaret, smiling faintly through her tears.

'By no means. What I do exclude is the remorse afterwards. Blot your misdeeds out (if you are particularly conscientious), by a good deed, as soon as you can; just as we did a correct sum at school on the slate, where an incorrect one was only half rubbed out. It was better than wetting our sponge with our tears; both less loss of time where tears had to be waited for, and a better effect at last.'

If Margaret thought Frederick's theory rather a rough one at first, she saw how he worked it out into continual production of kindness in fact. After a bad night with his mother (for he insisted on taking his turn as a sitter-up) he was busy next morning before breakfast, contriving a leg-rest for Dixon, who was beginning to feel the fatigues of watching. At breakfast-time, he interested Mr. Hale with vivid, graphic, rattling accounts of the wild life he had led in Mexico, South America, and elsewhere. Margaret would have given up the effort in despair to rouse Mr.

Hale out of his dejection; it would even have affected herself and rendered her incapable of talking at all. But Fred, true to his theory, did something perpetually; and talking was the only thing to be done, besides eating, at breakfast.

Before the night of that day, Dr. Donaldson's opinion was proved to be too well founded. Convulsions came on; and when they ceased, Mrs. Hale was unconscious. Her husband might lie by her shaking the bed with his sobs; her son's strong arms might lift her tenderly up into a comfortable position; her daughter's hands might bathe her face; but she knew them not. She would never recognise them again, till they met in Heaven.

Before the morning came all was over.

Then Margaret rose from her trembling and despondency, and became as a strong angel of comfort to her father and brother. For Frederick had broken down now, and all his theories were of no use to him. He cried so violently when shut up alone in his little room at night, that Margaret and Dixon came down in affright to warn him to be quiet: for the house partitions were but thin, and the next-door neighbours might easily hear his youthful passionate sobs, so different from the slower trembling agony of after-life, when we become inured to grief, and dare not be rebellious against the inexorable doom, knowing who it is that decrees.

Margaret sate with her father in the room with the dead. If he had cried, she would have been thankful. But he sate by the bed quite quietly; only, from time to time, he uncovered the face, and stroked it gently, making a kind of soft inarticulate noise, like that of some mother-animal caressing her young. He took no notice of Margaret's presence. Once or twice she came up to kiss him; and he submitted to it, giving her a little push away when she had done, as if her affection disturbed him from his absorption in the dead. He started when he heard Frederick's cries, and shook his head:—'Poor boy! poor boy!' he said, and took no more notice. Margaret's heart ached within her. She could not think of her own loss in thinking of her father's case. The night was wearing away, and the day was at hand, when, without a word of preparation, Margaret's voice broke upon the stillness of the room, with a clearness of sound that startled even herself: 'Let not your heart be troubled,' it said; and she went steadily on through all that chapter of unspeakable consolation.

CHAPTER XXXI - 'SHOULD AULD ACQUAINTANCE BE FORGOT?'

'Show not that manner, and these features all,
The serpent's cunning, and the sinner's fall?'
CRABBE.

The chill, shivery October morning came; not the October morning of the country, with soft, silvery mists, clearing off before the sunbeams that bring out all the gorgeous beauty of colouring, but the October morning of Milton, whose silver mists were heavy fogs, and where the sun could only show long dusky streets when he did break through and shine. Margaret went languidly about, assisting Dixon in her task of arranging the house. Her eyes were continually blinded by tears, but she had no time to give way to regular crying. The father and brother depended upon her; while they were giving way to grief, she must be working, planning, considering. Even the necessary arrangements for the funeral seemed to devolve upon her.

When the fire was bright and crackling—when everything was ready for breakfast, and the tea-kettle was singing away, Margaret gave a last look round the room before going to summon Mr. Hale and Frederick. She wanted everything to look as cheerful as possible; and yet, when it did so, the contrast between it and her own thoughts forced her into sudden weeping. She was kneeling by the sofa, hiding her face in the cushions that no one might hear her cry, when she was touched on the shoulder by Dixon.

'Come, Miss Hale—come, my dear! You must not give way, or where shall we all be? There is not another person in the house fit to give a direction of any kind, and there is so much to be done. There's who's to manage the funeral; and who's to come to it; and where it's to be; and all to be settled: and Master Frederick's like one crazed with crying, and master never was a good one for settling; and, poor gentleman, he goes about now as if he was lost. It's bad enough, my dear, I know; but death comes to us all; and you're well off never to have lost any friend till now.' Perhaps so. But this seemed a loss by itself; not to bear comparison with any other event in the world. Margaret did not take any comfort from what Dixon said, but the unusual tenderness of the prim old servant's manner touched her to the heart; and, more from a desire to show her gratitude for this than for any other reason, she roused herself up, and smiled in answer to Dixon's anxious look at her; and went to tell her father and brother that breakfast was ready.

Mr. Hale came—as if in a dream, or rather with the unconscious motion of a sleep-walker, whose eyes and mind perceive other things than what are present. Frederick came briskly in, with a forced cheerfulness, grasped her hand, looked into her eyes, and burst into tears. She had to try and think of little nothings to say all breakfast-time, in order to prevent the recurrence of her companions' thoughts too strongly to the last meal they had taken together, when there had been a continual strained listening for some sound or signal from the sick-room.

After breakfast, she resolved to speak to her father, about the funeral. He shook his head, and assented to all she proposed, though many of her propositions absolutely contradicted one another. Margaret gained no real decision from him; and was leaving the room languidly, to have a consultation with Dixon, when Mr. Hale motioned her back to his side.

'Ask Mr. Bell,' said he in a hollow voice.

'Mr. Bell!' said she, a little surprised. 'Mr. Bell of Oxford?'

'Mr. Bell,' he repeated. 'Yes. He was my groom's-man.'

Margaret understood the association.

'I will write to-day,' said she. He sank again into listlessness. All morning she toiled on, longing for rest, but in a continual whirl of melancholy business.

Towards evening, Dixon said to her:

'I've done it, miss. I was really afraid for master, that he'd have a stroke with grief. He's been all this day with poor missus; and when I've listened at the door, I've heard him talking to her, and talking to her, as if she was alive. When I went in he would be quite quiet, but all in a maze like. So I thought to myself, he ought to be roused; and if it gives him a shock at first, it will, maybe, be the better afterwards. So I've been and told him, that I don't think it's safe for Master Frederick to be here. And I don't. It was only on Tuesday, when I was out, that I met a Southampton man—the first I've seen since I came to Milton; they don't make their way much up here, I think. Well, it was young Leonards, old Leonards the draper's son, as great a scamp as ever lived—who plagued his father almost to death, and then ran off to sea. I never could abide him. He was in the *Orion* at the same time as Master Frederick, I know; though I don't recollect if he was there at the mutiny.'

'Did he know you?' said Margaret, eagerly.

'Why, that's the worst of it. I don't believe he would have known me but for my being such a fool as to call out his name. He were a Southampton man, in a strange place, or else I should never have been so ready to call cousins with him, a nasty, good-for-nothing fellow. Says he, "Miss Dixon! who would ha' thought of seeing you here? But perhaps I mistake, and you're Miss Dixon no longer?" So I told him he might still address me as an unmarried lady, though if I hadn't been so particular, I'd had good chances of matrimony. He was polite enough: "He couldn't look at me and doubt me." But I were not to be caught with such chaff from such a fellow as him, and so I told him; and, by way of being even, I asked him after his father (who I knew had turned him out of doors), as if they was the best friends as ever was. So then, to spite me—for you see we were getting savage, for all we were so civil to each other—he began to inquire after Master Frederick, and said, what a scrape he'd got into (as if Master Frederick's scrapes would ever wash George Leonards' white, or make 'em look otherwise than nasty, dirty black), and how he'd be hung for mutiny if ever he were caught, and how a hundred pound reward had been offered for catching him, and what a disgrace he had been to his family—all to spite me, you see, my dear, because before now I've helped old Mr. Leonards to give George a good rating, down in Southampton. So I said, there were other families be thankful if they could think they were earning an honest living as I knew, who had far more cause to blush for their sons, and to far away from home. To which he made answer, like the impudent chap he is, that he were in a confidential situation, and if I knew of any young man who had been so unfortunate as to lead vicious courses, and wanted to turn steady, he'd have no objection to lend him his patronage. He, indeed! Why, he'd corrupt a saint. I've not felt so bad myself for years as when I were standing talking to him the other day. I could have cried to think I couldn't spite him better, for he kept smiling in my face, as if he took all my compliments for earnest; and I couldn't see that he minded what I said in the least, while I was mad with all his speeches.'

'But you did not tell him anything about us—about Frederick?'

'Not I,' said Dixon. 'He had never the grace to ask where I was staying; and I shouldn't have told him if he had asked. Nor did I ask him what his precious situation was. He was waiting for a bus, and just then it drove up, and he hailed it. But, to plague me to the last, he turned back before he got in, and said, "If you can help me to trap Lieutenant Hale, Miss Dixon, we'll go partners in the reward. I know you'd like to be my partner, now wouldn't you? Don't be shy, but say yes." And he jumped on the bus, and I saw his ugly face leering at me with a wicked smile to think how he'd had the last word of plaguing.'

Margaret was made very uncomfortable by this account of Dixon's.

'Have you told Frederick?' asked she.

'No,' said Dixon. 'I were uneasy in my mind at knowing that bad Leonards was in town; but there was so much else to think about that I did not dwell on it at all. But when I saw master sitting so stiff, and with his eyes so glazed and sad, I thought it might rouse him to have to think of Master Frederick's safety a bit. So I told him all, though I blushed to say how a young man had been speaking to me. And it has done master good. And if we're to keep Master Frederick in hiding, he would have to go, poor fellow, before Mr. Bell came.'

'Oh, I'm not afraid of Mr. Bell; but I am afraid of this Leonards. I must tell Frederick. What did Leonards look like?'

'A bad-looking fellow, I can assure you, miss. Whiskers such as I should be ashamed to wear—they are so red. And for all he said he'd got a confidential situation, he was dressed in fustian just like a working-man.'

It was evident that Frederick must go. Go, too, when he had so completely vaulted into his place in the family, and promised to be such a stay and staff to his father and sister. Go, when his cares for the living mother, and sorrow for the dead, seemed to make him one of those peculiar people who are bound to us by a fellow-love for them that are taken away. Just as Margaret was thinking all this, sitting over the drawing-room fire—her father restless and uneasy under the pressure of this newly-aroused fear, of which he had not as yet spoken—Frederick came in, his brightness dimmed, but the extreme violence of his grief passed away. He came up to Margaret, and kissed her forehead.

'How wan you look, Margaret!' said he in a low voice. 'You have been thinking of everybody, and no one has thought of you. Lie on this sofa—there is nothing for you to do.'

'That is the worst,' said Margaret, in a sad whisper. But she went and lay down, and her brother covered her feet with a shawl, and then sate on the ground by her side; and the two began to talk in a subdued tone.

Margaret told him all that Dixon had related of her interview with young Leonards. Frederick's lips closed with a long whew of dismay.

'I should just like to have it out with that young fellow. A worse sailor was never on board ship—nor a much worse man either. I declare, Margaret—you know the circumstances of the whole affair?'

'Yes, mamma told me.'

'Well, when all the sailors who were good for anything were indignant with our captain, this fellow, to curry favour—pah! And to think of his being here! Oh, if he'd a notion I was within twenty miles of him, he'd ferret me out to pay off old grudges. I'd rather anybody had the hundred pounds they think I am worth than that rascal. What a pity poor old Dixon could not be persuaded to give me up, and make a provision for her old age!'

'Oh, Frederick, hush! Don't talk so.'

Mr. Hale came towards them, eager and trembling. He had overheard what they were saying. He took Frederick's hand in both of his:

'My boy, you must go. It is very bad—but I see you must. You have done all you could—you have been a comfort to her.'

'Oh, papa, must he go?' said Margaret, pleading against her own conviction of necessity.

'I declare, I've a good mind to face it out, and stand my trial. If I could only pick up my evidence! I cannot endure the thought of being in the power of such a blackguard as Leonards. I could almost have enjoyed—in other circumstances—this stolen visit: it has had all the charm which the French-woman attributed to forbidden pleasures.'

'One of the earliest things I can remember,' said Margaret, 'was your being in some great disgrace, Fred, for stealing apples. We had plenty of our own—trees loaded with them; but some one had told you that stolen fruit tasted sweetest, which you took au pied de la lettre, and off you went a-robbing. You have not changed your feelings much since then.'

'Yes—you must go,' repeated Mr. Hale, answering Margaret's question, which she had asked some time ago. His thoughts were fixed on one subject, and it was an effort to him to follow the zig-zag remarks of his children—an effort which he did not make.

Margaret and Frederick looked at each other. That quick momentary sympathy would be theirs no longer if he went away. So much was understood through eyes that could not be put into words. Both coursed the same thought till it was lost in sadness. Frederick shook it off first:

'Do you know, Margaret, I was very nearly giving both Dixon and myself a good fright this afternoon. I was in my bedroom; I had heard a ring at the front door, but I thought the ringer must have done his business and gone away long ago; so I was on the point of making my appearance in the passage, when, as I opened my room door, I saw Dixon coming downstairs; and she frowned and kicked me into hiding again. I kept the door open, and heard a message given to some man that was in my father's study, and that then went away. Who could it have been? Some of the shopmen?'

'Very likely,' said Margaret, indifferently. 'There was a little quiet man who came up for orders about two o'clock.'

'But this was not a little man—a great powerful fellow; and it was past four when he was here.'

'It was Mr. Thornton,' said Mr. Hale. They were glad to have drawn him into the conversation.

'Mr. Thornton!' said Margaret, a little surprised. 'I thought—— '

'Well, little one, what did you think?' asked Frederick, as she did not finish her sentence.

'Oh, only,' said she, reddening and looking straight at him, 'I fancied you meant some one of a different class, not a gentleman; somebody come on an errand.'

'He looked like some one of that kind,' said Frederick, carelessly. 'I took him for a shopman, and he turns out a manufacturer.'

Margaret was silent. She remembered how at first, before she knew his character, she had spoken and thought of him just as Frederick was doing. It was but a natural impression that was made upon him, and yet she was a little annoyed by it. She was unwilling to speak; she wanted to make Frederick understand what kind of person Mr. Thornton was—but she was tongue-tied.

Mr. Hale went on. 'He came to offer any assistance in his power, I believe. But I could not see him. I told Dixon to ask him if he would like to see you—I think I asked her to find you, and you would go to him. I don't know what I said.'

'He has been a very agreeable acquaintance, has he not?' asked Frederick, throwing the question like a ball for any one to catch who chose.

'A very kind friend,' said Margaret, when her father did not answer.

Frederick was silent for a time. At last he spoke:

'Margaret, it is painful to think I can never thank those who have shown you kindness. Your acquaintances and mine must be separate. Unless, indeed, I run the chances of a court-martial, or unless you and my father would come to Spain.' He threw out this last suggestion as a kind of feeler; and then suddenly made the plunge. 'You don't know how I wish you would. I have a good position—the chance of a better,' continued he, reddening like a girl. 'That Dolores Barbour that I was telling you of, Margaret—I only wish you knew her; I am sure you would like—no, love is the right word, like is so poor—you would love her, father, if you knew her. She is not eighteen; but if she is in the same mind another year, she is to be my wife. Mr. Barbour won't let us call it an engagement. But if you would come, you would find friends everywhere, besides Dolores. Think of it, father. Margaret, be on my side.'

'No—no more removals for me,' said Mr. Hale. 'One removal has cost me my wife. No more removals in this life. She will be here; and here will I stay out my appointed time.'

'Oh, Frederick,' said Margaret, 'tell us more about her. I never thought of this; but I am so glad. You will have some one to love and care for you out there. Tell us all about it.'

'In the first place, she is a Roman Catholic. That's the only objection I anticipated. But my father's change of opinion—nay, Margaret, don't sigh.'

Margaret had reason to sigh a little more before the conversation ended. Frederick himself was Roman Catholic in fact, though not in profession as yet. This was, then, the reason why his sympathy in her extreme distress at her father's leaving the Church had been so faintly expressed in his letters. She had thought it was the carelessness of a sailor; but the truth was, that even then he was himself inclined to give up the form of religion into which he had been baptised, only that his opinions were tending in exactly the opposite direction to those of his father. How much love had to do with this change not even Frederick himself could have told. Margaret gave up talking about this branch of the subject at last; and, returning to the fact of the engagement, she began to consider it in some fresh light:

'But for her sake, Fred, you surely will try and clear yourself of the exaggerated charges brought against you, even if the charge of mutiny itself be true. If there were to be a court-martial, and you could find your witnesses, you might, at any rate, show how your disobedience to authority was because that authority was unworthily exercised.'

Mr. Hale roused himself up to listen to his son's answer.

'In the first place, Margaret, who is to hunt up my witnesses? All of them are sailors, drafted off to other ships, except those whose evidence would go for very little, as they took part, or sympathised in the affair. In the next place, allow me to tell you, you don't know what a court-martial is, and consider it as an assembly where justice is administered, instead of what it really is—a court where authority weighs nine-tenths in the balance, and evidence forms only the other tenth. In such cases, evidence itself can hardly escape being influenced by the prestige of authority.'

'But is it not worth trying, to see how much evidence might be discovered and arrayed on your behalf? At present, all those who knew you formerly, believe you guilty without any shadow of excuse. You have never tried to justify yourself, and we have never known where to seek for proofs of your justification. Now, for Miss Barbour's sake, make your conduct as clear as you can in the eye of the world. She may not care for it; she has, I am sure, that trust in you that we all have; but you ought not to let her ally herself to one under such a serious charge, without showing the world exactly how it is you stand. You disobeyed authority—that was bad; but to have stood by, without word or act, while the authority was brutally used, would have been infinitely worse. People know what you did; but not the motives that elevate it out of a crime into an heroic protection of the weak. For Dolores' sake, they ought to know.'

'But how must I make them know? I am not sufficiently sure of the purity and justice of those who would be my judges, to give myself up to a court-martial, even if I could bring a whole array of truth-speaking witnesses. I can't send a bellman about, to cry aloud and proclaim in the streets what you are pleased to call my heroism. No one would read a pamphlet of self-justification so long after the deed, even if I put one out.'

'Will you consult a lawyer as to your chances of exculpation?' asked Margaret, looking up, and turning very red.

'I must first catch my lawyer, and have a look at him, and see how I like him, before I make him into my confidant. Many a briefless barrister might twist his conscience into thinking that he could earn a hundred pounds very easily by doing a good action—in giving me, a criminal, up to justice.'

'Nonsense, Frederick!—because I know a lawyer on whose honour I can rely; of whose cleverness in his profession people speak very highly; and who would, I think, take a good deal of trouble for any of—of Aunt Shaw's relations. Mr. Henry Lennox, papa.'

'I think it is a good idea,' said Mr. Hale. 'But don't propose anything which will detain Frederick in England. Don't, for your mother's sake.'

'You could go to London to-morrow evening by a night-train,' continued Margaret, warming up into her plan. 'He must go to-morrow, I'm afraid, papa,' said she, tenderly; 'we fixed that, because of Mr. Bell, and Dixon's disagreeable acquaintance.'

'Yes; I must go to-morrow,' said Frederick decidedly.

Mr. Hale groaned. 'I can't bear to part with you, and yet I am miserable with anxiety as long as you stop here.'

'Well then,' said Margaret, 'listen to my plan. He gets to London on Friday morning. I will—you might—no! it would be better for me to give him a note to Mr. Lennox. You will find him at his chambers in the Temple.'

'I will write down a list of all the names I can remember on board the *Orion*. I could leave it with him to ferret them out. He is Edith's husband's brother, isn't he? I remember your naming him in your letters. I have money in Barbour's hands. I can pay a pretty long bill, if there is any chance of success. Money, dear father, that I had meant for a different purpose; so I shall only consider it as borrowed from you and Margaret.'

'Don't do that,' said Margaret. 'You won't risk it if you do. And it will be a risk only it is worth trying. You can sail from London as well as from Liverpool?'

'To be sure, little goose. Wherever I feel water heaving under a plank, there I feel at home. I'll pick up some craft or other to take me off, never fear. I won't stay twenty-four hours in London, away from you on the one hand, and from somebody else on the other.'

It was rather a comfort to Margaret that Frederick took it into his head to look over her shoulder as she wrote to Mr. Lennox. If she had not been thus compelled to write steadily and concisely on, she might have hesitated over many a word, and been puzzled to choose between many an expression, in the awkwardness of being the first to resume the intercourse of which the concluding event had been so unpleasant to both sides. However, the note was taken from her before she had even had time to look it over, and treasured up in a pocket-book, out of which fell a long lock of black hair, the sight of which caused Frederick's eyes to glow with pleasure.

'Now you would like to see that, wouldn't you?' said he. 'No! you must wait till you see her herself. She is too perfect to be known by fragments. No mean brick shall be a specimen of the building of my palace.'

CHAPTER XXXII - MISCHANCES

'What! remain to be
  Denounced—dragged, it may be, in chains.'
      WERNER.

All the next day they sate together—they three. Mr. Hale hardly ever spoke but when his children asked him questions, and forced him, as it were, into the present. Frederick's grief was no more to be seen or heard; the first paroxysm had passed over, and now he was ashamed of having been so battered down by emotion; and though his sorrow for the loss of his mother was a deep real feeling, and would last out his life, it was never to be spoken of again. Margaret, not so passionate at first, was more suffering now. At times she cried a good deal; and her manner, even when speaking on indifferent things, had a mournful tenderness about it, which was deepened whenever her looks fell on Frederick, and she thought of his rapidly approaching departure. She was glad he was going, on her father's account, however much she might grieve over it on her own. The anxious terror in which Mr. Hale lived lest his son should be detected and captured, far out-weighed the pleasure he derived from his presence. The nervousness had increased since Mrs. Hale's death, probably because he dwelt upon it more exclusively. He started at every unusual sound; and was never comfortable unless Frederick sate out of the immediate view of any one entering the room. Towards evening he said:

'You will go with Frederick to the station, Margaret? I shall want to know he is safely off. You will bring me word that he is clear of Milton, at any rate?'

'Certainly,' said Margaret. 'I shall like it, if you won't be lonely without me, papa.'

'No, no! I should always be fancying some one had known him, and that he had been stopped, unless you could tell me you had seen him off. And go to the Outwood station. It is quite as near, and not so many people about. Take a cab there. There is less risk of his being seen. What time is your train, Fred?'

'Ten minutes past six; very nearly dark. So what will you do, Margaret?'

'Oh, I can manage. I am getting very brave and very hard. It is a well-lighted road all the way home, if it should be dark. But I was out last week much later.'

Margaret was thankful when the parting was over—the parting from the dead mother and the living father. She hurried Frederick into the cab, in order to shorten a scene which she saw was so bitterly painful to her father, who would accompany his son as he took his last look at his mother. Partly in consequence of this, and partly owing to one of the very common mistakes in the 'Railway Guide' as to the times when trains arrive at the smaller stations, they found, on reaching Outwood, that they had nearly twenty minutes to spare. The booking-office was not open, so they could not even take the ticket. They accordingly went down the flight of steps that led to the level of the ground below the railway. There was a broad cinder-path diagonally crossing a field which lay along-side of the carriage-road, and they went there to walk backwards and forwards for the few minutes they had to spare.

Margaret's hand lay in Frederick's arm. He took hold of it affectionately.

'Margaret! I am going to consult Mr. Lennox as to the chance of exculpating myself, so that I may return to England whenever I choose, more for your sake than for the sake of any one else. I can't bear to think of your lonely position if anything should happen to my father. He looks sadly changed—terribly shaken. I wish you could get him to think of the Cadiz plan, for many reasons. What could you do if he were taken away? You have no friend near. We are curiously bare of relations.'

Margaret could hardly keep from crying at the tender anxiety with which Frederick was bringing before her an event which she herself felt was not very improbable, so severely had the cares of the last few months told upon Mr. Hale. But she tried to rally as she said:

'There have been such strange unexpected changes in my life during these last two years, that I feel more than ever that it is not worth while to calculate too closely what I should do if any future event took place. I try to think only upon the present.' She paused; they were standing still for a moment, close on the field side of the stile leading into the road; the setting sun fell on their faces. Frederick held her hand in his, and looked with wistful anxiety into her face, reading there more care and trouble than she would betray by words. She went on:

'We shall write often to one another, and I will promise—for I see it will set your mind at ease—to tell you every worry I have. Papa is'—she started a little, a hardly visible start—but Frederick felt the sudden motion of the hand he held, and turned his full face to the road, along which a horseman was slowly riding, just passing the very stile where they stood. Margaret bowed; her bow was stiffly returned.

'Who is that?' said Frederick, almost before he was out of hearing. Margaret was a little drooping, a little flushed, as she replied:

'Mr. Thornton; you saw him before, you know.'

'Only his back. He is an unprepossessing-looking fellow. What a scowl he has!'

'Something has happened to vex him,' said Margaret, apologetically. 'You would not have thought him unprepossessing if you had seen him with mamma.'

'I fancy it must be time to go and take my ticket. If I had known how dark it would be, we wouldn't have sent back the cab, Margaret.'

'Oh, don't fidget about that. I can take a cab here, if I like; or go back by the rail-road, when I should have shops and people and lamps all the way from the Milton station-house. Don't think of me; take care of yourself. I am sick with the thought that Leonards may be in the same train with you. Look well into the carriage before you get in.'

They went back to the station. Margaret insisted upon going into the full light of the flaring gas inside to take the ticket. Some idle-looking young men were lounging about with the stationmaster. Margaret thought she had seen the face of one of them before, and returned him a proud look of offended dignity for his somewhat impertinent stare of undisguised admiration. She went hastily to her brother, who was standing outside, and took hold of his arm. 'Have you got your bag? Let us walk about here on the platform,' said she, a little flurried at the idea of so soon being left alone, and her bravery oozing out rather faster than she liked to acknowledge even to herself. She heard a step following them along the flags; it stopped when they stopped, looking out along the line and hearing the whizz of the coming train. They did not speak; their hearts were too full. Another moment, and the train would be here; a minute more, and he would be gone. Margaret almost repented the urgency with which she had entreated him to go to London; it was throwing more chances of detection in his way. If he had sailed for Spain by Liverpool, he might have been off in two or three hours.

Frederick turned round, right facing the lamp, where the gas darted up in vivid anticipation of the train. A man in the dress of a railway porter started forward; a bad-looking man, who seemed to have drunk himself into a state of brutality, although his senses were in perfect order.

'By your leave, miss!' said he, pushing Margaret rudely on one side, and seizing Frederick by the collar.

'Your name is Hale, I believe?'

In an instant—how, Margaret did not see, for everything danced before her eyes—but by some sleight of wrestling, Frederick had tripped him up, and he fell from the height of three or four feet, which the platform was elevated above the space of soft ground, by the side of the railroad. There he lay.

'Run, run!' gasped Margaret. 'The train is here. It was Leonards, was it? oh, run! I will carry your bag.' And she took him by the arm to push him along with all her feeble force. A door was opened in a carriage—he jumped in; and as he leant out to say, 'God bless you, Margaret!' the train rushed past her; an she was left standing alone. She was so terribly sick and faint that she was thankful to be able to turn into the ladies' waiting-room, and sit down for an instant. At first she could do nothing but gasp for breath. It was such a hurry; such a sickening alarm; such a near chance. If the train had not been there at the moment, the man would have jumped up again and called for assistance to arrest him. She wondered if the man had got up: she tried to remember if she had seen him move; she wondered if he could have been seriously hurt. She ventured out; the platform was all alight, but still quite deserted; she went to the end, and looked over, somewhat fearfully. No one was there; and then she was glad she had made herself go, and inspect, for otherwise terrible thoughts would have haunted her dreams. And even as it was, she was so trembling and affrighted that she felt she could not walk home along the road, which did indeed seem lonely and dark, as she gazed down upon it from the blaze of the station. She would wait till the down train passed and take her seat in it. But what if Leonards recognised her as Frederick's companion! She peered about, before venturing into the booking-office to take her ticket. There were only some railway officials standing about; and talking loud to one another.

'So Leonards has been drinking again!' said one, seemingly in authority. 'He'll need all his boasted influence to keep his place this time.'

'Where is he?' asked another, while Margaret, her back towards them, was counting her change with trembling fingers, not daring to turn round until she heard the answer to this question.

'I don't know. He came in not five minutes ago, with some long story or other about a fall he'd had, swearing awfully; and wanted to borrow some money from me to go to London by the next up-train. He made all sorts of tipsy promises, but I'd something else to do than listen to him; I told him to go about his business; and he went off at the front door.'

'He's at the nearest vaults, I'll be bound,' said the first speaker. 'Your money would have gone there too, if you'd been such a fool as to lend it.'

'Catch me! I knew better what his London meant. Why, he has never paid me off that five shillings'—and so they went on.

And now all Margaret's anxiety was for the train to come. She hid herself once more in the ladies' waiting-room, and fancied every noise was Leonards' step—every loud and boisterous voice was his. But no one came near her until the train drew up; when she was civilly helped into a carriage by a porter, into whose face she durst not look till they were in motion, and then she saw that it was not Leonards'.

CHAPTER XXXIII - PEACE

'Sleep on, my love, in thy cold bed,
Never to be disquieted!
My last Good Night—thou wilt not wake
Till I thy fate shall overtake.'
DR. KING.

Home seemed unnaturally quiet after all this terror and noisy commotion. Her father had seen all due preparation made for her refreshment on her return; and then sate down again in his accustomed chair, to fall into one of his sad waking dreams. Dixon had got Mary Higgins to scold and direct in the kitchen; and her scolding was not the less energetic because it was delivered in an angry whisper; for, speaking above her breath she would have thought irreverent, as long as there was any one dead lying in the house. Margaret had resolved not to mention the crowning and closing affright to her father. There was no use in speaking about it; it had ended well; the only thing to be feared was lest Leonards should in some way borrow money enough to effect his purpose of following Frederick to London, and hunting him out there. But there were immense chances against the success of any such plan; and Margaret determined not to torment herself by thinking of what she could do nothing to prevent. Frederick would be as much on his guard as she could put him; and in a day or two at most he would be safely out of England.

'I suppose we shall hear from Mr. Bell to-morrow,' said Margaret.

'Yes,' replied her father. 'I suppose so.'

'If he can come, he will be here to-morrow evening, I should think.'

'If he cannot come, I shall ask Mr. Thornton to go with me to the funeral. I cannot go alone. I should break down utterly.'

'Don't ask Mr. Thornton, papa. Let me go with you,' said Margaret, impetuously.

'You! My dear, women do not generally go.'

'No: because they can't control themselves. Women of our class don't go, because they have no power over their emotions, and yet are ashamed of showing them. Poor women go, and don't care if they are seen overwhelmed with grief.

But I promise you, papa, that if you will let me go, I will be no trouble. Don't have a stranger, and leave me out. Dear papa! if Mr. Bell cannot come, I shall go. I won't urge my wish against your will, if he does.'

Mr. Bell could not come. He had the gout. It was a most affectionate letter, and expressed great and true regret for his inability to attend. He hoped to come and pay them a visit soon, if they would have him; his Milton property required some looking after, and his agent had written to him to say that his presence was absolutely necessary; or else he had avoided coming near Milton as long as he could, and now the only thing that would reconcile him to this necessary visit was the idea that he should see, and might possibly be able to comfort his old friend.

Margaret had all the difficulty in the world to persuade her father not to invite Mr. Thornton. She had an indescribable repugnance to this step being taken. The night before the funeral, came a stately note from Mrs. Thornton to Miss Hale, saying that, at her son's desire, their carriage should attend the funeral, if it would not be disagreeable to the family. Margaret tossed the note to her father.

'Oh, don't let us have these forms,' said she. 'Let us go alone—you and me, papa. They don't care for us, or else he would have offered to go himself, and not have proposed this sending an empty carriage.'

'I thought you were so extremely averse to his going, Margaret,' said Mr. Hale in some surprise.

'And so I am. I don't want him to come at all; and I should especially dislike the idea of our asking him. But this seems such a mockery of mourning that I did not expect it from him.' She startled her father by bursting into tears. She had been so subdued in her grief, so thoughtful for others, so gentle and patient in all things, that he could not understand her impatient ways to-night; she seemed agitated and restless; and at all the tenderness which her father in his turn now lavished upon her, she only cried the more.

She passed so bad a night that she was ill prepared for the additional anxiety caused by a letter received from Frederick. Mr. Lennox was out of town; his clerk said that he would return by the following Tuesday at the latest; that he might possibly be at home on Monday. Consequently, after some consideration, Frederick had determined upon remaining in London a day or two longer. He had thought of coming down to Milton again; the temptation had been very strong; but the idea of Mr. Bell domesticated in his father's house, and the alarm he had received at the last moment at the railway station, had made him resolve to stay in London. Margaret might be assured he would take every precaution against being tracked by Leonards. Margaret was thankful that she received this letter while her father was absent in her mother's room. If he had been present, he would have expected her to read it aloud to him, and it would have raised in him a state of nervous alarm which she would have found it impossible to soothe away. There was not merely the fact, which disturbed her excessively, of Frederick's detention in London, but there were allusions to the recognition at the last moment at Milton, and the possibility of a pursuit, which made her blood run cold; and how then would it have affected her father? Many a time did Margaret repent of having suggested and urged on the plan of consulting Mr. Lennox. At the moment, it had seemed as if it would occasion so little delay—add so little to the apparently small chances of detection; and yet everything that had since occurred had tended to make it so undesirable. Margaret battled hard against this regret of hers for what could not now be helped; this self-reproach for having said what had at the time appeared to be wise, but which after events were proving to have been so foolish. But her father was in too depressed a state of mind and body to struggle healthily; he would succumb to all these causes for morbid regret over what could not be recalled. Margaret summoned up all her forces to her aid. Her father seemed to have forgotten that they had any reason to expect a letter from Frederick that morning. He was absorbed in one idea—that the last visible token of the presence of his wife was to be carried away from him, and hidden from his sight. He trembled pitifully as the undertaker's man was arranging his crape draperies around him. He looked wistfully at Margaret; and, when released, he tottered towards her, murmuring, 'Pray for me, Margaret. I have no strength left in me. I cannot pray. I give her up because I must. I try to bear it: indeed I do. I know it is God's will. But I cannot see why she died. Pray for me, Margaret, that I may have faith to pray. It is a great strait, my child.'

Margaret sat by him in the coach, almost supporting him in her arms; and repeating all the noble verses of holy comfort, or texts expressive of faithful resignation, that she could remember. Her voice never faltered; and she herself gained strength by doing this. Her father's lips moved after her, repeating the well-known texts as her words suggested them; it was terrible to see the patient struggling effort to obtain the resignation which he had not strength to take into his heart as a part of himself.

Margaret's fortitude nearly gave way as Dixon, with a slight motion of her hand, directed her notice to Nicholas Higgins and his daughter, standing a little aloof, but deeply attentive to the ceremonial. Nicholas wore his usual fustian clothes, but had a bit of black stuff sewn round his hat—a mark of mourning which he had never shown to his daughter Bessy's memory. But Mr. Hale saw nothing. He went on repeating to himself, mechanically as it were, all the funeral service as it was read by the officiating clergyman; he sighed twice or thrice when all was ended; and then, putting his hand on Margaret's arm, he mutely entreated to be led away, as if he were blind, and she his faithful guide.

Dixon sobbed aloud; she covered her face with her handkerchief, and was so absorbed in her own grief, that she did not perceive that the crowd, attracted on such occasions, was dispersing, till she was spoken to by some one close at hand. It was Mr. Thornton. He had been present all the time, standing, with bent head, behind a group of people, so that, in fact, no one had recognised him.

'I beg your pardon,—but, can you tell me how Mr. Hale is? And Miss Hale, too? I should like to know how they both are.'

'Of course, sir. They are much as is to be expected. Master is terribly broke down. Miss Hale bears up better than likely.'

Mr. Thornton would rather have heard that she was suffering the natural sorrow. In the first place, there was selfishness enough in him to have taken pleasure in the idea that his great love might come in to comfort and console her; much the same kind of strange passionate pleasure which comes stinging through a mother's heart, when her drooping infant nestles close to her, and is dependent upon her for everything. But this delicious vision of what might have been—in which, in spite of all Margaret's repulse, he would have indulged only a few days ago—was miserably disturbed by the recollection of what he had seen near the Outwood station. 'Miserably disturbed!' that is not strong enough. He was haunted by the remembrance of the handsome young man, with whom she stood in an attitude of such familiar confidence; and the remembrance shot through him like an agony, till it made him clench his hands tight in order to subdue the pain. At that late hour, so far from home! It took a great moral effort to galvanise his trust—erewhile so perfect—in Margaret's pure and exquisite maidenliness, into life; as soon as the effort ceased, his trust dropped down dead and powerless: and all sorts of wild fancies chased each other like dreams through his mind. Here was a little piece of miserable, gnawing confirmation. 'She bore up better than likely' under this grief. She had then some hope to look to, so bright that even in her affectionate nature it could come in to lighten the dark hours of a daughter newly made motherless. Yes! he knew how she would love. He had not loved her without gaining that instinctive knowledge of what capabilities were in her. Her soul would walk in glorious sunlight if any man was worthy, by his power of loving, to win back her love. Even in her mourning she would rest with a peaceful faith upon his sympathy. His sympathy! Whose? That other man's. And that it was another was enough to make Mr. Thornton's pale grave face grow doubly wan and stern at Dixon's answer.

'I suppose I may call,' said he coldly. 'On Mr. Hale, I mean. He will perhaps admit me after to-morrow or so.'

He spoke as if the answer were a matter of indifference to him. But it was not so. For all his pain, he longed to see the author of it. Although he hated Margaret at times, when he thought of that gentle familiar attitude and all the attendant circumstances, he had a restless desire to renew her picture in his mind—a longing for the very atmosphere she breathed. He was in the Charybdis of passion, and must perforce circle and circle ever nearer round the fatal centre.

'I dare say, sir, master will see you. He was very sorry to have to deny you the other day; but circumstances was not agreeable just then.'

For some reason or other, Dixon never named this interview that she had had with Mr. Thornton to Margaret. It might have been mere chance, but so it was that Margaret never heard that he had attended her poor mother's funeral.

CHAPTER XXXIV - FALSE AND TRUE

'Truth will fail thee never, never!
  Though thy bark be tempest-driven,
  Though each plank be rent and riven,
  Truth will bear thee on for ever!'
              ANON.

The 'bearing up better than likely' was a terrible strain upon Margaret. Sometimes she thought she must give way, and cry out with pain, as the sudden sharp thought came across her, even during her apparently cheerful conversations with her father, that she had no longer a mother. About Frederick, too, there was great uneasiness. The Sunday post intervened, and interfered with their London letters; and on Tuesday Margaret was surprised and disheartened to find that there was still no letter. She was quite in the dark as to his plans, and her father was miserable at all this uncertainty. It broke in upon his lately acquired habit of sitting still in one easy chair for half a day together. He kept pacing up and down the room; then out of it; and she heard him upon the landing opening and shutting the bedroom doors, without any apparent object. She tried to tranquillise him by reading aloud; but it was evident he could not listen for long together. How thankful she was then, that she had kept to herself the additional cause for anxiety produced by their encounter with Leonards. She was thankful to hear Mr. Thornton announced. His visit would force her father's thoughts into another channel.

He came up straight to her father, whose hands he took and wrung without a word—holding them in his for a minute or two, during which time his face, his eyes, his look, told of more sympathy than could be put into words. Then he turned to Margaret. Not 'better than likely' did she look. Her stately beauty was dimmed with much watching and with many tears. The expression on her countenance was of gentle patient sadness—nay of positive present suffering. He had not meant to greet her otherwise than with his late studied coldness of demeanour; but he could not help going up to her, as she stood a little aside, rendered timid by the uncertainty of his manner of late, and saying the few necessary common-place words in so tender a voice, that her eyes filled with tears, and she turned away to hide her emotion. She took her work and sate down very quiet and silent. Mr.

Thornton's heart beat quick and strong, and for the time he utterly forgot the Outwood lane. He tried to talk to Mr. Hale: and—his presence always a certain kind of pleasure to Mr. Hale, as his power and decision made him, and his opinions, a safe, sure port—was unusually agreeable to her father, as Margaret saw.

Presently Dixon came to the door and said, 'Miss Hale, you are wanted.'

Dixon's manner was so flurried that Margaret turned sick at heart. Something had happened to Fred. She had no doubt of that. It was well that her father and Mr. Thornton were so much occupied by their conversation.

'What is it, Dixon?' asked Margaret, the moment she had shut the drawing-room door.

'Come this way, miss,' said Dixon, opening the door of what had been Mrs. Hale's bed-chamber, now Margaret's, for her father refused to sleep there again after his wife's death. 'It's nothing, miss,' said Dixon, choking a little. 'Only a police-inspector. He wants to see you, miss. But I dare say, it's about nothing at all.'

'Did he name—' asked Margaret, almost inaudibly.

'No, miss; he named nothing. He only asked if you lived here, and if he could speak to you. Martha went to the door, and let him in; she has shown him into master's study. I went to him myself, to try if that would do; but no—it's you, miss, he wants.'

Margaret did not speak again till her hand was on the lock of the study door. Here she turned round and said, 'Take care papa does not come down. Mr. Thornton is with him now.'

The inspector was almost daunted by the haughtiness of her manner as she entered. There was something of indignation expressed in her countenance, but so kept down and controlled, that it gave her a superb air of disdain. There was no surprise, no curiosity. She stood awaiting the opening of his business there. Not a question did she ask.

'I beg your pardon, ma'am, but my duty obliges me to ask you a few plain questions. A man has died at the Infirmary, in consequence of a fall, received at Outwood station, between the hours of five and six on Thursday evening, the twenty-sixth instant. At the time, this fall did not seem of much consequence; but it was rendered fatal, the doctors say, by the presence of some internal complaint, and the man's own habit of drinking.'

The large dark eyes, gazing straight into the inspector's face, dilated a little. Otherwise there was no motion perceptible to his experienced observation. Her lips swelled out into a richer curve than ordinary, owing to the enforced tension of the muscles, but he did not know what was their usual appearance, so as to recognise the unwonted sullen defiance of the firm sweeping lines. She never blenched or trembled. She fixed him with her eye. Now—as he paused before going on, she said, almost as if she would encourage him in telling his tale—'Well—go on!'

'It is supposed that an inquest will have to be held; there is some slight evidence to prove that the blow, or push, or scuffle that caused the fall, was provoked by this poor fellow's half-tipsy impertinence to a young lady, walking with the man who pushed the deceased over the edge of the platform. This much was observed by some one on the platform, who, however, thought no more about the matter, as the blow seemed of slight consequence. There is also some reason to identify the lady with yourself; in which case—'

'I was not there,' said Margaret, still keeping her expressionless eyes fixed on his face, with the unconscious look of a sleep-walker.

The inspector bowed but did not speak. The lady standing before him showed no emotion, no fluttering fear, no anxiety, no desire to end the interview. The information he had received was very vague; one of the porters, rushing out to be in readiness for the train, had seen a scuffle, at the other end of the platform, between Leonards and a gentleman accompanied by a lady, but heard no noise; and before the train had got to its full speed after starting, he had been almost knocked down by the headlong run of the enraged half intoxicated Leonards, swearing and cursing awfully. He had not thought any more about it, till his evidence was routed out by the inspector, who, on making some farther inquiry at the railroad station, had heard from the station-master that a young lady and gentleman had been there about that hour—the lady remarkably handsome—and said, by some grocer's assistant present at the time, to be a Miss Hale, living at Crampton, whose family dealt at his shop. There was no certainty that the one lady and gentleman were identical with the other pair, but there was great probability. Leonards himself had gone, half-mad with rage and pain, to the nearest gin-palace for comfort; and his tipsy words had not been attended to by the busy waiters there; they, however, remembered his starting up and cursing himself for not having sooner thought of the electric telegraph, for some purpose unknown; and they believed that he left with the idea of going there. On his way, overcome by pain or drink, he had lain down in the road, where the police had found him and taken him to the Infirmary: there he had never recovered sufficient consciousness to give any distinct account of his fall, although once or twice he had had glimmerings of sense sufficient to make the authorities send for the nearest magistrate, in hopes that he might be able to take down the dying man's deposition of the cause of his death. But when the magistrate had come, he was rambling about being at sea, and mixing up names of captains and lieutenants in an indistinct manner with those of his fellow porters at the railway; and his last words were a curse on the 'Cornish trick' which had, he said, made him a hundred pounds poorer than he ought to have been. The inspector ran all this over in his mind—the vagueness of the evidence to prove that Margaret had been at the station—the unflinching, calm denial which she gave to such a supposition. She stood awaiting his next word with a composure that appeared supreme.

'Then, madam, I have your denial that you were the lady accompanying the gentleman who struck the blow, or gave the push, which caused the death of this poor man?'

A quick, sharp pain went through Margaret's brain. 'Oh God! that I knew Frederick were safe!' A deep observer of human countenances might have seen the momentary agony shoot out of her great gloomy eyes, like the torture of some creature brought to bay. But the inspector though a very keen, was not a very deep observer. He was a little struck, notwithstanding, by the form of the answer, which sounded like a mechanical repetition of her first reply—not changed and modified in shape so as to meet his last question.

'I was not there,' said she, slowly and heavily. And all this time she never closed her eyes, or ceased from that glassy, dream-like stare. His quick suspicions were aroused by this dull echo of her former denial. It was as if she had forced herself to one untruth, and had been stunned out of all power of varying it.

He put up his book of notes in a very deliberate manner. Then he looked up; she had not moved any more than if she had been some great Egyptian statue.

'I hope you will not think me impertinent when I say, that I may have to call on you again. I may have to summon you to appear on the inquest, and prove an alibi, if my witnesses' (it was but one who had recognised her) 'persist in deposing to your presence at the unfortunate event.' He looked at her sharply. She was still perfectly quiet—no change of colour, or darker shadow of guilt, on her proud face. He thought to have seen her wince: he did not know Margaret Hale. He was a little abashed by her regal composure. It must have been a mistake of identity. He went on:

'It is very unlikely, ma'am, that I shall have to do anything of the kind. I hope you will excuse me for doing what is only my duty, although it may appear impertinent.'

Margaret bowed her head as he went towards the door. Her lips were stiff and dry. She could not speak even the common words of farewell. But suddenly she walked forwards, and opened the study door, and preceded him to the door of the house, which she threw wide open for his exit. She kept her eyes upon him in the same dull, fixed manner, until he was fairly out of the house. She shut the door, and went half-way into the study; then turned back, as if moved by some passionate impulse, and locked the door inside.

Then she went into the study, paused—tottered forward—paused again—swayed for an instant where she stood, and fell prone on the floor in a dead swoon.

CHAPTER XXXV - EXPIATION

'There's nought so finely spun
 But it cometh to the sun.'

Mr. Thornton sate on and on. He felt that his company gave pleasure to Mr. Hale; and was touched by the half-spoken wishful entreaty that he would remain a little longer—the plaintive 'Don't go yet,' which his poor friend put forth from time to time. He wondered Margaret did not return; but it was with no view of seeing her that he lingered. For the hour—and in the presence of one who was so thoroughly feeling the nothingness of earth—he was reasonable and self-controlled. He was deeply interested in all her father said,

'Of death, and of the heavy lull,
 And of the brain that has grown dull.'

It was curious how the presence of Mr. Thornton had power over Mr. Hale to make him unlock the secret thoughts which he kept shut up even from Margaret. Whether it was that her sympathy would be so keen, and show itself in so lively a manner, that he was afraid of the reaction upon himself, or whether it was that to his speculative mind all kinds of doubts presented themselves at such a time, pleading and crying aloud to be resolved into certainties, and that he knew she would have shrunk from the expression of any such doubts—nay, from him himself as capable of conceiving them—whatever was the reason, he could unburden himself better to Mr. Thornton than to her of all the thoughts and fancies and fears that had been frost-bound in his brain till now. Mr. Thornton said very little; but every sentence he uttered added to Mr. Hale's reliance and regard for him. Was it that he paused in the expression of some remembered agony, Mr. Thornton's two or three words would complete the sentence, and show how deeply its meaning was entered into. Was it a doubt—a fear—a wandering uncertainty seeking rest, but finding none—so tear-blinded were its eyes—Mr. Thornton, instead of being shocked, seemed to have passed through that very stage of thought himself, and could suggest where the exact ray of light was to be found, which should make the dark places plain. Man of action as he was, busy in the world's great battle, there was a deeper religion binding him to God in his heart, in spite of his strong wilfulness, through all his mistakes, than Mr. Hale had ever dreamed. They never spoke of such things again, as it happened; but this one conversation made them peculiar people to each other; knit them together, in a way which no loose indiscriminate talking about sacred things can ever accomplish. When all are admitted, how can there be a Holy of Holies?

And all this while, Margaret lay as still and white as death on the study floor! She had sunk under her burden. It had been heavy in weight and long carried; and she had been very meek and patient, till all at once her faith had given way, and she had groped in vain for help! There was a pitiful contraction of suffering upon her beautiful brows, although there was no other sign of consciousness remaining. The mouth—a little while ago, so sullenly projected in defiance—was relaxed and livid.

'E par che de la sua labbia si mova
Uno spirto soave e pien d'amore,
Chi va dicendo a l'anima: sospira!'

The first symptom of returning life was a quivering about the lips—a little mute soundless attempt at speech; but the eyes were still closed; and the quivering sank into stillness. Then, feebly leaning on her arms for an instant to steady herself, Margaret gathered herself up, and rose. Her comb had fallen out of her hair; and with an intuitive desire to efface the traces of weakness, and bring herself into order again, she sought for it, although from time to time, in the course of the search, she had to sit down and recover strength. Her head drooped forwards—her hands meekly laid one upon the other—she tried to recall the force of her temptation, by endeavouring to remember the details which had thrown her into such deadly fright; but she could not. She only understood two facts—that Frederick had been in danger of being pursued and detected in London, as not only guilty of manslaughter, but as the more unpardonable leader of the mutiny, and that she had lied to save him. There was one comfort; her lie had saved him, if only by gaining some additional time. If the inspector came again to-morrow, after she had received the letter she longed for to assure her of her brother's safety, she would brave shame, and stand in her bitter penance—she, the lofty Margaret—acknowledging before a crowded justice-room, if need were, that she had been as 'a dog, and done this thing.' But if he came before she heard from Frederick; if he returned, as he had half threatened, in a few hours, why! she would tell that lie again; though how the words would come out, after all this terrible pause for reflection and self-reproach, without betraying her falsehood, she did not know, she could not tell. But her repetition of it would gain time—time for Frederick.

She was roused by Dixon's entrance into the room; she had just been letting out Mr. Thornton.

He had hardly gone ten steps in the street, before a passing omnibus stopped close by him, and a man got down, and came up to him, touching his hat as he did so. It was the police-inspector.

Mr. Thornton had obtained for him his first situation in the police, and had heard from time to time of the progress of his protege, but they had not often met, and at first Mr. Thornton did not remember him.

'My name is Watson—George Watson, sir, that you got——'

'Ah, yes! I recollect. Why you are getting on famously, I hear.'

'Yes, sir. I ought to thank you, sir. But it is on a little matter of business I made so bold as to speak to you now. I believe you were the magistrate who attended to take down the deposition of a poor man who died in the Infirmary last night.'

'Yes,' replied Mr. Thornton. 'I went and heard some kind of a rambling statement, which the clerk said was of no great use. I'm afraid he was but a drunken fellow, though there is no doubt he came to his death by violence at last. One of my mother's servants was engaged to him, I believe, and she is in great distress today. What about him?'

'Why, sir, his death is oddly mixed up with somebody in the house I saw you coming out of just now; it was a Mr. Hale's, I believe.'

'Yes!' said Mr. Thornton, turning sharp round and looking into the inspector's face with sudden interest. 'What about it?'

'Why, sir, it seems to me that I have got a pretty distinct chain of evidence, inculpating a gentleman who was walking with Miss Hale that night at the Outwood station, as the man who struck or pushed Leonards off the platform and so caused his death. But the young lady denies that she was there at the time.'

'Miss Hale denies she was there!' repeated Mr. Thornton, in an altered voice. 'Tell me, what evening was it? What time?'

'About six o'clock, on the evening of Thursday, the twenty-sixth.'

They walked on, side by side, in silence for a minute or two. The inspector was the first to speak.

'You see, sir, there is like to be a coroner's inquest; and I've got a young man who is pretty positive,—at least he was at first;—since he has heard of the young lady's denial, he says he should not like to swear; but still he's pretty positive that he saw Miss Hale at the station, walking about with a gentleman, not five minutes before the time, when one of the porters saw a scuffle, which he set down to some of Leonards' impudence—but which led to the fall which caused his death. And seeing you come out of the very house, sir, I thought I might make bold to ask if—you see, it's always awkward having to do with cases of disputed identity, and one doesn't like to doubt the word of a respectable young woman unless one has strong proof to the contrary.'

'And she denied having been at the station that evening!' repeated Mr. Thornton, in a low, brooding tone.

'Yes, sir, twice over, as distinct as could be. I told her I should call again, but seeing you just as I was on my way back from questioning the young man who said it was her, I thought I would ask your advice, both as the magistrate who saw Leonards on his death-bed, and as the gentleman who got me my berth in the force.'

'You were quite right,' said Mr. Thornton. 'Don't take any steps till you have seen me again.'

'The young lady will expect me to call, from what I said.'

'I only want to delay you an hour. It's now three. Come to my warehouse at four.'

'Very well, sir!'

And they parted company. Mr. Thornton hurried to his warehouse, and, sternly forbidding his clerks to allow any one to interrupt him, he went his way to his own private room, and locked the door. Then he indulged himself in the torture of thinking it all over, and realising every detail. How could he have lulled himself into the unsuspicious calm in which her tearful image had mirrored itself not two hours before, till he had weakly pitied her and yearned towards her, and forgotten the savage, distrustful jealousy with which the sight of her—and that unknown to him—at such an hour—in such a place—had inspired him! How could one so pure have stooped from her decorous and noble manner of bearing! But was it decorous—was it? He hated himself for the idea that forced itself upon him, just for an instant—no more—and yet, while it was present, thrilled him with its old potency of attraction towards her image. And then this falsehood—how terrible must be some dread of shame to be revealed—for, after all, the provocation given by such a man as Leonards was, when excited by drinking, might, in all probability, be more than enough to justify any one who came forward to state the circumstances openly and without reserve! How creeping and deadly that fear which could bow down the truthful Margaret to falsehood! He could almost pity her. What would be the end of it? She could not have considered all she was entering upon; if there was an inquest and the young man came forward. Suddenly he started up. There should be no inquest. He would save Margaret. He would take the responsibility of preventing the inquest, the issue of which, from the uncertainty of the medical testimony (which he had vaguely heard the night before, from the surgeon in attendance), could be but doubtful; the doctors had discovered an internal disease far advanced, and sure to prove fatal; they had stated that death might have been accelerated by the fall, or by the subsequent drinking and exposure to cold. If he had but known how Margaret would have become involved in the affair—if he had but foreseen that she would have stained her whiteness by a falsehood, he could have saved her by a word; for the question, of inquest or no inquest, had hung trembling in the balance only the night before. Miss Hale might love another—was indifferent and contemptuous to him—but he would yet do her faithful acts of service of which she should never know. He might despise her, but the woman whom he had once loved should be kept from shame; and shame it would be to pledge herself to a lie in a public court, or otherwise to stand and acknowledge her reason for desiring darkness rather than light.

Very gray and stern did Mr. Thornton look, as he passed out through his wondering clerks. He was away about half an hour; and scarcely less stern did he look when he returned, although his errand had been successful.

He wrote two lines on a slip of paper, put it in an envelope, and sealed it up. This he gave to one of the clerks, saying:—

'I appointed Watson—he who was a packer in the warehouse, and who went into the police—to call on me at four o'clock. I have just met with a gentleman from Liverpool who wishes to see me before he leaves town. Take care to give this note to Watson when he calls.'

The note contained these words:

'There will be no inquest. Medical evidence not sufficient to justify it. Take no further steps. I have not seen the coroner; but I will take the responsibility.'

'Well,' thought Watson, 'it relieves me from an awkward job. None of my witnesses seemed certain of anything except the young woman. She was clear and distinct enough; the porter at the rail-road had seen a scuffle; or when he found it was likely to bring him in as a witness, then it might not have been a scuffle, only a little larking, and Leonards might have jumped off the platform himself;—he would not stick firm to anything. And Jennings, the grocer's shopman,—well, he was not quite so bad, but I doubt if I could have got him up to an oath after he heard that Miss Hale flatly denied it. It would have been a troublesome job and no satisfaction. And now I must go and tell them they won't be wanted.'

He accordingly presented himself again at Mr. Hale's that evening. Her father and Dixon would fain have persuaded Margaret to go to bed; but they, neither of them, knew the reason for her low continued refusals to do so. Dixon had learnt part of the truth—but only part. Margaret would not tell any human being of what she had said, and she did not reveal the fatal termination to Leonards' fall from the platform. So Dixon curiosity combined with her allegiance to urge Margaret to go to rest, which her appearance, as she lay on the sofa, showed but too clearly that she required. She did not speak except when spoken to; she tried to smile back in reply to her father's anxious looks and words of tender enquiry; but, instead of a smile, the wan lips resolved themselves into a sigh. He was so miserably uneasy that, at last, she consented to go into her own room, and prepare for going to bed. She was indeed inclined to give up the idea that the inspector would call again that night, as it was already past nine o'clock.

She stood by her father, holding on to the back of his chair.

'You will go to bed soon, papa, won't you? Don't sit up alone!'

What his answer was she did not hear; the words were lost in the far smaller point of sound that magnified itself to her fears, and filled her brain. There was a low ring at the door-bell.

She kissed her father and glided down stairs, with a rapidity of motion of which no one would have thought her capable, who had seen her the minute before. She put aside Dixon.

'Don't come; I will open the door. I know it is him—I can—I must manage it all myself.'

'As you please, miss!' said Dixon testily; but in a moment afterwards, she added, 'But you're not fit for it. You are more dead than alive.'

'Am I?' said Margaret, turning round and showing her eyes all aglow with strange fire, her cheeks flushed, though her lips were baked and livid still.

She opened the door to the Inspector, and preceded him into the study. She placed the candle on the table, and snuffed it carefully, before she turned round and faced him.

'You are late!' said she. 'Well?' She held her breath for the answer.

'I'm sorry to have given any unnecessary trouble, ma'am; for, after all, they've given up all thoughts of holding an inquest. I have had other work to do and other people to see, or I should have been here before now.'

'Then it is ended,' said Margaret. 'There is to be no further enquiry.'

'I believe I've got Mr. Thornton's note about me,' said the Inspector, fumbling in his pocket-book.

'Mr. Thornton's!' said Margaret.

'Yes! he's a magistrate—ah! here it is.' She could not see to read it—no, not although she was close to the candle. The words swam before her. But she held it in her hand, and looked at it as if she were intently studying it.

'I'm sure, ma'am, it's a great weight off my mind; for the evidence was so uncertain, you see, that the man had received any blow at all,—and if any question of identity came in, it so complicated the case, as I told Mr. Thornton—'

'Mr. Thornton!' said Margaret, again.

'I met him this morning, just as he was coming out of this house, and, as he's an old friend of mine, besides being the magistrate who saw Leonards last night, I made bold to tell him of my difficulty.'

Margaret sighed deeply. She did not want to hear any more; she was afraid alike of what she had heard, and of what she might hear. She wished that the man would go. She forced herself to speak.

'Thank you for calling. It is very late. I dare say it is past ten o'clock. Oh! here is the note!' she continued, suddenly interpreting the meaning of the hand held out to receive it. He was putting it up, when she said, 'I think it is a cramped, dazzling sort of writing. I could not read it; will you just read it to me?'

He read it aloud to her.

'Thank you. You told Mr. Thornton that I was not there?'

'Oh, of course, ma'am. I'm sorry now that I acted upon information, which seems to have been so erroneous. At first the young man was so positive; and now he says that he doubted all along, and hopes that his mistake won't have occasioned you such annoyance as to lose their shop your custom. Good night, ma'am.'

'Good night.' She rang the bell for Dixon to show him out. As Dixon returned up the passage Margaret passed her swiftly.

'It is all right!' said she, without looking at Dixon; and before the woman could follow her with further questions she had sped up-stairs, and entered her bedchamber, and bolted her door.

She threw herself, dressed as she was, upon her bed. She was too much exhausted to think. Half an hour or more elapsed before the cramped nature of her position, and the chilliness, supervening upon great fatigue, had the power to rouse her numbed faculties. Then she began to recall, to combine, to wonder. The first idea that presented itself to her was, that all this sickening alarm on Frederick's behalf was over; that the strain was past. The next was a wish to remember every word of the Inspector's which related to Mr. Thornton. When had he seen him? What had he said? What had Mr. Thornton done? What were the exact words of his note? And until she could recollect, even to the placing or omitting an article, the very expressions which he had used in the note, her mind refused to go on with its progress. But the next conviction she came to was clear enough;—Mr. Thornton had seen her close to Outwood station on the fatal Thursday night, and had been told of her denial that she was there. She stood as a liar in his eyes. She was a liar. But she had no thought of penitence before God; nothing but chaos and night surrounded the one lurid fact that, in Mr. Thornton's eyes, she was degraded. She cared not to think, even to herself, of how much of excuse she might plead. That had nothing to do with Mr. Thornton; she never dreamed that he, or any one else, could find cause for suspicion in what was so natural as her accompanying her brother; but what was really false and wrong was known to him, and he had a right to judge her. 'Oh, Frederick! Frederick!' she cried, 'what have I not sacrificed for you!' Even when she fell asleep her thoughts were compelled to travel the same circle, only with exaggerated and monstrous circumstances of pain.

When she awoke a new idea flashed upon her with all the brightness of the morning. Mr. Thornton had learnt her falsehood before he went to the coroner; that suggested the thought, that he had possibly been influenced so to do with a view of sparing her the repetition of her denial. But she pushed this notion on one side with the sick wilfulness of a child. If it were so, she felt no gratitude to him, as it only showed her how keenly he must have seen that she was disgraced already, before he took such unwonted pains to spare her any further trial of truthfulness, which had already failed so signally. She would have gone through the whole—she would have perjured herself to save Frederick, rather—far rather—than Mr. Thornton should have had the knowledge that prompted him to interfere to save her. What ill-fate brought him in contact with the Inspector? What made him be the very magistrate sent for to receive Leonards' deposition? What had Leonards said? How much of it was intelligible to Mr. Thornton, who might already, for aught she knew, be aware of the old accusation against Frederick, through their mutual friend, Mr. Bell? If so, he had striven to save the son, who came in defiance of the law to attend his mother's death-bed. And under this idea she could feel grateful—not yet, if ever she should, if his interference had been prompted by contempt. Oh! had any one such just cause to feel contempt for her? Mr. Thornton, above all people, on whom she had looked down from her imaginary heights till now! She suddenly found herself at his feet, and was strangely distressed at her fall. She shrank from following out the premises to their conclusion, and so acknowledging to herself how much she valued his respect and good opinion. Whenever this idea presented itself to her at the end of a long avenue of thoughts, she turned away from following that path—she would not believe in it.

It was later than she fancied, for in the agitation of the previous night, she had forgotten to wind up her watch; and Mr. Hale had given especial orders that she was not to be disturbed by the usual awakening. By and by the door opened cautiously, and Dixon put her head in. Perceiving that Margaret was awake, she came forwards with a letter.

'Here's something to do you good, miss. A letter from Master Frederick.'

'Thank you, Dixon. How late it is!'

She spoke very languidly, and suffered Dixon to lay it on the counterpane before her, without putting out a hand to lake it.

'You want your breakfast, I'm sure. I will bring it you in a minute. Master has got the tray all ready, I know.'

Margaret did not reply; she let her go; she felt that she must be alone before she could open that letter. She opened it at last. The first thing that caught her eye was the date two days earlier than she received it. He had then written when he had promised, and their alarm might have been spared. But she would read the letter and see. It was hasty enough, but perfectly satisfactory. He had seen Henry Lennox, who knew enough of the case to shake his head over it, in the first instance, and tell him he had done a very daring thing in returning to England, with such an accusation, backed by such powerful influence, hanging over him. But when they had come to talk it over, Mr. Lennox had acknowledged that there might be some chance of his acquittal, if he could but prove his statements by credible witnesses—that in such case it might be worth while to stand his trial, otherwise it would be a great risk. He would examine—he would take every pains. 'It struck me' said Frederick, 'that your introduction, little sister of mine, went a long way. Is it so? He made many inquiries, I can assure you. He seemed a sharp, intelligent fellow, and in good practice too, to judge from the signs of business and the number of clerks about him. But these may be only lawyer's dodges. I have just caught a packet on the point of sailing—I am off in five minutes. I may have to come back to England again on this business, so keep my visit secret. I shall send my father some rare old sherry, such as you cannot buy in England,—(such stuff as I've got in the bottle before me)! He needs something of the kind—my dear love to him—God bless him. I'm sure—here's my cab. P.S.—What an escape that was! Take care you don't breathe of my having been—not even to the Shaws.'

Margaret turned to the envelope; it was marked 'Too late.' The letter had probably been trusted to some careless waiter, who had forgotten to post it. Oh! what slight cobwebs of chances stand between us and Temptation! Frederick had been safe, and out of England twenty, nay, thirty hours ago; and it was only about seventeen hours since she had told a falsehood to baffle pursuit, which even then would have been vain. How faithless she had been! Where now was her proud motto, *'Fais ce que dois, advienne que pourra?'* If she had but dared to bravely tell the truth as regarded herself, defying them to find out what she refused to tell concerning another, how light of heart she would now have felt! Not humbled before God, as having failed in trust towards Him; not degraded and abased in Mr. Thornton's sight. She caught herself up at this with a miserable tremor; here was she classing his low opinion of her alongside with the displeasure of God. How was it that he haunted her imagination so persistently? What could it be? Why did she care for what he thought, in spite of all her pride in spite of herself? She believed that she could have borne the sense of Almighty displeasure, because He knew all, and could read her penitence, and hear her cries for help in time to come. But Mr. Thornton—why did she tremble, and hide her face in the pillow? What strong feeling had overtaken her at last?

She sprang out of bed and prayed long and earnestly. It soothed and comforted her so to open her heart. But as soon as she reviewed her position she found the sting was still there; that she was not good enough, nor pure enough to be indifferent to the lowered opinion of a fellow creature; that the thought of how he must be looking upon her with contempt, stood between her and her sense of wrongdoing. She took her letter in to her father as soon as she was drest. There was so slight an allusion to their alarm at the rail-road station, that Mr. Hale passed over it without paying any attention to it. Indeed, beyond the mere fact of Frederick having sailed undiscovered and unsuspected, he did not gather much from the letter at the time, he was so uneasy about Margaret's pallid looks. She seemed continually on the point of weeping.

'You are sadly overdone, Margaret. It is no wonder. But you must let me nurse you now.'

He made her lie down on the sofa, and went for a shawl to cover her with. His tenderness released her tears; and she cried bitterly.

'Poor child!—poor child!' said he, looking fondly at her, as she lay with her face to the wall, shaking with her sobs. After a while they ceased, and she began to wonder whether she durst give herself the relief of telling her father of all her trouble. But there were more reasons against it than for it. The only one for it was the relief to herself; and against it was the thought that it would add materially to her father's nervousness, if it were indeed necessary for Frederick to come to England again; that he would dwell on the circumstance of his son's having caused the death of a man, however unwittingly and unwillingly; that this knowledge would perpetually recur to trouble him, in various shapes of exaggeration and distortion from the simple truth. And about her own great fault—he would be distressed beyond measure at her want of courage and faith, yet perpetually troubled to make excuses for her. Formerly Margaret would have come to him as priest as well as father, to tell him of her temptation and her sin; but latterly they had not spoken much on such subjects; and she knew not how, in his change of opinions, he would reply if the depth of her soul called unto his. No; she would keep her secret, and bear the burden alone. Alone she would go before God, and cry for His absolution. Alone she would endure her disgraced position in the opinion of Mr. Thornton. She was unspeakably touched by the tender efforts of her father to think of cheerful subjects on which to talk, and so to take her thoughts away from dwelling on all that had happened of late. It was some months since he had been so talkative as he was this day. He would not let her sit up, and offended Dixon desperately by insisting on waiting upon her himself.

At last she smiled; a poor, weak little smile; but it gave him the truest pleasure.

'It seems strange to think, that what gives us most hope for the future should be called Dolores,' said Margaret. The remark was more in character with her father than with her usual self; but to-day they seemed to have changed natures.

'Her mother was a Spaniard, I believe: that accounts for her religion. Her father was a stiff Presbyterian when I knew him. But it is a very soft and pretty name.'

'How young she is!—younger by fourteen months than I am. Just, the age that Edith was when she was engaged to Captain Lennox. Papa, we will go and see them in Spain.'

He shook his head. But he said, 'If you wish it, Margaret. Only let us come back here. It would seem unfair—unkind to your mother, who always, I'm afraid, disliked Milton so much, if we left it now she is lying here, and cannot go with us. No, dear; you shall go and see them, and bring me back a report of my Spanish daughter.'

'No, papa, I won't go without you. Who is to take care of you when I am gone?'

'I should like to know which of us is taking care of the other. But if you went, I should persuade Mr. Thornton to let me give him double lessons. We would work up the classics famously. That would be a perpetual interest. You might go on, and see Edith at Corfu, if you liked.'

Margaret did not speak all at once. Then she said rather gravely: 'Thank you, papa. But I don't want to go. We will hope that Mr. Lennox will manage so well, that Frederick may bring Dolores to see us when they are married. And as for Edith, the regiment won't remain much longer in Corfu. Perhaps we shall see both of them here before another year is out.'

Mr. Hale's cheerful subjects had come to an end. Some painful recollection had stolen across his mind, and driven him into silence. By-and-by Margaret said:

'Papa—did you see Nicholas Higgins at the funeral? He was there, and Mary too. Poor fellow! it was his way of showing sympathy. He has a good warm heart under his bluff abrupt ways.'

'I am sure of it,' replied Mr. Hale. 'I saw it all along, even while you tried to persuade me that he was all sorts of bad things. We will go and see them to-morrow, if you are strong enough to walk so far.'

'Oh yes. I want to see them. We did not pay Mary—or rather she refused to take it, Dixon says. We will go so as to catch him just after his dinner, and before he goes to his work.'

Towards evening Mr. Hale said:

'I half expected Mr. Thornton would have called. He spoke of a book yesterday which he had, and which I wanted to see. He said he would try and bring it to-day.'

Margaret sighed. She knew he would not come. He would be too delicate to run the chance of meeting her, while her shame must be so fresh in his memory. The very mention of his name renewed her trouble, and produced a relapse into the feeling of depressed, pre-occupied exhaustion. She gave way to listless languor. Suddenly it struck her that this was a strange manner to show her patience, or to reward her father for his watchful care of her all through the day. She sate up and offered to read aloud. His eyes were failing, and he gladly accepted her proposal. She read well: she gave the due emphasis; but had any one asked her, when she had ended, the meaning of what she had been reading, she could not have told. She was smitten with a feeling of ingratitude to Mr. Thornton, inasmuch as, in the morning, she had refused to accept the kindness he had shown her in making further inquiry from the medical men, so as to obviate any inquest being held. Oh! she was grateful! She had been cowardly and false, and had shown her cowardliness and falsehood in action that could not be recalled; but she was not ungrateful. It sent a glow to her heart, to know how she could feel towards one who had reason to despise her. His cause for contempt was so just, that she should have respected him less if she had thought he did not feel contempt. It was a pleasure to feel how thoroughly she respected him. He could not prevent her doing that; it was the one comfort in all this misery.

Late in the evening, the expected book arrived, 'with Mr. Thornton's kind regards, and wishes to know how Mr. Hale is.'

'Say that I am much better, Dixon, but that Miss Hale—'

'No, papa,' said Margaret, eagerly—'don't say anything about me. He does not ask.'

'My dear child, how you are shivering!' said her father, a few minutes afterwards. 'You must go to bed directly. You have turned quite pale!'

Margaret did not refuse to go, though she was loth to leave her father alone. She needed the relief of solitude after a day of busy thinking, and busier repenting.

But she seemed much as usual the next day; the lingering gravity and sadness, and the occasional absence of mind, were not unnatural symptoms in the early days of grief. And almost in proportion to her re-establishment in health, was her father's relapse into his abstracted musing upon the wife he had lost, and the past era in his life that was closed to him for ever.

CHAPTER XXXVI - UNION NOT ALWAYS STRENGTH

'The steps of the bearers, heavy and slow,
 The sobs of the mourners, deep and low.'
 SHELLEY.

At the time arranged the previous day, they set out on their walk to see Nicholas Higgins and his daughter. They both were reminded of their recent loss, by a strange kind of shyness in their new habiliments, and in the fact that it was the first time, for many weeks, that they had deliberately gone out together. They drew very close to each other in unspoken sympathy.

Nicholas was sitting by the fire-side in his accustomed corner: but he had not his accustomed pipe. He was leaning his head upon his hand, his arm resting on his knee. He did not get up when he saw them, though Margaret could read the welcome in his eye.

'Sit ye down, sit ye down. Fire's welly out,' said he, giving it a vigorous poke, as if to turn attention away from himself. He was rather disorderly, to be sure, with a black unshaven beard of several days' growth, making his pale face look yet paler, and a jacket which would have been all the better for patching.

'We thought we should have a good chance of finding you, just after dinner-time,' said Margaret.

'We have had our sorrow too, since we saw you,' said Mr. Hale.

'Ay, ay. Sorrows is more plentiful than dinners just now; I reckon, my dinner hour stretches all o'er the day; yo're pretty sure of finding me.'

'Are you out of work?' asked Margaret.

'Ay,' he replied shortly. Then, after a moment's silence, he added, looking up for the first time: 'I'm not wanting brass. Dunno yo' think it. Bess, poor lass, had a little stock under her pillow, ready to slip into my hand, last moment, and Mary is fustian-cutting. But I'm out o' work a' the same.'

'We owe Mary some money,' said Mr. Hale, before Margaret's sharp pressure on his arm could arrest the words.

'If hoo takes it, I'll turn her out o' doors. I'll bide inside these four walls, and she'll bide out. That's a'.'

'But we owe her many thanks for her kind service,' began Mr. Hale again.

'I ne'er thanked yo'r daughter theer for her deeds o' love to my poor wench. I ne'er could find th' words. I'se have to begin and try now, if yo' start making an ado about what little Mary could sarve yo'.'

'Is it because of the strike you're out of work?' asked Margaret gently.

'Strike's ended. It's o'er for this time. I'm out o' work because I ne'er asked for it. And I ne'er asked for it, because good words is scarce, and bad words is plentiful.'

He was in a mood to take a surly pleasure in giving answers that were like riddles. But Margaret saw that he would like to be asked for the explanation.

'And good words are—?'

'Asking for work. I reckon them's almost the best words that men can say. "Gi' me work" means "and I'll do it like a man." Them's good words.'

'And bad words are refusing you work when you ask for it.'

'Ay. Bad words is saying "Aha, my fine chap! Yo've been true to yo'r order, and I'll be true to mine. Yo' did the best yo' could for them as wanted help; that's yo'r way of being true to yo'r kind; and I'll be true to mine. Yo've been a poor fool, as knowed no better nor be a true faithful fool. So go and be d—— d to yo'. There's no work for yo' here." Them's bad words. I'm not a fool; and if I was, folk ought to ha' taught me how to be wise after their fashion. I could mappen ha' learnt, if any one had tried to teach me.'

'Would it not be worth while,' said Mr. Hale, 'to ask your old master if he would take you back again? It might be a poor chance, but it would be a chance.'

He looked up again, with a sharp glance at the questioner; and then tittered a low and bitter laugh.

'Measter! if it's no offence, I'll ask yo' a question or two in my turn.'

'You're quite welcome,' said Mr. Hale.

'I reckon yo'n some way of earning your bread. Folk seldom lives i' Milton just for pleasure, if they can live anywhere else.'

'You are quite right. I have some independent property, but my intention in settling in Milton was to become a private tutor.'

'To teach folk. Well! I reckon they pay yo' for teaching them, dunnot they?'

'Yes,' replied Mr. Hale, smiling. 'I teach in order to get paid.'

'And them that pays yo', dun they tell yo' whatten to do, or whatten not to do wi' the money they gives you in just payment for your pains—in fair exchange like?'

'No; to be sure not!'

'They dunnot say, "Yo' may have a brother, or a friend as dear as a brother, who wants this here brass for a purpose both yo' and he think right; but yo' mun promise not give it to him. Yo' may see a good use, as yo' think, to put yo'r money to; but we don't think it good, and so if yo' spend it a-thatens we'll just leave off dealing with yo'." They dunnot say that, dun they?'

'No: to be sure not!'

'Would yo' stand it if they did?'

'It would be some very hard pressure that would make me even think of submitting to such dictation.'

'There's not the pressure on all the broad earth that would make me, said Nicholas Higgins. 'Now yo've got it. Yo've hit the bull's eye. Hamper's—that's where I worked—makes their men pledge 'emselves they'll not give a penny to help th' Union or keep turnouts fro' clemming. They may pledge and make pledge,' continued he, scornfully; 'they nobbut make liars and hypocrites. And that's a less sin, to my mind, to making men's hearts so hard that they'll not do a kindness to them as needs it, or help on the right and just cause, though it goes again the strong hand. But I'll ne'er forswear mysel' for a' the work the king could gi'e me. I'm a member o' the Union; and I think it's the only thing to do the workman any good. And I've been a turn-out, and known what it were to clem; so if I get a shilling, sixpence shall go to them if they axe it from me. Consequence is, I dunnot see where I'm to get a shilling.'

'Is that rule about not contributing to the Union in force at all the mills?' asked Margaret.

'I cannot say. It's a new regulation at ourn; and I reckon they'll find that they cannot stick to it. But it's in force now. By-and-by they'll find out, tyrants makes liars.'

There was a little pause. Margaret was hesitating whether she should say what was in her mind; she was unwilling to irritate one who was already gloomy and despondent enough. At last out it came. But in her soft tones, and with her reluctant manner, showing that she was unwilling to say anything unpleasant, it did not seem to annoy Higgins, only to perplex him.

'Do you remember poor Boucher saying that the Union was a tyrant? I think he said it was the worst tyrant of all. And I remember at the time I agreed with him.'

It was a long while before he spoke. He was resting his head on his two hands, and looking down into the fire, so she could not read the expression on his face.

'I'll not deny but what th' Union finds it necessary to force a man into his own good. I'll speak truth. A man leads a dree life who's not i' th' Union. But once i' the' Union, his interests are taken care on better nor he could do it for himsel', or by himsel', for that matter. It's the only way working men can get their rights, by all joining together. More the members, more chance for each one separate man having justice done him. Government takes care o' fools and madmen; and if any man is inclined to do himsel' or his neighbour a hurt, it puts a bit of a check on him, whether he likes it or no. That's all we do i' th' Union. We can't clap folk into prison; but we can make a man's life so heavy to be borne, that he's obliged to come in, and be wise and helpful in spite of himself. Boucher were a fool all along, and ne'er a worse fool than at th' last.'

'He did you harm?' asked Margaret.

'Ay, that did he. We had public opinion on our side, till he and his sort began rioting and breaking laws. It were all o'er wi' the strike then.'

'Then would it not have been far better to have left him alone, and not forced him to join the Union? He did you no good; and you drove him mad.'

'Margaret,' said her father, in a low and warning tone, for he saw the cloud gathering on Higgins's face.

'I like her,' said Higgins, suddenly. 'Hoo speaks plain out what's in her mind. Hoo doesn't comprehend th' Union for all that. It's a great power: it's our only power. I ha' read a bit o' poetry about a plough going o'er a daisy, as made tears come into my eyes, afore I'd other cause for crying. But the chap ne'er stopped driving the plough, I'se warrant, for all he were pitiful about the daisy. He'd too much mother-wit for that. Th' Union's the plough, making ready the land for harvest-time. Such as Boucher—'twould be settin' him up too much to liken him to a daisy; he's liker a weed lounging over the ground—mun just make up their mind to be put out o' the way. I'm sore vexed wi' him just now. So, mappen, I dunnot speak him fair. I could go o'er him wi' a plough mysel', wi' a' the pleasure in life.'

'Why? What has he been doing? Anything fresh?'

'Ay, to be sure. He's ne'er out o' mischief, that man. First of a' he must go raging like a mad fool, and kick up yon riot. Then he'd to go into hiding, where he'd a been yet, if Thornton had followed him out as I'd hoped he would ha' done. But Thornton, having got his own purpose, didn't care to go on wi' the prosecution for the riot. So Boucher slunk back again to his house. He ne'er showed himsel' abroad for a day or two. He had that grace. And then, where think ye that he went? Why, to Hamper's. Damn him! He went wi' his mealy-mouthed face, that turns me sick to look at, a-asking for work, though he knowed well enough the new rule, o' pledging themselves to give nought to th' Unions; nought to help the starving turn-out! Why he'd a clemmed to death, if th' Union had na helped him in his pinch. There he went, ossing to promise aught, and pledge himsel' to aught—to tell a' he know'd on our proceedings, the good-for-nothing Judas! But I'll say this for Hamper, and thank him for it at my dying day, he drove Boucher away, and would na listen to him—ne'er a word—though folk standing by, says the traitor cried like a babby!'

'Oh! how shocking! how pitiful!' exclaimed Margaret. 'Higgins, I don't know you to-day. Don't you see how you've made Boucher what he is, by driving him into the Union against his will—without his heart going with it. You have made him what he is!'

Made him what he is! What was he?

Gathering, gathering along the narrow street, came a hollow, measured sound; now forcing itself on their attention. Many voices were hushed and low: many steps were heard not moving onwards, at least not with any rapidity or steadiness of motion, but as if circling round one spot. Yes, there was one distinct, slow tramp of feet, which made itself a clear path through the air, and reached their ears; the measured laboured walk of men carrying a heavy burden. They were all drawn towards the house-door by some irresistible impulse; impelled thither—not by a poor curiosity, but as if by some solemn blast.

Six men walked in the middle of the road, three of them being policemen. They carried a door, taken off its hinges, upon their shoulders, on which lay some dead human creature; and from each side of the door there were constant droppings. All the street turned out to see, and, seeing, to accompany the procession, each one questioning the bearers, who answered almost reluctantly at last, so often had they told the tale.

'We found him i' th' brook in the field beyond there.'

'Th' brook!—why there's not water enough to drown him!'

'He was a determined chap. He lay with his face downwards. He was sick enough o' living, choose what cause he had for it.'

Higgins crept up to Margaret's side, and said in a weak piping kind of voice: 'It's not John Boucher? He had na spunk enough. Sure! It's not John Boucher! Why, they are a' looking this way! Listen! I've a singing in my head, and I cannot hear.'

They put the door down carefully upon the stones, and all might see the poor drowned wretch—his glassy eyes, one half-open, staring right upwards to the sky. Owing to the position in which he had been found lying, his face was swollen and discoloured besides, his skin was stained by the water in the brook, which had been used for dyeing purposes. The fore part of his head was bald; but the hair grew thin and long behind, and every separate lock was a conduit for water. Through all these disfigurements, Margaret recognised John Boucher. It seemed to her so sacrilegious to be peering into that poor distorted, agonised face, that, by a flash of instinct, she went forwards and softly covered the dead man's countenance with her handkerchief. The eyes that saw her do this followed her, as she turned away from her pious office, and were thus led to the place where Nicholas Higgins stood, like one rooted to the spot. The men spoke together, and then one of them came up to Higgins, who would have fain shrunk back into his house.

'Higgins, thou knowed him! Thou mun go tell the wife. Do it gently, man, but do it quick, for we canna leave him here long.'

'I canna go,' said Higgins. 'Dunnot ask me. I canna face her.'

'Thou knows her best,' said the man. 'We'n done a deal in bringing him here—thou take thy share.'

'I canna do it,' said Higgins. 'I'm welly felled wi' seeing him. We wasn't friends; and now he's dead.'

'Well, if thou wunnot thou wunnot. Some one mun, though. It's a dree task; but it's a chance, every minute, as she doesn't hear on it in some rougher way nor a person going to make her let on by degrees, as it were.'

'Papa, do you go,' said Margaret, in a low voice.

'If I could—if I had time to think of what I had better say; but all at once——' Margaret saw that her father was indeed unable. He was trembling from head to foot.

'I will go,' said she.

'Bless yo', miss, it will be a kind act; for she's been but a sickly sort of body, I hear, and few hereabouts know much on her.'

Margaret knocked at the closed door; but there was such a noise, as of many little ill-ordered children, that she could hear no reply; indeed, she doubted if she was heard, and as every moment of delay made her recoil from her task more and more, she opened the door and went in, shutting it after her, and even, unseen to the woman, fastening the bolt.

Mrs. Boucher was sitting in a rocking-chair, on the other side of the ill-redd-up fireplace; it looked as if the house had been untouched for days by any effort at cleanliness.

Margaret said something, she hardly knew what, her throat and mouth were so dry, and the children's noise completely prevented her from being heard. She tried again.

'How are you, Mrs. Boucher? But very poorly, I'm afraid.'

'I've no chance o' being well,' said she querulously. 'I'm left alone to manage these childer, and nought for to give 'em for to keep 'em quiet. John should na ha' left me, and me so poorly.'

'How long is it since he went away?'

'Four days sin'. No one would give him work here, and he'd to go on tramp toward Greenfield. But he might ha' been back afore this, or sent me some word if he'd getten work. He might—— '

'Oh, don't blame him,' said Margaret. 'He felt it deeply, I'm sure—— '

'Willto' hold thy din, and let me hear the lady speak!' addressing herself, in no very gentle voice, to a little urchin of about a year old. She apologetically continued to Margaret, 'He's always mithering me for "daddy" and "butty;" and I ha' no butties to give him, and daddy's away, and forgotten us a', I think. He's his father's darling, he is,' said she, with a sudden turn of mood, and, dragging the child up to her knee, she began kissing it fondly.

Margaret laid her hand on the woman's arm to arrest her attention. Their eyes met.

'Poor little fellow!' said Margaret, slowly; 'he *was* his father's darling.'

'He *is* his father's darling,' said the woman, rising hastily, and standing face to face with Margaret. Neither of them spoke for a moment or two. Then Mrs. Boucher began in a low, growling tone, gathering in wildness as she went on: He *is* his father's darling, I say. Poor folk can love their childer as well as rich. Why dunno yo' speak? Why dun yo' stare at me wi' your great pitiful eyes? Where's John?' Weak as she was, she shook Margaret to force out an answer. 'Oh, my God!' said she, understanding the meaning of that tearful look. She sank back into the chair. Margaret took up the child and put him into her arms.

'He loved him,' said she.

'Ay,' said the woman, shaking her head, 'he loved us a'. We had some one to love us once. It's a long time ago; but when he were in life and with us, he did love us, he did. He loved this babby mappen the best on us; but he loved me and I loved him, though I was calling him five minutes agone. Are yo' sure he's dead?' said she, trying to get up. 'If it's only that he's ill and like to die, they may bring him round yet. I'm but an ailing creature mysel'—I've been ailing this long time.'

'But he is dead—he is drowned!'

'Folk are brought round after they're dead-drowned. Whatten was I thinking of, to sit still when I should be stirring mysel'? Here, whisth thee, child—whisth thee!

tak' this, tak' aught to play wi', but dunnot cry while my heart's breaking! Oh, where is my strength gone to? Oh, John—husband!'

Margaret saved her from falling by catching her in her arms. She sate down in the rocking chair, and held the woman upon her knees, her head lying on Margaret's shoulder. The other children, clustered together in affright, began to understand the mystery of the scene; but the ideas came slowly, for their brains were dull and languid of perception. They set up such a cry of despair as they guessed the truth, that Margaret knew not how to bear it. Johnny's cry was loudest of them all, though he knew not why he cried, poor little fellow.

The mother quivered as she lay in Margaret's arms. Margaret heard a noise at the door.

'Open it. Open it quick,' said she to the eldest child. 'It's bolted; make no noise—be very still. Oh, papa, let them go upstairs very softly and carefully, and perhaps she will not hear them. She has fainted—that's all.'

'It's as well for her, poor creature,' said a woman following in the wake of the bearers of the dead. 'But yo're not fit to hold her. Stay, I'll run fetch a pillow and we'll let her down easy on the floor.'

This helpful neighbour was a great relief to Margaret; she was evidently a stranger to the house, a new-comer in the district, indeed; but she was so kind and thoughtful that Margaret felt she was no longer needed; and that it would be better, perhaps, to set an example of clearing the house, which was filled with idle, if sympathising gazers.

She looked round for Nicholas Higgins. He was not there. So she spoke to the woman who had taken the lead in placing Mrs. Boucher on the floor.

'Can you give all these people a hint that they had better leave in quietness? So that when she comes round, she should only find one or two that she knows about her. Papa, will you speak to the men, and get them to go away? She cannot breathe, poor thing, with this crowd about her.'

Margaret was kneeling down by Mrs. Boucher and bathing her face with vinegar; but in a few minutes she was surprised at the gush of fresh air. She looked round, and saw a smile pass between her father and the woman.

'What is it?' asked she.

'Only our good friend here,' replied her father, 'hit on a capital expedient for clearing the place.'

'I bid 'em begone, and each take a child with 'em, and to mind that they were orphans, and their mother a widow. It was who could do most, and the childer are sure of a bellyful to-day, and of kindness too. Does hoo know how he died?'

'No,' said Margaret; 'I could not tell her all at once.'

'Hoo mun be told because of th' Inquest. See! Hoo's coming round; shall you or I do it? or mappen your father would be best?'

'No; you, you,' said Margaret.

They awaited her perfect recovery in silence. Then the neighbour woman sat down on the floor, and took Mrs. Boucher's head and shoulders on her lap.

'Neighbour,' said she, 'your man is dead. Guess yo' how he died?'

'He were drowned,' said Mrs. Boucher, feebly, beginning to cry for the first time, at this rough probing of her sorrows.

'He were found drowned. He were coming home very hopeless o' aught on earth. He thought God could na be harder than men; mappen not so hard; mappen as tender as a mother; mappen tenderer. I'm not saying he did right, and I'm not saying he did wrong. All I say is, may neither me nor mine ever have his sore heart, or we may do like things.'

'He has left me alone wi' a' these children!' moaned the widow, less distressed at the manner of the death than Margaret expected; but it was of a piece with her helpless character to feel his loss as principally affecting herself and her children.

'Not alone,' said Mr. Hale, solemnly. 'Who is with you? Who will take up your cause?' The widow opened her eyes wide, and looked at the new speaker, of whose presence she had not been aware till then.

'Who has promised to be a father to the fatherless?' continued he.

'But I've getten six children, sir, and the eldest not eight years of age. I'm not meaning for to doubt His power, sir,—only it needs a deal o' trust;' and she began to cry afresh.

'Hoo'll be better able to talk to-morrow, sir,' said the neighbour. 'Best comfort now would be the feel of a child at her heart. I'm sorry they took the babby.'

'I'll go for it,' said Margaret. And in a few minutes she returned, carrying Johnnie, his face all smeared with eating, and his hands loaded with treasures in the shape of shells, and bits of crystal, and the head of a plaster figure. She placed him in his mother's arms.

'There!' said the woman, 'now you go. They'll cry together, and comfort together, better nor any one but a child can do. I'll stop with her as long as I'm needed, and if yo' come to-morrow, yo' can have a deal o' wise talk with her, that she's not up to to-day.'

As Margaret and her father went slowly up the street, she paused at Higgins's closed door.

'Shall we go in?' asked her father. 'I was thinking of him too.'

They knocked. There was no answer, so they tried the door. It was bolted, but they thought they heard him moving within.

'Nicholas!' said Margaret. There was no answer, and they might have gone away, believing the house to be empty, if there had not been some accidental fall, as of a book, within.

'Nicholas!' said Margaret again. 'It is only us. Won't you let us come in?'

'No,' said he. 'I spoke as plain as I could, 'bout using words, when I bolted th' door. Let me be, this day.'

Mr. Hale would have urged their desire, but Margaret placed her finger on his lips.

'I don't wonder at it,' said she. 'I myself long to be alone. It seems the only thing to do one good after a day like this.'

CHAPTER XXXVII - LOOKING SOUTH

'A spade! a rake! a hoe!
A pickaxe or a bill!
A hook to reap, or a scythe to mow,
A flail, or what ye will—
And here's a ready hand
To ply the needful tool,
And skill'd enough, by lessons rough,
In Labour's rugged school.'
HOOD.

Higgins's door was locked the next day, when they went to pay their call on the widow Boucher: but they learnt this time from an officious neighbour, that he was really from home. He had, however, been in to see Mrs. Boucher, before starting on his day's business, whatever that was. It was but an unsatisfactory visit to Mrs. Boucher; she considered herself as an ill-used woman by her poor husband's suicide; and there was quite germ of truth enough in this idea to make it a very difficult one to refute. Still, it was unsatisfactory to see how completely her thoughts were turned upon herself and her own position, and this selfishness extended even to her relations with her children, whom she considered as incumbrances, even in the very midst of her somewhat animal affection for them. Margaret tried to make acquaintances with one or two of them, while her father strove to raise the widow's thoughts into some higher channel than that of mere helpless querulousness. She found that the children were truer and simpler mourners than the widow. Daddy had been a kind daddy to them; each could tell, in their eager stammering way, of some tenderness shown some indulgence granted by the lost father.

'Is yon thing upstairs really him? it doesna look like him. I'm feared on it, and I never was feared o' daddy.'

Margaret's heart bled to hear that the mother, in her selfish requirement of sympathy, had taken her children upstairs to see their disfigured father. It was intermingling the coarseness of horror with the profoundness of natural grief. She tried to turn their thoughts in some other direction; on what they could do for mother; on what—for this was a more efficacious way of putting it—what father would have wished them to do. Margaret was more successful than Mr. Hale in her efforts. The children seeing their little duties lie in action close around them, began to try each one to do something that she suggested towards redding up the slatternly room. But her father set too high a standard, and too abstract a view, before the indolent invalid. She could not rouse her torpid mind into any vivid imagination of what her husband's misery might have been before he had resorted to the last terrible step; she could only look upon it as it affected herself; she could not enter into the enduring mercy of the God who had not specially interposed to prevent the water from drowning her prostrate husband; and although she was secretly blaming her husband for having fallen into such drear despair, and denying that he had any excuse for his last rash act, she was inveterate in her abuse of all who could by any possibility be supposed to have driven him to such desperation. The masters—Mr. Thornton in particular, whose mill had been attacked by Boucher, and who, after the warrant had been issued for his apprehension on the charge of rioting, had caused it to be withdrawn,—the Union, of which Higgins was the representative to the poor woman,—the children so numerous, so hungry, and so noisy—all made up one great army of personal enemies, whose fault it was that she was now a helpless widow.

Margaret heard enough of this unreasonableness to dishearten her; and when they came away she found it impossible to cheer her father.

'It is the town life,' said she. 'Their nerves are quickened by the haste and bustle and speed of everything around them, to say nothing of the confinement in these pent-up houses, which of itself is enough to induce depression and worry of spirits. Now in the country, people live so much more out of doors, even children, and even in the winter.'

'But people must live in towns. And in the country some get such stagnant habits of mind that they are almost fatalists.'

'Yes; I acknowledge that. I suppose each mode of life produces its own trials and its own temptations. The dweller in towns must find it as difficult to be patient and calm, as the country-bred man must find it to be active, and equal to unwonted emergencies. Both must find it hard to realise a future of any kind; the one because the present is so living and hurrying and close around him; the other because his life tempts him to revel in the mere sense of animal existence, not knowing of, and consequently not caring for any pungency of pleasure for the attainment of which he can plan, and deny himself and look forward.'

'And thus both the necessity for engrossment, and the stupid content in the present, produce the same effects. But this poor Mrs. Boucher! how little we can do for her.'

'And yet we dare not leave her without our efforts, although they may seem so useless. Oh papa! it's a hard world to live in!'

'So it is, my child. We feel it so just now, at any rate; but we have been very happy, even in the midst of our sorrow. What a pleasure Frederick's visit was!'

'Yes, that it was,' said Margaret; brightly. 'It was such a charming, snatched, forbidden thing.' But she suddenly stopped speaking. She had spoiled the remembrance of Frederick's visit to herself by her own cowardice. Of all faults the one she most despised in others was the want of bravery; the meanness of heart which leads to untruth. And here had she been guilty of it! Then came the thought of Mr. Thornton's cognisance of her falsehood. She wondered if she should have minded detection half so much from any one else. She tried herself in imagination with her Aunt Shaw and Edith; with her father; with Captain and Mr. Lennox; with Frederick. The thought of the last knowing what she had done, even in his own behalf, was the most painful, for the brother and sister were in the first flush of their mutual regard and love; but even any fall in Frederick's opinion was as nothing to the shame, the shrinking shame she felt at the thought of meeting Mr. Thornton again. And yet she longed to see him, to get it over; to understand where she stood in his opinion. Her cheeks burnt as she recollected how proudly she had implied an objection to trade (in the early days of their acquaintance), because it too often led to the deceit of passing off inferior for superior goods, in the one branch; of assuming credit for wealth and resources not possessed, in the other. She remembered Mr. Thornton's look of calm disdain, as in few words he gave her to understand that, in the great scheme of commerce, all dishonourable ways of acting were sure to prove injurious in the long run, and that, testing such actions simply according to the poor standard of success, there was folly and not wisdom in all such, and every kind of deceit in trade, as well as in other things. She remembered—she, then strong in her own untempted truth—asking him, if he did not think that buying in the cheapest and selling in the dearest market proved some want of the transparent justice which is so intimately connected with the idea of truth: and she had used the word chivalric—and her father had corrected her with the higher word, Christian; and so drawn the argument upon himself, while she sate silent by with a slight feeling of contempt.

No more contempt for her!—no more talk about the chivalric! Henceforward she must feel humiliated and disgraced in his sight. But when should she see him? Her heart leaped up in apprehension at every ring of the door-bell; and yet when it fell down to calmness, she felt strangely saddened and sick at heart at each disappointment. It was very evident that her father expected to see him, and was surprised that he did not come. The truth was, that there were points in their conversation the other night on which they had no time then to enlarge; but it had been understood that if possible on the succeeding evening—if not then, at least the very first evening that Mr. Thornton could command,—they should meet for further discussion. Mr. Hale had looked forward to this meeting ever since they had parted. He had not yet resumed the instruction to his pupils, which he had relinquished at the commencement of his wife's more serious illness, so he had fewer occupations than usual; and the great interest of the last day or so (Boucher's suicide) had driven him back with more eagerness than ever upon his speculations. He was restless all evening. He kept saying, 'I quite expected to have seen Mr. Thornton. I think the messenger who brought the book last night must have had some note, and forgot to deliver it. Do you think there has been any message left to-day?'

'I will go and inquire, papa,' said Margaret, after the changes on these sentences had been rung once or twice. 'Stay, there's a ring!' She sate down instantly, and bent her head attentively over her work. She heard a step on the stairs, but it was only one, and she knew it was Dixon's. She lifted up her head and sighed, and believed she felt glad.

'It's that Higgins, sir. He wants to see you, or else Miss Hale. Or it might be Miss Hale first, and then you, sir; for he's in a strange kind of way.

'He had better come up here, Dixon; and then he can see us both, and choose which he likes for his listener.'

'Oh! very well, sir. I've no wish to hear what he's got to say, I'm sure; only, if you could see his shoes, I'm sure you'd say the kitchen was the fitter place.

'He can wipe them, I suppose, said Mr. Hale. So Dixon flung off, to bid him walk up-stairs. She was a little mollified, however, when he looked at his feet with a hesitating air; and then, sitting down on the bottom stair, he took off the offending shoes, and without a word walked up-stairs.

'Sarvant, sir!' said he, slicking his hair down when he came into the room. 'If hoo'l excuse me (looking at Margaret) for being i' my stockings; I'se been tramping a' day, and streets is none o' th' cleanest.'

Margaret thought that fatigue might account for the change in his manner, for he was unusually quiet and subdued; and he had evidently some difficulty in saying what he came to say.

Mr. Hale's ever-ready sympathy with anything of shyness or hesitation, or want of self-possession, made him come to his aid.

'We shall have tea up directly, and then you'll take a cup with us, Mr. Higgins. I am sure you are tired, if you've been out much this wet relaxing day. Margaret, my dear, can't you hasten tea?'

Margaret could only hasten tea by taking the preparation of it into her own hands, and so offending Dixon, who was emerging out of her sorrow for her late mistress into a very touchy, irritable state. But Martha, like all who came in contact with Margaret—even Dixon herself, in the long run—felt it a pleasure and an honour to forward any of her wishes; and her readiness, and Margaret's sweet forbearance, soon made Dixon ashamed of herself.

'Why master and you must always be asking the lower classes up-stairs, since we came to Milton, I cannot understand. Folk at Helstone were never brought higher than the kitchen; and I've let one or two of them know before now that they might think it an honour to be even there.'

Higgins found it easier to unburden himself to one than to two. After Margaret left the room, he went to the door and assured himself that it was shut. Then he came and stood close to Mr. Hale.

'Master,' said he, 'yo'd not guess easy what I've been tramping after to-day. Special if yo' remember my manner o' talk yesterday. I've been a seeking work. I have' said he. 'I said to mysel', I'd keep a civil tongue in my head, let who would say what 'em would. I'd set my teeth into my tongue sooner nor speak i' haste. For that man's sake—yo' understand,' jerking his thumb back in some unknown direction.

'No, I don't,' said Mr. Hale, seeing he waited for some kind of assent, and completely bewildered as to who 'that man' could be.

'That chap as lies theer,' said he, with another jerk. 'Him as went and drownded himself, poor chap! I did na' think he'd got it in him to lie still and let th' water creep o'er him till he died. Boucher, yo' know.'

'Yes, I know now,' said Mr. Hale. 'Go back to what you were saying: you'd not speak in haste—— '

'For his sake. Yet not for his sake; for where'er he is, and whate'er, he'll ne'er know other clemming or cold again; but for the wife's sake, and the bits o' childer.'

'God bless you!' said Mr. Hale, starting up; then, calming down, he said breathlessly, 'What do you mean? Tell me out.'

'I have telled yo',' said Higgins, a little surprised at Mr. Hale's agitation. 'I would na ask for work for mysel'; but them's left as a charge on me. I reckon, I would ha guided Boucher to a better end; but I set him off o' th' road, and so I mun answer for him.'

Mr. Hale got hold of Higgins's hand and shook it heartily, without speaking. Higgins looked awkward and ashamed.

'Theer, theer, master! Theer's ne'er a man, to call a man, amongst us, but what would do th' same; ay, and better too; for, belie' me, I'se ne'er got a stroke o' work, nor yet a sight of any. For all I telled Hamper that, let alone his pledge—which I would not sign—no, I could na, not e'en for this—he'd ne'er ha' such a worker on his mill as I would be—he'd ha' none o' me—no more would none o' th' others. I'm a poor black feckless sheep—childer may clem for aught I can do, unless, parson, yo'd help me?'

'Help you! How? I would do anything,—but what can I do?'

'Miss there'—for Margaret had re-entered the room, and stood silent, listening—'has often talked grand o' the South, and the ways down there. Now I dunnot know how far off it is, but I've been thinking if I could get 'em down theer, where food is cheap and wages good, and all the folk, rich and poor, master and man, friendly like; yo' could, may be, help me to work. I'm not forty-five, and I've a deal o' strength in me, measter.'

'But what kind of work could you do, my man?'

'Well, I reckon I could spade a bit—— '

'And for that,' said Margaret, stepping forwards, 'for anything you could do, Higgins, with the best will in the world, you would, may be, get nine shillings a week; maybe ten, at the outside. Food is much the same as here, except that you might have a little garden—— '

'The childer could work at that,' said he. 'I'm sick o' Milton anyways, and Milton is sick o' me.'

'You must not go to the South,' said Margaret, 'for all that. You could not stand it. You would have to be out all weathers. It would kill you with rheumatism. The mere bodily work at your time of life would break you down. The fare is far different to what you have been accustomed to.'

'I'se nought particular about my meat,' said he, as if offended.

'But you've reckoned on having butcher's meat once a day, if you're in work; pay for that out of your ten shillings, and keep those poor children if you can. I owe it to you—since it's my way of talking that has set you off on this idea—to put it all clear before you. You would not bear the dulness of the life; you don't know what it is; it would eat you away like rust. Those that have lived there all their lives, are used to soaking in the stagnant waters. They labour on, from day to day, in the great solitude of steaming fields—never speaking or lifting up their poor, bent, downcast heads. The hard spade-work robs their brain of life; the sameness of their toil deadens their imagination; they don't care to meet to talk over thoughts and speculations, even of the weakest, wildest kind, after their work is done; they go home brutishly tired, poor creatures! caring for nothing but food and rest. You could not stir them up into any companionship, which you get in a town as plentiful as the air you breathe, whether it be good or bad—and that I don't know; but I do know, that you of all men are not one to bear a life among such labourers. What would be peace to them would be eternal fretting to you. Think no more of it, Nicholas, I beg. Besides, you could never pay to get mother and children all there—that's one good thing.'

'I've reckoned for that. One house mun do for us a', and the furniture o' t'other would go a good way. And men theer mun have their families to keep—mappen six or seven childer. God help 'em!' said he, more convinced by his own presentation of the facts than by all Margaret had said, and suddenly renouncing the idea, which had but recently formed itself in a brain worn out by the day's fatigue and anxiety. 'God help 'em! North an' South have each getten their own troubles. If work's sure and steady theer, labour's paid at starvation prices; while here we'n rucks o' money coming in one quarter, and ne'er a farthing th' next. For sure, th' world is in a confusion that passes me or any other man to understand; it needs fettling, and who's to fettle it, if it's as yon folks say, and there's nought but what we see?'

Mr. Hale was busy cutting bread and butter; Margaret was glad of this, for she saw that Higgins was better left to himself: that if her father began to speak ever so mildly on the subject of Higgins's thoughts, the latter would consider himself challenged to an argument, and would feel himself bound to maintain his own ground. She and her father kept up an indifferent conversation until Higgins, scarcely aware whether he ate or not, had made a very substantial meal. Then he pushed his chair away from the table, and tried to take an interest in what they were saying; but it was of no use; and he fell back into dreamy gloom. Suddenly, Margaret said (she had been thinking of it for some time, but the words had stuck in her throat), 'Higgins, have you been to Marlborough Mills to seek for work?'

'Thornton's?' asked he. 'Ay, I've been at Thornton's.'

'And what did he say?'

'Such a chap as me is not like to see the measter. Th' o'erlooker bid me go and be d—— d.'

'I wish you had seen Mr. Thornton,' said Mr. Hale. 'He might not have given you work, but he would not have used such language.'

'As to th' language, I'm welly used to it; it dunnot matter to me. I'm not nesh mysel' when I'm put out. It were th' fact that I were na wanted theer, no more nor ony other place, as I minded.'

'But I wish you had seen Mr. Thornton,' repeated Margaret. 'Would you go again—it's a good deal to ask, I know—but would you go to-morrow and try him? I should be so glad if you would.'

'I'm afraid it would be of no use,' said Mr. Hale, in a low voice. 'It would be better to let me speak to him.' Margaret still looked at Higgins for his answer. Those grave soft eyes of hers were difficult to resist. He gave a great sigh.

'It would tax my pride above a bit; if it were for mysel', I could stand a deal o' clemming first; I'd sooner knock him down than ask a favour from him. I'd a deal sooner be flogged mysel'; but yo're not a common wench, axing yo'r pardon, nor yet have yo' common ways about yo'. I'll e'en make a wry face, and go at it to-morrow. Dunna yo' think that he'll do it. That man has it in him to be burnt at the stake afore he'll give in. I do it for yo'r sake, Miss Hale, and it's first time in my life as e'er I give way to a woman. Neither my wife nor Bess could e'er say that much again me.'

'All the more do I thank you,' said Margaret, smiling. 'Though I don't believe you: I believe you have just given way to wife and daughter as much as most men.'

'And as to Mr. Thornton,' said Mr. Hale, 'I'll give you a note to him, which, I think I may venture to say, will ensure you a hearing.'

'I thank yo' kindly, sir, but I'd as lief stand on my own bottom. I dunnot stomach the notion of having favour curried for me, by one as doesn't know the ins and outs of the quarrel. Meddling 'twixt master and man is liker meddling 'twixt husband and wife than aught else: it takes a deal o' wisdom for to do ony good. I'll stand guard at the lodge door. I'll stand there fro' six in the morning till I get speech on him. But I'd liefer sweep th' streets, if paupers had na' got hold on that work. Dunna yo' hope, miss. There'll be more chance o' getting milk out of a flint. I wish yo' a very good night, and many thanks to yo'.'

'You'll find your shoe's by the kitchen fire; I took them there to dry,' said Margaret.

He turned round and looked at her steadily, and then he brushed his lean hand across his eyes and went his way.

'How proud that man is!' said her father, who was a little annoyed at the manner in which Higgins had declined his intercession with Mr. Thornton.

'He is,' said Margaret; 'but what grand makings of a man there are in him, pride and all.'

'It's amusing to see how he evidently respects the part in Mr. Thornton's character which is like his own.'

'There's granite in all these northern people, papa, is there not?'

'There was none in poor Boucher, I am afraid; none in his wife either.'

'I should guess from their tones that they had Irish blood in them. I wonder what success he'll have to-morrow. If he and Mr. Thornton would speak out together as man to man—if Higgins would forget that Mr. Thornton was a master, and speak to him as he does to us—and if Mr. Thornton would be patient enough to listen to him with his human heart, not with his master's ears—'

'You are getting to do Mr. Thornton justice at last, Margaret,' said her father, pinching her ear.

Margaret had a strange choking at her heart, which made her unable to answer. 'Oh!' thought she, 'I wish I were a man, that I could go and force him to express his disapprobation, and tell him honestly that I knew I deserved it. It seems hard to lose him as a friend just when I had begun to feel his value. How tender he was with dear mamma! If it were only for her sake, I wish he would come, and then at least I should know how much I was abased in his eyes.'

CHAPTER XXXVIII - PROMISES FULFILLED

'Then proudly, proudly up she rose,
  Tho' the tear was in her e'e,
  "Whate'er ye say, think what ye may,
  Ye's get na word frae me!"'
            SCOTCH BALLAD.

It was not merely that Margaret was known to Mr. Thornton to have spoken falsely,—though she imagined that for this reason only was she so turned in his opinion,—but that this falsehood of hers bore a distinct reference in his mind to some other lover. He could not forget the fond and earnest look that had passed between her and some other man—the attitude of familiar confidence, if not of positive endearment. The thought of this perpetually stung him; it was a picture before his eyes, wherever he went and whatever he was doing. In addition to this (and he ground his teeth as he remembered it), was the hour, dusky twilight; the place, so far away from home, and comparatively unfrequented. His nobler self had said at first, that all this last might be accidental, innocent, justifiable; but once allow her right to love and be beloved (and had he any reason to deny her right?—had not her words been severely explicit when she cast his love away from her?), she might easily have been beguiled into a longer walk, on to a later hour than she had anticipated. But that falsehood! which showed a fatal consciousness of something wrong, and to be concealed, which was unlike her. He did her that justice, though all the time it would have been a relief to believe her utterly unworthy of his esteem. It was this that made the misery—that he passionately loved her, and thought her, even with all her faults, more lovely and more excellent than any other woman; yet he deemed her so attached to some other man, so led away by her affection for him as to violate her truthful nature. The very falsehood that stained her, was a proof how blindly she loved another—this dark, slight, elegant, handsome man—while he himself was rough, and stern, and strongly made. He lashed himself into an agony of fierce jealousy. He thought of that look, that attitude!—how he would have laid his life at her feet for such tender glances, such fond detention! He mocked at himself, for having valued the mechanical way in which she had protected him from the fury of the mob; now he had seen how soft and bewitching she looked when with a man she really loved. He remembered, point by point, the sharpness of her words—'There was not a man in all that crowd for whom she would not have done as much, far more readily than for him.' He shared with the mob, in her desire of averting bloodshed from them; but this man, this hidden lover, shared with nobody; he had looks, words, hand-cleavings, lies, concealment, all to himself.

Mr. Thornton was conscious that he had never been so irritable as he was now, in all his life long; he felt inclined to give a short abrupt answer, more like a bark than a speech, to every one that asked him a question; and this consciousness hurt his pride: he had always piqued himself on his self-control, and control himself he would. So the manner was subdued to a quiet deliberation, but the matter was even harder and sterner than common. He was more than usually silent at home; employing his evenings in a continual pace backwards and forwards, which would have annoyed his mother exceedingly if it had been practised by any one else; and did not tend to promote any forbearance on her part even to this beloved son.

'Can you stop—can you sit down for a moment? I have something to say to you, if you would give up that everlasting walk, walk, walk.'

He sat down instantly, on a chair against the wall.

'I want to speak to you about Betsy. She says she must leave us; that her lover's death has so affected her spirits she can't give her heart to her work.'

'Very well. I suppose other cooks are to be met with.'

'That's so like a man. It's not merely the cooking, it is that she knows all the ways of the house. Besides, she tells me something about your friend Miss Hale.'

'Miss Hale is no friend of mine. Mr. Hale is my friend.'

'I am glad to hear you say so, for if she had been your friend, what Betsy says would have annoyed you.'

'Let me hear it,' said he, with the extreme quietness of manner he had been assuming for the last few days.

'Betsy says, that the night on which her lover—I forget his name—for she always calls him "he"—— '

'Leonards.'

'The night on which Leonards was last seen at the station—when he was last seen on duty, in fact—Miss Hale was there, walking about with a young man who, Betsy believes, killed Leonards by some blow or push.'

'Leonards was not killed by any blow or push.'

'How do you know?'

'Because I distinctly put the question to the surgeon of the Infirmary. He told me there was an internal disease of long standing, caused by Leonards' habit of drinking to excess; that the fact of his becoming rapidly worse while in a state of intoxication, settled the question as to whether the last fatal attack was caused by excess of drinking, or the fall.'

'The fall! What fall?'

'Caused by the blow or push of which Betsy speaks.'

'Then there was a blow or push?'

'I believe so.'

'And who did it?'

'As there was no inquest, in consequence of the doctor's opinion, I cannot tell you.'

'But Miss Hale was there?'

No answer.

'And with a young man?'

Still no answer. At last he said: 'I tell you, mother, that there was no inquest—no inquiry. No judicial inquiry, I mean.'

'Betsy says that Woolmer (some man she knows, who is in a grocer's shop out at Crampton) can swear that Miss Hale was at the station at that hour, walking backwards and forwards with a young man.'

'I don't see what we have to do with that. Miss Hale is at liberty to please herself.'

'I'm glad to hear you say so,' said Mrs. Thornton, eagerly. 'It certainly signifies very little to us—not at all to you, after what has passed! but I—I made a promise to Mrs. Hale, that I would not allow her daughter to go wrong without advising and remonstrating with her. I shall certainly let her know my opinion of such conduct.'

'I do not see any harm in what she did that evening,' said Mr. Thornton, getting up, and coming near to his mother; he stood by the chimney-piece with his face turned away from the room.

'You would not have approved of Fanny's being seen out, after dark, in rather a lonely place, walking about with a young man. I say nothing of the taste which could choose the time, when her mother lay unburied, for such a promenade. Should you have liked your sister to have been noticed by a grocer's assistant for doing so?'

'In the first place, as it is not many years since I myself was a draper's assistant, the mere circumstance of a grocer's assistant noticing any act does not alter the character of the act to me. And in the next place, I see a great deal of difference between Miss Hale and Fanny. I can imagine that the one may have weighty reasons, which may and ought to make her overlook any seeming Impropriety in her conduct. I never knew Fanny have weighty reasons for anything. Other people must guard her. I believe Miss Hale is a guardian to herself.'

'A pretty character of your sister, indeed! Really, John, one would have thought Miss Hale had done enough to make you clear-sighted. She drew you on to an offer, by a bold display of pretended regard for you,—to play you off against this very young man, I've no doubt. Her whole conduct is clear to me now. You believe he is her lover, I suppose—you agree to that.'

He turned round to his mother; his face was very gray and grim. 'Yes, mother. I do believe he is her lover.' When he had spoken, he turned round again; he writhed himself about, like one in bodily pain. He leant his face against his hand. Then before she could speak, he turned sharp again:

'Mother. He is her lover, whoever he is; but she may need help and womanly counsel;—there may be difficulties or temptations which I don't know. I fear there are. I don't want to know what they are; but as you have ever been a good—ay! and a tender mother to me, go to her, and gain her confidence, and tell her what is best to be done. I know that something is wrong; some dread, must be a terrible torture to her.'

'For God's sake, John!' said his mother, now really shocked, 'what do you mean? What do you mean? What do you know?'

He did not reply to her.

'John! I don't know what I shan't think unless you speak. You have no right to say what you have done against her.'

'Not against her, mother! I *could* not speak against her.'

'Well! you have no right to say what you have done, unless you say more. These half-expressions are what ruin a woman's character.'

'Her character! Mother, you do not dare—' he faced about, and looked into her face with his flaming eyes. Then, drawing himself up into determined composure and dignity, he said, 'I will not say any more than this, which is neither more nor less than the simple truth, and I am sure you believe me,—I have good reason to believe, that Miss Hale is in some strait and difficulty connected with an attachment which, of itself, from my knowledge of Miss Hale's character, is perfectly innocent and right. What my reason is, I refuse to tell. But never let me hear any one say a word against her, implying any more serious imputation than that she now needs the counsel of some kind and gentle woman. You promised Mrs. Hale to be that woman!'

'No!' said Mrs. Thornton. 'I am happy to say, I did not promise kindness and gentleness, for I felt at the time that it might be out of my power to render these to one of Miss Hale's character and disposition. I promised counsel and advice, such as I would give to my own daughter; I shall speak to her as I would do to Fanny, if she had gone gallivanting with a young man in the dusk. I shall speak with relation to the circumstances I know, without being influenced either one way or another by the "strong reasons" which you will not confide to me. Then I shall have fulfilled my promise, and done my duty.'

'She will never bear it,' said he passionately.

'She will have to bear it, if I speak in her dead mother's name.'

'Well!' said he, breaking away, 'don't tell me any more about it. I cannot endure to think of it. It will be better that you should speak to her any way, than that she should not be spoken to at all.—Oh! that look of love!' continued he, between his teeth, as he bolted himself into his own private room. 'And that cursed lie; which showed some terrible shame in the background, to be kept from the light in which I thought she lived perpetually! Oh, Margaret, Margaret! Mother, how you have tortured me! Oh! Margaret, could you not have loved me? I am but uncouth and hard, but I would never have led you into any falsehood for me.'

The more Mrs. Thornton thought over what her son had said, in pleading for a merciful judgment for Margaret's indiscretion, the more bitterly she felt inclined towards her. She took a savage pleasure in the idea of 'speaking her mind' to her, in the guise of fulfilment of a duty. She enjoyed the thought of showing herself untouched by the 'glamour,' which she was well aware Margaret had the power of throwing over many people. She snorted scornfully over the picture of the beauty of her victim; her jet black hair, her clear smooth skin, her lucid eyes would not help to save her one word of the just and stern reproach which Mrs. Thornton spent half the night in preparing to her mind.

'Is Miss Hale within?' She knew she was, for she had seen her at the window, and she had her feet inside the little hall before Martha had half answered her question.

Margaret was sitting alone, writing to Edith, and giving her many particulars of her mother's last days. It was a softening employment, and she had to brush away the unbidden tears as Mrs. Thornton was announced.

She was so gentle and ladylike in her mode of reception that her visitor was somewhat daunted; and it became impossible to utter the speech, so easy of arrangement with no one to address it to. Margaret's low rich voice was softer than usual; her manner more gracious, because in her heart she was feeling very grateful to Mrs. Thornton for the courteous attention of her call. She exerted herself to find subjects of interest for conversation; praised Martha, the servant whom Mrs. Thornton had found for them; had asked Edith for a little Greek air, about which she had spoken to Miss Thornton. Mrs. Thornton was fairly discomfited. Her sharp Damascus blade seemed out of place, and useless among rose-leaves. She was silent, because she was trying to task herself up to her duty. At last, she stung herself into its performance by a suspicion which, in spite of all probability, she allowed to cross her mind, that all this sweetness was put on with a view of propitiating Mr. Thornton; that, somehow, the other attachment had fallen through, and that it suited Miss Hale's purpose to recall her rejected lover. Poor Margaret! there was perhaps so much truth in the suspicion as this: that Mrs. Thornton was the mother of one whose regard she valued, and feared to have lost; and this thought unconsciously added to her natural desire of pleasing one who was showing her kindness by her visit. Mrs. Thornton stood up to go, but yet she seemed to have something more to say. She cleared her throat and began:

'Miss Hale, I have a duty to perform. I promised your poor mother that, as far as my poor judgment went, I would not allow you to act in any way wrongly, or (she softened her speech down a little here) inadvertently, without remonstrating; at least, without offering advice, whether you took it or not.'

Margaret stood before her, blushing like any culprit, with her eyes dilating as she gazed at Mrs. Thornton. She thought she had come to speak to her about the falsehood she had told—that Mr. Thornton had employed her to explain the danger she had exposed herself to, of being confuted in full court! and although her heart sank to think he had not rather chosen to come himself, and upbraid her, and receive her penitence, and restore her again to his good opinion, yet she was too much humbled not to bear any blame on this subject patiently and meekly.

Mrs. Thornton went on:

'At first, when I heard from one of my servants, that you had been seen walking about with a gentleman, so far from home as the Outwood station, at such a time of the evening, I could hardly believe it. But my son, I am sorry to say, confirmed her story. It was indiscreet, to say the least; many a young woman has lost her character before now—— '

Margaret's eyes flashed fire. This was a new idea—this was too insulting. If Mrs. Thornton had spoken to her about the lie she had told, well and good—she would have owned it, and humiliated herself. But to interfere with her conduct—to speak of her character! she—Mrs. Thornton, a mere stranger—it was too impertinent! She would not answer her—not one word. Mrs. Thornton saw the battle-spirit in Margaret's eyes, and it called up her combativeness also.

'For your mother's sake, I have thought it right to warn you against such improprieties; they must degrade you in the long run in the estimation of the world, even if in fact they do not lead you to positive harm.'

'For my mother's sake,' said Margaret, in a tearful voice, 'I will bear much; but I cannot bear everything. She never meant me to be exposed to insult, I am sure.'

'Insult, Miss Hale!'

'Yes, madam,' said Margaret more steadily, 'it is insult. What do you know of me that should lead you to suspect—Oh!' said she, breaking down, and covering her face with her hands—'I know now, Mr. Thornton has told you—— '

'No, Miss Hale,' said Mrs. Thornton, her truthfulness causing her to arrest the confession Margaret was on the point of making, though her curiosity was itching to hear it. 'Stop. Mr. Thornton has told me nothing. You do not know my son. You are not worthy to know him. He said this. Listen, young lady, that you may understand, if you can, what sort of a man you rejected. This Milton manufacturer, his great tender heart scorned as it was scorned, said to me only last night, "Go to her. I have good reason to know that she is in some strait, arising out of some attachment; and she needs womanly counsel." I believe those were his very words. Farther than that—beyond admitting the fact of your being at the Outwood station with a gentleman, on the evening of the twenty-sixth—he has said nothing—not one word against you. If he has knowledge of anything which should make you sob so, he keeps it to himself.'

Margaret's face was still hidden in her hands, the fingers of which were wet with tears. Mrs. Thornton was a little mollified.

'Come, Miss Hale. There may be circumstances, I'll allow, that, if explained, may take off from the seeming impropriety.'

Still no answer. Margaret was considering what to say; she wished to stand well with Mrs. Thornton; and yet she could not, might not, give any explanation. Mrs. Thornton grew impatient.

'I shall be sorry to break off an acquaintance; but for Fanny's sake—as I told my son, if Fanny had done so we should consider it a great disgrace—and Fanny might be led away—— '

'I can give you no explanation,' said Margaret, in a low voice. 'I have done wrong, but not in the way you think or know about. I think Mr. Thornton judges me more mercifully than you;'—she had hard work to keep herself from choking with her tears—'but, I believe, madam, you mean to do rightly.'

'Thank you,' said Mrs. Thornton, drawing herself up; 'I was not aware that my meaning was doubted. It is the last time I shall interfere. I was unwilling to consent to do it, when your mother asked me. I had not approved of my son's attachment to you, while I only suspected it. You did not appear to me worthy of him. But when you compromised yourself as you did at the time of the riot, and exposed yourself to the comments of servants and workpeople, I felt it was no longer right to set myself against my son's wish of proposing to you—a wish, by the way, which he had always denied entertaining until the day of the riot.' Margaret winced, and drew in her breath with a long, hissing sound; of which, however, Mrs. Thornton took no notice. 'He came; you had apparently changed your mind. I told my son yesterday, that I thought it possible, short as was the interval, you might have heard or learnt something of this other lover—— '

'What must you think of me, madam?' asked Margaret, throwing her head back with proud disdain, till her throat curved outwards like a swan's. 'You can say nothing more, Mrs. Thornton. I decline every attempt to justify myself for anything. You must allow me to leave the room.'

And she swept out of it with the noiseless grace of an offended princess. Mrs. Thornton had quite enough of natural humour to make her feel the ludicrousness of the position in which she was left. There was nothing for it but to show herself out. She was not particularly annoyed at Margaret's way of behaving. She did not care enough for her for that. She had taken Mrs. Thornton's remonstrance to the full as keenly to heart as that lady expected; and Margaret's passion at once mollified her visitor, far more than any silence or reserve could have done. It showed the effect of her words. 'My young lady,' thought Mrs. Thornton to herself; 'you've a pretty good temper of your own. If John and you had come together, he would have had to keep a tight hand over you, to make you know your place. But I don't think you will go a-walking again with your beau, at such an hour of the day, in a hurry. You've too much pride and spirit in you for that. I like to see a girl fly out at the notion of being talked about. It shows they're neither giddy, nor bold by nature. As for that girl, she might be bold, but she'd never be giddy. I'll do her that justice. Now as to Fanny, she'd be giddy, and not bold. She's no courage in her, poor thing!'

Mr. Thornton was not spending the morning so satisfactorily as his mother. She, at any rate, was fulfilling her determined purpose. He was trying to understand where he stood; what damage the strike had done him. A good deal of his capital was locked up in new and expensive machinery; and he had also bought cotton largely, with a view to some great orders which he had in hand. The strike had thrown him terribly behindhand, as to the completion of these orders. Even with his own accustomed and skilled workpeople, he would have had some difficulty in fulfilling his engagements; as it was, the incompetence of the Irish hands, who had to be trained to their work, at a time requiring unusual activity, was a daily annoyance.

It was not a favourable hour for Higgins to make his request. But he had promised Margaret to do it at any cost. So, though every moment added to his repugnance, his pride, and his sullenness of temper, he stood leaning against the dead wall, hour after hour, first on one leg, then on the other. At last the latch was sharply lifted, and out came Mr. Thornton.

'I want for to speak to yo', sir.'

'Can't stay now, my man. I'm too late as it is.'

'Well, sir, I reckon I can wait till yo' come back.'

Mr. Thornton was half way down the street. Higgins sighed. But it was no use. To catch him in the street was his only chance of seeing 'the measter;' if he had rung the lodge bell, or even gone up to the house to ask for him, he would have been referred to the overlooker. So he stood still again, vouchsafing no answer, but a short nod of recognition to the few men who knew and spoke to him, as the crowd drove out of the millyard at dinner-time, and scowling with all his might at the Irish 'knobsticks' who had just been imported. At last Mr. Thornton returned.

'What! you there still!'

'Ay, sir. I mun speak to yo'.'

'Come in here, then. Stay, we'll go across the yard; the men are not come back, and we shall have it to ourselves. These good people, I see, are at dinner;' said he, closing the door of the porter's lodge.

He stopped to speak to the overlooker. The latter said in a low tone:

'I suppose you know, sir, that that man is Higgins, one of the leaders of the Union; he that made that speech in Hurstfield.'

'No, I didn't,' said Mr. Thornton, looking round sharply at his follower. Higgins was known to him by name as a turbulent spirit.

'Come along,' said he, and his tone was rougher than before. 'It is men such as this,' thought he, 'who interrupt commerce and injure the very town they live in: mere demagogues, lovers of power, at whatever cost to others.'

'Well, sir! what do you want with me?' said Mr. Thornton, facing round at him, as soon as they were in the counting-house of the mill.

'My name is Higgins'—

'I know that,' broke in Mr. Thornton. 'What do you want, Mr. Higgins? That's the question.'

'I want work.'

'Work! You're a pretty chap to come asking me for work. You don't want impudence, that's very clear.'

'I've getten enemies and backbiters, like my betters; but I ne'er heerd o' ony of them calling me o'er-modest,' said Higgins. His blood was a little roused by Mr. Thornton's manner, more than by his words.

Mr. Thornton saw a letter addressed to himself on the table. He took it up and read it through. At the end, he looked up and said, 'What are you waiting for?'

'An answer to the question I axed.'

'I gave it you before. Don't waste any more of your time.'

'Yo' made a remark, sir, on my impudence: but I were taught that it was manners to say either "yes" or "no," when I were axed a civil question. I should be thankfu' to yo' if yo'd give me work. Hamper will speak to my being a good hand.'

'I've a notion you'd better not send me to Hamper to ask for a character, my man. I might hear more than you'd like.'

'I'd take th' risk. Worst they could say of me is, that I did what I thought best, even to my own wrong.'

'You'd better go and try them, then, and see whether they'll give you work. I've turned off upwards of a hundred of my best hands, for no other fault than following you and such as you; and d'ye think I'll take you on? I might as well put a firebrand into the midst of the cotton-waste.'

Higgins turned away; then the recollection of Boucher came over him, and he faced round with the greatest concession he could persuade himself to make.

'I'd promise yo', measter, I'd not speak a word as could do harm, if so be yo' did right by us; and I'd promise more: I'd promise that when I seed yo' going wrong, and acting unfair, I'd speak to yo' in private first; and that would be a fair warning. If yo' and I did na agree in our opinion o' your conduct, yo' might turn me off at an hour's notice.'

'Upon my word, you don't think small beer of yourself! Hamper has had a loss of you. How came he to let you and your wisdom go?'

'Well, we parted wi' mutual dissatisfaction. I wouldn't gi'e the pledge they were asking; and they wouldn't have me at no rate. So I'm free to make another engagement; and as I said before, though I should na' say it, I'm a good hand, measter, and a steady man—specially when I can keep fro' drink; and that I shall do now, if I ne'er did afore.'

'That you may have more money laid up for another strike, I suppose?'

'No! I'd be thankful if I was free to do that; it's for to keep th' widow and childer of a man who was drove mad by them knobsticks o' yourn; put out of his place by a Paddy that did na know weft fro' warp.'

'Well! you'd better turn to something else, if you've any such good intention in your head. I shouldn't advise you to stay in Milton: you're too well known here.'

'If it were summer,' said Higgins, 'I'd take to Paddy's work, and go as a navvy, or haymaking, or summut, and ne'er see Milton again. But it's winter, and th' childer will clem.'

'A pretty navvy you'd make! why, you couldn't do half a day's work at digging against an Irishman.'

'I'd only charge half-a-day for th' twelve hours, if I could only do half-a-day's work in th' time. Yo're not knowing of any place, where they could gi' me a trial, away fro' the mills, if I'm such a firebrand? I'd take any wage they thought I was worth, for the sake of those childer.'

'Don't you see what you would be? You'd be a knobstick. You'd be taking less wages than the other labourers—all for the sake of another man's children. Think how you'd abuse any poor fellow who was willing to take what he could get to keep his own children. You and your Union would soon be down upon him. No!

no! if it's only for the recollection of the way in which you've used the poor knob-sticks before now, I say No! to your question. I'll not give you work. I won't say, I don't believe your pretext for coming and asking for work; I know nothing about it. It may be true, or it may not. It's a very unlikely story, at any rate. Let me pass. I'll not give you work. There's your answer.'

'I hear, sir. I would na ha' troubled yo', but that I were bid to come, by one as seemed to think yo'd getten some soft place in yo'r heart. Hoo were mistook, and I were misled. But I'm not the first man as is misled by a woman.'

'Tell her to mind her own business the next time, instead of taking up your time and mine too. I believe women are at the bottom of every plague in this world. Be off with you.'

'I'm obleeged to yo' for a' yo'r kindness, measter, and most of a' for yo'r civil way o' saying good-bye.'

Mr. Thornton did not deign a reply. But, looking out of the window a minute after, he was struck with the lean, bent figure going out of the yard: the heavy walk was in strange contrast with the resolute, clear determination of the man to speak to him. He crossed to the porter's lodge:

'How long has that man Higgins been waiting to speak to me?'

'He was outside the gate before eight o'clock, sir. I think he's been there ever since.'

'And it is now—?'

'Just one, sir.'

'Five hours,' thought Mr. Thornton; 'it's a long time for a man to wait, doing nothing but first hoping and then fearing.'

CHAPTER XXXIX - MAKING FRIENDS

'Nay, I have done; you get no more of me:
And I am glad, yea glad with all my heart,
That thus so clearly I myself am free.'
DRAYTON.

Margaret shut herself up in her own room, after she had quitted Mrs. Thornton. She began to walk backwards and forwards, in her old habitual way of showing agitation; but, then, remembering that in that slightly-built house every step was heard from one room to another, she sate down until she heard Mrs. Thornton go safely out of the house. She forced herself to recollect all the conversation that had passed between them; speech by speech, she compelled her memory to go through with it. At the end, she rose up, and said to herself, in a melancholy tone:

'At any rate, her words do not touch me; they fall off from me; for I am innocent of all the motives she attributes to me. But still, it is hard to think that any one—any woman—can believe all this of another so easily. It is hard and sad. Where I have done wrong, she does not accuse me—she does not know. He never told her: I might have known he would not!'

She lifted up her head, as if she took pride in any delicacy of feeling which Mr. Thornton had shown. Then, as a new thought came across her, she pressed her hands tightly together.

'He, too, must take poor Frederick for some lover.' (She blushed as the word passed through her mind.) 'I see it now. It is not merely that he knows of my falsehood, but he believes that some one else cares for me; and that I—— Oh dear!—oh dear! What shall I do? What do I mean? Why do I care what he thinks, beyond the mere loss of his good opinion as regards my telling the truth or not? I cannot tell. But I am very miserable! Oh, how unhappy this last year has been! I have passed out of childhood into old age. I have had no youth—no womanhood; the hopes of womanhood have closed for me—for I shall never marry; and I anticipate cares and sorrows just as if I were an old woman, and with the same fearful spirit. I am weary of this continual call upon me for strength. I could bear up for papa; because that is a natural, pious duty. And I think I could bear up against—at any rate, I could have the energy to resent, Mrs. Thornton's unjust, impertinent suspicions. But it is hard to feel how completely he must misunderstand me. What has happened to make me so morbid to-day? I do not know. I only know I cannot help it. I must give way sometimes. No, I will not, though,' said she, springing to her feet. 'I will not—I *will* not think of myself and my own position. I won't examine into my own feelings. It would be of no use now. Some time, if I live to be an old woman, I may sit over the fire, and, looking into the embers, see the life that might have been.'

All this time, she was hastily putting on her things to go out, only stopping from time to time to wipe her eyes, with an impatience of gesture at the tears that would come, in spite of all her bravery.

'I dare say, there's many a woman makes as sad a mistake as I have done, and only finds it out too late. And how proudly and impertinently I spoke to him that day! But I did not know then. It has come upon me little by little, and I don't know where it began. Now I won't give way. I shall find it difficult to behave in the same way to him, with this miserable consciousness upon me; but I will be very calm and very quiet, and say very little. But, to be sure, I may not see him; he keeps out of our way evidently. That would be worse than all. And yet no wonder that he avoids me, believing what he must about me.'

She went out, going rapidly towards the country, and trying to drown reflection by swiftness of motion.

As she stood on the door-step, at her return, her father came up:

'Good girl!' said he. 'You've been to Mrs. Boucher's. I was just meaning to go there, if I had time, before dinner.'

'No, papa; I have not,' said Margaret, reddening. 'I never thought about her. But I will go directly after dinner; I will go while you are taking your nap.

Accordingly Margaret went. Mrs. Boucher was very ill; really ill—not merely ailing. The kind and sensible neighbour, who had come in the other day, seemed to have taken charge of everything. Some of the children were gone to the neighbours. Mary Higgins had come for the three youngest at dinner-time; and since then Nicholas had gone for the doctor. He had not come as yet; Mrs. Boucher was dying; and there was nothing to do but to wait. Margaret thought that she should like to know his opinion, and that she could not do better than go and see the Higginses in the meantime. She might then possibly hear whether Nicholas had been able to make his application to Mr. Thornton.

She found Nicholas busily engaged in making a penny spin on the dresser, for the amusement of three little children, who were clinging to him in a fearless manner. He, as well as they, was smiling at a good long spin; and Margaret thought, that the happy look of interest in his occupation was a good sign. When the penny stopped spinning, 'lile Johnnie' began to cry.

'Come to me,' said Margaret, taking him off the dresser, and holding him in her arms; she held her watch to his ear, while she asked Nicholas if he had seen Mr. Thornton.

The look on his face changed instantly.

'Ay!' said he. 'I've seen and heerd too much on him.'

'He refused you, then?' said Margaret, sorrowfully.

'To be sure. I knew he'd do it all long. It's no good expecting marcy at the hands o' them measters. Yo're a stranger and a foreigner, and aren't likely to know their ways; but I knowed it.'

'I am sorry I asked you. Was he angry? He did not speak to you as Hamper did, did he?'

'He weren't o'er-civil!' said Nicholas, spinning the penny again, as much for his own amusement as for that of the children. 'Never yo' fret, I'm only where I was. I'll go on tramp to-morrow. I gave him as good as I got. I telled him, I'd not that good opinion on him that I'd ha' come a second time of mysel'; but yo'd advised me for to come, and I were beholden to yo'.'

'You told him I sent you?'

'I dunno' if I ca'd yo' by your name. I dunnot think I did. I said, a woman who knew no better had advised me for to come and see if there was a soft place in his heart.'

'And he—?' asked Margaret.

'Said I were to tell yo' to mind yo'r own business.—That's the longest spin yet, my lads.—And them's civil words to what he used to me. But ne'er mind. We're but where we was; and I'll break stones on th' road afore I let these little uns clem.'

Margaret put the struggling Johnnie out of her arms, back into his former place on the dresser.

'I am sorry I asked you to go to Mr. Thornton's. I am disappointed in him.'

There was a slight noise behind her. Both she and Nicholas turned round at the same moment, and there stood Mr. Thornton, with a look of displeased surprise upon his face. Obeying her swift impulse, Margaret passed out before him, saying not a word, only bowing low to hide the sudden paleness that she felt had come over her face. He bent equally low in return, and then closed the door after her. As she hurried to Mrs. Boucher's, she heard the clang, and it seemed to fill up the measure of her mortification. He too was annoyed to find her there. He had tenderness in his heart—'a soft place,' as Nicholas Higgins called it; but he had some pride in concealing it; he kept it very sacred and safe, and was jealous of every circumstance that tried to gain admission. But if he dreaded exposure of his tenderness, he was equally desirous that all men should recognise his justice; and he felt that he had been unjust, in giving so scornful a hearing to any one who had waited, with humble patience, for five hours, to speak to him. That the man had spoken saucily to him when he had the opportunity, was nothing to Mr. Thornton. He rather liked him for it; and he was conscious of his own irritability of temper at the time, which probably made them both quits. It was the five hours of waiting that struck Mr. Thornton. He had not five hours to spare himself; but one hour—two hours, of his hard penetrating intellectual, as well as bodily labour, did he give up to going about collecting evidence as to the truth of Higgins's story, the nature of his character, the tenor of his life. He tried not to be, but was convinced that all that Higgins had said was true. And then the conviction went in, as if by some spell, and touched the latent tenderness of his heart; the patience of the man, the simple generosity of the motive (for he had learnt about the quarrel between Boucher and Higgins), made him forget entirely the mere reasonings of justice, and overleap them by a diviner instinct. He came to tell Higgins he would give him work; and he was more annoyed to find Margaret there than by hearing her last words, for then he understood that she was the woman who had urged Higgins to come to him; and he dreaded the admission of any thought of her, as a motive to what he was doing solely because it was right.

'So that was the lady you spoke of as a woman?' said he indignantly to Higgins. 'You might have told me who she was.

'And then, maybe, yo'd ha' spoken of her more civil than yo' did; yo'd getten a mother who might ha' kept yo'r tongue in check when yo' were talking o' women being at the root o' all the plagues.'

'Of course you told that to Miss Hale?'

'In coorse I did. Leastways, I reckon I did. I telled her she weren't to meddle again in aught that concerned yo'.'

'Whose children are those—yours?' Mr. Thornton had a pretty good notion whose they were, from what he had heard; but he felt awkward in turning the conversation round from this unpromising beginning.

'They're not mine, and they are mine.'

'They are the children you spoke of to me this morning?'

'When yo' said,' replied Higgins, turning round, with ill-smothered fierceness, 'that my story might be true or might not, bur it were a very unlikely one. Measter, I've not forgetten.'

Mr. Thornton was silent for a moment; then he said: 'No more have I. I remember what I said. I spoke to you about those children in a way I had no business to do. I did not believe you. I could not have taken care of another man's children myself, if he had acted towards me as I hear Boucher did towards you. But I know now that you spoke truth. I beg your pardon.'

Higgins did not turn round, or immediately respond to this. But when he did speak, it was in a softened tone, although the words were gruff enough.

'Yo've no business to go prying into what happened between Boucher and me. He's dead, and I'm sorry. That's enough.'

'So it is. Will you take work with me? That's what I came to ask.'

Higgins's obstinacy wavered, recovered strength, and stood firm. He would not speak. Mr. Thornton would not ask again. Higgins's eye fell on the children.

'Yo've called me impudent, and a liar, and a mischief-maker, and yo' might ha' said wi' some truth, as I were now and then given to drink. An' I ha' called you a tyrant, an' an oud bull-dog, and a hard, cruel master; that's where it stands. But for th' childer. Measter, do yo' think we can e'er get on together?'

'Well!' said Mr. Thornton, half-laughing, 'it was not my proposal that we should go together. But there's one comfort, on your own showing. We neither of us can think much worse of the other than we do now.'

'That's true,' said Higgins, reflectively. 'I've been thinking, ever sin' I saw you, what a marcy it were yo' did na take me on, for that I ne'er saw a man whom I could less abide. But that's maybe been a hasty judgment; and work's work to such as me. So, measter, I'll come; and what's more, I thank yo'; and that's a deal fro' me,' said he, more frankly, suddenly turning round and facing Mr. Thornton fully for the first time.

'And this is a deal from me,' said Mr. Thornton, giving Higgins's hand a good grip. 'Now mind you come sharp to your time,' continued he, resuming the master. 'I'll have no laggards at my mill. What fines we have, we keep pretty sharply. And the first time I catch you making mischief, off you go. So now you know where you are.'

'Yo' spoke of my wisdom this morning. I reckon I may bring it wi' me; or would yo' rayther have me 'bout my brains?'

''Bout your brains if you use them for meddling with my business; with your brains if you can keep them to your own.'

'I shall need a deal o' brains to settle where my business ends and yo'rs begins.'

'Your business has not begun yet, and mine stands still for me. So good afternoon.'

Just before Mr. Thornton came up to Mrs. Boucher's door, Margaret came out of it. She did not see him; and he followed her for several yards, admiring her light and easy walk, and her tall and graceful figure. But, suddenly, this simple emotion of pleasure was tainted, poisoned by jealousy. He wished to overtake her, and speak to her, to see how she would receive him, now she must know he was aware of some other attachment. He wished too, but of this wish he was rather ashamed, that she should know that he had justified her wisdom in sending Higgins to him to ask for work; and had repented him of his morning's decision. He came up to her. She started.

'Allow me to say, Miss Hale, that you were rather premature in expressing your disappointment. I have taken Higgins on.'

'I am glad of it,' said she, coldly.

'He tells me, he repeated to you, what I said this morning about—' Mr. Thornton hesitated. Margaret took it up:

'About women not meddling. You had a perfect right to express your opinion, which was a very correct one, I have no doubt. But,' she went on a little more eagerly, 'Higgins did not quite tell you the exact truth.' The word 'truth,' reminded her of her own untruth, and she stopped short, feeling exceedingly uncomfortable.

Mr. Thornton at first was puzzled to account for her silence; and then he remembered the lie she had told, and all that was foregone. 'The exact truth!' said he. 'Very few people do speak the exact truth. I have given up hoping for it. Miss Hale, have you no explanation to give me? You must perceive what I cannot but think.'

Margaret was silent. She was wondering whether an explanation of any kind would be consistent with her loyalty to Frederick.

'Nay,' said he, 'I will ask no farther. I may be putting temptation in your way. At present, believe me, your secret is safe with me. But you run great risks, allow me to say, in being so indiscreet. I am now only speaking as a friend of your father's: if I had any other thought or hope, of course that is at an end. I am quite disinterested.'

'I am aware of that,' said Margaret, forcing herself to speak in an indifferent, careless way. 'I am aware of what I must appear to you, but the secret is another person's, and I cannot explain it without doing him harm.'

'I have not the slightest wish to pry into the gentleman's secrets,' he said, with growing anger. 'My own interest in you is—simply that of a friend. You may not believe me, Miss Hale, but it is—in spite of the persecution I'm afraid I threatened you with at one time—but that is all given up; all passed away. You believe me, Miss Hale?'

'Yes,' said Margaret, quietly and sadly.

'Then, really, I don't see any occasion for us to go on walking together. I thought, perhaps you might have had something to say, but I see we are nothing to each other. If you're quite convinced, that any foolish passion on my part is entirely over, I will wish you good afternoon.' He walked off very hastily.

'What can he mean?' thought Margaret,—'what could he mean by speaking so, as if I were always thinking that he cared for me, when I know he does not; he cannot. His mother will have said all those cruel things about me to him. But I won't care for him. I surely am mistress enough of myself to control this wild, strange, miserable feeling, which tempted me even to betray my own dear Frederick, so that I might but regain his good opinion—the good opinion of a man who takes such pains to tell me that I am nothing to him. Come poor little heart! be cheery and brave. We'll be a great deal to one another, if we are thrown off and left desolate.'

Her father was almost startled by her merriment this afternoon. She talked incessantly, and forced her natural humour to an unusual pitch; and if there was a tinge of bitterness in much of what she said; if her accounts of the old Harley Street set were a little sarcastic, her father could not bear to check her, as he would have done at another time—for he was glad to see her shake off her cares. In the middle of the evening, she was called down to speak to Mary Higgins; and when she came back, Mr. Hale imagined that he saw traces of tears on her cheeks. But that could not be, for she brought good news—that Higgins had got work at Mr. Thornton's mill. Her spirits were damped, at any rate, and she found it very difficult to go on talking at all, much more in the wild way that she had done. For some days her spirits varied strangely; and her father was beginning to be anxious about her, when news arrived from one or two quarters that promised some change and variety for her. Mr. Hale received a letter from Mr. Bell, in which that gentleman volunteered a visit to them; and Mr. Hale imagined that the promised society of his old Oxford friend would give as agreeable a turn to Margaret's ideas as it did to his own. Margaret tried to take an interest in what pleased her father; but she was too languid to care about any Mr. Bell, even though he were twenty times her godfather. She was more roused by a letter from Edith, full of sympathy about her aunt's death; full of details about herself, her husband, and child; and at the end saying, that as the climate did not suit, the baby, and as Mrs. Shaw was talking of returning to England, she thought it probable that Captain Lennox might sell out, and that they might all go and live again in the old Harley Street house; which, however, would seem very incomplete with-out Margaret. Margaret yearned after that old house, and the placid tranquillity of that old well-ordered, monotonous life. She had found it occasionally tiresome while it lasted; but since then she had been buffeted about, and felt so exhausted by this recent struggle with herself, that she thought that even stagnation would be a rest and a refreshment. So she began to look towards a long visit to the Lennoxes, on their return to England, as to a point—no, not of hope—but of leisure, in which she could regain her power and command over herself. At present it seemed to her as if all subjects tended towards Mr. Thornton; as if she could not forget him with all her endeavours. If she went to see the Higginses, she heard of him there; her father had resumed their readings together, and quoted his opinions perpetually; even Mr. Bell's visit brought his tenant's name upon the tapis; for he wrote word that he believed he must be occupied some great part of his time with Mr. Thornton, as a new lease was in preparation, and the terms of it must be agreed upon.

CHAPTER XL - OUT OF TUNE

'I have no wrong, where I can claim no right,
  Naught ta'en me fro, where I have nothing had,
  Yet of my woe I cannot so be quite;
  Namely, since that another may be glad
  With that, that thus in sorrow makes me sad.'
      WYATT.

Margaret had not expected much pleasure to herself from Mr. Bell's visit—she had only looked forward to it on her father's account, but when her godfather came, she at once fell into the most natural position of friendship in the world. He said she had no merit in being what she was, a girl so entirely after his own heart; it was an hereditary power which she had, to walk in and take possession of his regard; while she, in reply, gave him much credit for being so fresh and young under his Fellow's cap and gown.

'Fresh and young in warmth and kindness, I mean. I'm afraid I must own, that I think your opinions are the oldest and mustiest I have met with this long time.'

'Hear this daughter of yours, Hale. Her residence in Milton has quite corrupted her. She's a democrat, a red republican, a member of the Peace Society, a socialist—'

'Papa, it's all because I'm standing up for the progress of commerce. Mr. Bell would have had it keep still at exchanging wild-beast skins for acorns.'

'No, no. I'd dig the ground and grow potatoes. And I'd shave the wild-beast skins and make the wool into broad cloth. Don't exaggerate, missy. But I'm tired of this bustle. Everybody rushing over everybody, in their hurry to get rich.'

'It is not every one who can sit comfortably in a set of college rooms, and let his riches grow without any exertion of his own. No doubt there is many a man here who would be thankful if his property would increase as yours has done, without his taking any trouble about it,' said Mr. Hale.

'I don't believe they would. It's the bustle and the struggle they like. As for sitting still, and learning from the past, or shaping out the future by faithful work done in a prophetic spirit—Why! Pooh! I don't believe there's a man in Milton who knows how to sit still; and it is a great art.'

'Milton people, I suspect, think Oxford men don't know how to move. It would be a very good thing if they mixed a little more.'

'It might be good for the Miltoners. Many things might be good for them which would be very disagreeable for other people.'

'Are you not a Milton man yourself?' asked Margaret. 'I should have thought you would have been proud of your town.'

'I confess, I don't see what there is to be proud of. If you'll only come to Oxford, Margaret, I will show you a place to glory in.'

'Well!' said Mr. Hale, 'Mr. Thornton is coming to drink tea with us to-night, and he is as proud of Milton as you of Oxford. You two must try and make each other a little more liberal-minded.'

'I don't want to be more liberal-minded, thank you,' said Mr. Bell.

'Is Mr. Thornton coming to tea, papa?' asked Margaret in a low voice.

'Either to tea or soon after. He could not tell. He told us not to wait.'

Mr. Thornton had determined that he would make no inquiry of his mother as to how far she had put her project into execution of speaking to Margaret about the impropriety of her conduct. He felt pretty sure that, if this interview took place, his mother's account of what passed at it would only annoy and chagrin him, though he would all the time be aware of the colouring which it received by passing through her mind. He shrank from hearing Margaret's very name mentioned; he, while he blamed her—while he was jealous of her—while he renounced her—he loved her sorely, in spite of himself. He dreamt of her; he dreamt she came dancing towards him with outspread arms, and with a lightness and gaiety which made him loathe her, even while it allured him. But the impression of this figure of Margaret—with all Margaret's character taken out of it, as completely as if some evil spirit had got possession of her form—was so deeply stamped upon his imagination, that when he wakened he felt hardly able to separate the Una from the Duessa; and the dislike he had to the latter seemed to envelope and disfigure the former. Yet he was too proud to acknowledge his weakness by avoiding the sight of her. He would neither seek an opportunity of being in her company nor avoid it. To convince himself of his power of self-control, he lingered over every piece of business this afternoon; he forced every movement into unnatural slowness and deliberation; and it was consequently past eight o'clock before he reached Mr. Hale's. Then there were business arrangements to be transacted in the study with Mr. Bell; and the latter kept on, sitting over the fire, and talking wearily, long after all business was transacted, and when they might just as well have gone upstairs. But Mr. Thornton would not say a word about moving their quarters; he chafed and chafed, and thought Mr. Bell a most prosy companion; while Mr. Bell returned the compliment in secret, by considering Mr. Thornton about as brusque and curt a fellow as he had ever met with, and terribly gone off both in intelligence and manner. At last, some slight noise in the room above suggested the desirableness of moving there. They found Margaret with a letter open before her, eagerly discussing its contents with her father.

On the entrance of the gentlemen, it was immediately put aside; but Mr. Thornton's eager senses caught some few words of Mr. Hale's to Mr. Bell.

'A letter from Henry Lennox. It makes Margaret very hopeful.'

Mr. Bell nodded. Margaret was red as a rose when Mr. Thornton looked at her. He had the greatest mind in the world to get up and go out of the room that very instant, and never set foot in the house again.

'We were thinking,' said Mr. Hale, 'that you and Mr. Thornton had taken Margaret's advice, and were each trying to convert the other, you were so long in the study.'

'And you thought there would be nothing left of us but an opinion, like the Kilkenny cat's tail. Pray whose opinion did you think would have the most obstinate vitality?'

Mr. Thornton had not a notion what they were talking about, and disdained to inquire. Mr. Hale politely enlightened him.

'Mr. Thornton, we were accusing Mr. Bell this morning of a kind of Oxonian mediaeval bigotry against his native town; and we—Margaret, I believe—suggested that it would do him good to associate a little with Milton manufacturers.'

'I beg your pardon. Margaret thought it would do the Milton manufacturers good to associate a little more with Oxford men. Now wasn't it so, Margaret?'

'I believe I thought it would do both good to see a little more of the other,—I did not know it was my idea any more than papa's.'

'And so you see, Mr. Thornton, we ought to have been improving each other down-stairs, instead of talking over vanished families of Smiths and Harrisons. However, I am willing to do my part now. I wonder when you Milton men intend to live. All your lives seem to be spent in gathering together the materials for life.'

'By living, I suppose you mean enjoyment.'

'Yes, enjoyment,—I don't specify of what, because I trust we should both consider mere pleasure as very poor enjoyment.'

'I would rather have the nature of the enjoyment defined.'

'Well! enjoyment of leisure—enjoyment of the power and influence which money gives. You are all striving for money. What do you want it for?'

Mr. Thornton was silent. Then he said, 'I really don't know. But money is not what *I* strive for.'

'What then?'

'It is a home question. I shall have to lay myself open to such a catechist, and I am not sure that I am prepared to do it.'

'No!' said Mr. Hale; 'don't let us be personal in our catechism. You are neither of you representative men; you are each of you too individual for that.'

'I am not sure whether to consider that as a compliment or not. I should like to be the representative of Oxford, with its beauty and its learning, and its proud old history. What do you say, Margaret; ought I to be flattered?'

'I don't know Oxford. But there is a difference between being the representative of a city and the representative man of its inhabitants.'

'Very true, Miss Margaret. Now I remember, you were against me this morning, and were quite Miltonian and manufacturing in your preferences.' Margaret saw the quick glance of surprise that Mr. Thornton gave her, and she was annoyed at the construction which he might put on this speech of Mr. Bell's. Mr. Bell went on—

'Ah! I wish I could show you our High Street—our Radcliffe Square. I am leaving out our colleges, just as I give Mr. Thornton leave to omit his factories in speaking of the charms of Milton. I have a right to abuse my birth-place. Remember I am a Milton man.

Mr. Thornton was annoyed more than he ought to have been at all that Mr. Bell was saying. He was not in a mood for joking. At another time, he could have enjoyed Mr. Bell's half testy condemnation of a town where the life was so at variance with every habit he had formed; but now, he was galled enough to attempt to defend what was never meant to be seriously attacked.

'I don't set up Milton as a model of a town.'

'Not in architecture?' slyly asked Mr. Bell.

'No! We've been too busy to attend to mere outward appearances.'

'Don't say *mere* outward appearances,' said Mr. Hale, gently. 'They impress us all, from childhood upward—every day of our life.'

'Wait a little while,' said Mr. Thornton. 'Remember, we are of a different race from the Greeks, to whom beauty was everything, and to whom Mr. Bell might speak of a life of leisure and serene enjoyment, much of which entered in through their outward senses. I don't mean to despise them, any more than I would ape them. But I belong to Teutonic blood; it is little mingled in this part of England to what it is in others; we retain much of their language; we retain more of their spirit; we do not look upon life as a time for enjoyment, but as a time for action and exertion. Our glory and our beauty arise out of our inward strength, which makes us victorious over material resistance, and over greater difficulties still. We are Teutonic up here in Darkshire in another way. We hate to have laws made for us at a distance. We wish people would allow us to right ourselves, instead of continually meddling, with their imperfect legislation. We stand up for self-government, and oppose centralisation.'

'In short, you would like the Heptarchy back again. Well, at any rate, I revoke what I said this morning—that you Milton people did not reverence the past. You are regular worshippers of Thor.'

'If we do not reverence the past as you do in Oxford, it is because we want something which can apply to the present more directly. It is fine when the study of the past leads to a prophecy of the future. But to men groping in new circumstances, it would be finer if the words of experience could direct us how to act in what concerns us most intimately and immediately; which is full of difficulties that must be encountered; and upon the mode in which they are met and conquered—not merely pushed aside for the time—depends our future. Out of the wisdom of the past, help us over the present. But no! People can speak of Utopia much more easily than of the next day's duty; and yet when that duty is all done by others, who so ready to cry, "Fie, for shame!"'

'And all this time I don't see what you are talking about. Would you Milton men condescend to send up your to-day's difficulty to Oxford? You have not tried us yet.'

Mr. Thornton laughed outright at this. 'I believe I was talking with reference to a good deal that has been troubling us of late; I was thinking of the strikes we have gone through, which are troublesome and injurious things enough, as I am finding to my cost. And yet this last strike, under which I am smarting, has been respectable.'

'A respectable strike!' said Mr. Bell. 'That sounds as if you were far gone in the worship of Thor.'

Margaret felt, rather than saw, that Mr. Thornton was chagrined by the repeated turning into jest of what he was feeling as very serious. She tried to change the conversation from a subject about which one party cared little, while, to the other, it was deeply, because personally, interesting. She forced herself to say something.

'Edith says she finds the printed calicoes in Corfu better and cheaper than in London.'

'Does she?' said her father. 'I think that must be one of Edith's exaggerations. Are you sure of it, Margaret?'

'I am sure she says so, papa.'

'Then I am sure of the fact,' said Mr. Bell. 'Margaret, I go so far in my idea of your truthfulness, that it shall cover your cousin's character. I don't believe a cousin of yours could exaggerate.'

'Is Miss Hale so remarkable for truth?' said Mr. Thornton, bitterly. The moment he had done so, he could have bitten his tongue out. What was he? And why should he stab her with her shame in this way? How evil he was to-night; possessed by ill-humour at being detained so long from her; irritated by the mention of some name, because he thought it belonged to a more successful lover; now ill-tempered because he had been unable to cope, with a light heart, against one who was trying, by gay and careless speeches, to make the evening pass pleasantly away,—the kind old friend to all parties, whose manner by this time might be well known to Mr. Thornton, who had been acquainted with him for many years. And then to speak to Margaret as he had done! She did not get up and leave the room, as she had done in former days, when his abruptness or his temper had annoyed her. She sat quite still, after the first momentary glance of grieved surprise, that made her eyes look like some child's who has met with an unexpected rebuff; they slowly dilated into mournful, reproachful sadness; and then they fell, and she bent over her work, and did not speak again. But he could not help looking at her, and he saw a sigh tremble over her body, as if she quivered in some unwonted chill. He felt as the mother would have done, in the midst of 'her rocking it, and rating it,' had she been called away before her slow confiding smile, implying perfect trust in mother's love, had proved the renewing of its love. He gave short sharp answers; he was uneasy and cross, unable to discern between jest and earnest; anxious only for a look, a word of hers, before which to prostrate himself in penitent humility. But she neither looked nor spoke. Her round taper fingers flew in and out of her sewing, as steadily and swiftly as if that were the business of her life. She could not care for him, he thought, or else the passionate fervour of his wish would have forced her to raise those eyes, if but for an instant, to read the late repentance in his. He could have struck her before he left, in order that by some strange overt act of rudeness, he might earn the privilege of telling her the remorse that gnawed at his heart. It was well that the long walk in the open air wound up this evening for him. It sobered him back into grave resolution, that henceforth he would see as little of her as possible,—since the very sight of that face and form, the very sounds of that voice (like the soft winds of pure melody) had such power to move him from his balance. Well! He had known what love was—a sharp pang, a fierce experience, in the midst of whose flames he was struggling! but, through that furnace he would fight his way out into the serenity of middle age,—all the richer and more human for having known this great passion.

When he had somewhat abruptly left the room, Margaret rose from her seat, and began silently to fold up her work; the long seams were heavy, and had an unusual weight for her languid arms. The round lines in her face took a lengthened, straighter form, and her whole appearance was that of one who had gone through a day of great fatigue. As the three prepared for bed, Mr. Bell muttered forth a little condemnation of Mr. Thornton.

'I never saw a fellow so spoiled by success. He can't bear a word; a jest of any kind. Everything seems to touch on the soreness of his high dignity. Formerly, he was as simple and noble as the open day; you could not offend him, because he had no vanity.'

'He is not vain now,' said Margaret, turning round from the table, and speaking with quiet distinctness. 'To-night he has not been like himself. Something must have annoyed him before he came here.'

Mr. Bell gave her one of his sharp glances from above his spectacles. She stood it quite calmly; but, after she had left the room, he suddenly asked,—

'Hale! did it ever strike you that Thornton and your daughter have what the French call a tendresse for each other?'

'Never!' said Mr. Hale, first startled and then flurried by the new idea. 'No, I am sure you are wrong. I am almost certain you are mistaken. If there is anything, it is all on Mr. Thornton's side. Poor fellow! I hope and trust he is not thinking of her, for I am sure she would not have him.'

'Well! I'm a bachelor, and have steered clear of love affairs all my life; so perhaps my opinion is not worth having. Or else I should say there were very pretty symptoms about her!'

'Then I am sure you are wrong,' said Mr. Hale. 'He may care for her, though she really has been almost rude to him at times. But she!—why, Margaret would never think of him, I'm sure! Such a thing has never entered her head.'

'Entering her heart would do. But I merely threw out a suggestion of what might be. I dare say I was wrong. And whether I was wrong or right, I'm very sleepy; so, having disturbed your night's rest (as I can see) with my untimely fancies, I'll betake myself with an easy mind to my own.'

But Mr. Hale resolved that he would not be disturbed by any such nonsensical idea; so he lay awake, determining not to think about it.

Mr. Bell took his leave the next day, bidding Margaret look to him as one who had a right to help and protect her in all her troubles, of whatever nature they might be. To Mr. Hale he said,—

'That Margaret of yours has gone deep into my heart. Take care of her, for she is a very precious creature,—a great deal too good for Milton,—only fit for Oxford, in fact. The town, I mean; not the men. I can't match her yet. When I can, I shall bring my young man to stand side by side with your young woman, just as the genie in the Arabian Nights brought Prince Caralmazan to match with the fairy's Princess Badoura.'

'I beg you'll do no such thing. Remember the misfortunes that ensued; and besides, I can't spare Margaret.'

'No; on second thoughts, we'll have her to nurse us ten years hence, when we shall be two cross old invalids. Seriously, Hale! I wish you'd leave Milton; which is a most unsuitable place for you, though it was my recommendation in the first instance. If you would; I'd swallow my shadows of doubts, and take a college living; and you and Margaret should come and live at the parsonage—you to be a sort of lay curate, and take the unwashed off my hands; and she to be our housekeeper—the village Lady Bountiful—by day; and read us to sleep in the evenings. I could be very happy in such a life. What do you think of it?'

'Never!' said Mr. Hale, decidedly. 'My one great change has been made and my price of suffering paid. Here I stay out my life; and here will I be buried, and lost in the crowd.'

'I don't give up my plan yet. Only I won't bait you with it any more just now. Where's the Pearl? Come, Margaret, give me a farewell kiss; and remember, my dear, where you may find a true friend, as far as his capability goes. You are my child, Margaret. Remember that, and 'God bless you!'

So they fell back into the monotony of the quiet life they would henceforth lead. There was no invalid to hope and fear about; even the Higginses—so long a vivid interest—seemed to have receded from any need of immediate thought. The Boucher children, left motherless orphans, claimed what of Margaret's care she could bestow; and she went pretty often to see Mary Higgins, who had charge of them. The two families were living in one house: the elder children were at humble schools, the younger ones were tended, in Mary's absence at her work, by the kind neighbour whose good sense had struck Margaret at the time of Boucher's death. Of course she was paid for her trouble; and indeed, in all his little plans and arrangements for these orphan children, Nicholas showed a sober judgment, and regulated method of thinking, which were at variance with his former more eccentric jerks of action. He was so steady at his work, that Margaret did not often see him during these winter months; but when she did, she saw that he winced away from any reference to the father of those children, whom he had so fully and heartily taken under his care. He did not speak easily of Mr. Thornton.

'To tell the truth,' said he, 'he fairly bamboozles me. He's two chaps. One chap I knowed of old as were measter all o'er. T'other chap hasn't an ounce of measter's flesh about him. How them two chaps is bound up in one body, is a craddy for me to find out. I'll not be beat by it, though. Meanwhile he comes here pretty often; that's how I know the chap that's a man, not a measter. And I reckon he's taken aback by me pretty much as I am by him; for he sits and listens and stares, as if I were some strange beast newly caught in some of the zones. But I'm none daunted. It would take a deal to daunt me in my own house, as he sees. And I tell him some of my mind that I reckon he'd ha' been the better of hearing when he were a younger man.'

'And does he not answer you?' asked Mr. Hale.

'Well! I'll not say th' advantage is all on his side, for all I take credit for improving him above a bit. Sometimes he says a rough thing or two, which is not agreeable to look at at first, but has a queer smack o' truth in it when yo' come to chew it. He'll be coming to-night, I reckon, about them childer's schooling. He's not satisfied wi' the make of it, and wants for t' examine 'em.'

'What are they'—began Mr. Hale; but Margaret, touching his arm, showed him her watch.

'It is nearly seven,' she said. 'The evenings are getting longer now. Come, papa.' She did not breathe freely till they were some distance from the house. Then, as she became more calm, she wished that she had not been in so great a hurry; for, somehow, they saw Mr. Thornton but very seldom now; and he might have come to see Higgins, and for the old friendship's sake she should like to have seen him to-night.

Yes! he came very seldom, even for the dull cold purpose of lessons. Mr. Hale was disappointed in his pupil's lukewarmness about Greek literature, which had but a short time ago so great an interest for him. And now it often happened that a hurried note from Mr. Thornton would arrive, just at the last moment, saying that he was so much engaged that he could not come to read with Mr. Hale that evening. And though other pupils had taken more than his place as to time, no one was like his first scholar in Mr. Hale's heart. He was depressed and sad at this partial cessation of an intercourse which had become dear to him; and he used to sit pondering over the reason that could have occasioned this change.

He startled Margaret, one evening as she sate at her work, by suddenly asking:

'Margaret! had you ever any reason for thinking that Mr. Thornton cared for you?'

He almost blushed as he put this question; but Mr. Bell's scouted idea recurred to him, and the words were out of his mouth before he well knew what he was about.

Margaret did not answer immediately; but by the bent drooping of her head, he guessed what her reply would be.

'Yes; I believe—oh papa, I should have told you.' And she dropped her work, and hid her face in her hands.

'No, dear; don't think that I am impertinently curious. I am sure you would have told me if you had felt that you could return his regard. Did he speak to you about it?'

No answer at first; but by-and-by a little gentle reluctant 'Yes.'

'And you refused him?'

A long sigh; a more helpless, nerveless attitude, and another 'Yes.' But before her father could speak, Margaret lifted up her face, rosy with some beautiful shame, and, fixing her eyes upon him, said:

'Now, papa, I have told you this, and I cannot tell you more; and then the whole thing is so painful to me; every word and action connected with it is so unspeakably bitter, that I cannot bear to think of it. Oh, papa, I am sorry to have lost you this friend, but I could not help it—but oh! I am very sorry.' She sate down on the ground, and laid her head on his knees.

'I too, am sorry, my dear. Mr. Bell quite startled me when he said, some idea of the kind—'

'Mr. Bell! Oh, did Mr. Bell see it?'

'A little; but he took it into his head that you—how shall I say it?—that you were not ungraciously disposed towards Mr. Thornton. I knew that could never be. I hoped the whole thing was but an imagination; but I knew too well what your real feelings were to suppose that you could ever like Mr. Thornton in that way. But I am very sorry.'

They were very quiet and still for some minutes. But, on stroking her cheek in a caressing way soon after, he was almost shocked to find her face wet with tears. As he touched her, she sprang up, and smiling with forced brightness, began to talk of the Lennoxes with such a vehement desire to turn the conversation, that Mr. Hale was too tender-hearted to try to force it back into the old channel.

'To-morrow—yes, to-morrow they will be back in Harley Street. Oh, how strange it will be! I wonder what room they will make into the nursery? Aunt Shaw will be happy with the baby. Fancy Edith a mamma! And Captain Lennox—I wonder what he will do with himself now he has sold out!'

'I'll tell you what,' said her father, anxious to indulge her in this fresh subject of interest, 'I think I must spare you for a fortnight just to run up to town and see the travellers. You could learn more, by half an hour's conversation with Mr. Henry Lennox, about Frederick's chances, than in a dozen of these letters of his; so it would, in fact, be uniting business with pleasure.'

'No, papa, you cannot spare me, and what's more, I won't be spared.' Then after a pause, she added: 'I am losing hope sadly about Frederick; he is letting us down gently, but I can see that Mr. Lennox himself has no hope of hunting up the witnesses under years and years of time. No,' said she, 'that bubble was very pretty, and very dear to our hearts; but it has burst like many another; and we must console ourselves with being glad that Frederick is so happy, and with being a great deal to each other. So don't offend me by talking of being able to spare me, papa, for I assure you you can't.'

But the idea of a change took root and germinated in Margaret's heart, although not in the way in which her father proposed it at first. She began to consider how desirable something of the kind would be to her father, whose spirits, always feeble, now became too frequently depressed, and whose health, though he never complained, had been seriously affected by his wife's illness and death. There were the regular hours of reading with his pupils, but that all giving and no receiving could no longer be called companion-ship, as in the old days when Mr. Thornton came to study under him. Margaret was conscious of the want under which he was suffering, unknown to himself; the want of a man's intercourse with men. At Helstone there had been perpetual occasions for an interchange of visits with neighbouring clergymen; and the poor labourers in the fields, or leisurely tramping home at eve, or tending their cattle in the forest, were always at liberty to speak or be spoken to. But in Milton every one was too busy for quiet speech, or any ripened intercourse of thought; what they said was about business, very present and actual; and when the tension of mind relating to their daily affairs was over, they sunk into fallow rest until next morning. The workman was not to be found after the day's work was done; he had gone away to some lecture, or some club, or some beer-shop, according to his degree of character. Mr. Hale thought of trying to deliver a course of lectures at some of the institutions, but he contemplated doing this so much as an effort of duty, and with so little of the genial impulse of love towards his work and its end, that Margaret was sure that it would not be well done until he could look upon it with some kind of zest.

CHAPTER XLI - THE JOURNEY'S END

'I see my way as birds their trackless way—
I shall arrive! what time, what circuit first,
I ask not: but unless God send his hail
Or blinding fire-balls, sleet, or stifling snow,
In some time—his good time—I shall arrive;
He guides me and the bird. In His good time!'
BROWNING'S PARACELSUS.

So the winter was getting on, and the days were beginning to lengthen, without bringing with them any of the brightness of hope which usually accompanies the rays of a February sun. Mrs. Thornton had of course entirely ceased to come to the house. Mr. Thornton came occasionally, but his visits were addressed to her father, and were confined to the study. Mr. Hale spoke of him as always the same; indeed, the very rarity of their intercourse seemed to make Mr. Hale set only the higher value on it. And from what Margaret could gather of what Mr. Thornton had said, there was nothing in the cessation of his visits which could arise from any umbrage or vexation. His business affairs had become complicated during the strike, and required closer attention than he had given to them last winter. Nay, Margaret could even discover that he spoke from time to time of her, and always, as far as she could learn, in the same calm friendly way, never avoiding and never seeking any mention of her name.

She was not in spirits to raise her father's tone of mind. The dreary peacefulness of the present time had been preceded by so long a period of anxiety and care—even intermixed with storms—that her mind had lost its elasticity. She tried to find herself occupation in teaching the two younger Boucher children, and worked hard at goodness; hard, I say most truly, for her heart seemed dead to the end of all her efforts; and though she made them punctually and painfully, yet she stood as far off as ever from any cheerfulness; her life seemed still bleak and dreary. The only thing she did well, was what she did out of unconscious piety, the silent comforting and consoling of her father. Not a mood of his but what found a ready sympathiser in Margaret; not a wish of his that she did not strive to forecast, and to fulfil. They were quiet wishes to be sure, and hardly named without hesitation and apology. All the more complete and beautiful was her meek spirit of obedience. March brought the news of Frederick's marriage. He and Dolores wrote; she in Spanish-English, as was but natural, and he with little turns and inversions of words which proved how far the idioms of his bride's country were infecting him.

On the receipt of Henry Lennox's letter, announcing how little hope there was of his ever clearing himself at a court-martial, in the absence of the missing witnesses, Frederick had written to Margaret a pretty vehement letter, containing his renunciation of England as his country; he wished he could unnative himself, and declared that he would not take his pardon if it were offered him, nor live in the country if he had permission to do so. All of which made Margaret cry sorely, so unnatural did it seem to her at the first opening; but on consideration, she saw rather in such expression the poignancy of the disappointment which had thus crushed his hopes; and she felt that there was nothing for it but patience. In the next letter, Frederick spoke so joyfully of the future that he had no thought for the past; and Margaret found a use in herself for the patience she had been craving for him. She would have to be patient. But the pretty, timid, girlish letters of Dolores were beginning to have a charm for both Margaret and her father. The young Spaniard was so evidently anxious to make a favourable impression upon her lover's English relations, that her feminine care peeped out at every erasure; and the letters announcing the marriage, were accompanied by a splendid black lace mantilla, chosen by Dolores herself for her unseen sister-in-law, whom Frederick had represented as a paragon of beauty, wisdom and virtue. Frederick's worldly position was raised by this marriage on to as high a level as they could desire. Barbour and Co. was one of the most extensive Spanish houses, and into it he was received as a junior partner. Margaret smiled a little, and then sighed as she remembered afresh her old tirades against trade. Here was her preux chevalier of a brother turned merchant, trader! But then she rebelled against herself, and protested silently against the confusion implied between a Spanish merchant and a Milton mill-owner. Well! trade or no trade, Frederick was very, very happy. Dolores must be charming, and the mantilla was exquisite! And then she returned to the present life.

Her father had occasionally experienced a difficulty in breathing this spring, which had for the time distressed him exceedingly. Margaret was less alarmed, as this difficulty went off completely in the intervals; but she still was so desirous of his shaking off the liability altogether, as to make her very urgent that he should accept Mr. Bell's invitation to visit him at Oxford this April. Mr. Bell's invitation included Margaret. Nay more, he wrote a special letter commanding her to come; but she felt as if it would be a greater relief to her to remain quietly at home, entirely free from any responsibility whatever, and so to rest her mind and heart in a manner which she had not been able to do for more than two years past.

When her father had driven off on his way to the railroad, Margaret felt how great and long had been the pressure on her time and her spirits. It was astonishing, almost stunning, to feel herself so much at liberty; no one depending on her for cheering care, if not for positive happiness; no invalid to plan and think for; she might be idle, and silent, and forgetful,—and what seemed worth more than all the other privileges—she might be unhappy if she liked. For months past, all her own personal cares and troubles had had to be stuffed away into a dark cupboard; but now she had leisure to take them out, and mourn over them, and study their nature, and seek the true method of subduing them into the elements of peace. All these weeks she had been conscious of their existence in a dull kind of way, though they were hidden out of sight. Now, once for all she would consider them, and appoint to each of them its right work in her life. So she sat almost motionless for hours in the drawing-room, going over the bitterness of every remembrance with an unwincing resolution. Only once she cried aloud, at the stinging thought of the faithlessness which gave birth to that abasing falsehood.

She now would not even acknowledge the force of the temptation; her plans for Frederick had all failed, and the temptation lay there a dead mockery,—a mockery which had never had life in it; the lie had been so despicably foolish, seen by the light of the ensuing events, and faith in the power of truth so infinitely the greater wisdom!

In her nervous agitation, she unconsciously opened a book of her father's that lay upon the table,—the words that caught her eye in it, seemed almost made for her present state of acute self-abasement:—

> 'Je ne voudrois pas reprendre mon cœur en ceste sorte: meurs de honte, aveugle, impudent, traistre et desloyal a ton Dieu, et sembables choses; mais je voudrois le corriger par voye de compassion. Or sus, mon pauvre cœur, nous voilà tombez dans la fosse, laquelle nous avions tant resolu d'éschapper. Ah! relevons-nous, et quittons-la pour jamais, reclamons la misericorde de Dieu, et esperons en elle qu'elle nous assistera pour desormais estre plus fermes; et remettons-nous au chemin de l'humilité. Courage, soyons meshuy sur nos gardes, Dieu nous aydera.'

'The way of humility. Ah,' thought Margaret, 'that is what I have missed! But courage, little heart. We will turn back, and by God's help we may find the lost path.'

So she rose up, and determined at once to set to on some work which should take her out of herself. To begin with, she called in Martha, as she passed the drawing-room door in going up-stairs, and tried to find out what was below the grave, respectful, servant-like manner, which crusted over her individual character with an obedience that was almost mechanical. She found it difficult to induce Martha to speak of any of her personal interests; but at last she touched the right chord, in naming Mrs. Thornton. Martha's whole face brightened, and, on a little encouragement, out came a long story, of how her father had been in early life connected with Mrs. Thornton's husband—nay, had even been in a position to show him some kindness; what, Martha hardly knew, for it had happened when she was quite a little child; and circumstances had intervened to separate the two families until Martha was nearly grown up, when, her father having sunk lower and lower from his original occupation as clerk in a warehouse, and her mother being dead, she and her sister, to use Martha's own expression, would have been 'lost' but for Mrs. Thornton; who sought them out, and thought for them, and cared for them.

'I had had the fever, and was but delicate; and Mrs. Thornton, and Mr. Thornton too, they never rested till they had nursed me up in their own house, and sent me to the sea and all. The doctors said the fever was catching, but they cared none for that—only Miss Fanny, and she went a-visiting these folk that she is going to marry into. So, though she was afraid at the time, it has all ended well.'

'Miss Fanny going to be married!' exclaimed Margaret.

'Yes; and to a rich gentleman, too, only he's a deal older than she is. His name is Watson; and his mills are somewhere out beyond Hayleigh; it's a very good marriage, for all he's got such gray hair.'

At this piece of information, Margaret was silent long enough for Martha to recover her propriety, and, with it, her habitual shortness of answer. She swept up the hearth, asked at what time she should prepare tea, and quitted the room with the same wooden face with which she had entered it. Margaret had to pull herself up from indulging a bad trick, which she had lately fallen into, of trying to imagine how every event that she heard of in relation to Mr. Thornton would affect him: whether he would like it or dislike it.

The next day she had the little Boucher children for their lessons, and took a long walk, and ended by a visit to Mary Higgins. Somewhat to Margaret's surprise, she found Nicholas already come home from his work; the lengthening light had deceived her as to the lateness of the evening. He too seemed, by his manners, to have entered a little more on the way of humility; he was quieter, and less self-asserting.

'So th' oud gentleman's away on his travels, is he?' said he. 'Little 'uns telled me so. Eh! but they're sharp 'uns, they are; I a'most think they beat my own wenches for sharpness, though mappen it's wrong to say so, and one on 'em in her grave. There's summut in th' weather, I reckon, as sets folk a-wandering. My measter, him at th' shop yonder, is spinning about th' world somewhere.'

'Is that the reason you're so soon at home to-night?' asked Margaret innocently.

'Thou know'st nought about it, that's all,' said he, contemptuously. 'I'm not one wi' two faces—one for my measter, and t'other for his back. I counted a' th' clocks in the town striking afore I'd leave my work. No! yon Thornton's good enough for to fight wi', but too good for to be cheated. It were you as getten me the place, and I thank yo' for it. Thornton's is not a bad mill, as times go. Stand down, lad, and say yo'r pretty hymn to Miss Margaret. That's right; steady on thy legs, and right arm out as straight as a shewer. One to stop, two to stay, three mak' ready, and four away!'

The little fellow repeated a Methodist hymn, far above his comprehension in point of language, but of which the swinging rhythm had caught his ear, and which he repeated with all the developed cadence of a member of parliament. When Margaret had duly applauded, Nicholas called for another, and yet another, much to her surprise, as she found him thus oddly and unconsciously led to take an interest in the sacred things which he had formerly scouted.

It was past the usual tea-time when she reached home; but she had the comfort of feeling that no one had been kept waiting for her; and of thinking her own thoughts while she rested, instead of anxiously watching another person to learn whether to be grave or gay. After tea she resolved to examine a large packet of letters, and pick out those that were to be destroyed.

Among them she came to four or five of Mr. Henry Lennox's, relating to Frederick's affairs; and she carefully read them over again, with the sole intention, when she began, to ascertain exactly on how fine a chance the justification of her brother hung. But when she had finished the last, and weighed the pros and cons, the little personal revelation of character contained in them forced itself on her notice. It was evident enough, from the stiffness of the wording, that Mr. Lennox had never forgotten his relation to her in any interest he might feel in the subject of the correspondence. They were clever letters; Margaret saw that in a twinkling; but she missed out of them all hearty and genial atmosphere. They were to be preserved, however, as valuable; so she laid them carefully on one side. When this little piece of business was ended, she fell into a reverie; and the thought of her absent father ran strangely in Margaret's head this night. She almost blamed herself for having felt her solitude (and consequently his absence) as a relief; but these two days had set her up afresh, with new strength and brighter hope. Plans which had lately appeared to her in the guise of tasks, now appeared like pleasures. The morbid scales had fallen from her eyes, and she saw her position and her work more truly. If only Mr. Thornton would restore her the lost friendship,—nay, if he would only come from time to time to cheer her father as in former days,—though she should never see him, she felt as if the course of her future life, though not brilliant in prospect, might lie clear and even before her. She sighed as she rose up to go to bed. In spite of the 'One step's enough for me,'—in spite of the one plain duty of devotion to her father,—there lay at her heart an anxiety and a pang of sorrow.

And Mr. Hale thought of Margaret, that April evening, just as strangely and as persistently as she was thinking of him. He had been fatigued by going about among his old friends and old familiar places. He had had exaggerated ideas of the change which his altered opinions might make in his friends' reception of him; but although some of them might have felt shocked or grieved or indignant at his falling off in the abstract, as soon as they saw the face of the man whom they had once loved, they forgot his opinions in himself; or only remembered them enough to give an additional tender gravity to their manner. For Mr. Hale had not been known to many; he had belonged to one of the smaller colleges, and had always been shy and reserved; but those who in youth had cared to penetrate to the delicacy of thought and feeling that lay below his silence and indecision, took him to their hearts, with something of the protecting kindness which they would have shown to a woman. And the renewal of this kindliness, after the lapse of years, and an interval of so much change, overpowered him more than any roughness or expression of disapproval could have done.

'I'm afraid we've done too much,' said Mr. Bell. 'You're suffering now from having lived so long in that Milton air.

'I am tired,' said Mr. Hale. 'But it is not Milton air. I'm fifty-five years of age, and that little fact of itself accounts for any loss of strength.'

'Nonsense! I'm upwards of sixty, and feel no loss of strength, either bodily or mental. Don't let me hear you talking so. Fifty-five! why, you're quite a young man.'

Mr. Hale shook his head. 'These last few years!' said he. But after a minute's pause, he raised himself from his half recumbent position, in one of Mr. Bell's luxurious easy-chairs, and said with a kind of trembling earnestness:

'Bell! you're not to think, that if I could have foreseen all that would come of my change of opinion, and my resignation of my living—no! not even if I could have known how *she* would have suffered,—that I would undo it—the act of open acknowledgment that I no longer held the same faith as the church in which I was a priest. As I think now, even if I could have foreseen that cruellest martyrdom of suffering, through the sufferings of one whom I loved, I would have done just the same as far as that step of openly leaving the church went. I might have done differently, and acted more wisely, in all that I subsequently did for my family. But I don't think God endued me with over-much wisdom or strength,' he added, falling back into his old position.

Mr. Bell blew his nose ostentatiously before answering. Then he said:

'He gave you strength to do what your conscience told you was right; and I don't see that we need any higher or holier strength than that; or wisdom either. I know I have not that much; and yet men set me down in their fool's books as a wise man; an independent character; strong-minded, and all that cant. The veriest idiot who obeys his own simple law of right, if it be but in wiping his shoes on a door-mat, is wiser and stronger than I. But what gulls men are!'

There was a pause. Mr. Hale spoke first, in continuation of his thought:

'About Margaret.'

'Well! about Margaret. What then?'

'If I die—— '

'Nonsense!'

'What will become of her—I often think? I suppose the Lennoxes will ask her to live with them. I try to think they will. Her aunt Shaw loved her well in her own quiet way; but she forgets to love the absent.'

'A very common fault. What sort of people are the Lennoxes?'

'He, handsome, fluent, and agreeable. Edith, a sweet little spoiled beauty. Margaret loves her with all her heart, and Edith with as much of her heart as she can spare.'

'Now, Hale; you know that girl of yours has got pretty nearly all my heart. I told you that before. Of course, as your daughter, as my god-daughter, I took great interest in her before I saw her the last time. But this visit that I paid to you at Milton made me her slave. I went, a willing old victim, following the car of the conqueror. For, indeed, she looks as grand and serene as one who has struggled, and may be struggling, and yet has the victory secure in sight. Yes, in spite of all her present anxieties, that was the look on her face. And so, all I have is at her service, if she needs it; and will be hers, whether she will or no, when I die. Moreover, I myself, will be her preux chevalier, sixty and gouty though I be. Seriously, old friend, your daughter shall be my principal charge in life, and all the help that either my wit or my wisdom or my willing heart can give, shall be hers. I don't choose her out as a subject for fretting. Something, I know of old, you must have to worry yourself about, or you wouldn't be happy. But you're going to outlive me by many a long year. You spare, thin men are always tempting and always cheating Death! It's the stout, florid fellows like me, that always go off first.'

If Mr. Bell had had a prophetic eye he might have seen the torch all but inverted, and the angel with the grave and composed face standing very nigh, beckoning to his friend. That night Mr. Hale laid his head down on the pillow on which it never more should stir with life. The servant who entered his room in the morning, received no answer to his speech; drew near the bed, and saw the calm, beautiful face lying white and cold under the ineffaceable seal of death. The attitude was exquisitely easy; there had been no pain—no struggle. The action of the heart must have ceased as he lay down.

Mr. Bell was stunned by the shock; and only recovered when the time came for being angry at every suggestion of his man's.

'A coroner's inquest? Pooh. You don't think I poisoned him! Dr. Forbes says it is just the natural end of a heart complaint. Poor old Hale! You wore out that tender heart of yours before its time. Poor old friend! how he talked of his—— Wallis, pack up a carpet-bag for me in five minutes. Here have I been talking. Pack it up, I say. I must go to Milton by the next train.'

The bag was packed, the cab ordered, the railway reached, in twenty minutes from the moment of this decision. The London train whizzed by, drew back some yards, and in Mr. Bell was hurried by the impatient guard. He threw himself back in his seat, to try, with closed eyes, to understand how one in life yesterday could be dead to-day; and shortly tears stole out between his grizzled eye-lashes, at the feeling of which he opened his keen eyes, and looked as severely cheerful as his set determination could make him. He was not going to blubber before a set of strangers. Not he!

There was no set of strangers, only one sitting far from him on the same side. By and bye Mr. Bell peered at him, to discover what manner of man it was that might have been observing his emotion; and behind the great sheet of the outspread 'Times,' he recognised Mr. Thornton.

'Why, Thornton! is that you?' said he, removing hastily to a closer proximity. He shook Mr. Thornton vehemently by the hand, until the gripe ended in a sudden relaxation, for the hand was wanted to wipe away tears. He had last seen Mr. Thornton in his friend Hale's company.

'I'm going to Milton, bound on a melancholy errand. Going to break to Hale's daughter the news of his sudden death!'

'Death! Mr. Hale dead!'

'Ay; I keep saying it to myself, "Hale is dead!" but it doesn't make it any the more real. Hale is dead for all that. He went to bed well, to all appearance, last night, and was quite cold this morning when my servant went to call him.'

'Where? I don't understand!'

'At Oxford. He came to stay with me; hadn't been in Oxford this seventeen years—and this is the end of it.'

Not one word was spoken for above a quarter of an hour. Then Mr. Thornton said:

'And she!' and stopped full short.

'Margaret you mean. Yes! I am going to tell her. Poor fellow! how full his thoughts were of her all last night! Good God! Last night only. And how immeasurably distant he is now! But I take Margaret as my child for his sake. I said last night I would take her for her own sake. Well, I take her for both.'

Mr. Thornton made one or two fruitless attempts to speak, before he could get out the words:

'What will become of her!'

'I rather fancy there will be two people waiting for her: myself for one. I would take a live dragon into my house to live, if, by hiring such a chaperon, and setting up an establishment of my own, I could make my old age happy with having Margaret for a daughter. But there are those Lennoxes!'

'Who are they?' asked Mr. Thornton with trembling interest.

'Oh, smart London people, who very likely will think they've the best right to her. Captain Lennox married her cousin—the girl she was brought up with. Good enough people, I dare say. And there's her aunt, Mrs. Shaw. There might be a way open, perhaps, by my offering to marry that worthy lady! but that would be quite a pis aller. And then there's that brother!'

'What brother? A brother of her aunt's?'

'No, no; a clever Lennox, (the captain's a fool, you must understand) a young barrister, who will be setting his cap at Margaret. I know he has had her in his mind this five years or more: one of his chums told me as much; and he was only kept back by her want of fortune. Now that will be done away with.'

'How?' asked Mr. Thornton, too earnestly curious to be aware of the impertinence of his question.

'Why, she'll have my money at my death. And if this Henry Lennox is half good enough for her, and she likes him—well! I might find another way of getting a home through a marriage. I'm dreadfully afraid of being tempted, at an unguarded moment, by the aunt.'

Neither Mr. Bell nor Mr. Thornton was in a laughing humour; so the oddity of any of the speeches which the former made was unnoticed by them. Mr. Bell whistled, without emitting any sound beyond a long hissing breath; changed his seat, without finding comfort or rest while Mr. Thornton sat immoveably still, his eyes fixed on one spot in the newspaper, which he had taken up in order to give himself leisure to think.

'Where have you been?' asked Mr. Bell, at length.

'To Havre. Trying to detect the secret of the great rise in the price of cotton.'

'Ugh! Cotton, and speculations, and smoke, well-cleansed and well-cared-for machinery, and unwashed and neglected hands. Poor old Hale! Poor old Hale! If you could have known the change which it was to him from Helstone. Do you know the New Forest at all?'

'Yes.' (Very shortly).

'Then you can fancy the difference between it and Milton. What part were you in? Were you ever at Helstone? a little picturesque village, like some in the Odenwald? You know Helstone?'

'I have seen it. It was a great change to leave it and come to Milton.'

He took up his newspaper with a determined air, as if resolved to avoid further conversation; and Mr. Bell was fain to resort to his former occupation of trying to find out how he could best break the news to Margaret.

She was at an up-stairs window; she saw him alight; she guessed the truth with an instinctive flash. She stood in the middle of the drawing-room, as if arrested in her first impulse to rush downstairs, and as if by the same restraining thought she had been turned to stone; so white and immoveable was she.

'Oh! don't tell me! I know it from your face! You would have sent—you would not have left him—if he were alive! Oh papa, papa!'

CHAPTER XLII - ALONE! ALONE!

'When some beloved voice that was to you
Both sound and sweetness, faileth suddenly,
And silence, against which you dare not cry,
Aches round you like a strong disease and new—
What hope? what help? what music will undo
That silence to your sense?'
MRS. BROWNING.

The shock had been great. Margaret fell into a state of prostration, which did not show itself in sobs and tears, or even find the relief of words. She lay on the sofa, with her eyes shut, never speaking but when spoken to, and then replying in whispers. Mr. Bell was perplexed. He dared not leave her; he dared not ask her to accompany him back to Oxford, which had been one of the plans he had formed on the journey to Milton, her physical exhaustion was evidently too complete for her to undertake any such fatigue—putting the sight that she would have to encounter out of the question. Mr. Bell sate over the fire, considering what he had better do. Margaret lay motionless, and almost breathless by him. He would not leave her, even for the dinner which Dixon had prepared for him down-stairs, and, with sobbing hospitality, would fain have tempted him to eat. He had a plateful of something brought up to him. In general, he was particular and dainty enough, and knew well each shade of flavour in his food, but now the devilled chicken tasted like sawdust. He minced up some of the fowl for Margaret, and peppered and salted it well; but when Dixon, following his directions, tried to feed her, the languid shake of head proved that in such a state as Margaret was in, food would only choke, not nourish her.

Mr. Bell gave a great sigh; lifted up his stout old limbs (stiff with travelling) from their easy position, and followed Dixon out of the room.

'I can't leave her. I must write to them at Oxford, to see that the preparations are made: they can be getting on with these till I arrive. Can't Mrs. Lennox come to her? I'll write and tell her she must. The girl must have some woman-friend about her, if only to talk her into a good fit of crying.'

Dixon was crying—enough for two; but, after wiping her eyes and steadying her voice, she managed to tell Mr. Bell, that Mrs. Lennox was too near her confinement to be able to undertake any journey at present.

'Well! I suppose we must have Mrs. Shaw; she's come back to England, isn't she?'

'Yes, sir, she's come back; but I don't think she will like to leave Mrs. Lennox at such an interesting time,' said Dixon, who did not much approve of a stranger entering the household, to share with her in her ruling care of Margaret.

'Interesting time be—' Mr. Bell restricted himself to coughing over the end of his sentence. 'She could be content to be at Venice or Naples, or some of those Popish places, at the last "interesting time," which took place in Corfu, I think. And what does that little prosperous woman's "interesting time" signify, in comparison with that poor creature there,—that helpless, homeless, friendless Margaret—lying as still on that sofa as if it were an altar-tomb, and she the stone statue on it. I tell you, Mrs. Shaw shall come. See that a room, or whatever she wants, is got ready for her by to-morrow night. I'll take care she comes.'

Accordingly Mr. Bell wrote a letter, which Mrs. Shaw declared, with many tears, to be so like one of the dear general's when he was going to have a fit of the gout, that she should always value and preserve it. If he had given her the option, by requesting or urging her, as if a refusal were possible, she might not have come—true and sincere as was her sympathy with Margaret. It needed the sharp uncourteous command to make her conquer her vis inertiae, and allow herself to be packed by her maid, after the latter had completed the boxes. Edith, all cap, shawls, and tears, came out to the top of the stairs, as Captain Lennox was taking her mother down to the carriage:

'Don't forget, mamma; Margaret must come and live with us. Sholto will go to Oxford on Wednesday, and you must send word by Mr. Bell to him when we're to expect you. And if you want Sholto, he can go on from Oxford to Milton. Don't forget, mamma; you are to bring back Margaret.'

Edith re-entered the drawing-room. Mr. Henry Lennox was there, cutting open the pages of a new Review. Without lifting his head, he said, 'If you don't like Sholto to be so long absent from you, Edith, I hope you will let me go down to Milton, and give what assistance I can.'

'Oh, thank you,' said Edith, 'I dare say old Mr. Bell will do everything he can, and more help may not be needed. Only one does not look for much *savoir-faire* from a resident Fellow. Dear, darling Margaret! won't it be nice to have her here, again? You were both great allies, years ago.'

'Were we?' asked he indifferently, with an appearance of being interested in a passage in the Review.

'Well, perhaps not—I forget. I was so full of Sholto. But doesn't it fall out well, that if my uncle was to die, it should be just now, when we are come home, and settled in the old house, and quite ready to receive Margaret? Poor thing! what a change it will be to her from Milton! I'll have new chintz for her bedroom, and make it look new and bright, and cheer her up a little.'

In the same spirit of kindness, Mrs. Shaw journeyed to Milton, occasionally dreading the first meeting, and wondering how it would be got over; but more frequently planning how soon she could get Margaret away from 'that horrid place,' and back into the pleasant comforts of Harley Street.

'Oh dear!' she said to her maid; 'look at those chimneys! My poor sister Hale! I don't think I could have rested at Naples, if I had known what it was! I must have come and fetched her and Margaret away.' And to herself she acknowledged, that she had always thought her brother-in-law rather a weak man, but never so weak as now, when she saw for what a place he had exchanged the lovely Helstone home.

Margaret had remained in the same state; white, motionless, speechless, tearless. They had told her that her aunt Shaw was coming; but she had not expressed either surprise or pleasure, or dislike to the idea. Mr. Bell, whose appetite had returned, and who appreciated Dixon's endeavours to gratify it, in vain urged upon her to taste some sweetbreads stewed with oysters; she shook her head with the same quiet obstinacy as on the previous day; and he was obliged to console himself for her rejection, by eating them all himself. But Margaret was the first to hear the stopping of the cab that brought her aunt from the railway station. Her eyelids quivered, her lips coloured and trembled. Mr. Bell went down to meet Mrs. Shaw; and when they came up, Margaret was standing, trying to steady her dizzy self; and when she saw her aunt, she went forward to the arms open to receive her, and first found the passionate relief of tears on her aunt's shoulder. All thoughts of quiet habitual love, of tenderness for years, of relationship to the dead,—all that inexplicable likeness in look, tone, and gesture, that seem to belong to one family, and which reminded Margaret so forcibly at this moment of her mother,—came in to melt and soften her numbed heart into the overflow of warm tears.

Mr. Bell stole out of the room, and went down into the study, where he ordered a fire, and tried to divert his thoughts by taking down and examining the different books. Each volume brought a remembrance or a suggestion of his dead friend. It might be a change of employment from his two days' work of watching Margaret, but it was no change of thought. He was glad to catch the sound of Mr. Thornton's voice, making enquiry at the door. Dixon was rather cavalierly dismissing him; for with the appearance of Mrs. Shaw's maid, came visions of former grandeur, of the Beresford blood, of the 'station' (so she was pleased to term it) from which her young lady had been ousted, and to which she was now, please God, to be restored. These visions, which she had been dwelling on with complacency in her conversation with Mrs. Shaw's maid (skilfully eliciting meanwhile all the circumstances of state and consequence connected with the Harley Street establishment, for the edification of the listening Martha), made Dixon rather inclined to be supercilious in her treatment of any inhabitant of Milton; so, though she always stood rather in awe of Mr. Thornton, she was as curt as she durst be in telling him that he could see none of the inmates of the house that night. It was rather uncomfortable to be contradicted in her statement by Mr. Bell's opening the study-door, and calling out:

'Thornton! is that you? Come in for a minute or two; I want to speak to you.' So Mr. Thornton went into the study, and Dixon had to retreat into the kitchen, and reinstate herself in her own esteem by a prodigious story of Sir John Beresford's coach and six, when he was high sheriff.

'I don't know what I wanted to say to you after all. Only it's dull enough to sit in a room where everything speaks to you of a dead friend. Yet Margaret and her aunt must have the drawing-room to themselves!'

'Is Mrs.—is her aunt come?' asked Mr. Thornton.

'Come? Yes! maid and all. One would have thought she might have come by herself at such a time! And now I shall have to turn out and find my way to the Clarendon.'

'You must not go to the Clarendon. We have five or six empty bed-rooms at home.'

'Well aired?'

'I think you may trust my mother for that.'

'Then I'll only run up-stairs and wish that wan girl good-night, and make my bow to her aunt, and go off with you straight.'

Mr. Bell was some time up-stairs. Mr. Thornton began to think it long, for he was full of business, and had hardly been able to spare the time for running up to Crampton, and enquiring how Miss Hale was.

When they had set out upon their walk, Mr. Bell said:

'I was kept by those women in the drawing-room. Mrs. Shaw is anxious to get home—on account of her daughter, she says—and wants Margaret to go off with her at once. Now she is no more fit for travelling than I am for flying. Besides, she says, and very justly, that she has friends she must see—that she must wish good-bye to several people; and then her aunt worried her about old claims, and was she forgetful of old friends? And she said, with a great burst of crying, she should be glad enough to go from a place where she had suffered so much. Now I must return to Oxford to-morrow, and I don't know on which side of the scale to throw in my voice.'

He paused, as if asking a question; but he received no answer from his companion, the echo of whose thoughts kept repeating—

'Where she had suffered so much.' Alas! and that was the way in which this eighteen months in Milton—to him so unspeakably precious, down to its very bitterness, which was worth all the rest of life's sweetness—would be remembered. Neither loss of father, nor loss of mother, dear as she was to Mr. Thornton, could have poisoned the remembrance of the weeks, the days, the hours, when a walk of two miles, every step of which was pleasant, as it brought him nearer and nearer to her, took him to her sweet presence—every step of which was rich, as each recurring moment that bore him away from her made him recall some fresh grace in her demeanour, or pleasant pungency in her character. Yes! whatever had happened to him, external to his relation to her, he could never have spoken of that time, when he could have seen her every day—when he had her within his grasp, as it were—as a time of suffering. It had been a royal time of luxury to him, with all its stings and contumelies, compared to the poverty that crept round and clipped the anticipation of the future down to sordid fact, and life without an atmosphere of either hope or fear.

Mrs. Thornton and Fanny were in the dining-room; the latter in a flutter of small exultation, as the maid held up one glossy material after another, to try the effect of the wedding-dresses by candlelight. Her mother really tried to sympathise with her, but could not. Neither taste nor dress were in her line of subjects, and she heartily wished that Fanny had accepted her brother's offer of having the wedding clothes provided by some first-rate London dressmaker, without the endless troublesome discussions, and unsettled wavering, that arose out of Fanny's desire to choose and superintend everything herself. Mr. Thornton was only too glad to mark his grateful approbation of any sensible man, who could be captivated by Fanny's second-rate airs and graces, by giving her ample means for providing herself with the finery, which certainly rivalled, if it did not exceed, the lover in her estimation. When her brother and Mr. Bell came in, Fanny blushed and simpered, and fluttered over the signs of her employment, in a way which could not have failed to draw attention from any one else but Mr. Bell. If he thought about her and her silks and satins at all, it was to compare her and them with the pale sorrow he had left behind him, sitting motionless, with bent head and folded hands, in a room where the stillness was so great that you might almost fancy the rush in your straining ears was occasioned by the spirits of the dead, yet hovering round their beloved. For, when Mr. Bell had first gone upstairs, Mrs. Shaw lay asleep on the sofa; and no sound broke the silence.

Mrs. Thornton gave Mr. Bell her formal, hospitable welcome. She was never so gracious as when receiving her son's friends in her son's house; and the more unexpected they were, the more honour to her admirable housekeeping preparations for comfort.

'How is Miss Hale?' she asked.

'About as broken down by this last stroke as she can be.'

'I am sure it is very well for her that she has such a friend as you.'

'I wish I were her only friend, madam. I daresay it sounds very brutal; but here have I been displaced, and turned out of my post of comforter and adviser by a fine lady aunt; and there are cousins and what not claiming her in London, as if she were a lap-dog belonging to them. And she is too weak and miserable to have a will of her own.'

'She must indeed be weak,' said Mrs. Thornton, with an implied meaning which her son understood well. 'But where,' continued Mrs. Thornton, 'have these relations been all this time that Miss Hale has appeared almost friendless, and has certainly had a good deal of anxiety to bear?' But she did not feel interest enough in the answer to her question to wait for it. She left the room to make her household arrangements.

'They have been living abroad. They have some kind of claim upon her. I will do them that justice. The aunt brought her up, and she and the cousin have been like sisters. The thing vexing me, you see, is that I wanted to take her for a child of my own; and I am jealous of these people, who don't seem to value the privilege of their right. Now it would be different if Frederick claimed her.'

'Frederick!' exclaimed Mr. Thornton. 'Who is he? What right—?' He stopped short in his vehement question.

'Frederick,' said Mr. Bell in surprise. 'Why don't you know? He's her brother. Have you not heard—'

'I never heard his name before. Where is he? Who is he?'

'Surely I told you about him, when the family first came to Milton—the son who was concerned in that mutiny.'

'I never heard of him till this moment. Where does he live?'

'In Spain. He's liable to be arrested the moment he sets foot on English ground. Poor fellow! he will grieve at not being able to attend his father's funeral. We must be content with Captain Lennox; for I don't know of any other relation to summon.'

'I hope I may be allowed to go?'

'Certainly; thankfully. You're a good fellow, after all, Thornton. Hale liked you. He spoke to me, only the other day, about you at Oxford. He regretted he had seen so little of you lately. I am obliged to you for wishing to show him respect.'

'But about Frederick. Does he never come to England?'

'Never.'

'He was not over here about the time of Mrs. Hale's death?'

'No. Why, I was here then. I hadn't seen Hale for years and years and, if you remember, I came—No, it was some time after that that I came. But poor Frederick Hale was not here then. What made you think he was?'

'I saw a young man walking with Miss Hale one day,' replied Mr. Thornton, 'and I think it was about that time.'

'Oh, that would be this young Lennox, the Captain's brother. He's a lawyer, and they were in pretty constant correspondence with him; and I remember Mr. Hale told me he thought he would come down. Do you know,' said Mr. Bell, wheeling round, and shutting one eye, the better to bring the forces of the other to bear with keen scrutiny on Mr. Thornton's face, 'that I once fancied you had a little tenderness for Margaret?'

No answer. No change of countenance.

'And so did poor Hale. Not at first, and not till I had put it into his head.'

'I admired Miss Hale. Every one must do so. She is a beautiful creature,' said Mr. Thornton, driven to bay by Mr. Bell's pertinacious questioning.

'Is that all! You can speak of her in that measured way, as simply a "beautiful creature"—only something to catch the eye. I did hope you had had nobleness enough in you to make you pay her the homage of the heart. Though I believe—in fact I know, she would have rejected you, still to have loved her without return would have lifted you higher than all those, be they who they may, that have never known her to love. "Beautiful creature" indeed! Do you speak of her as you would of a horse or a dog?'

Mr. Thornton's eyes glowed like red embers.

'Mr. Bell,' said he, 'before you speak so, you should remember that all men are not as free to express what they feel as you are. Let us talk of something else.' For though his heart leaped up, as at a trumpet-call, to every word that Mr. Bell had said, and though he knew that what he had said would henceforward bind the thought of the old Oxford Fellow closely up with the most precious things of his heart, yet he would not be forced into any expression of what he felt towards Margaret. He was no mocking-bird of praise, to try because another extolled what he reverenced and passionately loved, to outdo him in laudation. So he turned to some of the dry matters of business that lay between Mr. Bell and him, as landlord and tenant.

'What is that heap of brick and mortar we came against in the yard? Any repairs wanted?'

'No, none, thank you.'

'Are you building on your own account? If you are, I'm very much obliged to you.'

'I'm building a dining-room—for the men I mean—the hands.'

'I thought you were hard to please, if this room wasn't good enough to satisfy you, a bachelor.'

'I've got acquainted with a strange kind of chap, and I put one or two children in whom he is interested to school. So, as I happened to be passing near his house one day, I just went there about some trifling payment to be made; and I saw such a miserable black frizzle of a dinner—a greasy cinder of meat, as first set me a-thinking. But it was not till provisions grew so high this winter that I bethought me how, by buying things wholesale, and cooking a good quantity of provisions together, much money might be saved, and much comfort gained. So I spoke to my friend—or my enemy—the man I told you of—and he found fault with every detail of my plan; and in consequence I laid it aside, both as impracticable, and also because if I forced it into operation I should be interfering with the independence of my men; when, suddenly, this Higgins came to me and graciously signified his approval of a scheme so nearly the same as mine, that I might fairly have claimed it; and, moreover, the approval of several of his fellow-workmen, to whom he had spoken. I was a little "riled," I confess, by his manner, and thought of throwing the whole thing overboard to sink or swim. But it seemed childish to relinquish a plan which I had once thought wise and well-laid, just because I myself did not receive all the honour and consequence due to the originator. So I coolly took the part assigned to me, which is something like that of steward to a club. I buy in the provisions wholesale, and provide a fitting matron or cook.'

'I hope you give satisfaction in your new capacity. Are you a good judge of potatoes and onions? But I suppose Mrs. Thornton assists you in your marketing.'

'Not a bit,' replied Mr. Thornton. 'She disapproves of the whole plan, and now we never mention it to each other. But I manage pretty well, getting in great stocks from Liverpool, and being served in butcher's meat by our own family butcher. I can assure you, the hot dinners the matron turns out are by no means to be despised.'

'Do you taste each dish as it goes in, in virtue of your office? I hope you have a white wand.'

'I was very scrupulous, at first, in confining myself to the mere purchasing part, and even in that I rather obeyed the men's orders conveyed through the housekeeper, than went by my own judgment. At one time, the beef was too large, at another the mutton was not fat enough. I think they saw how careful I was to leave them free, and not to intrude my own ideas upon them; so, one day, two or three of the men—my friend Higgins among them—asked me if I would not come in and take a snack. It was a very busy day, but I saw that the men would be hurt if, after making the advance, I didn't meet them half-way, so I went in, and I never made a better dinner in my life. I told them (my next neighbours I mean, for I'm no speech-maker) how much I'd enjoyed it; and for some time, whenever that especial dinner recurred in their dietary, I was sure to be met by these men, with a "Master, there's hot-pot for dinner to-day, win yo' come?" If they had not asked me, I would no more have intruded on them than I'd have gone to the mess at the barracks without invitation.'

'I should think you were rather a restraint on your hosts' conversation. They can't abuse the masters while you're there. I suspect they take it out on non-hot-pot days.'

'Well! hitherto we've steered clear of all vexed questions. But if any of the old disputes came up again, I would certainly speak out my mind next hot-pot day. But you are hardly acquainted with our Darkshire fellows, for all you're a Darkshire man yourself. They have such a sense of humour, and such a racy mode of expression! I am getting really to know some of them now, and they talk pretty freely before me.'

'Nothing like the act of eating for equalising men. Dying is nothing to it. The philosopher dies sententiously—the pharisee ostentatiously—the simple-hearted humbly—the poor idiot blindly, as the sparrow falls to the ground; the philosopher and idiot, publican and pharisee, all eat after the same fashion—given an equally good digestion. There's theory for theory for you!'

'Indeed I have no theory; I hate theories.'

'I beg your pardon. To show my penitence, will you accept a ten pound note towards your marketing, and give the poor fellows a feast?'

'Thank you; but I'd rather not. They pay me rent for the oven and cooking-places at the back of the mill: and will have to pay more for the new dining-room. I don't want it to fall into a charity. I don't want donations. Once let in the principle, and I should have people going, and talking, and spoiling the simplicity of the whole thing.'

'People will talk about any new plan. You can't help that.'

'My enemies, if I have any, may make a philanthropic fuss about this dinner-scheme; but you are a friend, and I expect you will pay my experiment the respect of silence. It is but a new broom at present, and sweeps clean enough. But by-and-by we shall meet with plenty of stumbling-blocks, no doubt.'

CHAPTER XLIII - MARGARET'S FLITTIN'

'The meanest thing to which we bid adieu,
Loses its meanness in the parting hour.'
ELLIOTT.

Mrs. Shaw took as vehement a dislike as it was possible for one of her gentle nature to do, against Milton. It was noisy, and smoky, and the poor people whom she saw in the streets were dirty, and the rich ladies over-dressed, and not a man that she saw, high or low, had his clothes made to fit him. She was sure Margaret would never regain her lost strength while she stayed in Milton; and she herself was afraid of one of her old attacks of the nerves. Margaret must return with her, and that quickly. This, if not the exact force of her words, was at any rate the spirit of what she urged on Margaret, till the latter, weak, weary, and broken-spirited, yielded a reluctant promise that, as soon as Wednesday was over she would prepare to accompany her aunt back to town, leaving Dixon in charge of all the arrangements for paying bills, disposing of furniture, and shutting up the house. Before that Wednesday—that mournful Wednesday, when Mr. Hale was to be interred, far away from either of the homes he had known in life, and far away from the wife who lay lonely among strangers (and this last was Margaret's great trouble, for she thought that if she had not given way to that overwhelming stupor during the first sad days, she could have arranged things otherwise)—before that Wednesday, Margaret received a letter from Mr. Bell.

'MY DEAR MARGARET:—I did mean to have returned to Milton on Thursday, but unluckily it turns out to be one of the rare occasions when we, Plymouth Fellows, are called upon to perform any kind of duty, and I must not be absent from my post. Captain Lennox and Mr. Thornton are here. The former seems a smart, well-meaning man; and has proposed to go over to Milton, and assist you in any search for the will; of course there is none, or you would have found it by this time, if you followed my directions. Then the Captain declares he must take you and his mother-in-law home; and, in his wife's present state, I don't see how you can expect him to remain away longer than Friday. However, that Dixon of yours is trusty; and can hold her, or your own, till I come. I will put matters into the hands of my Milton attorney if there is no will; for I doubt this smart captain is no great man of business. Nevertheless, his moustachios are splendid. There will have to be a sale, so select what things you wish reserved. Or you can send a list afterwards. Now two things more, and I have done. You know, or if you don't, your poor father did, that you are to have my money and goods when I die. Not that I mean to die yet; but I name this just to explain what is coming. These Lennoxes seem very fond of you now; and perhaps may continue to be; perhaps not. So it is best to start with a formal agreement; namely, that you are to pay them two hundred and fifty pounds a year, as long as you and they find it pleasant to live together. (This, of course, includes Dixon; mind you don't be cajoled into paying any more for her.) Then you won't be thrown adrift, if some day the captain wishes to have his house to himself, but you can carry yourself and your two hundred and fifty pounds off somewhere else; if, indeed, I have not claimed you to come and keep house for me first. Then as to dress, and Dixon, and personal expenses, and confectionery (all young ladies eat confectionery till wisdom comes by age), I shall consult some lady of my acquaintance, and see how much you will have from your father before fixing this. Now, Margaret, have you flown out before you have read this far, and wondered what right the old man has to settle your affairs for you so cavalierly? I make no doubt you have. Yet the old man has a right. He has loved your father for five and thirty years; he stood beside him on his wedding-day; he closed his eyes in death. Moreover, he is your godfather; and as he cannot do you much good spiritually, having a hidden consciousness of your superiority in such things, he would fain do you the poor good of endowing you materially. And the old man has not a known relation on earth; "who is there to mourn for Adam Bell?" and his whole heart is set and bent upon this one thing, and Margaret Hale is not the girl to say him nay. Write by return, if only two lines, to tell me your answer. But *no thanks*.'

Margaret took up a pen and scrawled with trembling hand, 'Margaret Hale is not the girl to say him nay.' In her weak state she could not think of any other words, and yet she was vexed to use these. But she was so much fatigued even by this slight exertion, that if she could have thought of another form of acceptance, she could not have sate up to write a syllable of it. She was obliged to lie down again, and try not to think.

'My dearest child! Has that letter vexed or troubled you?'

'No!' said Margaret feebly. 'I shall be better when to-morrow is over.'

'I feel sure, darling, you won't be better till I get you out of this horrid air. How you can have borne it this two years I can't imagine.'

'Where could I go to? I could not leave papa and mamma.'

'Well! don't distress yourself, my dear. I dare say it was all for the best, only I had no conception of how you were living. Our butler's wife lives in a better house than this.'

'It is sometimes very pretty—in summer; you can't judge by what it is now. I have been very happy here,' and Margaret closed her eyes by way of stopping the conversation.

The house teemed with comfort now, compared to what it had done. The evenings were chilly, and by Mrs. Shaw's directions fires were lighted in every bedroom. She petted Margaret in every possible way, and bought every delicacy, or soft luxury in which she herself would have burrowed and sought comfort. But Margaret was indifferent to all these things; or, if they forced themselves upon her attention, it was simply as causes for gratitude to her aunt, who was putting herself so much out of her way to think of her. She was restless, though so weak. All the day long, she kept herself from thinking of the ceremony which was going on at Oxford, by wandering from room to room, and languidly setting aside such articles as she wished to retain. Dixon followed her by Mrs. Shaw's desire, ostensibly to receive instructions, but with a private injunction to soothe her into repose as soon as might be.

'These books, Dixon, I will keep. All the rest will you send to Mr. Bell? They are of a kind that he will value for themselves, as well as for papa's sake. This—— I should like you to take this to Mr. Thornton, after I am gone. Stay; I will write a note with it.' And she sate down hastily, as if afraid of thinking, and wrote:

> 'DEAR SIR,—The accompanying book I am sure will be valued by you for the sake of my father, to whom it belonged.
>
> 'Yours sincerely,
>
> 'MARGARET HALE.'

She set out again upon her travels through the house, turning over articles, known to her from her childhood, with a sort of caressing reluctance to leave them—old-fashioned, worn and shabby, as they might be. But she hardly spoke again; and Dixon's report to Mrs. Shaw was, that 'she doubted whether Miss Hale heard a word of what she said, though she talked the whole time, in order to divert her attention.' The consequence of being on her feet all day was excessive bodily weariness in the evening, and a better night's rest than she had had since she had heard of Mr. Hale's death.

At breakfast time the next day, she expressed her wish to go and bid one or two friends good-bye. Mrs. Shaw objected:

'I am sure, my dear, you can have no friends here with whom you are sufficiently intimate to justify you in calling upon them so soon; before you have been at church.'

'But to-day is my only day; if Captain Lennox comes this afternoon, and if we must—if I must really go to-morrow—— '

'Oh, yes; we shall go to-morrow. I am more and more convinced that this air is bad for you, and makes you look so pale and ill; besides, Edith expects us; and she may be waiting me; and you cannot be left alone, my dear, at your age. No; if you must pay these calls, I will go with you. Dixon can get us a coach, I suppose?'

So Mrs. Shaw went to take care of Margaret, and took her maid with her to take care of the shawls and air-cushions. Margaret's face was too sad to lighten up into a smile at all this preparation for paying two visits, that she had often made by herself at all hours of the day. She was half afraid of owning that one place to which she was going was Nicholas Higgins'; all she could do was to hope her aunt would be indisposed to get out of the coach, and walk up the court, and at every breath of wind have her face slapped by wet clothes, hanging out to dry on ropes stretched from house to house.

There was a little battle in Mrs. Shaw's mind between ease and a sense of matronly propriety; but the former gained the day; and with many an injunction to Margaret to be careful of herself, and not to catch any fever, such as was always lurking in such places, her aunt permitted her to go where she had often been before without taking any precaution or requiring any permission.

Nicholas was out; only Mary and one or two of the Boucher children at home. Margaret was vexed with herself for not having timed her visit better. Mary had a very blunt intellect, although her feelings were warm and kind; and the instant she understood what Margaret's purpose was in coming to see them, she began to cry and sob with so little restraint that Margaret found it useless to say any of the thousand little things which had suggested themselves to her as she was coming along in the coach. She could only try to comfort her a little by suggesting the vague chance of their meeting again, at some possible time, in some possible place, and bid her tell her father how much she wished, if he could manage it, that he should come to see her when he had done his work in the evening.

As she was leaving the place, she stopped and looked round; then hesitated a little before she said:

'I should like to have some little thing to remind me of Bessy.'

Instantly Mary's generosity was keenly alive. What could they give? And on Margaret's singling out a little common drinking-cup, which she remembered as the one always standing by Bessy's side with drink for her feverish lips, Mary said:

'Oh, take summut better; that only cost fourpence!'

'That will do, thank you,' said Margaret; and she went quickly away, while the light caused by the pleasure of having something to give yet lingered on Mary's face.

'Now to Mrs. Thornton's,' thought she to herself. 'It must be done.' But she looked rather rigid and pale at the thought of it, and had hard work to find the exact words in which to explain to her aunt who Mrs. Thornton was, and why she should go to bid her farewell.

They (for Mrs. Shaw alighted here) were shown into the drawing-room, in which a fire had only just been kindled. Mrs. Shaw huddled herself up in her shawl, and shivered.

'What an icy room!' she said.

They had to wait for some time before Mrs. Thornton entered. There was some softening in her heart towards Margaret, now that she was going away out of her sight. She remembered her spirit, as shown at various times and places even more than the patience with which she had endured long and wearing cares. Her countenance was blander than usual, as she greeted her; there was even a shade of tenderness in her manner, as she noticed the white, tear-swollen face, and the quiver in the voice which Margaret tried to make so steady.

'Allow me to introduce my aunt, Mrs. Shaw. I am going away from Milton to-morrow; I do not know if you are aware of it; but I wanted to see you once again, Mrs. Thornton, to—to apologise for my manner the last time I saw you; and to say that I am sure you meant kindly—however much we may have misunderstood each other.'

Mrs. Shaw looked extremely perplexed by what Margaret had said. Thanks for kindness! and apologies for failure in good manners! But Mrs. Thornton replied:

'Miss Hale, I am glad you do me justice. I did no more than I believed to be my duty in remonstrating with you as I did. I have always desired to act the part of a friend to you. I am glad you do me justice.'

'And,' said Margaret, blushing excessively as she spoke, 'will you do me justice, and believe that though I cannot—I do not choose—to give explanations of my conduct, I have not acted in the unbecoming way you apprehended?'

Margaret's voice was so soft, and her eyes so pleading, that Mrs. Thornton was for once affected by the charm of manner to which she had hitherto proved herself invulnerable.

'Yes, I do believe you. Let us say no more about it. Where are you going to reside, Miss Hale? I understood from Mr. Bell that you were going to leave Milton. You never liked Milton, you know,' said Mrs. Thornton, with a sort of grim smile; 'but for all that, you must not expect me to congratulate you on quitting it. Where shall you live?'

'With my aunt,' replied Margaret, turning towards Mrs. Shaw.

'My niece will reside with me in Harley Street. She is almost like a daughter to me,' said Mrs. Shaw, looking fondly at Margaret; 'and I am glad to acknowledge my own obligation for any kindness that has been shown to her. If you and your husband ever come to town, my son and daughter, Captain and Mrs. Lennox, will, I am sure, join with me in wishing to do anything in our power to show you attention.'

Mrs. Thornton thought in her own mind, that Margaret had not taken much care to enlighten her aunt as to the relationship between the Mr. and Mrs. Thornton, towards whom the fine-lady aunt was extending her soft patronage; so she answered shortly,

'My husband is dead. Mr. Thornton is my son. I never go to London; so I am not likely to be able to avail myself of your polite offers.'

At this instant Mr. Thornton entered the room; he had only just returned from Oxford. His mourning suit spoke of the reason that had called him there.

'John,' said his mother, 'this lady is Mrs. Shaw, Miss Hale's aunt. I am sorry to say, that Miss Hale's call is to wish us good-bye.'

'You are going then!' said he, in a low voice.

'Yes,' said Margaret. 'We leave to-morrow.'

'My son-in-law comes this evening to escort us,' said Mrs. Shaw.

Mr. Thornton turned away. He had not sat down, and now he seemed to be examining something on the table, almost as if he had discovered an unopened letter, which had made him forget the present company. He did not even seem to be aware when they got up to take leave. He started forwards, however, to hand Mrs. Shaw down to the carriage. As it drove up, he and Margaret stood close together on the door-step, and it was impossible but that the recollection of the day of the riot should force itself into both their minds. Into his it came associated with the speeches of the following day; her passionate declaration that there was not a man in all that violent and desperate crowd, for whom she did not care as much as for him. And at the remembrance of her taunting words, his brow grew stern, though his heart beat thick with longing love. 'No!' said he, 'I put it to the touch once, and I lost it all. Let her go,—with her stony heart, and her beauty;—how set and terrible her look is now, for all her loveliness of feature! She is afraid I shall speak what will require some stern repression. Let her go. Beauty and heiress as she may be, she will find it hard to meet with a truer heart than mine. Let her go!'

And there was no tone of regret, or emotion of any kind in the voice with which he said good-bye; and the offered hand was taken with a resolute calmness, and dropped as carelessly as if it had been a dead and withered flower. But none in his household saw Mr. Thornton again that day. He was busily engaged; or so he said.

Margaret's strength was so utterly exhausted by these visits, that she had to submit to much watching, and petting, and sighing 'I-told-you-so's,' from her aunt. Dixon said she was quite as bad as she had been on the first day she heard of her father's death; and she and Mrs. Shaw consulted as to the desirableness of delaying the morrow's journey. But when her aunt reluctantly proposed a few days' delay to Margaret, the latter writhed her body as if in acute suffering, and said:

'Oh! let us go. I cannot be patient here. I shall not get well here. I want to forget.'

So the arrangements went on; and Captain Lennox came, and with him news of Edith and the little boy; and Margaret found that the indifferent, careless conversation of one who, however kind, was not too warm and anxious a sympathiser, did her good. She roused up; and by the time that she knew she might expect Higgins, she was able to leave the room quietly, and await in her own chamber the expected summons.

'Eh!' said he, as she came in, 'to think of th' oud gentleman dropping off as he did! Yo' might ha' knocked me down wi' a straw when they telled me. "Mr. Hale?" said I; "him as was th' parson?" "Ay," said they. "Then," said I, "there's as good a man gone as ever lived on this earth, let who will be t' other!" And I came to see yo', and tell yo' how grieved I were, but them women in th' kitchen wouldn't tell yo' I were there. They said yo' were ill,—and butter me, but yo' dunnot look like th' same wench. And yo're going to be a grand lady up i' Lunnon, aren't yo'?'

'Not a grand lady,' said Margaret, half smiling.

'Well! Thornton said—says he, a day or two ago, "Higgins, have yo' seen Miss Hale?" "No," says I; "there's a pack o' women who won't let me at her. But I can bide my time, if she's ill. She and I knows each other pretty well; and hoo'l not go doubting that I'm main sorry for th' oud gentleman's death, just because I can't get at her and tell her so." And says he, "Yo'll not have much time for to try and see her, my fine chap. She's not for staying with us a day longer nor she can help. She's got grand relations, and they're carrying her off; and we sha'n't see her no more." "Measter," said I, "if I dunnot see her afore hoo goes, I'll strive to get up to Lunnun next Whissuntide, that I will. I'll not be baulked of saying her good-bye by any relations whatsomdever." But, bless yo', I knowed yo'd come. It were only for to humour the measter, I let on as if I thought yo'd mappen leave Milton without seeing me.'

'You're quite right,' said Margaret. 'You only do me justice. And you'll not forget me, I'm sure. If no one else in Milton remembers me, I'm certain you will; and papa too. You know how good and how tender he was. Look, Higgins! here is his bible. I have kept it for you. I can ill spare it; but I know he would have liked you to have it. I'm sure you'll care for it, and study what is in it, for his sake.'

'Yo' may say that. If it were the deuce's own scribble, and yo' axed me to read in it for yo'r sake, and th' oud gentleman's, I'd do it. Whatten's this, wench? I'm not going for to take yo'r brass, so dunnot think it. We've been great friends, 'bout the sound o' money passing between us.'

'For the children—for Boucher's children,' said Margaret, hurriedly. 'They may need it. You've no right to refuse it for them. I would not give you a penny,' she said, smiling; 'don't think there's any of it for you.'

'Well, wench! I can nobbut say, Bless yo'! and bless yo'!—and amen.'

CHAPTER XLIV - EASE NOT PEACE

'A dull rotation, never at a stay,
  Yesterday's face twin image of to-day.'
          COWPER.

'Of what each one should be, he sees the form and rule,
  And till he reach to that, his joy can ne'er be full.'
          RUCKERT.

It was very well for Margaret that the extreme quiet of the Harley Street house, during Edith's recovery from her confinement, gave her the natural rest which she needed. It gave her time to comprehend the sudden change which had taken place in her circumstances within the last two months. She found herself at once an inmate of a luxurious house, where the bare knowledge of the existence of every trouble or care seemed scarcely to have penetrated. The wheels of the machinery of daily life were well oiled, and went along with delicious smoothness. Mrs. Shaw and Edith could hardly make enough of Margaret, on her return to what they persisted in calling her home. And she felt that it was almost ungrateful in her to have a secret feeling that the Helstone vicarage—nay, even the poor little house at Milton, with her anxious father and her invalid mother, and all the small household cares of comparative poverty, composed her idea of home. Edith was impatient to get well, in order to fill Margaret's bed-room with all the soft comforts, and pretty nick-knacks, with which her own abounded. Mrs. Shaw and her maid found plenty of occupation in restoring Margaret's wardrobe to a state of elegant variety. Captain Lennox was easy, kind, and gentlemanly; sate with his wife in her dressing-room an hour or two every day; played with his little boy for another hour, and lounged away the rest of his time at his club, when he was not engaged out to dinner. Just before Margaret had recovered from her necessity for quiet and repose—before she had begun to feel her life wanting and dull—Edith came down-stairs and resumed her usual part in the household; and Margaret fell into the old habit of watching, and admiring, and ministering to her cousin. She gladly took all charge of the semblances of duties off Edith's hands; answered notes, reminded her of engagements, tended her when no gaiety was in prospect, and she was consequently rather inclined to fancy herself ill. But all the rest of the family were in the full business of the London season, and Margaret was often left alone. Then her thoughts went back to Milton, with a strange sense of the contrast between the life there, and here. She was getting surfeited of the eventless ease in which no struggle or endeavour was required. She was afraid lest she should even become sleepily deadened into forgetfulness of anything beyond the life which was lapping her round with luxury. There might be toilers and moilers there in London, but she never saw them; the very servants lived in an underground world of their own, of which she knew neither the hopes nor the fears; they only seemed to start into existence when some want or whim of their master and mistress needed them. There was a strange unsatisfied vacuum in Margaret's heart and mode of life; and, once when she had dimly hinted this to Edith, the latter, wearied with dancing the night before, languidly stroked Margaret's cheek as she sat by her in the old attitude,—she on a footstool by the sofa where Edith lay.

'Poor child!' said Edith. 'It is a little sad for you to be left, night after night, just at this time when all the world is so gay. But we shall be having our dinner-parties soon—as soon as Henry comes back from circuit—and then there will be a little pleasant variety for you. No wonder it is moped, poor darling!'

Margaret did not feel as if the dinner-parties would be a panacea. But Edith piqued herself on her dinner-parties; 'so different,' as she said, 'from the old dowager dinners under mamma's regime;' and Mrs. Shaw herself seemed to take exactly the same kind of pleasure in the very different arrangements and circle of acquaintances which were to Captain and Mrs. Lennox's taste, as she did in the more formal and ponderous entertainments which she herself used to give. Captain Lennox was always extremely kind and brotherly to Margaret. She was really very fond of him, excepting when he was anxiously attentive to Edith's dress and appearance, with a view to her beauty making a sufficient impression on the world. Then all the latent Vashti in Margaret was roused, and she could hardly keep herself from expressing her feelings.

The course of Margaret's day was this; a quiet hour or two before a late breakfast; an unpunctual meal, lazily eaten by weary and half-awake people, but yet at which, in all its dragged-out length, she was expected to be present, because, directly afterwards, came a discussion of plans, at which, although they none of them concerned her, she was expected to give her sympathy, if she could not assist with her advice; an endless number of notes to write, which Edith invariably left to her, with many caressing compliments as to her eloquence du billet; a little play with Sholto as he returned from his morning's walk; besides the care of the children during the servants' dinner; a drive or callers; and some dinner or morning engagement for her aunt and cousins, which left Margaret free, it is true, but rather wearied with the inactivity of the day, coming upon depressed spirits and delicate health.

She looked forward with longing, though unspoken interest to the homely object of Dixon's return from Milton; where, until now, the old servant had been busily engaged in winding up all the affairs of the Hale family. It had appeared a sudden famine to her heart, this entire cessation of any news respecting the people amongst whom she had lived so long. It was true, that Dixon, in her business-letters, quoted, every now and then, an opinion of Mr. Thornton's as to what she had better do about the furniture, or how act in regard to the landlord of the Crampton Terrace house. But it was only here and there that the name came in, or any Milton name, indeed; and Margaret was sitting one evening, all alone in the Lennoxes's drawing-room, not reading Dixon's letters, which yet she held in her hand, but thinking over them, and recalling the days which had been, and picturing the busy life out of which her own had been taken and never missed; wondering if all went on in that whirl just as if she and her father had never been; questioning within herself, if no one in all the crowd missed her, (not Higgins, she was not thinking of him,) when, suddenly, Mr. Bell was announced; and Margaret hurried the letters into her work-basket, and started up, blushing as if she had been doing some guilty thing.

'Oh, Mr. Bell! I never thought of seeing you!'

'But you give me a welcome, I hope, as well as that very pretty start of surprise.'

'Have you dined? How did you come? Let me order you some dinner.'

'If you're going to have any. Otherwise, you know, there is no one who cares less for eating than I do. But where are the others? Gone out to dinner? Left you alone?'

'Oh yes! and it is such a rest. I was just thinking—But will you run the risk of dinner? I don't know if there is anything in the house.'

'Why, to tell you the truth, I dined at my club. Only they don't cook as well as they did, so I thought, if you were going to dine, I might try and make out my dinner. But never mind, never mind! There aren't ten cooks in England to be trusted at impromptu dinners. If their skill and their fires will stand it, their tempers won't. You shall make me some tea, Margaret. And now, what were you thinking of? you were going to tell me. Whose letters were those, god-daughter, that you hid away so speedily?'

'Only Dixon's,' replied Margaret, growing very red.

'Whew! is that all? Who do you think came up in the train with me?'

'I don't know,' said Margaret, resolved against making a guess.

'Your what d'ye call him? What's the right name for a cousin-in-law's brother?'

'Mr. Henry Lennox?' asked Margaret.

'Yes,' replied Mr. Bell. 'You knew him formerly, didn't you? What sort of a person is he, Margaret?'

'I liked him long ago,' said Margaret, glancing down for a moment. And then she looked straight up and went on in her natural manner. 'You know we have been corresponding about Frederick since; but I have not seen him for nearly three years, and he may be changed. What did you think of him?'

'I don't know. He was so busy trying to find out who I was, in the first instance, and what I was in the second, that he never let out what he was; unless indeed that veiled curiosity of his as to what manner of man he had to talk to was not a good piece, and a fair indication of his character. Do you call him good looking, Margaret?'

'No! certainly not. Do you?'

'Not I. But I thought, perhaps, you might. Is he a great deal here?'

'I fancy he is when he is in town. He has been on circuit now since I came. But—Mr. Bell—have you come from Oxford or from Milton?'

'From Milton. Don't you see I'm smoke-dried?'

'Certainly. But I thought that it might be the effect of the antiquities of Oxford.'

'Come now, be a sensible woman! In Oxford, I could have managed all the landlords in the place, and had my own way, with half the trouble your Milton landlord has given me, and defeated me after all. He won't take the house off our hands till next June twelvemonth. Luckily, Mr. Thornton found a tenant for it. Why don't you ask after Mr. Thornton, Margaret? He has proved himself a very active friend of yours, I can tell you. Taken more than half the trouble off my hands.'

'And how is he? How is Mrs. Thornton?' asked Margaret hurriedly and below her breath, though she tried to speak out.

'I suppose they're well. I've been staying at their house till I was driven out of it by the perpetual clack about that Thornton girl's marriage. It was too much for Thornton himself, though she was his sister. He used to go and sit in his own room perpetually. He's getting past the age for caring for such things, either as principal or accessory. I was surprised to find the old lady falling into the current, and carried away by her daughter's enthusiasm for orange-blossoms and lace. I thought Mrs. Thornton had been made of sterner stuff.'

'She would put on any assumption of feeling to veil her daughter's weakness,' said Margaret in a low voice.

'Perhaps so. You've studied her, have you? She doesn't seem over fond of you, Margaret.'

'I know it,' said Margaret. 'Oh, here is tea at last!' exclaimed she, as if relieved. And with tea came Mr. Henry Lennox, who had walked up to Harley Street after a late dinner, and had evidently expected to find his brother and sister-in-law at home. Margaret suspected him of being as thankful as she was at the presence of a third party, on this their first meeting since the memorable day of his offer, and her refusal at Helstone. She could hardly tell what to say at first, and was thankful for all the tea-table occupations, which gave her an excuse for keeping silence, and him an opportunity of recovering himself. For, to tell the truth, he had rather forced himself up to Harley Street this evening, with a view of getting over an awkward meeting, awkward even in the presence of Captain Lennox and Edith, and doubly awkward now that he found her the only lady there, and the person to whom he must naturally and perforce address a great part of his conversation. She was the first to recover her self-possession. She began to talk on the subject which came uppermost in her mind, after the first flush of awkward shyness.

'Mr. Lennox, I have been so much obliged to you for all you have done about Frederick.'

'I am only sorry it has been so unsuccessful,' replied he, with a quick glance towards Mr. Bell, as if reconnoitring how much he might say before him. Margaret, as if she read his thought, addressed herself to Mr. Bell, both including him in the conversation, and implying that he was perfectly aware of the endeavours that had been made to clear Frederick.

'That Horrocks—that very last witness of all, has proved as unavailing as all the others. Mr. Lennox has discovered that he sailed for Australia only last August; only two months before Frederick was in England, and gave us the names of—— '

'Frederick in England! you never told me that!' exclaimed Mr. Bell in surprise.

'I thought you knew. I never doubted you had been told. Of course, it was a great secret, and perhaps I should not have named it now,' said Margaret, a little dismayed.

'I have never named it to either my brother or your cousin,' said Mr. Lennox, with a little professional dryness of implied reproach.

'Never mind, Margaret. I am not living in a talking, babbling world, nor yet among people who are trying to worm facts out of me; you needn't look so frightened because you have let the cat out of the bag to a faithful old hermit like me. I shall never name his having been in England; I shall be out of temptation, for no one will ask me. Stay!' (interrupting himself rather abruptly) 'was it at your mother's funeral?'

'He was with mamma when she died,' said Margaret, softly.

'To be sure! To be sure! Why, some one asked me if he had not been over then, and I denied it stoutly—not many weeks ago—who could it have been? Oh! I recollect!'

But he did not say the name; and although Margaret would have given much to know if her suspicions were right, and it had been Mr. Thornton who had made the enquiry, she could not ask the question of Mr. Bell, much as she longed to do so.

There was a pause for a moment or two. Then Mr. Lennox said, addressing himself to Margaret, 'I suppose as Mr. Bell is now acquainted with all the circumstances attending your brother's unfortunate dilemma, I cannot do better than inform him exactly how the research into the evidence we once hoped to produce in his favour stands at present. So, if he will do me the honour to breakfast with me to-morrow, we will go over the names of these missing gentry.'

'I should like to hear all the particulars, if I may. Cannot you come here? I dare not ask you both to breakfast, though I am sure you would be welcome. But let me know all I can about Frederick, even though there may be no hope at present.'

'I have an engagement at half-past eleven. But I will certainly come if you wish it,' replied Mr. Lennox, with a little afterthought of extreme willingness, which made Margaret shrink into herself, and almost wish that she had not proposed her natural request. Mr. Bell got up and looked around him for his hat, which had been removed to make room for tea.

'Well!' said he, 'I don't know what Mr. Lennox is inclined to do, but I'm disposed to be moving off homewards. I've been a journey to-day, and journeys begin to tell upon my sixty and odd years.'

'I believe I shall stay and see my brother and sister,' said Mr. Lennox, making no movement of departure. Margaret was seized with a shy awkward dread of being left alone with him. The scene on the little terrace in the Helstone garden was so present to her, that she could hardly help believing it was so with him.

'Don't go yet, please, Mr. Bell,' said she, hastily. 'I want you to see Edith; and I want Edith to know you. Please!' said she, laying a light but determined hand on his arm. He looked at her, and saw the confusion stirring in her countenance; he sate down again, as if her little touch had been possessed of resistless strength.

'You see how she overpowers me, Mr. Lennox,' said he. 'And I hope you noticed the happy choice of her expressions; she wants me to "see" this cousin Edith, who, I am told, is a great beauty; but she has the honesty to change her word when she comes to me—Mrs. Lennox is to "know" me. I suppose I am not much to "see," eh, Margaret?'

He joked, to give her time to recover from the slight flutter which he had detected in her manner on his proposal to leave; and she caught the tone, and threw the ball back. Mr. Lennox wondered how his brother, the Captain, could have reported her as having lost all her good looks. To be sure, in her quiet black dress, she was a contrast to Edith, dancing in her white crape mourning, and long floating golden hair, all softness and glitter. She dimpled and blushed most becomingly when introduced to Mr. Bell, conscious that she had her reputation as a beauty to keep up, and that it would not do to have a Mordecai refusing to worship and admire, even in the shape of an old Fellow of a College, which nobody had ever heard of. Mrs. Shaw and Captain Lennox, each in their separate way, gave Mr. Bell a kind and sincere welcome, winning him over to like them almost in spite of himself, especially when he saw how naturally Margaret took her place as sister and daughter of the house.

'What a shame that we were not at home to receive you,' said Edith. 'You, too, Henry! though I don't know that we should have stayed at home for you. And for Mr. Bell! for Margaret's Mr. Bell—— '

'There is no knowing what sacrifices you would not have made,' said her brother-in-law. 'Even a dinner-party! and the delight of wearing this very becoming dress.'

Edith did not know whether to frown or to smile. But it did not suit Mr. Lennox to drive her to the first of these alternatives; so he went on.

'Will you show your readiness to make sacrifices to-morrow morning, first by asking me to breakfast, to meet Mr. Bell, and secondly, by being so kind as to order it at half-past nine, instead of ten o'clock? I have some letters and papers that I want to show to Miss Hale and Mr. Bell.'

'I hope Mr. Bell will make our house his own during his stay in London,' said Captain Lennox. 'I am only so sorry we cannot offer him a bed-room.'

'Thank you. I am much obliged to you. You would only think me a churl if you had, for I should decline it, I believe, in spite of all the temptations of such agreeable company,' said Mr. Bell, bowing all round, and secretly congratulating himself on the neat turn he had given to his sentence, which, if put into plain language, would have been more to this effect: 'I couldn't stand the restraints of such a proper-behaved and civil-spoken set of people as these are: it would be like meat without salt. I'm thankful they haven't a bed. And how well I rounded my sentence! I am absolutely catching the trick of good manners.'

His self-satisfaction lasted him till he was fairly out in the streets, walking side by side with Henry Lennox. Here he suddenly remembered Margaret's little look of entreaty as she urged him to stay longer, and he also recollected a few hints given him long ago by an acquaintance of Mr. Lennox's, as to his admiration of Margaret. It gave a new direction to his thoughts. 'You have known Miss Hale for a long time, I believe. How do you think her looking? She strikes me as pale and ill.'

'I thought her looking remarkably well. Perhaps not when I first came in—now I think of it. But certainly, when she grew animated, she looked as well as ever I saw her do.'

'She has had a great deal to go through,' said Mr. Bell.

'Yes! I have been sorry to hear of all she has had to bear; not merely the common and universal sorrow arising from death, but all the annoyance which her father's conduct must have caused her, and then——'

'Her father's conduct!' said Mr. Bell, in an accent of surprise. 'You must have heard some wrong statement. He behaved in the most conscientious manner. He showed more resolute strength than I should ever have given him credit for formerly.'

'Perhaps I have been wrongly informed. But I have been told, by his successor in the living—a clever, sensible man, and a thoroughly active clergyman—that there was no call upon Mr. Hale to do what he did, relinquish the living, and throw himself and his family on the tender mercies of private teaching in a manufacturing town; the bishop had offered him another living, it is true, but if he had come to entertain certain doubts, he could have remained where he was, and so had no occasion to resign. But the truth is, these country clergymen live such isolated lives—isolated, I mean, from all intercourse with men of equal cultivation with themselves, by whose minds they might regulate their own, and discover when they were going either too fast or too slow—that they are very apt to disturb themselves with imaginary doubts as to the articles of faith, and throw up certain opportunities of doing good for very uncertain fancies of their own.'

'I differ from you. I do not think they are very apt to do as my poor friend Hale did.' Mr. Bell was inwardly chafing.

'Perhaps I used too general an expression, in saying "very apt." But certainly, their lives are such as very often to produce either inordinate self-sufficiency, or a morbid state of conscience,' replied Mr. Lennox with perfect coolness.

'You don't meet with any self-sufficiency among the lawyers, for instance?' asked Mr. Bell. 'And seldom, I imagine, any cases of morbid conscience.' He was becoming more and more vexed, and forgetting his lately-caught trick of good manners. Mr. Lennox saw now that he had annoyed his companion; and as he had talked pretty much for the sake of saying something, and so passing the time while their road lay together, he was very indifferent as to the exact side he took upon the question, and quietly came round by saying: 'To be sure, there is something fine in a man of Mr. Hale's age leaving his home of twenty years, and giving up all settled habits, for an idea which was probably erroneous—but that does not matter—an untangible thought. One cannot help admiring him, with a mixture of pity in one's admiration, something like what one feels for Don Quixote. Such a gentleman as he was too! I shall never forget the refined and simple hospitality he showed to me that last day at Helstone.'

Only half mollified, and yet anxious, in order to lull certain qualms of his own conscience, to believe that Mr. Hale's conduct had a tinge of Quixotism in it, Mr. Bell growled out—'Aye! And you don't know Milton. Such a change from Helstone! It is years since I have been at Helstone—but I'll answer for it, it is standing there yet—every stick and every stone as it has done for the last century, while Milton! I go there every four or five years—and I was born there—yet I do assure you, I often lose my way—aye, among the very piles of warehouses that are built upon my father's orchard. Do we part here? Well, good night, sir; I suppose we shall meet in Harley Street to-morrow morning.'

CHAPTER XLV - NOT ALL A DREAM

'Where are the sounds that swam along
The buoyant air when I was young?
The last vibration now is o'er,
And they who listened are no more;
Ah! let me close my eyes and dream.'
W. S. LANDOR.

The idea of Helstone had been suggested to Mr. Bell's waking mind by his conversation with Mr. Lennox, and all night long it ran riot through his dreams. He was again the tutor in the college where he now held the rank of Fellow; it was again a long vacation, and he was staying with his newly married friend, the proud husband, and happy Vicar of Helstone. Over babbling brooks they took impossible leaps, which seemed to keep them whole days suspended in the air. Time and space were not, though all other things seemed real. Every event was measured by the emotions of the mind, not by its actual existence, for existence it had none. But the trees were gorgeous in their autumnal leafiness—the warm odours of flower and herb came sweet upon the sense—the young wife moved about her house with just that mixture of annoyance at her position, as regarded wealth, with pride in her handsome and devoted husband, which Mr. Bell had noticed in real life a quarter of a century ago. The dream was so like life that, when he awoke, his present life seemed like a dream. Where was he? In the close, handsomely furnished room of a London hotel! Where were those who spoke to him, moved around him, touched him, not an instant ago? Dead! buried! lost for evermore, as far as earth's for evermore would extend. He was an old man, so lately exultant in the full strength of manhood. The utter loneliness of his life was insupportable to think about. He got up hastily, and tried to forget what never more might be, in a hurried dressing for the breakfast in Harley Street.

He could not attend to all the lawyer's details, which, as he saw, made Margaret's eyes dilate, and her lips grow pale, as one by one fate decreed, or so it seemed, every morsel of evidence which would exonerate Frederick, should fall from beneath her feet and disappear. Even Mr. Lennox's well-regulated professional voice took a softer, tenderer tone, as he drew near to the extinction of the last hope. It was not that Margaret had not been perfectly aware of the result before. It was only that the details of each successive disappointment came with such relentless minuteness to quench all hope, that she at last fairly gave way to tears. Mr. Lennox stopped reading.

'I had better not go on,' said he, in a concerned voice. 'It was a foolish proposal of mine. Lieutenant Hale,' and even this giving him the title of the service from which he had so harshly been expelled, was soothing to Margaret, 'Lieutenant Hale is happy now; more secure in fortune and future prospects than he could ever have been in the navy; and has, doubtless, adopted his wife's country as his own.'

'That is it,' said Margaret. 'It seems so selfish in me to regret it,' trying to smile, 'and yet he is lost to me, and I am so lonely.' Mr. Lennox turned over his papers, and wished that he were as rich and prosperous as he believed he should be some day. Mr. Bell blew his nose, but, otherwise, he also kept silence; and Margaret, in a minute or two, had apparently recovered her usual composure. She thanked Mr. Lennox very courteously for his trouble; all the more courteously and graciously because she was conscious that, by her behaviour, he might have probably been led to imagine that he had given her needless pain. Yet it was pain she would not have been without.

Mr. Bell came up to wish her good-bye.

'Margaret!' said he, as he fumbled with his gloves. 'I am going down to Helstone to-morrow, to look at the old place. Would you like to come with me? Or would it give you too much pain? Speak out, don't be afraid.'

'Oh, Mr. Bell,' said she—and could say no more. But she took his old gouty hand, and kissed it.

'Come, come; that's enough,' said he, reddening with awkwardness. 'I suppose your aunt Shaw will trust you with me. We'll go to-morrow morning, and we shall get there about two o'clock, I fancy. We'll take a snack, and order dinner at the little inn—the Lennard Arms, it used to be,—and go and get an appetite in the forest. Can you stand it, Margaret? It will be a trial, I know, to both of us, but it will be a pleasure to me, at least. And there we'll dine—it will be but doe-venison, if we can get it at all—and then I'll take my nap while you go out and see old friends. I'll give you back safe and sound, barring railway accidents, and I'll insure your life for a thousand pounds before starting, which may be some comfort to your relations; but otherwise, I'll bring you back to Mrs. Shaw by lunch-time on Friday. So, if you say yes, I'll just go up-stairs and propose it.'

'It's no use my trying to say how much I shall like it,' said Margaret, through her tears.

'Well, then, prove your gratitude by keeping those fountains of yours dry for the next two days. If you don't, I shall feel queer myself about the lachrymal ducts, and I don't like that.'

'I won't cry a drop,' said Margaret, winking her eyes to shake the tears off her eye-lashes, and forcing a smile.

'There's my good girl. Then we'll go up-stairs and settle it all.' Margaret was in a state of almost trembling eagerness, while Mr. Bell discussed his plan with her aunt Shaw, who was first startled, then doubtful and perplexed, and in the end, yielding rather to the rough force of Mr. Bell's words than to her own conviction; for to the last, whether it was right or wrong, proper or improper, she could not settle to her own satisfaction, till Margaret's safe return, the happy fulfilment of the project, gave her decision enough to say, 'she was sure it had been a very kind thought of Mr. Bell's, and just what she herself had been wishing for Margaret, as giving her the very change which she required, after all the anxious time she had had.'

CHAPTER XLVI - ONCE AND NOW

'So on those happy days of yore
 Oft as I dare to dwell once more,
 Still must I miss the friends so tried,
 Whom Death has severed from my side.

 But ever when true friendship binds,
 Spirit it is that spirit finds;
 In spirit then our bliss we found,
 In spirit yet to them I'm bound.'
 UHLAND.

Margaret was ready long before the appointed time, and had leisure enough to cry a little, quietly, when unobserved, and to smile brightly when any one looked at her. Her last alarm was lest they should be too late and miss the train; but no! they were all in time; and she breathed freely and happily at length, seated in the carriage opposite to Mr. Bell, and whirling away past the well-known stations; seeing the old south country-towns and hamlets sleeping in the warm light of the pure sun, which gave a yet ruddier colour to their tiled roofs, so different to the cold slates of the north. Broods of pigeons hovered around these peaked quaint gables, slowly settling here and there, and ruffling their soft, shiny feathers, as if exposing every fibre to the delicious warmth. There were few people about at the stations, it almost seemed as if they were too lazily content to wish to travel; none of the bustle and stir that Margaret had noticed in her two journeys on the London and North-Western line. Later on in the year, this line of railway should be stirring and alive with rich pleasure-seekers; but as to the constant going to and fro of busy trades-people it would always be widely different from the northern lines. Here a spectator or two stood lounging at nearly every station, with his hands in his pockets, so absorbed in the simple act of watching, that it made the travellers wonder what he could find to do when the train whirled away, and only the blank of a railway, some sheds, and a distant field or two were left for him to gaze upon. The hot air danced over the golden stillness of the land, farm after farm was left behind, each reminding Margaret of German Idyls—of Herman and Dorothea—of

Evangeline. From this waking dream she was roused. It was the place to leave the train and take the fly to Helstone. And now sharper feelings came shooting through her heart, whether pain or pleasure she could hardly tell. Every mile was redolent of associations, which she would not have missed for the world, but each of which made her cry upon 'the days that are no more,' with ineffable longing. The last time she had passed along this road was when she had left it with her father and mother—the day, the season, had been gloomy, and she herself hopeless, but they were there with her. Now she was alone, an orphan, and they, strangely, had gone away from her, and vanished from the face of the earth. It hurt her to see the Helstone road so flooded in the sun-light, and every turn and every familiar tree so precisely the same in its summer glory as it had been in former years. Nature felt no change, and was ever young.

Mr. Bell knew something of what would be passing through her mind, and wisely and kindly held his tongue. They drove up to the Lennard Arms; half farm-house, half-inn, standing a little apart from the road, as much as to say, that the host did not so depend on the custom of travellers, as to have to court it by any obtrusiveness; they, rather, must seek him out. The house fronted the village green; and right before it stood an immemorial lime-tree benched all round, in some hidden recesses of whose leafy wealth hung the grim escutcheon of the Lennards. The door of the inn stood wide open, but there was no hospitable hurry to receive the travellers. When the landlady did appear—and they might have abstracted many an article first—she gave them a kind welcome, almost as if they had been invited guests, and apologised for her coming having been so delayed, by saying, that it was hay-time, and the provisions for the men had to be sent a-field, and she had been too busy packing up the baskets to hear the noise of wheels over the road, which, since they had left the highway, ran over soft short turf.

'Why, bless me!' exclaimed she, as at the end of her apology, a glint of sunlight showed her Margaret's face, hitherto unobserved in that shady parlour. 'It's Miss Hale, Jenny,' said she, running to the door, and calling to her daughter. 'Come here, come directly, it's Miss Hale!' And then she went up to Margaret, and shook her hands with motherly fondness.

'And how are you all? How's the Vicar and Miss Dixon? The Vicar above all! God bless him! We've never ceased to be sorry that he left.'

Margaret tried to speak and tell her of her father's death; of her mother's it was evident that Mrs. Purkis was aware, from her omission of her name. But she choked in the effort, and could only touch her deep mourning, and say the one word, 'Papa.'

'Surely, sir, it's never so!' said Mrs. Purkis, turning to Mr. Bell for confirmation of the sad suspicion that now entered her mind. 'There was a gentleman here in the spring—it might have been as long ago as last winter—who told us a deal of Mr. Hale and Miss Margaret; and he said Mrs. Hale was gone, poor lady. But never a word of the Vicar's being ailing!'

'It is so, however,' said Mr. Bell. 'He died quite suddenly, when on a visit to me at Oxford. He was a good man, Mrs. Purkis, and there's many of us that might be thankful to have as calm an end as his. Come Margaret, my dear! Her father was my oldest friend, and she's my god-daughter, so I thought we would just come down together and see the old place; and I know of old you can give us comfortable rooms and a capital dinner. You don't remember me I see, but my name is Bell, and once or twice when the parsonage has been full, I've slept here, and tasted your good ale.'

'To be sure; I ask your pardon; but you see I was taken up with Miss Hale. Let me show you to a room, Miss Margaret, where you can take off your bonnet, and wash your face. It's only this very morning I plunged some fresh-gathered roses head downward in the water-jug, for, thought I, perhaps some one will be coming, and there's nothing so sweet as spring-water scented by a musk rose or two. To think of the Vicar being dead! Well, to be sure, we must all die; only that gentleman said, he was quite picking up after his trouble about Mrs. Hale's death.'

'Come down to me, Mrs. Purkis, after you have attended to Miss Hale. I want to have a consultation with you about dinner.'

The little casement window in Margaret's bed-chamber was almost filled up with rose and vine branches; but pushing them aside, and stretching a little out, she could see the tops of the parsonage chimneys above the trees; and distinguish many a well-known line through the leaves.

'Aye!' said Mrs. Purkis, smoothing down the bed, and despatching Jenny for an armful of lavender-scented towels, 'times is changed, miss; our new Vicar has seven children, and is building a nursery ready for more, just out where the arbour and tool-house used to be in old times. And he has had new grates put in, and a plate-glass window in the drawing-room. He and his wife are stirring people, and have done a deal of good; at least they say it's doing good; if it were not, I should call it turning things upside down for very little purpose. The new Vicar is a teetotaller, miss, and a magistrate, and his wife has a deal of receipts for economical cooking, and is for making bread without yeast; and they both talk so much, and both at a time, that they knock one down as it were, and it's not till they're gone, and one's a little at peace, that one can think that there were things one might have said on one's own side of the question. He'll be after the men's cans in the hay-field, and peeping in; and then there'll be an ado because it's not ginger beer, but I can't help it. My mother and my grandmother before me sent good malt liquor to haymakers; and took salts and senna when anything ailed them; and I must e'en go on in their ways, though Mrs. Hepworth does want to give me comfits instead of medicine, which, as she says, is a deal pleasanter, only I've no faith in it. But I must go, miss, though I'm wanting to hear many a thing; I'll come back to you before long.

Mr. Bell had strawberries and cream, a loaf of brown bread, and a jug of milk, (together with a Stilton cheese and a bottle of port for his own private refreshment,) ready for Margaret on her coming down stairs; and after this rustic luncheon they set out to walk, hardly knowing in what direction to turn, so many old familiar inducements were there in each.

'Shall we go past the vicarage?' asked Mr. Bell.

'No, not yet. We will go this way, and make a round so as to come back by it,' replied Margaret.

Here and there old trees had been felled the autumn before; or a squatter's roughly-built and decaying cottage had disappeared. Margaret missed them each and all, and grieved over them like old friends. They came past the spot where she and Mr. Lennox had sketched. The white, lightning-scarred trunk of the venerable beech, among whose roots they had sate down was there no more; the old man, the inhabitant of the ruinous cottage, was dead; the cottage had been pulled down, and a new one, tidy and respectable, had been built in its stead. There was a small garden on the place where the beech-tree had been.

'I did not think I had been so old,' said Margaret after a pause of silence; and she turned away sighing.

'Yes!' said Mr. Bell. 'It is the first changes among familiar things that make such a mystery of time to the young, afterwards we lose the sense of the mysterious. I take changes in all I see as a matter of course. The instability of all human things is familiar to me, to you it is new and oppressive.'

'Let us go on to see little Susan,' said Margaret, drawing her companion up a grassy road-way, leading under the shadow of a forest glade.

'With all my heart, though I have not an idea who little Susan may be. But I have a kindness for all Susans, for simple Susan's sake.'

'My little Susan was disappointed when I left without wishing her goodbye; and it has been on my conscience ever since, that I gave her pain which a little more exertion on my part might have prevented. But it is a long way. Are you sure you will not be tired?'

'Quite sure. That is, if you don't walk so fast. You see, here there are no views that can give one an excuse for stopping to take breath. You would think it romantic to be walking with a person "fat and scant o' breath" if I were Hamlet, Prince of Denmark. Have compassion on my infirmities for his sake.'

'I will walk slower for your own sake. I like you twenty times better than Hamlet.'

'On the principle that a living ass is better than a dead lion?'

'Perhaps so. I don't analyse my feelings.'

'I am content to take your liking me, without examining too curiously into the materials it is made of. Only we need not walk at a snail's' pace.'

'Very well. Walk at your own pace, and I will follow. Or stop still and meditate, like the Hamlet you compare yourself to, if I go too fast.'

'Thank you. But as my mother has not murdered my father, and afterwards married my uncle, I shouldn't know what to think about, unless it were balancing the chances of our having a well-cooked dinner or not. What do you think?'

'I am in good hopes. She used to be considered a famous cook as far as Helstone opinion went.'

'But have you considered the distraction of mind produced by all this haymaking?'

Margaret felt all Mr. Bell's kindness in trying to make cheerful talk about nothing, to endeavour to prevent her from thinking too curiously about the past. But she would rather have gone over these dear-loved walks in silence, if indeed she were not ungrateful enough to wish that she might have been alone.

They reached the cottage where Susan's widowed mother lived. Susan was not there. She was gone to the parochial school. Margaret was disappointed, and the poor woman saw it, and began to make a kind of apology.

'Oh! it is quite right,' said Margaret. 'I am very glad to hear it. I might have thought of it. Only she used to stop at home with you.'

'Yes, she did; and I miss her sadly. I used to teach her what little I knew at nights. It were not much to be sure. But she were getting such a handy girl, that I miss her sore. But she's a deal above me in learning now.' And the mother sighed.

'I'm all wrong,' growled Mr. Bell. 'Don't mind what I say. I'm a hundred years behind the world. But I should say, that the child was getting a better and simpler, and more natural education stopping at home, and helping her mother, and learning to read a chapter in the New Testament every night by her side, than from all the schooling under the sun.'

Margaret did not want to encourage him to go on by replying to him, and so prolonging the discussion before the mother. So she turned to her and asked,

'How is old Betty Barnes?'

'I don't know,' said the woman rather shortly. 'We'se not friends.'

'Why not?' asked Margaret, who had formerly been the peacemaker of the village.

'She stole my cat.'

'Did she know it was yours?'

'I don't know. I reckon not.'

'Well! could not you get it back again when you told her it was yours?'

'No! for she'd burnt it.'

'Burnt it!' exclaimed both Margaret and Mr. Bell.

'Roasted it!' explained the woman.

It was no explanation. By dint of questioning, Margaret extracted from her the horrible fact that Betty Barnes, having been induced by a gypsy fortune-teller to lend the latter her husband's Sunday clothes, on promise of having them faithfully returned on the Saturday night before Goodman Barnes should have missed them, became alarmed by their non-appearance, and her consequent dread of her husband's anger, and as, according to one of the savage country superstitions, the cries of a cat, in the agonies of being boiled or roasted alive, compelled (as it were) the powers of darkness to fulfil the wishes of the executioner, resort had been had to the charm. The poor woman evidently believed in its efficacy; her only feeling was indignation that her cat had been chosen out from all others for a sacrifice. Margaret listened in horror; and endeavoured in vain to enlighten the woman's mind; but she was obliged to give it up in despair. Step by step she got the woman to admit certain facts, of which the logical connexion and sequence was perfectly clear to Margaret; but at the end, the bewildered woman simply repeated her first assertion, namely, that 'it were very cruel for sure, and she should not like to do it; but that there were nothing like it for giving a person what they wished for; she had heard it all her life; but it were very cruel for all that.' Margaret gave it up in despair, and walked away sick at heart.

'You are a good girl not to triumph over me,' said Mr. Bell.

'How? What do you mean?'

'I own, I am wrong about schooling. Anything rather than have that child brought up in such practical paganism.'

'Oh! I remember. Poor little Susan! I must go and see her; would you mind calling at the school?'

'Not a bit. I am curious to see something of the teaching she is to receive.'

They did not speak much more, but thridded their way through many a bosky dell, whose soft green influence could not charm away the shock and the pain in Margaret's heart, caused by the recital of such cruelty; a recital too, the manner of which betrayed such utter want of imagination, and therefore of any sympathy with the suffering animal.

The buzz of voices, like the murmur of a hive of busy human bees, made itself heard as soon as they emerged from the forest on the more open village-green on which the school was situated. The door was wide open, and they entered. A brisk lady in black, here, there, and everywhere, perceived them, and bade them welcome with somewhat of the hostess-air which, Margaret remembered, her mother was wont to assume, only in a more soft and languid manner, when any rare visitors strayed in to inspect the school. She knew at once it was the present Vicar's wife, her mother's successor; and she would have drawn back from the interview had it been possible; but in an instant she had conquered this feeling, and modestly advanced, meeting many a bright glance of recognition, and hearing many a half-suppressed murmur of 'It's Miss Hale.' The Vicar's lady heard the name, and her manner at once became more kindly. Margaret wished she could have helped feeling that it also became more patronising. The lady held out a hand to Mr. Bell, with—

'Your father, I presume, Miss Hale. I see it by the likeness. I am sure I am very glad to see you, sir, and so will the Vicar be.'

Margaret explained that it was not her father, and stammered out the fact of his death; wondering all the time how Mr. Hale could have borne coming to revisit Helstone, if it had been as the Vicar's lady supposed. She did not hear what Mrs. Hepworth was saying, and left it to Mr. Bell to reply, looking round, meanwhile, for her old acquaintances.

'Ah! I see you would like to take a class, Miss Hale. I know it by myself. First class stand up for a parsing lesson with Miss Hale.'

Poor Margaret, whose visit was sentimental, not in any degree inspective, felt herself taken in; but as in some way bringing her in contact with little eager faces, once well-known, and who had received the solemn rite of baptism from her father, she sate down, half losing herself in tracing out the changing features of the girls, and holding Susan's hand for a minute or two, unobserved by all, while the first class sought for their books, and the Vicar's lady went as near as a lady could towards holding Mr. Bell by the button, while she explained the Phonetic system to him, and gave him a conversation she had had with the Inspector about it.

Margaret bent over her book, and seeing nothing but that—hearing the buzz of children's voices, old times rose up, and she thought of them, and her eyes filled with tears, till all at once there was a pause—one of the girls was stumbling over the apparently simple word 'a,' uncertain what to call it.

'A, an indefinite article,' said Margaret, mildly.

'I beg your pardon,' said the Vicar's wife, all eyes and ears; 'but we are taught by Mr. Milsome to call "a" an—who can remember?'

'An adjective absolute,' said half-a-dozen voices at once. And Margaret sate abashed. The children knew more than she did. Mr. Bell turned away, and smiled.

Margaret spoke no more during the lesson. But after it was over, she went quietly round to one or two old favourites, and talked to them a little. They were growing out of children into great girls; passing out of her recollection in their rapid development, as she, by her three years' absence, was vanishing from theirs. Still she was glad to have seen them all again, though a tinge of sadness mixed itself with her pleasure. When school was over for the day, it was yet early in the summer afternoon; and Mrs. Hepworth proposed to Margaret that she and Mr. Bell should accompany her to the parsonage, and see the—the word 'improvements' had half slipped out of her mouth, but she substituted the more cautious term 'alterations' which the present Vicar was making. Margaret did not care a straw about seeing the alterations, which jarred upon her fond recollection of what her home had been; but she longed to see the old place once more, even though she shivered away from the pain which she knew she should feel.

The parsonage was so altered, both inside and out, that the real pain was less than she had anticipated. It was not like the same place. The garden, the grass-plat, formerly so daintily trim that even a stray rose-leaf seemed like a fleck on its exquisite arrangement and propriety, was strewed with children's things; a bag of marbles here, a hoop there; a straw-hat forced down upon a rose-tree as on a peg, to the destruction of a long beautiful tender branch laden with flowers, which in former days would have been trained up tenderly, as if beloved. The little square matted hall was equally filled with signs of merry healthy rough childhood.

'Ah!' said Mrs. Hepworth, 'you must excuse this untidiness, Miss Hale. When the nursery is finished, I shall insist upon a little order. We are building a nursery out of your room, I believe. How did you manage, Miss Hale, without a nursery?'

'We were but two,' said Margaret. 'You have many children, I presume?'

'Seven. Look here! we are throwing out a window to the road on this side. Mr. Hepworth is spending an immense deal of money on this house; but really it was scarcely habitable when we came—for so large a family as ours I mean, of course.' Every room in the house was changed, besides the one of which Mrs. Hepworth spoke, which had been Mr. Hale's study formerly; and where the green gloom and delicious quiet of the place had conduced, as he had said, to a habit of meditation, but, perhaps, in some degree to the formation of a character more fitted for thought than action. The new window gave a view of the road, and had many advantages, as Mrs. Hepworth pointed out. From it the wandering sheep of her husband's flock might be seen, who straggled to the tempting beer-house, unobserved as they might hope, but not unobserved in reality; for the active Vicar kept his eye on the road, even during the composition of his most orthodox sermons, and had a hat and stick hanging ready at hand to seize, before sallying out after his parishioners, who had need of quick legs if they could take refuge in the 'Jolly Forester' before the teetotal Vicar had arrested them. The whole family were quick, brisk, loud-talking, kind-hearted, and not troubled with much delicacy of perception. Margaret feared that Mrs. Hepworth would find out that Mr. Bell was playing upon her, in the admiration he thought fit to express for everything that especially grated on his taste. But no! she took it all literally, and with such good faith, that Margaret could not help remonstrating with him as they walked slowly away from the parsonage back to their inn.

'Don't scold, Margaret. It was all because of you. If she had not shown you every change with such evident exultation in their superior sense, in perceiving what an improvement this and that would be, I could have behaved well. But if you must go on preaching, keep it till after dinner, when it will send me to sleep, and help my digestion.'

They were both of them tired, and Margaret herself so much so, that she was unwilling to go out as she had proposed to do, and have another ramble among the woods and fields so close to the home of her childhood. And, somehow, this visit to Helstone had not been all—had not been exactly what she had expected. There was change everywhere; slight, yet pervading all. Households were changed by absence, or death, or marriage, or the natural mutations brought by days and months and years, which carry us on imperceptibly from childhood to youth, and thence through manhood to age, whence we drop like fruit, fully ripe, into the quiet mother earth. Places were changed—a tree gone here, a bough there, bringing in a long ray of light where no light was before—a road was trimmed and narrowed, and the green straggling pathway by its side enclosed and cultivated. A great improvement it was called; but Margaret sighed over the old picturesqueness, the old gloom, and the grassy wayside of former days. She sate by the window on the little settle, sadly gazing out upon the gathering shades of night, which harmonised well with her pensive thought. Mr. Bell slept soundly, after his unusual exercise through the day. At last he was roused by the entrance of the tea-tray, brought in by a flushed-looking country-girl, who had evidently been finding some variety from her usual occupation of waiter, in assisting this day in the hayfield.

'Hallo! Who's there! Where are we? Who's that,—Margaret? Oh, now I remember all. I could not imagine what woman was sitting there in such a doleful attitude, with her hands clasped straight out upon her knees, and her face looking so steadfastly before her. What were you looking at?' asked Mr. Bell, coming to the window, and standing behind Margaret.

'Nothing,' said she, rising up quickly, and speaking as cheerfully as she could at a moment's notice.

'Nothing indeed! A bleak back-ground of trees, some white linen hung out on the sweet-briar hedge, and a great waft of damp air. Shut the window, and come in and make tea.'

Margaret was silent for some time. She played with her teaspoon, and did not attend particularly to what Mr. Bell said. He contradicted her, and she took the same sort of smiling notice of his opinion as if he had agreed with her. Then she sighed, and putting down her spoon, she began, apropos of nothing at all, and in the high-pitched voice which usually shows that the speaker has been thinking for some time on the subject that they wish to introduce—'Mr. Bell, you remember what we were saying about Frederick last night, don't you?'

'Last night. Where was I? Oh, I remember! Why it seems a week ago. Yes, to be sure, I recollect we talked about him, poor fellow.'

'Yes—and do you not remember that Mr. Lennox spoke about his having been in England about the time of dear mamma's death?' asked Margaret, her voice now lower than usual.

'I recollect. I hadn't heard of it before.'

'And I thought—I always thought that papa had told you about it.'

'No! he never did. But what about it, Margaret?'

'I want to tell you of something I did that was very wrong, about that time,' said Margaret, suddenly looking up at him with her clear honest eyes. 'I told a lie;' and her face became scarlet.

'True, that was bad I own; not but what I have told a pretty round number in my life, not all in downright words, as I suppose you did, but in actions, or in some shabby circumlocutory way, leading people either to disbelieve the truth, or believe a falsehood. You know who is the father of lies, Margaret? Well! a great number of folk, thinking themselves very good, have odd sorts of connexion with lies, left-hand marriages, and second cousins-once-removed. The tainting blood of falsehood runs through us all. I should have guessed you as far from it as most people. What! crying, child? Nay, now we'll not talk of it, if it ends in this way. I dare say you have been sorry for it, and that you won't do it again, and it's long ago now, and in short I want you to be very cheerful, and not very sad, this evening.'

Margaret wiped her eyes, and tried to talk about something else, but suddenly she burst out afresh.

'Please, Mr. Bell, let me tell you about it—you could perhaps help me a little; no, not help me, but if you knew the truth, perhaps you could put me to rights—that is not it, after all,' said she, in despair at not being able to express herself more exactly as she wished.

Mr. Bell's whole manner changed. 'Tell me all about it, child,' said he.

'It's a long story; but when Fred came, mamma was very ill, and I was undone with anxiety, and afraid, too, that I might have drawn him into danger; and we had an alarm just after her death, for Dixon met some one in Milton—a man called Leonards—who had known Fred, and who seemed to owe him a grudge, or at any rate to be tempted by the recollection of the reward offered for his apprehension; and with this new fright, I thought I had better hurry off Fred to London, where, as you would understand from what we said the other night, he was to go to consult Mr. Lennox as to his chances if he stood the trial. So we—that is, he and I,—went to the railway station; it was one evening, and it was just getting rather dusk, but still light enough to recognise and be recognised, and we were too early, and went out to walk in a field just close by; I was always in a panic about this Leonards, who was, I knew, somewhere in the neighbourhood; and then, when we were in the field, the low red sunlight just in my face, some one came by on horseback in the road just below the field-style by which we stood. I saw him look at me, but I did not know who it was at first, the sun was so in my eyes, but in an instant the dazzle went off, and I saw it was Mr. Thornton, and we bowed,'——

'And he saw Frederick of course,' said Mr. Bell, helping her on with her story, as he thought.

'Yes; and then at the station a man came up—tipsy and reeling—and he tried to collar Fred, and over-balanced himself as Fred wrenched himself away, and fell over the edge of the platform; not far, not deep; not above three feet; but oh! Mr. Bell, somehow that fall killed him!'

'How awkward. It was this Leonards, I suppose. And how did Fred get off?'

'Oh! he went off immediately after the fall, which we never thought could have done the poor fellow any harm, it seemed so slight an injury.'

'Then he did not die directly?'

'No! not for two or three days. And then—oh, Mr. Bell! now comes the bad part,' said she, nervously twining her fingers together. 'A police inspector came and taxed me with having been the companion of the young man, whose push or blow had occasioned Leonards' death; that was a false accusation, you know, but we had not heard that Fred had sailed, he might still be in London and liable to be arrested on this false charge, and his identity with the Lieutenant Hale, accused of causing that mutiny, discovered, he might be shot; all this flashed through my mind, and I said it was not me. I was not at the railway station that night. I knew nothing about it. I had no conscience or thought but to save Frederick.'

'I say it was right. I should have done the same. You forgot yourself in thought for another. I hope I should have done the same.'

'No, you would not. It was wrong, disobedient, faithless. At that very time Fred was safely out of England, and in my blindness I forgot that there was another witness who could testify to my being there.'

'Who?'

'Mr. Thornton. You know he had seen me close to the station; we had bowed to each other.'

'Well! he would know nothing of this riot about the drunken fellow's death. I suppose the inquiry never came to anything.'

'No! the proceedings they had begun to talk about on the inquest were stopped. Mr. Thornton did know all about it. He was a magistrate, and he found out that it was not the fall that had caused the death. But not before he knew what I had said. Oh, Mr. Bell!' She suddenly covered her face with her hands, as if wishing to hide herself from the presence of the recollection.

'Did you have any explanation with him? Did you ever tell him the strong, instinctive motive?'

'The instinctive want of faith, and clutching at a sin to keep myself from sinking,' said she bitterly. 'No! How could I? He knew nothing of Frederick. To put myself to rights in his good opinion, was I to tell him of the secrets of our family, involving, as they seemed to do, the chances of poor Frederick's entire exculpation? Fred's last words had been to enjoin me to keep his visit a secret from all. You see, papa never told, even you. No! I could bear the shame—I thought I could at least. I did bear it. Mr. Thornton has never respected me since.'

'He respects you, I am sure,' said Mr. Bell. 'To be sure, it accounts a little for——. But he always speaks of you with regard and esteem, though now I understand certain reservations in his manner.'

Margaret did not speak; did not attend to what Mr. Bell went on to say; lost all sense of it. By-and-by she said:

'Will you tell me what you refer to about "reservations" in his manner of speaking of me?'

'Oh! simply he has annoyed me by not joining in my praises of you. Like an old fool, I thought that every one would have the same opinions as I had; and he evidently could not agree with me. I was puzzled at the time. But he must be perplexed, if the affair has never been in the least explained. There was first your walking out with a young man in the dark—'

'But it was my brother!' said Margaret, surprised.

'True. But how was he to know that?'

'I don't know. I never thought of anything of that kind,' said Margaret, reddening, and looking hurt and offended.

'And perhaps he never would, but for the lie,—which, under the circumstances, I maintain, was necessary.'

'It was not. I know it now. I bitterly repent it.'

There was a long pause of silence. Margaret was the first to speak.

'I am not likely ever to see Mr. Thornton again,'—and there she stopped.

'There are many things more unlikely, I should say,' replied Mr. Bell.

'But I believe I never shall. Still, somehow one does not like to have sunk so low in—in a friend's opinion as I have done in his.' Her eyes were full of tears, but her voice was steady, and Mr. Bell was not looking at her. 'And now that Frederick has given up all hope, and almost all wish of ever clearing himself, and returning to England, it would be only doing myself justice to have all this explained. If you please, and if you can, if there is a good opportunity, (don't force an explanation upon him, pray,) but if you can, will you tell him the whole circumstances, and tell him also that I gave you leave to do so, because I felt that for papa's sake I should not like to lose his respect, though we may never be likely to meet again?'

'Certainly. I think he ought to know. I do not like you to rest even under the shadow of an impropriety; he would not know what to think of seeing you alone with a young man.'

'As for that,' said Margaret, rather haughtily, 'I hold it is "Honi soit qui mal y pense." Yet still I should choose to have it explained, if any natural opportunity for easy explanation occurs. But it is not to clear myself of any suspicion of improper conduct that I wish to have him told—if I thought that he had suspected me, I should not care for his good opinion—no! it is that he may learn how I was tempted, and how I fell into the snare; why I told that falsehood, in short.'

'Which I don't blame you for. It is no partiality of mine, I assure you.'

'What other people may think of the rightness or wrongness is nothing in comparison to my own deep knowledge, my innate conviction that it was wrong. But we will not talk of that any more, if you please. It is done—my sin is sinned. I have now to put it behind me, and be truthful for evermore, if I can.'

'Very well. If you like to be uncomfortable and morbid, be so. I always keep my conscience as tight shut up as a jack-in-a-box, for when it jumps into existence it surprises me by its size. So I coax it down again, as the fisherman coaxed the genie. "Wonderful," say I, "to think that you have been concealed so long, and in so small a compass, that I really did not know of your existence. Pray, sir, instead of growing larger and larger every instant, and bewildering me with your misty outlines, would you once more compress yourself into your former dimensions?" And when I've got him down, don't I clap the seal on the vase, and take good care how I open it again, and how I go against Solomon, wisest of men, who confined him there.'

But it was no smiling matter to Margaret. She hardly attended to what Mr. Bell was saying. Her thoughts ran upon the idea, before entertained, but which now had assumed the strength of a conviction, that Mr. Thornton no longer held his former good opinion of her—that he was disappointed in her. She did not feel as if any explanation could ever reinstate her—not in his love, for that and any return on her part she had resolved never to dwell upon, and she kept rigidly to her resolution—but in the respect and high regard which she had hoped would have ever made him willing, in the spirit of Gerald Griffin's beautiful lines,

> 'To turn and look back when thou hearest
> The sound of my name.'

She kept choking and swallowing all the time that she thought about it. She tried to comfort herself with the idea, that what he imagined her to be, did not alter the fact of what she was. But it was a truism, a phantom, and broke down under the weight of her regret. She had twenty questions on the tip of her tongue to ask Mr. Bell, but not one of them did she utter. Mr. Bell thought that she was tired, and sent her early to her room, where she sate long hours by the open window, gazing out on the purple dome above, where the stars arose, and twinkled and disappeared behind the great umbrageous trees before she went to bed. All night long too, there burnt a little light on earth; a candle in her old bedroom, which was the nursery with the present inhabitants of the parsonage, until the new one was built. A sense of change, of individual nothingness, of perplexity and disappointment, over-powered Margaret. Nothing had been the same; and this slight, all-pervading instability, had given her greater pain than if all had been too entirely changed for her to recognise it.

'I begin to understand now what heaven must be—and, oh! the grandeur and repose of the words—"The same yesterday, to-day, and for ever." Everlasting! "From everlasting to everlasting, Thou art God." That sky above me looks as though it could not change, and yet it will. I am so tired—so tired of being whirled on through all these phases of my life, in which nothing abides by me, no creature, no place; it is like the circle in which the victims of earthly passion eddy continually. I am in the mood in which women of another religion take the veil. I seek heavenly steadfastness in earthly monotony. If I were a Roman Catholic and could deaden my heart, stun it with some great blow, I might become a nun. But I should pine after my kind; no, not my kind, for love for my species could never fill my heart to the utter exclusion of love for individuals. Perhaps it ought to be so, perhaps not; I cannot decide to-night.'

Wearily she went to bed, wearily she arose in four or five hours' time. But with the morning came hope, and a brighter view of things.

'After all it is right,' said she, hearing the voices of children at play while she was dressing. 'If the world stood still, it would retrograde and become corrupt, if that is not Irish. Looking out of myself, and my own painful sense of change, the progress all around me is right and necessary. I must not think so much of how circumstances affect me myself, but how they affect others, if I wish to have a right judgment, or a hopeful trustful heart.' And with a smile ready in her eyes to quiver down to her lips, she went into the parlour and greeted Mr. Bell.

'Ah, Missy! you were up late last night, and so you're late this morning. Now I've got a little piece of news for you. What do you think of an invitation to dinner? a morning call, literally in the dewy morning. Why, I've had the Vicar here already, on his way to the school. How much the desire of giving our hostess a teetotal lecture for the benefit of the haymakers, had to do with his earliness, I don't know; but here he was, when I came down just before nine; and we are asked to dine there to-day.'

'But Edith expects me back—I cannot go,' said Margaret, thankful to have so good an excuse.

'Yes! I know; so I told him. I thought you would not want to go. Still it is open, if you would like it.'

'Oh, no!' said Margaret. 'Let us keep to our plan. Let us start at twelve. It is very good and kind of them; but indeed I could not go.'

'Very well. Don't fidget yourself, and I'll arrange it all.'

Before they left Margaret stole round to the back of the Vicarage garden, and gathered a little straggling piece of honeysuckle. She would not take a flower the day before, for fear of being observed, and her motives and feelings commented upon. But as she returned across the common, the place was reinvested with the old enchanting atmosphere. The common sounds of life were more musical there than anywhere else in the whole world, the light more golden, the life more tranquil and full of dreamy delight. As Margaret remembered her feelings yesterday, she said to herself:

'And I too change perpetually—now this, now that—now disappointed and peevish because all is not exactly as I had pictured it, and now suddenly discovering that the reality is far more beautiful than I had imagined it. Oh, Helstone! I shall never love any place like you.

A few days afterwards, she had found her level, and decided that she was very glad to have been there, and that she had seen it again, and that to her it would always be the prettiest spot in the world, but that it was so full of associations with former days, and especially with her father and mother, that if it were all to come over again, she should shrink back from such another visit as that which she had paid with Mr. Bell.

CHAPTER XLVII - SOMETHING WANTING

'Experience, like a pale musician, holds
A dulcimer of patience in his hand;
Whence harmonies we cannot understand,
Of God's will in His worlds, the strain unfolds
In sad, perplexed minors.'
MRS. BROWNING.

About this time Dixon returned from Milton, and assumed her post as Margaret's maid. She brought endless pieces of Milton gossip: How Martha had gone to live with Miss Thornton, on the latter's marriage; with an account of the bridesmaids, dresses and breakfasts, at that interesting ceremony; how people thought that Mr. Thornton had made too grand a wedding of it, considering he had lost a deal by the strike, and had had to pay so much for the failure of his contracts; how little money articles of furniture—long cherished by Dixon—had fetched at the sale, which was a shame considering how rich folks were at Milton; how Mrs. Thornton had come one day and got two or three good bargains, and Mr. Thornton had come the next, and in his desire to obtain one or two things, had bid against himself, much to the enjoyment of the bystanders, so as Dixon observed, that made things even; if Mrs. Thornton paid too little, Mr. Thornton paid too much. Mr. Bell had sent all sorts of orders about the books; there was no understanding him, he was so particular; if he had come himself it would have been all right, but letters always were and always will be more puzzling than they are worth. Dixon had not much to tell about the Higginses. Her memory had an aristocratic bias, and was very treacherous whenever she tried to recall any circumstance connected with those below her in life. Nicholas was very well she believed. He had been several times at the house asking for news of Miss Margaret—the only person who ever did ask, except once Mr. Thornton. And Mary? oh! of course she was very well, a great, stout, slatternly thing! She did hear, or perhaps it was only a dream of hers, though it would be strange if she had dreamt of such people as the Higginses, that Mary had gone to work at Mr. Thornton's mill, because her father wished her to know how to cook; but what nonsense that could mean she didn't know. Margaret rather agreed with her that the story was incoherent enough to be like a dream. Still it was pleasant to have some one now with whom she could talk of Milton, and Milton people. Dixon was not over-fond of the subject, rather wishing to leave that part of her life in shadow. She liked much more to dwell upon speeches of Mr. Bell's, which had suggested an idea to her of what was really his intention—making Margaret his heiress. But her young lady gave her no encouragement, nor in any way gratified her insinuating enquiries, however disguised in the form of suspicions or assertions.

All this time, Margaret had a strange undefined longing to hear that Mr. Bell had gone to pay one of his business visits to Milton; for it had been well understood between them, at the time of their conversation at Helstone, that the expla-explanation she had desired should only be given to Mr. Thornton by word of mouth, and even in that manner should be in nowise forced upon him. Mr. Bell was no great correspondent, but he wrote from time to time long or short letters, as the humour took him, and although Margaret was not conscious of any definite hope, on receiving them, yet she always put away his notes with a little feeling of disappointment. He was not going to Milton; he said nothing about it at any rate. Well! she must be patient. Sooner or later the mists would be cleared away. Mr. Bell's letters were hardly like his usual self; they were short, and complaining, with every now and then a little touch of bitterness that was unusual. He did not look forward to the future; he rather seemed to regret the past, and be weary of the present. Margaret fancied that he could not be well; but in answer to some enquiry of hers as to his health, he sent her a short note, saying there was an old-fashioned complaint called the spleen; that he was suffering from that, and it was for her to decide if it was more mental or physical; but that he should like to indulge himself in grumbling, without being obliged to send a bulletin every time.

In consequence of this note, Margaret made no more enquiries about his health. One day Edith let out accidentally a fragment of a conversation which she had had with Mr. Bell, when he was last in London, which possessed Margaret with the idea that he had some notion of taking her to pay a visit to her brother and new sister-in-law, at Cadiz, in the autumn. She questioned and cross-questioned Edith, till the latter was weary, and declared that there was nothing more to remember; all he had said was that he half-thought he should go, and hear for himself what Frederick had to say about the mutiny; and that it would be a good opportunity for Margaret to become acquainted with her new sister-in-law; that he always went somewhere during the long vacation, and did not see why he should not go to Spain as well as anywhere else. That was all. Edith hoped Margaret did not want to leave them, that she was so anxious about all this. And then, having nothing else particular to do, she cried, and said that she knew she cared much more for Margaret than Margaret did for her. Margaret comforted her as well as she could, but she could hardly explain to her how this idea of Spain, mere *château en Espagne* as it might be, charmed and delighted her. Edith was in the mood to think that any pleasure enjoyed away from her was a tacit affront, or at best a proof of indifference. So Margaret had to keep her pleasure to herself, and could only let it escape by the safety-valve of asking Dixon, when she dressed for dinner, if she would not like to see Master Frederick and his new wife very much indeed?

'She's a Papist, Miss, isn't she?'

'I believe—oh yes, certainly!' said Margaret, a little damped for an instant at this recollection.

'And they live in a Popish country?'

'Yes.'

'Then I'm afraid I must say, that my soul is dearer to me than even Master Frederick, his own dear self. I should be in a perpetual terror, Miss, lest I should be converted.'

'Oh' said Margaret, 'I do not know that I am going; and if I go, I am not such a fine lady as to be unable to travel without you. No! dear old Dixon, you shall have a long holiday, if we go. But I'm afraid it is a long "if."'

Now Dixon did not like this speech. In the first place, she did not like Margaret's trick of calling her 'dear old Dixon' whenever she was particularly demonstrative. She knew that Miss Hale was apt to call all people that she liked 'old,' as a sort of term of endearment; but Dixon always winced away from the application of the word to herself, who, being not much past fifty, was, she thought, in the very prime of life. Secondly, she did not like being so easily taken at her word; she had, with all her terror, a lurking curiosity about Spain, the Inquisition, and Popish mysteries. So, after clearing her throat, as if to show her willingness to do away with difficulties, she asked Miss Hale, whether she thought if she took care never to see a priest, or enter into one of their churches, there would be so very much danger of her being converted? Master Frederick, to be sure, had gone over unaccountable.

'I fancy it was love that first predisposed him to conversion,' said Margaret, sighing.

'Indeed, Miss!' said Dixon; 'well! I can preserve myself from priests, and from churches; but love steals in unawares! I think it's as well I should not go.'

Margaret was afraid of letting her mind run too much upon this Spanish plan. But it took off her thoughts from too impatiently dwelling upon her desire to have all explained to Mr. Thornton. Mr. Bell appeared for the present to be stationary at Oxford, and to have no immediate purpose of going to Milton, and some secret restraint seemed to hang over Margaret, and prevent her from even asking, or alluding again to any probability of such a visit on his part. Nor did she feel at liberty to name what Edith had told her of the idea he had entertained,—it might be but for five minutes,—of going to Spain. He had never named it at Helstone, during all that sunny day of leisure; it was very probably but the fancy of a moment,—but if it were true, what a bright outlet it would be from the monotony of her present life, which was beginning to fall upon her.

One of the great pleasures of Margaret's life at this time, was in Edith's boy. He was the pride and plaything of both father and mother, as long as he was good; but he had a strong will of his own, and as soon as he burst out into one of his stormy passions, Edith would throw herself back in despair and fatigue, and sigh out, 'Oh dear, what shall I do with him! Do, Margaret, please ring the bell for Hanley.'

But Margaret almost liked him better in these manifestations of character than in his good blue-sashed moods. She would carry him off into a room, where they two alone battled it out; she with a firm power which subdued him into peace, while every sudden charm and wile she possessed, was exerted on the side of right, until he would rub his little hot and tear-smeared face all over hers, kissing and caressing till he often fell asleep in her arms or on her shoulder. Those were Margaret's sweetest moments. They gave her a taste of the feeling that she believed would be denied to her for ever.

Mr. Henry Lennox added a new and not disagreeable element to the course of the household life by his frequent presence. Margaret thought him colder, if more brilliant than formerly; but there were strong intellectual tastes, and much and varied knowledge, which gave flavour to the otherwise rather insipid conversation. Margaret saw glimpses in him of a slight contempt for his brother and sister-in-law, and for their mode of life, which he seemed to consider as frivolous and purposeless. He once or twice spoke to his brother, in Margaret's presence, in a pretty sharp tone of enquiry, as to whether he meant entirely to relinquish his profession; and on Captain Lennox's reply, that he had quite enough to live upon, she had seen Mr. Lennox's curl of the lip as he said, 'And is that all you live for?'

But the brothers were much attached to each other, in the way that any two persons are, when the one is cleverer and always leads the other, and this last is patiently content to be led. Mr. Lennox was pushing on in his profession; cultivating, with profound calculation, all those connections that might eventually be of service to him; keen-sighted, far-seeing, intelligent, sarcastic, and proud. Since the one long conversation relating to Frederick's affairs, which she had with him the first evening in Mr. Bell's presence, she had had no great intercourse with him, further than that which arose out of their close relations with the same household. But this was enough to wear off the shyness on her side, and any symptoms of mortified pride and vanity on his. They met continually, of course, but she thought that he rather avoided being alone with her; she fancied that he, as well as she, perceived that they had drifted strangely apart from their former anchorage, side by side, in many of their opinions, and all their tastes.

And yet, when he had spoken unusually well, or with remarkable epigrammatic point, she felt that his eye sought the expression of her countenance first of all, if but for an instant; and that, in the family intercourse which constantly threw them together, her opinion was the one to which he listened with a deference,—the more complete, because it was reluctantly paid, and concealed as much as possible.

CHAPTER XLVIII - 'NE'ER TO BE FOUND AGAIN'

'My own, my father's friend!
I cannot part with thee!
I ne'er have shown, thou ne'er hast known,
How dear thou art to me.'
ANON.

The elements of the dinner-parties which Mrs. Lennox gave, were these; her friends contributed the beauty, Captain Lennox the easy knowledge of the subjects of the day; and Mr. Henry Lennox and the sprinkling of rising men who were received as his friends, brought the wit, the cleverness, the keen and extensive knowledge of which they knew well enough how to avail themselves without seeming pedantic, or burdening the rapid flow of conversation.

These dinners were delightful; but even here Margaret's dissatisfaction found her out. Every talent, every feeling, every acquirement; nay, even every tendency towards virtue was used up as materials for fireworks; the hidden, sacred fire, exhausted itself in sparkle and crackle. They talked about art in a merely sensuous way, dwelling on outside effects, instead of allowing themselves to learn what it has to teach. They lashed themselves up into an enthusiasm about high subjects in company, and never thought about them when they were alone; they squandered their capabilities of appreciation into a mere flow of appropriate words. One day, after the gentlemen had come up into the drawing-room, Mr. Lennox drew near to Margaret, and addressed her in almost the first voluntary words he had spoken to her since she had returned to live in Harley Street.

'You did not look pleased at what Shirley was saying at dinner.'

'Didn't I? My face must be very expressive,' replied Margaret.

'It always was. It has not lost the trick of being eloquent.'

'I did not like,' said Margaret, hastily, 'his way of advocating what he knew to be wrong—so glaringly wrong—even in jest.'

'But it was very clever. How every word told! Do you remember the happy epithets?'

'Yes.'

'And despise them, you would like to add. Pray don't scruple, though he is my friend.'

'There! that is the exact tone in you, that—' she stopped short.

He listened for a moment to see if she would finish her sentence; but she only reddened, and turned away; before she did so, however, she heard him say, in a very low, clear voice,—

'If my tones, or modes of thought, are what you dislike, will you do me the justice to tell me so, and so give me the chance of learning to please you?'

All these weeks there was no intelligence of Mr. Bell's going to Milton. He had spoken of it at Helstone as of a journey which he might have to take in a very short time from then; but he must have transacted his business by writing, Margaret thought, ere now, and she knew that if he could, he would avoid going to a place which he disliked, and moreover would little understand the secret importance which she affixed to the explanation that could only be given by word of mouth. She knew that he would feel that it was necessary that it should be done; but whether in summer, autumn, or winter, it would signify very little. It was now August, and there had been no mention of the Spanish journey to which he had alluded to Edith, and Margaret tried to reconcile herself to the fading away of this illusion.

But one morning she received a letter, saying that next week he meant to come up to town; he wanted to see her about a plan which he had in his head; and, moreover, he intended to treat himself to a little doctoring, as he had begun to come round to her opinion, that it would be pleasanter to think that his health was more in fault than he, when he found himself irritable and cross. There was altogether a tone of forced cheerfulness in the letter, as Margaret noticed afterwards; but at the time her attention was taken up by Edith's exclamations.

'Coming up to town! Oh dear! and I am so worn out by the heat that I don't believe I have strength enough in me for another dinner. Besides, everybody has left but our dear stupid selves, who can't settle where to go to. There would be nobody to meet him.'

'I'm sure he would much rather come and dine with us quite alone than with the most agreeable strangers you could pick up. Besides, if he is not well he won't wish for invitations. I am glad he has owned it at last. I was sure he was ill from the whole tone of his letters, and yet he would not answer me when I asked him, and I had no third person to whom I could apply for news.'

'Oh! he is not very ill, or he would not think of Spain.'

'He never mentions Spain.'

'No! but his plan that is to be proposed evidently relates to that. But would you really go in such weather as this?'

'Oh! it will get cooler every day. Yes! Think of it! I am only afraid I have thought and wished too much—in that absorbing wilful way which is sure to be disappointed—or else gratified, to the letter, while in the spirit it gives no pleasure.'

'But that's superstitious, I'm sure, Margaret.'

'No, I don't think it is. Only it ought to warn me, and check me from giving way to such passionate wishes. It is a sort of "Give me children, or else I die." I'm afraid my cry is, "Let me go to Cadiz, or else I die."'

'My dear Margaret! You'll be persuaded to stay there; and then what shall I do? Oh! I wish I could find somebody for you to marry here, that I could be sure of you!'

'I shall never marry.'

'Nonsense, and double nonsense! Why, as Sholto says, you're such an attraction to the house, that he knows ever so many men who will be glad to visit here next year for your sake.'

Margaret drew herself up haughtily. 'Do you know, Edith, I sometimes think your Corfu life has taught you—— '

'Well!'

'Just a shade or two of coarseness.'

Edith began to sob so bitterly, and to declare so vehemently that Margaret had lost all love for her, and no longer looked upon her as a friend, that Margaret came to think that she had expressed too harsh an opinion for the relief of her own wounded pride, and ended by being Edith's slave for the rest of the day; while that little lady, overcome by wounded feeling, lay like a victim on the sofa, heaving occasionally a profound sigh, till at last she fell asleep.

Mr. Bell did not make his appearance even on the day to which he had for a second time deferred his visit. The next morning there came a letter from Wallis, his servant, stating that his master had not been feeling well for some time, which had been the true reason of his putting off his journey; and that at the very time when he should have set out for London, he had been seized with an apoplectic fit; it was, indeed, Wallis added, the opinion of the medical men—that he could not survive the night; and more than probable, that by the time Miss Hale received this letter his poor master would be no more.

Margaret received this letter at breakfast-time, and turned very pale as she read it; then silently putting it into Edith's hands, she left the room.

Edith was terribly shocked as she read it, and cried in a sobbing, frightened, childish way, much to her husband's distress. Mrs. Shaw was breakfasting in her own room, and upon him devolved the task of reconciling his wife to the near contact into which she seemed to be brought with death, for the first time that she could remember in her life. Here was a man who was to have dined with them to-day lying dead or dying instead! It was some time before she could think of Margaret. Then she started up, and followed her upstairs into her room. Dixon was packing up a few toilette articles, and Margaret was hastily putting on her bonnet, shedding tears all the time, and her hands trembling so that she could hardly tie the strings.

'Oh, dear Margaret! how shocking! What are you doing? Are you going out? Sholto would telegraph or do anything you like.'

'I am going to Oxford. There is a train in half-an-hour. Dixon has offered to go with me, but I could have gone by myself. I must see him again. Besides, he may be better, and want some care. He has been like a father to me. Don't stop me, Edith.'

'But I must. Mamma won't like it at all. Come and ask her about it, Margaret. You don't know where you're going. I should not mind if he had a house of his own; but in his Fellow's rooms! Come to mamma, and do ask her before you go. It will not take a minute.'

Margaret yielded, and lost her train. In the suddenness of the event, Mrs. Shaw became bewildered and hysterical, and so the precious time slipped by. But there was another train in a couple of hours; and after various discussions on propriety and impropriety, it was decided that Captain Lennox should accompany Margaret, as the one thing to which she was constant was her resolution to go, alone or otherwise, by the next train, whatever might be said of the propriety or impropriety of the step. Her father's friend, her own friend, was lying at the point of death; and the thought of this came upon her with such vividness, that she was surprised herself at the firmness with which she asserted something of her right to independence of action; and five minutes before the time for starting, she found herself sitting in a railway-carriage opposite to Captain Lennox.

It was always a comfort to her to think that she had gone, though it was only to hear that he had died in the night. She saw the rooms that he had occupied, and associated them ever after most fondly in her memory with the idea of her father, and his one cherished and faithful friend.

They had promised Edith before starting, that if all had ended as they feared, they would return to dinner; so that long, lingering look around the room in which her father had died, had to be interrupted, and a quiet farewell taken of the kind old face that had so often come out with pleasant words, and merry quips and cranks.

Captain Lennox fell asleep on their journey home; and Margaret could cry at leisure, and bethink her of this fatal year, and all the woes it had brought to her. No sooner was she fully aware of one loss than another came—not to supersede her grief for the one before, but to re-open wounds and feelings scarcely healed. But at the sound of the tender voices of her aunt and Edith, of merry little Sholto's glee at her arrival, and at the sight of the well-lighted rooms, with their mistress pretty in her paleness and her eager sorrowful interest, Margaret roused herself from her heavy trance of almost superstitious hopelessness, and began to feel that even around her joy and gladness might gather. She had Edith's place on the sofa; Sholto was taught to carry aunt Margaret's cup of tea very carefully to her; and by the time she went up to dress, she could thank God for having spared her dear old friend a long or a painful illness.

But when night came—solemn night, and all the house was quiet, Margaret still sate watching the beauty of a London sky at such an hour, on such a summer evening; the faint pink reflection of earthly lights on the soft clouds that float tranquilly into the white moonlight, out of the warm gloom which lies motionless around the horizon. Margaret's room had been the day nursery of her childhood, just when it merged into girlhood, and when the feelings and conscience had been first awakened into full activity. On some such night as this she remembered promising to herself to live as brave and noble a life as any heroine she ever read or heard of in romance, a life sans peur et sans reproche; it had seemed to her then that she had only to will, and such a life would be accomplished. And now she had learnt that not only to will, but also to pray, was a necessary condition in the truly heroic. Trusting to herself, she had fallen. It was a just consequence of her sin, that all excuses for it, all temptation to it, should remain for ever unknown to the person in whose opinion it had sunk her lowest. She stood face to face at last with her sin. She knew it for what it was; Mr. Bell's kindly sophistry that nearly all men were guilty of equivocal actions, and that the motive ennobled the evil, had never had much real weight with her. Her own first thought of how, if she had known all, she might have fearlessly told the truth, seemed low and poor. Nay, even now, her anxiety to have her character for truth partially excused in Mr. Thornton's eyes, as Mr. Bell had promised to do, was a very small and petty consideration, now that she was afresh taught by death what life should be. If all the world spoke, acted, or kept silence with intent to deceive,—if dearest interests were at stake, and dearest lives in peril,—if no one should ever know of her truth or her falsehood to measure out their honour or contempt for her by, straight alone where she stood, in the presence of God, she prayed that she might have strength to speak and act the truth for evermore.

CHAPTER XLIX - BREATHING TRANQUILLITY

'And down the sunny beach she paces slowly,
With many doubtful pauses by the way;
Grief hath an influence so hush'd and holy.'
HOOD.

'Is not Margaret the heiress?' whispered Edith to her husband, as they were in their room alone at night after the sad journey to Oxford. She had pulled his tall head down, and stood upon tiptoe, and implored him not to be shocked, before she had ventured to ask this question. Captain Lennox was, however, quite in the dark; if he had ever heard, he had forgotten; it could not be much that a Fellow of a small college had to leave; but he had never wanted her to pay for her board; and two hundred and fifty pounds a year was something ridiculous, considering that she did not take wine. Edith came down upon her feet a little bit sadder; with a romance blown to pieces.

A week afterwards, she came prancing towards her husband, and made him a low curtsey:

'I am right, and you are wrong, most noble Captain. Margaret has had a lawyer's letter, and she is residuary legatee—the legacies being about two thousand pounds, and the remainder about forty thousand, at the present value of property in Milton.'

'Indeed! and how does she take her good fortune?'

'Oh, it seems she knew she was to have it all along; only she had no idea it was so much. She looks very white and pale, and says she's afraid of it; but that's nonsense, you know, and will soon go off. I left mamma pouring congratulations down her throat, and stole away to tell you.'

It seemed to be supposed, by general consent, that the most natural thing was to consider Mr. Lennox henceforward as Margaret's legal adviser. She was so entirely ignorant of all forms of business that in nearly everything she had to refer to him. He chose out her attorney; he came to her with papers to be signed. He was never so happy as when teaching her of what all these mysteries of the law were the signs and types.

'Henry,' said Edith, one day, archly; 'do you know what I hope and expect all these long conversations with Margaret will end in?'

'No, I don't,' said he, reddening. 'And I desire you not to tell me.'

'Oh, very well; then I need not tell Sholto not to ask Mr. Montagu so often to the house.'

'Just as you choose,' said he with forced coolness. 'What you are thinking of, may or may not happen; but this time, before I commit myself, I will see my ground clear. Ask whom you choose. It may not be very civil, Edith, but if you meddle in it you will mar it. She has been very *farouche* with me for a long time; and is only just beginning to thaw a little from her Zenobia ways. She has the making of a Cleopatra in her, if only she were a little more pagan.'

'For my part,' said Edith, a little maliciously, 'I am very glad she is a Christian. I know so very few!'

There was no Spain for Margaret that autumn; although to the last she hoped that some fortunate occasion would call Frederick to Paris, whither she could easily have met with a convoy. Instead of Cadiz, she had to content herself with Cromer. To that place her aunt Shaw and the Lennoxes were bound. They had all along wished her to accompany them, and, consequently, with their characters, they made but lazy efforts to forward her own separate wish. Perhaps Cromer was, in one sense of the expression, the best for her. She needed bodily strengthening and bracing as well as rest.

Among other hopes that had vanished, was the hope, the trust she had had, that Mr. Bell would have given Mr. Thornton the simple facts of the family circumstances which had preceded the unfortunate accident that led to Leonards' death. Whatever opinion—however changed it might be from what Mr. Thornton had once entertained, she had wished it to be based upon a true understanding of what she had done; and why she had done it. It would have been a pleasure to her; would have given her rest on a point on which she should now all her life be restless, unless she could resolve not to think upon it. It was now so long after the time of these occurrences, that there was no possible way of explaining them save the one which she had lost by Mr. Bell's death. She must just submit, like many another, to be misunderstood; but, though reasoning herself into the belief that in this hers was no uncommon lot, her heart did not ache the less with longing that some time—years and years hence—before he died at any rate, he might know how much she had been tempted. She thought that she did not want to hear that all was explained to him, if only she could be sure that he would know. But this wish was vain, like so many others; and when she had schooled herself into this conviction, she turned with all her heart and strength to the life that lay immediately before her, and resolved to strive and make the best of that.

She used to sit long hours upon the beach, gazing intently on the waves as they chafed with perpetual motion against the pebbly shore,—or she looked out upon the more distant heave, and sparkle against the sky, and heard, without being conscious of hearing, the eternal psalm, which went up continually. She was soothed without knowing how or why. Listlessly she sat there, on the ground, her hands clasped round her knees, while her aunt Shaw did small shoppings, and Edith and Captain Lennox rode far and wide on shore and inland. The nurses, sauntering on with their charges, would pass and repass her, and wonder in whispers what she could find to look at so long, day after day. And when the family gathered at dinner-time, Margaret was so silent and absorbed that Edith voted her moped, and hailed a proposal of her husband's with great satisfaction, that Mr. Henry Lennox should be asked to take Cromer for a week, on his return from Scotland in October.

But all this time for thought enabled Margaret to put events in their right places, as to origin and significance, both as regarded her past life and her future. Those hours by the sea-side were not lost, as any one might have seen who had had the perception to read, or the care to understand, the look that Margaret's face was gradually acquiring. Mr. Henry Lennox was excessively struck by the change.

'The sea has done Miss Hale an immense deal of good, I should fancy,' said he, when she first left the room after his arrival in their family circle. 'She looks ten years younger than she did in Harley Street.'

'That's the bonnet I got her!' said Edith, triumphantly. 'I knew it would suit her the moment I saw it.'

'I beg your pardon,' said Mr. Lennox, in the half-contemptuous, half-indulgent tone he generally used to Edith. 'But I believe I know the difference between the charms of a dress and the charms of a woman. No mere bonnet would have made Miss Hale's eyes so lustrous and yet so soft, or her lips so ripe and red—and her face altogether so full of peace and light.—She is like, and yet more,'—he dropped his voice,—'like the Margaret Hale of Helstone.'

From this time the clever and ambitious man bent all his powers to gaining Margaret. He loved her sweet beauty. He saw the latent sweep of her mind, which could easily (he thought) be led to embrace all the objects on which he had set his heart. He looked upon her fortune only as a part of the complete and superb character of herself and her position: yet he was fully aware of the rise which it would immediately enable him, the poor barrister, to take. Eventually he would earn such success, and such honours, as would enable him to pay her back, with interest, that first advance in wealth which he should owe to her. He had been to Milton on business connected with her property, on his return from Scotland; and with the quick eye of a skilled lawyer, ready ever to take in and weigh contingencies, he had seen that much additional value was yearly accruing to the lands and tenements which she owned in that prosperous and increasing town. He was glad to find that the present relationship between Margaret and himself, of client and legal adviser, was gradually superseding the recollection of that unlucky, mismanaged day at Helstone. He had thus unusual opportunities of intimate intercourse with her, besides those that arose from the connection between the families.

Margaret was only too willing to listen as long as he talked of Milton, though he had seen none of the people whom she more especially knew. It had been the tone with her aunt and cousin to speak of Milton with dislike and contempt; just such feelings as Margaret was ashamed to remember she had expressed and felt on first going to live there. But Mr. Lennox almost exceeded Margaret in his appreciation of the character of Milton and its inhabitants. Their energy, their power, their indomitable courage in struggling and fighting; their lurid vividness of existence, captivated and arrested his attention. He was never tired of talking about them; and had never perceived how selfish and material were too many of the ends they proposed to themselves as the result of all their mighty, untiring endeavour, till Margaret, even in the midst of her gratification, had the candour to point this out, as the tainting sin in so much that was noble, and to be admired. Still, when other subjects palled upon her, and she gave but short answers to many questions, Henry Lennox found out that an enquiry as to some Darkshire peculiarity of character, called back the light into her eye, the glow into her cheek.

When they returned to town, Margaret fulfilled one of her sea-side resolves, and took her life into her own hands. Before they went to Cromer, she had been as docile to her aunt's laws as if she were still the scared little stranger who cried herself to sleep that first night in the Harley Street nursery. But she had learnt, in those solemn hours of thought, that she herself must one day answer for her own life, and what she had done with it; and she tried to settle that most difficult problem for women, how much was to be utterly merged in obedience to authority, and how much might be set apart for freedom in working. Mrs. Shaw was as good-tempered as could be; and Edith had inherited this charming domestic quality; Margaret herself had probably the worst temper of the three, for her quick perceptions, and over-lively imagination made her hasty, and her early isolation from sympathy had made her proud; but she had an indescribable childlike sweetness of heart, which made her manners, even in her rarely wilful moods, irresistible of old; and now, chastened even by what the world called her good fortune, she charmed her reluctant aunt into acquiescence with her will. So Margaret gained the acknowledgment of her right to follow her own ideas of duty.

'Only don't be strong-minded,' pleaded Edith. 'Mamma wants you to have a footman of your own; and I'm sure you're very welcome, for they're great plagues. Only to please me, darling, don't go and have a strong mind; it's the only thing I ask. Footman or no footman, don't be strong-minded.'

'Don't be afraid, Edith. I'll faint on your hands at the servants' dinner-time, the very first opportunity; and then, what with Sholto playing with the fire, and the baby crying, you'll begin to wish for a strong-minded woman, equal to any emergency.'

'And you'll not grow too good to joke and be merry?'

'Not I. I shall be merrier than I have ever been, now I have got my own way.'

'And you'll not go a figure, but let me buy your dresses for you?'

'Indeed I mean to buy them for myself. You shall come with me if you like; but no one can please me but myself.'

'Oh! I was afraid you'd dress in brown and dust-colour, not to show the dirt you'll pick up in all those places. I'm glad you're going to keep one or two vanities, just by way of specimens of the old Adam.'

'I'm going to be just the same, Edith, if you and my aunt could but fancy so. Only as I have neither husband nor child to give me natural duties, I must make myself some, in addition to ordering my gowns.'

In the family conclave, which was made up of Edith, her mother, and her husband, it was decided that perhaps all these plans of hers would only secure her the more for Henry Lennox. They kept her out of the way of other friends who might have eligible sons or brothers; and it was also agreed that she never seemed to take much pleasure in the society of any one but Henry, out of their own family. The other admirers, attracted by her appearance or the reputation of her fortune, were swept away, by her unconscious smiling disdain, into the paths frequented by other beauties less fastidious, or other heiresses with a larger amount of gold. Henry and she grew slowly into closer intimacy; but neither he nor she were people to brook the slightest notice of their proceedings.

CHAPTER L - CHANGES AT MILTON

'Here we go up, up, up;
And here we go down, down, downee!'
NURSERY SONG.

Meanwhile, at Milton the chimneys smoked, the ceaseless roar and mighty beat, and dizzying whirl of machinery, struggled and strove perpetually. Senseless and purposeless were wood and iron and steam in their endless labours; but the persistence of their monotonous work was rivalled in tireless endurance by the strong crowds, who, with sense and with purpose, were busy and restless in seeking after—What? In the streets there were few loiterers,—none walking for mere pleasure; every man's face was set in lines of eagerness or anxiety; news was sought for with fierce avidity; and men jostled each other aside in the Mart and in the Exchange, as they did in life, in the deep selfishness of competition. There was gloom over the town. Few came to buy, and those who did were looked at suspiciously by the sellers; for credit was insecure, and the most stable might have their fortunes affected by the sweep in the great neighbouring port among the shipping houses. Hitherto there had been no failures in Milton; but, from the immense speculations that had come to light in making a bad end in America, and yet nearer home, it was known that some Milton houses of business must suffer so severely that every day men's faces asked, if their tongues did not, 'What news? Who is gone? How will it affect me?' And if two or three spoke together, they dwelt rather on the names of those who were safe than dared to hint at those likely, in their opinion, to go; for idle breath may, at such times, cause the downfall of some who might otherwise weather the storm; and one going down drags many after. 'Thornton is safe,' say they. 'His business is large—extending every year; but such a head as he has, and so prudent with all his daring!' Then one man draws another aside, and walks a little apart, and, with head inclined into his neighbour's ear, he says, 'Thornton's business is large; but he has spent his profits in extending it; he has no capital laid by; his machinery is new within these two years, and has cost him—we won't say what!—a word to the wise!' But that Mr. Harrison was a croaker,—a man who had succeeded to his father's trade-made fortune, which he had feared to lose by altering his mode of business to any having a larger scope; yet he grudged every penny made by others more daring and far-sighted.

But the truth was, Mr. Thornton was hard pressed. He felt it acutely in his vulnerable point—his pride in the commercial character which he had established for himself. Architect of his own fortunes, he attributed this to no special merit or qualities of his own, but to the power, which he believed that commerce gave to every brave, honest, and persevering man, to raise himself to a level from which he might see and read the great game of worldly success, and honestly, by such far-sightedness, command more power and influence than in any other mode of life. Far away, in the East and in the West, where his person would never be known, his name was to be regarded, and his wishes to be fulfilled, and his word pass like gold. That was the idea of merchant-life with which Mr. Thornton had started. 'Her merchants be like princes,' said his mother, reading the text aloud, as if it were a trumpet-call to invite her boy to the struggle. He was but like many others—men, women, and children—alive to distant, and dead to near things. He sought to possess the influence of a name in foreign countries and far-away seas,—to become the head of a firm that should be known for generations; and it had taken him long silent years to come even to a glimmering of what he might be now, to-day, here in his own town, his own factory, among his own people. He and they had led parallel lives—very close, but never touching—till the accident (or so it seemed) of his acquaintance with Higgins. Once brought face to face, man to man, with an individual of the masses around him, and (take notice) out of the character of master and workman, in the first instance, they had each begun to recognise that 'we have all of us one human heart.' It was the fine point of the wedge; and until now, when the apprehension of losing his connection with two or three of the workmen whom he had so lately begun to know as men,—of having a plan or two, which were experiments lying very close to his heart, roughly nipped off without trial,—gave a new poignancy to the subtle fear that came over him from time to time; until now, he had never recognised how much and how deep was the interest he had grown of late to feel in his position as manufacturer, simply because it led him into such close contact, and gave him the opportunity of so much power, among a race of people strange, shrewd, ignorant; but, above all, full of character and strong human feeling.

He reviewed his position as a Milton manufacturer. The strike a year and a half ago,—or more, for it was now untimely wintry weather, in a late spring,—that strike, when he was young, and he now was old—had prevented his completing some of the large orders he had then on hand. He had locked up a good deal of his capital in new and expensive machinery, and he had also bought cotton largely, for the fulfilment of these orders, taken under contract. That he had not been able to complete them, was owing in some degree to the utter want of skill on the part of the Irish hands whom he had imported; much of their work was damaged and unfit to be sent forth by a house which prided itself on turning out nothing but first-rate articles. For many months, the embarrassment caused by the strike had been an obstacle in Mr. Thornton's way; and often, when his eye fell on Higgins, he could have spoken angrily to him without any present cause, just from feeling how serious was the injury that had arisen from this affair in which he was implicated. But when he became conscious of this sudden, quick resentment, he re-resolved to curb it. It would not satisfy him to avoid Higgins; he must convince himself that he was master over his own anger, by being particularly careful to allow Higgins access to him, whenever the strict rules of business, or Mr. Thornton's leisure permitted. And by-and-bye, he lost all sense of resentment in wonder how it was, or could be, that two men like himself and Higgins, living by the same trade, working in their different ways at the same object, could look upon each other's position and duties in so strangely different a way. And thence arose that intercourse, which though it might not have the effect of preventing all future clash of opinion and action, when the occasion arose, would, at any rate, enable both master and man to look upon each other with far more charity and sympathy, and bear with each other more patiently and kindly. Besides this improvement of feeling, both Mr. Thornton and his workmen found out their ignorance as to positive matters of fact, known heretofore to one side, but not to the other.

But now had come one of those periods of bad trade, when the market falling brought down the value of all large stocks; Mr. Thornton's fell to nearly half. No orders were coming in; so he lost the interest of the capital he had locked up in machinery; indeed, it was difficult to get payment for the orders completed; yet there was the constant drain of expenses for working the business. Then the bills became due for the cotton he had purchased; and money being scarce, he could only borrow at exorbitant interest, and yet he could not realise any of his property. But he did not despair; he exerted himself day and night to foresee and to provide for all emergencies; he was as calm and gentle to the women in his home as ever; to the workmen in his mill he spoke not many words, but they knew him by this time; and many a curt, decided answer was received by them rather with sympathy for the care they saw pressing upon him, than with the suppressed antagonism which had formerly been smouldering, and ready for hard words and hard judgments on all occasions. 'Th' measter's a deal to potter him,' said Higgins, one day, as he heard Mr. Thornton's short, sharp inquiry, why such a command had not been obeyed; and caught the sound of the suppressed sigh which he heaved in going past the room where some of the men were working. Higgins and another man stopped over-hours that night, unknown to any one, to get the neglected piece of work done; and Mr. Thornton never knew but that the overlooker, to whom he had given the command in the first instance, had done it himself.

'Eh! I reckon I know who'd ha' been sorry for to see our measter sitting so like a piece o' grey calico! Th' ou'd parson would ha' fretted his woman's heart out, if he'd seen the woeful looks I have seen on our measter's face,' thought Higgins, one day, as he was approaching Mr. Thornton in Marlborough Street.

'Measter,' said he, stopping his employer in his quick resolved walk, and causing that gentleman to look up with a sudden annoyed start, as if his thoughts had been far away.

'Have yo' heerd aught of Miss Marget lately?'

'Miss—who?' replied Mr. Thornton.

'Miss Marget—Miss Hale—th' oud parson's daughter—yo known who I mean well enough, if yo'll only think a bit—' (there was nothing disrespectful in the tone in which this was said).

'Oh yes!' and suddenly, the wintry frost-bound look of care had left Mr. Thornton's face, as if some soft summer gale had blown all anxiety away from his mind; and though his mouth was as much compressed as before, his eyes smiled out benignly on his questioner.

'She's my landlord now, you know, Higgins. I hear of her through her agent here, every now and then. She's well and among friends—thank you, Higgins.' That 'thank you' that lingered after the other words, and yet came with so much warmth of feeling, let in a new light to the acute Higgins. It might be but a will-o'-th'-wisp, but he thought he would follow it and ascertain whither it would lead him.

'And she's not getten married, measter?'

'Not yet.' The face was cloudy once more. 'There is some talk of it, as I understand, with a connection of the family.'

'Then she'll not be for coming to Milton again, I reckon.'

'No!'

'Stop a minute, measter.' Then going up confidentially close, he said, 'Is th' young gentleman cleared?' He enforced the depth of his intelligence by a wink of the eye, which only made things more mysterious to Mr. Thornton.

'Th' young gentleman, I mean—Master Frederick, they ca'ad him—her brother as was over here, yo' known.'

'Over here.'

'Ay, to be sure, at th' missus's death. Yo' need na be feared of my telling; for Mary and me, we knowed it all along, only we held our peace, for we got it through Mary working in th' house.'

'And he was over. It was her brother!'

'Sure enough, and I reckoned yo' knowed it or I'd never ha' let on. Yo' knowed she had a brother?'

'Yes, I know all about him. And he was over at Mrs. Hale's death?'

'Nay! I'm not going for to tell more. I've maybe getten them into mischief already, for they kept it very close. I nobbut wanted to know if they'd getten him cleared?'

'Not that I know of. I know nothing. I only hear of Miss Hale, now, as my landlord, and through her lawyer.'

He broke off from Higgins, to follow the business on which he had been bent when the latter first accosted him; leaving Higgins baffled in his endeavour.

'It was her brother,' said Mr. Thornton to himself. 'I am glad. I may never see her again; but it is a comfort—a relief—to know that much. I knew she could not be unmaidenly; and yet I yearned for conviction. Now I am glad!'

It was a little golden thread running through the dark web of his present fortunes; which were growing ever gloomier and more gloomy. His agent had largely trusted a house in the American trade, which went down, along with several others, just at this time, like a pack of cards, the fall of one compelling other failures. What were Mr. Thornton's engagements? Could he stand?

Night after night he took books and papers into his own private room, and sate up there long after the family were gone to bed. He thought that no one knew of this occupation of the hours he should have spent in sleep. One morning, when daylight was stealing in through the crevices of his shutters, and he had never been in bed, and, in hopeless indifference of mind, was thinking that he could do without the hour or two of rest, which was all that he should be able to take before the stir of daily labour began again, the door of his room opened, and his mother stood there, dressed as she had been the day before. She had never laid herself down to slumber any more than he. Their eyes met. Their faces were cold and rigid, and wan, from long watching.

'Mother! why are not you in bed?'

'Son John,' said she, 'do you think I can sleep with an easy mind, while you keep awake full of care? You have not told me what your trouble is; but sore trouble you have had these many days past.'

'Trade is bad.'

'And you dread—'

'I dread nothing,' replied he, drawing up his head, and holding it erect. 'I know now that no man will suffer by me. That was my anxiety.'

'But how do you stand? Shall you—will it be a failure?' her steady voice trembling in an unwonted manner.

'Not a failure. I must give up business, but I pay all men. I might redeem myself—I am sorely tempted—'

'How? Oh, John! keep up your name—try all risks for that. How redeem it?'

'By a speculation offered to me, full of risk; but, if successful, placing me high above water-mark, so that no one need ever know the strait I am in. Still, if it fails—'

'And if it fails,' said she, advancing, and laying her hand on his arm, her eyes full of eager light. She held her breath to hear the end of his speech.

'Honest men are ruined by a rogue,' said he gloomily. 'As I stand now, my creditors, money is safe—every farthing of it; but I don't know where to find my own—it may be all gone, and I penniless at this moment. Therefore, it is my creditors' money that I should risk.'

'But if it succeeded, they need never know. Is it so desperate a speculation? I am sure it is not, or you would never have thought of it. If it succeeded—'

'I should be a rich man, and my peace of conscience would be gone!'

'Why! You would have injured no one.'

'No; but I should have run the risk of ruining many for my own paltry aggrandisement. Mother, I have decided! You won't much grieve over our leaving this house, shall you, dear mother?'

'No! but to have you other than what you are will break my heart. What can you do?'

'Be always the same John Thornton in whatever circumstances; endeavouring to do right, and making great blunders; and then trying to be brave in setting to afresh. But it is hard, mother. I have so worked and planned. I have discovered new powers in my situation too late—and now all is over. I am too old to begin again with the same heart. It is hard, mother.'

He turned away from her, and covered his face with his hands.

'I can't think,' said she, with gloomy defiance in her tone, 'how it comes about. Here is my boy—good son, just man, tender heart—and he fails in all he sets his mind upon: he finds a woman to love, and she cares no more for his affection than if he had been any common man; he labours, and his labour comes to nought. Other people prosper and grow rich, and hold their paltry names high and dry above shame.'

'Shame never touched me,' said he, in a low tone: but she went on.

'I sometimes have wondered where justice was gone to, and now I don't believe there is such a thing in the world,—now you are come to this; you, my own John Thornton, though you and I may be beggars together—my own dear son!'

She fell upon his neck, and kissed him through her tears.

'Mother!' said he, holding her gently in his arms, 'who has sent me my lot in life, both of good and of evil?'

She shook her head. She would have nothing to do with religion just then.

'Mother,' he went on, seeing that she would not speak, 'I, too, have been rebellious; but I am striving to be so no longer. Help me, as you helped me when I was a child. Then you said many good words—when my father died, and we were sometimes sorely short of comforts—which we shall never be now; you said brave, noble, trustful words then, mother, which I have never forgotten, though they may have lain dormant. Speak to me again in the old way, mother. Do not let us have to think that the world has too much hardened our hearts. If you would say the old good words, it would make me feel something of the pious simplicity of my childhood. I say them to myself, but they would come differently from you, remembering all the cares and trials you have had to bear.'

'I have had a many,' said she, sobbing, 'but none so sore as this. To see you cast down from your rightful place! I could say it for myself, John, but not for you. Not for you! God has seen fit to be very hard on you, very.'

She shook with the sobs that come so convulsively when an old person weeps. The silence around her struck her at last; and she quieted herself to listen. No sound. She looked. Her son sate by the table, his arms thrown half across it, his head bent face downwards.

'Oh, John!' she said, and she lifted his face up. Such a strange, pallid look of gloom was on it, that for a moment it struck her that this look was the forerunner of death; but, as the rigidity melted out of the countenance and the natural colour returned, and she saw that he was himself once again, all worldly mortification sank to nothing before the consciousness of the great blessing that he himself by his simple existence was to her. She thanked God for this, and this alone, with a fervour that swept away all rebellious feelings from her mind.

He did not speak readily; but he went and opened the shutters, and let the ruddy light of dawn flood the room. But the wind was in the east; the weather was piercing cold, as it had been for weeks; there would be no demand for light summer goods this year. That hope for the revival of trade must utterly be given up.

It was a great comfort to have had this conversation with his mother; and to feel sure that, however they might henceforward keep silence on all these anxieties, they yet understood each other's feelings, and were, if not in harmony, at least not in discord with each other, in their way of viewing them. Fanny's husband was vexed at Thornton's refusal to take any share in the speculation which he had offered to him, and withdrew from any possibility of being supposed able to assist him with the ready money, which indeed the speculator needed for his own venture.

There was nothing for it at last, but that which Mr. Thornton had dreaded for many weeks; he had to give up the business in which he had been so long engaged with so much honour and success; and look out for a subordinate situation. Marlborough Mills and the adjacent dwelling were held under a long lease; they must, if possible, be relet. There was an immediate choice of situations offered to Mr. Thornton. Mr. Hamper would have been only too glad to have secured him as a steady and experienced partner for his son, whom he was setting up with a large capital in a neighbouring town; but the young man was half-educated as regarded information, and wholly uneducated as regarded any other responsibility than that of getting money, and brutalised both as to his pleasures and his pains. Mr. Thornton declined having any share in a partnership, which would frustrate what few plans he had that survived the wreck of his fortunes. He would sooner consent to be only a manager, where he could have a certain degree of power beyond the mere money-getting part, than have to fall in with the tyrannical humours of a moneyed partner with whom he felt sure that he should quarrel in a few months.

So he waited, and stood on one side with profound humility, as the news swept through the Exchange, of the enormous fortune which his brother-in-law had made by his daring speculation. It was a nine days' wonder. Success brought with it its worldly consequence of extreme admiration. No one was considered so wise and far-seeing as Mr. Watson.

CHAPTER LI - MEETING AGAIN

'Bear up, brave heart! we will be calm and strong;
Sure, we can master eyes, or cheek, or tongue,
Nor let the smallest tell-tale sign appear
She ever was, and is, and will be dear.'
RHYMING PLAY.

It was a hot summer's evening. Edith came into Margaret's bedroom, the first time in her habit, the second ready dressed for dinner. No one was there at first; the next time Edith found Dixon laying out Margaret's dress on the bed; but no Margaret. Edith remained to fidget about.

'Oh, Dixon! not those horrid blue flowers to that dead gold-coloured gown. What taste! Wait a minute, and I will bring you some pomegranate blossoms.'

'It's not a dead gold-colour, ma'am. It's a straw-colour. And blue always goes with straw-colour.' But Edith had brought the brilliant scarlet flowers before Dixon had got half through her remonstrance.

'Where is Miss Hale?' asked Edith, as soon as she had tried the effect of the garniture. 'I can't think,' she went on, pettishly, 'how my aunt allowed her to get into such rambling habits in Milton! I'm sure I'm always expecting to hear of her having met with something horrible among all those wretched places she pokes herself into. I should never dare to go down some of those streets without a servant. They're not fit for ladies.'

Dixon was still huffed about her despised taste; so she replied, rather shortly:

'It's no wonder to my mind, when I hear ladies talk such a deal about being ladies—and when they're such fearful, delicate, dainty ladies too—I say it's no wonder to me that there are no longer any saints on earth——'

'Oh, Margaret! here you are! I have been so wanting you. But how your cheeks are flushed with the heat, poor child! But only think what that tiresome Henry has done; really, he exceeds brother-in-law's limits. Just when my party was made up so beautifully—fitted in so precisely for Mr. Colthurst—there has Henry come, with an apology it is true, and making use of your name for an excuse, and asked me if he may bring that Mr. Thornton of Milton—your tenant, you know—who is in London about some law business. It will spoil my number, quite.'

'I don't mind dinner. I don't want any,' said Margaret, in a low voice. 'Dixon can get me a cup of tea here, and I will be in the drawing-room by the time you come up. I shall really be glad to lie down.'

'No, no! that will never do. You do look wretchedly white, to be sure; but that is just the heat, and we can't do without you possibly. (Those flowers a little lower, Dixon. They look glorious flames, Margaret, in your black hair.) You know we planned you to talk about Milton to Mr. Colthurst. Oh! to be sure! and this man comes from Milton. I believe it will be capital, after all. Mr. Colthurst can pump him well on all the subjects in which he is interested, and it will be great fun to trace out your experiences, and this Mr. Thornton's wisdom, in Mr. Colthurst's next speech in the House. Really, I think it is a happy hit of Henry's. I asked him if he was a man one would be ashamed of; and he replied, "Not if you've any sense in you, my little sister." So I suppose he is able to sound his h's, which is not a common Darkshire accomplishment—eh, Margaret?'

'Mr. Lennox did not say why Mr. Thornton was come up to town? Was it law business connected with the property?' asked Margaret, in a constrained voice.

'Oh! he's failed, or something of the kind, that Henry told you of that day you had such a headache,—what was it? (There, that's capital, Dixon. Miss Hale does us credit, does she not?) I wish I was as tall as a queen, and as brown as a gipsy, Margaret.'

'But about Mr. Thornton?'

'Oh I really have such a terrible head for law business. Henry will like nothing better than to tell you all about it. I know the impression he made upon me was, that Mr. Thornton is very badly off, and a very respectable man, and that I'm to be very civil to him; and as I did not know how, I came to you to ask you to help me. And now come down with me, and rest on the sofa for a quarter of an hour.'

The privileged brother-in-law came early and Margaret reddening as she spoke, began to ask him the questions she wanted to hear answered about Mr. Thornton.

'He came up about this sub-letting the property—Marlborough Mills, and the house and premises adjoining, I mean. He is unable to keep it on; and there are deeds and leases to be looked over, and agreements to be drawn up. I hope Edith will receive him properly; but she was rather put out, as I could see, by the liberty I had taken in begging for an invitation for him. But I thought you would like to have some attention shown him: and one would be particularly scrupulous in paying every respect to a man who is going down in the world.' He had dropped his voice to speak to Margaret, by whom he was sitting; but as he ended he sprang up, and introduced Mr. Thornton, who had that moment entered, to Edith and Captain Lennox.

Margaret looked with an anxious eye at Mr. Thornton while he was thus occupied. It was considerably more than a year since she had seen him; and events had occurred to change him much in that time. His fine figure yet bore him above the common height of men; and gave him a distinguished appearance, from the ease of motion which arose out of it, and was natural to him; but his face looked older and care-worn; yet a noble composure sate upon it, which impressed those who had just been hearing of his changed position, with a sense of inherent dignity and manly strength. He was aware, from the first glance he had given round the room, that Margaret was there; he had seen her intent look of occupation as she listened to Mr. Henry Lennox; and he came up to her with the perfectly regulated manner of an old friend. With his first calm words a vivid colour flashed into her cheeks, which never left them again during the evening. She did not seem to have much to say to him. She disappointed him by the quiet way in which she asked what seemed to him to be the merely necessary questions respecting her old acquaintances, in Milton; but others came in—more intimate in the house than he—and he fell into the background, where he and Mr. Lennox talked together from time to time.

'You think Miss Hale looking well,' said Mr. Lennox, 'don't you? Milton didn't agree with her, I imagine; for when she first came to London, I thought I had never seen any one so much changed. To-night she is looking radiant. But she is much stronger. Last autumn she was fatigued with a walk of a couple of miles. On Friday evening we walked up to Hampstead and back. Yet on Saturday she looked as well as she does now.

'We!' Who? They two alone?

Mr. Colthurst was a very clever man, and a rising member of parliament. He had a quick eye at discerning character, and was struck by a remark which Mr. Thornton made at dinner-time. He enquired from Edith who that gentleman was; and, rather to her surprise, she found, from the tone of his 'Indeed!' that Mr. Thornton of Milton was not such an unknown name to him as she had imagined it would be. Her dinner was going off well. Henry was in good humour, and brought out his dry caustic wit admirably. Mr. Thornton and Mr. Colthurst found one or two mutual subjects of interest, which they could only touch upon then, reserving them for more private after-dinner talk. Margaret looked beautiful in the pomegranate flowers; and if she did lean back in her chair and speak but little, Edith was not annoyed, for the conversation flowed on smoothly without her. Margaret was watching Mr. Thornton's face. He never looked at her; so she might study him unobserved, and note the changes which even this short time had wrought in him. Only at some unexpected mot of Mr. Lennox's, his face flashed out into the old look of intense enjoyment; the merry brightness returned to his eyes, the lips just parted to suggest the brilliant smile of former days; and for an instant, his glance instinctively sought hers, as if he wanted her sympathy. But when their eyes met, his whole countenance changed; he was grave and anxious once more; and he resolutely avoided even looking near her again during dinner.

There were only two ladies besides their own party, and as these were occupied in conversation by her aunt and Edith, when they went up into the drawing-room, Margaret languidly employed herself about some work. Presently the gentlemen came up, Mr. Colthurst and Mr. Thornton in close conversation. Mr. Lennox drew near to Margaret, and said in a low voice:

'I really think Edith owes me thanks for my contribution to her party. You've no idea what an agreeable, sensible fellow this tenant of yours is. He has been the very man to give Colthurst all the facts he wanted coaching in. I can't conceive how he contrived to mismanage his affairs.'

'With his powers and opportunities you would have succeeded,' said Margaret. He did not quite relish the tone in which she spoke, although the words but expressed a thought which had passed through his own mind. As he was silent, they caught a swell in the sound of conversation going on near the fire-place between Mr. Colthurst and Mr. Thornton.

'I assure you, I heard it spoken of with great interest—curiosity as to its result, perhaps I should rather say. I heard your name frequently mentioned during my short stay in the neighbourhood.' Then they lost some words; and when next they could hear Mr. Thornton was speaking.

'I have not the elements for popularity—if they spoke of me in that way, they were mistaken. I fall slowly into new projects; and I find it difficult to let myself be known, even by those whom I desire to know, and with whom I would fain have no reserve. Yet, even with all these drawbacks, I felt that I was on the right path, and that, starting from a kind of friendship with one, I was becoming acquainted with many. The advantages were mutual: we were both unconsciously and consciously teaching each other.'

'You say "were." I trust you are intending to pursue the same course?'

'I must stop Colthurst,' said Henry Lennox, hastily. And by an abrupt, yet apropos question, he turned the current of the conversation, so as not to give Mr. Thornton the mortification of acknowledging his want of success and consequent change of position. But as soon as the newly-started subject had come to a close, Mr. Thornton resumed the conversation just where it had been interrupted, and gave Mr. Colthurst the reply to his inquiry.

'I have been unsuccessful in business, and have had to give up my position as a master. I am on the look out for a situation in Milton, where I may meet with employment under some one who will be willing to let me go along my own way in such matters as these. I can depend upon myself for having no go-ahead theories that I would rashly bring into practice. My only wish is to have the opportunity of cultivating some intercourse with the hands beyond the mere "cash nexus." But it might be the point Archimedes sought from which to move the earth, to judge from the importance attached to it by some of our manufacturers, who shake their heads and look grave as soon as I name the one or two experiments that I should like to try.'

'You call them "experiments" I notice,' said Mr. Colthurst, with a delicate increase of respect in his manner.

'Because I believe them to be such. I am not sure of the consequences that may result from them. But I am sure they ought to be tried. I have arrived at the conviction that no mere institutions, however wise, and however much thought may have been required to organise and arrange them, can attach class to class as they should be attached, unless the working out of such institutions bring the individuals of the different classes into actual personal contact. Such intercourse is the very breath of life. A working man can hardly be made to feel and know how much his employer may have laboured in his study at plans for the benefit of his workpeople. A complete plan emerges like a piece of machinery, apparently fitted for every emergency. But the hands accept it as they do machinery, without understanding the intense mental labour and forethought required to bring it to such perfection. But I would take an idea, the working out of which would necessitate personal intercourse; it might not go well at first, but at every hitch interest would be felt by an increasing number of men, and at last its success in working come to be desired by all, as all had borne a part in the formation of the plan; and even then I am sure that it would lose its vitality, cease to be living, as soon as it was no longer carried on by that sort of common interest which invariably makes people find means and ways of seeing each other, and becoming acquainted with each others' characters and persons, and even tricks of temper and modes of speech. We should understand each other better, and I'll venture to say we should like each other more.'

'And you think they may prevent the recurrence of strikes?'

'Not at all. My utmost expectation only goes so far as this—that they may render strikes not the bitter, venomous sources of hatred they have hitherto been. A more hopeful man might imagine that a closer and more genial intercourse between classes might do away with strikes. But I am not a hopeful man.'

Suddenly, as if a new idea had struck him, he crossed over to where Margaret was sitting, and began, without preface, as if he knew she had been listening to all that had passed:

'Miss Hale, I had a round-robin from some of my men—I suspect in Higgins' handwriting—stating their wish to work for me, if ever I was in a position to employ men again on my own behalf. That was good, wasn't it?'

'Yes. Just right. I am glad of it,' said Margaret, looking up straight into his face with her speaking eyes, and then dropping them under his eloquent glance. He gazed back at her for a minute, as if he did not know exactly what he was about. Then sighed; and saying, 'I knew you would like it,' he turned away, and never spoke to her again until he bid her a formal 'good night.'

As Mr. Lennox took his departure, Margaret said, with a blush that she could not repress, and with some hesitation,

'Can I speak to you to-morrow? I want your help about—something.'

'Certainly. I will come at whatever time you name. You cannot give me a greater pleasure than by making me of any use. At eleven? Very well.'

His eye brightened with exultation. How she was learning to depend upon him! It seemed as if any day now might give him the certainty, without having which he had determined never to offer to her again.

CHAPTER LII - 'PACK CLOUDS AWAY'

'For joy or grief, for hope or fear,
For all hereafter, as for here,
In peace or strife, in storm or shine.'
ANON.

Edith went about on tip-toe, and checked Sholto in all loud speaking that next morning, as if any sudden noise would interrupt the conference that was taking place in the drawing-room. Two o'clock came; and they still sate there with closed doors. Then there was a man's footstep running down stairs; and Edith peeped out of the drawing-room.

'Well, Henry?' said she, with a look of interrogation.

'Well!' said he, rather shortly.

'Come in to lunch!'

'No, thank you, I can't. I've lost too much time here already.'

'Then it's not all settled,' said Edith despondingly.

'No! not at all. It never will be settled, if the "it" is what I conjecture you mean. That will never be, Edith, so give up thinking about it.'

'But it would be so nice for us all,' pleaded Edith. 'I should always feel comfortable about the children, if I had Margaret settled down near me. As it is, I am always afraid of her going off to Cadiz.'

'I will try, when I marry, to look out for a young lady who has a knowledge of the management of children. That is all I can do. Miss Hale would not have me. And I shall not ask her.'

'Then, what have you been talking about?'

'A thousand things you would not understand: investments, and leases, and value of land.'

'Oh, go away if that's all. You and she will be unbearably stupid, if you've been talking all this time about such weary things.'

'Very well. I'm coming again to-morrow, and bringing Mr. Thornton with me, to have some more talk with Miss Hale.'

'Mr. Thornton! What has he to do with it?'

'He is Miss Hale's tenant,' said Mr. Lennox, turning away. 'And he wishes to give up his lease.'

'Oh! very well. I can't understand details, so don't give them me.'

'The only detail I want you to understand is, to let us have the back drawing-room undisturbed, as it was to-day. In general, the children and servants are so in and out, that I can never get any business satisfactorily explained; and the arrangements we have to make to-morrow are of importance.'

No one ever knew why Mr. Lennox did not keep to his appointment on the following day. Mr. Thornton came true to his time; and, after keeping him waiting for nearly an hour, Margaret came in looking very white and anxious.

She began hurriedly:

'I am so sorry Mr. Lennox is not here,—he could have done it so much better than I can. He is my adviser in this'——

'I am sorry that I came, if it troubles you. Shall I go to Mr. Lennox's chambers and try and find him?'

'No, thank you. I wanted to tell you, how grieved I was to find that I am to lose you as a tenant. But, Mr. Lennox says, things are sure to brighten'——

'Mr. Lennox knows little about it,' said Mr. Thornton quietly. 'Happy and fortunate in all a man cares for, he does not understand what it is to find oneself no longer young—yet thrown back to the starting-point which requires the hopeful energy of youth—to feel one half of life gone, and nothing done—nothing remaining of wasted opportunity, but the bitter recollection that it has been. Miss Hale, I would rather not hear Mr. Lennox's opinion of my affairs. Those who are happy and successful themselves are too apt to make light of the misfortunes of others.'

'You are unjust,' said Margaret, gently. 'Mr. Lennox has only spoken of the great probability which he believes there to be of your redeeming—your more than redeeming what you have lost—don't speak till I have ended—pray don't!' And collecting herself once more, she went on rapidly turning over some law papers, and statements of accounts in a trembling hurried manner. 'Oh! here it is! and—he drew me out a proposal—I wish he was here to explain it—showing that if you would take some money of mine, eighteen thousand and fifty-seven pounds, lying just at this moment unused in the bank, and bringing me in only two and a half per cent.—you could pay me much better interest, and might go on working Marlborough Mills.' Her voice had cleared itself and become more steady. Mr. Thornton did not speak, and she went on looking for some paper on which were written down the proposals for security; for she was most anxious to have it all looked upon in the light of a mere business arrangement, in which the principal advantage would be on her side. While she sought for this paper, her very heart-pulse was arrested by the tone in which Mr. Thornton spoke. His voice was hoarse, and trembling with tender passion, as he said:—

'Margaret!'

For an instant she looked up; and then sought to veil her luminous eyes by dropping her forehead on her hands. Again, stepping nearer, he besought her with another tremulous eager call upon her name.

'Margaret!'

Still lower went the head; more closely hidden was the face, almost resting on the table before her. He came close to her. He knelt by her side, to bring his face to a level with her ear; and whispered-panted out the words:—

'Take care.—If you do not speak—I shall claim you as my own in some strange presumptuous way.—Send me away at once, if I must go;—Margaret!—'

At that third call she turned her face, still covered with her small white hands, towards him, and laid it on his shoulder, hiding it even there; and it was too delicious to feel her soft cheek against his, for him to wish to see either deep blushes or loving eyes. He clasped her close. But they both kept silence. At length she murmured in a broken voice:

'Oh, Mr. Thornton, I am not good enough!'

'Not good enough! Don't mock my own deep feeling of unworthiness.'

After a minute or two, he gently disengaged her hands from her face, and laid her arms as they had once before been placed to protect him from the rioters.

'Do you remember, love?' he murmured. 'And how I requited you with my insolence the next day?'

'I remember how wrongly I spoke to you,—that is all.'

'Look here! Lift up your head. I have something to show you!' She slowly faced him, glowing with beautiful shame.

'Do you know these roses?' he said, drawing out his pocket-book, in which were treasured up some dead flowers.

'No!' she replied, with innocent curiosity. 'Did I give them to you?'

'No! Vanity; you did not. You may have worn sister roses very probably.'

She looked at them, wondering for a minute, then she smiled a little as she said—

'They are from Helstone, are they not? I know the deep indentations round the leaves. Oh! have you been there? When were you there?'

'I wanted to see the place where Margaret grew to what she is, even at the worst time of all, when I had no hope of ever calling her mine. I went there on my return from Havre.'

'You must give them to me,' she said, trying to take them out of his hand with gentle violence.

'Very well. Only you must pay me for them!'

'How shall I ever tell Aunt Shaw?' she whispered, after some time of delicious silence.

'Let me speak to her.'

'Oh, no! I owe to her,—but what will she say?'

'I can guess. Her first exclamation will be, "That man!"'

'Hush!' said Margaret, 'or I shall try and show you your mother's indignant tones as she says, "That woman!"'

Five Novels by Thomas Hardy - Far From The Madding Crowd, The Return of the Native, The Mayor of Casterbridge, Tess of the d'Urbervilles, Jude the Obscure (complete and unabridged)
Thomas Hardy
Benediction Classics, 2013
1114 pages
ISBN: 978-1-78139-356-7

Available from www.amazon.com, www.amazon.co.uk

Thomas Hardy, (1840 - 1928) was an English novelist and poet. He was highly critical of Victorian society and focussed mainly on the declining rural communities.

Four Notable Works: Sons and Lovers, the Rainbow, Women in Love and Lady Chatterley's Lover
D. H. Lawrence
Benediction Classics, 2013
1130 pages
ISBN: 978-1-78139-403-8

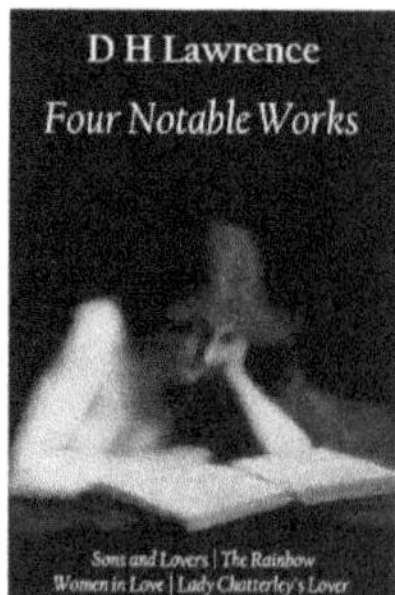

Available from www.amazon.com, www.amazon.co.uk

Lawrence is best known for his novels Sons and Lovers, The Rainbow, Women in Love and Lady Chatterley's Lover. Within all of these novels, Lawrence contrasts living with existing, within an industrial setting. In particular, he explores the nature of relationships. What is love? Is it physical? Is it emotional? Can you have one without the other? Finally, Lawrence explores the class system and the strange behaviours generated within it. He is a philosopher at heart. The sexual exploits of his characters, although shocking at the time, emphasise Lawrence's belief that society had over-emphasised the place of the mind and forgotten the importance of physical intimacy.

E M Forster - Collected Works, including A Room with a View, Howards End, The Longest Journey, Where Angels Fear to Tread and The Celestial Omnibus and other Stories
E M Forster
Oxford City Press, 2013
808 pages
ISBN: 978-1-78139-373-4

Available from www.amazon.com, www.amazon.co.uk

Edward Morgan Forster (1879 - 1970) is best known for his beautiful novels - ironic with delicious plots, highlighting the hypocrisy and discrimination in early 20th-century British society.

Henry James - Notable Works, including (complete and unabridged): The American, The Turn of the Screw, The Portrait of a Lady, The Wings of the Dove, Daisy Miller and The Ambassadors
Henry James
Benediction Classics, 2013
1128 pages
ISBN: 978-1-78139-371-0

Available from www.amazon.com, www.amazon.co.uk

Henry James (1843 - 1916) was born in American but eventually settled in England. He is considered to be a key figure of 19th-century literary realism. His writing explores the perceptions of a character, and his works have been compared with impressionist paintings. His novels brought new life and interest into narrative fiction.

This omnibus edition includes his notable works:

The American,
The Turn of the Screw,
The Portrait of a Lady,
The Wings of the Dove,
Daisy Miller,
The Ambassadors

Also from Benediction Books ...

Wandering Between Two Worlds: Essays on Faith and Art
Anita Mathias
Benediction Books, 2007
152 pages
ISBN: 0955373700

Available from www.amazon.com, www.amazon.co.uk

In these wide-ranging lyrical essays, Anita Mathias writes, in lush, lovely prose, of her naughty Catholic childhood in Jamshedpur, India; her large, eccentric family in Mangalore, a sea-coast town converted by the Portuguese in the sixteenth century; her rebellion and atheism as a teenager in her Himalayan boarding school, run by German missionary nuns, St. Mary's Convent, Nainital; and her abrupt religious conversion after which she entered Mother Teresa's convent in Calcutta as a novice. Later rich, elegant essays explore the dualities of her life as a writer, mother, and Christian in the United States-- Domesticity and Art, Writing and Prayer, and the experience of being "an alien and stranger" as an immigrant in America, sensing the need for roots.

About the Author

Anita Mathias is the author of *Wandering Between Two Worlds: Essays on Faith and Art*. She has a B.A. and M.A. in English from Somerville College, Oxford University, and an M.A. in Creative Writing from the Ohio State University, USA. Anita won a National Endowment of the Arts fellowship in Creative Non-fiction in 1997. She lives in Oxford, England with her husband, Roy, and her daughters, Zoe and Irene.

Anita's website:
http://www.anitamathias.com, and
Anita's blog Dreaming Beneath the Spires:
http://dreamingbeneaththespires.blogspot.com

The Church That Had Too Much
Anita Mathias
Benediction Books, 2010
52 pages
ISBN: 9781849026567

Available from www.amazon.com, www.amazon.co.uk

The Church That Had Too Much was very well-intentioned. She wanted to love God, she wanted to love people, but she was both hampered by her muchness and the abundance of her possessions, and beset by ambition, power struggles and snobbery. Read about the surprising way The Church That Had Too Much began to resolve her problems in this deceptively simple and enchanting fable.

About the Author

Anita Mathias is the author of *Wandering Between Two Worlds: Essays on Faith and Art*. She has a B.A. and M.A. in English from Somerville College, Oxford University, and an M.A. in Creative Writing from the Ohio State University, USA. Anita won a National Endowment of the Arts fellowship in Creative Non-fiction in 1997. She lives in Oxford, England with her husband, Roy, and her daughters, Zoe and Irene.

Anita's website:
http://www.anitamathias.com, and
Anita's blog Dreaming Beneath the Spires:
http://dreamingbeneaththespires.blogspot.com

www.ingramcontent.com/pod-product-compliance
Lightning Source LLC
Chambersburg PA
CBHW081130300726
48982CB00005B/908

* 9 7 8 1 7 8 1 3 9 4 3 0 4 *